THE MAN WITHOUT Q

ROBERT MUSIL was born in Klagenfurt, Austria, in 1880. Trained in science and philosophy, he left a career in the military to turn to writing. The publication of his novel *Young Törless* in 1906 brought him international recognition; to this day it remains a classic parable on the misuse of power. After serving in the First World War, Musil lived alternately in Vienna and Berlin, with much of his time being dedicated to the slow writing of his masterwork, *The Man Without Qualities*. In 1938, when Hitler's rise to power threatened Musil's work with being banned in both Austria and Germany, he emigrated to Switzerland, where he and his wife lived until his death in 1942. The first complete German edition of *The Man Without Qualities* finally appeared in 1978.

ROBERT MUSIL

THE MAN

WITHOUT

QUALITIES

TRANSLATED BY SOPHIE WILKINS AND BURTON PIKE

PICADOR

A SORT OF INTRODUCTION
PSEUDOREALITY PREVAILS
INTO THE MILLENNIUM

TRANSLATED FROM THE GERMAN BY SOPHIE WILKINS

EDITORIAL CONSULTANT: BURTON PIKE

First published 1995 by Alfred A. Knopf, Inc.

First published in Great Britain 1995 by Picador

First published in paperback 1997 by Picador

This edition first published 2011 by Picador
an imprint of Pan Macmillan, a division of Macmillan Publishers Limited
Pan Macmillan, 20 New Wharf Road, London N1 9RR
Basingstoke and Oxford
Associated companies throughout the world
www.panmacmillan.com

ISBN 978-1-4472-1187-7

Originally published in German as *Der Mann ohne Eigenschaften*,
Neu-Edition, edited by Prof. Adolf Frisé
Copyright © 1978 by Rowohlt Verlag GmbH, Reinbek bei Hamburg.

3 5 7 9 8 6 4

A CIP catalogue record for this book is available from
the British Library.

Printed and bound by CPI Group (UK) Ltd, Croydon, CR0 4YY

Visit **www.picador.com** to read more about all our books
and to buy them. You will also find features, author interviews and
news of any author events, and you can sign up for e-newsletters
so that you're always first to hear about our new releases.

CONTENTS

PART I: A SORT OF INTRODUCTION

PART II: PSEUDOREALITY PREVAILS

PART III: INTO THE MILLENNIUM
(THE CRIMINALS)

PART I

A SORT OF INTRODUCTION

From which, remarkably enough, nothing develops

A barometric low hung over the Atlantic. It moved eastward toward a high-pressure area over Russia without as yet showing any inclination to bypass this high in a northerly direction. The isotherms and isotheres were functioning as they should. The air temperature was appropriate relative to the annual mean temperature and to the aperiodic monthly fluctuations of the temperature. The rising and setting of the sun, the moon, the phases of the moon, of Venus, of the rings of Saturn, and many other significant phenomena were all in accordance with the forecasts in the astronomical yearbooks. The water vapor in the air was at its maximal state of tension, while the humidity was minimal. In a word that characterizes the facts fairly accurately, even if it is a bit old-fashioned: It was a fine day in August 1913.

Automobiles shot out of deep, narrow streets into the shallows of bright squares. Dark clusters of pedestrians formed cloudlike strings. Where more powerful lines of speed cut across their casual haste they clotted up, then trickled on faster and, after a few oscillations, resumed their steady rhythm. Hundreds of noises wove themselves into a wiry texture of sound with barbs protruding here and there, smart edges running along it and subsiding again, with clear notes splintering off and dissipating. By this noise alone, whose special quality cannot be captured in words, a man returning after years of absence would have been able to tell with his eyes shut that he was back in the Imperial Capital and Royal City of Vienna. Cities, like people, can be recognized by their walk. Opening his eyes, he would know the place by the rhythm of movement in the streets long before he caught any characteristic detail. It would not matter even if he only imagined that he could do this. We overestimate the importance of knowing where we are because in nomadic times it was essential to recognize the tribal feeding grounds. Why are we satisfied to speak vaguely of a red nose, without specifying what shade of red, even though degrees of red can be stated precisely to the micromillimeter of a wavelength, while with something so infinitely more complicated as what city one happens to be in, we always insist on knowing it exactly? It merely distracts us from more important concerns.

So let us not place any particular value on the city's name. Like all big cities it was made up of irregularity, change, forward spurts, failures to keep step, collisions of objects and interests, punctuated by unfathomable silences; made up of pathways and untrodden ways, of one great rhythmic beat as well as the chronic discord and mutual displacement of all its contending rhythms. All in all, it was like a boiling bubble inside a pot made of the durable stuff of buildings, laws, regulations, and historical traditions.

The two people who were walking up one of its wide, bustling avenues naturally were not thinking along these lines. They clearly belonged to a privileged social class, with their distinguished bearing, style of dress, and conversation, the initials of their names embroidered on their underwear, and just as discreetly, which is to say not for outward show but in the fine underwear of their minds, they knew who they were and that they belonged in a European capital city and imperial residence. Their names might have been Ermelinda Tuzzi and Arnheim—but then, they couldn't be, because in August Frau Tuzzi was still in Bad Aussee with her husband and Dr. Arnheim was still in Constantinople; so we are left to wonder who they were. People who take a lively interest in what goes on often wonder about such puzzling sights on the street, but they soon forget them again, unless they happen to remember during their next few steps where they have seen those other two before. The pair now came to a sudden stop when they saw a rapidly gathering crowd in front of them. Just a moment earlier something there had broken ranks; falling sideways with a crash, something had spun around and come to a skidding halt—a heavy truck, as it turned out, which had braked so sharply that it was now stranded with one wheel on the curb. Like bees clustering around the entrance to their hive people had instantly surrounded a small spot on the pavement, which they left open in their midst. In it stood the truck driver, gray as packing paper, clumsily waving his arms as he tried to explain the accident. The glances of the newcomers turned to him, then warily dropped to the bottom of the hole where a man who lay there as if dead had been bedded against the curb. It was by his own carelessness that he had come to grief, as everyone agreed. People took turns kneeling beside him, vaguely wanting to help; unbuttoning his jacket, then closing it again; trying to prop him up, then laying him down again. They were really only marking time while waiting for the ambulance to bring someone who would know what to do and have the right to do it.

The lady and her companion had also come close enough to see something of the victim over the heads and bowed backs. Then they stepped back and stood there, hesitating. The lady had a queasy feeling in the pit of her stomach, which she credited to compassion, although she mainly felt irresolute and helpless. After a while the gentleman said: "The brakes on these heavy trucks take too long to come to a full stop." This datum gave the lady some relief, and she thanked him with an appreciative glance. She did not really understand, or care to understand, the technology involved, as long as his explanation helped put this ghastly incident into perspective by reducing it to a technicality of no direct personal concern to her. Now the siren of an approaching ambulance could be heard. The speed with which it was coming to the rescue filled all the bystanders with satisfaction: how admirably society was functioning! The victim was lifted onto a stretcher and both together were then slid into the ambulance. Men in a sort of uniform were attending to him, and the inside of the vehicle, or what one could see of it, looked as clean and tidy as a hospital ward. People dispersed almost as if justified in feeling that they had just witnessed something entirely lawful and orderly.

"According to American statistics," the gentleman said, "one hundred ninety thousand people are killed there every year by cars and four hundred fifty thousand are injured."

"Do you think he's dead?" his companion asked, still on the unjustified assumption that she had experienced something unusual.

"I expect he's alive," he answered, "judging by the way they lifted him into the ambulance."

2

HOUSE AND HOME OF
THE MAN WITHOUT QUALITIES

The street where this little mishap had occurred was one of those long, winding rivers of traffic radiating outward from the heart of the city to flow through its surrounding districts and empty into the suburbs. Had the distinguished couple followed its course a little longer, they would have come upon a sight that would certainly have pleased them: an old garden, still retaining some of its eighteenth- or even seventeenth-century character, with wrought-iron railings through which one could glimpse, in passing, through the trees on a well-clipped lawn, a sort of little château with short wings, a hunting lodge or rococo love nest of times past. More specifically, it was basically seventeenth-century, while the park and the upper story showed an eighteenth-century influence and the façade had been restored and somewhat spoiled in the nineteenth century, so that the whole had something blurred about it, like a double-exposed photograph. But the general effect was such that people invariably stopped and said: "Oh!" When this dainty little white gem of a house had its windows open one could see inside the elegant serenity of a scholar's study with book-lined walls.

This dwelling and this house belonged to the man without qualities.

He was standing behind a window gazing through the fine green filter of the garden air to the brownish street beyond, and for the last ten minutes he had been ticking off on his stopwatch the passing cars, trucks, trolleys, and pedestrians, whose faces were washed out by the distance, timing everything whirling past that he could catch in the net of his eye. He was gauging their speeds, their angles, all the living forces of mass hurtling past that drew the eye to follow them like lightning, holding on, letting go, forcing the attention for a split second to resist, to snap, to leap in pursuit of the next item . . . then, after doing the arithmetic in his head for a while, he slipped the watch back into his pocket with a laugh and decided to stop all this nonsense.

If all those leaps of attention, flexings of eye muscles, fluctuations of the psyche, if all the effort it takes for a man just to hold himself upright within the flow of traffic on a busy street could be measured, he thought—as he toyed with calculating the incalculable—the grand total would surely dwarf the energy needed by Atlas to hold up the world, and one could then estimate the enormous undertaking it is nowadays merely to be a person who does nothing at all. At the moment, the man without qualities was just such a person.

And what of a man who does do something?

There are two ways to look at it, he decided:

A man going quietly about his business all day long expends far more muscular energy than an athlete who lifts a huge weight once a day. This has been proved physiologically, and so the social sum total of everybody's little everyday efforts, especially when added together, doubtless releases far more energy into the world than do rare heroic feats. This total even makes the single heroic feat look positively minuscule, like a grain of sand on a mountaintop with a megalomaniacal sense of its own importance. This thought pleased him.

But it must be added that it did not please him because he liked a solid middle-class life; on the contrary, he was merely taking a perverse pleasure in thwarting his own inclinations, which had once taken him in quite another direction. What if it is precisely the philistine who is alive with intimations of a colossally new, collective, ant-like heroism? It will be called a rationalized heroism, and greatly admired. At this point, who can tell? There were at that time hundreds of such open questions of the greatest importance, hovering in the air and burning underfoot. Time was on the move. People not yet born in those days will find it hard to believe, but even then time was racing along like a cavalry camel, just like today. But nobody knew where time was headed. And it was not always clear what was up or down, what was going forward or backward.

"No matter what you do," the man without qualities thought with a shrug, "within this mare's nest of forces at work, it doesn't make the slightest difference!" He turned away like a man who has learned to resign himself—indeed, almost like a sick man who shrinks from every strong physical contact; yet in crossing the adjacent dressing room he hit a punching bag that was hanging there a hard, sudden blow that seemed not exactly in keeping with moods of resignation or conditions of weakness.

3

EVEN A MAN WITHOUT QUALITIES HAS A FATHER WITH QUALITIES

When the man without qualities had returned from abroad sometime before, it was a certain exuberance as well as his loathing for the usual kind of apartment that led him to rent the little château, a former summer house outside the city gates that had lost its vocation when it was engulfed by the spreading city and had finally become no more than a run-down, untenanted piece of real estate waiting for its value to go up. The rent was correspondingly low, but to get everything repaired and brought up to modern standards had cost an unexpectedly large sum. It had become an adventure that resulted in driving him to ask his father for help—by no means pleasant for a man who cherishes his independence. He was thirty-two, his father sixty-nine.

The old gentleman was aghast. Not really on account of the surprise attack, though that entered into it because he detested rash conduct; nor did he mind the contribution levied on him, as he basically approved of his son's announcing an interest in domesticity and putting his life in order. But to take on a house that had to be called a château, even if only in the diminutive, affronted his sense of propriety and worried him as a baleful tempting of fate.

He himself had started out as a tutor in the houses of the high aristocracy while still working for his degree, and he had continued tutoring even as a young law clerk—not really from necessity, for *his* father was quite well off. But those carefully nurtured connections

paid off later on when he became a university lecturer and law professor, and they led to his gradually rising to become the legal adviser
to almost all the feudal nobility in the country, although by this time
he had no need of a professional sideline at all. Even long after the
fortune he had made could stand comparison with the dowry
brought him by his wife—the daughter of a powerful industrial family in the Rhineland, his son's mother, who had died all too soon—he
never allowed these connections, formed in his youth and strengthened in his prime, to lapse. Even after retiring from his practice, except for the occasional special consultation at a high fee, the old
scholar who had achieved distinction made a careful catalog of every
event concerning his circle of former patrons, extended with great
precision from fathers to sons to grandsons. No honor, wedding,
birthday, or name day passed without a letter of congratulation from
him, always a subtle blend of perfectly measured deference and
shared reminiscence. He received just as promptly in return brief
letters of acknowledgment, which thanked the dear friend and esteemed scholar. So his son was aware, from boyhood on, of the aristocratic knack for meting out almost unconsciously and with
unfailing condescension the exact degree of affability called for, and
Ulrich had always been irritated by the subservience of a man who
was, after all, a member of the intellectual aristocracy toward the
owners of horses, fields, and traditions. If his father was insensitive
on this point, it was not because of any calculation; it had been a natural instinct for him to build a great career in this way, so that he
became not only a professor and a member of academies and many
learned and official committees but was also made a Knight, and
then a Commander, the recipient of the Grand Cross of various high
orders. His Majesty finally raised him to the hereditary nobility, having already previously named him to membership in the House of
Lords. There the distinguished man joined the liberal wing, which
sometimes opposed the leading peers; yet none of his noble patrons
seemed to mind or even to wonder at this; they had never regarded
him as anything but the personified spirit of the rising middle class.
The old gentleman participated keenly in the technical work of legislation, and even if a controversial issue had him voting on the liberal
side the other side bore him no grudge; their sense of the matter was,
rather, that he had not been invited to join them. What he did in

politics was no different from what he had always done: combine his superior knowledge—which sometimes entailed working toward a gentle improvement of conditions—with the demonstration that his personal loyalty was always to be relied upon; and so he had risen quite unchanged, as his son maintained, from the role of tutor to the upper class to that of tutor to the Upper House.

When he learned about his son's acquisition of the château it struck him as a transgression against limits all the more sacred for not being legally defined, and he rebuked his son even more bitterly than on the many previous occasions he had found it necessary to do so, almost in terms of prophesying a bad end of which this purchase was the beginning. The basic premise of his life was affronted. As with many men who achieve distinction, this feeling was far from self-serving but consisted in a deep love of the general good above personal advantage—in other words, he sincerely venerated the state of affairs that had served him so well, not because it was to his advantage, but because he was in harmony and coexistent with it, and on general principles. This is a point of great importance: even a pedigreed dog searches out his place under the dining table, regardless of kicks, not because of canine abjection but out of loyalty and faith; and even coldly calculating people do not succeed half so well in life as those with properly blended temperaments who are capable of deep feeling for those persons and conditions that happen to serve their own interests.

4

IF THERE IS A SENSE OF REALITY, THERE MUST ALSO BE A SENSE OF POSSIBILITY

To pass freely through open doors, it is necessary to respect the fact that they have solid frames. This principle, by which the old professor had always lived, is simply a requisite of the sense of reality. But if there is a sense of reality, and no one will doubt that it has its justification for existing, then there must also be something we can call a sense of possibility.

Whoever has it does not say, for instance: Here this or that has happened, will happen, must happen; but he invents: Here this or that might, could, or ought to happen. If he is told that something is the way it is, he will think: Well, it could probably just as well be otherwise. So the sense of possibility could be defined outright as the ability to conceive of everything there might be just as well, and to attach no more importance to what is than to what is not. The consequences of so creative a disposition can be remarkable, and may, regrettably, often make what people admire seem wrong, and what is taboo permissible, or, also, make both a matter of indifference. Such possibilists are said to inhabit a more delicate medium, a hazy medium of mist, fantasy, daydreams, and the subjunctive mood. Children who show this tendency are dealt with firmly and warned that such persons are cranks, dreamers, weaklings, know-it-alls, or troublemakers.

Such fools are also called idealists by those who wish to praise them. But all this clearly applies only to their weak subspecies, those who cannot comprehend reality or who, in their melancholic condition, avoid it. These are people in whom the lack of a sense of reality is a real deficiency. But the possible includes not only the fantasies of people with weak nerves but also the as yet unawakened intentions of God. A possible experience or truth is not the same as an actual experience or truth minus its "reality value" but has—according to its partisans, at least—something quite divine about it, a fire, a soaring, a readiness to build and a conscious utopianism that does not shrink from reality but sees it as a project, something yet to be invented. After all, the earth is not that old, and was apparently never so ready as now to give birth to its full potential.

To try to readily distinguish the realists from the possibilists, just think of a specific sum of money. Whatever possibilities inhere in, say, a thousand dollars are surely there independently of their belonging or not belonging to someone; that the money belongs to a Mr. Me or a Mr. Thee adds no more to it than it would to a rose or a woman. But a fool will tuck the money away in his sack, say the realists, while a capable man will make it work for him. Even the beauty of a woman is undeniably enhanced or diminished by the man who possesses her. It is reality that awakens possibilities, and nothing would be more perverse than to deny it. Even so, it will always be the same possibilities, in sum or on the average, that go on repeating themselves until a man comes along who does not value the actuality above the idea. It is he who first gives the new possibilities their meaning, their direction, and he awakens them.

But such a man is far from being a simple proposition. Since his ideas, to the extent that they are not idle fantasies, are nothing but realities as yet unborn, he, too, naturally has a sense of reality; but it is a sense of possible reality, and arrives at its goal much more slowly than most people's sense of their real possibilities. He wants the forest, as it were, and the others the trees, and forest is hard to define, while trees represent so many cords of wood of a definable quality. Putting it another and perhaps better way, the man with an ordinary sense of reality is like a fish that nibbles at the hook but is unaware of the line, while the man with that sense of reality which can also be called a sense of possibility trawls a line through the water and has no idea whether there's any bait on it. His extraordinary indifference to the life snapping at the bait is matched by the risk he runs of doing utterly eccentric things. An impractical man—which he not only seems to be, but really is—will always be unreliable and unpredictable in his dealings with others. He will engage in actions that mean something else to him than to others, but he is at peace with himself about everything as long as he can make it all come together in a fine idea. Today he is still far from being consistent. He is quite capable of regarding a crime that brings harm to another person merely as a lapse to be blamed not on the criminal but on the society that produced the criminal. But it remains doubtful whether he would accept a slap in the face with the same detachment, or take it impersonally as one takes the bite of a dog. The chances are that he would first hit back and then on reflection decide that he shouldn't have. Moreover, if someone were to take away his beloved, it is most unlikely that he would today be quite ready to discount the reality of his loss and find compensation in some surprising new reaction. At present this development still has some way to go and affects the individual person as a weakness as much as a strength.

And since the possession of qualities assumes a certain pleasure in their reality, we can see how a man who cannot summon up a sense of reality even in relation to himself may suddenly, one day, come to see himself as a man without qualities.

5

ULRICH

The man without qualities whose story is being told here was called Ulrich, and Ulrich—his family name must be suppressed out of consideration for his father—had already given proof of his disposition while still on the borderline between childhood and adolescence, in a class paper on a patriotic theme. Patriotism in Austria was quite a special subject. German children simply learned to despise the wars sacred to Austrian children, and were taught to believe that French children, whose forebears were all decadent lechers, would turn tail by the thousands at the approach of a German soldier with a big beard. Exactly the same ideas, with roles reversed and other desirable adjustments, were taught to French, English, and Russian children, who also had often been on the winning side. Children are, of course, show-offs, love to play cops and robbers, and are naturally inclined to regard the X family on Y Street as the greatest family in the world if it happens to be their own. So patriotism comes easily to children. But in Austria, the situation was slightly more complicated. For although the Austrians had of course also won all the wars in their history, after most of them they had had to give something up.

This was food for thought, and Ulrich wrote in his essay on love of country that anyone who really loved his country must never regard it as the best country in the world. Then, in a flash of inspiration that seemed to him especially fine, although he was more dazzled by its splendor than he was clear about its implications, he added to this dubious statement a second, that God Himself probably preferred to speak of His world in the subjunctive of possibility (*hic dixerit quispiam*—"here someone might object that . . ."), for God creates the world and thinks while He is at it that it could just as well be done differently. Ulrich gloried in this sentence, but he must not have expressed himself clearly enough, because it caused a great uproar and nearly got him expelled from school, although nothing happened because the authorities could not make up their minds whether to regard his brazen remark as calumny against the Fatherland or as blasphemy against God. At the time, he was attending the Theresianum, that select school for the sons of the aristocracy and gentry that supplied the noblest pillars of the state. His father, furious at the humiliation brought upon him by this unrecognizable chip off the old block, packed him off abroad to a Belgian town nobody had ever heard of, where a small, inexpensive private school run on shrewd and efficient business lines did a roaring trade in black sheep. There Ulrich learned to give his disdain for other people's ideals international scope.

Since that time sixteen or seventeen years had passed, as the clouds drift across the sky. Ulrich neither regretted them nor was proud of them; he simply looked back at them in his thirty-second year with astonishment. He had meanwhile been here and there, including brief spells at home, and engaged in this or that worthwhile or futile endeavor. It has already been mentioned that he was a mathematician, and nothing more need be said of that for the moment; in every profession followed not for money but for love there comes a moment when the advancing years seem to lead to a void. After this moment had lasted for some time, Ulrich remembered that a man's native country is supposed to have the mysterious power of making the mind take root and thrive in its true soil, and so he settled there with the feeling of a hiker who sits down on a bench for eternity, but with the thought that he will be getting up again immediately.

When he set about putting his house in order, as the Bible has it, it turned out to be the experience he had actually been waiting for. He had got himself into the pleasant position of having to restore his run-down little property from scratch. He was free to follow any principle, from the stylistically pure to total recklessness, free to choose any style from the Assyrians to cubism. What should he choose? Modern man is born in a hospital and dies in a hospital, so he should make his home like a clinic. So claimed a leading architect of the moment; and another reformer of interior decoration advocated movable partitions in homes instead of fixed walls so that people would learn to trust their housemates instead of shutting themselves off from one another. Time was making a fresh start just then (it does so all the time), and a new time needs a new style. Luckily for Ulrich, the little château already had three styles superimposed on one another, setting limits on what he could do to meet all these new demands. Yet he felt quite shaken by the responsibility of having the opportunity to renovate a house, what with the threat hovering over his head of "Show me how you live and I will tell you who you are!"—which he had read repeatedly in art magazines. After intensive study of these periodicals he decided that he had best take the extension of his personality into his own hands, and began to design his future furniture himself. But no sooner had he come up with an impressively massive form than it occurred to him that something spare, and strictly functional, could just as easily be put in its place; and when he had sketched a form of reinforced concrete that looked emaciated by its own strength, he was reminded of the thin, vernal lines of a thirteen-year-old girl's body and drifted off into a reverie instead of making up his mind.

He was in that familiar state—not that the occasion mattered too seriously to him—of incoherent ideas spreading outward without a center, so characteristic of the present, and whose strange arithmetic adds up to a random proliferation of numbers without forming a unit. Finally he dreamed up only impracticable rooms, revolving rooms, kaleidoscopic interiors, adjustable scenery for the soul, and his ideas grew steadily more devoid of content. He had now finally reached the point to which he had been drawn all along. His father would have put it something like this: "Give a fellow a totally free hand and he will soon run his head into a wall out of sheer confusion." Or this: "A man who can have anything he wants will soon be at a loss as to what to wish for." Ulrich repeated these sayings to himself with great enjoyment. Their hoary wisdom appeared to him as an extraordinary new thought. For a man's possibilities, plans, and feelings must first be hedged in by prejudices, traditions, obstacles, and barriers of all sorts, like a lunatic in his straitjacket, and only then can whatever he is capable of doing have perhaps some value, substance, and staying power. Here, in fact, was an idea with incalculable implications. Now the man without qualities, who had come back to his own country, took the second step toward letting himself be shaped by the outward circumstances of life: at this point in his deliberations he simply left the furnishing of his house to the genius of his suppliers, secure in the knowledge that he could safely leave the traditions, prejudices, and limitations to them. All he did himself was to touch up the earlier lines, the dark antlers under the white vaultings of the little hall, the formal ceiling in the salon, and whatever else that seemed to him useful and convenient.

When it was all done he could shake his head and wonder: "Is this the life that is going to be mine?" What he possessed was a charming little palace; one must almost call it that because it was exactly the way one imagines such places, a tasteful residence for a resident as conceived by furniture dealers, carpet sellers, and interior decorators who were leaders in their fields. All that was missing was for this charming clockwork to be wound up, for then carriages bringing high dignitaries and noble ladies would come rolling up the driveway, and footmen would leap from their running boards to ask, looking Ulrich over dubiously: "Where is your master, my good man?"

He had returned from the moon and had promptly installed himself on the moon again.

6

LEONA, OR A CHANGE IN VIEWPOINT

Once a man has put his house in order it is time to go courting. Ulrich's girlfriend in those days was a chanteuse in a small cabaret who went by the name of Leontine. She was tall, curvaceously slender, provocatively lifeless, and he called her Leona.

He had been struck by the moist darkness of her eyes, the dolefully passionate expression on her handsome, regular, long face, and the songs full of feeling that she sang instead of risqué ones. All these old-fashioned little songs were about love, sorrow, abandonment, faithfulness, forest murmurs, and shining trout. She stood tall and lonely to the marrow on the tiny stage and patiently sang at the public with a housewife's voice, and even if something suggestive did slip in now and then, the effect was all the more ghostlike because she spelled out all the feelings of the heart, the tragic as well as the teasing, with the same wooden gestures. Ulrich was immediately reminded of old photographs or engravings of dated beauties in ancient issues of forgotten women's magazines. As he thought himself into this woman's face he saw in it a large number of small traits that simply could not be real, yet they made the face what it was. There are, of course, in all periods all kinds of countenances, but only one type will be singled out by a period's taste as its ideal image of happiness and beauty while all the other faces do their best to copy it, and with the help of fashion and hairdressers even the ugly ones manage to approximate the ideal. But there are some faces that never succeed, faces born to a strange distinction of their own, unyieldingly expressing the regal and banished ideal beauty of an earlier period. Such faces wander about like corpses of past desires in the great void of love's traffic, and the men who gaped into the vast tedium of Leontine's singing, unaware of what was happening to them, felt their nostrils twitch with feelings quite different from those aroused by brazen petite chanteuses with tango spit curls. So Ulrich decided to call her Leona and desired to possess her, as he might have wanted to possess a luxurious lion-skin rug.

But after their acquaintance had begun, Leona developed another anachronistic quality: she was an incredible glutton, and this is a vice whose heyday had passed a very long time ago. Its origin was in the craving she had suffered as a poor child for rich, costly delicacies; now, finally liberated, it had the force of an ideal that has broken out of its cage and seized power. Her father had apparently been a respectable little man who beat her every time she went out with admirers, but she did it only because there was nothing she liked better than to sit at one of those sidewalk tables in front of a little pastry shop, spooning up her sherbet while genteelly watching the passing parade. It could not be maintained that she took no interest in sex, but it could be said that she was, in this respect as in every other, downright lazy and hated to work. In her ample body every stimulus took an astonishingly long time to reach the brain, and it happened that her eyes began to glaze over for no apparent reason in midafternoon, although the night before they had been fixed on a point on the ceiling as though she were observing a fly. Or else in the midst of a complete silence she might begin to laugh at a joke she just now understood, having listened to it days ago without any sign of understanding it. When she had no particular reason to be otherwise, she was completely ladylike. She could never be made to tell how she had got into her line of work in the first place. She apparently did not quite remember this herself. But it was clear that she regarded the work of a cabaret singer as a necessary part of life, bound up with everything she had ever heard about greatness in art and artists, so that it seemed to her altogether right, uplifting, and refined to step out every evening onto a tiny stage enveloped in billowing cigar haze to sing songs known for their heartrending appeal. If things needed livening up a bit she did not, of course, shrink from slipping in something gamy now and then, but she was quite sure that the prima donna at the Imperial Opera did exactly the same.

Of course, if the art of trading for money not the entire person, as usual, but only the body must be called prostitution, then Leona occasionally engaged in prostitution. But if you have lived for nine years, as she had from the age of sixteen, on the miserable pay of the lowest dives, with your head full of the prices of costumes and underwear, the deductions, greediness, and caprices of the owners, the commissions on the food and drink of the patrons warming up to their fun, and the price of a room in the nearby hotel, day after day, including the fights and the business calculations, then everything the layman enjoys as a night on the town adds up to a profession full of its own logic, objectivity, and class codes. Prostitution especially is a matter in which it makes all the difference whether you see it from above or from below.

But even though Leona's attitude toward sexual questions was completely businesslike, she had her romantic side as well. Only with her, everything high-flown, vain, and extravagant, all her feelings of pride, envy, lust, ambition, and self-abandonment, in short, the driving forces of her personality and upward social mobility, were anchored by some freak of nature not in the so-called heart but in the gut, the eating processes—which in fact were regularly associated in earlier times and still are today, as can be seen among primitives and the carousing peasantry, who manage to express social standing and all sorts of other human distinctions at their ritual feasts by overeating, with all the side effects. At the tables in the honky-tonk where she worked, Leona did her job; but what she dreamed of was a cavalier who would sweep her away from all this by means of an affair as long as one of her engagements and allow her to sit grandly in a grand restaurant studying a grand menu. She would then have preferred to eat everything on the menu at once, yet the pain of having to choose was sweetened by the satisfaction of having a chance to show that she knew how one had to choose, how one put together an exquisite repast. Only in the choice of desserts could she let herself go, so that reversing the usual order she ended up turning dessert into an extensive second supper. With black coffee and stimulating quantities of drink Leona restored her capacities, then egged herself on through a sequence of special treats until her passion was finally quenched. Her body was now so stuffed with choice concoctions that it was ready to split at the seams. She then looked around in indolent triumph and, though never talkative, enjoyed reminiscing about the expensive delights she had consumed. She would speak of *Polmone à la Torlogna* or *Pommes à la Melville* with the studied casualness with which some people affectedly let drop the name of a prince or a lord of the same name they have met.

Because public appearances with Leona were not exactly to Ulrich's taste, he usually moved her feedings to his house, with the antlers and the stylish furniture for an audience. Here, however, she felt cheated of her social satisfaction, and whenever the man without qualities tempted her to these private excesses with the choicest fare ever supplied by a restaurant chef she felt ill-used, exactly like a woman who realizes she is not being loved for her soul. She was a beauty, she was a singer, she had no reason to hide, as several dozen men she aroused every evening would have testified. Yet this man, although he wanted to be alone with her, would not even give her the satisfaction of moaning "Leona, you devil, your ass is driving me crazy!" and licking his mustache with desire when he so much as looked at her, as she was accustomed to expect from her gallants. Although she stuck to him faithfully Leona despised him a little, and Ulrich knew it. He also knew well what was expected of him, but the days when he could have brought himself to say such things and still had a mustache were too long gone. To be no longer able to do something one used to be able to do, no matter how foolish it was, is exactly as if apoplexy has struck an arm and a leg. His eyeballs twitched when he looked at her after food and drink had gone to her head. Her beauty could be gently lifted off her. It was the beauty of that duchess whom Scheffel's Saint Ekkehard had carried over the convent's threshold, the beauty of the great lady with the falcon on her glove, the beauty of the legendary Empress Elizabeth of Austria, with her heavy crown of braids, a delight for people who were all dead. And to put it precisely, she also brought to mind the divine Juno—not the eternal and imperishable goddess herself, but the quality that a vanished or vanishing era called "Junoesque." Thus was the dream of life only loosely draped over its substance.

But Leona knew that such elegant entertainment entitled the host to something more than a guest who was merely there to be gaped at, even when he asked for nothing more; so she rose to her feet as soon as she was able and serenely broke into full-throated song. Her friend regarded such an evening as a ripped-out page, alive with all sorts of suggestions and ideas but mummified, like everything torn from its context, full of the tyranny of that eternally fixed stance that accounts for the uncanny fascination of tableaux vivants, as though life had suddenly been given a sleeping pill and was now standing there stiff, full of inner meaning, sharply outlined, and yet, in sum, making absolutely no sense at all.

7

IN A WEAK MOMENT ULRICH
ACQUIRES A NEW MISTRESS

One morning Ulrich came home looking a mess. His clothes hung in shreds, he had to wrap his bruised head in a cold towel, his watch and wallet were gone. He had no idea whether he had been robbed by the three men with whom he had got into a fight or whether a passing Samaritan had quietly lifted them while he lay unconscious on the pavement. He went to bed, and while his battered limbs, tenderly borne up and enveloped, were restored to being, he mulled over his adventure once more.

The three heads had suddenly loomed up in front of him; perhaps he had brushed up against one of the men at that late, lonely hour, for his thoughts had been wandering. But these faces were already set in anger and moved scowling into the circle of the lamplight. At that point he made a mistake. He should have instantly recoiled as if in fear, backing hard into the fellow who had stepped into him, or jabbing an elbow into his stomach, and tried to escape; he could not take on three strong men single-handed. He resisted the idea that the three faces suddenly glaring at him out of the night with rage and scorn were simply after his money, but chose to see them as a spontaneous materialization of free-floating hostility. Even as the hooligans were cursing at him he toyed with the notion that they might not perhaps be hooligans at all but citizens like himself, only slightly tipsy and freed of their inhibitions, whose attention had fastened on his passing form and who now discharged on him the hatred that is always ready and waiting for him or for any stranger, like a thunderstorm in the atmosphere. There were times when he felt something of the sort himself. Regrettably, a great many people nowadays feel antagonistic toward a great many other people. It is a basic trait of civilization that man deeply mistrusts those who are outside his own circle, so it is not only the Teuton who looks down on the Jew but also the soccer player who regards the pianist as an incomprehensible and inferior creature. Ultimately a thing exists only by virtue of its boundaries, which means by a more or less hostile act against its surroundings: without the Pope there would have been no Luther, and without the pagans no Pope, so there is no getting away from the fact that man's deepest social instinct is his antisocial instinct. Not that Ulrich thought this out in such detail, but he knew this condition of vague atmospheric hostility with which the air of our era is charged, and when it suddenly comes to a head in the form of three strangers who lash out like thunder and lightning and then afterward vanish again forever, it is almost a relief.

In any case, facing three such louts, he apparently indulged in too much thinking. For although the first one who jumped him, anticipated by Ulrich with a blow on the chin, went flying back, the second, who should have been felled in a flash immediately afterward, was only grazed by Ulrich's fist because a blow from behind with a heavy object had nearly cracked Ulrich's skull. Ulrich's knees buckled, and he felt a hand grabbing at him; recovering with that almost unnatural lucidity of the body that usually follows an initial collapse, he struck out at the tangle of strange bodies but was hammered down by fists growing larger all the time.

Satisfied with his analysis of what had gone wrong as primarily an athlete's slipup—anyone can jump too short on occasion—Ulrich, whose nerves were still in excellent shape, quietly fell asleep, with precisely the same delight in the descending spirals of fading consciousness that he had dimly felt during his defeat.

When he woke up again he checked to make sure he had not been seriously hurt, and considered his experience once again. A brawl always leaves a bad taste in the mouth, that of an overhasty intimacy, as it were, and leaving aside the fact that he had been the one attacked, Ulrich somehow felt that he had behaved improperly. But in what way? Close by those streets where there is a policeman every three hundred paces to avenge the slightest offense against law and order lie other streets that call for the same strength of body and mind as a jungle. Mankind produces Bibles and guns, tuberculosis and tuberculin. It is democratic, with kings and nobles; builds churches and, against the churches, universities; turns cloisters into barracks, but assigns field chaplains to the barracks. It naturally arms hoodlums with lead-filled rubber truncheons to beat a fellow man within an inch of his life and then provides featherbeds for the lonely, mistreated body, like the one now holding Ulrich as if filled with respect and consideration. It is the old story of the contradictions, the inconsistency, and the imperfection of life. It makes us smile or sigh. But not Ulrich. He hated this mixture of resignation and infatuation in regard to life that makes most people put up with its inconsistencies and inadequacies as a doting maiden aunt puts up with a young nephew's boorishness. Still, he did not immediately leap out of bed when it looked as though he were profiting from the disorderliness of human affairs by lingering there, because in many ways it is only a premature compromise with one's conscience at the expense of the general cause, a short circuit, an evasion into the private sphere, when one avoids doing wrong and does the right thing for one's own person instead of working to restore order in the whole scheme of things. In fact, after his involuntary experience Ulrich saw desperately little value even in doing away with guns here, with monarchs there, in making some lesser or greater progress in cutting down on stupidity and viciousness, since the measure of all that is nasty and bad instantly fills up again, as if one leg of the world always slips back when the other pushes forward. One had to find the cause of this, the secret mechanism behind it! How incomparably more important that would be than merely being a good person in accordance with obsolescent moral principles, and so in matters of morality Ulrich was attracted more to service on the general staff than to the everyday heroism of doing good.

At this point he went back in his mind to the sequel of last night's adventure. As he regained his senses from the beating he had suffered, a cab stopped at the curb; the driver tried to lift up the wounded stranger by the shoulders, and a lady was bending over him with an angelic expression on her face. This child's picture-book vision, natural to moments of consciousness rising from the depths, soon gave way to reality: the presence of a woman busying herself with him had the effect on Ulrich of a whiff of cologne, superficial and quickening, so that he also instantly knew that he had not been too badly damaged, and tried to rise to his feet with good grace. In this he did not succeed as smoothly as he would have liked, and the lady anxiously offered to drive him somewhere to get help. Ulrich asked to be taken home, and as he really still looked dazed and helpless, she granted his request. Once inside the cab, he quickly recovered his poise. He felt something maternally sensuous beside him, a fine cloud of solicitous idealism, in the warmth of which tiny crystals of doubt were already hatching, filling the air like softly falling snow and generating the fear of some impulsive act as he felt himself becoming a man again. He told his story, and the beautiful woman, only slightly younger than himself, around thirty, perhaps, lamented what brutes people were and felt terribly sorry for him.

Of course he now launched into a lively defense of his experience, which was not, as he explained to the surprised motherly beauty, to be judged solely by its outcome. The fascination of such a fight, he said, was the rare chance it offered in civilian life to perform so many varied, vigorous, yet precisely coordinated movements in response to barely perceptible signals at a speed that made conscious control quite impossible. Which is why, as every athlete knows, training must stop several days before a contest, for no other reason than that the muscles and nerves must be given time to work out the final coordination among themselves, leaving the will, purpose, and consciousness out of it and without any say in the matter. Then, at the moment of action, Ulrich went on, muscles and nerves leap and fence with the "I"; but this "I"—the whole body, the soul, the will, the central and entire person as legally distinguished from all others—is swept along by his muscles and nerves like Europa riding the Bull. Whenever it does not work out this way, if by some unlucky chance the merest ray of reflection hits this darkness, the whole effort is invariably doomed.

Ulrich had talked himself into a state of excitement. Basically, he now maintained, this experience of almost total ecstasy or transcendence of the conscious mind is akin to experiences now lost but known in the past to the mystics of all religions, which makes it a kind of contemporary substitution for an eternal human need. Even if it is not a very good substitute it is better than nothing, and boxing or similar kinds of sport that organize this principle into a rational system are therefore a species of theology, although one cannot expect this to be generally understood as yet.

Ulrich's lively speech to his companion was probably inspired, in part, by vanity, to make her forget the sorry state in which she had found him. Under these circumstances it was hard for her to tell whether he was being serious or sardonic. In any case it might have seemed quite natural, perhaps even interesting, to her that he should try to explain theology in terms of sport, since sport is a timely topic while nobody really knows anything about theology, although there were undeniably still a great many churches around. All in all, she decided that by some lucky chance she had come to the rescue of a brilliant man, even though she did wonder, betweenwhiles, whether he might have suffered a concussion.

Ulrich, who now wanted to say something comprehensible, took the opportunity to point out in passing that even love must be regarded as one of the religious and dangerous experiences, because it lifts people out of the arms of reason and sets them afloat with no ground under their feet.

True enough, the lady said, but sports are so rough.

So they are, Ulrich hastened to concur, sports are rough. One could say they are the precipitations of a most finely dispersed general hostility, which is deflected into athletic games. Of course, one could also say the opposite: sports bring people together, promote the team spirit and all that—which basically proves only that brutality and love are no farther apart than one wing of a big, colorful, silent bird is from the other.

He had put the emphasis on the wings and on that bright, mute bird—a notion that did not make much sense but was charged with some of that vast sensuality with which life simultaneously satisfies all the rival contradictions in its measureless body. He now noticed that his neighbor had no idea what he was talking about, and that the soft snowfall she was diffusing inside the cab had grown thicker. So he turned to face her completely and asked whether she was perhaps repelled by such talk of physical matters? The doings of the body, he went on, were really too much in fashion, and they included a feeling of horror: because a body in perfect training has the upper hand, it responds automatically in its finely tuned way to every stimulus, so surely that its owner is left with an uncanny sensation of having to watch helplessly as his character runs off with some part of his anatomy, as it were.

It indeed seemed that this question touched the young woman deeply; she appeared excited by his words, was breathing hard, and cautiously moved away a little. A mechanism similar to the one he had just described—heavy breathing, a flushed skin, a stronger beating of the heart, and perhaps some other symptoms as well—seemed to have been set off inside her. But just then the cab stopped at Ulrich's gate, and there was only time for him to ask with a smile for his rescuer's address so that he could thank her properly. To his astonishment, this favor was not granted. And so the black wrought-iron gate banged shut behind a baffled stranger. What she presumably saw were the trees of an old park rising tall and dark in the light of electric streetlights and lamps going on in windows, and the low wings of a boudoir-like, dainty little château spreading out on a well-shorn emerald lawn, and a glimpse of an interior hung with pictures and lined with colorful bookshelves, as her erstwhile companion disappeared into an unexpectedly delightful setting.

So concluded the events of last night, and as Ulrich was still thinking how unpleasant it would have been if he had had to spend more time on yet another of those love affairs he had long since grown tired of, a lady was announced who would not give her name and who now entered his room heavily veiled. It was she herself, who had not wanted to give him her name and address, but had now come in person to carry on the adventure in her own romantically charitable fashion, on the pretext of being concerned about his health.

Two weeks later Bonadea had been his mistress for fourteen days.

8

KAKANIA

At the age when one still attaches great importance to everything connected with tailors and barbers and enjoys looking in the mirror, one also imagines a place where one would like to spend one's life, or at least where it would be smart to stay even if one did not care for it too much personally. For some time now such an obsessive daydream has been a kind of super-American city where everyone rushes about, or stands still, with a stopwatch in hand. Air and earth form an anthill traversed, level upon level, by roads live with traffic. Air trains, ground trains, underground trains, people mailed through tubes special-delivery, and chains of cars race along horizontally, while express elevators pump masses of people vertically from one traffic level to another; at the junctions, people leap from one vehicle to the next, instantly sucked in and snatched away by the rhythm of it, which makes a syncope, a pause, a little gap of twenty seconds during which a word might be hastily exchanged with someone else. Questions and answers synchronize like meshing gears; everyone has only certain fixed tasks to do; professions are located in special areas and organized by group; meals are taken on the run. Other parts of the city are centers of entertainment, while still others contain the towers where one finds wife, family, phonograph, and soul. Tension and relaxation, activity and love, are precisely timed and weighed on the basis of exhaustive laboratory studies. If anything goes wrong in any of these activities the whole thing is simply dropped; something else or sometimes a better way will be found or someone else will find the way one has missed; there's nothing wrong with that, while on the other hand nothing is so wasteful of the social energies as the presumption that an individual is called upon to cling for all he is worth to some specific personal goal. In a community coursed through by energies every road leads to a worthwhile goal, provided one doesn't hesitate or reflect too long. Targets are short-term, but since life is short too, results are maximized, which is all people need to be happy, because the soul is formed by what you accomplish, whereas what you desire without achieving it merely warps the soul. Happiness depends very little on what we want, but only on achieving whatever it is. Besides, zoology teaches that a number of flawed individuals can often add up to a brilliant social unit.

It is by no means certain that this is the way it has to be, but such ideas belong to those travel fantasies reflecting our sense of incessant movement that carries us along. These fantasies are superficial, restless, and brief. God knows what will really happen. Presumably it is up to us to make a new start at any given moment and come up with a plan for us all. If all that high-speed business doesn't suit us, let's do something else! For instance, something quite slow-moving, with a veiled, billowing, sea-slug-like, mysterious happiness and the deep, cow-eyed gaze the ancient Greeks admired. But that is not how it really is; we are at the mercy of our condition. We travel in it day and night, doing whatever else we do, shaving, eating, making love, reading books, working at our jobs, as though those four walls around us were standing still; but the uncanny fact is that those walls are moving along without our noticing it, casting their rails ahead like long, groping, twisted antennae, going we don't know where. Besides, we would like to think of ourselves as having a hand in making our time what it is. It is a very uncertain part to play, and sometimes, looking out the window after a fairly long pause, we find that the landscape has changed. What flies past flies past, it can't be helped, but with all our devotion to our role an uneasy feeling grows on us that we have traveled past our goal or got on a wrong track. Then one day the violent need is there: Get off the train! Jump clear! A homesickness, a longing to be stopped, to cease evolving, to stay put, to return to the point before the thrown switch put us on the wrong track. And in the good old days when the Austrian Empire still existed, one could in such a case get off the train of time, get on an ordinary train of an ordinary railroad, and travel back to one's home.

There, in Kakania, that state since vanished that no one understood, in many ways an exemplary state, though unappreciated, there was a tempo too, but not too much tempo. Whenever one thought of that country from someplace abroad, the memory that hovered before one's eyes was of white, wide, prosperous-looking roads dating from the era of foot marches and mail coaches, roads that crisscrossed the country in every direction like rivers of order, like ribbons of bright military twill, the paper-white arm of the administration holding all the provinces in its embrace. And what provinces they were! Glaciers and sea, Karst limestone and Bohemian fields of grain, nights on the Adriatic chirping with restless cicadas, and Slovakian villages where the smoke rose from chimneys as from upturned nostrils while the village cowered between two small hills as if the earth had parted its lips to warm its child between them. Of course cars rolled on these roads too, but not too many! The conquest of the air was being prepared here too, but not too intensively. A ship would now and then be sent off to South America or East Asia, but not too often. There was no ambition for world markets or world power. Here at the very center of Europe, where the world's old axes crossed, words such as "colony" and "overseas" sounded like something quite untried and remote. There was some show of luxury, but by no means as in such overrefined ways as the French. People went in for sports, but not as fanatically as the English. Ruinous sums of money were spent on the army, but only just enough to secure its position as the second-weakest among the great powers. The capital, too, was somewhat smaller than all the other biggest cities of the world, but considerably bigger than a mere big city. And the country's administration was conducted in an enlightened, unobtrusive manner, with all sharp edges cautiously smoothed over, by the best bureaucracy in Europe, which could be faulted only in that it regarded genius, and any brilliant individual initiative not backed by noble birth or official status, as insolent and presumptuous. But then, who welcomes interference from unqualified outsiders? And in Kakania, at least, it would only happen that a genius would be regarded as a lout, but never was a mere lout taken—as happens elsewhere—for a genius.

All in all, how many amazing things might be said about this vanished Kakania! Everything and every person in it, for instance, bore the label of *kaiserlich-königlich* (Imperial-Royal) or *kaiserlich* und *königlich* (Imperial *and* Royal), abbreviated as "k.k." or "k.&k.," but to be sure which institutions and which persons were to be designated by "k.k." and which by "k.&k." required the mastery of a secret science. On paper it was called the Austro-Hungarian Monarchy, but in conversation it was called Austria, a name solemnly abjured officially while stubbornly retained emotionally, just to show that feelings are quite as important as constitutional law and that regulations are one thing but real life is something else entirely. Liberal in its constitution, it was administered clerically. The government was clerical, but everyday life was liberal. All citizens were equal before the law, but not everyone was a citizen. There was a Parliament, which asserted its freedom so forcefully that it was usually kept shut; there was also an Emergency Powers Act that enabled the government to get along without Parliament, but then, when everyone had happily settled for absolutism, the Crown decreed that it was time to go back to parliamentary rule. The country was full of such goings-on, among them the sort of nationalist movements that rightly attracted so much attention in Europe and are so thoroughly misunderstood today. They were so violent that they jammed the machinery of government and brought it to a dead stop several times a year, but in the intervals and during the deadlocks people got along perfectly well and acted as if nothing had happened. And in fact, nothing really *had* happened. It was only that everyone's natural resentment of everyone else's efforts to get ahead, a resentment we all feel nowadays, had crystallized earlier in Kakania, where it can be said to have assumed the form of a sublimated ceremonial rite, which could have had a great future had its development not been cut prematurely short by a catastrophe.

For it was not only the resentment of one's fellow citizens that had become intensified there into a strong sense of community; even the lack of faith in oneself and one's own fate took on the character of a deep self-certainty. In this country one acted—sometimes to the highest degree of passion and its consequences—differently from the way one thought, or one thought differently from the way one acted. Uninitiated observers have mistaken this for charm, or even for a weakness of what they thought to be the Austrian character. But they were wrong; it is always wrong to explain what happens in a country by the character of its inhabitants. For the inhabitant of a country has at least nine characters: a professional, a national, a civic, a class, a geographic, a sexual, a conscious, an unconscious, and possibly even a private character to boot. He unites them in himself, but they dissolve him, so that he is really nothing more than a small basin hollowed out by these many streamlets that trickle into it and drain out of it again, to join other such rills in filling some other basin. Which is why every inhabitant of the earth also has a tenth character that is nothing else than the passive fantasy of spaces yet unfilled. This permits a person all but one thing: to take seriously what his at least nine other characters do and what happens to them; in other words, it prevents precisely what should be his true fulfillment. This interior space—admittedly hard to describe—is of a different shade and shape in Italy from what it is in England, because everything that stands out in relief against it is of a different shade and shape; and yet it is in both places the same: an empty, invisible space, with reality standing inside it like a child's toy town deserted by the imagination.

Insofar as this can become visible to all eyes it had happened in Kakania, making Kakania, unbeknownst to the world, the most progressive state of all; a state just barely able to go along with itself. One enjoyed a negative freedom there, always with the sense of insufficient grounds for one's own existence, and lapped around by the great fantasy of all that had not happened or at least not yet happened irrevocably as by the breath of those oceans from which mankind had once emerged.

Events that might be regarded as momentous elsewhere were here introduced with a casual *"Es ist passiert . . ."*—a peculiar form of "it happened" unknown elsewhere in German or any other language, whose breath could transform facts and blows of fate into something as light as thistledown or thought. Perhaps, despite so much that can be said against it, Kakania was, after all, a country for geniuses; which is probably what brought it to its ruin.

9

THE FIRST OF THREE ATTEMPTS TO BECOME A GREAT MAN

This man who had returned could not remember any time in his life when he had not been fired with the will to become a great man; it was a desire Ulrich seemed to have been born with. Such a dream may of course betray vanity and stupidity, but it is no less true that it is a fine and proper ambition without which there probably would not be very many great men in the world.

The trouble was that he knew neither how to become one nor what a great man is. In his school days his model had been Napoleon, partly because of a boy's natural admiration for the criminal and partly because his teachers had made a point of calling this tyrant, who had tried to turn Europe upside down, the greatest evildoer in history. This led directly to Ulrich's joining the cavalry as an ensign as soon as he was able to escape from school. The chances are that even then, had anyone asked him why he chose this profession, he would no longer have replied: "In order to become a tyrant." But such wishes are Jesuits: Napoleon's genius began to develop only after he became a general. But how could Ulrich, as an ensign, have convinced his colonel that becoming a general was the necessary next step for him? Even at squadron drill it seemed often enough that he and the colonel did not see eye-to-eye. Even so, Ulrich would not have cursed the parade ground—that peaceful common on which pretensions are indistinguishable from vocations—had he not been so ambitious. Pacifist euphemisms such as "educating the people to bear arms" meant nothing to him in those days; instead, he surrendered himself to an impassioned nostalgia for heroic conditions of lordliness, power, and pride. He rode in steeplechases, fought duels, and recognized only three kinds of people: officers, women, and civilians, the last-named a physically underdeveloped and spiritually contemptible class of humanity whose wives and daughters were the legitimate prey of army officers. He indulged in a splendid pessimism: it seemed to him that because the soldier's profession was a sharp, white-hot instrument, this instrument must be used to sear and cut the world for its salvation.

As luck would have it he came to no harm, but one day he made a discovery. At a social gathering he had a slight misunderstanding with a noted financier, which Ulrich was going to clear up in his usual dashing style; but it turned out that there are men in civilian clothes also who know how to protect their women. The financier had a word with the War Minister, whom he knew personally, and soon thereafter Ulrich had a lengthy interview with his colonel, in which the difference between an archduke and a simple army officer was made clear to him. From then on the profession of warrior lost its charm for him. He had expected to find himself on a stage of world-shaking adventures with himself as hero, but now saw nothing but a drunken young man shouting on a wide, empty square, answered only by the paving stones. When he realized this, he took his leave of this thankless career, in which he had just been made lieutenant, and quit the service.

10

The second attempt. Notes toward a morality for the man without qualities

But when Ulrich switched from the cavalry to civil engineering, he was merely swapping horses. The new horse had steel legs and ran ten times faster.

In Goethe's world the clattering of looms was still considered a disturbing noise. In Ulrich's time people were just beginning to discover the music of machine shops, steam hammers, and factory sirens. One must not believe that people were quick to notice that a skyscraper is bigger than a man on a horse. On the contrary, even today those who want to make an impression will mount not a skyscraper but a high horse; they are swift like the wind and sharp-sighted, not like a giant refractor but like an eagle. Their feelings have not yet learned to make use of their intellect; the difference in development between these two faculties is almost as great as that between the vermiform appendix and the cerebral cortex. So it was no slight advantage to realize, as Ulrich did when barely out of his teens, that a man's conduct with respect to what seem to him the Higher Things in life is far more old-fashioned than his machines are.

From the moment Ulrich set foot in engineering school, he was feverishly partisan. Who still needed the Apollo Belvedere when he had the new forms of a turbodynamo or the rhythmic movements of a steam engine's pistons before his eyes! Who could still be captivated by the thousand years of chatter about the meaning of good and evil when it turns out that they are not constants at all but functional values, so that the goodness of works depends on historical circumstances, while human goodness depends on the psychotechnical skills with which people's qualities are exploited? Looked at from a technical point of view, the world is simply ridiculous: impractical in all that concerns human relations, and extremely uneconomic and imprecise in its methods; anyone accustomed to solving his problems with a slide rule cannot take seriously a good half of the assertions people make. The slide rule is two systems of numbers and lines combined with incredible ingenuity; the slide rule is two white-enameled sticks of flat trapezoidal cross section that glide past each other, with whose help the most complex problems can be solved in an instant without needlessly losing a thought; the slide rule is a small symbol carried in one's breast pocket and sensed as a hard white line over one's heart. If you own a slide rule and someone comes along with big statements or great emotions, you say: "Just a moment, please—let's first work out the margin for error and the most-probable values."

This was without doubt a powerful view of what it meant to be an engineer. It could serve as the frame for a charming future self-portrait, showing a man with resolute features, a shag pipe clenched between his teeth, a tweed cap on his head, traveling in superb riding boots between Cape Town and Canada on daring missions for his business. Between trips there would always be time to draw on his technical knowledge for advice on world organization and management, or time to formulate aphorisms like the one by Emerson that ought to hang over every workbench: "Mankind walks the earth as a prophecy of the future, and all its deeds are tests and experiments, for every deed can be surpassed by the next." Actually, Ulrich had written this himself, putting together several of Emerson's pronouncements.

It is hard to say why engineers don't quite live up to this vision. Why, for instance, do they so often wear a watch chain slung on a steep, lopsided curve from the vest pocket to a button higher up, or across the stomach in one high and two low loops, as if it were a metrical foot in a poem? Why do they favor tiepins topped with stag's teeth or tiny horseshoes? Why do they wear suits constructed like the early stages of the automobile? And why, finally, do they never speak of anything but their profession, or if they do speak of something else, why do they have that peculiar, stiff, remote, superficial manner that never goes deeper inside than the epiglottis? Of course this is not true of all of them, far from it, but it is true of many, and it was true of all those Ulrich met the first time he went to work in a factory office, and it was true of those he met the second time. They all turned out to be men firmly tied to their drawing boards, who loved their profession and were wonderfully efficient at it. But any suggestion that they might apply their daring ideas to themselves instead of to their machines would have taken them aback, much as if they had been asked to use a hammer for the unnatural purpose of killing a man.

And so Ulrich's second and more mature attempt to become a man of stature, by way of technology, came quickly to an end.

11

THE MOST IMPORTANT ATTEMPT OF ALL

Thinking over his time up to that point today, Ulrich might shake his head in wonder, as if someone were to tell him about his previous incarnations; but his third effort was different. An engineer may understandably become absorbed in his specialty instead of giving himself up to the freedom and vastness of the world of thought, even though his machines are delivered to the ends of the earth, for he is no more called upon to adapt the daring and innovative soul of his technology to his private soul than a machine can be expected to apply to itself the differential calculus upon which it is based. But the same cannot be said of mathematics, which is the new method of thought itself, the mind itself, the very wellspring of the times and the primal source of an incredible transformation.

If it is the fulfillment of man's primordial dreams to be able to fly, travel with the fish, drill our way beneath the bodies of towering mountains, send messages with godlike speed, see the invisible and hear the distant speak, hear the voices of the dead, be miraculously cured while asleep, see with our own eyes how we will look twenty years after our death, learn in flickering nights thousands of things above and below this earth no one ever knew before; if light, warmth, power, pleasure, comforts, are man's primordial dreams, then present-day research is not only science but sorcery, spells woven from the highest powers of heart and brain, forcing God to open one fold after another of his cloak; a religion whose dogma is permeated and sustained by the hard, courageous, flexible, razor-cold, razor-keen logic of mathematics.

Of course there is no denying that all these primordial dreams appear, in the opinion of nonmathematicians, to have been suddenly realized in a form quite different from the original fantasy. Baron Münchhausen's post horn was more beautiful than our canned music, the Seven-League Boots more beautiful than a car, Oberon's kingdom lovelier than a railway tunnel, the magic root of the mandrake better than a telegraphed image, eating of one's mother's heart and then understanding birds more beautiful than an ethologic study of a bird's vocalizing. We have gained reality and lost dream. No more lounging under a tree and peering at the sky between one's big and second toes; there's work to be done. To be efficient, one cannot be hungry and dreamy but must eat steak and keep moving. It is exactly as though the old, inefficient breed of humanity had fallen asleep on an anthill and found, when the new breed awoke, that the ants had crept into its bloodstream, making it move frantically ever since, unable to shake off that rotten feeling of antlike industry. There is really no need to belabor the point, since it is obvious to most of us these days that mathematics has taken possession, like a demon, of every aspect of our lives. Most of us may not believe in the story of a Devil to whom one can sell one's soul, but those who must know something about the soul (considering that as clergymen, historians, and artists they draw a good income from it) all testify that the soul has been destroyed by mathematics and that mathematics is the source of an evil intelligence that while making man the lord of the earth has also made him the slave of his machines. The inner drought, the dreadful blend of acuity in matters of detail and indifference toward the whole, man's monstrous abandonment in a desert of details, his restlessness, malice, unsurpassed callousness, money-grubbing, coldness, and violence, all so characteristic of our times, are by these accounts solely the consequence of damage done to the soul by keen logical thinking! Even back when Ulrich first turned to mathematics there were already those who predicted the collapse of European civilization because no human faith, no love, no simplicity, no goodness, dwelt any longer in man. These people had all, typically, been poor mathematicians as young people and at school. This later put them in a position to prove that mathematics, the mother of natural science and grandmother of technology, was also the primordial mother of the spirit that eventually gave rise to poison gas and warplanes.

The only people who actually lived in ignorance of these dangers were the mathematicians themselves and their disciples the scientists, whose souls were as unaffected by all this as if they were racing cyclists pedaling away for dear life, blind to everything in the world except the back wheel of the rider ahead of them. But one thing, on the other hand, could safely be said about Ulrich: he loved mathematics because of the kind of people who could not endure it. He was in love with science not so much on scientific as on human grounds. He saw that in all the problems that come within its orbit, science thinks differently from the laity. If we translate "scientific outlook" into "view of life," "hypothesis" into "attempt," and "truth" into "action," then there would be no notable scientist or mathematician whose life's work, in courage and revolutionary impact, did not far outmatch the greatest deeds in history. The man has not yet been born who could say to his followers: "You may steal, kill, fornicate— our teaching is so strong that it will transform the cesspool of your sins into clear, sparkling mountain streams." But in science it happens every few years that something till then held to be in error suddenly revolutionizes the field, or that some dim and disdained idea becomes the ruler of a new realm of thought. Such events are not merely upheavals but lead us upward like a Jacob's ladder. The life of science is as strong and carefree and glorious as a fairy tale. And Ulrich felt: People simply don't realize it, they have no idea how much thinking can be done already; if they could be taught to think a new way, they would change their lives.

Now, it is a question whether the world is so topsy-turvy that it always needs turning around. The world itself has always had a twofold answer to this question. From the beginning of the world most people, in their youth, have been in favor of turning the world around. They have always felt it was ridiculous the way their elders clung to convention and thought with the heart—a lump of flesh— instead of with the brain. To the young, the moral stupidity of their elders has always looked like the same inability to make new connections that constitutes ordinary intellectual stupidity, and their own natural morality has always been one of achievement, heroism, and change. But they have no sooner reached their years of accomplishment than they no longer remember this, and even less do they want to be reminded of it. Which is why many of those for whom mathematics or science is a true profession are bound to disapprove of anyone taking up science for reasons such as Ulrich's.

Nevertheless, experts judged his achievements in this third profession, in the few years since he had taken it up, to have been not inconsiderable.

12

THE LADY WHOSE LOVE ULRICH WON AFTER A CONVERSATION ABOUT SPORTS AND MYSTICISM

It turned out that Bonadea, too, yearned for great ideas.

Bonadea was the lady who had rescued Ulrich on the night of his ill-fated boxing match and who had visited him the next morning shrouded in veils. He had baptized her Bonadea, "the Good Goddess," for the way she had entered his life and also after that goddess of chastity whose ancient temple in Rome had become, by an odd reversal of fate, a center for all the vices. She did not know that story. She was pleased at the euphonious nickname Ulrich had conferred on her, and wore it on her visits to him as if it were a sumptuously embroidered housedress. "Am I really your good goddess," she asked, "your own *bona dea*?" And the correct pronunciation of these two words demanded that she throw her arms around his neck and lift her face up to his with a gaze full of feeling.

She was the wife of a prominent man and the fond mother of two handsome boys. Her favorite phrase was "highly respectable," applied to people, messengers, shops, and feelings, when she wanted to praise them. She could utter the words "truth, goodness, and beauty" as often and as casually as someone else might say "Thursday." Her intellectual needs were most deeply satisfied by her concept of a peaceful, idyllic life in the bosom of her family, its radiant happiness toned down to a gentle lamplight by the hovering presence far beneath of the dark realm of "Lead me not into temptation." She had only one fault: she could become inordinately aroused at the mere sight of a man. She was not lustful; she was sensual, as other people have other afflictions, for instance suffering from sweaty hands or blushing too readily. It was something she had apparently been born with and could never do anything to curb. Meeting Ulrich in circumstances so like a novel, so firing to the imagination, she had been destined from the first moment to fall prey to a passion that began as sympathy, then led, after a brief though intense inner struggle, to forbidden intimacies, and continued as a seesaw between pangs of sinful desire and pangs of remorse.

But Ulrich was only the most recent of God knows how many men in her life. Once they have caught on, men tend to treat such nymphomaniac women no better than morons for whom the cheapest tricks are good enough and who can be tripped up in the same way time and again. The tenderer feelings of male passion are something like the snarling of a jaguar over fresh meat—he doesn't like to be disturbed. Consequently, Bonadea often led a double life, like any other respectable citizen who, in the dark interstices of his consciousness, is a train robber. Whenever no one was holding her in his arms, this quiet, regal woman was oppressed by self-hatred for the lies and humiliations she had to risk in order to be held in someone's arms. When her senses were aroused she was subdued and gentle; her blend of rapture and tears, crude directness shadowed by predictable remorse, mania bolting in panic from the lurking depression that threatened, heightened her attraction, arousing excitement much like a ceaseless tattoo on a drum hung with black crêpe. But between lapses, in her intervals of calm, in the remorse that made her aware of her helplessness, she was full of the claims of respectability, and this made life with her far from simple. A man was expected to be truthful and kind, sympathetic toward every misfortune, devoted to the Imperial House, respectful toward everything respected, and, morally, to conduct himself with all the delicacy of a visitor at a sickbed.

Not that it made any difference if these expectations were disappointed. To justify her conduct, she had made up a tale of how her husband had caused her unfortunate condition in the innocent early years of their marriage. This husband, considerably older and physically bigger than she, was cast as a ruthless monster in the sad, portentous account she gave to Ulrich during the very first hours of their new love. It was only sometime afterward that he discovered that the man was a well-known and respected judge, of high professional competence, who was also given to the form of hunting that consists in the harmless gunning down of wild game; a welcome figure at various pubs and clubs frequented by hunters and lawyers, where male topics rather than art or love were the subject of conversation. The only failing of this rather unaffected, good-natured, and jovial man was that he was married to his wife, so that he found himself more often than other men engaged with her in what is referred to in the language of the law courts as a casual encounter. The psychological effect of submitting for years to a man she had married from motives of the head rather than the heart had fostered in Bonadea the illusion that she was physically overexcitable, and fantasy made it almost independent of her consciousness. She was chained to this man, so favored by circumstance, by some compulsion she could not fathom; she despised him for her own spinelessness and felt spineless in order to despise him; she was unfaithful to him as a means of escape but always chose the most awkward moments to speak of him or of their children; and she was never able to let go of him completely. Like many unhappy wives, she ended up with an attitude—in an otherwise rather unstable personal environment—determined by resentment of her solidly rooted husband, and she carried her conflict with him into every new experience that was supposed to free her from him.

What could a man do to silence her lamentations but transport her with all possible speed from the depressive to the manic state? She would promptly charge the doer of this deed with taking advantage of her weakness and with being devoid of all finer sensibilities, but her affliction laid a veil of moist tenderness over her eyes when she, as she put it with scientific detachment, "inclined" to this man.

13

A RACEHORSE OF GENIUS CRYSTALLIZES THE RECOGNITION OF BEING A MAN WITHOUT QUALITIES

It is not immaterial that Ulrich could say to himself that he had accomplished something in his field. His work had in fact brought him recognition. Admiration would have been too much to ask, for even in the realm of truth, admiration is reserved for older scholars on whom it depends whether or not one gets that professorship or professorial chair. Strictly speaking, he had remained "promising," which is what, in the Republic of Learning, they call the republicans, that is, those who imagine that they should give all their energies to their work rather than reserve a large part of them for getting ahead. They forget that individual achievement is limited, while on the other hand everybody wants to get ahead, and they neglect the social duty of climbing, which means beginning as a climber so as to become in turn a prop and stay to other climbers on the way up.

And one day Ulrich stopped wanting to be promising. The time had come when people were starting to speak of genius on the soccer field or in the boxing ring, although there would still be at most only one genius of a halfback or great tennis-court tactician for every ten or so explorers, tenors, or writers of genius who cropped up in the papers. The new spirit was not yet quite sure of itself. But just then Ulrich suddenly read somewhere, like a premonitory breath of ripening summer, the expression "the racehorse of genius." It stood in the report of a sensational racing success, and the author was probably not aware of the full magnitude of the inspiration his pen owed to the communal spirit. But Ulrich instantly grasped the fateful connection between his entire career and this genius among racehorses. For the horse has, of course, always been sacred to the cavalry, and as a youth Ulrich had hardly ever heard talk in barracks of anything but horses and women. He had fled from this to become a great man, only to find that when as the result of his varied exertions he perhaps could have felt within reach of his goal, the horse had beaten him to it.

No doubt this has a certain temporal justification, since it is not so very long ago that our idea of an admirable masculine spirit was exemplified by a person whose courage was moral courage, whose strength was the strength of a conviction, whose steadfastness was of the heart and of virtue, and who regarded speed as childish, feinting as not permissible, and agility and verve as contrary to dignity. Ultimately no such person could be found alive, except on the faculty of prep schools and in all sorts of literary pronouncements; he had become an ideological phantasm, and life had to seek a new image of manliness. As it looked around, it found that the tricks and dodges of an inventive mind working on logical calculations do not really differ all that much from the fighting moves of a well-trained body. There is a general fighting ability that is made cold and calculating by obstacles and openings, whether one is trained to search out the vulnerable spot in a problem or in a bodily opponent. A psychotechnical analysis of a great thinker and a champion boxer would probably show their cunning, courage, precision and technique, and the speed of their reactions in their respective fields to be the same. It is probably a safe assumption that the qualities and skills by which they succeed do not differ from those of a famous steeplechaser—for one should never underestimate how many major qualities are bought into play in clearing a hedge. But on top of this, a horse and a boxer have an advantage over a great mind in that their performance and rank can be objectively measured, so that the best of them is really acknowledged as the best. This is why sports and strictly objective criteria have deservedly come to the forefront, displacing such obsolete concepts as genius and human greatness.

As for Ulrich, he must even be credited with being a few years ahead of his time on this point. He had conducted his scientific work in precisely this spirit of improving the record by a victory, an inch or a pound. He meant his mind to prove itself keen and strong, and it had performed the work of the strong. This pleasure in the power of the mind was a state of expectancy, a warlike game, a kind of vague masterful claim on the future. What this power would enable him to accomplish was an open question; he could do everything with it or nothing, become a savior of mankind or a criminal. This is probably the nature of the mind that provides the world of machines and discoveries its constant flow of new supplies. Ulrich had regarded science as a preparation, a toughening, and a kind of training. If it turned out that this way of thinking was too dry, hard, narrow, and blinkered, it would have to be accepted, like the grimace of extreme exertion and tension that show on the face when the body and the will are being pushed to great accomplishments. He had for years gladly endured spiritual hardship. He despised those who could not follow Nietzsche's dictum to "let the soul starve for the truth's sake," those who turn back, the fainthearted, the softheaded who comfort their souls with spiritual nonsense and feed it—because reason allegedly gives it stones instead of bread—on religious, metaphysical, and fictitious pap, like rolls soaked in milk. It was his opinion that in this century, together with everything human, one was on an expedition, which required as a matter of pride that one cut off all useless questions with a "not yet," and that life be conducted on a provisional basis, but with awareness of the goal to be reached by those who will come after. The fact is, science has developed a concept of hard, sober intelligence that makes the old metaphysical and moral ideas of the human race simply intolerable, even though all it has to put in their place is the hope that a distant day will come when a race of intellectual conquerors will descend into the valleys of spiritual fruitfulness.

But this works only so long as the eye is not forced to abandon visionary distance for present nearness, or made to read a statement that in the meantime a racehorse has become a genius. The next morning Ulrich got out of bed on his left foot and fished halfheartedly for his slipper with his right. That had been in another city and street from where he was now, but only a few weeks ago. On the brown, gleaming asphalt under his windows cars were already speeding past. The pure morning air was filling up with the sourness of the day, and as the milky light filtered through the curtains it seemed to him unspeakably absurd to start bending his naked body forward and backward as usual, to strain his abdominal muscles to push it up off the ground and lower it again, and finally batter away at a punching bag with his fists, as so many people do at this hour before going to the office. One hour daily is a twelfth of a day's conscious life, enough to keep a trained body in the condition of a panther alert for any adventure; but this hour is sacrificed for a senseless expectation, because the adventures worthy of such preparation never come along. The same is true of love, for which people get prepared in the most monstrous fashion. Finally, Ulrich realized that even in science he was like a man who has climbed one mountain range after another without ever seeing a goal. He had now acquired bits and pieces of a new way to think and feel, but the glimpse of the New, so vivid at first, had been lost amid the ever-proliferating details, and if he had once thought that he was drinking from the fountain of life, he had now drained almost all his expectations to the last drop. At this point he quit, right in the middle of an important and promising piece of work. He now saw his colleagues partly as relentless, obsessive public prosecutors and security chiefs of logic, and partly as opium eaters, addicts of some strange pale drug that filled their world with visions of numbers and abstract relations. "God help me," he thought, "surely I never could have meant to spend all my life as a mathematician?"

But what had he really meant to do? At this point he could have turned only to philosophy. But the condition philosophy found itself in at the time reminded him of the oxhide being cut into strips in the story of Dido, even as it remained highly doubtful that these strips would ever measure out a kingdom, and what was new in philosophy resembled what he had been doing himself and held no attraction for him. All he could say was that he now felt further removed from what he had really wanted to be than he had in his youth, if indeed he had ever known what it was. With wonderful clarity he saw in himself all the abilities and qualities favored by his time—except for the ability to earn his living, which was not necessary—but he had lost the capacity to apply them. And since, now that genius is attributed to soccer players and horses, a man can save himself only by the use he makes of genius, he resolved to take a year's leave of absence from his life in order to seek an appropriate application for his abilities.

14

Boyhood friends

Since his return, Ulrich had already been a few times to see his friends Walter and Clarisse, for these two had not left town, although it was summer, and he had not seen them for a number of years. Whenever he got there, they were playing the piano together. It was understood that they would take no notice of him until they had finished the piece; this time it was Beethoven's jubilant "Ode to Joy." The millions sank, as Nietzsche describes it, awestruck in the dust; hostile boundaries shattered, the gospel of world harmony reconciled and unified the sundered; they had unlearned walking and talking and were about to fly off, dancing, into the air. Faces flushed, bodies hunched, their heads jerked up and down while splayed claws banged away at the mass of sound rearing up under them. Something unfathomable was going on: a balloon, wavering in outline as it filled up with hot emotion, was swelling to the bursting point, and from the excited fingertips, the nervously wrinkling foreheads, the twitching bodies, again and again surges of fresh feeling poured into this awesome private tumult. How often they had been through this!

Ulrich could never stand this piano, always open and savagely baring its teeth, this fat-lipped, short-legged idol, a cross between a dachshund and a bulldog, that had taken over his friends' lives even as far as the pictures on their walls and the spindly design of their arty reproduction furniture; even the fact that there was no live-in maid, but only a woman who came in daily to cook and clean, was part of it. Beyond the windows of this household the slopes of vineyards with clumps of old trees and crooked shacks rose as far as the sweeping forests beyond; but close in, everything was untidy, bare, scattered, and corroded, as it is wherever the edges of big cities push forward into the countryside. The arc that spanned such a foreground and the lovely distance was created by the instrument; gleaming black, it sent fiery pillars of tenderness and heroism out through the walls, even if these pillars, pulverized into a fine ash of sound, collapsed only a hundred yards away without ever reaching the hillside with the fir trees where the tavern stood halfway up the path leading to the forest. But the house was able to make the piano resound, forming one of those megaphones through which the soul cries into the cosmos like a rutting stag, answered only by the same, competing cries of thousands of other lonely souls roaring into the cosmos. Ulrich's strong position in this household rested on his insistence that music represented a failure of the will and a confusion of the mind; he spoke of it with less respect than he actually felt. Since at that time music was, for Walter and Clarisse, the source of their keenest hope and anxiety, they partly despised him for his attitude and partly revered him as an evil spirit.

When they had finished this time, Walter did not move but sat there, drooping, drained and forlorn on his half-turned piano stool, but Clarisse got up and gave the intruder a lively greeting. Her hands and face were still twitching with the electric charge of the music, and her smile forced its way through a tension between ecstasy and disgust.

"Frog Prince!" she said, with a nod backward at the music or Walter. Ulrich felt the elastic bond between himself and Clarisse tense again. On his last visit she had told him of a terrible dream in which a slippery creature, big-belly soft, tender and gruesome, had tried to overpower her in her sleep, and this huge frog symbolized Walter's music. The two of them had few secrets from Ulrich. Now, having barely said hello to Ulrich, Clarisse turned away from him and quickly back to Walter, again uttered her war cry—"Frog Prince!"— which Walter evidently did not understand, and, her hands still trembling from the music, gave a pained and painfully wild pull at her husband's hair. He made an amiably puzzled face and came back one step closer out of the slippery void of the music.

Then Clarisse and Ulrich took a walk through the slanting arrows of the evening sun, without Walter; he remained behind at the piano. Clarisse said:

"The ability to fend off harm is the test of vitality. The spent is drawn to its own destruction. What do you think? Nietzsche maintains it's a sign of weakness for an artist to be overly concerned about the morality of his art." She had sat down on a little hummock.

Ulrich shrugged. When Clarisse married his boyhood friend three

years ago she was twenty-two, and it was he him...
her Nietzsche's works as a wedding present. He sr...

"If I were Walter, I'd challenge Nietzsche to a d...

Clarisse's slender, hovering back, in delicate lines...
stretched like a bow; her face, too, was tense with...
she kept it anxiously averted from her friend.

"You are still both maidenly and heroic at the same ..., Ulrich
added. It might or might not have been a question, a bit of a joke, but
there was also a touch of affectionate admiration in his words. Clarisse did not quite understand what he meant, but the two words,
which she had heard from him before, bored into her like a flaming
arrow into a thatched roof.

Intermittent waves of random churning sounds reached them. Ulrich knew that Clarisse refused her body to Walter for weeks at a
time when he played Wagner. He played Wagner anyway, with a bad
conscience; like a boyhood vice.

Clarisse would have liked to ask Ulrich how much he knew of this:
Walter could never keep anything to himself. But she was ashamed
to ask. So she finally said something quite different to Ulrich, who
had sat down on a small nearby mound.

"You don't care about Walter," she said. "You're not really his
friend." It sounded like a challenge, though she said it with a laugh.

Ulrich gave her an unexpected answer. "We're just boyhood
friends. You were still a child, Clarisse, when the two of us were already showing the unmistakable signs of a fading schoolboy friendship. Countless years ago we admired each other, and now we
mistrust each other with intimate understanding. Each of us would
like to shake off the painful sense of having once mistaken himself
for the other, so now we perform the mutual service of a pitilessly
honest distorting mirror."

"So you don't think he will ever amount to anything?" Clarisse
asked.

"There is no second such example of inevitability as that offered
by a gifted young man narrowing himself down into an ordinary
young man, not as the result of any blow of fate but through a kind of
preordained shrinkage."

Clarisse closed her lips firmly. The old youthful pact between
them, that conviction should come before consideration, made her

eat high, but the truth still hurt. Music! The sounds continued
churn toward them. She listened. Now, in their silence, the seething of the piano was distinctly audible; if they listened without paying
attention, the sound might seem to be boiling upward out of the
grassy hummocks, like Brünnhilde's flickering flames.

It would have been hard to say what Walter really was. Even today
he was an engaging person with richly expressive eyes, no doubt
about it, although he was already over thirty-four and had been for
some time holding down a government job vaguely concerned with
the fine arts. His father had got him this berth in the civil service,
threatening to stop his allowance if he did not accept it. Walter was
actually a painter. While studying the history of art at the university,
he had worked in a painting class at the academy; afterward he had
lived for a time in a studio. He had still been a painter when he
moved with Clarisse into this house under the open sky, shortly after
they were married. But now he seemed to be a musician again, and
in the course of his ten years in love he had sometimes been the one,
sometimes the other, and a poet as well, during a period when he had
edited a literary publication with marriage in mind; he had then
taken a job with a theatrical concern but had dropped it after a few
weeks; sometime later, again in order to be able to marry, he became
the conductor of a theater orchestra, saw the impossibility of this,
too, after six months, and became a drawing master, a music critic, a
recluse, and many other things until his father and his future father-
in-law, broad-minded as they were, could no longer take it. Such
older people were accustomed to say that he simply lacked willpower, but it would have been equally valid to call him a lifelong,
many-sided dilettante, and it was quite remarkable that there were
always authorities in the worlds of music, painting, and literature
who expressed enthusiastic views about Walter's future. In Ulrich's
life, by contrast, even though he had a few undeniably noteworthy
achievements to his credit, it had never happened that someone
came up to him and said: "You are the man I have always been looking for, the man my friends are waiting for." In Walter's life this had
happened every three months. Even though these were not necessarily the most authoritative people in the field, they all had some
influence, a promising idea, projects under way, jobs open, friendships, connections, which they placed at the service of the Walter

they had discovered, whose life as a result took such a colorful zigzag course. He had an air about him that seemed to matter more than any specific achievement. Perhaps he had a particular genius for passing as a genius. If this is dilettantism, then the intellectual life of the German-speaking world rests largely upon dilettantism, for this is a talent found in every degree up to the level of those who really *are* highly gifted, in whom it usually seems, to all appearances, to be missing.

Walter even had the gift of seeing through all this. While he was, naturally, as ready as the next person to take credit for his successes, his knack for being borne upward with such ease by every lucky chance had always troubled him as a terrifying sign that he was a lightweight. As often as he moved on to new activities and new people, he did it not simply from instability but in great inner turmoil, driven by anxiety that he had to move on to safeguard his spiritual integrity before he took root where the ground was already threatening to give way under him. His life had been a series of convulsive experiences from which emerged the heroic struggle of a soul resisting all compromise, never suspecting that in this way it was only creating its own dividedness. For all the time he was suffering and struggling for his intellectual integrity, as befits a genius, and investing all he had in his talent, which was not quite a great talent, his fate had silently led him in an inward full circle back to nothing. He had at long last reached the point where no further obstacles stood in his way. The quiet, secluded, semi-scholarly job that sheltered him from the corruptions of the art market gave him all the time and independence he needed to listen exclusively to his inner call. The woman he loved was his, so there were no thorns in his heart. The house "on the brink of solitude" they had taken after they married could not have been more suitable for creative work. But now that there was no longer anything left to be overcome, the unexpected happened: the works promised for so long by the greatness of his mind failed to materialize. Walter seemed no longer able to work. He hid things and destroyed things; he locked himself in every morning, and every afternoon when he came home; he went for long walks, with his sketchbook shut; but the little that came of all this he never showed to anyone, or else tore it up. He had a hundred different reasons for this. His views also underwent a conspicuous change at this time. He no longer spoke of "art of our time" and "the art of the future"—concepts Clarisse had associated with him since she was fifteen, but drew a line somewhere—in music it might be with Bach, in literature with Stifter, in painting with Ingres—and declared that whatever came later was bombastic, degenerate, oversubtle, or dissolute. With mounting vehemence he insisted that in a time so poisoned in its intellectual roots as the present, a pure talent must abstain from creation altogether. But although such stringent pronouncements came from his mouth, he was betrayed by the sounds of Wagner, which began to penetrate the walls of his room more and more often as soon as he shut himself in—the music he had once taught Clarisse to despise as the epitome of a philistine, bombastic, degenerate era but to which he was now addicted as to a thickly brewed, hot, benumbing drug.

Clarisse fought against this. She hated Wagner, if for nothing else for his velvet jacket and beret. She was the daughter of a painter world-famous for his stage designs. She had spent her childhood in the realm of stage sets and greasepaint; amid three different kinds of art jargon—of the theater, the opera, and the painter's studio; surrounded by velvets, carpets, genius, panther skins, knickknacks, peacock feathers, chests, and lutes. She had come to loathe from the depths of her soul everything voluptuary in art, and was drawn to everything lean and austere, whether it was the metageometry of the new atonal music or the clarified will of classic form, stripped of its skin, like a muscle about to be dissected. It was Walter who had first brought this new gospel into her virginal captivity. She called him "my prince of light," and even when she was still a child, she and Walter had vowed to each other not to marry until he had become a king. The story of his various metamorphoses and projects was also a chronicle of infinite sufferings and raptures, for all of which she was to be the trophy. Clarisse was not as gifted as Walter; she had always felt it. But she saw genius as a question of willpower. With ferocious energy she set out to make the study of music her own. It was not impossible that she was completely unmusical, but she had ten sinewy fingers and resolution; she practiced for days on end and drove her ten fingers like ten scrawny oxen trying to tear some overwhelming weight out of the ground. She attacked painting in the same fashion. She had considered Walter a genius since she was fifteen, because she had always intended to marry only a genius. She would not let him fail her in this, and when she realized that he was failing she put up a frantic struggle against the suffocating, slow change in the atmosphere of their life. It was at just this point that Walter could have used some human warmth, and when his helplessness tormented him he would clutch at her like a baby wanting milk and sleep; but Clarisse's small, nervous body was not maternal. She felt abused by a parasite trying to ensconce itself in her flesh, and she refused herself to him. She scoffed at the steamy laundry warmth in which he sought to be comforted. It is possible that that was cruel, but she wanted to be the wife of a great man and was wrestling with destiny.

Ulrich had offered Clarisse a cigarette. What more could he have said, after so brusquely telling her what he thought? The smoke from their cigarettes drifted up the rays of the evening sun and mingled some distance away from them.

How much does Ulrich know about this? Clarisse wondered on her hummock. Anyway, what can he possibly know about such struggles? She remembered how Walter's face fell apart with pain, almost to extinction, when the agonies of music and lust beset him and her resistance left him no way out. No, she decided, Ulrich couldn't know anything of their monstrous love-game on the Himalayas of love, contempt, fear, and the obligations of the heights. She had no great opinion of mathematics and had never considered Ulrich to be as talented as Walter. He was clever, he was logical, he knew a lot—but was that any better than barbarism? She had to admit that his tennis used to be incomparably better than Walter's, and she could remember sometimes watching his ruthless drives with a passionate feeling of "he'll get what he wants" such as she had never felt about Walter's painting, music, or ideas. Now she thought: "What if he knows all about us and just isn't saying anything?" Only a moment ago he had, after all, distinctly alluded to her heroism. The silence between them had now become strangely exciting.

But Ulrich was thinking: "How nice Clarisse was ten years ago—half a child, blazing with faith in the future of the three of us." She had been actually unpleasant to him only once, when she and Walter had just got married and she had displayed that unattractive selfish-ness-for-two that so often makes young women who are ambitiously in love with their husbands so insufferable to other men. "That's got a lot better since," he thought.

15

CULTURAL REVOLUTION

Walter and he had been young in that now-forgotten era just after the turn of the last century, when many people imagined that the century was young too.

The just-buried century in Austria could not be said to have cov-ered itself with glory during its second half. It had been clever in technology, business, and science, but beyond these focal points of its energy it was stagnant and treacherous as a swamp. It had painted like the Old Masters, written like Goethe and Schiller, and built its houses in the style of the Gothic and the Renaissance. The demands of the ideal ruled like a police headquarters over all expressions of life. But thanks to the unwritten law that allows mankind no imita-tion without tying it to an exaggeration, everything was produced with a degree of craftsmanship the admired prototypes could never have achieved, traces of which can still be seen today in our streets and museums; and—relevant or not—the women of the period, who were as chaste as they were shy, had to wear dresses that covered them from the ears down to the ground while showing off a billowing bosom and a voluptuous behind. For the rest, there is no part of the past we know so little about, for all sorts of reasons, as the three to five decades between our own twentieth year and the twentieth year of our fathers. So it may be useful to be reminded that in bad periods the most appalling buildings and poems are constructed on princi-ples just as fine as in good periods; that all the people involved in destroying the achievements of a preceding good epoch feel they are improving on them; and that the bloodless youth of such inferior periods take just as much pride in their young blood as do the new generations of all other eras.

And each time it is like a miracle when after such a shallow, fading period all at once there comes a small upward surge. Suddenly, out of the becalmed mentality of the nineteenth century's last two decades, an invigorating fever rose all over Europe. No one knew exactly what was in the making; nobody could have said whether it was to be a new art, a new humanity, a new morality, or perhaps a reshuffling of society. So everyone said what he pleased about it. But everywhere people were suddenly standing up to struggle against the old order. Everywhere the right man suddenly appeared in the right place and—this is so important!—enterprising men of action joined forces with enterprising men of intellect. Talents of a kind that had previously been stifled or had never taken part in public life suddenly came to the fore. They were as different from each other as could be, and could not have been more contradictory in their aims. There were those who loved the overman and those who loved the under-man; there were health cults and sun cults and the cults of consumptive maidens; there was enthusiasm for the hero worshipers and for the believers in the Common Man; people were devout and skeptical, naturalistic and mannered, robust and morbid; they dreamed of old tree-lined avenues in palace parks, autumnal gardens, glassy ponds, gems, hashish, disease, and demonism, but also of prairies, immense horizons, forges and rolling mills, naked wrestlers, slave uprisings, early man, and the smashing of society. These were certainly opposing and widely varying battle cries, but uttered in the same breath. An analysis of that epoch might produce some such nonsense as a square circle trying to consist of wooden iron, but in reality it all blended into shimmering sense. This illusion, embodied in the magical date of the turn of the century, was so powerful that it made some people hurl themselves with zeal at the new, still-unused century, while others chose one last quick fling in the old one, as one runs riot in a house one absolutely has to move out of, without anyone feeling much of a difference between these two attitudes.

If one does not want to, there is no need to make too much of this bygone "movement." It really affected only that thin, unstable layer of humanity, the intellectuals, who are unanimously despised by all those who rejoice in impregnable views, no matter how divergent from one another (the kind of people who are back in the saddle today, thank God); the general population was not involved. Still, even though it did not become a historical event, it was an eventlet, and the two friends, Walter and Ulrich, in their early youth had just caught its afterglow. Something went through the thicket of beliefs in those days like a single wind bending many trees—a spirit of heresy and reform, the blessed sense of an arising and going forth, a mini-renaissance and -reformation, such as only the best of times experience; whoever entered the world then felt, at the first corner, the breath of this spirit on his cheek.

16

A MYSTERIOUS MALADY OF THE TIMES

So they had actually been two young men, not so long ago—Ulrich thought when he was alone again—who, oddly enough, not only had the most profound insights before anyone else did, but even had them simultaneously, for one of them had only to open his mouth to say something new to find that the other had been making the same tremendous discovery. There is something special about youthful friendships: they are like an egg that senses in its yolk its glorious future as a bird, even while it presents to the world only a rather expressionless egg shape indistinguishable from any other. He vividly remembered the boy's and student's room where they had met whenever he returned for a few weeks from his first outings into the world: Walter's desk, covered with drawings, notes, and sheets of music, like the early rays of the glory of a famous man's future; facing it, the narrow bookcase where Walter sometimes stood in his ardor like Sebastian at the stake, the lamplight on his beautiful hair, which Ulrich had always secretly admired. Nietzsche, Peter Altenberg, Dostoyevsky or whoever they had just been reading had to resign themselves to being left lying on the floor or the bed when they had served their purpose and the flood of talk would not suffer the petty interruption of putting a book tidily back in place. The arrogance of the young, who find the greatest minds just good enough to serve their own occasions, now seemed to Ulrich strangely endearing. He tried to remember these conversations. It was like reaching on awakening for the last vanishing, dreamlike thoughts of sleep. And he thought, in mild astonishment: When we were assertive in those days, the point was not to be right—it was to assert ourselves! A young man needs to shine, far more than he needs to see something in the light. He now felt the memory of the feeling of being young, that hovering on rays of light, as an aching loss.

It seemed to Ulrich that with the beginning of his adult life a general lull had set in, a gradual running down, in spite of occasional eddies of energy that came and went, to an ever more listless, erratic rhythm. It was very hard to say what this change consisted of. Were there suddenly fewer great men? Far from it! And besides, they don't matter; the greatness of an era does not depend on them. The intellectually lackluster 1860s and 1880s, for instance, could no more prevent the rise of a Nietzsche or a Hebbel than either of these men could raise the intellectual level of his contemporaries. Had life in general reached a standstill? No, it had become more powerful! Were there more paralyzing contradictions than before? There could hardly be more! Had the past not known any absurdities? Heaps! Just between ourselves: people threw their support to the weak and ignored the strong; sometimes blockheads played leading roles while brilliant men played the part of eccentrics; the good Germanic citizen, untroubled by history's labor pains, which he dismissed as decadent and morbid excrescences, went on reading his family magazines and visited the crystal palaces and academies in vastly greater numbers than he did the avant-garde exhibitions. Least of all did the political world pay attention to the New Men's views and publications; and the great public institutions resisted everything new as if surrounded by a *cordon sanitaire* against the plague. Could one not say, in fact, that things have got better since then? Men who once merely headed minor sects have become aged celebrities; publishers and art dealers have become rich; new movements are constantly being started; everybody attends both the academic and the avant-garde

shows, and even the avant-garde of the avant-garde; the family magazines have bobbed their hair; politicians like to sound off on the cultural arts, and newspapers make literary history. So what has been
lost?

Something imponderable. An omen. An illusion. As when a magnet releases iron filings and they fall in confusion again. As when a
ball of string comes undone. As when a tension slackens. As when an
orchestra begins to play out of tune. No details could be adduced
that would not also have been possible before, but all the relationships had shifted a little. Ideas whose currency had once been lean
grew fat. Persons who would before never have been taken seriously
became famous. Harshness mellowed, separations fused, intransi-
gents made concessions to popularity, tastes already formed relapsed
into uncertainties. Sharp boundaries everywhere became blurred
and some new, indefinable ability to form alliances brought new people and new ideas to the top. Not that these people and ideas were
bad, not at all; it was only that a little too much of the bad was mixed
with the good, of error with truth, of accommodation with meaning.
There even seemed to be a privileged proportion of this mixture that
got furthest on in the world; just the right pinch of makeshift to bring
out the genius in genius and make talent look like a white hope, as a
pinch of chicory, according to some people, brings out the right coffee flavor in coffee. Suddenly all the prominent and important positions in the intellectual world were filled by such people, and all
decisions went their way. There is nothing one can hold responsible
for this, nor can one say how it all came about. There are no persons
or ideas or specific phenomena that one can fight against. There is no
lack of talent or goodwill or even of strong personalities. There is just
something missing in everything, though you can't put your finger on
it, as if there had been a change in the blood or in the air; a mysterious disease has eaten away the previous period's seeds of genius, but
everything sparkles with novelty, and finally one has no way of knowing whether the world has really grown worse, or oneself merely
older. At this point a new era has definitively arrived.

So the times had changed, like a day that begins radiantly blue and
then by degrees clouds over, without having the kindness to wait for
Ulrich. He evened the score by holding the cause of these mysterious
changes that made up the disease eating away genius to be simple,

common stupidity. By no means in an insulting sense. For if stupidity, seen from within, did not so much resemble talent as possess the ability to be mistaken for it, and if it did not outwardly resemble progress, genius, hope, and improvement, the chances are that no one would want to be stupid, and so there would be no stupidity. Or fighting it would at least be easy. Unfortunately, stupidity has something uncommonly endearing and natural about it. If one finds that a reproduction, for instance, seems more of an artistic feat than a hand-painted original, well, there is a certain truth in that, and it is easier to prove than that van Gogh was a great artist. It is also easy and profitable to be a more powerful playwright than Shakespeare or a less uneven storyteller than Goethe, and a solid commonplace always contains more humanity than a new discovery. There is, in short, no great idea that stupidity could not put to its own uses; it can move in all directions, and put on all the guises of truth. The truth, by comparison, has only one appearance and only one path, and is always at a disadvantage.

But after a while Ulrich had a curious notion in this connection. He imagined that the great churchman and thinker Thomas Aquinas (d. 1274), after taking infinite pains to put the ideas of his own time in the best possible order, had then continued through history to go even deeper to the bottom of things, and had just finished. Now, still young by special dispensation, he stepped out of his arched doorway with many folios under his arm, and an electric trolley shot right past his nose. Ulrich chuckled at the dumbstruck amazement on the face of the *doctor universalis,* as the past had called the celebrated Thomas.

A motorcyclist came up the empty street, thundering up the perspective bow-armed and bow-legged. His face had the solemn self-importance of a howling child. It reminded Ulrich of a photo he had seen a few days ago in a magazine of a famous woman tennis player poised on tiptoe, one leg exposed to above the garter, the other flung up toward her head as she reached for a high ball with her racket, on her face the expression of an English governess. In the same issue there was also a picture of a champion swimmer being massaged after a contest. Two women dressed in street clothes, one at the swimmer's feet, the other at her head, were solemnly looking down at her as she lay on a bed, naked on her back, one knee drawn up in a posture of sexual abandon, the masseur standing alongside resting his hands on it. He wore a doctor's gown and gazed out of the picture as though this female flesh had been skinned and hung on a meat hook. Such were the things people were beginning to see at the time, and somehow they had to be acknowledged, as one acknowledges the presence of skyscrapers and electricity. A man can't be angry at his own time without suffering some damage, Ulrich felt. Ulrich was also always ready to love all these manifestations of life. But he could never bring himself to love them wholeheartedly, as one's general sense of social well-being requires. For a long time now a hint of aversion had lain on everything he did and experienced, a shadow of impotence and loneliness, an all-encompassing distaste for which he could not find the complementary inclination. He felt at times as though he had been born with a talent for which there was at present no objective.

17

EFFECT OF A MAN WITHOUT QUALITIES
ON A MAN WITH QUALITIES

While Ulrich and Clarisse were talking, they did not notice that the music in the house behind them broke off now and again. At those moments Walter had gone to the window. He could not see them, but felt that they were just beyond his field of vision. Jealousy tormented him. The cheap intoxicant of sluggishly sensual music was luring him back to the piano. It lay behind him, open like a bed rumpled by a sleeper resisting consciousness in order to avoid facing reality. He was racked by the jealousy of a paralyzed man who can sense how the healthy walk, yet he could not bring himself to join them, for his anguish offered no possibility of defending himself against them.

When Walter got up in the morning and had to rush to the office, when he talked with people during the day and rode home among them in the afternoon, he felt he was an important person, called upon to do great things. He believed then that he saw things differently: he was moved where others passed by unresponsively, and where others reached for a thing without thinking, for him the very act of moving his own arm was fraught with spiritual adventure, or else it was paralyzed in loving contemplation of itself. He was sensitive, and his feelings were constantly agitated by brooding, depressions, billowing ups and downs; he was never indifferent, always seeing joy or misery in everything, so he always had something exciting to think about. Such people exercise an unusual attraction, because the moral flaw in which they incessantly live communicates itself to others. Everything in their conversation takes on a personal significance, and one feels free in their company to be constantly preoccupied with oneself, so that they provide a pleasure otherwise obtainable only from an analyst or therapist for a fee, with the further difference that with the psychiatrist one feels sick, while Walter helped a person to feel very important for reasons that had previously escaped one's attention. With this talent for encouraging self-preoccupation, he had in fact conquered Clarisse and in time driven all his rivals from the field. Since everything became for him an ethical movement, he could hold forth convincingly on the immorality of ornament, the hygiene of simple forms, and the beery fumes of Wagner's music, in accord with the new taste in the arts, terrorizing even his future father-in-law, whose painter's brain was like a peacock's tail unfurled. So there could be no question that Walter had his successes to look back on.

And yet, when he got home full of impressions and plans, ripe and new as perhaps never before, a demoralizing change took place in him. Merely putting a canvas on the easel or a sheet of paper on the table was the sign of a terrible flight from his heart. His head remained clear, and the plan inside it hovered as if in a very transparent and distinct atmosphere; indeed, the plan split and became two or more plans, all ready to compete for supremacy—but the connection between his head and the first movements needed to carry it out seemed severed. Walter could not even make up his mind to lift a finger. He simply did not get up from where he happened to be sitting, and his thoughts slid away from the task he had set himself like snow evaporating as it falls. He didn't know where the time went, but all of a sudden it was evening, and since after several such experiences he had learned to start dreading them on his way home, whole series of weeks began to slip, and passed away like a troubled half-sleep. Slowed down by a sense of hopelessness in all his decisions and movements, he suffered from bitter sadness, and his incapacity solidified into a pain that often sat like a nosebleed behind his forehead the moment he tried to make up his mind to do something. Walter was fearful, and the symptoms he recognized in himself not only hampered him in his work but also filled him with anxiety, for they were apparently so far beyond his control that they often gave him the impression of an incipient mental breakdown.

But as his condition had grown steadily worse in the course of the last year, he found a miraculous refuge in a thought he had never valued enough before. The idea was none other than that the Europe in which he was forced to live was hopelessly decadent. During ages in which things seem to be going well outwardly, while inwardly they undergo the kind of regression that may be the fate of all things, including cultural development—unless special efforts are made to keep them supplied with new ideas—the obvious question was, presumably, what one could do about it. But the tangle of clever, stupid, vulgar, and beautiful is at such times so particularly dense and intricate that many people obviously find it easier to believe that there is something occult at the root of things, and proclaim the fated fall of one thing or another that eludes precise definition and is portentously vague. It hardly matters whether the doomed thing is the human race, vegetarianism, or the soul; all that a healthy pessimism needs is merely something inescapable to hold on to. Even Walter, who in better days used to be able to laugh at such doctrines, soon discovered their advantages once he began to try them out. Instead of *his* feeling bad and unable to work, it was now the times that were sick, while he was fine. His life, which had come to nothing, was now, all at once, tremendously accounted for, justified on a world-historical scale that was worthy of him, so that picking up a pen or pencil and laying it down again virtually took on the aura of a great sacrifice.

With all this, however, Walter still had to struggle with himself, and Clarisse kept on tormenting him. She turned a deaf ear to his critical discussions of the times; with her it was genius or nothing.

What it was she did not know, but whenever the subject came up her whole body began to tremble and tense up. "You either feel it or you don't" was all the proof she could offer. For him she always remained the same cruel little fifteen-year-old girl. She had never quite understood his way of feeling, nor could he ever control her. But cold and hard as she was, and then again so spirited, with her ethereal, flaming will, she had a mysterious ability to influence him, as though shocks were coming through her from a direction that could not be fitted into the three dimensions of space. This influence sometimes bordered on the uncanny. He felt it most keenly when they played the piano together. Clarisse's playing was hard and colorless, prompted by stirrings in her that he did not share, and that frightened him as they reached him when their bodies glowed till the soul burned through. Something indefinable then tore itself loose inside her and threatened to fly away with her spirit. It came out of some secret hollow in her being that had to be anxiously kept shut up tight. He had no idea what made him feel this, or what it was, but it tortured him with an unutterable fear and the need to do something decisive against it, which he could not do because no one but him noticed anything.

As he stood at the window watching Clarisse coming back alone, he dimly knew that he would again not be able to resist the urge to make disparaging remarks about Ulrich. Ulrich had returned from abroad at a bad time. He was bad for Clarisse. He ruthlessly exacerbated something inside Clarisse that Walter dared not touch: the cavern of disaster, the pitiful, the sick, the fatal genius in her, the secret empty space where something was tearing at chains that might someday give way. Now she had entered and was standing bareheaded before him, sunhat in hand, and he looked at her. Her eyes were mocking, tender, clear—perhaps a little too clear. Sometimes he felt that she simply had a certain strength he lacked. Even when she was a child he had felt her as a thorn that would never let him find peace, and evidently he had never wanted her to be otherwise; perhaps this was the secret of his life, which the other two did not understand.

"How deeply we suffer," he thought. "I don't think it can happen often that two people love each other as deeply as we must."

And he began to speak without preamble: "I don't want to know what Ulo has been telling you, but I can tell you that the strength you marvel at in him is pure emptiness." Clarisse looked at the piano and smiled; he had involuntarily sat down again beside the open instrument. "It must be easy to feel heroic," he went on, "when one is naturally insensitive, and to think in miles when you've no idea what riches can be hidden in an inch!" They sometimes called him Ulo, his boyhood nickname, and he liked them for it, as one may keep a smiling respect for one's old nanny. "He's come to a dead end!" Walter added. "You don't see it, but don't imagine that I don't know him."

Clarisse had her doubts.

Walter said vehemently: "Today it's all decadence! A bottomless pit of intelligence! He is intelligent, I grant you that, but he knows nothing at all about the power of a soul in full possession of itself. What Goethe calls personality, what Goethe calls mobile order—those are things he doesn't have a clue about! 'This noble concept of power and restraint, of choice and law, of freedom and measure, mobile order . . .' " The poet's lines came in waves from his lips. Clarisse regarded these lips in amiable wonder, as though they had just let fly a pretty toy. Then she collected herself and interjected like a good little housewife: "Would you like a beer?" "Yes. Why not? Don't I always have one?" "Well, there is none in the house." "I wish you hadn't asked," Walter sighed. "I might never have thought of it."

And that was that, as far as Clarisse was concerned. But Walter had been thrown off the track and didn't know how to continue.

"Do you remember our conversation about the artist?" he asked tentatively.

"Which one?"

"The one we had a few days ago. I explained to you what a living principle of form in a person means. Don't you remember, I came to the conclusion that in the old days, instead of death and logical mechanization, blood and wisdom reigned?"

"No."

Walter was stymied; he groped, wavered. Suddenly he burst out: "He's a man without qualities!"

"What is that?" Clarisse asked, giggling.

"Nothing. That's just it, it's nothing."

But Clarisse found the phrase intriguing.

"There are millions of them nowadays," Walter declared. "It's the human type produced by our time!" He was pleased with the term he had hit upon so unexpectedly. As if he were starting a poem, he let the expression drive him on even before its meaning was clear to him. "Just look at him! What would you take him for? Does he look like a doctor, a businessman, a painter, or a diplomat?"

"He's none of those," Clarisse said dryly.

"Well, does he look like a mathematician?"

"I don't know—how should I know what a mathematician is supposed to look like?"

"You've hit the nail on the head! A mathematician looks like nothing at all—that is, he is likely to look intelligent in such a general way that there isn't a single specific thing to pin him down! Except for the Roman Catholic clergy, no one these days looks the way he should, because we use our heads even more impersonally than our hands. But mathematics is the absolute limit: it already knows as little about itself as future generations, feeding on energy pills instead of bread and meat, will be likely to know about meadows and young calves and chickens!"

Clarisse had meanwhile put their simple supper on the table, and Walter was already digging into it, which may have suggested the analogy to him. Clarisse was watching his lips. They reminded her of his late mother's. They were strong feminine lips that ate as if they were getting the housework done, and were topped off by a small clipped mustache. His eyes shone like freshly peeled chestnuts, even when he was merely looking for a piece of cheese on the platter. Although he was short, and flabby rather than delicate of build, he was a man of striking appearance, the kind who always seem to be standing in a good light. He now continued:

"His appearance gives no clue to what his profession might be, and yet he doesn't look like a man without a profession either. Consider what he's like: He always knows what to do. He knows how to gaze into a woman's eyes. He can put his mind to any question at any time. He can box. He is gifted, strong-willed, open-minded, fearless, tenacious, dashing, circumspect—why quibble, suppose we grant him all those qualities—yet he has none of them! They've made him what he is, they've set his course for him, and yet they don't belong to him. When he is angry, something in him laughs. When he is sad, he is up to something. When something moves him, he turns against it. He'll

always see a good side to every bad action. What he thinks of anything will always depend on some possible context—nothing is, to
him, what it is; everything is subject to change, in flux, part of a
whole, of an infinite number of wholes presumably adding up to a
superwhole that, however, he knows nothing about. So every answer
he gives is only a partial answer, every feeling only an opinion, and he
never cares *what* something is, only 'how' it is—some extraneous
seasoning that somehow goes along with it, that's what interests him.
I don't know whether I'm making myself clear—?"

"Quite clear," Clarisse said, "but I think that's all very nice of
him."

Walter had unintentionally spoken with signs of growing dislike;
his old boyhood sense of being weaker than his friend increased his
jealousy. For although he was convinced that Ulrich had never really
achieved anything beyond a few proofs of naked intellect and capacity, he could never shake off a secret sense of always having been
Ulrich's physical inferior. The portrait he was sketching freed him,
like bringing off a work of art, as if it were not his own doing at all but
something that had begun as a mysterious inspiration, with word
after word coming to him, while inwardly something dissolved without his being conscious of it. By the time he finished he had recognized that Ulrich stood for nothing but this state of dissolution that
all present-day phenomena have.

"So you like it, do you?" he said, painfully surprised. "You can't be
serious?"

Clarisse was chewing bread and soft cheese; she could only smile
with her eyes.

"Oh well," Walter said, "I suppose we used to think that way ourselves, in the old days. But surely it can't be regarded as anything
more than a preliminary phase? Such a man is not really a human
being!"

Clarisse had swallowed her mouthful. "That's what he says himself!" she affirmed.

"What does he say himself?"

"Oh, I don't know—that today everything is coming apart. Everything has come to a standstill, he says, not just him. But he doesn't
take it as hard as you do. He once gave me a long talk about it: If you
analyze a thousand people, you will find two dozen qualities, emo-

tions, forms of development, types of structure and so on, which are what they all consist of. And if you do a chemical analysis of your body, all you get is water with a few dozen little heaps of matter swimming in it. The water rises inside us just as it does inside trees, and it forms the bodies of animals just as it forms the clouds. I think that's neatly put. But it doesn't help you to know what to say about yourself. Or what to do." Clarisse giggled. "So then I told him that you go fishing for days when you have time off, and lie around by the water."

"So what? I'd like to know if he could stand that for even ten minutes. But *human beings,*" Walter said firmly, "have been doing that for ten thousand years, staring up at the sky, feeling the warmth of the earth, without trying to analyze it any more than you'd analyze your own mother."

Clarisse couldn't help giggling again. "He says things have become more complicated meanwhile. Just as we swim in water, we also swim in a sea of fire, a storm of electricity, a firmament of magnetism, a swamp of warmth, and so on. It's just that we can't feel it. All that finally remains is formulas. What they mean in human terms is hard to say; that's all there is. I've forgotten whatever I learned about it at school, but I think that's what it amounts to. Anybody nowadays, says Ulrich, who wants to call the birds 'brothers,' like Saint Francis or you, can't do it so easily but must be prepared to be cast into a furnace, plunge into the earth through the wires of an electric trolley, or gurgle down the drain with the dishwater into the sewer."

"Oh sure, sure," Walter interrupted this report. "First, four elements are turned into several dozen, and finally we're left floating around on relationships, processes, on the dirty dishwater of processes and formulas, on something we can't even recognize as a thing, a process, a ghost of an idea, of a God-knows-what. Leaving no difference anymore between the sun and a kitchen match, or between your mouth at one end of the digestive tract and its other end either. Every thing has a hundred aspects, every aspect a hundred connections, and different feelings are attached to every one of them. The human brain has happily split things apart, but things have split the human heart too." He had leapt to his feet but remained standing behind the table.

"Clarisse," he said, "the man is a danger for you! Look, Clarisse,

what every one of us needs today more than anything else is simplicity, closeness to the earth, health—and yes, definitely, say what you
like, a child as well, because a child keeps us anchored to the ground.
Everything Ulo tells you is inhuman. I promise you I *have* the courage, when I come home, simply to have a cup of coffee with you,
listen to the birds, take a little walk, chat with a neighbor, and let the
day fade out quietly: that's human life!"

The tenderness of these sentiments had brought him slowly closer
to her. But the moment fatherish feelings could be detected raising
their gentle bass voice from afar, Clarisse balked. As he drew near,
her face became expressionless and tilted defensively.

When he had reached her side he radiated a gentle glow like a
good country stove. In this warm stream Clarisse wavered for a moment. Then she said: "Nothing doing, my dear!" She grabbed a
piece of bread and some cheese from the table and kissed him
quickly on the forehead. "I'm going out to see if there are any nocturnal butterflies."

"But Clarisse," Walter pleaded. "All the butterflies are gone this
time of year."

"Oh, you never can tell."

Nothing was left of her in the room but her laughter. With her
bread and cheese she roamed the meadows; it was a safe neighborhood and she needed no escort. Walter's tenderness collapsed like a
soufflé taken too soon from the oven. He heaved a deep sigh. Then
he hesitantly sat down again at the piano and struck a few keys. Willy-
nilly his playing turned into improvisations on themes from Wagner's
operas, and in the splashings of this dissolutely tumescent substance
he had refused in the days of his pride, his fingers cleared a path and
gurgled through the fields of sound. Let them hear it, far and wide!
The narcotic effect of this music paralyzed his spine and eased his
fate.

18

MOOSBRUGGER

The Moosbrugger case was currently much in the news. Moosbrugger was a carpenter, a big man with broad shoulders and no excess fat on him, a head of hair like brown lamb's wool, and good-natured strong paws. His face also expressed a good-natured strength and right-mindedness, qualities one would have smelled (had one not seen them) in the blunt, plain, dry workaday smell that belonged to this thirty-four-year-old man and came from the wood he worked with and a job that called as much for mindfulness as for exertion.

Anyone who came up against this face for the first time, a face blessed by God with every sign of goodness, would stop as if rooted to the spot, because Moosbrugger was usually flanked by two armed guards, his hands shackled with a small, strong steel chain, its grip held by one of his escorts.

When he noticed anyone staring at him a smile would pass over his broad, good-natured face with the unkempt hair and a mustache and the little chin tuft. He wore a short black jacket with light gray trousers, his bearing was military, and he planted his feet wide apart; but it was that smile that most fascinated the reporters in the courtroom. It might be an embarrassed smile or a cunning smile, an ironic, malicious, pained, mad, bloodthirsty, or terrifying smile: they were groping visibly for contradictory expressions and seemed to be searching desperately in that smile for something they obviously could find nowhere else in the man's entire upright appearance.

For Moosbrugger had killed a woman, a prostitute of the lowest type, in a horrifying manner. The reporters described in detail a knife wound in the throat from the larynx to the back of the neck, also the two stab wounds in the breast that penetrated the heart, and the two in the back on the left side, and how both breasts were sliced through so that they could almost be lifted off. The reporters had expressed their revulsion at this, but they did not stop until they had counted thirty-five stabs in the belly and explained the deep slash that reached from the navel to the sacrum, continuing up the back in numerous lesser cuts, while the throat showed marks of strangulation. From such horrors they could not find their way back to Moosbrugger's good-natured face, although they were themselves good-natured men who had nevertheless described what had happened in a factual, expert manner and, evidently, in breathless excitement. They hardly availed themselves of even the most obvious explanation, that the man before them was insane—for Moosbrugger had already been in various mental hospitals several times for similar crimes—even though a good reporter is very well informed on such questions these days; it looked as though they were still reluctant to give up the idea of the villain, to banish the incident from their own world into the world of the insane. Their attitude was matched by that of the psychiatrists, who had already declared him normal just as often as they had declared him not accountable for his actions. There was also the amazing fact that no sooner had they become known than Moosbrugger's pathological excesses were regarded as "finally something interesting for a change" by thousands of people who deplore the sensationalism of the press, from busy officeholders to fourteen-year-old sons to housewives befogged by their domestic cares. While these people of course sighed over such a monstrosity, they were nevertheless more deeply preoccupied with it than with their own life's work. Indeed, it might happen that a punctilious department head or bank manager would say to his sleepy wife at bedtime: "What would you do now if I were a Moosbrugger?"

When Ulrich first laid eyes on that face with its signs of being a child of God above handcuffs, he quickly turned around, slipped a few cigarettes to the sentry at the nearby court building, and asked him about the convoy that had apparently just left the gates; he was told . . . Well, anyway, this is how something of the sort must have happened in earlier times, since it is often reported this way, and Ulrich almost believed it himself; but the contemporary truth was that he had merely read all about it in the newspaper. It was to be a long time before he met Moosbrugger in person, and before that happened he caught sight of him only once during the trial. The probability of experiencing something unusual through the newspapers is much greater than that of experiencing it in person; in other words, the more important things take place today in the abstract, and the more trivial ones in real life.

What Ulrich learned of Moosbrugger's story in this fashion was more or less the following:

Moosbrugger had started out in life as a poor devil, an orphan shepherd boy in a hamlet so small that it did not even have a village street, and his poverty was such that he never dared speak to a girl. Girls were something he could always only look at, even later on when he became an apprentice and then when he was a traveling journeyman. One only need imagine what it must mean when something one craves as naturally as bread or water can only be looked at. After a while one desires it unnaturally. It walks past, skirts swaying around its calves. It climbs over a stile and is visible up to the knees. One looks into its eyes, and they turn opaque. One hears it laugh and turns around quickly, only to look into a face as immovably round as a hole in the ground into which a mouse has just slipped.

So it is understandable that Moosbrugger justified himself even after the first time he killed a girl by saying that he was constantly haunted by spirits calling to him day and night. They threw him out of bed when he slept and bothered him at his work. Then he heard them talking and quarreling with one another day and night. This was no insanity, and Moosbrugger could not bear being called insane, although he himself sometimes dressed up his story a little with bits of remembered sermons, or trimmed it in accordance with the advice on malingering one picks up in prison. But the material to work with was always there, even if it faded a little when his attention wandered.

It had been the same during his years as a journeyman. Work is not easy for a carpenter to find in winter, and Moosbrugger often had no roof over his head for weeks on end. He might have trudged along the road all day to reach a village, only to find no shelter. He would have to keep on marching late into the night. With no money for a meal, he drinks schnapps until two candles light up behind his eyes and the body keeps walking on its own. He would rather not ask for a cot at the shelter, regardless of the hot soup, partly because of the bedbugs and partly because of the offensive red tape; better to pick up a few pennies by begging and crawl into some farmer's haystack for the night. Without asking, of course; what's the point of spending a long time asking when you're only going to be insulted? In the morning, of course, there is often an argument and a charge of assault, vagrancy, and begging, and finally there is an ever-thickening file of such convictions. Each new magistrate opens this file with much pomposity, as if it explained Moosbrugger.

And who considers what it means to go for days and weeks without a proper bath? The skin gets so stiff that it allows only the clumsiest movements, even when one tries to be delicate; under such a crust the living soul itself hardens. The mind may be less affected, it goes on doing the needful after a fashion, burning like a small light in a huge walking lighthouse full of crushed earthworms and grasshoppers, with everything personal squashed inside, and only the fermenting organic matter stalking onward. As he wandered on through the villages, or even on the deserted roads, Moosbrugger would encounter whole processions of women, one now, and another one half an hour later, but even if they appeared at great intervals and had nothing to do with each other, on the whole they were still processions. They were on their way from one village to another, or had just slipped out of the house; they wore thick shawls or jackets that stood out in stiff, snaky lines around their hips; they stepped into warm rooms or drove their children ahead of them, or were on the road so alone that one could have thrown a stone at them like shying at a crow. Moosbrugger asserted that he could not possibly be a sex murderer, because these females had inspired only feelings of aversion in him. This is not implausible—we think we understand a cat, for instance, sitting in front of a cage staring up at a fat, fair canary hopping up and down, or batting a mouse, letting it go, then batting it again, just to see it run away once more; and what is a dog running after a bicycle, biting at it only in play—man's best friend? There is in this attitude toward the living, moving, silently rolling or flitting fellow creature enjoying its own existence something that suggests a deep innate aversion to it. And then what could one do when she started screaming? One could only come to one's senses, or else, if one simply couldn't do that, press her face to the ground and stuff earth into her mouth.

Moosbrugger was only a journeyman carpenter, a man utterly alone, and while he got on well enough with the other men wherever he worked, he never had a friend. Every now and then the most powerful of instincts turned his inner being cruelly outward. But he may have lacked only, as he said, the education and the opportunity to make something different out of this impulse, an angel of mass destruction or a great anarchist, though not the anarchists who band together in secret societies, whom he contemptuously called fakes. He was clearly ill, but even if his obviously pathological nature provided the basis for his attitude, and this isolated him from other men, it somehow seemed to him a stronger and higher sense of his own self. His whole life was a comically and distressingly clumsy struggle to gain by force a recognition of this sense of himself. Even as an apprentice he had once broken the fingers of one master who tried to beat him. He ran away from another with the master's money—in simple justice, as he said. He never stayed anywhere for long. As long as he could keep others at arm's length, as he always did at first, working peacefully, with his big shoulders and few words, he stayed. But as soon as they began to treat him familiarly and without respect, as if they had caught on to him, he packed up and left, seized by an uncanny feeling as though he were not firmly settled inside his skin. Once, he had waited too long. Four bricklayers on a building site had got together to show him who was boss—they would make the scaffolding around the top story give way under him. He could hear them tittering behind his back as they came closer; he hurled himself at them with all his boundless strength, threw one down two flights of stairs, and cut all the tendons in the arms of two others. To be punished for this, he said, had been a shock to his system. He emigrated to Turkey but came back again, because the world was in league against him everywhere; no magic word and no kindness could prevail against this conspiracy.

He had eagerly picked up such phrases in the mental wards and prisons, with scraps of French and Latin stuck in the most unsuitable places as he talked, ever since he had discovered that it was the possession of these languages that gave those in power the right to decide his fate with their "findings." For the same reason, he also did his utmost during hearings to express himself in an exaggerated High German, saying such things as "This must be regarded as the basis for my brutality" or "I had imagined her to be even more vicious than the others of her kind in my usual estimation of them." But when he saw that this failed to make an impression he could rise to the heights of a grand theatrical pose, declaring disdainfully that he was a "theoretical anarchist" whom the Social Democrats were ready to rescue at a moment's notice if he chose to accept a favor from those utterly pernicious Jewish exploiters of the ignorant working class. This would show them that he too had a "discipline," a field of his own where the learned presumption of his judges could not follow him.

Usually this kind of talk brought him high marks for "remarkable intelligence" in the court's judgment, respectful attention to his words during the proceedings, and tougher sentences; yet deep down, his flattered vanity regarded these hearings as the high points of his life. Which is why he hated no one as fervently as he hated the psychiatrists who imagined they could dismiss his whole complex personality with a few foreign words, as if it were for them an everyday affair. As always in such cases, the medical diagnoses of his mental condition fluctuated under the pressure of the superior world of juridical concepts, and Moosbrugger never missed a chance to demonstrate in open court his own superiority over the psychiatrists, unmasking them as puffed-up dupes and charlatans who knew nothing at all, and whom he could trick into placing him in a mental institution instead of sending him to prison, where he belonged. For he did not deny what he had done, but simply wanted his deeds understood as the mishaps of an important philosophy of life. It was those snickering women who were in the forefront of the conspiracy against him. They all had their skirt-chasers and turned up their noses at a real man's straight talk, if they didn't take it as a downright insult. He gave them a wide berth as long as he could, so as not to let them provoke him, but it was not possible all the time. There are days when a man feels confused and can't get hold of anything because his hands are sweating with restlessness. If one then has to give in, he can be sure that at the first step he takes there will be, far up the road like an advance patrol sent out by the others, one of those poisons on two feet crossing his path, a cheat who secretly laughs at the man while she saps his strength and puts on her act for him, if she doesn't do something much worse to him in her unscrupulousness!

And so the end of that night had come, a night of listless boozing, with lots of noise to keep down the inner restlessness. The world can be unsteady even when you aren't drunk. The street walls waver like stage sets behind which something is waiting for its cue. It gets quieter at the edge of town, where you come into the open fields lit by the moon. That was where Moosbrugger had to circle back to get home, and it was there, by the iron bridge, that the girl accosted him. She was one of those girls who hire themselves out to men in the fields, a jobless, runaway housemaid, a little thing of whom all you could see were two gleaming little mouse eyes under her kerchief. Moosbrugger turned her down and quickened his step, but she begged him to take her home with him. Moosbrugger walked: straight ahead, then around a corner, finally helplessly, this way and that; he took big strides, and she ran alongside him; he stopped, she stood there like a shadow. It was as if he were drawing her along behind him. He made one more attempt to drive her off: he suddenly turned around and spat twice in her face. It was no use; she was invulnerable.

This happened in the immense park, which they had to cross at its narrowest part. Moosbrugger began to feel sure that the girl had a protector nearby—how else would she have the nerve to keep after him despite his exasperation? He reached for the knife in his pants pocket; he wasn't anyone's fool! They might jump him together; behind those bitches the other man was always hiding to jeer at you. Come to think of it, didn't she look like a man in disguise? He saw shadows move and heard crackling in the bushes, while this schemer beside him repeated her plea again and again, at regular intervals like a gigantic pendulum. But he could see nothing to hurl his giant's strength at, and the uncanny way nothing at all was happening began to frighten him.

By the time they turned into the first, still very dark street, there were beads of sweat on his forehead, and he was trembling. He kept his eyes straight ahead and walked into the first café that was still open. He gulped down a black coffee and three brandies and could sit there in peace, for fifteen minutes or so; but when he paid his check the worry was there again: what would he do if she was waiting for him outside? There are such thoughts, like string winding in endless snares around arms and legs. He had hardly taken a few steps on the dark street when he felt the girl at his side. Now she was no longer humble but cocky and self-confident; nor did she plead anymore but merely kept silent. Then he realized that he would never get rid of her, because it was he himself who was drawing her after him. His throat filled up with tearful disgust. He kept walking, and that creature, trailing him, was himself again. It was just the same as when he was always meeting those processions of women in the road. Once, he had cut a big wooden splinter out of his own leg because he was too impatient to wait for the doctor; in the same way, he now felt his knife lying long and hard in his pocket.

But by a superhuman exertion of his moral sense, Moosbrugger hit upon one more way out. Behind the board fence along which the road now led was a playing field; one couldn't be seen there, and so he went in. He lay down in the cramped ticket booth and pushed his head into the corner where it was darkest; the soft, accursed second self lay down beside him. So he pretended to fall asleep right away, in order to be able to sneak out later on. But when he started to creep out softly, feet first, there it was again, winding its arms around his neck. Then he felt something hard, in her pocket or his. He tugged it out. He couldn't say whether it was a scissors or a knife; he stabbed her with it. He had claimed it was only a pair of scissors, but it was his own knife. She fell with her head inside the booth. He dragged her partway outside, onto the soft ground, and kept on stabbing her until he had completely separated her from himself. Then he stood there beside her for maybe another quarter of an hour, looking down at her, while the night grew calmer again and wonderfully smooth. Now she could never again insult a man and trail after him. He finally carried the corpse across the street and laid it down in front of a bush so that it could be more easily found and buried, as he stated, because now it was no longer her fault.

During his trial Moosbrugger created the most unpredictable problems for his lawyer. He sat relaxed on his bench, like a spectator, and called out "Bravo!" every time the prosecutor made a point of what a public menace the defendant was, which Moosbrugger regarded as worthy of him, and gave out good marks to witnesses who declared that they had never noticed anything about him to indicate that he could not be held responsible for his actions.

"You're quite a character," the presiding judge flattered him from time to time, humoring him along as he conscientiously tightened the noose the accused had put around his own neck. At such moments Moosbrugger looked astonished, like a harried bull in the arena, let his eyes wander, and noticed in the faces around him, though he could not understand it, that he had again worked himself one level deeper into his guilt.

Ulrich was especially taken with the fact that Moosbrugger's defense was evidently based on some dimly discernible principle. He had not gone out with intent to kill, nor did his dignity permit him to plead insanity. There could be no question of lust as a motive—he had felt only disgust and contempt. The act could accordingly only be called manslaughter, to which he had been induced by the suspicious conduct of "this caricature of a woman," as he put it. If one understood him rightly, he even wanted the killing to be regarded as a political crime, and he sometimes gave the impression that he was fighting not for himself but for this view of the legal issue. The judge's tactics against him were based on the usual assumption that he was dealing with a murderer's obvious, cunning efforts to evade responsibility.

"Why did you wipe the blood off your hands? Why did you throw the knife away? Why did you change into fresh underwear and clean clothes afterward? Because it was Sunday? Not because you were covered with blood? Why did you go out looking for entertainment? So the crime didn't prevent you from doing so? Did you feel any remorse at all?" Ulrich well understood the deep resignation with which Moosbrugger at such moments lamented his lack of an education, which left him helpless to undo the knots in this net woven of incomprehension. The judge translated this into an emphatic reproof: "You always find a way to shift the blame to others!"

This judge added it all up, starting with the police record and the vagrancy, and presented it as Moosbrugger's guilt, while to Moosbrugger it was a series of completely separate incidents having nothing to do with one another, each of which had a different cause that lay outside Moosbrugger somewhere in the world as a whole. In the judge's eyes, Moosbrugger was the source of his acts; in Moosbrugger's eyes they had perched on him like birds that had flown in from somewhere or other. To the judge, Moosbrugger was a special case; for himself he was a universe, and it was very hard to say something convincing about a universe. Two strategies were here locked in combat, two integral positions, two sets of logical consistency. But Moosbrugger had the less favorable position; even a much cleverer man could not have expressed the strange, shadowy reasonings of his mind. They rose directly out of the confused isolation of his life, and while all other lives exist in hundreds of ways—perceived the same way by those who lead them and by all others, who confirm them—his own true life existed only for him. It was a vapor, always losing and changing shape. He might, of course, have asked his judges whether their lives were essentially different. But he thought no such thing. Standing before the court, everything that had happened so naturally in sequence was now senselessly jumbled up inside him, and he made the greatest efforts to make such sense of it as would be no less worthy than the arguments of his distinguished opponents. The judge seemed almost kindly as he lent support to this effort, offering a helpful word or idea, even if these turned out later to have the most terrible consequences for Moosbrugger.

It was like the struggle of a shadow with a wall, and in the end Moosbrugger's shadow was reduced to a lurid flickering. Ulrich was present on the last day of the trial. When the presiding judge read out the psychiatrists' findings that the accused was responsible for his actions, Moosbrugger rose to his feet and announced to the court: "I am satisfied with this opinion and have achieved my purpose." The response of scornful incredulity in the eyes around him made him add angrily: "Since it is I who forced the indictment, I declare myself satisfied with the conduct of the case." The presiding judge, who had now become all strictness and retribution, reprimanded him with the remark that the court was not concerned with giving him satisfaction. Then he read him the death sentence, exactly as if it were now time to answer seriously the nonsense Moosbrugger had been spouting throughout the trial, to the amusement of the spectators. Moosbrugger said nothing to this, so that he would not appear to be frightened. Then the proceedings were concluded and it was all over. His mind reeled; he fell back, helpless against the arrogance of those who failed to understand. Even as the guards were leading him out, he turned around, struggling for words, raised his hands in the air, and cried out, in a voice that shook him free of his guards' grip: "I am satisfied, even though I must confess to you that you have condemned a madman."

That was a non sequitur, but Ulrich sat there breathless. This was clearly madness, and just as clearly it was no more than a distortion of our own elements of being. Cracked and obscure it was; it somehow occurred to Ulrich that if mankind could dream as a whole, that dream would be Moosbrugger. Ulrich came back to reality only when "that miserable clown of a lawyer," as Moosbrugger ungratefully referred to him during the trial, announced that he would appeal to have the verdict set aside on grounds of some detail or other, while his towering client was led away.

19

A LETTER OF ADMONITION AND A CHANCE TO ACQUIRE QUALITIES. RIVALRY OF TWO ACCESSIONS TO THE THRONE

So the time passed, until one day Ulrich received a letter from his father.

"My dear son, once again several months have gone by without my being able to deduce from your scanty communications that you have taken the slightest step forward in your career or have made any preparations to do so.

"I will joyfully acknowledge that in the course of the last few years the satisfaction has been vouchsafed me of hearing your achievements praised in various esteemed quarters, with predictions on that basis of a promising future for you. But on the one hand, the tendency you have inherited, though not from me, to make enthusiastic first strides in some new endeavor that attracts you, only to forget soon afterward, so to speak, what you owe yourself and those who have rested their hopes on you, and on the other hand, my inability to detect in your communications the slightest sign of a plan for your future, fill me with grave concern.

"It is not only that at your age other men have already secured a solid position in life, but also that I may die at any time, and the property I shall bequeath in equal shares to you and your sister, though not negligible, is not sufficiently ample, under present circumstances, to secure unaided that social position which you will now, at last, have to establish for yourself. What fills me with grave concern is the thought that ever since you took your degree, you have only vaguely talked of plans to be realized in various fields, and which you, in your usual way, may considerably overestimate, but that you never write of taking any interest in a university appointment, nor of any preliminary approach to one or another university with regard to such plans, nor of making any other contact with influential circles. No one can possibly suspect me of denigrating a scholar's need for independence, considering that it was I who was the first, forty-seven years ago, to break with the other schools of criminal jurisprudence on that point in my book on Samuel Pufendorf's *Theory of the Responsibility for Moral Actions and Its Relation to Modern Jurisprudence*, which you know and which is now going into its twelfth edition, where I brought the true context of the problem to light. Just as little can I accept, after the experiences of a hardworking life, that a man rely on himself alone and neglect the academic and social connections that provide the support by means of which alone the individual's work prospers as part of a fruitful and beneficial whole.

"I therefore hope and trust that I shall be hearing from you at your earliest convenience, and that the expenditures I have made on behalf of your advancement will be rewarded by your taking up such connections, now that you have returned home, and by your ceasing to neglect them. I have also written in this vein to my old and trusted friend and patron, the former President of the Treasury and present Chairman of the Imperial Family Court Division, Office of the Court Chamberlain, His Excellency Count Stallburg, asking him to give his beneficent attention to the request you will in due course soon present to him. My highly placed friend has already been so kind as to reply by return mail. It is your good fortune that he will not only see you but expresses a warm interest in your personal progress as depicted by myself. This means that your future is assured, insofar as it is in my power and estimation to do so, assuming that you understand how to make a favorable impression on His Excellency, while also strengthening the esteem in which you are held by the leading academic circles.

"As regards the request I am certain you will be glad to lay before

His Excellency, as soon as you know what it is about, its object is the following:

"There will take place in Germany in 1918, specifically on or about the 15th of June, a great celebration marking the jubilee of Emperor Wilhelm II's thirtieth year upon the throne, to impress upon the world Germany's greatness and power. Although that is still several years away, a reliable source informs us that preparations are already being made, though for the time being quite unofficially, of course. Now you are certainly aware that in the same year our own revered Emperor Franz Josef will be celebrating the seventieth jubilee of his accession and that this date falls on December 2nd. Given the modesty which we Austrians display far too much in all questions concerning our own fatherland, there is reason to fear, I must say, that we will experience another Sadowa, meaning that the Germans, with their trained methodical aim for effect, will anticipate us, just as they did in that campaign, when they introduced the needle gun and took us by surprise.

"Fortunately, the anxiety I have just expressed has already been anticipated by other patriotic personages with good connections, and I can tell you confidentially that there is a campaign under way in Vienna to forestall the eventuality of such a coup and to bring to bear the full weight of a seventy-year reign, so rich in blessings and sorrows, against a jubilee of a mere thirty years. Inasmuch as December 2nd cannot of course possibly be moved ahead of June 15th, someone came up with the splendid idea of declaring the entire year of 1918 as a jubilee year for our Emperor of Peace. I am, however, only insofar apprised of this as the institutions of which I am a member have had occasion to express their views on this proposal. You will learn the details as soon as you present yourself to Count Stallburg, who intends to place you on the Planning Committee in a position of considerable distinction for so young a man as yourself.

"Let me also prevail upon you not to continue neglecting—as, to my acute embarrassment, you have—the relations I have so long recommended to you with Section Chief Tuzzi of the Imperial Foreign Office, but to call at once upon his wife, who, as you know, is the daughter of a cousin of my late brother's widow, and hence your cousin. I am told she occupies a prominent position in the project I have just described. My revered friend Count Stallburg has already had the extraordinary kindness to inform her of your intended visit to her, which is why you must not delay it a moment longer.

"As regards myself, there is nothing much to report; other than my lectures, work on the new edition of my aforementioned book takes up all of my time, as well as the remainder of energy one still has at one's disposal in old age. One has to make good use of one's time, for it is short.

"From your sister I hear only that she is in good health. She has a fine, capable husband, although she will never admit that she is satisfied with her lot and feels happy in it.

"With my blessing, your loving

Father."

PART II

PSEUDOREALITY PREVAILS

20

A TOUCH OF REALITY. IN SPITE OF THE
ABSENCE OF QUALITIES, ULRICH TAKES
RESOLUTE AND SPIRITED ACTION

That Ulrich actually decided to call on Count Stallburg was prompted not least, though not only, by curiosity.

Count Stallburg had his office in that Imperial and Royal citadel the Hofburg, and the Emperor and King of Kakania was a legendary old gentleman. A great many books have of course been written about him since, and exactly what he did, prevented, or left undone is now known, but then, in the last decade of his and Kakania's life, the younger people who kept abreast of the arts and sciences sometimes wondered whether he actually existed. The number of his portraits one saw was almost as large as the number of his kingdom's inhabitants; on his birthday as much food and drink was consumed as on that of the Savior, bonfires blazed on the mountains, and the voices of millions vowed that they loved him as a father; an anthem in his honor was the only work of poetry or music of which every Kakanian knew at least a line. But this popularity and publicity was so superconvincing that believing in his existence was rather like believing in stars that one sees though they ceased to exist thousands of years ago.

The first thing that happened when Ulrich arrived in his cab at the Imperial Hofburg was that the cabbie stopped in the outer courtyard and asked to be paid, claiming that although he was allowed to drive through the inner courtyard, he was not permitted to stop there. Ulrich was annoyed at the cabbie, whom he took for a cheat or a coward, but his protests were powerless against the man's timid refusal, which suddenly made him sense the aura of a power mightier than he. When he walked into the inner courtyard he was much impressed with the numerous red, blue, white, and yellow coats, trousers, and helmet plumes that stood there stiffly in the sun like birds on a sandbank. Up to that moment he had considered "His Majesty" one of those meaningless terms which had stayed in use, as one may be an atheist and still say "Thank God." But now his gaze wandered up high walls and he saw an island—gray, self-contained, and armed—lying there while the city's speed rushed blindly past it.

After he had presented himself he was led up stairways and along corridors, through rooms large and small. Although he was very well dressed, he felt that his exact measure was being taken by every eye he encountered. It would apparently occur to no one here to confuse intellectual aristocracy with the real thing, and against this Ulrich had no recourse but ironic protest and bourgeois criticism. He ascertained that he was walking through a vast shell with little content; the great public rooms were almost unfurnished, but this empty taste lacked the bitterness of a great style. He passed a casual sequence of individual guardsmen and servants, who formed a guard more haphazard than magnificent; a half dozen well-trained and well-paid private detectives might have served far more effectively. One kind of servant, in a gray uniform and cap like a bank messenger's, shuttling between the lackeys and the guardsmen, made him think of a lawyer or dentist who does not keep his office and his living quarters sufficiently separate. "One feels clearly through all this how it must have awed the Biedermeier generation with its splendor," Ulrich thought, "but today it can't even compete with the attractiveness and comfort of a hotel, so it continues to fall back on being all noble restraint and stiffness."

But when he entered Count Stallburg's presence, Ulrich was received by His Excellency inside a great hollow prism of the best proportions, in the center of which this unpretentious, bald-headed, somewhat stooped man, his knees bent like an orangutan's, stood facing Ulrich in a manner that could not possibly be the way an eminent Imperial Court functionary of noble birth would naturally look—it had to be an imitation of something. His Excellency's shoulders were bowed, his underlip drooped, he resembled an aged beagle or a worthy accountant. Suddenly there could be no doubt as to whom he reminded one of; Count Stallburg became transparent, and Ulrich realized that a man who has been for seventy years the All-Highest Center of supreme power must find a certain satisfaction in retreating behind himself and looking like the most subservient of his subjects. Consequently it simply became good manners and a natural form of discretion for those in the vicinity of this All-Highest personage not to look more personal than he did. This seems to be why kings so often like to call themselves the first servants of their country, and a quick glance confirmed for Ulrich that His Excellency indeed wore those short, ice-gray muttonchop whiskers framing a clean-shaven chin that were sported by every clerk and railway porter in Kakania. The belief was that they were emulating the appearance of their Emperor and King, but the deeper need in such cases is reciprocity.

Ulrich had time for such reflections because he had to wait awhile for His Excellency to speak. The theatrical instinct for disguise and transformation, one of life's pleasures, could here be seen in all its purity, without the least taint or awareness of a performance; so strongly did it manifest itself here in this unconscious, perennial art of self-representation that by comparison the middle-class custom of building theaters and staging plays as an art that can be rented by the hour struck him as something quite unnatural, decadent, and schizoid. And when His Excellency finally parted his lips and said to him: "Your dear father . . . ," only to come to a halt, there was something in his voice that made one notice his remarkably beautiful yellowish hands and something like an aura of finely tuned morality surrounding the whole figure, which charmed Ulrich into forgetting himself, as intellectuals are apt to do. For His Excellency now asked him what he did, and when Ulrich said "Mathematics" responded with "Indeed, how interesting, at which school?" When Ulrich assured him that he had nothing to do with schools, His Excellency said, "Indeed, how interesting, I see, research, university." This seemed to Ulrich so natural and precise, just the way one imagines a fine piece of conversation, that he inadvertently took to behaving as though he were at home here and followed his thoughts instead of the protocol demanded by the situation. He suddenly thought of Moosbrugger. Here was the Power of Clemency close at hand; nothing seemed to him simpler than to make a stab at using it.

"Your Excellency," he said, "may I take this favorable opportunity to appeal to you on behalf of a man who has been unjustly condemned to death?"

The question made Count Stallburg's eyes open wide.

"A sex murderer, to be sure," Ulrich conceded, though he realized at once that he was entirely out of order. "The man's insane, of course," he hastily added to save the situation, and was about to add "Your Excellency must be aware that our penal code, dating from the middle of the last century, is outdated on this point," but he had to swallow and got stuck. It was a blunder to impose on this man a discussion of a kind that people used to intellectual activity engage in, often quite without purpose. Just a few words, adroitly planted, can be as fruitful as rich garden loam, but in this place their effect was closer to that of a little clump of dirt one has inadvertently brought into the room on the sole of one's shoe. But now Count Stallburg, noticing Ulrich's embarrassment, showed him his truly great benevolence.

"Yes, yes, I remember," he said with a slight effort after Ulrich had given him the man's name, "and so you say he is insane, and you would like to help him?"

"He can't be held responsible for what he does."

"Quite so, those are always especially unpleasant cases."

Count Stallburg seemed much distressed by the difficulties involved. Looking bleakly at Ulrich, he asked, as if nothing else were to be expected, whether Moosbrugger's sentence was final. Ulrich had to admit that it was not.

"Ah, in that case," he went on, sounding relieved, "there's still time," and he began to speak of Ulrich's "papa," leaving the Moosbrugger case in amiable ambiguity.

Ulrich's slip had momentarily made him lose his presence of mind, but oddly enough his mistake seemed not to have made a bad impression on Count Stallburg. His Excellency had been nearly speechless at first, as though someone had taken off his jacket in his presence, but then such spontaneity from a man so well recommended came to seem to him refreshingly resolute and high-spirited. He was pleased to have found these two words, intent as he was on forming a favorable impression. He wrote them immediately ("We hope that we have found a resolute and high-spirited helper") in his letter of introduction to the chairman of the great patriotic campaign. When Ulrich received this document a few moments later, he felt like a child who is dismissed with a piece of chocolate pressed into its little hand. He now held something between his fingers and received instructions to come again, in a manner that left him uncertain whether it was an order or an invitation, but without giving him an opportunity to protest. "There must be some misunderstanding—I really had no intention whatever . . . ," he would have liked to say, but by this time he was already on his way out, back along the great corridors and through the vast salons. He suddenly came to a stop, thinking, "That picked me up like a cork and set me down somewhere I never meant to go!" He scrutinized the insidious simplicity of the décor with curiosity, and felt quite certain in deciding that even now he was still unimpressed by it. This was simply a world that had not yet been cleared away. But still, what was that strong, peculiar quality it had made him feel? Damn it all, there was hardly any other way to put it: it was simply amazingly real.

21

THE REAL INVENTION OF THE PARALLEL CAMPAIGN BY COUNT LEINSDORF

The real driving force behind the great patriotic campaign—to be known henceforth as the Parallel Campaign, both for the sake of abbreviation and because it was supposed to "bring to bear the full weight of a seventy-year reign, so rich in blessings and sorrows, against a jubilee of a mere thirty years"—was not, however, Count Stallburg, but his friend His Grace the Imperial Liege-Count Leinsdorf.

At the time Ulrich was making his visit in the Hofburg, Count Leinsdorf's secretary was standing in that great nobleman's beautiful, tall-windowed study, amid multiple layers of tranquillity, devotion, gold braid, and the solemnity of fame, with a book in his hand from which he was reading aloud to His Grace a passage he had been directed to find. This time it was something out of Johann Gottlieb Fichte that he had dug up in the *Addresses to the German Nation* and considered most appropriate:

To be freed from the original sin of sloth [he read] and the cowardice and duplicity that follow in its wake, men need models, such as the founders of the great religions actually were, to prefigure for them the enigma of freedom. The necessary teaching of moral conviction is the task of the Church, whose symbols must be regarded not as homilies but only as the means of instruction for the proclamation of the eternal verities.

He stressed the words "sloth," "prefigure," and "Church." His Grace listened benevolently, had the book shown to him, but then shook his head.

"No," said the Imperial Count, "the book may be all right, but this Protestant bit about the Church won't do."

The secretary looked frustrated, like a minor official whose fifth draft of a memo has been returned to him by the head of his department, and cautiously demurred: "But wouldn't Fichte make an excellent impression on nationalistic circles?"

"I think," His Grace replied, "we had better do without him for the present." As he clapped the book shut his face clapped shut too, and at this wordless command the secretary clapped shut with a deep bow and took back his Fichte, as if removing a dish from the table, which he would file away again on the shelf with all the other philosophic systems of the world. One does not do one's own cooking but has it taken care of by the servants.

"So, for the time being," Count Leinsdorf said, "we keep to our four points: Emperor of Peace, European Milestone, True Austria, Property and Culture. You will draw up the circular letter along those lines."

Just then a political thought had struck His Grace, which translated into words came to, more or less, "They'll come along of their own accord." He meant those sectors of his Fatherland who felt they belonged less to Austria than to the greater German nation. He regarded them with disfavor. Had his secretary found a more acceptable quotation with which to flatter their sensibilities—hence the choice of J. G. Fichte—he might have let him write it down. But the moment that offensive note about the Church gave him a pretext to drop it, he did so with a sigh of relief.

His Grace was the originator of the great patriotic campaign. When the disturbing news reached him from Germany, it was he who had come up with the slogan "Emperor of Peace." This phrase instantly evoked the image of an eighty-eight-year-old sovereign—a true father of his people—and an uninterrupted reign of seventy years. The image naturally bore the familiar features of his Imperial Master, but its halo was not that of majesty but of the proud fact that his Fatherland possessed the oldest sovereign with the longest reign in the world. Foolish people might be tempted to see in this merely his pleasure in a rarity—as if Count Leinsdorf, had, for instance, rated the possession of the far rarer horizontally striped "Sahara" stamp with watermark and one missing perforation over the posses-sion of an El Greco, as in fact he did, even though he owned both and was not unmindful of his family's celebrated collection of paintings—but this is simply because these people don't understand what en-riching power a symbol has, even beyond that of the greatest wealth.

For Count Leinsdorf, his allegory of the aged ruler held the thought both of his Fatherland, which he loved, and of the world to which it should be a model. Count Leinsdorf was stirred by great and aching hopes. He could not have said what moved him more, grief at not seeing his country established in quite the place of honor among the family of nations which was her due, or jealousy of Prussia, which had thrust Austria down from that place of eminence (in 1866, by a stab in the back!), or else whether he was simply filled with pride in the nobility of a venerable state and the desire to show the world just how exemplary it was. In his view, the nations of Europe were help-lessly adrift in the whirlpool of materialistic democracy. What hov-ered before him was an inspiring symbol that would serve both as a warning and as a sign to return to the fold. It was clear to him that something had to be done to put Austria in the vanguard, so that this "splendorous rally of the Austrian spirit" would prove a "milestone" for the whole world and enable it to find its own true being again; and all of this was connected with the possession of an eighty-eight-year-old Emperor of Peace.

Anything more, or more specific, Count Leinsdorf did not yet know. But he was certain that he was in the grip of a great idea. Not only did it kindle his passion—which should have put him on his guard, as a Christian of strict and responsible upbringing—but with dazzling conclusiveness this idea flowed directly into such sublime and radiant conceptions as that of the Sovereign, the Fatherland, and the Happiness of Mankind. Whatever obscurity still clung to his vision could not upset His Grace. He was well acquainted with the theological doctrine of the *contemplatio in caligine divina*, the contemplation in divine darkness, which is infinitely clear in itself but a dazzling darkness to the human intellect. Besides, he had always believed that a man who does something truly great usually doesn't know why. As Cromwell had said: "A man never gets as far as when he does not know where he is going!" So Count Leinsdorf serenely indulged himself in enjoying his symbol, whose uncertainty aroused him far more powerfully than any certainties.

Symbols apart, his political views were of an extraordinary solidity and had that freedom of great character such as is made possible only by a total absence of doubts. As the heir to a feudal estate he was a member of the Upper House, but he was not politically active, nor did he hold a post at Court or in the government. He was "nothing but a patriot." But precisely because of this, and because of his independent wealth, he had become the focus for all other patriots who followed with concern the development of the Empire and of mankind. The ethical obligation not to remain a passive onlooker but to "offer a helping hand from above" permeated his life. He was convinced that "the people" were "good." Since not only his many officials, employees, and servants but countless others depended on him for their economic security, he had never known "the people" in any other respect, except on Sundays and holidays, when they poured out from behind the scenery as a cheerful, colorful throng, like an opera chorus. Anything that did not fit in with this image he attributed to "subversive elements," the work of irresponsible, callow, sensation-seeking individuals. Brought up in a religious and feudal spirit, never exposed to contradiction through having to deal with middle-class people, not unread, but as an aftereffect of the clerical instruction of his sheltered youth prevented for the rest of his life from recognizing in a book anything other than agreement with or mistaken divergence from his own principles, he knew the outlook of more up-to-date people only from the controversies in Parliament or in the newspapers. And since he knew enough to recognize the many superficialities there, he was daily confirmed in his prejudice that the true bourgeois world, more deeply understood, was basically nothing other than what he himself conceived it to be. In general, "the true" prefixed to political convictions was one of his aids for finding his way in a world that although created by God too often denied Him. He was firmly convinced that even true socialism fitted in with his view of things. He had had from the beginning, in fact, a deeply personal notion, which he had never fully acknowledged even to himself, to build a bridge across which the socialists were to come marching into his own camp. It is obvious that helping the poor is a proper chivalric task, and that for the true high nobility there was really no very great difference between a middle-class factory owner and his workers. "We're all socialists at heart" was one of his pet sayings, meaning no more and no less than that there were no social distinctions in the hereafter. In this world, however, he considered them necessary facts of life, and expected the working class, after due attention to its material welfare, to resist the unreasonable slogans imported by foreign agitators and to accept the natural order of things in a world where everyone finds duty and prosperity in his allotted place. The true aristocrat accordingly seemed as important to him as the true artisan, and the solution of political and economic questions was subsumed for him in a harmonious vision he called "Fatherland."

His Grace could not have said how much of all this had run through his mind in the quarter of an hour since his secretary had left the room. All of it, perhaps. The medium-tall man, some sixty years old, sat motionless at his desk, his hands clasped in his lap, and did not know that he was smiling. He wore a low collar because of a tendency to goiter, and a handlebar mustache, either for the same reason or because it gave him a look slightly reminiscent of certain portraits of Bohemian noblemen of the Wallenstein era. A high-ceilinged room stood around him, and this in turn was surrounded by the huge empty spaces of the anteroom and the library, around which, shell upon shell, further rooms, quiet, deference, solemnity, and the wreath of two sweeping stone staircases arranged themselves. Where the staircases led to the entrance gate, a tall doorkeeper stood in a heavy braided coat, his staff in his hand, gazing through the hole of the archway into the bright fluidity of the day, where pedestrians floated past like goldfish in a bowl. On the border between these two worlds rose the playful tendrils of a rococo façade, famed among art historians not only for its beauty but because its height exceeded its width. It is now considered the first attempt to draw the skin of an expensive, comfortable country manor over the skeleton of a town house, grown tall because of the middle-class urban constriction of its ground plan, and represents one of the most important examples of the transition from feudal landed splendor to the style of middle-class democracy. It was here that the existence of the Leinsdorfs, art-historically certified, made the transition into the spirit of the age. But whoever did not know that saw as little of it as a drop of water shooting by sees of its sewer wall; all he would notice was the mellow grayish hole made by the archway breaking the otherwise solid façade of the street, a surprising, almost exciting recess in whose cavernous depth gleamed the gold of the braid and the large knob on the doorkeeper's staff. In fine weather, this man stood in front of the entrance like a flashing jewel visible from afar, intermingled with a row of housefronts that no one noticed, even though it was just these walls that imposed the order of a street upon the countless, nameless, passing throngs. It is a safe bet that most of the common people over whose order Count Leinsdorf kept anxious and ceaseless vigil linked his name, when it came up, with nothing but their recollection of this doorkeeper.

His Grace would not have felt pushed into the background; he would rather have been inclined to consider the possession of such a doorkeeper as the "true selflessness" that best becomes a nobleman.

22

THE PARALLEL CAMPAIGN, IN THE FORM OF AN INFLUENTIAL LADY OF INEFFABLE SPIRITUAL GRACE, STANDS READY TO DEVOUR ULRICH

It was this Count Leinsdorf whom Ulrich should have gone to see next, as Count Stallburg wished, but he had decided to visit instead the "great cousin" recommended by his father, because he was curious to see her with his own eyes. He had never met her but had taken a special dislike to her ever since all the well-meaning people who knew they were related had begun saying: "There's a woman you must get to know." It was always said with that marked emphasis on the "you" intended to single out the person addressed as exceptionally well placed to appreciate such a jewel, and which can be a sincere compliment or a cloak for the conviction that he was just the sort of fool for such an acquaintance. Ulrich's frequent requests for a detailed description of this lady's qualities never brought satisfying replies. It was either "She has such an ineffable spiritual grace" or "She is our loveliest and cleverest woman" or, as many would say, simply, "She's an ideal woman." "How old is she?" Ulrich would ask, but nobody knew her age and the person thus asked was usually amazed that it had never occurred to him to give it a thought. "Well then, who is her lover?" "An affair?" The not inexperienced young man he asked this of looked at him in wonder: "You're quite right. No one would ever suspect her of such a thing."

"I see—a high-minded beauty," Ulrich concluded, "a second Diotima." And from that day forth that was what he called her in his thoughts, after the celebrated female teacher of love.

But in reality her name was Ermelinda Tuzzi, and in truth it was just plain Hermine. Now, Ermelinda is, to be sure, not even a translation of Hermine, but she had earned the right to this beautiful name one day through a flash of intuition, when it suddenly stood before her spiritual ear as a higher form of truth, even though her husband went on being called Hans, and not Giovanni. Despite his surname he had first learned Italian at the consular school. Ulrich was no less prejudiced against this Section Chief Tuzzi than against his wife. He was the only commoner in a position of authority in the Imperial Ministry of Foreign Affairs, which was even more feudal than the other government departments. There Tuzzi was the head of the most influential section, was considered the right hand—even the brains, it was rumored—of his Minister, and was one of the few men who could influence the fate of Europe. But when a commoner rises to such a position in such exalted surroundings, he may reasonably be supposed to possess qualities favorably combining personal indispensability with a knack for keeping modestly in the background. Ulrich was close to imagining this influential section chief as a kind of upright regimental sergeant major in the cavalry obliged to drill one-year conscripts from the high nobility. The fitting complement, Ulrich thought, would be a spouse who, despite the extolling of her beauty, was ambitious, no longer young, and encased in a middle-class corset of culture.

But Ulrich was mightily surprised when he made his visit. Diotima received him with the indulgent smile of an eminent lady who knows that she is also beautiful and has to forgive men, superficial creatures that they are, for always thinking of her beauty first.

"I've been expecting you," she said, leaving Ulrich uncertain whether she meant this as a kindness or a rebuke. The hand she gave him was plump and weightless.

He held it a moment too long, his thoughts unable to let go of this hand at once. It rested in his own like a fleshy petal; its pointed nails, like beetle wings, seemed poised to fly off with her at any moment into the improbable. He was overwhelmed by the exaltation of this female hand, basically a rather shameless human organ that, like a dog's muzzle, will touch anything and yet is publicly considered the seat of fidelity, nobility, and tenderness. During these few seconds, he noted that there were several rolls of fat on Diotima's neck, covered with the finest skin; her hair was wound into a Grecian knot, which stood out stiffly and in its perfection resembled a wasp's nest.

Ulrich felt a hostile impulse, an urge to offend this smiling woman, and yet he could not quite resist her beauty.

Diotima, for her part, also gave him a long and almost searching gaze. She had heard things about this cousin that to her ear had a slight tinge of the scandalous, and besides, he was related to her. Ulrich noticed that she, too, could not quite resist the impression of his physical appearance. He was used to this. He was clean-shaven, tall, well-built, and supplely muscular; his face was bright but impenetrable; in a word, he sometimes regarded himself as the preconceived idea most women have of an impressive and still young man; he simply did not always have the energy to disabuse them. Diotima resisted this impression by deciding to feel compassion for him. Ulrich could see that she was constantly studying his appearance and, obviously not moved by unfavorable feelings, was probably telling herself that the noble qualities he so palpably seemed to possess must be suffocated by a vicious life and could be saved. Although she was not much younger than Ulrich and physically in full open bloom, her appearance emanated something withheld and virginal that formed a strange contrast to her self-confidence. So they went on surveying each other even after they had begun to talk.

Diotima began by calling the Parallel Campaign a unique, never-to-recur opportunity to bring into existence what must be regarded as the greatest and most important thing in the world. "We must and will bring to life a truly great idea. We have the opportunity, and we must not fail to use it."

"Do you have something specific in mind?" Ulrich asked naïvely.

No, Diotima did not have anything specific in mind. How could she? No one who speaks of the greatest and most important thing in the world means anything that really exists. What peculiar quality of the world would it be equivalent to? It all amounts to one thing being greater and more important, or more beautiful and sadder, than another; in other words, the existence of a hierarchy of values and the comparative mode, which surely implies an end point and a superlative? But if you point this out to someone who happens at that very moment to be speaking of the greatest and most important thing in the world, that person will suspect that she is dealing with an individual devoid of feelings and ideals. This was Diotima's reaction, and so had Ulrich spoken.

As a woman admired for her intellect, Diotima found Ulrich's objection irreverent. After a moment she smiled and replied: "There is so much that is great and good that has not yet been realized that the choice will not be easy. But we will set up committees from all sectors of the population, which will help us in our work. Or don't you think, Herr von ———, that it is an incredible privilege to be in a position to call on a whole nation—indeed, on the whole world—on such an occasion, to awaken it in the midst of its materialistic preoccupations to the life of the spirit? You must not assume that we have in mind something 'patriotic' in the long-outdated sense."

Ulrich was humorously evasive.

Diotima did not laugh, but barely smiled. She was accustomed to witty men, but they were all something else besides. Paradox for the sake of paradox struck her as immature, and aroused the need to remind her cousin of the seriousness of the reality that lent to this great national undertaking dignity as well as responsibility. In a tone of finality, she made a fresh start. Ulrich involuntarily sought between her words those black-and-yellow tapes that are used for interleaving and fastening official papers in Austrian government offices; but what came from Diotima's lips were by no means only bureaucratic formulas but also such cultural code words as "soulless age, dominated only by logic and psychology" or "the present and eternity," and suddenly there was mention of Berlin, too, and the "treasure of feeling" Austria had still preserved, in contrast to Prussia.

Ulrich attempted several times to interrupt these ex cathedra pronouncements, but the vestry incense of high bureaucracy instantly clouded over the interruption, gently veiling its tactlessness. Ulrich was astonished. He rose. His first visit was clearly at an end.

During these moments of his retreat Diotima treated him with that bland courtesy, carefully and pointedly a little overdone, which she had learned by imitating her husband. He used it in his dealings with young aristocrats who were his subordinates but might one day be his ministers. There was, in her manner of inviting him to come again, a touch of that supercilious uneasiness of the intellectual when faced with a ruder vitality. When he held her gentle, weightless hand in his own once more, they looked into each other's eyes. Ulrich had the distinct impression that they were destined to cause each other considerable annoyance through love.

"Truly," he thought, "a hydra of a beauty." He had meant to let the great patriotic campaign wait for him in vain, but it seemed to have become incarnate in the person of Diotima and stood ready to swallow him up. It was a semi-comical feeling: despite his maturity and experience, he felt like a destructive little worm being eyed attentively by a large chicken. "For heaven's sake," he thought, "I can't let myself be provoked to petty derelictions by this giantess of the soul!" He had had enough of his affair with Bonadea, and he committed himself to exercise the utmost restraint.

As he was leaving the apartment, he was cheered by a pleasant impression he had already had on his arrival. A little chambermaid with dreamy eyes showed him out. In the darkness of the entrance hall her eyes, fluttering up to his for the first time, had been like black butterflies; now, as he left, they floated down through the darkness like black snowflakes. There was something Arabian or Algerian-Jewish about the little girl, something so unobtrusively sweet that Ulrich again forgot to take a good look at her. It was only when he was out in the street again that he felt what an uncommonly alive and refreshing sight the little maid was after Diotima's presence.

23

A GREAT MAN'S INITIAL INTERVENTION

Ulrich's departure had left both Diotima and her maid in a state of vague excitement. But while the little black lizard always felt as though she had been allowed to flit up a high, shimmering wall whenever she saw a distinguished visitor to the door, Diotima handled her impression of Ulrich with the conscientiousness of a woman who doesn't really mind feeling touched though she should because she has the ability to keep herself gently in check. Ulrich did not know that on that same day another man had entered her life to lift her up like a giant mountain offering a tremendous view.

Dr. Paul Arnheim had called on her soon after arriving in town.

He was immeasurably rich. His father was the mightiest mogul of "Iron Germany," that is, Bismarck's Germany, to which even Section Chief Tuzzi had condescended. Tuzzi was laconic on principle. He felt that puns and the like, even if one could not do entirely without them in witty conversation, had better not be too good, because that would be middle-class. He had advised his wife to treat this visitor with marked distinction, for even if his kind were not yet on top in the German Reich, and their influence at Court was not to be compared with that of the Krupps, they might, in his opinion, be on top tomorrow. He also passed on to her a confidential rumor that the son—a man well into his forties, incidentally—was aiming not merely at his father's position but was preparing himself, based on the trend of the times and his international connections, to become a Reichsminister someday. Tuzzi of course regarded this as completely out of the question, unless a world cataclysm were to pave the way.

He had no idea what a tempest his words unleashed in his wife's imagination. In her circle it was a matter of principle not to think too highly of "men in trade," but like every person of bourgeois outlook, she admired wealth in those depths of the heart that are quite immune to convictions, and the prospect of actually meeting so incredibly rich a man made her feel as if golden angel's wings had come down to her from on high. Ever since her husband's rise, Ermelinda Tuzzi was not entirely unaccustomed to consorting with fame and riches. But fame based on intellectual achievements melts away with surprising speed as one becomes socially involved with its bearers, and feudal wealth manifests itself either in the foolish debts of young attachés or is constrained by a traditional style of living without ever attaining the brimming profusion of freely piled-up mountains of money and the brilliant cascading showers of gold with which the great banks and industrial combines fuel their business. All Diotima knew of banks was that even their middle-echelon executives traveled first-class on business, while she always had to go second-class unless accompanied by her husband. This was the standard by which she imagined the luxury that must surround the top despots of financial operations on so oriental a scale.

Her little maid, Rachel—it goes without saying that Diotima pronounced it in the French style—had heard fantastic things. The least she had to report was that the nabob had arrived in his own private train, had reserved an entire hotel, and had brought a little black slave with him. The truth was considerably more modest, if only because Paul Arnheim never acted conspicuously. Only the little blackamoor was real. Some years ago, on a trip in southernmost Italy, Arnheim had picked him out of a traveling dance troupe, partly for show and partly from an impulse to raise a fellow creature from the depths and carry out God's work by opening up the life of the mind to him. He soon enough lost interest and used the now sixteen-year-old boy only as a servant, even though before the boy was fourteen Arnheim had been giving him Stendhal and Dumas to read.

But even though the rumors her maid brought home were so childish in their extravagance that Diotima had to smile, she made her repeat them word for word, because she found it charming and unspoiled, as was only possible in this one great city, which was "rife with culture to the point of innocence." And the little black boy surprisingly caught even her imagination.

Diotima was the eldest of three daughters of a secondary-school teacher without private means, so that Tuzzi had been considered a good catch for her even before he had been anything but an as yet unknown middle-class vice-consul. In her girlhood she had had nothing but her pride, and since her pride had nothing to be proud about, it was only a rolled-up propriety bristling with feelers of sensitivity. But even such a posture may conceal ambition and daydreams, and can be an unpredictable force.

If Diotima had at first been lured by the prospect of distant entanglements in distant lands, she was soon disappointed. After a few years her experience served only as a discreetly exploited advantage over women friends who envied her her slight aura of the exotic, and it could not ward off the realization that at such foreign posts life remains, by and large, the life one has brought along with the rest of one's baggage. For a long time, Diotima's ambitions had been close to ending up in the genteel hopelessness of the fifth service grade, until by chance her husband's career took a sudden upward turn when a benevolent minister of a "progressive" cast of mind took this bourgeois into the central office of the ministry itself. In this position, Tuzzi was now approached by many people who wanted something from him, and from this moment something came alive in Diotima, almost to her own amazement, a treasure of memories of "spiritual beauty and grandeur" ostensibly gathered in a cultured home and the great world centers, but which in fact she had probably acquired in a girls' private school as a model student, and this she began turning cautiously to account. Her husband's sober but uncommonly dependable intelligence inevitably attracted attention to her as well, and as soon as she noticed that her cultural advantages were being appreciated, she joyfully began to slip little "highminded" ideas into the conversation in the right places, as completely guileless as a damp little sponge releasing the moisture it had previously soaked up for no particular purpose. And gradually, as her husband rose further in rank, more and more people were drawn into association with him, and her home became a "salon" which enjoyed a reputation as a place where "society and intellect" met. Now that she was seeing persons of consequence in many fields, Diotima began as well to seriously discover herself. Her feeling for what was correct, still on the alert as it had been in school, still adept at remembering its lessons and at bringing things together into an amiable unity, simply by extension, turned into a form of intellect in itself, and the Tuzzi house won a recognized position.

24

CAPITAL AND CULTURE. DIOTIMA'S FRIENDSHIP WITH COUNT LEINSDORF, AND THE OFFICE OF BRINGING DISTINGUISHED VISITORS INTO ACCORD WITH THE SOUL

But it took Diotima's friendship with Count Leinsdorf to make her salon an institution.

Among the parts of the body after which friends are named, Count

Leinsdorf's was so situated between the head and the heart that Diotima would have to be considered a bosom friend, if such a term were still in use. His Grace revered Diotima's mind and beauty without permitting himself any unseemly intentions. His patronage not only gave Diotima's salon an unassailable position but conferred on it—as he liked to say—an official status.

For his own person, His Grace the Imperial Liege-Count Leinsdorf was "nothing but a patriot." But the state does not consist only of the Crown and the people, with the administrative machinery in between; there is something else besides: thought, morality, principle! Devout as His Grace was, as a man permeated with a sense of responsibility who, incidentally, also ran factories on his estates, he never closed his mind to the realization that the human mind these days has in many respects freed itself from the tutelage of the Church. He could not imagine how a factory, for example, or a stock-exchange deal in wheat or sugar could be conducted on religious principles; nor was there any conceivable way to run a modern, large-scale landed estate rationally without the stock exchange and industry. When His Grace's business manager showed him how a certain deal could be made more profitably with a group of foreign speculators than in partnership with the local landed nobility, in most cases His Grace had to choose the former, because objective conditions have a rationale of their own, and this cannot be defied for sentimental reasons by the head of a huge economic enterprise who bears the responsibility not only for himself but for countless other lives as well. There is such a thing as a professional conscience that in some cases contradicts the religious conscience, and Count Leinsdorf was convinced that in such a case even the Cardinal Archbishop would not act differently than he. Of course, Count Leinsdorf was always willing to deplore this state of affairs at public sessions of the Upper House and to express the hope that life would find its way back to the simplicity, naturalness, supernaturalness, soundness, and necessity of Christian principles. Whenever he opened his mouth to make such pronouncements, it was as though an electric contact had been opened, and he flowed in a different circuit. The same thing happens to most people, in fact, when they express themselves in public, and if anyone had reproached Count Leinsdorf with doing in private what he denounced in public, he would, with saintly conviction, have branded it the demagogic babble of subversives who lacked even a clue about the extent of life's responsibilities. Nevertheless, he realized the prime importance of establishing a connection between the eternal verities and the world of business, which is so much more complicated than the lovely simplicity of tradition, and he also recognized that such a connection could not be found anywhere but in the profundities of middle-class culture. With its great ideas and ideals in the spheres of law, duty, morality, and beauty, it reached even the common everyday struggles and contradictions of life, and seemed to him like a bridge made of tangled living plants. It did not, of course, offer as firm and secure a foothold as the dogmas of the Church, but it was no less necessary and responsible, which is why Count Leinsdorf was not only a religious idealist but also a passionate civilian idealist.

These convictions of His Grace's corresponded to the composition of Diotima's salons. These gatherings were celebrated for the fact that on her "great days" one ran into people one could not exchange a single word with because they were too well known in some special field or other for small talk, while in many cases one had never even heard the name of the specialty for which they were world-famous. There were Kenzinists and Canisians, a grammarian of Bo might come up against a partigen researcher, a tokontologist against a quantum physicist, not to mention the representatives of new movements in arts and literature that changed their labels every year, all permitted to circulate in limited numbers along with their better-recognized colleagues. In general, things were so arranged that a random mixture blended harmoniously, except for the young intellectuals, whom Diotima usually kept apart by means of special invitations, and those rare or special guests whom she had a way of unobtrusively singling out and providing with a special setting. What distinguished Diotima's gatherings from all similar affairs was, incidentally, if one may say so, the lay element; people from the world of applied ideas, the kind who—in Diotima's words—had once spread out around a core of theological studies as a flock of faithful doers, really an entire community of lay brothers and sisters—in short, the element of *action*. But now that theology has been displaced by economics and physics, and Diotima's list of administrators of the spirit on earth who were to be invited had grown with time to resemble the

Catalogue of Scientific Papers of the Royal Society, the new lay brothers and sisters were correspondingly a collection of bank directors, technicians, politicians, high officials, and ladies and gentlemen of society with their hangers-on.

Diotima made a particular point of cultivating the women, although she gave preference to the "ladies" over the "intellectuals" among them. "Life is much too overburdened with knowledge these days," she was accustomed to say, "for us to be able to do without the 'unfragmented woman.'" She was convinced that only the unfragmented woman still possessed the fated power to embrace the intellect with those vital forces that, in her opinion, it obviously sorely needed for its salvation. This concept of the entwining woman and the power of Being, incidentally, redounded greatly to her credit among the young male nobility who attended regularly because it was considered the thing to do and because Tuzzi was not unpopular; for the unfragmented Being is something the nobility really takes to, and more specifically, at the Tuzzis' couples could become deeply absorbed in conversation without attracting attention; so that for tender rendezvous and long heart-to-heart talks, her house—though Diotima had no inkling of this—was even more popular than a church.

His Grace the Liege-Count Leinsdorf summed up these two social elements, so various in themselves, which mingled at Diotima's— when he did not simply call them "the true elite"—as "capital and culture." But he liked best of all to think of them in terms of "official public service," a concept that had pride of place in his thinking. He regarded every accomplishment, that of the factory worker or the concert singer as well as that of the civil servant, as a form of official service.

"Every person," he would say, "performs an office within the state; the worker, the prince, the artisan, are all civil servants." This was an emanation of his always and under all circumstances impartial way of thinking, ignorant of bias, and in his eyes even the ladies and gentlemen of the highest society performed a significant if not readily definable office when they chatted with learned experts on the Bogazköy inscriptions or the question of lamellibranchiate mollusks, while eyeing the wives of prominent financiers. This concept of official public service was his version of what Diotima referred to as the religious unity, lost since the Middle Ages, of all human activity.

All enforced sociability, such as that at the Tuzzis', beyond a certain naïve and crude level, springs basically from the need to simulate a unity that could govern all of humanity's highly varied activities and that is never there. This simulation was what Diotima called culture, usually, with special amplification, "our Old Austrian culture." As her ambition had expanded to embrace intellect, she had learned to use this term more and more often. She understood by it: the great paintings of Velázquez and Rubens hanging in the Imperial Museum; the fact that Beethoven was, so to speak, an Austrian; Mozart, Haydn, St. Stephen's Cathedral, the Burgtheater; the weighty traditional ceremonials at the Imperial Court; Vienna's central district, where the smartest dress and lingerie shops of an empire with fifty million inhabitants were crowded together; the discreet manners of high officials; Viennese cuisine; the aristocracy, which considered itself second to none except the English, and their ancient palaces; high society's tone of sometimes genuine, mostly sham, aestheticism. She also understood by it the fact that in this country so eminent a gentleman as Count Leinsdorf had taken her under his wing and made her house the center of his own cultural endeavors. She did not know that His Grace was also moved by the consideration that it was not quite the thing to open his own noble house to innovations that might easily get out of hand. Count Leinsdorf was often secretly horrified by the freedom and indulgence with which his beautiful friend spoke of human passions and the turmoil they cause, or of revolutionary ideas. But Diotima did not notice this. She drew a line, as it were, between public immodesty and private modesty, like a female physician or a social worker. She was acutely sensitive to any word that touched her too personally, but impersonally she would talk freely about anything, and could only feel that Count Leinsdorf found the mixture most appealing.

Nothing in life is built, however, without the stones having to be broken out from somewhere else. To Diotima's painful surprise some tiny, dreamy-sweet almond kernel of imagination, once the core of her existence when there was nothing else in it, and which had still been there when she decided to marry Vice-Consul Tuzzi, who looked like a leather steamer trunk with two dark eyes, had vanished in the years of success. She realized that much of what she understood by "our Old Austrian culture," like Haydn or the

Habsburgs, had once been only a boring school lesson, while to be actually living in the midst of it all now seemed enchanting and quite as heroic as the midsummer humming of bees. In time, however, it became not only monotonous but also a strain on her, and even hopeless. Diotima's experience with her famous guests was no different from that of Count Leinsdorf with his banking connections; however much one might try to get them into accord with one's soul, it did not succeed. One can talk about cars and X rays, of course, with a certain amount of feeling, but what else can one do about the countless other inventions and discoveries that nowadays every single day brings forth, other than to marvel at human inventiveness in general, which in the long run gets to be too tiresome!

His Grace would drop in occasionally, and spoke with a political figure or had himself introduced to a new guest. It was easy for him to enthuse about the profound reaches of culture, but when you were as closely involved with it as Diotima, the insoluble problem was not its depths but its breadth! Even questions of such immediate concern as the noble simplicity of Greece or the meaning of the Prophets dissolved, in conversation with specialists, into an incalculable multiplicity of doubts and possibilities. Diotima found that even the celebrities always talked in twos, because the time had already come when a person could talk sensibly and to the point with at most one other person—and she herself could not really find anyone at all. At this point Diotima had discovered in herself the well-known suffering caused by that familiar malady of contemporary man known as civilization. It is a frustrating condition, full of soap, radio frequencies, the arrogant sign language of mathematical and chemical formulas, economics, experimental research, and the inability of human beings to live together simply but on a high plane. And even the relationship of her own innate nobility of mind to the social nobility, whom she had to handle with great care and who brought her, with all her successes, many a disappointment, gradually came to seem to her more and more typical of an age not of culture but merely of civilization.

Civilization, then, meant everything that her mind could not control. Including, for a long time now, and first of all, her husband.

25

Sufferings of a married soul

In her misery she read a great deal, and discovered that she had lost something she had previously not really known she had: a soul.

What's that? It is easy to define negatively: It is simply that which sneaks off at the mention of algebraic series.

But positively? It seems successfully to elude every effort to pin it down. There may once have been in Diotima something fresh and natural, an intuitive sensibility wrapped in the propriety she wore like a cloak threadbare from too much brushing, something she now called her soul and rediscovered in Maeterlinck's batik-wrapped metaphysics, or in Novalis, but most of all in the ineffable wave of anemic romanticism and yearning for God that, for a while, the machine age squirted out as an expression of its spiritual and artistic misgivings about itself. It might also be that this original freshness in Diotima could be defined more precisely as a blend of quiet, tenderness, devotion, and kindness that had never found a proper path and in the foundry in which Fate casts our forms had happened to pour itself into the comical mold of her idealism. Perhaps it was imagination; perhaps an intuition of the instinctive vegetative processes at work every day beneath the covering of the body, above which the soulful expression of a beautiful woman gazes at us. Possibly it was only the coming of certain indefinable hours when she felt warm and expansive, when her sensations were keener than usual, when ambition and will were becalmed and she was seized by a hushed rapture and fullness of life while her thoughts, even the slightest ones, turned away from the surface and toward the inward depths, leaving the world's events far away, like noise beyond a garden wall. At such times Diotima felt as if she had a direct vision of the truth within herself without having to strain for it; tender experiences that as yet bore no name raised their veils, and she felt—to cite only a few of the many descriptions of it she had found in the literature on the subject—harmonious, humane, religious, and close to that primal source that sanctifies everything arising from it and leaves sinful everything that does not. But even though it was all quite lovely to think about, Diotima could never get beyond such hints and intimations of this peculiar condition; nor did the prophetic books she relied on for help, which spoke of the same thing in the same mysterious and imprecise language. Diotima was reduced to blaming this, too, on a period of civilization that had simply filled up with rubble the access to the soul.

What she called "soul" was probably nothing more than a small amount of capital in love she had possessed at the time of her marriage. Section Chief Tuzzi was not the right business opportunity to invest in. His advantage over Diotima, at first and for a long time, was that of the older man; to this was later added the advantage of the successful man in a mysterious position, who gives his wife little insight into himself even as he looks on indulgently at the trivia that keep her busy. And apart from the tendernesses of courtship, Tuzzi had always been a practical man of common sense who never lost his balance. Even so, the well-cut assurance of his actions and his suits, the—one could say—urbanely grave aroma of his body and his beard, the guardedly firm baritone in which he spoke, all gave him an aura that excited the soul of the girl Diotima as the nearness of his master excites the retriever who lays his muzzle on the master's knees. And just as the dog trots along behind, his feelings safe and fenced in, so Diotima, too, under such serious-minded, matter-of-fact guidance, entered upon the infinite landscape of love.

Here Section Chief Tuzzi preferred the straight paths. His daily habits were those of an ambitious worker. He rose early, either to ride or, preferably, to take an hour's walk, which not only preserves the body's elasticity but also represents the kind of pedantic, simple routine that, strictly adhered to, consorts perfectly with an image of responsible achievement. It also goes without saying that on those evenings when they were not invited out and had no guests he immediately withdrew to his study; for he was forced to maintain his great stock of expert information at the high level that constituted his advantage over his aristocratic colleagues and superiors. Such a life sets firm restraints, and ranges love with the other activities. Like all those whose imagination is not consumed by the erotic, Tuzzi in his bachelor days—apart from having to show himself occasionally because of his diplomatic profession in the company of friends taking out little chorus girls—had been a quiet visitor at one brothel or another, and carried the regular rhythm of this habit over into his marriage. Thus Diotima learned to know love as something violent, assaultive, and brusque that was released only once every week by an even greater power. This change in the nature of two people, which always began promptly on time, to be followed, a few minutes later, by a short exchange on those events of the day that had not come up before and then a sound sleep, and which was never mentioned in the times between, except perhaps in hints and allusions—like making a diplomatic joke about the *"partie honteuse"* of the body—nevertheless had unexpected and paradoxical consequences for her.

On the one hand, it was the cause of that extravagantly swollen ideality—that officious, outwardly-oriented personality—whose power of love, whose spiritual longing, reached out for all things great and noble that turned up in her environment, and that so intensely spread itself and bound itself to these that Diotima evoked the impression, so confusing to males, of a mightily blazing yet Platonic sun of love, the description of which had made Ulrich curious to meet her. On the other hand, however, this broad rhythm of marital contact had developed, purely physiologically, into a habit that asserted itself quite independently and without connection to the loftier parts of her being, like the hunger of a farmhand whose meals are infrequent but heavy. With time, as tiny hairs began to sprout on Diotima's upper lip and the masculine independence of the mature female woman mingled with the traits of the girl, she became aware of this split as something horrible. She loved her husband, but this was mingled with a growing revulsion, a dreadful affront to her soul, which could only be compared to what Archimedes, deeply absorbed in his mathematical problems, might have felt if the enemy soldier had not killed him but made sexual demands on him. And since her husband was not aware of this—nor would he have thought about it if he had been—and since her body always ended up betraying her to him against her will, she felt enslaved; it was a slavery that might not be considered unvirtuous but was just as tormenting as she imagined the appearance of a nervous tic or the inescapability of a vice to be. Now, this might perhaps have made Diotima slightly melancholy and even more idealistic, but unfortunately it happened just at the time that her salon began to cause her some spiritual difficulties.

Section Chief Tuzzi encouraged his wife's intellectual endeavors because he was not slow to see how they might serve to bolster his own position, but he had never taken part in them, and it is safe to say that he did not take them seriously. For the only things this experienced man took seriously were power, duty, high social status, and, at a certain remove, reason. He even warned Diotima repeatedly against being too ambitious in her aesthetic affairs of state, because even if culture is, so to speak, the spice in the food of life, the best people did not go in for an oversalted diet. He said this quite without irony, as it was what he believed, but Diotima felt belittled. She constantly felt that her husband followed her idealistic endeavors with a hovering smile; and whether he was at home or not, and whether this smile—if indeed he did smile; she could never be quite sure—was for her personally or merely part of the facial expression of a man who for professional reasons always had to look superior, as time went on it became increasingly unbearable to her, yet she could not shake off its infamous appearance of being in the right. At times, Diotima would try to blame a materialistic age that had turned the world into an evil, purposeless game in which atheism, socialism, and positivism left no freedom for a person with a rich inner life to rise to true being; but even this was not often of much use.

Such was the situation in the Tuzzi household when the great patriotic campaign quickened the pace of events. Ever since Count Leinsdorf had established his campaign headquarters in Diotima's house so as not to involve the aristocracy, an unspoken sense of responsibility had reigned there, for Diotima had made up her mind to prove to her husband, now or never, that her salon was no plaything. His Grace had confided in her that the great patriotic campaign needed a crowning idea, and it was her burning ambition to find it. The thought of creating something with the resources of an empire and before the attentive eyes of the world, an embodiment of culture at its greatest or, more modestly circumscribed, perhaps something that would reveal the innermost being of Austrian culture—this thought moved Diotima as if the door to her salon had suddenly sprung open and the boundless ocean were lapping at her threshold like an extension of the floor.

There is no denying that her first reaction to this vision was the sense of the momentary gaping of an illimitable void.

First impressions are so often right! Diotima felt sure that something incomparable was going to happen, and she summoned up her many ideals; she mobilized all the pathos of her schoolgirl history lessons, through which she had learned to think in terms of empires and centuries; she did absolutely everything one has to do in such a situation. But after a few weeks had passed in this fashion, she had to face the fact that no inspiration whatsoever had come her way. What Diotima felt toward her husband at this point would have been hatred, had she been at all capable of hatred—such a base impulse! Instead, she became depressed, and began to feel a "resentment against everything" such as she had never known before.

It was at this point that Dr. Arnheim arrived, accompanied by his little black servant, and shortly thereafter paid his momentous call on Diotima.

26

THE UNION OF SOUL AND ECONOMICS. THE MAN WHO CAN ACCOMPLISH THIS WANTS TO ENJOY THE BAROQUE CHARM OF OLD AUSTRIAN CULTURE. AND SO AN IDEA FOR THE PARALLEL CAMPAIGN IS BORN

Diotima never had an improper thought, but on this day there must have been all sorts of goings-on in her mind as it dwelled on the innocent little black boy, after she had sent "Rachelle" out of the room. She had willingly listened once again to the maid's story after Ulrich had left the house of his "great cousin," and the beautiful, ripe woman was feeling young and as if she were playing with a tinkling toy. There had once been a time when the aristocracy had kept black servants—delightful images of sleigh rides with gaily caparisoned horses, plumed lackeys, and frost-powdered trees passed through her mind—but all this picturesque aspect of high life had perished long ago. "The soul has gone out of society these days," she thought. Something in her heart sided with the dashing outsider who still dared keep a blackamoor, this improperly aristocratic bourgeois, this intruder who put to shame the propertied heirs of tradition, as the learned Greek slave had once shamed his Roman masters. Cramped as her self-confidence was by all sorts of considerations, it took wing and gladly deserted to his colors as a sister spirit, and this feeling, so natural compared with her other feelings, even made her overlook that Dr. Arnheim—the rumors were still contradictory, nothing was yet known for certain—was presumed to be of Jewish descent; at least on his father's side, it was reported with certainty. His mother had been dead so long that it would take some time for the facts to be established. It might even have been possible that a certain cruel Weltschmerz in Diotima's heart was not at all interested in a denial.

She had cautiously permitted her thoughts to stray from the blackamoor and approach his master. Dr. Paul Arnheim was not only a rich man but also a man of notable intellect. His fame went beyond the fact that he was heir to world-spanning business interests; the books he had written in his leisure hours were regarded in advanced circles as extraordinary. The people who form such purely intellectual groups are above social and financial considerations, but one must not forget that precisely for that reason they are especially fascinated by a rich man who joins their ranks; furthermore, Arnheim's pamphlets and books proclaimed nothing less than the merger of soul and economics, or of ideas and power. The sensitive minds of the time, those with the finest antennae for what was in the wind, spread the report that he combined these normally opposite poles in his own person, and they encouraged the rumor that here was a man for the times, who might be called on one day to guide for the better the destinies of the German Reich and perhaps—who could tell?— even the world. For there had long been a widespread feeling that the principles and methods of old-style politics and diplomacy were steering Europe right into the ditch, and besides, the period of turning away from specialists had already begun.

Diotima's condition, too, could have been expressed as rebellion against the thinking of the older school of diplomacy, which is why she instantly grasped the marvelous similarity between her own position and that of this brilliant outsider. Besides, the famous man had called on her at the first possible moment; her house was the first by far to receive this mark of distinction, and his letter of introduction from a mutual woman friend mentioned the venerable culture of the Habsburg capital and its people, which this hardworking man hoped to enjoy between unavoidable business engagements. Diotima felt singled out like a writer who is being translated into the language of a foreign country for the first time, when she learned from the letter that this renowned foreigner knew the reputation of her intellect. She noted that he did not look in the least Jewish but was a noble-looking, reserved man of the classic-Phoenician type. Arnheim, too, was delighted to find in Diotima not only a woman who had read his books but who, as a classical beauty on the plump side, corresponded to his Hellenic ideal of beauty, with a bit more flesh on her, perhaps, to soften those strict classical lines. It could not long remain concealed from Diotima that the impression she was able to make in a twenty-minute conversation on a man of real worldwide connections was enough to completely dispel all those doubts through which her own husband, caught up as he was in his rather dated diplomatic ways, had insulted her importance.

She took quiet satisfaction in repeating that conversation to herself. It had barely begun when Arnheim was already saying that he had come to this ancient city only to recuperate a little, under the baroque spell of the Old Austrian culture, from the calculations, materialism, and bleak rationalism in which a civilized man's busy working life was spent nowadays.

There is such a blithe soulfulness in this city, Diotima had answered, as she was pleased to recall.

"Yes," he had said, "we no longer have any inner voices. We know too much these days; reason tyrannizes our lives."

To which she had replied: "I like the company of women. They don't know anything and are unfragmented."

And Arnheim had said: "Nevertheless, a beautiful woman understands far more than a man, who, for all his logic and psychology, knows nothing at all of life."

At which point she had told him that a problem similar to that of freeing the soul from civilization, only on a monumental and national scale, was occupying influential circles here.

"We must—" she had said, and Arnheim interrupted with "That is quite wonderful!"—"bring new ideas, or rather, if I may be permitted to say so"—here he gave a faint sigh—"bring ideas for the very first time into the domains of power." And she had gone on: Committees drawn from all sectors of the population were to be set up in order to ascertain what these ideas should be.

But just at this point Arnheim had said something most important, and in such a tone of warm friendship and respect that the warning left a deep mark on Diotima's mind.

It would not be easy, he had explained, to accomplish anything significant in this way. No democracy of committees but only strong individual personalities, with experience in both reality and the realm of ideas, would be able to direct such a campaign!

Up to this point, Diotima had gone over the conversation in her mind word for word, but here it dissolved into splendor—she could no longer remember what she had answered. A vague, thrilling feeling of joy and expectancy had been lifting her higher and higher all this time; now her mind resembled a small, brightly colored child's balloon that had broken loose and, shining gloriously, was floating upward toward the sun. And in the next instant it burst.

Thus was an idea it had lacked hitherto born to the great Parallel Campaign.

27

NATURE AND SUBSTANCE OF A GREAT IDEA

It would be easy to say what this idea consisted of, but no one could possibly describe its significance. For what distinguishes a great, stirring idea from an ordinary one, possibly even from an incredibly ordinary and mistaken one, is that it exists in a kind of molten state through which the self enters an infinite expanse and, inversely, the expanse of the universe enters the self, so that it becomes impossible to differentiate between what belongs to the self and what belongs to the infinite. This is why great, stirring ideas consist of a body, which like the human body is compact yet frail, and of an immortal soul, which constitutes its meaning but is not compact; on the contrary, it dissolves into thin air at every attempt to grab hold of it in cold words.

After this preamble it must be said that Diotima's great idea amounted to nothing more than that the Prussian, Arnheim, was the man to assume the spiritual leadership of the great Austrian patriotic endeavor, even though this Parallel Campaign contained a barb of jealousy aimed at Prussia-Germany. But this was only the dead verbal body of the idea, and whoever finds it incomprehensible or absurd is kicking a corpse. As concerns the soul of this idea, it was chaste and proper, and in any case her decision contained, so to speak, a codicil for Ulrich. She did not know that her cousin had also made an impression on her, although on a far deeper level than Arnheim, and overshadowed by the impression Arnheim had made; had she realized this, she would probably have despised herself for it. But she had instinctively guarded herself against such knowledge by declaring before her conscious mind that Ulrich was "immature," even though he was older than she was. She took the position that she felt sorry for him, which facilitated her conviction that it was a duty to choose Arnheim instead of Ulrich for the responsibilities of leading the campaign. On the other hand, after she had given birth to this resolution, feminine logic dictated that the slighted party now needed and deserved her help. If he felt shortchanged somehow, there was no better way to make up for it than by taking part in the great campaign, where he would have occasion to be much in her and Arnheim's company. So Diotima decided on that, too, but only as one tucks in a loose end.

28

A CHAPTER THAT MAY BE SKIPPED BY ANYONE NOT PARTICULARLY IMPRESSED BY THINKING AS AN OCCUPATION

Ulrich, meanwhile, was at home, sitting at his desk, working. He had got out the research paper he had interrupted in the middle weeks ago when he had decided to return from abroad; he did not intend to finish it, but it diverted him to see that he could still do that sort of thing. The weather was fine, but in the last few days he had gone out only on brief errands; he had not even set foot in the garden. He had drawn the curtains and was working in the subdued light like an acrobat in a dimly lit circus arena rehearsing dangerous new somersaults for a panel of experts before the public has been let in. The precision, vigor, and sureness of this mode of thinking, which has no equal anywhere in life, filled him with something like melancholy.

He now pushed back the sheets of paper covered with symbols and formulas, the last thing he had written down being an equation for the state of water as a physical example to illustrate the application of a new mathematical process; but his thoughts must have strayed a while before.

"Wasn't I telling Clarisse something about water?" he mused, but could not recall the particulars. But it didn't really matter, and his thoughts roamed idly.

Unfortunately, nothing is so hard to achieve as a literary representation of a man thinking. When someone asked a great scientist how he managed to come up with so much that was new, he replied: "Because I never stop thinking about it." And it is surely safe to say that unexpected insights turn up for no other reason than that they are expected. They are in no small part a success of character, emotional stability, unflagging ambition, and unremitting work. What a bore such constancy must be! Looking at it another way, the solution of an intellectual problem comes about not very differently from a dog with a stick in his mouth trying to get through a narrow door; he will turn his head left and right until the stick slips through. We do much the same thing, but with the difference that we don't make indiscriminate attempts but already know from experience approximately how it's done. And if a clever fellow naturally has far more skill and experience with these twistings and turnings than a dim one, the slipping-through takes the clever fellow just as much by surprise; it is suddenly there, and one perceptibly feels slightly disconcerted because one's ideas seem to have come of their own accord instead of waiting for their creator. This disconcerted feeling is nowadays called intuition by many people who would formerly, believing that it must be regarded as something suprapersonal, have called it inspiration; but it is only something impersonal, namely the affinity and coherence of the things themselves, meeting inside a head.

The better the head, the less evident its presence in this process. As long as the process of thinking is in motion it is a quite wretched state, as if all the brain's convolutions were suffering from colic; and when it is finished it no longer has the form of the thinking process as one experiences it but already that of what has been thought, which is regrettably impersonal, for the thought then faces outward and is dressed for communication to the world. When a man is in the process of thinking, there is no way to catch the moment between the personal and the impersonal, and this is manifestly why thinking is such an embarrassment for writers that they gladly avoid it.

But the man without qualities was now thinking. One may draw the conclusion from this that it was, at least in part, not a personal affair. But then what is it? World in, and world out; aspects of world falling into place inside a head. Nothing of any importance had occurred to him; after he had thought about water as an example, nothing had occurred to him except that water is something three times the size of the land, even counting only what everyone recognizes as water: rivers, seas, lakes, springs. It was long thought to be akin to air. The great Newton thought so, and yet most of his other ideas are still as up-to-date as if they had been thought today. The Greeks thought that the world and life had arisen from water. It was a god: Okeanos. Later, water sprites, elves, mermaids, and nymphs were invented. Temples and oracles were built by the water's edge. The cathedrals of Hildesheim, Paderborn, and Bremen were all built over springs, and behold, are these cathedrals not still standing today? And isn't water still used for baptism? And aren't there devotees of water and apostles of natural healing, whose souls are in such oddly sepulchral health? So there was a place in the world like a blurred spot or grass trodden flat. And of course the man without qualities also had modern scientific concepts in his head, whether he happened to be thinking of them or not. According to them water is a colorless liquid, blue only in thick layers, odorless and tasteless, as you recited over and over in school until you can never forget it, although physiologically it also contains bacteria, vegetable matter, air, iron, calcium sulfate, and calcium bicarbonate, and although physically this archetype of liquids is not basically a liquid at all but, depending on circumstances, a solid, a liquid, or a gas. Ultimately it all dissolves into systems of formulas, all somehow interlinked, and there were only a few dozen people in the whole wide world who thought alike about even so simple a thing as water; all the rest talk about it in languages that belong somewhere between today and some thousands of years ago. So one must say that as soon as a man begins to reflect even a little, he falls into disorderly company!

Now Ulrich remembered that he had, in fact, told all this to Clarisse, who was no better educated than a little animal; but notwithstanding the superstitions she was made of, one had a vague feeling of oneness with her. The thought pricked him like a hot needle.

He was annoyed with himself.

The well-known ability of thought as recognized by doctors to dissolve and dispel those deep-raging, morbidly tangled and matted conflicts generated in the dank regions of the self apparently rests on nothing other than its social and worldly nature, which links the individual creature to other people and objects. But unfortunately the healing power of thought seems to be the same faculty that diminishes the personal sense of experience. A casual reference to a hair on a nose weighs more than the most important concept, and acts, feelings, and sensations, when reported in words, can make one feel one has been present at a more or less notable personal event, however ordinary and impersonal the acts, feelings, and sensations may be.

"It's idiotic," Ulrich thought, "but that's how it is." It made him think of that dumb but deep, exciting sensation, touching immediately on the self, when one sniffs one's own skin. He stood up and pulled the curtains back from the window.

The bark of the trees was still moist from the morning. On the street outside a violet haze of gasoline fumes hovered. The sun shone through it, and people were moving along briskly. It was an asphalt spring, a seasonless spring day in autumn such as only cities can conjure up.

29

EXPLANATION AND DISRUPTIONS OF A
NORMAL STATE OF AWARENESS

Ulrich and Bonadea had agreed on a signal to let her know that he was at home alone. He was always alone, but he gave no signal. He must have expected for some time that Bonadea, hatted and veiled, would show up unbidden. For Bonadea was madly jealous. When she came to see a man—even if it was only to tell him how much she despised him—she always arrived full of inner weakness, what with the impressions of the street and the glances of the men she passed on the way still rocking in her like a faint seasickness. But when the man sensed her weakness and made straight for her body, even though he had callously neglected her for so long, she was hurt, picked a quarrel, delayed with reproachful remarks what she herself could hardly bear to wait for any longer, and had the air of a duck shot through the wings that has fallen into the sea of love and is trying to save itself by swimming.

And all of a sudden she really was sitting here, crying and feeling mistreated.

At such moments when she was angry at her lover, she passionately begged her husband's forgiveness for her lapses. In accordance with a good old rule of unfaithful women, which they apply so as not to betray themselves by an untimely slip of the tongue, she had told her husband about the interesting scholar she sometimes ran into on her visits to a woman friend, although she was not inviting him over because he was too spoiled socially to come from his house to hers and she did not find him interesting enough to invite anyway. The half-truth in this story made it an easier lie, and the other half she used as a grievance against her lover.

How was she supposed to explain to her husband, she asked Ulrich, why she was suddenly visiting her friend less and less? How could she make him understand such fluctuations in her feelings? She cared about the truth because she cared about all ideals, but Ulrich was dishonoring her by forcing her to deviate further from them than was necessary!

She put on a passionate scene, and when it was over, reproaches, avowals, and kisses flooded the ensuing vacuum. When these, too, were over, nothing had happened; the chitchat gushed back to fill the void, and time blew little bubbles like a glass of stale water.

"How much more beautiful she is when she goes wild," Ulrich thought, "but how mechanically it all finished again." The sight of her had excited him and enticed him to make love to her, but now that it was done he felt again how little it had to do with him personally. Another abundantly clear demonstration of how a healthy man can be turned with incredible speed into a frothing lunatic. But this erotic transformation of the consciousness seemed only a special instance of something much more general: for an evening at the theater, a concert, a church service, all such manifestations of the inner life today are similar, quickly dissolving islands of a second state of consciousness that is sometimes interpolated into the ordinary one.

"Only a little while ago," he thought, "I was still working, and before that I was on the street and bought some paper. I said hello to a man I know from the Physics Society, a man with whom I had a serious talk not so long ago. And now, if only Bonadea would hurry up a little, I could look something up in those books I can see from here through the crack in the door. Yet in between we flew through a cloud of insanity, and it is just as uncanny how solid experiences close over this vanishing gap again and assert themselves in all their tenacity."

But Bonadea did not hurry up, and Ulrich was forced to think of something else. His boyhood friend Walter, little Clarisse's husband, who had become so odd, had once said of him: "Ulrich always puts tremendous energy into doing only whatever he considers unnecessary." He happened to remember it at this moment and thought, "The same thing could be said about all of us nowadays." He remembered quite well! A wooden balcony ran all around the country house; Ulrich was the guest of Clarisse's parents; it was a few days before the wedding, and Walter was jealous of him. It was amazing how jealous Walter could be. Ulrich was standing outside in the sunshine when Clarisse and Walter came into the room that lay behind the balcony. He overheard their conversation without trying to keep out of sight. All he remembered of it now was that one sentence. And the scene: the shadowy depths of the room hung like a wrinkled, slightly open pouch on the sunny glare of the outside wall. In the folds of this pouch Walter and Clarisse appeared. Walter's face was painfully drawn and looked as if it had long yellow teeth. Or one could also say that a pair of long yellow teeth lay in a jeweler's box lined with black velvet and that these two people stood spookily by. The jealousy was nonsense, of course; Ulrich did not desire his friends' wives. But Walter had always had a quite special ability to experience intensely. He never got what he was after because he was so swamped by his feelings. He seemed to have a built-in, highly melodious amplifier of the minor joys and miseries of life. He was always paying out emotional small change in gold and silver, while Ulrich operated on a larger scale, with, so to speak, intellectual checks made out for vast sums—but it was only paper, after all. When Ulrich visualized Walter at his most characteristic, he saw him reclining at a forest's edge. He was wearing shorts and, oddly enough, black socks. Walter did not have a man's legs, neither the strong muscular kind nor the skinny sinewy kind, but the legs of a girl; a not particularly attractive girl with soft, plain legs. With his hands behind his head he gazed at the landscape, and heaven forbid he should be disturbed. Ulrich did not remember actually having seen Walter like this on any specified occasion which stamped itself on his mind; it was more of an image that slowly hardened over a decade and a half, like a great seal. And the memory that Walter had been jealous of him at that time was somehow pleasantly stimulating. It had all happened at that time of life when one still takes delight in oneself. It occurred to Ulrich that he had now been to see them several times, "and Walter hasn't been to see me once. But what of it? I might just go out there again this evening."

He planned, after Bonadea at last finished dressing and left, to send them word of his coming. It was not advisable to do that sort of thing in her presence because of the tedious cross-examination that would inevitably follow.

And since thoughts come and go quickly and Bonadea was far from finished, he had yet another idea. This time it was a little theory, simple, illuminating, and time-killing. "A young man with an active mind," Ulrich reflected, probably still thinking of his boyhood friend Walter, "is constantly sending out ideas in every direction. But only those that find a resonance in his environment will be reflected back to him and consolidate, while all the other dispatches are scattered in space and lost!" Ulrich took it as a matter of course that a man who has intellect has all kinds of intellect, so that intellect is more original than qualities. He himself was a man of many contradictions and supposed that all the qualities that have ever manifested themselves in human beings lie close together in every man's mind, if he has a mind at all. This may not be quite right, but what we know about the origin of good and evil suggests that while everyone has a mind of a certain size, he can still probably wear a great variety of clothing in that size, if fate so determines. And so Ulrich felt that what he had just thought was not entirely without significance. For if, in the course of time, commonplace and impersonal ideas are automatically reinforced while unusual ideas fade away, so that almost everyone, with a mechanical certainty, is bound to become increasingly mediocre, this explains why, despite the thousandfold possibilities available to everyone, the average human being is in fact average. And it also explains why even among those privileged persons who make a place for themselves and achieve recognition there will be found a certain mixture of about 51 percent depth and 49 percent shallowness, which is the most successful of all. Ulrich had perceived this for a long time as so intricately senseless and unbearably sad that he would have gladly gone on thinking about it.

He was put off by Bonadea's still giving no sign that she was done. Peering cautiously through the half-open door to the bedroom, he saw that she had stopped dressing. She felt it was indelicate of him to be so absentminded when they should be savoring the last drops of their precious time together; hurt by his silence, she was waiting to see what he would do. She had picked up a book that had in it, luckily, beautiful pictures from the history of art.

Ulrich was irritated by her waiting and pursued his meditations in a state of vague impatience.

30

ULRICH HEARS VOICES

Suddenly his thoughts focused, and as though he were looking through a chink between them, he saw Christian Moosbrugger, the carpenter, and his judges.

In a manner that was painfully ridiculous to anyone not of his mind, the judge spoke:

"Why did you wipe the blood off your hands?—Why did you throw the knife away?—Why did you change into a clean suit and underwear and clean clothes afterward?—Because it was Sunday? Not because they were bloodstained?—How could you go to a dance that same evening? What you had done did not prevent you from going out for a good time? Did you feel no remorse whatsoever?"

Something flickers in Moosbrugger's mind—old prison wisdom: Feign remorse. The flicker gives a twist to his mouth and he says: "Of course I did!"

"But at the police station you said: 'I feel no remorse at all, only such hate and rage I could explode!'" the judge caught him out.

"That may be so," Moosbrugger says, recovering himself and his dignity, "it may be that I had no other feelings then."

"You are a big, strong man," the prosecutor cuts in, "how could you possibly have been afraid of a girl like Hedwig?"

"Your Honor," Moosbrugger answers with a smile, "she was making up to me. She threatened to be even more treacherous than I usually expected women of her sort to be. I may look strong, and I am—"

"Well then," the presiding judge growls, leafing through his files.

"But in certain situations," Moosbrugger says loudly, "I am very shy, even cowardly."

The judge's eyes dart up from the file; like two birds taking off from a branch, they abandon the sentence they had just been perching on.

"But the time you picked that fight with the men on the building site you weren't at all cowardly!" the judge says. "You threw one of them down two floors, you pulled a knife on the others—"

"Your Honor," Moosbrugger cries out in a threatening voice, "I still stand today on the standpoint—"

The presiding judge waves this away.

"Injustice," Moosbrugger says, "must be the basis of my brutality. I have stood before the court, a simple man, and thought Your Honors must know everything anyway. But you have let me down!"

The judge's face had long been buried again in the file.

The prosecutor smiles and says in a kindly tone: "But surely Hedwig was a perfectly harmless girl?"

"Not to me she wasn't!" Moosbrugger says, still indignant.

"It seems to *me*," the presiding judge says emphatically, "that you always manage to put the blame on someone else."

"Now tell me, why did you start stabbing her?" the prosecutor gently begins at the beginning again.

31

WHOSE SIDE ARE YOU ON?

Was it something he had heard at the session of the trial he attended, or had he just picked it up from the reports he had read? He remembered it all so vividly now, as though he could actually hear these voices. He had never in his life "heard voices"—by God, he was not like that. But if one does hear them, then something descends like the quiet peace of a snowfall. Suddenly walls are there, from the earth to the sky; where before there was air, one strides through thick soft walls, and all the voices that hopped from one place to another in the cage of the air now move about freely within the white walls that have fused together down to their inmost essence.

He was probably overstimulated from work and boredom; such things happen sometimes; anyway, he didn't find it half bad, hearing voices. Suddenly he was saying under his breath, "We have a second home, where everything we do is innocent."

Bonadea was lacing up a string. She had meanwhile come into his room. She was displeased with their conversation; she found it in poor taste. She had long since forgotten the name of the man who had killed that girl, the case the papers had been so full of, and it all came back to mind only reluctantly when Ulrich began to speak of him.

"But if Moosbrugger can evoke this disturbing impression of innocence," he said after a while, "how much more innocent that poor, ragged, shivering creature was, with those mouse eyes under that kerchief, that Hedwig, who begged him for a night's shelter in his room and got herself killed for it."

"Must you?" Bonadea offered and shrugged her white shoulders. For when Ulrich gave this turn to the conversation, it came at the maliciously chosen moment when the clothes his offended friend had half put on when she came into his room, thirsting for reconciliation, were once more heaped on the carpet, forming a small, charmingly mythological crater of foam like the one that had given birth to Aphrodite. Bonadea was therefore ready to detest Moosbrugger, and to pass over the fate of his victim with a fleeting shudder. But Ulrich would not let it go at that, and insisted on vividly depicting for her Moosbrugger's impending fate.

"Two men who have no bad feelings against him at all will put the noose around his neck, only because that is what they are paid for. Perhaps a hundred people will be watching, some because it is their job, others because everyone wants to have seen an execution once in his life. A solemn gentleman in a top hat, frock coat, and black gloves will then tighten the noose, while at the same moment his helpers grab hold of Moosbrugger's legs and pull, to break his neck. Then the man with the black gloves plays doctor, and lays a hand on Moosbrugger's heart to check whether it is still beating—because if it is, the whole procedure has to be gone through once again, more impatiently and with less solemnity. Now, are you really for Moosbrugger or against him?" Ulrich asked.

Slowly and painfully, like a person awakened at the wrong time, Bonadea had lost "the mood," as she was accustomed to calling her fits of adultery. Now, after her hands had irresolutely held her slipping clothes and open corset for a while, she had to sit down. Like every woman in a similar situation, she had firm confidence in an established public order of such a degree of justice that one could go about one's private affairs without having to think about it. But now, reminded of the opposite, compassionate partisanship for Moosbrugger as victim took hold of her, sweeping aside any thought of Moosbrugger the criminal.

"Then you are always for the victim," Ulrich insisted, "and against the act?"

Bonadea expressed the obvious feeling that such a conversation in such a situation was not appropriate.

"But if your judgment is so consistent in condemning the act," Ulrich replied, instead of instantly apologizing, "then how can you justify your adulteries, Bonadea?"

It was the plural that was in such especially bad taste! Bonadea said nothing but sat down, with a disdainful look, in one of the luxurious armchairs and stared up, insulted, at the dividing line between wall and ceiling.

32

THE FORGOTTEN, HIGHLY RELEVANT STORY
OF THE MAJOR'S WIFE

It is not advisable to feel kinship with an obvious lunatic, nor did Ulrich do so. And yet why did one expert maintain that Moosbrugger was a lunatic and the other that he was not? Where had the reporters got their slickly factual account of the work of Moosbrugger's knife? And by what qualities did Moosbrugger arouse that excitement and horror that made half of the two million people who lived in this city react to him as if he were a family quarrel or a broken engagement, something so personally exciting that it stirred normally dormant areas of the soul, while his story was a more indifferent novelty in the country towns and meant nothing at all in Berlin or Breslau, where from time to time they had their own Moosbruggers, the Moosbruggers in their own families, to think about. The awful way society had of toying with its victims preoccupied Ulrich. He felt an echo of it in himself too. No impulse stirred in him either to free Moosbrugger or to assist justice, and his feelings stood on end like a cat's fur. For some unknown reason Moosbrugger concerned him more deeply than the life he himself was leading. Moosbrugger seized him like an obscure poem in which everything is slightly distorted and displaced, and reveals a drifting meaning fragmented in the depths of the mind.

"Thrill-seeking!" He pulled himself up short. To be fascinated with the gruesome or the taboo, in the admissible form of dreams and neuroses, seemed quite in character for the people of the bourgeois age. "Either/or!" he thought. "Either I like you or I don't. Either I defend you, freakishness and all, or I ought to punch myself in the jaw for playing around with this monstrosity!" And finally, a cool but energetic compassion would also be appropriate here. There was a lot that could be done in this day and age to prevent such events and such characters from happening, if only society would make half the moral effort it demands of such victims. But then it turned out that there was yet another angle from which the matter could be considered, and strange memories rose up in Ulrich's mind.

We never judge an act by that aspect of it which is pleasing or displeasing to God. It was Luther, oddly enough, who had said that, probably under the influence of one of the mystics with whom he was friends for a while. It could certainly have been said by many another religious. They were, in the bourgeois sense, all immoralists. They distinguished between the sins and the soul, which can remain immaculate despite the sins, almost as Machiavelli distinguished the ends from the means. The "human heart" had been "taken from them." "In Christ too there was an outer and an inner man, and everything he did with regard to outward things he did as the outer man, while his inner man stood by in immovable solitude," says Eckhart. Such saints and believers would in the end have been capable of acquitting even Moosbrugger! Mankind has certainly made progress since then, but even though it will kill Moosbrugger, it still has the weakness to venerate those men who might—who knows?—have acquitted him.

And now Ulrich remembered a sentence, which was preceded by a wave of uneasiness: "The soul of the Sodomite might pass through the throng without misgiving, and with a child's limpid smile in its eyes; for everything depends on an invisible principle." This was not so very different from the other sayings, yet in its slight exaggeration it had the sweet, sickly breath of corruption. And as it turned out, a space belonged to this saying, a room with yellow French paperbacks on the tables and glass-bead curtains instead of doors; and a feeling stirred in his chest as when a hand reaches inside the split carcass of a chicken to pull out the heart: It was Diotima who had uttered that sentence the last time he saw her. It came, moreover, from a contemporary author Ulrich had loved in his youth but whom he had since learned to regard as a parlor philosopher, and aphorisms like this taste like bread doused with perfume, so that for decades one doesn't want to have anything to do with any of it.

Yet however strong the distaste that this aroused in Ulrich, he thought it disgraceful that he had let it keep him all his life from returning to the other, authentic statements of that mysterious language. For he had a special, instinctive understanding for them, which might rather be called a familiarity that leapt over the understanding, although he could never make up his mind to embrace them wholeheartedly as tenets of faith. They lay—such statements, which spoke to him with a fraternal sound, with a gentle, dark inwardness that was the opposite of the hectoring tones of mathematical or scientific language, though otherwise indefinable—like islands scattered among his preoccupations, without connection and rarely visited; yet, when he surveyed them, to the extent that he had come to know them, it seemed to him that he could feel their coherence, as if these islands, only a little separated from each other, were the outposts of a coast hidden behind them, or represented the remains of a continent that had perished primordial eras ago.

He felt the softness of sea, mist, and low black ridges of land asleep in a yellowish-gray light. He remembered a little sea voyage, an escape along the lines of "A trip will do you good!" or "Try a change of scene!" and he knew precisely what a strange, absurdly magical experience had superimposed itself by its deterrent force once and for all, on all others of its kind. For an instant the heart of a twenty-year-old beat in his breast, whose hairy skin had thickened and coarsened with the years. The beating of a twenty-year-old heart inside his thirty-two-year-old chest felt like an improper kiss given by a boy to a man. Nevertheless, this time he did not shrink from the memory. It was the memory of a passion that had come to a strange end, a passion he had felt at twenty for a woman considerably older than he, not only in years but by virtue of her settled domestic state.

Characteristically, he remembered only imprecisely what she looked like. A stilted photograph and his memory of the hours he had spent alone thinking of her took the place of live impressions of the face, clothes, voice, and movements of this woman. He had in the meantime become so estranged from her world that the fact of her having been the wife of an army major struck him as so incredible, it was funny. By this time, he thought, she will long have been a retired colonel's wife. According to the regimental scuttlebutt she was a trained artist, a virtuoso pianist who had never performed publicly out of deference to the wishes of her family; later on, in any case, her marriage made such a career impossible. She did, in fact, play the piano beautifully at regimental parties, with all the radiance of a well-gilded sun floating above chasms of feelings, and from the first Ulrich had fallen in love not so much with this woman's sensual presence as with what she stood for. The lieutenant who at that time had borne his name was not shy; his eye had already practiced on female small game and even espied the faintly beaten poacher's path leading to this or that respectable woman. But for such twenty-year-old officers a "grand passion," if they thought of such a thing at all, was something else entirely; it was a concept, something that lay outside their range of activity and was as devoid of experienced content, hence as luminously vacuous, as only a really grand concept can be. So when for the first time in his life Ulrich saw in himself the possibility of applying this concept, it was as good as done; the part played in this by the major's wife was no more than that of the last contributory cause that triggers the outbreak of a disease. Ulrich became lovesick. And since true lovesickness is not a desire for possession but the world's gentle self-unveiling, for the sake of which one willingly renounces possession of the beloved, the lieutenant proceeded to explain the world to the major's wife in an unaccustomed and persistent manner such as she had never heard before. Constellations, bacteria, Balzac, and Nietzsche whirled around in a vortex of ideas the point of which, as she sensed with growing clarity, was directed at certain differences—not considered a proper subject of conversation in those days—between her own body and that of the lieutenant. She was bewildered by his insistence on linking love with subjects that, as far as she knew, had never had anything to do with love. One day, when they had gone out riding, as they walked beside their horses she left her hand in his for a moment and was appalled to find that her hand stayed there as if in a swoon. In the next second flames ran through them from their wrists to their knees and a bolt of lightning felled both of them so that they almost tumbled by the wayside, where they found themselves sitting on the moss, wildly kissing and then overcome with embarrassment, because love was so great and out of the ordinary that, to their surprise, they could find nothing to say or do other than what people usually do in such embraces. The horses, growing restive, at last released the lovers from this predicament.

The love between the major's wife and this too-young lieutenant remained short and unreal throughout its course. They both marveled at it; they held each other close a few more times, both sensing that something was wrong and would not let them come fully to-gether, body to body in their embraces, even if they shed all obsta-cles of clothing and morality. The major's wife did not want to deny herself a passion she felt to be beyond her power to judge, but she was throbbing with secret reproaches on account of her husband and the difference in age. When Ulrich told her one day, on some thread-bare pretext, that he had to take a long furlough, the officer's lady breathed a tearful sigh of relief. By this time Ulrich was so far gone in love that he had no more pressing need than to get away as quickly and as far as possible from the vicinity of the cause of this love. He traveled blindly at random, until a coast put an end to the railroad tracks, took a boat to the nearest island, and there, in some place he had never heard of, minimally provided with bed and board, he wrote that first night the first of a series of long letters to his beloved, which he never mailed.

These letters, written in the dead of night after filling his thoughts all day, were later lost—as they were probably meant to be. At first he had still had much to say about his love for her and all sorts of thoughts she inspired in him, but all that was soon and increasingly displaced by the scenery. Mornings the sun raised him from his sleep, and when the fishermen were out on the water, the women and children near their houses, he and a donkey who was grazing among the shrubs and hillocks between the island's two little villages seemed to be the only higher forms of life on this adventurous out-post of the world. Ulrich followed his companion's example and climbed up on a hillock or lay down on the island's rim in the com-pany of sea, rock, and sky. He had no sense of presuming, because the difference in size did not seem to matter, nor did the difference between mind and nature, animate and inanimate; this communion diminished all kinds of differences. To put it quite soberly, these dif-ferences were neither lost nor lessened, but their meaning fell away; one was no longer "subject to those divisions that afflict mankind" as described by those religious seized by the mysticism of love, of whom the young cavalry lieutenant at that time knew absolutely nothing. Nor did he reflect on these phenomena—as a hunter on the track of wild game might track down an observation and follow it up—in-deed, he hardly noticed them, but he took them into himself. He sank into the landscape, although it was just as much an inexpressible being borne up by it, and when the world surpassed his eyes, its meaning lapped against him from within in soundless waves. He had penetrated the heart of the world; from it to his far-off love was no farther than the nearest tree. In-feeling linked living beings without space, as in a dream two beings can pass through each other without mingling, and altered all their relations. Other than this, however, his state of mind had nothing in common with dreaming. It was clear, and brimful of clear thoughts; however, nothing in him was moved by cause, purpose, or physical desire, but everything went rippling out in circle after ever-renewed circle, as when an infinite jet falls on a basin's surface. This was what he also described in his letters, and nothing else.

Life's very shape was completely altered. Not placed in the focus of ordinary attention but freed from sharpness. Seen this way, everything seemed a little scattered and blurred, and being infused all the while with a delicate clarity and certainty from other centers. All of life's questions and occurrences took on an incomparable mildness, gentleness, and serenity, while their meaning was utterly transformed. If in this state of being a beetle, for instance, should run past the hand of a man deep in thought, it was not an approach, a passing by, a moving off, nor was it beetle and man, but a happening that ineffably touched the heart, and not even a happening but, although it was happening, a condition. And with the help of such tranquil experiences everything that usually makes up an ordinary life was endowed with a radical new meaning for Ulrich at every turn.

In this condition even his love for the major's wife quickly took on its predestined form. Thinking of her incessantly, he sometimes tried to visualize her doing whatever she might be doing at that very moment, aided by his thorough knowledge of her circumstances. But as soon as he succeeded in seeing his beloved as if she were physically present, his feeling for her, which had grown so infinitely clairvoyant, became blind, and he had to quickly reduce her image to that blissful certainty of her-being-there-for-him-somewhere proper to a Great Love. It was not very long before she had turned entirely into that impersonal center of energy, the underground dynamo that kept his lights going, and he wrote her a final letter, setting forth that the great ideal of living for love actually had nothing to do with physical possession and the wish "Be mine!" that came from the sphere of thrift, appropriation, and gluttony. This was the only letter he mailed, and approximately the high point of his lovesickness, from which it soon declined and suddenly ended.

33

BREAKING WITH BONADEA

Meanwhile Bonadea, who could not go on staring continually at the ceiling, had stretched out on her back on the divan, her tender maternal belly in white batiste free to breathe unhampered by whalebone and laces. She called this position "thinking." It flashed through her mind that her husband was not only a judge but also a hunter, whose eyes sometimes sparkled when he spoke of the beasts that preyed on game; she felt there might be something in this to help both Moosbrugger and his judges. Yet she did not want her husband put in the wrong by her lover, except *as* a lover; her family feeling demanded that the head of her household be seen as dignified and respected. So she came to no decision. And while this conflict was drowsily darkening her horizon like two banks of clouds amorphously merging with each other, Ulrich enjoyed being free to follow his thoughts. But this had lasted for quite a while, and as nothing had occurred to Bonadea that would have given matters a new turn, she reverted to feeling aggrieved that Ulrich had negligently insulted her, and the time he was letting pass without making it up to her began to weigh on her as a provocation.

"So you think I am doing wrong in coming here to see you?" she finally asked him, with grave emphasis, sadly, but ready for battle.

Ulrich gave no answer but shrugged his shoulders. He had long since forgotten what she was talking about, but he simply couldn't stand her at this moment.

"So you are really capable of blaming *me* for our passion?"

"Every such question has as many answers hanging on it as there are bees in a hive," Ulrich replied. "All human spiritual disorder, with its never-resolved problems, hangs on every single one of them in some disgusting way."

He was only saying aloud what he had been thinking, off and on, all day. But Bonadea took "spiritual disorder" as referring to herself and decided that this was too much. She would have liked to draw the curtains again and so do away with this quarrel, but she would just as gladly have howled with grief. All at once she understood that Ulrich had grown tired of her. Given her temperament, she had hitherto never lost her lovers except as one mislays something and forgets it when attracted to something new, or in that other easy-come, easy-go fashion that, no matter how personally irritating sometimes, still had something of the air of the workings of a higher power. And so her first reaction to Ulrich's quiet resistance was the feeling that she had grown old. She was humiliated by her helpless and obscene position, half-naked on a sofa, an easy target for insults. Without stopping to think, she got up and grabbed her clothes. But the rustling and swishing of the silken chalices into which she was slipping back did not move Ulrich to remorse. Right above her eyes, Bonadea felt the stabbing pain of helplessness. "He's a brute," she said to herself over and over. "He said it on purpose to hurt me! He's not lifting a finger!" With every ribbon she tied and every hook she fastened, she sank deeper into that abysmally black well of a long-forgotten childish anguish at being abandoned. Darkness welled up around her; Ulrich's face was visible as if in the waning light, set hard and brutal against the dark of her misery. "How could I ever have loved that face?" Bonadea asked herself, but at the same moment the words "Lost forever!" tightened her whole chest in a spasm.

Ulrich, who guessed that she had made up her mind never to come back, did nothing to stop her. In front of the mirror, Bonadea firmly smoothed her hair put on her hat, and tied her veil. Now that the veil was fastened in front of her face it was all over; it was as solemn as a death sentence, or when the lock snaps shut on a suitcase. He was to have no last kiss, nor even to realize that he was missing his last chance ever to kiss her again!

At this thought she almost threw her arms around his neck in pity, and could have cried her eyes out on his chest.

34

A HOT FLASH AND CHILLED WALLS

After Ulrich had escorted Bonadea out and was alone again, he no longer had any desire to go on working. He went out to the street with the intention of sending a message to Walter and Clarisse that he would come to see them this evening. As he was crossing the small foyer, he noticed a pair of antlers on the wall; somehow they reminded him of Bonadea's movements when she had tied her veil before the mirror, except that here there was no resigned smile. He looked around, contemplating his environment. All these circular lines, intersecting lines, straight lines, curves and wreaths of which a domestic interior is composed and that had piled up around him were neither nature nor inner necessity but bristled, to the last detail, with baroque overabundance. The current and heartbeat that constantly flows through all the things in our surroundings had stopped for a moment. "I'm only fortuitous," Necessity leered. "Observed without prejudice, my face doesn't look much different from a leper's," Beauty confessed. Actually, it did not take much to produce this effect: a varnish had come off, a power of suggestion had lost its hold, a chain of habit, expectation, and tension had snapped; a fluid, mysterious equilibrium between feeling and world was upset for the space of a second. Everything we feel and do is somehow oriented "lifeward," and the least deviation away from this direction toward something beyond is difficult or alarming. This is true even of the simple act of walking: one lifts one's center of gravity, pushes it forward, and lets it drop again—and the slightest change, the merest hint of shrinking from this letting-oneself-drop-into-the-future, or even of stopping to wonder at it—and one can no longer stand upright! Stopping to think is dangerous. It occurred to Ulrich that every decisive point in his life had left behind a similar feeling.

He found a messenger and sent him off with his note. It was about four in the afternoon, and he decided to walk there, taking his time. It was a deliciously late-spring kind of fall day. There was a ferment in the air. People's faces were like spindrift. After the monotonous tension of his thoughts in the last few days he felt as if he were exchanging a prison for a warm bath. He made a point of walking in an amiable, relaxed manner. A gymnastically well trained body holds so much readiness to move and fight that today it gave him an unpleasant feeling, like the face of an old clown, full of oft-repeated false passions. In the same way, his truth-seeking had filled his being with capacities for mental agility, divided into troops of thoughts exercising each other, and given him that—strictly speaking—false clown expression that everything, even sincerity itself, assumes when it becomes a habit. So Ulrich thought. He flowed like a wave among its fellow waves, if one may say so, and why not, when a man who has been wearing himself out with lonely work at last rejoins the community and delights in flowing along with it?

At such a moment nothing may seem so remote as the thought that people are not much concerned, inwardly, with the life they lead and are led by. And yet we all know this as long as we are young. Ulrich remembered how such a day had looked to him in these same streets ten or fifteen years ago. It had all been twice as glorious then, and yet there had quite definitely been in all that seething desire an aching sense of being taken captive; an uneasy feeling that "Everything I think I am attaining is attaining me," a gnawing surmise that in this world the untrue, uncaring, personally indifferent statements will echo more strongly than the most personal and authentic ones. "This beauty," one thought, "is all well and good, but is it mine? And is the truth I am learning *my* truth? The goals, the voices, the reality, all this seductiveness that lures and leads us on, that we pursue and plunge into—is this reality itself or is it no more than a breath of the real, resting intangibly on the surface of the reality the world offers us? What sharpens our suspicions are all those prefabricated compartments and forms of life, semblances of reality, the molds set by earlier generations, the ready-made language not only of the tongue but also of sensations and feelings."

Ulrich had stopped in front of a church. Good heavens, if a gigantic matron were to have been sitting here in the shade, with a huge belly terraced like a flight of steps, her back resting against the houses behind her, and above, in thousands of wrinkles, warts, and pimples, the sunset in her face, couldn't he have found *that* beautiful

too? Lord, yes, it was beautiful! He didn't want to weasel out of this
by claiming he was put on earth with the obligation to admire this
sort of thing; however, there was nothing to prevent him from finding these broad, serenely drooping forms and the filigree of wrinkles
on a venerable matron beautiful—it is merely simpler to say that she
is old. And this transition from finding the world old to finding it
beautiful is about the same as that from a young person's outlook to
the higher moral viewpoint of the mature adult, which remains absurdly didactic until one suddenly espouses it oneself. It was only
seconds that Ulrich stood outside the church, but they rooted in him
and compressed his heart with all the resistance of primal instinct
against this world petrified into millions of tons of stone, against this
frozen moonscape of feeling where, involuntarily, he had been set
down.

It may be a convenience and a comfort for most people to find the
world ready-made, apart from a few minor personal details, and
there is no disputing that whatever endures is not only conservative
but also the foundation of all advances and revolutions; but it must
be said that this casts a feeling of deep, shadowy unease on those who
live according to their own lights. It flashed on Ulrich with surprising
suddenness, as he appreciated the architectural fine points of the sacred edifice, that one could just as easily devour people as build such
monuments or allow them to stand. The houses beside it, the firmament above, the indescribable harmony of all the lines and spaces
that caught and guided the eye, the look and expression of the people
passing below, their books, their morals, the trees along the street
. . . it all seems at times as stiff as folding screens, as hard as a
printer's die stamp, complete—there is no other way of putting it—
so complete and finished that one is mere superfluous mist beside it,
a small, exhaled breath God has no time for anymore.

At this moment he wished he were a man without qualities. But it
is probably not so very different for anyone. Few people in mid-life
really know how they got to be what they are, how they came by their
pastimes, their outlook, their wife, their character, profession, and
successes, but they have the feeling that from this point on nothing
much can change. It might even be fair to say that they were tricked,
since nowhere is a sufficient reason to be found why everything
should have turned out the way it did; it could just as well have

turned out differently; whatever happened was least of all their own doing but depended mostly on all sorts of circumstances, on moods, the life and death of quite different people; these events converged on one, so to speak, only at a given point in time. In their youth, life lay ahead of them like an inexhaustible morning, full of possibilities and emptiness on all sides, but already by noon something is suddenly there that may claim to be their own life yet whose appearing is as surprising, all in all, as if a person had suddenly materialized with whom one had been corresponding for some twenty years without meeting and whom one had imagined quite differently. What is even more peculiar is that most people do not even notice it; they adopt the man who has come to them, whose life has merged with their own, whose experiences now seem to be the expression of their own qualities, and whose fate is their own reward or misfortune. Something has done to them what flypaper does to a fly, catching it now by a tiny hair, now hampering a movement, gradually enveloping it until it is covered by a thick coating that only remotely suggests its original shape. They then have only vague recollections of their youth, when there was still an opposing power in them. This opposing power tugs and spins, will not settle anywhere and blows up a storm of aimless struggles to escape; the mockery of the young, their revolt against institutions, their readiness for everything that is heroic, for martyrdom or crime, their fiery earnestness, their instability—all this means nothing more than their struggles to escape. Basically, these struggles merely indicate that nothing a young person does is done from an unequivocal inner necessity, even though they behave as if whatever they are intent upon at the moment must be done, and without delay. Someone comes up with a splendid new gesture, an outward or inward—how shall we translate it?—vital pose? A form into which inner meaning streams like helium into a balloon? An expression of impression? A technique of being? It can be a new mustache or a new idea. It is playacting, but like all playacting it tries to say something, of course—and like the sparrows off the rooftops when someone scatters crumbs on the ground, young souls instantly pounce on it. Imagine, if you will, what it is to have a heavy world weighing on tongue, hands, and eyes, a chilled moon of earth, houses, mores, pictures, and books, and inside nothing but an unstable, shifting mist; what a joy it must be whenever someone brings out a slogan in which one thinks one can recognize oneself. What is more natural than that every person of intense feeling get hold of this new form before the common run of people does? It offers that moment of self-realization, of balance between inner and outer, between being crushed and exploding.

There is no other basis, Ulrich thought—and all this, of course, touched him personally as well—as he stood with his hands in his pockets, his face looking as peaceful and contentedly asleep as if he were dying in the sun's rays that whirled about him, a gentle death in snow—no other basis, he thought, for that everlasting phenomenon variously called the new generation, fathers and sons, intellectual revolution, change of style, evolution, fashion, and revival. What makes this craving for the renovation of life into a *perpetuum mobile* is nothing but the discomfort at the intrusion, between one's own misty self and the alien and already petrified carapace of the self of one's predecessors, of a pseudoself, a loosely fitting group soul. With a little attention, one can probably always detect in the latest Future signs of the coming Old Times. The new ideas will then be a mere thirty years older but contented and with a little extra fat on their bones or past their prime, much as one glimpses alongside a girl's shining features the extinguished face of the mother; or they have had no success, and are down to skin and bones, shrunken to a re-form proposed by some old fool who is called the Great So-and-so by his fifty admirers.

He came to a halt again, this time in a square where he recognized some of the houses and remembered the public controversies and intellectual ferment that had accompanied their construction. He thought of the friends of his youth; they had all been the friends of his youth, whether he knew them personally or only by name, whether they were the same age as he or older, all the rebels who wanted to bring new things and new people into the world, whether here or scattered over all the places he had ever known. Now these houses stood in the late, already fading afternoon light, like kindly aunts in outmoded hats, quite proper and irrelevant and anything but exciting. He was tempted to a little smile. But the people who had left these unassuming relics behind had meanwhile become professors, celebrities, names, recognized participants in the recognized development of progress; they had made it by a more or less direct path from the mist to the petrifact, and for that reason history may report of them someday, in giving its account of the century: "Among those present were . . ."

35

BANK DIRECTOR LEO FISCHEL AND THE PRINCIPLE OF INSUFFICIENT CAUSE

At this moment Ulrich was interrupted by an acquaintance addressing him out of nowhere. Before leaving home that morning this acquaintance had had the unpleasant surprise of finding in a side pocket of his briefcase a circular from Count Leinsdorf, which he had received some time ago and forgotten to answer because his sound business sense disinclined him from having anything to do with patriotic movements originating in high social circles. "Rotten business," he doubtless said to himself at the time, though that was not at all what he would have wanted to say publicly; but, as memory will, his had played a dirty trick on him by taking orders from this first, unofficial reaction of his feelings and letting the matter drop, instead of waiting for a considered decision. When he opened the form letter this time, he saw something he had previously overlooked and that now caused him acute embarrassment; it was really only a phrase, two little words that turned up in all sorts of places throughout the text, but these two words had cost the portly man several minutes of indecision as he stood, briefcase in hand, before leaving his house. They were: "the true."

Bank Director Fischel—for that is what he was called, Director Leo Fischel of the Lloyd Bank, though he was only a manager with the title of director—(Ulrich, though much younger, could regard himself as a friend from earlier days; he had been quite close to

Fischel's daughter, Gerda, the last time he had stayed in the city, though he had called on her only once since his return)—Director Fischel knew Count Leinsdorf as a man who made his money work for him and kept up with modern methods; in fact, running his mind over the account (Count Leinsdorf used Lloyd's, among other banks, for his dealings on the stock exchange), he recognized Count Leinsdorf for a man of consequence, as they say in business. Therefore Leo Fischel could not understand how he could have been so careless about so important an invitation, in which His Grace appealed to a select circle to take part in a great and communal undertaking. Fischel himself had been included in this circle only because of some very special circumstances, to be gone into later, and all this was the reason he had rushed up to Ulrich the moment he caught sight of him. He had heard that Ulrich had something to do with the affair, was indeed in a "prominent position"—one of those inexplicable but not uncommon rumors that anticipate the facts—and fired off three questions at him like a three-barreled pistol:

"What is really meant by 'the true patriotism,' 'the true progress,' and 'the true Austria'?"

Startled out of his mood but continuing its spirit, Ulrich replied in the manner he always fell into in his conversations with Fischel: "The P.I.C."

"The what?" Director Fischel innocently spelled the letters out after him, this time not suspecting a joke, because such abbreviations, while not so numerous then as they are now, were familiar from cartels and trusts, and radiated confidence. But then he said: "Please, no jokes just now, I'm in a hurry and late for a meeting."

"The Principle of Insufficient Cause," Ulrich elucidated. "You are a philosopher yourself and know about the Principle of Sufficient Cause. The only exception we make is in our own individual cases: in our real, I mean our personal, lives, and in our public-historical lives, everything that happens happens for no good or sufficient reason."

Leo Fischel wavered between disputing this and letting it pass. Director Leo Fischel of the Lloyd Bank loved to philosophize (there still are such people in the practical professions) but he actually was in a hurry, so he said: "You are dodging the issue. I know what progress is, I know what Austria is, and I probably know what it is to love my country too, but I'm not quite sure what true patriotism is, or what the true Austria, or true progress may be, and that's what I'm asking you."

"All right. Do you know what an enzyme is? Or a catalyst?"

Leo Fischel only raised a hand defensively.

"It doesn't contribute anything materially, but it sets processes in motion. You must know from history that there has never been such a thing as the true faith, the true morality, and the true philosophy. But the wars, the viciousness, and the hatreds unleashed in their name have transformed the world in a fruitful way."

"Some other time!" Fischel implored him, and then tried another tack: cards on the table. "Look, I have to cope with this on the Exchange, and I really would like to know what Count Leinsdorf actually has in mind: just what does he mean by that additional 'true' of his?"

"I give you my solemn word," Ulrich said gravely, "that neither I nor anyone else knows what 'the true' anything is, but I can assure you that it is on the point of realization."

"You're a cynic!" Director Fischel declared as he dashed off, but after the first step he turned back and amended himself: "Quite recently I was saying to Gerda that you would have made a first-rate diplomat. I hope you'll come see us again soon."

36

THANKS TO THE ABOVE-MENTIONED PRINCIPLE THE PARALLEL CAMPAIGN BECOMES A TANGIBLE REALITY BEFORE ANYONE KNOWS WHAT IT IS

Director Leo Fischel of the Lloyd Bank, like all bank directors before the war, believed in progress. As a capable man in his field he knew, of course, that only where one has a thorough knowledge of the facts can one have a conviction on which one would be willing to stake one's own money. The immense expansion of activities does not allow for such competence outside one's own field. Accordingly, efficient, hardworking people have no convictions beyond the limits of their own narrow specialties; none, that is, they will not instantly abandon under pressure from the outside. One might go so far as to say that conscientiousness forces them to act differently from the way they think. Director Fischel, for instance, could form no concept at all of true patriotism or the true Austria, but he did have his own opinion of true progress, which was certainly different from Count Leinsdorf's opinion. Exhausted by stocks and bonds or whatever it was he had to deal with, his only recreation an evening at the opera once a week, he believed in a progress of the whole that must somehow resemble his bank's progressively increasing profitability. But now that Count Leinsdorf claimed to know better even in this respect, and thus began to put pressure on Leo Fischel's conscience, Fischel felt that "you can never know, after all" (except, of course, with stocks and bonds), and since one might not know but on the other hand would rather not miss out on anything, he decided to informally sound out his general manager on the matter.

When he did, the general manager had for quite similar reasons already had a talk with the chief executive of the National Bank and knew all about it. For not only the general manager of the Lloyd Bank but, it goes without saying, the chief executive of the National Bank had also received an invitation from Count Leinsdorf. Leo Fischel, who was only a head of department, owed his invitation entirely to his wife's family connections: she came from the upper reaches of the government/bureaucracy and never forgot it, either in her social relations or in her domestic quarrels with Leo. He therefore contented himself, as he and his superior talked about the Parallel Campaign, with wagging his head significantly, as if to say "big proposition," though it might in other circumstances have meant "rotten business"—either way it couldn't hurt, but on account of his wife Fischel would probably have been happier if it had turned out to be a "rotten business."

So far, however, von Meier-Ballot, the chief executive who had been consulted by the general manager, had himself formed an excellent impression of the undertaking. When he received Count Leinsdorf's "suggestion," he went over to the mirror—naturally, though not for that reason—and there he saw, above the tailcoat and the little gold chain of his order, the composed face of a middle-class government minister, in which the hardness of money was at most barely visible somewhere far back in the eyes. His fingers hung down like flags in a calm, as though they had never in their life had to carry out the hasty movements with which an apprentice bank teller counts his cash. This bureaucratically overbred high financier who had hardly a thing in common any longer with the hungry, roaming wild dogs of the stock-exchange game, saw vague but pleasingly modulated possibilities ahead, an outlook he had an opportunity of confirming that same evening in conversation with the former Ministers of State von Holtzkopf and Baron Wisnieczky at the Industrialists' Club.

These two gentlemen were well-informed, distinguished, and discreet persons in some kind of high positions into which they had been shunted after the brief caretaker government between two political crises in which they had participated had become superfluous. They were men who had spent their lives in the service of the State and the Crown, with no taste for the limelight unless ordered into it by His Majesty himself. They had heard the rumor that the great campaign was to have a subtle barb aimed at Germany. They were still convinced, as they had been before the failure of their mission, that the lamentable manifestations that had even then been making the political life of the Dual Monarchy a focus of infection for Europe were extraordinarily complicated. But just as they had felt duty-bound to regard these problems as solvable when they received the order to solve them, so they would declare that it was not outside the realm of possibility that something might be achieved by the means Count Leinsdorf was suggesting. Specifically, they felt that "a landmark," "a splendid show of vitality," "a commanding role on the world stage that would have a bracing effect on the situation here at home," were goals so well formulated by Count Leinsdorf that one could no more refuse them than refuse a call for every man who desired the Good to step forward.

It is of course possible that von Holtzkopf and Wisnieczky, as men informed and experienced in public affairs, felt some qualms, especially as they might assume that they themselves would be expected to play a part in the further development of this campaign. But it is easy for people who live on the ground floor to be choosy and turn down whatever does not suit them. One whose gondola in life is nine thousand feet up in the air, however, can't simply step outside, even if one is not in accord with everything going on. And since persons in such high circles really are loyal and—as opposed to the previously mentioned bourgeois dither—do not like to act otherwise than they think, they must in many cases avoid giving too much careful thought to an issue. The banker von Meier-Ballot accordingly found his own favorable impression of the affair confirmed by what the two other gentlemen had to say about it; while he personally and professionally was given to caution, he had heard enough to decide that this was an affair to which he would lend his presence in any case, but without committing himself.

At this time the Parallel Campaign was not yet in existence, and not even Count Leinsdorf had any idea what form it would take. It can be said with certainty that at the moment, the only definite thing that had occurred to him was a list of names.

But even this is a great deal. It meant that even at this stage, without anyone needing to have a clear conception of anything, a network of readiness that covered a great many connections was in place; and one can certainly maintain that this is the proper sequence. For first it was necessary to invent knife and fork, and *then* mankind learned to eat properly. This was how Count Leinsdorf explained it.

37

By launching the slogan "Year of Austria," a journalist makes a lot of trouble for Count Leinsdorf, who issues a frantic call for Ulrich

Although Count Leinsdorf had sent out invitations in many directions "to start people thinking," he might not have made headway so quickly had not an influential journalist who had heard that something was in the wind quickly published two long articles in his paper offering as his own ideas everything he had guessed to be in the works. He did not know much—where, indeed, could he have found out?—but no one noticed; indeed, this was just what made it possible for his articles to be so irresistibly effective. He was really the inventor of the idea of the "Year of Austria" that he wrote about in his columns, without himself knowing what he meant by it but writing sentence after sentence in which this phrase combined with others as in a dream and took on new forms and unleashed storms of enthusiasm. Count Leinsdorf was horrified at first, but he was wrong. The phrase "Year of Austria" showed what it means to be a journalistic genius, for it was a triumph of true instinct. It caused vibrations to sound that would have remained dumb at the mention of an "Austrian Century"; the call to bring about such an era would have struck sensible people as impossible to take seriously. Why this is so would be hard to say. Perhaps a certain vagueness, a metaphorical quality that lessens realistic perceptions, lent wings to the feelings of more people than just Count Leinsdorf. For vagueness has an elevating and magnifying power.

It seems that the bona fide, practical realist just doesn't love reality or take it seriously. As a child he crawls under the table when his parents are out, converting their living room by this simple yet inspired trick into an adventure. As a boy he longs for a watch; as a young man with a gold watch, for a wife to go with it; as a man with watch and wife, for a promotion; and yet, when he has happily achieved this little circle of desires and should be peacefully swinging back and forth in it like a pendulum, his supply of unsatisfied yearnings does not seem to have diminished at all. For if he wants to elevate himself above the daily rut, he resorts to figures of speech. Since to him snow is evidently unpleasant at times, he compares it to a woman's shimmering bosom, and as soon as he begins to tire of his wife's breasts, he likens them to shimmering snow. He would be horrified if the beaks of his wife's nipples actually turned to coral, or their billing and cooing turned out to come from the horny beak of a real dove, but poetically it excites him. He is capable of turning everything into something else—snow to skin, skin to flower petals, petals to sugar, sugar to powder, powder to drifting snow again—as long as he can make it out to be something it is not, which may be taken to prove that he cannot bear to stay in the same place for long, no matter where he may find himself. Most of all, no true Kakanian could, in his soul, bear Kakania for long. To ask of him an "Austrian Century" would be tantamount to asking him to sentence himself and the world to the punishments of hell by an absurdly voluntary effort. An Austrian Year, on the other hand, was quite something else. It meant: Let's show them, for once, who we could be!—but, so to speak, only until further notice, and for a year at most. One could understand by it whatever one liked, it wasn't for eternity, and this somehow touched the heart. It stirred to life the deepest love of one's country.

And so Count Leinsdorf had an undreamed-of success. After all, his original idea had also come to him as such a figure of speech, but a number of names had occurred to him as well, and his moral nature aspired to something beyond such intangibles. He had a well-defined concept of the way the imagination of the common people or, as he now put it to a faithful journalist, the imagination of the public, must be directed to a goal that was clear, sound, reasonable, and in harmony with the true aims of mankind and their own country. This journalist, spurred on by his colleague's success, wrote all this down immediately, and as he had the advantage of having it from "an authentic source," it was part of the technique of his profession to draw attention to this by attributing his information in large type to "influential circles." This was precisely what Count Leinsdorf had expected of him, for His Grace attached great importance to being no ideologue but an experienced practical statesman, and he wanted a fine line drawn between a "Year of Austria" as the brainchild of a clever member of the press and the circumspection of responsible circles. To this end he borrowed the technique of someone he would not normally have liked to regard as a model—Bismarck—to let newsmen serve as the mouthpiece for his actual intentions so as to be able to acknowledge or disavow them as circumstances might dictate.

But while Count Leinsdorf acted with such shrewdness, he overlooked something. For it was not only a man like himself who saw the Truth we so much need; innumerable other people saw themselves as possessing it as well. It may be defined as a calcification of the previously described state of mind, in which one still makes metaphors. Sooner or later even the desire for these metaphors disappears, and many of the people who still retain a supply of definitively unfulfilled dreams create for themselves a point at which they stare in secret, as though it marks the beginning of a world that life still owes them. In almost no time after he had sent out his statement to the press, His Grace had intimations that all those who have no money harbor inside them an unpleasant crank. This opinionated man-within-the-man goes with him to the office every morning and has absolutely no way to air his protest against the way things are done in the world; so instead he keeps his eyes glued to a lifelong secret point of his own that everyone else refuses to see, although it is obviously the source of all the misery in a world that will not recognize its savior. Such fixed points, where the center of a person's equilibrium coincides with the world's center of equilibrium, may be, for instance, a spittoon that can be shut with a simple latch; or the abolition of open salt cellars in restaurants, the kind people poke their knives into, so as to stop at one stroke the spread of that scourge of mankind, tuberculosis; or the adoption of Oehl's system of shorthand, so effective a time-saver it can solve the problems of society once and for all; or conversion to a natural mode of living that would halt the present random destruction of the environment; not to mention a metaphysical theory of the motions of celestial bodies, simplification of the administrative apparatus, and a reform of sex life. In the right circumstances a man can help himself by writing a book about his point, or a pamphlet, or at least a letter to the editor, thereby putting his protest on the historical record, which is marvelously comforting even if nobody ever reads it. Usually, however, it can be counted on to attract the attention of a few readers who assure the author that he is a new Copernicus, whereupon they introduce themselves as unrecognized Newtons. This custom of picking the points out of each other's fur is widespread and a great comfort, but it is without lasting effect because the participants soon fall to quarreling and find themselves isolated again. However, it can also happen that a small circle of admirers gathers around one prophet or another, and with united energy accuses heaven of being remiss in not sufficiently supporting its anointed son. And if a ray of hope should suddenly fall from on high upon such little piles of points, as it did when Count Leinsdorf issued a public statement that a "Year of Austria"— if it should materialize, which was still not yet settled—would in any case have to be in accord with the true aims of existence, they receive it like saints vouchsafed a divine vision.

Count Leinsdorf had aimed at bringing about a powerful demonstration arising spontaneously out of the midst of the people themselves, meaning the universities, the clergy, certain names never absent from the rosters of charity affairs, and even the press. He was counting on the patriotic parties, the "sound sense" of the middle class, which hung out flags on the Emperor's birthday, and the support of leading financiers; he even included the politicians, because he hoped in his heart that his great work would render politics superfluous by bringing it all down to the common denominator of "our fatherland," from which he subsequently intended to subtract the "land," leaving the fatherly ruler as the only remainder. But the one thing His Grace had not reckoned with and that surprised him was the widespread need to improve the world, which was hatched out by the warmth of a great occasion as insect eggs are hatched by a fire. His Grace had not counted on this; he had expected a great amount of patriotism but was not prepared for inventions, theories, schemes for world unity, and people demanding that he release them from intellectual prisons. They besieged his palace, hailed the Parallel Campaign as a chance to help make the truth prevail at last, and Count Leinsdorf did not know what to do with them. In awareness of his social position he could not, after all, sit down at table with all these people, yet, given a mind filled with intense morality, he did not want to avoid meeting them, either; but since his education had been in politics and philosophy to the exclusion of science and technology, he had no way of telling whether there was anything to their proposals or not.

In this situation he felt an increasingly desperate need for Ulrich, who had been recommended to him as the very man for the occasion; obviously, his secretary or any ordinary secretary could not cope with such exigencies. Once, when he had been very annoyed with his secretary, he had even prayed to God—though he was ashamed of it the next day—for Ulrich to come. And when this did not happen, he personally took systematic steps to find him. He ordered the directory to be checked, but Ulrich was not yet in it. He then went to his friend Diotima, who could usually be counted on for advice, and it turned out that the admirable woman had actually seen Ulrich already, but she had forgotten to ask for his address, or pretended she had in order to use the opportunity to propose a new and far better candidate for secretary of the great campaign. But Count Leinsdorf was quite agitated and declared most positively that he had already grown used to Ulrich, that a Prussian was out of the question, even a reformed Prussian, and that he wanted to hear nothing at all about still further complications. Dismayed to see that he had apparently hurt his friend's feelings, he came up with an idea of his own—he told her that he would drive straight to his friend the Commissioner of Police, who should certainly be able to dig up the address of any citizen whatever.

38

CLARISSE AND HER DEMONS

When Ulrich's note arrived Walter and Clarisse were again playing the piano so violently that the spindly reproduction furniture rattled and the Dante Gabriel Rossetti prints on the walls trembled. The aged messenger who had found house and doors open without being challenged was met by a full blast of thunder in the face as he fought his way into the sitting room, and the holy uproar he had wandered into left him nailed to the wall with awe. It was Clarisse who finally discharged the onrushing musical excitement with two powerful crashes and set him free. While she read the note, the interrupted outpouring still writhed under Walter's hands; a melody ran along jerkily like a stork and then spread its wings. Clarisse kept a mistrustful ear on this while she deciphered Ulrich's handwriting.

When she announced their friend's impending arrival, Walter said: "Too bad!"

She sat down again beside him on her little revolving piano stool, and a smile that for some reason struck Walter as cruel parted her lips, which looked sensual. It was that moment when the players rein in their blood in order to be able to release it in the same rhythm, eyes blazing out of their heads in four long parallel axes while their buttocks tense and grip the little stools that keep trying to wobble on the long necks of their wooden screws.

The next instant, Clarisse and Walter were off like two locomotives racing side by side. The piece they were playing came rushing at their eyes like flashing rails, vanished under the thundering engine, and spread out behind them as a ringing, resonant, marvelously present landscape. In the course of this ride these two people's separate feelings were compressed into a single entity; hearing, blood, muscles, were all swept along irresistibly by the same experience; shimmering, bending, curving walls of sound forced their bodies onto the same track, bent them as one, and expanded and contracted their chests in the same breath. In a fraction of a second, gaiety, sadness, anger, and fear, love and hatred, desire and satiety, passed through Walter and Clarisse. They became one, just as in a great panic hundreds of people who a moment before had been distinct in every way suddenly make the same flailing movements of flight, utter the same senseless screams, their gaping mouths and staring eyes the same, all swept backward and forward, left and right, by the same aimless force, howling, twitching, tangling, trembling. But this union did not have the same dull, overwhelming force as life itself, where this kind of thing does not happen so easily, although it blots out everything personal when it does. The anger, love, joy, gaiety, and sadness that Clarisse and Walter felt in their flight were not full emotions but little more than physical shells of feelings that had been worked up into a frenzy. They sat stiffly in a trance on their little stools, angry, in love, or sad, at nothing, with nothing, about nothing, or each of them at, with, about something else, thinking and meaning different things of their own; the dictate of music united them in highest passion, yet at the same time it left them with something absent, as in the compulsive sleep of hypnosis.

Each of these two people felt it in his own way. Walter was happy and excited. Like most musical people, he considered these billowing surges and emotional stirrings, all this cloudy, churned-up, somatic sediment of the soul, to be the simple language of the eternal that binds all mankind together. It delighted him to press Clarisse to himself with the powerful arm of primal emotion. On this day, he had come home earlier than usual from the office, where he had been cataloging works of art that still bore the imprint of great, unfragmented times and emitted a mysterious strength of will. Clarisse had given him a friendly welcome, and now in the awesome world of music she was firmly bound to him. It was a day of mysterious successes, a soundless march as if gods were approaching. "Perhaps today is the day?" Walter thought. He wanted to bring Clarisse back, but not by force; the realization would have to rise up from her innermost self and incline her gently to him.

The piano was hammering glinting note heads into a wall of air. Although the origin of this process was entirely real, the walls of the room soon disappeared, and there arose in their place golden partitions of music, that mysterious space in which self and world, perception and feeling, inside and outside, plunge into one another in the most indefinable way, while the space itself consists entirely of sensation, certainty, precision, a whole hierarchy of ordered detail of glory. It was to these sensual details that the threads of feeling were fastened, spun from the billowing haze of their souls, and this haze was mirrored in the precision of these walls of sound and appeared clear to itself. The two players' souls hung like cocoons in these threads and rays. The more tightly they became enwrapped and the farther their beams were spread, the cozier Walter felt; his dreams were assuming so much of the shape of a small child that he was beginning here and there to strike the notes with a false and too sentimental emphasis.

But before it came to the point of making a spark of ordinary feeling strike through the golden mist and bring them back to an earthly relationship to each other, Clarisse's thoughts had diverged as far from Walter's as is possible for two people who are storming along side by side with twinned gestures of desperation and rapture. In fluttering mists, images sprang up, overlapped, fused, faded—that was Clarisse's thinking. She had her own way of thinking; sometimes several ideas were intertwined simultaneously, sometimes none at all, but then one could feel the thoughts lurking like demons behind the stage. The temporal sequence of events that gives such real support to most people became in Clarisse a veil that threw its folds one over the other, only to dissolve them into a barely visible puff of air.

This time, three people were around Clarisse: Walter, Ulrich, and the woman-killer Moosbrugger.

Ulrich had told her about Moosbrugger.

Attraction and repulsion blended into a peculiar spell.

Clarisse was gnawing at the root of love. It is a forked root, with kisses and bites, glances clinging and a tormented last-minute aversion of the gaze. "Does getting along well together lead to hate?" she wondered. "Does a decent life crave brutality? Does peacefulness need cruelty? Does orderliness long to be torn apart?" Such were, and were not, the thoughts provoked by Moosbrugger. Beneath the thunder of the music a world was suspended around her, a conflagration on the verge of breaking out, inwardly eating away at the timbers. But it was also like a metaphor, where the things compared are the same yet on the other hand quite different, and from the dissimilarity of the similar as from the similarity of the dissimilar two columns of smoke drift upward with the magical scent of baked apples and pine twigs strewn on the fire.

"We should never have to stop playing," she said to herself, and flicking the pages back she started again at the beginning when they reached the end. Walter smiled self-consciously and joined in.

"What is Ulrich actually doing with his mathematics?" she asked him.

Walter shrugged his shoulders while playing, as if he were at the wheel of a racing car.

"One would have to go on and on playing, till the very end," Clarisse thought. "If one could go on playing uninterruptedly to the end of one's life, what would Moosbrugger be then? A horror? An idiot? A black bird in the sky?" She did not know.

She knew nothing at all. One fine day—she could have calculated to the day when it happened—she had awakened from the sleep of childhood and found the conviction ready-made that she was called upon to accomplish something, to play a special role, perhaps even chosen for some great purpose. At the time, she knew nothing of the world. Nor did she believe what she was told about it—by her parents, her older brothers; their chattering was all well and good, but one could not assimilate what they said, one simply couldn't, any more than a chemical substance can absorb another that does not "fit" it. Then came Walter; that was the day; from that day on everything "fit." Walter wore a little mustache, a toothbrush on his upper lip; he called her "Fräulein," and all at once the world was no longer a barren, chaotic, parched plain but a gleaming circle, with Walter at the center, herself at the center, two centers coinciding in one. Earth, buildings, fallen leaves not swept away, aching lines of perspective (she remembered the moment as one of the most tormenting of her childhood, when she stood with her father looking at a scenic view, and her father, the painter, went into endless raptures over it, while for her, gazing into the world along those long aerial lines of perspective only hurt, as if she had to run her finger along the sharp edge of a ruler)—these were the things that had made up life before. Now, all at once, it had become hers, flesh of her flesh.

She knew then that she would do something gigantic, though what it would be she did not yet know. Meanwhile she felt it most powerfully with music, and hoped then that Walter would become an even greater genius than Nietzsche, to say nothing of Ulrich, who arrived on the scene later and who had merely given her Nietzsche's works as a present.

From then on things had progressed. How fast, it was now impossible to say. How badly she had played the piano before; how little she had known about music! Now she played better than Walter. And all the books she had read! Where had they all come from? She saw it all before her like swarms of black birds fluttering around a little girl standing in the snow. But somewhat later she saw a black wall with white spots in it; black stood for all she didn't know, and while the white ran together to form little, and sometimes larger, islands, the black remained unchangingly infinite. This blackness emitted fear and agitation. "Is this the devil?" she thought. "Has the devil turned into Moosbrugger?" Between the white spots she now noticed thin gray tracks; on these she had moved from one thing to the next in her life; they were events: departures, arrivals, excited discussions, battling with her parents, the marriage, the house, the incredible struggle with Walter. The thin gray tracks coiled like snakes. "Snakes!" Clarisse thought. "Snakes!" These events entangled her, trapped her, kept her from getting where she wanted to go, were slippery, and made her aim at a target she did not want.

Snakes, snares, slippery; that was life's way. Her thoughts began to race like life. Her fingertips dipped into the torrent of music. In the streambed of music snakes and snares came slithering down. Then the prison where they kept Moosbrugger hidden opened like the refuge of a quiet bay. Clarisse's thoughts entered his cell with a shudder. "One must make music to the end," she repeated to herself for encouragement, but her heart was trembling violently. When it had calmed down the entire cell was filled with her self. It was as gentle a feeling as salve on a wound, but when she tried to hang on to it forever it began to open and spread apart like a fairy tale or a dream. Moosbrugger sat with his head in his hand, and she freed him from his fetters. As her fingers moved, and as if at their summons, strength, courage, virtue, kindness, beauty, and riches entered the cell like a breeze from many meadows. "It doesn't matter at all why I am doing this, it doesn't matter why I feel like doing this," Clarisse felt, "what counts is that now I am doing it." She laid her hands, a part of her own body, on his eyes, and when she withdrew her fingers Moosbrugger had turned into a handsome youth and she stood beside him as an incredibly beautiful woman with a body as sweet and soft as a southern wine, not at all recalcitrant, as little Clarisse's body usually was. "This is the form of our innocence," she noted in some deep-down thinking layer of consciousness.

But why couldn't Walter be like this? Emerging from the depths of her music fantasy, she remembered what a child she still had been, already in love with Walter at fifteen, and prepared to save him by her courage, strength, and kindness from all the dangers that threatened his genius. And how beautiful it had been when Walter glimpsed those deep spiritual pitfalls everywhere. She wondered whether it had all been mere childishness. Their marriage had irradiated it with a disturbing light. Somehow their marriage was suddenly creating a great embarrassment for their love. Not that things hadn't also been wonderful of late, perhaps even richer in meaning and substance than formerly; still, that huge conflagration, those flames everywhere flickering across the sky, had dwindled to the difficulties of a fire of the hearth that is reluctant to burn. Clarisse was not quite sure whether her struggles with Walter still mattered. Meanwhile life was racing by like this music that was vanishing under her hands. In a wink it would be over! She was gradually overcome by hopeless terror. At this moment she noticed that Walter's playing was becoming unsure. His feelings were splashing like big raindrops on the keys. She instantly guessed what he was thinking of: the child. She knew that he wanted to bind her to himself with a child. They argued about it day in, day out. And the music did not stop for a second. The music knew no denial. Like a net whose entangling meshes she had not noticed, it was pulling shut with lightning speed.

Clarisse leapt up in mid-chord and banged the piano shut; Walter barely managed to save his fingers.

Oh, how that hurt! Still shocked, he understood everything. It was Ulrich's coming, the mere news of which was enough to throw her mind into a frenzy! Ulrich was bad for Clarisse in that he callously roused in her something that Walter himself hardly dared touch, that wretched streak of genius in Clarisse. The secret cavern where something calamitous was tearing at chains that might one day give way.

He did not stir, but only gave Clarisse a dumbfounded stare.

And Clarisse offered no explanations, stood there, and breathed hard.

She was definitely not at all in love with Ulrich, she assured Walter after he had spoken. If she were in love with him, she would say so at once. But she did feel kindled by him, like a light. She felt she shone more herself, amounted to more, when he was near; Walter on the other hand always wanted only to close the shutters. Besides, her feelings were nobody else's business, not Ulrich's and not Walter's!

Yet Walter thought that between the fury and indignation that breathed from her words he could scent a narcotic, deadly kernel of something that was not fury.

Dusk had fallen. The room was black. The piano was black. The silhouettes of two people who loved each other were black. Clarisse's eyes gleamed in the dark, kindled like a light, and in Walter's mouth, restless with pain, the enamel on a tooth shone like ivory. Regardless of the greatest affairs of state occurring in the world outside, and despite its vexations, this seemed to be one of those moments for which God had created the earth.

39

A MAN WITHOUT QUALITIES CONSISTS OF QUALITIES WITHOUT A MAN

But Ulrich did not come that evening. After Director Fischel had left him in such haste, he fell to mulling over the question of his youth: why the world so uncannily favored inauthentic and—in a higher sense—untrue statements. "One always gets one step ahead precisely when one lies," he thought. "That's another thing I should have told him."

Ulrich was a passionate man, but not in the sense of passions as commonly understood. There must indeed have been something that drove him again and again into this state, and it was perhaps passion, but when he was actually excited or behaving in an excited manner, his attitude was both passionate and detached at the same time. He had run the gamut of experience, more or less, and felt that he might still now at any time plunge into something that need not mean anything to him personally so long as it stimulated his urge to action. So without much exaggeration he was able to say of his life that everything in it had fulfilled itself as if it belonged together more than it belonged to him. *B* had always followed *A*, whether in battle or in love. Therefore he had to suppose that the personal qualities he had achieved in this way had more to do with one another than with him; that every one of them, in fact, looked at closely, was no more intimately bound up with him than with anyone else who also happened to possess them.

Nevertheless, one is undoubtedly conditioned by one's qualities and is made up of them, even if one is not identical with them, and so one can sometimes seem just as much a stranger to oneself at rest as in motion. If Ulrich had been asked to say what he was really like he would have been at a loss, for like so many people he had never tested himself other than by a task and his relation to it. His self-confidence had not been damaged, nor was it coddled and vain; it never needed that overhauling and lubrication that is called probing one's conscience. Was he a strong person? He didn't know; on that point he was perhaps fatefully mistaken. But he had surely always been a person with faith in his own strength. Even now he did not doubt that the differences between identifying with one's own experiences and qualities and distancing oneself from them was only a difference in attitude, in a sense a deliberate decision or a choice of the degree to which one saw one's life as a general manifestation or an individual one. Put simply, one can take what one does or what happens to one either personally or impersonally. One can feel a blow as an insult as well as a pain, in which case it becomes unbearably intensified; but one can also take it in a sporting sense, as a setback by which one should not let oneself be either intimidated or enraged, and then, often enough, one never even notices it. But in this second case, all that has happened is that the blow has been put in a general context, that of combat, so that it is seen to depend on the purpose it is meant to serve. And it is just this—that an experience derives its meaning, even its content, only from its position in a chain of logically consistent events—which is apparent when a man sees his experience not only as a personal event but as a challenge to his spiritual powers. He will also be less emotionally affected by what he does. But oddly enough, what we consider a sign of superior intelligence in a boxer is judged to be cold and callous in people who can't box but incline to an intellectual way of life. Whether we apply and demand a general or a personal attitude in a given situation is governed by all sorts of distinctions. A murderer who goes coolly about his business is likely to be judged particularly vicious; a professor who continues to work out a problem in the arms of his wife is seen as a dry-as-dust pedant; a politician who climbs to high office over the bodies of those he has destroyed will be called a monster or a hero, depending on his success; but soldiers, hangmen, or surgeons, on the other hand, are expected to behave with the same impassivity that is condemned in others. Without going further into the morality of these examples, we cannot overlook the uncertainty that leads in every case to a compromise between the objectively and the subjectively proper attitude.

This uncertainty gave Ulrich's personal problem a broader context. In earlier times, one had an easier conscience about being a person than one does today. People were like cornstalks in a field, probably more violently tossed back and forth by God, hail, fire, pestilence, and war than they are today, but as a whole, as a city, a region, a field, and as to what personal movement was left to the individual stalk—all this was clearly defined and could be answered for. But today responsibility's center of gravity is not in people but in circumstances. Have we not noticed that experiences have made themselves independent of people? They have gone on the stage, into books, into the reports of research institutes and explorers, into ideological or religious communities, which foster certain kinds of experience at the expense of others as if they are conducting a kind of social experiment, and insofar as experiences are not actually being developed, they are simply left dangling in the air. Who can say nowadays that his anger is really his own anger when so many people talk about it and claim to know more about it than he does? A world of qualities without a man has arisen, of experiences without the person who experiences them, and it almost looks as though ideally private experience is a thing of the past, and that the friendly burden of personal responsibility is to dissolve into a system of formulas of possible meanings. Probably the dissolution of the anthropocentric point of view, which for such a long time considered man to be at the center of the universe but which has been fading away for centuries, has finally arrived at the "I" itself, for the belief that the most important thing about experience is the experiencing, or of action the doing, is beginning to strike most people as naïve. There are probably people who still lead personal lives, who say "We saw the So-and-sos yesterday" or "We'll do this or that today" and enjoy it without its needing to have any content or significance. They like everything that comes in contact with their fingers, and are purely private persons insofar as this is at all possible. In contact with such people, the world becomes a private world and shines like a rainbow. They may be very happy, but this kind of people usually seems absurd to the others, although it is still not at all clear why.

And suddenly, in view of these reflections, Ulrich had to smile and admit to himself that he was, after all, a character, even without having one.

40

A MAN WITH ALL THE QUALITIES, BUT HE IS INDIFFERENT TO THEM. A PRINCE OF INTELLECT IS ARRESTED, AND THE PARALLEL CAMPAIGN GETS ITS HONORARY SECRETARY

It is not difficult to describe the basic traits of this thirty-two-year-old man Ulrich, even though all he knows about himself is that he is as close to as he is far from all qualities, and that they are all, whether or not he has made them his own, in a curious fashion indifferent to him. With a suppleness of mind, owing simply to his being gifted in various directions, he combines a certain aggressiveness. His is a masculine mind. He is not sensitive toward other people and rarely puts himself in their place, except to get to know them for his own purposes. He is no respecter of rights unless he respects the person whose rights they are, which is not very often. With the passage of time, a certain inclination toward the negative has developed in him, a flexible dialectic of feeling that easily leads him to discover a flaw in something widely approved or, conversely, to defend the forbidden and to refuse responsibilities with a resentment that springs from the desire to create his own responsibilities. Despite this need, however, and apart from certain self-indulgences, he lets himself be guided morally by the chivalrous code that is followed by almost all men as long as they live in secure circumstances in middle-class society, and so, with all the arrogance, ruthlessness, and negligence of a man called to his vocation, he leads the life of another man who has made of his inclinations and abilities more or less ordinary, practical and social use. He was accustomed, instinctively and without vanity, to regard himself as the instrument of a not unimportant purpose, which he intended to discover in good time; even now, early in this year of groping unrest, after he realized how his life had been drifting, the feeling that he was on his way somewhere was soon restored, and he made no special effort with his plans. It is none too easy to recognize in such a temperament the passion that drives it; ambiguously formed by predisposition and circumstances, its fate has not yet been laid bare by any really tough counterpressure. But the main thing is that the missing element needed in order to crystallize a decision is still unknown. Ulrich was a man forced somehow to live against himself, though outwardly he appeared to be indulging his inclinations without constraint.

Comparing the world to a laboratory had rekindled an old idea in his mind. Formerly he had thought of the kind of life that would appeal to him as a vast experimental station for trying out the best ways of being a man and discovering new ones. That the great existing laboratory was functioning rather haphazardly, lacking visible directors or theoreticians at the top, was another matter. It might even be said that he himself would have wanted to become something like a philosopher king; who wouldn't? It is so natural to regard the mind as the highest power, the supreme ruler of everything. That is what we are taught. Anybody who can dresses up in intellect, decks himself out in it. Mind and spirit, in combination with a numinous other something, is the most ubiquitous thing there is. The spirit of loyalty, the spirit of love, a masculine mind, a cultivated mind, the greatest living mind, keeping up the spirit of one cause or another, acting in the spirit of this or that movement: how solid and unexceptionable it sounds, right down to its lowest levels. Beside it everything else, be it humdrum crime or the hot pursuit of profits, seems inadmissible, the dirt God removes from His toenails.

But what of "spirit" standing by itself, a naked noun, bare as a ghost to whom one would like to lend a sheet? One can read the poets, study the philosophers, buy paintings, hold all-night discussions—does all this bestow spirit on us?° If it does, do we then possess it? And even if we should, this spirit is so firmly bound up with the accidental form in which it happens to manifest itself! It passes right through the person who wants to absorb it, leaving only a small tremor behind. What can we do with all this spirit? It is constantly being spewed out in truly astronomical quantities on masses of paper, stone, and canvas, and just as ceaselessly consumed at a tremendous cost in nervous energy. But what becomes of it then? Does it vanish like a mirage? Does it dissolve into particles? Does it evade the earthly law of conservation? The motes of dust that sink and slowly settle down to rest inside us bear no relation to all that expense. Where has it gone, where and what is it? If we knew more about it there might be an awkward silence around this noun, "spirit."

Evening had come; buildings as if broken out of pure space, asphalt, steel rails, formed the cooling shell that was the city. The mother shell, full of childlike, joyful, angry human movement. Where every drop begins as a droplet sprayed or squirted; a tiny explosion caught by the walls, cooling, calming, and slowing down, hanging quietly, tenderly, on the slope of the mother shell, hardening at last into a little grain on its wall.

"Why," Ulrich thought suddenly, "didn't I become a pilgrim?" A

°The German word *Geist* is variously rendered in this chapter as "mind," "spirit," and "intellect." A powerful concept in German culture, *Geist* embraces all three. —ED.

pure, uncontingent way of life, as piercingly fresh as ozone, presented itself to his senses; whoever cannot say "Yes" to life should at least utter the "No" of the saint. And yet it was simply impossible to consider this seriously. Nor could he see himself becoming an adventurer, though it might feel rather like an everlasting honeymoon, and appealed to his limbs and his temperament. He had not been able to become a poet or one of those disillusioned souls who believe only in money and power, although he had the makings of either. He forgot his age, he imagined he was twenty, but even so, something inside him was just as certain that he could become none of those things; every possibility beckoned him, but something stronger kept him from yielding to the attraction. Why was he living in this dim and undecided fashion? Obviously, he said to himself, what was keeping him spellbound in this aloof and nameless way of life was nothing other than the compulsion to that loosening and binding of the world that is known by a word we do not care to encounter by itself: spirit, or mind. Without knowing why, Ulrich suddenly felt sad, and thought: "I simply don't love myself." Within the frozen, petrified body of the city he felt his heart beating in its innermost depths. There was something in him that had never wanted to remain anywhere, had groped its way along the walls of the world, thinking: There are still millions of other walls; it was this slowly cooling, absurd drop "I" that refused to give up its fire, its tiny glowing core.

The mind has learned that beauty makes things or people good, bad, stupid, or enchanting. It dissects a sheep and a penitent and finds humility and patience in both. It analyzes a substance and notes that it is a poison in large quantities, a stimulant in smaller ones. It knows that the mucous membrane of the lips is related to the mucous membrane of the intestine, but also knows that the humility of those lips is related to the humility of all that is saintly. It jumbles things up, sorts them out, and forms new combinations. To the mind, good and evil, above and below, are not skeptical, relative concepts, but terms of a function, values that depend on the context they find themselves in. The centuries have taught it that vices can turn into virtues and virtues into vices, so the mind concludes that basically only ineptitude prevents the transformation of a criminal into a useful person within the space of a lifetime. It does not accept anything as permissible or impermissible, since everything may have some quality that may someday make it part of a great new context. It secretly detests everything with pretensions to permanence, all the great ideals and laws and their little fossilized imprint, the well-adjusted character. It regards nothing as fixed, no personality, no order of things; because our knowledge may change from day to day, it regards nothing as binding; everything has the value it has only until the next act of creation, as a face changes with the words we are speaking to it.

And so the mind or spirit is the great opportunist, itself impossible to pin down, take hold of, anywhere; one is tempted to believe that of all its influence nothing is left but decay. Every advance is a gain in particular and a separation in general; it is an increase in power leading only to a progressive increase in impotence, but there is no way to quit. Ulrich thought of that body of facts and discoveries, growing almost by the hour, out of which the mind must peer today if it wishes to scrutinize any given problem closely. This body grows away from its inner life. Countless views, opinions, systems of ideas from every age and latitude, from all sorts of sick and sound, waking and dreaming brains run through it like thousands of small sensitive nerve strands, but the central nodal point tying them all together is missing. Man feels dangerously close to repeating the fate of those gigantic primeval species that perished because of their size; but he cannot stop himself.

This reminded Ulrich of that rather dubious notion in which he had long believed and even now had not quite uprooted from himself: that the world would be best governed by a senate of the wisest, the most advanced. It is after all very natural to think that man, who calls in professionally trained doctors rather than shepherds to treat him when sick, has no reason, when well, to let public affairs be conducted by windbags no better qualified than shepherds. This is why the young, who care about the essentials in life, begin by regarding everything in the world that is neither true nor good nor beautiful, such as the Internal Revenue Service or a debate in the legislature, as irrelevant; at least they used to. Nowadays, thanks to their education in politics and economics, they are said to be different. But even at that time, as one got older and on longer acquaintance with the smokehouse of the mind, in which the world cures the bacon of its daily affairs, one learned to adapt oneself to reality, and a person with a trained mind would finally end up limiting himself to his specialty and spend the rest of his life convinced that the whole of life should perhaps be different, but there was no point in thinking about it. This is more or less how people who follow intellectual pursuits maintain their equilibrium. Suddenly Ulrich saw the whole thing in the comical light of the question whether, given that there was certainly an abundance of mind around, the only thing wrong was that mind itself was devoid of mind.

He felt like laughing. He was himself, after all, one of those specialists who had renounced responsibility for the larger questions. But disappointed, still-burning ambition went through him like a sword. At this moment there were two Ulrichs, walking side by side. One took in the scene with a smile and thought: So this is the stage on which I once hoped to play a part. One day I woke up, no longer snug in mother's crib, but with the firm conviction that there was something I had to accomplish. They gave me cues, but I felt they had nothing to do with me. Like a kind of feverish stagefright, everything in those days was filled with my own plans and expectations. Meanwhile the stage has continued revolving unobtrusively, I am somewhat farther along on my way, and I may already be standing near the exit. Soon I shall be turned out, and the only lines of my great part that I will have uttered are "The horses are saddled! The devil take all of you!"

But while the Ulrich smiling at these reflections walked on through the hovering evening, the other had his fists clenched in pain and rage. He was the less visible of the two and was searching for a magic formula, a possible handle to grasp, the real mind of the mind, the missing piece, perhaps only a small one, that would close the broken circle. This second Ulrich had no words at his disposal. Words leap like monkeys from tree to tree, but in that dark place where a man has his roots he is deprived of their kind mediation. The ground streamed away under his feet. He could hardly open his eyes. Can a feeling rage like a storm and yet not be a stormy feeling at all? By a storm of feeling we mean something that makes our trunk groan and our branches flail to the verge of breaking. But this storm left the surface quite undisturbed. It was almost a state of conversion, of turning back. There was no flicker of change in his facial expression, yet inside him not an atom seemed to stay in place. Ulrich's senses were unclouded, and yet each person he passed was perceived in some out-of-the-ordinary way by his eye, each sound differently by his ear. He could not have said more sharply, nor more deeply either, nor more softly, nor more naturally or unnaturally. Ulrich could not say anything at all, but at this moment he thought of that curious experience, "spirit," as he would of a beloved who had deceived him all his life without his loving her less, and it bound him to everything that came his way. For in love everything is love, even pain and revulsion. The tiny twig on the tree and the pale windowpane in the evening light became an experience deeply embedded in his own nature, barely expressible in words. Things seemed to consist not of wood and stone but of some grandiose and infinitely tender immorality that, the moment it came in contact with him, turned into a deep moral shock.

All this lasted no longer than a smile, and just as Ulrich was thinking, "Now for once I shall remain wherever it has carried me," he had the misfortune to run into an obstacle that shattered this tension.

What happened now came out of a wholly different world than the one in which Ulrich had just been experiencing trees and stones as a sensitive extension of his own body.

A left-wing tabloid had slavered its venomous spittle all over the Great Idea, as Count Leinsdorf might have put it, calling it just another sensation for the ruling class in the wake of the latest sex murder, and this caused an honest workingman who had been drinking to lose his temper. He had brushed up against two solid citizens pleased with their day's business who, convinced that a contented frame of mind could express itself anywhere, were rather loudly airing their approval of the great patriotic campaign they had read about in *their* paper. Words were exchanged, and as the proximity of a policeman encouraged the citizens as much as it provoked their attacker, the scene became increasingly impassioned. The policeman began by watching it over his shoulder, subsequently turning to face it and then coming closer; he attended as an observer, like a protruding offshoot of the iron machinery of the state, which ends in buttons and other metal trim. There is always something ghostly about living constantly in a well-ordered state. You cannot step into the street or drink a glass of water or get on a streetcar without touching the balanced levers of a gigantic apparatus of laws and interrelations, setting

them in motion or letting them maintain you in your peaceful existence; one knows hardly any of these levers, which reach deep into
the inner workings and, coming out the other side, lose themselves in
a network whose structure has never yet been unraveled by anyone.
So one denies their existence, just as the average citizen denies the
air, maintaining that it is empty space. But all these things that one
denied, these colorless, odorless, tasteless, weightless, and morally
indefinable things such as water, air, space, money, and the passing
of time, turn out in truth to be the most important things of all, and
this gives life a certain spooky quality. Sometimes a man may be
seized by panic, helpless as in a dream, thrashing about wildly like an
animal that has blundered into the incomprehensible mechanism of
a net. Such was the effect of the policeman's buttons on the workingman, and it was at this moment that the arm of the state, feeling that
it was not being respected in the proper manner, proceeded to make
an arrest.

It was not made without resistance and repeated pronouncements
of rebellious sentiments. Flattered by the sensation he was creating,
the drunk unleashed a previously hidden, total antipathy toward his
fellowman. An impassioned struggle for self-assertion began. A
heightened sense of self had to contend in him with the uncanny
feeling that he was not settled inside his own skin. The world, too,
was unsettled; it was a wavering mist continually losing and changing
shape. Buildings stood slanted, broken out of space; between them
people were ridiculous, swarming, yet fraternal ninnies. I have been
called to straighten things out here, the staggering drunk felt. The
whole scene was filled with something shimmering, and some piece
of what was happening was clearly getting through to him, but then
the walls started spinning again. His eyes were popping out of his
head like stalks, while the soles of his feet still clung to the ground.
An amazing stream had begun to pour from his mouth; words came
from somewhere deep inside; there was no comprehending how they
had ever got in there in the first place; possibly they were abusive. It
was hard to tell. Outside and inside were all tangled up together. The
anger was not an inner anger, but only the physical shell of anger
roused to frenzy, and the face of a policeman came very slowly forward to meet a clenched fist until it bled.

But the policeman, too, had meanwhile turned into three policemen. With the other policemen a crowd had come running; the drunk had thrown himself to the ground and was resisting arrest. Ulrich now did something rash. He had picked up the words "offense against the Crown" and remarked that the man was in no condition to be held responsible for insulting anyone and should be sent home to sleep it off. He said it casually enough, but to the wrong people. The fellow now shouted that Ulrich was welcome to join His Majesty in kissing his————! and a policeman who obviously blamed this relapse on Ulrich's interference barked at him to clear out. But Ulrich was unaccustomed to regarding the state as other than a hotel in which one was entitled to polite service, and objected to being addressed in such a tone; whereupon the police unexpectedly decided that one drunk did not justify the presence of three policemen and arrested Ulrich as well.

The hand of a uniformed man now clutched his arm. Ulrich's arm was considerably stronger than this offensive grip, but he did not dare break it; it would have meant letting himself in for a hopeless boxing match with the armed power of the state, so he had no other recourse than a polite request that they let him go along voluntarily. The station was in the district headquarters, and as he entered, Ulrich was reminded by the floor and walls of an army barracks. They were filled with the same grim struggle between relentlessly dragged-in dirt and crude detergents. The next thing he noticed was the appointed symbol of civil authority, two writing desks—writing crates, really—topped by a balustrade with several of its little columns missing, and covered with torn and scorched cloth and resting on very low, ball-shaped feet with only the last peeling traces of brownish-yellow varnish clinging to the wood it had once coated, back in the reign of the Emperor Ferdinand. Third, the place was filled with a heavy intimation that here one was expected to wait, without asking any questions. His policeman, after stating the grounds of the arrest, stood beside Ulrich like a column. Ulrich immediately tried to give some sort of explanation. The sergeant in command of this fortress raised an eye from the form he had been filling in when the convoy arrived, looked Ulrich up and down, then dropped his eye again and without a word went on filling in his form. Ulrich had a sense of infinity. Then the sergeant pushed the form aside, took a volume from the shelf, made an entry, sprinkled sand on it, put the book back, took down another, made an entry, sprinkled sand, pulled a file out of a bundle of similar files, and continued as before. Ulrich felt a second infinity unfolding during which the constellations moved in their predetermined orbits and he did not exist.

From this office an open door led into a corridor lined with cells. Ulrich's protégé had been taken there immediately on arrival, and as nothing more was heard from him, his intoxication had probably blessed him with sleep. But there was a sense of ominous other things going on. The corridor with the cells must have had a second entrance; Ulrich kept hearing heavy-footed comings and goings, doors slamming, muffled voices, and suddenly, as someone else was brought in, one of those voices rose in a desperate plea: "If you have a spark of human feeling, don't arrest me!" The voice broke, and there was something curiously out of place, almost ridiculous, in this appeal to a functionary's feelings, since functions are only carried out impersonally. The sergeant raised his head for a moment, without entirely abandoning his file. Ulrich heard the determined shuffle of many feet, whose bodies were presumably mutely pushing a resistant body along. Then came the sound of two feet alone, stumbling as after a shove. A door slammed shut loudly, a bolt clicked, the uniformed man at the desk had bent his head again, and in the air lay the silence of a full stop set in its proper place at the end of a sentence.

Ulrich seemed to have been mistaken, however, in assuming that he himself did not yet exist in the cosmos of the police, for the next time the sergeant raised his head he looked straight at Ulrich; the last lines he had written gleamed damply, unblotted with sand, and Ulrich's case suddenly appeared to have been officially in this bureaucratic existence for some time. Name? Age? Occupation? Address? Ulrich was being questioned.

He felt as though he had been sucked into a machine that was dismembering him into impersonal, general components before the question of his guilt or innocence came up at all. His name, the most intellectually meaningless yet most emotionally charged words in the language for him, meant nothing here. His works, which had secured his reputation in the scientific world, a world ordinarily of such solid standing, here did not exist; he was not asked about them even once. His face counted only as an aggregate of officially describable features—it seemed to him that he had never before pondered the fact that his eyes were gray eyes, one of the four officially recognized kinds of eyes, one pair among millions; his hair was blond, his build tall, his face oval, and his distinguishing marks none, although he had his own opinion on that point. His own feeling was that he was tall and broad-shouldered, with a chest curving like a filled sail on the mast, and joints fastening his muscles like small links of steel whenever he was angry or fighting or when Bonadea was clinging to him; but that he was slender, fine-boned, dark, and as soft as a jellyfish floating in the water whenever he was reading a book that moved him or felt touched by a breath of that great homeless love whose presence in the world he had never been able to understand. So he could, even at such a moment as this, himself appreciate this statistical demystification of his person and feel inspired by the quantitative and descriptive procedures applied to him by the police apparatus as if it were a love lyric invented by Satan. The most amazing thing about it was that the police could not only dismantle a man so that nothing was left of him, they could also put him together again, recognizably and unmistakably, out of the same worthless components. All this achievement takes is that something imponderable be added, which they call "suspicion."

All at once, Ulrich realized that it would take the coolest wit he could muster to extricate himself from the fix his foolishness had got him into. The questioning continued. He tried to imagine their reaction if he were to answer that his address was that of a stranger. Or if he replied, in answer to the question why he had done what he had done, that he always did something other than what he was really interested in doing? But outwardly he gave the proper answers as to street and house number, and tried to make up an acceptable version of his conduct. The feebleness of his mind's inward authority vis-à-vis the police sergeant's outward authority was acutely embarrassing; nevertheless, he finally glimpsed a chance of saving the situation. Even as he responded to the query "Occupation?" with "Independent"—he could not have brought himself to say "Engaged in independent research"—he saw, in the eye that was fixed on him, the same lackluster expression as if he had said "homeless," but then, when in the list of particulars his father's status came up and it appeared that his father was a member of the Upper House, the look changed. It was still mistrustful, but something in it immediately gave Ulrich the feeling of a swimmer, tossed this way and that by huge waves, who suddenly feels his big toe scraping solid ground.

With quickening presence of mind he seized his advantage. He instantly qualified everything he had so far admitted; he confronted this authority of ears bound by their oath of office with the express demand to be heard by the Commissioner himself, and when this merely evoked a smile he lied—quite casually, with a happily recovered naturalness, prepared to talk himself out of it if threatened with a noose of demands for precise details—and said that he was a friend of Count Leinsdorf's and secretary of the great patriotic campaign one read so much about in the newspapers. He could see immediately that this had the effect, previously unaroused, of causing him to be taken seriously as a person, and he pressed his advantage.

The result was that the sergeant now eyed him indignantly, because he did not want to take the responsibility either of detaining this catch or of letting it go. As there was no higher official in the building at this hour he resorted to an expedient that showed, to the simple sergeant's credit, how much he had learned from his superiors about handling awkward cases. He made a solemn face and expressed grave misgivings that Ulrich apparently not only had been guilty of insulting an officer of the law and interfering with the execution of his duty but, considering the position he claimed to hold, also came under suspicion of being involved in obscure, possibly political, machinations and would therefore have to submit to being transferred to the political division at central police headquarters.

So a few minutes later Ulrich was on his way through the night, in a cab he had been permitted to hire, at his side a plainclothesman not much inclined to conversation. As they approached police headquarters the prisoner saw the brightly lit windows on the second floor, where at this late hour an important conference was still going on in the Chief Commissioner's office. This building was no gloomy hole but rather more like a Ministry, and Ulrich was already breathing a more familiar air. He soon noticed, too, that the officer on night duty quickly recognized what an absurd blunder the exasperated peripheral apparatus had made in arresting Ulrich; still, it was quite inadvisable to release from the clutches of the law someone so reckless as to run into them uninvited. The next-higher official at headquarters also had an iron machine for a face and insisted that the prisoner's own rashness made it extremely difficult for the police to take responsibility for his release. Ulrich had already twice gone over all the points that had worked so well with the sergeant, but with no effect on this higher official, and he was about to give up hope when suddenly his judge's face underwent a remarkable, almost happy, change. Reading the charge again with care, he asked Ulrich to repeat his name, made sure of his address, politely asked him to wait a moment, and left the room. After ten minutes he came back, looking like a man who had remembered something that pleased him, and with striking courtesy invited the arrested gentleman to follow him. At the door of one of the well-lit rooms on the upper floor he said only: "The Chief Commissioner would like to speak with you personally," and the next moment Ulrich found himself facing a gentleman with the muttonchop whiskers he knew so well by now, who had just come from the conference room next door.

He was about to explain, in a tone of gentle reproach, his presence as the consequence of an error at the local police office but was anticipated by the Chief Commissioner, who greeted him with the words: "An unfortunate misunderstanding, my dear Herr Doktor, the Inspector has already told me all about it. All the same, a slight penalty is in order, in view of . . . ," and he looked at Ulrich roguishly (if such a word may be used at all of the highest police official), as though giving him a chance to guess the answer himself.

Ulrich was totally stumped by the riddle.

"His Grace!" the Commissioner offered by way of assistance.

"His Grace Count Leinsdorf," he went on, "asked me most urgently for your whereabouts, just a few hours ago."

Ulrich still did not quite follow.

"You are not in the directory, my dear sir," the Commissioner explained in a tone of mock reproach, and as though this were Ulrich's only crime.

Ulrich bowed, with a formal smile.

"I gather that you are expected to call on His Grace tomorrow on a matter of great public importance, and I cannot bring myself to prevent you from doing so by locking you up," the master of the iron machine concluded his little joke.

It may be assumed that the Chief Commissioner would have regarded Ulrich's arrest as unwarranted in any case, since the Inspec-

tor who had happened to recall Ulrich's name coming up the first
time at central police headquarters a few hours before had represented the incident to the Chief Commissioner in such a way as to
make the conclusion inevitable that no one had actually interfered
with the law arbitrarily. His Grace, incidentally, never heard how Ulrich had been tracked down. Ulrich felt obliged to pay his call the day
following this evening of lèse-majesté, and during this visit was immediately appointed Honorary Secretary to the great patriotic campaign. Count Leinsdorf, had he known how it had all come about,
would not have been able to say otherwise than that it was like a
miracle.

41

RACHEL AND DIOTIMA

Shortly afterward the first session of the great patriotic campaign was
held at Diotima's.

The dining room had been transformed into a conference room.
The dining table, fully extended and covered with green baize, occupied the center of the room. Sheets of bone-white ministry paper
with pencils of varying degrees of hardness were laid at each place.
The sideboard had been removed. The corners of the room were
empty and austere. The walls were reverently bare but for a portrait
of His Majesty hung by Diotima and that of a wasp-waisted lady
which Tuzzi in his consular days had brought home from somewhere
and which might pass for an ancestral portrait. Diotima would have
loved to put a crucifix at the head of the table, but Tuzzi had laughed
her out of it before tactfully absenting himself from his house for the
day.

For the Parallel Campaign was to be inaugurated quite privately.
No government ministers or official bigwigs appeared, nor any politicians. The intention was to start with a small, select group of none

but selfless servants of the Idea: The head of the International Bank, Herr von Holtzkopf and Baron Wisnieczky, a few ladies of the high nobility, some well-known figures associated with the city's great charities, and, in accord with Count Leinsdorf's principle of "capital and culture," representatives of the great universities, the art academies, industry, the landowning families, and the Church were expected. The government was represented by a few unobtrusive young ministry officials who fitted into this social circle and enjoyed their chiefs' confidence. This mixture was in keeping with the wishes of Count Leinsdorf, who had dreamed of a spontaneous manifestation arising from the midst of the people but who found it a great relief, after his experience with their reformist zeal, to know with whom one was dealing.

The little maid Rachel (somewhat freely translated by her mistress into a French "Rachelle") had been up and about since six o'clock that morning. She had extended the big dining table, pushed two card tables up to it, covered the whole with green baize, and dusted with special care, carrying out all these burdensome tasks in great excitement. Diotima had said to her the previous evening: "Tomorrow we may be making world history here!" and Rachel's whole body was aglow with happiness at being part of a household where such an event could take place—a great compliment to the event, since Rachel's body, beneath its black uniform, was as exquisite as Meissen porcelain.

Rachel was nineteen and believed in miracles. She had been born in a squalid shack in Poland, where a mezuzah hung on the doorpost and the soil came up through the cracks in the floorboards. She had been cursed and driven out of the door, her mother standing by with a helpless look on her face, her brothers and sisters grinning with fear. She had pleaded for mercy on her knees, her heart strangled with shame, but to no avail. An unscrupulous young fellow had seduced her; she no longer knew how; she had had to give birth to her child in the house of strangers and then had left the country. Rachel had traveled; despair rolled along with her under the filthy cart in which she rode until, wept out, she saw the capital city, toward which some instinct had driven her, as some great wall of fire into which she wanted to hurl herself to die. But—oh true miracle—this wall parted and took her in. Since then, Rachel had always felt as though she were living in the interior of a golden flame. Chance had brought her to Diotima's house, and Diotima regarded running away from home in Galicia as quite natural, if it led to her. After they had got to know each other well, Diotima sometimes told the little girl about the famous and important people who regularly visited the house where "Rachelle" had the privilege of serving; she had even told her a few things about the Parallel Campaign for the pleasure of seeing Rachel's eyes light up like a pair of golden mirrors radiantly reflecting her mistress's image.

For even if she had been cursed by her father because of some unscrupulous fellow, Rachel was an honorable girl and loved simply everything about Diotima: her soft dark hair, which Rachel was allowed to brush mornings and evenings; the dresses she helped her into; the Chinese lacquerwork and the little carved Indian tables; the books in foreign languages lying about, of which she understood not a word; she also loved Herr Tuzzi and, most recently, the nabob who had paid a call on her mistress the second day after his arrival in town—she made it out to be the first day. Rachel had stared at him in the hall with a rapture worthy of the Christian Savior descending from his golden shrine, and the only thing that vexed her was that he had not brought along his Soliman to pay his respects to her mistress.

But today, with so historic an event in the offing, she felt confident that something wonderful would happen to her too, and she supposed that this time Soliman would probably be in attendance, as the solemnity of the occasion demanded. Not that everything hinged on this expectation, but it was a necessary flourish, part of the plot of amorous intrigue present in every novel Rachel read to improve her mind. For Rachel was allowed to read the novels Diotima had put aside, just as she was allowed to cut down and alter for herself Diotima's discarded lingerie. Rachel sewed well and read fluently— that was her Jewish heritage—but when she was reading a novel Diotima had recommended as a great work of art (these were her favorites) she understood what was happening in it only as one perceives a lively event from a distance, or in a strange country; she was engrossed and moved by goings-on she did not understand and that she could not influence, and this she enjoyed enormously. She enjoyed in the same way, when sent out on an errand or when distinguished visitors came to the house, the imposing and exciting demeanor of an imperial city, its superabundance of brilliant detail, surpassing her understanding, in which she shared simply by being in a privileged place in its midst. She was not at all interested in understanding it better; she had forgotten, in her anger, the basic teachings of her Jewish home, the wise maxims heard there, and felt as little need for them as a flower needs a spoon and fork in order to nourish itself with the juices of earth and air.

So now she collected all the pencils once more and carefully slipped their shiny points into the little machine affixed to the corner of the table, which peeled off the wood so perfectly when you turned the handle that, when you repeated the process, not the tiniest chip fell off. Then she put the pencils back beside the velvety sheets of paper, three different kinds in each place, reflecting that this perfect machine she was allowed to use had been brought over yesterday evening with the pencils and the paper from the Foreign Ministry and the Imperial household by a uniformed messenger. It was now seven o'clock. Rachel quickly cast a general's glance over all the details of the arrangement and hurried out of the room to waken Diotima, for the meeting was set for a quarter past ten, and Diotima had stayed in bed awhile after the master had left the house.

These mornings with Diotima were a special treat for Rachel. The word "love" does not fit the case; the word "veneration" is closer, if one pictures it in its full meaning, in which the honor conferred so completely penetrates a person that it fills his inmost being and pushes him, so to speak, out of his own place within himself. From her adventure back home Rachel had a little daughter, now eighteen months old, whom she saw when she regularly took a large portion of her wages to the foster mother on the first Sunday of every month. But although she did not neglect her duty as a mother, she saw in it only a punishment incurred in the past, and her feelings had again become those of a girl whose chaste body had not yet been opened by love.

She approached Diotima's bed, and her gaze, adoring as that of a mountain climber catching sight of the snowy peak rising out of the morning darkness into the first blue of dawn, glided over Diotima's shoulder before she touched the tender mother-of-pearl warmth of her mistress's skin with her fingers. Then she savored the subtly mingled scent of the hand that came sleepily out from under the covers to be kissed, smelling of the previous day's colognes but also of the faint steaminess of the night's rest. Rachel held the slipper for the groping, naked foot and received the awakening glance. But the sensual contact with that magnificent female body would not have been so thrilling by far had it not been wholly irradiated by Diotima's moral significance.

"Did you remember to place the chair with the armrests for His Grace? And the little silver bell for me? Did you put out twelve sheets of paper for the secretary? And six pencils, Rachelle, six, not just three, for him?" was what Diotima said on this occasion. At each of these questions, Rachel inwardly ticked off on her fingers all she had done, with a frightened thrill of ambition, as though her life were at stake. Her mistress had thrown on a dressing gown and went into the conference room. Her way of training "Rachelle" involved reminding her that it was not enough to regard everything done or undone as one's personal concern, but to consider its general import. If Rachel broke a glass, "Rachelle" was told that the damage in itself signified nothing but that the transparent glass was a symbol of the daily little duties the eye barely perceived because it gladly dwelled on higher things, which was all the more reason that one had to pay the most particular attention to these duties. To find herself treated with such ministerial courtesy could bring remorse and happiness to Rachel's eyes as she swept up the fragments. Her cooks, from whom Diotima expected right thinking and recognition of errors they had committed, had come and gone often enough since Rachel had entered her service, but Rachel loved Diotima's sublime phrases with all her heart, just as she loved the Emperor, the state funerals, and the flaming candles in the darkness of the Catholic churches. She might fib a little to get out of a scrape, but she was thoroughly ashamed of herself afterward. Perhaps she even took a perverse pleasure in her little lies because they made her feel how really bad she was, compared with Diotima; but she usually indulged herself in this only when she hoped to be able to turn the falsehood, secretly and quickly, into a truth.

When one human being looks up to another so much in every way, it happens that his body is, so to speak, taken away from him and plunges like a little meteorite into the sun of the other body. Diotima had no fault to find with Rachel's performance and kindly patted her little maid on the shoulder. Then they both went into the bathroom to dress Diotima for the great day. When Rachel tempered the bathwater, lathered the soap, and was permitted to rub Diotima's body down with the bath towel as boldly as though it were her own, it gave her much more pleasure than if it really were merely her own, which seemed of no account, inspired no confidence; she was far from thinking of it even for comparison, but felt, in touching Diotima's statuesque abundance, rather like an oaf of a recruit who belonged to a dazzling regiment.

So was Diotima girded for the great day.

42

THE GREAT SESSION

On the minute of the appointed hour, Count Leinsdorf appeared, accompanied by Ulrich. Rachel, already aglow from admitting an uninterrupted stream of guests for whom she had to open the door and help with their coats, recognized Ulrich at once and noted with satisfaction that he, too, had been no casual visitor but a man brought to her mistress's house by a significant chain of events, as was now demonstrated by his arrival in the company of His Grace. She fluttered to the door, which she opened ceremoniously, and then crouched down at the keyhole to see what would now happen inside. It was a large keyhole, and she saw the banker's clean-shaven chin and the prelate Niedomansky's violet neckband, as well as the golden sword knot of General Stumm von Bordwehr, who had been sent by the War Ministry although it really had not been invited; the Ministry had declared, in a letter to Count Leinsdorf, that it did not wish to be absent on "so highly patriotic" an occasion, though not directly involved in bringing it about or in the foreseeable course it would take. Diotima had forgotten to mention this to Rachel, who was quite excited by the presence of a general at this gathering but could make out nothing more, for the present, about what was going on.

Diotima, meanwhile, had welcomed His Grace, not paying much attention to Ulrich, as she was introducing other guests to the Count, beginning with Dr. Paul Arnheim. She explained to His Grace that a lucky chance had brought this distinguished friend of her house, and even though as a non-Austrian he could not expect to take a formal part in their conference, she hoped he would be permitted to stay as her personal adviser, because—here she appended a gentle threat— his great experience and connections in the field of international culture and its relations with economic questions were an invaluable support to her, considering that she had so far been obliged to take sole responsibility for covering these areas and could not soon be replaced even in the future, although she was only too aware of her inadequacy.

Count Leinsdorf found himself ambushed; it was the first time since he had known her that his middle-class friend had surprised him by committing an indiscretion. Arnheim, too, felt taken aback, like a sovereign whose entrance has not been staged with the proper fanfare; he had of course been certain that Count Leinsdorf had known and approved of his being invited. But Diotima, with an obstinate look on her flushed face, did not give an inch; like all women with too clear a conscience in the matter of marital fidelity, she could develop an insufferable feminine persistence in a good cause.

She was at that time already in love with Arnheim, who had by this time called on her more than once, but in her inexperience she had no inkling of the nature of her feeling. They talked about what it is that moves the soul, that ennobles the flesh between the sole of the foot and the crown of the head and transforms the confused impressions of civilized life into harmonious spiritual vibrations. But even this was a great deal, and because Diotima was inclined to caution and always on guard against compromising herself, this intimacy struck her as too sudden, and she had to mobilize truly great emotions, the very greatest, in fact, and where were they most likely to be found? Where everyone has shifted them, to the drama of history. For Diotima and Arnheim, the Parallel Campaign was, so to speak, a safety island in the swelling traffic of their souls. They regarded it as clearly fated that they should have been brought together at such an important moment, and they could not agree more that the great patriotic enterprise was an immense opportunity and responsibility for intellectual people. Arnheim said so too, though he never forgot to add that it depended primarily upon people with strong personalities who had experience in economics as well as the world of ideas, and only secondarily on the scope of the organization. So in Diotima the Parallel Campaign had become inextricably bound up with Arnheim; the void it had presented to her imagination at the beginning had given way to a copious abundance. Her hope that the great treasures of feeling embodied in the Austrian heritage could be strengthened by Prussian intellectual discipline was now most happily justified, and these impressions were so strong that this normally very correct woman had not realized what a breach of protocol she had committed in undertaking to invite Arnheim to the inaugural conference. Now there was no retreat; anyway, Arnheim, who sensed how it had happened, found it essentially disarming, however annoyed he was at finding himself in a false position; and His Grace was basically too fond of his friend Diotima to show his surprise beyond his first, involuntary, recoil. He met Diotima's explanation with silence and after an awkward little pause amiably held out his hand to Arnheim, assuring him in the most civil and complimentary terms that he was welcome, as in fact he was. Most of the others present had probably noticed the little scene and wondered about Arnheim's presence insofar as they knew who he was; but among well-bred people it is generally assumed that there is a sufficient reason for everything, and it is considered poor taste to ask too many prying questions.

Diotima had meanwhile recovered her statuesque impassivity. After a few moments she called the meeting to order and asked His Grace to honor her house by taking a chair.

His Grace made a speech. He had been preparing it for days, and his cast of mind was much too fixed to let him change anything at the last minute; he could only just manage to tone down the most outspoken allusions to the Prussian needle gun, which (an underhanded trick) had got the better of the Austrian muzzle-loaders in '66.

"What has brought us together," Count Leinsdorf said, "is the shared conviction that a great testimonial arising from the midst of the people themselves must not be left to chance but needs guidance by an influence that sees far into the future from a place with a broad perspective—in other words, from the top. His Majesty, our beloved Emperor and Sovereign, will in the year 1918 celebrate the almost unique jubilee of the seventieth year since his richly blessed ascent to the throne with all the strength and vigor, please God, we have always been accustomed to admire in him. We are certain that this occasion will be celebrated by the grateful people of Austria in a manner to show the world not only our deep love for him, but also that the Austro-Hungarian Monarchy stands together, grouped firm as a rock around its Sovereign."

At this point Count Leinsdorf wavered, wondering whether to mention anything about the signs of decay to which this rock, even at a unified celebration of its Emperor and King, was exposed; resistance by Hungary, which recognized only a King, had to be reckoned with. This was why His Grace had originally meant to speak of two firm rocks. But somehow this also failed to do justice to his sense of the Austro-Hungarian state.

This sense of the Austro-Hungarian state was so oddly put together that it must seem almost hopeless to explain it to anyone who has not experienced it himself. It did not consist of an Austrian part and a Hungarian part that, as one might expect, complemented each other, but of a whole and a part; that is, of a Hungarian and an Austro-Hungarian sense of statehood, the latter to be found in Austria, which in a sense left the Austrian sense of statehood with no country of its own. The Austrian existed only in Hungary, and there as an object of dislike; at home he called himself a national of the kingdoms and lands of the Austro-Hungarian Monarchy as represented in the Imperial Council, meaning that he was an Austrian plus a Hungarian minus that Hungarian; and he did this not with enthusiasm but only for the sake of a concept that was repugnant to him, because he could bear the Hungarians as little as they could bear him, which added still another complication to the whole combination. This led many people to simply call themselves Czechs, Poles, Slovenes, or Germans, and this was the beginning of that further decay and those well-known "unpleasant phenomena of an internal political kind," as Count Leinsdorf called them, which according to him were "the work of irresponsible, callow, sensation-seeking elements" not kept sufficiently in check by the politically unenlightened mass of inhabitants. As the subject here touched upon has since been dealt with in many well-informed and clever books, the reader will be glad to be reassured that neither at this point nor later will any serious attempt be made to paint a historical canvas and enter into competition with reality. It is fully sufficient to note that the mysteries of this Dualism (the technical term for it) were at the very least as recondite as those of the Trinity, for the historical process nearly everywhere resembles a juridical one, with hundreds of clauses, appendices, compromises, and protests, and it is only to this that attention should be drawn. The common man lives and dies among these complications all unsuspecting, which is just as well for him, because if he were to realize in what sort of a trial, with what lawyers, costs, and conflicting motives, he was entangled, he might be seized by paranoia no matter what country he lived in. Understanding reality is exclusively a matter for the philosopher of political history. For him the present period follows upon the Battle of Mohács or Lietzen as the roast the soup; he knows all the proceedings and has at every moment the sense of necessity arising out of lawful process. If he is, moreover, like Count Leinsdorf an aristocratic philosopher trained in political history, whose forebears, wielding sword or spindle, had personally played their parts in the preliminaries, he can survey the result as a smoothly ascending line.

And so His Grace Count Leinsdorf had said to himself before the conference: "We must not forget that His Majesty's noble and generous resolve to let the people take part in the conduct of their own affairs, up to a point, has not been in effect long enough to have produced everywhere the kind of political maturity in every respect worthy of the confidence so magnanimously placed in the people by His Majesty. So we will not discern, as does the grudging world beyond our frontiers, signs of senile decay in such execrable demonstrations as we are now unfortunately experiencing, but rather signs of a still immature, hence inexhaustible, youthful strength of the Austrian people."

He had meant to bring all this up at the meeting, but because Arnheim was present he did not say everything he had thought out beforehand but contented himself with hinting at the ignorance abroad of true conditions in Austria, leading to exaggeration where certain unpleasant phenomena were concerned. "For," His Grace concluded, "if we wish to give unmistakable proof of our strength and unity, we do so entirely in the interests of the wider world, since a happy relationship among the European family of nations is based upon mutual esteem and respect for one another's power." He then repeated only once more that such a forceful, blunt display of strength must truly come from the midst of the people and hence be directed from above, the purpose of this meeting being to find ways and means of so doing. Considering that only a short time ago Count Leinsdorf had thought of nothing more than a list of names, to which only the suggestion of a "Year of Austria" had been added from outside, this could be characterized as great progress, even though His Grace had not even expressed everything in his mind.

After this speech, Diotima took the floor to clarify the chairman's objectives. The great patriotic campaign, she explained, must find a great aim that would emerge, as His Grace had said, from the midst of the people. "We who are gathered here today for the first time do not feel called upon to define this aim as of now, but we are assembled to create first of all an organization to prepare the way for the framing of suggestions leading toward this aim." With these words she opened the discussion.

At first there was silence. Shut birds of different species and song patterns, none of whom have any idea what is going to happen to them, together in a cage, and they will initially be silent exactly the same way.

Finally, a professor asked for permission to speak. Ulrich did not know him. His Grace had presumably got his secretary to invite this gentleman at the last moment. He spoke of the path of history. When we look ahead, he said, we see an impenetrable wall. If we look left and right, we see an overwhelming mass of important events without recognizable direction. To cite just a few instances: the present conflict with Montenegro, the Spanish ordeals in battle in Morocco, the obstructionism of the Ukrainians in the Austrian Imperial Council. But looking back, everything, as if by a miracle, has become order and purpose. . . . Therefore, if he might say so, we experience at every moment the mystery of a miraculous guidance. So he wanted to welcome as a great idea opening the eyes of a nation, as it were, to this, to let it look consciously into the ways of Providence by calling upon it on a definite occasion of rare sublimity. . . . This was all he had wanted to say. It was much like modern methods of teaching, letting the pupil work out the answers together with the teacher, rather than imposing on him ready-made results.

The assembled company stared stonily, but with a pleasant expression, at the green tablecloth; even the prelate representing the Archbishop reacted to this clerical performance by a layman with the same polite reserve as the gentlemen from the ministries, without allowing his face to betray a hint of cordial agreement. It was like the way people feel when someone on the street suddenly begins to address all and sundry at the top of his voice; everyone, even those who had been thinking of nothing at all, feels suddenly that he is out on serious business, or that someone is making improper use of the street. As he spoke, the professor had been struggling with a sense of embarrassment, squeezing out his words with jerky constraint, as if a strong wind were snatching away his breath; he waited for an answering echo, then slowly withdrew the expectant look from his face, not without dignity.

It was a relief to all when the representative of the Imperial Privy Purse came to the rescue by quickly giving them a list of foundations and endowments to be expected, in that jubilee year, from His Majesty's private funds. It began with the donation of a sum for the building of a pilgrims' church, a foundation for the support of deacons without private means, gifts to the Archduke Karl and Field Marshal Radetzky Veterans' Clubs, to the soldiers' widows and orphans from the campaigns of '66 and '78, followed by funds for pensioned noncommissioned officers, for the Academy of Sciences, and so it went, on and on. There was nothing exciting about these lists; they simply had their place and took their course as a public expression of Imperial benevolence. The moment they had all been read off a Frau Weghuber, a manufacturer's wife with an impressive record of charitable works, rose promptly to her feet, quite impervious to any idea that there might be something more pressing than the objects of her concern. She advanced a proposal for a Greater Austrian Franz Josef Soup Kitchen, which was received sympathetically. However, the delegate from the Ministry of Public Worship and Education pointed out that his own department had received a somewhat similar suggestion, namely, the publication of a monumental work, *Emperor Franz Josef I and His Time*. But after this happy start silence again prevailed, and most of those present felt trapped in an awkward situation.

Had they been asked on their way to this meeting whether they knew what historical events or great events or things of that sort were, they would certainly have replied in the affirmative; but confronted with the weighty imperative of making up such an event on the spot, they slowly began to feel faint, and something like rumblings of a very natural kind stirred inside them.

At this dangerous moment the ever-tactful Diotima, who had prepared refreshments, interrupted the meeting.

43

ULRICH MEETS THE GREAT MAN FOR THE FIRST TIME. NOTHING IRRATIONAL HAPPENS IN WORLD HISTORY, BUT DIOTIMA CLAIMS THAT THE TRUE AUSTRIA IS THE WHOLE WORLD

During the pause for refreshments, Arnheim observed that the more all-inclusive the organization, the further the various proposals would diverge from one another. This was a characteristic symptom of its present state of development, based, as it was, only on reason. Yet it was just this that made it a tremendous undertaking, to force a whole people into awareness of the will, inspiration, and all that was basic, which lay far deeper than reason.

Ulrich replied by asking him whether he really believed that anything would come of this campaign.

"No doubt about it," Arnheim said, "great events are always the expression of a general situation." The mere fact that a meeting such as this had been possible anywhere was proof of its profound necessity.

And yet discrimination in such matters seems difficult, Ulrich said. Suppose, for instance, that the composer of the latest worldwide musical hit happened to be a political schemer and managed to become president of the world—which was certainly conceivable, given his enormous popularity—would this be a leap forward in history or an expression of the cultural situation?

"That's quite impossible!" Arnheim said seriously. "Such a composer couldn't possibly be either a schemer or a politician—otherwise, his genius for musical comedy would be inexplicable, and nothing absurd happens in world history."

"But so much that's absurd happens in the world, surely?"

"In world history, never!"

Arnheim was visibly on edge. Diotima and Count Leinsdorf stood nearby in lively, low-voiced conversation. His Grace had, after all, expressed to his friend his amazement at meeting a Prussian on this markedly Austrian occasion. For reasons of discretion, if nothing else, he regarded it as wholly out of the question to let an alien play a leading part in the Parallel Campaign, although Diotima pointed out the splendid and confidence-inspiring impression such freedom from political egotism would inevitably make abroad. She then changed her tactics, giving her plan a surprising new dimension. She spoke of a woman's tact, an intuitive certainty deeply immune to society's prejudices. If His Grace would only listen, just this once, to that voice. Arnheim was a European, an intellectual force known throughout Europe; precisely because he was not an Austrian, his participation would prove that the intellect as such was at home in Austria. Suddenly she came out with the pronouncement that the True Austria was the whole world. The world, she explained, would find no peace until its nations learned to live together on a higher plane, like the Austrian peoples in their Fatherland. A Greater Austria, a Global Austria—that was the idea His Grace had inspired in her at this happy moment—the crowning idea the Parallel Campaign had been missing all along!

Irresistible, commanding her pacifist zeal, the beautiful Diotima stood before her noble friend. Count Leinsdorf could not yet make up his mind to surrender his objections, but he again admired this woman's fiery idealism and breadth of vision, and pondered whether it might not be more advantageous to sound out Arnheim first rather than deal on the spot with suggestions of such weighty consequence.

Arnheim was restless, sensing the nature of this conversation yet unable to influence it. He and Ulrich were surrounded by the curious, drawn by the presence of this Croesus, and Ulrich was just saying:

"There are several thousand occupations in which people lose themselves, where they invest all their wits. But if you are looking for the universal human element, for what they all have in common, there are really only three possibilities left: stupidity, money, or, at most, some leftover memory of religion."

"Quite right, religion!" Arnheim broke in emphatically, and asked Ulrich whether he really believed that it had all died out, down to the roots. He had stressed the word "religion" so loudly that Count Leinsdorf was bound to hear.

His Grace seemed to have come to terms, meanwhile, with Diotima, for led by her he now approached the group, which tactfully made way, and addressed Arnheim.

Ulrich suddenly found himself alone, and bit his lip.

He began, for some reason—perhaps to kill time or not to stand there so awkwardly—to think of the drive to this meeting. As a man who moved with the times, Count Leinsdorf, who had brought him along, owned several cars, but inasmuch as he also clung to tradition, he occasionally used a pair of superb chestnut horses that he kept, together with a coachman and a light carriage; so when his major-domo had come for his instructions, His Grace had decided that it would be fitting to drive these two beautiful, almost historical creatures to the inaugural meeting of the Parallel Campaign.

"This one is Pepi, and that one is Hans," Count Leinsdorf had explained on the way, as they watched the dancing brown hillocks of the horses' cruppers and now and then one of the nodding heads moving rhythmically sideways so that the foam flew from its mouth. It was hard to comprehend what was going on inside the animals; it was a beautiful morning and they moved at a fast trot. Perhaps fodder and speed were the only passions left to horses, since Pepi and Hans were geldings and knew nothing of love as a tangible desire, but only as a breath and a haze that sometimes veiled their vision of the world with thin, lucent clouds. The passion for fodder was preserved in a marble manger full of delicious oats, a hayrack full of fresh hay, the sound of the stable halter rubbing on its ring, and, concentrated in the warm, steamy stable smell, a spicy, steady aroma needled with the ammonia-charged strong sense of self: Here are horses! Speed was something else again. In this, the poor soul is still bound to the herd, where motion suddenly takes possession of the lead stallion, or all of them together, and the lot of them goes galloping off into the wind and the sun; for when the animal is alone and free to charge off to all four points of the compass, often a mad shudder will run through its skull and it will go storming off aimlessly, plunging into a terrible freedom as empty in one direction as another, until it comes to a bewildered halt and can be lured back with a bucket of oats. Pepi and Hans were well-trained horses, used to running in harness; they moved forward eagerly, their hooves beating the sunny street fenced in by houses. People were gray swarms for them, causing them neither joy nor fear; the bright window displays, the women parading in their colorful finery—patches of meadow no good for grazing; hats, neckties, books, diamonds along the street: a desert. Only the two dream-islands of stable and trotting rose up, and sometimes, as though in a dream or in play, Hans and Pepi shied at a shadow, pressed against the shafts, were revived by a flick of the whip, and leaned gratefully into the reins.

Suddenly Count Leinsdorf had sat up straight in the cushions and asked Ulrich: "Stallburg tells me, Herr Doktor, that you are taking an interest in someone?" Ulrich was so taken by surprise that he did not immediately grasp the connection, and Leinsdorf went on: "Very good of you. I know all about it. I'm afraid there's not much to be done—such a terrible fellow. But that intangible personal something in need of grace, which every Christian has in him, often shows itself in just such an individual. And when a man sets out to do something great, he should think most humbly of the helpless. Perhaps this fellow can be given another physical examination."

After Count Leinsdorf had delivered himself of this long speech, sitting upright in the jolting carriage, he let himself drop back into the upholstery and added: "But we cannot forget that at this moment we owe all our energies to the realization of a historic event!"

Ulrich really felt a liking for this naïve old aristocrat, who was standing there still talking with Diotima and Arnheim, and felt almost a twinge of jealousy. For the conversation seemed to be quite lively; Diotima was smiling; Count Leinsdorf's eyes were popping with alarm as he tried to follow Arnheim, who was holding forth with noble composure. Ulrich caught the phrase "bringing ideas into the spheres of power." He could not stand Arnheim, simply as a model of existence, on principle. This combination of intellect, business, good living, and learning was absolutely insufferable. He was convinced that Arnheim had organized everything the previous evening so that he would be neither the first nor the last to arrive at the session this morning; and yet he had certainly not looked at his watch before he left home but had probably done so for the last time before sitting down to breakfast and receiving the report of his secretary, who had handed him the mail; then he had transformed the time at his disposal into the precise amount of mental activity he intended to do before he had to leave, and when he dispassionately gave himself up to that activity, he was certain it would fill up the time exactly; for the right thing and the time it takes are mysteriously connected, like a sculpture and the space it inhabits, or a javelin thrower and the target he hits without looking at it. Ulrich had already heard a great deal about Arnheim and had read some of his works. In one of them, Arnheim had written that a man who inspects his suit in the mirror is incapable of fearless conduct, because the mirror, originally created to give pleasure—as Arnheim explained it—had become an instrument of anxiety, like the clock, which is a substitute for the fact that our activities no longer follow a natural sequence.

Ulrich had to force himself to look away in order not to be seen staring rudely at the nearby group, and his eyes came to rest on the little maid who was moving about among the chatting groups, offering refreshments with respectful glances. But little Rachel did not notice him; she had forgotten him and even neglected to bring her tray over to him. She was approaching Arnheim and presenting her refreshments to him as to a god; she longed to kiss the short, masterful hand that reached out for the lemonade and held the glass absentmindedly, without the nabob's taking a sip. Once this high point was passed she continued on her rounds like a dazed little robot and made her way as quickly as she could out of this world-historical room, where everything was filled with legs and talk, back into the hall again.

44

CONTINUATION AND CONCLUSION OF THE
GREAT SESSION. ULRICH TAKES A LIKING TO
RACHEL, AND RACHEL TO SOLIMAN. THE
PARALLEL CAMPAIGN GETS ORGANIZED

Ulrich liked girls like this: ambitious, well-behaved, in their well-trained timidity like little fruit trees whose sweet ripe fruit is destined to fall one day into the mouth of some young knight of Cockaigne as soon as he deigns to open his lips. "They have to be brave and tough," he thought, "like Stone Age women who shared their hunter's bed by night and carried his weapons and household gear on marches by day," although he himself had never gone on such an expedition except in the distant prehistoric age of his awakening manhood. With a sigh he sat down again, for the session had resumed. In remembering, he was struck that the black-and-white vestments one put on these maids were the same colors as nuns' habits; this had never occurred to him before, and he wondered at it. But the divine Diotima was speaking again, saying that the Parallel Campaign must culminate in a great symbol. That meant that it would not do to have just any sort of goal, no matter how widely visible, no matter how patriotic. This goal would have to seize the heart of the world. It could not be just practical, it also had to be a poem. It had to be a landmark. It had to be a mirror in which the world would see itself and blush. And not just blush but, as in a fairy tale, see its own true countenance and never again be able to forget it. His Grace had suggested for this symbol "Emperor of Peace."

This being the premise, there could be no mistaking that the suggestions considered thus far had been wide of the mark, Diotima went on. When she spoke of symbols earlier in the meeting, she had naturally meant not soup kitchens but that nothing less was at stake than the need to recover that unity of mankind that had been lost because the disparity of interests in society had grown so great. The question arises whether at the present time the peoples of today are still at all capable of such great, unifying ideas? All the suggestions made so far were splendid, of course, but they diverged so widely, which already showed that none of them had unifying power.

As she spoke, Ulrich was watching Arnheim. His dislike did not attach itself to any particular details of that physiognomy but quite simply to the totality. Not that the individual features—the industrial baron's hard Phoenician skull, the sharp face that seemed to be formed of too little material, so that it had a certain flatness, the lordly, English-tailor repose of the figure, and, at the second place where a man peeks out of his suit, the rather too-short-fingered hands—were not in themselves sufficiently noteworthy. What irritated Ulrich was the harmony in which all of this coexisted. Arnheim's books also had the same kind of self-assurance; the world was in order, as soon as Arnheim had given it his due consideration. As he sat watching Arnheim being so dramatically attentive to the foolishness they were having to sit through, Ulrich suddenly felt a slum kid's impulse to throw rocks or mud at this man who had grown up in all that wealth and perfection. Arnheim was drinking it all in like a connoisseur whose face says: Without going overboard, I must say this is a noble vintage!

Diotima had now come to the end of her speech. Right after the intermission, when they had all sat down again, everyone had looked confident that something conclusive was about to occur. Nobody had given it any real thought, but they all had that look of waiting for something important to happen. And now Diotima concluded: So when the question imposed itself whether the present time and the peoples of today's world were at all capable of such great, unifying ideas, it was necessary and proper to add: The idea of the power to redeem. For it was a question of redemption, of a redeeming upsurge. In short: even if we could not yet imagine it in any detail. It must come out of the total community, or it would not come at all. And so she would take it upon herself, after having consulted with His Grace, to conclude today's meeting with the following proposal: As His Grace had rightly observed, the august ministerial departments already represented a division of the world in accordance with its main aspects, such as religion and education, commerce, industry, law, and so on. If those present would therefore agree to set up committees, each headed by a delegate from a government department, with representatives of the respective institutions and sectors of the population at his side, the resulting organization would already embody the major moral forces of the world in their proper order and would serve as an instrument through which these forces could flow in and be filtered. The final determination would be made by an executive committee, and the entire structure would then need only several special committees and subcommittees, such as a publicity committee, a fund-raising committee, and the like, while she would like to reserve to herself personally the forming of a special committee for the further elaboration of the campaign's fundamental ideas, of course in constant cooperation with all the other committees.

Again there was a general silence, but this time of palpable relief. Count Leinsdorf nodded his head several times. Someone asked as a point of further clarification how the specifically Austrian note would come into the campaign as thus conceived.

In response to this question, General Stumm von Bordwehr rose to speak, even though all the preceding speakers had remained seated. He was well aware, he said, that the soldier's role in the council chamber was a modest one. If he spoke nevertheless, it was not to inject his own opinion into the unsurpassable critical remarks and suggestions already made, all of them excellent, but only to offer one more idea at the end, for everyone's indulgent consideration. The planned demonstration was intended to impress the outside world. But what impressed the outside world was the power of a people. And in view of the present situation in the European family of nations, as His Grace had said, a demonstration of this kind would certainly not be pointless. The idea of the state was, after all, the idea of power; as Treitschke said, the state is the power of self-preservation in the struggle for national survival. The general was only touching on a well-known sore spot in mentioning the condition of our artillery and our navy, both in unsatisfactory condition owing to the apathy of Parliament. Which is why he hoped they would consider, in case no other goal should be found, which was still an open question, that a broadly based popular concern with the problems of the army and its equipment would be a decidedly worthy aim. *Si vis pacem, para bellum!* Strength in peace wards off war, or at least shortens its span. He could therefore confidently maintain that steps taken in that direction would have a conciliatory effect on other nations and would make for an impressive demonstration of peaceable intentions.

At this moment there was a curious feeling in the room. Most of those present had at first felt that this speech was not in keeping with the meeting's real purpose, but as the General became more dominant acoustically, the effect on his listeners was like the reassuring tramp of well-ordered battalions. The original impulse of the Parallel Campaign, "Better than Prussia," shyly raised its head, as though some distant regimental band were trumpeting the march about Prince Eugène riding against the Turks, or the anthem "God Save the Emperor," . . . though of course if His Grace had now stood up to propose—as he was far from intending to do—that they should put their Prussian brother Arnheim at the head of the regimental band, they might have believed, in the state of vague exaltation in which they found themselves, that they were hearing the Prussian anthem instead, and would hardly have been able to object.

At the keyhole, "Rachelle" reported: "Now they're talking about war."

Her quick return to the hall at the end of the intermission owed a little to the fact that this time Arnheim had actually brought Soliman in his wake. As bad weather was threatening, the little African boy had followed his master, carrying an overcoat. When Rachel opened the door he had made an impudent face, since he was a spoiled young Berliner who was used to women fussing over him in a way he had not yet learned to take advantage of. But Rachel had assumed that he must be spoken to in his native African language; it simply never occurred to her to try German. Since she absolutely had to make herself understood, she had put her arm around the sixteen-year-old's shoulder and pointed the way to the kitchen, where she gave him a chair and pushed in front of him whatever cakes and drinks were within reach. She had never done this sort of thing in her life, and when she straightened up from the table her heart was pounding like sugar being pulverized in a mortar.

"What's your name?" Soliman asked; so he spoke German!

"Rachelle, Rachel," she said, and ran off.

In the kitchen, Soliman made the most of the cake, wine, and hors d'oeuvres, lit a cigarette, and started a conversation with the cook.

Seeing this when she came back from waiting on the guests gave Rachel a stab.

"In there," she said, "they'll be talking about something very important again any minute now."

But Soliman was not impressed, and the cook, an older woman, laughed.

"It might even mean war!" Rachel added excitedly—and was able to cap this a little later with her news from the keyhole that it had almost reached that point.

Soliman pricked up his ears. "Are there any Austrian generals in there?" he asked.

"See for yourself," Rachel said. "There's one, at least." And they went together to the keyhole.

Their glance fell now on some white paper, then on a nose; a big shadow passed by, a ring flashed. Life broke up into bright details. Green baize stretching away like a lawn; a white hand at rest somewhere, without a context, pale as in a waxworks; peering in slantwise, one could see the golden tassel of the General's sword gleaming in a corner. Even the pampered Soliman showed some excitement. Seen through the crack of a door and an imagination, life swelled to weird and fairy-tale dimensions. The stooping position made the blood buzz in one's ears, and the voices behind the door now rumbled like falling rocks, now glided as on greased planks. Rachel slowly straightened up. The floor seemed to heave under her feet; she was enveloped by the spirit of the occasion as though she had put her head under one of those black cloths used by conjurors and photographers. Soliman stood up too, and the blood drained fluttering from their heads. The little black boy smiled, and behind his bluish lips his scarlet gums shimmered.

While this instant in the hall, among the hanging overcoats of influential personages, faded slowly like a bugle call, a resolution was being passed in the conference room after Count Leinsdorf had thanked the General for his important and valuable suggestions, though the time had not yet come for examining proposals on their merits, as the organizational groundwork must be laid first. To this end, all that was needed now—apart from suiting the plan to the realities as represented by the ministries—was a final resolution to the effect that those present had unanimously agreed to submit the wishes of the people, as soon as these could be determined by the Parallel Campaign, to His Majesty, with the most humble petition to be allowed to dispose freely of the means for their material fulfillment (which would have to be raised by then) if such were His Majesty's most gracious pleasure.

This had the advantage that the people would be placed in the position of setting the worthiest possible aim for themselves, but through the agency of the Sovereign's most gracious will. The resolution was passed at His Grace's special request; for although it was only a matter of form, he considered it important that the people not take action on their own and without the consent of constitutional authority—not even to honor it.

The other participants would not have made such a point of this, but by the same token they had no objection to it. And it was in order, too, that the meeting should end with the passing of a resolution. For whether one sets a final period to a brawl with a knife, or ends a musical piece by crashing all ten fingers simultaneously down on the keyboard a few times, or whether the dancer bows to his lady, or whether one passes a resolution, it would be an uncanny world if events simply slunk off, if there were not a final ceremony to assure that they had indeed taken place. And that is why it is done.

45

SILENT ENCOUNTER OF TWO MOUNTAIN PEAKS

When the session was over, Arnheim had quietly maneuvered, at a hint from Diotima, to be left behind, alone. Section Chief Tuzzi was observing a respectful margin of time to be sure of not returning home before the end of the session.

In these minutes between the departure of the guests and the settling down of the house, as her passage from room to room was interrupted by brief, sometimes conflicting, orders, considerations, and the general unrest that a fading great event leaves behind, Arnheim smiled as his eyes followed Diotima's movements. She felt that her domicile was in a state of tremulous movement; all the things that had had to abandon their customary places because of the great event returned piece by piece, like a big wave ebbing from the sand in countless little hollows and runnels. While Arnheim waited in urbane silence until she and the commotion around her settled down again, it struck Diotima that no matter how many people had gone in and out of her house, no man—other than Section Chief Tuzzi—had ever been so domestically alone with her that one palpably felt the mute life of the empty apartment. And suddenly her chaste mind was troubled by a bizarre notion: her empty apartment, in the absence of even her husband, seemed like a pair of trousers Arnheim had just slipped into. There are such moments, when chastity itself may be visited by such abortive flashes from the pit of darkness, and so the wonderful dream of a love in which body and soul are entirely one bloomed in Diotima.

Arnheim had no inkling of this. His trousers made an impeccably perpendicular line to the gleaming parquet; his morningcoat, his cravat, his serenely smiling patrician head, said nothing, so perfect were they. Actually, he had intended to complain to Diotima about the incident on his arrival, to make sure that no such thing happened in future. But there was at this moment something that made this man, who hobnobbed with American money magnates as an equal, who had been received by emperors and kings, this nabob who could offer any woman her weight in platinum, something that made him, instead of complaining, stare entranced at Diotima, whose name was really Ermelinda, or actually only Hermine Tuzzi, the mere wife of a ranking official. For this something it is here once again necessary to resort to the word "soul."

The word has already turned up more than once, though not in the clearest contexts; as, for instance, something lost in our time, or incompatible with civilization; as something at odds with physical urges and connubial habits; something that is moved, and not only to repugnance, by a murderer; something that was to be liberated by the Parallel Campaign; as a subject for religious meditations and *contemplatio in caligine divina* by Count Leinsdorf; as, with many people, a love of metaphor; and so on. The most peculiar of all the peculiarities of the word "soul," however, is that young people cannot pronounce it without laughing. Even Diotima and Arnheim were shy of using it without a modifier, for it is still possible to speak of having a great, noble, craven, daring, or debased soul, but to come right out with "my soul" is something one simply cannot bring oneself to do. It is distinctly an older person's word, and this can only be understood by assuming that in the course of life people become more and more aware of something for which they urgently need a name they cannot find until they finally resort, reluctantly, to the name they had originally despised.

How to describe it, then? Whether one is at rest or in motion, what matters is not what lies ahead, what one sees, hears, wants, takes, masters. It forms a horizon, a semicircle before one, but the ends of this semicircle are joined by a string, and the plane of this string goes right through the middle of the world. In front, the face and hands look out of it; sensations and strivings run ahead of it, and no one doubts that whatever one does is always reasonable, or at least passionate. In other words, outer circumstances call for us to act in a way everyone can understand; and if, in the toils of passion, we do something incomprehensible, that too is, in its own way, understandable. Yet however understandable and self-contained everything seems, this is accompanied by an obscure feeling that it is only half the story. Something is not quite in balance, and a person presses forward, like a tightrope walker, in order not to sway and fall. And as he presses on through life and leaves lived life behind, the life ahead and the life already lived form a wall, and his path in the end resembles the path of a woodworm: no matter how it corkscrews forward or even backward, it always leaves an empty space behind it. And this horrible feeling of a blind, cutoff space behind the fullness of everything, this half that is always missing even when everything is a whole, this is what eventually makes one perceive what one calls the soul.

We always include it, of course, in our thoughts, intuitions, feelings, in all sorts of surrogate ways and according to our individual temperament. In youth it manifests itself as a distinct feeling of insecurity about whether everything one does is really the right thing, after all; in old age as a sense of wonder at how little one has done of all one had really meant to do. In between, one takes comfort in the thought that one is a hell of a good, capable fellow, even if every little thing can't be justified; or that the world is not the way it ought to be either, so that one's failures come to represent a fair enough compromise. Then there are always some people who think beyond all this of a God who has their missing piece in His pocket. Only love has a special position in this; in this exceptional case the missing half grows back: the beloved seems to stand where ordinarily something was always missing. The souls unite "dos-à-dos," as it were, making themselves superfluous in the process. This is why most people, after the one great love in their youth is over, no longer feel the absence of their soul, so that this so-called foolishness fulfills a useful social function.

Neither Diotima nor Arnheim had ever loved. We already know this about Diotima, but the great financier also had, in a wider sense, a chaste soul. He had always been afraid that the feelings he aroused in women might not be for himself but for his money, and so he lived only with women to whom he also gave, not love, but money. He had never had a friend for fear of being used; he had only business friends, even if the business happened to be an intellectual exchange. This shrewd man, although imbued with experience of life, was still untouched and in danger of being permanently alone when he met Diotima, whom destiny had intended for him. The mysterious forces within them converged. It could be compared only with the movement of the trade winds, the Gulf Stream, the volcanic tremors of the earth's crust; forces vastly superior to those of man, akin to the stars, were set in motion from one to the other, overriding such barriers as hours and days, measureless currents. At such moments the actual words spoken are supremely unimportant. Rising from the vertical creases of his trousers, Arnheim's body seemed to stand there in the godlike solitude of a towering mountain. United with him through the valley between them, Diotima rose on its other side, luminous with solitude, in her fashionable dress of the period with its puffed sleeves on the upper arms, the artful pleats over the bosom widening above the stomach, the skirt narrowing again below the knees to cling to her calves. The glass-bead curtains at the doors cast moving reflections like ponds, the javelins and arrows on the walls trembled with their feathered and deadly passions, and the yellow volumes of Calman-Lévy on the tables were as silent as lemon groves. We will reverently pass over the first words spoken.

46

IDEALS AND MORALITY ARE THE BEST MEANS FOR FILLING THAT BIG HOLE CALLED SOUL

Arnheim was the first to shake off the spell. To linger in such a state was, to his way of thinking, impossible, without either sinking into a dull, vacuous, lethargic brooding or else foisting on one's devotion a solid framework of ideas and convictions that could not but distort its nature.

This method, which admittedly kills the soul but then, so to speak, preserves it for general consumption by canning it in small quantities, has always been its bridge to rational thought, convictions, and practical action, in their successful conduct of all moralities, philosophies, and religions. God knows, as we have already said, what a soul is anyway. There can be no doubt whatsoever that the burning desire to obey only the call of one's soul leaves infinite scope for action, a true state of anarchy, and there are cases of chemically pure souls actually committing crimes. But the minute a soul has morals, religion, philosophy, a well-grounded middle-class education, ideals in the spheres of duty and beauty, it has been equipped with a system of rules, conditions, and directives that it must obey before it can think of being a respectable soul, and its heat, like that of a blast furnace, is directed into orderly rectangles of sand. All that remains are only logical problems of interpretation, such as whether an action falls under this or that commandment, and the soul presents the tranquil panorama of a battlefield after the fact, where the dead lie still and one can see at once where a scrap of life still moves or groans. Which is why we cross that bridge as quickly as we can. If a person is plagued by religious doubts, as many are in their youth, he takes to persecuting unbelievers; if troubled by love, he turns it into marriage; and when overcome by some other enthusiasm, he takes refuge from the impossibility of living constantly *in* its fire by beginning to live *for* that fire. That is, he fills the many moments of his day, each of which needs a content and an impetus, not with his ideal state but with the many ways of achieving it by overcoming obstacles and incidents—which guarantees that he will never need to attain it. For only fools, fanatics, and mental cases can stand living at the highest pitch of soul; a sane person must be content with declaring that life would not be worth living without a spark of that mysterious fire.

Arnheim's life was filled to the brim with activity. He was a realist and had listened with an indulgent smile and not without appreciation for the good form shown by these representatives of the old Austrian tradition in the session he witnessed as they spoke of an Imperial Franz-Josef Soup Kitchen and the link between duty and military marches. He was far from making fun of it, as Ulrich had done, for he was convinced that it took far less courage and superiority to pursue great ideas than to recognize the touching kernel of idealism in such average, slightly absurd people of good appearance.

But when in the midst of all this, Diotima, this classical beauty with a Viennese plus, uttered her term "Global Austria," a phrase as hot and almost as incomprehensible to the human mind as a flame, something had seized his heart.

There was a story told about him that he had in his Berlin house a splendid room full of Baroque and Gothic sculptures. As it happens, the Catholic Church (for which Arnheim had a great love) depicts its saints and standard-bearers of Goodness mostly in poses of joy, even ecstasy. Here were saints dying in all kinds of postures, with the soul wringing out the body as if it were squeezing water out of a piece of laundry. All those gestures of arms crossed like sabers, of twisted necks, taken from their original surroundings and brought together in an alien space, gave the impression of a catatonics' ward in a lunatic asylum.

This collection was highly esteemed and brought many art historians to Arnheim, with whom he conversed knowledgeably; but often he sat alone and lonely in his gallery, with a quite different feeling, a kind of horrified amazement, as though he were looking at a half-demented world. He felt how morality had once glowed with an ineffable fire, but now even a mind like his own could do no more than stare into the burned-out clinkers. This dark vision of what all religions and myths express in the tale of commandments given originally to men by the gods, this intuition of a pristine state of the soul, somewhat uncanny and yet presumably pleasing to the gods, formed a strange fringe of uneasiness around the otherwise complacent expanse of his thoughts. Arnheim also had an assistant gardener, a simple but deep man, as Arnheim put it, with whom he often talked about the life of the flowers because one can learn more from such a man than from the experts. Until one day Arnheim discovered that this gardener's helper was stealing from him. It seems that he made off with everything he could lay his hands on, in a kind of desperation, saving the proceeds to set up on his own; this was the one idea that obsessed him day and night. But one day a small sculpture disappeared, and the police who were called in exposed the whole operation. The evening Arnheim was informed of this, he sent for the man and reproached him all night long for having allowed his passionate acquisitiveness to lead him astray. It was said that he was extremely upset himself and at times came close to weeping in a dark adjoining room. For he envied this man, for reasons he could not explain to himself. The next morning, he had the police take him away.

This story was confirmed by close friends of Arnheim's. Now, standing alone with Diotima in this room, he felt rather as he had felt then, sensing something like the soundless flames of the world leaping all around them along its four walls.

47

What all others are separately, Arnheim is rolled into one

In the following weeks Diotima's salon experienced a tremendous upsurge. People came to hear the latest news of the Parallel Campaign and to see the new man Diotima was reported to have prescribed for herself: variously, a German nabob, a rich Jew, and an eccentric who wrote poetry, dictated the price of coal, and was the German Kaiser's personal friend. It was not only the highborn ladies and gentlemen from Count Leinsdorf's world and diplomatic circles who came; the upper-middle-class figures who controlled the economy and led the world of culture seemed also increasingly attracted. And so specialists in the Ewe language and composers who had never heard a note of one another's music ran into one another here, shooting box met confessional box, and people to whom the word "course" meant the race course, the course of the stock exchange, or a university course.

And now something unheard of came to pass: there was a man who could speak with everyone in their own language, and that man was Arnheim.

After the embarrassment he had suffered at the beginning of the first meeting he held himself aloof from the official sessions, nor did he attend all the social gatherings, as he was often out of town. There was, of course, no further mention of the secretarial post; he had himself explained to Diotima that this idea could not be acceptable to the other side, and she yielded to Arnheim's judgment, although she could never look at Ulrich without regarding him as a usurper. Arnheim came and went. Three or five days would pass in a flash, he would be back from Paris, Rome, Berlin; what was going on at Diotima's was only a small slice of his life. But he favored it, and took part in it with all his energy.

That he could discuss industry with industrial giants and the economy with bankers was to be expected, but he could also chat just as freely about molecular physics, mysticism, and pigeon shooting. He was an extraordinary talker; once he was off, he never stopped, like a book one cannot close until everything in it demanding utterance has been said. But he had a quietly dignified, fluent manner of speaking, with a touch of sadness about it like a stream overhung by dark bushes, and this gave the flow of his words an air of necessity. His reading and his memory were of truly extraordinary compass; he could give experts the subtlest cues in their own fields, but he also knew every person of note in the English, French, and Japanese nobility, and was at home at racetracks and golf links not only in Europe but in Australia and America as well. So even the chamois hunters, champion horsemen, and holders of boxes at the Imperial Theater, who had come to see a crazy rich Jew (something a little different, as they put it), left Diotima's house shaking their heads with respect.

His Grace once took Ulrich aside and said to him:

"You know, our ducal houses have had bad luck with their tutors these last hundred years. They used to get the kind of people many of whom would later get into the encyclopedia, and these tutors would bring along music masters and drawing masters who showed their appreciation by creating things we now refer to as our old culture. But ever since we have had the new, universal education, and people from my own circles—forgive me—go in for academic degrees, our tutors have somehow fallen off. Our sons are quite right, of course, to shoot pheasant and boar, ride, and chase pretty girls—there's little to be said against that if one is young. But in the old days, it was the tutors who channeled part of that youthful energy into the necessity of cultivating the mind and the arts as well as the pheasants, and this no longer happens."

It was only an idea that just crossed His Grace's mind, as such things did from time to time; suddenly he turned to face Ulrich and concluded: "You see, it was that fateful year 1848 that drove a wedge between the middle class and the aristocracy, to the loss of both sides." He looked at the assembled company with concern. He was irked every time the opposition speakers in Parliament boasted of culture as middle class; he would have liked true middle-class culture to be found in the aristocracy, but the poor aristocracy could see nothing in it; it was a weapon invisible to them with which they were being trounced, and since they had been increasingly losing power all along, there was finally nothing left for them to do but come to Diotima's and see the thing for themselves. Count Leinsdorf sometimes felt this way with a heavy heart as he observed the hubbub, wishing that the high office this house had been given the opportunity to serve were taken more seriously.

"Excellency, the middle class is having exactly the same experience with the intellectuals now as the high nobility had with its tutors then," Ulrich tried to comfort him. "They don't know what to make of them. Just look at all these people gaping at Dr. Arnheim."

But all along Count Leinsdorf had only been looking at Arnheim anyway.

"That's no longer intellect," Ulrich said, explaining the general amazement, "it is a phenomenon like a rainbow with a foot you can take hold of and actually feel. He talks about love and economics, chemistry and trips in kayaks; he is a scholar, a landowner, and a stockbroker; in short, what the rest of us are separately, he is rolled into one; of course we're amazed. You shake your head, Excellency? But I'm convinced the cloud of so-called temporal progress, into which no one of us can see, has set him down on the parquet in our midst."

"I was not shaking my head over you," His Grace elucidated. "I was thinking of Dr. Arnheim. All in all, one has to admit he's an interesting figure."

48

THE THREE CAUSES OF ARNHEIM'S FAME AND THE MYSTERY OF THE WHOLE

But that was simply the way Arnheim usually affected people.

He was a man of stature.

His activity spread over terrestrial continents and continents of knowledge. He knew everything: philosophers, economics, music, the world, sports. He expressed himself fluently in five languages. The world's most famous artists were his friends, and he bought the art of tomorrow when it was still green on the vine, at prices that were not yet inflated. He was received at the Imperial Court and knew how to talk with workers. He owned a villa in the latest style, which appeared in photographs in all the publications on contemporary architecture, and also, somewhere in the sandiest wastes of Prussia, a ramshackle old castle that actually looked like the decomposed cradle of Prussian chauvinism.

Such expansiveness and receptivity are seldom accompanied by personal achievement; but in this respect, too, Arnheim was an exception. Once or twice a year he secluded himself on his country estate and there wrote down the experiences of his intellectual life. These books and articles, by now quite an imposing number of them, were widely read, enjoyed large printings, and were translated into many languages. A sick physician inspires no confidence, but when a man who has known how to do so well for himself speaks, there must be something in it. This was the first source of Arnheim's fame.

The second had its origin in the nature of science and scholarship. We hold knowledge in high esteem, and rightly so. But though a man's life may be completely filled by research into the functioning of the kidneys, there will be moments, humanistic moments, so to speak, when he may ponder the relationship between the kidneys and his country. This is why Goethe is so widely quoted in Germany. But when a scholar wants to show expressly that he is not only a man of learning but also possesses a lively mind with an interest in the future, he will do well to show himself acquainted with works it not only does him credit to know but promises to bring even more credit in the future—like a stock appreciating in value with time—and in such cases quotations from Paul Arnheim were enjoying increasing popularity. His excursions into scientific areas for support of his general views did not, it is true, always satisfy the strictest criteria; while they showed an easy command of the literature, the specialist would invariably find in them those little slips and misconceptions that betray the dilettante, just as surely as the stitching of a single seam betrays the homemade dress as compared with the product of the couturier's studio. But one should by no means think that this prevented the specialists from admiring Arnheim. They smiled complacently; he impressed them as a true product of the new age, a man whose name was in all the newspapers, an economic king, a man whose intellectual achievements, at least compared with those of earlier kings, were astonishing; and if they might be allowed to note that in their own sphere they represented something considerably different from him, they nevertheless showed their appreciation by calling him a brilliant man, a man of genius, or, quite simply, a universal man, which among specialists amounts to the same thing as when men say to each other of a woman that she is a woman's idea of a beauty.

The third source of Arnheim's fame was economics. He managed not at all badly with the old salts, the seasoned captains of industry; in a big deal, he could outsmart the craftiest of them. They did not regard him as much of a businessman, in any case, and called him the "Crown Prince," to distinguish him from his father, whose short, thick tongue was not so adroit in conversation but made up for it by picking up the flavor of a good business deal at whatever distance and by the subtlest chemistry. Him they feared, and revered, but when they heard of the philosophical demands the Crown Prince made on the business class, which he would weave even into the most matter-of-fact discussions, they smiled. He was notorious for quoting poets at board meetings, and for insisting that the economy could not be separated from other human activities and could be dealt with only within the larger context of all vital problems, national, intellectual, and even spiritual.

But even while they smiled at this sort of thing, they could not quite overlook that precisely by adding such frills to business, Arnheim junior was cutting an increasingly important figure in public opinion. News of him would turn up now in the financial, now in the political, now in the literary and art columns of leading newspapers throughout the world, whether it was a review of a work from his pen, the report of a notable speech he had given somewhere, or notice of his reception by some ruler or art association, until there was no man in the circle of industrial movers and shakers, who operate in silence and behind double-locked doors, as much talked about outside that circle as he was. All these presidents, board chairmen, directors, top managers, heads of banks, corporations, mine works, shipping companies, are by no means, in their hearts, the evil manipulators they are often represented to be. Apart from their highly developed sense of family, the inner rationale of their lives is that of money, and that is a rationale with very sound teeth and a healthy appetite. They were all convinced that the world would be much better off if left to the free play of supply and demand rather than to armored warships, bayonets, potentates, and diplomats ignorant of economics. But the world being what it is, with its ingrained prejudice against a life dedicated primarily to its own self-interest and only secondarily to the public good, and its preference for chivalry, public-spiritedness, and public missions above private enterprise, these magnates were the last people in the world to leave this out of their calculations, and they energetically made use of the advantages offered to the public good through customs negotiations backed by armed force, or the use of the military against strikers. On this road, however, business leads directly to philosophy, for nowadays only criminals dare to harm others without philosophy, and so they accustomed themselves to regarding Arnheim junior as a kind of papal legate for their affairs. Despite the irony with which they were always ready to regard his tendencies, they were pleased to have in him a man who could take their case as readily before a conclave of bishops as to a sociological conference; ultimately he won influence over them like a beautiful and cultivated wife who regards her husband's everlasting office work as a bore but is useful to the business because everyone admires her. Now, beyond this one need only imagine the effect of Maeterlinckian or Bergsonian philosophy applied to questions about the price of coal or to cartel politics, to estimate how depressing Arnheim junior's presence could be to industrialists' conferences and directors' meetings in Paris or St. Petersburg or Cape Town when he turned up as his father's ambassador and had to be heard out from beginning to end. His resulting successes in business were as impressive as they were mysterious, and out of all this grew the well-known report of the man's towering stature and his lucky hand.

A good deal more could be said about Arnheim's successes. With diplomats, for instance, who handled the important but alien field of economics with the circumspection of men charged with the care of an unpredictable elephant, while Arnheim treated it with the nonchalance of a native keeper. With artists, for whom he hardly ever did anything, which did not prevent them from seeing him as a Maecenas. And lastly with journalists, who should in all fairness have been the first to be mentioned, because it was they who through their admiration had first created Arnheim's image as a great man, though they did not realize how much he was their own creation; for someone had whispered in their ear and they consequently believed they could hear the grass of history growing. The basic pattern of his success was everywhere the same: Surrounded by the magic aura of his wealth and the legend of his importance, he always had to deal with people who towered over him in their own fields but who liked him as an outsider with a surprising knowledge of their subject and were daunted by his personally representing a link between their world and other worlds of which they had no idea. So it had come to seem quite natural for him to appear in a world of specialists as a whole man, and to have the effect of a harmonious entity. At times he dreamed of a new Weimar or Florentine renaissance of industry and trade, a new prosperity under the leadership of strong personalities, each of whom would have to be capable of combining individual achievements in technology, science, and the arts, and able to guide them from the highest standpoint. He felt he had this capacity. He possessed the gift of never being superior in any specific, provable respect but, owing to some fluid, perpetually self-renewing equilibrium, of still coming out on top in every situation. It was probably the fundamental talent of a politician, but Arnheim was also convinced that it was a profound mystery. He called it "the Mystery of the Whole." For even the beauty of a person consists of almost nothing demonstrable, or any specific feature, but rather that magical something that makes even small defects useful, just as the profound goodness and love, the dignity and greatness, of a person are almost independent of what he does, are indeed capable of ennobling everything he does. In this life, in some mysterious fashion, the whole always takes precedence over its parts. While ordinary people may indeed be the sum of their virtues and faults, the great man is he who first bestows rank on his qualities. And if the secret of his success is that it cannot quite be explained as the result of his achievements and his qualities, then the presence of a force greater than its manifestations is the mystery upon which all greatness in life rests. This is how Arnheim had phrased it in one of his books, and as he set down these words he almost felt that he had touched the hem of the supernatural, and this, too, he allowed to shine through in the text.

49

ANTAGONISM SPROUTS BETWEEN THE OLD AND THE NEW DIPLOMACY

His association with persons whose specialty was to have been born to the hereditary nobility constituted no exception. Arnheim so muted his own high distinction, so modestly laid claim only to a certain intellectual nobility, which knows its own merits and limits, that beside him the bearers of the most venerable noble names seemed after a while to be bowed down under their burden like gnarled laborers. It was Diotima who appreciated this most keenly. She recognized the Mystery of the Whole with the eye of an artist who sees the dream of his life realized in an unsurpassable way.

She was now wholly reconciled to her salon again. Arnheim warned her against putting too much emphasis on formal organization; crude material interests would take over, stifling the original pure intention; he preferred keeping the salon as it was.

Section Chief Tuzzi, on the other hand, expressed his misgivings that this would never get them beyond endless floods of talk.

He had crossed one leg over the other and clasped one knee with his heavily veined, lean, dark hands. Next to Arnheim, who sat upright in a flawlessly cut suit of some soft fabric, Tuzzi, with his trim little beard and southern eyes, looked like a Levantine pickpocket beside a Hanseatic merchant prince. It was an encounter between two kinds of distinction, and the Austrian, a mosaic of highly cultivated cosmopolitanism, with its casual dash, certainly did not regard itself as the lesser. Section Chief Tuzzi had an engaging manner of asking how the Parallel Campaign was coming along, as though he was not supposed to know at first hand what was going on in his own house.

"We would love to know as soon as possible what your plans are," he said with an amiable smile at his wife and Arnheim, as if to say that he was of course only an outsider in this matter. Then he explained that this joint enterprise of his wife's and Count Leinsdorf's was already causing grave concern in official quarters. At his most recent briefing session with His Majesty, the Minister of Foreign Affairs had taken soundings as to what kind of public demonstrations in honor of the jubilee might be acceptable to His Majesty, namely, up to what point His Majesty might be graciously willing to countenance a plan anticipating the trend of the times by taking a lead in an international peace program. Which was the only way, Tuzzi pointed out, to translate into political terms the idea of a Global Austria that had come up in His Grace's speech. But His Gracious Majesty, with his world-famous punctiliousness and reserve, Tuzzi went on, had instantly waved the suggestion aside, saying firmly: "Oh, I don't like being pushed into the limelight," and now no one could say whether this meant His Majesty was definitely opposed to the idea or not.

Such was Tuzzi's discreet way of being indiscreet about the little secrets of his profession, as only a man who knows how to keep the big secrets can be. He ended by saying that it was now up to the various embassies to sound out their respective courts abroad, as we were not sure of our own ground but had to find some solid point of departure somewhere. Technically, after all, there were all sorts of given possibilities, from calling a general peace conference, to a summit meeting for twenty sovereigns, all the way down to decorating the Peace Palace at The Hague with frescoes by Austrian artists, or a foundation for the benefit of the children and orphans of The Hague's domestic staff. At this point he asked Arnheim what they were thinking about the jubilee year at the Prussian court. Arnheim disclaimed having any information in this regard. He was repelled by this Austrian cynicism. He, who knew how to chat so elegantly, froze up in Tuzzi's company like a man who wants it clearly understood that affairs of state must be discussed with the utmost gravity and coolness. In this fashion two contrasting kinds of urbanity, two national- and two life-styles, not without a touch of sexual rivalry, presented themselves to Diotima. But place a greyhound beside a pug, a willow beside a poplar, a glass of wine on a freshly plowed field, a portrait in a sailboat instead of in an art gallery—in short, place side by side two highbred and distinct forms of life, and a void will come into being between them; they will cancel each other out, with the effect of a quite malicious, bottomless absurdity. Diotima felt this with her eyes and ears without understanding it, but she was sufficiently alarmed to give a turn to the conversation by telling her husband firmly that she intended to achieve something spiritually great with the Parallel Campaign, and would allow only the needs of truly modern minds to influence its leadership.

Arnheim was grateful to her for restoring the dignity of the concept, especially because he had to be on his guard, at times, against going under; he could no more afford to be facetious about the events that so nobly justified his being with Diotima than a drowning man can be about his life jacket. Yet he surprised himself by asking Diotima, his voice betraying some uncertainty, whom she would include, in that case, in the intellectual spearhead of the Parallel Campaign.

Diotima was of course quite unprepared to give a clear answer to this question. The days she spent with Arnheim had given her such an abundance of suggestions and ideas that she had not yet got around to sorting them out, and while he had repeated to her more than once that the democracy of the committees mattered far less than strong personalities with a comprehensive view of things, all it meant to her was simply "You and I"—though she was still far from deciding anything, or even from having the necessary insight. It was probably just this of which she was reminded by the pessimism in Arnheim's voice, because she answered: "Do we have anything at all nowadays that we can regard as truly important and great, something worth working for with all our might?"

"It is the mark of a time that has lost the inner certainty of healthier times," Arnheim responded, "that it is hard for something to crystallize as the greatest and most important thing of all."

Section Chief Tuzzi had lowered his eyes to a speck of dust on his trousers, so that one might interpret his smile as a sign of agreement.

"And indeed, what should it be?" Arnheim went on tentatively. "Religion?"

Section Chief Tuzzi now directed his smile upward; Arnheim had pronounced the word this time not quite so emphatically and unskeptically as before in His Grace's presence, but with sonorous gravity nonetheless.

Diotima, defending herself against her husband's smile, threw in: "Why not? Religion too!"

"Of course. But since we must come to a practical decision: Have you ever thought of appointing a bishop to the committee, who should come up with a modern goal for the campaign? God is profoundly unmodern: we simply cannot imagine him in tails, clean-shaven, with neatly parted hair; our image of him is still patriarchal. And what is there apart from religion? The nation? The state?"

Diotima was pleased at this, because Tuzzi regarded the state as a masculine subject one did not discuss with women. But now he was silent, only his eyes still hinting that there might be something further to be said on that score.

"Science?" Arnheim went on. "Culture? That leaves art. Truly, it is art that should first reflect the unity of existence and its inner order. But we know the picture art presents today. Fragmentation everywhere; extremes without connections. Stendhal, Balzac, and Flaubert have already created the epic of the new mechanized social and inner life, while the demonic substrata of our lives have been laid bare by Dostoyevsky, Strindberg, and Freud. We who live today have a deep sense that there is nothing left for us to do."

Here Section Chief Tuzzi interjected that when he wanted to read something solid, he took down his Homer, or Peter Rosegger.

Arnheim took up the suggestion: "You should include the Bible. With the Bible, Homer, and Rosegger or Reuter, one can manage. And this takes us right to the heart of the problem. What if a new Homer should come along, would we, frankly, be at all capable of listening to him? I believe the answer is no. We don't have him because we don't need him!" Arnheim was now in the saddle and riding high. "If we needed him, we would have him! For in the final analysis, nothing negative happens in world history. What can it mean that we place everything that is truly great and essential in the past? Homer and Christ have never again been equaled, to say nothing of being surpassed; there is nothing more beautiful than the Song of Songs. The Gothic age and the Renaissance stand before modern times like mountain ranges at the entrance to a great plain, and where, today, are the great rulers? How short-winded even the deeds of Napoleon look beside those of the pharaohs, the work of Kant beside that of the Buddha, that of Goethe beside Homer! But here we are, and we must live for something. What does it all add up to? Nothing but—" But here Arnheim broke off and confessed that he was reluctant to put it into words, because he was forced to conclude that all we regard as great and important in life has nothing to do with the innermost force of our lives.

"And that would be?" Tuzzi inquired. He had hardly any objection to the implication that most things were taken far too seriously.

"No one today knows the answer," Arnheim replied. "The problem of civilization can be solved only by the heart. By the appearance of a new type of man. By an inner vision and a pure will. The intellect has achieved nothing but watering down the great past into liberalism. But perhaps we do not see far enough, perhaps we reckon on too small a scale; every moment may be that of a great historic turning point!"

Diotima had been on the point of objecting that this would leave nothing for the Parallel Campaign to do. But in some peculiar way she found herself enthralled by Arnheim's somber visions. Perhaps there was a residue of "too much homework" in her that burdened her when she always had to read the newest books and talk about the newest pictures; pessimism toward art liberated her from all sorts of beauty she had not really liked at all, just as a pessimistic view of science eased her anxiety in the face of culture, the overabundance of the knowable and the influential. Thus Arnheim's despairing judgment of the times came, as she suddenly realized, as a release. And the thought flitted pleasantly through her heart that Arnheim's melancholy somehow had something to do with herself.

50

FURTHER DEVELOPMENTS.
SECTION CHIEF TUZZI DECIDES TO INFORM
HIMSELF ABOUT ARNHEIM

Diotima had guessed right. From the moment Arnheim had noticed that the bosom of this enchanting woman who had read his books on the soul was lifted and moved by a force of an unmistakable kind, he had suffered a loss of nerve otherwise foreign to him. Putting it briefly and in his own terms, it was the faintheartedness of the moralist who suddenly and unexpectedly meets heaven on earth. To empathize with him, one need only imagine how it would be if we were surrounded by nothing but this quiet blue puddle with soft white wads of feathers floating in it.

The moral person as such is ridiculous and unpleasant, as we know by the odor of those poor, resigned people who have nothing they can call their own but their morality. Morality needs great tasks from which to derive its significance, which is why Arnheim had always striven to complement his nature, which inclined to moralizing, by drawing on world events and history, and saturating his activities with ideology. That was his favorite concept: carrying ideas into the spheres of power and talking business only in connection with cultural questions. He liked to draw analogies from history in order to fill it with new life; the role of present-day finance seemed to him similar to that of the Catholic Church: a great influence behind the scenes; unyielding yet yielding in its dealings with the ruling powers; and he sometimes saw himself functioning like a cardinal.

But on this occasion he had come to Austria more on a whim, and even though he never traveled wholly without a purpose, even on a whim, he could not quite remember how the plan—incidentally, a plan of some scope—had originally entered his mind. The inspiration for this trip seemed to have come out of the blue, an instant resolve, and it may have been this small circumstance of freedom about it that a trip to Bombay would hardly have made a less exotic impression on him than this out-of-the-way German-language metropolis in which he had landed. The thought, inconceivable in Prussia, of playing a leading role in the Parallel Campaign had done the rest and made him feel illogically fantastic, like a dream, whose absurdity his practical good sense recognized but whose spell he was powerless to break. He could probably have accomplished the business purpose of his trip far more simply and directly, but he regarded it as a holiday from reason to keep coming back here, and for these excursions into fairyland he was punished by his business sense in that he smudged the black good-conduct mark he should have given himself into a gray blur over everything.

There was no repetition, at least, of that far-reaching contemplation in the dark as had happened in Tuzzi's presence, if only because Section Chief Tuzzi turned up only in passing, and Arnheim had to parcel out his words to all sorts of persons whom he found amazingly receptive in this beautiful country. In His Grace's presence he called criticism sterile and the present age godless, once more letting it be understood that redemption from so negative an existence could come only through the heart; for Diotima's sake he added that the German spirit, and perhaps the world as well, could be freed from the excesses of rationalism and petty bookkeeping only by the rich culture of its southern lands. Encircled by ladies, he spoke of the need to organize the inner resources of human tenderness, in order to save mankind from arms races and soullessness. To a circle of active professionals he expounded Hölderlin's saying that there were no longer human beings in Germany but only professionals, winding up with: "And no one can achieve anything in his profession without a sense of some overarching purpose, least of all the financier!"

People listened to him gladly because it was so nice that a man with so many ideas also had money, and the circumstance that all those who spoke with him came away with the impression that an undertaking like the Parallel Campaign was a most dubious affair, riddled with the most explosive intellectual contradictions, also reinforced in everyone the notion that no one else was as obviously cut out as he was for taking the helm in this adventure.

However, Section Chief Tuzzi would not have been, in his quiet way, one of his country's leading diplomats had he noticed nothing of

Arnheim's pervasive presence in his house; he simply could not make head or tail of it. He did not let on, because a diplomat never shows what he is thinking. Personally, and also in principle, so to speak, he found this outsider most irritating, and that he had blatantly chosen the salon of Tuzzi's wife as the scene of operations for some secret objective Tuzzi regarded as a challenge. Not for an instant did he believe Diotima's assurances that the nabob visited the Imperial City on the Danube so often because his mind felt most at home in its ancient culture. Tuzzi's problem was that he had no clue to help him solve this mystery, because in all his official experience he had never come across a person like Arnheim.

And since Diotima had announced that she intended to give Arnheim a leading position in the Parallel Campaign, and had complained about His Grace's resistance to this idea, Tuzzi was seriously concerned. He did not think much of either the Parallel Campaign or Count Leinsdorf, but he regarded his wife's idea as politically so amazingly tactless that he was overcome with the feeling that all these years of patient husbandly training such as he flattered himself to have given her had collapsed like a house of cards. He had in fact used exactly this figure of speech in thinking about it, even though Section Chief Tuzzi never indulged himself in figures of speech because they are too literary and, socially, smell of poor taste; but this time he felt quite shaken by it.

However, Diotima strengthened her position again as things went on by her stubbornness. She had become gently aggressive and spoke of a new kind of person who could no longer passively leave the spiritual responsibility for the course of world events to the professional leaders. Then she spoke of feminine tact that could sometimes be a visionary gift perhaps capable of penetrating distances beyond the daily routine of professionals. Finally, she said that Arnheim was a European, a thinker known throughout Europe, that the conduct of affairs of state in Europe was not sufficiently European, not spiritual enough, and that the world would find no peace until it was as permeated by a universally Austrian spirit as the ancient Austrian culture that embraced all the peoples, with their different languages, within the borders of the monarchy.

She had never before dared to stand up so resolutely against her husband's authority, but Section Chief Tuzzi was temporarily reassured by it, because he had never regarded his wife's strivings as higher in significance than problems with her dressmaker, was delighted when she was admired by others, and could now take a less alarming view of her current goings-on, much as if a woman who loved color had for once chosen too gaudy a ribbon. So he confined himself to going over again, with grave courtesy, all the reasons why in a man's world decisions on Austrian affairs could not be publicly entrusted to a Prussian, even though he could see that there might be some advantage in being on friendly terms with a man in so unique a position. He assured Diotima that she would be misunderstanding his scruples if she inferred from them that he was not pleased to see Arnheim in her company as often as possible. Privately he hoped that this would give him the opportunity, sooner or later, to set a trap for the outsider.

Only when Tuzzi had to stand by and see Arnheim sweeping from success to success everywhere did he come back to the idea that she seemed overinvolved with this man—only to find again that she did not respect his wishes as of old but argued with him and declared his misgivings chimerical. He decided as a man not to struggle against the dialectics of a woman but to bide his time and wait for circumstances to prove him right in the end. But then something happened to give him a powerful incentive.

One night, something like the sound of very distant weeping aroused him from his sleep. It barely disturbed him at first; he simply did not understand what it was. But from time to time the spiritual distance lessened by a jump, until suddenly the menacing disturbance was quite close to his ears, and he started so violently out of his sleep that he sat bolt upright in bed. Diotima lay on her side facing away from him and gave no sign of being awake, but something made him feel that she was. He whispered her name once, then again, and tenderly tried to turn her white shoulder to him. But as he turned her around and her face rose above her shoulder in the dark, it looked at him angrily, expressed defiance, and had been crying. Unfortunately, Tuzzi's sound sleep was reclaiming him and dragging him relentlessly back into his pillows, while Diotima's face hovered above him as a painfully bright distortion he could make no sense of. "Whatsamatter?" he muttered in the soft bass of returning unconsciousness, and received a clear, irritable, unwelcome answer that stamped itself on his ear, fell into his drowsiness, and lay there like a sparkling coin in the water.

"You toss about so much in your sleep, no one can sleep next to you!" Diotima had said harshly and distinctly; his ear had taken it in, but he had already slipped back into sleep without being able to utter a word in his own defense.

He merely felt that he was the victim of a grave injustice. Quiet, restful sleep was in his opinion one of a diplomat's chief virtues, for it was a condition of all success. It was a point on which he was acutely sensitive, and Diotima's remark was a serious challenge to his very existence. He realized that something in her had changed. While it never occurred to him even in his sleep to suspect his wife of any tangible infidelity, he never doubted for a moment that the personal discomfort inflicted on him must be connected with Arnheim. He slept on angrily, as it were, till morning and awakened with the firm resolve to find out all he could about this disturbing person.

51

THE HOUSE OF FISCHEL

Director Fischel of the Lloyd Bank was that bank director, or, more properly, manager with the title of director, who had somehow unaccountably forgotten to acknowledge Count Leinsdorf's invitation and had thereafter not been invited again. And even that first invitation he had owed only to the connections of his wife, Clementine. Clementine Fischel's family were old civil service. Her father had been Accountant General, her grandfather had been a senior official in the finance department, and three of her brothers held high positions in various ministries. Twenty-four years ago she had married Leo Fischel, for two reasons: first, because families high in the civil service sometimes have more children than means; but second, for a romantic reason, because compared with the relentlessly thrifty tightness of her parental home, banking seemed a liberal-minded, modern profession, and in the nineteenth century a cultivated person did not judge another person's value according to whether he was a Jew or a Catholic; indeed, as matters stood then, she almost felt there was something particularly refined in rising above the crude anti-Semitic prejudice of the common people.

Later the poor woman was destined to see a nationalist spirit welling up all over Europe, and with it a surge of Jew-baiting, transforming her husband in her very arms, as it were, from a respected free spirit into a corrosive spawn of an alien race. In the beginning she had resisted this transformation with all the indignation of a "magnanimous heart," but as the years passed she was worn down by the naïvely cruel and steadily growing hostility and intimidated by the general prejudice. In time, as the differences between herself and her husband gradually became acrimonious—when, for reasons he would never quite go into, he never rose above the rank of manager and lost all prospects of ever being appointed a bank director—she came to justify to herself, with a shrug, many things that wounded her by remembering that Leo's character was, after all, alien to her own, though toward outsiders she never abandoned the principles of her youth.

Their differences, however, were basically nothing more than a lack of understanding; as in many marriages, a natural misfortune, as it were, surfaced as soon as the couple ceased to be rapturously happy. Ever since Leo's career had hesitantly ground to a halt at what was in effect a stockbroker's desk, Clementine was no longer able to excuse certain of his peculiarities by taking into account that he was not ensconced in the glassy calm of a ministerial office but was sitting at the "roaring loom of time"—and who knows whether she had not married him just on account of this quotation from Goethe? His side-whiskers, which, with the pince-nez riding the middle of his nose, had once reminded her of an English lord with muttonchops, now suggested a stockbroker, and some of his mannerisms of gesture and turns of phrase became positively insufferable to her. At first Clementine tried to improve her husband, but she ran into terrible snags as it became apparent that nowhere in the world was there a standard by which to judge whether muttonchop whiskers rightly suggested a lord or a broker, or at what point on the nose a pince-nez, combined with a wave of the hand, expressed enthusiasm or cynicism. Besides, Leo Fischel was simply not the man to let himself be improved. He dismissed as social tomfoolery the faultfinding that tried to turn him into the Christian-Teutonic beau ideal of a high ministry official, and rejected her arguments as unworthy of a reasonable man; for the more his wife took offense at certain details, the more he stressed the great guidelines of reason. And so the Fischel household was gradually transformed into the battleground of two contending philosophies of life.

Director Fischel of the Lloyd Bank enjoyed philosophizing, but only for ten minutes a day. He enjoyed thinking that human life had a solid rational basis and that it paid off intellectually; he imagined this on the pattern of the harmonious hierarchy of a great bank and noted with satisfaction the daily signs of progress he read about in the papers.

This faith in the immutable guidelines of reason and progress had for a long time enabled him to dismiss his wife's carpings with a shrug or a cutting retort. But since misfortune had decreed that in the course of this marriage the mood of the times would shift away from the old principles of liberalism that had favored Leo Fischel— the great guiding ideals of tolerance, the dignity of man, and free trade—and reason and progress in the Western world would be displaced by racial theories and street slogans, he could not remain untouched by it either. He started by flatly denying the existence of these changes, just as Count Leinsdorf was accustomed to deny the existence of certain "unpleasant political manifestations" and waited for them to disappear of their own accord. Such waiting is the first, almost imperceptible degree of the torture of exasperation that life inflicts on men of principle. The second degree is usually called, and was therefore also called by Fischel, "poison." This poison is the appearance, drop by drop, of new views on morals, art, politics, the family, newspapers, books, and social life, already accompanied by the helpless feeling that there is no turning back and by indignant denials, which cannot avoid a certain acknowledgment of the thing denied. Nor was Director Fischel spared the third and final degree, when the isolated showers and sprinklings of the New turn into a steady, drenching rain. In time this becomes one of the most horrible torments that a man who has only ten minutes a day to spare for philosophy can experience.

Leo came to know on how many points people can have differences of opinion. The drive to be right, a need almost synonymous with human dignity, began to celebrate excesses in the Fischel household. For millennia this drive has produced thousands of admirable philosophies, works of art, books, deeds, and partisan alliances, and when this admirable, but also fanatical and monstrous, innate human drive has to make do with ten minutes on practical philosophy or a debate on the basic principles of the household, it cannot fail to burst, like a drop of molten lead, into innumerable sharp splinters that inflict the most painful wounds. It burst over the question of whether a maid was to be given notice or not, and whether toothpicks belonged on the table or not; but whatever made it burst, it had the capacity to reconstitute itself immediately into two infinitely detailed opposing views of the world.

This was all very well by day, since Director Fischel was in his office then, but at night he was only human, and this gravely worsened the relations between him and Clementine. Things today are so complicated that a person can really keep fully informed only in one field, basically, which in his case was stocks and bonds, and so he was inclined at night to be of a generally yielding disposition. Clementine, on the contrary, remained sharp and unyielding, raised as she had been in a strict civil-service household with its constant emphasis on duty. Besides, her class consciousness would not permit them separate bedrooms, which would have made their already inadequate apartment even smaller. But a shared bedroom, with the lights out, puts a man in the situation of an actor having to play before an invisible house the rewarding but by now worn-out role of a hero impersonating a growling lion. For years now, Leo's dark auditorium had not let slip the faintest hint of applause, nor yet the smallest sign of disapproval, and this was surely enough to shatter the strongest nerves. In the morning at breakfast, which the couple took together in accordance with time-honored tradition, Clementine was stiff as a frozen corpse and Leo twitchy with nerves. Even their daughter, Gerda, noticed something of this every time and had come to imagine married life with dread and bitter loathing, as a catfight in the dark of night.

Gerda was twenty-three, and the favorite bone of contention of both her progenitors. Leo Fischel thought it was time to start thinking of a good match for her. But Gerda said, "You're old-fashioned, Papa," and had chosen her friends in a swarm of Christian nationalists her own age, none of whom offered the slightest prospect of being able to support a wife; instead, they despised capitalism and maintained that no Jew had yet proved capable of serving as a great symbol of humanity. Leo Fischel called them anti-Semitic louts and would have forbidden them the house, but Gerda said, "You don't understand, Papa, they only mean it symbolically"; and nervous and anemic as she was, Gerda immediately got upset if she was not handled with care. So Fischel suffered her friends' society, as once Odysseus had had to suffer Penelope's suitors in his house, for Gerda was the ray of sunshine in his life. But he did not suffer in silence, because that was not in his nature. He thought he knew all about morality and great ideas himself, and held forth on them at every opportunity in order to exert a good influence on Gerda. Every time he did so Gerda answered: "Yes, Papa, you would be absolutely right if the whole thing did not have to be looked at from a wholly different point of view from the one you still cling to!"

What did Clementine do when Gerda talked like this? Not a thing. She made a resigned face and kept her own counsel, but Leo could be sure that behind his back she would be on Gerda's side—as if she knew what symbols were! Leo Fischel had always had every reason to assume that his good Jewish head was superior to his wife's, and nothing outraged him so much as to observe that she was using Gerda's craziness to her own advantage. Why should he, of all people, suddenly no longer be capable of keeping up with the times? They were in this together! Then he remembered last night. This was no longer sniping at a man's self-esteem, it was digging it up by the roots! At night a man has only his nightshirt on, and right underneath that is his character. No expertise, no professional shrewdness, can protect him. Here a man stakes his whole life, nothing less. So what did it mean that Clementine, whenever the conversation turned to Christian-Germanic ideas, made a face as if he were fresh from the jungle?

Now, man is a being who can stand mistrust as little as tissue paper can the rain. Since Clementine had ceased to find Leo attractive she found him unbearable, and since Leo began to feel that Clementine doubted him he saw at every turn a conspiracy in his own house. At the same time Clementine and Leo deluded themselves, like everyone whose mind has been formed by the prevailing customs and literature, that their passions, characters, destinies, and actions made them dependent on each other. In truth, of course, more than half of life consists not of actions but of formulas, of opinions we make our own, of on-the-one-hands and on-the-other-hands, and of all the piled-up impersonality of everything one has heard and knows. The fate of this husband and wife depended mostly on a murky, persistent, confused structuring of ideas that were not even their own but belonged to public opinion and shifted with it, without their being able to defend themselves against it. Compared with this dependence their personal dependence on each other represented only a tiny fraction, a wildly overestimated residue. And while they deluded themselves that they had their own private lives, and questioned each other's character and will, the agonizing difficulty lay in the unreality of their conflict, which they covered with every possible peevishness.

It was Leo Fischel's bad luck that he neither played cards nor found pleasure in taking out pretty girls, but, worn out by his work, suffered from a marked craving for family life, whereas his wife, who had nothing to do day or night but be the bosom of the family, was no longer subject to any romantic illusions about that. There were times when Leo Fischel felt he was suffocating, attacked by nothing he could put his finger on from all sides at once. He was a hardworking small cell in the body politic, doing its duty with a will, but receiving from all sides poisoned juices. And so, though it far exceeded his need for philosophy, the aging man, left in the lurch by his life-partner and seeing no grounds for abandoning the rational fashion of his youth, began to sense the profound emptiness of emotional life, its formlessness which is eternally changing its forms, its slow but relentless overturning that pulls everything with it.

It was on one such morning, his head occupied with family problems, that Fischel had forgotten to answer His Grace's invitation, and on many subsequent mornings he had to listen to accounts of what was going on in Section Chief Tuzzi's wife's circle, which made it appear most regrettable not to have seized such a chance for Gerda to enter the best society. Fischel's conscience was none too clear, since his own general manager and the chief executive of the National Bank attended those gatherings, but as everyone knows, a man will defend himself most violently against reproaches the more strongly he is torn between guilt and innocence. But every time Fischel tried, with all the superiority of a practical man, to make fun of these patriotic goings-on, he was advised that a financier who was abreast of the times, such as Paul Arnheim, evidently thought otherwise. It was amazing how much Clementine, and even Gerda—who normally, of course, took the opposite line from her mother's—had found out about this man, and as the stock exchange, too, was buzzing with all sorts of stories about him, Fischel felt driven onto the defensive, unable to keep up with them or to come out and say about so eminent a businessman that he was not to be taken seriously.

But when Fischel was on the defensive he adopted a suitably bearish stance, in this instance keeping up an impenetrable silence in the face of all allusions to the Tuzzi household, Arnheim, the Parallel Campaign, and his own failure. He tried to find out where and how long Arnheim was staying in town, and furtively hoped for an event that would at one blow expose the hollow pretense of it all and bring down his family's high rating of those stocks with a crash.

52

SECTION CHIEF TUZZI FINDS A BLIND SPOT IN THE WORKINGS OF HIS MINISTRY

After he had decided to find out all about Arnheim, Section Chief Tuzzi soon made the satisfying discovery of a large blind spot in the workings of the Ministry of Foreign Affairs and of the Imperial House, which were his special concern: it had not been designed to deal with persons like Arnheim. Other than memoirs, Tuzzi read no literary works but the Bible, Homer, and Rosegger, priding himself that this saved him from dissipating his mental forces. But that not a single man was to be found in the whole Foreign Ministry who had read a book of Arnheim's he recognized as an error.

Section Chief Tuzzi had the right to summon the heads of other departments to his own office, but on the morning after that night disturbed by tears, he had gone himself to see the chief of the press department, impelled by a feeling that the occasion which led him to seek a discussion did not warrant full official status. The chief of the press department admired Section Chief Tuzzi for knowing so many personal details about Arnheim, admitted that he, too, had frequently heard the name mentioned, but promptly warded off any intimation that the man could possibly be found in any of his departmental files, since Arnheim had not, as far as he recalled, ever been the object of official consideration and since the processing of news material could not, of course, be extended to cover the public expressions of private individuals. Tuzzi conceded that this was as it should be, but pointed out that these days the borderline between the official and the private status of persons and events was not always clearly definable, which the chief of the press department found a most acute observation, whereupon the two section chiefs agreed that they had before them a most intriguing flaw in the system.

It was clearly a morning on which Europe was enjoying a little peace and quiet, because the two officials sent for the head clerk and instructed him to start a file headed *Arnheim, Dr. Paul*, though there was as yet nothing in it. After the head clerk came the chief file clerk and the clerk in charge of news clippings, both of whom were able to state on the spot, all aglow with efficiency, that no Arnheim was to be found in their files. Finally the press secretaries were called in, whose job it was to go through the newspapers every day and lay their clippings before the various chiefs. When asked about Arnheim they all made serious faces, and testified that he was indeed mentioned often and most favorably in the papers they read, but that they could not say what his writings were about because his activities—as they could immediately affirm—were not included within the sphere of their official concern with the news. Thus the flawless functioning of the Foreign Ministry's apparatus was demonstrated whenever one touched a button, and all these officials left the room with the sense of having made the best show of their reliability.

"It's exactly as I told you," the chief of the press department said to Tuzzi with satisfaction. "Nobody knows a thing."

The two section chiefs had listened to the reports with smiling dignity, sitting—as if embalmed forever by their surroundings, like flies in amber—in luxurious leather armchairs, on the deep-pile red carpet, framed by the tall windows draped in dark red in that white-and-gold room dating from the time of Maria Theresa, and acknowledged that the blind spot in the system, which they now had at least spotted, would be hard to cure.

"In this department," its chief said with satisfaction, "we deal with every public utterance, but a borderline must be drawn somewhere around the term 'public.' I can guarantee that every 'Hear, hear' shouted by some deputy at one of this year's regional council meetings can be located in our files within ten minutes, and every such interjection made in the last ten years, as far as it concerns foreign affairs, within half an hour at most. The same applies to every political newspaper article; my men do painstaking work. But those are tangible, so to speak responsible, utterances, in connection with well-defined conditions, powers, and concepts. However, if I have to decide, from a purely professional point of view, under which heading the clerk who compiles the excerpts or the catalog is to file some personal effusion by—let's see, whom could we use as an example?"

Tuzzi helpfully gave him the name of one of the latest writers to frequent Diotima's salon. The chief of the press department glanced up at him uneasily, as if he were hard of hearing.

"All right, him, let's say—but where do we draw the line between what to note and what to pass over? We've even had political poems. Does this mean that every versifier—or perhaps only authors who write for our Burgtheater . . . ?"

Both laughed.

"How is one to deduce what these people mean, even if they were Schiller and Goethe? Of course there's always a higher meaning in it, but for all practical purposes they contradict themselves with every second word they say."

By this time the two men had become aware that they were running the risk of becoming involved in something "impossible," a word with the added nuance of something socially ridiculous, to which diplomats are so keenly sensitive.

"Of course we can't bring a whole staff of literary and drama critics into the ministry," Tuzzi said with a smile, "but on the other hand, once we've become aware of it, there's no denying that such people are not without influence on world opinion and consequently do affect politics."

"It isn't done in any Foreign Office in the world," the press chief said helpfully.

"Agreed. But drop after drop will hollow out stone." Tuzzi found that this proverb served nicely to express a certain danger. "Shouldn't we try to set up a way of handling this?"

"I don't know. I have qualms," the other section chief said.

"So do I, of course!" Tuzzi replied. As the conversation neared its end he felt ill at ease, as if his tongue were coated, uncertain whether he had been talking nonsense or whether it would turn out after all to be another instance of that perspicacity for which he was celebrated. The press chief was equally undecided, and so they ended by assuring each other that they would have another talk on the subject later.

The press chief issued instructions to order Arnheim's complete works for the ministry library, by way of concluding the matter, and Tuzzi went to a political department, where he requested a detailed report on the man Arnheim from the Austrian Embassy in Berlin. This was the only thing left for him to do at the moment, and until the report arrived his only source of information about Arnheim was his wife, a source he now felt strongly disinclined to use. He recalled Voltaire's saying that people use words only to hide their thoughts and use thoughts only to justify the wrongs they have done. Certainly, that is what diplomacy had always been. But that a person spoke and wrote as much as Arnheim did, to hide his real intentions behind words, was something new; it made Tuzzi uneasy, and he would have to get to the bottom of it.

53

MOOSBRUGGER IS MOVED TO ANOTHER PRISON

The killer of a prostitute, Christian Moosbrugger, had been forgotten a few days after the newspapers stopped printing the reports of his trial, and the public had turned to other things for excitement. Only a circle of experts still took an interest in him. His lawyer had entered a plea to have the trial invalidated, demanded a new psychiatric examination, and taken other steps as well: the execution was indefinitely postponed and Moosbrugger moved to another prison.

The precautions with which this was done flattered him: loaded guns, many people, arms and legs in irons. They were paying attention to him, they were afraid of him, and Moosbrugger loved it. When he climbed into the prison van, he glanced around for admiration and tried to catch the surprised gaze of the passersby. Cold wind, blowing down the street, played with his curly hair; the air drained him. Two seconds; then a guard shoved his behind into the van.

Moosbrugger was vain. He did not like to be pushed like that; he was afraid that the guards would punch him, shout or laugh at him. The fettered giant did not dare to look at any of his escort and slid to the front of the van of his own accord.

But he was not afraid of death. Life is full of things that must be endured, and that certainly hurt more than being hanged, and whether a man has a few years more or less to live really doesn't matter. The passive pride of a man who has been locked up for long stretches would not let him fear his punishment; but in any case, he did not cling to life. What was there in life that he should love? Surely not the spring breeze, or the open road, or the sun? They only make a man tired, hot, and dusty. No one loves life who really knows it. "If I could say to someone," Moosbrugger thought, " 'Yesterday I had some terrific roast pork at the corner restaurant!' that might be something." But one could do without even that. What would have pleased him was something that could satisfy his ambition, which had always come up against nothing but stupid insults.

An uneven jolting ran from the wheels through the bench into his body. Behind the bars in the door the cobblestones were running backward; heavy wagons were left behind; at times, men, women, or children stumbled diagonally across the bars; a distant cab was gaining on them, growing, coming closer, beginning to spray out life as an anvil throws off sparks; the horses' heads seemed to be about to push through the door; then the clatter of hooves and the soft sound of rubber-tired wheels ran on past behind the wall of the van. Moosbrugger slowly turned his head back to stare again at the ceiling where it met the van's side in front of him. The noises outside roared, blared, were stretched like a canvas over which now and then flitted the shadow of something happening. Moosbrugger took the ride as a change, without paying much attention to its meaning. Between two dark, inert stretches in prison a quarter of an hour's opaque, white, foaming time was shooting by. This was how he had always experienced his freedom. Not really pretty. "That business about the last meal," he thought, "the prison chaplain, the hangmen, the quarter hour before it's all over, won't be too different. It will bounce along on wheels too; I'll be kept busy all the time, like now, trying to keep from sliding off this bench at every jolt, and I won't be seeing or hearing much of anything with all those people hopping around me. It's the best thing that can happen: finally I'll get some peace."

A man who has liberated himself from wanting to live feels immensely superior. Moosbrugger remembered the superintendent who had been his first interrogator at the police station. A real gent, who spoke in a low voice.

"Look here, Mr. Moosbrugger," he had said, "I beseech you: grant me success!" And Moosbrugger had replied, "Well, if success means that much to you, let's draw up a statement."

The judge, later on, was skeptical, but the superintendent had confirmed it in court. "Even if you don't care about relieving your conscience on your own account, please give me the personal satisfaction that you are doing it for my sake." The superintendent had repeated this before the whole court, even the presiding judge had looked pleased, and Moosbrugger had risen to his feet:

"My deep respect to His Honor the superintendent for making

this statement!" he had loudly proclaimed, then added, with a graceful bow: "Although the superintendent's last words to me were 'We will probably never see each other again,' it is an honor and a privilege to see you, the superintendent, again today."

A smile of self-approval transformed Moosbrugger's face, and he forgot the guards sitting opposite him, flung to and fro like himself by the jolting van.

54

IN CONVERSATION WITH WALTER AND CLARISSE, ULRICH TURNS OUT TO BE REACTIONARY

Clarisse said to Ulrich: "Something must be done for Moosbrugger; this murderer is musical!"

Ulrich had finally, on a free afternoon, paid them a visit to make up for the one so fatefully prevented by his arrest.

Clarisse was clutching at his lapel; Walter stood beside her with a look on his face that was not quite sincere.

"What do you mean, musical?" Ulrich asked with a smile.

Clarisse looked merrily shamefaced. Unintentionally. As if she had to clap a tight comic grin on her face to hold back the embarrassment oozing from every pore. She let go of his lapel.

"Oh, nothing special," she said. "You seem to have become an influential man!" It was not always easy to make her out.

Walter had already made a start, and then stopped again. Here, outside the city, there was still some snow on the ground; white fields and between them, like dark water, black earth. The sun washed over everything equitably. Clarisse wore an orange jacket and a blue wool cap. The three of them were out for a walk, and Ulrich, in the midst of nature's desolate disarray, had to explain Arnheim's writings to her. These dealt with algebraic series, benzol rings, the materialist as well as the universalist philosophy of history, bridge supports, the evolution of music, the essence of the automobile, Hata 606, the theory of relativity, Bohr's atomic theory, autogeneous welding, the flora of the Himalayas, psychoanalysis, individual psychology, experimental psychology, physiological psychology, social psychology, and all the other achievements that prevent a time so greatly enriched by them from turning out good, wholesome, integral human beings. However, Arnheim dealt with all these subjects in his writing in the most soothing fashion, assuring his readers that whatever they did not understand represented only an excess of sterile intellect, while the truth was always simplicity itself, like human dignity and that instinct for transcendent realities within reach of everyone who lived simply and was in league with the stars.

"Plenty of people are saying this kind of thing nowadays," Ulrich explained, "but Arnheim is the one whom people believe because they see him as a big, rich man who really knows whatever it is he is talking about, who has actually been to the Himalayas, owns automobiles, and can wear as many benzol rings as he likes."

Clarisse, prompted by a vague notion of carnelian rings, wanted to know what benzol rings looked like.

"You're a dear girl, Clarisse, all the same!" Ulrich said.

Walter came to her defense. "Thank heaven she doesn't have to understand all that chemical gobbledygook." But then he proceeded to defend the works of Arnheim, which he had read. He would not claim that Arnheim was the best one could imagine, but he was still the best the present age had produced; this was a new spirit! Scientifically sound, yet also capable of going beyond technical knowledge.

Thus their walk came to an end. The result for all of them was wet feet, an irritated brain—as though the thin, bare branches on the trees, sparkling in the winter sun, had turned to splinters stuck in the retina—a vulgar craving for hot coffee, and the feeling of human forlornness.

Steaming snow rose from their shoes; Clarisse enjoyed the mess they were making on the floor, and Walter kept his femininely sensuous lips pursed the whole time, because he was itching to start an argument. Ulrich told them about the Parallel Campaign. When Arnheim's name cropped up again the argument began.

"I'll tell you what I hold against him," Ulrich persisted. "Scientific man is an entirely inescapable thing these days; we can't not want to know! And at no time has the difference between the expert's experience and that of the layman been as great as it is now. Everyone can see this in the ability of a masseur or a pianist. No one would send a horse to the races these days without special preparation. It is only on the problems of being human that everyone feels called upon to pronounce judgment, and there's an ancient prejudice to the effect that one is born and dies a human being. But even if I know that five thousand years ago women wrote the same love letters, word for word, that they write today, I can't read such letters any longer without wondering whether it isn't ever going to change!"

Clarisse seemed inclined to agree. Walter, however, smiled like a fakir preparing not to bat an eyelash while someone runs a hatpin through his cheeks.

"Meaning only, presumably, that until further notice you refuse to be a human being?" he broke in.

"More or less. It has an unpleasant feeling of dilettantism about it."

"But I'll grant you something quite different," Ulrich went on after some thought. "The experts never finish anything. Not only are they not finished today, but they are incapable of conceiving an end to their activities. Even incapable, perhaps, of wishing for one. Can you imagine that man will still have a soul, for instance, once he has learned to understand it and control it biologically and psychologically? Yet this is precisely the condition we are aiming for! That's the trouble. Knowledge is a mode of conduct, a passion. At bottom, an impermissible mode of conduct: like dipsomania, sex mania, homicidal mania, the compulsion to know forms its own character that is off-balance. It is simply not so that the researcher pursues the truth; it pursues him. He suffers it. What is true is true, and a fact is real, without concerning itself about him: he's the one who has a passion for it, a dipsomania for the factual, which marks his character, and he doesn't give a damn whether his findings will lead to something human, perfect, or anything at all. Such a man is full of contradictions and misery, and yet he is a monster of energy!"

"And—?" Walter asked.

"What do you mean, 'And—?' "

"Surely you're not suggesting that we can leave it at that?"

"I would like to leave it at that," Ulrich said calmly. "Our conception of our environment, and also of ourselves, changes every day. We live in a time of passage. It may go on like this until the end of the planet if we don't learn to tackle our deepest problems better than we have so far. Even so, when one is placed in the dark, one should not begin to sing out of fear, like a child. And it is mere singing in the dark to act as though we knew how we are supposed to conduct ourselves down here; you can shout your head off, it's still nothing but terror. All I know for sure is: we're galloping! We're still a long way from our goals, they're not getting any closer, we can't even see them, we're likely to go on taking wrong turns, and we'll have to change horses; but one day—the day after tomorrow, or two thousand years from now—the horizon will begin to flow and come roaring toward us!"

Dusk had fallen. "No one can see my face now," Ulrich thought. "I don't even know myself whether I'm lying." He spoke as one does when making an uncertain snap judgment about the results of decades of certainty. It occurred to him that this youthful dream he had just unfurled for Walter had long since turned hollow. He didn't want to go on talking.

"Meaning," Walter said sharply, "that we should give up trying to make any sense of life?"

Ulrich asked him why he needed to make sense of it. It seemed to be doing nicely without that, it seemed to him.

Clarisse giggled. She didn't mean to mock Walter; Ulrich's question had struck her as funny.

Walter turned on the light, as he saw no reason why Ulrich should exploit the advantage, with Clarisse, of being the dark man. An irritating glare enveloped the three of them.

Ulrich stubbornly expanded on his point: "What one needs in life is merely the conviction that one's business is doing better than one's neighbor's. Your pictures, my mathematics, somebody else's wife and children—everything that can assure a person that he is in no way unusual but that in this way of being in no way unusual he will not so easily find his equal!"

Walter had not yet sat down again. He was full of unrest. Triumph.

"Do you realize what you're talking about?" he shouted. "Muddling through! You're simply an Austrian, and you're expounding the Austrian national philosophy of muddling through!"

"That may not be as bad as you think," Ulrich replied. "A passionate longing for keenness and precision, or beauty, may very well bring one to prefer muddling through to all those exertions in the modern spirit. I congratulate you on having discovered Austria's world mission."

Walter wanted to make some retort. But it turned out that the unrest that had kept him on his feet was not only a sense of triumph but—how to put it?—also the need to leave the room. He hesitated between the two impulses, but they were irreconcilable, and his gaze slid away from Ulrich's eyes toward the door.

When they were alone, Clarisse said: "This murderer is musical. I mean . . ." She paused, then went on mysteriously: "I can't explain it, but you must do something for him."

"But what can I do?"

"Set him free."

"You must be dreaming."

"You can't mean all those things you say to Walter?" Clarisse asked, and her eyes seemed to be urging him to an answer whose content he could not guess.

"I don't know what you want," he said.

Clarisse kept her eyes stubbornly on his lips; then she came back to her point: "You ought to do what I said, anyway; you would be transformed."

Ulrich observed her, trying to understand. He must have missed something—an analogy, or some "as if" that might have given a meaning to what she was saying. It sounded strange to hear her speaking so naturally without making sense, as though referring to some commonplace experience she had had.

But Walter was back. "I'm prepared to admit—" he began. The interruption had taken the edge off the argument.

He perched on his piano stool again and noticed with satisfaction some soil clinging to his shoes. "Why is there no dirt on Ulrich's shoes?" he thought. "It's the last hope of salvation for European man."

But Ulrich was looking above Walter's shoes at his legs, sheathed in black cotton, with their unlovely shape of the soft legs of young girls.

"A man today who still aspires to integrity deserves a lot of credit," Walter said.

"There's no such thing anymore," Ulrich countered. "You only have to look in a newspaper. It's filled with an immeasurable opacity. So many things are being talked about, it would surpass the intellectual capacity of a Leibniz. But we don't even notice; we have changed. There's no longer a whole man confronting a whole world, only a human something moving about in a general culture-medium."

"Quite so," Walter shot back. "There is in fact no complete education anymore, in Goethe's sense. Which is why today every idea has its opposite. Every action and its opposite are accompanied by the subtlest arguments, which can be defended or attacked with equal ease. How on earth can you champion such a state of affairs?"

Ulrich shrugged.

"One has to withdraw completely," Walter said softly.

"Or just go along," his friend replied. "Perhaps we're on our way to the termite state, or some other un-Christian division of labor." Ulrich thought privately that it would be just as easy to agree as to argue. Contempt showed as clearly through the politeness as a tidbit in aspic. He knew that Walter would again be annoyed with what he had just said, but he was beginning to long for a conversation with someone with whom he could agree completely, for once. There had been a time when he and Walter had had such conversations: the words are drawn from the breast by some mysterious power, and not one word misses its mark. But when one talks with antipathy the words rise like fog from an icy plain. He looked at Walter without resentment, certain that Walter also felt that the further this conversation went the more it was deforming his inner convictions, but that he was blaming Ulrich for it. "Everything we think is either sympathy or antipathy!" Ulrich thought. At this moment he was so vividly struck by the truth of this that he felt it as a physical pressure, like the bodily contact of people swaying in unison when they are jammed together. He looked around for Clarisse.

But Clarisse seemed to have stopped listening some time ago; at some point she had picked up the newspaper that had lain in front of her on the table and had begun asking herself why she found this so pleasurable. She felt herself looking at the boundless opacity Ulrich had spoken of before, with the paper between her hands. Her arms unfolded the darkness and opened out. Her arms formed two cross-beams with the trunk of her body, with the newspaper hanging between them. That was the pleasure, but the words to describe it were nowhere within her. She knew only that she was looking at the paper without reading it, and that it seemed to her there must be some savage mystery inside Ulrich, a power akin to her own, though she could not pin it down. Her lips had opened as if she were about to smile, but it was unconscious, a loosening of a still-frozen tension.

Walter continued in a low voice: "You're right when you say there's nothing serious, rational, or even intelligible left; but why can't you see that it is precisely this growing rationality, infecting everything like a disease, that is to blame? Everyone's brain is seized with this craving to become more and more rational, to rationalize and compartmentalize life more than ever, but unable to imagine what's to become of us when we know everything and have it all analyzed, classified, mechanized, standardized. It can't go on like this."

"Well," Ulrich said with composure, "when the monks were in charge, a Christian had to be a believer, even though the only heaven he could conceive of, with its clouds and harps, was rather boring; and now we are confronted with the Heaven of Reason, which reminds us of our school days with its rulers, hard benches, and horrible chalk figures."

"I have the feeling there will be a reaction of an unbridled excess of fantasy," Walter added thoughtfully. There was a hint of cowardice and cunning in this remark. He was thinking of Clarisse's mysterious irrationality, and as he spoke of reason threatening to drive the irrational to excess he was thinking of Ulrich. The two others did not catch on, which made him feel, in triumph and pain, that they did not understand him. He would have loved to ask Ulrich not to set foot in this house so long as he stayed in town, if only he could have done so without provoking Clarisse to mutiny.

The two men watched Clarisse in silence.

Clarisse suddenly noticed that they were no longer arguing, rubbed her eyes, and blinked amiably at Ulrich and Walter, who sat in the rays of yellow light against the dusky blue of the windowpanes like exhibits in a glass case.

55

SOLIMAN AND ARNHEIM

Meanwhile Christian Moosbrugger, the murderer of the young woman, had acquired yet another female admirer. The question of his guilt or his affliction had captured her heart a few weeks before as vividly as it had those of many others, and she had her own view of the case, which diverged somewhat from that of the court. The name "Christian Moosbrugger" appealed to her, evoking a tall, lonely man sitting by a mill overgrown with moss, listening to the roar of the water. She firmly believed that the accusations against him would be cleared up in some entirely unexpected way. As she sat in the kitchen or the dining room with her needlework, a Moosbrugger who had somehow shaken off his chains would appear beside her—and wild fantasies spun themselves out. It was far from impossible that Christian, had he only met Rachel in time, would have given up his career as a killer of girls and revealed himself as a robber chieftain with an immense future.

The poor man in his prison never dreamed of the heart that was beating for him as it bent over the mending of Diotima's underwear. It was no great distance from the apartment of Section Chief Tuzzi to the court building. From one roof to the other an eagle would have needed only a few wingbeats, but for the modern soul, which playfully spans oceans and continents, nothing is as impossible as finding its way to souls who live just around the corner.

And so the magnetic currents had dissipated again, and for some time Rachel had loved the Parallel Campaign instead of Moosbrugger. Even if things were not going as well as they might inside the reception rooms, a great deal was going on in the antechambers. Rachel, who had always managed to read the newspapers that passed from her employer's quarters to the kitchen, no longer had the time, since she was standing from dawn to dusk as a small guard post in front of the Parallel Campaign. She loved Diotima, Section Chief Tuzzi, His Grace Count Leinsdorf, the nabob, and, once she had noticed that he was beginning to play a role in the household, even Ulrich, as a dog loves his master's friends with a single love, though excitingly varied by their different smells. But Rachel was intelligent. In Ulrich's case, for instance, she was well aware that he was always somewhat at variance with the others, and her imagination started trying to think up some special, unexplained part he must play in the Parallel Campaign. He always looked at her in a friendly fashion, and little Rachel noticed that he kept on looking at her most particularly when he thought she was not aware of it. She felt sure that he wanted something from her; well, she had nothing against it; her little white pelt twitched with expectation, and a tiny golden dart would shoot at him out of her fine black eyes from time to time. Ulrich, without being able to figure it out, sensed the sparks flying from this little person as she flitted around the furniture and the stately visitors, and it offered him some distraction.

He owed his place in Rachel's attention not least to certain secret talks in the antechamber, which tended to undermine Arnheim's dominant position. That dazzling figure was quite unaware that he had a third enemy, besides Ulrich and Tuzzi, in the person of his little page Soliman. This small black fellow was the glittering buckle on the magic belt with which the Parallel Campaign had engirdled Rachel. A funny little creature, who had followed his master from magic climes to the street where Rachel worked, he was simply appropriated by her as that part of the fairy tale intended for her, in accordance with the social law that made the nabob the sun who belonged to Diotima, while Soliman, an enchanting colorful fragment of stained glass sparkling in that sun, was Rachel's booty. The boy, however, saw things somewhat differently. Although physically small he was sixteen going on seventeen, a creature full of romantic notions, malice, and personal pretension. Arnheim had plucked him out of a traveling dance troupe in southern Italy and taken him into his household. The strangely restless little fellow with the mournful monkey's eyes had touched his heart, and the rich man decided to open higher vistas to him. It was a longing for a close, faithful companionship, such as not infrequently overcame the solitary man—a weakness he usually hid behind increased activity. And so Arnheim treated Soliman, until his fourteenth year, on more or less those same terms of equality as rich families once casually brought up their wet nurse's offspring side by side with their own, letting them share the games and fun, until the moment when it appears that the same milk is of a lower grade when it is a mother's milk compared with that of a wet nurse. Soliman used to crouch day and night at his master's desk or at his feet, behind his back or on his knees, during Arnheim's long hours of conversation with famous visitors. He had read Scott, Shakespeare, and Dumas when Scott, Shakespeare, and Dumas had happened to be lying around on the tables, and had learned to spell from the *Handbook on the Humanities*. He ate his master's sweets, and when no one was looking soon took to smoking his cigarettes as well. A private tutor came and gave him—though somewhat erratically, because of all the traveling they did—an elementary education. It was all terribly boring to Soliman, who loved nothing more than serving as a valet, which he was also allowed to do, and which was serious, grown-up work, satisfying his need for action. But one day— not so long ago either—his master had called him in and told him, in a friendly way, that he had not quite fulfilled the hopes set on him. Now he was no longer a child, and Arnheim, his master, was responsible for seeing that Soliman, the little servant, turned into a decent citizen; which is why he had decided to treat him henceforth as exactly what he would have to be, so that he could learn to get used to it. Many successful men, Arnheim added, had begun as bootblacks and dishwashers; this beginning had indeed been the source of their strength, because the most important thing in life was to do whatever one does with all one's heart.

That hour, when he was promoted from the undefined status of a pet kept in luxury to that of a servant with free board and lodging and a small wage, ravaged Soliman's heart to a degree of which Arnheim had no notion at all. Arnheim's statements had gone clear over Soliman's head, but Soliman's feelings made him guess what they meant, and he had hated his master ever since the change had been imposed on him. Not that he stopped helping himself to books, sweets, and cigarettes, but while he had formerly taken merely what gave him pleasure, he now deliberately stole from Arnheim, with so insatiable a vengefulness that he sometimes simply broke things, or hid them, or threw them away—things Arnheim obscurely thought he remembered, puzzled that they never turned up again. While Soliman was revenging himself like a goblin, he pulled himself together remarkably in carrying out his duties and presenting a pleasing appearance. He continued to be a sensation with all the cooks, housemaids, hotel staff, and female visitors; was spoiled by their glances and smiles, gaped at by jeering ragamuffins on the street; and generally felt like a fascinating and important personage, even when oppressed. His master, too, occasionally favored him with a pleased or complacent glance, or with a kind, wise word. Everyone praised Soliman as a handy, obliging boy, and if it happened that such praise came just after he had got something especially awful on his conscience he grinned obsequiously, enjoying his triumph as if he had swallowed a searingly cold lump of ice.

Rachel had won this boy's trust the moment she told him that what was going on in the house might be preparations for war; ever since, she had been subjected by him to the most scandalous revelations about her idol, Arnheim. Despite Soliman's blasé airs, his imagination was like a pincushion bristling with swords and daggers, and the tales he poured into Rachel's ear about Arnheim were full of thundering horses' hooves and swaying torches and rope ladders. He revealed that his name was not really Soliman, rattling off a long exotic name with such speed that she could never catch it. He later imparted the secret that he was the son of an African prince, kidnapped as a baby from his father, whose warriors, cattle, slaves, and jewels numbered in the thousands. Arnheim had bought him only in order to sell him back to his father for a staggering sum, but Soliman was going to run away, and would have done it sooner were his father not so far away.

Rachel was not fooled by these stories, but she believed them because nothing connected with the Parallel Campaign could be incredible enough. She would also have liked to forbid Soliman such talk about Arnheim, but had to stop short of regarding his presump-

tion with horrified mistrust because his assurance that his master was
not to be trusted promised, for all her doubts, a tremendous imminent, thrilling complication for the Parallel Campaign.

Such were the storm clouds behind which the tall man brooding
by the moss-grown millrace disappeared, and a pallid light gathered
in the wrinkled grimaces of Soliman's little monkey face.

56

THE PARALLEL CAMPAIGN COMMITTEES SEETHE WITH ACTIVITY. CLARISSE WRITES TO HIS GRACE PROPOSING A NIETZSCHE YEAR

At about this time Ulrich had to report to His Grace two or three
times a week. A high-ceilinged, shapely room, delightful in its very
proportions, had been set aside for him. At the window stood a large
Maria Theresa desk. On the wall hung a dark picture, mutely glowing
with patches of red, blue, and yellow, of some horsemen or other
driving their lances into the bellies of other, fallen horsemen. On the
opposite wall hung the portrait of a solitary lady whose vulnerable
body was carefully armored in a gold-embroidered, wasp-waisted
corset. There seemed no reason why she had been banished all by
herself to this wall, as she was obviously a Leinsdorf; her young, powdered face resembled the Liege-Count's as closely as a footprint in
dry snow matches one in wet loam. Ulrich, incidentally, had little opportunity to study Count Leinsdorf's face. Since the last meeting,
the Parallel Campaign had received such a boost that His Grace
never found leisure to devote to the great ideas anymore but had to
spend his time reading correspondence, receiving people, discussions, and expeditions. He had already had a consultation with the
Prime Minister, a talk with the Archbishop, a conference at the
Chamberlain's office, and had more than once sounded out a number of the high aristocracy and the ennobled commoners in the

Upper House. Ulrich had not been invited to these discussions and gathered only that all sides expected strong political resistance from the opposition, so they all declared they would be able to support the Parallel Campaign the more vigorously the less their names were linked with it, and for the time being only sent observers to represent them at the committee meetings.

The good news was that these committees were making great strides from week to week. As agreed at the inaugural sessions, they had divided up the world according to the major aspects of religion, education, commerce, agriculture, and so on; every committee already contained a representative of the corresponding ministry, and all committees were already devoting themselves to their task, to wit, that every committee in accord with all the other committees was waiting for the representatives of the respective organizations and sectors of the population to present their wishes, suggestions, and petitions, which would be screened and passed on to the executive committee. In this fashion it was hoped that a steady stream of the country's principal moral forces could be channeled, in an ordered and concentrated way, to the executive committee, an expectation already gratified by the swelling tide of written communications. Very shortly the flood of memoranda from the various committees to the executive committee were able to refer to their own earlier memoranda, previously transmitted to the executive committee, so that they took to beginning with a sentence that gained in importance from one instance to the next and started with the words: "With reference to our mem. no. so-and-so, ref. to no. such-and-such/XYZ, no. this-and-that"; all these numbers grew larger with each communication. This in itself was already a sign of healthy growth. In addition, even the embassies began to report through semi-official channels on the impression being made abroad by this vigorous display of Austrian patriotism; the foreign ambassadors were already sending out cautious feelers for information; alerted deputies were asking questions in Parliament; and private enterprise manifested itself by way of inquiries from business firms that took the liberty of making suggestions or seeking a way in which they could link their firms with patriotism. The apparatus was set up, and because it was there it had to function, and once it was functioning, it began to accelerate; once a car starts rolling in an open field, even if no one is at the wheel, it will always take a definite, even a very impressive and remarkable course of its own.

And so a great force had been set in motion, and Count Leinsdorf began to feel it. He put on his pince-nez and read all the incoming mail with great seriousness from beginning to end. It was no longer the proposals and desires of unknown, passionate individuals, such as had inundated him at the outset, before things had been set on a regular course, and even though these applications or inquiries still came from the heart of the people, they were now signed by the chairmen of alpine clubs, leagues for free thought, girls' welfare associations, workingmen's organizations, social groups, citizens' clubs, and other such nondescript clusterings that run ahead of the transition from individualism to collectivism like little heaps of street sweepings before a stiff breeze. And even if His Grace was not in sympathy with everything they asked for, he felt that, all in all, important progress had been made. He took off his pince-nez, handed the communication back to the official who had presented it to him, and nodded his satisfaction without saying a word; he felt that the Parallel Campaign was in good order and clearly on its way, and in due time would find its proper form.

The ministry official who took the letter back usually placed it on a pile of other letters, and when the last one of the day lay on top, he read for His Grace's eyes. Then His Grace's mouth would speak: "Excellent, but we can't say yes and we can't say no as long as we have no really firm idea what our central goal is." But this was just what the official had read in His Grace's eyes after every previous letter, and it was precisely what he thought himself, and he had his gold-plated pocket pencil ready to write what he had already written at the bottom of every previous letter, the magic formula: "Fi." This magic formula, widely used in the Kakanian civil service, stood for "Filed for later decision," and was a model of that circumspection that loses sight of nothing, and rushes into nothing. "Fi," for instance, took care of a minor civil servant's application for an emergency grant-in-aid to pay for his wife's impending confinement by filing it away until the child was grown and old enough to earn a living, simply because the matter might be in the process of being dealt with by pending legislation, and in the meantime the senior official did not have the heart to turn down his subordinate's petition out of hand. The same treatment would also be accorded an application from an influential personage or a government bureau that one could not afford to offend by a refusal, even though one knew some other influential quarter was opposed to this application. And basically, everything that came to the department's attention for the first time was kept on file on principle, until a similar case came up to serve as a precedent.

But it would be quite wrong to make fun of this administrative custom, since a great deal more is filed for later decision in the world outside government offices. How little it means that monarchs on their accession still take an oath to make war on Turks or other infidels, considering that in all the history of mankind no sentence has ever been completely crossed out or quite completed, which at times gives rise to that bewildering tempo of progress exactly resembling a flying ox. In government offices, at least, a few things get lost, but nothing ever gets lost in the world. "Fi" is indeed one of the basic formulas of the structure of our life. When, however, something struck His Grace as particularly urgent, he had to choose another method. He would then send the proposal to Court, to his friend Count Stallburg, with the query whether it might be regarded as "tentatively definitive," as he put it. After some time he would receive a reply, always to the effect that His Majesty's wishes on this point could not as of now be conveyed, but in the meantime it seemed desirable to begin by letting public opinion follow its own direction and then to reconsider the proposal in due course, depending on how it had been received and on any other contingencies that might arise in the meantime. This reply caused the proposal to become a duly constituted file, and as such it was passed on to the proper ministerial department, whence it returned with the note that the department did not consider itself authorized to arrive at an independent decision in the matter, and when this happened Count Leinsdorf made a note to propose at one of the next meetings of the executive committee that an interdepartmental subcommittee be set up to study the problem.

In only one case was His Grace's mind inexorably made up, that of a letter not signed by the chairman of any society or any officially recognized religious, scientific, or artistic body. Such a letter had come recently from Clarisse, using Ulrich's name as a reference, and proposing the proclamation of an Austrian Nietzsche Year, in conjunction with which something would have to be done for the murderer of women, Moosbrugger. She wrote that, as a woman, she felt called upon to make this suggestion, and also because of the significant coincidence that Nietzsche had been a mental case and so was Moosbrugger. Ulrich barely managed a joke to conceal his annoyance when Count Leinsdorf showed him this letter, which he had already recognized by its oddly immature handwriting crisscrossed with heavy horizontal T-bar strokes and underlinings. Count Leinsdorf, however, sensing his embarrassment, said seriously and kindly: "This is not without interest. One might say that it shows ardor and energy, but I'm afraid we must shelve all such personal suggestions, or we shall never get anywhere. As you know the writer personally, perhaps you would like to pass this letter on to your cousin?"

57

GREAT UPSURGE. DIOTIMA DISCOVERS THE STRANGE WAYS OF GREAT IDEAS

Ulrich slipped the letter into his pocket to make it disappear, but in any case it would not have been easy to take it up with Diotima. Ever since the newspaper article about the "Year of Austria" had appeared, she had been swept along by a rising tide of incoherent activity. Not only did Ulrich hand over to her, preferably unread, all the files he received from Count Leinsdorf, but every day the mail brought heaps of letters and press clippings, and masses of books on approval came from booksellers; her house swelled with people as the sea swells when moon and wind tug at it together, and the telephone never stopped ringing. Had little Rachel not taken charge of it with seraphic zeal, and given most of the information herself because she said she could not bother her mistress incessantly, Diotima would have collapsed under the burden.

Yet this nervous breakdown that never happened, even as it kept quivering and pulsating in her body, brought Diotima a kind of happiness she had never known before. It was a shudder, a being endlessly showered with significance, a crackling like that of the pressure in the capstone of the world arch, a prickling like the awareness of nothingness when one stands on the summit of the highest mountain peak for miles around. It was, in short, a sense of position that was awakening in this daughter of a modest secondary-school teacher and this young wife of a middle-class vice-consul, which she had remained in the freshness of her heart despite her rise in society. Such a sense of position belongs to the unnoticed but essential conditions of life, like not noticing the revolutions of the earth or the part our personality plays in directing our perceptions. Since man is taught not to bear vanity in his heart, he keeps most of it underfoot, in that he walks on the soil of a great fatherland, religion, or income-tax bracket; or else, lacking such a vantage point, he makes do with a place anyone can have, on the momentarily highest point reached by the pillar of time as it rises out of the void; in other words, we take pride in living in and for the present moment, when all our predecessors have turned to dust and no successors have yet appeared. But if for some reason this vanity, of which we are usually unconscious, suddenly mounts from the feet to the head, it can cause a mild craziness, like that of those virgins who imagine they are pregnant with the globe of the earth itself.

Even Section Chief Tuzzi now paid Diotima the tribute of inquiring how things were going, sometimes even asking her to oversee one minor matter or another; at such times the smile with which he usually referred to her salon was replaced by a dignified seriousness. It was still not known to what extent the idea of finding himself placed in the forefront of an international pacifist movement would be agreeable to His Gracious Majesty, but on this point Tuzzi repeatedly asked Diotima not to take the slightest step into the field of foreign affairs without first consulting him. He even suggested on the spot that if ever any serious move should be made toward an international peace campaign, every precaution first immediately be taken against any possible political complications that might ensue. Such a noble idea should in no way be rejected, he explained to his wife, not even if there might be some possibility of realizing it, but it was abso-

lutely necessary to keep open one's options for going ahead or retreating from the very beginning. He then laid out for Diotima the
differences between disarmament, a peace conference, a summit
meeting, and so on, all the way down to the already mentioned foundation for decorating the Peace Palace at The Hague with murals by
Austrian artists; he had never before spoken with his wife in this factual manner. Sometimes he would even come back to the bedroom
with his briefcase to supplement his remarks, in case he had forgotten to add, for instance, that he personally could regard everything
having to do with a Global Austria as conceivable only, of course, as
part of a pacifist or humanitarian undertaking of some kind; anything
else could only make one look dangerously irresponsible, or some
such thing.

Diotima answered with a patient smile: "I shall do my best to do as
you wish, but you should not exaggerate the importance of foreign
affairs for us. There is a tremendous upsurge, an inner sense of redemption, coming from the anonymous depths of the people; you
can't imagine the floods of petitions and suggestions that overwhelm
me every day."

She was admirable, for she gave no hint of the enormous difficulties she actually had to contend with. In the deliberations of the great
central committee, which was organized under the headings of Religion, Justice, Agriculture, Education, and so forth, all idealistic
suggestions met with that icy and timorous reserve so familiar to Diotima from her husband in the days before he had become so attentive. There were times when she felt quite discouraged from sheer
impatience, when she could not conceal from herself that this iner-
tial resistance of the world would be hard to break. However clearly
she herself could see the Year of Austria as the Year of a Global
Austria, and the Austrian nations as the model for the nations of the
world—all it took was to prove that Austria was the true home of
the human spirit everywhere—it was equally clear that for the slow-
witted this concept would have to be fleshed out with a particular
content and supplemented by some inspired symbol, something less
abstract, with more sense-appeal, to help them understand. Diotima
pored for hours over many books, searching for the right image, and
it would have to be a uniquely Austrian symbolic image, of course.

But now Diotima was having strange experiences with the nature of great ideas.

It appeared that she was living in a great age, since the age was full of great ideas. But one would not believe how hard it was to translate the greatest and most important of them into reality, considering that all the conditions for doing so existed except one: knowing which of them was the greatest and most important. Every time Diotima had almost opted in favor of some idea, she could not help noticing that its opposite was equally great and equally worthy of realization. That's the way it is, after all, and she couldn't help it. Ideals have curious properties, and one of them is that they turn into their opposites when one tries to live up to them. Take Tolstoy, for instance, and Bertha Suttner, two writers whose ideas were about equally discussed at the time—but how, Diotima thought, can mankind even have roast chicken without violence? And if one should not kill, as these two writers demanded, what was to be done with the soldiers? They would be unemployed, poor devils, and the criminals would see the dawn of a golden age. Such proposals had actually been made, and signatures were said to be in the process of being collected. Diotima could never have imagined a life without eternal verities, but now she found to her amazement that there are two, or more, of every eternal verity. Which is why every reasonable person—Section Chief Tuzzi, in this case, who was to that extent vindicated—has a deeply rooted mistrust of eternal verities. Of course he will never deny that they are indispensable, but he is convinced that people who take them literally must be mad. According to his way of thinking—which he helpfully offered to his wife—ideals make excessive demands on human nature, with ruinous consequences, unless one refuses at the outset to take them quite seriously. The best proof of this that Tuzzi could offer was that such words as "ideal" and "eternal verity" never occur at all in government offices, which deal with serious matters. A civil servant who would think of using such an expression in an official communication would instantly be advised to see a doctor to request a medical leave. But even if Diotima listened to him sadly, she always drew new strength from such moments of weakness, and plunged back into her researches.

Even Count Leinsdorf marveled at her mental energy when he

finally found the time to come for a consultation with her. His Grace wanted a spontaneous testimonial arising from the midst of the people. He sincerely wanted to find out the will of the people and to refine it by cautiously influencing it from above, for he hoped one day to submit it to His Majesty, not as a ritual offering from a Byzantine monarchy but as a sign of true self-awareness achieved by nations adrift in the vortex of democracy. Diotima knew that His Grace still clung to the "Emperor of Peace" concept and that of a splendid testimonial demonstration of the True Austria, even though he did not in principle reject the idea of a Global Austria, but only so long as it properly expressed the sense of a family of nations gathered around their patriarch. From this political family His Grace covertly and tacitly excluded Prussia, even though he had nothing against Dr. Arnheim personally and even made a point of referring to him as "an interesting person."

"We certainly don't want anything patriotic in the outworn sense of the word," he offered. "We must shake up the nation, the world. A Year of Austria is a fine idea, it seems to me, and I have in fact already told the fellows from the press myself that the public imagination should be steered in that direction. But once we've agreed on that, what do we do in this Austrian Year—have you thought of that, my dear? That, you see, is the problem! That's what we really need to know. Unless we help things along a little from above, the immature elements will gain the upper hand. And I simply haven't the time to think of anything!"

Diotima thought His Grace seemed worried, and said vivaciously: "The campaign is no good at all unless it culminates in a great symbol. That much is certain. It must seize the heart of the world, but it also needs some influence from above; there is no denying that. An Austrian Year is a brilliant suggestion, but in my opinion a World Year would be still finer, a World-Austrian Year, in which Europe could recognize Austria as its true spiritual home."

"Not so fast! Not so fast!" warned Count Leinsdorf, who had often been startled by his friend's spiritual audacity. "Aren't your ideas always perhaps a little excessive, Diotima? This is not the first time you've brought this up, but one can't be too careful. What have you come up with to do in this World Year?"

With this question, however, Count Leinsdorf, led by the bluntness that made his thinking so full of character, had touched Diotima at precisely her most vulnerable point. "Count," she said after some hesitation, "that is the hardest question in the world to answer. I intend as soon as possible to invite a circle of the most distinguished men, poets and philosophers, and I will wait to hear what this group has to say before I say anything."

"Good!" His Grace exclaimed, instantly won over for a postponement. "How right you are! One can never be careful enough. If you only knew what I have to listen to day in and day out!"

58

QUALMS ABOUT THE PARALLEL CAMPAIGN. BUT IN THE HISTORY OF MANKIND THERE IS NO VOLUNTARY TURNING BACK

On one occasion His Grace also had time to go into it more deeply with Ulrich.

"I can't say I care too much for this Dr. Arnheim," he said confidentially. "A brilliant man, of course; no wonder your cousin is impressed with him. But he is, after all, a Prussian. He has a way of looking on. You know, when I was a little boy, in '65 it was, my sainted father had a shooting party at Chrudim Castle and one of the guests had the same way of looking on, and a year later it turned out that no one had the remotest idea who had brought him along and that he was a major on the Prussian general staff! Not, of course, that I'm suggesting anything, but I don't altogether like this fellow Arnheim knowing all about us."

"Your Grace," Ulrich said, "I'm glad you offer me a chance to speak my mind on the subject. It's time something was done; things are going on that make me wonder and that aren't suitable for a foreign observer to see. After all, the Parallel Campaign is supposed to raise everyone's spirits, isn't it? Surely that is what Your Grace intended?"

"Well of course, naturally."

"But the opposite is happening!" Ulrich exclaimed. "I have the impression it's making all the best people look unusually concerned, even downhearted!"

His Grace shook his head and twiddled his thumbs, as he always did when his mood darkened. He had, in fact, made similar observations himself.

"Ever since it got around that I have some connection with the Parallel Campaign," Ulrich went on, "whenever I get into conversation with someone it doesn't take three minutes before he says to me: 'What is it you're really after with this Parallel Campaign? There's no such thing nowadays as great achievements or great men!' "

"Well, themselves excepted, of course," Count Leinsdorf interjected. "I know all about that; I hear it all the time too. The big industrialists grumble that the politicians don't give them enough protective tariffs, and the politicians grumble about industry for not coming up with enough money for their election campaigns."

"Quite so!" Ulrich proceeded with his exposition. "The surgeons clearly believe that surgery has made progress since the days of Billroth, but they say that medicine as a whole, and science in general, are doing too little for surgery. I would even go so far, if you will permit me, as to suppose that the theologians believe theology has made advances since the time of Christ—"

Count Leinsdorf raised a hand in mild protest.

"Excuse me if I said something inappropriate, especially as it was quite unnecessary; my point is a quite general one. The surgeons, as I said, claim that scientific research is not fulfilling its promise, but if you talk to a research scientist about the present, he will complain that, much as he would like to broaden his outlook a bit, the theater bores him and he can't find a novel that entertains and stimulates him. Talk to a poet, and he'll tell you that there is no faith. Talk to a painter—since I want to leave the theologians out of it—and he'll be pretty sure to tell you that painters can't give their best in a period that has such miserable literature and philosophy. Of course the sequence in which they blame one another is not always the same, but it always reminds one a bit of musical chairs, if you know what I mean, sir, or Puss in the Corner, and I've no idea what the law or the rule is at the bottom of it. I'm afraid it looks as though each individual may still be satisfied with himself, more or less, but collectively, for some universal reason, mankind seems ill at ease inside its own skin, and the Parallel Campaign seems destined to bring this condition to light."

"Good heavens," His Grace said in response to this analysis, without its being quite clear what he meant by it, "nothing but ingratitude!"

"I have already, incidentally," Ulrich continued, "two folders full of general proposals, which I've had no previous opportunity to return to Your Grace. One of them I've headed: *Back to—!* It's amazing how many people tell us that the world was better off in earlier times and want the Parallel Campaign to take us back there. Without counting the understandable slogan, Back to Religion!, we still have a Back to the Baroque, Back to Gothic, Back to Nature, Back to Goethe, to Ancient Germanic Law, to Moral Purity, and quite a few more."

"Hmm, yes. But perhaps there is a real idea in there somewhere, which it would be a mistake to discourage?" Count Leinsdorf offered.

"That's possible, but how should one deal with it? 'After careful consideration of your esteemed letter of such-and-such a date, we regret that we do not regard the present moment as suitable . . .'? Or 'We have read your letter with interest, please supply details on how restoration of the world as it was in the Baroque, the Gothic, et cetera, et cetera, is to be effected . . . and so on'?"

Ulrich was smiling, but Count Leinsdorf felt he was treating the situation with a little too much levity, and twiddled his thumbs with renewed vigor to ward it off. His face, with its handlebar mustache, assumed a hardness reminiscent of the Wallenstein era, and then he came out with a most noteworthy statement:

"Dear Doctor," he said, "in the history of mankind there is no voluntary turning back!"

This statement surprised no one more than Count Leinsdorf himself, who had actually intended to say something quite different. As a conservative, he had been annoyed with Ulrich, and had wanted to point out to him that the middle classes had spurned the universal spirit of the Catholic Church and were now suffering the consequences. He was also on the point of praising the times of absolute centralism, when the world was still led by persons aware of their responsibilities in accordance with fixed principles. But while he was still groping for words, it suddenly occurred to him what a nasty surprise it would be to wake up one morning without a hot bath and trains, with an Imperial town crier riding through the streets instead of the morning papers. And so Count Leinsdorf thought: "Things can never again be what they were, the way they were," and as he thought this he was quite astonished. For one assumed that if there was indeed no voluntary going back in history, then mankind was like a man driven along by some inexplicable wanderlust, a man who could neither go back nor arrive anywhere, and this was a quite remarkable condition.

Now, while His Grace had an extraordinary knack for keeping apart two ideas that might contradict each other so that they never came together in his consciousness, he should have firmly rejected this particular idea, which was inimical to all his principles. However, he had taken rather a liking to Ulrich, and as far as time permitted, he enjoyed explaining political matters on a strictly logical basis to this intellectually alert young man who had come to him so well recommended, whose only drawback was his middle-class status, which made him something of an outsider when it came to the really great issues. But once one begins with logic, where one idea follows from the immediately preceding one, one never knows where it may all come out at the end. And so Count Leinsdorf did not retract his statement but merely gazed at Ulrich in intense silence.

Ulrich picked up a second folder and took advantage of the pause to hand both files to His Grace.

"I had to head the second one *Forward to—!*" he began to explain, but His Grace started to his feet and found that his time was up. He urged Ulrich to leave the continuation of their talk for another time, when there would be more leisure to give it some thought.

"By the way," he said, already on his feet, "your cousin is going to have a gathering of our most distinguished thinkers to discuss all these problems. Do go; please be sure to go; I don't know whether I shall be permitted to be there."

Ulrich put back his folders, and Count Leinsdorf, in the shadow of the open door, turned around once more. "A great experiment naturally makes everyone nervous. But we'll shake them up!" His sense of propriety would not let him leave Ulrich behind without some word of comfort.

59

MOOSBRUGGER REFLECTS

Moosbrugger had meanwhile settled down in his new prison as best he could. The gate had hardly shut behind him when he was bellowed at. He had been threatened with a beating when he protested, if he remembered rightly. He had been put in solitary. For his walk in the yard he was handcuffed, and the guards' eyes were glued to him. They had shaved his head, even though his sentence was under appeal and not yet legally in force, because, they said, they had to take his measurements. They had lathered him all over with a stinking soft soap, on the pretext of disinfecting him. As an old hand, he knew that all this was against regulations, but behind that iron gate it is not so easy to maintain one's dignity. They did as they pleased with him. He demanded to see the warden, and complained. The warden had to admit that some things were not in accordance with regulations, but it was not a punishment, he said, only a precaution. Moosbrugger complained to the prison chaplain, but the chaplain was a kindly old man whose amiable ministry was anachronistically flawed by his inability to cope with sexual crimes. He abhorred them with the lack of understanding of a body that had never even touched the periphery of such feelings, and was even dismayed that Moosbrugger's honest appearance moved him to the weakness of feeling personally sorry for him. He sent Moosbrugger to the prison doctor, and for his own part, as in all such cases, sent up to the Creator an omnibus prayer that did not go into detail but dealt in such general terms with man's proneness to error that Moosbrugger was included in the moment of prayer along with the freethinkers and atheists. The prison doctor told Moosbrugger that he was making a mountain out of a molehill, gave him a friendly slap on the back, and absolutely refused to pay any attention to his complaints, on the grounds that— if Moosbrugger understood him right—it was all beside the point as long as the question of whether he was insane or only malingering had not been settled by the medical authorities. Infuriated, Moosbrugger suspected that all these people spoke to suit themselves, and that it was this trick with words that gave them the power to do as they pleased with him. He had the feeling of simple people that the educated ought to have their tongues cut out. He looked at the doctor's face with its dueling scars; at the priest's face, withered from the inside; at the austerely tidy office face of the warden; saw each face looking back at him in its own way, and saw in all of them something beyond his reach that they had in common, which had been his lifelong enemy. The constricting pressure that in the outside world forces every person, with all his self-conceit, to wedge himself with effort among all that other flesh, was somewhat eased—despite all the discipline—under the roof of the prison, where everything lived for waiting, and the interaction of the inmates, even when it was coarse and violent, was undermined by a shadow of unreality. Moosbrugger reacted with his whole powerful body to the slackening of tension after the trial. He felt like a loose tooth. His skin itched. He felt miserable, as if he had caught an infection. It was a self-pitying, tenderly nervous hypersensitivity that came over him sometimes: the woman who lay underground and who had got him into this mess seemed to him a crude, nasty bitch contrasted with a child, if he compared her to himself.

Just the same, Moosbrugger was not altogether dissatisfied. He could tell in many ways that he was a person of some importance here, and it flattered him. Even the attention given to all convicts alike gave him satisfaction. The state had to feed them, bathe them, clothe them, and concern itself with their work, their health, their books, and their songs from the moment they had broken the law; it had never done these things before. Moosbrugger enjoyed this attention, even if it was strict, like a child who has succeeded in forcing its mother to notice it with anger. But he did not want it to continue much longer. The idea that his sentence might be commuted to life in prison or in a lunatic asylum sparked in him the resistance we feel when every effort to escape from our circumstances only leads us back to them, time and again. He knew that his lawyer was trying to get the case reopened, that he was to be interrogated all over again, but he made up his mind to oppose that as soon as he could and insist that they kill him.

Above all, he had to make a dignified exit, for his life had been a battle for his rights. In solitary, Moosbrugger considered what his rights were. He couldn't say. But they were everything he had been cheated of all his life. The moment he thought of that he swelled with emotion. His tongue arched and started to move like a Lippizaner stallion in his zeal to pronounce the word nobly enough. "My right," he thought, drawing the word out as long as he could, to realize this concept, and thought, as if he were speaking to someone: "It's when you haven't done anything wrong, or something like that, isn't it?" Suddenly he had it: "Right is justice." That was it. His right was his justice! He looked at his wood-plank bed in order to sit on it, turned awkwardly around to tug at it—in vain, as it was screwed to the floor—then slowly sat down.

He had been cheated of his justice! He remembered his master's wife, when he was sixteen. He had dreamed that something cold was blowing on his belly, then it had disappeared inside his body; he had yelled and fallen out of bed, and the next morning felt as if he had been beaten black-and-blue. Other apprentices had once told him that you could always get a woman by showing her your fist with the thumb sticking out between the middle and the forefinger. He didn't know what to make of it; they all said they had tried it, but when he thought about it the ground gave way under him, or his head seemed to be screwed on wrong; in short, something was going on inside him that separated him by a hairbreadth from the natural order and was not quite steady. "Missus," he said, "I'd like to do something nice to you. . . ." They were alone; she looked into his eyes and must have seen something there; she said: "You just clear out of this kitchen!" He then held up his fist with the thumb sticking out. But the magic worked only halfway: her face turned dark red and she hit him with the wooden ladle in her hand, too fast for him to dodge the blow, right across the face; he realized it only when the blood began to trickle over his lips. But he remembered that instant vividly now, for the blood suddenly turned and flowed upward, up above his eyes, and he threw himself on the strapping woman who had so viciously insulted him; the master came in; and what happened then, until the moment he stood in the street with his legs buckling and his things thrown after him, was like a big red cloth being ripped to shreds. That was how they made a mockery and a shambles of his right, and he took to the road again. Can a man find his rights on the road? All the women were already somebody else's right, and so were all the apples and all the beds. And the police and the judges were worse than the dogs.

But what it really was that always gave people a hold on him, and why they were always throwing him in jails or madhouses, Moosbrugger could never really figure out. He stared long and hard at the floor, at the corners of his cell; he felt like a man who has dropped a key on the floor. But he couldn't find it; the floor and the corners turned day-gray and ordinary again, though just a while ago they had been a dreamscape where a thing or a person springs up at the drop of a word.

Moosbrugger mustered all his logic. He could only remember distinctly all the places it began. He could have ticked them off on his fingers and described them. Once, it had been in Linz, another time in Braila. Years had passed between. And the last time it was here in the city. He could see every stone so sharply outlined, as stones usually aren't. He also remembered the rotten feeling that always went with it, as if he had poison instead of blood in his veins, or something like that. For instance, he was working outdoors and women passed by; he didn't want to look at them, because they bothered him, but new ones kept constantly passing by, so finally his eyes would follow them with loathing, and that slow turning of his eyes this way and that felt as if his eyes were stirring in tar or in setting cement inside him. Then he noticed that his thoughts were growing heavy. He thought slowly anyway, the words gave him trouble, he never had enough words, and sometimes, when he was talking to someone, the other man would look at him in surprise: he wouldn't understand how much was being said in the one word Moosbrugger was uttering so slowly. He envied all those people who had learned to talk easily when they were young. His own words seemed to stick to his gums to spite him just when he needed them most, and it sometimes took forever to tear out the next syllable so he could go on from there. There was no getting around it: this couldn't be due to natural causes. But when he said in court that it was the Freemasons or the Jesuits or the Socialists who were torturing him this way, nobody understood what he was talking about. Those lawyers and judges could outtalk him, all right, and had all sorts of things to say against him, but none of them had a clue to what was really going on.

When this sort of thing had continued for some time, Moosbrugger got frightened. Just try standing in the street with your hands tied, waiting to see what people will do! He knew that his tongue, or something deep inside him, was glued down, and it made him miserably unsure of himself, a feeling he had to struggle for days to hide. But then there came a sharp, one could almost say soundless, boundary. Suddenly a cold breeze was there. Or else a big balloon rose up in the air right in front of him and flew into his chest. At the same instant he felt something in his eyes, his lips, the muscles of his face; everything around him seemed to fade, to turn black, and while the houses lay down on the trees, some cats quickly leapt from the bushes and scurried away. This lasted only for an instant, then it was over.

This was the real beginning of the time they all wanted to know about and never stopped talking about. They pestered him with the most pointless questions; unfortunately, he could remember his experiences only dimly, through what they meant to him. Because these periods were all meaning! They sometimes lasted for minutes, sometimes for days on end, and sometimes they changed into other, similar experiences that could last for months. To begin with the latter, because they are simpler, and in Moosbrugger's opinion even a judge could understand then: Moosbrugger heard voices or music or a wind, or a blowing and humming, a whizzing and rattling, or shots, thunder, laughing, shouts, speaking, or whispering. It came at him from every direction; the sounds were in the walls, in the air, in his clothes, in his body. He had the impression he was carrying it in his body as long as it was silent; once it was out, it hid somewhere in his surroundings, but never very far from him. When he was working, the voices would speak at him mostly in random words or short phrases, insulting and nagging him, and when he thought of something they came out with it before he could, or spitefully said the opposite of what he meant. It was ridiculous to be declared insane on this account; Moosbrugger regarded these voices and visions as mere monkeyshines. It entertained him to hear and see what they did; that was ever so much better than the hard, heavy thoughts he had himself. But of course he got very angry when they really annoyed him, that was only natural. Moosbrugger knew, because he always paid close attention to all the expressions that were applied to him, that this was called hallucinating, and he was pleased that he had this knack for hallucination that others lacked; it enabled him to see all sorts of things others didn't, such as lovely landscapes and hellish monsters. But he found that they always made far too much of it, and when the stays in mental hospitals became too unpleasant, he maintained outright that he was only pretending. The know-it-alls would ask him how loud the sounds were; a senseless question, because of course what he heard was sometimes as loud as a thunderclap, and sometimes the merest whisper. Even the physical pains that sometimes plagued him could be unbearable or slight enough to be imaginary. That wasn't the important thing. Often he could not have described exactly what he saw, heard, and felt, but he knew what it was. It could be very blurred; the visions came from outside, but a shimmer of observation told him at the same time that they were really something inside himself. The important thing was that it is not at all important whether something is inside or outside; in his condition, it was like clear water on both sides of a transparent sheet of glass.

When he was feeling on top of things Moosbrugger paid no attention at all to his voices and visions but spent his time in thinking. He called it thinking because he had always been impressed with the word. He thought better than other people because he thought both inside and outside. Thinking went on inside him against his will. He said that thoughts were planted in him. He was hypersensitive to the merest trifles, as a woman is when her breasts are tight with milk, but this did not interfere with his slow, manly reflectiveness. At such times his thoughts flowed like a stream running through a lush meadow swelled by hundreds of leaping brooks.

Now Moosbrugger had let his head drop and was looking down at the wood between his fingers. "A squirrel in these parts is called a tree kitten," it occurred to him, "but just let somebody try to talk about a tree cat with a straight face! Everyone would prick up their ears as if a real shot had gone off among the farting sound of blanks on maneuvers. In Hesse, on the other hand, it's called a tree fox. Any man who's traveled around knows such things."

But oh, how curious the psychiatrists got when they showed him a picture of a squirrel and he said: "That's a fox, I guess, or it could be a hare, or maybe a cat or something." They'd always shoot a question right back at him then: "How much is fourteen plus fourteen?" and he would say in his deliberate way, "Oh, about twenty-eight to forty." This "about" gave them trouble, which made Moosbrugger grin. It was really so simple. He knew perfectly well that you get twenty-eight when you go on from fourteen to another fourteen; but who says you have to stop there? Moosbrugger's gaze would always range a little farther ahead, like that of a man who has reached the top of a ridge outlined against the sky and finds that behind it there are other, similar ridges. And if a tree kitten is no cat and no fox, and has teeth like a hare's, and the fox eats the hare, you don't have to be so particular about what you call it; you just know it's somehow sewn together out of all those things and goes scampering over the trees. Moosbrugger's experience and conviction were that no thing could be singled out by itself, because things hang together. It had happened that he said to a girl, "Your sweet rose lips," but suddenly the words gave way at their seams and something upsetting happened: her face went gray, like earth veiled in a mist, there was a rose sticking out of it on a long stem, and the temptation to take a knife and cut it off, or punch it back into the face, was overwhelming. Of course, Moosbrugger did not always go for his knife; he only did that when he couldn't get rid of the temptation any other way. Usually he used all his enormous strength to hold the world together.

In a good mood, he could look a man in the face and see in it his own face, as it might gaze back at him from among the minnows and bright pebbles of a shallow stream; in a bad mood, he could tell by a fleeting glance at a man's face that here was the same man who always gave him trouble, everywhere, no matter how differently he disguised himself each time. How can anyone object to this? We all have trouble with the same man almost every time. If we were to investigate who the people are we get so idiotically fixated on, it is bound to turn out to be the one with the lock to which we have the key. And in love? How many people look at the same beloved face day in, day out, yet when they shut their eyes can't say what it looks like? Or even aside from love and hate; how incessantly things are subject to change, depending on habit, mood, point of view! How often joy burns out and an indestructible core of sadness emerges! How often a man calmly beats up another, whom he might as easily leave in peace. Life forms a surface that acts as if it could not be otherwise, but under its skin things are pounding and pulsing. Moosbrugger always kept his legs solidly planted on real earth, holding them together, sensibly trying to avoid whatever might confuse him. But sometimes a word burst in his mouth, and what a revolution, what a dream of things then welled up out of such a cold, burned-out double word as tree kitten or rose lips!

Sitting on that plank in his cell that was both his bed and his table, he deplored his education, which had not taught him to express himself properly. The little creature with her mouse eyes who was still making so much trouble for him, even though she'd been underground for some time, made him angry. They were all on her side. He lumbered to his feet. He felt fragile, like charred wood. He was hungry again; the prison fare fell far short of satisfying a huge man like him, and he had no money for better. In such a state it was impossible for him to think of everything they wanted to know. One of these changes had come on, for days and weeks, the way March comes, or April, and then this business had happened. He knew nothing more about it than the police already had in their files; he didn't even know how it had got into their files. The reasons, the considerations he could remember, he had already stated in court anyway. But what had really happened seemed to him as if he had suddenly said fluently in a foreign language something that made him feel good but that he could no longer repeat.

"I just want it over and done with as soon as possible!" Moosbrugger thought.

60

EXCURSION INTO THE REALM OF LOGIC
AND MORALS

Legally, Moosbrugger's case could be summed up in a sentence. He was one of those borderline cases in law and forensic medicine known even to the layman as a case of diminished responsibility.

These unfortunates typically suffer not only substandard health but also have a substandard disease. Nature has a peculiar preference for producing such people in droves. *Natura non fecit saltus,* she makes no jumps but prefers gradual transitions; even on the grand scale she keeps the world in a transitional state between imbecility and sanity. But the law takes no notice of this. It says: *Non datur tertium sive medium inter duo contradictoria,* or in plain language, a person is either capable or not capable of breaking the law; between two contraries there is no third or middle state. It is this ability to choose that makes a person liable to punishment. His liability to punishment makes him legally a person, and as a person in the legal sense he shares in the suprapersonal benefaction of the law. Anyone who cannot grasp this right away should think of the cavalry. A horse that goes berserk every time someone attempts to mount it is treated with special care, given the softest bandages, the best riders, the choicest fodder, and the most patient handling. But if a cavalryman is guilty of some lapse, he is put in irons, locked in a flea-ridden cage, and deprived of his rations. The reasoning behind this difference is that the horse belongs merely to the empirical animal kingdom, while the dragoon belongs to the logical and moral kingdom. So understood, a person is distinguished from the animals—and, one may add, from the insane—in that he is capable, according to his intellectual and moral faculties, of acting against the law and of committing a crime. Since a person's liability to punishment is the quality that elevates him to the status of a moral being in the first place, it is understandable that the pillars of the law grimly hang on to it.

There is also the unfortunate complication that court psychiatrists, who would be called upon to oppose this situation, are usually far more timid professionally than the jurists. They certify as really insane only those persons they cannot cure—which is a modest exaggeration, since they cannot cure the others either. They distinguish between incurable mental diseases, the kind that with God's help will improve after a while of their own accord, and the kind that the doctor cannot cure either but that the patient could have avoided, assuming of course that the right influences and considerations had providentially been brought to bear on him in time. These second and third groups supply those lesser patients whom the angel of medicine treats as sick people when they come to him in his private practice, but whom he shyly leaves to the angel of law when he encounters them in his forensic practice.

Such a case was Moosbrugger. In the course of his life, respectable enough except when interrupted by those unaccountable fits of bloodthirstiness, he had as often been confined in mental institutions as he had been let go, and had been variously diagnosed as a paralytic, paranoiac, epileptic, and manic-depressive psychotic, until at his recent trial two particularly conscientious forensic psychiatrists had restored his sanity to him. Of course, there was not a single person in that vast crowded courtroom, the doctors included, who was not convinced that Moosbrugger was insane, one way or another; but it was not a way that corresponded to the conditions of insanity laid down by the law, so this insanity could not be acknowledged by conscientious minds. For if one is partly insane, one is also, juridically, partly sane, and if one is partly sane one is at least partly responsible for one's actions, and if one is partly responsible one is wholly responsible; for responsibility is, as they say, that state in which the individual has the power to devote himself to a specific purpose of his own free will, independently of any compelling necessity, and one cannot simultaneously possess and lack such self-determination.

Not that this excludes the existence of persons whose circumstances and predispositions make it hard for them to "resist immoral impulses" and "opt for the good," as the lawyers put it, and Moosbrugger was such a person, in whom circumstances that would have no effect at all on others were enough to trigger the "intent" to commit an offense. First, however, his powers of reasoning and judgment were sufficiently intact, in the view of the court, so that an effort on his part could just as well have left the crime uncommitted, and there was no reason to exclude him from the moral estate of responsibility. Second, a well-ordered judicial system demands that every culpable act that is wittingly and willingly performed be punished. And third, judicial logic assumes that in all insane persons—with the exception of the most unfortunate, who when asked to multiply 7 times 7 stick out their tongue, or answer "Me" when asked to name His Imperial and Royal Majesty—there is still present a minimal power of discrimination and self-control and that it would only have taken a special effort of intelligence and willpower to recognize the criminal nature of the deed and to resist the criminal impulses. It is surely the least one has a right to expect from such dangerous persons!

Law courts resemble wine cellars in which the wisdom of our forefathers lies in bottles. One opens them and could weep at how unpalatable the highest, most effervescent, degree of the human striving for precision can be before it reaches perfection. And yet it seems to intoxicate the insufficiently seasoned mind. It is a well-known phenomenon that the angel of medicine, if he has listened too long to lawyers' arguments, too often forgets his own mission. He then folds his wings with a clatter and conducts himself in court like a reserve angel of law.

61

THE IDEAL OF THE THREE TREATISES, OR THE UTOPIA OF EXACT LIVING

This is how Moosbrugger had come by his death sentence. It was only thanks to the influence of Count Leinsdorf and His Grace's friendship for Ulrich that there was now a chance to review Moosbrugger's mental condition one more time. Ulrich actually had no intention of taking any further interest in Moosbrugger's fate, then or later. The depressing mixture of brutality and suffering that is the

nature of such people was as distasteful to him as the blend of precision and sloppiness that characterized the judgments usually pronounced upon them. He knew precisely what he had to think of
Moosbrugger, if he took a sober view of the case, and what measures
one might try with such people who belong neither in prison nor in
freedom and for whom the mental hospitals were not the answer either. He also realized that thousands of other people knew this, too,
and were constantly discussing every such problem from the aspects
that each of them was interested in; he also knew that the state would
eventually kill Moosbrugger because in the present state of incompleteness this was simply the cleanest, cheapest, and safest solution.
It may be callous to resign oneself to this; but then, our speeding
traffic claims more victims than all the tigers of India, yet the ruthless, unscrupulous, and casual state of mind in which we put up with
it is what also enables us to achieve our undeniable successes.

This state of mind, so perceptive in detail and so blind to the total
picture, finds its most telling expression in a certain ideal that might
be called the ideal of a life's work and that consists of no more than
three treatises. There are intellectual activities where it is not the big
books but the short monographs or articles that constitute a man's
proud achievement. If someone were to discover, for instance, that
under hitherto unobserved circumstances stones were able to speak,
it would take only a few pages to describe and explain so earth-shat-
tering a phenomenon. On the other hand, one can always write yet
another book about positive thinking, and this is far from being of
only academic interest, since it involves a method that makes it impossible ever to arrive at a clear resolution of life's most important
questions. Human activities might be graded by the quantity of
words required: the more words, the worse their character. All the
knowledge that has led our species from wearing animal skins to people flying, complete with proofs, would fill a handful of reference
books, but a bookcase the size of the earth would not suffice to hold
all the rest, quite apart from the vast discussions that are conducted
not with the pen but with the sword and chains. The thought suggests itself that we carry on our human business in a most irrational
manner when we do not use those methods by which the exact
sciences have forged ahead in such exemplary fashion.

Such had in fact been the mood and the tendency of a period—a number of years, hardly of decades—of which Ulrich was just old enough to have known something. At that time people were thinking—"people" is a deliberately vague way of putting it, as no one could say who and how many thought that way; let us say it was in the air—that perhaps life could be lived with precision. Today one wonders what they could have meant by that. The answer would possibly be that a life's work can as easily be imagined as consisting of three poems or three actions as of three treatises, in which the individual's capacity for achievement is intensified to its highest degree. It would more or less come down to keeping silent when one has nothing to say, doing only the necessary where one has nothing special to do, and, most important, remaining indifferent unless one has that ineffable sense of spreading one's arms wide, borne aloft on a wave of creation. One will observe that this would be the end of most of our inner life, but that might not be such a painful loss. The thesis that the huge quantities of soap sold testify to our great cleanliness need not apply to the moral life, where the more recent principle seems more accurate, that a strong compulsion to wash suggests a dubious state of inner hygiene. It would be a useful experiment to try to cut down to the minimum the moral expenditure (of whatever kind) that accompanies all our actions, to satisfy ourselves with being moral only in those exceptional cases where it really counts, but otherwise not to think differently from the way we do about standardizing pencils or screws. Perhaps not much good would be done that way, but some things would be done better; there would be no talent left, only genius; the washed-out prints that develop from the pallid resemblance of actions to virtues would disappear from the image of life; in their place we would have these virtues' intoxicating fusion in holiness. In short, from every ton of morality a milligram of an essence would be left over, a millionth part of which is enough to yield an enchanting joy.

But the objection will be raised that this is a utopia. Of course it is. Utopias are much the same as possibilities; that a possibility is not a reality means nothing more than that the circumstances in which it is for the moment entangled prevent it from being realized—otherwise it would be only an impossibility. If this possibility is disentangled from its restraints and allowed to develop, a utopia arises. It is like what happens when a scientist observes the change of an element within a compound and draws his conclusions. Utopia is the experiment in which the possible change of an element may be observed, along with the effects of such a change on the compound phenomenon we call life. If the element under observation is precision itself, one isolates it and allows it to develop, considering it as an intellectual habit and way of life, allowed to exert its exemplary influence on everything it touches. The logical outcome of this should be a human being full of the paradoxical interplay of exactitude and indefiniteness. He is incorruptibly, deliberately cold, as required by the temperament of precision; but beyond this quality, everything else in him is indefinite. The stable internal conditions guaranteed by a system of morality have little value for a man whose imagination is geared to change. Ultimately, when the demand for the greatest and most exact fulfillment is transferred from the intellectual realm to that of the passions, it becomes evident—as already indicated—that the passions disappear and that in their place arises something like a primordial fire of goodness.

Such is the utopia of precision. One doesn't know how such a man will spend the day, since he cannot continually be poised in the act of creation and will have sacrificed the domestic hearth fire of limited sensations to some imaginary conflagration. But this man of precision exists already! He is the inner man who inhabits not only the scientist but the businessman, the administrator, the sportsman, and the technician, though for the present only during those daytime hours they call not their life but their profession. This man, given to taking everything seriously and without bias, is biased to the point of abhorrence against the idea of taking himself seriously, and there is, alas, no doubt that he would regard the utopia of himself as an immoral experiment on persons engaged in serious business.

Which is why Ulrich, in his concern with the question of whether everything else should be subordinated to the most powerful forms of inner achievement—in other words, whether a goal and a meaning can be found for what is happening and has happened to us—had always, all his life, been quite alone.

62

THE EARTH TOO, BUT ESPECIALLY ULRICH, PAYS HOMAGE TO THE UTOPIA OF ESSAYISM

Precision, as a human attitude, demands precise action and precise being. It makes maximal demands on the doer and on life. But here a distinction must be made.

In reality, as we all know, there is not only an imaginary precision (not yet present in reality at all) but also a pedantic kind, the difference being that the imaginary kind sticks to the facts and the pedantic kind to imaginary constructs. The precision, for instance, with which Moosbrugger's peculiar mentality was fitted into a two-thousand-year-old system of legal concepts resembled a madman's pedantic insistence on trying to spear a free-flying bird with a pin; this precision was concerned not at all with the facts but only with the imaginary concept of cumulative law. But with respect to the big question of whether Moosbrugger could be legally condemned to death, the psychiatrists were absolutely precise: they did not dare say more than that Moosbrugger's clinical picture did not exactly correspond to any hitherto observed syndrome, and left any further conclusions entirely to the jurists.

The courtroom on that occasion offered an image of life itself, in that all those energetic up-to-the-minute characters who wouldn't dream of driving a car more than five years old, or letting a disease be treated by methods that had been the best ten years ago, and who further give all their time, willy-nilly, to promoting the latest inventions and fervently believe in rationalizing everything in their domain . . . these people nevertheless abandon questions of beauty, justice, love, and faith—that is, all the questions of humanity—as long as their business interests are not involved, preferably to their wives or, where their wives are not quite up to it, to a subspecies of men given to intoning thousand-year-old phrases about the chalice and sword of life, to whom they listen casually, irritably, and skeptically, without believing any of it but also without considering the possibility that it might be done some other way. Thus there are really two kinds of outlook, which not only conflict with each other but, which is worse, usually coexist side by side in total noncommunication except to assure each other that they are both needed, each in its place. The one is satisfied to be precise and stick to the facts, while the other is not, but always looks at the whole picture and derives its insights from so-called great and eternal truths. The first achieves success, the other scope and prestige. Clearly, a pessimist could say that the results in the first case are worth nothing and in the second case are not true. For what use will it be on the Day of Judgment, when all human achievements are weighed, to offer up three articles on formic acid, or even thirty? On the other hand, what do we know of the Day of Judgment if we do not even know what may have become of formic acid by then?

It was between these two poles of Neither and Nor that the pendulum of evolution was swinging when mankind first learned, more than eighteen but not quite twenty centuries ago, that there would be such a spiritual court at the end of the world. It corresponds to the experience that a swing in one direction is always followed by a swing in the opposite direction. And while it might be conceivable and desirable for such a revolution to proceed as a spiral, which climbs higher with every change of direction, for unknown reasons evolution seldom gains more than it loses through detours and destruction. So Dr. Paul Arnheim was quite right when he told Ulrich that world history never allows the negative to prevail; world history is optimistic, it always decides enthusiastically for the one, and only afterward for its opposite! And so, too, the pioneer dreams of precision were followed by no attempt whatever to realize them but were abandoned to the unwinged uses of engineers and scientists, while everyone else reverted to a more worthy and far-reaching frame of mind.

Ulrich could still remember quite well how uncertainty had made its comeback. Complaints were heard in ever greater number from people who followed a somewhat uncertain calling—writers, critics, women, and those practicing the profession of being the new generation—all protesting that pure knowledge tore apart every sublime achievement of mankind without ever being able to put it back together, and they demanded a new humane faith, a return to inner primal values, a spiritual revival, and all sorts of things of that kind. At first Ulrich had naïvely assumed that the outcries came from hard-riding people who had dismounted, limping, screaming to have their sores rubbed with soul; but he gradually realized that these repetitive calls for a new dispensation, which had struck him as so comical at first, were being echoed far and wide. Science had begun to be outdated, and the unfocused type of person that dominates the present had begun to assert itself.

Ulrich had refused to take this seriously and went on developing his intellectual bent in his own way.

From the earliest youthful stirrings of self-confidence, which are often so touching, even moving, to look back upon in later years, all sorts of once-cherished notions lingered in his memory even now, among them the expression "living hypothetically." It still expressed the courage and the inescapable ignorance of life that makes every step an act of daring without experience; it showed the desire for grand connections and the aura of revocability a young man feels as he hesitantly ventures into life. Ulrich felt that none of this really needed to be taken back. A thrilling sense of having been chosen for something is the best and the only certain thing in one whose glance surveys the world for the first time. If he monitors his feelings, he finds nothing he can accept without reservation. He seeks a possible beloved but can't tell whether it's the right one; he is capable of killing without being sure that he will have to. The drive of his own nature to keep developing prevents him from believing that anything is final and complete, yet everything he encounters behaves as though it were final and complete. He suspects that the given order of things is not as solid as it pretends to be; no thing, no self, no form, no principle, is safe, everything is undergoing an invisible but ceaseless transformation, the unsettled holds more of the future than the settled, and the present is nothing but a hypothesis that has not yet been surmounted. What better can he do than hold himself apart from the world, in the good sense exemplified by the scientist's guarded attitude toward facts that might be tempting him to premature conclusions? Hence he hesitates in trying to make something of himself; a character, a profession, a fixed mode of being, are for him concepts that already shadow forth the outlines of the skeleton, which is all that will be left of him in the end. He seeks to understand himself differently, as someone inclined and open to everything that may enrich him inwardly, even if it should be morally or intellectually taboo; he feels like a stride, free to move in any direction, from equilibrium to equilibrium, but always forward. And when he sometimes thinks he has found the right idea, he perceives that a drop of indescribable incandescence has fallen into the world, with a glow that makes the whole earth look different.

Later, when Ulrich's intellectual capacity was more highly developed, this became an idea no longer connected with the vague word "hypothesis" but with a concept he oddly termed, for certain reasons, "essay." It was more or less in the way an essay, in the sequence of its paragraphs, explores a thing from many sides without wholly encompassing it—for a thing wholly encompassed suddenly loses its scope and melts down to a concept—that he believed he could most rightly survey and handle the world and his own life. The value of an action or a quality, and indeed its meaning and nature, seemed to him to depend on its surrounding circumstances, on the aims it served; in short, on the whole—constituted now one way, now another—to which it belonged. This is only a simple description of the fact that a murder can appear to us as a crime or a heroic act, and making love as a feather that has fallen from the wing of an angel or that of a goose. But Ulrich generalized this: all moral events take place in a field of energy whose constellation charges them with meaning. They contain good and evil the way an atom contains the possibilities of certain chemical combinations. They are what they will become, so to speak; and just as the word "hard" denotes four entirely different essences, depending on whether it is connected with love, brutality, zeal, or discipline, the significance of all moral events seemed to him to be the function of other events on which they depended. In this way an open-ended system of relationships arises, in which independent meanings, such as are ascribed to actions and qualities by way of a rough first approximation in ordinary life, no longer exist at all. What is seemingly solid in this system becomes a porous pretext for many possible meanings; the event occurring becomes a symbol of something that perhaps may not be happening but makes itself felt through the symbol; and man as the quintessence of his possibilities, potential man, the unwritten poem of his existence, confronts man as recorded fact, as reality, as character. Accordingly, Ulrich felt that he was basically capable of every virtue and every baseness; the fact that in a balanced social order virtues as well as vices are tacitly regarded as equally burdensome attested for him to what happens in nature generally, that every play of forces tends in time toward an average value and average condition, toward compromise and inertia. Ulrich regarded morality as it is commonly understood as nothing more than the senile form of a system of energies that cannot be confused with what it originally was without losing ethical force.

It is possible that these views also reflected some uncertainty about life, but uncertainty is sometimes nothing more than mistrust of the usual certainties, and anyway, it is good to remember that even so experienced a person as mankind itself seems to act on quite similar principles. In the long run it revokes everything it has done, to replace it with something else; what it used to regard as a crime it regards as a virtue, and vice versa; it builds up impressive frameworks of meaningful connections among events, only to allow them to collapse after a few generations. However, all this happens in succession instead of as a single, homogeneous experience, and the chain of mankind's experiments shows no upward trend. By contrast, a conscious human essayism would face the task of transforming the world's haphazard awareness into a will. And many individual lines of development indicate that this could indeed happen soon. The hospital aide clothed in lily-white, who, with the help of acids, thins out a patient's stool in a white china dish in order to obtain a purple smear, rubbing it until the right hue rewards her attention, is already living, whether she knows it or not, in a world more open to change than is the young lady who shudders at the sight of the same stuff in the street. The criminal, caught up in the moral magnetic field of his act, can only move like a swimmer who has to go with the current that sweeps him along, as every mother knows whose child has ever suffered this fate, though no one would believe her, because there was no place for such a belief. Psychiatry calls great elation "a hypomanic disturbance," which is like calling it a hilarious distress, and regards all heightened states, whether of chastity or sensuality, scrupulosity or carelessness, cruelty or compassion, as pathologically suspect— how little would a healthy life mean if its only goal were a middle condition between two extremes! How drab it would be if its ideal were really no more than the denial of the exaggeration of its ideals! To recognize this is to see the moral norm no longer as a set of rigid commandments but rather as a mobile equilibrium that at every moment requires continual efforts at renewal. We are beginning to regard as too limiting the tendency to ascribe involuntarily acquired habits of repetitiveness to a man as his character, and then to make his character responsible for the repetitions. We are learning to recognize the interplay between inner and outer, and it is precisely our understanding of the impersonal elements in man that has given us new clues to the personal ones, to certain simple patterns of behavior, to an ego-building instinct that, like the nest-building instinct of birds, uses a few techniques to build an ego out of many various materials. We are already so close to knowing how to use certain influences to contain all sorts of pathological conditions, as we can a wild mountain stream, and it will soon be a mere lapse of social responsibility or a lingering clumsiness if we fail to transform criminals into archangels at the right time. And there is so much more one could add, scattered manifestations of things that have not yet coalesced to act together, the general effect of which is to make us tired of the crude approximations of simpler times, gradually to make us experience the necessity of altering the basic forms and foundations of a moral order that over two thousand years has adjusted only piecemeal to evolving tastes and exchanging it for a new morality capable of fitting more closely the mobility of facts.

Ulrich was convinced that the only thing missing was the right formula, the expression that the goal of a movement must find in some happy moment before it is achieved, in order that the last lap can be accomplished. Such an expression is always risky, not yet justified by the prevailing state of affairs, a combination of exact and inexact, of precision and passion. But it was in just those years that should have spurred him on that something peculiar happened to Ulrich. He was no philosopher. Philosophers are despots who have no armies to command, so they subject the world to their tyranny by locking it up in a system of thought. This apparently also accounts for the presence of great philosophers in times of great tyrants, while epochs of progressive civilization and democracy fail to bring forth a convincing philosophy, at least to judge by the disappointment one hears so widely expressed on the subject. Hence today we have a terrifying amount of philosophizing in brief bursts, so that shops are the only places where one can still get something without Weltanschauung, while philosophy in large chunks is viewed with decided mistrust. It is simply regarded as impossible, and even Ulrich was by no means innocent of this prejudice; indeed, in the light of his scientific background, he took a somewhat ironic view of philosophy. This put him in a position where he was always being provoked to think about what he was observing, and yet at the same time was burdened with a certain shyness about thinking too hard.

But what finally determined his attitude was still another factor. There was something in Ulrich's nature that in a haphazard, paralyzing, disarming way resisted all logical systematizing, the single-minded will, the specifically directed drives of ambition; it was also connected with his chosen term, "essayism," even though it contained the very elements he had gradually and with unconscious care eliminated from that concept. The accepted translation of "essay" as "attempt" contains only vaguely the essential allusion to the literary model, for an essay is not a provisional or incidental expression of a conviction capable of being elevated to a truth under more favorable circumstances or of being exposed as an error (the only ones of that kind are those articles or treatises, chips from the scholar's workbench, with which the learned entertain their special public); an essay is rather the unique and unalterable form assumed by a man's inner life in a decisive thought. Nothing is more foreign to it than the irresponsible and half-baked quality of thought known as subjectivism. Terms like true and false, wise and unwise, are equally inapplicable, and yet the essay is subject to laws that are no less strict for appearing to be delicate and ineffable. There have been more than a few such essayists, masters of the inner hovering life, but there would be no point in naming them. Their domain lies between religion and knowledge, between example and doctrine, between *amor intellectualis* and poetry; they are saints with and without religion, and sometimes they are also simply men on an adventure who have gone astray.

Nothing is more revealing, by the way, than one's involuntary experience of learned and sensible efforts to interpret such essayists, to turn their living wisdom into knowledge to live by and thus extract some "content" from the motion of those who were moved: but about as much remains of this as of the delicately opalescent body of a jellyfish when one lifts it out of the water and lays it on the sand. The rationality of the uninspired will make the teachings of the inspired crumble into dust, contradiction, and nonsense, and yet one has no right to call them frail and unviable unless one would also call an elephant too frail to survive in an airless environment unsuited to its needs. It would be regrettable if these descriptions were to evoke an impression of mystery, or of a kind of music in which harp notes and sighing glissandi predominate. The opposite is the case, and the underlying problem presented itself to Ulrich not at all intuitively but quite soberly, in the following form: A man who wants the truth becomes a scholar; a man who wants to give free play to his subjectivity may become a writer; but what should a man do who wants something in between? Examples of what lies in between can be found in every moral precept, such as the well-known and simple: Thou shalt not kill. One sees right off that that is neither a fact nor a subjective experience. We know that we adhere to it strictly in some respects, while allowing for a great many, if sharply defined, exceptions; but in a very large number of cases of a third kind, involving imagination, desires, drama, or the enjoyment of a news story, we vacillate erratically between aversion and attraction. What we cannot classify as either a fact or a subjective experience we sometimes call an imperative. We have attached such imperatives to the dogmas of religion and the law and thereby give them the status of deduced truth. But the novelists tell us about the exceptions, from Abraham's sacrifice of Isaac to the most recent beauty who shot her lover, and dissolve it again into something subjective. We can cling to one of these poles or let ourselves be swept back and forth between them by the tide—but with what feelings? The feeling of most people for this precept is a mixture of wooden obedience (including that of the "wholesome type" that flinches from even thinking of such a thing but, only slightly disoriented by alcohol or passion, promptly does it) and a mindless paddling about in a wave of possibilities. Is there really no other approach to this precept? Ulrich felt that as things stood, a man longing to do something with all his heart does not know whether he should do it or leave it undone. And yet he suspected that it could be done, or not done, wholeheartedly. In themselves, an impulse to act and a taboo were equally meaningless to him. Linking them to a law from above or within aroused his critical intelligence; more than that, the need to ennoble a self-sufficient moment by giving it a noble pedigree diminished its value. All this left his heart silent, while only his head spoke; but he felt that there might be another way to make his choice coincide with his happiness. He might be happy because he didn't kill, or happy because he killed, but he could never be the indifferent fulfiller of an imperative demanded of him. What he felt at this moment was not a commandment; it was a region he had entered. Here, he realized, everything was already decided, and soothed the mind like mother's milk. But what gave him this insight was no longer thinking, nor was it feeling in the usual incoherent way: it was a "total insight" and yet again only a message carried to him from far away by the wind, and it seemed to him neither true nor false, neither rational nor irrational; it seized him like a faint, blissful hyperbole dropped into his heart.

And as little as one can make a truth out of the genuine elements of an essay can one gain a conviction from such a condition—at least not without abandoning the condition, as a lover has to abandon love in order to describe it. The boundless emotion that sometimes stirred Ulrich without activating him contradicted his urge to act, which insisted on limits and forms. Now, it may be only right and natural to want to *know* before letting one's feelings speak; he involuntarily imagined that what he wanted to find and someday would, even if it should not be truth, would be no less firm than truth. But in his special case, this made him rather like a man busily getting equipment together while losing interest in what it is meant for. If someone had asked him at any point while he was writing treatises on mathematical problems or mathematical logic, or engaged in some scientific project, what it was he hoped to achieve, he would have answered that there was only one question worth thinking about, the question of the right way to live. But if one holds up an imperative for a long time without anything happening, the brain goes to sleep, just as the arm does that has held something up for too long; our thoughts cannot be expected to stand at attention indefinitely any more than soldiers on parade in summer; standing too long, they will simply fall down in a faint. As Ulrich had settled on his view of life around his twenty-sixth year, it no longer seemed quite genuine in his thirty-second. He had not elaborated his ideas any further, and apart from a vague, tense feeling such as one has when waiting for something with one's eyes closed, there was not much sign of personal emotion in him, since the days of his tremulous earliest revelations had gone. Yet it was probably an underground movement of this kind that gradually slowed him down in his scientific work and kept him from giving it all he had. This generated a curious conflict in him. One must not forget that basically the scientific cast of mind is more God-oriented than the aesthetic mind, ready to submit to "Him" the moment "He" deigns to show Himself under the conditions it prescribes for recognizing Him, while our aesthetes, confronted with His manifestation, would find only that His talent was not original and that His view of the world was not sufficiently intelligible to rank Him with really God-given talents. Ulrich could not abandon himself to vague intimations as readily as anyone of that species could, but neither could he conceal from himself that in all those years of scientific scrupulosity he had merely been living against his grain. He wished something unforeseen would happen to him, for when he took what he somewhat wryly called his "holiday from life" he had nothing, in one direction or the other, that gave him peace.

Perhaps one could say on his behalf that at a certain age life begins to run away with incredible speed. But the day when one must begin to live out one's final will, before leaving the rest behind, lies far ahead and cannot be postponed. This had become menacingly clear to him now that almost six months had gone by and nothing had changed. He was waiting: all the time, he was letting himself be pushed this way and that in the insignificant and silly activity he had taken on, talking, gladly talking too much, living with the desperate tenacity of a fisherman casting his nets into an empty river, while he was doing nothing that had anything to do with the person he after all signified; deliberately doing nothing: he was waiting. He waited hiding behind his person, insofar as this word characterizes that part of a human being formed by the world and the course of life, and his quiet desperation, dammed up behind that façade, rose higher every day. He felt himself to be in the worst crisis of his life and despised himself for what he had left undone. Are great ordeals the privilege of great human beings? He would have liked to believe it, but it isn't so, since even the dullest neurotics have their crises. So all he really had left in the midst of his deep perturbation was that residue of imperturbability possessed by all heroes and criminals—it isn't courage, willpower, or confidence, but simply a furious tenacity, as hard to drive out as it is to drive life out of a cat even after it has been completely mangled by dogs.

If one wants to imagine how such a man lives when he is alone, the most that can be said is that at night his lighted windows afford a view of his room, where his used thoughts sit around like clients in the waiting room of a lawyer with whom they are dissatisfied. Or one could perhaps say that Ulrich once, on such a night, opened the window and looked out at the snake-smooth trunks of the trees, so black and sleekly twisted between the blankets of snow covering their tops and the ground, and suddenly felt an urge to go down into the garden just as he was, in his pajamas; he wanted to feel the cold in his hair. Downstairs he turned out the light, so as not to stand framed in the lighted doorway; a canopy of light projected into the shadow only from his study. A path led to the iron gate fronting the street; a second crossed it, darkly outlined. Ulrich walked slowly toward it. And then the darkness towering up between the treetops suddenly, fantastically, reminded him of the huge form of Moosbrugger, and the naked trees looked strangely corporeal, ugly and wet like worms and yet somehow inviting him to embrace them and sink down with them in tears. But he didn't do it. The sentimentality of the impulse revolted him at the very moment it touched him. Just then some late passersby walked through the milky foam of the mist outside the garden railing, and he may have looked like a lunatic to them, as his figure in red pajamas between black tree trunks now detached itself from the trees. But he stepped firmly onto the path and went back into his house fairly content, feeling that whatever was in store for him would have to be something quite different.

63

BONADEA HAS A VISION

When Ulrich got up on the morning following this night, late and feeling as if he had been badly beaten up, he was told that Bonadea had come to call; it was the first time since their quarrel that they would see each other.

During the period of their separation, Bonadea had shed many tears. She often felt in this time that she had been ill-treated. She had often resounded like a muffled drum. She had had many adventures and many disappointments. And although the memory of Ulrich sank into a deep well with every adventure, after every disappointment it emerged again, helpless and reproachful as the desolate pain in a child's face. In her heart, Bonadea had already asked her friend a hundred times to forgive her jealousy, "castigating her wicked pride," as she put it, until at last she decided to sue for peace.

She sat before him, charming, melancholy, and beautiful, and feeling sick to her stomach. He stood in front of her "like a youth," his skin polished like marble from the great events and high diplomacy she believed him engaged in. She had never before noticed how strong and determined his face looked. She would gladly have surrendered herself to him entirely, but she dared not go so far, and he showed no disposition to encourage her. This coldness saddened her beyond words, but had the grandeur of a statue. Unexpectedly, Bonadea seized his dangling hand and kissed it. Ulrich stroked her hair pensively. Her legs turned to water in the most feminine way in the world, and she was about to fall to her knees. But Ulrich gently pushed her back in her chair, brought whiskey and soda, and lit a cigarette.

"A lady does not drink whiskey in the morning!" Bonadea protested. For an instant she regained enough energy to be offended, and her heart rose to her head with the suspicion that the matter-of-fact offer of such a strong and, as she thought, licentious drink contained a heartless implication.

But Ulrich said kindly: "It will do you good. All the women who have played a major role in politics have drunk whiskey." For in order to justify her visit, Bonadea had said how impressed she was with the great patriotic campaign, and that she would like to lend a hand in it.

That was her plan. She always believed several things at the same time, and half-truths made it easier for her to lie.

The whiskey was pale gold and warming like the sun in May.

Bonadea felt like a seventy-year-old woman sitting on a garden bench outside her house. She was getting old. Her children were growing up. The eldest was already twelve. It was certainly disgraceful to follow a man one didn't even know very well into his house, just because he had eyes that looked at one like a man behind a window. One notices, she thought, little details about this man one doesn't like and that could be a warning. One could, in fact—if only there were something to hold one back at such times!—break it off, flushed with shame and perhaps even flaming with anger; but because this doesn't happen, this man grows more and more passionately into his role. And one feels oneself very clearly like a stage set in the glare of artificial light; what one has before one is stage eyes, a stage mustache, the buttons of a costume being unbuttoned, and the whole scene from the first entrance into the room to the first horrible moment of being sober again all takes place inside a consciousness that has stepped outside one's head and papered the walls with pure hallucination. Bonadea did not use precisely these words—her thought was only partly verbal anyway—but even as she was trying to visualize it she felt herself at the mercy of this change in consciousness. "Whoever could describe it would be a great artist—no, a pornographer!" she thought, looking at Ulrich. She never for an instant lost her good intentions, her determination to hold on to decency, even in this condition; only then they stood outside and waited but had absolutely nothing to say in a world transformed by desire. When Bonadea's reason returned, this was her worst anguish. The change of consciousness during sexual arousal, which people pass over as something natural, was in her so overpowering in the depth and suddenness not only of her ecstasy but also of her remorse that it frightened her in retrospect as soon as she had returned to the peace of her family circle. She thought she must be going mad. She hardly dared look at her children, for fear of harming them with her corrupt glance. And she winced whenever her husband looked at her with more than his usual warmth, but was afraid of freedom from constraint in being alone. All this led her, in the weeks of separation, to plan that henceforth she would have no other lover beside Ulrich; he would be her mainstay and would save her from excesses with strangers.

"How could I have allowed myself to find fault with him?" she now thought as she sat facing him for the first time in so long. "He is so much more complete than I am." She gave him credit for her having been a much improved person during their embraces, and was probably also thinking that he would have to introduce her to his new social circle at the next charity affair. Bonadea inwardly swore an oath of allegiance, and tears of emotion came to her eyes as she turned all this over in her mind.

Ulrich meanwhile was finishing his whiskey with the deliberateness of a man who has to act on a hard decision. For the time being, he told her, it was not yet possible to introduce her to Diotima.

Bonadea naturally wanted to know exactly why it was not possible; and then she wanted to know exactly when it would be possible.

Ulrich had to point out to her that she was not a person of prominence in the arts, nor in the sciences, nor in organized charity, so that it would take a very long time before he could convince Diotima of the need for Bonadea's assistance.

Bonadea had in the meantime been filled with curious feelings toward Diotima. She had heard enough about Diotima's virtues not to be jealous; rather, she envied and admired this woman, who could hold the interest of Bonadea's beloved without making improper concessions to him. She ascribed the statuesque serenity she thought she saw in Ulrich to this influence. Her term for herself was "passionate," by which she understood both her dishonorable state and an honorable excuse for it. But she admired cool women with much the same feeling with which unfortunate owners of perpetually damp hands put their hands in a hand that is particularly dry and lovely. "It is her doing!" she thought. "It is she who has changed Ulrich so much!" A hard drill in her heart, a sweet drill in her knees: these two drills whirring simultaneously and in opposite directions made Bonadea feel almost ready to faint as she came up against Ulrich's resistance. So she played her trump card: Moosbrugger.

She had realized on agonizing reflection that Ulrich must have a strange liking for this horrible character. She herself simply felt revolted by "the brutal sensuality," as she saw it, expressed in Moosbrugger's acts of violence. In this respect her feeling was much the same—though of course she did not know this—as that of the prostitutes who quite single-mindedly, untainted by bourgeois romanticism, see in the sex murderer simply a hazard of their profession. But what she needed, including her unavoidable lapses, was a tidy and credible world, and Moosbrugger would help her to restore it. Since Ulrich had a weakness for him, and she had a husband who was a judge and could supply useful information, the thought had ripened of its own accord in her forlorn state that she might link her weakness to Ulrich's weakness by way of her husband; this yearning image had the comforting power of sensuality sanctioned by a feeling of justice. But when she approached her spouse on the subject, he was astounded at her juridical fervor, although he knew how easily she got carried away by everything great and good in human nature. But since he was not only a judge but a hunter too, he put her off good-humoredly by saying that the only way to deal with such vermin was to exterminate them wherever one came across them without a lot of sentimental fuss, and he did not respond to further inquiries. On her second try, some time later, all Bonadea could get out of him was the supplementary opinion that childbearing was a woman's affair while killing was a job for men, and as she did not want to stir up any suspicions by being overzealous on this dangerous subject she was debarred, for the time being, from the path of the law. This left mercy as the only way of pleasing Ulrich by doing something for Moosbrugger, and this way led her—one can hardly call this a surprise, more a kind of attraction—to Diotima.

In her mind she could see herself as Diotima's friend, and she granted herself her own wish to be forced to make her admired rival's acquaintance for the sake of the cause, which brooked no delay, although of course she was too proud to seek it for herself. She was going to win Diotima over to Moosbrugger's cause—something Ulrich had clearly not succeeded in doing, as she had instantly guessed—and her imagination painted the situation in beautiful scenes. The tall, marmoreal Diotima would put her arm around Bonadea's warm shoulders, bowed down by sins, and Bonadea expected that her own role would more or less be to anoint that divinely untouched heart with a drop of mortal fallibility. This was the stratagem she proposed to her lost friend.

But today Ulrich was impervious to any suggestion of saving Moosbrugger. He knew Bonadea's noble sentiments and knew how easily the flaring up of a single worthy impulse could turn into a raging fire consuming her whole body. He made it clear that he did not have the slightest intention of meddling in the Moosbrugger case.

Bonadea looked up at him with hurt, beautiful eyes in which the water rose above the ice like the borderline between winter and spring.

Ulrich had never entirely lost a certain gratitude for the childlike beauty of their first meeting, that night he lay senseless on the pavement with Bonadea crouching by his head, and the wavering, romantic vagueness of the world, of youth, of emotion, came trickling into his returning consciousness from this young woman's eyes. So he tried to soften his offending refusal, to dissipate it in talk.

"Imagine yourself walking across a big park at night," he suggested, "and two ruffians come at you. Would your first thought be to feel pity for them and that their brutality is society's fault?"

"But I never walk through a park at night," Bonadea promptly parried.

"But suppose a policeman came along: wouldn't you ask him to arrest them?"

"I would ask him to protect me."

"Which means that he would arrest them."

"I don't know what he would do with them. Anyway, Moosbrugger is not a ruffian."

"All right, then, let's assume he is working as a carpenter in your house. You're alone with him in the place, and his eyes start to slither from side to side."

Bonadea protested: "What an awful thing you're making me do!"

"Of course," Ulrich said, "but I'm only trying to show you how extremely unpleasant the kind of people are who lose their balance so easily. One can only indulge in an impartial attitude toward them when someone else takes the beating. In that case, I grant you, as the victims of society or fate they bring out our tenderest feelings. You must admit that no one can be blamed for his faults, as seen through his own eyes; from his point of view they are, at worst, mistakes or bad qualities in a whole person who is no less good because of them, and of course he's perfectly right."

Bonadea had to adjust her stocking and felt compelled as she did so to look up at Ulrich with her head slightly tilted back, so that— unguarded by her eye—a richly contrasting life of lacy frills, smooth stocking, tensed fingers, and the gentle pearly gleam of skin emerged around her knee.

Ulrich hastily lit a cigarette and went on:

"Man is not good, but he is always good; that's a tremendous difference, don't you see? We find a sophistry of self-love amusing, but we ought to conclude from it that a human being can really do no wrong; what is wrong can only be an effect of something he does. This insight could be the right starting point for a social morality."

With a sigh, Bonadea smoothed her skirt back in place, straightened, and sought to calm herself with a sip of the pale golden fire.

"And now let me explain to you," Ulrich went on with a smile, "why it is possible to have all sorts of feeling for Moosbrugger but not to do anything for him. Basically, all these cases are like the loose end of a thread—if you pull at it, the whole fabric of society starts to unravel. I can illustrate this, for a start, by some purely rational problems."

Somehow or other, Bonadea lost a shoe. Ulrich bent down for it, and the foot with its warm toes came up to meet the shoe in his hand like a small child. "Don't bother, don't, I'll do it myself," Bonadea said, holding out her foot to him.

"There are, to begin with, the psychiatric-juridical questions," Ulrich continued relentlessly, even as the whiff of diminished responsibility rose from her leg to his nostrils. "We know that medicine has already practically reached the point of being able to prevent most such crimes if only we were prepared to spend the necessary amounts of money. So now it's only a social question."

"Oh please, not that again!" Bonadea pleaded, now that he had said "social" for the second time. "When they get started on that at home, I leave the room; it bores me to death."

"All right," Ulrich conceded, "I meant to say that just as we already have the technology to make useful things out of corpses, sewage, scrap, and toxins, we almost have the psychological techniques too. But the world is taking its time in solving these questions. The government squanders money on every kind of foolishness but hasn't a penny to spare for solving the most pressing moral problems. That's in its nature, since the state is the stupidest and most malicious person there is."

He spoke with conviction. But Bonadea tried to lead him back to the heart of the matter.

"Dearest," she said longingly, "isn't it the best thing for Moosbrugger that he's not responsible?"

Ulrich fought her off: "It would probably be more important to execute several responsible people than to save one irresponsible person from execution!"

He was now pacing the floor in front of her. Bonadea found him revolutionary and inflaming. She managed to catch his hand, and laid it on her bosom.

"Fine," he said. "I shall now explain to you the emotional questions."

Bonadea opened his fingers and spread his hand over her breast. The accompanying glance would have melted a heart of stone. For the next few moments Ulrich felt as if he had two hearts in his breast, like the confusion of clocks ticking in a watchmaker's shop. Mustering all his willpower, he restored order in his breast and said gently: "No, Bonadea."

Bonadea was now on the brink of tears, and Ulrich spoke to her: "Isn't it contradictory that you get yourself worked up about this one affair just because I happened to tell you about it, whereas you don't even notice the millions of equally unjust things that happen every day?"

"What difference does that make?" Bonadea protested. "The point is, I do happen to know about this one, and I would be a bad person if I stayed calm!"

Ulrich said that one had to keep calm; absolutely, passionately calm, he added. He had repossessed his hand and sat down some distance from Bonadea. "Nowadays everything is done 'meanwhile' and 'for the time being,' " he observed. "It can't be helped. We are driven by the scrupulousness of our reason into an atrocious un-scrupulousness of our hearts." He poured another whiskey for himself, too, and put his feet up on the sofa. He was beginning to feel tired.

"Everyone starts out wanting to understand life as a whole," he said, "but the more accurately one thinks about it, the more it narrows down. When he's mature, a person knows more about one particular square millimeter than all but at most two dozen other people in the world; he knows what nonsense people talk who know less about it, but he doesn't dare move because if he shifts even a micromillimeter from his spot he will be talking nonsense too."

His weariness was now the same transparent gold as his drink on the table. I've been talking nonsense for the last half hour too, he thought. But this diminished state was comfortable enough. The only thing he feared was that it might occur to Bonadea to come and sit down next to him. There was only one way to forestall this: keep talking. He had propped up his head on his hands and lay stretched at full length like the effigies on the tombs in the Medici Chapel. He suddenly became aware of this, and as he assumed his pose he actually felt a certain grandeur flowing through his body, a hovering in their serenity, and he felt more powerful than he was. For the first time he thought he distantly understood these works of art, which he had previously only looked at as foreign objects. Instead of saying anything, he fell silent. Even Bonadea felt something. It was a "moment," as one calls it, that defies characterization. Some dramatic exaltation united the two of them, and left them mute.

"What is left of me?" Ulrich thought bitterly. "Possibly someone who has courage and is not for sale, and likes to think that for the sake of his inner freedom he respects only a few external laws. But this inner freedom consists of being able to think whatever one likes; it means knowing, in every human situation, why one doesn't need to be bound by it, but never knowing what one wants to be bound by!" In this far from happy moment, when the curious little wave of feeling that had held him for an instant ebbed away again, he would have been ready to admit that he had nothing but an ability to see two sides to everything—that moral ambivalence that marked almost all his contemporaries and was the disposition of his generation, or perhaps their fate. His connections to the world had become pale, shadowy, and negative. What right did he have to treat Bonadea badly? It was always the same frustrating talk they had, over and over again; it arose from the inner acoustics of emptiness, where a shot resounds twice as loudly and echoes on and on. It burdened him that he could no longer speak to her except like this. For the special misery this caused them both, he came up with an almost witty, appealing name: Baroque of the Void. He sat up to say something nice to her.

"It just struck me," he said to Bonadea, who had kept her seat and dignified position. "It's a funny thing. A remarkable difference: a person able to be responsible for what he does can always do something different, but a person who isn't *never* can."

Bonadea responded with something quite profound: "Oh, Ulrich!" she said. That was the only interruption, and silence closed around them once more.

When Ulrich spoke in generalities in her presence, she did not like it at all. She felt quite rightly that despite her many lapses, she lived surrounded by people like herself, and she had a sound instinct for the unsociable, eccentric, and solipsistic way he had of treating her with ideas instead of feelings. Still, crime, love, and sadness had linked themselves in her mind, a highly dangerous mixture. Ulrich now seemed to her not nearly as intimidating, as much of a paragon, as he had at the beginning of their meeting; by way of compensation she now saw in him a boyish quality that aroused her idealism, the air of a child not daring to run past some obstacle in order to throw itself into its mother's arms. She had felt for the longest time a free-floating, almost uncontrollable tenderness for him. But after Ulrich had checked her first hint of this, she forced herself with great effort to hold back. The memory of how she had lain undressed and powerless on his sofa on her previous visit still rankled, and she was resolved to sit, if she had to, on that chair in her hat and veil to the very end in order to teach him that he had before him a person who knew how to control herself as much as her rival, Diotima. Bonadea always missed the great idea that was supposed to go along with the great excitement she felt through the nearness of a lover. Unfortunately, this can, of course, be said of life itself, which contains a lot of excitement and little sense, but Bonadea did not know this, and she tried to express some great idea. Ulrich's thoughts lacked the dignity she needed, to her way of thinking, and she was probably searching for something finer, more deeply felt. But refined hesitancy and vulgar attraction, attraction and a terrible dread of being attracted prematurely, all became part of the stimulus of the silence in which the suppressed actions twitched, and mingled, too, with the memory of the great peace that had so united her with her lover for a second. It was, in the end, like when rain hangs in the air but cannot fall; a numbness that spread over her whole skin and terrified her with the idea that she might lose her self-control without noticing it.

Suddenly a physical illusion sprang from all this: a flea. Bonadea could not tell whether it was reality or imagination. She felt a shudder in her brain, a dubious impression as if an idea had detached itself from the shadowy bondage of all the rest but was still only a fantasy—and at the same time she felt an undeniable, quite realistic shudder on her skin. She held her breath. When one hears something coming, pit-a-pat, up the stairs, knowing there is no one there but quite distinctly hearing pit-a-pat—that's how it is. Bonadea realized in a flash that this was an involuntary continuation of the lost shoe. A desperate expedient for a lady. But just as she was trying to banish the spook, she felt a sharp sting. She gave a little shriek, her cheeks flushed a bright red, and she called upon Ulrich to help her look for it. A flea favors the same regions as a lover; her stocking was searched down to the shoe; her blouse had to be unbuttoned in front. Bonadea declared that she must have picked it up in the streetcar or from Ulrich. But it was not to be found, and had left no traces behind.

"I can't imagine what it could have been!" Bonadea said.

Ulrich smiled with unexpected friendliness.

Bonadea burst into tears, like a little girl who has misbehaved.

64

GENERAL STUMM VON BORDWEHR
VISITS DIOTIMA

General Stumm von Bordwehr had paid his first call on Diotima. He was the army officer sent by the War Ministry as their observer to the great inaugural meeting, where he made an impressive speech, which, however, could not prevent the War Ministry from being passed over—for obvious reasons—when the committees for the great peace campaign were set up, one for each ministry.

He was a not very imposing general, with his little paunch and the little toothbrush on his upper lip in place of a real mustache. His face was round and expressed something of the family man with no money beyond the funds for the statutory bond required when an officer wanted to marry. He said to Diotima that a soldier could expect to play only a modest role in the council chamber. Besides, it went without saying that for political reasons the Ministry of War could not be included in the roster of committees. Nevertheless, he dared maintain that the proposed campaign should have an effect abroad, and what had an influence abroad was the might of a people. He repeated the celebrated philosopher Treitschke's observation that the state is the power to survive in the struggle of nations. Power displayed in peace kept war at bay, or at least shortened its cruelty. He went on like this for another quarter of an hour, slipping in classical quotations he fondly remembered from his school days; maintained that those years of humanistic studies had been the happiest of his life; tried to make Diotima feel that he admired her and was delighted with the way she had conducted the great conference; wanted only to repeat once again that, rightly understood, the building up of the armed forces that lagged far behind those of the other great powers could be the most impressive demonstration of peaceful intentions; and for the rest declared his confident expectation that a widespread popular concern for the country's military problems was bound to arise of its own accord.

This amiable general gave Diotima the fright of her life. There were in those days in Kakania families whose houses were frequented socially by army officers because their daughters married army officers, and then there were families whose daughters did not marry army officers, either because there was no money for the mandatory security bond or on principle, so they did not receive army officers socially. Diotima's family had belonged to the second sort for both reasons, with the consequence that this conscientiously beautiful woman had gone out into life with a concept of the military that was something like an image of Death decked out in motley.

She replied that there was so much that was great and good in the world that the choice was not easy. It was a great privilege to be allowed to give a great sign in the midst of the world's materialistic bustle, but also a grave responsibility. And the demonstration was meant, after all, to arise spontaneously from the midst of the people themselves, for which reason she had to keep her own wishes a little in the background. She placed her words with care, as though stitching them together with threads in the national colors, and burned the mild incense of high bureaucratic phraseology upon her lips.

But when the General had left, the sublime woman suffered an inner breakdown. Had she been capable of so vulgar a sentiment as hatred she would have hated the pudgy little man with his waggling eyes and the gold buttons on his belly, but since this was impossible she felt vaguely insulted but could not say why. Despite the wintry cold she opened the windows and paced the room several times, her silks rustling. When she shut the windows again there were tears in her eyes. She was quite amazed. This was now the second time she was weeping without reason. She remembered the night when, in bed at her husband's side, she had shed tears without being able to explain them. This time the purely nervous character of the process, unrelated to any tangible cause, was even more evident; this fat general caused tears to gush from her eyes like an onion, without any sensible feeling being involved. She had good cause to be worried; a shadowy fear told her that a wolf was prowling round her flocks and that it was high time to exorcise it by the power of the Idea. This is how it happened that after the General's visit Diotima made up her mind to organize with the greatest speed the planned gathering of great minds who would help her define the proper content of the patriotic campaign.

65

FROM THE CONVERSATIONS BETWEEN ARNHEIM AND DIOTIMA

It greatly eased Diotima's heart that Arnheim had just returned from a trip and was at her disposal.

"Your cousin and I were talking about generals just a few days ago," he instantly responded, with the air of a man alluding to a suspicious coincidence without wanting to be specific. Diotima received the impression that her contradictory cousin, with his unenthusiastic view of the great campaign, also favored the vague menaces emanating from the General.

"I wouldn't like to expose this to ridicule in the presence of your cousin," Arnheim went on, changing the subject, "but I would like to be able to make you feel something you would hardly come upon by yourself, far away as you are from such things: the connection between business and poetry. Of course, I mean business in the largest sense, the world's business, such as I have been fated to conduct by the position to which I was born; it is related to poetry, it has irrational, even mystical aspects. I might even say that business is quite particularly endowed with those aspects. You see, money is an extraordinarily intolerant power."

"There is probably a certain intolerance in everything people stake their lives on," Diotima said hesitantly, her mind still on the unfinished first part of the conversation.

"Especially with money!" Arnheim quickly said. "Foolish people imagine it's a pleasure to have money. It is in fact a terrible responsibility. I won't speak of the countless lives dependent on me, for whom I represent a sort of fate; let me just mention that my grandfather started by picking up garbage in a middle-sized town in the Rhineland."

At these words Diotima actually felt a sudden shiver of what she thought was economic imperialism, but this was an error; since she was not quite without the prejudice of her social circle, she associated garbage removal with what was called in her regional dialect the dungman, and so her friend's courageous confession made her blush.

"With this refining process for waste," he continued his confession, "my grandfather laid the groundwork for the influence of the Arnheims. But even my father was a self-made man, if you consider that it was he who in forty years expanded the firm into a worldwide concern. Two years at a trade school was all he had, but he can see through the most tangled world affairs at a glance, and knows everything he needs to know before anyone else does. I myself studied economics and every conceivable branch of science, all quite beyond his ken, and no one has any idea how he does it, but he never misses a detail. That is the mystery of a vigorous, simple, great, and healthy life!"

Arnheim's voice, as he spoke of his father, took on a special, reverential tone, as though its magisterial calm had a small crack somewhere. It struck Diotima all the more because Ulrich had told her that old Arnheim was supposed to be a short, broad-shouldered fellow with a bony face and a button nose, who always wore a gaping swallowtail coat and handled his investments with the dogged circumspection of a chess player moving his pawns. Without waiting for her response, Arnheim continued after a brief pause:

"Once a business has expanded to the degree reached only by the very few I speak of, there is hardly anything in life it is not somehow involved with. It is a little cosmos. You would be amazed if you knew what seemingly quite uncommercial problems—artistic, moral, political—I sometimes have to bring up in conferring with my managing director. But the firm is no longer mushrooming the way it did in its early days, which I'd like to call its heroic days. No matter how prosperous a business firm may be, there is a mysterious limit to its growth, as there is with everything organic. Have you ever asked yourself why no animal in our time grows bigger than an elephant? You'll find the same mystery in the history of art and in the strange relationships of the life of peoples, cultures, and epochs."

Diotima was now ashamed of herself for having shrunk from the refining process for waste disposal, and felt confused.

"Life is full of such mysteries. There is something that defies all reason. My father is in league with it. But a man like your cousin,"

Arnheim said, "an activist with a head full of ideas how things could be done differently and better, has no feeling for it."

Diotima responded to this second reference to Ulrich with a smile suggesting that a man like her cousin had no claim to exert any influence on her. Arnheim's even, somewhat sallow skin, which in his face was as smooth as a pear, had flushed over the cheekbones. He had succumbed to a curious urge Diotima had been arousing in him for some time now to let down his guard and confide in her totally, down to the last hidden detail. Now he locked himself up again, picked up a book from the table, read its title without taking it in, impatiently laid it down again, and said in his usual voice—it moved Diotima as deeply at this moment as the gesture of a man who, in gathering up his clothes, reveals that he has been naked—"I have wandered from the point. What I have to say to you about the General is that you could do nothing better than to realize your plan as quickly as possible and raise the level of our campaign with the help of humanistic ideas and their recognized representatives. But there's no need to turn the General away on principle. Personally he may be a man of goodwill, and you know my principle of not missing any opportunity to bring the life of the spirit into a sphere of mere power."

Diotima seized his hand and summed up the conversation in her good-bye: "Thank you for being so frank with me."

Arnheim irresolutely let that gentle hand rest in his own for a moment, staring down at it thoughtfully as though there were something he had forgotten to say.

66

ALL IS NOT WELL BETWEEN ULRICH AND ARNHEIM

Her cousin often took pleasure, at that time, in reporting to Diotima his experiences as His Grace's aide-de-camp, and always made a special point of showing her the files with all the proposals that kept pouring into Count Leinsdorf's office.

"Almighty cousin," he reported, with a fat folder in his hand, "I can no longer handle this alone. The whole world seems to expect improvements from us. Half of them begin with the words 'No more of . . .' and the other half with 'Forward to . . .' Here is a batch of demands starting with 'No more Rome!' and going all the way to 'Forward to kitchen gardens!' What would you want to choose?"

It was not easy to sort out all the petitions the world was addressing to Count Leinsdorf, but two kinds surpassed all the rest in volume. One blamed the troubles of the times on one particular detail and demanded its abolition; such details were nothing less than the Jews or the Church of Rome, socialism or capitalism, mechanistic thinking or the neglect of technical possibilities, miscegenation or segregation, big landed estates or big cities, overemphasis on intellect or inadequate popular education. The second group, on the other hand, pointed to a goal just ahead that, when reached, would suffice to take care of everything. These desirable goals of the second persuasion differed from the specific evils denounced by the first mostly by nothing more than the emotional plus or minus signs attached, obviously because the world is made up of both critical and affirming temperaments. So there were letters of the second category that joyfully took the negative line that it was high time to break with the ridiculous cult of the arts, because life was a far greater poet than all the scribblers. These letters demanded courtroom reports and travel books for general use; while letters on the same subject from the first category would be joyfully positive in maintaining that the mountaineer's ecstasy upon reaching the summit outdid all the sublimities of art, philosophy, and religion, so instead of these one should support mountain-climbing clubs. In this double-jointed fashion the public demanded a slowing down of the tempo of the times just as much as a competition for the best short essay, because life was unbearably/exquisitely short, and there was a desperate need for the liberation of mankind from/by garden apartments, the emancipation of women, dancing, sports, interior decoration, and from any number of other burdens by any number of other panaceas.

Ulrich closed his folder and spoke privately.

"Mighty cousin," he said, "it is amazing that half of them seek salvation in the future and the other half in the past. I don't know what we are to make of that. His Grace would say that the present is without salvation."

"Is His Grace thinking in terms of the Church?" Diotima asked.

"He has only just come up with the discovery that in the history of mankind there is no turning back voluntarily. What makes it difficult is that going forward is not much use either. Permit me to say that we're in a very peculiar situation, unable to move either forward or backward, while the present moment is felt to be unbearable too."

When Ulrich talked like this Diotima barricaded herself in her tall body as in a tower marked with three stars in Baedeker.

"Do you believe, dear lady, that anyone fighting for or against a cause today," Ulrich asked, "who tomorrow by some miracle were to become the all-powerful ruler of the world, would instantly do what he had been clamoring for all his life? I am convinced he would grant himself a few days' delay."

Ulrich paused. Diotima suddenly turned to him without responding and asked him sternly:

"Why did you encourage the General about our campaign?"

"What general?"

"General von Stumm!"

"Do you mean that round little general from the first big meeting? Me? I haven't even seen him since, let alone encouraged him!"

Ulrich's astonishment was convincing and called for an explanation on her part. Since it was impossible that a man like Arnheim should be guilty of a falsehood, there had to be a misunderstanding somewhere, and Diotima gave him the reason for her assumption.

"So I am supposed to have spoken with Arnheim about General

von Stumm? I never did that either," Ulrich assured her. "I did talk with Arnheim—just a moment . . ." He searched his memory, then broke into a laugh. "It would be very flattering if Arnheim attached so much importance to every word I say. We have had several discussions lately—if that's the word for our differences—and I did once say something about a general, but not any particular one, only incidentally to illustrate a point. I maintained that a general who for strategic reasons sends his battalions to certain doom is a murderer, if you think of them as thousands of mothers' sons, but that he immediately becomes something else seen from some other perspective, such as, for example, the necessity of sacrifice, or the insignificance of life's short span. I used a lot of other examples. But here you must allow me to digress. For quite obvious reasons, every generation treats the life into which it is born as firmly established, except for those few things it is interested in changing. This is practical, but it's wrong. The world can be changed in all directions at any moment, or at least in any direction it chooses; it's in the world's nature. Wouldn't it be more original to try to live, not as a definite person in a definite world where only a few buttons need adjusting—what we call evolution—but rather to behave from the start as someone born to change surrounded by a world created to change, roughly like a drop of water inside a cloud? Are you annoyed with me for being so obscure again?"

"I'm not annoyed with you, but I can't understand you." Diotima commanded: "Do tell me the whole conversation!"

"Well, Arnheim started it. He stopped me and formally challenged me to a conversation," Ulrich began. " 'We businessmen,' he said to me with a rather puckish smile, quite in contrast to his usual quiet pose, but still very majestic, 'we businessmen are not as calculating as you might think. Actually, we—I mean the leading men, of course; the small fry may spend all their time calculating—we come to regard our really successful ideas as something that defies all calculation, like the personal success of a politician, and, in the last analysis, like the artist's too.' Then he asked me to judge what he was going to say next with the indulgence we grant the irrational: from the first day he saw me, he confided, he'd had certain ideas about me—and it seems, gracious cousin, that you also told him many things about me, which he assured me he had not needed to hear to form his opinion, which was that strangely enough I had made a mistake in choosing a purely abstract, conceptual profession, because no matter how gifted I was in that direction, I was basically a scientist, and no matter how surprised I might be to hear it, my real talent lay in the field of action and personal effectiveness!"

"Oh really?" Diotima said.

"I quite agree with you," Ulrich hastened to say. "There is nothing I am less fit for than being myself."

"You are always making fun of things instead of devoting yourself to life," Diotima said, still annoyed with him over the files.

"Arnheim maintains the opposite. I am under a compulsion to think my way to excessively thorough conclusions about life—he says."

"You're always sardonic and negative, always leaping into the impossible and avoiding every real decision," Diotima maintained.

"It is simply my conviction," Ulrich replied, "that thinking is a world of its own, and real life is another. The difference between their respective levels of development at the present time is too great. Our brain is some thousands of years old, but if it had worked out only half of everything and forgotten the other half, its true image would be our reality. All one can do is refuse intellectual participation in it."

"Aren't you making things much too easy for yourself?" Diotima asked, without any offensive intention, rather like a mountain looking down on a little brook at its foot. "Arnheim enjoys theorizing too, but I think he lets hardly anything pass without examining all its aspects. Don't you feel that the point of thinking is to be a concentrated capacity for applying—"

"No," Ulrich said.

"I'd like to hear what answer Arnheim gave you."

"He told me that the intellect today is the helpless spectator of real developments because it is dodging the great tasks of life. He asked me to look at what subjects the arts treat, at what trivia the churches concern themselves with, at how narrow even the perspective of the scholars is—and I should consider that all the while, the earth is being literally carved up! Then he said that this was precisely what he wanted to talk with me about."

"And what was your answer?" Diotima asked eagerly, supposing that Arnheim had been trying to appeal to her cousin's conscience about his indifferent attitude to the problems of the Parallel Campaign.

"I told him that realizing a potential always attracts me less than the unrealized, and I mean not only the future but also the past and missed opportunities. It seems to me our history has been that every time we have fulfilled some small part of an idea, we are so pleased that we leave the much greater remainder unfinished. Magnificent institutions are usually the bungled drafts of their ideas; so, incidentally, are magnificent personalities. That's what I answered. A difference in the angle of perspective, so to speak."

"How argumentative of you!" said Diotima, with a sense of injury.

"He retaliated by telling me his impression of me when I resist the active life because of some unfulfilled intellectual element in the general scheme. Would you like to hear it? Like a man who lies down on the ground beside a bed that has been prepared for him. A squandering of energy, something physically immoral, is what he called it, to make sure I didn't miss the point. He kept at me to make me see that great goals can be reached only by using the existing economic, political, and, not least, intellectual structure of power. For his own part, he considers it more ethical to make use of it than to neglect it. He really hammered away at me. He called me a man of action in a defensive stance, a cramped defensive stance. I think he has some sinister reason for wanting to gain my respect."

"He wants to be helpful!" Diotima cried out in reproof.

"Oh no," Ulrich said. "I may be only a little pebble, and he is a splendid, puffed-out glass ball. But I have the impression he's afraid of me."

Diotima made no answer. What Ulrich had said might be presumptuous, but it had occurred to her that the conversation he had just recounted was not at all what it should have been according to the impression she had got from Arnheim. It even worried her a bit. Although she thought Arnheim quite incapable of intrigue, Ulrich was gaining her confidence, and so she asked him what she should do about the case of General Stumm.

"Keep him off!" was Ulrich's answer, and Diotima could not spare herself the reproach that she was well pleased with it.

67

DIOTIMA AND ULRICH

Diotima's relationship to Ulrich had much improved, now that they had formed the habit of getting together regularly. They often had to drive out together to call on people, and he came to see her several times a week, often unannounced and at unconventional hours. In the circumstances, their being related was convenient for a domestic relaxation of the strict social code. Diotima did not always receive him in the drawing room armored in full panoply from chignon to skirt hem, but sometimes in slight domestic disarray, even if only a very cautious disarray. A kind of fellowship had grown up between them that lay mainly in the form of their association, but forms have their inward effects, and the emotions that create them can also be awakened by them.

Ulrich sometimes felt with great intensity that Diotima was very beautiful. On these occasions he saw her as a young, tall, plump heifer of good stock, surefooted and studying with a deep gaze the dry grasses she was feeding on. In other words, even then he did not look on her without the malice and irony that revenged themselves on her spiritual nobility by drawing on images from the animal kingdom and that arose from a deep annoyance less against this foolish paragon than against the school where her performances were a success. "How likable she could be," he thought, "if she were uneducated and careless and as good-natured as a big warm female body always is when it doesn't flatter itself that it has any special ideas!" The celebrated wife of the much-whispered-about Section Chief Tuzzi evaporated from her body, leaving it behind like a dream that, together with pillows, bed, and dreamer, turned into a white cloud all alone in the world with its tenderness.

But when Ulrich came back to earth from such a flight of the imagination, what he found before him was an ambitious middle-class mind eager to associate with aristocratic ideas. Physical kinship together with a strong difference in temperament, incidentally, is disturbing; sometimes the mere idea of kinship is enough, the consciousness of self; siblings often cannot bear each other in a way that goes far beyond anything that might be justified; it derives merely from the existence of the one throwing into doubt the existence of the other, from the slightly distorted mirror image they have of each other. Sometimes Diotima's being about the same height as Ulrich was enough to remind him that they were related and made him feel repugnance for her body. He had transferred to her, with some differences, a function usually reserved for his boyhood friend Walter—that of humbling and irritating his pride, much as seeing ourselves again in certain unpleasant old photographs has the power to humiliate us and at the same time challenge our pride. It followed that even in the mistrust Ulrich felt for Diotima there had to be something of a bond and a drawing together, in short a touch of genuine affection, just as his old warm allegiance with Walter still survived in the form of mistrust. But since he did not like Diotima, this baffled him for a long time without his being able to get to the bottom of it. They sometimes set off on little expeditions together. With Tuzzi's encouragement they took advantage of the fine weather, despite the unfavorable time of year, to show Arnheim "the lovely sights around Vienna"—Diotima never used any other expression but this cliché—and Ulrich always felt that he was being taken along in the role of an elderly female relation serving as chaperone because Section Chief Tuzzi could not spare the time. Later it happened that Ulrich also drove out alone with Diotima when Arnheim was out of town. For such expeditions, as well as for the immediate purposes of the campaign, Arnheim had made available as many automobiles as might be needed, since His Grace's carriage, ornate with its coat of arms, was too well known about town and too conspicuous. These cars, incidentally, were not necessarily Arnheim's own; the rich always can find others who are only too pleased to oblige.

Such excursions served not merely for diversion but also served the purpose of winning support for the campaign from influential or wealthy persons, so they took place more often within the city limits than in the countryside. The cousins saw many beautiful things together: Maria Theresa furniture, Baroque palaces, people still borne through life on the hands of their many servants, modern houses with great suites of rooms, palatial banks, and the blend of Spanish austerity and middle-class domestic habits in the homes of high-ranking civil servants. All in all, it was, for the aristocracy, what was left of the grand manner with no running water, repeated in paler imitation in the houses and conference rooms of the wealthy middle class with improved hygiene and, on the whole, better taste. A ruling caste always remains slightly barbaric. In the castles of the nobility, cinders and leftovers not burned away by the slow smoldering of time were still lying where they had fallen. Close beside magnificent staircases one stepped on boards of soft wood, and hideous new furniture stood carelessly alongside magnificent old pieces. The new rich, on the other hand, in love with the imposing and grandiose moments of their predecessors, had instinctively made a fastidious and refined selection. Wherever a castle had passed into middle-class hands, was it not merely seen to be provided with modern comfort, like an heirloom chandelier through which electric wiring had been threaded, but the inferior furnishings had also been cleared out and valuable pieces brought in, chosen either by the owner or according to the unassailable recommendation of experts. It was not, incidentally, in the castles where this refinement showed itself most impressively but in the town houses that, in keeping with the times, had been furnished with all the impersonal luxury of an ocean liner and yet had preserved, in this country of subtly refined social ambition, through some ineffable breath, some hardly perceptible widening of the space between the pieces of furniture or the dominant position of a painting on a wall, the tender, clear echo of a great sound that had faded away.

Diotima was enchanted by so much "culture." She had always known that her native country harbored such treasures, but even she was amazed at their abundance. They would be invited together to visit in the country, and Ulrich noticed, among other things, that the fruit here was not infrequently picked up in the fingers and eaten unpeeled, whereas in the houses of the upper bourgeoisie the ceremonial of knife and fork was strictly observed. The same could also be said about conversation, which tended to be flawlessly distinguished only in the middle-class homes, while among the nobility the well-known, relaxed idiom reminiscent of cabdrivers prevailed. Diotima presented her cousin with an enthusiastic defense of all this. She conceded that the bourgeois estates had better plumbing and showed more intelligence in their appointments, while at the nobility's country seats one froze in winter, there were often narrow, worn stairs, stuffy, low-ceilinged bedrooms were the behind-the-scenes counterpart of magnificent public rooms, and there were no dumbwaiters or bathrooms for the servants. But that was just what made it all, in a sense, more heroic, this feeling for tradition and this splendid nonchalance! she wound up ecstatically.

Ulrich used these excursions to examine the feeling that bound him to Diotima. But there were so many digressions along the way that it is necessary to follow them awhile before coming to the point.

At that time, women were encased in clothes from throat to ankle. Men's clothes today are like what they were then, but they used to be more appropriate because they still represented an organic outward sign of the flawless cohesion and strict reserve that marked a man of the world. In those days, even a person of few prejudices, unhampered by shame in appreciating the undraped human body, would have regarded a display of nudity as a relapse into the animal state, not because of the nakedness but because of the loss of the civilized aphrodisiac of clothing. Actually, it would then have been considered below the animal state, for a three-year-old Thoroughbred and a playing greyhound are far more expressive in their nakedness than a human body can ever be. But animals can't wear clothes; they have only the one skin, while human beings in those days had many skins. In full dress, with frills, puffs, bell skirts, cascading draperies, laces, and gathered pleats, they had created a surface five times the size of the original one, forming a many-petaled chalice heavy with an erotic charge, difficult of access, and hiding at its core the slim white animal that had to be searched out and that made itself terribly desirable. It was the prescribed process Nature herself uses when she bids her creatures fluff out their plumage or spray out clouds of ink, so that desire and terror raised to a degree of unearthly frenzy will mask the matter-of-fact proceedings that are the heart of the matter.

For the first time in her life Diotima felt herself more than superficially affected by this game, though in the most decorous way. Coquetry was not wholly unknown to her, since it was one of the social accomplishments a lady had to master. Nor had she ever failed to notice when a young man looked at her with a glance that expressed something besides respect; in fact she rather liked it, because it made her feel the gentle power of feminine reproof when she forced the eyes of a man, intent on her like the horns of a bull, to turn away by uttering high-minded sentiments. But Ulrich, in the security of their kinship and his selfless services to the Parallel Campaign, and protected, too, by the codicil established in his favor, permitted himself liberties that pierced straight through the tangled weavings of her idealism. On one occasion, for instance, as they were driving through the countryside, they passed some delightful valleys where hillsides covered with dark pine woods sloped down toward the road, and Diotima pointed to them with the lines "Who planted you, O lovely woods, so high up there above?" She of course quoted these lines as poetry, without any hint of the tune that went along with them; she would have considered that old hat and inane. Ulrich was quick to answer: "The Landbank of Lower Austria. Don't you know, cousin, that all the forests hereabouts belong to the Landbank? The master you are about to praise in the next line is a forester on the bank's payroll. Nature in these parts is a planned product of the forestry industry, a storehouse of serried ranks of cellulose for the manufacturers, as you can see at a glance."

His answers were quite often like that. When she spoke of beauty, he spoke of the fatty tissue supporting the epidermis. When she mentioned love, he responded with the statistical curve that indicates the automatic rise and fall in the annual birthrate. When she spoke of the great figures in art, he traced the chain of borrowings that links these figures to one another. Somehow it always began with Diotima talking as if on the sixth day of Creation God had placed man as a pearl in the shell of the world, whereupon Ulrich reminded her that mankind was a tiny pile of dots on the outermost crust of a dwarf globe. She was not quite sure what Ulrich was up to, though it was obviously an attack on that sphere of greatness with which Diotima felt allied, and most of all she felt that he was rudely showing off. She found it hard to take that her cousin, whom she regarded as an intellectual enfant terrible, imagined he knew more than she did, and his materialistic arguments, which meant nothing to her, drawn as they were from the lower culture of facts and figures, annoyed her mightily.

"Thank heaven," she once came back at him sharply, "there are still people capable of believing in simple things, no matter how great their experience!"

"Your husband, for instance," Ulrich said. "I've been meaning to tell you for a long time that I much prefer him to Arnheim."

They had got into the habit of exchanging ideas by speaking about Arnheim. For like all people in love, Diotima derived pleasure from talking about the object of her love without, at least so she believed, betraying herself; and since Ulrich found this insufferable, as does any man who has no ulterior motive in yielding the stage to another, it often happened on such occasions that he lashed out against Arnheim. Between Arnheim and himself a relationship of a peculiar kind had developed. When Arnheim was not traveling, they met almost every day. Ulrich knew that Section Chief Tuzzi regarded the Prussian with suspicion, as he did himself from observing Arnheim's effect on Diotima since the very beginning. Not that there was yet anything improper between them, so far as could be judged by a third party who was confirmed in this judgment by the revolting excess of propriety between these lovers, who were evidently emulating the loftiest examples of a Platonic union of souls. Yet Arnheim showed a striking inclination to draw his friend's cousin (or was she his lover after all?, Ulrich wondered, but considered it most probably something like lover plus friend divided by two) into this intimate relationship. He often addressed Ulrich in the manner of an older friend, a tone made permissible by the difference in age between them but that became unpleasantly tainted with condescension because of the difference in their position. Ulrich's response was almost always standoffish in a rather challenging way: he made a point of not seeming in the least impressed by speaking with a man who might just as easily have been speaking with kings and chancellors instead. Annoyed with himself because of his lack of propriety, he contradicted Arnheim with impolite frequency and unseemly irony, as a substitute for which he would have done better to enjoy himself as a silent observer. He was astonished that Arnheim irritated him so violently. Ulrich saw in him, fattened by favorable circumstances, the model example of an intellectual development he hated. For this celebrated writer was shrewd enough to grasp the questionable situation man had got himself into ever since he ceased looking for his image in the mirror of a stream, and sought it instead in the sharp, broken surfaces of his intelligence; but this writing iron magnate blamed the predicament on intelligence itself and not on its imperfections. There was a con game in this union between the soul and the price of coal, a union that at the same time purposefully served to keep apart what Arnheim did with his eyes wide open and what he said and wrote in his cloud of intuition. Added to this, to exacerbate Ulrich's uneasiness, was something new to him, the combination of intellect and wealth. When Arnheim talked about some particular subject almost like a specialist and then suddenly, with a casual wave of his hand, made all the details disappear in the light of a "great thought," he might be acting on some not unjustified need of his own, but at the same time this manner of freely disposing of things in two directions at once was too suggestive of the rich man who can afford the best and most expensive of everything. He had a wealth of ideas that was always slightly reminiscent of the ways of real wealth. But perhaps it was not even this that most provoked Ulrich into creating difficulties for the celebrated man; perhaps it was rather the inclination of Arnheim's mind toward a dignified mode of holding court and keeping house that of itself led to an association with the best brands of the traditional as well as of the unusual. For in the mirror of this Epicurean connoisseurship Ulrich saw the affected grimace that is the face of the times, if one subtracts the few really strong lines of passion and thought in it; all this left him with hardly a chance to reach a better understanding of the man, who could probably be credited with all sorts of merits as well. It was, of course, an utterly senseless battle he was waging, in an environment predisposed in Arnheim's favor, and in a cause that had no importance at all; the most that could be said for it was that this senselessness gave the sense of the total expenditure of his own energies. It was also a quite hopeless struggle, for if Ulrich actually once managed to wound his opponent, he had to recognize that he had hit the wrong Arnheim; if Arnheim the thinker lay defeated on the ground, Arnheim the master of reality rose like a winged being with an indulgent smile, and hastened from the idle games of such conversations to Baghdad or Madrid.

This invulnerability made it possible for him to counter the younger man's bad manners with that amiable camaraderie the source of which Ulrich could never quite pinpoint. Besides, Ulrich was himself concerned not to go too far in tearing Arnheim down, because he was determined not to slip again into one of those half-baked and demeaning adventures in which his past had been far too rich; and the progress he observed between Arnheim and Diotima served as an effective insurance against weakening. So he generally directed the points of his attacks like the points of a foil, which yield on impact and are shielded with a friendly little rubber button to soften the blow. It was Diotima who had come up with this comparison. She found herself mystified by this cousin of hers. His candid face with the clear brow, his quietly breathing chest, the ease in all his movements, all clearly indicated to her that no malicious, spiteful, sadistic-libidinous impulses could dwell in such a body. Nor was she quite without pride in so personable a member of her family; she had made up her mind from the beginning of their acquaintance to take him under her wing. Had he had black hair, a crooked shoulder, a muddy skin, or a low forehead, she would have said that his views accorded with his looks. But as it was, she was struck by a certain discrepancy between his looks and his ideas that made itself felt as an inexplicable uneasiness. The antennae of her famed intuition groped in vain for the cause, but she enjoyed the groping at the other end of the antennae. In a sense, though not of course seriously, she sometimes even preferred Ulrich's company to Arnheim's. Her need to feel superior was more gratified by him, she felt more sure of herself, and to regard him as frivolous, eccentric, or immature gave her a certain satisfaction that balanced the idealism, becoming increasingly dangerous from day to day, that she saw taking on incalculable dimensions in her feelings for Arnheim. Soul is a terribly grave affair, and materialism by contrast is lighthearted. The conduct of her relationship with Arnheim was sometimes as much of a strain as her salon, and her contempt for Ulrich made her life easier. She did not understand herself, but she noticed this effect, and this enabled her whenever she was annoyed with her cousin over one of his remarks to give him a sideways look that was only a tiny smile in the corner of her eye, while the eye itself, idealistically untouched and indeed even slightly disdainful, gazed straight ahead.

Anyway, whatever their reasons may have been, Diotima and Arnheim behaved toward Ulrich like two fighters clinging to a third per-

son whom in their alternating fear they shove back and forth between themselves; a situation not without its dangers for Ulrich, for
through Diotima the question arose: Must people be in accord with
their bodies or not?

68

A DIGRESSION: MUST PEOPLE BE IN ACCORD WITH THEIR BODIES?

Independently of what their faces were talking about, the motion of
the car on those long drives rocked the two cousins so that their
clothes touched, overlapped a bit, and moved apart again. One could
only see this from their shoulders, because the rest of them was enveloped by a shared blanket, but the bodies felt this contact, muffled
by their clothing, as delicately indistinct as things seen in moonlight.
Ulrich was not unreceptive to this kind of flirting, without taking it
too seriously. The overrefined transmission of desire from the body
to the clothes, from the embrace to the obstacles, or, in short, from
the goal to the approach, answered to his nature, whose sensuality
drove him toward the woman; but its critical faculties held him back
from the alien, uncongenial person it suddenly, with relentless lucidity, perceived her to be, and this made for a lively tug-of-war between inclination and aversion. But this meant that the body's
sublime beauty, its human beauty, the moment when the spirit's
song rises from nature's instrument, or that other moment when the
body is like a goblet filling up with a mystic potion, was something he
had never known, leaving aside those dreams of the major's wife that
had for the longest time put an end to such inclinations in him.

All his relationships with women, since then, had somehow not
been right. With a certain amount of goodwill on both sides that happens, unfortunately, all too easily. From the moment they first began
to think about it, a man and a woman find a ready-made matrix of

feelings, acts, and complications waiting to take them in charge, and beneath this matrix the process takes its course in reverse; the stream no longer flows from the spring; the last things to happen push their way to the front of consciousness; the pure pleasure two people have in each other, this simplest and deepest of all feelings in love, and the natural source of all the rest, disappears completely in this psychic reversal.

So on his trips with Diotima, Ulrich not infrequently remembered their leave-taking after his first visit. He had taken her mild hand, an artfully and nobly perfected weightless hand, in his own as they gazed into each other's eyes. They both undoubtedly felt some aversion, and yet it occurred to them that they might nevertheless fuse to the point of extinction. Something of this vision had remained between them. Thus two heads above cast a horrible chill on each other while the bodies below helplessly melt together at white heat. There is in this something nastily mythical, as in a two-headed god or the devil's cloven hoof, and it had often led Ulrich astray in his youth, when he had experienced it fairly often; but with the years it had proved to be no more than a very bourgeois aphrodisiac, in exactly the same way that the unclothed body substitutes for the nude. Nothing so inflames the middle-class lover as the flattering discovery of the power to drive another person into an ecstasy so wild that to be the cause of such changes by any other means one would have to become a murderer.

And truly, that there can be such changes in civilized people, that we actually can produce such effects!—isn't this the question and the amazement in the bold, glazed eyes of all those who dock at the lonely island of lust, where they are murderer, destiny, and God, and experience the maximum irrationality and adventurousness in the greatest comfort?

The repugnance he came to acquire with time against this kind of love eventually extended to his own body too, which had always encouraged these misbegotten affairs by giving women the illusion of a reliable virility, for which Ulrich was too cerebral and too conflicted. At times he was as downright jealous of his own appearance as if it were a rival using cheap tricks against him—in which a contradiction emerged that is also present in others who are not aware of it. For he was the one who kept his body trim by exercising it, giving it the shape, expression, and readiness for action that influence the mind no less than an ever-smiling or an ever-solemn face can. Oddly enough, the majority of people have either a neglected body, formed and deformed by chance circumstances, which seems to have almost no relation at all to their mind and character, or else a body disguised by the mask of sports, giving it the look of those hours when it is on vacation from itself. Those are the hours when a person spins out the daydream of his appearance, casually picked up from the magazines of the smart, great world. All those bronzed and muscular tennis players, horsemen, and race-car drivers, who look like world-record holders though usually they are merely competent; those ladies all dressed up or all undressed; they are all daydreamers, differing from common daydreamers only in that their dream doesn't stay in their brain but comes out into the open air as a projection of the mass soul—physically, dramatically, and (as one might say in the idiom of more-than-dubious occult phenomena) ideoplastically. But in common with the usual spinners of fantasies they have a certain shallowness of the dream, both as to its content and its nearness to the waking state. The problem of the integral physiognomy still eludes us, even though we have learned to draw conclusions about man's nature, sometimes even amazingly correct conclusions, from his handwriting, voice, sleeping position, and God knows what else; yet for the body as a whole we have only the fashionable models on which it forms itself, or at most a kind of nature-cure philosophy.

But is this the body of our mind, our ideas, intimations, plans, or—the pretty ones included—the body of our follies? That Ulrich had loved those follies and still to some extent had them did not prevent him from feeling not at home in the body they had created.

69

Diotima and Ulrich, continued

And it was above all Diotima who confirmed in a new way his sense that the surface and depths of his person were not one and the same. This came through clearly for him on these trips with her, which sometimes felt like drives through moonlight, when the young woman's beauty detached itself from her person altogether and momentarily veiled his eyes like gossamer spun by a dream. He knew, of course, that Diotima compared everything he said with the conventional wisdom on the subject—the higher conventional wisdom, to be sure—and was pleased that she found it "immature," so that he constantly sat there as if he were before the wrong end of a telescope trained on him. He became smaller and smaller, and believed when he spoke with her (or at least was not far from believing) in his role of devil's advocate and materialist that he could hear in his own words conversations from his last terms at school, when he and his classmates had idolized all the villains and monsters of world history because the teachers had presented them in tones of idealistic abhorrence. And when Diotima looked at him indignantly he grew smaller still, regressing from the morality of heroism and the drive for expansion to the defiant lies, callousness, and wavering excesses of adolescence—only quite figuratively, of course, as one can detect in a gesture or a word some distant similarity with gestures and words one has long since discarded, or only dreamed, or seen and disliked in others. In any event, this all resonated in his delight in shocking Diotima. The mind of this woman, who would have been so beautiful without her mind, aroused an inhuman feeling in him, perhaps a fear of mind itself, an aversion for all great things, a feeling that was quite faint, hardly detectable—and perhaps feeling was a much too pretentious expression for something that was but a mere breath. But if one magnified it into words, they would have gone something like this: at times he saw not only this woman's idealism but all the idealism in the world, in all its extent and ramifications,

appear bodily in the form of an image hovering just above that Grecian head—it only just missed being the horns of the Devil! Then
Ulrich grew even smaller still and—again figuratively speaking—re-
gressed to the first hotly moral state of childhood, in whose eyes
temptation and terror lie as in the stare of a gazelle. The tender emotions of that age can in a single moment of yielding cause the whole,
still-tiny world to burst into flames, since they have neither an aim
nor the ability to make anything happen, but are a completely
boundless fire. It was quite unlike him, and yet in Diotima's company Ulrich ended up longing for these childhood feelings, though
he could barely imagine them because they have so little in common
with the conditions under which an adult lives.

At one point he very nearly confessed it to her. On one of their
trips they had left the car to walk into a small valley that was like a
river delta of meadows with steep forested banks and that formed a
crooked triangle with a winding brook in its center stilled by a light
frost. The slopes had been partly cleared of timber, with a few trees
left standing like feather dusters stuck in the bare hillsides and hill-
tops. This scene had tempted them to take a walk. It was one of those
wistful, snowless days that seem in the middle of winter like a faded,
no-longer-fashionable summer gown. Diotima abruptly asked her
cousin: "Why does Arnheim call you an activist? He says that you're
always full of ideas how to do things differently and better." She had
suddenly remembered that her talk with Arnheim about Ulrich and
the General had ended inconclusively.

"I don't understand," she went on. "It always seems to me that you
hardly ever mean anything seriously. But I must ask you, because we
are involved together in such a responsible task. Do you remember
our last conversation? There was something you said: you maintained
that nobody, if he had the necessary power, would do what he wants
to do. Now I would like to know what you meant by that. Wasn't it a
horrible idea?"

Ulrich did not reply at once. And during this silence, after she had
spoken as impudently as possible, she realized how much she had
been preoccupied with the forbidden question of whether Arnheim
and she would do what each of them secretly wanted. She suddenly
thought she had given herself away to Ulrich. She blushed, tried to
stop herself, blushed even more, and did her best to gaze out over

the valley, away from him, with the most unconcerned expression she could muster.

Ulrich had observed the process. "I'm very much afraid that the only reason Arnheim, as you say, calls me an activist is that he overestimates my influence with the Tuzzi family," he answered. "You know yourself how little attention you pay to what I say. But now that you have asked me, I realize what my influence on you ought to be. May I tell you without your instantly criticizing me again?"

Diotima nodded silently as a sign of assent and tried to pull herself together behind an appearance of absentmindedness.

"So I said," Ulrich began, "that nobody would turn his dreams into realities even if he could. You remember our file folders full of suggestions? And now I ask you: Is there anyone who would not be embarrassed if something he had passionately demanded all his life were suddenly to come true? If, for instance, the Kingdom of God were suddenly to burst on the Catholics, or the classless society of the future on the socialists? But perhaps this doesn't prove anything. We get used to demanding things and aren't quite ready to have our wishes realized; it's only natural, many people would say. Let me go on: Music must be the most important thing in the world to a musician, and painting to a painter, and probably even the building of cement houses to a cement specialist. Do you think that this will induce him to imagine God as a specialist in reinforced concrete and that the others will prefer a painted world, or a world blown on the bugle, to the real one? You'll call it a silly question, but what makes it serious is that we are expected to insist on just this kind of silliness!

"Now please don't think," he said, turning to her in all seriousness, "that all I mean by this is that everyone wants what is hard to get, and despises the attainable. What I mean is this: Within reality there is a senseless craving for unreality."

He had inconsiderately led Diotima a long way into the little valley; the snow trickling down the slopes was perhaps what made the ground wetter the higher they went, and they had to hop from one small clump of grass to the next, which punctuated their talk and forced Ulrich to go on with it by fits and starts. There were, as a result, so many obvious objections to what he was saying that Diotima did not know where to begin. She had got her feet wet and stood still on a grassy mound, led astray and anxious, clutching at her skirts.

Ulrich turned back and laughed. "You've started something exceedingly dangerous, great cousin. People are vastly relieved to be left in a position where they can't put their ideas into practice."

"And what would *you* do," Diotima asked irritably, "if you could rule the world for a day?"

"I suppose I would have no choice but to abolish reality."

"I'd love to know how you'd go about it."

"I don't know either. I hardly know what I mean by it. We wildly overestimate the present, the sense of the present, the here and now; like you and me being here in this valley, as if we'd been put in a basket and the lid of the present had fallen on it. We make too much of it. We'll remember it. Even a year from now we may be able to describe how we were standing here. But what really moves us—me anyway—is always—putting it cautiously; I don't want to look for an explanation or a name for it—opposed in a sense to this way of experiencing things. It is displaced by so much here and now, so much Present. So it can't become the present in its turn."

In the narrow valley Ulrich's words sounded loud and confused. Diotima suddenly felt uneasy and moved to get back to the car. But Ulrich made her stay and look at the landscape.

"Some thousands of years ago this was a glacier," he explained. "Even the earth isn't altogether what it's pretending to be for the moment. This well-rounded character is a hysteric. Today it is acting the good middle-class mother feeding her children. Back then the world was frigid and icy, like a spiteful girl. Several thousand years before that it luxuriated in hot fern forests, sultry swamps, and demonic beasts. We can't say that it has evolved toward perfection, nor what its true condition is. And the same goes for its daughter, mankind. Imagine the clothes in which people have stood here through the ages, right where we are standing now. Expressed in terms of the madhouse, it suggests long-standing obsessions with suddenly erupting manic ideas; after these run their course, a new concept of life is there. So you see, reality does away with itself!

"There's something else I'd like to tell you"—Ulrich made a fresh start after a while. "That sense of having firm ground underfoot and a firm skin all around, which appears so natural to most people, is not very strongly developed in me. Think back to how you were as a child; all gentle glow. And then a teenager, lips burning with longing. Something in me rebels against the idea that so-called mature adulthood is the peak of such a development. In a sense it is, and in a sense it isn't. If I were a myrmeleonina, the ant predator that resembles a dragonfly, I'd be horrified to think that the year before I had been the squat gray myrmeleon, the ant lion, running backward and living at the edge of the forest, dug in at the bottom of a funnel-shaped hole in the sand, catching ants by the waist with invisible pincers after first exhausting them by somehow bombarding them with grains of sand. There are times when the thought of my youth horrifies me in quite the same way, even though I may have been a dragonfly then and may be a monster now."

He did not really know what he was aiming at. With his myrmeleon and myrmeleonina he had only been aping Arnheim's cultured omniscience a little. But he had it on the tip of his tongue to say: "Please, won't you make love to me, just to be nice? We are kindred, not wholly separate, certainly not one; in any case, the polar opposite of a dignified and formal relationship."

But Ulrich was mistaken. Diotima was the kind of person who is satisfied with herself and therefore regards each age she passes through as a step on a stairway leading upward from below. She had no way of understanding what Ulrich was talking about, especially as she did not know what he had left unsaid. But they had meanwhile returned to the car, so she felt serene again, taking in what he was saying as his usual kind of chatter, somewhere between amusing and irritating, commanding no more of her attention than at most the corner of an eye. At this moment he really had no influence whatsoever on her except that of bringing her down to earth. A filmy cloud of shyness, risen from some hidden corner of her heart, had dissipated in a dry void. For the first time, perhaps, she had a hard, clear glimpse of the fact that her relations with Arnheim would force her, sooner or later, to make a choice that could change her whole life. One could not say that she was happy about this just now, but it had the weighty presence of a real mountain range. A weak moment had passed. That "not to do what one wants to do" had had for an instant an absurd glow she no longer understood.

"Arnheim is altogether the opposite of me. He is always overestimating the happiness with which time and space rendezvous with him to form the present moment," Ulrich sighed with a smile, moved to bring what he had been saying to an orderly conclusion. But he said nothing further about childhood, so it never came to the point where Diotima would have found out that he had a tender side.

70

CLARISSE VISITS ULRICH TO
TELL HIM A STORY

Redecorating old castles was the specialty of the well-known painter van Helmond, whose masterpiece was his daughter Clarisse, and one day she unexpectedly walked in on Ulrich.

"Papa sends me," she informed him, "to find out whether you couldn't use your splendid aristocratic connections just a little for him too." She eyed the room with interest, threw herself into one chair and her hat onto another. Then she held out her hand to Ulrich.

"Your Papa overestimates me," he started to say, but she cut him short.

"Nonsense. You know perfectly well the old man always needs money. Business simply isn't what it used to be!" She laughed. "Elegant place you've got here. Nice!" She scrutinized her surroundings again and then looked at Ulrich. Her whole bearing had something of the endearing shyness of a pet dog whose bad conscience makes its skin twitch.

"Anyway, if you can do it, you will. If not, then you won't. Of course, I promised him you would. But I came for another reason. His asking me to see you put an idea into my head. It's about a certain problem in my family. I'd like to hear what you think." Her mouth and eyes hesitated and flickered for an instant; then she took her leap over the initial hurdle. "Would the term 'beauty doctor' suggest anything to you? A painter is a beauty doctor."

Ulrich understood; he knew her parents' house.

"Dark, distinguished, splendid, luxurious, upholstered, pennanted, and tasseled," she went on. "Papa is a painter, a painter is a kind of beauty doctor, and visiting our house has always been regarded as quite the thing socially, like going to the newest spa. You understand what I'm talking about. And one of Papa's main sources of income has always been decorating palaces and big country houses. Do you know the Pachhofens?"

Ulrich was not acquainted with this patrician family except for a Fräulein Pachhofen he had met once, years ago, in Clarisse's company.

"She was my friend," Clarisse said. "She was seventeen, and I was fifteen. Papa was supposed to renovate the castle and do the interiors. The Pachhofen place, of course. We were all invited. Walter too; it was the first time he came along with us. And Meingast."

"Meingast?" Ulrich did not know who Meingast was.

"But of course you know him; Meingast, who went to Switzerland later on. He wasn't yet a philosopher in those days, but a rooster in every family with daughters."

"I've never met him," Ulrich said. "But now I do know who he is."

"All right, then." Clarisse did some strenuous mental arithmetic. "Just a minute! Walter was then twenty-three and Meingast somewhat older. Walter was a great secret admirer of Papa's, and it was the first time he'd ever been invited to stay at a castle. Papa often had an air of wearing inner royal robes. I think at first Walter was more in love with Papa than with me. And Lucy—"

"Slow down, Clarisse, for heaven's sake!" Ulrich pleaded. "I seem to have lost the connection."

"Lucy," Clarisse said, "is Lucy Pachhofen, of course, the daughter of the Pachhofens with whom we were staying. Now do you understand? All right, then, you understand. Papa wrapped Lucy in velvet or brocade with a long train and posed her on one of her horses; she imagined he must be a Titian or Tintoretto. They were absolutely mad about each other."

"Papa about Lucy, and Walter about Papa?"

"Give me a chance, will you? At that time, there was Impressionism. Papa was still painting old-fashioned/musical, the way he still does today, brown gravy and peacocks' tails. But Walter was all for open air, the clean lines of English functionalism, the new and sincere. In his heart, Papa found him as insufferable as a Protestant sermon; he couldn't stand Meingast either, but he had two daughters to marry off; he had always spent more than he made, so he was long-suffering with the souls of the two young men. Walter, for his part, secretly loved Papa, as I said, but publicly he had to criticize him because of the new art movements, and Lucy never understood anything about art at all, but she was afraid of making a fool of herself in front of Walter, and she was afraid that Walter might turn out to be right, in which case Papa would only be a ridiculous old man. Do you get the picture?"

Before committing himself, Ulrich wanted to know where Mama had been.

"Mama was there too, of course. They quarreled every day as always, no more and no less. You can see that in these circumstances Walter enjoyed a favorable position. Everthing converged on Walter: Papa feared him, Mama egged him on, and I was beginning to fall in love with him. But Lucy played up to him. So Walter had a certain power over Papa, which he was beginning to savor in a cautiously lascivious way. I mean, it was then that Walter began to have a sense of his own importance; without Papa and me he would have been nothing. Do you see how it all hangs together?"

Ulrich felt it was safe to say he did.

"But I wanted to tell you something else!" Clarisse exclaimed. She took some time to think before she said: "Listen. Let's just start with me and Lucy: that was complicated in an exciting way. I was naturally worried about Papa, whose infatuation was on the point of ruining the whole family. But I was also curious about how this kind of thing happens. They were both out of their minds. Lucy's friendship for me was of course mixed up with the feeling that she had a man for a lover whom I still obediently called 'Papa.' She was more than a little proud, but at the same time it made her terribly ashamed to face me. I don't think the old castle had sheltered such complications under its roof since it was built. All day long Lucy hung around Papa whenever she could, and then at night she came to me in the tower to confess. I slept in the tower, and we had the lights on almost all night long."

"How far did Lucy actually go with your father?"

"That was the only thing I could never find out. But just think of those summer nights! The owls whimpering, the night moaning, and when it all got too spooky we both got into my bed so we could go on talking. We couldn't see how a man in the grip of so fatal a passion could do anything but shoot himself. We were really waiting for it to happen from one day to the next—".

"It strikes me," Ulrich interrupted, "that nothing much had really happened between them."

"That's what I think too—not everything. Yet things did happen. You'll see in a minute. All of a sudden, Lucy had to leave because her father arrived unexpectedly and took her off on a trip to Spain. You should have seen Papa then, when he was left on his own. I think there were times he came awfully close to strangling Mama. He was off on horseback from dawn to dusk, with a folding easel strapped behind his saddle, but he never painted a stroke, and he never touched a brush at home either. The point is, he usually paints like a robot, but in those days I'd find him sitting in one of those huge, empty rooms with a book he hadn't even opened. He would sometimes brood like this for hours, then he'd get up and do the same thing in some other room or in the garden, sometimes all day long. Well, he was an old man, and youth had left him in the lurch; it's understandable, isn't it? And I suppose the image of Lucy and me, seeing us all the time as two girlfriends with their arms around each other's waists, chatting confidentially, must have sprouted in him then—like some wild seed. Perhaps he knew that Lucy always used to join me in the tower. So one night, around eleven, all the lights in the castle were out, and there he was. That was quite something!" Clarisse was carried away with the import of her own story. "You hear this tapping and scraping on the stairs, and don't know what to make of it; then you hear the clumsy fiddling with the door handle, and the door opening spookily—"

"Why didn't you call out for help?"

"That's what was so peculiar about it. I knew from the first sound who it was. He must have stood still in the doorway, because I didn't hear anything for quite a while. He was probably frightened too. Then he slowly, carefully shut the door and whispered my name. I was absolutely stunned. I had no intention of answering him, but this weird thing happened: from somewhere deep inside me, as though I were a deep space, came a sound like a whimper. Have you ever heard of such a thing?"

"No. Go on!"

"Well, that's all; the next instant he was clutching at me with infinite despair; he almost fell on my bed, and his head was lying on the pillow beside mine."

"Tears?"

"Dry spasms. An old body, abandoned. I understood that at once. Oh, I tell you, if it were possible to tell afterward all one felt at such a moment, it would be something really enormous. I think he was beside himself with fury against the whole world of propriety, because of what it had made him miss. Suddenly I sense that he is himself again, and I know right away, although it's pitch-dark, that he's absolutely convulsed with a ruthless hunger for me. I know there is not going to be any mercy or consideration for me; there hasn't been a sound since that moan of mine; my body was blazing dry and his was like a piece of paper one sets at the edge of a fire. He became incredibly light. I felt his arm snaking down my body, away from my shoulder. And now there's something I want to ask you. It's why I came. . . ."

Clarisse broke off.

"What? You haven't asked anything!" Ulrich prompted her after a short pause.

"No. There's something else I have to say first: The idea that he must be taking my keeping so still as a sign of consent made me loathe myself. Yet I lay there, my mind a blank, petrified with fear. What do you make of that?"

"I don't know what to say."

"With one hand he kept stroking my face; the other wandered around. Trembling, pretending it wasn't up to anything, passing over my breast like a kiss, then, as if waiting, listening for some response. Then finally it moved—well, you know, and at the same time his face sought mine. But at that point I pulled myself away with all my strength and turned on my side; and again that sound came out of my chest, a sound I didn't know, something halfway between pleading and moaning. You see, I have a birthmark, a black medallion—"

"And what did your father do?" Ulrich interrupted coolly.

But Clarisse refused to be interrupted. "Right here," she said with a tense smile, pointing through her dress to a spot inward from her hip. "This is how far he got, to the medallion. This medallion has a magic power, or anyway, there's something special about it."

Suddenly the blood rushed to her face. Ulrich's silence had sobered her and dissipated the idea that had kept her under its spell. With an embarrassed smile she quickly finished:

"My father? He instantly sat up. I couldn't see what was going on in his face; embarrassment, I suppose. Maybe gratitude. After all, I had saved him at the last moment. You must understand: an old man, and a young girl has the strength to do that! He must have thought I was strange somehow, because he pressed my hand quite tenderly, and stroked my head twice with his other hand. Then he went away, without a word. So I hope you'll do what you can for him? After all, I had to tell you, so you'd understand."

Trim and correct, in a tailored dress she wore only when she came into town, she stood there, ready to leave, and held out her hand to say good-bye.

71

THE COMMITTEE TO DRAFT GUIDELINES FOR HIS MAJESTY'S SEVENTIETH JUBILEE CELEBRATION OPENS ITS FIRST SESSION

About her letter to Count Leinsdorf and her request that Ulrich save Moosbrugger, Clarisse had not said a word; she seemed to have forgotten all that. But for Ulrich, too, some time had to pass before he remembered it. For Diotima had at last come to the point in her preparations where, within the framework of the "Enquiry to Draft Guidelines and Ascertain the Wishes of All Sectors of the Population in Connection with His Majesty's Seventieth Jubilee Celebration," a meeting of the special "Committee to Draft Guidelines in Connection with His Majesty's Seventieth Jubilee Celebration" could be called, whose leadership Diotima had personally reserved for herself. His Grace had composed the invitation himself, Tuzzi had edited it, and Arnheim had been shown Tuzzi's suggestions before it was finally approved. In spite of all that, it contained everything that weighed on His Grace's mind.

"What brings us together in this meeting," it read, "is our mutual understanding that a powerful demonstration arising from the midst of the people must not be left to chance, but calls for a farsighted influence from a quarter commanding a broad, panoramic view, that is, an influence from above." This was followed by "the extremely rare occasion of this seventieth anniversary of an accession to the throne so richly blessed," the "grateful throng of peoples," the Emperor of Peace, the lack of political maturity, the Global Year of Austria, and finally the appeal to "Property and Culture" to fashion all this into a glorious manifestation of the True Austrian spirit, but only after giving it the most painstaking consideration.

From Diotima's lists, the groups for Art, Literature, and Science were chosen and with great care and effort augmented, while, on the other hand, of those who might be allowed to attend although not expected to take an active part, only a very small number had remained after the most thorough sifting. But the number of invited guests was still so large that there could be no question of a regular sit-down dinner at the green baize table; the only alternative was an informal evening reception with a cold buffet. The guests sat or stood however it could be arranged, and Diotima's rooms resembled the encampment of a spiritual army, supplied with sandwiches, pastries, wines, liqueurs, and tea in such quantities as could only have been made possible by special budgeting concessions Tuzzi granted to his wife—with, it must be added, not a word of protest, from which it may be inferred that he proposed to make use of new, intellectual methods of diplomacy.

The handling of such a throng made great demands on Diotima as a hostess, and she might perhaps have taken exception to many things had her head not resembled a superb fruit bowl with words constantly falling over the edge of its superabundance; words with which the lady of the house welcomed each arriving guest, enchanting him with detailed knowledge of his latest work. Her preparations for this had been extraordinary and could only have been accomplished with Arnheim's help; he had placed his private secretary at her disposal to arrange the material and make extracts of the most important texts. The splendid slag left behind by this volcanic endeavor was a large library bought with funds Count Leinsdorf had provided to start the Parallel Campaign, and together with Diotima's own books they had been set up as the only decoration in the last of the emptied rooms. The flowered wallpaper, or what could still be seen of it, betrayed the boudoir, a stimulus to flattering reflections about its occupant. This library turned out to have other advantages as well: every one of the invitees, after having been graciously greeted by Diotima, wandered aimlessly through the rooms and was drawn without fail to the wall of books at the far end as soon as he caught sight of it. A cluster of scrutinizing backs constantly rose and sank before it, like bees in front of a flowering hedge, and even if the cause was only the noble curiosity every creative person feels for book collections, delicious contentment seeped into the marrow of his bones when the viewer finally discovered his own works, and the patriotic campaign benefited from it.

Diotima at first allowed the assembly to drift, intellectually, at its own sweet will, though she made a point of assuring the poets in particular that all life, even the world of business, rested on an inner poetry if one "regarded it magnanimously." This surprised no one, but it turned out that most of those singled out for such confidences had come on the assumption that they were expected to launch the Parallel Campaign with some brief words of advice—somewhere between five and forty-five minutes' worth—which, if heeded, would guarantee its success, even if subsequent speakers squandered time with pointless and misguided suggestions. This almost drove Diotima to tears at first, and it was only with great effort that she kept her unruffled look, for she realized that each one of them was saying something different and she would never be able to pull it all together. She was still inexperienced in coping with such high concentrations of superior minds, and since so universal a gathering of great men would not come about again so easily, it could only be assimilated laboriously and methodically, step by step. There are many things in the world, incidentally, that taken singly mean something quite different to people from what they mean in the mass. Water, for instance, is less of a pleasure in excessive than in small doses, by exactly the difference between drowning and drinking, and the same can be said of poisons, amusements, leisure, piano playing, ideals, indeed probably everything, so that what something is depends on its degree of density and other circumstances. It is only necessary to add that even genius is no exception, lest the following impressions appear to suggest some sort of denigration of the eminent personages who had placed themselves so selflessly at Diotima's disposal.

For even at this first gathering one could receive the impression that every great mind feels extremely insecure as soon as it leaves the refuge of its treetop aerie and has to make itself understood on common ground. The extraordinary language that passed over Diotima's head like some movement in the skies as long as she conversed alone with one of the powerful turned, as soon as they were joined by a third or a fourth person and several lines of discourse got entangled in contradiction, into a distressing inability to arrive at any kind of order. Whoever does not shrink from such similes might try to visualize a swan that, after its proud flight, waddles along on the ground. But on longer acquaintance this, too, becomes quite understandable. The lives of great minds today are founded on a certain "no one knows what for." They enjoy great veneration, expressed on their fiftieth to their hundredth birthdays, or on the tenth anniversary of some agricultural college that garlands itself with honorary doctorates, or on various other occasions when speeches must be made about the country's cultural treasures. We have a history of great men, and we regard it as an institution that belongs to us, just like prisons or the army; having it means we have to have people to put into it. And so, with a certain automatism inherent in such social needs, we always pick the next in line and shower him with the honors ripe to be handed out. But this veneration is not quite sincere; at its base lies the gaping, generally accepted conviction that there is really not a single person who deserves it, and it is hard to tell whether the mouth opens to acclaim someone or to yawn. To call a man a genius nowadays, with the unspoken gloss that there is really no longer any such thing, smacks of some cult of the dead, something like hysterical love making a great to-do for no other reason than that there is no real feeling present.

For sensitive people this is of course not a pleasant situation, and they try to get rid of it in various ways. Some are driven in their despair to get rich by learning to exploit the demand not only for great minds but also for wild men, profound novelists, puffed-up lovers, and leaders of the new generation; others wear an invisible royal crown on their heads that they will not remove under any circumstances, prepared with embittered modesty not to expect the value of their creation to be seen in its true light before two to ten centuries have passed. They all feel that it is a terrible tragedy for the nation that its truly great men can never become a part of its living culture because they are too far ahead of it.

It must be emphasized, however, that the minds under consideration so far have been those of an aesthetic bent, since there is a considerable difference in the ways the mind relates to the world. While the aesthetic mind wants the same sort of admiration accorded to Goethe and Michelangelo, Napoleon and Luther, hardly anyone today knows the name of the man who gave humanity the untold blessing of anesthesia; nobody searches the lives of Gauss, Euler, or Maxwell for an Immortal Beloved, and hardly anyone cares where Lavoisier and Cardanus were born and died. Instead, we learn how their ideas and inventions were further developed by the ideas and inventions of other, equally uninteresting people, and continually concentrate on their achievements, which live on through others long after the brief flame of the individual has burned out. One is amazed at first to see how sharp the distinction is between two kinds of human endeavor, but soon enough counterexamples come to mind, and it begins to look like the most natural of differentiations. Familiar custom assures us it is the difference between person and work, between the greatness of a human being and that of a cause, between culture and knowledge, humanity and nature. Work and outstanding productivity do not increase moral stature, nor being a man in the eyes of heaven, nor those unanalyzable lessons of life that are handed down only by the example of statesmen, heroes, saints, singers, and, one must admit, movie actors—in short, that great irrational power in which the poet, too, feels he has a part, as long as he believes in what he says and holds fast to his belief that whatever his circumstances, his voice is the voice of the inner life, the blood, the heart, the nation, Europe, or all mankind. It is the mysterious whole of which he feels himself to be the medium, while the others are merely rummaging around in the comprehensible—and this is a mission one must believe in before one can learn to see it! What assures us of this is a voice of truth, certainly, but isn't there something odd about this truth? For where one looks less at the person than at the cause, there is, remarkably, always a fresh person to carry on the cause, while on the other hand, wherever the emphasis is on the person, there is always the feeling after a certain level has been reached that there is no longer anyone who measures up anymore, and that true greatness lies in the past.

Each and every one of the men gathered at Diotima's that night was a vessel of the whole, and that was a lot all at once. Writing and thinking, activities as natural to man as swimming is to a duckling, was something they practiced as a profession, and they were, in fact, really better at it than most. But what was it all for? What they did was beautiful, it was great, it was unique, but so much uniqueness bore the collective breath of mortality and the graveyard, having no evident meaning or purpose, ancestors or progeny. Countless remembered experiences, myriads of crisscrossing vibrations of the spirit, were gathered in these heads, which were stuck like a carpet weaver's needles in a carpet extending without seams or edges all around them in every direction and somewhere, at some random place, creating a pattern that seemed to repeat itself elsewhere but was actually a little different. But is this the proper use of oneself, to set such a little patch on eternity?

It would probably be saying far too much to say that Diotima had grasped all this, but she felt the wind of the grave over the fields of the spirit, and the nearer this first day drew to its close, the deeper she slipped into discouragement. Luckily, it brought to her mind a certain hopelessness Arnheim had expressed on another occasion, when they had spoken of such things, though at the time she had not quite grasped his meaning; now her friend was away on a trip, but she remembered how he had warned her not to place too great hopes in this gathering. So it was actually Arnheim's melancholy into which she was drifting, which made it ultimately an almost sensuously pensive and flattering pleasure. Musing on his prophetic words, she wondered: "Isn't it, deep down, the pessimism people of action are always bound to feel when they come in contact with those who traffic in words?"

72

SCIENCE SMILING INTO ITS BEARD, OR A
FIRST FULL-DRESS ENCOUNTER WITH EVIL

Now for a few necessary words about a smile, specifically a man's smile, and about a beard, created for the male act of smiling into one's beard; the smile of the scholars who had accepted Diotima's invitation and were listening to the famous artists. Although they were smiling, they were absolutely not to be suspected of doing so ironically. On the contrary, it was their way of expressing deference and incompetence, as has already been explained. But this, too, should fool no one. They were sincere in this, consciously; but subconsciously, to use a fashionable term, or, better still, in the sum of their being, they were people in whom a propensity for Evil crackled like a fire under a caldron.

This has a paradoxical ring, of course, and any of our university professors in whose presence one attempted to assert it would probably counter that he was a humble servant of truth and progress and otherwise knew nothing about anything. That is his professional ideology. But high-mindedness is the mark of every professional ideology. Hunters, for instance, would never dream of calling themselves the butchers of wild game; they prefer to call themselves the duly licensed friends of nature and animals; just as businessmen uphold the principle of an honorable profit, while the businessman's god, Mercury, that distinguished promoter of international relations, is also the god of thieves. So the image of a profession in the minds of its practitioners is not too reliable.

If we ask ourselves dispassionately how science has arrived at its present state—an important question in itself, considering how entirely we are in its power and how not even an illiterate is safe from its domination, since he has to learn to live with countless things born of science—we get a different picture. Credible received wisdom indicates that it all began in the sixteenth century, a time of the greatest spiritual turbulence, when people ceased trying to penetrate the deep mysteries of nature as they had done through two millennia of religious and philosophical speculation, but were instead satisfied with exploring the surface of nature in a manner that can only be called superficial. For instance the great Galileo Galilei, always the first to be mentioned in this connection, eliminated the question of what were nature's deep intrinsic reasons for abhorring a vacuum and consequently letting a falling body penetrate space after space until it finally comes to rest on solid ground, and settled for something more common: he simply established how quickly such a body falls, the course it takes, the time it takes, and what is its rate of downward acceleration. The Catholic Church made a grave error in threatening this man with death and forcing him to recant instead of summarily executing him without much ceremony, since it was from his way of looking at things, and that of others of like mind, that afterward—in next to no time, in the scale of history—there arose railway timetables, industrial machines, physiological psychology, and our era's moral decay against which the Church no longer stands a chance. The Church probably erred in being overprudent, because Galileo was not only the discoverer of the law of falling bodies and the motion of the earth, but also an inventor in whom, as we would say today, major capital took an interest; besides, he was not the only one in his time who was seized by the new spirit. On the contrary, historical accounts show that the matter-of-factness that inspired him raged and spread like an infection. However disconcerting it may sound nowadays to speak of someone as inspired by matter-of-factness, believing as we do that we have far too much of it, in Galileo's day the awakening from metaphysics to the hard observation of reality must have been, judging by all sorts of evidence, a veritable orgy and conflagration of matter-of-factness! But should one ask what mankind was thinking of when it made this change, the answer is that it did no more than what every sensible child does after trying to walk too soon; it sat down on the ground, contacting the earth with a most dependable if not very noble part of its anatomy, in short, that part on which one sits. The amazing thing is that the earth showed itself to be uncommonly receptive, and ever since that moment of contact has allowed men to entice inventions, conveniences, and discoveries out of it in quantities bordering on the miraculous.

Such preliminaries might lead one to think, with some justice, that it is the miracle of the Antichrist we now find ourselves in the midst of; for the metaphor of "contact" used here is to be interpreted not only in the sense of dependability, but also just as much in the sense of the unseemly and disreputable. And in truth, before intellectuals discovered their pleasure in "facts," facts were the sole preserve of soldiers, hunters, and traders—people by nature full of violence and cunning. The struggle for existence makes no allowance for sentimental considerations; it knows only the desire to kill one's opponent in the quickest, most factual way; here everyone is a positivist. Nor is it a virtue in business to let oneself be taken in instead of going for the solid facts, since a profit is ultimately a psychological overpowering of your opponent arising from the circumstances. If, on the other hand, one looks at the qualities that lead to the making of discoveries, one finds freedom from traditional considerations and inhibitions, courage, as much initiative as ruthlessness, the exclusion of moral considerations, patience in haggling for the smallest advantage, dogged endurance on the way to the goal, if necessary, and a veneration for measure and number that expresses the keenest mistrust of all uncertainty. In other words, we find just those ancient vices of soldiers, hunters, and traders, here merely translated into intellectual terms and interpreted as virtues. This raises them above the pursuit of personal and relatively vulgar advantage, but even in this transformation the element of primal evil is not lost; it is seemingly indestructible and everlasting, at least as everlasting as everything humanly sublime, since it consists of nothing less and nothing else than the urge to trip up that sublimity and watch it fall on its face. Who has never felt a nasty itch, looking at a beautifully glazed, luxuriantly curved vase, at the thought of smashing it to bits with a single blow of one's stick? This temptation, raised to its full heroic bitterness—that nothing in life can be relied on unless it is firmly nailed down—is a basic feeling embedded in the sobriety of science; and though we are too respectable to call it the Devil, a whiff of burned horsehair still clings to it.

We can begin at once with the peculiar predilection of scientific thinking for mechanical, statistical, and physical explanations that have, as it were, the heart cut out of them. The scientific mind sees kindness only as a special form of egotism; brings emotions into line with glandular secretions; notes that eight or nine tenths of a human being consists of water; explains our celebrated moral freedom as an automatic mental by-product of free trade; reduces beauty to good digestion and the proper distribution of fatty tissue; graphs the annual statistical curves of births and suicides to show that our most intimate personal decisions are programmed behavior; sees a connection between ecstasy and mental disease; equates the anus and the mouth as the rectal and the oral openings at either end of the same tube—such ideas, which expose the trick, as it were, behind the magic of human illusions, can always count on a kind of prejudice in their favor as being impeccably scientific. Certainly they demonstrate the love of truth. But surrounding this clear, shining love is a predilection for disillusionment, compulsiveness, ruthlessness, cold intimidation, and dry rebuke, a spiteful predilection, or at least an involuntary emanation of such a kind.

To put it differently, the voice of truth is accompanied by a suspicious static noise to which those most closely involved turn a deaf ear. Well, contemporary psychology knows many such repressed phenomena and is ready with advice to haul them out and make them as clear as possible to oneself, to prevent their having harmful effects. How about putting it to the test, then, and trying to make an open display of that ambiguous taste for the truth, with its malicious undertones of human spitefulness, its hound-of-hell attitude, letting it take its chances in life, as it were? What might come of this is, more or less, that lack of idealism already discussed under the heading of a utopia of exact living, an attitude of experiment and revocation, but subject to the iron laws of warfare involved in all intellectual conquests. This approach to shaping life is of course in no way nurturing or appeasing. It would regard everything worthy of life not with simple veneration but rather as a line of demarcation being constantly redrawn in the battle for inner truth. It would question the sanctity of the world's momentary condition, not from skepticism but rather in the conviction of the climber that the foot with the firmer hold is always the lower one. In the fire of such a Church Militant, which hates doctrine for the sake of revelation yet to come and sets aside law and values in the name of an exacting love for their imminent new configurations, the Devil would find his way back to God or, more simply, truth would again be the sister of virtue and would no longer have to play tricks on goodness behind its back, like a young niece with an old maiden aunt.

All that sort of thing is absorbed more or less consciously by a young man in the lecture halls of learning, along with the basics of a great, constructive way of thinking capable of bringing together with ease such disparate phenomena as a falling stone and an orbiting star, and of analyzing something as seemingly whole and indivisible as the origin of a simple act within the depths of consciousness into currents whose inner sources lie thousands of years apart. But should anyone presume to use such an approach outside the limits of specific professional problems, he would quickly be given to understand that the needs of life are different from the requirements of thought. What happens in life is more or less the opposite of whatever the trained mind is accustomed to. Life places a very high value on natural distinctions and congenialities; whatever exists, no matter what it is, is regarded up to a point as the natural thing, and not to be lightly tampered with; changes that become necessary proceed reluctantly and in a kind of two-steps-forward, one-step-back rhythm. If someone of purely vegetarian convictions, say, were to address a cow as "Ma'am"—on the perfectly reasonable assumption that one is likely to behave more brutally toward someone addressed with "Hey there!"—he would be called a conceited ass or even a crackpot, but not because of his vegetarian convictions or his respect for animals, which are regarded as most humane, but because he was acting them out directly in the real world. In short, what we think and what we do coexist in an intricate compromise whereby the claims of the intellect are paid off at the rate of no more than 50 percent of every thousand, while to make up for the rest it is adorned with the title of honorary creditor.

But if the human mind, in the imposing shape that is its most recent manifestation, is indeed, as we have suggested, a very masculine saint with warlike and hunterlike ancillary vices, one might conclude from the circumstances described above that the mind's inherent tendency toward depravity, grandiose as it is, can neither reveal itself nor find any occasion to purge itself through contact with reality, with the result that it is likely to turn up on all sorts of quite strange, unsupervised paths by which it evades its sterile captivity. Whether everything up to this point has been merely a play of conceits is an open question, but there is no denying that this last surmise has its own peculiar confirmation. There is a nameless mood abroad in the world today, a feeling in the blood of more than a few people, an expectation of worse things to come, a readiness to riot, a mistrust of everything one reveres. There are those who deplore the lack of idealism in the young but who, the moment they must act themselves, automatically behave no differently from someone with a healthy mistrust of ideas who backs up his gentle persuasiveness with the effect of some kind of blackjack. Is there, in other words, any pious intent that does not have to equip itself with a little bit of corruption and reliance on the lower human qualities in order to be taken in this world as serious and seriously meant? Terms like "bind," "force," "put the screws on," "don't be afraid to smash windows," "take strong measures," all have the pleasant ring of dependability. Propositions of the kind that the greatest philosopher, after a week in barracks, will learn to spring to attention at the drill sergeant's voice, or that a lieutenant and eight men are enough to arrest any parliament in the world, achieved their classic form only somewhat later, in the discovery that a few spoonfuls of castor oil poured down the throat of an idealist can make the sternest convictions look ridiculous; but long before that, and although they were disclaimed with indignation, such ideas had the savage buoyancy of sinister dreams.

It just so happens that the second thought, at the very least, of every person today confronted by an overwhelming phenomenon, even if it should be its beauty that so overwhelms him, is "You can't fool me! I'll cut you down to size!" And this mania for cutting things down to size, typical of an era that not only flees with the fox but also pursues with the hounds, has hardly anything to do any longer with life's natural separation of the raw from the sublime; it is, rather, much more a self-tormenting bent of mind, an inadmissible lust at the spectacle of the good being humiliated and too easily destroyed altogether. It is not dissimilar from some passionate desire to give the lie to oneself, and perhaps there are bleaker prospects than believing in a time that has come into the world coccyx-first and merely needs the Creator's hands to turn it around.

Much of this sort of thing may be expressed by a man's smile, even when the man is not himself aware of it or it has never even gone through his consciousness at all, and this was the sort of smile with which most of the invited celebrated experts lent themselves to Diotima's praiseworthy efforts. It began as a prickling sensation moving up the legs, which did not quite know in which direction they should turn, and finally landed as a look of benevolent amazement on the face. With relief one spotted an acquaintance or a colleague one could speak to. One had the feeling that going home, outside the gate, one would have to stamp firmly a few times to test the ground. Still, it was a very pleasant occasion. Such general undertakings never find a proper content, of course, like all universal and elevated concepts. One cannot even imagine the concept "dog"; the word is only a reference to particular dogs and canine qualities, and this is even more the case with "patriotism" or the loftiest patriotic ideas. But even if it has no content, it certainly has a meaning, and it is surely desirable from time to time to bring that meaning to life! This was what most of those present were communicating to one another, although mostly within the silence of the unconscious. But Diotima, still standing in the main reception room and favoring stragglers with her little speeches of welcome, was astonished to hear what appeared to be lively conversations starting up on such subjects as the difference between Bohemian and Bavarian beer, or publishers' royalties.

It was too bad that she could not watch her reception from the street. From out there it looked marvelous. The light shone brightly through the curtains of the tall windows along the façade of the house, heightened by the additional glow of authority and distinction emanating from the waiting cars, as well as by the gaping passersby who stopped to look up for a while without quite knowing why. Diotima would have been pleased by the sight. There were people constantly standing in the half-light the festivity cast on the street; behind their backs, the great darkness began that within a short distance quickly became impenetrable.

73

LEO FISCHEL'S DAUGHTER GERDA

In all this hubbub, Ulrich kept putting off fulfilling his promise to Fischel that he would pay the family a visit. He actually never did get around to it until something unexpected happened: Fischel's wife, Clementine, came to see him.

She had phoned to announce her visit, and Ulrich awaited her not without apprehension. It had been three years since he had regularly come to their house, during a stay of some months in town; since his return he had been there only once, not wanting to stir up a past flirtation and dreading having to deal with a mother's disappointment. But Clementine Fischel was a woman of "magnanimous spirit," with so little opportunity to exercise it in her daily petty struggles with her husband, Leo, that for special occasions, regrettably so rare in her life, she had reserves of truly heroic high-mindedness to draw upon. Even so, this thin woman with her austere, rather care-worn face felt a bit embarrassed when she found herself face-to-face with Ulrich, saying she needed to speak to him privately, even though they were alone as it was. But he was the only person Gerda would still listen to, she said, adding that she hoped he would not misunderstand her request.

Ulrich was aware of the Fischel family's situation. Not only were the father and mother constantly at war, but their daughter, Gerda, already twenty-three, had surrounded herself with a swarm of odd young people who had somehow co-opted Papa Leo, who ground his teeth, as a most grudging Maecenas and backer of their "new movement" because his house was the most convenient for their get-togethers. Gerda was so nervous and anemic, and got so terribly upset every time anyone tried to make her see less of these friends—Clementine reported—who were, after all, just silly boys without real breeding; still, the way they insisted on parading their mystical anti-Semitism was not only in poor taste, it revealed an inner brutality. Not that she had come to complain about anti-Semitism, she added, which was a sign of the times, one simply had to resign oneself to it—she was even prepared to admit that in some respects there might be something in it. Clementine paused and would have dried a tear with her handkerchief had she not worn a veil; but as it was she refrained from dropping the tear, contenting herself with merely pulling her white handkerchief out of her little handbag.

"You know what Gerda's like," she said, "a beautiful and gifted girl but—"

"A bit rebellious." Ulrich finished it for her.

"Yes, Heaven help us, always going to extremes."

"So she's still a German Nationalist?"

Clementine spoke of the parents' feelings. "A mother's errand of mercy" was what she somewhat pathetically called her visit, which had as its secondary aim to entice Ulrich back as a regular visitor to their family circle, now that he was known to have risen to such eminence in the Parallel Campaign. "I hate myself," she went on, "for the way I encouraged Gerda's friendship with these boys in recent years, against Leo's will. I thought nothing of it; these youngsters are idealists in their way, and an open-minded person can let the occasional offensive word pass. . . . But Leo—you know how he is—is upset by anti-Semitism, whether it's merely mystical or symbolic or not."

"And Gerda, in her free-spirited, Germanic, blond fashion, won't recognize the problem?" Ulrich rounded it out.

"She's the same as I was at her age in this respect. Do you think, by the way, that Hans Sepp has any prospects?"

"Is Gerda engaged to him?" Ulrich asked cautiously.

"That boy has no means whatever of providing for her," Clementine sighed. "How can you talk of an engagement? But when Leo ordered him out of the house Gerda ate so little for three weeks running that she turned to skin and bone." All at once, she broke out angrily: "You know, it seems to me like hypnosis, like some sort of spiritual infection! That boy incessantly expounds his philosophy under our roof, and Gerda never notices the continual insult to her parents in it, even though she's always been a good and affectionate child otherwise. But whenever I say anything, she answers: 'You're so old-fashioned, Mama.' So I thought—you're the only man who counts for something with her, and Leo thinks the world of you!—couldn't you come over and try to open Gerda's eyes to the callowness of Hans and his cronies?"

For such a model of propriety as Clementine to resort to so aggressive a tactic could only mean that she was seriously worried. Whatever their conflicts, she was inclined to a certain solidarity with her husband in this situation. Ulrich raised his eyebrows in concern.

"I'm afraid Gerda will call me old-fashioned too. These new young people pay no attention to us elders on such matters of principle."

"It occurred to me that the easiest way to distract Gerda might be your finding something for her to do in that patriotic campaign of yours everyone is talking about," Clementine offered, and Ulrich hastened to promise her a visit, even while assuring her that the Parallel Campaign was far from being ready for such uses.

When Gerda saw him coming through the door a few days afterward, two circular red spots appeared on her cheeks, but she energetically shook his hand. She was one of those charmingly purposeful young women of our time who would instantly become bus drivers if some higher purpose called for it.

Ulrich had not been mistaken in the assumption that he would find her alone; it was the hour when Mama was out shopping and Papa was still at the office. Ulrich had hardly taken his first steps into the room when he was overcome with a sense of déjà vu, everything so reminded him of a particular day during their earlier times together. It had been a few weeks later in the year then, still spring but one of those piercingly hot days that sometimes precede the summer like burning embers, hard for the still unseasoned body to bear. Gerda's face had looked haggard and thin. She was dressed in white and smelled white, like linen dried on meadow grass. The blinds were down in all the rooms, and the whole apartment was full of rebellious half-lights and arrows of heat whose points were broken off from piercing through the sack-gray barrier. Ulrich felt that Gerda's body was made up entirely of the same freshly washed linen hangings as her dress. He felt this quite without emotion and could have calmly peeled layer after layer off her, without needing the least erotic stimulus to egg him on. He had the very same feeling again this time. Theirs seemed to be a perfectly natural but pointless intimacy, and they both feared it.

"Why did it take you so long to come see us?" Gerda asked.

Ulrich told her straight out that her parents would surely not wish them to be so close unless they intended to marry.

"Oh, Mama," Gerda said. "Mama's absurd. So we're not supposed to be friends if we don't instantly think about that! But Papa wants you to come often; you're said to be quite somebody in that big affair."

She came out with this quite openly, this foolishness of the old folk, secure in her assumption that she and Ulrich were naturally in league against it.

"I'll come," Ulrich replied, "but now tell me, Gerda, where does that leave us?"

The point was, they did not love each other. They had played a lot of tennis together, met at social functions, gone out together, taken an interest in each other, and thus unawares had crossed the borderline that separates an intimate friend whom we allow to see us in all our inward disorder from those for whom we cultivate our appearance. They had unexpectedly become as close as two people who have loved each other for a long time, who in fact almost no longer love each other, without actually going through love. They were always arguing, so it looked as if they did not care for each other, but it was both an obstacle and a bond between them. They knew that with all this it would only take one spark to start a big fire. Had there been less of a difference in their ages, or had Gerda been a married woman, then "opportunity would probably have created the thief," and the theft might have led, at least afterward, to passion, since we talk ourselves into love as we talk ourselves into a rage, by making the proper gestures. But just because they knew all this, they did not do it. Gerda had remained a virgin, and furiously resented it.

Instead of answering Ulrich's question, she had busied herself about the room, when suddenly he stood beside her. That was reckless of him, because one can't stand so close to a girl at such a moment and just start talking about something. They followed the path of least resistance, like a brook that, avoiding obstacles, flows down a meadow, and Ulrich put his arm around Gerda's hip so that his fingertips reached the precipitate downward line of the inside elastic that follows from garter belt to stocking. He turned up Gerda's face, with its confused and slightly sweaty look, and kissed her on the lips. Then they stood still, unable to let go or come together. His finger-tips connected with the broad elastic of her garter belt and let it snap gently against her thigh a few times. Then he tore himself away and with a shrug asked her again:

"Where do we go from here, Gerda?"

Gerda fought down her excitement and said: "Is this how it has to be?"

She rang for refreshments; she set the household in motion.

"Tell me something about Hans," Ulrich asked her gently, when they had sat down and had to begin the conversation again. Gerda, who had not quite regained her poise, did not answer at first, but after a while she said: "You're so pleased with yourself, you'll never understand younger people like us."

"Sticks and stones . . . ," Ulrich said evasively. "I think, Gerda, that I'm done with science now. Which means that I am making common cause with the younger generation. Is it enough to swear to you that knowledge is akin to greed? That it is a shabby form of thriftiness? A supercilious kind of spiritual capitalism? There is more feeling in me than you think. But I want to spare you the kind of talk that amounts to nothing but words."

"You must get to know Hans better," Gerda replied weakly, then she erupted again: "Anyway, you'd never understand that it's possi-ble to fuse with others into a community, without any thought of yourself!"

"Does Hans still come so often?" Ulrich asked warily. Gerda shrugged her shoulders.

Her shrewd parents had refrained from forbidding Hans Sepp the house altogether; he was allowed to come a few days every month. In turn Hans Sepp, the student who was nothing and had as yet no pros-pect of becoming something, had to promise not to make Gerda do anything she shouldn't, and to suspend his propagandizing for some mystical, Germanic action. In this way they hoped to rob him of the charm of forbidden fruit. And Hans Sepp in his chastity (only the sensual man wants to possess, but then sensuality is a Jewish-capital-istic trait) had calmly given his word as requested, without, however, taking it to mean that he would give up his frequent secret comings and goings, making incendiary speeches, hotly pressing Gerda's hands or even kissing her, all of which still comes naturally to soulmates, but only that he would refrain from advocating sexual union without benefit of clergy or civic authority, which he had been advocating, but on a purely theoretical plane. He had pledged his word all the more readily as he did not feel that he and Gerda were spiritually mature enough as yet to turn his principles into action; setting up a barrier to the temptations of the baser instincts was quite in line with his way of thinking.

But the two young people naturally suffered under these restraints imposed on them before they had found their own inner discipline. Gerda especially would not have put up with such interference from her parents, had it not been for her own uncertainties; this made her resentment all the greater. She did not really love her young friend all that much; it was more a matter of translating her opposition to her parents into an attachment to him. Had Gerda been born some years later than she was, her papa would have been one of the richest men in town, even if not too highly regarded as a result, and her mother would have admired him again, before Gerda could have been of an age to experience the bickerings of her progenitors as a conflict within herself. She would then probably have taken pride in being of "racially mixed" parentage; but as things stood, she rebelled against her parents and their problems, did not want to be genetically tainted by them, and was blond, free, Germanic, and forceful, as if she had nothing at all to do with them. This solution, as good as it looked, had the disadvantage that she had never got around to bringing the worm that was gnawing at her inwardly out into the light of day. In her home, nationalism and racism were treated as nonexistent, even though they were convulsing half of Europe with hysterical ideas and everything in the Fischel household in particular turned on nothing else. Whatever Gerda knew of it had come to her from the outside, in the dark form of rumors, suggestion, and exaggeration. The paradox of her parents—who normally reacted strongly to anything talked about by many people—making so notable an exception in this case had made a deep impression early in her life, and since she attached no definite, objective meaning to this ghostly presence, she tended to connect with it everything disagreeable and peculiar in her home life, especially during her adolescence.

One day she met the Christian-Germanic circle of young people to which Hans Sepp belonged, and suddenly felt she had found her true home. It would be hard to say what these young people actually believed in; they formed one of those innumerable undefined "free-spirited" little sects that have infested German youth ever since the breakdown of the humanistic ideal. They were not racial anti-Semites but opponents of "the Jewish mind," by which they meant capitalism and socialism, science, reason, parental authority and parental arrogance, calculation, psychology, and skepticism. Their basic doctrinal device was the "symbol"; as far as Ulrich could make out, and he had, after all, some understanding of such things, what they meant by "symbol" was the great images of grace, which made everything that is confused and dwarfed in life, as Hans Sepp put it, clear and great, images that suppress the noise of the senses and dip the forehead in streams of transcendence. Such symbols were the Isenheim Altar, the Egyptian pyramids, and Novalis; Beethoven and Stefan George were acceptable approximations. But they did not state, in so many words, what a symbol was: first, because a symbol cannot be expressed in so many words; second, because Aryans do not deal in dry formulas, which is why they achieved only approximations of symbols during the last century; and third, because some centuries only rarely produce the transcendent moment of grace in the transcendent human being.

Gerda, who was no fool, secretly felt not a little distrust toward these overblown sentiments, but she also distrusted her distrust, in which she thought she detected the legacy of her parents' rationalism. Behind her façade of independence she was anxiously at pains to disobey her parents, in dread that her bloodlines might hinder her from following Hans's ideas. She felt deeply mutinous against the taboos girding the morals of her so-called good family and against the arrogant parental rights of intrusion that threatened to suffocate her personality, while Hans, who had "no family at all," as her mother put it, suffered much less than she did; he had emerged from her circle of companions as Gerda's "spiritual guide," passionately harangued the girl, who was as old as he was, trying to transport her, with his tirades accompanied by kisses, into the "region of the Unconditional," though in practice he was quite adept at coming to terms with the conditioned state of the Fischel household, as long as he was permitted to reject it "on principle," which of course always led to rows with Papa Leo.

"My dear Gerda," Ulrich said after a while, "your friends torment you about your father—they really are the worst kind of blackmailers!"

Gerda turned pale, then red. "You are no longer young yourself," she replied. "You think differently from us." She knew that she had stung Ulrich's vanity, and added in a conciliatory tone: "I don't expect much from love anyway. Maybe I am wasting my time with Hans, as you say; maybe I have to resign myself altogether to the idea that I'll never love anyone enough to open every crevice of my soul to him: my thoughts and feelings, work and dreams; I don't even think that would be so very awful."

"How wise beyond your years you sound, Gerda, when you talk like your friends," Ulrich broke in.

Gerda was annoyed. "When I talk with my friends," she said, "our thoughts flow from one to the other, and we know that we live and speak as one with our people—do you have any idea what this means? We stand with countless others of our own kind, we feel their presence, in a sensory, physical way I'm sure you've never . . . In fact, you can't even imagine such a thing, can you? Your desire has always been for a *single* person; you think like a beast of prey!"

Why a beast of prey? Her words hung in midair, giving her away; she realized their senselessness and felt ashamed of her eyes, wide with fear, which were staring at Ulrich.

"Let's not go into that," Ulrich said gently. "Let me tell you a story instead. Do you know"—he drew her closer with his hand, inside which her wrist disappeared like a child among high crags—"the sensational story of the capture of the moon? You know, of course, that long ago our earth had several moons. And there's a very popular theory that such moons are not what we take them for, cosmic bodies that have cooled like the earth itself, but great globes of ice rushing through space that have come too close to the earth and are held fast by it. Our moon is said to be the last of them. Come and have a look at it!"

Gerda had followed him to the window and looked for the pale moon in the sunny sky.

"Doesn't it look like a disk of ice?" Ulrich asked. "That's no source of light. Have you ever wondered why the man in the moon always faces us the same way? Our last moon is no longer turning on its axis, that's why; it's already fixed in place! You see, once the moon has come into the earth's power it doesn't merely revolve around the earth but is drawn steadily closer. We don't notice it because it takes thousands of years or even longer for the screw to tighten. But there's no getting away from it, and there must have been thousands of years in the history of the earth during which the previous moons were drawn very close and went on racing in orbit with incredible speed. And just as our present moon pulls a tide from three to six feet high after it, an earlier one would have dragged in its wake whole mountain ranges of water and mud, tumbling all over the globe. We can hardly imagine the terror in which generation after generation must have lived on such a crazy earth for thousands upon thousands of years."

"But were there human beings on earth already?" Gerda asked.

"Certainly. In the end, such an ice moon cracks up, comes crashing down like giant hailstones, and the mountainous flood it has been dragging along in its orbit collapses and covers the whole globe with one vast tidal wave before it settles down again: That's none other than the great biblical Flood, meaning a great universal inundation! How else could all the myths be in such agreement, if mankind hadn't experienced it all? And since we have one moon left, such ages are bound to come once more. It's a strange thought. . . ."

Gerda gazed breathlessly out of the window and up at the moon; her hand was still resting in his, the moon was a pale, ugly stain on the sky, and it was precisely this unassuming presence that made this fantastic cosmic adventure—of which she somehow saw herself as the victim—look like an ordinary, everyday reality.

"But there's no truth at all to this story," Ulrich said. "The experts call it a crackpot theory, and the moon isn't really coming any closer to the earth; it is, in fact, thirty-two kilometers farther from us than it should be, according to our calculations, if I remember it right."

"Then why did you tell me this story?" Gerda asked, and tried to extricate her hand from his. But her defiance had quite run out of steam, as it always did when she spoke with this man, who was certainly not Hans's intellectual inferior and yet managed to keep from going to extremes in his views, to keep his fingernails clean and his hair combed. Ulrich noticed the fine black down growing like a contradiction on Gerda's fair skin; the tiny hairs sprouting from her body seemed to bespeak the variously composite nature of poor modern mankind.

"I don't really know," he replied. "Shall I come and see you again?"

Gerda took out the excitement of her liberated hand on various small objects, which she pushed this way and that, without saying anything.

"See you soon, then," Ulrich promised, although this had not been his intention before he came.

74

THE FOURTH CENTURY B.C. VERSUS THE YEAR 1797. ULRICH RECEIVES ANOTHER LETTER FROM HIS FATHER

The rumor had quickly spread that the meetings at Diotima's were an extraordinary success. And now Ulrich received an unusually long letter from his father, stuffed with enclosed pamphlets and offprints. The letter read more or less like this:

My dear son:

Your extended silence . . .

However, I have had the pleasure of hearing from another source that my efforts on your behalf . . . my kind friend Count Stallburg . . . His Grace Count Leinsdorf . . . our kinswoman the wife of Section Chief Tuzzi . . . And now I must ask you, if you will, to use all your influence in your new circle in the following matter:

The world would come apart if everything held to be true were indeed to be accepted as such and every will could have its way as long as it seems to itself legitimate. All of us are therefore duty-bound to determine the one truth and the proper aim; then, insofar as we have succeeded in so doing, to take care, with an unflinching sense of our duty, that it is set down in the clear form of scientific thought. You may gather from this what it means when I tell you that in lay circles, but also, sad to say, in scientific circles susceptible to the promptings of a confused age, an extremely dangerous movement has been afoot for a long time to bring about certain presumed reforms and ameliorations in the proposed revision of the penal code. To fill you in, a committee of noted experts has been in existence for a number of years, appointed by the Minister of Justice to draw up such a proposed revision, to which committee I have the honor to belong, as does my university colleague Professor Schwung, whom you may remember from earlier days before I had seen through him, so that for many years he could pass as my best friend. As regards the liberalizations mentioned above, a rumor has reached me—unfortunately only too likely to be true!—that in the approaching jubilee year of our revered and merciful sovereign, exploiting, as it were, all inclinations to magnanimity, special efforts are likely to be made to pave the way for just such a disastrous emasculation of our legal system. It goes without saying that Professor Schwung and I are equally resolved to forestall this.

I realize that you are not versed in legal matters, but the chances are you know that the method of breaching our fortifications most favored by the present tendency to legal obfuscation, which falsely dubs itself humanitarianism, consists in the effort to extend the concept of mental impairment, for which punishment is not in order, in the vague form of diminished responsibility, even to those numerous individuals who are neither insane nor morally normal: that army of inferior persons the morally feebleminded, which sadly enough constitutes one of the ever-growing diseases of our civilization. You will see for yourself that this concept of diminished responsibility—if you can call it a concept, which I contest—is most intimately connected with the manner in which we interpret the concepts of full responsibility, or irresponsibility, as the case may be, and this brings me to the point of this letter:

Proceeding from already existing formulations of the law, and in view of the circumstances cited, I have proposed to the previously mentioned planning committee the following version of Paragraph 318 of our future penal code:

"No criminal act has been committed if the perpetrator was in a state of unconsciousness or pathological disturbance of his mind at the time he was engaged in the act under consideration, so that—" and Professor Schwung submitted a proposal beginning with exactly the same words.

But then *he* continued as follows: "so that he could not exercise his free will," while mine was to read: "so that he did not have the capacity to perceive the wrongfulness of his act." I must admit that I did not at first realize the malicious intent of this contradiction. My personal view has always been this, that as the intellect and reasoning power develops, the will comes to dominate desires or instincts by way of considered thoughts and the decisions springing from them. Any willed act is accordingly always the result of prior thought and not purely instinctive. Man is free insofar as he has the power of choice in the exercise of his will; when under the influence of human cravings, that is to say, cravings prompted by his sensual nature which interfere with his ability to think clearly, then he is not free. Volition is simply not a matter of chance but an act of self-determination arising necessarily from within the person, and so the will is determined by thought, and when the thought process is disturbed, the will is no longer the will, as the man's action is prompted only by his natural cravings. I am of course aware that the opposite view is also represented in the literature, i.e., that thought is regarded as being determined by the will. This is a view, however, that has its adherents among modern jurists only since 1797, while the one I hold has stood up to all attacks since the fourth century B.C. But to show that I was willing to meet my colleague halfway, I put forward a formulation that would join both proposals, as follows:

"No criminal act shall have been committed if the offender was at the time of his act in a state of unconsciousness or a morbid disturbance of his mental activity, so that he did not have the capacity to perceive the wrongfulness of his act and could not exercise his free will."

But here Professor Schwung revealed himself in his true colors! Showing no appreciation whatsoever of my willingness to meet him halfway, he arrogantly insisted that the "and" in my statement had to be replaced with an "or." You see the point? What differentiates the thinker from the layman is precisely this fine distinction of an "or" where the layman simply puts an "and," and Schwung was trying to stigmatize me as a superficial thinker by exposing my readiness to find a compromise, using the "and" to unite both formulations, exposing it to the suspicion that I had failed to grasp the full magnitude of the difference to be bridged, with all its implications!

It goes without saying that from that moment on I have rigorously opposed him on every point.

I immediately withdrew my compromise proposal and have had to insist on the acceptance of my first version without any compromise whatsoever; since when, however, Schwung has been making trouble for me with a most perfidious ingenuity. He claims, for instance, that under my proposed version, which is based on the capacity to recognize a wrongful act as such, a person who suffers from special delusions but is otherwise normal, as sometimes happens, could be exonerated on grounds of mental illness only if it could be proved that this person had assumed, because of his delusions, the existence of circumstances under which his act would be justified or not punishable under the law, so that he would have been acting correctly, although within a false concept of reality. This objection has no merit at all, however, for while empirical logic recognizes the existence of persons who are partly insane and partly sane, the logic of the law must never admit such a mixture of juridical states; before the law, a person is either responsible for his actions or not responsible, and we may assume that even in persons suffering from special kinds of delusions, a general capacity to know right from wrong still exists. If this is blurred by delusions in a specific instance, it needs only a special effort of the intelligence to bring it into harmony with the rest of the personality, and there is no reason to see any special problem in that.

And so I immediately pointed out to Professor Schwung that if the state of being responsible and that of not being responsible for one's actions cannot logically exist simultaneously, these states must be assumed to follow each other in rapid alternation, giving rise to the problem, especially where his theory is concerned, from which of these alternating states has the act in question resulted? To determine this, you would have to cite all the influences to which the accused has been subjected since his birth, and everything that may have influenced the actions of all his forebears, from whom his good and bad traits are inherited.

You will hardly believe this, but Schwung actually had the cheek to retort that this was quite so, as the logic of the law must never admit a mixture of two juridical states with respect to one and the same act, so that it is necessary to decide even with regard to each specific act of volition whether it was possible for the accused, in the light of his psychological history, to control his will or not. He chooses to claim that we are far more clearly aware of our free will than of the fact that everything that happens has a cause, and as long as we are basically free, we are also free with respect to specific causes, so that we must assume that in such a case it only requires a special effort of the will to resist the causally determined criminal impulses.

At this point Ulrich desisted from further exploration of his father's plans and pensively hefted in his hand the many enclosures cited in the letter's margin. Casting one more hasty glance at the letter's conclusion, he learned that his father expected him to use his "objective influence" on Counts Leinsdorf and Stallburg, and strongly advised him to warn the appropriate committees of the Parallel Campaign in good time of the dangers to the spiritual foundation of the entire government should so important a problem be wrongly formulated and resolved in the Year of the Jubilee.

75

GENERAL STUMM VON BORDWEHR CONSIDERS VISITS TO DIOTIMA AS A DELIGHTFUL CHANGE FROM HIS USUAL RUN OF DUTY

The tubby little General had paid Diotima another visit. Although the soldier has but a modest part to play in the council chamber, he began by saying, he would take it upon himself to predict that the state is the power to hold one's own in the struggle among nations, and that the military strength displayed in peacetime wards off war. But Diotima had instantly pulled him up short.

"General," she said, quivering with indignation, "all of life depends upon the forces of peace; even the life of business, rightly regarded, is a form of poetry."

The little General stared at her for a moment, dumbfounded, but soon regained his seat in the saddle.

"Your Excellency . . . ," he hastened to agree. In order to understand this form of address, we must remember that Diotima's husband was a ministerial section chief, and that in Kakania a section chief held the same rank as divisional commanders, who alone were entitled to be addressed as Excellency and only when on duty, at that; but since the soldier's profession is a knightly one, no soldier could expect to advance his career without so addressing them even when off duty, and in the spirit of chivalrous striving one also addressed their wives as Excellency, without wasting much thought on the question of when *they* were on duty. Such intricate considerations flashed through the little General's mind and enabled him to reassure Diotima instantly, with his first words, of his unqualified agreement and humble devotion, as he said, "Your Excellency takes the words out of my mouth. It goes without saying that, for political reasons, the War Ministry could not have been considered when the committees were set up, but we heard that the great movement is to be pacifist in its aims—an international peace campaign, they say, or perhaps the donation of Austrian murals to the Peace Palace at The Hague—and I can assure Your Excellency of our entire sympathy with such an aim. People generally tend to have certain misconceptions about the military; of course I won't deny that a young lieutenant is likely to yearn for a war, but all responsible quarters are most deeply convinced that the sphere of force, which we unfortunately do represent, must be linked with the blessings of the human spirit, precisely as Your Excellency has just put it."

He now dug a little brush out of his trouser pocket and went over his little mustache with it a number of times; it was a bad habit dating back to his time as a cadet, a phase during which the mustache still stands for life's impatiently awaited great hope, and he was totally unaware of it. His big brown eyes were fixed on Diotima's face, trying to read the effect of his words. Diotima seemed mollified, though in his presence she never quite was, and deigned to fill him in on what had been going on since the first meeting. The general showed enthusiasm, especially for the Great Council, expressed his admiration for Arnheim, and declared his conviction that such a gathering was bound to bear splendid fruit.

"There are so many people, after all, who don't realize how little order there is in the world of the mind," he explained. "I am even convinced, if Your Excellency will permit me to say so, that most people suppose they are seeing some progress in the order of things every day. They see order everywhere: in the factories, the offices, the railway timetables, the schools—here I may also mention proudly our own barracks, which in their modest way positively recall the discipline of a good orchestra—and no matter where you look, you will see order of some kind, rules and regulations for pedestrians, drivers, taxation, churches, business, social protocol, etiquette, morality, and so on. I'm sure that almost everyone considers our era the best-ordered of all time. Don't you have this feeling too, deep down, Your Excellency? I certainly do. If I'm not very careful, I let myself be overcome by the feeling that the modern spirit rests precisely on such a greater order, and that the great empires of Nineveh and Rome fell only because somehow they let things slide. That's what I think most people feel; they go on the unspoken assumption that the past is dead and gone as a punishment for something that got out of order. But of course that's a delusion that people who know their history shouldn't succumb to. It's why, unfortunately, we can't do without power and the soldier's profession."

It was deeply gratifying to the General to chat like this with this brilliant young woman; what a delightful change from the usual run of his official duties. But Diotima had no idea how to answer him, so she fell back on repeating herself:

"We really do hope to bring the most distinguished minds to bear on it, though our task even then will be a hard one. You can't imagine what a great variety of suggestions keep pouring in, and we do want to make the best choices. But you were speaking of order, General. We will never reach our goal through order, by a sober weighing of pros and cons, comparisons and tests. Our solution must come as a flash of lightning, a fire, an intuition, a synthesis! Looking at the history of mankind, we see no logical development; what it does suggest, with its sudden flashes of inspiration, the meaning of which emerges only later on, is a great poem!"

"If I may say so, Your Excellency," the General replied, "a soldier knows very little about poetry; but if anyone can breathe lightning and fire into a movement, it is Your Excellency; that much an old army officer can understand."

76

COUNT LEINSDORF HAS HIS DOUBTS

So far the tubby little General had been quite urbane, even though he had come uninvited to see her, and Diotima had confided more to him than she had intended. What made her fear him nonetheless, so that she afterward regretted again her amiability to him, was not really his doing but, as Diotima told herself, her old friend Count Leinsdorf's. Could His Grace be jealous? And if so, of whom? Although he always put in a brief appearance at meetings, Leinsdorf did not seem as favorably inclined to the Council as Diotima had expected. His Grace was decidedly averse to what he called mere literature. It stood for something he associated with Jews, newspapers, sensation-hungry booksellers, and the liberal, hopelessly garrulous paid hirelings of the bourgeoisie; the expression "mere literature" had positively become his new signature phrase. Every time Ulrich offered to read him the latest proposals that had come in the mail, including all the suggestions for moving the world forward or backward, he would cut him off with the words everyone uses when in addition to his own plans he hears about those everyone else has:

"No, no, I'm busy today, and all that is mere literature anyway."

What he was thinking of, in contrast to mere literature, was fields, the men who worked them, little country churches, and that great order of things which God had bound as firmly together as the sheaves on a mown field, an order at once comely, sound, and rewarding, even if it did sometimes tolerate distilleries on country estates because one had to keep pace with the times. Given this tranquil breadth of outlook, gun clubs and dairy cooperatives, no matter how far from the great centers they were to be found, must appear as part and parcel of that solid order and community; and if they should be moved to make a claim on general philosophical principles, that claim must enjoy the priority of a duly registered spiritual property, as it were, over any spiritual claims put forward by private individuals. This is why, every time Diotima wanted to speak with him seriously about something she had gleaned from her Great Minds, Count Leinsdorf was usually holding in his hand, or pulling out of his pocket, some petition from a club of five simpletons, saying that this paper weighed more in the world of real problems than the bright ideas of some genius.

This attitude resembled the one praised by Section Chief Tuzzi, as embodied in his ministerial archives, which withheld their official recognition of the Council's existence while taking every fleabite from the most insignificant provincial news sheet in deadly earnest; and Diotima, when beset by such problems, had no one she could confide in except Arnheim. But Arnheim, of all people, took His Grace's part in the matter. It was he who explained to her about that grandseigneur's tranquil breadth of outlook, when she complained to him about Count Leinsdorf's predilection for crack shots and co-op dairies.

"His Grace believes that we must take our direction from the land and the times," he explained gravely. "Believe me, it comes naturally of owning land. The soil uncomplicates life, just as it purifies water. Even I feel its effect every time I stay on my own very modest country estate. Real life makes everything simple." And after a slight hesitation he added: "The grand scale on which His Grace's life takes place also makes him extremely tolerant, not to say recklessly indulgent. . . ."

This side of her noble patron was new to Diotima, so she looked up expectantly.

"I wouldn't wish to state as a certainty," Arnheim went on with a vague emphasis, "that Count Leinsdorf is aware how very much your cousin, as his secretary, abuses his confidence—in principle only, I hasten to add—by his skepticism toward lofty schemes, by his sarcasm as a form of sabotage. I would be inclined to fear that his influence on His Grace was not a wholesome one, if this true peer were not so firmly entrenched in the great traditional feelings and ideas that support real life, so that he can probably afford to risk this confidence."

These were strong words, and Ulrich had deserved them. But Diotima did not pay as much attention to them as she might have, because she was so impressed with the other aspect of Arnheim's outlook, his owning landed estates not as a landowner but rather as a kind of spiritual massage; she thought it was magnificent, and mused on what it might be like to find oneself the lady of such a manor.

"I sometimes marvel," she said, "at the generosity with which you yourself judge His Grace. All of that is surely part of a vanishing chapter of history?"

"And so it is," Arnheim replied, "but the simple virtues of courage, chivalry, and self-discipline, which his caste developed to such an exemplary degree, will always keep their value. In a word, the ideal of the Master! I have learned to value the principle of the Master more and more in my business life as well."

"Then the ideal of the Master would, in the end, amount to almost the same thing as that of the Poem?" Diotima asked pensively.

"That's a wonderful way of putting it!" her friend agreed. "It's the secret of a vigorous life. Reason alone is not enough for a moral or a political life. Reason has its limits; what really matters always takes place above and beyond it. Great men have always loved music, poetry, form, discipline, religion, and chivalry. I would go so far as to say, in fact, that they and only they can succeed! Those are the so-called imponderables that make the master, make the man, and there is something, some obscure residue of this, in what the populace admires in the actor. But to return to your cousin: Of course it isn't simply a matter of turning conservative when we begin to prefer our comforts to sowing wild oats. But even if we were all born as revolutionaries, there comes a day when we notice that a simple, good person, regardless of what we think of his intelligence—a dependable, cheerful, brave, loyal human being, in other words—is not only a rare delight but also the true soil from which all life springs. Such wisdom is as old as the hills, but it denotes a change in taste, which in our youth naturally favors the exotic, to that of the mature man. I admire your cousin in many respects, or if this is saying too much, because there is little he says that is defensible, I could almost say that I love him, for something that is extraordinarily free and independent in his nature, together with much that is inwardly rigid and eccentric; it is just this mixture of freedom and mental rigidity that may account for his special charm, by the way. But he is a dangerous man, with his infantile moral exoticism and his highly developed intelligence that is always on the lookout for some adventure without knowing what, exactly, is egging him on."

77

ARNHEIM AS THE DARLING OF THE PRESS

Diotima repeatedly had occasion to contemplate the imponderables of Arnheim's attitude.

It was on his advice, for instance, that the representatives of the leading newspapers were sometimes invited to the sessions of the Council (as Section Chief Tuzzi had somewhat sarcastically dubbed the Committee to Draft a Guiding Resolution with Regard to the Seventieth Jubilee of His Majesty's Reign), and Arnheim, who was only a guest without any official status, enjoyed a degree of attention from them that put all other celebrities in the shade. For some reason newspapers are not the laboratories and experimental stations of the mind that they could be, to the public's great benefit, but usually only its warehouses and stock exchanges. If he were alive today, Plato—to take him as an example, because along with a dozen others he is regarded as the greatest thinker who ever lived—would certainly be ecstatic about a news industry capable of creating, exchanging, refining a new idea every day; where information keeps pouring in from the ends of the earth with a speediness he never knew in his own lifetime, while a staff of demiurges is on hand to check it all out instantaneously for its content of reason and reality. He would have supposed a newspaper office to be that *topos uranios,* that heavenly realm of ideas, which he has described so impressively that to this day all the better class of people are still idealists when talking to their children or employees. And of course if Plato were to walk suddenly into a news editor's office today and prove himself to be indeed that great author who died over two thousand years ago, he would be a tremendous sensation and would instantly be showered with the most lucrative offers. If he were then capable of writing a volume of philosophical travel pieces in three weeks, and a few thousand of his well-known short stories, perhaps even turn one or the other of his older works into a film, he could undoubtedly do very well for himself for a considerable period of time. The moment his return had ceased to be news, however, and Mr. Plato tried to put into practice one of his well-known ideas, which had never quite come into their own, the editor in chief would ask him to submit only a nice little column on the subject now and then for the Life and Leisure section (but in the easiest and most lively style possible, not heavy: remember the readers), and the features editor would add that he was sorry, but he could use such a contribution only once a month or so, because there were so many other good writers to be considered. And both of these gentlemen would end up feeling that they had done quite a lot for a man who might indeed be the Nestor of European publicists but still was a bit outdated, and certainly not in a class for current newsworthiness with a man like, for instance, Paul Arnheim.

Arnheim himself would of course never concur in this, because his reverence for all greatness would be offended by it, yet in many respects he was bound to find it understandable. These days, with everything in the world being talked about helter-skelter, when prophets and charlatans rely on the same phrases, except for certain subtle differences no busy man has the time to keep track of, and editors are constantly pestered with alarms that someone or other may be a genius, it is very hard to recognize the true value of a man or an idea; all one can do is keep an ear cocked for the moment when all the murmurs and whispers and shufflings at the editor's door grow loud enough to be admitted as the voice of the people. From that moment on, however, genius does enter a new state. It ceases to be a windy business of book or drama reviews, with all their contradictions, which the paper's ideal reader will take no more seriously than the babble of children, but has achieved the status of a fact, with all the consequences that entails.

Fools who keep inveighing against such realities overlook the desperate need for idealism behind all this. The world of those who write and have to write is chockablock with big terms and concepts that have lost their referent. The attributes of great men and great causes tend to outlive whatever it was that gave rise to them, and so a great many attributes are left over. They had once been coined by a distinguished man for another distinguished man, but these men are long dead, and the surviving concepts must be put to some use. Writers are in consequence always searching for the right man for the words. Shakespeare's "powerful imagination," Goethe's "universality," Dostoyevsky's "psychological depth," and all the other legacies of a long literary history hang like endless laundry in the heads of writers, and the resulting mental overstock reduces these people to calling every tennis player a profound strategist and every fashionable writer a great man of letters. Obviously they will always be grateful for a chance to use up their surplus without reducing its value. But it must always be applied to a man whose distinction is already an established fact, so that everyone understands that the words can be pinned on him, and it hardly matters where. And such a man was Arnheim, because Arnheim was Arnheim, whose very birth as the heir of his father was already an event, and there could be no doubt about the news value of anything he said. All he had to do was to take just enough trouble to say something that, with a little goodwill, could be regarded as significant. Arnheim himself formulated it as a principle: "Much of a man's real importance," he used to say, "lies in his ability to make himself understood by his contemporaries."

So now once again he got along beautifully, as always, with the papers, which fastened on him. He could afford to smile at those ambitious financiers or politicians who stand ready to buy up whole forests of newspapers. Such an effort to influence public opinion seemed to him as uncouth and timid as offering to pay for a woman's love when it could be had so much more cheaply just by stimulating her imagination. He had told the reporters who asked him about the Council that the very fact of its convocation proved its profound necessity, because nothing in world history happened without a rational cause; a sentiment that so fully corresponded to their professional outlook that it was quoted appreciatively in several newspapers. It was in fact, on closer scrutiny, a good statement. For the kind of people who take everything that happens seriously would feel nauseated if they could assume that not every event has a good cause; on the other hand, they would also rather bite their tongues, as we know, than take anything too seriously, even significance itself. The pinch of pessimism in Arnheim's statement greatly contributed to the solid dignity of their professional endeavors, and even the fact that he was a foreigner could be read as a sign that the whole world was concerning itself with these enormously interesting movements in Austria.

The other celebrities in attendance did not have the same instinctive flair for pleasing the press, but they noticed its effect; and since celebrities in general know little about each other and in that train to immortality in which they are traveling together usually set eyes on each other only in the dining car, the special public recognition Arnheim enjoyed had its unexamined effect on them too; and even though he continued to stay away from all official committee meetings, in the Council itself he came quite automatically to play the role of a central figure. The further this meeting of minds progressed, the clearer it became that he was the really sensational element in it, although he basically did nothing to create that effect other than, possibly, by expressing in conversation with its famous members his judgment, which could be interpreted as an openhearted pessimism, that the Council could hardly be expected to accomplish much of anything, but that, on the other hand, so noble a task merited all the trustful devotion one could muster. So subtle a pessimism inspires confidence even in great minds, for the idea that the intellect nowadays cannot really accomplish much is, for some reason, more congenial than the possibility that the intellect of some colleague might succeed in accomplishing something, and Arnheim's reserved judgment about the Council could be taken as leaning toward the more acceptable negative chance.

78

Diotima's metamorphoses

Diotima's feelings did not develop in quite the same straight ascending line as Arnheim's success.

It sometimes happened, in the midst of a social gathering in her transformed apartment, with its rooms stripped of their usual furnishings, that she felt as though she were awakening in some dreamland. She would be standing there, surrounded by space and people, the light of the chandelier flowing over her hair and on down her shoulders and hips so that she seemed to feel its bright flood, and she was all statue, like some figure on a fountain, at the epicenter of the world, drenched in sublime spiritual grace. She saw it as a once-in-a-lifetime chance to bring about everything that she had always held to be most important and supremely great, and she no longer cared particularly that she had no very clear idea what this might be. The whole apartment, the presence of the people in it, the whole evening, enveloped her like a dress lined in yellow silk; she felt it on her skin, though she did not see it. From time to time she turned her gaze to Arnheim, who was usually standing somewhere in a group of men, talking; but then she realized that her gaze had been resting on him all along, and it was only her awakening that now followed her eyes. Even when she was not looking at him, the outermost wingtips of her soul, so to speak, always rested on his face and told her what was going on in it.

And as long as we're on the subject of feathers, one might add that there was also something dreamlike in his appearance, something of a businessman with golden angel's wings who had descended into the midst of this gathering. The rattle of express and luxury trains, the humming of limousines, the peace of hunting lodges, the flapping of sails on a yacht, were all in these invisible, folded plumes that rustled softly whenever he raised his arm in a gesture, in these wings with which her feelings had dressed him. Arnheim was often away on his trips, as always, and this gave his presence a permanent air of reaching out beyond the present moment and local events, important as they were for Diotima. She knew that while he was in town a secret coming and going of telegrams, visitors, and emissaries in charge of his business affairs was constantly afoot. She had gradually formed an idea, perhaps even an exaggerated one, of the importance of a firm with global interests and its involvement in world affairs on the highest level. Arnheim sometimes told breathtaking stories about the ramifications of international finance, overseas trade, and their connection with politics; quite new horizons, indeed first-ever horizons, opened up for Diotima; all it took was to hear him once on the subject of Franco-German confrontation, of which Diotima knew not much more than that almost everyone she knew felt slightly anti-German while acknowledging a certain burdensome fraternal duty. In Arnheim's presentation it became a Gallo-Celtic–East European–Transalpine complex interlinked with the problems of the coal mines of Lorraine and the oil fields of Mexico as well as the antagonism between Anglo- and Latin America. Of such ramifications Section Chief Tuzzi had no idea, or showed none. He confined himself to pointing out to Diotima yet again, from time to time, that in his opinion Arnheim's presence and marked preference for their home was definitely inexplicable without ulterior motives, but he did not say what these might be, and did not know himself.

And so his wife was deeply impressed with the superiority of a new breed of men over the methods of an obsolete diplomacy. She had not forgotten the moment of her decision to make Arnheim the head of the Parallel Campaign. It had been the first great idea of her life, accompanied by the most amazing sensations of dreaming and melting all at once, and as the idea broadened out into marvelous distances, everything that had made up Diotima's life hitherto melted toward it. What little part of this state of mind could be put into words did not amount to much: a glittering, a flickering, a strange emptiness and flight of ideas; nor did she mind admitting—Diotima thought—that its nucleus, the thought of placing Arnheim at the head of the unprecedented patriotic campaign, would be impossible. Arnheim was a foreigner in Austria, there was no getting around it. To put him in charge from the start, as she had presented it to her husband and Count Leinsdorf, was simply not feasible. Nevertheless, everything had turned out as, in her spellbound state, she had known it would. For all her other efforts to inject a truly inspiring content into the campaign had remained fruitless so far; the great first session, all the committee work, even this special council, against which Arnheim, by some strange irony of fate, had actually warned her himself, had so far led to nothing other than . . . Arnheim, whom people were always crowding around, who had to keep talking endlessly, who formed the secret focus of all their hopes. He was the New Man, destined to take over the helm of history from the old powers. She could flatter herself that it was she who had discovered him on sight, talked with him about the entrance of the New Man into the spheres of power, and helped him against all resistance to follow his path here. Even if Arnheim did have ulterior motives, as Tuzzi suspected, Diotima would in any case have felt almost justified in supporting him all the way; at such a fateful moment one cannot stop to split hairs, and Diotima felt with absolute certainty that her life had reached a pinnacle.

Apart from the born losers and the lucky devils of this world, one human being is about as badly off as the next, but they lead their lives on different levels. For the man of today, who has on the whole not much perspective on the meaning of his life, the confident sense of his own level is a most desirable second best. In exceptional cases this confidence can rise to an ecstasy of height or power, just as there are those who turn giddy when they know themselves to be high up in a building, even though they are standing in the middle of a room with the windows shut. When Diotima reflected that one of the most influential men in Europe was working together with her to infuse ideas into the strongholds of power, and how destiny itself must have

brought them together, and what was going on, even if on this particular day nothing special was actually happening on this high floor
of a World-Austrian humanitarian undertaking: when she reflected
on it, her tangled thoughts soon resembled knots that had slackened
into loops; they came more easily and were soon racing along,
accompanied by an unusual sense of joy and success, as though
streaming toward her and bringing flashes of amazing insights. Her
self-confidence rose; successes she would never have dreamed of lay
within reach; she felt more cheerful than was her habit, sometimes
even a daring joke would occur to her, and something she had never
known in all her life, waves of gaiety, even of exuberance, coursed
through her. She felt as though she were high up in a turret, in a
room with many windows. But it was also a queer, scary feeling. She
felt plagued by an indefinable, general, indescribable sense of well-
being that made her want to do things, do something, anything,
though she couldn't imagine what. It was as if she had suddenly
become aware of the globe turning under her feet and could not
shake this awareness off; or as if all this excitement without tangible
cause were as inhibiting as a dog leaping about at one's feet, though
how it had got there no one could say. And so Diotima sometimes
worried about the change she had undergone without her own express permission, and her condition, all in all, most resembled that
bright, nervous gray, the color of the faint, weightless sky at the hour
of utter hopelessness, when the heat is at its worst.

At this point Diotima's striving toward the ideal underwent a significant change. This striving had never been clearly distinguishable
from the proper admiration for all greatness; it was a noble idealism,
a decorous high-mindedness, a disciplined exaltation, and since, in
these more robust times of ours, we hardly recognize any of this anymore, perhaps it should be laid out briefly once more. This idealism
had nothing to do with realities, because reality always involves working at something, which means getting your hands dirty. It was more
like the flower paintings done by archduchesses, for whom flowers
were the only seemly choice of life study, and quite typical of this
idealism was the term "culture"; it regarded itself as the vessel of
culture. But this idealism could also be described as harmonious, because it detested everything unbalanced and saw the task of education as reconciling all the crude antagonisms sadly so prevalent in the

world; in short, it was not perhaps so very different from what we still mean—though of course only wherever the great middle-class traditions are still upheld—by a sound and pure idealism, the kind that distinguishes most carefully between conflicts worthy of its concern and those that aren't, and which, because of its faith in a higher humanity, does not share the conviction of the saints (along with doctors and engineers) that even moral garbage may contain unused heavenly fuels. Formerly, had Diotima been roused from her sleep and asked what she wanted, she would have said, without having to think, that a living soul's powers of love felt the need to share itself with all the world; but after being awake for a while she would have modified this by noting that in our present world, with its overgrowth of civilization and intellect, it would perhaps be safer to speak more cautiously, even in cases of the highest sensibilities, of a force analogous to the power of love. And she would really have meant it. Even today there are still thousands of people who are like atomizers, spraying the power of love around like a perfume.

When Diotima sat down to read her books she brushed her lovely hair back from her forehead, which gave her a logical air, and proceeded to read responsibly, with a view to extracting from what she called culture whatever might help her in the none too easy social situation in which she found herself; and this was how she lived, distributing herself in tiny droplets of rarefied love among all the things that deserved it, condensing as a cloudy breath upon them at some distance from herself, so that she was actually left with nothing but the empty bottle of her body, one of the household effects of Section Chief Tuzzi. Before Arnheim appeared on the scene this had finally led to moods of deep depression, when Diotima was still alone between her husband and that most incandescent event of her life, the Parallel Campaign; since then, however, her energies had quite naturally regrouped. The power of love had firmly pulled itself together and had reentered her body, as it were, and the "analogous" force had become something very selfish and unmistakable. The feeling her cousin had been the first to evoke, that she was about to take some kind of action and that something she could not yet bring herself to imagine was about to happen between herself and Arnheim, had now grown so much more intense than anything she had ever known that she felt exactly as if she had passed from dreaming to waking. A void, typical of the first stage of that transition, had opened up in Diotima, and she seemed to remember descriptions she had read that suggested it might herald the beginning of a great passion. She thought she could understand in that light much of what Arnheim had been saying to her recently. Everything he told her about his position, the qualities needed and the duties laid upon him by his life, was in preparation for something inexorable, and Diotima, surveying everything that had been her ideal hitherto, felt the pessimism that casts its shadow on every act, just as, with one's trunks all packed, one casts a last look around the rooms that have been home for years and are now seen with the life nearly gone out of them. The unexpected effect was that Diotima's soul, temporarily unsupervised by the higher faculties, behaved like a truant schoolboy boisterously careening around until he is overcome by the sadness of his pointless liberty; and owing to this curious situation something briefly entered into her relations with her husband, despite the increasing distance between them, that bore a strange resemblance, if not to a late springtime of love, then at least to a potpourri of all love's seasons.

The little Section Chief, with his pleasant aroma of tanned dry skin, was baffled by what was happening. He had noticed several times that his wife, when guests were present, seemed strangely dreamy, withdrawn, remote, and highly nervous, truly nervous and yet far away at the same time; still, when they were alone again and he approached her, somewhat intimidated and disconcerted, to ask her about it, she would suddenly throw her arms around him with inexplicable exuberance, and the pair of lips she pressed on his forehead were so hot they reminded him of the barber's curling irons on his mustache when they got too close to his skin. Such unscheduled affection was not to his taste, and he stealthily wiped away its traces when Diotima was not looking. But whenever he felt like taking her in his arms, or had actually done so, which made it even worse, she hotly accused him of never having loved her, of only pouncing on her like an animal. Now, from the days of his youth, a certain degree of touchiness and moodiness had of course formed part of his image of a desirable woman who would complement a man's nature, and the ineffable grace with which Diotima proffered a cup of tea, picked up a new book, or passed judgment on a problem that, in his opinion, she could not possibly understand, had always delighted him with its formal perfection. It all affected him like perfect background music by which to dine, something he dearly loved; but then, Tuzzi was also sure that the detachment of music from dining (or from church services) and the endeavor to cultivate it for its own sake was a sign of middle-class presumption, even though he knew that one should never say so; anyway, it was not the sort of thing he ever seriously concerned himself with. But what was he to do when Diotima hugged him one minute and the next denounced him as a man beside whom a person with a soul of her own could never be free to fulfill herself? What could a man say in answer to exhortations that he give more thought to the oceanic depths of beauty within, instead of fastening on her body? All of a sudden he was supposed to see the difference between Eros, the free spirit of love unburdened by lust, and mechanical sex. It was all, of course, stuff she had read somewhere, and comical at that, but when a woman lectures a man in this fashion as she is undressing in front of him!—Tuzzi thought—it becomes downright insulting. For he could not fail to notice that Diotima's underwear had evolved in the direction of a certain worldly frivolity. She had always dressed with care and deliberation, since her social position required her to be smart without dressing above her station. But within the gradations from respectable durability to filmy, frilly provocation she was now making concessions to beauty she would once have called unworthy of an intelligent woman. However, when Giovanni (Tuzzi's name was really Hans, but he had been stylishly rechristened in keeping with his surname) noticed, she blushed down to her shoulders and brought up Frau von Stein, who had made no concessions even to a Goethe! So now Section Chief Tuzzi was no longer free, when *he* felt that the time had come, to escape from those weighty concerns of state beyond the private sphere and find release in the very lap of his own household; he found himself instead at Diotima's mercy; instead of the former clear line between mental exertion at the office and physical relaxation at home, he was faced with a virtual return to the strenuous and slightly ridiculous union of mind and body appropriate to courtship, to carrying on like a cock pheasant or some lovesick, versifying youth.

It is hardly too much to say that he found this utterly revolting at times, and that because of it his wife's public success at this time caused him physical pain. Diotima had public opinion on her side, something Section Chief Tuzzi respected so unconditionally that he shied away from asserting his authority or meeting her incomprehensible moods with sarcasm, lest he seem unappreciative. It began to dawn on him that being the husband of a distinguished woman was a painful affliction that had to be carefully hidden from the world, much like an accidental castration. He took great pains to show nothing of what he felt, came and went inconspicuously, always in a cloud of amiable official impenetrability, whenever Diotima had visitors or meetings, dropping the occasional politely helpful suggestion or comforting ironic remark, and seemed to lead his life in a separate but friendly adjoining world, always in accord with Diotima, even entrusting her with a little mission now and then when they were alone, publicly encouraging Arnheim's visits to his home; in whatever spare time he had from the weighty cares of office, he studied Arnheim's publications, and hated men who published their writings as the cause of his troubles.

For this was the question to which the main question—why was Arnheim frequenting his house?—sometimes reduced itself: Why did Arnheim write? Writing is a particular form of chatter, and Tuzzi couldn't stand men who chatter. They made him want to clench his jaws and spit through his teeth like a sailor. There were exceptions, of course; that he granted. He knew some high-ranking civil servants who had written their memoirs after they retired, and others who sometimes wrote for the newspapers. As Tuzzi saw it, a civil servant wrote only when he was dissatisfied or when he was a Jew, because Tuzzi held that Jews were ambitious and dissatisfied. Then there were also men of achievement who had written books about their experiences, but only in their old age and in America or, at most, in England. Besides, Tuzzi was of course versed in literature and, like all diplomats, had a preference for memoirs, from which one could pick up witty remarks and insights into the workings of men's minds. Still, that such works were no longer being written must signify something, so perhaps his was an old-fashioned taste, not in keeping with an age of functionalism. Finally, people wrote because it was their profession. Tuzzi could accept this without reservation, so long as it brought in enough money, or fell into the after all recognized category of "poet." He even felt quite honored to receive the leading men in this profession, in which he had hitherto included those writers supported by the Foreign Office's Save the Reptile Fund, but without giving it much thought he would also have counted the *Iliad* and the Sermon on the Mount, both of which he certainly revered, among those achievements we owe to a profession that may either be practiced independently or have to be subsidized. But why a man like Arnheim, who had no need whatsoever to write at all, should write so much was a problem behind which Tuzzi, now more than ever, suspected something that persisted in eluding him.

79

SOLIMAN IN LOVE

Soliman, the little black slave or African prince, as the case may be, had meanwhile managed to convince Rachel, Diotima's little maid or, alternatively, confidante, that they would have to keep a sharp eye on what went on in the house, in order to forestall a sinister plan of Arnheim's when the time came. Not that she was entirely convinced, but the two of them kept watch like conspirators, and always eavesdropped when there were visitors. Soliman talked endlessly about couriers coming and going and mysterious visitors to his master at the hotel, and said he was prepared to give his oath as an African prince that he would get to the bottom of it. The African princely oath entailed Rachel's slipping her hand between the buttons of his jacket and shirt so she could lay it on his bare chest while he recited the vow, and his hand doing the same to her; this Rachel declined. All the same, little Rachel, who dressed and undressed her mistress and took her telephone calls, and through whose hands Diotima's black hair flowed every morning and evening while golden words from her mistress's lips flowed through her ears: this ambitious little creature who had been living as though posed atop a pillar ever since the Parallel Campaign had started, trembling with adoration that flowed upward from her eyes to the goddess she served day after day, had for some time taken pleasure in spying on her, plain and simple.

Through open doors from neighboring rooms or the crack of a slowly closing door or simply while lingering over some small task nearby, she tried to overhear everything said by Diotima and Arnheim, Tuzzi and Ulrich, and picked up glances, sighs, hand-kissings, words, laughter, gestures, like scraps of a torn-up document she could not fit together again. But most of all it was the little keyhole that opened up vistas which curiously, somehow, reminded Rachel of the long-forgotten time when she lost her virtue. That tiny opening let her gaze slip deep inside the room's interior, where people broken up into sections flat as cardboard moved about, their voices no longer held within the fine borders of words but proliferating into meaningless sound; the awe, reverence, and admiration that bound Rachel to these people then came wildly undone, dissolving in excitement as when a lover suddenly penetrates, with all his being, so deeply into the beloved that everything grows dark before her eyes, and behind the drawn curtain of her skin the light flares up. Little Rachel crouched at the keyhole, her black dress tight over her knees, throat, and shoulders; Soliman cowered beside her in his livery, like hot chocolate in a dark-green cup; when he happened to lose his balance he would steady himself against Rachel's shoulder, knee, or skirt with a quick movement of his hand, letting it rest there for an instant till he let go until only his fingertips still touched her; then these, too, were slowly, caressingly, withdrawn. He couldn't help giggling, and then Rachel would lay her soft fingers on the swelling bolsters of his lips.

Unlike Rachel, Soliman was not interested in the Council, and whenever he could dodged the chore of helping her serve the guests. He preferred coming along on Arnheim's private visits to Diotima. This meant waiting in the kitchen for Rachel to be free again, to the annoyance of the cook, who had so enjoyed his first visit, because he had since then apparently lost his tongue. But Rachel never had time to sit in the kitchen for long, and when she was gone again the cook, a single woman in her thirties, paid him little motherly attentions. He put up with that for a while, with an extremely haughty look on his chocolate face; then he would get up, like someone who has forgotten something or is looking for something, his eyes rolled up to the ceiling, his back to the door, walking backward as if to see the ceiling better. The cook already knew this clumsy act was coming, as soon as he stood up and rolled his eyes, showing the whites; but she was too annoyed and jealous to let on that she noticed, until Soliman finally ceased bothering about his act, now reduced to a formula that took him to the threshold of the brightly lit kitchen, where he would hesitate with a most ingenuous expression on his face. The cook then made a point of not looking in his direction. Soliman glided backward into the dark foyer, like a dark image in dark water, listening for another second, quite unnecessarily, and then suddenly took to pursuing Rachel with fantastic leaps throughout the strange house.

Section Chief Tuzzi was never at home, and Soliman was not worried about Arnheim and Diotima, knowing that they had ears only for each other. He had even tested this now and then, by knocking something over, without being noticed. He lorded it throughout the rooms like a stag in the forest. His blood pressed upward through his head like antlers with eighteen dagger points. The tips of these antlers brushed walls and ceilings. The blinds were usually drawn in all the rooms not in use, to save the colors of the furnishings from being faded by the sunlight, and so Soliman rowed through this twilit world with wide movements of his arms, as if through leafy undergrowth. He enjoyed making a dramatic dance of it. He was intent on violence. This youngster, whom women tended to spoil out of curiosity, had never actually had intercourse with a woman but only picked up all the vices of European boys, and his cravings were as yet so unappeased by experience, so unbridled and flaring in every direction, that his lust did not know whether it was supposed to be quenched by Rachel's blood or her kisses, or else by a freezing up of all the veins in his body the moment he set eyes on his beloved.

Wherever Rachel might be hiding, he suddenly turned up, with a smile of triumph at his own cleverness. He would bar her way, respecting the sanctity of neither the master's study nor Diotima's bedroom; he popped up from behind curtains, desk, closets, beds, making Rachel's heart stand still every time, in horror at such impudence, such a tempting of fate, whenever the dimness somewhere condensed into a black face in which two white rows of teeth gleamed. But the moment Soliman found himself face-to-face with Rachel in the flesh, he was instantly recalled to propriety. This girl was so much older than he, and so beautiful, like a fine shirt of his master's one couldn't bring oneself to soil the very first moment it came fresh from the laundry, and anyway she was so real that all his fantasies paled in her presence. She scolded him for carrying on like a little savage, and tried to teach him some respect for Diotima, Arnheim, and the great honor of having a share in the Parallel Campaign; Soliman, for his part, always had little presents for her, whether it was a flower plucked from his master's bouquet for Diotima, a cigarette stolen at the hotel, or a handful of bonbons he had scooped up in passing from a bowl; he only pressed Rachel's fingers and, as he gave her his gift, laid her hand on his heart, which was flaming inside his black body like a red torch in a dark night.

There was also the time Soliman had made his way right into Rachel's room, where she had been banished with her sewing on strict orders from Diotima, who had been disturbed the previous day by some scuffling in the hall while Arnheim was with her. Before entering on her house arrest she had quickly looked around for him without finding him, but when she stepped sadly into her little room, there he was, seated on her bed with a radiant expression on his face. Rachel hesitated before shutting the door, but Soliman leapt up and did it for her. Then he rummaged in his pockets, pulled something out, blew on it to clean it off, and approached the girl like a hot flatiron.

"Hold out your hand!" he ordered.

Rachel held it out to him. He had some twinkling shirt studs in his hand and tried to fit them into her cuff. Rachel thought they were glass.

"Diamonds!" he explained proudly.

The girl, sensing that something was wrong, hastily pulled her arm back. Not that she had any definite suspicion; the son of an African prince, even if he had been kidnapped, might still have a few gemstones sewed secretly into his shirt; one never knew. Yet some instinct made her afraid of these buttons, as if Soliman were offering her poison, and suddenly all the flowers and candies he had already given her took on in retrospect a sinister air. She pressed her hands to her body and looked at him aghast. It was time to speak to him seriously; she was older than he and in service with a kind mistress. But all she could think of was old saws like "Honesty is the best policy" or "Give the Devil your little finger and he'll take your whole hand." She turned pale; such sayings were not enough. It was the wisdom she had been raised on at home; it was upright, proper, and simple as old pots and pans, but there was not much you could do with it; such a saying was usually just one sentence, with a period at the end. At this moment she felt ashamed of parading such childhood maxims, as one feels ashamed of old, threadbare clothes. That the ancient clothes chest from some poor man's attic turns up, a hundred years later, as a decorative item in the salons of the rich was beyond her ken; like all respectable simple people, she admired a new chair made of wickerwork. She tried hard to come up with something she had learned in her new life, but of all the thrilling scenes of love and terror she remembered from the books Diotima had given her, none fitted the present case; all those fine words and feelings were tied to their contexts and would be as much use here as a key in the wrong lock. It was the same with the great pronouncements and admonitions she had from Diotima. Rachel felt a red mist swirling around her and was close to tears. At length she said hotly: "I don't steal from *my* mistress!"

"Why not?" Soliman flashed his teeth at her.

"I just don't."

"I didn't either. This is mine!" Soliman shouted.

A good mistress takes care of the likes of us, Rachel felt. Love was what she felt for Diotima. Boundless respect for Arnheim. Deep loathing for those mischievous and mutinous types who are called subversive elements by the good police. But she could not find the words for all this; like a huge farm wagon overloaded with hay and fruit, with its brakes out of order, this huge ballast of feelings went rolling out of control inside her.

"It's mine! Take it!" Soliman repeated, grabbing for Rachel's hand again. She snatched her arm away, and as he tried to hang on to it, with his anger mounting as he sensed he would have to let go because his boyish strength was no match for Rachel's resistance—she was pulling away from his grasp with the whole weight of her body—he lost his head, bent over, and bit her ferociously in the arm.

Rachel gave a scream, but had to stifle it, and hit Soliman in the face.

But by this time his eyes were brimming with tears; he threw himself to his knees, pressed his lips to Rachel's dress, and cried so hard that Rachel felt the hot wetness coming through to her thighs.

There she stood, helpless in the clutch of the kneeling boy who had taken hold of her skirt and was digging his head into her body. She had never in her life known such a feeling, and gently stroked the soft wiry mop of his hair with her fingers.

80

GETTING TO KNOW GENERAL STUMM, WHO TURNS UP UNACCOUNTABLY AT THE COUNCIL

Meanwhile the Council had been enriched by a remarkable addition: despite the rigorous weeding out of those asked to attend, the General had turned up one evening, thanking Diotima effusively for the honor of her invitation. A soldier had only a modest part to play in the council chamber, he averred, but to be allowed to be present at so eminent a gathering, even if only as a silent bystander, was a dream he had cherished since his youth. Diotima gazed around over his head in silence, looking for the guilty party: Arnheim was talking, as one statesman to another, with His Grace; Ulrich, looking unutterably bored, stared at the buffet as though he were counting the cakes on it; the familiar scene presented a solid front without the slightest opening for the intrusion of such an unusual suspicion. Yet there was nothing Diotima was so sure of as that she herself had not invited the General, unless she had taken to walking in her sleep or having fits of amnesia. It was an awkward moment. Here stood the little General, undoubtedly with an invitation in the breast pocket of his forget-me-not-blue uniform tunic, for a man in his position could not possibly be suspected of so outrageous a gamble as coming without being asked; on the other hand, there in the library stood Diotima's graceful desk, with all the leftover printed invitations in a locked drawer to which Diotima almost alone had access. Tuzzi? she briefly wondered, but this, too, was unlikely. How the invitation and the General had come together remained something of a spiritualistic conundrum, and since Diotima was inclined to believe in the supernatural where she personally was concerned, she felt a shiver go through her from head to foot. But she had no choice, in any case, other than to bid the General welcome.

He had wondered a little at the invitation himself, incidentally, late as it was in coming, since Diotima had regrettably given him not the slightest sign of such an intention on his two visits, and he had noticed that the address, obviously written by an underling, showed inaccuracies as to his rank and the style of salutation not to be expected from a lady of Diotima's social position. But the General was an easygoing man, not inclined to suspect anything out of the ordinary, let alone anything out of this world. He assumed that there had been some little slip-up, which was not going to stop him from enjoying his success.

For Major General Stumm von Bordwehr, Chief of the War Ministry's Department for Military Education and Cultural Affairs, was sincerely pleased with the official mission that had come his way. On the eve of the great inaugural meeting of the Parallel Campaign, the Chief of Administration had sent for him and said: "Stumm, old man, you're the scholarly type. We're going to write you a letter of introduction, and off you go. Just give it the once-over and tell us what they're up to." No amount of protesting afterward did any good; the fact that he had not succeeded in gaining a foothold in the Parallel Campaign was a mark against him in his file, which he had tried in vain to erase by his visits to Diotima. So he had hotfooted it to Administration when the invitation arrived after all, and daintily setting one foot before the other under his paunch, with a touch of nonchalant impudence, but a little out of breath, he reported that his carefully planned initiatives had led to the expected result, after all.

"There you are, then," Lieutenant General Frost von Aufbruch said. "I always knew you'd make it." He offered Stumm a chair and a cigarette, switched on the electric sign over the door that said "In Conference, No Admittance," then briefed Stumm on his mission, mainly a matter of reconnaissance and reporting back. "There's really nothing special we're after, you see, so long as you just show up there as often as you can and let them see we're in the picture; not being on any of the committees is probably in order, at this point, but there's no reason we shouldn't be in on any plans to honor our Supreme Commander and Sovereign with some spiritual sort of present on his birthday. That's why I picked you, personally, and proposed you to His Excellency the Minister for this detail; nobody can have any objection. So good luck to you, old man, and do a good job." Lieutenant General Frost von Aufbruch dismissed him with a friendly nod, and General Stumm von Bordwehr forgot that a soldier is supposed to show no emotion, clicked his heels from the bottom of his heart, so to speak, and said, snapping to attention: "At your service, Excellency, and thanks!"

If there are civilians of warlike temperament, why can't there be military men who love the arts of peace? Kakania had them in quantity. They painted, collected insects, started stamp albums, or studied world history. Their isolation in all those tiny garrisons, and the fact that regulations did not permit officers to publish their intellectual findings except with the approval of their superiors, tended to give their efforts the appearance of something peculiarly personal. General Stumm, too, had gone in for such hobbies in his earlier years. He had originally served with the cavalry, but his small hands and short legs were ill-suited to clutching and controlling so unreasonable a beast as a horse, and he so conspicuously lacked the qualities needed for giving military orders that his superiors used to say that if a squadron were positioned on the barracks square with their horses' heads rather than their tails, as usual, toward the stable wall, he would be incapable of getting them out through the gates. In revenge, little Stumm grew a beard, dark brown and rounded; he was the only officer in the Emperor's cavalry with a full beard, but regulations did not specifically forbid it. And he took to collecting pocketknives, in a scientific spirit. On his pay he could not afford a collection of weapons, but of knives, classified according to their make, possession of corkscrew and nail file, grade of steel, place of origin, the casing material and so on, he soon had a large number; in his room stood tall cabinets with many shallow drawers, all neatly labeled, which brought him a reputation for learning. He could also make verses, and even as a cadet at the military academy he had always got the best grades in religion and composition; and so one day the colonel called him into the office.

"You'll never make a passable cavalry officer," he said. "If I stuck a suckling babe on a horse and sent it to the front, he'd put up about as much of a show as you do. But it's a long time since the regiment has had anyone at staff college. Why don't you apply, Stumm?"

So Stumm had two glorious years at the staff college in the capital. While he again failed to show the intellectual keenness needed to ride a horse, he attended every military concert, visited the museums, and collected theater programs. He decided to switch to a civilian career but did not know how to go about it. In the end, he was found neither suited nor definitely unfit for service on the general staff; he was regarded as clumsy and unambitious, but something of a philosopher, so for the next two years he was tentatively assigned to the general staff in command of an infantry division, which ended in his belonging, as a captain of cavalry, to the large number of those who, as the general staff's auxiliary reserve, never get away from the line unless something unusual happens. Captain Stumm now served with another regiment, where he passed for an expert in military theory as well. But it did not take his new superiors long to catch on that in practical matters he was a babe-in-the-saddle. His career was a martyrdom, all the way up to lieutenant colonel; but even as a major he no longer dreamed of anything but a long furlough on half pay until he could be put on the retired list as an acting colonel, with the title and the uniform but not the pension of a colonel. He was through with giving any thought to promotion, which in line regiments went by seniority, in excruciating slow motion; through with those mornings when, with the sun still rising, a man comes in from the barracks quadrangle, chewed out from head to foot, in dusty boots, and goes into the mess hall to add some empty wine bottles to the long emptiness of the day ahead; through with the so-called social life, the regimental stories, and those regimental amazons who spend their lives at their uniformed husbands' sides, echoing their progress up the ladder of rank on a social scale of silvery precision, tones so inexorably refined as to be only just within range of the human ear. And he was through with those nights when dust, wine, boredom, the expanses of fields crossed on horseback, and the tyranny of the endless talk about horses drove every officer, married and unmarried alike, to those parties behind drawn curtains where women were stood on their heads to have champagne poured into their petticoats, and they got the inevitable Jew of those godforsaken little Galician garrison towns, who was a one-man institution like some small weather-beaten country store, where you could get everything from love to saddle soap on credit, with interest—to procure girls trembling with awe, fear, and curiosity. His only self-indulgence in those days was the studious enrichment of his collection of knives and corkscrews, many of them brought personally to the crackbrained lieutenant colonel by the same Jew, who polished them on his sleeve before he placed them on the table, with a reverent look on his face as though they were prehistoric relics.

The unexpected breakthrough came when a fellow alumnus from the staff college remembered Stumm and proposed his transfer to the War Office, where the Department of Education was looking for an assistant to its chief; they wanted someone with an outstanding grasp of the civilian world. Two years later Stumm, by now advanced to colonel, had been entrusted with running the department. Now that he was mounted on a desk chair instead of the beast sacred to the cavalry, he was a different man. He made major general and could be fairly certain of making it to lieutenant general. He had of course shaved off his beard long ago, but now, with advancing age, he was growing a forehead, and his tendency to tubbiness gave him the look of a well-rounded man in every sense of the term. He even became happy, and happiness can do wonders for a man's latent possibilities. He had been meant for a life at the top, and it showed in every way. Be it the sight of a stylishly dressed woman, the showy bad taste of the latest Viennese architecture, the outspread colors of a great produce market, be it the grayish-brown asphalt air of the streets, that mild atmospheric asphalt full of miasmas, smells, and fragrances, or the noise that broke apart for a few seconds to let out one specific sound, be it the endless variety of the civilian world, even those little white restaurant tables that are so incredibly individual although they undeniably all look alike: he took a delight in them all that was like the jingling of spurs in his head. His was a happiness such as civilians find only in taking a train ride into the country, knowing that they will pass a day green, happy, and overarched by something or other. This feeling included a sense of his own significance, that of the War Office, of culture, of the meaningfulness of everyone else, and was so intense that Stumm had not once, since his arrival, thought of visiting the museums or going to the theater again. It was the sort of feeling of which one is hardly ever fully aware, though it permeates everything, from the general's gold braid to the voices of the carillons, and is itself a kind of music without which the dance of life would instantly come to a dead stop.

What the devil, he had certainly made his way! So Stumm thought as he now stood here, his cup brimming over, in these rooms, a part of this brilliant assemblage of great minds. Here he was, at last! The only uniform, where all else was steeped in intellect! And there was something more to fill him with amazement. Imagine the sky-blue sphere of the earth, slightly brightened by the forget-me-not blue of Stumm's military tunic, filled to bursting with happiness, with significance, with the mysterious brain-phosphorus of inward illumination, and at the very center of this sphere the General's heart, upon which was poised, like the Virgin Mary upon the serpent's head, a goddess of a woman whose smile is interwoven with everything and is in fact the mysterious magnetic center of all things: then you have, more or less, the impression Diotima made on Stumm von Bordwehr from the moment her image first filled his widening eyes. Actually, General Stumm cared as little for women as he did for horses. His rather short, plump legs had never felt quite at home on horseback, and when he'd had to talk horses too, even when off duty, he used to dream of nights that he had ridden himself sore, down to the bone, and couldn't dismount; in the same fashion his comfort-loving nature had always disposed him against sexual athleticism, and the daily grind of his duties was sufficiently fatiguing to leave him with no need for letting off excess steam at night. Not that he had been a spoilsport in his day, but when he had to spend his evenings not with his knife collection but with his fellow officers, he usually resorted to a wise expedient; his sense of bodily harmony had soon taught him to drink himself through the riotous state into the sleepy one, which suited him far better than the risks and disappointments of love. It was only later on, after he had married and soon had two children as well as their ambitious mother to support, that he fully appreciated how sensible his habits had been before he succumbed to the temptation to marry, lured into it no doubt by the somewhat unmilitary aura attaching to the notion of a married warrior. Since then he had developed a vivid ideal of woman outside marriage, something that had evidently been germinating in his unconscious long before and consisted in a mild infatuation with the kind of woman by whom he felt intimidated, so that there was no question of having to exert himself in any form of courtship. When he looked over the pictures of women he had clipped from popular periodicals in his bachelor days—never more than a sideline among his activities as a collector—they all had in common that daunting quality, though he had not realized it at the time; and he had never known such overwhelming adoration until his first meeting with Diotima. Quite apart from the impact of her beauty, he had looked up her name in his encyclopedia as soon as he heard that she was a second Diotima, and though he still did not quite understand what a Diotima might be, he gathered it had something to do with that great sphere of civilian culture of which he still knew far too little, sad to say, despite his official position, and the world's intellectual superiority fused with this woman's physical grace. Nowadays, when relations between the sexes have become so simplified, it is probably necessary to point out that this is likely to be the most sublime experience a man can have. General Stumm felt that his arms were too short to embrace Diotima's lofty voluptuousness, while at the same time his mind felt the same about the world and its culture, so that he experienced everything that came his way in a state of gently pervasive infatuation, just as his rounded body took on something of the suspended roundness of the globe itself.

It was this infatuation that brought Stumm von Bordwehr, soon after Diotima had dismissed him from her presence, irresistibly back to her. He planted himself close to the object of his admiration, especially as he knew no one else among those present, and listened in on her conversations with the other guests. He would have loved to take notes, for he would hardly have believed the sovereign ease with which she handled such intellectual riches, like someone toying with a string of priceless pearls, had his own ears not borne witness to her skill as she welcomed, one after another, such a variety of celebrities. It was only when she had given him a look after ungraciously turning away from him several times, that he realized the unseemliness of a general's eavesdropping on his hostess in that fashion, and backed away. He made a few lonely tours of the overcrowded premises, drank a glass of wine, and was just about to find a decorative place to stand against a wall when he noticed Ulrich, whom he had seen once before, at the first meeting, and his memory lit up; Ulrich had been a bright, restless lieutenant in one of the two squadrons General Stumm had once gently led as a lieutenant colonel.

"A man of my own sort," Stumm thought. "And to think how young he still is, to have made it to so high a position!" He made a beeline for Ulrich, and after they had shaken hands and compared notes for a while, Stumm indicated the assembled company and said: "An incredible opportunity for me to learn about the most important problems in the civilian world."

"You'll be amazed, General," Ulrich said.

The General, who needed an ally, warmly shook his hand. "You were a lieutenant in the Ninth Uhlans," he said significantly, "and someday that will turn out to have been a great honor for us, even if the others don't yet realize it as I do."

81

COUNT LEINSDORF'S VIEWS OF *REALPOLITIK.*
ULRICH FOSTERS ORGANIZATIONS

While the Council did not yet give the slightest sign of coming up with any answers, the Parallel Campaign was making great strides at the Palais Leinsdorf: it was there that the threads of reality meshed. Ulrich came twice a week.

He had never dreamed that such numbers of organizations existed. Organizations for field sports and water sports, temperance clubs and drinking clubs, were heard from—in short, organizations and counterorganizations of every kind. They worked to promote the interests of their members and to hamper those of the others. Everyone in the world seemed to belong to at least one organization. Ulrich in his amazement said:

"Your Grace, this goes far beyond what we, in our innocence, have always regarded as natural manifestations of the social instinct. We're faced with the monstrous fact that in the kind of state we have invented, with its law and order, everybody is also a member of a gang. . . ."

But Count Leinsdorf was in favor of organizations. "Remember," he said, "that no good has ever come of ideological politics; we must go in for practical politics. I won't deny that I even regard the far too intellectual concerns of your cousin's circle as potentially dangerous!"

"Could you give me some guidelines, sir?" Ulrich asked.

Count Leinsdorf looked at him, wondering whether the inexperienced young man was ready for so daring a disclosure. But then he decided to risk it.

"Well now, you see," he began cautiously, "I'll tell you something that may be new to you, because you are young: *realpolitik* means *not* doing the very thing you would love to do; however, you can win people over by letting them have their way in little things!"

His listener's eyes popped; Count Leinsdorf smiled complacently.

"So you see," he explained, "all I am saying is that in practice, politics must be guided not by the power of an idea but always by some actual need. Of course everyone would like to make the great ideas come true, that goes without saying. So one should never do what one would like to do. Kant was the first to say so."

"Really!" Ulrich exclaimed in amazement. "But one must aim at something, surely?"

"Aim? Bismarck wanted to make the King of Prussia great; that was his aim. He didn't know from the start that to achieve it, he would have to make war on Austria and France, and that he would found the German Empire."

"Is Your Grace suggesting that we should aim at a great and powerful Austria and nothing else?"

"We still have four years to go. In four years all sorts of things can happen. You can put a people on its feet, but it must do its own walking. Do you see what I mean? Put it on its feet—that's what we must do. But a people's feet are its firm institutions, its political parties, its organizations, and so on, and not a lot of talk."

"Your Grace! Even if it doesn't exactly sound like it, you have just uttered a truly democratic idea!"

"Well, it may be aristocratic too, even though my fellow peers don't see eye-to-eye with me on this. Old Hennenstein and Türckheim told me they expected nothing but a filthy mess to come of all this. So we must watch our step. We must start building on a small scale, so be very nice to the people who come to us."

Consequently Ulrich for some time after this turned no one away. One man who came to him talked a great deal about stamp collecting. To begin with, he said, it made for international understanding; second, it satisfied the need for property and position on which society was unquestionably based; third, it not only called for considerable knowledge but also required decisions on a level that it was not too much to call artistic. Ulrich looked the man over, with his careworn and rather shabby appearance; but the man caught the question in Ulrich's glance and countered it by saying that stamps were also commercially valuable, a factor not to be underrated; millions were made in trading them; the great stamp auctions attracted dealers and collectors from all over the world. It was one way to get rich. But as for himself, he was an idealist; he was putting together a special collection for which there was no commercial interest as yet. All he asked was that a great stamp exhibition be held in the Jubilee Year, when he could be depended upon to bring his specialty to public attention.

After him came a man with the following story: On his walks through the streets—though it was even more exciting when one rode a trolley—he had for years been in the habit of counting the number of straight strokes in the big block letters of the shop signs (there were three strokes in an *A*, for instance, and four in an *M*) and dividing the sum total by the number of letters counted. His average so far had been consistently two and a half strokes to a letter, but this was obviously not invariable, since it could change with every new street. Now, deviations from the norm could be quite distressing, while there was great satisfaction every time the numbers came out right—an effect quite like the catharsis said to be achieved while watching classical tragedy on the stage. If you considered the letters themselves, however—anyone could check this out—divisibility by three was a rare bit of luck, which is why most inscriptions tended to leave you with a noticeable sense of frustration, except for those consisting of several letters each composed of four strokes, as in *M*, *E*, *W*, for instance, which could be depended upon to leave one feeling remarkably happy. So what to do? the visitor asked. Simply this, an order issued by the Public Health Office favoring four-stroke letter series in shop signs and discouraging as far as possible the use of one-stroke letters, such as *O*, *S*, *I*, *C*, which lead to poor and therefore depressing results.

Ulrich looked the man over and took care to keep a distance between them; yet he did not really look like a mental case, but was a well-dressed person in his thirties with an intelligent and amiable expression. He went on calmly explaining that mental arithmetic was an indispensable skill in every line of work, that to teach by means of games was in keeping with modern educational methods, that statistics had often revealed deep connections between things long before these could be explained, that everyone knew the damage done by an education based on book learning alone, and, in conclusion, that the excitement his findings had aroused in all those who had chosen to repeat his experiments spoke for itself. If the Public Health Office could be induced to adopt his discovery, other countries would soon follow suit, and the Jubilee Year could turn out to be a blessing for all mankind.

Ulrich advised all these people to organize: "You still have almost four years' time, and if you succeed, His Grace will be sure to use all his influence on your behalf."

Most of them, however, were already organized, which of course changed matters. It was relatively simple when a soccer club wanted an honorary professorship for its outside right, to demonstrate the importance of modern physical culture; one could always promise to take the matter under consideration. But it was hard in such cases as the following: A man in his fifties presented himself as a senior executive in a government department; his forehead shone with the light of martyrdom when he identified himself as the founder and president of the Oehl Shorthand Association, hoping to draw the attention of the great patriotic campaign's Secretary to the Oehl short-hand system.

Oehl shorthand was an Austrian system, he went on to explain, which was all you needed to know to understand why it was not widely adopted or encouraged. Was the Secretary himself a practic-ing stenographer, by any chance? No? Then he was perhaps not aware of the advantages of any stenographic system: the saving in time, in mental energy. Did he have any idea what a tremendous waste of mental effort was entailed by all those curlicues and prolixi-ties, the imprecision and the bewildering repetition of similar parts, and the confusion that arose between truly expressive, significant graphic components and merely ritualistic and arbitrarily idiosyn-cratic flourishes of the pen?

Ulrich was amazed to meet a man so implacably determined to stamp out ordinary, presumably harmless, handwriting. When it came to saving mental effort, shorthand was a vital necessity for a rapidly growing world that had to get things done quickly. But even from a moral standpoint the question of Short or Long was crucial. The long-eared script, as the senior official bitterly termed it because of the senseless loops it was full of, encouraged tendencies to im-precision, arbitrariness, and wastefulness, especially the waste of time, while shorthand inculcated precision, willpower, manliness. Shorthand, he said, taught people to do what was necessary and to avoid what was unnecessary and irrelevant. Surely there was a lesson in practical morality here, of the greatest possible significance espe-cially for any Austrian. And then there was the aesthetic side of it. Wasn't prolixity rightly considered an ugly quality? Had not the great classical authors rightly declared economy of means to be an essen-tial element of beauty? But even regarding it from the public-health angle, the senior executive official went on, it was most important to shorten the time spent sitting hunched over one's desk. After having in this fashion illuminated the subject of shorthand from various other scientific-scholarly angles as well, to his listener's edification, the visitor finally began to dilate upon the Oehl system's immense superiority over all other systems of shorthand. He showed that from every one of the points of view under consideration, all other systems of shorthand were a mere betrayal of the very principle of shorthand.

He then unfolded the story of his own personal martyrdom to the cause. There were all the older, more powerful systems, which had had time to ally themselves with all sorts of vested interests. All the trade schools were teaching the Vogelbauch system and stood pat against any change, backed up, in accordance with the laws of inertia, by the business community. The newspapers, which obviously profit enormously from the advertisements of the trade schools, would not hear of any proposals for reform. And the Education Office? What a sad joke that was, according to Herr Oehl. Five years ago, when shorthand was first made a required subject in the secondary schools, the Office of Education had set up a committee of advisers on the system to be chosen; the committee was naturally packed with representatives of the trade schools and the business community and with government stenographers, who were of course hand in glove with the press, and that was that! It was all too obvious that the Vogelbauch system was slated to win! The Oehl Shorthand Association had issued a warning and a protest against such criminal indifference to the public interest. But its delegates could no longer get anyone at the Education Office to see them!

Ulrich took cases of this kind to His Grace. "Oehl?" Count Leinsdorf said. "An official, you say?" His Grace rubbed his nose for a long time but came to no decision. "Perhaps you should see his head of department and find out if there's anything to what he says," he mused after a while, but he was feeling creative and canceled this suggestion. "No, I'll tell you what we'll do: we'll draw up a memorandum. Let's find out what they have to say for themselves." And he added confidentially, to give Ulrich an insight into the deeper workings of things: "With any of these things, you can never tell whether they are nonsense or not," he said. "But you see, my dear fellow, you can always depend on something important coming of the fact that somebody attaches importance to it. Take the case of Dr. Arnheim, that darling of all the newspapers. The newspapers could just as easily pursue some other hare. But given that they pursue him, that makes Arnheim important. You said, didn't you, that this man Oehl has an organization behind him? Not that it proves anything, of course, but on the other hand, as I said, we must keep up with the times, and when a good many people are for something, the chances are that something will come of it."

82

Clarisse calls for an Ulrich Year

There was really no reason for Ulrich to pay Clarisse a visit other than his having to give her a good talking-to about the letter she had written to Count Leinsdorf; when she had come to see him a few days earlier, he had forgotten all about it. On his way there, however, it occurred to him that Walter was definitely jealous of him and would be upset about the visit when he heard of it. But there was nothing Walter could do about it. The majority of men find themselves in this funny situation if they happen to be jealous: they cannot keep an eye on their women until after office hours.

The time of day Ulrich had chosen to go there made it unlikely that he would find Walter at home. It was quite early in the afternoon. He had phoned to say he was coming. The snowy whiteness of the landscape outside shone so intensely into the room that it was as though there were no curtains at all on the windows. In this merciless light that glittered off every object stood Clarisse, greeting Ulrich with a laugh from the center of the room. On the side toward the window, the minimal curvature of her boyish body flashed in vivid colors, while the side in shadow was a bluish-brown mist from which her forehead, nose, and chin jutted out like snowy ridges whose edges are blurred by wind and sun. The impression she gave was less that of a human being than of the meeting of ice and light in the spectral solitude of an Alpine winter. Ulrich caught some of the spell she must cast on Walter at times, and his mixed feelings for his boyhood friend briefly gave way to an insight into the image two people presented to each other, whose life he perhaps knew hardly at all.

"I don't know whether you told Walter anything about the letter you wrote to Count Leinsdorf," he began, "but I've come to speak to you alone, and to warn you never to do that kind of thing again." Clarisse pushed two chairs together and made him sit down.

"Don't tell Walter," she asked him, "but tell me what you have against it. You mean the Nietzsche Year? What did your Count say to that?"

"What do you suppose he could have said? The way you tied it in with Moosbrugger was utterly crazy. And even without that he'd probably have thrown your letter away."

"Oh, really?" Clarisse was very disappointed. Then she said: "Luckily, you have some say in it too!"

"But don't you see, you're simply out of your mind!"

Clarisse smiled, accepting this as a compliment. She laid her hand on his arm and asked him: "But an Austrian Year is nonsense, isn't it?"

"Of course it is."

"But a Nietzsche Year would be a fine thing. Why should it be wrong to want something just because we happen to like the idea ourselves?"

"And what exactly is your idea of a Nietzsche Year?"

"That's your affair."

"Very funny."

"Not at all. Why does it seem funny to you to try to put into practice something you take seriously as an intellectual matter? Tell me that."

"I'll be glad to," Ulrich said, freeing his arm from her hand. "After all, Nietzsche isn't the issue; it could just as well be Christ or Buddha."

"Or you. Why not get to work on an Ulrich Year!" She said this with the same casual air as when she had urged him to free Moosbrugger. This time, however, his attention had not strayed, and he was looking at her face while he listened to her words. All he saw was Clarisse's usual smile, that funny little grimace that was the unintended result of the mental effort she was making.

"Oh well," he thought, "she doesn't mean any harm."

But Clarisse drew closer to him again. "Why don't you make it You Year? You might just be in a position to do it now. Only don't say anything to Walter about it—I've told you that already—nor about my Moosbrugger letter. Not a word, ever, that I've talked to you about it. But I assure you, this murderer is musical, even though he can't actually compose. Haven't you ever noticed that every human being is the center of a cosmic sphere? When the person moves, the sphere moves with him. That's the way to make music, without thinking about it, simple as the cosmic sphere around you. . . ."

"And you feel that I should work on something of that sort for a year of my own, do you?"

"No," Clarisse answered, playing it safe. Her fine lips seemed about to say something but held their peace, and the flame blazed silently from her eyes. It was hard to say what it was that emanated from her at such moments. One felt scorched, as if one had come too close to something red hot. Now she smiled, but it was a smile that curled on her lips like an ash left behind in the wake of the burned-out flare from her eyes.

"Still, that is the sort of thing I could do, if I had to," Ulrich went on, "but I'm afraid you think I should make a coup d'état?"

Clarisse thought it over. "Let's say a Buddha Year, then," she said evasively. "I don't know what Buddha stood for, or only vaguely, but let's accept it, and if we think it matters, then we should do something about it. It either deserves our faith in it or it doesn't!"

"Fine. Now . . . a Nietzsche Year was what you said. But what was it Nietzsche actually wanted?"

Clarisse reconsidered. "Well, of course I don't mean a Nietzsche monument or a Nietzsche street," she said in some embarrassment. "But people should try to live as he—"

"As he wanted?" he interrupted her. "But what did he want?"

Clarisse started to answer, hesitated, and finally said: "Oh come on, you know all that yourself. . . ."

"I don't know a thing," he teased her. "But I can tell you this: You can set up a Kaiser Franz Josef Soup Kitchen, and you can meet the needs of a Society for the Protection of the House Cat, but you cannot turn great ideas into reality any more than you can do it with music. Why is that? I don't know. But that's how it is."

He had finally found refuge on the little sofa behind the little table; it was a position easier to defend than the chair. In the open space in the middle of the room, on the far bank, as it were, of an illusory prolongation of the shining tabletop, Clarisse was still standing and talking. Her whole slender body was involved; she actually felt everything she wanted to say with her whole body first of all, and was always needing to do something with it. Ulrich had always thought of her body as hard and boyish, but now, as it gently swayed on legs pressed close together, he saw Clarisse as a Javanese dancer. Suddenly it occurred to him that he would not be surprised if she fell into a trance. Or was he in a trance himself? He launched into a long speech:

"You want to organize your life around an idea," he began. "And you'd like to know how to do that. But an idea is the most paradoxical thing in the world. The flesh in the grip of an idea is like a fetish. Bonded to an idea, it becomes magical. An ordinary slap in the face, bound up with ideas of honor, or of punishment and the like, can kill a man. And yet ideas can never maintain themselves in the state in which they are most powerful; they're like the kind of substance that, exposed to the air, instantly changes into some other, more lasting, but corrupted form. You've been through this often yourself. Because an idea is what *you* are: an idea in a particular state. You are touched by a breath of something, and it's like a note suddenly emerging from the humming of strings; in front of you there is something like a mirage; out of the confusion of your soul an endless parade is taking shape, with all the world's beauty looking on from the roadside. All this can be the effect of a single idea. But after a while it comes to resemble all your previous ideas, it takes its place among them, becomes part of your outlook and your character, your principles or your moods; in the act of taking shape it has lost its wings and its mystery."

Clarisse answered: "Walter is jealous of you. Not on my account, I'm sure. It's because you look as though you could do what he wishes he could do. Do you see what I mean? There is something about you that cuts him down. I wish I knew how to put it." She scrutinized him.

Their two speeches intertwined.

Walter had always been life's special pet, always held on its lap. He transformed everything that happened to him and gave it a tender vitality. Walter had always been the one whose life had been the richer in experiences. "But having more of a life is one of the earliest and subtlest signs of mediocrity," Ulrich thought. "Seen in context, an experience loses its personal venom or sweetness." That was how it was, more or less. Even the assertion that this was the case established a context, and one got no kiss of welcome or good-bye for it.

And despite all that, Walter was jealous of him? He was glad to hear it.

"I told him he ought to kill you," Clarisse reported.

"What?"

"Exterminate him! I said. Suppose you're not really all you think you are, and suppose Walter is the better man and has no other way to gain his peace of mind: it would make sense, wouldn't it? Besides, you can always fight back."

"No half measures for you, I see," Ulrich said, somewhat shaken.

"Well, we were only talking. How do you feel about it, by the way? Walter says it's wrong even to think such things."

"Oh no, thinking is quite in order," he replied hesitantly, taking a good look at Clarisse. She had a peculiar charm all her own. Was it as though she were somehow standing side by side with herself? She was not quite there, yet all there, both in close proximity.

"Bah, thinking!" she cut in. Her words were addressed to the wall behind him, as though her eyes were fixed on a point somewhere between. "You're every bit as passive as Walter." These words, too, fell somewhere midway between them, keeping their distance like an insult, yet sounding conciliatory, because of the confidential closeness they implied. "What *I* say is, if you can think something, you should be able to do it too," she insisted dryly.

Then she moved off, walked to the window, and stood there with her hands clasped behind her back.

Ulrich stood up quickly, went over to her, and placed an arm around her shoulders.

"Dear little Clarisse," he said, "you're being a bit strange today, aren't you? But I must put in a good word for myself; you're not really concerned with me anyway, are you?"

Clarisse was staring out the window. But now her gaze sharpened; she was focusing on something specific out there, for support. She felt as if her thoughts had strayed outside and had only just returned. This feeling of being like a room, with the sense of the door just having shut, was nothing new to her. On and off she had days, even weeks, when everything around her was brighter and lighter than usual, as though it would take hardly any effort to slip out of herself and go traipsing about the world unencumbered; then again there were the bad times, when she felt imprisoned, and though these times usually passed quickly, she dreaded them like a punishment, because everything closed in on her and was so sad. Just now she was aware of a lucid, sober peacefulness, and it worried her a little; she was not sure what it was she had wanted just a while ago, and this sense of leaden clarity and quiet control was often a prelude to the time of punishment. She pulled herself together with the feeling that if she could keep this conversation going with conviction, she would be back on safe ground.

"Don't say 'dear little' to me," she said, pouting, "or I might end up killing you myself." It came out like a joke, so she felt she had made one. She stole a cautious look at him, to see how he was taking it. "Of course, it was only a way of putting it, but you must realize that I'm serious. Where were we? You said it wasn't possible to live by an idea. There's no real energy in you, neither you nor Walter!"

"You horrified me by calling me a passivist! But there are two kinds. There's a passive passivism, like Walter's and then there's the active kind!"

"What is active passivism?" Clarisse was intrigued.

"A prisoner waiting for his chance to break out!"

"Bah!" said Clarisse. "Excuses."

"Well, yes," he conceded. "Maybe."

Clarisse still held her hands clasped behind her back and stood with her legs wide apart, as though in riding boots.

"You know what Nietzsche says? Wanting to know for sure is like wanting to know where the ground is for your next step, mere cowardice. One has to start somewhere to act on one's intentions, not just talk about it. And I've always expected you of all people to do something special someday!"

Suddenly she had taken hold of a button on his vest and started twisting it, her face lifted up to his. Instinctively he laid his hand on hers to save the button.

"I've been thinking for a long time," she went on shyly, "that the really rotten, vile things that go on happen not because someone is doing them but because we are letting them happen. They expand to fill a void!" After this coup she looked at him expectantly. Then she burst out: "Letting things happen is ten times more dangerous than doing them, don't you see?" She struggled inwardly for a more exact formulation, but then she only added: "You know exactly what I mean, don't you? Even though you are always saying that we have to let things go their own way. But I understand what you're saying. It's occurred to me more than once that you're the Devil himself!" These words had slipped out of Clarisse's mouth like a lizard. They frightened her. All she had been thinking of at the outset was Walter's begging her to have a child by him. Ulrich caught a flicker in her eyes; she wanted him. Her upturned face was suffused with something—nothing at all lovely, something ugly but touching. Something like a violent outbreak of sweat blurring the features. But it was disembodied, purely imaginary. He felt infected by it against his will and overcome by a slight absentmindedness. He was losing his power to hold out against her craziness, and so he grabbed her hand to make her sit down on the sofa, and sat down beside her.

"Let me tell you now why I do nothing," he began, and fell silent.

Clarisse, who had become herself again the moment she felt his touch, urged him on.

"There's nothing a man can do, because . . . but I can't really expect you to understand this," he began, then he extracted a cigarette and devoted himself to lighting it.

"Go on," Clarisse prompted him. "What are you trying to say?"

But he kept silent. She pushed her arm behind his back and shook him, like a boy showing how strong he can be. With her, there was no need to say anything; the mere suggestion of something out of the ordinary was enough to set her imagination going. "You're really evil!" she said, and tried in vain to hurt him. But at this moment they were unpleasantly interrupted by Walter's return.

83

PSEUDOREALITY PREVAILS; OR, WHY DON'T WE MAKE HISTORY UP AS WE GO ALONG?

What could Ulrich have said to Clarisse anyway?

He had kept it to himself because she had somehow brought him to the verge of actually saying "God." He had been about to say, more or less: God does not really mean the world literally; it is a metaphor, an analogy, a figure of speech that He has to resort to for some reason or other, and it never satisfies Him, of course. We are not supposed to take Him at his word, it is we ourselves who must come up with the answer for the riddle He sets us. He wondered whether Clarisse would have agreed to regard the whole thing as a game of Cowboys and Indians or Cops and Robbers. Of course she would. Whoever took the first step, she would stick by him like a she-wolf and keep a sharp lookout.

But there was something else he had also had on the tip of his tongue, something about mathematical problems that do not admit of a general solution but do allow for particular solutions, which one could combine to come nearer to a general solution. He might have added that he regarded the problem of human life as that kind of problem. What we call an age—without specifying whether we mean centuries, millennia, or the time span between schoolchild and grandparent—that broad unregulated flow of conditions would come to mean a more or less chaotic succession of unsatisfactory and, in themselves, false answers out of which there might emerge the right and whole solution only when mankind had learned to put all the pieces together.

On his way home in the streetcar, it all came back to him, but he was rather ashamed of such thoughts in the presence of the other passengers riding into town with him. One could tell by looking at them that they were on their way home from definite occupations or setting out toward definite entertainments; even just by looking at their clothes one could tell where they had come from or were going.

He studied the woman next to him; clearly a wife and mother, forty-ish, probably the wife of an academic, and she had small opera glasses on her lap. Sitting beside her, toying with those ideas, he felt like a little boy at play, and playing something slightly improper, at that.

For to think without pursuing some practical purpose is surely an improper, furtive occupation; especially those thoughts that take huge strides on stilts, touching experience only with tiny soles, are automatically suspect of having disreputable origins. There was a time when people talked of their thoughts taking wing; in Schiller's time such intellectual highfliers would have been widely esteemed, but in our own day such a person seems to have something the matter with him, unless it happens to be his profession and source of income. There has obviously been a shift in our priorities. Certain concerns have been taken out of people's hearts. For high-flown thoughts a kind of poultry farm has been set up, called philosophy, theology, or literature, where they proliferate in their own way beyond anyone's ability to keep track of them, which is just as well, because in the face of such expansion no one need feel guilty about not bothering with them personally. With his respect for professionalism and expertise, Ulrich was basically determined to go along with any such division of labor. Nevertheless, he still indulged in thinking for himself, even though he was no professional philosopher, and at the moment he could see that to do otherwise was to take the road leading to the beehive state. The queen would lay her eggs, the drones would devote themselves to lust and the life of the mind, and the specialists would toil. It was quite possible to imagine the world so organized; total productivity might even go up as a result. For the present, every human being is still a microcosm of all humanity, as it were, but this has clearly become too much to bear and it no longer works, so that the humane element has become a transparent fraud. For the new division of labor to succeed, it might be necessary to arrange for at least one set of workers to evolve an intellectual synthesis. After all, without mind . . . What Ulrich meant was that it would give him nothing to look forward to. But this was of course a prejudice. No one really knows what life depends on. He shifted in his seat and studied the reflection of his face in the windowpane opposite, looking for something else to think about. But there was his head floating along in the fluid glass, midway between the inside and the outside, becoming remarkably compelling after a while in its insistence on some kind of completion.

Was there a war actually going on in the Balkans or not? Some sort of intervention was undoubtedly going on, but whether it was war was hard to tell. So much was astir in the world. There was another new record for high-altitude flight; something to be proud of. If he was not mistaken, the record now stood at 3,700 meters and the man's name was Jouhoux. A black boxer had beaten the white champion; the new holder of the world title was Johnson. The President of France was going to Russia; there was talk of world peace being at stake. A newly discovered tenor was garnering fees in South America that had never been equaled even in North America. A terrible earthquake had devastated Japan—the poor Japanese. In short, much was happening, there was great excitement everywhere around the turn of 1913–1914. But two years or five years earlier there had also been much excitement, every day had had its sensations, and yet it was hard, not to say impossible, to remember what it was that had actually happened. A possible synopsis: The new cure for syphilis was making . . . Research into plant metabolism was moving . . . The conquest of the South Pole seemed . . . Professor Steinach's experiments with monkey glands were arousing . . . Half the details could easily be left out without making much difference. What a strange business history was! We could safely say of this or that event that it had already found its place in history, or certainly would find it; but whether this event had actually taken place was not so sure! Because for anything to happen, it has to happen at a certain date and not at some other date or even not at all; also, the thing itself has to happen and not by chance something merely approximating it or something related. But this is precisely what no one can say of history, unless he happens to have written it down at the time, as the newspapers do, or it's a matter of one's professional or financial affairs, since it is of course important to know how many years one has to go till retirement or when one will come into a certain sum of money or when one will have spent it, and in such a context even wars can become memorable occurrences. Examined close up, our history looks rather vague and messy, like a morass only partially made safe for pedestrian traffic, though oddly enough in the end there does seem to be a path across it, that very "path of history" of which nobody knows the starting point. This business of serving as "the stuff of history" infuriated Ulrich. The luminous, swaying box in which he was riding seemed to be a machine in which several hundred kilos of people were being rattled around, by way of being processed into "the future." A hundred years earlier they had sat in a mail coach with the same look on their faces, and a hundred years hence, whatever was going on, they would be sitting as new people in exactly the same way in their updated transport machines—he was revolted by this lethargic acceptance of changes and conditions, this helpless contemporaneity, this mindlessly submissive, truly demeaning stringing along with the centuries, just as if he were suddenly rebelling against the hat, curious enough in shape, that was sitting on his head.

Instinctively he got to his feet and made the rest of his way on foot. In the more generous human confines of the city, in which he now found himself, his uneasiness gave way to good humor again. What a crazy notion of little Clarisse's, to want a year of the mind. He concentrated his attention on this point. What made it so senseless? One might just as well ask why Diotima's patriotic campaign was senseless.

Answer Number One: Because world history undoubtedly comes into being like all the other stories. Authors can never think of anything new, and they all copy from each other. This is why all politicians study history instead of biology or whatever. So much for authors.

Answer Number Two: For the most part, however, history is made without authors. It evolves not from some inner center but from the periphery. Set in motion by trifling causes. It probably doesn't take nearly as much as one would think to turn Gothic man or the ancient Greek into modern civilized man. Human nature is as capable of cannibalism as it is of the *Critique of Pure Reason;* the same convictions and qualities will serve to turn out either one, depending on circumstances, and very great external differences in the results correspond to very slight internal ones.

Digression One: Ulrich recalled a similar experience dating from his army days. The squadron rides in double file, and "Passing on orders" is the drill; each man in turn whispers the given order to the next man. So if the order given up front is: "Sergeant major move to the head of the column," it comes out the other end as "Eight troopers to be shot at once," or something like that. And this is just how world history is made.

Answer Number Three: If, therefore, we were to transplant a generation of present-day Europeans at a tender age into the Egypt of 5000 B.C., world history would begin afresh in the year 5000 B.C., repeat itself for a while, and then, for reasons nobody could fathom, gradually begin to deviate from its established course.

Digression Two: The law of world history—it now occurred to him—was none other than the fundamental principle of government in old Kakania: "muddling through." Kakania was an incredibly clever state.

Digression Three or Answer Number Four: The course of history was therefore not that of a billiard ball—which, once it is hit, takes a definite line—but resembles the movement of clouds, or the path of a man sauntering through the streets, turned aside by a shadow here, a crowd there, an unusual architectural outcrop, until at last he arrives at a place he never knew or meant to go to. Inherent in the course of history is a certain going off course. The present is always like the last house of a town, which somehow no longer counts as a house in town. Each generation wonders "Who am I, and what were my forebears?" It would make more sense to ask "Where am I?" and to assume that one's predecessors were not different in kind but merely in a different place; that would be a move in the right direction, he thought.

He had been numbering his own answers and digressions as he went along, while glancing now into some passing face, now into a shop window, to keep his thoughts from running away with him entirely, but had nevertheless gone slightly astray and had to stop for a moment to see where he was and find the best way home. Before taking this route, he tried once more to get his question straight in his mind. Crazy little Clarisse was quite right in saying that we should make history, make it up, even though he had argued against it with her. But why didn't we?

All that occurred to him in answer at the moment was Director Fischel of Lloyd's Bank, his friend Leo Fischel, with whom years ago he had sometimes sat outside a café in the summer. For if Ulrich had been talking to Fischel instead of to himself, Fischel would typically have said: "I should only have your worries!" Ulrich appreciated this refreshing answer Fischel would have given. "My dear Fischel," he immediately replied in his mind, "it's not that simple. When I say history, I mean, if you recall, our life. And I did admit from the start that it's in very bad taste for me to ask: Why don't people create history—that is, why do they attack history like so many beasts only when they are wounded, when their shirttails are on fire, in short, only in an emergency? So why is this question in such bad taste? What do we have against it, when all it means is that people shouldn't let their lives drift as they do?"

"Everybody knows the answer," Director Fischel would retort. "We're lucky when the politicians and the clergy and the big shots with nothing to do, and everybody else who runs around with all the answers, keep their hands off our daily lives. Besides which, we're a civilized people. If only so many people nowadays weren't so uncivilized!" And of course Director Fischel was right. A man is lucky if he knows his way around stocks and bonds, and other people refrain from dabbling so much in history just because they think they know how it works. We couldn't live without ideas, God forbid, but we have to aim at a certain equilibrium among them, a balance of power, an armed truce of ideas, so that none of the contending parties can get too much done. Fischel's sedative was civilization. It was the fundamental sentiment of civilization, in fact. And yet there is also the contrary sentiment, asserting itself more and more, that the times of heroic-political history, made by chance and its champions, have become largely obsolete and must be replaced by a planned solution to all problems, a solution in which all those concerned must participate.

At this point the Ulrich Year came to an end with Ulrich's arrival on his own doorstep.

84

ASSERTION THAT ORDINARY LIFE, TOO, IS UTOPIAN

At home he found the usual stack of mail forwarded from Count Leinsdorf's. An industrialist was offering an outsize cash award for the best results in the military training of young civilians. The archbishopric opposed the founding of a great orphanage, on the grounds that it had to be on guard against creeping interdenominationalism. The Committee on Public Worship and Education reported on the progress of the definitive suggestion, tentatively announced, to erect a great Emperor of Peace and Austrian Peoples Monument near the Imperial Residence; after consultation with the Imperial and Royal Office for Public Worship and Education, and after sounding out the leading art, engineering, and architectural associations, the Committee had found the differences of opinion such that it saw itself constrained—without prejudice to eventual future requirements and subject to the Central Executive Committee's consent—to announce a competition for the best plan for a competition with regard to such an eventual monument. The Chamberlain's Office, having taken due cognizance of the proposals submitted three weeks earlier, was returning them to the Central Executive Committee with regrets that no decision thereon by His Most Gracious Majesty could be passed on at this time, but that it was in any case desirable for the time being to let public opinion continue to crystallize on these as well as other points. The Imperial and Royal Office for Public Worship and Education stated in response to the Committee's communication ref. no. so-and-so that it was not in a position to favor any special action in support of the Oehl Shorthand Association. The Block Letter Society for Mental Health announced its foundation and applied for a grant.

And so it went. Ulrich pushed aside this packet of "realities" and brooded on it for a while. Suddenly he got to his feet, called for his hat and coat, left word that he would be back in an hour or so, phoned for a cab, and returned to Clarisse.

Darkness had fallen. A little light fell onto the road from only one window of her house; footprints in the snow had frozen, making holes to stumble over; the outer door was locked and the visitor unexpected, so that his shouts, knocking, and hand clapping went unheard for the longest time. When at last Ulrich was back inside, it did not seem to be the same room he had left such a short time ago but seemed another world, surprised to see him, with a table laid for a simple private meal for two, every chair occupied by something that had settled down on it, and walls that offered the intruder a certain resistance.

Clarisse was wearing a plain woolen bathrobe and laughing. Walter, who had let the latecomer in, blinked his eyes and slipped the huge house key into a table drawer. Without beating about the bush, Ulrich said, "I'm back because I owe Clarisse an answer." Then he resumed talking at the point where Walter's arrival had interrupted their conversation. After a while, the room, the house, and all sense of time had vanished, and the conversation was hanging somewhere up in the blue of space, in the net of the stars.

Ulrich presented them with his scheme for living the history of ideas instead of the history of the world. The difference, he said to begin with, would have less to do with what was happening than with the interpretation one gave it, with the purpose it was meant to serve, with the system of which the individual events were a part. The prevailing system was that of reality, and it was just like a bad play. It's not for nothing that we speak of a "theater of world events"—the same roles, complications, and plots keep turning up in life. People make love because there is love to be made, and they do it in the prevailing mode; people are proud as the Noble Savage, or as a Spaniard, a virgin, or a lion; in ninety out of a hundred cases even murder is committed only because it is perceived as tragic or grandiose. Apart from the truly notable exceptions, the successful political molders of the world in particular have a lot in common with the hacks who write for the commercial theater; the lively scenes they create bore us by their lack of ideas and novelty, but by the same token they lull us into that sleepy state of lowered resistance in which we acquiesce in everything put before us. Seen in this light, history arises out of routine ideas, out of indifference to ideas, so that reality comes primarily of nothing being done for ideas. This might be briefly summed up, he claimed, by saying that we care too little about what is happening and too much about to whom, when, and where it is happening, so that it is not the essence of what happens that matters to us but only the plot; not the opening up of some new experience of life but only the pattern of what we already know, corresponding precisely to the difference between good plays and merely successful plays. Which means that we must do the opposite of what we do, and first of all give up being possessive about our experiences. We should look upon our experiences less as something personal and real and more as something general and abstract, or with the detachment with which we look at a painting or listen to a song. They should not be turned in upon ourselves but upward and outward. And if this was true on the personal plane, something more would have to be done on the collective plane, something that Ulrich could not quite pin down and that he called a pressing of the grapes, cellaring the wine, concentrating the spiritual juices, and without all of which the individual could not feel other than helpless, of course, abandoned to his own resources. As he talked on in this vein, he remembered the moment when he had told Diotima that reality ought to be done away with.

Almost as a matter of course, Walter began by declaring all this to be an obvious commonplace. As if the whole world, literature, art, science, religion, were not already a "pressing and cellaring" in any case! As if any literate person denied the value of ideas or failed to pay homage to the spirit, to beauty and goodness! As if education were anything other than an initiation into the world of the human spirit!

Ulrich clarified his position by suggesting that education was merely an initiation into the contemporary and prevalent modes and manners, which are random creations, so that those who seek to acquire a mind of their own must first of all realize that they have none as yet. An entirely open mind, poetically creative and morally experimental on a grand scale, was what he called it.

Now Walter said that Ulrich was being impossible. "You paint a charming picture," he said, "as though we had any choice between living our ideas or living our lives. But you may remember the lines

I am no syllogism nor a fiction—
I am a man, with all his contradiction!

Why not go a step further? Why not demand that we get rid of the belly to make space for the mind? But I say to you: A man is made of common clay! That we stretch out an arm and draw it back again, that we have to decide whether to turn right or left, that we are made of habits, prejudices, and earth, and nevertheless make our way as best we can—that is what makes us fully human. What you are saying, tested even slightly against reality, shows it up as being, at best, mere literature."

"If you will let me include all the other arts under that heading too," Ulrich conceded, "all the teachings on how to live, the religions, and so on, then I do mean something like that: namely, that our existence should consist wholly of literature."

"Really? You call the Savior's mercy or the life of Napoleon *literature?*" Walter exclaimed. But then he had a better idea, and he turned to his friend with all the aplomb of the man holding trumps and said: "You are the kind of man who regards canned vegetables as the raison d'être of fresh greens."

"You're absolutely right. And you could also say that I am one of those who will only cook with salt," Ulrich coolly admitted. He was tired of talking about it.

At this point Clarisse joined in, turning to Walter:

"Why do you contradict him? Aren't you the one who always says, whenever something special happens: Here is something we should be able to put on the stage, for everyone to see and understand?" And turning to Ulrich in agreement, she said: "What we really ought to do is sing! We ought to sing ourselves!"

She had stood up and entered the little circle formed by the chairs. She held herself with a certain awkwardness, as though about to demonstrate her idea by going into a dance. Ulrich, who found such displays of naked emotion distasteful, remembered at this point that most people or, bluntly speaking, the average sort, whose minds are stimulated without their being able to create, long to act out their own selves. These are of course the same people who are so likely to find, going on inside them, something "unutterable"—truly a word that says it all for them and that is the clouded screen upon which whatever they say appears vaguely magnified, so that they can never tell its real value. To put a stop to this, he said: "This was not what I meant, but Clarisse is right; the theater proves that intense personal feelings may serve an impersonal purpose, a complex of meaning and metaphor that makes them more or less transcend the merely personal."

"I know exactly what Ulrich means," Clarisse chimed in again. "I can't remember ever getting a special pleasure out of something because it was happening to *me*. It was *happening*, that was the thing! Like music, for instance," she said, turning to her husband. "You don't want to own it; the joy of it is that it's there! We absorb our experiences and expand them into something beyond ourselves in a single movement; we seek to realize ourselves, yes, but not the way a shopkeeper realizes a profit!"

Walter clutched his head, but for Clarisse's sake he switched to another argument. He did his best to make his words come with the force of a steady, cold jet. "If you value an experience only to the degree that it generates spiritual energy," he said to Ulrich, "then let me ask you this: Doesn't that presuppose a life that has no other aim than to produce spiritual energy and power?"

"It is the life that all existing societies claim as their goal," Ulrich replied.

"In such a world the people would presumably lead their lives under the influence of great passions and ideas, philosophies and novels," Walter continued. "Let me take it a step further: Would they live so as to make great philosophy and poetry possible, or would their lives *be* philosophy and poetry in the flesh, as it were? I'm sure I know which you mean, since the first case would be exactly what we mean by a civilization in the first place. But if you mean the second, aren't you overlooking the fact that such a life-as-art, or whatever you'd call it, unimaginable as it is to begin with, would make philosophy and art quite superfluous; it means one thing only, the end of art!" He flashed this trump card for Clarisse's benefit.

It took the trick. Even Ulrich needed a while to marshal his forces. Then he laughed and said: "Don't you know that every perfect life would be the end of art? It seems to me that you yourself are on the way to perfecting your life at the expense of your art."

He had intended no sarcasm, but Clarisse pricked up her ears.

Ulrich went on: "Every great book breathes this spirit of love for the fate of individuals at odds with the forms the community tries to impose on them. It leads to decisions that cannot be decided; there is nothing to be done but to give a true account of their lives. Extract the meaning out of all literature, and what you will get is a denial, however incomplete, but nonetheless an endless series of individual examples all based on experience, which refute all the accepted rules, principles, and prescriptions underpinning the very society that loves these works of art! In the end, a poem, with its mystery, cuts through to the point where the meaning of the world is tied to thousands of words in constant use, severs all these strings, and turns it into a balloon floating off into space. If this is what we call beauty, as we usually do, then beauty is an indescribably more ruthless and cruel upheaval than any political revolution ever was."

Walter had turned pale to the lips. He hated this view of art as a negation of life, of art against life. He regarded it as offensively bohemian, the dregs of an outdated impulse to shock the conventional mind. He caught the irony of the self-evident fact that in a perfect world there would be no more beauty because it would be superfluous, but he did not hear his friend's unspoken question. For Ulrich was aware of having oversimplified his case. He could just as easily have said the opposite, that art is subversive because art is love; it beautifies its object by loving it, and there may be no other way in this world to beautify a thing or a creature than by loving it. And it is only because even our love consists of mere fragments that beauty works by intensification and contrast. And it is only in the sea of love that the concept of perfection, beyond all intensification, fuses with the concept of beauty, which depends on intensification. Once again Ulrich's thoughts had brushed against "the realm," and he stopped short, annoyed with himself. Walter had meanwhile pulled himself together, and after having rejected his friend's suggestion that people should live more or less as they read, as a commonplace idea as well as an impossible one, he proceeded to prove it evil and vulgar too.

"If a man," he began in the same artfully controlled fashion as before, "were to live his life as you suggest, he would have to accept—not to mention other impossible implications—everything that gave him a good idea, in fact everything even capable of doing so. This would of course mean universal decadence, but since you don't mind that side of it, presumably—unless you are thinking of those vague general arrangements about which you haven't gone into detail—let me ask you only about the personal consequences. It seems to me that such a man is bound to be, in every case in which he doesn't happen to be the poet of his own life, worse off than an animal; if he couldn't come up with an idea, then he couldn't come to any decision either, so that for a great part of his life he would simply be at the mercy of all his impulses, moods, the usual banal passions—in short, at the mercy of all the most impersonal elements of which a man consists, and for as long as the channel leading upward remained blocked, he would have to let himself be the toy of everything that came into his head!"

"Then he would have to refuse to do anything," Clarisse answered in Ulrich's stead. "This is the active passivism of which a person must be capable in some circumstances."

Walter could not make himself look at her. Her capacity for refusal was, after all, a major factor in their life together; Clarisse, looking like a little angel in the long nightgown that covered her feet, had stood on her bed declaiming Nietzschean sentiments, with her teeth flashing: "I toss my question like a plumb line into your soul! You want a child and marriage, but I ask you: Are you the man to have a child? Are you the victorious master of his own powers? Or is it merely the voice of the animal in you, the slave of nature, speaking?" In the twilight of the bedroom this had made a rather gruesome spectacle, while Walter had tried in vain to coax her back down under the bedclothes. And now here she was, armed for the future with a new slogan: active passivism, of which a person had to be capable if need be—a phrase that clearly smacked of a man without qualities. Had she been confiding in Ulrich? Was he encouraging her in her eccentricities? These questions were writhing like worms in Walter's heart, so that he almost felt sick to his stomach. His face turned ashen and all the tension went out of it, leaving it a mass of helpless wrinkles.

Ulrich saw this and asked him warmly if anything was wrong?

With an effort, Walter said no and brightly smiling, invited Ulrich to go on with his nonsense.

"Oh well," Ulrich conceded, "you're not so wrong there. But in a spirit of good sportsmanship we often tolerate actions that are harmful to ourselves, if our opponent performs them in an attractive way; the quality of the performance somehow contends with the quality of the damage done. Very often, too, we have an idea that takes us a step farther along, but all too soon habit, inertia, selfish promptings, and so on take its place, because that's the way things go. So I may have been describing a condition that can never be carried to its proper conclusion, but there's no denying that it is wholly the condition of the world in which we live."

Walter had regained his equanimity. "If you turn the truth upside down, you can always say something that is just as true as it is topsy-turvy," he said gently, without disguising his reluctance for any further argument. "It's just like you to call something impossible but real."

Clarisse, however, was rubbing her nose hard. "And yet it seems very important to me," she said, "that there's something impossible in every one of us. It explains so many things. While I was listening to you both, it seemed to me that if we could be cut open our entire life might look like a ring, just something that goes around something." She had already, earlier on, pulled off her wedding ring, and now she peered through it at the lamplit wall. "There's nothing inside, and yet it looks as though that were precisely what matters most. Ulrich can't be expected to express this perfectly the first time he tries."

And so this discussion ended after all, sad to say, with Walter getting hurt once again.

85

GENERAL STUMM TRIES TO BRING SOME ORDER INTO THE CIVILIAN MIND

Ulrich had probably been out an hour longer than he had indicated on leaving, and was told on his return that a military gentleman had been waiting for him for quite some time. Upstairs, to his surprise, he found General Stumm, who greeted him as an old comrade in arms.

"Do forgive me, old friend," the General called out to him in welcome, "for barging in on you so late, but I couldn't get off duty any
sooner, so I've been sitting here for a good two hours, surrounded by
your books—what terrifying heaps of them you've got!"

After an exchange of courtesies, it turned out that Stumm had
come for help with an urgent problem. Sitting there with one leg
flung jauntily over the other, not an easy posture for a man with his
waistline, and holding out his arm with its little hand, he said: "Urgent? When one of my aides comes along with an urgent piece of
business I usually tell him there's nothing urgent in this world except
making it in time to a certain closet. But jokes aside, I had to come
and see you about something most important. I've already told you
that I regard your cousin's house as a special opportunity for me to
learn more about the civilian world and its major concerns. Something nonmilitary, for a change, and I can assure you that I am enormously impressed. On the other hand, while we brass hats may have
our weaknesses, we're not nearly as stupid as most people seem to
think. I hope you'll agree that when we get something done, we make
a good job of it. You do agree? I knew I could trust you to see that,
which is why I can confess to you frankly that even so, I am ashamed
of our army mentality. Ashamed, I say! Other than our Chaplain
General, I seem to be the man in our army who has most to do with
the spiritual and mental side of things. But I don't mind telling you
that if you take a good look at the military mind, outstanding as it is, it
seems to me like a morning roll call. You do remember what a morning roll call is like? The duty officer puts down on his report: So many
men and horses present, so many men and horses absent, sick or
whatever, Uhlan Leitomischl absent without leave, and so on. But
why such and such numbers of men and horses are present or sick
or whatever, that he never puts down. And it's precisely the sort of
thing you need to know when dealing with a civilian administration.
When a soldier has something to say, he keeps it short, simple, and to
the point, but I often have to confer with those civilian types from
the various ministries, and they always want to know, at every
turn, the whys and wherefores of every proposal I make, with reference to considerations and interactions on a higher plane. So what I
did—this is just between ourselves, you understand—I proposed to
my chief, His Excellency General Frost von Aufbruch, or rather I

hope to surprise him with it . . . anyhow, my idea is to use my opportunities at your cousin's to get the hang of it all, all these higher considerations and significations, and put them to use, if I may say so without blowing my own horn, to upgrade our military mentality. After all, the army has its doctors, vets, pharmacists, clergy, auditors, commissary officers, engineers, and bandmasters, but what it hasn't got yet is a Central Liaison for the civilian mind.

Only now did Ulrich notice that Stumm von Bordwehr had brought along a briefcase, which he had propped against the desk, one of those leather bags with a shoulder strap for carrying official files through the mazes of government corridors and from one government building to another. The General must have come with an orderly who was waiting for him downstairs, although Ulrich had not seen anyone, for it was costing Stumm quite an effort to pull the heavy bag onto his knees, so as to spring the little steel lock with its imposing air of battlefield technology.

"I haven't been wasting any time since I started attending your meetings"—he smiled, while the light-blue tunic of his uniform tightened around its gold buttons as he stooped—"but there are things, you see, I'm still not quite sure about." He fished out of the bag a number of sheets covered with odd-looking notes and lines.

"Your cousin," he elucidated, "your cousin and I had a quite exhaustive talk about it, and what she wants, understandably enough, is that her efforts to raise a spiritual monument to our Gracious Sovereign should lead to an idea, an idea outranking, as it were, all of the current ideas. But I've noticed already, much as I admire all these people she's invited to work on it, that it's a very tall order. The minute one man says something, another will come up with the opposite—haven't you noticed it?—but what strikes me, for one, as even worse is that the civilian mind seems to be what we call, speaking of a horse, a poor feeder. You remember, don't you? You can stuff that kind of beast with double rations, but it never gets any fatter! Or if it does," he qualified, in response to a mild objection from his host, "even if it does gain weight, its bones don't develop, and its coat stays dull; all it gets is a grass belly. I find that fascinating, you see, and I've made up my mind to look into it, to figure out why we can't get some order into this business."

Stumm smiled as he handed his former lieutenant the first of his papers. "They can say what they like about us," he said, "but we army men have always known how to get things in order. Here's my outline of the main ideas I got out of those fellows at your cousin's meetings. As you'll see, every one of them, when you ask him privately, places top priority on something different." Ulrich looked at the paper in astonishment. It was drawn up like a registration form or, in fact, a military list, divided by horizontal and vertical lines into sections, with entries in words that somehow resisted the format, for what he read here, written in military calligraphy, were the names of Jesus Christ; Buddha, Gautama, aka Siddhartha; Lao-tzu; Luther, Martin; Goethe, Wolfgang; Ganghofer, Ludwig; Chamberlain, and evidently many more, running on to another page. In a second column he read the words "Christianity," "Imperialism," "Century of Interchange," and so on, with yet more columns of words beyond.

"I might even call it a page from the Domesday Book of modern culture," Stumm commented, "because we have expanded it further, and it now contains the names of the ideas, plus their originators, that have moved us in the last twenty-five years. I had no idea what a job it would be!" When Ulrich asked him how he had got this inventory together, he was glad to explain his system.

"I had to commandeer a captain, two lieutenants, and five noncoms to get it done in such short order. If we'd been able to do it in a really up-to-date fashion, we'd simply have sent around a questionnaire to all the regiments: 'Who do you think is the greatest man?' The way it's done nowadays when the papers take a poll and all that, you know, together with an order to report the results in percentages. But of course you can't do that sort of thing in the army, because no unit would be allowed to report any answer other than 'His Majesty the Emperor.' So then I thought of going into which books are the most widely read and have the biggest printings, but there we soon found out that next to the Bible it's the Post Office New Year's booklet, with the new postal rates and the old jokes, which every 'occupant' gets free from his postman in return for his annual tip, which again made us realize what a tricky thing the civilian mind is, since those books that appeal to everyone are generally rated the best, or at least, as they tell me, an author in Germany must have an awful lot of like-minded readers before he can pass for an impressive thinker. So we couldn't take that route either, and how we finally did it I couldn't tell you right now; it was an idea of Corporal Hirsch's, together with Lieutenant Melichar, but we did it."

General Stumm put the sheet of paper aside and, with an expression eloquent with disappointment, pulled out another. After taking inventory of the Central European stock of ideas, he had not only discovered to his regret that it consisted of nothing but contradictions but also been amazed to find that these contradictions, on closer scrutiny, tended to merge into one another.

"By now I'm used to being told something different by each of the famous men at your cousin's when I ask them to enlighten me about something," he said, "but every time I've been talking to them for a while, they still seem to be saying the same thing—that's what I can't get into my head, and it could be that my army-issue brain isn't up to it." The problem that was worrying General Stumm was no trifle and actually should not have been left in the War Office's lap, even though it could be shown that it was intimately related to war. Our times rejoice in a number of great ideas, and by a special kindness of fate each idea is paired with its opposite, so that individualism and collectivism, nationalism and internationalism, socialism and capitalism, imperialism and pacifism, rationalism and superstition, are all equally at home in them, together with the unused remnants of countless opposites of an equal or lesser contemporary value. By now this seems as natural as day and night, hot and cold, love and hate, and, for every tensor muscle in the body, the presence of its opposing extensor muscle, nor would it have occurred to General Stumm—or anyone else—to see anything unusual in any of this, had his ambition not taken the plunge into this adventure because of his love for Diotima. Love cannot settle for a unity of Nature based upon opposites; its need for tenderness demands a unity without contradictions, and so the General had tried in every possible way to establish such a unity.

"Here I have," he told Ulrich as he showed him the relevant pages of his report, "a list I've made up of all the Commanders in Chief of Ideas, i.e., all the names in recent times that have led sizable battalions of ideas to victory. On this other page here you see the battle order; this one is a strategical plan; and this last one is an attempt to establish depots or ordnance bases from which to move further supplies of ideas up to the front. Now, I'm sure you can see—I've made certain that the drawing shows this clearly—when looking at any set of ideas in action, that it draws its supplies of additional troops and intellectual matériel not only from its own depots but also from those of its opponents; you see how it keeps shifting positions and how it suddenly turns unaccountably against its own backup forces; you can see ideas constantly crossing over to the other side and back again, so that you will find them now in one line of battle, now in the other. In short, there's no way to draw up a decent plan of communications or line of demarcation or anything else, and the whole thing is—though I can't actually believe what I'm saying!—what any one of our commanding officers would be bound to call one hell of a mess!"

Stumm slipped several dozen pages into Ulrich's hands. They were covered with strategic plans, railway lines, networks of roads, charts of range and firing power, symbols for different units and for brigade headquarters, circles, squares, crosshatched areas; just like a regular General Staff's plan of operations, it had red, green, yellow, and blue lines running this way and that, with all sorts of little flags, meaning a variety of things (such as were to become so popular the following year), painted in all over the place.

"It's no use," Stumm sighed. "I've tried doing it differently, by representing the problem from a military-geographical angle instead of a strategic one, in the hope of getting at least a clearly defined field of operations, but that didn't work either. Have a look at the oro- and hydrographic sketches." Ulrich saw symbols for mountain peaks branching out and massing together again elsewhere, and for springs, networks of streams, lakes. "I've experimented with all sorts of other ways of trying to pull the whole thing together," the General said, with a gleam of irritation or panic in his normally merry gaze. "But do you know what it's like? It's like traveling second class in Galicia and picking up crab lice. I've never felt so filthy helpless! When you spend a lot of time with ideas you end up itching all over, and you can scratch till you bleed, without getting any relief." His vivid description made Ulrich laugh.

"No, no, don't laugh!" the General pleaded. "I've been thinking that you, now that you've become a leading civilian, would understand this stuff and that you'd understand my problem too. So I've come to you for help. I have far too much respect for the world of the intellect to believe that I can be right about all this."

"You take thinking far too seriously, Colonel," Ulrich said to comfort him. The "Colonel" had just slipped out, and he apologized: "Sorry, General; for a minute you had me back in the days when you sometimes ordered me to join you in a philosophical chat in the corner of the mess hall. I can only repeat, a man shouldn't take the art of thinking as seriously as you are doing."

"Not take it seriously!" Stumm groaned. "But I can't go back to just getting along in the mindless way I used to live. Don't you see that? It makes me shudder to think how long I lived between the parade ground and the barracks, with nothing but my messmates' dirty jokes and their stories about their sexual exploits."

They sat down to supper. Ulrich was touched by the General's childlike ideas, on which he then acted with such manly courage, and by the inexhaustible youthfulness that comes from having lived in small garrison towns at the right time of life. He had invited his companion of those years long gone to share his evening meal, and the General was so obsessed by his desire to enter into Ulrich's arcane world that he picked up each slice of sausage with utmost concentration.

"Your cousin," he said, raising his wineglass, "is the most marvelous woman I know. They rightly call her a second Diotima; I've never known anyone like her. You know, my wife . . . you haven't met her. I've nothing to complain of, and then we have the children, but a woman like Diotima . . . well, there's no comparison! When she's receiving I sometimes position myself behind her—what majestic feminine curves!—while at the same time she's talking up front with some outstanding civilian on so high a level that I honestly wish I could take notes! And that Section Chief she's married to has absolutely no idea how lucky he is to have her! I'm sorry if this fellow Tuzzi happens to be someone you like, but I personally can't stand him! All he ever does is slink around with a smirk on his face as if he knew all the answers and won't tell. But I'm not buying that, because with all my respect for the civilian world, government officials are the lowest on my totem pole; they're nothing but a kind of civilian army that try to get the better of us every chance they have, with the outrageous politeness of a cat sitting high up in a tree and looking down at a dog. Your Dr. Arnheim now, that's a man of a different caliber entirely," Stumm went on, "though he may be a bit conceited too, but there's no denying his superiority." He had evidently been drinking too fast, after so much talking, because he was now warming up and growing confidential.

"I don't know what it is," he said. "Maybe the reason I don't understand is that a fellow's mind gets so complicated nowadays, but even though I admire your cousin myself as if—I must say, as if I had a great lump sticking in my throat—still, it's a relief to me that she's in love with Arnheim."

"What? Are you sure there's something going on between them?" Ulrich burst out, although it should not really have been any concern of his; Stumm goggled at him mistrustfully with his shortsighted eyes, still misty with emotion, and snapped on his pince-nez.

"I never said he'd had her," was his straight, soldierly retort. He put his pince-nez back in his pocket and added in quite unsoldierly fashion: "But I wouldn't mind if he had either; devil take me, I've told you already that a man's mind gets complicated in that company. I'm certainly no lover boy, but when I imagine the tenderness Diotima could offer this man I feel a tenderness for him myself, and vice versa, as if the kisses he gave her were my own."

"He gives her kisses?"

"How do I know? I don't go around spying on them. I only mean, if he did. I don't really know what I mean. But I did see him once catching her hand, when they thought nobody was looking, and then for a while they were so quiet together, the kind of stillness you get on the command 'All helmets off, kneel for prayer!' and then she whispered something, it sounded like an appeal, and he answered something. I remember what they said word for word, because it was so hard to understand; what she said was: 'If only we could find the right idea to save us,' and he said: 'Only a pure, unflawed idea of love can save us.' He seemed to have taken her words too personally, because she must have meant the saving idea she needs for her great campaign—What are you laughing at? But feel free to laugh; I've always had my own funny ways, I guess, and now I've made up my mind to help her. There must be something one can do; there are so many ideas floating around, one of them will have to be the saving idea in the end. But I'll need you to give me a hand!"

"My dear General," Ulrich said, "I can only tell you again that you take thinking too seriously. But since you care so much, I'll try to explain as best I can how the civilian mind works." By now they had lighted their cigars, and he began: "First of all, General, you're on the wrong track. The civilian world has no more of a monopoly on the spiritual life than the military has on the physical side, as you think. If anything, it's exactly the other way around. The mind stands for order, and where will you find more order than in the army, where every collar is exactly four centimeters high, the number of buttons on your tunic never varies, and even on nights made for dreams the beds are lined up straight along the wall? The deployment of a squadron in battle formation, the lining up of a regiment, the proper position of bridle and bit—if all these are not significant spiritual achievements, there is no such thing as spiritual achievement!"

"Go teach your grandmother to suck eggs," the General growled warily, uncertain whether to mistrust his ears or the wine.

"Just a minute," Ulrich persisted. "Science is possible only where situations repeat themselves, or where you have some control over them, and where do you have more repetition and control than in the army? A cube would not be a cube if it were not just as rectangular at nine o'clock as at seven. The same kind of rules work for keeping the planets in orbit as in ballistics. We'd have no way of understanding or judging anything if things flitted past us only once. Anything that has to be valid and have a name must be repeatable, it must be represented by many specimens, and if you had never seen the moon before, you'd think it was a flashlight. Incidentally, the reason God is such an embarrassment to science is that he was seen only once, at the Creation, before there were any trained observers around."

But Stumm von Bordwehr, whose entire life had been prescribed for him since his military-school days, from the shape of his cap to permission to marry, was hardly inclined to listen to such doctrines with an open mind.

"My dear fellow," he said craftily. "Maybe so, but what has that to do with me? Very witty of you to suggest that science was invented by us army men, but I wasn't speaking of science at all but, as your cousin says, of the soul, and when she speaks of the soul I feel like taking off all my clothes because the uniform clashes so with it!"

"Stumm, old man," Ulrich went on doggedly, "a great many people accuse science of being soulless and mechanical and of making everything it touches the same. Yet they don't notice that there's much more mechanical or predictable regularity in sentimental matters than in intellectual ones. For when is a feeling really natural and simple? When it can be automatically expected to manifest itself in everybody, given the same circumstances. How could we expect people to behave in a virtuous manner if a virtuous act were not repeatable at will? I could give you many more examples, and if you escape from this drab repetitiveness into the darkest recesses of your being, where the uncontrolled impulses live, those sticky animal depths that save us from evaporating under the glare of reason, what do you find? Stimuli and strings of reflexes, entrenched habits and skills, reiteration, fixation, imprints, series, monotony! That's the same as uniforms, barracks, and regulations, my dear Stumm; and the civilian soul shows an amazing kinship to the military. You might say that it desperately clings to this model, though it can never quite equal it. And where it can't do that, it feels like a child left entirely on its own. Take a woman's beauty, for instance: the beauty that takes you by surprise and bowls you over as if you were seeing it for the first time in your life is really something you have known and sought forever, an image your eyes have long since anticipated, which now comes into full daylight, as it were. But when it's really a case of love at first sight, a kind of beauty you have never perceived before, you simply don't know what to do about it. Nothing like it has ever come your way, you have no name for it, you are not prepared to respond to it, you're hopelessly bewildered, dazzled, reduced to a state of blind amazement, a kind of idiocy that seems to have very little to do with happiness. . . ."

The General could no longer contain his excitement. He had been listening with that expertise one acquired during military exercises when subjected to critical and edifying remarks by superior officers that one must be able to repeat at command but should not really take to heart, or else one might just as well ride home bareback on a porcupine. But now Ulrich had touched him to the quick, and he broke in: "I must say, what you're describing is amazingly on target! When I lose myself in admiration for your cousin, everything inside me seems just to dissolve! And when I do my utmost to pull myself together and come up with some useful idea, my mind turns into an agonizing blank again—'idiotic' may be too strong a word for it, but it's close enough. And so you're saying, as I understand it, that we

army men do use our heads, that the civilian mind . . . of course I
can't accept your suggestion that they model their thinking on ours;
that's just one of your jokes . . . but that we have just as good a mind,
well, that's what I sometimes think too. And everything that goes
above and beyond thinking, as you say, all that stuff we soldiers regard as so notably civilian, such as the soul, virtue, deep feeling, sentiment—the kind of thing this fellow Arnheim handles with such
flair—anyway, you're saying that it's of course part of the human
spirit and in fact involves those so-called considerations of a higher
sort we've been talking about, but you're also saying that it's quite
stupefying, and I must say I totally agree with you, but when all's said
and done, the civilian intellect is indisputably the superior one, and
so I must ask you, how does it all add up?"

"What I said just now was, *first of all*—you forgot that—first of all,
I said, the military life is intellectual by nature, and second, the civilian life is physical by nature. . . ."

"But that's nonsense, surely?" Stumm objected mistrustfully. The
physical superiority of the military was a dogma, like the conviction
that the officer caste stands nearest to the throne, and even though
Stumm had never regarded himself as an athlete, the moment any
doubt was cast upon his physical superiority he felt sure that a comparable civilian paunch had to be several degrees flabbier than his
own.

"No more and no less nonsense than everything else," Ulrich defended himself. "But let me finish. About a hundred years ago, you
see, the leading brains in German civilian life believed that a man
using his head could deduce the world's laws while sitting at his desk,
like so many geometric theorems about triangles. And the typical
thinker was a man in homespun who tossed his long hair back from
his forehead and hadn't even heard of the oil lamp, much less of electricity and the phonograph. Such arrogance has been purged out of
our system since then; in these last hundred years we've become
much better acquainted with ourselves and with nature and everything, but as a result, the better we understand things in detail, the
less we understand the whole, as it were, so what we get is a great
many more systems of order and much less order over all."

"That fits in with my own findings," Stumm agreed.

"Only most people aren't as keen as you are on making sense of it,"

Ulrich continued. "After so many struggles, we're on a downward slide now. Just think what's happening today: As soon as some leading thinker comes up with an idea it is immediately pulled apart by the sympathies and antipathies generated: first its admirers rip large chunks out of it to suit themselves, wrenching their masters' minds out of shape the way a fox savages his kill, and then his opponents destroy the weak links so that soon there's nothing left but a stock of aphorisms from which friend and foe alike help themselves at will. The result is a general ambiguity. There's no Yes without a No dangling from it. Whatever you do, you can find twenty of the finest ideas in support and another twenty against it. It's much like love or hatred or hunger, where tastes have to differ so that each can find his own."

"You've said it!" Stumm exclaimed, in wholehearted agreement again. "I myself have already put something like it to Diotima. But don't you think that all this confusion seems to justify the military position—though I'd be mortified to have to believe it even for a minute!"

"I'd advise you," Ulrich said, "to tip off Diotima that God, for reasons still unknown to us, seems to be leading us into an era of physical culture, for the only thing that gives ideas some sort of foothold is the body to which they belong—which gives you, as an army officer, something of an advantage."

The tubby little General winced. "On the plane of physical culture I look about as beautiful as a peeled peach," he said after a while, with bitter satisfaction. "And I'd better make it clear that I think of Diotima only in an honorable way, and hope to pass muster in her eyes in the same fashion."

"Too bad," Ulrich said. "Your aims would be worthy of a Napoleon, but you won't find this the right century for them."

The General swallowed this gentle gibe with the dignity of a man conscious of suffering for the lady of his heart, and only said, after a moment's thought: "Thank you, in any case, for your interesting advice."

86

The industrial potentate and the merger of Soul with Business. Also, All roads to the mind start from the soul, but none lead back again

At this time, when the General's love for Diotima took a back seat to his admiration for Diotima and Arnheim as a pair, Arnheim should long since have made up his mind never to come back. Instead, he made arrangements to prolong his stay; he kept his suite at the hotel, and the great mobility of his life seemed to have come to a standstill. It was a time when the world was being shaken up in various ways, and those who kept themselves well informed toward the end of the year 1913 lived on the edge of a seething volcano, although the peaceful processes of production everywhere suggested that it could never really erupt again. The power of this suggestion was not equally strong everywhere. The windows of the handsome old palace on the Ballhausplatz where Section Chief Tuzzi held sway often lit up the bare trees in the gardens across the way until late into the night, giving a thrill of awe to the better class of strollers who might be passing by in the darkness. For just as his sainthood permeates the figure of the humble carpenter Joseph, so the name Ballhausplatz permeated that palace with the aura of being one of a half-dozen mysterious kitchens where, behind drawn curtains, the fate of mankind was being dished up. Dr. Arnheim was quite well informed of what was going on. He received coded telegrams and, from time to time, a visit from one of his managers, bringing confidential information from company headquarters; the windows of his hotel suite, too, were often lit up till all hours, and an imaginative observer might easily have thought that a secondary or counter-government was here in nightly session, a modern, apocryphal battle station of economic diplomacy.

Nor did Arnheim for his part ever neglect to produce such an impression; without the power of suggestion in his appearance, a man is only a sweet watery fruit without a peel. Even at breakfast, which for this reason he never took in private but in the hotel restaurant, open to all, he dictated his orders for the day to his shorthand-scribbling secretary with the authoritative air of the experienced ruler and the courteous poise of a man who knows all eyes are upon him. Arnheim would have found none of the details inspiring in themselves, but since they not only combined to lay claim to his attention but also made room for the charms of breakfast, they produced a heightened sense of things. Human talent, he liked to think, probably needs to be somewhat restricted if it is to unfold to its best potential; the really fertile borderland between reckless freedom of thought and a dispirited blankness of mind is, as everyone who knows life is aware, a very narrow strip of territory. Besides, he never doubted that it made all the difference *who* had an idea. Everyone knows that new and important ideas seldom arise in only one mind at a time, while, on the other hand, the brain of a man who is accustomed to thinking is constantly breeding thoughts of unequal value, so that the end result, its final effective form, always comes to an idea from the outside, not merely from the thinker's mind but from the whole concatenation of his circumstances. A question from the secretary, a glance at a nearby table, a greeting from someone entering the room, or some such thing would always remind Arnheim, at just the right moment, that he must keep up an imposing presence, and this perfecting of his appearance carried over to his thinking as well. It all culminated in his conviction, suiting his needs, that the thinking man must always be simultaneously a man of action.

Nevertheless, he attached no great importance to his present occupation; even though it was designed to achieve something that might, under certain circumstances, be remarkably profitable, he still felt that he was overstaying his time here. He repeatedly reminded himself of that cold breath of ancient wisdom, *Divide et impera,* which applies to every transaction and calls for a certain subordination of each individual instance to the whole, for the secret of the successful approach to any undertaking is the same as that of the man who is loved by many women while himself careful to play no favorites. But it was no use. Fully mindful of the demands the world imposes on a man born to action on a grand scale, and no matter how often he took pains to search his soul, he could not close his eyes to the fact that he was in love. It was an awkward fix, because a heart turned fifty is a tough muscle, not so easily stretched as that of a twenty-year-old in love's springtime, and it caused him considerable vexation.

It troubled him, to begin with, that his interest in his far-flung international concerns was withering like a flower cut off at the root, while everyday trivia like a sparrow on his windowsill or a waiter's smile positively blossomed into significance for him. As to his moral concepts, normally a comprehensive system for being always in the right, without any loopholes, he saw them shrinking in scope while taking on a certain physical quality. It could be called devotion, but this again was a word that usually had a much wider and anyway a quite different meaning, for without devotion nothing can be achieved in any sphere: devotion to duty, to a superior or a leader, even devotion to life itself, in all its richness and variety, seen as a manly quality, had always seemed to him to be uprightness itself, which for all its openness had more to do with restraint than with a yielding up of the self. And the same might be said of faithfulness, which, confined to a woman, smacks of limitation, as was true of chivalry and gentleness, unselfishness and delicacy, all of them virtues usually thought of in association with her but losing their richest quality thereby, so that it is hard to say whether a man's experience of love only flows toward a woman as water tends to collect in the lowest, generally not the most acceptable spot, or whether the love of a woman is the volcanic center whose warmth sustains all life on earth. A supreme degree of male vanity therefore feels more at ease in male rather than female company, and when Arnheim compared the wealth of ideas he had brought to the spheres of power with the state of bliss he owed to Diotima, he could not shake off the sense of having slipped somehow.

At times he longed for embraces and kisses like a boy ready to fling himself passionately at the feet of the coldhearted beloved refusing him, or else he caught himself wanting to burst out sobbing, or hurl a challenge to the world and, finally, carry off the beloved in his arms. Now, we all know that the irresponsible margin of the conscious personality that breeds stories and poems is also the home base of all sorts of childish memories that surface on those rare occasions when the intoxication of fatigue, the release of alcohol, or some other disturbance brings them to light. Arnheim's bursts of feeling were no more substantial than these phantoms, so that he need not have been upset by them (thereby considerably increasing his original agitation), if these infantile regressions had not forced him to realize that his inner life was swarming with faded moral stereotypes. The stamp of general validity he was always at pains to give to his actions, as a man conscious of living with the eyes of all Europe upon him, suddenly showed itself as having nothing to do with his inner life. This may be quite natural for anything supposed to be valid for everyone, but what troubled him was the implication that if what is generally valid is not the inward truth, then contrariwise the inward man is not generally valid. And so Arnheim now felt haunted at every step not only by the urge to sound some deafening wrong note, or perform some foolishly illegitimate act, but also by the annoying thought that on some irrational level this would be the right thing to do. Ever since he had come to know again the fire that makes the tongue go dry in the mouth, he was overcome with the sense of having lost a path he had always followed, the feeling that the whole ideology of the great man he lived by was only an emergency substitute for something that was missing.

This naturally brought his childhood to mind. In his early portraits he had big, dark, round eyes, like the paintings of the boy Jesus disputing with the doctors in the Temple, and he saw all his governesses and tutors standing around him in a circle, marveling at his precocity, because he had been a clever boy who had always had clever teachers. He had also proved himself to be a warmhearted, sensitive child who would tolerate no unfairness; since his life was far too sheltered to let any unfairness come his way, he made the wrongs of others his own where he came across them, and got himself into fights on their account. This was quite an achievement, considering what obstacles were put in his way to prevent this very thing, so that it never took more than a minute for someone to come rushing up to pry him loose from his opponent. Because such fights lasted just long enough to give him a taste of some painful experience but were always interrupted in time to leave him with the impression of his own unflinching courage, Arnheim still remembered them with self-satisfaction; and this lordly quality of courage that would shrink from nothing passed later into his books and his principles, as becomes a man who needs to tell his contemporaries how to conduct themselves for self-respect and happiness.

This childhood state was still vividly present to his mind, while another condition, of a somewhat later period, that had succeeded and partly transformed it now appeared to be dormant or on the verge of petrifaction—if this is understood as turning not to stone, in the ordinary sense, but to diamonds. It was love, now startled into a new life by his contact with Diotima, and it was characteristic of Arnheim that his first youthful experience of love had nothing to do with women, or indeed any specific persons; this was a rather perplexing business he had never quite resolved for himself, even though in the course of time he had come to learn the most up-to-date explanations for it.

"What he meant was perhaps only the baffling manifestation of something still absent, like those rare expressions that appear on faces with which they have no connection, belonging rather to other, different faces suddenly intuited beyond the horizon of the visible; simple melodies in the midst of mere noise, feelings inside people, feelings he sensed inside himself, in fact, that were not yet real feelings when he tried to capture them in words, but only something inside him reaching outward, its tips already breaking the surface, getting wet, as things sometimes do reach out on fever-bright spring days when their shadows creep beyond them and come to rest so quietly, all flowing in one direction, like reflections in a stream."

This was how it was expressed, much later on and in other accents, by a poet Arnheim esteemed because to know of this reclusive man who avoided all notoriety made one an insider; not that Arnheim understood him, for he associated such allusions with the talk about the awakening of a new soul that had been in fashion during his youth, or with the then popular pictures of reedy girls, painted with a pair of lips that looked like fleshy flower buds.

At that time, around the year 1887—"good heavens, almost a generation ago!" Arnheim thought—he appeared in photographs as the "new man" of the period, in a high-buttoned black satin waistcoat with a wide, heavy silk cravat deriving from the Biedermeier style but meant to suggest the Baudelairean, with the help of an orchid (the latest thing) in his buttonhole, exerting a malevolent fascination on all who saw Arnheim junior on his way to dine and impress his youth-

ful person on some robust businessmen friends of his father's. Portraits of young Arnheim at work ran to a slide rule peeping decora-
tively from the breast pocket of a tweedy English sport jacket, worn
quite comically with a towering stiff collar, which nevertheless
heightened the effect of the head. That was how Arnheim had
looked, and he still could not keep from looking at his image with a
certain approval. He had played good tennis when it was still played
on lawns, with all the zeal of a passion as yet reserved for the few;
surprised his father by openly attending workers' meetings, after a
student year in Zurich where he had become unsuitably acquainted
with socialist ideas, which did not prevent him from galloping his
horse recklessly through a working-class quarter of town on another
day. In short, it had all been a whirl of contradictory but challenging
new experiences which gave him the enchanting illusion of having
been born at just the right time, an illusion so important to a young
man, even though he realizes later on that its value does not lie in its
rarity, exactly. As time went on and Arnheim came to think more and
more conservatively, he did wonder whether this ever-renewed feeling of being the last word wasn't part of nature's wastefulness; but he
never gave it up, because he never did like to give up anything that
had ever belonged to him, and his collector's nature had carefully
preserved within him all there was at the time. But today it seemed
to him, however rounded and various his life appeared to be, that he
had been most particularly moved and most lastingly influenced by
what had seemed at first the most unreal element of all: precisely
that romantically expectant state of mind whispering to him that he
belonged not only to the world of bustling activity but to yet another
world, suspended inside it, as if holding its breath.

This dreamy expectancy, restored to him in its full original freshness by Diotima's influence, becalmed all activity and busyness now;
the tumult of youthful conflict and hopeful, ever-changing vistas
gave way to a daydream in which all words, events, and needs were
basically the same deep down, away from their surface differences.
At such moments even ambition was hushed; the world was a distant
noise beyond the garden wall, as though his soul had overflowed its
banks and was truly present to him for the first time. It cannot be too
strongly emphasized that this was not a philosophy but as physical an
experience as seeing the moon, though overwhelmed by daylight,

hovering mutely in the morning sky. In such a state of mind even the young Paul Arnheim had calmly dined at select restaurants, dressed with care to attend all the social functions, done everything that had to be done but always, as it were, with no greater or lesser distance from one part of himself to the other than to or from the next person or object; somehow the outer world did not leave off at his skin, and his inner world did not merely shine out through the window of reflection, but both blended into a single undivided state of separateness and presence, as mild, calm, and lofty as a dreamless sleep. Morally it felt like a truly great indifference, a sense of all values being equal; nothing was minor or major: a poem and a kiss on a woman's hand were the equal in significance of a scholarly work in several volumes or some great act of statesmanship, and just as everything evil was meaningless, so, basically, everything good had become superfluous in this immersion in the tender primal kinship of all created things. Arnheim behaved quite normally, except that he was doing it in an intangible atmosphere of special significance, behind the tremulous flame of which the inner man stood motionless, watching the outer man eating an apple or being measured for a new suit.

Was it illusion, then, or the shadow of a reality never to be quite understood? The only possible answer is that all religions, at certain stages of their development, have asserted the reality of this shadow, and so have all lovers, all romantics, all those with a hankering for the moon, for springtime, and the blissful dying of the days in early fall. Eventually it fades away, however, it evaporates and dries up, one cannot say which—until one day something else has taken its place and it is instantly forgotten as only unreal experiences, dreams, and illusions are forgotten. Since this primal and cosmic love experience is normally encountered the first time one falls in love, one usually thinks even later in life that one knows just what to make of it, regarding it as part of the foolishness one may indulge in before one is old enough to vote. So this was how it was with him, but since for Arnheim it had never been associated with a woman, it could never quite leave his heart in the usual way, along with her; instead, it was overlaid by impressions received, after completing his schooling, when he entered his father's business. Since he did nothing by halves, he soon discovered here that the productive and well-balanced life is a poem greater by far than any hatched out by a poet in his garret, and a different sort of thing altogether.

Now for the first time he showed his talent for being an exemplary character. The poem of life has this advantage over all other poems, that it is set in all capital letters, as it were, no matter what its content may be. Even the youngest trainee in a firm of world rank has the whole world circling around him, with continents peering over his shoulder, so that nothing he does is without significance, while the lone writer in his seclusion has at most flies circling around him no matter how hard he tries to get something done. This is so obvious that many people, from the moment they begin to work in the medium of life itself, regard everything that used to move them before as "mere literature," meaning that the effect it has is at best weak and muddled, generally contradictory so that it cancels itself out, and anyway not in proportion to the fuss made over it. Arnheim was not quite like that, of course; he neither denied the noble influence of art nor was capable of regarding anything that had once strongly moved him as foolishness or a delusion. When he recognized the superiority of his adult responsibilities over the dreamy outlook of his youth he took steps, guided by his new mature insights, to effect a fusion of both kinds of experience. He did, in fact, what so many, certainly the majority of the professional classes, do after beginning their careers: far from wishing to turn their backs entirely on their former interests, they find themselves for the first time in a serene, mature relationship to the enthusiastic impulses of their younger years. Discovering the great poem of life, knowing their own part in it, restores to them the courage of the dilettante they had lost when they burned their own poems. Working on the poem of their own life, they can at last regard themselves as *born* experts and set about permeating their daily round with a sense of intellectual responsibility, feeling themselves faced with a thousand small decisions in making it moral and attractive, modeling themselves on their notion of how Goethe led his life and giving everyone to understand that without music, without the beauties of nature and the sight of animals and children at play, and without a good book, life would not be worth having. This soulful middle class is still, among Germans, the leading consumer of the arts and of all literature that is not too heavy; but its members understandably look down upon art and literature, which they once regarded as the ultimate fulfillment, as upon an earlier stage of development, even though it may have been more perfect in its way than what fate allotted to them; or else they regard it much as a manufacturer of sheet metal, say, might regard a sculptor of plaster statues if he were weak enough to see any beauty in that sort of product.

Now Arnheim resembled this cultural middle class as a glorious hothouse double carnation resembles a weedy little pink growing wild at the roadside. He never thought in terms of a cultural revolution or radical innovation, but thought only of the interweaving of the new into the traditional, a taking over, with gentle modifications and a moral reanimation, of the faded privileges of the powers that were. He was no snob, no worshiper of those who outranked him in society. Received at court and on terms with the high nobility and the leading government officialdom, he adjusted himself to this environment not at all as an imitator but only as an amateur of the conservative feudal manner, one who never forgets or seeks to make others forget his patrician, quasi-Goethean-Frankfurt, origins. But with this concession his capacity for resistance was exhausted, and any greater distancing of himself from greatness would have seemed to him untrue to life. He was deeply convinced that the creators of wealth—led by the businessmen who directed life and would be shaping a new era— were destined to take over at some point from the ruling powers, and this gave him a certain quiet arrogance, which had been proved valid enough by the subsequent course of events. But taking money's claim to power as a given, the question was still how the desired power was to be rightly used. The bank directors' and industrial magnates' predecessors had no problem; they were feudal knights who made literal mincemeat of their enemies, leaving the clergy to handle the morals. But while contemporary man has in money, as Arnheim saw it, the surest control of society, a means as tough and precise as the guillotine, it can also be as vulnerable as an arthritic— how painfully the money market limps and aches all over at the slightest draft!—and is most delicately involved with everything it controls. Because he understood this subtle interdependence of all the forms of life, which only the blind arrogance of the ideologue can overlook, Arnheim came to see the regal man of business as the synthesis of change and permanence, power and civility, sensible risk-

taking and strong-minded reliance on information, but essentially as
the symbolic figure of democracy-in-the-making. By the persistent
and disciplined honing of his own personality, by his intellectual
grasp of the economic and social complexes at hand, and by giving
thought to the leadership and structure of the state as a whole, he
hoped to help bring the new era to birth, that age where the social
forces made unequal by fate and nature would be properly and fruit-
fully organized and where the ideal would not be shattered by the
inevitable limitations of reality, but be purified and strengthened instead. Objectively put, he had brought about the fusion of interests
between business and the soul by working out the overall concept of
the Business King, and that feeling of love that had once taught him
the unity of all things now formed the nucleus of his conviction that
culture and all human interests formed a harmonious whole.

It was at about this time, too, that Arnheim began to publish his
writings, and in them surfaced the term "soul." He presumably resorted to it as a device, a flying start, a royal motto, since princes and
generals certainly have no souls, and as for financiers, he was the very
first to have one. It undoubtedly also played a part in his need to set
up defenses that could not be breached by the business mentality of
those forming his intimate circle, and more specifically by the imperious nature and greater business sense of his father, beside whom
he was beginning to assume the role of the aging crown prince. And
it is equally certain that his ambition to master all worthwhile knowledge—a taste for polyhistory so consuming that no single man could
have lived up to the goals he set himself—found in the soul a means
to rise above all that his intellect could not encompass. In this he was
a man of his time, which had recently developed a strong religious
bent, not because it had a call to religion but only, it seems, out of an
irritable feminine revolt against money, science, and calculation, to
all of which it succumbed with a passion. What was questionable and
uncertain, however, was whether Arnheim, in speaking of the soul,
believed in it; whether it was real to him, like his stock portfolio. He
used the word to express something for which he had no other term.
Driven by his need to use it in conversation—Arnheim was a talker
who did not easily let anyone else get a word in—and finding that he
made an impression, he came to use it more and more in his writings,
referring to it as though its existence were as assured as that of one's

own back, even though one never gets to see it. And so he wrote with real fervor of something vague and portentous that is interwoven with the all-too-factual world of business affairs as a profound silence is interwoven with vivid speech. He did not deny the usefulness of knowledge; quite the contrary, he was himself an impressively busy compiler of data, as only a man who has all the resources at his command can be, but once he had proved himself in that arena he would say that above and beyond this level of keenness and precision there was a higher realm of wisdom that was accessible only to the visionary. He spoke of the will by which nation-states and international business giants are founded, so as to let it be understood that with all his greatness he was nothing but an arm that could be moved only by a heart beating somewhere beyond the range of human vision. He held forth on technological advances or moral values in the most down-to-earth fashion, in terms familiar to the man in the street, only to add that such exploitation of nature and man's spiritual energies amounted to nothing more than a fatal ignorance if the sense was lacking that they were merely the surface ripples of an ocean the immense depths of which were hardly touched by them. He delivered such sentiments in the manner of the regent of an exiled queen who had received her personal instructions and orders the world accordingly.

This keeping the world in order was perhaps his truest and fiercest passion, a craving for power far surpassing everything even a man in his position could afford, which drove this man who was so powerful in the real world to withdraw at least once a year to his castle in East Prussia, where he dictated a whole book to his secretary. The strange sense of mission that had surfaced first and most vividly in his early days of youthful enthusiasm and still afflicted him from time to time, though with lessened intensity, had found this outlet for itself. In the thick of his global undertakings it came over him like a sweet trance, a longing for the cloister, murmuring to him that all the contradictions, all the great ideas, all worldly experience and effort, were a unity, not only as vaguely understood by what we call culture and humanity but also in a wildly literal and shimmeringly passive sense, as when on a morbidly lovely day one might gaze out over river and meadows, hands crossed in one's lap, unwilling to tear oneself away, evermore. In this sense, his writing was a compromise. And because there is only one soul, not within reach but in exile, from which it has only one way to make itself known to us in all its hazy ambiguity, while there are such countless, endless problems in the world to which its royal message can be applied, so, as the years went by, he found himself in that grave embarrassment suffered by all legitimists and prophets when it is all taking too long to happen. Arnheim had only to sit down alone to write for his pen to start leading him, with a truly uncanny flow of words, from the soul to the problems of the mind, the moral life, economics, and politics, all brilliantly lighted from some invisible source and appearing in a clear and magically unifying illumination. There was something intoxicating in this expansiveness, but it depended on that split consciousness which alone makes creative composition possible for so many writers, in that the mind shuts out and forgets whatever does not happen to fit into its scheme. Speaking to another person, whose presence was a link to the rest of the world, Arnheim would never have let himself go so recklessly; but bent over a sheet of paper that was ready to reflect his views, he joyfully abandoned himself to a metaphoric expression of his convictions, only a small portion of which had any basis in fact, while the greater part was a billowing cloud of words whose sole— and incidentally not inconsiderable—claim to reality was that it always arose spontaneously in the same places.

Anyone inclined to find fault should remember that having a split personality has long since ceased to be a trick reserved for lunatics; at the present-day tempo, our capacity for political insight, for writing a piece for the newspapers, for faith in the new movements in art and literature, and for countless other things, depends wholly on a knack for being, at times, convinced against our own convictions, splitting off a part of our mind and stretching it to form a brand-new wholehearted conviction. So it was another point in Arnheim's favor that he never quite honestly believed what he was saying. As a man in his prime he had already had his say on anything and everything; he had his convictions, which covered much ground, and saw no barriers to going on spinning new convictions smoothly out of the old ones, indefinitely. A man whose mind worked to such good effect and who could switch it in other states of consciousness to checking balance sheets and estimating profits to be made on his deals could not fail to notice that there was no shape or set course to his activity, though it continued to expand almost inexhaustibly in every direction; it was bounded only by the unity of his person, and although Arnheim could hold a large amount of self-esteem, this was not for him an intellectually satisfactory state of affairs. He tried blaming it on the residual element of irrationality that the informed observer can detect everywhere in life; he tried to shrug it off on the grounds that in our time everything tends to overflow its borders, and since no man can quite transcend the weaknesses of his century, he saw in this a welcome chance to practice that modesty typical of all great men by setting up above himself, quite unenviously, such figures as Homer and Buddha, because they had lived in more favorable eras. But as time went on and his literary success peaked without making any real difference to his crown-princely state, that element of irrationality, the absence of tangible results, and his troubling sense of having missed his target and lost his original resolve became more oppressive. He surveyed his work, and even though he saw that it was good, he felt as though all these ideas were setting up a barrier between some haunting primal home and himself, like a wall of diamonds growing daily more encrusted.

Something unpleasant of this sort had happened and left its mark on him just recently. He had made use of the leisure he currently indulged himself in more frequently than was his habit, to dictate to his secretary an essay on the essential accord between government architecture and the concept of the state, and he had broken off a sentence intended to run "Contemplating this edifice, we see the silence of the walls" after the word "silence," in order to linger for a moment over the image of the Cancelleria in Rome, which had just risen up unbidden before his inner eye. But as he looked at the typescript over his secretary's shoulder he noticed that, anticipating him as usual, the secretary had already written: ". . . we see the silence of the soul." That day Arnheim dictated no more, and on the following day he had the sentence deleted.

Compared with experiences that reached so far and so deep, what price the ordinary physical love for a woman? Sadly, Arnheim had to admit to himself that it mattered just as much as the realization, summing up his life, that all roads to the mind start in the soul, but none lead back there again. There were of course many women who had enjoyed close relations with him, but other than the parasitic species they tended to be professionally engaged, educated women or artists, for with these two kinds, the kept women and the self-sustaining types, it was possible to have a clear-cut understanding. His moral nature had always guided him into relationships where instinct and the consequent inevitable arrangements with women could somehow be dealt with rationally. But Diotima was the first woman to penetrate into his pre-moral, secret inner life, and this almost made him look at her askance. She was only the wife of a government official, after all, socially most presentable, of course, but without that supreme degree of cultivation that comes only with power, while Arnheim could marry a daughter of American high finance or of an English duke. He had moments of recoiling with a primitive nursery antagonism, the naïvely cruel arrogance and dismay of the well-bred child taken for the first time to a city school, so that his growing infatuation seemed to threaten him with disgrace. When at such moments he resumed his business activities with the icy superiority of a spirit that had died to the world and been reborn to it, then the cool rationality of money, immune to contamination, seemed an extraordinarily clean force compared with love.

But this only meant that for him the time had come when the prisoner wonders how he could have let himself be robbed of his freedom without putting up a life-and-death struggle. For when Diotima said: "What do the affairs of the world amount to? *Un peu de bruit autour de notre âme . . . ,*" he felt a tremor go through the edifice of his life.

87

MOOSBRUGGER DANCES

Meanwhile Moosbrugger was still sitting in a detention cell at the district courthouse while his case was under study. His counsel had got fresh wind in his sails and was using delaying tactics with the authorities to keep the case from coming to a final conclusion.

Moosbrugger smiled at all this. He smiled from boredom.

Boredom rocked his mind like a cradle. Ordinarily boredom blots out the mind, but his was rocked by it, this time anyway. He felt like an actor in his dressing room, waiting for his cue.

If Moosbrugger had had a big sword, he'd have drawn it and chopped the head off his chair. He would have chopped the head off the table and the window, the slop bucket, the door. Then he would have set his own head on everything, because in this cell there was only one head, his own, and that was as it should be. He could imagine his head sitting on top of things, with its broad skull, its hair like a fur cap pulled down over his forehead; he liked that.

If only the room were bigger and the food better!

He was quite glad not to see people. People were hard to take. They often had a way of spitting, or of hunching up a shoulder, that made a man feel down in the mouth and ready to drive a fist through their back, like punching a hole in the wall. Moosbrugger did not believe in God, only in what he could figure out for himself. His contemptuous terms for the eternal truths were: the cop, the bench, the preacher. He knew he could count on no one but himself to take care of things, and such a man sometimes feels that others are there only to get in his way. He saw what he had seen so often: the inkstands, the green baize, the pencils, the Emperor's portrait on the wall, the way they all sat there around him: a booby trap camouflaged, not with grass and green leaves, just with the feeling: That's how it is. Then remembered things would pop into his head—the way a bush stood at the river bend, the creak of a pump handle, bits of different landscapes all jumbled up, an endless stock of memories of things he hadn't realized he'd noticed at the time. "I bet I could tell them a thing or two," he thought. He was daydreaming like a youngster: a man they had locked up so often he never grew older. "Next time I'll have to take a closer look at it," Moosbrugger thought, "otherwise they'll never understand." Then he smiled sternly and spoke to the judges about himself, like a father saying about his son: "Just you lock him up, that good-for-nothing, he needs to be taught a lesson."

Sometimes he felt annoyed, of course, with the prison regulations. Or he was hurting somewhere. But then he could ask to see the prison doctor or the warden, and things fell into place again, like water closing over a dead rat that had fallen in. Not that he thought of it quite in these terms, but he kept having the sense almost constantly these days, even if he did not have the words for it, that he was like a great shining sheet of water, not to be disturbed by anything.

The words he did have were: hm-hm, uh-uh.

The table was Moosbrugger.

The chair was Moosbrugger.

The barred window and the bolted door were himself.

There was nothing at all crazy or out of the ordinary in what he meant. It was just that the rubber bands were gone. Behind every thing or creature, when it tries to get really close to another, is a rubber band, pulling. Otherwise, things might finally go right through one another. Every movement is reined in by a rubber band that won't let a person do quite what he wants. Now, suddenly, all those rubber bands were gone. Or was it just the feeling of being held in check, as if by rubber bands?

Maybe one just can't cut it so fine? "For instance, women keep their stockings up with elastic. There it is!" Moosbrugger thought. "They wear garters on their legs like amulets. Under their skirts. Just like the rings they paint around fruit trees to stop the worms from crawling up."

But we mention this only in passing. Lest anyone suppose that Moosbrugger felt he had to stay on good terms with everything. It wasn't really like that. It was only that he was both inside and outside.

He was the boss now, and he acted bossy. He was putting things in order before they killed him off. The moment he thought of anything, anything he pleased, it obeyed him like a well-trained dog to whom you say: "Down, boy!" Locked up though he was, he had a tremendous sense of power.

On the dot, his soup was brought. On the dot, he was awakened and taken out for his walk. Everything in his cell was on the mark, strict and immovable. This sometimes seemed incredible to him. He had the strangely topsy-turvy impression that all this order emanated from him, even though he knew that it was being imposed on him.

Other people have this sort of experience when they are stretched out in the summery shade of a hedge, the bees are buzzing, and the sun rides small and hard in the milky sky: the world revolves around them like a mechanical toy. Moosbrugger felt it when he merely looked at the geometric scene presented by his cell.

At such times he noticed that he had a mad craving for good food; he dreamed of it, and by day the outlines of a good plate of roast pork kept rising up before his eyes with an uncanny persistence the moment his mind turned back from other preoccupations. "Two portions!" Moosbrugger then ordered. "No, make it three!" He thought this so hard, and heaped up his imaginary plate so greedily, that he instantly felt full to bursting, to the point of nausea; he gorged himself in his imagination. "Why," he wondered, wagging his head, "why do I feel so stuffed, so soon after wanting to eat? Between eating and bursting lie all the pleasures of this world! Hell, what a world! There are hundreds of examples to prove how little space it gives you. To take just one, for instance: a woman you don't have is like the moon at night climbing higher and higher, sucking and sucking at your heart; but once you've had her, you feel like trampling on her face with your boots. Why is it like that?" He remembered being asked about it lots of times. One could answer: Women are women *and* men too, because men chase after them. But it was only one more thing that the people who asked all the questions wouldn't really understand. So they asked him why he thought that people were in cahoots against him. As if even his own body wasn't in cahoots with them! This was quite obvious where women were concerned, of course, but even with men his body understood things better than he did himself. One word leads to another, you know what's what, you're in each other's pocket all day long, and then, in a flash, you've somehow crossed that narrow borderline where you get along with them without any trouble. But if his body had got him into this, it had better get him out of it again! All Moosbrugger could remember was that he'd been vexed or frightened, and his chest with its arms flailing had rushed at them like a big dog on command. That was all Moosbrugger could understand anyway; between getting along and being fed up there's only a thin line, that's all, and once something gets started it soon gets scary and tight.

Those people who were always using those foreign words and were always sitting in judgment on him would keep throwing this up to him: "But you don't go and kill a man just for that, surely!" Moosbrugger only shrugged. People have been done in for a few pennies, or for nothing at all, when someone happened to feel like it. But he had more self-respect than that, he wasn't one of that kind. In time the rebuke registered with him; he found himself wondering why he felt the world closing in on him, or whatever you might call it, time and again, so that he had to clear a space for himself by force, in order that the blood could drain out of his head again. He thought it over. But wasn't it just the same with thinking too? Whenever he felt in the right mood for doing some thinking, the pleasure of it made him want to smile. Then his thoughts stopped itching under the skull, and suddenly there was just one idea there. It was like the difference between an infant's toddling along and a fine figure of a woman dancing. It was like being under a spell. There's the sound of an accordion being played, a lamp stands on the table, butterflies come inside, out of the summer night—that was how his thoughts came fluttering into the light of the one idea, or else Moosbrugger grabbed them with his big fingers as they came and crushed them, looking for one breathtaking moment like little dragons caught there. A drop of Moosbrugger's blood had fallen into the world. You couldn't see it because it was dark, but he could feel what was going on out there. The tangled mess smoothed itself out. A soundless dance replaced the intolerable buzzing with which the world so often tormented him. Everything that happened was lovely now, just as a homely girl can be lovely when she no longer stands alone but is taken by the hand and whirled around in a dance, her face turned upward to a staircase from which others are looking down at her. It was a strange business. When Moosbrugger opened his eyes and looked at the people who happened to be nearby at such a moment, when everything was dancing to his tune, as it were, they, too, seemed lovely to him. They were no longer in league against him, they did not form a wall against him, and he realized that it was only the strain of getting the better of him that twisted the look of people and things like some crushing weight. At such times Moosbrugger danced for them. He danced with dignity and invisibly, he who never danced with anyone in real life, moved by a music that increasingly turned into self-communion and sleep, the womb of the Mother of God, and finally the peace of God himself, a wondrously incredible state of deathlike release; he danced for days, unseen by anyone, until it was all outside, all out of him, clinging to things around him like a cobweb stiffened and made useless by the frost.

How could anyone who had never been through all this judge the rest? After those days and weeks when Moosbrugger felt so light he could almost slip out of his skin, there always came those long stretches of imprisonment. The public prisons were nothing by comparison. Then when he tried to think, everything inside him shriveled up, bitter and empty. He hated the workingmen's study centers and the night schools where they tried to tell him how to think—after all, he knew the heady feeling of his thoughts taking off with long strides, as if on stilts! They made him feel as if he had to drag himself through the world on leaden feet, hoping to find some place where things might be different again.

Now he thought back to that hope with no more than a pitying smile. He had never managed to find a possible resting point midway between his two extremes. He was fed up. He smiled grandly at oncoming death.

He had, after all, seen quite a bit of the world. Bavaria and Austria, all the way to Turkey. And a great deal had happened during his lifetime that he had read about in the papers. An eventful time, on the whole. Deep down he was quite proud to have been a part of it all. Thinking it over bit by bit, he had to take it as a troubled and dreary business, but his own track did run right across it; looking back, you could see it clearly, from birth to death. Moosbrugger was far from feeling that he would actually be executed; he was executing himself, with the help of those other people, that was the way he looked at what was coming. It all added up to a whole, of sorts: the highways, the towns, the cops and the birds, the dead and his own death. It wasn't altogether clear to him, and the others understood it even less, though they could talk more glibly about it.

He spat and thought of the sky, which looks like a mousetrap covered in blue. "The kind they make in Slovakia, those round, high mousetraps," he thought.

88

ON BEING INVOLVED WITH MATTERS OF CONSEQUENCE

It is now high time to consider something previously touched upon in various connections, which might be formulated as: There is nothing so hazardous to the mind as its involvement with matters of great consequence.

A man wanders through a forest, climbs a mountain and sees the world spread out below him, stares at his infant just put into his arms for the first time, or enjoys the good fortune of holding a position in life envied by all. And we ask: What is it like for him? Surely, he thinks, this is all many-layered, deep, important; it's just that he doesn't have the presence of mind to take it at its word, so to speak. The marvel that is facing him and outside him, enclosing him like a magnetic casing, drains his mind and leaves it a blank. While his gaze is held fast by a thousand details, he secretly feels as if he had spent all his ammunition. Outwardly the soul-drenched, sun-drenched, deepened or heightened moment glazes the world with a galvanic silver coating, down to the tiniest leaflets and their capillaries, but here inside, at the world's personal end, a certain lack of inner substance makes itself felt, in the form of a big, vacuous, round O. This condition is the classic symptom of making contact with all that is eternal and great, like dwelling upon the peaks of humanity and nature. Those of us who prefer to live with greatness—first and foremost among whom will be found those great souls for whom little things simply don't exist—find their inward life drawn out of them involuntarily and stretched into an extended superficiality.

The danger of having to do with great things may therefore also be regarded as a law of the conservation of spiritual energy, and it seems to be more or less generally valid. The utterances of socially prominent persons of great influence are usually more vacuous than our own. Ideas closely involved with particularly estimable subjects usually look as though it is only their privileged status that saves them from being regarded as not up to snuff. The causes dearest to our hearts—the nation, peace, humanity, character, and similarly sacred objectives—sprout on their backs the cheapest flora of the mind. This would make ours a topsy-turvy world, unless we assume that the more significant the subject, the more inanely it may be discussed, in which case the world is turned right side up again.

This law, however, helpful as it was toward our understanding of European culture, is not always clearly in evidence, and in times of transition from one group of great causes to another, the mind that seeks to serve some great cause may even seem subversive, although it is only changing its uniform. A transition of this kind was already noticeable when the people we are speaking of were having their anxieties and triumphs. There were already, for instance—to start with a subject of special concern to Arnheim—books enjoying huge sales, though these were not yet the books most respected, even though great respect was reserved only for those books that had impressive sales. Football and lawn tennis had already become influential industries, but there was still some hesitation at the institutes of advanced technology when it came to setting up professorial chairs for teaching them. All in all, whether it was in fact the late lamented rakehell and admiral Drake who introduced the potato from America, heralding the end of recurrent famines throughout Europe, or the less lamented, highly cultivated, and equally pugnacious Admiral Raleigh, or some anonymous Spanish sailors, or even that worthy rascal and slave trader Hawkins, it was a long time before it occurred to anyone to consider these men more important, thanks to the potato, than, say, the physicist Al Shirazi, who is known only for his correct explanation of the rainbow. But with the bourgeois era a revaluation of such achievements began, which in Arnheim's time was far advanced and hindered only by some residual old-fashioned prejudices. The quantity of the effect, and the effect of quantity, as the new, self-evident object of veneration, still struggled against an aging, blind, aristocratic regard for quality, but in the popular imagination this struggle had already spawned fantastic hybrids, quite like the concept of the "great mind" itself, which, in the form we have come to know it in the last generation, is a blend of its significance-as-such and its potato-significance, for we lived in expectation of a man who would personify the solitary genius and yet be instantly understandable to all and sundry like a nightingale.

It was hard to tell what to expect along these lines, since the hazardousness of being involved with greatness is usually not perceived until such greatness is halfway past and gone. Nothing is easier than to look down on the flunky who visibly condescends to His Majesty's guests in His Majesty's name, but whether the man who treats Today respectfully in the name of Tomorrow is a flunky or not is usually not known until the day after Tomorrow. The hazard of being involved with great things includes the unpleasant certainty that while the things change, the hazard remains the same.

89

ONE MUST MOVE WITH THE TIMES

Dr. phil. Arnheim had received a scheduled visit from two top executives of his firm and had held a long conference with them; in the morning, all the papers and calculations still lay in disorder in his sitting room, for his secretary to deal with. Arnheim had decisions to make before his firm's emissaries left by the afternoon train, and he always enjoyed this sort of situation for the pleasurable tension it never failed to arouse. In ten years' time, he reflected, technology will have reached the point when our firm will have its own business planes, and I shall be able to direct my team long distance during a summer vacation in the Himalayas. As he had reached his decisions overnight and had only to go over them and confirm them in the light of day, he was at the moment free. He had ordered his breakfast sent up and was relaxing with his first cigar of the day, mulling over last night's gathering at Diotima's, which he had been obliged to leave rather early.

This time, it had been a most entertaining party, with a large num-

ber of the guests under thirty, few over thirty-five, almost still
bohemians but already beginning to be famous and noticed in the
newspapers: not only native talents but visitors from all over the
world attracted by word that in Kakania a lady who moved in
the highest circles was blazing a trail for the spirit to penetrate the
world. It was, at times, like finding oneself in a literary café, and Arnheim had to smile at the thought of Diotima looking almost intimidated under her own roof; but it had been quite stimulating on the
whole and in any case an extraordinary experiment, he felt. His
friend Diotima, disappointed with the fruitless meetings of the very
eminent, had made a determined effort to give the Parallel Campaign an infusion of the latest trends in thought and had made good
use of Arnheim's contacts for the purpose. He merely shook his head
when he remembered the conversations he had been obliged to listen to, crazy enough, in his opinion, but one must give way to youth,
he told himself; to simply reject them puts one in an impossible position. So he felt as it were seriously amused by the whole thing, which
had been a bit much all at once.

They had said to hell with . . . what was it, now? Oh yes, experience. That personal sensory experience the earthy warmth and immediacy of which the Impressionists had apostrophized fifteen years
earlier, as though it were some miraculous flower. Flabby and mindless, was their verdict on Impressionism now. They wanted sensuality curbed and a spiritual synthesis.

Now, synthesis probably meant the opposite of skepticism, psychology, scientific study, and analysis, all the literary tendencies of
their fathers' generation.

So far as could be gathered, theirs was not so much a philosophical
stance as, rather, the craving of young bones and muscles to move
freely, to leap and dance, unhampered by criticism. When they felt
like it they would not hesitate to consign synthesis to the devil too,
along with analysis and all reflection. Then they maintained that the
mind needed the sap of immediate experience to make it grow. Usually it was members of some other group who took this position, of
course, but sometimes in the heat of argument it could turn out to be
the same people.

What fine slogans they came up with! They called for the intellectual temperament. And lightning thought, ready to leap at the

world's throat! Cosmic man's sharply honed brain! And what else had he heard?

A new human race, restyled on the basis of an American world plan for production by mechanized power.

Lyricism allied to the most intense dramatism of life.

Technicism—a spirit worthy of the machine age.

Blériot—one of them had cried out—was at that very moment soaring over the English Channel at thirty-five miles an hour! If we could write this "Thirty-five Mile" poem we would be able to chuck all the rest of our moth-eaten literature into the garbage!

What was needed was accelerationism, the ultimate speeding up of experience based on the biomechanics learned in sports training and the circus acrobat's precision of movement!

Photogenic rejuvenation, by means of film . . .

Someone pointed out that a man was a mysterious innerspace, who should be helped to find his place in the cosmos by means of the cone, the sphere, the cylinder, and the cube. Whereupon an opposing voice made itself heard, to the effect that the individualistic view of art underlying that statement was on its way out and that a future humanity must be given a new sense of habitation by means of communal housing and settlements. While an individualistic faction and a socialistic one were forming along these lines, a third one began by voicing the opinion that only religious artists were truly social-minded. At this point a group of New Architects was heard from, claiming leadership on the grounds that religion was at the heart of architecture, besides which it promoted love of one's country and stability, attachment to the soil. The religious faction, reinforced by the geometric one, averred that art was not a peripheral but a central concern, a fulfillment of cosmic laws; but as the discussion went on, the religionists lost the cubists to the architects, whom they joined in insisting that man's relation to the cosmos was, after all, best expressed through spatial forms that gave validity and character to the individual element. The statement was made that one had to project oneself deep into the human soul and give it a fixed three-dimensional form. Then an angry voice dramatically asked all and sundry what they really thought: What was more important, ten thousand starving human beings or a work of art? Since almost all of them were artists of one kind or another, they did in fact believe that art alone could heal the soul of man; they had merely been unable to agree on the nature of this healing process, or on what claims for it should be put to the Parallel Campaign. But now the original social group came to the fore again, led by fresh voices: the question whether a work of art was more important than the misery of ten thousand people raised the question whether ten thousand works of art could make up for the misery of a single human being. Some rather robust artists proposed that artists should take themselves less seriously, become less narcissistic. Let the artist go hungry and develop some social concern! they demanded. Life was the greatest and the only work of art, someone said. A voice boomed out that it was not art but hunger that brought people together! A mediating voice reminded everyone that the best antidote to the overestimation of the self in art was a thorough grounding in craftsmanship. After this offer of a compromise, someone made use of the pause, born of fatigue and mutual revulsion, to ask serenely whether anyone present really supposed that anything at all could be done before the contact between man and space had even been defined? This became the signal for technologists, accelerationists, and the rest to take the floor again, and the debate flowed on, this way and that, for a good while longer. Eventually an accord was struck, however, because everyone wanted to go home, but not without reaching some kind of conclusion, so they all fell in with a statement to the general effect that while the present time was full of expectation, impatient, wayward, and miserable, the messiah for whom it was hoping and waiting was not yet in sight.

Arnheim reflected for a moment.

He had been the center of a circle throughout all this; whenever those on the outer fringe who could not hear or make themselves heard slipped away, others immediately took their place; he had clearly become the center of this gathering too, even when this was not always apparent during the somewhat unmannerly debate. After all, he had for a long time been well up on the subjects discussed. He knew all about the cube and its applications; he had built garden housing for his employees; he knew machines, what made them work, their tempo; he spoke effectively on gaining insight into the self; he had money invested in the burgeoning film industry. Reconstructing the drift of the discussion, he realized besides that it had by no means gone as smoothly as his memory had represented it. Such discussions move in odd ways, as though the contending parties had been assembled blindfolded in a polyhedron, each armed with a stick and ordered to go straight ahead. A confused and wearisome spectacle devoid of logic. But isn't this an image of the way things generally go in life? Here, too, control is gained not by the restraints and dictates of logic, which at most function like a police force, but only by the untamed dynamic forces of the mind. Such were Arnheim's reflections as he remembered the attention that had been paid to him, and he decided that the new style in thinking could be likened to the process of free association, when the conscious mind relaxed its controls, all undeniably very stimulating.

He made an exception and lit a second cigar, though he did not normally give in to such sensual self-indulgence. And even as he was still holding up the match and needed to contract his facial muscles to suck in the first smoke, he could not help smiling as he thought of the little General, who had started a conversation with him at the party the night before. Since the Arnheims owned a cannon and armor-plate works and were prepared to turn out vast quantities of munitions, if it came to that, Arnheim was ready to listen when the slightly funny but likable General (who sounded quite different from a Prussian general, far more unbuttoned in his speech but also, one might say, more expressive of an ancient culture—though, one would have to say, a declining culture) turned to him confidentially and—with such a sigh, downright philosophic!—commented on the discussion going on around them, which at least in part, one had to admit, was radically pacifist in tone.

The General, as the only military officer present, obviously felt a little out of place and bemoaned the fickleness of public opinion, because some comments on the sanctity of human life had just met with general approbation.

"I don't understand these people," were the words with which he turned to Arnheim, seeking enlightenment from a man of internationally recognized intellect. "I simply don't see why these new men in all their ignorance keep talking about generals drenched in blood! I think I understand quite well the older men who usually come here, even though they're rather unmilitary in their outlook as well. When, for instance, that famous poet—what's his name?—that tall older gentleman with the paunch, who's supposed to have written those verses about the Greek gods, the stars, and our timeless emotions: our hostess told me he's a real poet in an age that turns out nothing but intellectuals . . . well, as I was saying, I haven't read any of his works, but I'm sure I'd understand him, if it's true that he's noted mainly for not wasting his time on petty stuff, because that's what we in the army call a strategist. A sergeant—if I may resort to such a humble example—must of course concern himself with the welfare of every single man in his company; the strategist, on the other hand, deals with at least a thousand men at a time and must be prepared to sacrifice ten such units at once if a higher purpose demands it. I see no logic in calling this sort of thing a blood-drenched general in one case and a sense of timeless values in the other! I wish you'd help me understand this if you can."

Arnheim's peculiar position in this city and its society had stung him into a certain, otherwise carefully watched, impulse to mockery. He knew whom the little military gentleman meant, though he did not let on; besides, it didn't matter, since he himself could have mentioned several other varieties of such eminences who had unmistakably made a poor showing this evening.

Glumly thinking it over, Arnheim held back the smoke of his cigar between parted lips. His own situation in this circle had also been none too easy. Despite all his prominence, he had overheard quite a number of nasty remarks that could have been aimed at him personally, and what they condemned was often nothing less than what he had loved in his youth, just as these young men now cherished the pet ideas of their own generation. It was a strange feeling, almost spooky, to find himself revered by young men who, almost in the same breath, savagely ridiculed a past in which he had a secret share of his own; it gave him a sense of his own elasticity, adaptability, and enterprising spirit—almost, one might say, the reckless daring of a well-hidden bad conscience. He swiftly pondered what it was that differentiated him from this younger generation. These young men were at odds with one another on every single point at issue; all they unambiguously had in common was their joint assault on objectivity, intellectual responsibility, and the balanced personality.

There was one thing in particular that enabled Arnheim to take a kind of spiteful joy in this situation. The overestimation of certain of his contemporaries, in whom the personal element was especially conspicuous, had always irked him. To name names, even in his thoughts, was a self-indulgence that so distinguished an opponent as himself would never permit, of course, but he knew exactly whom he meant. "A sober and modest young fellow, lusting for illustrious delights," to quote Heine, whom Arnheim secretly cherished, and whom he recruited for the occasion. "One is bound to extol his aims and his dedication to his craft as a poet . . . his bitter toil, the indescribable doggedness, the grim exertions with which he shapes his verses. . . . The muses do not smile upon him, but he holds the genius of the language in his hand . . . the terrifying discipline to which he must subject himself, he calls a great deed in words." Arnheim had an excellent memory and could recite pages by heart. He let his thoughts wander. He marveled at Heine, who, in attacking a man of his own time, had anticipated phenomena that had only now come fully into their own, and it inspired him to emulate this achievement as he now turned his thoughts to the second representative of the great German idealistic outlook, the General's poet. This was now, after the lean, the fat intellectual kine. This poet's portentous idealism corresponded to those big deep brass instruments in the orchestra that resemble upended locomotive boilers and produce an unwieldy grunting and rumbling. With a single note they muffle a thousand possibilities. They huff and puff out huge bales of timeless emotions. Anyone capable of trumpeting poetry on such a scale— Arnheim thought, not without bitterness—is nowadays rated by us as a poet, as compared with a mere literary man. Then why not rate him as a general as well? Such people after all live on the best of terms with death and constantly need several thousand dead to make them enjoy their brief moment of life with dignity.

But just then someone had made the point that even the General's dog, howling at the moon some rose-scented night, might if challenged defend himself by saying: "So what, it's the moon, isn't it? I am expressing the timeless emotions of my race!" quite like one of those gentlemen so famous for doing the very same. The dog might even add that his emotion was unquestionably a powerful experience, his expression richly moving, and yet so simple that his public could understand him perfectly, and as for his ideas playing second fiddle to his feelings, that was entirely in keeping with prevailing standards and had never yet been regarded as a drawback in literature.

Arnheim, discomfited by this echoing of his thoughts, again held back the cigar smoke between lips that for a moment remained half open, as a token barrier between himself and his surroundings. He had praised some of these especially pure poets on every occasion, because it was the thing to do, and had sometimes even supported them with cash, though in fact, as he now realized, he could not stand them and their inflated verses. "These heraldic figures who can't even support themselves," he thought, "really belong in a game preserve, together with the last of the bison and eagles." And since, as this evening had proved, it was not in keeping with the times to support them, Arnheim's reflections ended not without some profit for himself.

90

DETHRONING THE IDEOCRACY

It probably makes sense that times dominated by the spirit of the marketplace see as their true counterpart those poets who have nothing at all to do with their time, who do not besmirch themselves with the topical concerns of their day but supply only pure poetry, as it were, addressing their faithful in obsolete idioms on great subjects, as though they were just passing through on earth, coming from eternity, where they live, like the man who went to America three years ago and is already speaking broken German on his first visit home. This is much the same as compensating for a big hole by setting a hollow dome on top of it, and since the higher hollowness only enlarges the ordinary one below, nothing is more natural, after all, than that such a period fostering the cult of personality should be followed by one that turns its back on all this fuss over responsibility and greatness.

Arnheim tried cautiously, experimentally, and with the cozy sense of being personally insured against damage, to feel his way into this conjectured future development. This was certainly no minor undertaking. He had to take into account everything he had seen in recent years in America and Europe: the new dance fanatics, whether they were jazzing up Beethoven or transposing the new sensualism into fresh rhythms; the new painters, who tried to express a maximum of meaning by a minimum of lines and colors; the art of the film, where a gesture universally understood, presented with a new little twist, took the world by storm; and finally he thought of the common man, who already, as a great believer in sports, was kicking like a furious baby in his efforts to take possession of Nature's bosom. What is so striking about all this is a certain tendency to allegory, if this is understood as an intellectual device to make everything mean more than it has any honest claim to mean. Just as the world of the Baroque saw in a helmet and a pair of crossed swords all the Greek gods and their myths, and it was not Count Harry who kissed Lady Harriet but a god of war kissing the goddess of chastity, so today, when Harry and Harriet are smooching, they are experiencing the temper of our times, or something out of our array of ten dozen contemporary myths, which of course no longer depict an Olympus floating above formal gardens but present the entire modern hodgepodge itself. On screen and on stage, on the dance floor and at concerts, in cars, on planes, on the water and in the sun, at the tailor's and in the business office, there is constantly in the making an immense new surface consisting of im- and expressions, of gestures, role-playing, and experiences. All these goings-on, each with its distinct outward forms, in the aggregate suggest a body in lively circular motion, with everything inside it thrusting out toward the surface, where it enters into combination with all the rest, while the interior goes on seething and heaving with amorphous life. Had Arnheim been able to see only a few years into the future, he would have seen that 1,920 years of Christian morality, millions of dead men in the wake of a shattering war, and a whole German forest of poetry rustling in homage to the modesty of Woman could not hold back the day when women's skirts and hair began to grow shorter and the young girls of Europe slipped off eons of taboos to emerge for a while naked, like peeled bananas. He would have seen other changes as well, which he would hardly have believed possible, nor does it matter which of those would last and which would disappear, if we consider what vast and probably wasted efforts would have been needed to effect such revolutions in the way people lived by the slow, responsible, evolutionary road traveled by philosophers, painters, and poets, instead of tailors, fashion, and chance; it enables us to judge just how much creative energy is generated by the surface of things, compared with the barren conceit of the brain.

Such is the dethronement of ideocracy, of the brain, the displacement of the mind to the periphery: the ultimate problem, Arnheim thought. This has always been life's way with man, of course, restructuring humankind from the surface inward; the only difference is that people used to feel that they in turn should contribute something from their inside to their outside. Even the General's dog, which Arnheim now kindly remembered, would never have understood any other line of development, for this loyal friend of man's character had still been formed by the stable, docile man of the previous century, in that man's image; but its cousin the prairie wolf, or the prairie rooster, would have understood readily enough. When that wild fowl, dancing for hours on end, plumes itself and claws the ground, there is probably more soul generated than by a scholar linking one thought to another at his desk. For in the last analysis, all thoughts come out of the joints, muscles, glands, eyes, and ears, and from the shadowy general impressions that the bag of skin to which they belong has of itself as a whole. Bygone centuries were probably sadly mistaken in attaching too much importance to reason and intelligence, convictions, concepts, and character; like regarding the record office and the archives as the most important part of a government department because they are housed at headquarters, although they are only subordinate functions taking orders from elsewhere.

All at once, Arnheim—stimulated perhaps by a certain dissolving of tensions under the influence of love—found his way to the redeeming idea that would put all these complications in perspective; it was somehow pleasantly associated with the concept of increased turnover. An increased turnover of ideas and experiences was undeniably characteristic of the new era, if only as the natural consequence of bypassing the time-consuming process of intellectual assimilation. He pictured the brain of the age replaced by the mechanism of supply and demand, the painstaking thinker replaced, as the regulating factor, by the businessman, and he could not help enjoying the moving vision of a vast production of experiences freely mingling and parting, a sort of pudding with a nervous life of its own, quivering all over with sensations; or a huge tom-tom booming with immense resonance at even the lightest tap. The fact that these images did not quite jell, as it were, was already owing to the state of reverie they had induced in Arnheim, who felt that it was just such a life that could be compared with a dream in which one finds oneself simultaneously outside, witnessing the strangest events, and quietly inside, at the very center of things, one's ego rarefied, a vacuum through which all the feelings glow like blue neon tubes. It is life that does the thinking all around us, forming with playful ease the connections our reason can only laboriously patch together piecemeal, and never to such kaleidoscopic effect. So it was that Arnheim mused as a man of business, while at the same time electrified to the twenty tips of his fingers and toes by his sense of the free-flowing psychophysical traffic of the dawning age. It seemed to him far from impossible that a great, superrational collectivity was coming to birth and that, abandoning an outworn individualism, we were on our way back, with all the superiority and ingenuity of the white race, to a Paradise Reformed, bringing a modern program, a rich variety of choices, to the rural backwardness of the Garden of Eden.

There was only one fly in the ointment. Just as in dreams we are able to inject an inexplicable feeling that cuts through the whole personality into some happening or other, we are able to do this while awake—but only at the age of fifteen or sixteen, while still in school. Even at that age, as we all know, we live through great storms of feeling, fierce urgencies, and all kinds of vague experiences; our feelings are powerfully alive but not yet well defined; love and anger, joy and scorn, all the general moral sentiments, in short, go jolting through us like electric impulses, now engulfing the whole world, then again shriveling into nothing; sadness, tenderness, nobility, and generosity of spirit form the vaulting empty skies above us. And then what happens? From outside us, out of the ordered world around us, there appears a ready-made form—a word, a verse, a demonic laugh, a Napoleon, Caesar, Christ, or perhaps only a tear shed at a father's grave—and the "work" springs into being like a bolt of lightning. This sophomore's "work" is, as we too easily overlook, line for line the complete expression of what he is feeling, the most precise match of intention and execution, and the perfect blending of a young man's experience with the life of the great Napoleon. It seems, however, that the movement from the great to the small is somehow not reversible. We experience it in dreams as well as in our youth: we have just given a great speech, with the last words still ringing in our ears as we awaken, when, unfortunately, they do not sound quite as marvelous as we thought they were. At this point we do not see ourself as quite the weightlessly shimmering phenomenon of that dancing prairie cock, but realize instead that we have merely been howling with much emotion at the moon, like the General's much-cited fox terrier.

So there was something not quite in order here, Arnheim thought, arousing himself from his trance—but in any case, a man must move with the times, he added, now fully alert; for what, after all, should come more naturally to him than to apply this tried-and-true principle of production to the fabrication of life as well?

91

SPECULATIONS ON THE INTELLECTUAL
BULL AND BEAR MARKET

The gatherings at the Tuzzis now resumed their regular and crowded course.

At a meeting of the Council, Section Chief Tuzzi turned to the "cousin," saying: "Do you realize that all this has been done before?"

With a glance, he indicated the seething human contents of the home of which he was currently dispossessed.

"In the early days of Christianity, the centuries around the birth of Christ. In that Christian-Levantine-Hellenistic-Judaic melting pot

where innumerable sects crystallized." He launched on a list: "Ada-
mites, Cainites, Ebionites, Collyridians, Archontians, Euchites, Oph-
ites . . ." With a funny, hasty deliberateness of tempo that comes of
slowing the pace in order to conceal one's fluency on a subject, he
recited a long series of pre- and early-Christian sect names, as if he
were trying to give his wife's cousin to understand that he knew more
about what was going on in his house than, for reasons of his own, he
usually cared to show.

He then went on to specify that one of the sects named opposed
marriage because of the high value it placed on chastity, while another, also prizing chastity above all, had a funny way of attaining this
aim by means of ritual debauchery. One sect practiced self-mutilation because they regarded female flesh as an invention of the Devil,
while another made its men and women attend services stark naked.
There were those who, brooding on their creed and coming to the
conclusion that the Serpent who had seduced Eve was a divine person, went in for sodomy, while others tolerated no virgins among
their flock because their studies proved that the Mother of God had
borne other children besides Jesus, so that virginity was a dangerous
heresy. Some were always doing the opposite of what others were
doing, for more or less the same reasons and on the same principles.

Tuzzi delivered himself of all this with the gravity appropriate to a
historical disquisition, however peculiar the facts, yet with an undertone of what were then called smoking-room stories. They were
standing close to the wall; the Section Chief threw his cigarette stub
into an ashtray with a grim little smile, still absentmindedly eyeing
the throng of guests, as though he had meant to say only enough to
last the time it takes to finish a cigarette, and ended with: "It seems
to me that the differences of opinion and points of view in those days
show a state of affairs not too dissimilar to the controversies among
our intellectuals today. They'll be gone with the wind tomorrow. If
various historical circumstances had not given rise at the right moment to an ecclesiastical bureaucracy with the necessary political
powers, hardly a trace of the Christian faith would be left today. . . ."

Ulrich agreed. "Properly paid officials in charge of the faith can be
trusted to uphold the regulations with the necessary firmness. In
general I feel that we never do justice to the value of our vulgar
qualities; if they were not so dependable, no history would be made

at all, because our purely intellectual efforts are incurably controversial and shift with every breeze."

The Section Chief glanced up at him mistrustfully and then immediately shifted his gaze away again. That sort of comment was too unbuttoned for his taste. He nevertheless acted in a noticeably friendly and congenial fashion, even on such short acquaintance, toward this cousin of his wife's. He came and went and had the air, amid all that was going on in his house, of living in some other, closed world, the loftier significance of which he kept hidden from all eyes; yet there were always times when he could hold out no longer and had to reveal himself to somebody, if only indistinctly, for an instant, and then it was always this cousin with whom he struck up a conversation. It was the natural human consequence of feeling neglected by his wife, despite her occasional fits of tenderness for him. At such times Diotima kissed him like a little girl, a girl of perhaps fourteen, who out of heaven knows what affectation suddenly smothers an even littler boy with kisses. Tuzzi's upper lip, under its curled mustache, would then instinctively draw back in embarrassment. The new conditions in his household got him and his wife into impossible situations. He had certainly not forgotten Diotima's complaint about his snoring, and had also, meanwhile, read the works of Arnheim and was prepared to discuss them with her; they contained some things he could accept, a great deal that struck him as all wrong, and a certain amount he did not understand, though serene in the assumption that this was the author's problem rather than his own. But he had always been accustomed in such matters simply to state the authoritative opinion of a man experienced in these things, and the present likelihood of Diotima's contradicting him every time, of having to debate with her points he considered to be beneath him, struck him as so unfair a change in his private life that he could not bring himself to have it out with her; he even caught himself in vague fantasies of having it out in a duel with Arnheim instead.

Tuzzi suddenly narrowed his beautiful brown eyes in irritation and told himself that he must keep a sharper watch on his moods. The cousin beside him—not at all the sort of man Tuzzi would normally want to become too closely involved with—only reminded him of his wife through an association of ideas that hardly had any real content, the mere fact of their being blood relatives. He had also noticed for some time that Arnheim seemed, rather cautiously, to be favoring this young man, who for his own part did not conceal his marked antipathy to Arnheim: two observations that did not really amount to much, yet were enough to make Tuzzi aware of his own inexplicable liking for Ulrich. He opened his eyes again and stared briefly like an owl across the room, without really looking at anything.

His wife's cousin, incidentally, was staring straight ahead just as Tuzzi was, bored but at ease with him, and had not even noticed the pause in their exchange. Tuzzi felt obliged to say something, like a man who fears that his silence might give away his inwardly troubled condition.

"You like to take a cynical view," he said with a smile, as if Ulrich's remark about the bureaucratic administration of religious faith had only just been allowed to come to his attention, "and I daresay my wife is not unjustified in fearing to count on your support, despite her sympathies for you as a cousin. If I may say so, your views on your fellowmen tend to be on the bearish side."

"What an excellent term for it!" Ulrich said, clearly pleased. "Even though I'm afraid I don't quite live up to it. It's really history that has always taken a bearish or a bullish line with all mankind—bearish when it is using trickery or violence, and bullish more or less in your wife's manner, by trying to have faith in the power of ideas. Dr. Arnheim, too, if you can believe what he says, is a bull. While you, as a professional bear amid this choir of angels, must have feelings I would be interested to hear about."

He regarded the Section Chief with a sympathetic expression. Tuzzi drew his cigarette case from his pocket and shrugged his shoulders. "What makes you think that my outlook must be different from that of my wife?" he countered. He had meant to discourage the personal turn the conversation had taken, but his retort had only reinforced it. Luckily, Ulrich had not noticed this, and went on: "We're made of stuff that takes on the shape of every mold it gets into, one way or another."

"That's over my head," Tuzzi replied evasively.

Ulrich was glad to hear it. Tuzzi's way was the opposite of his own, and he took real pleasure in talking with a man who refused to be goaded into an intellectual discussion and had no other defense, or would use no other, than to interpose his whole person as a shield.

His original dislike of Tuzzi had long since reversed itself under the pressure of his far greater dislike of the doings under Tuzzi's roof; he simply couldn't understand why Tuzzi put up with it, and could only try to guess. He was getting to know him only very slowly, as one keeps an animal under observation, outwardly, without the ease of insight their words give us into people, who talk because they are clearly impelled to. What appealed to him at first was the dessicated look of the man, who was of just middle height, and the dark, intense eye, betraying much uneasy feeling, not at all the eye of a bureaucrat, nor did it seem to fit in with Tuzzi's present personality as revealed in conversation; unless one assumed something not altogether unusual, that it was a boy's eye peering out from among the man's features, like a window opening out of an unused, locked-up, and long-forgotten part of the interior. The next thing Ulrich had noticed was Tuzzi's body odor, something of china or dry wooden boxes or a mix of sun, sea, exotic landscapes, an obdurate hardness and a discreet whiff of the barbershop. This odor gave Ulrich pause; he had come across only two people with a distinct personal odor; the other one was Moosbrugger. When he called to mind Tuzzi's sharp yet subtle smell and also thought of Diotima, whose ample surface emanated a fine powdery scent that did not seem to mask anything, it came to contrasting kinds of passion that seemed to have nothing to do with the actual life this rather incongruous couple shared. Ulrich now had to make an effort to call his thoughts to order before he could respond to Tuzzi's cool disclaimer.

"It's presumptuous of me," he resumed, in that faintly bored but resolute tone in which one apologizes for having to be a bore in one's turn, because the situation leaves one no alternative, "it certainly is presumptuous of me to offer you my definition of diplomacy, but I do it in the hope that you will straighten me out. Let me put it this way: diplomacy assumes that a dependable social order can be achieved only by mendacity, cowardice, cannibalism, in short, the predictable baseness of human nature. It is based on a bearish idealism, to resort once more to your admirable expression. This is sad in a fascinating way, because it goes with the assumption that our higher faculties are so ambiguous in nature that they can lead us equally well to cannibalism as to the *Critique of Pure Reason.*"

"It really is too bad," the Section Chief protested, "that you have so romantic a view of diplomacy and, like so many others, you confuse politics with intrigue. There may have been something in what you say when diplomacy was still being conducted by highborn dilettantes, but it no longer applies in an age of responsible social leadership. We are not sad, we are optimistic. We must have faith in the future, or we could not live with our conscience, which is no different from everyone else's. If you must talk of cannibalism, then all I can say is that diplomacy can take credit for keeping the world from turning cannibalistic; but to do so, one has to believe in something higher."

"What do you believe in?" Ulrich demanded bluntly.

"Oh, come now," Tuzzi said. "I'm no longer a boy, who might answer such a question point-blank. All I meant was that the more a diplomat can identify himself with the spiritual currents of his time, the easier he will find his profession. And vice versa: we have learned in the course of a few generations that the more progress we make in every direction, the greater our need for diplomacy—but that's only natural, after all."

"Natural? But then you're saying just what I've said!" Ulrich exclaimed, with all the animation consistent with the image they wished to present, of two civilized men engaged in casual conversation. "I pointed out with regret that our spiritual and moral values cannot sustain themselves in the long run without support from what is material and evil, and you reply, more or less, that the more spiritual energy is at work, the more caution is needed. Let us say, then, that we can treat a man as a worm and by this means get him to do not quite everything, and we can appeal to what is best in him and by this means get him to do not quite everything. So we waver between these two approaches, we mix them, that's all there is to it. It seems to me that I may flatter myself on being in far greater accord with you than you're willing to admit."

Section Chief Tuzzi turned to his inquisitor; a tiny smile lifted his little mustache, and his gleaming eyes took on an ironically indulgent expression as he tried to find a way to end this conversation, which was as unsafe as an icy pavement underfoot, and as pointlessly childish as boys skidding on such a pavement. "You know," he answered, "I hope you don't regard this as too crude of me, but I must say that philosophizing should be left to the professors. Always excepting our official great philosophers, whom I hold in greatest esteem and all of whom I've read; they're what we've got to live with. And our professors, well, it's their job, there doesn't have to be any more to it than that; we have to have teachers, to keep things going. But other than that, the fine old Austrian principle that a good citizen shouldn't rack his brains over everything still holds water. It hardly ever does any good, and it is a touch presumptuous too."

The Section Chief rolled himself a cigarette and held his peace; he felt no further need to apologize for his "crudeness." Ulrich, watching his slender brown fingers at their work, was delighted with Tuzzi's half-witted effrontery.

"You have just stated the same, very modern principle that the churches have applied to their members for nearly two thousand years, and which the socialists have begun to follow too," he said politely.

Tuzzi shot him a glance to see what the cousin meant by this analogy; expecting Ulrich to expatiate on it further, he was already annoyed in anticipation of such interminable intellectual indiscretion. But the cousin contented himself with indulgently scrutinizing the man at his side with his pre-1848 mentality. Ulrich had long assumed that Tuzzi must have his reasons for tolerating his wife's relationship with Arnheim within certain limits, and would have liked to know what he hoped to gain by it. It still mystified him. Was Tuzzi acting on the same principle as the banks with respect to the Parallel Campaign (they were keeping as aloof from it as they could without quite giving up their chance to have a finger in the pie) and meanwhile being blind to Diotima's new springtide of love, which was becoming so obvious? Ulrich was inclined to doubt it. He took a certain pleasure in scrutinizing the deep furrows and seams in the man's face and watching the hard modeling of the jaw muscles when those teeth bit into the cigarette holder. Here was an image of pure masculinity. Ulrich was a bit fed up with talking to himself so much, and enjoyed trying to imagine what it must be like to be a man of few words. He supposed that even as a boy Tuzzi had disliked other boys who talked too much, the kind who grow up to be intellectuals, while the boys who would rather spit through their teeth than open their mouths turn into men who prefer not to waste their time, but seek to compensate in action or intrigue, in simple endurance and self-defense, for not indulging any more than they can help in those inescapable acts of feeling and thinking which they somehow find so profoundly embarrassing that they wish they could use thoughts and feelings only to mislead other people. Had anyone said such a thing to Tuzzi, he would naturally have denied it, just as he would deny anything too emotional, because he would not, on principle, tolerate exaggerations and eccentricities in any direction. It was simply out of order to speak to him about what he so admirably represented in person, just as it was to ask a musician, an actor, or a dancer what he was really getting at, and Ulrich was tempted at this point to pat the Section Chief on his shoulder or gently run a hand through his hair, some wordless pantomime or other for the sympathetic understanding between them.

The one thing that Ulrich did not take fully into account was that Tuzzi, not only as a boy but now, that very moment, felt the urge to spit between his teeth in a blast of masculinity. For he sensed something of that vague benevolence at his side, and he felt ill at ease with it. He realized that his remark about philosophy contained an admixture of elements it was not advisable to risk on an outsider, and he didn't know what had possessed him to let himself go so rashly with this cousin (for some reason this was what he always called Ulrich). He couldn't stand voluble men, and wondered with dismay whether he might unconsciously be trying to win this man over as an ally where his wife was concerned; the thought darkened his skin with shame, because such help was unacceptable, and he involuntarily took several steps away from Ulrich, masking his impulse with some awkward excuse.

But then he changed his mind, moved back, and asked: "Incidentally, have you wondered at all why Dr. Arnheim is staying with us so long?" He suddenly imagined that such a question would be the best proof that he regarded any connection between Arnheim's stay and his wife as out of the question.

The cousin gave him an outrageously dumbfounded stare. The answer was so obvious that it was hard to think what else to say. "Do you think," he said haltingly, "that there must be a special reason for it? If so, it would be business, surely?"

"I have nothing to go on," Tuzzi answered, feeling every inch the diplomat again. "But could there be another reason?"

"Of course there can't actually be any other reason," Ulrich conceded civilly. "How very observant of you. For my part I must admit that I never gave it any thought at all; I assumed that it had more or less to do with his literary bent. Wouldn't that be another possibility?"

The Section Chief favored this with no more than an absent smile. "In that case you would have to give me some notion why a man like Arnheim has literary interests in the first place," he said, to his instant regret, because he could see the cousin winding up for one of his lengthy answers.

"Have you never noticed," Ulrich began, "that an incredible lot of people can be seen these days talking to themselves on the street?"

Tuzzi gave a shrug.

"There's something the matter with people. It seems they're unable to take in their experiences or else to wholly enter into them, so they have to pass along what's left. An excessive need to write, it seems to me, comes from the same thing. You may not be able to spot this in the written product, which tends to turn into something far removed from its origin, depending on talent and experience, but it shows up quite unambiguously in the reading of it; hardly anyone reads anymore today; everyone just uses the writer to work off his own excess on him, in some perverse fashion, whether by agreeing or disagreeing."

"So you think there's something the matter with Arnheim's life?" Tuzzi asked, all attention again. "I've been reading his books lately, out of curiosity, because so many people seem to think he has great political prospects, but I must say I can't see what need they fill, or any purpose to them."

"Putting this question in more general terms," the cousin said, "when a man is so rich in money and influence that he can have anything he wants, why does he write at all? It boils down to the naïve question Why do professional storytellers write? They write about something that never happened as if it had actually happened, obviously. Does this mean that they admire life as a beggar admires the rich, whose indifference to him he never tires of describing? Or is it a form of chewing the cud? Or a way of stealing a little happiness by creating in imagination what cannot be attained or endured in reality?"

"Have you never written anything yourself?" Tuzzi broke in.

"Much as it troubles me, never. Since I am far from being so happy that I have no need of it, I am resolved that if I do not soon feel the urge to write, I shall kill myself for being constitutionally so totally abnormal."

He said this with such grave amiability that his little joke unintentionally rose up from the flow of the conversation like a flooded stone surfacing as the water recedes.

Tuzzi noticed, and tactfully covered it over. "All in all, then," he concluded, "you are only confirming my point that government officials begin to write only when they retire. But how does that apply to Arnheim?"

The cousin remained silent.

"Do you know that Arnheim's view of this undertaking to which he is sacrificing so much of his expensive time is totally pessimistic and not at all bullish?" Tuzzi suddenly said, lowering his voice. He had just remembered how Arnheim, in conversation with himself and his wife, had at the very outset expressed grave doubts about the prospects of the Parallel Campaign, and the fact that he happened to recall this at this particular moment, after so long a time, struck him somehow as a diplomatic coup on his own part, even though he had been able to find out virtually nothing, so far, about the reasons for Arnheim's prolonged stay.

The cousin's face actually registered astonishment.

Perhaps he was only accommodating Tuzzi with this look, because he preferred to go on saying nothing. In any case, both gentlemen, who were separated the next moment by guests coming up to them, were in this fashion left with the sense of having had a stimulating talk.

92

SOME OF THE RULES GOVERNING
THE LIVES OF THE RICH

Having so much attention and admiration lavished on him might have made any man other than Arnheim suspicious and unsure of himself, on the assumption that he owed it all to his money. But Arnheim regarded suspicion as the mark of an ignoble character, permissible to a man in his position only on the basis of unequivocal financial reports, and anyway he was convinced that being rich was a personal quality. Every rich man regards being rich as a personal quality. So does every poor man. There is a universal tacit understanding on the point. This general accord is troubled only slightly by the claims of logic that having money, while capable of conferring certain traits of character on whoever has it, is not in itself a human quality. Such an academic quibble need not detain us. Every human nose instantly smells the subtle scent of independence, the habit of command, the habit of always choosing the best of everything for oneself, the whiff of misanthropy, and the unwavering sense of responsibility that goes with power, that rises up, in short, from a large and secure income. Everyone can see at a glance that such a person is nourished and daily renewed by quintessential cosmic forces. Money circulates visibly just under his skin like the sap in a blossom. Here there is no such thing as conferred traits, acquired habits; nothing indirect or secondhand! Destroy his bank account and his credit, and the rich man has not merely lost his money but has become, on the very day he realizes what has happened, a withered flower. With the same immediacy with which his riches were once seen as one of his personal qualities, the indescribable quality of his nothingness is now perceived, smelling like a smoldering cloud of uncertainty, irresponsibility, incapacity, and poverty. Riches are simply a personal, primary quality that cannot be analyzed without being destroyed.

But the effect and the functions of this rare property are most complicated, and it takes great spiritual strength to control them.

Only people with no money imagine riches as a dream fulfilled; those who have it never tire of explaining to those who do not have it how much trouble it gives them. Arnheim, for instance, had often pondered the fact that every technical or administrative executive in his firm had a great deal more specialized knowledge than he did, and he had to reassure himself every time that, seen from a sufficiently lofty perspective, such things as ideas, knowledge, loyalty, talent, prudence, and the like can be bought because they are available in abundance, while the ability to make use of them presupposes qualities given only to the few who happen to have been born and bred on the heights.

Another equally burdensome problem of the rich is that everyone wants money from them. Money doesn't matter, of course, and a few thousands or tens of thousands more or less make hardly any difference to a rich man, and so rich people like to emphasize at every opportunity that money does not affect a human being's value one way or the other, meaning that they would be equally valuable even without their money, and their feelings are apt to be hurt when they feel misunderstood on this point. It is really too bad that such misunderstandings keep arising, particularly in their dealings with gifted people. Such people remarkably often have no money, just projects and talent, which does not lessen their sense of their own value, and nothing seems more natural to them than to ask a rich friend who doesn't care about money to put his surplus at the service of some good cause or other. They don't seem to understand that their rich friend would like to support them with his ideas, his abilities, his charisma. Besides, their expectations place him in a false position with respect to money, the nature of which demands increase, just as animal nature is set on procreation. Money can be put into bad investments, where it perishes on the monetary field of honor; it will buy a new car, even though the old one is still as good as new, or enable its owner to stay at the most expensive hotels in world-famous resorts, accompanied by his polo ponies, or to establish prizes for horse races or art, or to give a party for a hundred guests that costs enough in one evening to feed a hundred families for a year: with all this, one throws one's money out the window like a farmer casting out seed, so that it will come back with interest through the door. But to give it away quietly for purposes and people who are of no use to it is simply to commit murder most foul upon one's money. The purposes may be good, and the people incomparable, in which case they should be given every kind of help—except with money. This was a principle with Arnheim, and his consistent application of it had gained him a reputation for taking a creative and active part in the intellectual advancement of his time.

Arnheim could also claim that he thought like a socialist, and many rich people do think like socialists. They don't mind their capital being decreed to them by a natural law of society, and are firmly convinced that it is the man who confers value on property, not vice versa. They can calmly discuss a future when they will no longer be around, which will see the end of property, and are further confirmed in regarding themselves as social-minded by the frequency with which upright socialists prefer to await the inevitable revolution in the company of the rich rather than that of the poor. One could go on like this for a long time, describing all the functions of money Arnheim had mastered. Economic activity cannot really be separated from the other intellectual activities, and it was surely natural for him to give money as well as good advice to his intellectual and artistic friends when their need was urgent, but he did not always give it, and he never gave them much. They assured him that he was the only man in the whole world they could ask for money, because he alone had the necessary intellectual grasp of the matter, and he believed them, because he was convinced that the need for capital permeates all human functions much like the need for air to breathe, but he also met them halfway in their vision of money as a spiritual force by applying it only with the most tactful restraint.

Why is it, anyway, that a man is admired and loved? Isn't it an almost unfathomable mystery, rounded and fragile as an egg? Is a man more truly loved for his mustache than for his car? Is the love aroused by a sun-bronzed son of the South more personal than that aroused by a son of a leading industrial magnate? In a period when almost all well-dressed men were clean-shaven, Arnheim went on sporting a Vandyke beard and a clipped mustache; this small, extraneous, yet familiar presence on his face reminded him somehow, rather agreeably, whenever he was letting himself go a bit in talking to his always eager listeners, of his money.

93

EVEN THROUGH PHYSICAL CULTURE IT IS HARD TO GET A HOLD ON THE CIVILIAN MIND

For a long time the General had been sitting on one of the chairs that lined the walls around the intellectual arena, his "sponsor," as he liked to call Ulrich, occupying the next chair but one, while the free chair between them held refreshments in the form of two wine-glasses they had carried away from the buffet. The General's light-blue tunic had been creeping upward, until it now formed furrows over his paunch, like a worried forehead. They were absorbed in listening to a conversation going on just in front of them.

"Beaupré's game," somebody was saying, "is positively touched with genius; I watched him here this summer, and the previous winter on the Riviera. Even when he slips up, luck stays on his side and makes up for it. And he slips up fairly often, because the actual structure of his game negates a really sound tennis style—but then, he's a truly inspired player, which evidently exempts him from the normal laws of tennis."

"As for me, I prefer scientific tennis to the intuitive kind," someone objected. "Braddock, for instance. There may be no such thing as perfection, but Braddock comes close."

The first speaker: "Beaupré's genius, his dazzling unpredictability, is at its peak at the point where science fails."

A third voice: "Isn't calling it genius overdoing it a bit?"

"What would you call it? Genius is what inspires a man to return the ball just right at the most unlikely moment!"

"I'm bound to agree," the Braddockian said in support, "that a personality must make itself felt whether a man is holding a tennis racket or the fate of a nation in his hand."

"No, no, 'genius' is going too far," the third man protested.

The fourth man was a musician. He said: "You're quite wrong. You're overlooking the physical thinking involved in sport, because you're evidently still in the habit of overvaluing the logical, systematic kind of thinking. That's practically as out of date as the prejudice that music enriches the emotional life, and sport is a discipline of the will. But physical movement in itself is so magical that we can't stand it without some kind of buffer. You can see that in films when there's no music. Music is inward motion, it supports the kinetic imagination. Once you have grasped the sorcery in music, you can see the genius in sports without a second's hesitation. It's only science that's devoid of genius; it's mere mental acrobatics."

"So then I'm right," Beaupré's fan said, "when I say that Braddock's scientific game shows no genius."

"You're not taking into account that we would need to start by revitalizing the term 'science,' " the Braddock fan said defensively.

"Incidentally, which of them outranks the other one?" someone wondered.

No one knew the answer. Each of them had frequently beaten the other, but no one knew the exact figures.

"Let's ask Arnheim!" someone suggested.

The group dispersed. The silence in the area of the three chairs lingered on. At last General Stumm said pensively: "Well, I was listening to all that the whole time, you know, and it seems to me you could say the same thing about a victorious general, leaving out the music, perhaps. So why do they call it genius when it's a tennis player and barbarism when it's a general?"

Ever since his sponsor had suggested that he try getting through to Diotima by advocating physical culture as his particular cause, he had given considerable thought to the question of how he could best use this promising approach to the civilian mind, despite his personal aversion to the actual practice of it; but the difficulties, as he was forced to observe again and again, were inordinately large.

94

Diotima's nights

Diotima wondered how Arnheim could stand all these people, visibly enjoying himself, when her own feelings corresponded all too closely to what she had expressed a number of times in saying that the world's business was no more than *un peu de bruit autour de notre âme*.

There were times when she looked around and saw her house filled with the cream of society and culture—and felt bewildered. It reduced the story of her life to nothing but that extreme contrast between the depths and the heights, between the young girl's anxiety inside a tight middle-class world and now this blinding life at the summit. Already poised on a dizzily high narrow ledge, she felt the call to lift up her foot once more, toward an even greater height. The risk was seductive. She wrestled with the resolve to enter into a life where action, mind, soul, and dream are one. Basically she no longer fretted over the failure of a crowning idea for the Parallel Campaign to emerge; nor did her vision of a World Austria still matter quite so much; even her discovery that for every great projection of the human mind there was an equally valid opposite had lost its terrors for her. The really important movements of life have less to do with logic than with lightning and fire, and she had grown used to not trying to make sense of all the greatness by which she felt surrounded. She would gladly have dropped her campaign altogether and married Arnheim, as a little girl solves her problems by forgetting all about them and leaping into her father's arms. But the incredible ramification of her project had her trapped. She could take no time to think. The outer chain of events and the inward one ran on independently side by side, even as she tried in vain to link them up. Just like her marriage, outwardly appearing happier than ever, when in fact everything was inwardly dissolving.

Had Diotima been able to act in character, she would have spoken frankly with her husband; but there was nothing she could tell him. Was it love she felt for Arnheim? What they were to each other could be given so many names that even this trivial one occasionally surfaced among her thoughts. They had never even kissed, and an utmost intermingling of souls was something Tuzzi would not understand even if such a thing were confessed to him. Diotima herself sometimes wondered at the fact that nothing more reportable was going on between herself and Arnheim. But she had never dropped her good-girl's tendency to look up, ambitiously, to older men, and she could more easily have imagined something at least describable if not actually tangible going on between herself and her cousin, who seemed younger than herself and upon whom she looked down just a little, rather than with the man she loved and who seemed so to appreciate her ability to dissipate her feelings into general reflections on the loftiest plane. Diotima knew that one had to let oneself tumble headlong into radical changes in one's circumstances and wake up amid one's new four walls without quite knowing how one got there, but she felt exposed to influences that kept her wide awake. She was not entirely free from the distaste the typical Austrian of her period felt toward his German kin. In its classical form, which has become a rarity in our day, this distaste corresponded more or less to an image of the venerated heads of Goethe and Schiller planted guilelessly on bodies that had been fed on sticky puddings and gravies, and shared something of their nonhuman inwardness. And great as Arnheim's success was in her circle, it did not escape her that after the first surprise certain resistances made themselves felt, never taking on form or coming out into the open, yet by their whispering presence undermining her self-assurance and making her aware of the differences between her own bias and the reservations felt by many persons upon whom she had been accustomed to model her own conduct. Now, ethnic prejudice is usually nothing more than self-hatred, dredged up from the murky depths of one's own conflicts and projected onto some convenient victim, a traditional practice from time immemorial when the shaman used a stick, said to be the repository of the demon's power, to draw the sickness out of the afflicted. That her beloved was a Prussian troubled Diotima's heart with further terrors, of which she could form no clear image, so she was surely not quite unjustified in perceiving her wavering condition, so sharply different from the brute simplicity of her married state, as a passion.

Diotima suffered sleepless nights, during which she was torn between a Prussian industrial autocrat and an Austrian bureaucrat. In the state between trance and dream, Arnheim's great, luminous life passed in parade before her. She saw herself airborne at this adored man's side through a heaven of new honors, but it was a heaven of a distasteful Prussian blue. Meantime, in the black Austrian night, the yellow body of Section Chief Tuzzi still lay beside her own. She was only dimly aware of this, as of a black-and-yellow symbol of the old Kakanian culture, though he had little enough of that. It was backed by the Baroque façade of her noble friend Count Leinsdorf's great town residence, and the shades of Beethoven, Mozart, and Haydn, and of Prince Eugene of Savoy, Austria's liberator from the Turks, hovered over it, like homesickness anticipating actual exile. Diotima could not make up her mind to take such a step outside her own world, just like that, even though she almost hated her husband for being the obvious obstacle. Inside her beautiful big body, her soul felt helplessly trapped as in a vast landscape in full flower.

"I mustn't be unfair," Diotima thought. "The government official, the man given over to his work, may no longer be awake and open and receptive, but in his youth he might have been capable of it." She remembered certain moments when they were still engaged to be married, though even then Section Chief Tuzzi had been no longer exactly a youth. "He achieved his position and his personality by hard work and devotion to duty," she thought tolerantly, "and he has no suspicion that it has cost him his own personal life."

Ever since she had achieved her social triumph she thought more indulgently of her husband, and so she now made him yet another inward concession. "No one is a born rationalist and utilitarian," she reflected. "We all start out as a living soul. But ordinary, everyday existence silts us up, the usual human passions go through us like a firestorm, and the cold world brings out that coldness in us that freezes the soul." Perhaps she had been too reticent to force him into facing up to this. How sad it was. It seemed to her that she could never summon up the courage to involve Section Chief Tuzzi in the scandal of a divorce, such a shattering blow to anyone as wrapped up as he was in his public role.

"Even adultery is preferable!" she suddenly told herself.

Adultery was what Diotima had been considering for some time.

To do one's duty in one's appointed place is a sterile notion; quantities of energy are poured out to no purpose! The right course is to choose one's place and shape one's circumstances deliberately. If she was going to condemn herself to staying with her husband, there still remained a choice between a useless and a fruitful martyrdom, and it was her choice to make. So far Diotima had been hampered by the moral sleaziness and the unattractive air of irresponsibility that were inseparable from all the stories of adultery that had ever come her way. She simply couldn't imagine herself in such a situation. To touch the doorknob of a certain kind of hotel room seemed tantamount to diving into a cesspool. To slip, with rustling skirts, up some strange staircase—a certain moral complacency of her body resisted the thought. Hasty kisses went against her grain, as did clandestine words of love. Catastrophe was more in her line. Those last walks together, choked good-byes, torn between a mother's duty and love, were much more her style. But owing to her husband's thrifty disposition she had no children, and catastrophe was precisely the thing to be avoided. So she opted, if it should come to that, for a Renaissance model. A love that had to live with a dagger through the heart. While she could form no very clear image of this, there was something decidedly upright about it, with a background of classic ruins under fleeting clouds. Guilt and its transcendence, passion expiated by suffering, trembled in this image and filled Diotima with an unutterable intensity and awe. "Wherever a person finds her highest potential and the richest field for her energies is where she belongs," she thought, "because it is there that she can do the most to intensify life as a whole!"

She looked at her husband as best she could in the dark. Just as the eye does not register the ultraviolet rays of the spectrum, so this rationalist would never notice certain emotional realities of the inner life!

Section Chief Tuzzi was breathing evenly, suspecting nothing, cradled by the assumption that during his well-earned eight hours of

mental absence nothing of importance could be happening in
Europe. Such tranquillity did not fail to impress Diotima, and more
than once she pondered the idea: Renunciation! good-bye to Arnheim! great, noble words of anguish, heaven-storming resignation,
leave-taking on the scale of a Beethoven; the powerful muscle of her
heart tensed up under these demands made on it. The future bil-
lowed with conversations full of a tremulous, autumnal brilliance,
the poignancy of far-off blue mountain ranges. But could renunciation coexist with the double marriage bed? Diotima started up from
her pillows, her black hair flying in wild ringlets. Section Chief
Tuzzi's sleep was no longer the sleep of innocence but rather that of
a serpent with a rabbit in its belly. She came dangerously close to
waking him up and, in view of this new dilemma, shrieking in his face
that she must, she must and would, leave him! Such a flight into hysteria in her conflicted situation would certainly have been understandable, but her body was too healthy for that; she felt that it
simply did not react with the requisite horror to Tuzzi's proximity.
She faced the absence of this horror with a dry shudder. No tears
succeeded in running down her cheeks, but oddly enough it was the
thought of Ulrich that gave her a certain comfort in this particular
situation. These days she normally never gave him a thought, but his
peculiar remarks about wanting to abolish reality, while Arnheim
overestimated it, had a mysterious overtone, a hovering note Diotima had ignored at the time, only to have it surface in her mind
during these night watches of hers. "All it means is that one shouldn't
worry too much about what is going to happen," she told herself irritably. "It's the most commonplace idea in the world!" Yet even as she
phrased this thought so badly and simplistically, she realized that it
contained something she did not understand, the very thing that
acted on her like a sedative, paralyzing her despair along with her
consciousness. Time flitted away like a dark shadow line, as she comforted herself that somehow her inability to muster a lasting despair
might also redound to her credit; but this consoling thought no longer took hold.

At night thoughts keep flowing through alternately bright and dark
patches, like water in high mountains, and when they quietly reappeared after a while Diotima felt as though she had merely dreamed
all that earlier frothing. The boiling little stream behind the dark

mountain range was not the same as the quiet river she slid into at the end. Anger, loathing, courage, fear, all had drained away, there must be no such feelings, they didn't exist: In the soul's struggles with itself there is no one to blame! Ulrich, too, slipped back into oblivion. All that was left now were the ultimate mysteries, the soul's eternal longings. Their moral worth does not depend on what one does. It does not depend on the movements of consciousness or of passion. Even the passions are only *un peu de bruit autour de notre âme*. Kingdoms may be won or lost while the soul does not stir, and one can do nothing to attain one's destiny; in its own time it grows out of the depths of one's being, serene and everyday, like the music of the spheres. Then Diotima lay awake more than ever, but full of confidence. Such thoughts, with their final period somewhere out of sight, had the beauty of putting her to sleep very quickly, even on the most sleepless nights. Like a velvety vision, she felt her love fusing with the infinite darkness that reaches out beyond the stars, inseparable from herself, inseparable from Paul Arnheim, immune to all schemes and set purposes. She hardly found the time to reach for the tumbler of sweetened water she kept on her little night table for her insomnia but used only at the very last moment of consciousness, because it always slipped her mind when she was agitated. The soft sound of her drinking purled, like lovers' whisperings behind a wall, beside her husband's sleep, unheard by him; then Diotima lay back reverently on her pillows and sank into the silence of unconscious being.

95

THE GREAT MAN OF LETTERS: REAR VIEW

It is almost too familiar a phenomenon to be worth mentioning: Once her celebrated guests had realized that the seriousness of her campaign did not call for any great effort on their part, they behaved like mere people, and Diotima, her house filled with noise and high ideas, was disappointed. High-minded as she was, she was ignorant of that law of circumspection which makes a man's conduct in private the opposite of his professional conduct. She did not know that politicians who had called each other liars and crooks in the assembly hall went amicably to lunch side by side in the dining hall. That judges who, in their juridical capacity, have just imposed a heavy fine on some unfortunate may press his hands in sympathy at the end of the proceedings she knew, but saw nothing out of the way in that. That female entertainers sometimes lead irreproachable domestic lives behind the scenes of their dubious public displays she had heard, and even found touching. She also saw a fine symbolism in princes laying aside their crowns on occasion to be simple human beings. But when she saw princes of the cultural realm enjoying themselves as if they were just anybody, she found it hard to make allowances for such a double standard. What is the underlying need, the psychological law behind this common tendency that makes men turn their backs on who they are in their professional lives? Every man is two people, and one hardly knows whether it is in the morning or in the evening that he reverts to his real self.

And so, however pleased she was to see her soul mate so popular with all the men of her circle, and in particular to see him singling out the younger men for his attention, it sometimes depressed her to see him so caught up in all this social activity. A truly great mind, she felt, should not care quite so much to mingle with the ordinary cultural elite, nor be so ready to traffic in the fluctuating marketplace of ideas.

The truth was that Arnheim was not a great mind but only a great man of letters.

In our cultural landscape, the great man of letters has replaced the great mind just as the plutocrats have replaced royalty in the political world. Just as the regal intellect and imagination had its place in the days of reigning princes, the great man of letters has his place in the days of great political campaigns and great department stores. The leading man of letters represents a special form of the connection between the mind and all large-scale operations. The least one may therefore expect of a great author is that he should drive a great car. He has to be a great traveler, be received by high officials, give lectures, and be a moral force not to be underestimated by the leaders of public opinion; he is the keeper of a nation's soul, the upholder of its humanitarian aspirations before the rest of the world; at home, he must receive notable visitors, and with all that, there is still his work to be done, which must be turned out with the agility of a circus performer who never shows the strain of doing his act. A great author is by no means the same thing as a writer who makes lots of money. He need not necessarily write the best-seller of the year or the book of the month himself, as long as he doesn't challenge this sort of evaluation, because it is he who sits on all the award committees, signs all the manifestos, writes all the introductions, delivers all the commencement addresses, pronounces on all the important events, and is called in whenever it is necessary to demonstrate what new heights of progress have just been achieved. For in all his activities, the literary eminence represents not his country as a whole but only its vanguard, its great elite, which already almost constitutes a majority, and so he lives within a magnetic field of chronic intellectual tension. It is of course our present forms of social life that make culture a mega-industry, just as for its part our mega-industrial complex aims to control culture, politics, and the public conscience; the two phenomena meet halfway. Which is why this description is not aimed at anyone in particular but serves only to represent a standard figure on the social chessboard, subject to rules and to making moves as they have evolved in the course of history. Our well-meaning contemporaries take the stand that having intelligence in itself is not enough (there is so much of it around that a little more or less makes no real difference; anyway, everyone thinks he has enough for his own needs), because our first priority is the struggle against stupidity, which means that intelligence must be displayed, made highly visible and operative, and since the Great Author suits this purpose better than an even greater author whom the largest number might not find quite so easy to understand, everyone does his level best to make the visibly Great even greater.

With this understanding, no one could seriously hold it against Arnheim that he was one of the first, experimental, though already quite perfected embodiments of such a public figure, though a certain innate fitness for the role was understood. After all, most writers would like to be Great Authors, but it is the same with them as with mountains; between the Austrian towns of Graz and St. Pölten, for instance, there are many mountains that could look exactly like Monte Rosa, if only they were high enough. The most indispensable condition for being a Great Author is always that one has to write books or plays that will do equally well for high and low. To effect the desired good, one must be an effective writer to begin with; this is the basic principle of every Great Author's life. It is a strange and wonderful principle too, a fine antidote to the temptations of solitude, Goethe's very own principle of effective action: if you will just get things done in a good world, everything else will fall into place. For once a writer has made his effect, his life undergoes a remarkable sea change. His publisher stops saying that a businessman who goes into publishing is a sort of tragic idealist because he could do so much better for himself by dealing in textiles or unspoiled paper. The critics discover him as a worthy subject for their labors, because critics are often not really bad people at heart but former poets who, because times are bad, have to pin their hearts to something that will inspire them to speak out; they are war poets or love poets, depending on the nature of the inward gleanings for which they must find a market, so their preference for the work of a Great Author rather than just any author is quite understandable. There is really only so much work a critic can do, and so the best of this limited output tends to be distributed over the annual publications from the pens of Great Authors, whose works consequently become the savings banks, as it were, of the national cultural economy, in that each of them brings in its train critical commentaries which are in no way mere explications but virtual deposits, and there is correspondingly less capital left over for all the rest. But where this really mounts up is with the essayists, biographers, and instant historians, who relieve themselves all over the great man. Meaning no offense, but dogs prefer a busy street corner to a lonely cliff for their calls of nature, so why should human beings who feel the higher urge to leave their names behind choose a cliff that is obviously unfrequented? Before he knows it, the Great Author ceases to be a separate entity and has become a symbiosis, a collective national product in the most delicate sense of the term, and enjoys the most gratifying assurance life can offer that his prosperity is most intimately bound up with that of countless others.

This may also be why the Great Author is so often noted for his pronounced sense of good form. He resorts to open combat only when his position is threatened; in all other circumstances his conduct is admirably serene and good-natured. He can put up gracefully with any number of trivialities uttered in his praise. Great men of letters do not lightly deign to discuss other writers, but when they do, they seldom flatter a man of true distinction but prefer to encourage one of those unobtrusive talents made up of 49 percent ability and 51 percent inability, which, thanks to this mixture, are very good at everything that needs strength to get done but might be damaged by a strong personality, so that every one of them sooner or later achieves an influential position in the literary world. But with this description we may already have gone beyond what is peculiar to the Great Author alone. The proverb has it that nothing succeeds like success, and nowadays even an ordinary man of letters is likely to have an inordinate fuss made over him long before he has become a Great Author, when he is still a reviewer, columnist, radio scriptwriter, screenwriter, or the editor of some little magazine; some of them resemble those little rubber pigs or donkeys with a hole in their back where you blow them up.

When we see our Great Authors carefully sizing up this situation and doing their best to mold it into an image of an alert population honoring its great personalities, shall we not be grateful to them? They ennoble life as they find it by their sympathetic interest in it. Just try to imagine the opposite, a writer who did none of the above. He would have to decline cordial invitations, rebuff people, assess praise not as a grateful recipient but as a critic, tear up what comes naturally, treat great opportunities as suspect, simply for being so great, and would have nothing of his own to offer in recompense other than processes going on inside his head, hard to express, hard to assess, merely a writer's achievement of which a time that already has its Great Authors has no great need. Would such a man not remain a total outsider and have to withdraw from reality, with all the inevitable consequences?

This was, in any case, Arnheim's opinion.

96

THE GREAT MAN OF LETTERS: FRONT VIEW

A Great Author's problem arises from the fact that even a creative life has to be conducted in a businesslike way, but the language in which it is done is traditionally idealistic, and it was this very blend of business and idealism that played so crucial a part in Arnheim's lifework.

Such anachronistic mixtures turn up everywhere nowadays. Even as our dead, for instance, are being trotted off to their resting place by internal combustion engine, we can't forgo dressing up the top of such a handsome motorized hearse with a medieval helmet and two crossed swords, and that's how it goes with everything; human evolution is a long-drawn-out process. Only two generations ago business letters affected flowery turns of phrase, while today we can already state all sorts of things from love to pure logic in the language of supply and demand, security and discount, at least as well as we can in psychological and religious terms; however, we don't do that yet. That's because our new language is not yet quite sure of itself. The ambitious moneyman finds himself in a difficult spot these days. To place himself on a level with the established powers, he must dress up his activities in great ideas. But great ideas that command instant allegiance no longer exist, because our skeptical contemporaries believe in neither God nor humanity, kings nor morality—unless they believe in all of them indiscriminately, which amounts to the same thing. So the captain of industry, disinclined to forgo greatness, which serves him as a compass, must resort to the democratic dodge of replacing the immeasurable influence of greatness by the measurable greatness of influence. So now whatever counts as great *is* great; but this means that eventually whatever is most loudly hawked as great is also great, and not all of us have the knack of swallowing this innermost truth of our times without gagging a little. Arnheim had been trying conscientiously to find a way.

In such a fix a cultivated man might for instance be reminded of the link between the world of learning and the Church in the Middle Ages. A philosopher who wanted to succeed and influence the thought of his contemporaries had to get along with the Church in those days, which might lead the vulgar freethinker to suppose that such constraints must have kept the philosopher from rising to greatness. But the opposite was the case. Our experts assure us that the result was nothing less than an incomparable Gothic beauty of thought, and if it was possible to make allowances for the Church without harming one's intellectual quality, why shouldn't it be possible to do the same for advertising? Can't a man who wants to get something done get it done under these conditions as well? Arnheim was convinced that it was a sign of greatness in a man not to be overly critical of his times. The best rider on the best horse who is fighting it will not take his hurdles as smoothly as the horseman who manages to move as one with his mount.

Take Goethe, for another example: Now, there was a genius such as the earth is not likely to produce again, but he was also the knighted son of a prosperous business family and, as Arnheim felt, the very first Great Author his nation had ever produced. Arnheim modeled himself on the great poet in many ways. But his favorite story about him was the well-known incident when Goethe, while secretly sympathizing, left poor Johann Gottlieb Fichte in the lurch when the philosopher was fired from the University of Jena for having spoken of the Deity and divine matters "grandly, but perhaps not with the proper decorum," and went about his defense in an "impassioned" manner rather than extricating himself from the affair "in the smoothest possible way," as the urbane master poet observes in his memoirs. Arnheim not only would have done exactly as Goethe did, but would have cited Goethe's example to try to convince all and sundry that this alone was the Goethean, the meaningful way to act. He would hardly have contented himself with the fact that, oddly enough, we are more likely to feel sympathy when a great man does the wrong thing than when a lesser man does the right thing, but would have gone beyond it to point out that an obstinate insistence on principle not only is fruitless but shows a lack of depth and historical irony, what he would also have called the Goethean irony of making the best of it with dignity, showing a sense of humor in action, a mode of conduct that time always proves to have been right in the end. Considering that today, barely two life spans later, the injustice done to the worthy, upright, and slightly excessive Fichte has long since dwindled to a private matter of no consequence to his reputation, while the reputation of Goethe, despite his behaving badly, has suffered equally little in the long run, we must admit that the wisdom of time in fact accords with the wisdom of Arnheim.

And a third example—Arnheim always had quantities of good examples at his disposal—illustrating the deep meaning of the first two: Napoleon. Heine in his *Travel Pictures* describes him in a manner in such perfect accordance with Arnheim's views that we may as well cite his own words, which Arnheim knew by heart:

"Such a mind," Heine wrote, referring to Napoleon—though he might as easily have said it of Goethe, whose diplomatic nature he always defended with the acuity of a lover who knows deep down that he is not really in accord with the object of his admiration— "Such a mind is what Kant means when he asks us to imagine one that works, not intellectually, like our own, but intuitively. The knowledge that our intellect acquires by slow analytic study and laborious deduction, the intuitive mind sees and grasps in one and the same movement. Hence his gift for understanding his time and the moment and for cajoling its spirit, never crossing it, always using it. But since this spirit of the age is not merely revolutionary but is formed by the confluence of both revolutionary and reactionary aspects, Napoleon never acted in a purely revolutionary or counterrevolutionary manner but always in the spirit of both views, both principles, both tendencies, which in him came together, and so he always acted in a manner that was natural, simple, great, never fitful or harsh, always calm and temperate. He never had the need to indulge in petty intrigue, and his coups always resulted from his skill in understanding and moving the masses. Petty, analytical minds incline to slow, intricate scheming, while synthesizing intuitive minds have their own miraculous ways of so combining the possibilities held out by the times that they can take speedy advantage of them for their own ends."

Heine may have meant that a little differently from the way his admirer Arnheim understood it, but Arnheim felt that these words virtually described him as well.

97

CLARISSE'S MYSTERIOUS POWERS
AND MISSIONS

Clarisse indoors . . . Walter seems to have been mislaid somehow, but she has an apple and her bathrobe. The apple and the bathrobe are the two sources from which an unnoticed fine ray of reality streams into her consciousness. What made her think that Moosbrugger was musical? She didn't know. Possibly all murderers are musical. She knows that she wrote a letter on this subject to His Grace Count Leinsdorf; she also remembers what she wrote, approximately, but she has no real access to it.

But was the Man Without Qualities unmusical?

As no good answer came to her, she dropped the question and passed on to other things.

After a while it did come to her: Ulrich is the Man Without Qualities. A man without qualities can't be musical, of course; but he can't be unmusical, either. . . .

He had said to her: You are virginal and heroic.

She reiterated: Virginal and heroic! A glow came into her cheeks. She felt called upon to do something, but she didn't know what.

Her thoughts were driving in two directions, as in a hand-to-hand struggle. She felt attracted and repelled, without knowing toward or by what. This ended in a faint feeling of tenderness that was somehow left over from the struggle and that moved her to go looking for Walter. She stood up and put the apple down.

She was sorry that she was always tormenting Walter. She was only fifteen when she first noticed that she had the power to torment him. All she had to do was to say loudly and firmly that something he had said was not so, and he would flinch, no matter how right what he had said was. She knew he was afraid of her. He was afraid she might go crazy. He had let it slip once and then quickly tried to cover up; but she had known ever since that it was in his mind. She thought it was really lovely. Nietzsche says: "Is there a pessimism of the strong?

An intellectual leaning toward what is hard, horrifying, evil? A deep instinct against morality? A craving for the terrible as the worthy enemy?" When such words came to mind they gave her a sensual thrill in her mouth, gentle and strong as milk, so that she could hardly swallow.

She thought of the child Walter wanted from her. He was afraid of that too. Made sense, if he thought she might one day go mad. It made a tenderness rise up for him, though she violently fought it down. She had forgotten that she meant to go looking for Walter. There was something going on in her body. Her breasts were filling up, the blood flowed thickly through the veins in her arms and legs, there was a vague pressure on her bladder and bowels. Her slim body deepened inside, grew sensitive, alive, strange, step by step; a child lay bright and smiling in her arms; from her shoulders the Mother of God's golden cloak fell in radiant folds to the floor, and the congregation was singing. It was out of her hands: the Lord had been born unto the world!

But no sooner had this happened than her body snapped shut, closing the gap over the image, like a split log ejecting the entering wedge; she was her own slim self again, feeling disgust and a cruel merriment. She was not going to make it so easy for Walter. "Let it be thy victory and thy freedom that long for offspring": she recited Nietzsche to herself. "Thou shalt build living memorials to thyself. But before that, thou must build up thine own body and soul." Clarisse smiled; it was her special smile, licking upward like a slender flame from a fire under a great stone.

Then she remembered that her father had been afraid of Walter. Her mind went back to years ago. It was something she was in the habit of doing; she and Walter would ask each other: "Do you remember . . . ?" and the light of the past flowed magically from the far distance into the present. It was fun, they enjoyed it. It was perhaps like turning around, after having doggedly trudged along a road for hours, to see all the empty distance one has covered transformed into a grand vista, to one's genuine satisfaction; but they never saw it in that light; they took their reminiscing very seriously. And so it seemed to her incredibly titillating and curious that her father, the aging painter, at that time an authority figure in her life, had been afraid of Walter, who had brought a new era into his house, while

Walter was afraid of her. It was like putting her arm around her friend Lucy Pachhofen and having to say "Papa" to him, while knowing that Papa was Lucy's lover, for that was going on during that same period.

Again Clarisse's cheeks flushed. She was intensely absorbed in trying to bring to mind that peculiar whimpering sound, that strange whimpering she had told Ulrich about. She picked up her mirror and tried to make the face, with lips pressed together in fear, that she must have made the night her father came to her bed. She couldn't manage to imitate the sound that had escaped from her breast in that state of temptation. She thought that the same sound must still be there, inside her chest, as it was then. It was a sound without restraint or scruple, but it had never surfaced again. She put down the mirror and looked around warily, touching everything with her eyes to assure herself that she was alone. Then she felt with her fingertips through her robe, searching for that velvety-black birthmark that had so strange a power. There it was, in the hollow of her groin, half hidden on the inside of the thigh and close to where the pubic hairs somewhat raggedly made room for it; she let her hand rest on it, made her mind a blank, and waited for the sensation she remembered. She felt it at once. It was not the gentle streaming of lust, but her arm grew stiff and taut like a man's arm; she felt that if she could just lift it high enough she would be able to smash everything with it! She called this spot on her body the Devil's Eye. It was the spot at which her father had stopped and turned back. The Devil's Eye had a gaze that pierced through any clothing and "caught" men's eyes and drew them to her, spellbound but unable to move as long as Clarisse willed it. Clarisse thought certain words in quotation marks, with special emphasis, just as she heavily underlined them in writing; the words thus emphasized tensed up with meaning, just as her arm was tensed up now; who would even have supposed that one could really "catch" something, someone, with the eye? Well, she was the first person who held this word in her hand like a stone to be flung at a target. It was all part of the smashing force in her arm. All this had made her forget the whimpering sound she had started out to consider; instead, she thought about her younger sister, Marion. When she was four years old, Marion's hands had to be tied up at night, to keep them from slipping, in all innocence, under the covers, only be-

cause they were drawn toward a pleasing sensation like two baby
bears drawn to a honeycomb in a hollow tree. And some time later
Clarisse had once had to tear Walter away from Marion. Her family
was possessed by sensuality as vintners are by wine. It was fated, a
heavy burden she had to bear. Just the same, her thoughts went on
wandering in the past, the tension in her arm relaxed, and her hand
rested obliviously in her lap. In those days she had still been on terms
of formality with Walter. Actually, she owed him a lot. It was he who
had brought the news that there were modern people who insisted
on plain, cool furniture and hung pictures on their walls that showed
the truth. He read new things to her, Peter Altenberg, little stories of
young girls who rolled their hoops in the love-crazed tulip beds and
had eyes that shone with sweet innocence like glazed chestnuts.
From that time on Clarisse knew that her slender legs, still a child's
legs, she had thought, were quite as important as a scherzo by "someone or other."

At the time, they were all staying in a summer place together, a
large group; several families of their acquaintance had rented cottages by a lake, and all the bedrooms were filled up with invited
friends, male and female. Clarisse had to double up with Marion, and
around eleven Dr. Meingast sometimes dropped by on his secret
moonlight rounds, for a chat. He—who was now a famous man in
Switzerland—had then been the life of the party and the idol of all
the mothers. How old was she then?—between fifteen and sixteen,
or maybe fourteen and fifteen?—when he had brought his student
George Gröschl along, who was only a little older than Marion and
Clarisse. Dr. Meingast had been somewhat absentminded that evening, rambling a little about moonbeams, parents who slept through
everything and didn't care, and people with a modern outlook; suddenly he was gone, as if he had come only to leave stocky little
George, his great admirer, behind with the girls. George was silent,
probably too shy to talk, and the girls, who had been talking to Meingast, also kept quiet. But George must have clenched his teeth in the
dark and stepped over to Marion's bed. A little light fell into the
room from outside, but in the corners, where the bed stood, impenetrable masses of shadow loomed, so Clarisse could not make out
what was going on, except that George seemed to be standing upright beside the bed, looking down at Marion; but he had his back to

Clarisse, and there was not a sound from Marion, as though she were not in the room at all. A long time went by. But in the end, while Marion remained motionless, George detached himself from the shadows like a murderer; for a moment his shoulder and side showed pale in the bright patch of moonlight in the middle of the room, as he moved toward Clarisse, who had quickly lain down again and pulled the covers up to her chin. She knew that the secret thing that had been going on at Marion's bed would now happen again and was rigid with suspense as George stood silently by her bedside. His lips seemed pressed unnaturally tight together. Finally his hand came, like a snake, and busied itself with Clarisse. What else he was doing she had no idea, and could make no sense of the little she perceived of his movements, despite her excitement. She herself did not feel aroused—that came later—but at the moment felt only a strong, indefinable, anxious excitement; she kept still like a trembling stone in a bridge over which a heavy vehicle is passing so slowly there seems no end to it; she felt unable to speak, and let it all be done to her. After George had let her go he disappeared without a word, and neither of the two sisters could be sure that the other had experienced the same thing as herself; they had not called to each other for help or asked for sympathy, and years went by before they exchanged a word about the incident.

Clarisse had recovered her apple, gnawed off a little piece, and chewed on it. George had never given himself away or made any acknowledgment of what had happened, except perhaps at first to make stonily portentous eyes now and then. By this time he had turned into a smart rising young lawyer in government service, and Marion was married. Much more, however, had happened with Dr. Meingast. On going abroad, he had shed his cynicism and become what is called, outside the universities, a famous philosopher, always surrounded by a throng of students of both sexes. Walter and Clarisse had recently received a letter from him to the effect that he was about to visit his native land in order to get some work done, undisturbed by his followers. Would they be able to put him up? He had heard that they were living "on the border between nature and the big city."

This news might in fact have been what had triggered Clarisse's line of thought that day. "Oh Lord, what a weird time it was!" she thought, and realized, too, that it had been the summer before the summer with Lucy. Meingast had taken to kissing her whenever he felt like it. "If you please, I shall kiss you now," he said politely before he did it, and he also kissed every one of her girlfriends; there was one of them whose skirt Clarisse had never again been able to look at without having to think of eyelids lowered in false modesty. Meingast had told her about it himself, and Clarisse, who was only fifteen, after all, had said to the fully adult Dr. Meingast, when he told her of his exploits with her young friends: "You're a pig!" She got a kick out of calling him such a crude name to his face—it felt like being booted and spurred—though it did not prevent her from being afraid that she would not be able to resist him either, in the end, and when he asked her for a kiss she did not dare refuse, for fear of seeming silly.

But when Walter kissed her for the first time, she said gravely: "I promised Mama never to do this kind of thing." And that was the difference in a nutshell. Walter talked like an angel and he talked a lot, he was swathed in art and philosophy like the moon swathed in a broad bank of clouds. He read aloud to her. But what he mostly did was look at her constantly, only at her among all her friends, that was all there was between them at first; it was just like having the moon look down on you: all you do is fold your hands. Actually, holding hands was the next step, quietly clasping hands without a word spoken, and what an amazingly strong bond it was! Clarisse felt her whole body purified by the touch of his hand; if he happened to seem absentminded and cool in taking her hand, she felt destroyed. "You can't imagine what it means to me!" she said pleadingly. By that time they were very close, in secret. He taught her a new appreciation of mountains and beetles; all she had ever seen in nature before was a landscape that Papa or one of his colleagues would paint and sell. Now all of a sudden she began to regard her family with a critical eye; she felt all new and different.

Suddenly she had a clear recollection of that business with the scherzo. "Your legs, Miss Clarisse," Walter had said, "have more to do with real art than all of your papa's paintings." There was a piano in the house where they were staying that summer, on which they used to play duets. Clarisse was learning things from him; she wanted to rise above her girlfriends and her family; none of them understood how anyone could spend such lovely summer days playing the piano instead of going out boating or swimming; but she had pinned her hopes on Walter, she had already, even then, decided she would be "his mate," she would marry him, and when he snapped at her for playing a wrong note, she would be boiling inwardly, but her pleasure outweighed the hurt. Walter did snap at her sometimes, in fact, because the spirit is uncompromising; but only at the piano. Music apart, it still happened sometimes that Meingast kissed her, and on one moonlight expedition, when Walter was rowing, she nestled her head on Meingast's chest quite of her own accord as they sat in the stern together. Meingast had such a way with him in these matters, she had no way of knowing what would come of it, while Walter, the second time he grabbed her, right after their piano lesson, at the very last moment when they had already reached the doorway and he pounced on her from behind and kissed her hard, had only given her the unpleasant feeling that she had to struggle for air, to tear herself away from him. Nevertheless, her mind was made up; no matter what happened between her and the other one, she must never let go of this one.

It was a funny thing, all that, anyway; there was something about Meingast's breath that made all resistance melt away—it was like pure, light air that makes you feel happy for no reason—while Walter, who suffered from a halting digestion, as Clarisse had known for some time, just like the halting way he had of making up his mind about anything, had a stuffy kind of breath, a little too hot, a little musty and paralyzing. Such psychosomatic factors had played a strange part all along, and Clarisse could take it in stride, because nothing seemed more natural to her than Nietzsche's saying that a person's body *is* the soul. Her legs had no more genius than her head, they had exactly as much, they *were* her genius; her hand, at Walter's touch, instantly released a stream of intentions and assurances that flowed from head to toe, without a word; and her youth—once it had come to know itself—rebelled against all the convictions and other foolishness of her parents with the simple freshness of a hard young body that despises all the feelings remotely connected with the voluptuous marriage beds and lush Turkish carpets so popular with the morally strict older generation. And so the physical continued to play a part she understood differently from the way others might see it.

But here Clarisse broke off her reminiscences, or it was rather her reminiscences that on the instant, without the bump of a landing, dropped her back into the present. It was all this, and what was to follow, that she had wanted to tell her friend, the Man Without Qualities. Perhaps there was too much of Meingast in it, who had after all disappeared soon after that exciting summer. He had fled abroad; that incredible inward transformation of his had begun that was to make a famous philosopher out of the frivolous womanizer; and thereafter Clarisse had seen him only in passing, when neither of them had been reminded of the past. But as she saw it, her own part in his transformation was perfectly clear to her. A good deal more had happened between them in the weeks before his disappearance. In Walter's absence—and in his jealous presence too, cutting Walter out and driving him to outdo himself—she and Meingast went through emotional storms and even crazier times, in those hours before a storm that can drive a man and a woman out of their minds, followed by the hours after the storm, all passion spent, that are like green meadows after a rain, in the pure air of friendship. Clarisse had let a lot of things be done to her, not unwillingly, but, eager as she was to know everything, the child had fought back in her own way afterward, by telling her licentious friend exactly what she thought of him. And because, in that last period before he left, Meingast's mood had already sobered into friendship and a noble resignation in his rivalry with Walter, she was now convinced that she had drawn onto herself all that had troubled his spirit before he went off to Switzerland, helping him toward that unexpected self-transformation. She was confirmed in this idea by what had happened between Walter and herself immediately afterward. Clarisse could no longer distinguish between those long-gone years and months, but what did it matter just when one thing or another had happened? The point was that when she and Walter had grown close, despite much resistance on her part, there came a dreamy time of long walks and confessions, of taking spiritual possession of one another with countless agonizing yet blissful little orgies of soul-probing to which lovers are tempted when they are still lacking that very amount of resolute courage which they have already lost in chastity. It was just as if Meingast had bequeathed them his sins, to be relived on a higher plane, until their ultimate meaning had been extracted by exhausting it; and they both perceived it thus. And now, when Clarisse cared so little for Walter's love that she often found herself repelled by it, she saw even more clearly that the ecstatic thirst for love that had driven her out of her mind to such a degree could have been nothing other than an incarnation, that is, she knew, a manifestation in the flesh of something not of the flesh: a meaning, a mission, a destiny, such as is written in the stars for the elect.

She was not ashamed, she felt more like crying when she compared the Then and Now, but Clarisse could never cry but pressed her lips together hard, and it turned into something that looked rather more like her smile. Her arm, covered with kisses up to the armpit; her leg, guarded by the Devil's Eye; her pliant body, twisted over and over by her lover's yearning and twisting back like a rope, all harbored the marvelous feeling that goes with love: the sense that every movement is of mysterious importance. Clarisse sat there feeling like an actress during intermission. To be sure, she did not know what lay ahead, but she felt it was the unremitting duty of lovers to always be to each other what they had been in their finest moments. And here was her arm, here were her legs, her head was poised on her body, in awesome readiness to be the first in recognizing the sign that could not fail to appear.

It may be hard to understand what Clarisse meant, but it was all perfectly plain to her. She had written a letter to Count Leinsdorf calling for a Nietzsche Year and also asking for the release of the sex murderer and perhaps his exhibition before the public as a reminder of the calvaries endured by those who are doomed to take upon themselves the widespread sins of all mankind; and now she also knows why she did it. Someone must be the first to speak. She may not have expressed it too well, but no matter, the point was to make a start and end this putting up with everything and letting things take their course. History proves that the world needs such people from time to time—the words *eon to eon* echoed in her mind like two bells one can't see, although they are nearby—people who simply cannot fall into line and go on lying like all the rest and who have to make a nuisance of themselves. So much was clear.

It was also clear that people who make a nuisance of themselves are going to feel the pressure of the world. Clarisse knows that mankind's great geniuses have always had to suffer, and she doesn't wonder that many days and weeks in her life pass under some leaden weight, as if a heavy slab had been laid on them, but she has come through every time so far, and it's the same for everybody; the Church in its wisdom has even instituted formal times of mourning and mortification so as to concentrate all the sadness into a day or a week rather than let a half century be flooded with hopelessness and callousness, as has also been known to happen. More of a problem in Clarisse's life have been certain other phases, all too buoyant and unrestrained, when a word may sometimes be enough to make her go off the rails altogether. At such times she is so beside herself that she can't tell where she is, except that she is definitely not absent; on the contrary, she could be said to be more inwardly present than ever, inside some deep inner space somehow contained inside the space her body occupies in the world, something indefinable in ordinary words—but then, why struggle for words where words don't apply; she will soon be back with the others again in any case, with only a little tickle left in her head, like after a nosebleed. Clarisse realizes that these phases she sometimes goes through are dangerous. Evidently she is being tested and prepared for something special. She tends to think of several things at a time anyway, like a fan opening and shutting, with one fold partly beside, partly underneath the other, and when this gets too confusing it is only natural to wish one could just pull out altogether, with one jerk; lots of people feel like that; they just don't make it, that's all.

So Clarisse enjoys intimations and forebodings as other people pride themselves on their memory or on their strong stomach when they say they could eat splintered glass. Besides, Clarisse has already proved more than once that she has what it takes; she has tested her strength against her father, against Meingast, against George Gröschl. With Walter her struggle was still ongoing, things were still in movement, albeit haltingly. But for some time now Clarisse had been meaning to try her strength on the Man Without Qualities. She could not have said exactly since when; perhaps since the time Walter had come up with that name and Ulrich had accepted it; before that, she had to admit, in those early years, she had never paid him any serious attention, though they had been good enough friends. But "Man Without Qualities" reminded her, for instance, of playing the piano, that is, of all those blue moods, leaps of joy, fits of anger, one races through on the keyboard without their quite being real passions. She felt a kinship with all that. From this point one could only move straight as an arrow to refusing to do anything one could not do wholeheartedly, which took her right back to the deep turbulence in her marriage. A man without qualities doesn't say No to life, he says Not yet! and saves himself for the right moment; she had understood this with her whole body. What if the meaning of all those times when she moved outside herself was that she was meant to become the Mother of God? She remembered the vision that had come to her, not fifteen minutes ago. "Maybe every mother could become the Mother of God," she thought, "if she refuses to give in, to lie, to take action, but only brings out what is deepest inside her as her child? Provided she gets nothing for herself out of it," she added sadly. For the idea was far from being altogether attractive; it was more like having that sense, split between torment and bliss, of serving as a sacrifice for something. For her vision had been like an image appearing between the branches of a tree, with the leaves suddenly flickering like candle flames, but gone in an instant as the branches snap together again; but now her mood was changed for good. The very next moment it occurred to her by chance that the word "birth" was contained in the word "birthmark"—a point that would have been lost on anyone else, but to Clarisse portended no less than that her destiny was written in the stars. The wondrous thought that a woman, both as a lover and as a mother, must take a man into herself made her feel at once yielding and excited. Without knowing its source, she felt it melt away her resistance even as she sensed her power.

But she was still far from trusting the Man Without Qualities. He didn't always mean everything he said. When he insisted that ideas could not be carried out, or that he took nothing quite seriously, he was only covering up; she understood that clearly; they had sniffed each other out and recognized each other by secret signs, while Walter was thinking that Clarisse had her crazy spells. Still, there was something bitterly evil in Ulrich, a devilish bent for going the world's self-indulgent way. He had to be set free. She had to go and get him.

She had said to Walter: Kill him. It didn't really mean anything, she didn't really know what she meant by it, but if anything, it meant that something had to be done to tear him out of himself, at any cost.

She would have to wrestle with him for his soul.

She laughed, rubbed her nose, paced back and forth in the dark. Something had to be done about the Parallel Campaign. What? she didn't know.

98

FROM A COUNTRY THAT CAME TO GRIEF BECAUSE OF A DEFECT IN LANGUAGE

The train of events is a train that lays down its own tracks as it goes along. The river of time carries its own banks along with it. The traveler moves on a solid floor between solid walls, but the floor and the walls are strongly influenced by the movements of the travelers, though they do not notice it. What a stroke of luck for Clarisse's peace of mind that along with all her other notions, this one had not yet occurred to her.

But Count Leinsdorf was also safe from it. He was shielded from this notion by his view of himself as a practitioner of *realpolitik.*

The days rocked along and turned into weeks. The weeks did not stop moving, either, but formed links in a chain. Something was happening every minute. And when something is happening every minute, it is easy to imagine that one is actually getting real things done. The sumptuous reception rooms at the Leinsdorf town residence, for instance, were to be thrown open to the public invited to a festival for the benefit of consumptive children, an event preceded by exhaustive conferences between His Grace and His Grace's majordomo, fixing certain dates by which certain preparations had to be completed. The police simultaneously organized an anniversary exhibition, to which all of high society was invited, and the High Commissioner had called on His Grace personally to deliver the invitation. When Count Leinsdorf arrived, the High Commissioner recognized his volunteer assistant and honorary secretary, who was quite superfluously introduced to him again, giving the High Commissioner a chance to show off his legendary memory for faces; he was said to be acquainted personally with every tenth citizen, or at least to be informed about him. Diotima also came, accompanied by her husband, and all those present awaited the arrival of a member of the Royal and Imperial House, to whom some of them were to be presented, and everyone without exception agreed that the exhibition was a huge success and simply fascinating. It consisted of a great many pictures crowded together on the walls, and mementos of great crimes arranged in glass-fronted cabinets and showcases. These included burglars' tools, forgers' apparatus, lost buttons that had provided clues, and the tragic weapons of notorious murderers, captioned with their respective stories, while the pictures on the walls contrasted with this arsenal of horror by showing edifying scenes of police activities. Here you could see the kindly policeman guiding the little old lady across the street, the solemn policeman looking down at a corpse washed up from the river, the brave policeman flinging himself at the bridle of a shying horse, an allegorical painting of the Police Force as Guardian Angel to the City, the lost child surrounded by motherly policemen at the station, the policeman in flames carrying a young girl out of a burning house, and many, many more, such as "First Aid" and "Alone on the Beat," as well as the portraits of policemen with years of service dating back to 1869, captioned with inspiring accounts of their careers, and framed poems extolling the work of the police force as a whole or its individual functionaries. Its highest official, the ministerial head of the police division that was called, in Kakania, by the psychological designation Ministry for Inner Concerns, in his welcoming speech drew his listeners' attention to these pictures, which, he said, showed the spirit of the police as a true manifestation of the people. The natural admiration for a spirit of such helpfulness and discipline was a fountain of moral renewal in an age such as this, when art and life only too often sank into mindless sensuality and self-indulgence. Diotima, standing beside Count Leinsdorf, felt uneasily that this ran counter to her own efforts on behalf of modern art, and was gazing intently into the art with a gentle yet unyielding expression on her face, to register upon the general atmosphere her dissent from this particular Kakanian official's point of view. Her cousin, watching her

from a slight distance with the sentiments proper to an honorary secretary of the Parallel Campaign, suddenly within all this packed
crowd felt a gingerly touch on his arm and was surprised to find at his
side Bonadea, who had arrived with her husband, the eminent judge,
and was using the moment when all necks were craned toward the
august speaker, with the Archduke by his side, to work her way close
to her fickle lover. This bold move was the fruit of long scheming.
Hard hit by her lover's desertion at a time when she was sadly struggling to tie down, as it were, even the freely fluttering fringes of the
banner of her lust, all her thoughts in these last weeks had been
focused on winning him back. He had been avoiding her, and forcing
him to "have it out" with her only put her in the unbecoming role of
the pursuer of someone who would rather be left alone, so she had
decided to force her way into the circle where he was to be found day
after day. She had in her favor, after all, her husband's professional
connection with the case of the loathsome killer Moosbrugger, as
well as her friend's intention to do something for that murderer,
which made her a natural factor in effecting a liaison. She had consequently been making quite a nuisance of herself to her husband
lately, with her references to concern in influential circles for the
welfare of the criminally insane, and had made him take her along to
the opening of the police exhibition, where, something told her, she
would at last get to meet Diotima. When the Minister had concluded
his speech and the mass of visitors began to circulate, she never
budged from the side of her reluctant lover, accompanying him on a
tour of the awful bloodstained weapons despite her nearly insurmountable horror of them.

"You said all this sort of thing could be prevented if people only
wanted to," she whispered, like an obedient child showing off how
earnestly it has been paying attention to something once explained to
her. Letting the crowd press her close to him a while later, she
smiled and used the opportunity to murmur in his ear: "You once
said that in the right circumstances anyone is capable of any
weakness."

Her ostentatious insistence on clinging to his side was a great embarrassment to Ulrich, whom she was purposefully steering, despite
all he could do to distract her from this aim, toward Diotima, and
since he couldn't lecture her in front of all these people on the im-

propriety of what she was up to, he realized that the day had come when he had no choice but to bring about just what he had always tried to prevent, the acquaintance of these two women with each other. They were already close to a group of which Diotima and His Grace formed the center when Bonadea cried out, in front of a display case: "Oh look, there's Moosbrugger's knife!" And so it was. Bonadea stared at it joyfully, as if she had just come upon Grandma's first party favor in some drawer at home. So Ulrich quickly made up his mind and found a suitable pretext for asking his cousin's permission to present a lady who longed to meet her and whom he knew to be passionately interested in all efforts on behalf of the good, the true, and the beautiful.

So no one could really say that nothing much was happening as the days and weeks rocked along; actually, the police exhibit and all that went with it was the least of it. In England, for instance, they had something far more magnificent, much talked of in society hereabouts: a doll's house that was presented to the Queen, built by a famous architect, with a dining room three feet long, its walls hung with miniature portraits by famous contemporary painters, with bedrooms where hot and cold water came from real taps, and a library that included a little album made entirely of gold, in which the Queen could paste tiny photographs of the royal family, a microscopically printed railway timetable and shipping schedule, and about two hundred tiny volumes in which famous authors had with their own hands written poems and stories for the Queen. Diotima had a two-volume set of the deluxe edition of the English book about it that had only just appeared, with expensive color prints of everything worth seeing, to which rarity she owed an increased participation in her soirees by the highest-ranking personages in society. And there was more, one thing coming so quickly on the heels of another that it was hard to find words to keep up with it all, so that it felt like a flurry of drumbeats in the soul preceding something just around the corner that had not yet come into view. There was, for instance, the first strike ever of the Imperial and Royal Telegraph, conducted in a most disquieting fashion that came to be known as passive resistance, and consisted simply of everyone involved going about their work punctiliously by the book; it turned out that everything could be brought to a standstill far more speedily by the strictest observance of all the official regulations than by the most ruthless anarchy. Like the story of the Captain of Kopenick in Prussia—a man still remembered for conferring that military rank on himself by dint of putting on a secondhand uniform, then stopping a patrol in the street and using it, together with the Prussian virtue of unconditional obedience to orders from anyone in uniform, to liberate the municipal treasury—passive resistance was something that tickled the imagination, but it also subliminally undermined the principles that inspired the disapproval one felt obliged to express. The newspapers reported among other items that His Majesty's Government had signed an agreement with another majesty's government to keep the peace, revive the economy, and work sincerely together to establish and respect the rights of all, and listed the measures to be taken if these were or might be threatened. Section Chief Tuzzi's superior, the Foreign Minister, made a speech, a few days afterward, in which he urged the need for close collaboration among the three continental empires, which could not afford to ignore modern social developments but must, in the joint interests of the dynasties, make common cause against social innovations. Italy was involved in a military campaign in Libya. Germany and England had a problem in Baghdad. Kakania was making certain military preparations in the south, to show the world that it would not allow Serbia to expand to the sea but would permit it only a railway line to the coast. And reported on a par with all the events of this magnitude was the world-famous Swedish actress Vogelsang's confession that she had never in all her life slept as well as on this, her first night in Kakania, and her delight at the policeman who had rescued her from the delirious crowd and then asked permission to press her hand in both of his.

This, then, brings us back to the police exhibition. A great deal was happening everywhere, and people were certainly aware of it. It was regarded as a good thing when we were the ones doing it, and aroused apprehensiveness when it was done by others. Every schoolboy could understand each thing as it happened, but as to what it all meant in general, nobody really knew except for a very few persons, and even they were not sure. Only a short time later it might as well have happened in a different sequence, or the other way around, and nobody would have known the difference, except for a few changes that inexplicably establish themselves in the course of time and so constitute the slimy track made by the snail of history.

In such circumstances a foreign embassy may well be facing a hard task when trying to find out what is actually going on. The diplomatic representatives would gladly have drawn their wisdom from Count Leinsdorf, but His Grace placed obstacles in their way. In his work he found anew day by day the contentment that solid achievement leaves in its wake, and what foreign observers beheld in his countenance was the beaming serenity that comes from operations proceeding in good order. Department One sent a memorandum; Department Two replied; when Department One had been notified of Department Two's reply, it was usually advisable to suggest talking it over in person, and when an agreement had been reached in this fashion, it was decided that nothing could be done about the matter; and so there was always something to do. In addition there were those countless minor considerations that must not be overlooked. After all, one was always working hand in glove with all the various ministries; one did not want to give offense to the Church; one had to take account of certain persons and social considerations; in short, even on those days when one wasn't doing anything in particular, there were so many things one had to guard against doing that one had the sense of being kept frantically busy at all times. His Grace fully appreciated these facts of life.

"The higher a man is placed by destiny," he used to say, "the better he sees that everything depends on only a few simple principles, but above all on a firm will and well-planned activity." Once, when speaking to his "young friend," he went even more deeply into this subject. Apropos of the German struggle for national unity, he admitted that between 1848 and 1866 quite a number of the best brains in the country had had their say in politics. "But then," he went on, "that fellow Bismarck came along, and there was one good thing he did if he did nothing else: he showed them how politics should be done. It isn't done with a lot of talk and clever ideas! Despite his seamy side, he did see to it that ever since his time, wherever the German tongue is spoken, everyone knows that in politics there is no hope to be had from cleverness and speechmaking, only from silent thought and action."

Count Leinsdorf also expressed himself along these lines at Diotima's Council meetings, and the representatives of foreign powers that sometimes sent along their observers had a hard time trying to fathom his meaning. Arnheim's part in it was regarded as worth watching, and so was the position of Section Chief Tuzzi, and there came to be a general consensus that there was a secret understanding between these two men and Count Leinsdorf, the political aim of which was for the present concealed behind lively attention-stealing devices such as Frau Section Chief Tuzzi's pancultural endeavors. Considering how Count Leinsdorf succeeded in hoodwinking even those hardened observers without even trying, there is no denying the gift he felt he had for realism in politics.

But even those gentlemen who on festive occasions wear gold-embroidered foliage and other rank growths on their tailcoats held to the *realpolitisch* prejudices of their game, and since they could discover no solid clues behind the scenes of the Parallel Campaign, they soon turned their attention to something that was the cause of most of the obscure phenomena in Kakania, called "the unliberated national minorities." We all talk as if nationalism were purely the invention of the arms dealers, but we really should try for a more comprehensive explanation, and to this end Kakania makes an important contribution. The inhabitants of this Imperial and Royal Imperial–Royal Dual Monarchy had a serious problem: they were supposed to feel like Imperial and Royal Austro-Hungarian patriots, while at the same time being Royal Hungarian or Imperial Royal Austrian patriots. Their understandable motto in the face of such complexities was "United we stand" (from *viribus unitis,* "with forces joined"). But the Austrians needed to take a far stronger stand than the Hungarians, because the Hungarians were, first and last, simply Hungarians and were regarded only incidentally, by foreigners who did not know their language, as Austro-Hungarians too; the Austrians, however, were, to begin with and primarily, nothing at all, and yet they were supposed by their leaders to feel Austro-Hungarian and be Austrian-Hungarians—they didn't even have a proper word for it. Nor was there an Austria. Its two components, Hungary and Austria, made a match like a red-white-and-green jacket with black-and-yellow trousers. The jacket was a jacket, but the trousers were the relic of an extinct black-and-yellow outfit that had been ripped apart in the year 1867. The trousers, or Austria, were since then officially referred to as "the kingdoms and countries represented in the Imperial Council of the Realm," meaning nothing at all, of course, because it was only a phrase concocted from various names, for even those kingdoms referred to, such wholly Shake-spearean kingdoms as Lodomeria and Illyria, were long gone, even when there was still a complete black-and-yellow outfit worn by ac-tual soldiers. So if you asked an Austrian where he was from, of course he couldn't say: I am a man from one of those nonexistent kingdoms and countries; so for that reason alone he preferred to say: I am a Pole, a Czech, an Italian, Friulian, Ladino, Slovene, Croat, Serb, Slovak, Ruthenian, or Wallachian—and this was his so-called nationalism. Imagine a squirrel that doesn't know whether it is a squirrel or a chipmunk, a creature with no concept of itself, and you will understand that in some circumstances it could be thrown into fits of terror by catching sight of its own tail. So this was the way Kakanians related to each other, with the panic of limbs so united as they stood that they hindered each other from being anything at all. Since the world began, no creature has as yet died of a language defect, and yet the Austrian and Hungarian Austro-Hungarian Dual Monarchy can nevertheless be said to have perished from its inexpressibility.

A stranger to Kakanian history might be interested to learn just how so seasoned and eminent a Kakanian as Count Leinsdorf coped with this problem. He began by excising Hungary altogether from his watchful mind; as a wise diplomat, he simply never mentioned it, just as parents avoid speaking of a son who has struck out for inde-pendence against their wish and who, they keep expecting, will yet live to regret it; the rest he referred to as the "nationalities," or else as the "Austrian ethnic stocks." This was a most subtle device. His Grace had studied constitutional law and had found a definition ac-cepted more or less worldwide, to the effect that a people could claim to count as a nation only if it had its own constitutional state, from which he deduced that the Kakanian nations were simply na-tional minorities, at most. On the other hand, Count Leinsdorf knew that man finds his full, true destiny only within the overarching com-munal framework of a nation, and since he did not like the thought of anyone being deprived in this respect, he concluded that it was necessary to subordinate the nationalities and ethnic breeds to an all-embracing State. Besides, he believed in a divine order, even if that order was not always discernible to the human eye, and in the revolutionary modernist moods that sometimes overcame him he was even capable of thinking that the idea of the State, which was coming so strongly into its own these days, was perhaps nothing other than the Divine Right of Kings just beginning to manifest itself in a rejuvenated form. However that might be—as a realist in politics he took good care never to overdo the theorizing, and would even have settled for Diotima's view that the idea of the Kakanian State was synonymous with that of World Peace—the point was that there *was* a Kakanian State, even if its name was a dubious one, and that a Kakanian nation had to be invented to go with it. He liked to illustrate this by pointing out, for instance, that nobody was a schoolboy if he didn't go to school, but that the school remained a school even when it stood empty. The more the minorities balked against the Kakanian school's efforts to bind them into one nation, the more necessary the school, in the given circumstances. The more they insisted that they were separate nations, the more they demanded the restoration of their so-called long-lost historic rights, the more they flirted with their ethnic brothers and cousins across the borders and openly called the Empire a prison from which they must be released, the more Count Leinsdorf tried to calm them down by calling them ethnic stocks and agreed with their own emphasis on their underdeveloped state; only he offered to improve it by raising them up to be part of one Austrian nation. Whatever they wanted that did not fit in with his plan or that was overly mutinous, he blamed in his familiar diplomatic way on their failure so far to transcend their political immaturity, which was to be dealt with by a wise blend of shrewd tolerance and gently punitive restraints.

And so when Count Leinsdorf created the Parallel Campaign, the various ethnicities immediately perceived it as a covert Pan-Germanic plot. His Grace's participation in the police exhibition was linked with the secret police and interpreted as proof positive of his sympathies with that politically repressive body. This was all known to the foreign observers, who had heard all the horror stories about the Parallel Campaign they could want. They kept it in mind while listening to the stories about the reception of the actress Vogelsang, the English Queen's dollhouse, and the striking telegraphers, or when they were asked what they thought of the recently published international agreements; and although the Minister's praise of the disciplinary spirit could be taken as an announcement of a policy if one so desired, they probably felt that to the unprejudiced eye the opening of the police exhibition, despite all the talk about it, had produced nothing worth noticing, though they also had the impression like everyone else that something was brewing in a general way, though it could not yet be pinned down.

99

OF THE MIDDLING INTELLIGENCE AND ITS FRUITFUL COUNTERPART, THE HALFWIT; THE RESEMBLANCE BETWEEN TWO ERAS; LOVABLE AUNT JANE; AND THE DISORDER CALLED MODERN TIMES

It really was impossible to gain a clear idea of what went on when Diotima's Council was in session. The general tendency among the avant-garde in those days was in favor of taking action; people who lived by their brains felt it incumbent upon themselves to take over the leadership from those who lived for their bellies. There was also something known as Expressionism. Nobody could say just what it was, but the word suggests some kind of squeezing-out; constructive visions, perhaps, but inasmuch as the contrast with traditional art revealed them as being destructive, too, we might simply call them structive, which commits one to nothing either way, and a structive outlook sounds pretty good. Nor is that all.

The general orientation was toward the Now and the real world, the inside turning toward the outside, but there was also a movement turning from the outside inward; the intellect and individualism were already seen as outmoded and egocentric, love was once again discredited, and the salutary effect of artistic trash on the masses, when injected into the cleansed souls of men of action, was about to be rediscovered. "What people are" evidently keeps changing as rapidly as "What people are wearing," and both have in common the fact that no one, not even those in the fashion business, knows the real secret of who "these people" are. But anyone trying to run counter to this would look silly, like a person caught between the opposing currents of an electric therapy machine, wildly twitching and jerking without anyone's being able to see his attacker. For the enemy is not those quick-witted enough to take advantage of the given business situation; it's the gaseous fluidity and instability of the general state of affairs itself, the confluence of innumerable currents from all directions that constitute it, its unlimited capacity for new combinations and permutations, plus, on the receiving end, the absence or breakdown of valid, sustaining, and ordering principles.

To find a secure foothold in this flow of phenomena is like trying to hammer a nail into a fountain's jet of water; and yet there is a certain constant in it. What is actually going on when that agile species man calls a tennis player a genius? Something unstated is at work here. And when they attribute genius to a racehorse? Something more is left unsaid. Whether they call a football player a scientist of the game, or admire a fencer's intellectual style, or speak of a boxer's tragic defeat, there is always something undeclared going on. They exaggerate, but the exaggeration is a form of imprecision, the sort of fuzziness of mind that makes the denizens of a small town regard the son of the department store owner as a man of the world. There is bound to be a grain of truth in it, and anyway, why shouldn't the surprises an athletic champion pulls off suggest those we get from a genius, or his strategies seem analogous to those of a seasoned explorer of the unknown? Even though there is something else, something far more important, that is quite wrong with such analogies, of course, this is not perceived, or perceived only with reluctance, by those given to making them. At bottom there is an uncertainty of values, passed over and ignored; it is probably less its idea of genius that makes this era attribute genius to a tennis player or a racehorse than its general distrust for the world of the mind, of the intellect, to which the term rightly belongs.

This might be the moment to bring up Aunt Jane, of whom Ulrich was reminded when he was leafing through some old family albums Diotima had lent him, comparing the faces he saw in them with the faces seen in her house. As a boy, Ulrich had often stayed with a great-aunt who'd had a friend, Aunt Jane, from time immemorial. Jane was not really an aunt, originally. She had come into the house as the children's piano teacher and had not exactly achieved any wonders in that line, either, but she had won their love because it was a principle with her that there was not much point in doing one's piano practice if one was not born for music, as she put it. She got more enjoyment out of seeing the children climb trees, and in this fashion she became an aunt to two generations as well as—through the retroactive effect of the passage of years—her disappointed employer's lifelong friend.

"Ah yes, dear Mucki!" Aunt Jane would say, for instance, full of feeling impervious to time, her voice so charged with indulgence and admiration for little Nepomuk, who was by then an uncle in his forties, that it still lived for anyone who had heard it once. That voice of Aunt Jane's sounded as if it had been dusted with flour; absolutely as if one had dipped one's bare arm into the finest flour. It was a husky voice, crumb-coated, all because she drank lots of black coffee and smoked long, thin, strong Virginia cigars, which, as she aged, had blackened and eroded her teeth. When you looked at her face you might also feel that the sound of her voice had something to do with those innumerable little fine lines that covered her skin like the lines of an etching. Her face was long and gentle, and to the later generations seemed never to have changed, like everything else about Aunt Jane. She wore one and the same dress all her life, even if, as seems likely, it was a series of reproductions of the original; it was a long, tight casing of black ribbed silk from neck to toe, making no allowance for any excessive mobility of the body, with an endless row of little black buttons, like a priest's cassock. At the top there was a low, stiff stand-up collar with turned-down corners, between which her Adam's apple formed active gullies in the fleshless skin of her neck every time she pulled on her cigar; the tight sleeves ended in stiff white cuffs, and for a roof she had a reddish-blond slightly curly man's wig, parted in the middle. With the passing of the years that part showed a little more of the canvas, but more affecting than that were the two spots where the gray temples could be seen from under the bright wig, the only sign that Aunt Jane had not remained the same age all her life.

She might seem to have anticipated by many decades the masculine kind of woman who has since come into fashion, but that is not really the case, because in her manly breast there beat a most feminine heart. She might also be thought to have once been a famous pianist who later lost touch with her time, for that is how she looked. But this was not so either, because she had never been more than a piano teacher, and both that mannish hairdo and her priestly garb could be traced to the fact that as a girl Aunt Jane had been infatuated with the Abbé Franz Liszt, whom she had met socially several times during one short period, and that was when her name had somehow assumed its English form. With that encounter she kept faith, like a lovesick knight wearing his lady's colors into his gray old age without ever having asked for more, and in Aunt Jane's case this was more touching than if it had been some uniform of her own great days she had worn in her retirement.

When the children were considered old enough, they were made privy to Aunt Jane's deep secret, after many solemn admonitions to respect it; much as if it had been a rite of passage. Jane had no longer been a young girl (a fastidious soul takes its time in making such a choice) when she found the man she loved and married, against her family's will; he had of course been an artist, although, because of the rotten luck of small-town, provincial circumstances, only a photographer. But a short time after they were married he was already running up debts like a genius and drinking furiously. Aunt Jane made sacrifices for him, she fetched him home from the tavern, she wept in secret and openly at his knees. He looked like a genius, with an imperious mouth and flamboyant hair, and if Aunt Jane had been able to infect him with the passion of her despair, he would have become, with his disastrous vices, as great as Lord Byron. But the photographer proved recalcitrant to such a transfer of feeling, abandoned Jane after a year of marriage, leaving with her maid, a peasant girl who was pregnant by him, and he died not much later, in misery. Jane cut a lock of hair from his superb head and kept it; she took the child born to him out of wedlock and raised it as her own, under great deprivation; she rarely spoke of her past; a life given over to passion is not an easy one, or easy to talk about.

Aunt Jane's life had held its share of romantic eccentricity. But later on, when the photographer in his earthly imperfection had long ceased to hold her under his spell, the imperfect substance of her love for him had somehow also moldered away, leaving behind only the eternal form of love and inspiration, so that at a great remove in time her experience had become indistinguishable from a truly earthshaking kind of emotion. Aunt Jane's mind was probably not supercharged intellectually, but its form was beautiful. Her attitude was heroic, but such a stance is unattractive only as long as it is falsely motivated; once it has become quite empty of content, it again turns to flickering flames and true faith. Aunt Jane lived on tea, black coffee, and two cups of beef bouillon a day, but no one in that little town stopped and stared after her on the streets when she passed by in her black cassock, because the people knew her, they knew she was a proper lady, they even looked up to her for being a proper lady and having the determination to dress as she pleased, even though they did not know the reasons for it.

So this is more or less the story of Aunt Jane, who died a long time ago, at a great age, and my great-aunt is dead too, and so is Uncle Nepomuk, and what were their lives all about anyway? Ulrich asked himself. But just then he would have given a lot to be able to talk with Aunt Jane again. He turned the pages of the thick old albums with those family photographs that had somehow ended up in Diotima's possession, and the closer he came to the beginnings of that new art of picture-taking, the more proudly, it seemed to him, the subjects faced the camera. There they were, with one foot placed on a pile of cardboard boulders wreathed in paper ivy or, if they were officers, with a saber posed between their straddled legs; the girls had their hands folded in their laps and their eyes opened wide; the emancipated men stood their ground in creaseless trousers that rose up like curling smoke, in coats with a bold romantic sweep to them, as though a gale had blown away the dignified stiffness of the bourgeois frock coat. The time must have been somewhere between 1860 and 1870, when photography had emerged from its earliest stages, when the revolutionary forties were remembered as a wild, chaotic time long gone and life had become subtly different, though no one could say exactly what the new elements were; even the tears, embraces, and confessions in which the new middle class had tried to find its soul in its early days were no more, but as a wave runs out over the sands, this noble impulse had now come to express itself in the way people dressed and in a certain personal buoyancy for which there may be a better word, but for the moment all we have is the photographs. The photographers then wore velvet jackets and handlebar mustaches, to make them look like painters, and the painters designed huge cartoons on which they put whole regiments of important figures through their paces; people in general felt it was just the right time for a technology capable of immortalizing them as well. All that remains to be said is that at no other time could they all have felt so full of genius and stature as the people of this particular period, which produced fewer uncommon individuals—unless it was harder for such individuals to become visible in the midst of so many?—than ever before.

As he turned the pages, Ulrich wondered whether there was some connection between that era, when a photographer could feel like a genius because he drank, wore an open-necked shirt, and, with the aid of the latest techniques, was able to project his sense of his own greatness of spirit onto all those of his contemporaries who posed before his lens, and Ulrich's own time, when only racehorses were truly felt to have genius because of their all-surpassing ability to stretch their legs and contract them again. The two periods look different. The present looks proudly down upon the past, which, if it had happened to occur later, would have looked proudly down upon the present. Yet it mainly amounted to the same thing, because in both cases the major role is played by muddled thinking and an ignoring of the telling differences. A single aspect of greatness is taken for the whole, a distant analogy for a truth, and the flayed hide of a significant word is stuffed with something modish. It works, though not for long. The talkers in Diotima's salon were never entirely wrong about anything, for their concepts were as misty as the outlines of bodies in a steambath. "These ideas, on which life hangs as the eagle hangs on his wings," Ulrich thought, "our countless moral and artistic notions of life, by nature as delicate as mountain ranges of granite blurred by distance." On such tongues as these the ideas multiplied by being turned over and over; it was impossible to discuss one of them for any length of time without suddenly finding oneself caught up in the next.

These were the kind of people who had throughout history regarded themselves as the New Era, a term like a sack in which to catch all the winds of the compass, always serving as an excuse for not placing things in their own objective order but fitting them into an illusory compound with a chimera. And yet it holds a confession of faith, the oddly living conviction that it is up to them to bring order into the world. If we were to judge what they were trying to do along those lines as halfway intelligent, it might be worth saying that it is precisely the other half, the unnamed or—to come straight out with it—the stupid, never exact or complementary part of that middling intelligence that held an inexhaustible power of self-renewal and fruitfulness. There was life in it, mutability, restlessness, freedom to adopt a fresh perspective. They probably had their own sense of how it was with them. They were shaken up by it, it blew in gusts through their heads, those children of a nerve-racked age, aware that something was wrong, each feeling intelligent enough and yet all of them together feeling somehow barren. If they also happened to have talent—and their intellectual woolliness certainly did not exclude this possibility—then what was going on in their heads was like seeing the weather, the clouds, trains, telegraph wires, trees and animals and the whole moving panorama of our dear world, through a narrow, dirt-encrusted window; and no one was very quick to notice the state of his own window, but everyone noticed it about the window next door.

Ulrich had once asked them, for the fun of it, just what they meant by what they were saying. They gave him jaundiced looks, told him he had a mechanistic view of life and was too skeptical, and stated that the most complicated problems must be made to yield the simplest solutions, so that the New Era—once it had shucked the confusing present—would turn out to be simplicity itself. Compared with Arnheim, Ulrich did not strike them as impressive at all, and Aunt Jane would have patted him on the cheek, saying, "I know just how they feel. You put them off with your seriousness."

100

GENERAL STUMM INVADES THE STATE
LIBRARY AND LEARNS ABOUT THE WORLD
OF BOOKS, THE LIBRARIANS GUARDING IT,
AND INTELLECTUAL ORDER

General Stumm had noticed the rebuff to his "comrade in arms" and undertook to comfort him. "What a lot of useless palaver," he said in indignant dismissal of the Council members; then, without any encouragement from Ulrich, he started to talk about himself, with a certain excitement mixed with self-satisfaction:

"You remember, don't you," he said, "that I'd made up my mind to find that great redeeming idea Diotima wants and lay it at her feet. It turns out that there are lots of great ideas, but only one of them can be the greatest—that's only logical, isn't it?—so it's a matter of putting them in order. You said yourself that this is a resolve worthy of a Napoleon, right? You even gave me a number of excellent suggestions, as was to be expected of you, but I never got to the point of using them. In short, I have to go about it my own way."

He took his horn-rimmed glasses out of his pocket and put them on in place of the pince-nez, a sign that he wanted to look closely at someone or something.

"One of the foremost rules for a good general is to find out the enemy's strength," he said. "So I asked them to get me a card to our world-famous Imperial Library, and with the help of a librarian who very charmingly put himself at my disposal when I told him who I was, I have now penetrated the enemy's lines. We marched down the ranks in that colossal storehouse of books, and I don't mind telling you I was not particularly overwhelmed; those rows of books are no worse than a garrison on parade. Still, after a while I couldn't help starting to do some figuring in my head, and I got an unexpected answer. You see, I had been thinking that if I read a book a day, it would naturally be exhausting, but I would be bound to get to the end sometime and then, even if I had to skip a few, I could claim a certain position in the world of the intellect. But what d'you suppose that librarian said to me, as we walked on and on, without an end in sight, and I asked him how many books they had in this crazy library? Three and a half million, he tells me. We had just got to the seven hundred thousands or so, but I kept on doing these figures in my head; I'll spare you the details, but I checked it out later at the office, with pencil and paper: it would take me ten thousand years to carry out my plan.

"I felt nailed to the spot—the whole world seemed to be one enormous practical joke! And I'm telling you, even though I'm feeling a bit calmer about it, there's something radically wrong somewhere!

"You may say that it isn't necessary to read every last book. Well, it's also true that in war you don't have to kill every last soldier, but we still need every one of them. You may say to me that every book is needed too. But there, you see, you wouldn't be quite right, because that isn't so. I asked the librarian.

"It occurred to me, you see, that the fellow lives among those millions of books, he knows each one, he knows where to find them, he ought to be able to help me. Of course I wasn't going to ask him point-blank: Where do I find the finest idea in the world? That sounds too much like the opening of a fairy tale, even I know that much; besides, I never liked fairy tales, even as a child. But what to do? I had to ask him something of the sort in the end anyway. But I never told him why I wanted to know, not a word about our Campaign and having to find the most inspiring aim for it—discretion, you know; I didn't feel I was authorized to go that far. So I finally tried a little stratagem. 'By the way,' I said casually, 'how on earth do you go about finding the right book somewhere in this immense collection . . . ?' I tried to say it as I imagined Diotima might, and I dropped a few pennies' worth of admiration into my voice, and sure enough, he started to purr and fell all over himself with helpfulness, and what was the Herr General interested in finding out?

" 'Oh, all sorts of things,' I said, as if he were prying into state secrets; I was playing for time.

" 'I only meant what subject or what author,' he asked. 'Is it military history?'

" 'Oh no,' I said, 'more on the lines of the history of peace.'

" 'History as such? Or current pacifist literature?'

"No, I said, it wasn't that simple. 'Might there be, for instance, something like a compendium of all the great humanitarian ideas or anything like that?' You remember how much research I've already got my people to do on those lines. He didn't say a word. 'Or a book on realizing the most important aims of all?' I say to him.

" 'Something in theological ethics?' he suggests.

" 'Theological ethics too,' I said, 'but it would have to include something about our old Austrian culture and a bit about Grillparzer,' I specified. My eyes must have been blazing with such a thirst for knowledge that the fellow suddenly took fright, as if I was about to suck him dry altogether. I went on a little longer about needing a kind of timetable that would enable me to make connections among all kinds of ideas in every direction—at which point he turns so polite it's absolutely unholy, and offers to take me into the catalog room and let me do my own searching, even though it's against the rules, because it's only for the use of the librarians. So I actually found myself inside the holy of holies. It felt like being inside an enormous brain. Imagine being totally surrounded by those shelves, full of books in their compartments, ladders all over the place, all those book stands and library tables piled high with catalogs and bibliographies, the concentrate of all knowledge, don't you know, and not one sensible book to read, only books about books. It positively reeked of brain phosphorus, and I felt that I must have really got somewhere. But of course a funny feeling came over me when the man was going to leave me there on my own—I felt both awestruck and uneasy as hell. Up the ladder he scoots, like a monkey, aiming straight at a book from below, fetches it down, and says: 'Here it is, General, a bibliography of bibliographies for you'—you know about that? In short, the alphabetical list of alphabetical lists of the titles of all the books and papers of the last five years dealing with ethical problems, exclusive of moral theology and literature, or however he put it, and he tries to slip away. I barely had time to grab his lapel and hang on to him.

" 'Just a moment, sir,' I cried, 'you can't leave me here without telling me your secret, how you manage to . . .' I'm afraid I let slip the word 'madhouse,' because that's how I suddenly felt about it. 'How do you find your way in this madhouse of books?' He must have got the wrong impression—it occurred to me later that crazy people are given to calling others crazy—anyway, he just kept staring at my saber, and I could hardly keep hold of him. And then he gave me a real shock. When I didn't let go of him he suddenly pulled himself up, rearing up in those wobbly pants of his, and said in a slow, very emphatic way, as though the time had come to give away the ultimate secret: 'General,' he said, 'if you want to know how I know about every book here, I can tell you: Because I never read any of them.'

"It was almost too much, I tell you! But when he saw how stunned I was, he explained himself. The secret of a good librarian is that he never reads anything more of the literature in his charge than the titles and the tables of contents. 'Anyone who lets himself go and starts reading a book is lost as a librarian,' he explained. 'He's bound to lose perspective.'

" 'So,' I said, trying to catch my breath, 'you never read a single book?'

" 'Never. Only the catalogs.'

" 'But aren't you a Ph.D.?'

" 'Certainly I am. I teach at the university, as a special lecturer in Library Science. Library Science is a special field leading to a degree, you know,' he explained. 'How many systems do you suppose there are, General, for the arrangement and preservation of books, cataloging of titles, correcting misprints and misinformation on title pages, and the like?'

"I must admit that when he left me there alone, after that, I felt like doing one of two things: bursting into tears, or lighting a cigarette—neither of which I was allowed to do there. But what do you think happened? As I'm standing there, totally at a loss, an old attendant who must have been watching us all along pads around me respectfully a few times, then he stops, looks me in the face, and starts speaking to me in a voice quite velvety, from either the dust on the books or the foretaste of a tip: 'Is there anything in particular, sir, you are looking for?' he asks me. I try to shake my head, but the old fellow goes on: 'We get lots of gentlemen from the Staff College in here. If you'll just tell me, sir, what subject you're interested in at the moment, sir . . . Julius Caesar, Prince Eugene of Savoy, Count Daun? Or is it something contemporary? Military statutes? The budget?' I swear the man sounded so sensible and knew so much about what was inside those books that I gave him a tip and asked him how he did it. And what do you think? He tells me again that the students at the Staff College come to him when they have a paper to write, 'And when I bring the books,' he goes on, 'they often cuss a bit, and gripe about all the nonsense they have to learn, and that's how the likes of us pick up all sorts of things. Or else it's the Deputy who has to draw up the budget for the Department of Education, and he asks me what material was used by the Deputy the year before. Or it might be the Bishop, who's been writing about certain types of beetles for the last fifteen years, or one of the university professors, who complains that he's been waiting three weeks to get a certain book, and we have to look for it on all the adjoining shelves, in case it's been misplaced, and then it turns out he's had it at home for the last two years. That's the way it's been, sir, for nigh on forty years; you develop an instinct for what people want, and what they read for it.'

" 'Well,' I said, 'be that as it may, my friend, it still isn't so simple for me to tell you what I'm looking for.'

"And what do you think he comes back with? He gives me a quiet look, and nods, and says: 'That happens all the time too, General, if I may say so. There was a lady who came in, not so long ago, who said exactly the same thing to me. Perhaps you know her, sir, she's the wife of Section Chief Tuzzi, of the Foreign Office?'

"Now, what do you think of that? You could have knocked me over with a feather. And when the old fellow caught on, he just went and fetched all the books Diotima has on reserve there, so now, when I come to the library, it's practically like a secret mystical marriage; now and then I make a discreet pencil mark in the margin, or I write a word in, and I know she'll see it the very next day, and she won't have a clue who it is that's inside her own head, when she wonders what's going on."

The General paused blissfully. But then he pulled himself together, his face took on a look of grim seriousness, and he continued: "Now brace yourself and give me your full attention, because I'm going to ask you something. We're all convinced—aren't we?—that we're living in the best-ordered times the world has ever seen. I know I once said in Diotima's presence that it's a prejudice, but it's a prejudice I naturally share. And now I have to face the fact that the only people with a really reliable *intellectual* order are the library attendants, and I ask you—no, I don't ask you; after all, we've talked about this before, and naturally I've thought it over again in the light of my recent experiences. So let me put it this way: Suppose you're drinking brandy, right? A good thing to do in some circumstances. But you keep on, and on, and on, drinking brandy—are you with me?—and the first thing is, you get drunk; next, you get the d.t.'s; and finally, you get conducted with military honors to your last resting place, where the chaplain testifies to your unflinching devotion to duty and so on. Do you get the picture? Good, you've got it, nothing to it. So now let's take water. Imagine drinking water until you drown in it. Or imagine going on eating until your intestines are tied into knots. Or you go on taking drugs—quinine, arsenic, opium. What for? you ask. Well, my friend, I'm coming to the most extraordinary proposition: Take *order*. Or rather, start imagining a great idea, and then another still greater, and then another even greater than that one, and so on; and in the same style, try to increase the concept of order in your head. At first it's as neat and tidy as an old maid's room and as clean as a Horse Guards stable. Then it's as splendid as a brigade in battle formation. Next, it's crazy, like coming out of the casino late at night and commanding the stars: 'Universe, 'ten*shun*, eyes right!' Or let's put it this way: At first order is like a new recruit still falling over his own feet, and you straighten him out. Then it's like dreaming you've suddenly been promoted, over everybody's head, to Minister of War. Next, just imagine a total universal order embracing all mankind—in short, the perfect civilian state of order: that, I say, is death by freezing, it's rigor mortis, a moonscape, a geometric plague!

"I discussed that with my library attendant. He suggested that I read Kant or somebody, all about the limits of ideas and perceptions. But frankly, I don't want to go on reading. I have a funny feeling that I now understand why those of us in the army, where we have the highest degree of order, also have to be prepared to lay down our lives at any moment. I can't exactly explain why. Somehow or other, order, once it reaches a certain stage, calls for bloodshed. And now I am honestly worried that your cousin is carrying all her efforts too far, to the point where she is likely to go and do something that might do her a lot of harm—and I'll be less able than ever to help her! Do you see what I mean? As for the arts and sciences and all they can offer in terms of great and admirable ideas, of course I have nothing but the greatest respect for all that; I wouldn't dream of saying anything against it."

101

COUSINS IN CONFLICT

At about this time Diotima turned to her cousin again. She did it at one of her evenings, coming like a tired dancer through the eddies swirling persistently, unremittingly, through her rooms, to sit down beside him in a pool of quiet where he had parked himself on a little settee against the wall. It was a long time since she had done anything like it. She had avoided seeing him "off duty" ever since those drives in the country together, and as if because of them.

From heat or fatigue, her face looked slightly blotchy.

She propped her hands on the settee, said, "How are you?" and nothing more, even though there was clearly something more needing to be said, and stared straight ahead, with her head slightly bowed. She looked a bit groggy, to borrow a term from the boxing ring, not even bothering to smooth down her dress properly as she sat there, hunched over.

It made her cousin think of tousled hair and bare legs under a peasant skirt. Strip away the frosting, and what was left was a handsome, sturdy creature, and he had to restrain himself from simply taking her hand in his fist, like a peasant.

"So Arnheim isn't making you happy," he said evenly.

Perhaps she should have put him in his place, but she felt strangely moved; after a while, she said: "His friendship makes me very happy."

"I thought his friendship distresses you a little."

"What nonsense!" Diotima pulled herself up and recovered her ladylike poise. "Do you know who really distresses me?" she asked, trying for an easy, chatty tone. "Your friend the General. What does that man want? Why does he keep coming here? Why is he always staring at me?"

"He's in love with you," her cousin replied.

Diotima gave a nervous laugh. She went on: "Do you realize that I shudder from head to foot when I set eyes on him? He makes me think of death."

"An uncommonly life-loving figure of Death, if you look at him without prejudice."

"Evidently I'm not unprejudiced. I don't know why, but I go into a panic every time he comes up to me and informs me that I make 'outstanding' ideas 'stand out' on an 'outstanding occasion.' He makes my skin crawl with an indescribable, incomprehensible, dreamlike fear."

"Of him?"

"Who else? The man's a hyena."

Her cousin had to laugh. She went on with her scolding like a child out of control. "He goes creeping around, just waiting to see our best efforts come to nothing!"

"Which is probably exactly what you are so afraid of. Dear cousin, don't you remember that I foretold the collapse of your undertaking from the first? It can't be helped; you simply have to face it."

Diotima looked at him haughtily. She remembered only too well, even to the words she had spoken to him the first time he came to see her, words that it now hurt her to think about. She had lectured him on what a privilege it was to call upon a whole nation, indeed upon the world, to take up its spiritual mission in the midst of its material-istic concerns. She had wanted nothing outworn, nothing of the old mind-sets, and yet the look she was now giving her cousin was more that of someone who had risen above all that, than of someone who had got above herself. She had considered a Year of the World, a universal rebirth, something to crown all of Western culture; there were times when she had come close, others when her goal seemed to recede from her grasp; she had gone through many ups and downs, and she had suffered. The last few months had been like a long sea voyage, first lifted up by huge waves, then dropped into deep troughs, over and over again, so that by now she could hardly tell what had come first and what later. Now she was sitting here, after her immense efforts, glad that the bench she sat on was not moving, content to do nothing but perhaps watch the smoke curling upward from a man's pipe; so intensely did she feel this that she had, in fact, chosen the image herself—an old man's pipe smoke in the light of the sinking sun. She seemed to herself like someone with great frenzied battles behind him. In a weary tone, she said to her cousin: "I have been through such a great deal; I have changed, I'm afraid."

"In my favor, I hope?"

Diotima shook her head and smiled without looking at him.

"In that case you should know that it's Arnheim who's behind the General, not me!" Ulrich said suddenly. "You've been putting all the blame for bringing in the General on me, all along. But don't you remember what I told you the first time you called me on the carpet about it?"

Diotima remembered. "Keep him away," her cousin had said. But Arnheim had told her to make the General feel welcome. She felt something she could not put into words, as if she were sitting inside a cloud that was quickly rising above her eyes. But the next instant the settee again felt hard and solid under her body, and she said: "I don't know how this General came to us in the first place. I never invited him. And Dr. Arnheim, whom I asked about it, naturally knows nothing about it either. Something must have gone wrong."

Her cousin was not very helpful. "I knew the General years ago, but this is the first time I've seen him in ages," he said. "Of course, he's probably spying here a little for the War Office, but he's sincere about wanting to help you, too. And I have it from his own lips that Arnheim makes quite a point of being attentive to him."

"Because Arnheim takes an interest in everything!" Diotima retorted. "He advised me not to rebuff the General, because he believes in the man's good faith and because he may be useful to us, in his influential position."

Ulrich vehemently shook his head. "Just listen to all the cackling going on around him!" he burst out so sharply that guests nearby turned their heads, to his hostess's embarrassment. "He can take it—

he's rich! He has money, he agrees with every one of them, and he knows that they're all acting as his unpaid press agents."

"Why should he bother?" Diotima asked critically.

"Because of his vanity. He's a monster of vanity. How can I make you see the full extent of it? I mean vanity in the biblical sense: all cymbals and sounding brass to hide a vacuum. A man is vain when he prides himself on having seen the moon rise over Asia on his left while on his right Europe fades away in the sunset—this is how he once described to me his crossing of the Sea of Marmara. The moon probably rises far more beautifully behind the flowerpot on the windowsill of a lovesick young girl than it does over Asia."

Diotima was thinking about where they might go to talk without being overheard. "You find his popularity irritating," she said in a low voice as she led him away through the various rooms, all filled with guests, until she had deftly maneuvered him into the foyer. Here she resumed the conversation with: "Why are you so set against him? You make it so hard for me."

"I make it hard for you?" Ulrich asked with raised eyebrows.

"How can I talk freely with you about everything, as long as you persist in this attitude?" They had come to a stop in the middle of the foyer.

"Please feel free to tell me anything, whatever it is," he said warmly. "You two are in love, I know that much. Will he marry you?"

"He has asked me," Diotima replied without regard to their exposed position as they stood there. She was overcome by her feelings and took no offense at her cousin's bluntness.

"And what about you?" he asked.

She blushed like a schoolgirl. "Oh, for me it's a heavy responsibility," she said hesitantly. "I can't let myself be rushed into doing something unfair. And where the really great things in life are concerned, it doesn't matter so much what one does."

Ulrich was mystified by these words, since he knew nothing of the long nights in which Diotima had learned to overcome the voice of passion and attained that serene evenhandedness of the soul where love floats in the horizontal position of a seesaw equally weighted at both ends. But he sensed that for the moment it would be best to abandon the direct line of straight talk, and took a diplomatic turn:

"I'd be glad to tell you about my attitude to Arnheim, because in the circumstances I shouldn't want you to feel that I'm against him in any way. I think I understand Arnheim quite well. You must realize that whatever is happening in your house—let's call it a kind of synthesis—it is something he has already experienced many times before. Wherever you have intellectual ferment taking the form of convictions, it also appears almost immediately in the form of the opposing convictions. And where it is embodied in a so-called leading intellectual personality, then the moment that personality is not freely saluted on all sides, it feels as insecure as if it were in a cardboard box tossed into the water. We have a tendency in this country to fall in love with noted personalities, like the drunks who throw their arms around a stranger's neck, only to push him away again after a while, for equally obscure reasons. So I have a vivid idea of what Arnheim must be feeling—a form of seasickness, I'd say. And when he remembers in such circumstances what money can do if you know how to use it, he feels firm ground under his feet for the first time after a long sea voyage. He is bound to notice how each suggestion, proposal, wish, service, accomplishment, struggles to enter the orbit of wealth, which is in that sense an image of the mind itself. Ideas striving for power tend to attach themselves to ideas that already have power. I hardly know how to put it to you; the difference between ideas that aim high and those that are merely ambitious is hard to pin down. But once the genuinely great, with its usual material poverty and purity of spirit, is displaced by the mere label of greatness, all sorts of spurious candidates for the label push their way in—quite understandably—and then you also get the kind of greatness that can be conferred by publicity and business acumen. And there you have your Arnheim in all his innocence and guilt."

"You're being very holy all of a sudden," Diotima said acidly.

"You're right, it's none of my business, but that way he has of accepting the mixed effects of inward and outward greatness and trying to make it all look like a model of humanitarianism could in fact exasperate me to a frantic degree of holiness."

"Oh, you are so wrong!" Diotima broke in. "You see him only as a blasé rich man. But Arnheim sees wealth as an absolutely all-pervasive responsibility. He devotes himself to his business as another man might give himself over to a human being entrusted to his care. He deeply needs to make a real difference in the world. If he makes himself available to people, it is because, as he says, a man must keep moving if he wants to be moved. Or was it Goethe who said that? He once explained it to me at length. His point is that to do good, you must, to begin with, *do something*. Of course, I admit that I have also been known to feel that he sometimes mixes too freely with all sorts of people."

As they talked, they were walking back and forth in the empty foyer, with its mirrors and all the coats on the racks. Now Diotima stopped and put her hand on her cousin's arm, saying:

"This man, so highly favored by fate in every way, has the modest notion that a man alone is no stronger than a sick person left on his own. Don't you agree with him there? To be alone is to fall prey to a thousand fantasies." She dropped her eyes as though she were searching the floor for something, even as she felt her cousin's eyes on her lowered eyelids.

"Oh, I suppose I might be talking about myself. I have been so lonely of late. But so are you! I can tell. You have an embittered look; you're not at all happy, are you? Everything you say shows that you're on bad terms with everything in your own life. You're jealous by nature, and you have a chip on your shoulder, you're against everything. I don't mind telling you that Arnheim has complained to me that you refuse to be friends with him."

"Has he actually told you that he wants us to be friends? If so, he's lying!"

Diotima looked up at him and laughed. "There you go again, making a mountain out of a molehill. We both want your friendship. Perhaps we do because you are just as you are. But I'd have to go back a bit to explain: Arnheim came up with such examples as . . ." She hesitated, then thought better of it. "No, that would take us too far afield. In brief, Arnheim says that we have to make use of whatever means our times afford us. The thing is to act on the basis of two different attitudes, never quite revolutionary and never quite antirevolutionary, never quite out of love or out of hate nor out of some particular inclination of our own, but always trying to develop every possibility one has. But that isn't being clever, as you see it; it merely shows a simple, all-embracing character, someone with a gift for bringing disparate things together by seeing through their superficial differences—the personality of a born leader!"

"And what has that to do with me?" Ulrich asked.

His challenge had the effect of tearing through her reminiscences of a long conversation about scholasticism, the Church, Goethe and Napoleon, and the whole fog of cultural ambiguities that had thickened around Diotima's head, and she suddenly saw herself clearly, sitting beside her cousin on the long shoe cupboard where, in the heat of argument, she had made him sit down with her; his back was stubbornly avoiding the coats hanging in rows behind them, which had badly mussed her hair. As she patted it in place, she replied:

"But you're his exact opposite! You'd like to re-create the whole world in your own image. You're always opposing everything with that passive resistance of yours, or whatever that horrid expression is." She was delighted to tell him just what she thought, for once. But all this while she kept thinking that they had better not stay where they were, in case other guests started leaving or coming through the foyer for some reason.

"You're always so hypercritical," she went on. "I don't recall you ever having a good word to say about anything, except to praise everything that's intolerable nowadays, out of sheer contrariness. Every time one tries to hold on to a feeling or an intuition in the midst of this desert of our godless age, one can count on your fervent defense of specialization, disorder, all the negative side of life." So saying, she stood up and gave him to understand, with a smile, that they must find a better place to sit. It was either rejoining the others or finding a hiding place where they could go on with their talk. The Tuzzis' bedroom could be entered even from here, through a door covered with wallpaper, but Diotima felt it was too intimate a place to take her cousin, especially as every time the apartment was rearranged for a reception there was no telling how much of a mess the bedroom had been left in. So there was no refuge left but one of the two maids' rooms. The thought that it would be a funny mixture of taking liberties and of her housewifely duty to subject Rachel's room, where she never set foot, to an impromptu inspection decided her. As they went there, and even as she apologized for taking him there, and once they were inside the little room, she intently went on talking to Ulrich:

"I get the feeling that you are always out to undermine Arnheim, every chance you get. Your opposition hurts him. He is an outstanding contemporary, which is why he is and needs to be in touch with present-day realities. While you are always on the point of taking a leap into the impossible. He is all affirmation and perfect balance; you are, frankly, asocial. He strives for unity, intent to his fingertips upon achieving some clear decision; you oppose him with nothing but your formless outlook. He has a feeling for everything that has taken a long time to become what it is; and you? What about you? You act as though the world were about to begin tomorrow. Why don't you answer me? From the very first day, when I told you we had been given a chance to do something truly great, your attitude has been the same. And when I see this chance as a predestined moment that has brought us all together for a purpose, waiting, as it were, with an unspoken question in our eyes, for an answer, you carry on like a brat who wants only to disrupt everything." She was choosing her words with care to gloss over their awkward situation in the maid's room, fortifying her position by giving her cousin the most elaborate scolding.

"If that's how I am, how can I possibly be of any use to you?" Ulrich asked. He had sat down on Rachel's little iron bedstead, an arm's length from Diotima, facing him on the little wicker chair. The answer she gave him was admirable.

"If you ever saw me doing something horrible, something really awful," she said unexpectedly, "I'm sure you'd be an angel about it." She was startled to hear herself say it. She had only meant to point up his love of contradiction by joking that he could be expected to be most kind and considerate when she least deserved it; but a spring had suddenly bubbled up in her unconscious, making her say things that sounded rather silly, and yet it was amazing how they seemed to apply to her and her relationship to this cousin of hers!

Ulrich sensed it. He looked at her without speaking; then, after a pause, he responded with a question: "Are you very much . . . are you madly in love with him?"

Diotima looked at the floor. "What an absurd way to put it! I'm not a schoolgirl with a crush, you know."

But her cousin would not be put off. "I am asking you this for a reason: I am wondering whether you have already come to know that longing that we all have—including even the most detestable creatures among tonight's guests next door—to strip off our clothes, put our arms around each other's shoulders, and sing instead of talking; then you would have to go from one of us to the other and kiss him like a sister on the lips. If this is a bit much, I might let them wear nightshirts."

Diotima answered at random: "What lovely ideas you indulge in."

"But don't you see, I have known what it feels like, myself, though it was a long time ago. And there have been very respectable persons who claimed that this was precisely the way life should be on earth."

"Then it's your own fault if you don't act accordingly," Diotima interrupted. "Besides, there's no need to make it look so ridiculous." She had remembered that her adventure with Arnheim eluded classification and made one long for a life without social differences, where action, soul, mind, and body would all be one.

Ulrich did not answer. He offered his cousin a cigarette. She accepted it. As the cramped little room filled with smoke, Diotima wondered what Rachel would think when she sniffed the evidence of this intrusion. Should they open the window? Or should she explain to the little servant in the morning? Oddly enough, it was precisely the thought of Rachel that decided her to stay; she had been on the point of putting an end to this increasingly awkward tête-à-tête, but the sense of her intellectual superiority and the cigarette smoke that would mystify her maid somehow coalesced into something she was rather enjoying.

Ulrich was watching her. He was surprised at himself for having spoken to her as he did, but he went on with it; he felt a need for companionship. "I'll tell you," he resumed, "under what conditions I might be so seraphic—seraphic is probably not too grand a term for not merely enduring another person but feeling that person if I may put it like this—under his psychological loincloth, without a shudder."

"Unless the other is a woman," Diotima said, in view of her cousin's dubious reputation in the family.

"Not even excepting that."

"You're right. What I call loving the human being in a woman is a great rarity." Diotima felt that Ulrich had been, for some time now, expressing views closer to her own, and yet there was always something amiss and whatever he said never came quite close enough.

"Seriously now," he said stubbornly, leaning forward, his forearm resting on his muscular thighs, his gloomy gaze fixed on the floor. "We still say, nowadays, I love this woman, and I hate this man, instead of saying I find that person attractive or repellent. It would be a step closer to the truth to say that it is I, myself, who arouses in the other the capacity for attracting or repelling me, and even more accurate to say that the other somehow brings out in me the requisite qualities, and so on. We can never know where it begins; the whole thing is a functional interdependence, like the one between two bouncing balls or two electric circuits. We've known all that for a long time now, but we still prefer to regard ourselves as the cause, the primal cause, in the magnetic fields of emotion around us; even when someone admits that he is merely imitating someone else, he makes it sound like an active achievement of his own. And this is why I ask you again whether you have ever been uncontrollably in love, or furious, or desperate. Because it is at such times that you can see clearly, if you are at all perceptive, that in such an overwrought state we behave no differently from a bee on a windowpane or an amoeba in poisoned water: we are caught in a storm of movement, we dash off blindly in every direction at once, we beat our brains out against brick walls, until, by some lucky chance, we find an opening to freedom, which we promptly attribute, as soon as our consciousness has crystallized again, to a calculated plan of action."

"I must say," Diotima objected, "that this is a dismal and demeaning view of emotions that have the power to decide a person's whole life."

"Are you thinking of the boring old argument about whether or not we are masters of our own fate?" Ulrich replied, with a quick glance upward. "If everything is determined by a cause, then no one is responsible for anything, and so on? I must confess that I've never given as much as fifteen minutes of thought to that question in my whole life. It belongs to a period that became obsolete while nobody was looking. It comes from theology, and apart from jurists, who still have a lot of theology and the smell of burning heretics in their nostrils, the only people who still think in terms of causation are those members of your family who are likely to say: 'You are the cause of my sleepless nights' or 'The sudden drop in the price of wheat was the cause of his misfortune.' "

Diotima drew herself up. "Why are you always talking about criminals? Crime seems to hold a special fascination for you. What do you suppose that means?"

"Oh no," her cousin said. "It doesn't mean a thing. A certain degree of excitement, at most. Our ordinary state is an averaging out of all the crimes of which we are capable. But now that the word 'theology' has come up, let me ask you something. . . ."

"Whether I've ever been madly in love or jealous, again?"

"No. Think about this: If God has ordained whatever happens and always knows what will happen, how can a human being commit a sin? It's an old question, but it's still as good as new. What kind of trickster God would it be who sets us up to commit offenses against him, with his own prior knowledge and consent? He doesn't merely know in advance what we are likely to do: there are plenty of examples of such resigned love; oh no, he makes us do wrong! That's the situation in which we find ourselves today, with respect to each other. The self is losing its status as a sovereign making its own laws. We are learning to know the rules by which it develops, the influence of its environment, its structural types, its disappearance in moments of the most intense activity: in short, the laws regulating its formation and its conduct. Think of it, cousin, the laws of personality! It's like talking of a trade union for lonely rattlesnakes or a robbers' chamber of commerce. What with laws being the most impersonal thing in the world, the personality becomes no more than the imaginary meeting point of all that's impersonal, so that it's hard to find for it that honorable standpoint you don't want to relinquish. . . ."

So he spoke, and Diotima took occasion to object: "But, my dear friend, surely one ought to do everything as personally as one can. . . ." Finally, she said: "You really are being very theological today; I've never known that side of your character." Again she sat there like a tired dancer. Such a strong and handsome woman! She somehow felt this herself, in all her bones. She had been avoiding her cousin for weeks, perhaps even months by now. But she rather liked this man of her own age. He looked dashing in evening dress, in the dimly lit room, black and white like a knight templar; there was something of the passion of the Cross in this black and white. She glanced around the modest little bedroom. The Parallel Campaign was far away, she had gone through a great emotional struggle, and here she was in this little room, as plain as duty itself, with only the grace notes of some pussy willows and the unused picture postcards stuck in the frame of the mirror—so it was between these, framed by images of the great city, that the little maid saw her face in the glass! Where did she wash, come to think of it? Ah, in that narrow cupboard, there must be a basin under the lid, Diotima now remembered, and then the thought crossed her mind: "This man wants to and yet he doesn't want to."

She looked at him calmly, with the air of a friendly listener. "Does Arnheim really want to marry me?" she asked herself. He had said so. But then he had not persisted. There was always so much else to talk about. But her cousin too, instead of going on and on in that impersonal fashion, should have asked her: How are you doing, then? Why didn't he ask? She felt that he would understand if she could tell him all about her inner struggles. "Is it a good thing for me?" he had asked her, all too predictably, when she told him how she had changed. The insolence! Diotima smiled.

Both of these men were a bit peculiar, come to think of it. Why did her cousin never have a good word to say for Arnheim? She knew that Arnheim wanted his friendship; but Ulrich too, judging by his own irritable remarks, had Arnheim much on his mind. "And how totally he misunderstands him!" she thought again. There was nothing to be done about it. Besides, at this point it was not only her soul that mutinied against her body, married as it was to Section Chief Tuzzi, but at times her body mutinied against her soul, made to languish, by Arnheim's hesitant and high-strung love, at the rim of a desert where what she saw ahead was perhaps a mirage, only the quivering reflection of her yearning. She would have liked to confide her misery and her helplessness to her cousin. She liked the decisive, one-track mind he usually showed on such occasions. Arnheim's balanced many-sidedness certainly rated higher, but at a moment of decision Ulrich would not waver so much, despite his theorizing, which tended toward an absolute suspension in uncertainty. She sensed this, without knowing why; it was probably part of what she had felt for him from their first encounter. If at this moment Arnheim felt like a huge effort, a royal burden laid upon her soul, too much to bear in every sense, then everything Ulrich was saying tended toward a single effect, that of losing responsibility as one contemplated hundreds of interactions, so that she felt suspiciously free. She suddenly needed to make herself heavier than she was; she couldn't say how, but was immediately reminded of an incident when, as a young girl, she had carried a little boy away from some danger, and how he had kept hitting her in the belly with his knees to make her let him go. The force of this memory—which had occurred to her as unexpectedly as if it had suddenly come down the chimney into this lonely little room—quite threw her off balance. "Madly in love?" she thought. Why did he keep asking her that? As if she were incapable of really letting herself go. Her mind had wandered from what he was saying, so, without any idea whether it would be apropos or not, she simply interrupted him and told him once and for all, without regard to anything he might have been saying, with a laugh (unless her sense of laughing as she spoke was not quite reliable in the sudden, heedless excitement of it): "But I *am* madly in love!"

Ulrich openly smiled at this. "You're quite incapable of it," he said.

She had stood up, her hands on her hair, staring at him in amazement.

"In order to lose control," he specified calmly, "one has to be quite precise and objective. Two selves, aware of how dubious a thing it is these days to be a self, cling to each other—or so I imagine, if it's love at any price and not merely the usual kind of thing and they become so enmeshed with each other that the one feels like the cause for the other one's existence, as they feel themselves changing into greatness and begin to float like a veil. It is incredibly hard, in such a state, to make no false moves, even though one has been making all the right moves for some time. It is simply very hard to feel the right thing in this world! Quite contrary to the general preconception, it almost calls for a certain pedantry. Incidentally, that's just what I wanted to say to you. You flatter me, you know, when you say I could be expected to behave like an angel. A human being would have to be wholly objective—which is almost the same as being impersonal, after all—to be wholly a personification of love. This means being all feeling and sensibility and thought. Now, all the elements that make up a human being are tender, since they yearn toward each other;

only the human being itself is not. So being madly in love is something you might not even want for yourself. . . ."

He had done his best to speak as casually as possible; he even lit another cigarette to keep his face from looking too solemn as he spoke, and Diotima also accepted another from him to hide her embarrassment. She made a comically defiant face and blew the smoke high into the air, to show her independence, because she hadn't quite understood what he was talking about. But their situation as a whole was having a strong effect on her: that her cousin was suddenly saying all these things to her, in this room where they were alone together, without making the slightest move to take her hand or touch her hair, a move so natural in the circumstances, even though they were feeling the magnetic attraction their two bodies exerted on each other in this confined space. What if they . . . , she wondered. But what could one do in this maid's room? She looked around. Act like a whore? But how does one do that? Suppose she started blubbering? Blubbering: that was a schoolgirl expression that had suddenly come back to her. Suppose she suddenly did what he had talked about before, took off her clothes, put her arm around his shoulder, and sang . . . sang what? Played the harp? She looked at him, smiling. It was like being with a wayward brother, in whose company one could do anything that came into one's head. Ulrich was smiling too. But his smile was like a blind window, because now that he had indulged himself in this sort of talk with Diotima he merely felt ashamed of himself. Still, she had an intimation of the possibility of loving this man; it would be something like her idea of modern music, that is, quite unsatisfying and yet full of something excitingly different.

And even though she took it for granted that she was more aware of all this than he was, the thought of it as she stood there facing him sent a hidden glow up her legs, which made her say rather abruptly to her cousin, with the face of a woman who feels the conversation has been running on too long: "My dear, we're really being quite impossible. Do stay here a bit longer while I go ahead and show myself to our guests again."

102

LOVE AND WAR AMONG THE FISCHELS

Gerda waited in vain for Ulrich's visit. He had, in fact, forgotten his promise to see her, or remembered it only when he had other things to do.

"Forget about him," Clementine said, whenever Director Fischel grumbled about it. "We used to be good enough for him, but he's probably setting his social sights higher these days. If you go after him you'll only make matters worse; you're much too clumsy to carry it off."

Gerda missed this older friend. She wished he would come and knew that if he did come, she would wish him away. For all her twenty-three years, nothing had yet happened in her life other than the cautious wooing of a certain Herr Glanz, who had her father on his side, and her Christian-Germanic friends, whom she sometimes regarded as schoolboys rather than real men. "Why doesn't he ever come to see me?" she wondered, whenever she thought of Ulrich. Among her friends, the Parallel Campaign was seen as beyond any doubt the opening salvo in the spiritual destruction of the German people, and she felt embarrassed by Ulrich's involvement in it; she longed to hear his side of it, however, hoping that he would be able to exonerate himself.

Her mother said to her father: "You missed your chance to be in this affair. It would have been a good thing for Gerda, and she'd have had something else to think about; a lot of people go to the Tuzzis'." It had come to light that he had neglected to respond to His Grace's invitation. Now he had to suffer for it.

The young men whom Gerda called her spiritual comrades in arms had settled down in his house like Penelope's suitors, debating what a young man of German blood should do about the Parallel Campaign.

"A financier must be able, at times, to act in the spirit of a Maecenas," Frau Clementine exhorted her husband when he fumed that he had not hired Hans Sepp, Gerda's "spiritual guide," as a tutor, for good money, only to have *this* situation come of it.

Hans Sepp, the graduate student, who had not the slightest prospect of being able to keep a wife, had come into the household as a tutor but, owing to the conflicts that were tearing the family apart, had become its tyrant. Now he was discussing with his friends, who had become Gerda's friends, at the Fischels', how to save the German aristocracy from being ensnared by Diotima—of whom it was said that she made no distinction between persons of her own race and those of an alien race—and caught up in the nets of the Jewish spirit. While in the presence of Leo Fischel this sort of talk was usually tempered with a certain philosophic objectivity, he still heard enough of certain terms and principles for it to get on his nerves. They worried that such a campaign, which was bound to lead to total catastrophe, should have surfaced in an era not destined to bring forth great symbols, and the recurrent expressions "deeply meaningful," "upward humanization," and "free personhood" were enough by themselves to make the pince-nez quiver on Fischel's nose every time he heard them. He had to stand by while there proliferated in his own house such concepts as "the art of living thought," "the graph of spiritual growth," and "action on the wing." He discovered that a biweekly "hour of purification" was held regularly under his roof. He demanded an explanation. It turned out that what they meant by this was reading the poems of Stefan George together. Leo Fischel searched his old encyclopedia in vain for the poet's name. But what irritated him most of all, old-style liberal that he was, was that these green pups referred to all the high government officials, bank presidents, and leading university figures in the Parallel Campaign as "puffed-up little men"; then there were the world-weary airs they gave themselves, complaining that the times had become devoid of great ideas, if there was anyone left who was ready for great ideas; that even "humanity" had become a mere buzzword, as far as they were concerned, and that only "the nation" or, as they called it, "folk and folkways" still really had any meaning.

"The word 'humanity' is meaningless to me, Papa," Gerda said, when he tried to reason with her. "The life seems to have gone out of it. But 'my nation'—now, that's a physical reality."

"*Your* nation!" Leo Fischel began, meaning to say something

about the biblical prophets and his own father, who had been a lawyer in Trieste.

"I know," Gerda interrupted, "but my nation in a spiritual sense is
what I am talking about."

"I'm going to lock you up in your room till you come to your
senses!" Papa Leo said. "And I won't have those friends of yours in
my house. They're undisciplined characters who spend all their time
brooding over their consciences instead of going to work and making
something of themselves."

"I know, Papa, how your mind works," Gerda replied. "Your generation feels entitled to humiliate us just because you're supporting
us. You're all patriarchal capitalists."

Such debates were no rarity, given a father's tendency to worry.

"And what would you live on, if I were not a capitalist?" the master
of the house wanted to know.

Gerda usually cut short any such ramifications. "I can't be expected to know everything; all I know is that we already have scientists, teachers, religious leaders, political leaders, and other men of
action engaged in creating new values."

At this point Bank Director Fischel might bother to ask ironically:
"And by these religious and political leaders I suppose you mean
yourselves?" but he did it only to have the last word; in the end, he
was always relieved that Gerda didn't notice how resigned he was,
how he had learned to expect that her nonsense would always lead to
his giving in. He was finally driven to conclude such arguments more
than once by cautiously praising the reasonableness of the Parallel
Campaign, in contrast to the rabid countermoves advocated in his
own house; but he did it only when Clementine was out of earshot.

What gave Gerda's resistance to her father's admonitions an air of
stubborn martyrdom, something that even Leo and Clementine
vaguely sensed, was that breath of innocent lust wafting through this
house. The young people discussed among themselves many things
about which the elders kept a resentful silence. Even what they
called their nationalism, this fusion of their constantly warring egos
into an imaginary unity they called their Christian-Germanic commune, had, compared with the festering love life of their elders,
something of the winged Eros about it. Wiser than their years, they
disdained "lust" and "the inflated lie about the crude enjoyment of

animal existence," as they called it, but talked so much about su-
prasensuality and mystical desire that the startled listener reacted
willy-nilly by feeling a certain tenderness for sensuality and physical
desires, and even Leo Fischel had to admit that the unbridled ardor
of their language sometimes made the listener feel the roots of their
ideas shooting down his legs, though he disapproved, because in his
opinion great ideas were meant to be uplifting.

Clementine, for her part, said: "You shouldn't simply turn your
back on everything, Leo."

"How can they say 'Property kills the spirit'?" he started to argue.
"Do I lack spirit? Maybe you do, insofar as you take their nonsense
seriously."

"You don't understand, Leo. They mean it in a Christian sense;
they want to leave the old life behind, to have a higher life on earth."

"That's not Christian, that's just crackbrained," Leo said stubbornly.

"What if it is not the realists who see reality, but those who look
inward?" Clementine suggested.

"That's a laugh!" Fischel claimed. But he was wrong; he was crying
inwardly, overwhelmed by the uncontrollable changes all around
him.

These days Director Fischel felt the need for fresh air more often
than he used to; at the end of the day's work he was in no hurry to get
home, and if there was still some daylight he loved to wander a bit in
one of the parks, even in winter. His liking for these city parks dated
back to his days as a junior assistant. For no reason he could see, the
city administration had ordered the iron folding stools freshly
painted in late autumn; now they stood there, bright green, piled up
against each other along the snowy paths, pricking the imagination
with their springtime color. At times, Leo Fischel would sit down on
one of these chairs, all alone and muffled up to the ears at the edge of
a playground or a promenade, and watch the nursemaids with their
charges, flaunting their winter health in the sun. The children played
with their yo-yos or threw snowballs, and the little girls made big
eyes like grown women—ah, Fischel thought, the very same eyes
that in the face of a beautiful woman delight you with the thought
that she has the eyes of a child! It did him good to watch the little
girls at play—in their eyes love still floated as in a pond in fairyland,

where the stork comes to get it later on—and sometimes to watch their governesses too. He had often enjoyed this spectacle in his youth, when he was still standing *outside* life's shop window, without the money to walk in, and all he could do was wonder what fate might have in store for him. What a sorry mess it had turned out to be, he thought, and for an instant he felt as if he were sitting on the green grass amid white crocuses with all the tension of youth. When his sense of reality recalled him to the sight of snow and green paint, his thoughts oddly enough kept coming back to his income. Money means independence, but all his salary went for the needs of the family and the savings required by common sense, so a man really had to do something more, apart from his job, to make himself independent; possibly turn to account his knowledge of the stock exchange, like the top executives at the bank.

But such thoughts came to Leo only while he was watching the little girls at play, and then he rejected them, because he certainly did not feel that he had the necessary temperament for speculation. He was a head of department, with the honorary title of a director and no prospect of rising above this, so he instantly chastened himself with the thought that so toilworn a back as his own was already too hunched over ever to straighten up again. He did not know that he was using such thoughts solely to erect an insurmountable barrier between himself and the pretty children and their maids, who, at such moments in the park, meant the charms of life to him, for he was, even in the disgruntled mood that kept him from going home, an incorrigible family man who would have given anything if only he could have transformed that Circle of Hell at home into a garland of angels around the father-god, the titular bank director.

Ulrich also liked the parks and walked across them whenever he could on his way somewhere, which was now he happened again to run into Fischel, who at the sight of him immediately recollected all he had already had to suffer at home on account of the Parallel Campaign. He expressed his dissatisfaction at his young friend's taking so lightly the invitations of old friends, a point he could make with all the more sincerity since time passing makes even the most casual friendships grow as old as the closest ones.

Fischel's young old friend said that he was truly delighted to see

Fischel again and deplored the foolishness that was keeping him too busy to have done so before.

Fischel complained that everything was going to the dogs and that business was bad. Anyway, the old moral order was losing its grip, what with all the materialism and the hastiness in which everything had to be done.

"And here I was just thinking that I could envy you!" Ulrich countered. "A businessman's work is surely a veritable refuge of sanity? At least it's the only profession resting on a theoretically sound basis."

"That it is!" Fischel agreed. "The businessman serves the cause of human progress, asking only for a reasonable profit. And yet he is just as badly off as everyone else, when it comes to that," he added gloomily.

Ulrich had agreed to walk him home.

On their arrival, they found a mood already strained to the breaking point.

All Gerda's friends were present, and a tremendous battle of words was in full swing. Most of the young people were still at school or in their first or second term at the university, though a few had jobs in business. How they had come to form this group was something they themselves no longer knew. One by one. Some had met in nationalist student fraternities, others in the socialist or Catholic youth movement, and others out hiking with a horde of *Wandervögel.*

It would not be wholly out of order to suppose that the only thing they all had in common was Leo Fischel. To endure, a spiritual movement needs a physical basis, and this physical basis was Fischel's apartment, together with the refreshments provided by Frau Clementine, along with a certain regulation of the traffic. Gerda went with the apartment, Hans Sepp went with Gerda, and Hans Sepp, the student with the impure complexion and all-the-purer soul, though not their leader, because these young people acknowledged no leader, was the most impassioned of them all. They might meet elsewhere occasionally, where the hostess would be someone other than Gerda, but the nucleus of their movement was basically as described.

Still, the source of these young people's inspiration was as remarkable an enigma as the appearance of a previously unknown disease, or a sequence of winning numbers in a game of chance. When the sun of old-style European idealism began to fade and its white blaze darkened, many torches were passed from hand to hand—ideas, torches of the mind, stolen from Heaven knows where, or invented by whom?—and flaring up here and there, they became that dancing pool of fire a little spiritual community. And so there was much talk, those last few years before the great war carried all of it to its foregone conclusion, among the younger generation, about love and fellowship—and the young anti-Semites who met at Bank Director Fischel's felt themselves to be most particularly under the sign of an all-embracing love and fellowship. True fellowship is the work of an inner law, and the deepest, simplest, most perfect, and foremost of these is the law of love. Love, as already noted, not in its base, sensual form, for physical possession is an invention of Mammon that in the end only disrupts the community and strips it of its meaning. And one can't, of course, love just everybody and anybody. But one can respect the character of every individual, as long as that person truthfully strives to keep growing, with an unremitting inner responsibility. And so they fiercely argued about everything, in the name of love.

But on this particular day a united front had formed against Frau Clementine, who was so pleased at feeling young again, and inwardly agreed that married love really did have something in common with interest paid on capital, but drew the line at tolerating harsh criticism of the Parallel Campaign on the grounds that Aryans could create viable symbols only if they kept alien elements out of it. Clementine was just on the verge of losing her temper, and Gerda's cheeks were aflame with round red spots because her mother would take no hint to leave the room. When Leo Fischel had entered with Ulrich, she was pleading in sign language with Hans Sepp to break it off, and Hans said in a conciliating tone: "These days, no one can create anything great!" supposing that he had thereby reduced everything to the customary impersonal formula acceptable to all those present.

Unluckily, Ulrich joined in at this point and asked Hans—poking a little malicious fun at Fischel—whether he did not believe in any kind of progress at all.

"Progress?" Hans Sepp retorted with a patronizing air. "You need only think of the kind of men we had a hundred years ago, before progress set in: Beethoven! Goethe! Napoleon! Hebbel!"

"Hmm," Ulrich said. "The last-named was only just born a hundred years ago."

"Our young friends dismiss numerical precision," Director Fischel gloated.

Ulrich did not pursue this. He knew that Hans Sepp held him in jealous contempt, yet he felt a certain sympathy for Gerda's peculiar friends. So he sat down among them and went on: "We're undeniably making so much progress in the several branches of human capability that we actually feel we can't keep up with it! Isn't it possible that this can also make us feel that there is no progress? After all, progress is surely the product of all our joint efforts, so we can practically predict that any real progress is likely to be precisely what nobody wanted."

Hans Sepp's dark shock of hair turned into a tremulous horn pointed at Ulrich. "There, now you've said it yourself: what nobody wanted! A lot of cackling back and forth, a hundred ways, but no way to go! Ideas, of course, but no soul! And no character! The sentence leaps off the page, the word leaps from the sentence, the whole is no longer a whole, as Nietzsche has already said. Never mind that Nietzsche's egomania is another minus value for existence! Can you tell me one single, solid, ultimate value from which you, for instance, take your bearings in life?"

"Just like that—on demand!" Fischel protested, but Ulrich asked Hans: "Is it really utterly impossible for you to live without some ultimate value?"

"Utterly," said Hans, "but I admit that I am bound to be unhappy as a result."

"The hell you say!" Ulrich laughed. "Everything we can do depends on our not being overly perfectionist, not waiting for the ultimate inspiration. That's what the Middle Ages did, and ignorant they stayed."

"Did they, now?" Hans Sepp retorted. "I'd say that we're the ignorant ones."

"But you must admit that our ignorance is manifestly of a very rich and varied sort?"

A drawling voice was heard muttering at the back: "Variety . . .

knowledge . . . relative progress! All concepts from the mechanistic outlook of an era corrupted by capitalism. There's hardly more to be said. . . ."

Leo Fischel was also muttering to himself; something to the effect that in his opinion Ulrich was being far too indulgent with these juvenile misfits. He took cover behind the newspaper he unfolded.

But Ulrich was enjoying himself. "Is the modern house, with its six rooms, maid's bath, vacuum cleaner, and all that, progress, compared with the old houses with their high ceilings, thick walls, and handsome archways, or not?"

"No!" Hans Sepp shouted.

"Is the airplane progress, compared with the mail coach?"

"Yes!" Director Fischel shouted.

"The machine compared with handicrafts?"

"Handicrafts!" from Hans, and "Machine!" from Leo.

"It seems to me," Ulrich said, "that every step forward is also a step backward. Progress always exists in only one particular sense. And since there's no sense in our life as a whole, neither is there such a thing as progress as a whole."

Leo Fischel lowered his paper. "Would you say that it's better to be able to cross the Atlantic in six days rather than having to spend six weeks on it?"

"I'd be inclined to say that it's definitely progress to have the choice. But our young Christians wouldn't agree to that, either."

The circle of friends sat still, taut as a drawn bow. Ulrich had paralyzed their tongues but not their fighting spirit. He went on evenly: "But you can also say the opposite: If our life makes progress in the particular instance, it also makes sense in the particular instance. But once it has made sense to offer up human sacrifice to the gods, say, or burn witches, or wear powdered wigs, then that remains one of life's valid possibilities, even when more hygienic habits and more humane customs represent progress. The trouble is that progress always wants to do away with the old meaning."

"Do you mean to say," Fischel asked, "that we should go back to human sacrifice after we have succeeded in putting such abominable acts of darkness behind us?"

"Is it darkness, necessarily?" Hans Sepp replied in Ulrich's place. "When you devour an innocent rabbit, that's darkness, but when a cannibal dines reverently and with religious rites on a stranger, we simply cannot know what goes on inside him."

"There certainly must have been something to be said for the ages we have left behind," Ulrich agreed, "otherwise so many nice people would never have gone along with them. I wonder if we could turn that to account for ourselves, without sacrificing too much? And perhaps we are still sacrificing so many human beings today only because we never clearly faced the problem of the right way to overcome mankind's earlier answers. The way in which everything hangs together is extremely obscure and hard to express."

"But to your way of thinking, the ideal aim must always be some sort of bottom line or balanced books, right?" Hans Sepp burst out, against Ulrich this time. "You believe in bourgeois progress every bit as much as Director Fischel, you just manage to express it in the most twisted and perverted words you can find, so that you can't be pinned down." Hans had been the spokesman for his friends. Ulrich turned to look at Gerda's face. He intended to pick up casually where he had left off, ignoring the fact that Fischel and the young men were as ready to pounce on him as on each other.

"But aren't you striving toward some goal yourself, Hans?" he asked doggedly.

"*Something* is striving. Inside me. Through me," Hans rapped out.

"And is it going to get there?" Leo Fischel indulged himself in sarcasm, thereby, as all but himself realized, going over to Ulrich's side.

"I wouldn't know," Hans answered gloomily.

"You should take your exams—that would be progress." Fischel could not refrain from piling it on, so irritated was he, no less by his friend than by these callow youths.

At this moment the room seemed to explode. Frau Clementine cast an imploring look at her husband; Gerda tried to forestall Hans as he struggled for words, which finally came bursting out as yet another attack on Ulrich.

"You may be sure," he shouted, "that basically even you don't have a single idea that Director Fischel couldn't come up with just as well!"

With this parting shot he rushed out of the room, followed by his cohorts, making their bows in angry haste. Director Fischel, bludgeoned by the looks he was getting from his wife, pretended to remember his duties as a host and trudged grumpily into the foyer to speed his guests on their way. Clementine heaved a sigh of relief, now that the air was cleared, then she rose too, and Ulrich suddenly found himself alone with Gerda.

103

THE TEMPTATION

Gerda was visibly upset when they were left alone together. He took her hand; her arm started trembling, and she broke away from him.

"You have no idea what it means to Hans to have a goal," she said. "You make fun of all that; that's cheap enough. It seems to me your mind is more disgusting than ever!" She had been groping for the harshest possible word and was startled by what she had come up with. Ulrich tried to catch hold of her hand again; she pulled her arm close to her side. "That's no longer good enough for us!" She hurled her words with a fierce disdain, but her body swayed toward him.

"I know," Ulrich said sarcastically. "Everything you people do must meet the highest standards. That's exactly what makes me behave the way you've just described so amiably. You probably wouldn't believe how much it meant to me to talk to you quite differently back in the old days."

"You were never any different!" Gerda answered quickly.

"I've always been undecided," Ulrich said simply, searching her face. "Would you be interested in hearing about what's going on at my cousin's?"

Something now flickered in Gerda's eyes that was clearly distinct from her uneasiness at Ulrich's proximity: she was burning to find out all she could on that subject, for Hans's sake, and was trying to hide her eagerness. Ulrich perceived this with a certain satisfaction, and like an animal scenting danger, he instinctively changed course and began to talk of something else.

"Do you still remember my story about the moon?" he asked. "First I'd like to tell you something else like that."

"More of your lies, I'm sure!" she snapped.

"Not if I can possibly help it. . . . You must remember, from the lectures you've attended, how people go about deciding whether something is a law or not? Either you start out with reasons for believing that it is a law, as in physics or chemistry, and even though your observations never quite add up to the precise results you're looking for, they come fairly close in some definite pattern, and you work it out from there. Or else, as happens so often in life, you have no such reasons and find yourself facing a phenomenon about which you can't quite tell whether it is a law or pure chance; that's where things acquire a human interest. Then you translate a series of observations into a series of figures, which you divide into ca⸱ ⸱gories to see which numbers lie between this value and that, and the next, and so on; you arrange them in series where the frequency with which something happens shows or doesn't show a systematic increase or decrease, and you get either a stable series or a distributive function. You then calculate the degree of aberration, the mean deviation, the degree of deviation from some arbitrary value, the central value, the normal value, the average value, the dispersion, and so forth, and with the help of all these concepts you study your given phenomenon."

Ulrich laid all this out in so casual a tone that it would have been hard to tell whether he was only just working it out in his own mind or hypnotizing Gerda with a display of science for the fun of it. Gerda had moved away from him, leaning forward in an armchair with a furrow of concentration between her eyebrows as she looked down at the floor. To be spoken to in this matter-of-fact tone, an appeal to her intellect, put a damper on her rebelliousness, which she now felt fading away, together with the self-assurance it had given her. Her schooling had taken her through a few semesters at the university, skimming a vast body of new knowledge that could no longer be contained in the old framework of classic and humanistic studies. Such an education leaves many young people feeling powerless in facing a new time, a new world where the soil can no longer be worked with the old tools. She had no idea where Ulrich's line of reasoning was taking her. She believed him because she was in love with him, and doubted him because she was ten years younger than he and belonged to a new generation keenly aware of its fresh energies; the two conflicting strands of feeling mingled hazily within her as she listened.

"Besides which, you see, we have data that are indistinguishable from those that demonstrate a natural law, yet they have no such basis. Statistical series can sometimes have the same regularity that we associate with natural law. I'm sure you can think of examples you've heard in some sociology lecture, like the statistics about divorce in America, let's say. Or the ratio between male and female births, one of the most stable factors of the kind. Or the number of conscripts annually who try to evade their military service by some form of self-mutilation, also a relative constant, or the suicide statistics; even theft, rape, and bankruptcy occur, as far as I know, at more or less the same annual rate. . . ."

At this point Gerda's resistance tried to break through. "Are you trying to explain progress to me?" she cried out, doing her best to sound sarcastic.

"But of course," Ulrich came back at her, without breaking stride. "It's called the law of large numbers, a bit nebulously. Meaning that one person may commit suicide for this reason and another for that reason, but when a great number is involved, then the accidental and the personal elements cancel each other out, and what's left . . . but that's just it: what *is* left? I ask you. Because you see, what's left is what each one of us as laymen calls, simply, the average, which is a "something," but nobody really knows exactly *what*. Let me add that efforts have been made to find a logical and formal explanation for this law of large numbers, as an accepted fact, as it were. But there are also those who say that such regularity of phenomena which are not casually related to each other cannot be explained at all by conventional logic, and the point has been made, among others, that such phenomena must be analyzed not as individual instances but as involving some unknown laws of aggregates or collectives. I don't want to bother you with the details, which I no longer have at my fingertips anyway, but I would certainly love to know, for myself, whether there are such laws of the collective phenomenon, or whether it is simply by some irony of nature that the particular instance arises from the happening of nothing in particular, and that the ultimate meaning turns out to be something arrived at by taking the average of what is basically meaningless. It would certainly make a radical difference to our sense of ourselves if we knew the answer, one way or another! Whichever it turns out to be, any possibility of leading an ordered life depends on this law of large numbers. If there were no such law of averages, we might have a year with nothing at all happening, followed by one in which you could count on nothing for certain, famine alternating with oversupply, no births followed by too many, and we would all be fluttering to and fro between our heavenly and our hellish possibilities like little birds when someone suddenly comes up to their cage."

"Is all this true?" Gerda asked hesitantly.

"You ought to know it yourself."

"Of course I do, as far as the details go! But what I don't know is whether this is what you meant before, when they were all arguing. What you were saying about progress simply sounded like a deliberate provocation."

"That's what you always think about me. But what do we really know about the nature of our progress? Not a thing. There are all sorts of possibilities for the way things might turn out, and I simply mentioned just one more."

"How things *might* turn out! That's always the way with you; it would never occur to you to wonder how things *should* be."

"You and your friends—always jumping the gun. There's always got to be a supreme goal, an ideal, a program—an absolute. Yet in the end, all that ever comes of it is a compromise, some common denominator. Isn't it tiring and ridiculous to be always reaching for the heights and always ending up settling for some mediocre result?"

It was essentially the same conversation he had had with Diotima, with only superficial differences. Nor did it make much difference which woman happened to be sitting there facing him; a body, introduced into a given magnetic field, invariably sets certain processes in motion. Ulrich studied Gerda, who was not answering his last question. There she sat, a skinny girl, with a little furrow of resentment between her eyes. Another hollow, vertical furrow could be seen in the V of her low-cut blouse. Her arms and legs were long and delicate. She suggested a limp springtime, aglow with a premature summer heat, together with the full impact of the willfulness locked in so young a body. He felt a strange mixture of aversion and detachment at the thought that he was closer to a decision than he had realized and that this young girl was destined to play a part in it. Willy-nilly he suddenly found himself telling her his impressions of the so-called younger generation in the Parallel Campaign, ending with words that took Gerda by surprise:

"These younger people are also very radical, and I'm not popular with them either. But I pay them back in the same coin, because I, too, am radical in my own way, and I can put up with any kind of disorder more easily than the intellectual kind. I like to see ideas not only developed but brought together. I want not only the oscillation but also the density of an idea. This is what you, my indispensable friend, criticize as my tendency to describe only what might be, instead of what ought to be. Well, I do know the difference. This is probably the most anachronistic attitude one can have nowadays, when intellectual rigor and the emotional life are at the farthest remove from each other, but our precision in technology has unfortunately advanced to such a point that it seems to regard the imprecision of life as its proper complement. Why won't you understand? The chances are you're incapable of understanding me, and it's perverse of me to try to confuse a mind so well attuned to the times. Still, Gerda, I sometimes honestly wonder whether I might be wrong, after all. Possibly the very people I can't stand are carrying out what I once hoped to accomplish myself. They may be doing it all wrong, not using their heads, one running this way and the other that way, each spouting an idea that he regards as the only possible idea in the world; each one of them feels tremendously clever, and they all agree in regarding our times as cursed with sterility. But suppose it's the other way around, and every one of them is stupid, but all of them together are pregnant with the future? Every one of our truths seems to be born split into two opposing falsehoods, and this, too, can be a way of arriving at a result that transcends the merely personal. In that case the final balance, the sum total of all the experiments, no longer rests with the individual, who becomes unbearably one-sided, but with the experimental collective. In short, I ask you to make allowances for an old man whose loneliness sometimes drives him to excess."

"You've certainly given me a lot to think about," Gerda said grimly. "Why don't you write a book? That way, you might be able to help yourself and us, too."

"Why on earth should I feel called upon to write a book?" Ulrich objected. "I was born of my mother, after all, not an inkwell."

Gerda was wondering whether a book by Ulrich would really help anyone. Like all the young people in her circle, she overrated the power of the printed word. A total silence had fallen in the apartment since they had stopped talking, as if the elder Fischels had left the house in the wake of their indignant guests. And Gerda sensed the force emanating from the more powerful male body beside her, as she always did, contrary to all her resolutions, when they were alone together; the effort to resist made her tremble. Ulrich noticed it; he stood up, laid his hand on Gerda's frail shoulder, and said to her: "Look at it this way, Gerda. Suppose the moral sphere works more or less like the physical, as suggested by the kinetic theory of gases: everything whirling around at random, each element doing what it will, but as soon as you work out rationally what is least likely to result from all this, that's precisely the result you get! Such correspondences, strange as they are, do exist. So suppose we also assume that there is a certain number of ideas circulating in our day, resulting in some average value that keeps shifting, very slowly and automatically—it's what we call progress, or the historical situation. What matters most about this, however, is that our personal, individual share in all this makes no difference; whether we individually move to the right or to the left, whether we think and act on a high or a low level, in an unpredictable or a calculated fashion, a new or an old style, does not affect this average term, which is all that God and the world care about."

As he spoke he tried to put his arm around her, though it was palpably costing him an effort.

Gerda was furious. "You always begin by philosophizing," she cried out, "and it always turns into the usual rooster's cock-a-doodle-doo!" Her face was aflame, with flecks of color in it. Her lips seemed to be sweating, but there was something attractive about her indignation. "What you make of it is precisely what *we* don't want!"

Now Ulrich could not resist the temptation to ask her, in a low voice: "Is possession so deadly?"

"I don't want to talk about that," Gerda retorted in an equally low tone.

"It's all the same, whether it's a person you own or a thing, I know that," Ulrich went on. "Gerda, I understand you and Hans better than you think. So what is it that you and Hans want? Tell me."

"Nothing! That's just it," Gerda exclaimed triumphantly. "There's no way to state it. Papa also keeps on saying: 'You must make clear to yourself what it is you actually want. Then you will see what nonsense it is.' Well, everything is nonsense when you make it clear to yourself. To be sensible is never to get beyond the commonplace. I know you'll have something to say about that, you and your sensible way of thinking."

Ulrich shook his head. "And what about this demonstration against Count Leinsdorf?" he asked gently, as though he were not changing the subject.

"Oh, so you spy on us!" Gerda exclaimed.

"Call it spying if you like, I don't mind; but tell me about it, Gerda."

Gerda showed some embarrassment. "Nothing special. Just some sort of demonstration by the Young Germans—marching past his residence, yelling 'Shame!' and things like that. The Parallel Campaign is a shame!"

"In what way?"

Gerda shrugged.

"Do sit down again," Ulrich pleaded. "You're making far too much of it. Let's have a quiet talk about it, shall we?"

Gerda obeyed.

"Now listen to me, and tell me if you think I'm on the right track. You say that possession kills. You're thinking of money, to begin with, and of your parents. I agree that they're dead souls. . . ."

Gerda looked offended.

"Very well, let's not talk about money but of 'having' in other ways. Take the man who 'has' himself in hand; the man who 'has' his convictions; the man who lets himself be 'had' by another person or by his own passions or merely his own habits or successes; the man who wants to conquer something, the man who wants anything at all: you reject all that? You want to be nomads, nomads forever on the move, as Hans once called it, if I remember. Moving on toward some other meaning, or state of being? Am I right so far?"

"All you're saying is quite right, in an awful sort of way; the intelligence doing a good imitation of the soul."

"And intelligence is implicated in all that 'having', isn't it? The intelligence is what measures, weighs, classifies, and collects everything, like an old banker. But what about all the things I talked with you about today that have quite a lot to do with our souls?"

"A cold kind of soul."

"You're absolutely right, Gerda. Now all I have to do is to tell you why I'm taking the part of the cold souls or even the bankers."

"Because you're a coward." Ulrich noticed that as she spoke she bared her teeth like a terrified little animal.

"So be it," he replied. "But surely you believe me capable, if nothing else, of being man enough to escape by, if necessary, climbing a lightning rod or down the tiniest foothold on a wall, if I were not so sure that every attempt at breaking out only leads back to Papa."

Gerda had refused to enter into this conversation with Ulrich ever since their last talk on a similar subject. The feelings he was talking about were hers and Hans's alone, and she dreaded, even more than Ulrich's sarcasm, his coming over to her side, which merely left her at his mercy before she could tell whether he meant what he said or was just acting the Devil quoting scripture. From the moment, earlier on, when she had been taken by surprise at the sadness in his words—she was now enduring the consequences of having so briefly let down her guard—she had been visibly engaged in a violent inner struggle. But Ulrich was in a similar fix himself. He was far from taking a perverse pleasure in his power over the girl; he simply did not take Gerda seriously, and since this involved a certain element of dislike, he generally expressed himself freely to her, without regard for her feelings. But for some time now, the more zestfully he took the world's part against her, the more he felt curiously inclined to confide in her, to let her see him as he really was, without deceit or making himself look good, and wanting to see her true inner self as naked as a garden slug. He now looked at her thoughtfully and said: "I feel like letting my eyes rest between your cheeks like clouds in the sky. I don't really know how clouds feel in the sky, but then, I know as much as anybody about those moments when God seizes us like a glove and slowly turns us inside out on his fingers. You and your friends make it too easy for yourselves. You sense the negative side of the world we all live in, and you loudly proclaim that the positive world belongs to your parents and elders, and the world of the shadowy negative to you, the new generation. I don't exactly relish playing the spy for your parents, my dear Gerda, but I put it to you that in choosing between the banker and an angel, the more realistic character of the banker's profession counts for something too."

"Would you like some tea?" Gerda said sharply. "What can I do to make you comfortable here? I want you to see me at my best as the perfect daughter of the house." She had pulled herself together again.

"Then suppose you marry Hans?"

"But I don't want to marry him!"

"You must have some plan or other—you can't go on living forever on your opposition to your parents."

"One of these days I shall leave home, make myself independent, and he and I will remain friends."

"Please, Gerda, let's suppose that you and Hans will be married or something like it; it can hardly be avoided if things keep going the way they are. And now try to imagine yourself brushing your teeth in the morning, and Hans making out the income tax return, in an otherworldly state of mind."

"Do I have to know that?"

"Your Papa would say so, if he had any notion of otherworldly states of mind; most people on life's voyage, I'm sorry to say, know very well how to stow their uncommon experiences so deep in the hold of their ship that they never perceive them at all. But let me ask a simpler question: Will you be expecting Hans to be faithful to you? Marital fidelity is part and parcel of the ownership complex, you know. You would have to accept Hans's finding inspiration in another woman. Indeed, according to your principles, you would have to see it as an enrichment of your own life."

"Don't suppose for a minute that we never discuss these questions ourselves," Gerda replied. "You can't become a new human being overnight; but it is very bourgeois to consider this an argument against making the effort."

"What your father wants is actually something quite different from what you think. He doesn't even claim to know more about all that than you and Hans; he merely says that he can't understand what you're up to. But he does know that power is a very sensible thing. He believes there's more sense in it than in you and him and Hans all rolled into one. What if he were to offer Hans enough money to let him finish his course and get his degree, without having to worry? And if he promised him, after a fair trial period, not that the marriage would take place, but at least that he would not stand in its way on principle? On only one condition: namely, that until the end of the trial period you two stop seeing each other, or keeping in touch, even to the extent you do now?"

"So this is what you're lending yourself to, is it?"

"I merely want to help you understand your father. He is a sinister deity who wields uncanny powers. He thinks he can make Hans see things his way by using money. In his opinion, a Hans with a limited monthly income couldn't possibly go on exceeding every limit of foolishness. But your father may be a dreamer, in his own way. I admire him, just as I admire compromises, averages, dry facts, dead numbers. I don't believe in the Devil, but if I did I should think of him as the trainer who drives Heaven to break its own records. Anyway, I promised him to keep at you until there was nothing left of your fantasies—only reality."

Ulrich was far from saying all this with a clear conscience. Gerda stood facing him as if in flames, the anger in her eyes overlaid with tears. All at once, a way had been opened up for her and Hans. But had Ulrich betrayed her, or did he want to help them? She had no idea, but whichever it was, it was likely to make her as unhappy as it made her happy. In her confusion she mistrusted him, and yet she felt with a passion that there was a sacred bond between them, if only he would admit it.

He now added: "Your father of course harbors a secret hope that I may use the opportunity to win you for myself and change your mind altogether."

"That's out of the question!" Gerda forced herself to say.

"As far as you and I are concerned, I suppose that is out of the question," Ulrich said gently. "But we can't go on like this, either. I've already gone too far." He tried to smile, but felt extreme self-loathing as he did so. He really wanted none of this. He sensed the irresolution in her and despised himself for the cruelty it aroused in him.

At that very instant Gerda stared at him with horrified eyes. Suddenly she was beautiful, like a fire one has approached too closely; almost without form, only a warmth that paralyzes the will.

"You must come to see me," he suggested. "We can't speak freely here." Male ruthlessness shone out of his eyes in a blaze of empty light.

"No," Gerda said defensively. But she averted her eyes, and Ulrich sadly saw—as though by turning away she had again presented herself to his scrutiny—the body of this young girl, neither beautiful nor ugly, breathing hard. He gave a deep and wholly sincere sigh.

104

RACHEL AND SOLIMAN ON THE WARPATH

In the Tuzzi household, charged as it was with a high mission as a gathering place of ideas, there was a light-footed, quick, ardent, un-German creature in service. The little lady's maid, Rachel, was like a chambermaid in Mozart. She opened the front door and stood ready with arms half outstretched to receive the visitor's overcoat. At such times Ulrich sometimes wondered whether she had any idea of his connection with the Tuzzis and tried to catch her eye, but Rachel either turned her eyes away or let them meet his blankly, like two blind little patches of black velvet. He seemed to remember her eyes meeting his with quite a different expression at their first encounter, and several times noticed another pair of eyes, like two big white snails, aiming at Rachel from a dark corner of the entrance hall, Soliman's eyes, but whether this boy might be the reason for Rachel's reserve was an open question, because Rachel responded as little to that gaze as to Ulrich's, and quietly withdrew as soon as she had announced the visitor.

The truth was more romantic than curiosity could suppose. Ever since Soliman had succeeded, with his willful innuendos against Arnheim, in lending that radiant presence a shadowy aura of obscure machinations, tarnishing even Rachel's childlike admiration for Diotima, all her passionate need to outdo herself in correct and devoted service had concentrated on Ulrich. Convinced by Soliman that a strict watch had to be kept on everything that went on in the house, she had become a zealous eavesdropper at keyholes, and while waiting on the guests had overheard more than one private conversation between Section Chief Tuzzi and his wife; nor had Ulrich's position midway between Diotima and Arnheim, as a man they both distrusted and desired, escaped her notice, and this corresponded entirely to her own feeling, wavering between rebellion and remorse, for her unsuspecting mistress. Now she also realized that she had known for a long time that Ulrich wanted something from her. It never entered her mind that he might find her attractive. Driven from home as she had been, and longing to prove to her family back in Galicia how great a success she could make of herself despite all that, she naturally dreamed of striking it lucky, something like an unexpected inheritance, the discovery that she was of noble birth, a chance to save the life of a prince . . . but the simple possibility that a gentleman who came to her mistress's house as a visitor might take a liking to her and want her to be his lover or even his wife would never have occurred to her. And so she simply held herself ready to do Ulrich some great service. It was she and Soliman who had sent the General an invitation when they learned that he was a friend of Ulrich's, though there was no denying they also did it to get things moving; considering what they thought they knew, a general certainly seemed the right person to turn the trick. Rachel, in her obscure, elfin sympathy with Ulrich, inevitably developed an overwhelming identification with him, as she secretly watched every movement of his lips, his eyes, his fingers, as if these were actors to whom she was bound with the passion of someone who sees her own insignificant self brought by them onto a vast stage. The more she realized that this mutual involvement constricted her breathing like a tight dress when crouching at a keyhole, the more depraved she felt for not resisting with greater firmness Soliman's simultaneous dark pursuit of her; this was the reason, of which Ulrich had no inkling, why she met his curiosity about her with that subservient passion for acting the well-trained, model maidservant.

Ulrich wondered in vain why this creature who seemed to be made for tender love play was so chaste that she might be almost a case of that rebellious frigidity not uncommonly found among some fine-boned women. He changed his mind, however, and was even a bit disappointed when he came upon a surprising scene one day. Arnheim had just arrived and gone in to see Diotima; Soliman was squatting on his haunches in the foyer, and Rachel had slipped away again as usual. Ulrich took advantage of the momentary stir caused by Arnheim's arrival to return to the hall for the handkerchief in his overcoat pocket. The light was out again, and Soliman did not realize that Ulrich, in the shadow of the doorway, had not returned to the reception room. Soliman got to his feet stealthily and, with great care, produced a large flower from under his jacket, a lovely white calla lily, which he contemplated for a while, then he set off on tiptoe past the kitchen door. Ulrich quietly followed him until Soliman stopped at Rachel's door, pressed the flower to his lips, and fixed it to the handle by twisting the stem around twice and squeezing its end into the keyhole.

It had not been easy to extract this lily from the bouquet on the way over with Arnheim and hide it for Rachel, and Rachel fully appreciated such attentions. Getting caught and fired would have meant Death and Judgment Day as far as Rachel was concerned, so it was naturally a great nuisance to have to watch out for Soliman all the time, wherever she might be, nor did she like being suddenly pinched in the leg without daring to cry out whenever she passed some hiding place where he might be lying in wait for her. Still, the fact that somebody was taking terrible chances just to be attentive to her, to spy devotedly on her every step and put her character to the test under the most difficult circumstances, could hardly fail to make an impression. The little ape was rushing her quite needlessly and dangerously, and yet, against all her principles and at odds with her crumpled dreams of great things in store, she sometimes felt a guilty craving to make the most of this African king's son whose thick lips were waiting at every turn to serve her, the serving maid, as if made for her alone.

One day, Soliman asked her right out if she was game. Arnheim had gone to the mountains with Diotima and some friends for two days and had left Soliman behind. It was the cook's day off, and Section Chief Tuzzi was taking his meals at a restaurant. Rachel had told Soliman about the cigarette stubs she had found in her room, and Diotima's unspoken question what would the little maid make of it was answered by Rachel's and Soliman's agreeing that something seemed to be afoot in the Council, something that called for the two of them to take some action of their own. When Soliman asked her if she was game, he announced that he meant to take the documents proving his noble birth from where Arnheim had locked them up. Rachel did not believe in these documents, but life amid so many tempting mysteries had given her a craving for something to happen. They decided that she would keep on her maid's cap and frilled apron when Soliman fetched her and took her to Arnheim's hotel, as if she had been sent on an errand there by her employers. When they stepped out on the street, such a smoldering heat rose up from behind the lacy bib of her apron that it almost blurred her vision, but Soliman boldly stopped a cab; he had plenty of money these days, when Arnheim was so often absentminded. This stiffened Rachel's spine too, and she stepped into the carriage in the sight of all the world as if she were charged and employed to ride in style with little black boys. The midmorning streets, with the well-dressed idlers to whom they belonged, flew by, and again Rachel's heart was thumping as if she were a thief. She tried to lean back properly, as she had seen Diotima do, but could not keep her body from bouncing up and down in the rich upholstery as the closed carriage rocked along, while Soliman took advantage of her reclining position to press the broad stamp pads of his lips on hers, risking their being seen through the windows, and a sensation like the simmering of some scented fluid poured from the billowing cushions into Rachel's back.

Nor was the young Moor disposed to forgo the pomp of driving right up to the hotel entrance. The porters in their black silk sleeves and green aprons grinned when Rachel stepped out of the carriage, the doorman peered through the glass door as Soliman paid the fare, and Rachel felt as though the pavement were giving way under her feet. But when no one stopped them as they walked through the vast pillared lobby, she thought that Soliman must enjoy a certain status in the hotel. Again she flushed with embarrassment when she felt the eyes of some armchair loungers following her as she passed by, but going up the stairs, she saw many chambermaids dressed in black with their white caps, like herself, if not perhaps as smartly, and she began to feel quite like an explorer wandering over an unknown, possibly dangerous island, who encounters human beings at last.

Then Rachel found herself for the first time in her life inside the rooms of a distinguished hotel. Soliman immediately locked all the doors and then felt called upon to kiss his little friend again. The kisses these two had been giving each other of late had something of the glow of a child's kiss, intended more for mutual reassurance than as any assault upon the moral fiber, and even now, when they were for the first time alone together in a locked room, Soliman's most pressing concern was to find even more romantic ways of hiding themselves away. He pulled down the blinds and stopped up all the keyholes giving on the corridor. Rachel was much too excited by all these preparations to think of anything other than her own daring and the disgrace of a possible discovery.

Next, Soliman led her to Arnheim's closets and trunks, all open except for one. This was clearly the one harboring the secret. He took the keys from all the open trunks and tried them one by one, with no success, while chattering nonstop, pouring out all his reserves of camels, princes, mysterious couriers, and insinuations against Arnheim. He borrowed one of Rachel's hairpins and tried to pick the lock with it. When this failed him, he ripped all the keys from all the closet doors and drawers, spread them out between his knees as he squatted on the floor, and paused to brood over this collection, trying to think of a fresh expedient. "Now you can see how he hides things from me!" he said to Rachel, rubbing his forehead. "But I may as well show you everything else first."

And so he simply spread the bewildering riches from Arnheim's trunks and closets out before Rachel, who was crouching on the floor, with her hands clasped between her knees, staring at these things with curiosity. The intimate wardrobe of a man accustomed to the choicest of luxuries was something she had never seen before. Her own master was certainly not poorly dressed, but he had neither the money nor the need for the ultrasophisticated concoctions of the best tailors and shirtmakers, the creators of luxuries for home and travel. Even her mistress had nothing to compare with the exquisite things, feminine in their delicacy and complicated in their uses, that belonged to this immensely rich man. Something of Rachel's original awe for the nabob came to life again, even as Soliman puffed himself up with pride in the stunning impression he was making on her as he dragged out everything, showing off all the gadgets and eagerly explaining all the mysteries. Rachel was beginning to tire of the endless display, when she was suddenly struck by an odd coincidence. She realized that things of this kind had been cropping up lately among Diotima's lingerie and household things. They were not as numerous or as expensive as Arnheim's, but compared to Diotima's former monastic simplicity, they were certainly closer to what she was seeing here than to her austere past. Rachel was overcome by the outrageous notion that the link between her mistress and Arnheim might be less spiritual than she had supposed.

She blushed to the roots of her hair.

Never since she had entered Diotima's service had her thoughts wandered into this area. Her eyes had gulped down the glory of her mistress's body without giving any thought to the possible uses of such beauties, like gulping down a powder with its paper envelope. Her satisfaction at being permitted to share the life of persons of such exalted station had been so great that in all this time Rachel, who was so easily seduced, had never thought of any man as a sexual being, but only as someone different in a romantic way, like in a novel. Her high-mindedness had made her a child again, transporting her, as it were, back to the stage before puberty, that time of selfless enthusiasms for the greatness of others. This was in fact how Rachel had come to swallow Soliman's tall stories so willingly, in such a trance of gullibility, that it made the cook laugh at her. But now, as Rachel crouched on the floor and saw the suggestive tokens of an adulterous union between Arnheim and Diotima spread out before her in broad daylight, a long-impending change took place inside her—the awakening from an unnatural state of exaltation into the mistrustful state of the actual world of the flesh.

Gone in a flash was her romanticism; she was a down-to-earth little body with a somewhat irritated notion that even a servant girl had some rights in life. Soliman was squatting beside her before his outspread bazaar, having collected up all the things she had especially admired, and was trying to stuff into her pockets whatever was not too big, as presents from him. Now he leapt up and made another quick attack with a pocketknife on the locked trunk, while rattling on about having to get a lot of money from the bank before Arnheim returned, using his master's checkbook—in money matters the mad little devil had quite lost his innocence—so that he and Rachel could run away together, but not before he had his papers.

Rachel abruptly stood up, firmly emptied her pockets of all the "presents" he had stuffed into them, and said, "Don't talk such nonsense! I have to go now. What time is it?" Her voice sounded deeper. She smoothed her apron and adjusted her cap. Soliman instantly realized that she was through with playing the game, and that she was suddenly much older than he. But before he could reassert himself, Rachel was kissing him good-bye. This time her lips did not tremble but pressed hard into the luscious fruit of his face as she bent over him, forcing the boy's head back and keeping at it so long that he almost choked. Soliman struggled, and when she finally let go he felt as if a taller, stronger boy had been holding him under water, so that his first impulse was to get even with her for an unfair trick played on him. But Rachel had slipped out the door, and the look he sent after her—for that was all of him that caught up with her—as inflamed as the red-hot tip of a burning arrow, gradually faded to a soft ash. Soliman then picked up his master's belongings from the floor to put them back in order; he had now turned into a young man who could look forward to something that had ceased to be unattainable.

105

LOVE ON THE HIGHEST LEVEL IS NO JOKE

Following their excursion to the mountains, Arnheim had gone abroad for longer than usual. "Gone abroad"—as he had come to think of it himself—was certainly an odd expression to use, considering that it should have been "gone home." It was because of this and other such reasons that it was in fact becoming urgently necessary for him to come to a decision. He was haunted by unpleasant daydreams such as had never before entered his disciplined head. One especially persistent one was of seeing himself standing with Diotima on a tall church steeple, where they gazed briefly at the green landscape stretched far below and then jumped off. A vision of forcing his way unchivalrously into the Tuzzis' bedroom at night to shoot the Section Chief obviously came to the same thing. He could perhaps have chosen to finish him off in a duel, but this seemed less natural; the fantasy was already loaded down with too many realistic rituals, and the closer Arnheim approached reality, the more troublesome the increase of inhibitions. Asking Tuzzi simply and openly for the hand of his wife in marriage was conceivable, but what would Tuzzi be likely to say to that? It simply meant opening oneself up to all sorts of ridicule. And even if Tuzzi were to be civilized about it and there was a minimum of scandal, or possibly no scandal at all, divorce having come to be tolerated even in the best circles, there was still the fact that an old bachelor always made himself a bit ridiculous by a late marriage, much like a couple having a baby for their silver wedding anniversary. And if Arnheim really had to do such a thing, he owed it to the firm to marry a prominent American widow at the very least, or a great lady of ancient lineage with connections at court, and not the divorced wife of a middle-class government official. He could not make a move, even if it were merely of a sensual nature, that was not permeated with responsibility. In a time like the present, when responsibility for one's acts or thoughts plays so slight a role, it was by no means mere personal ambition that raised such objections, but a truly suprapersonal need to bring the power fostered by the Arnheims (a formation rooted in simple greed, which it had long since outgrown, however; it now had a mind of its own, a will of its own, it had to keep growing, to solidify its position, lest it sicken, lest it become rusted when it rested!) into accord with the forces and hierarchies of life itself, nor had he ever knowingly made a secret of this to Diotima. An Arnheim was of course free to marry even some peasant if he chose, but free only as regarded his own person; he would still be betraying a cause for a personal weakness.

It was nevertheless true that he had proposed marriage to Diotima. He had done it, if only to forestall the kind of adulterous goings-on that do not consort well with the disciplined conduct of life on a high level. Diotima had gratefully pressed his hand and, with a smile reminiscent of the finest such smiles in the history of art, she had responded to his proposal with the words: "It is never those we embrace that we love most deeply. . . ." After this answer, as equivocal as the seductive yellow deep inside the chaste lily, Arnheim could never bring himself to go once more into the breach. Instead, they went in for general conversations in which the words "divorce," "marriage," "adultery," and the like showed a strange tendency to crop up. More than once, for instance, Arnheim and Diotima talked in depth about the treatment of adultery in contemporary literature, and Diotima felt that this problem was invariably handled without any appreciation for the great values of self-discipline, renunciation, or heroic self-denial, but purely from a sensual point of view. Arnheim's view was precisely the same, unfortunately, so that he could only add that there was hardly anyone left these days capable of fully appreciating the deep moral mystery of the individual. This mystery consisted in having to keep a tight rein on the tendency to self-indulgence. Historic periods of permissiveness have never failed, so far, in making all those who lived in them miserable. All discipline, abstinence, chivalry, music, morality, poetry, form, taboo, had no deeper purpose than to give the correct limits, a definite shape, to life. There is no such thing as boundless happiness. There is no great happiness without great taboos. Even in business, to pursue one's advantage at all costs is to risk getting nowhere. Keeping within one's limits is the secret of all phenomena, of power, happiness, faith, and the key to the task of maintaining oneself as a tiny human creature within the universe. Such was Arnheim's statement of the case, and Diotima could not but agree. It was in a sense a regrettable consquence of such insights that they lent to legitimacy a richness of meaning that is no longer available to most people. But great souls cannot do without legitimacy. At peak moments of perception, one senses how the cosmos turns on an axis of vertical austerity. And the businessman, even as he rules the world, respects kingship, aristocracy, and the church as pillars of the irrational. The legitimate is simple, as all greatness is simple, open to anyone's understanding. Homer was simple, Christ was simple. The truly great minds always come down to simple basics; one must have the courage to admit, in fact, that they always come back to moral commonplaces, which is why it is hardest of all for the truly free spirit to defy tradition.

Such insights, true as they are, are not much help to a man bent on intruding into someone else's marriage. So these two people found themselves in the position of being linked by a splendid bridge with a hole at its center, just a few yards wide, so that they cannot come together. Arnheim was deeply sorry that he had no spark of that desire which is the same, whatever its object, and as likely to catapult a man into a rash business deal as into a rash love affair; his regret moved him to talk at length about desire. According to him, desire was precisely the feeling that best corresponds to the merely intellectual culture of our era. No other feeling aims so unequivocally at its specific object. It strikes and sticks like an arrow, rather than swarming on into ever greater distances like a flock of birds. It impoverishes the soul, just like arithmetic and mechanics and brutality. In this fashion Arnheim spoke with disapproval of desire, even as he felt it struggling like a blinded slave in the cellar.

Diotima took a different tack. She held out her hand to him and beseeched him: "Let us say no more! Words can do much, but there are things beyond words. The real truth between two people cannot be put into words. The moment we speak, certain doors begin to close; language works best for what doesn't really matter; we talk in lieu of living. . . ."

Arnheim concurred. "You're so right. The word, in its arrogance, gives an arbitrary and impoverished form to the invisible movements of our inner being."

"Say no more, please," Diotima repeated, laying a hand on his arm. "I feel that we give each other a moment of life when we are silent together." After a while, she withdrew her hand again and sighed: "There are instants when all the hidden jewels of the soul lie revealed."

"There may come a time," Arnheim complemented this,"—and there are many signs that it is near already—when souls will behold each other without the mediation of the senses. Souls come together when one pair of lips withdraws from the other."

Diotima pursed her lips so that they suggested a crooked little tube such as butterflies dip into blossoms. She was totally besotted.

Like all heightened states of emotion, love brings out a certain madness about the supposed connectedness of things so that any words uttered tended to light up with richly ramifying significance, which manifested itself like a veiled deity before it dissolved in silence. Diotima knew this phenomenon from her lonely hours of lofty meditation, but never before with this intensity to the very edge of barely endurable joy; she was brimming over with uncontrollable feeling, with something godlike inside her that moved as if on skates, and more than once she felt that she was about to crash down in a dead faint.

Arnheim buoyed her up with his great pronouncements. He gave her time to recover, to catch her breath. Then he again spread the safety net of ideal considerations beneath them.

The torment of this expansive joy was that it militated against concentration. It kept emitting tremulous new waves that rippled outward in widening circles but never pressed together to form a current of action. Diotima had after all reached the point of regarding the risks of an affair as the more considerate and civilized alternative to the crude catastrophe of smashed lives, while Arnheim had long since opted morally against accepting such a sacrifice and was ready to marry her. They could have each other, one way or another, at any moment, and they both knew it, but they did not know which form it should take, for their happiness swept their souls, made for it as they were, to such solemn heights that the fear of spoiling everything by some awkward move paralyzed them: a natural state of anxiety for people with a cloud under their feet.

Their minds had never failed to drink in all the grandeur and beauty life had poured out for them, and yet, at its very apex, their joy was strangely curtailed. All the wishes and vanities that had normally filled their lives now lay far beneath them, like toy houses and farmyards deep in the valley, with all the clucking, barking, and other excitements swallowed up in the stillness, leaving only the sense of silent deep space.

"Can it be that we have a mission?" Diotima wondered, surveying the emotional pinnacle on which she found herself with a foreboding of some agonizing and unimaginable turn up ahead. Not only had she experienced lesser degrees of such exaltation herself, but even an emotional lightweight like her cousin had been known to speak of such things, and much had been written about them of late. But if there was any truth to the reports, there were times, every thousand years or so, when the soul was closer to an awakening than usual, born into the real world, as it were, via certain individuals upon whom it imposes tests far beyond mere reading and talking. In this connection, even the inexplicable appearance on the scene of the uninvited General suddenly popped into her mind. And so she murmured to her friend, who was groping for new words as their agitation formed a trembling arc between them: "Two people can understand each other without always finding some rational formula for it."

And Arnheim responded, as his eye met hers straight as a ray from the sinking sun, "You're right. As you said before, the real truth between two people cannot be put into words; every effort of that kind only creates a further obstacle between them."

106

DOES MODERN MAN BELIEVE IN GOD OR IN THE HEAD OF THE WORLDWIDE CORPORATION? ARNHEIM WAVERING

Arnheim alone. Deep in thought, he stands at the window of his hotel suite, gazing down on the leafless treetops, their bare branches forming a grille, beneath which the passersby, bright and dark, brushing against each other, form the two serpentine lines of the informal street parade that starts at this hour. A smile of annoyance parts the great man's lips.

Up to now he had never had any difficulty in defining what he considered soulless. What was not soulless these days? It was easy enough to spot the rare exceptions, too. A far-off evening of chamber music came to mind, played by friends visiting his castle in Prussia, young musicians who were rather hard up, and yet whose spirited harmonies rang out on the evening air, amid the fragrance of the northern linden trees; that was soulful. Or to take another case: He had recently refused to go on paying an allowance to a certain artist. He had fully expected that the artist would be angry at him and feel he had been left in the lurch before he had been given a chance to make his reputation; he would have to be told that there were other artists in need of support and all that sort of thing, something Arnheim did not look forward to doing. Instead, this man, the next time he met Arnheim, had merely looked hard into his eyes and then shaken his hand, saying: "You've left me in a tough spot, but I'm sure a man like you never does anything without a good reason." Now, there was a manly soul, and Arnheim was not disinclined to do something for him again, some other time.

So there still was such a thing as soul in many instances, even these days. It had always been a point of importance to Arnheim. But when one has to deal with it directly and unconditionally, a man's sincerity is put to a hard test. Was a time really coming when souls would be able to commune together without the mediation of the senses? Was there any purpose, of the same value and importance as the realistic aims of life, to be accomplished in communing together as he and this marvelous woman had been inwardly driven to do lately? While in his sober senses he never believed it for an instant, yet he was sure that he was encouraging Diotima to believe it.

Arnheim was in a peculiar state of conflict. Moral wealth is closely related to the financial kind; he was well aware of it, and it is easy to understand. For morality replaces the soul with logic; once a soul is thoroughly moral, it no longer has any moral problems, only logical ones; it asks itself whether something it wants to do is governed by this commandment or that, whether its intention is to be understood one way or another, and so on, all of which is like a wildly scrambling mob that has been whipped into shape by a gymnastics coach so that it responds to signals such as Right turn, Arms out, Bend knees, and so on. But logic presupposes repeatable experiences. In a vortex of events that never repeat themselves, we could obviously never formulate the profound insight that A equals A, or that the greater is not the lesser, but would be living in a kind of dream, a condition abhorred by every thinker. And the same is true of morality: if our acts were unrepeatable, then there would be nothing to be expected of us, and a morality that could not tell people what was expected of them would be no fun at all. This quality of repetitiveness that inheres in the workings of the mind and morality inheres also, and to the highest degree, in money. Money positively consists of this quality. As long as it keeps its value, it carves up all the world's pleasures into those little building blocks of purchasing power that can then be combined into whatever one pleases. Money is accordingly both moral and rational; and since we all know that the converse is not the case, i.e., not every moral and reasonable person has money, we may conclude that money is the original source of these qualities, or at least that money is the crowning reward of a moral and rational life.

Not that Arnheim of course thought precisely along the lines that education and religion were the natural consequence of wealth, but he did assume that wealth obliged its owner to have them, while liking to point out that the spiritual powers did not always understand enough of the effective powers in life and were rarely quite free of certain traces of unworldliness. As a man with a large overview, he came to all sorts of conclusions beyond this too. Every act of weighing something, taking account of it or measuring it, presupposes that the object in question will not change in the process; where such a change occurs nonetheless, the mind must be exerted to its utmost to find something unchangeable even within the change, and so money is akin to all the powers of the mind, serving as a model to the world's scientists for dividing up the world into atoms, laws, hypotheses, and curious mathematical symbols, and the technicians use all these fictions to build up a world of new things. All of this was as familiar to this owner of a gigantic industrial complex, who so thoroughly understood the nature of the forces at his disposal, as the moral assumptions of the Bible are to the average reader of novels.

This inward need for the unequivocal, the repeatable, and the solid, upon which the success of all thinking and planning depends— so Arnheim reflected as he stood gazing down on the street from his window—is always appeased by some form of violence. Anyone who wants to build on rock in dealing with human beings has to rely on the baser qualities and passions, for only what is most closely bound up with egotism endures and can always be counted on; the higher aims are unreliable, contradictory, and fleeting as the wind. The man who knew that empires would sooner or later have to be run just like factories gazed upon the swarms of uniforms and proud faces no bigger than nits down there, with a smile that was a blend of superiority and sadness. There could be no doubt that if God returned this very day to set up the Millennium on earth, not a single practical, experienced man would take any stock in it unless the Last Judgment came fully equipped with a punitive apparatus of prison fortresses, police, armies, sedition laws, government departments, and whatever else was needed in order to rein in the incalculable potential of the human soul by relying on the two basic facts that the future tenant of heaven can be made to do what is needed only by intimidation and tightening the screws or else by bribery—in a word, by "strong measures."

But then Paul Arnheim would step forward and speak to the Lord: "Lord, why bother? Egotism is the most reliable factor in human life. It enables the politician, the soldier, the king, to keep order in the world by cunning and force. Mankind dances to its tune, as You and I must admit. To do away with force is to weaken the world order. Our task is to make man capable of greatness, although he is a mongrel cur!" So saying, Arnheim would smile modestly at the Lord, with composure, in token of the importance for every man of recognizing the great mysteries, in all humility. And then he would continue his address as follows: "But money is surely just as safe a means of managing human relationships as physical force, the crude uses of which it allows us to discontinue. Money is power in the abstract, a pliant, highly developed, and creative form, a unique form, of power. Isn't business really based on cunning and force, on outwitting and exploiting others, except that in business, cunning and force have become wholly civilized, internalized in fact, so that they are actually clothed in the guise of man's liberty? Capitalism, as the organization of egotism based on a hierarchy in which one's rank depends on one's capacity for getting money, is simply the greatest and yet the most humane order we have been able to devise, to Your everlasting glory. There is no more precise measure than this for all human action."

And so Arnheim would have advised the Lord to organize the Millennium on business principles and entrust its administration to a leading businessman; a man, it went without saying, who would also have the mental capacities of a philosopher. After all, religion unaided had always got the worst of it in this world, and compared with the insecurity of its existence in times of armed power struggles, there was much to be gained for it under a business administration.

So Arnheim would have spoken, for a deep inner voice told him distinctly that money was as indispensable as reason and morality. But another, equally deep inner voice told him just as sharply that a man must dare to jettison reason, morality, and the whole of his rationalized existence without a backward glance. At those dizzy moments when he felt no greater urge than to plunge, like some errant meteor, into the blazing solar mass that was Diotima, this voice was almost the more powerful. At such times the wild proliferation of his thoughts seemed to him as alien and extraneous as the self-impelled growth of nails and hair. The moral life then looked dead, and a secret aversion to morality and order made him blush. Arnheim was suffering the fate of his whole era. This era worships money, order, knowledge, calculation, measures and weights—the spirit of money and everything related to it, in short—but also deplores all that. Even as it goes on hammering and calculating during working hours, and at all other times carries on like a horde of children driven from one excess to another by the challenge What's next? with its bitter, sickening aftertaste, it cannot shake off an inward warning to repent. It deals with this conflict by a division of labor, assigning to certain intellectuals, the confessers and confessors of their period, dealers in absolutions and indulgences, literary Savonarolas and evangelists, whose presence is the most reassuring to those not personally in a position to live up to their precepts, the task of recording all such premonitions and inward lamentations. Of course, all the lip service and government funds dropped annually by the State into their bottomless cultural schemes are much the same kind of moral ransom money.

This functional split manifested itself inside Arnheim himself as well. Sitting at one of this executive desks checking sales figures, he would have been ashamed to think otherwise than as a businessman and technician; but once it was no longer the firm's money that was involved, he would have been ashamed not to think otherwise, not to insist that mankind must be made capable of self-improvement by some other means than pursuit of the chimera of going by the book, regulations, orders, norms, and all that, with results so devoid of inward meaning and so ephemeral. This Other Way was unquestionably what is called religion, and he had written books about it, in which he had also called it myth, the return to simplicity, the realm of the soul, the spiritualization of the economy, the nature of action, and so on, because it had many aspects, as many, to be specific, as he found in himself when he was selflessly analyzing himself, as a man must do when facing the prospect of great tasks. But it seemed to be fated that this functional split should fail him in the hour of decision. At the very moment when he longed to entrust himself to the flame of his passion, or had the urge to be as great and singlehearted as the heroic figures of old, as untrammeled as only the true aristocrat can be, as wholly religious as the quintessential nature of love demands; at the very moment, in short, when he yearned to fling himself at Diotima's feet without regard to the crease of his trousers or his future, an inner voice held him back. It was the untimely voice of reason or, as he irritably told himself, the instinct for calculating and hoarding that nowadays stands everywhere in the way of life on the grand scale, the dream of ecstasy. He hated this voice even as he was forced to acknowledge its validity. For, assuming that there was a honeymoon, what form would life with Diotima take after that honeymoon? He would return to his business affairs, and they would cope with the other tasks of a lifetime together. The year would alternate between financial operations and recuperation in the arms of nature, in the animal and vegetative part of one's own being. It might even turn into a great, truly humanistic marriage of action and repose, of human need and beauty. That would be fine; it was doubtless what he vaguely had in mind as a goal. Arnheim believed that no one could muster the strength for great financial operations who was incapable of letting go entirely, of abandoning himself altogether, beyond all desire, far from the madding crowd, with only a loincloth to cover his nakedness, as it were. Still, Arnheim was filled with some savage wordless state of satisfaction, because all this was the opposite of what he felt first and last for Diotima. Every time he laid eyes on this Classical beauty with those modern rounded curves, he was thrown into confusion, felt his strength melting away, unequal to his need to absorb into his own inner being this poised, self-sufficient creature so serenely moving in her own orbit. There was nothing loftily humane about this feeling, nothing even merely humane. It was a taste of the whole cosmic void of eternity. He stared at the beauty of his beloved with a gaze that seemed to have been seeking her for a thousand years and now, having found her, was suddenly unemployed, helpless in a kind of stupor, an almost idiotic amazement. So excessive a demand on emotion left it nearly incapable of responding; it corresponded to nothing so much as a longing for both of them to be shot together from a cannon into intergalactic space!

The tactful Diotima found the right words again even for this condition. In one such moment she recalled that even in his day the great Dostoyevsky had noted a connection between love, idiocy, and inner holiness. But people of our own time, lacking the supportive presence of a devout Russia at their shoulders, probably needed a special dispensation to live by such an idea.

Her words might have come straight from Arnheim's heart.

The moment when they were spoken was one of those times engaged with both self-awareness and object awareness, like a stopped-up trumpet that refuses to emit a sound no matter how hard one blows into it, bringing all the blood to one's head; everything in it was charged with significance, from the tiniest cup on a shelf asserting its presence in the room like one of van Gogh's objects, to the human bodies, swollen and supercharged by the unutterable, which seemed to press into space.

Startled by her own words, Diotima said: "I wish we could just talk in fun. Humor is so wonderful; it floats free beyond desire, completely unconcerned with appearances."

Arnheim smiled at this. He had risen from his chair and started to pace the room. What if I tore her to pieces, he wondered, if I started to roar and dance, if I reached down my throat to tear out my heart for her; could I make a miracle happen? But as he cooled down, he came to a stop.

It was this scene that had just come vividly to mind. His glance again rested icily on the street below. It really would take some sort of redemptive miracle, he thought, the world would have to be populated by a new breed of men, before one could begin to think of putting such thoughts into practice. He dropped the effort of determining how and from what the world was to be redeemed; in any case, everything would have had to be different from the way it was. He went back to his desk, which he had abandoned half an hour since, back to his letters and telegrams, and rang for Soliman to fetch his secretary.

As he awaited the secretary's arrival, already engaged in formulating the first sentences of a statement for dictation on economic conditions, the remembered experience crystallized into a beautiful, richly significant moral form. After all, Arnheim said to himself firmly, a man who is aware of his responsibilities, even when giving his soul away, sacrifices only the interest, never the capital.

107

COUNT LEINSDORF ACHIEVES AN UNEXPECTED POLITICAL SUCCESS

When His Grace spoke of a European family of nations that was to throng joyfully around the venerable Emperor Patriarch, he always tacitly excluded Prussia. Perhaps he was now doing it with more feeling than ever, for Count Leinsdorf was undeniably bothered by his awareness of Dr. Arnheim; every time he arrived at his friend Diotima's he would find either the man himself or traces of his recent presence, and he knew no more than Section Chief Tuzzi what to make of it. As for Diotima, every time she turned her soulful gaze on him, she noticed as never before the swollen veins on His Grace's hands and neck and the faded-tobacco colored skin from which emanated the characteristic smell of an aging man. Even though she never failed to treat the great nobleman with all due reverence, something had gone out of her radiance toward him, something like the change from a summer sun to a winter sun. Count Leinsdorf was not given to fantasies or to music, but ever since Dr. Arnheim had become so persistent a presence it was strange how often he had a faint ringing in his ears, like the kettledrums and cymbals of an Austrian military march, or a visual sensation, whenever he closed his eyes, of a great billowing of black-and-yellow flags, vast numbers of them, in motion. Similar patriotic hallucinations seemed to be afflicting other friends of the Tuzzis' as well. At least, though Germany was always spoken of with the utmost respect whenever he happened to be within earshot, if he ever dropped a hint that the great patriotic project might eventually take on a certain pointedness against the brother empire, this respect was irradiated with a heartfelt smile.

His Grace had apparently stumbled upon an important phenomenon within his special field of interest. There are certain family feelings of a special intensity, and one of these was the widespread dislike of Germany among the European family of states before 1914. Perhaps Germany was spiritually the least unified country, so that everyone could find something there to suit his own distaste; its early culture had been the first to fall under the wheels of the new era, to be shredded into high-flown slogans for the promotion of the bogus and the commercial; it was also grasping, aggressive, full of bluster, and dangerously irresponsible, like every great mass in ferment—but all this was ultimately merely European, and might at most have seemed all-too-European to the Europeans. The world apparently needs its negative entities, images of the unwanted, which attract to themselves all the disgust and disharmony, all the slag of a smoldering fire, such as life tends to leave behind. Out of all that "could be" there suddenly crystallizes, to the stunned amazement of everyone concerned, the "it is," and whatever drops away during this disorderly process, whatever is unsuitable, superfluous, unsatisfying, seems to coagulate into the vibrant universal hatred agitating all living creatures that is apparently so characteristic of our present civilization, which compensates for all our lack of satisfaction with ourselves by allowing us to feel that easy dissatisfaction so readily inspired by everyone else. Trying to isolate specific scapegoats for this displeasure is merely part of the oldest psychotechnical bag of tricks known to man. Just as the medicine man drew the carefully prepared fetish from his patient's body, the good Christian projects his own faults onto the good Jew, whom he accuses of seducing him into committing advertisements, high interest rates, newspapers, and all that sort of thing. In the course of time people have blamed their troubles on bad weather, witches, socialists, intellectuals, generals, and in the years before the Great War, Austrians saw a most welcome scapegoat of this sort in Prussian Germany. Unfortunately, the world has lost not only God but the Devil as well. As it projects its unwanted evil onto the scapegoat, so it projects its desired good onto ad hoc ideal figures, which it reveres for doing what it finds inconvenient to do for itself. We let others perform the hard tricks as we watch from our seats: that is sport. We let others talk themselves into the most one-sided exaggerations: that's idealism. We shake off evil and make those who are spattered by it our scapegoats. It is one way of creating an order in the world, but this technique of hagiolatry and fattening the scapegoats by projection is not without danger, because it fills the world with all the tensions of unresolved inner conflicts. People alternately kill each other or swear eternal brotherhood without quite knowing just how real any of it is, because they have projected part of themselves onto the outer world, and everything seems to be happening partly out there in reality and partly behind the scenes, so that we have an illusory fencing match between love and hate. The ancient belief in demons, which made heavenly-hellish spirits responsible for all the good and bad that came one's way, worked much better, more accurately, more tidily, and we can only hope that, as we advance in psychotechnology, we shall make our way back to it.

Kakania was a country exceptionally well qualified for this game with living symbols of what was Wanted or Unwanted; life in Kakania had a certain unreality anyway, so that the most cultivated persons, who regarded themselves as the heirs and standard-bearers of the celebrated Kakanian culture from Beethoven to Lehár, felt it was quite natural to think of the Germans of the Reich as allies and brothers even while cordially detesting them. Seeing them get their occasional comeuppance did not upset anyone here, while their successes always left one a bit concerned about affairs at home. Affairs at home mostly meant that Kakania, a country that had originally been as good as any and sometimes better than most, had in the course of the centuries somewhat lost interest in itself. Several times in the course of the Parallel Campaign it could be perceived that world history is made up much as all other stories are—i.e., the authors seldom come up with anything really new and are rather given to copying each other's plots and ideas. But there is also something else involved which has not yet been mentioned, and that is the delight in storytelling itself; it takes the shape of that conviction so common to authors that they are working on a good story, that passion of authorship that lengthens an author's ears and makes them glow, so that all criticism simply melts away. Count Leinsdorf had this conviction and this passion, and so did some of his friends, but it had been lost in the farther reaches of Kakania, where the search for a substitute had been under way for the longest time now. There the history of Kakania had been replaced by that of the nation; the authors were at work on it even now, formulating it in that European taste that finds historical novels and costume dramas edifying. This resulted in a situation not yet perhaps sufficiently appreciated, which was that persons who had to deal with some commonplace problem such as building a school or appointing a stationmaster found themselves discussing this in connection with the year 1600 or 400, arguing about which candidate was preferable in the light of what settlements arose in the Lower Alps during the great Gothic or Slavic migrations, and about battles fought during the Counter-Reformation, and injecting into all this talk the notions of high-mindedness and rascality, homeland, truth, and manliness, and so on, which more or less corresponded to the sort of stuff the majority were currently reading. Count Leinsdorf, who attached no importance to literature, never ceased to wonder at this circumstance, especially considering how well off, basically, he found all the peasants, artisans, and townsfolk he encountered on his trips through the countryside to visit his Bohemian estates settled by generations of Germans and Czechs. He blamed it on some special virus, the detestable work of agitators, that there would be these sudden outbursts of violent dissatisfaction with each other and with the wisdom of the government, which were all the more puzzling in that these people got on so peacefully and contentedly with everyone in the long intervals between such fits, when nothing happened to remind them of their ideals.

The government's policy, that well-known Kakanian policy for dealing with national minorities, was one of alternating, every six months or so, between taking a punitive line against some mutinous minority and then again wisely giving ground to it; just as the fluid in a U-tube rises on one side when it sinks on the other, so government policy fluctuated vis-à-vis the German minority. This minority played a special part in Kakania, since it tended on the whole to want just one thing: that the State should be powerful. It had clung longer than any other minority to the belief that the history of Kakania must have some meaning, and it was only after it gradually caught on to the fact that in Kakania a man could begin as a traitor and end as a cabinet minister, and could then continue his ministerial career by going in for high treason, that it, too, began to regard itself as an oppressed nationality. It may be that this sort of thing was going on elsewhere too, but in Kakania it needed no revolutions or other upheavals to produce this effect, because here it came about of its own accord, naturally, like the quiet swinging of a pendulum from side to side, simply by virtue of the general vagueness of the ideas involved, until in the end there was nothing left in Kakania except oppressed nationalities, the oppressors being represented by a supreme circle of personages who saw themselves as being constantly baited and plagued by the oppressed. In this high circle people were deeply troubled because nothing was happening, troubled by an absence of history, so to speak, and a strong feeling that something must be done at long last. And if this meant turning against Germany, as the Parallel Campaign seemed inclined to do, it was not an altogether unwelcome eventuality; first of all, because there was that feeling of always being put in the shade by the brothers in the Reich, and second, because persons in government circles were themselves Germans, so there was actually no better way for them to demonstrate Kakania's impartiality than by joining in such a selfless gesture.

It was therefore entirely understandable that in these circumstances nothing could be farther from His Grace's mind than any suspicion that his undertaking was Pan-Germanic. But that it was so regarded could be deduced from the gradual disappearance of the Slavic groups from among the "officially recognized minorities" whose claims should command the attention of the Parallel Campaign committees, and the foreign envoys came to hear such terrible reports about Arnheim, Tuzzi, and a German plot against the Slavic element that some of all this even reached His Grace's ears in the muted form of rumor, confirming his fears that even on those days when nothing special was happening one had to be hard at work to make sure that so many things that were not supposed to happen did not happen. But being a practical politician, he was now slow to make his countermove, though in so doing he unfortunately acted on such a magnanimous calculation that it looked at first like an error in statesmanship. As the Propaganda Committee, in charge of popularizing the Parallel Campaign, did not yet have a chairman, Count Leinsdorf decided to choose Baron Wisnieczky for the post, in special consideration of the fact that Wisnieczky had some years before been a member of a cabinet brought down by the German nationalist parties on suspicion that it was carrying out an insidious anti-German policy. His Grace was in this instance following a scheme of his own. From the very start of the Parallel Campaign it had been one of his ideas to win over precisely those of the German Kakanians who felt less allegiance to their own country than to the German nation. However much the other "ethnic" elements might refer to Kakania as a prison, and however publicly they avowed their love for France, Italy, or Russia, no serious politician could ever put such quasi-exotic predilections on a level with the predilection of certain German Kakanians for the German Reich, which held Kakania in a geographic stranglehold and had been one with it historically until a mere generation ago. It was to these German apostates, whose intrigues hurt Count Leinsdorf most because he was German himself, that he had been referring when he pronounced his well-known dictum: "They'll come along of their own accord!" This dictum had meanwhile attained the rank of a political prophecy in which much confidence was placed by members of the patriotic campaign, signifying more or less that once the other ethnic groups had been won over to patriotism, the German elements would feel constrained to join in, for as everyone knows, it is much harder to hold aloof from something everyone else is doing than to refuse to be first in line. Therefore the way to get the Germans in was to move against them by favoring the other nationalities. Count Leinsdorf had known this for quite a while, and now that the time had come to act, he carried it through and placed Baron Wisnieczky, who was a Pole by birth but a Kakanian by conviction, at the head of the Propaganda Committee.

It would be hard to say whether His Grace was aware that this choice was an affront to the German cause, as his critics later said; the chances are that he thought he was serving the true German interest in this fashion. But the immediate consequence of his move was that the Parallel Campaign was now being intensely attacked in German circles as well, so that it ended up being regarded on the one side as an anti-German plot and being openly resisted as such, while on the other side it had long been regarded as pro-German and had therefore been avoided, with diplomatic excuses, from the outset. The unexpected effect did not escape His Grace's attention, of course, and was a matter of intense concern everywhere. This further tribulation only stiffened Count Leinsdorf's resolve, however, and when Diotima and other leading figures anxiously questioned him about it, time after time, he turned an impenetrable but determined face toward such feeble-spirited creatures and said: "This move has not met with immediate success, I know, but you cannot let a great aim depend on whether or not you achieve instant success with any measure along the way; meanwhile we have achieved a more widespread interest in the Parallel Campaign, and the rest will fall into place if we simply hold firm."

108

THE UNREDEEMED NATIONALITIES AND GENERAL STUMM'S REFLECTIONS ABOUT THE TERMINOLOGY OF REDEMPTION

No matter how many words are spoken at every moment in a great city to express the personal concerns of its inhabitants, there is one word that is never among them: "redeem." All other words, from the most impassioned to the most discriminating, even those dealing with extreme situations, may be assumed to be heard more than once, whether shouted or whispered, expressions such as, for instance: "You're the worst crook that ever lived" or "No other woman could be as beautiful as you," so that these most personal sentiments could in fact be charted in sweeping statistical curves representing their mass distribution throughout the city. But no living man ever says to another: "You can redeem me" or "Be my redeemer." He can be tied to a tree and left to starve, or marooned on a desert island with the woman he had been courting in vain for months, or rescued from being jailed for forging checks, and every word in the dictionary may come pouring from his lips, but as long as he is experiencing real emotion he will never utter the words "redeem," "redeemer," or "redemption," even though these are perfectly acceptable terms as such.

And yet the peoples united under the Crown of Kakania called themselves Unredeemed Nations.

General Stumm von Bordwehr was thinking about it. In his position at the War Office, he had ample knowledge of Kakania's problems with nationalism, because the military were the first to feel the effects, at the budget hearings, of the seesawing policies resulting from the hundreds of conflicting considerations by which the State was hamstrung. Only a little while ago an urgent money bill had had to be withdrawn, to the War Minister's white fury, because an Unredeemed Nationality had demanded in return for its support such concessions as the government could not possibly make without dangerously arousing the yearning for redemption of other nationalities. So Kakania was left naked to its enemies, as the budgetary outlay had been proposed to replace the army's hopelessly obsolete guns—whose range could be compared with the guns of other powers as a knife compares with a spear—with new guns that would be as a spear to a knife compared with those of the other powers. This necessary purchase had now once again been prevented, for who knew how long. To say that this setback made General Stumm consider suicide would be going too far, but a deep depression is sometimes heralded by any number of random, trivial symptoms, and Stumm's brooding over the redeemed and the unredeemed was certainly connected with Kakania's defenseless, disarmed state—to which it was condemned by its intolerable domestic squabbles—the more so because in his semi-civilian status at Diotima's he had been hearing about redemption until he was sick and tired of it.

His first reaction was that the term was one of those verbal inflations not yet classified by linguistic science. So his common sense as a soldier told him, but apart from the fact that his sound instinct had already been disoriented by Diotima—it was after all from her lips that Stumm had heard the word "redemption" for the first time and had been charmed by it, and even today, in spite of the failed artillery bill, the word when uttered by Diotima was still enveloped in a kind of magic, so that the General's first reaction could really more properly be described as the second of his life! And there was another reason why the theory of verbal inflation didn't seem to hold water: it was only necessary to salt the individual units of the word group "redemption" with a small, innocent lack of gravity, and they instantly came trippingly from the tongue. "You've just saved my soul!" or some such; who has not said something of the sort at one time or another, provided of course that it refers to nothing more than the relief after a ten-minute wait or some equally slight inconvenience that has been brought to an end. Now the General realized that it was not so much the words that offended a healthy common sense as their absurd claim to being taken literally. When Stumm asked himself where he had ever come across such talk of redemption or salvation, other than at Diotima's or in politics, he realized that it had been in churches or cafés, in art journals, and in the books of Dr. Arnheim, which he had read with admiration. He now realized that such words refer not to a simple, natural human occurrence but to something abstract, some general complication or other; to redeem and to yearn for redemption is definitely a spiritual transaction.

The General nodded with amazement at the fascinating insights this special duty of his seemed to be bringing him. He switched on the red light over his office door as a signal that he was in conference, and while his officers who came bearing files in their arms turned back from his door with a sigh, he went on with his speculations. The intellectual types he kept running into nowadays wherever he went were chronically dissatisfied, finding fault because there was either too little or too much being done about this or that; to hear them tell it, nothing ever seemed to go as it should. He was becoming quite fed up with them. They were in a class with those miserable specimens susceptible to cold who always find themselves sitting in a draft. When they were not complaining about the preponderance of scientific attitudes, they were excoriating illiteracy, general boorishness or general overrefinement, fanaticism or indifference: whichever way they turned, they found something wrong. Their minds never came to rest, but were fixated on the ceaseless wanderings of that residual element in things that never finds its proper place anywhere. So they ended up convinced that their era was fated to be a spiritual wasteland that could be redeemed only by some special

event or some very special personage. It was among the so-called intellectuals that the word "redemption" and its kin came into vogue at
this time. They did not see how things could go on unless a messiah
came quickly. Depending on circumstances, he would be a medical
messiah who would redeem the art of healing from the specialized
research teams that pursued their experiments while human beings
sickened and died around them, or a messianic poet capable of writing a drama that would sweep millions of people into the theaters
despite its ineffable sublimity; besides the belief that every kind of
human endeavor needed a messiah to restore it to its pristine purpose, there was of course also the simple and unadulterated longing
for a leader sent to put *everything* to rights with his strong right arm.
The age before the Great War was a messianic age, and the fact that
entire nations wanted to be redeemed in a lump was really nothing
special or unusual for its time.

Not that the General regarded this as something to be taken any
more literally than anything else people were saying. "If the Redeemer were to come again today," he said to himself, "they would
bring down his Government just like any other." Judging by his own
personal experience, he supposed that this came of too many people
writing too many books and newspaper articles. "How wise of the
army to forbid officers to write books without special permission," he
thought, and was startled to feel a hot wave of loyalty for the first
time in ages. He was obviously starting to think too much! It all came
of keeping company with the civilian mind, which had evidently lost
the advantage of having a firm perspective on the world. The General saw this clearly now, and it enabled him to understand all that
palaver about redemption from yet another angle. The General's
mind strayed back to distant memories of his classes in religion and
history for support along this new line of thought, and if his welter of
ideas could have been lifted bodily out of his head and ironed out, it
would have looked more or less as follows: To begin briefly with the
ecclesiastical aspect of things, as long as one believed in religion, one
could defenestrate a good Christian or a pious Jew from any story in
the castle of hope or prosperity, and he would always land on his spiritual feet, as it were, because all religions included in their view of
life an irrational, incalculable element they called God's inscrutable
will. Whenever a man could not make sense of things, he merely had

to remember this rogue element in the equation, and his spirit could rub its hands with satisfaction, as it were. This falling on one's feet and rubbing one's hands is called having a working philosophy of life, and this is what modern man has lost. He must either give up thinking about his life altogether, which is what many people are quite content to do, or else he finds himself strangely torn between having to think and yet never quite seeming to arrive at a satisfactory resolution of his problems. This conflict has in the course of history taken on the form of a total skepticism as often as it has that of a renewed subjection to faith, and its most prevalent form today is probably the conviction that without a spiritual dimension there can be no human life worthy of the name, but with too much of it there can be none either. It is on this conviction that our civilization as a whole is based. It takes great care to provide for education and research, but never too well, only enough money to keep education and research properly subordinated to the great sums expended on entertainment, cars, and guns. It clears the way for talent but sees to it that it should be a talent for business. Every idea is given due recognition, after some resistance, but this always works out so as to benefit equally the opposite idea. It looks like some tremendous weakness and carelessness, but it is probably also a quite deliberate effort to put the spiritual dimension in its place, for if any one of the ideas that motivate our lives were ever carried out seriously, so seriously that nothing would be left of its opposite, then our civilization would hardly be our civilization.

The General had a pudgy little baby fist; he clenched it and whacked the top of his desk with it as if it were a padded glove; a man had to have a strong fist. As an officer, he knew what to think! The irrational element was known as honor, obedience, the Supreme Commander in Chief, Part III of the Service Regulations, and to sum it all up, the conviction that war is nothing but the continuation of peace by stronger measures, a forceful kind of order, without which the world cannot survive. The gesture with which the General had thumped his desk would have been slightly ludicrous if a fist were not as much a spiritual manifestation as an athletic one, a kind of indispensable extension of the mind. Stumm von Bordwehr was a bit fed up with the whole civilian nexus. He had discovered that library attendants were the only people left who had a sound general overview of the civilian mind. He had hit upon the paradox of excessive order, the perfection of which inevitably brought inaction in its train. He had a funny feeling, something like an insight into why it was the army where the greatest order was to be found at the same time as the greatest readiness to lay down one's life. For some indefinable reason, order seems to bring on bloodshed! This worried him, and he decided that he must not go on working at such pressure. Anyway, he wondered mutinously, what is this spiritual dimension? It doesn't walk around in a bedsheet at midnight, so what can it be but a certain order we impose on our impressions and experiences? But in that case, he concluded firmly, on a happy inspiration, if the spirit is nothing more than the order of our experience, then in a properly ordered world we don't need it at all!

With a sigh of relief, Stumm von Bordwehr switched off the "in conference" light outside his door, stepped up to the mirror, and smoothed his hair down, in order to efface all signs of emotional stress before his subordinates came in.

109

BONADEA, KAKANIA; SYSTEMS OF HAPPINESS AND BALANCE

If there was anyone in Kakania who understood nothing of politics, and was quite happy that way, it was Bonadea; and yet there was a connection between her and the Unredeemed Nationalities. Bonadea—not to be confused with Diotima; Bonadea the Good Goddess, Goddess of Chastity, whose temple by one of those twists of fate ended up as the scene of orgies; Bonadea, wife of a presiding county judge or some such legal eminence, and the frustrated mistress of a man who was neither worthy of her nor sufficiently attached to her—had a system, which was more than could be said of Kakanian politics.

Bonadea's system had so far consisted in leading a double life. Her social status was assured in that she belonged to a family of distinction and enjoyed the reputation of a cultivated and notable woman in her own social circle; that she gave way to certain temptations she could ascribe to being constitutionally overexcitable, or having a heart given to folly, since the follies of the heart, like romantic political crimes, enjoy a certain esteem, even when committed under dubious circumstances. Here the heart plays about the same role as honor, obedience, and Service Regulations, Part III, played in the General's life, or as the irrational element in every well-ordered life that ultimately puts to rights whatever baffles the unaided rational mind.

But Bonadea's system had a flaw, in that it split her life into two different conditions, the transition from one to the other of which could not be achieved without paying a heavy price. For however eloquent her heart could be before one of her lapses, it was equally deflated afterward, and she was constantly alternating between a maniacally effervescent state of mind and one that drained away in inky blackness, hardly ever coming into equilibrium. All the same, it was a system, that is, it was no mere play of uncontrolled instincts—the way life used to be seen as the automatic squaring of accounts between pleasure and pain, with a certain profit registered on the side of pleasure, but a system that included quite a number of psychological moves designed to fake these accounts.

Everyone has some such method of jockeying one's psychological accounts in one's own favor, aiming at a minimum balance of pleasure that should ordinarily get one through the day. A person's pleasure in life can also consist of displeasure; such differences in kind don't matter much, since as everyone knows there are as many contented melancholics as there are funeral marches that float as lightly in their element as a dance tune does in its own. The opposite is probably equally valid, in that many normally cheerful persons are no whit happier than many habitually sad ones, because happiness is just as much of a strain as unhappiness, more or less like flying on the principle of lighter or heavier than air. But there is another objection to be made. Would the rich not consider themselves justified in their perennial insistence that the poor need not envy them, because the happiness to be got out of money is illusory? Money merely sets a man the problem of working out another system of life, the pleasure surplus of which can at best be no greater than any other. According to this principle, the family without a roof over its head, provided it survives an icy winter night, should theoretically be just as happy with the first rays of the morning sun as the rich man who has to get out of his warm bed. In practice it comes down to this, that everyone bears his burden with the patience of a donkey, since a donkey whose strength slightly exceeds the demands of his burden is happy enough. And this is, in fact, the soundest available definition of personal happiness, as long as we restrict ourselves to donkeys. In reality, however, personal happiness (or equilibrium, contentment, whatever we may choose to call the innermost reflex aim of the personality) is self-contained only as a stone is in a wall, or a drop of water in a river, which are permeated by the forces and tensions of the whole. What a person does and feels is a negligible part of what he must assume many others normally do and feel with him. A human being never lives only in his own equilibrium but depends on that of the surrounding strata of humanity, so that the individual's little pleasure factory is affected by a most complicated moral credit system, about which more will have to be said later on, being as much a part of the community's psychic balance sheet as of the individual's.

Since Bonadea's efforts to win her lover back were unsuccessful, making her think that Diotima's intellect and energy had robbed her of Ulrich, she was consumed with jealousy; and yet, as is the way with weak personalities, her admiration for her rival provided a certain justification and compensation for her loss, which partially reconciled her to it. In this condition she had managed for some time now to be received by Diotima occasionally, on the pretext of having some modest contribution to offer to the Parallel Campaign, without achieving an entrance into the circles that frequented the house; on this point she imagined there must be a certain understanding between Diotima and Ulrich. So she felt herself to be a victim of their cruelty, and since she also loved them, the illusion of an ineffable purity and selflessness flowered inside her. In the mornings, when her husband had left the house—a moment she could hardly wait for—she often sat down at her mirror like a bird ready to groom its feathers. She tied, curled, and twisted her hair until it took on a form

not unlike Diotima's Grecian knot. She combed out and brushed little curls into place, and if the total effect was a bit silly, she never
noticed, because the face that smiled back at her from the mirror did
bear a faint resemblance to the goddess. The poise and beauty of her
idol, and the latter's sense of fulfillment, then rippled upward inside
her like the tiny, shallow, warm waves of a mysterious if not yet
deeply consummated union, much like sitting at the ocean's rim dabbling one's feet in the surf. What she did was akin to an act of religious worship—from the times when primitive man crept bodily into
the masks of the gods down to the rites and ceremonies of civilization, so carnal a joy of faithful mimicry has never quite lost its
power!—and had all the greater hold on Bonadea because of her
compulsive love of clothes and adornments. When Bonadea studied
her appearance in a new dress in her mirror, she could never have
imagined a time to come when leg-of-mutton sleeves, little curls
framing the forehead, and long bell-shaped skirts would be replaced
by knee-length skirts and hair cut like a boy's. Nor would she have
argued against it; her brain was simply incapable of imagining such a
possibility. She had always dressed like a lady and contemplated the
latest fashions, every six months, with reverence, as though she were
face-to-face with eternity. Even though an appeal to her intelligence
could have brought her to admit that such things were transitory, it
would in no way have lessened her reverence for them. The tyranny
of the mundane entered her bloodstream unnoticed, and the times
when one turned down the corner of one's visiting cards, or sent
one's friends New Year's greetings, or slipped off one's gloves at a
ball, were so long gone by the time one did *not* do any of these things
that they might as well have been a hundred years in the past: that is,
wholly unimaginable, impossible, and outdated. Which is why Bonadea without her clothes on was such a comical sight, stripped as she
was of all her ideological protection too, the naked victim of an inexorable compulsion that was sweeping her off her feet with the inhuman force of an earthquake.

But her periodic Fall from Civilization amid the vicissitudes of a
dull reality had been missing from her life of late, and ever since
Bonadea had been devoting such ritualistic care to her appearance,
the illegitimate portion of her life, for the first time since she was
twenty, was being lived as if she were a widow. In general, women

who are overly careful of their appearance may be presumed to be leading relatively chaste lives, because the means become the ends, just as great sports figures often make poor lovers, all-too-martial-looking officers make bad soldiers, and exceptionally intellectual-looking men are often blockheads. But with Bonadea it was not only a matter of where she chose to invest her energies but the amazing intensity with which she had turned to her new life. She penciled her eyebrows with a painter's loving care and enameled her forehead and cheeks for a heightened effect that reached beyond naturalism and mere reality into the style of religious art. Shaking her body into place inside a pliant corset, she suddenly felt a sisterly affection for her large breasts, which she had hitherto regarded as an embarrassing, because overly feminine, handicap. Her husband was quite taken aback when he tickled her neck with a finger and was told: "Please don't, you're spoiling my coiffure!" or when he tried to take her hand and she said: "Not now, I'm wearing my new dress!" But the power of sin had slipped from its physical mooring in the body and was drifting like a nova across the sky in the transfigured new world of a Bonadea who, in this unaccustomed softer radiance, felt released from her "excitability" as though the scales of some leprous disease had fallen away from her. For the first time since they were married, her spouse wondered whether there might be some third party threatening his domestic peace.

All that had happened was merely a phenomenon from the realm of vital systems. Clothes, when abstracted from the flow of present time and their transmogrifying function on the human body, and seen as forms in themselves, are strange tubes and excrescences worthy of being classed with such facial decorations as the ring through the nose or the lip-stretching disk. But how enchanting they become when seen together with the qualities they bestow on their wearer! What happens then is no less than the infusion, into some tangled lines on a piece of paper, of the meaning of a great word. Imagine a man's invisible kindness and moral excellence suddenly looming as a halo the size of the full moon and golden as an egg yolk right over his head, the way it does in old religious paintings, as he happens to be strolling down the avenue or heaping little tea sandwiches on his plate—what an overwhelming, shattering sensation it would be! And just such a power to make the invisible, and even the nonexistent, *visible* is what a well-made outfit demonstrates every day of the week.

Such things are like debtors who repay our investment in them with fantastic interest, and in that sense all things are indebted to us. For it is not only clothes that have such power, but convictions, prejudices, theories, hopes, faith in something or other, ideas, even thoughtlessness insofar as it is its quality of self-reflexiveness that gives it a sense of its own rightness. All these, by endowing us with the properties we lend them, serve the aim of presenting the world in a light that emanates from ourselves, and this is basically the task for which everyone has a method of his own. With great and varied skills we create a delusion that enables us to coexist serenely with the most monstrous things, simply because we recognize these frozen grimaces of the universe as a table or a chair, a shout or an outstretched arm, a speed or a roast chicken. We are capable of living between one open chasm of sky above our heads and another, slightly camouflaged chasm of sky beneath our feet, feeling as untroubled on earth as if we were in a room with the door closed. We know that our life is ebbing away both outward into the inhuman distances of cosmic space and downward into the inhuman microspace of the atom, while we go on dealing with a middle stratum, the things that make up our world, without troubling ourselves at all over the fact that this proves only a preference for impressions received in the middle distance, as it were. Such an attitude is considerably beneath our intellectual level, but that alone proves what a large part our feelings play in our intelligence. Our most important psychological machinery is, in fact, kept in motion to maintain us in a certain equilibrium, and all the emotions, all the passions in the world are nothing compared with the immense but wholly unconscious effort human beings make just to preserve their peace of mind. This works so well that there seems no point in drawing attention to it. But looked at closely, it does seem to be an extremely artificial state of mind that enables a man to walk upright among the circling constellations and permits him, surrounded as he is by an almost infinite unknown, to slip his hand with aplomb between the second and third buttons of his jacket. Not only does every human being, the idiot as much as the sage, apply his special skills to make this happen; all these personal stratagems are also cleverly built into society's moral and intellectual systems for maintaining its inner equilibrium, so that they serve the same purpose on a larger scale. This interlocking of systems resembles that of nature itself, where all the magnetic fields of the cosmos affect those of the earth without anyone noticing it, because the result is simply whatever happens on earth. The consequent psychological relief is so great that the wisest of men and the most ignorant of little girls, if left undisturbed, feel very clever and pleased with themselves.

But such states of satisfaction that might also be called compulsive states of feeling and volition, in a sense, are sometimes followed by the contrary; to resort again to the terminology of the madhouse, there is a sudden great flight of ideas worldwide, which leaves in its wake a repolarization of all human life around new centers and axes. The final cause of all great revolutions, which lies deeper than their effective cause, is not the accretion of intolerable conditions, but the loss of cohesion that bolstered the society's artificial peace of mind. There is an applicable saying by a famous early scholastic, *"Credo ut intelligam,"* which might be freely translated into a prayer for our times as "O Lord, please grant my spirit a production credit!" since every human creed is probably only a special instance of the credit system. In love as in business, in science as in the long jump, one has to believe before one can win and score, so how can it be otherwise for life as a whole? However well founded an order may be, it always rests in part on a voluntary faith in it, a faith that, in fact, always marks the spot where the new growth begins, as in a plant; once this unaccountable and uninsurable faith is used up, the collapse soon follows; epochs and empires crumble no differently from business concerns when they lose their credit.

And so this reflection on the principle of psychic equilibrium leads us from the beautiful example of Bonadea to the sad case of Kakania. For Kakania was the first country in our present historical phase from which God withdrew His credit: the love of life, faith in itself, and the ability of all civilized nations to disseminate the useful illusion that they have a mission to fulfill. It was an intelligent country, it housed cultivated people who, like cultivated people all over the globe, ran around in an unsettled state of mind amid a tremendous whirl of noise, speed, innovation, conflict, and whatever goes to make up the optical-acoustical landscape of our lives; like everybody else, they read and heard every day dozens of news items that made their hair stand on end, and were willing to work themselves up over them, even to intervene, but they never got around to it because a few minutes afterward the stimulus had already been displaced in their minds by more recent ones; like everyone else, they felt surrounded by murder, killings, passion, self-sacrifice, and greatness, all somehow going on within the Gordian knot that was forming around them, but they could never break through to these adventures because they were trapped in an office or somewhere, at work, and by evening, when they were free, their unresolved tensions exploded into forms of relaxation that failed to relax them. There was the special problem for persons of cultivated sensibilities, at least for those who did not devote themselves so single-mindedly to love as Bonadea: they no longer had the gift of faith or credit, nor had they learned to fake it. They no longer knew what their smiles, their sighs, their ideas, were for. What exactly was the point of their thoughts, their smiles? Their opinions were haphazard, their inclinations an old story, the scheme of things seemed to be hanging in midair, one ran into it as into a net, and there was nothing to do or leave undone with all one's heart, because there was no unifying principle. And so the cultivated person was someone who felt steadily mounting up a debt that he would never be able to pay off, felt bankruptcy inexorably approaching; and either inveighed against the times in which he was condemned to live, even though he enjoyed living in them like anyone else, or else hurled himself with the courage of those who have nothing to lose at every idea that promised a change.

It was the same as anywhere else in the world, of course, but when God cut off Kakania's credit, He did it in so special a style that whole nations had their eyes opened to the high cost of civilization. Like bacteria they had been sitting pretty in their culture medium, without bothering their heads about the proper curvature of the sky above or anything, when suddenly things tightened up. Although men are not normally aware of it, they must believe that they are something more than they are in order to be capable of being what they are; they need to feel this something more above and around them, and there are times when they suddenly miss it. What is missed is something imaginary. Nothing at all had happened in Kakania, and formerly it would have been thought of as the old, unobtrusive Kakanian way of life, but this nothing had become as disturbing as getting no sleep or seeing no sense in anything. And so it was easy enough for the intellectuals, once they had persuaded themselves that an ethnically homogeneous culture was the answer, to make the Kakanian ethnic minorities believe it, as a kind of substitute for religion or for the ideal of the Good Emperor in Vienna, or simply as a way of understanding the incomprehensible fact that there are seven days in the week. There are so many inexplicable things in life, but one loses sight of them when singing the national anthem. It would naturally be at such a moment that a good Kakanian could have joyfully answered the question of what he was by saying: "Nothing," meaning that Something that could make of a Kakanian everything he had never yet been! But the Kakanians were not so stiff-necked a people and contented themselves with a compromise, in that every nationality tried only to do with every other nationality whatever suited its own purposes. It is naturally hard in these circumstances to empathize with grievances not one's own. After two thousand years of altruistic teachings, we have become so unselfish that even if it means you or I have to suffer, we are bound to take the part of the other fellow. But it would be wrong to think of the notorious Kakanian nationalist rivalries as particularly savage. It was more a historical process than a real one. The people actually quite liked each other; even though they did crack each other's heads and spit in each other's faces, it was done as a matter of higher cultural considerations, as when a man who normally wouldn't hurt a fly, for instance, will sit in court under the image of Christ Crucified and condemn another man to death. It is only fair to say that whenever their higher selves relaxed a bit, the Kakanians breathed a sigh of relief and, born consumers of food and drink as they were, looked with amazement upon their role as the tools of history.

110

MOOSBRUGGER DISSOLVED AND PRESERVED

Moosbrugger was still in prison, waiting for further psychiatric examinations. It felt like a solid stack of days. Each day made itself distinctly felt when it came, of course, but toward evening it already began to merge with the stack. Moosbrugger certainly registered the presence of convicts, guards, corridors, courtyards, a glimpse of blue sky, a passing cloud or two, food, water, and now and then an official checking up on him, but these impressions were too feeble to be lasting. He had no watch, no sun, no work, to tell him the time. He was always hungry. He was always tired, from pacing around his seven square yards, which is far more tiring than wandering freely for miles. He was bored with everything he did, as if he had to keep stirring a pot of glue. But when he considered it as a whole, it seemed to him that day and night, his cleaning his plate and again cleaning his plate, inspections and checkups, all droned along one after the other without a break, and he found that entertaining. His life clock had gone out of order; it could be turned ahead or back. He liked that; it was his sort of thing. Things long past and fresh happenings were no longer kept apart artificially, and when it was all the same, then what they called "at different times" no longer stuck to it like the red thread they tie to a twin baby's neck so they can tell it from the other one. All the irrelevancies vanished from his life. When he pondered this life of his, he talked with himself inwardly, slowly, laying equal stress on every syllable; in this way life sang a different tune from the one heard every day. He often let his mind linger on a word for a long time, and when he finally moved on, without quite knowing how, after a while the word would turn up again somewhere else. It tickled him to think how much was happening for him that nobody knew about. The sense of being inwardly at peace with himself that sometimes came to him is hard to describe. Anyone can conceive of a man's life flowing along like a brook, but what Moosbrugger felt was his life flowing like a brook through a vast, still lake. As it flowed onward it continued to mingle with what it was leaving behind and became almost indistinguishable from the movements on either side of it. Once, in a half-waking dream, he had a sense of having worn this life's Moosbrugger like an ill-fitting coat on his back; now, when he opened it a bit, the most curious sort of lining came billowing out silkily, endless as a forest.

He no longer cared what was going on outside. Somewhere a war was going on. Somewhere there was a big wedding. Now the King of Belukhastan is coming, he thought. Everywhere soldiers were being drilled, whores were walking their beat, carpenters were standing among rafters. In the taverns of Stuttgart the beer came pouring from the same curving yellow taps as in Belgrade. On the road there were always the police demanding to see your papers. Then they stamped them. Everywhere there are bedbugs or no bedbugs. Work or no work. The women are the same everywhere. The doctors in all the hospitals are the same. When a man leaves his work in the evening the streets are full of people with nothing to do. It's all the same, always and everywhere; nobody has any new ideas. When Moosbrugger saw his first plane overhead in the blue sky—now, that was something! But then there was one plane after another, and they all looked alike. The sameness of things out there was different from the way his thoughts were all alike in being wonderful. He couldn't figure it out, and anyway it had always got in his way. He shook his head. To hell with the world, he thought. Or to hell with him and let them hang him: whatever happened, what did he have to lose . . . ?

And yet he sometimes would walk as if absentmindedly to the door and quietly try the place where the lock was on the outside. Then an eye would glare through the peephole and an angry voice come from the corridor, calling him names. Such insults made Moosbrugger move quickly back into his cell, and it was then that he felt locked up and robbed. Four walls and an iron door are nothing when you can freely walk in and out. Bars on an unfamiliar window are nothing special, and a plank bed or wooden table always in its place is quite in order. It's only when a man can't do what he wants with them that something crazy happens. Here things, made by human beings to serve them, slaves whose appearance one doesn't even bother to notice, suddenly get uppity. They block one's way. When Moosbrugger noticed these things giving him orders he had a good mind to smash them, and it was a struggle to convince himself that it was beneath him to fight these minions of the law. But his hands were twitching so hard he was afraid he was going to have a fit.

Out of the whole wide world they had picked these seven square yards, and Moosbrugger was pacing them, back and forth. The minds of the sane people out there, incidentally, who were not locked up, worked much the same as his own. They who had taken such a lively interest in him not so long ago had quickly forgotten him. He had been put in this place like a nail driven into the wall; once in, nobody notices it anymore. Other Moosbruggers were taking their turn; they were not himself, not even the same person every time, but they served the same purpose. There had been a sex crime, a grim story, a horrible murder, the act of a madman, of a man not quite responsible, the sort of thing to watch out for, but then the police and the courts had done their job. . . . Such vague and vacuous generalizations and memory tags loosely held the now-desiccated remains of the incident somewhere in their wide net. Moosbrugger's name was forgotten, the details were forgotten. He might have been "a squirrel, a hare, or a fox," the public remembered nothing specific about him, there remained only dim, wide areas of overlapping general notions, like the gray shimmer in a telescope focused at too great a distance. This failure to make connections, the cruelty of a mind that shuffles concepts around without bothering about the burden of suffering and life that weighs down every decision, was what the general mind had in common with that of Moosbrugger; but what was in his crazed brain a dream, a fairy tale, that flawed or odd spot in the mirror of consciousness which does not reflect reality but lets the light through, was lacking in society as a whole, unless some individual, in his obscure excitement, showed a hint of it here and there.

And what did concern Moosbrugger specifically, this particular Moosbrugger and none other, the one temporarily stored on these seven square yards of the world—the feeding, surveillance, authorized treatment, final disposal of the case by life or death sentence—was all in the hands of a relatively small group of people with a wholly different attitude. Here eyes on duty spied on him, voices came down hard on him for the slightest misstep. Never did fewer than two guards enter his cell. He was always handcuffed when they took him through the corridors. They acted with the fear and caution that had to do with this particular Moosbrugger within this limited area but was in strange contrast with the treatment accorded to him in general. He often complained about these strict measures. But when he did, the captain, the warden, the doctor, the priest, whoever heard him, turned a frozen face on him and told him he was being treated according to regulations. So regulations had taken the place of the interest the world had once taken in him, and Moosbrugger thought: "You've got a long rope around your neck and you can't see who's pulling it." He was roped to the outside world but, as it were, around the corner, out of sight. People who mostly never gave him a thought, who did not even know he existed, or to whom he meant at best no more than what some chicken on a village street means to a university professor of zoology—they were all in it together, preparing the doom that he felt tugging at him in some ghostly way. Some skirt in an office was typing a memo for his record. A registrar was ingeniously classifying it for filing. Some high functionary of the court was drawing up the latest directive for implementing his sentence. Psychiatrists were debating how to draw the line between the purely psychopathic constitution in certain cases of epilepsy and its manifestations when combined with other syndromes. Jurists were analyzing the factors that mitigated culpability in relation to factors that might modify the sentence. A bishop denounced the unraveling of the moral fabric, and a game warden's complaint to Bonadea's husband, the judge, about the excessive increase in foxes was reinforcing that eminent legal mind's bias in favor of reinforcing the inflexibility of the law.

It is such impersonal matters that go into the making of personal happenings in a way that for the present eludes description. When Moosbrugger's case was shorn of all its individual romantic elements, of interest only to him and to the few people he had murdered, not much more was left of it than what could be gathered from the list of references to works cited that Ulrich's father had enclosed in a recent letter to his son. Such a list looks like this: AH. AMP. AAC. AKA. AP. ASZ. BKL. BGK. BUD. CN. DTJ. DJZ. FBvM. GA. GS. JKV. KBSA. MMW. NG. PNW. R. VSvM. WMW. ZGS. ZMB. ZP. ZSS. Addickes ibid. Beling ibid., and so on. Written out, these would read: Annales d'Hygiène Publique et de Médicine légale, ed. Brouardel, Paris; Annales Médico-Psychologiques, ed. Ritti . . . etc.,

etc., making a list a page long even when reduced to the briefest of abbreviations. The truth is not a crystal that can be slipped into one's pocket, but an endless current into which one falls headlong. Imagine every one of these abbreviations trailing a dozen or hundreds of printed pages, for each page a man with ten fingers writing it, and for each of his ten fingers ten disciples and ten opponents with ten fingers each, and at every fingertip a tenth of a personal idea, and you have a dim notion of what the truth is like. Without it not even that well-known sparrow can fall off the roof. Sun, wind, food brought it there, and illness, hunger, cold, or a cat killed it, but none of this could have happened without the operation of laws, biological, psychological, meteorological, physical, chemical, sociological, and all the rest, and it is much less of a strain to be merely looking for such laws than to have to make them up, as is done in the moral and judicial disciplines.

As for Moosbrugger himself, with his great respect for human knowledge, although he had, unfortunately, so small a portion of it: he never would have understood his situation completely even had he known exactly what it was. He had a dim sense of it. He felt that he was in an unstable condition. His big, powerful body was not as solid as it looked. Sometimes the open sky peered right into his skull. Just as it had, so often, in the old days on the road. And though he sometimes wished he could shake it off, he was never free, these days, of a certain solemn exaltation that streamed toward him, through the prison walls, from all the world. So there he sat, the wild, captive threat of a dreaded act, like an uninhabited coral island in a boundless sea of scientific papers that surrounded him invisibly on all sides.

111

To the Legal Mind, Insanity Is an All-or-Nothing Proposition

Still, a criminal's life can often be a picnic compared with the strenuous brainwork he imposes on the pundits of the law. The offender simply takes advantage of the fact that the transitions in nature from health to sickness are smooth and imperceptible, while to the jurist it is a case of "The arguments *pro* and *contra* freedom of the will or insight into the wrongful nature of the act so tend to cut across and cancel each other out that no system of logic can lead to other than a problematic verdict." A jurist has logical reasons for bearing in mind that "in regard to one and the same act there is no admissible possibility that it can arise from a mixture of two different mental states," and he will not permit "the principle of moral freedom in relation to physically conditioned states of mind to be lost in a vague mist of empirical thought." He is not beholden to Nature for his concepts, but penetrates Nature with the flame of his thinking and the sword of moral law. A heated debate on this point had broken out in the committee, of which Ulrich's father was a member, convoked by the Ministry of Justice to update the penal code; however, it had taken some time and several reminders from his father to bring Ulrich to the point of studying, like a good son, his father's position paper with all its enclosed documentation.

Ulrich's "affectionate father," as he signed even the most embittered of his letters, had declared and proposed that a partially insane person should be acquitted only when there was sufficient evidence that his delusory system contained ideas that, were they not delusory, would justify the act or exempt it from liability to punishment. Professor Schwung, on the other hand—possibly because he had been the old man's friend and colleague for forty years, which must after all lead to a violent difference of opinion sooner or later—had declared and proposed that such an individual, in whom the state of being responsible for his actions and not being responsible for his actions must occur in constant alternation, since from a legal point of view they could not coexist simultaneously, should be acquitted only if and when there was evidence, with respect to that specific act of the will, that at the precise moment of this act of the will the offender had been unable to control himself. So much for the point at issue. The layman can readily see that it may be no less difficult for the criminal not to overlook any moment of sane volition at the instant he performs the act in question than not to overlook any thought that might perhaps make him liable to punishment; but the law is not obliged to make thinking and moral conduct a bed of roses! And as both these learned jurists were equally zealous on behalf of the law's dignity, and neither could win a majority of the committee over to his side, they began by charging each other with error, and then in swift succession with illogical thinking, deliberate misunderstanding, and a lapse of standards. They did this at first within the privacy of the irresolute committee, but then, when the meetings came to a halt, had to be adjourned, and finally suspended indefinitely, Ulrich's father wrote two pamphlets, entitled "Paragraph 318 of the Penal Code and the True Spirit of the Law" and "Par. 318 of the Penal Code and the Muddied Wellsprings of Our Jurisprudence," which Ulrich found among the enclosures with his father's letter, together with the critical review of them published by Professor Schwung in the journal *The Legal Scholar*.

These pamphlets were full of "and"s and "or"s, because the question of whether these two views could be combined by an "and" or must be kept apart by an "or" had to be "cleared up." When after a long interval the committee finally reassembled, it, too, had split into an "and" and an "or" faction. There was also another fraction, which supported the simple proposal to let the degree of culpability and responsibility rise and fall in proportion to the rise and fall in the degree of the psychological effort that would suffice, in the given pathological circumstances, to maintain self-control. This grouping was opposed by a fourth faction, which insisted that before all else there must be a clear and definite decision as to whether a criminal could be said to be responsible for his actions at all; logically, where there was a lessened responsibility for an action, there had first to be a responsibility, and even if the criminal was only in part responsible for his actions he must still suffer the penalty with his entire person, because the guilty part was not otherwise accessible to the workings of the law. This met with opposition from yet another faction, which, while granting the principle, pointed out that nature did not follow it, in that nature produced half-crazy people upon whom the benefits of the law could be conferred only by modifying their punishment, in view of the circumstances, without at all condoning their guilt. This led to the formation of a "soundness of mind" faction as opposed to a "full responsibility" faction, and it was only when these also had split up into enough splinter groups that those aspects of the problem came to light which had not yet occasioned a difference of opinion.

Naturally, no professional man of our time bases his arguments on those of philosophy and theology, but as perspectives—empty, like space, and yet, like space, telescoping the objects in it—these two rivals for the last word of wisdom persist everywhere in invading the optics of each special field of knowledge. And so here, too, the carefully avoided question of whether a human being could be regarded as a free agent, that good old problem of the freedom of the will, provided the focus for all the differences of opinion, although it was not under consideration. For if a man is morally free, he must, in practice, be subjected by punishment to a compulsion in which no one, in theory, believes. If, on the other hand, he is regarded not as free but as the meeting ground for inexorably interlocking natural processes, then one cannot consider him morally accountable for what he does, even though one can effectively discourage him from doing it by inflicting punishment on him. This problem gave rise to still another faction, which proposed that the culprit be divided into two parts: a zoologic-psychological entity, which did not concern the judge, and a juridical entity, which, though only a fiction, was legally free and accountable. Fortunately, this proposal remained confined to theory.

It is hard to be brief in doing justice to justice. The commission consisted of about twenty legal pundits who were capable of adopting several thousand different points of view among themselves, as can easily be calculated. The laws to be updated had been in operation since the year 1852, so that on top of everything else they had proved highly durable, not lightly to be replaced by anything else. In any case, the fixed institution of the law cannot keep up with every brain wave of currently fashionable tendencies, as one participant rightly pointed out. The conscientiousness with which the commission's task had to be performed is best appreciated in the light of the fact that statistically, about seventy out of every hundred people who commit crimes that damage society may be sure of slipping through the meshes of the law. How clear this makes our duty to give all the more rigorous thought to the 25 percent or so who get caught! This situation may of course have improved slightly, and besides, it would be wrong to see the real purpose of this report as making fun of the ice flowers that logic brings so exquisitely to bloom in the heads of our legal pundits; this has been done already by innumerable people whose mental climate tends toward slush. On the contrary, it was masculine strictness, arrogance, moral soundness, impregnability, and complacency, all qualities of temperament and largely virtues that, as we say, we hope never to lose, which prevented the learned members of the commission from making an unprejudiced use of their intelligence. They dealt with men as boys, in the manner of elderly schoolteachers in charge of a pupil who needed only to be willing to learn and pay attention in order to "do well"—and thereby simply evoked the prerevolutionary sentiments of the generation before their own, that of 1848. No doubt their understanding of psychology was about fifty years out of date; that easily happens when one has to till one's own fields of expertise with the borrowed tools of a neighbor, and the deficiency is usually made good as soon as circumstances permit. The one thing that remains permanently behind the times, especially because it prides itself on its steadfastness, is the human heart, most of all that of the conscientious man. The mind is never so hard, dry, and twisted as when it has a slight chronic heart condition.

This ultimately led to a furious outburst. When the various skirmishes had worn down all the participants and kept the work from getting on, more and more voices were raised to suggest a compromise, which would look much as all formulas do when designed to cover up an unbridgeable gap with fine phrases. There was a tendency to agree on the familiar definition that termed "of sound mind" those criminals whose mental and moral qualities make them capable of committing a crime, but not those who lacked such qualities; a most extraordinary definition, which has the advantage of making it very hard for criminals to qualify, so that those who do would almost be entitled to wear their convict's uniform with the aura of an academic degree.

But at this point Ulrich's father, facing the threatening lull of the Jubilee Year, and a definition as round as an egg, which he regarded as a hand grenade aimed at his own person, took what he called his sensational turn to the social school of thought. The social view holds that the criminally "degenerate" individual must be judged not morally but only insofar as he is likely to harm society as a whole. Hence the more dangerous he is, the more responsible he is for his actions, with the inescapable logical consequence that those criminals who seem to be the most innocent, the mentally sick, who are by nature least susceptible to correction by punishment, must be threatened with the harshest penalties, harsher than those for sane persons, so that the deterrent factor of the punishment be equal for all. It might fairly be expected that Professor Schwung would have a hard time finding an objection to this social view of the matter. This expectation was borne out, which was why he resorted to expedients that drove Ulrich's father in turn to leave the path of jurisprudence, which was threatening to lose itself in the sands of controversy within the committee, and appeal to his son to turn to account those connections with high and even the highest circles, which he owed to his father, in his father's good cause. For instead of making any attempt at a sober refutation, his colleague Schwung had at once fastened maliciously on the term "social" to denounce it, in a new publication, as "materialistic" and suspect of being infected with "the Prussian idea of the State."

"My dear son," Ulrich's father wrote, "of course I immediately pointed out the Roman precedent for the social school of legal theory, which is by no means Prussian in origin, but this may be of no use against such a denunciation and defamation calculated with diabolical malice to create in *high quarters* the predictably loathsome impression only too easily linked there with the thought of materialism and Prussia. These are no longer the kind of allegations against which a man can defend himself. Rumors are being spread, so vague that they are hardly likely to be carefully scrutinized in *high quarters,* where being forced to deal with them at all may be held

against their innocent victim quite as much as against the unscrupulous slanderer. I, who have all my life scorned to use backstairs methods, now see myself driven to ask you . . ." And so on, and so the
letter ended.

112

ARNHEIM SETS HIS FATHER, SAMUEL, AMONG THE GODS AND DECIDES TO GET ULRICH INTO HIS POWER. SOLIMAN WANTS TO FIND OUT MORE ABOUT HIS OWN ROYAL FATHER

Arnheim had rung for Soliman. It was a long time since he had felt
like talking with the boy, and now that he did, the rascal seemed to
be wandering around in the hotel somewhere.

Ulrich's opposition had finally succeeded in wounding Arnheim.

Arnheim had of course not been blind to the fact that Ulrich was
working against him. Ulrich did it impersonally, with an effect like
that of water on fire, salt on sugar, undermining Arnheim's influence
almost without conscious intent. Arnheim felt sure that Ulrich even
took advantage of Diotima's reliance on him to drop unfavorable or
satiric remarks about Arnheim.

Nothing of the kind had happened to him in ages. His usual
method for keeping the upper hand failed him here. The effect of a
great man who is his own man is like that of a great beauty; deny it,
and it is a punctured balloon, or a Greek statue on which someone
has put a hat. A beautiful woman loses her looks when she ceases to
please, and a great man when ignored may become an even greater
one but ceases to be a great public figure. Not that Arnheim realized
it in these terms, but he thought: "I can't stand opposition, because
only the intellect thrives on it, and I despise anyone who is all
intellect."

Arnheim took it for granted that he could find a way to neutralize his opponent. But he wanted to win Ulrich over, to influence him, teach him, compel his admiration. In order to make this easier, he had talked himself into feeling a deep and paradoxical affection for Ulrich, though he would not have known how to account for this. He had nothing to fear from Ulrich, and there was nothing he wanted from him; he knew that neither Count Leinsdorf nor Section Chief Tuzzi was a friend, and otherwise things were going, if slowly, just as he wanted them to go. Ulrich's countereffect paled beside Arnheim's effect; all that was left of it was a wispy protest, which seemed to accomplish nothing except perhaps to delay Diotima's resolve by faintly paralyzing that marvelous woman's purpose. Arnheim had subtly pried it out of her and now could not help smiling when he thought of it. Was it a wistful smile or a malicious one? Such distinctions, in matters of this kind, are of no consequence. It was only fair, he thought, that his enemy's criticism and resistance should work unconsciously in his, Arnheim's, favor. It was the victory of the deeper cause, one of those marvelously lucid, self-resolving complications of life. It was destiny, Arnheim felt, that seemed to bring him and the younger man together and made him yield points to Ulrich, who did not understand. For Ulrich resisted all his blandishments; he seemed moronically insensitive to his own social advantage, either not noticing or not appreciating this offer of friendship.

There was something that Arnheim called Ulrich's wit. What he meant by it was, in part, this failure of a brilliant man to recognize his own advantage and to adjust his mind to the great aims and opportunities that would bring him status and a solid footing in life. Ulrich acted on the absurd contrary idea that life had to adjust itself to suit his mind. Arnheim called Ulrich's image to mind: as tall as himself, younger, without the softening of contour he could not fail to notice on his own body; something unconditionally independent in his look—something Arnheim attributed, not without envy, to Ulrich's coming of ascetic-scholarly stock, which was his idea of Ulrich's origins. The face showed less concern about money and appearances than a rising dynasty of experts in the processing of waste had permitted their descendants to feel. Yet there was something missing in this face. It was life that was missing here; the marks of experience were shockingly absent! As Arnheim perceived this in a flash of surreal clarity, he was so disturbed by it that it made him realize all over again how much he cared about Ulrich—why, here was a face almost visibly headed for disaster! He brooded over the conflicting sense of envy and anxiety this made him feel; there was a sad satisfaction in it, as when someone has taken a coward's refuge in a safe port. A sudden violent upsurge of envy and disapproval drove to the surface the thought he had been both seeking and avoiding, that Ulrich probably was a man capable of sacrificing not only the interest but all the capital of his soul, if circumstances called for it. Strangely enough, it was this, in fact, that Arnheim also meant by Ulrich's wit. At this moment, recalling the expression he had coined, it became perfectly clear to him: the idea that a man could let himself be swept away by passion, beyond the limits of the atmosphere where he could breathe, struck Arnheim as a witty notion, a joke.

When Soliman at last came sidling into the room and stood facing his master, Arnheim had almost forgotten why he had sent for him, but he found it soothing to have a living and devoted creature close by. He paced up and down the room, with a stern expression, and the black disk of the boy's face turned this way and that, watching him.

"Sit down!" Arnheim ordered; he had turned on his heel when he reached the corner and kept standing there as he spoke: "The great Goethe, somewhere in *Wilhelm Meister*, has a maxim charged with much feeling to guide our conduct in life: 'Think in order to act, act in order to think.' Can you understand this? No, I don't suppose you can understand it. . . ." He answered his own question and fell silent again. This prescription holds all of life's wisdom, he thought, and the man who wants to oppose me knows only half of it: namely, thinking. This, too, could be what he had meant by "merely witty." He recognized Ulrich's weakness. Wit comes from witting, or knowing; the wisdom of language itself here pointed to the intellectual origins of this quality, its ghostly, emotionally impoverished nature. The witty man is inclined to outsmart himself, to ignore those natural limits the man of true feeling respects. This insight brought the matter of Diotima and the soul's capital substance into a more pleasing light, and as he was thinking this, Arnheim said to Soliman: "This maxim holds all the wisdom life can give, and it has led me to take away your books and make you go to work."

Soliman said nothing and made a solemn face.

"You have seen my father several times," Arnheim said suddenly. "Do you remember him?"

Soliman responded to this by rolling his eyes so that the whites showed, and Arnheim said pensively, "You see, my father almost never reads a book. How old do you think my father is?" Again he did not wait for an answer and added: "He is already over seventy and still has a hand in everything in the world that might concern our firm." Arnheim resumed pacing the room in silence. He felt an irrepressible urge to talk about his father, but could not say everything that was on his mind. No one knew better than he that even his father sometimes lost out in a business deal; but nobody would have believed him, because once a man has the reputation of being Napoleon, even his lost battles count as victories. So there had never been any way for Arnheim of holding his own beside his father other than the one he had chosen, that of making culture, politics, and society serve business. Old Arnheim seemed pleased enough at the younger Arnheim's great knowledge and accomplishments, but whenever an important decision had to be made, and the problem had been discussed and analyzed for days on end, from the production angle and the financial angle and for its impact on the world economy and civilization, he thanked everyone, not infrequently ordered the exact opposite of what had been proposed, and responded to all objections with only a helpless, stubborn smile. Even the directors often shook their heads dubiously over this way he had, but then sooner or later it would always turn out that the old man had somehow been right. It was more or less like an old hunter or mountain guide having to listen to a meteorologists' conference but then always ending up in favor of the prophecies delivered by his own rheumatism; not so very odd, basically, since there are so many problems where one's rheumatism happens to be a surer guide than science, nor does having an exact forecast matter all that much in a world where things always turn out differently from what one had expected, anyway, and the thing is to be shrewd and tough in adapting oneself to their waywardness. So Paul Arnheim should have had no trouble in understanding that an old hand at the game knows a great deal that cannot be foreseen theoretically, and can do a great deal because of his knowledge; still, it was a fateful day for him when he discovered that old Samuel had intuition.

"Do you know what is meant by intuition?" Arnheim asked, from deep in his thoughts, as though groping for the shadow of an excuse to speak of it. Soliman blinked hard, as he always did when he was being cross-examined about something he had forgotten to do, and Arnheim again caught himself up. "I'm feeling a bit on edge today," he said, "as you can't be expected to know, of course. But please pay close attention to what I am about to tell you: Making money often gets us into situations in which we don't look too good, as you can imagine. All this having to watch your arithmetic and make sure you get a profit out of everything, all the time, runs strictly counter to the ideal of a great and noble life such as was possible fox a man to aim at in happier times long ago. In those days they could make of murder the noble virtue of bravery, but it seems doubtful to me that something of the sort can be done with bookkeeping: there is no real goodness, no dignity, no depth of feeling in it. Money turns everything into an abstraction, it is so coldly rational; whenever I see money I can't help thinking—I don't know whether you can follow me here—thinking of mistrustful fingers testing it, of loud arguments and much shrewd manipulation, all equally repulsive to me."

He broke off and fell back into his solitary musing, as he thought of those uncles who had patted him on the head when he was a child, saying what a good little head he had on his shoulders. A good little head for figures. How he hated that kind of attitude! Those shining gold coins reflected the mind of a family that had worked its way up in the world. Feeling ashamed of his family was beneath him; on the contrary, he made a point of acknowledging his origins with a fine modesty, especially in the highest circles, but he dreaded any show of the calculating family mind as though it were a taint, like speaking with too much intensity and gesturing with hands aflutter, which would make him impossible among the best people.

This was probably the root of his reverence for the irrational. The aristocracy was irrational—this might be taken as a witticism reflecting on the intellectual limitations of the nobility, but not as Arnheim meant it. It had to do with the fact that as a Jew he could not be appointed an officer in the Army Reserve, nor could he, as an Arnheim, occupy the lowly position of a noncom, so he was simply declared unfit for military service, and to this day he refused to see only the absurdity of this without duly appreciating the code of honor behind it. This recollection moved him to enrich his speech to Soliman with some further remarks.

"It is possible"—he picked up the thread, for despite his distaste for pedantry he was a methodical man, even in his digressions—"it is possible, even probable, that our noble families were not always paragons of what we today consider a noble bearing. To assemble all those huge landed estates upon which their titles of nobility came to be based, their forebears must have been no less calculating and sharp in their dealings than today's men of business; it is even possible that the modern businessman conducts his affairs with far more honesty. But there is a force in the earth itself, you know, something in the soil, in hunting, in warfare, in faith, in tilling the land—in short, in the physical life of people who used their heads far less than their arms and legs; it was nature itself that gave them the strength to which they ultimately owed their dignity, their nobility, their disinclination to demean themselves in any way whatsoever."

He wondered whether he had not allowed his mood to trick him into going too far. What if Soliman missed his master's meaning and misunderstood the words to suggest that he was entitled to think less highly of the upper classes? But something unexpected happened. Soliman had been fidgeting on his seat for a while, and he now interrupted his master with a question.

"If you please, sir," Soliman asked, "about my father: is he a king?"

Arnheim gave him a startled look. "I don't know anything about that," he said, still somewhat sternly, though inwardly a little amused. But as he gazed at Soliman's serious, almost resentful face, he found it touching. It pleased him to see the boy taking everything so seriously. He is a dimwit, he thought, and really a tragic case. Somehow he equated witlessness with a heavy feeling of well-being. In a gently didactic manner, he went on to give the boy something more of an answer to his question. "There is hardly any reason to assume that your father is a king. More likely he had a hard living to earn, because I found you in a troupe of jugglers on a beach."

"How much did I cost?" Soliman persisted.

"My dear boy, how can you expect me to remember that today? It couldn't have been much. But why worry about that now? We are born to create our own kingdom. Next year sometime I may let you take a commercial course, and then you could make a start as a trainee in one of our offices. Of course it will depend on you what you make of it, but I shall keep an eye on you. You might, for instance, aim at eventually representing our interests in places where the colored people already have some influence. We'd have to move with care, of course, but being a black man might turn out to have certain advantages for you. It is only in doing such work that you can come to understand fully how much these years under my immediate supervision have done for you already, and I can tell you one thing now: you belong to a race that still bears some of nature's own nobility. In our medieval tales of chivalry, black kings always played a distinguished role. If you cultivate what you have of spiritual quality—your dignity, your goodness of heart, your openness, your courageous love of the truth, and the even greater courage to resist intolerance, jealousy, resentment, and all the petty nervous spitefulness that stigmatizes most people nowadays—if you can do that, you will certainly make your way as a man of business, because we are called upon to bring the world not only our wares but a better life."

Arnheim had not talked so intimately with Soliman in a long time, and the idea that any onlooker might think him a fool made him uneasy, but there was no onlooker, and besides, what he was saying to Soliman was only the surface layer covering far deeper currents of thought he was keeping to himself. What he was saying about the aristocratic mind and the historic rise of the nobility was moving, deep inside him, in the opposite direction to his spoken words. Inwardly he could not repress the thought that never since the beginning of the world had anything sprung from spiritual purity and good intentions alone; everything was far more likely to spring from the common dirt, which in time sheds its crudeness and cleans itself up and eventually even gives rise to greatness and purity of thought. The rise of the nobility was not based on conditions pregnant with a lofty humanism, he thought, any more than was the growth of the garbage-moving business into a worldwide corporation, and yet the one had blossomed into the silver age of the eighteenth century, and the other had led directly to Arnheim. Life was facing him, in short, with an inescapable problem best formulated in the dilemma: How much common dirt is necessary and acceptable as the soil in which to propagate high-mindedness?

On another level, his thoughts had meanwhile intermittently pursued what he had been saying to Soliman about intuition and reason, and he suddenly had a vivid memory of the first time he had told his father that he—the old man—did business by intuition. Intuition was fashionable at the time with all those who could not justify what they did by logic; it was playing the same role, more or less, as is played today by having "flair." Every false or ultimately unsatisfactory move was credited to intuition, and intuition was used for everything from cooking to writing books, but the elder Arnheim had not heard of it, and he actually let himself go so far as to look up in surprise at his son, for whom it was a moment of triumph. "Making money," he said to his father, "forces us to think along lines that are not always in the best style. Still, it will probably be up to us men of big business to take over the leadership of the masses the next time there's a turning point in history, whether we are spiritually ready or not. But if there is anything in the world that can give me the courage to face such a burden, it is you; you have the vision and willpower of the kings and prophets of the great old days, who were still guided by God. Your way of tackling a deal is ineffable, a mystery, and I must say that all mysteries that elude calculation are in the same class, whether it is the mystery of courage or of invention or of the stars!" It was humiliating to see old Arnheim, who had been looking up at him, drop his eyes again, after his son's first sentences, back to his newspaper, from which he did not raise them on any subsequent occasion when the younger man talked of business and intuition. Such was the characteristic relationship between father and son, and on a third level of his thoughts, on the same screen with these remembered images, as it were, Arnheim was analyzing it even now. He regarded his father's superior gift for business, though it always depressed him to think of it, as a kind of primitive force that would forever elude the son, a more complicated man; this relieved him of having to keep striving in vain to emulate the inimitable, and at the same time provided him with letters patent of his own noble descent. This brilliant double maneuver turned money into a suprapersonal, mythical force for which only the most primitive originality could be a match, and it also set his forebear among the gods, quite as had the ancient heroes, who undoubtedly also thought of their mythical forefather, with all the awe he inspired, as just a shade more primitive than themselves.

But on a fourth level of his mind he knew nothing of the smile that hovered over that third level, and rethought the same idea in a serious vein, as he considered the role he still hoped to play on this earth. Such levels of thought are of course not to be taken literally, as if superimposed on each other like actual layers of the soil, but are merely meant to suggest currents of thought, flowing from various directions and perpetually crisscrossing under the influence of strong emotional conflicts. All his life, Arnheim had felt an almost morbidly sensitive dislike of wit and irony, a dislike probably motivated by a not inconsiderable hereditary tendency to both. He had suppressed this tendency because he felt it to be ignoble, a quality of the intellectual riffraff, yet it unaccountably popped up at this very moment, when he was feeling his most aristocratic and anti-intellectual, with regard to Diotima: just when his feelings were on tiptoe, ready to take flight, as it were, he felt a devilish temptation to give sublimity the slip by making one of those pointed lethal jokes about love he had heard often enough from the lips of low-ranking or coarse characters.

As his mind rose again to the surface through all these strata of thought, he abruptly found himself gazing at Soliman's gloomily listening face, like a black punchball on which unintelligible words of wisdom had come raining down like so many blows. What an absurd position I am getting myself into! Arnheim thought.

Soliman looked as if he had fallen asleep on his chair with his eyes wide open; as his master reached the end of that one-sided conversation, the eyes set themselves in motion, while the body refused to stir, as though still waiting for the word to wake up. Arnheim saw it and saw in the black boy's gaze the craving to hear more about whatever intrigues could have brought a king's son to be a valet. This gaze, lunging at him like claws outstretched for their prey, momentarily reminded Arnheim of that gardener's helper who had made off with pieces from his collection, and he said to himself with a sigh that he would probably always be lacking in the natural acquisitive instinct. It suddenly occurred to him that this would also sum up, in a word, his relation to Diotima. Painfully moved, he felt how, at the very summit of his life, a cold shadow separated him from everything he had ever touched. It was not an easy thought for a man who had just stated the principle that a man must think in order to act, and who had always striven to make all greatness his own and to transform whatever was less than great with the stamp of his own distinguished imprint. But the shadow had slipped between him and the objects of his desire, despite the willpower he had never lacked, and Arnheim surprised himself by thinking that he could see a connection between that shadow and those shimmers of awe that had cast their veils over his youth, as if, mishandled in some way, they had turned into an almost imperceptible skin of ice. Why this ice did not melt even when confronted with Diotima's unworldly heart he could not tell; but, like a most unwelcome jab of a pain that had only been waiting for a touch to awaken it, there came the sudden thought of Ulrich. It came with the realization that the same shadow rested on the other man's life, but with so different an effect! Within the range of human passions, that of a man jealous of another man's personality is seldom accorded the recognition its intensity has earned for it, and the discovery that his uncontrollable irritation with Ulrich resembled, on a deeper level, the hostile encounter of two brothers unaware of each other's identity gave him a rather pleasant jolt. Arnheim compared their two personalities from this angle with a new interest. Ulrich had even less of the crude acquisitive instinct for advantages in life, and his immunity to the sublime acquisitive instinct for status and recognition, whatever it was that mattered, was downright infuriating. This man needed none of the weight and substance of life. His sober zeal, which was undeniable, was not a self-serving passion; it came close to reminding Arnheim of the self-effacing manner in which his own staff did their work, except that Ulrich's selflessness came with such a flourish of arrogance. One might call him a man possessed who was not interested in possessing anything. Or perhaps a man fighting for a cause who had taken a vow of poverty. He could also be regarded as a man given entirely to theorizing, and yet this, too, fell short, because one could certainly not call him a theorist. Arnheim recalled having pointed out to Ulrich that his intellectual capacities were no match for his practical ones. Yet from a practical point of view, the man was utterly impossible.

So Arnheim's mind turned this way and that, not for the first time, but despite the day's mood of self-doubt, he could not possibly grant Ulrich superiority over himself on any one count; the crucial difference must be attributable to some deficiency of Ulrich's. And yet the man had such an air of freshness and freedom, which, Arnheim reluctantly admitted to himself, reminded him of that "Secret of Integrity" which he knew himself to possess, though this other man somehow shook his faith in it. How else would it have been possible, on a purely rational plane, to attribute, however uneasily, the same "wit" to this rootless phantom of a man as Arnheim had learned to fear in an all-too-expert realist such as his father? "There's something missing in the man," Arnheim thought, but as though this were merely the obverse of that truth, it occurred to him at almost the same moment and quite involuntarily that "the man has a soul!"

The man had reserves of soul as yet untapped. As this intuition had taken him by surprise, Arnheim was not ready to say just what he meant by it, but as time goes on, every man, as he knew, finds that his soul, by some irreversible process, has turned into intelligence, morality, and lofty ideas; in his friendly enemy this had not yet run its course, and he still had some of his original store of it, something with an indefinable ambiguous charm, which manifested itself in peculiar combinations with elements from the realm of the soulless, the rational, the mechanical—everything that could not quite be regarded as part of the cultural sphere itself.

While he was turning all this over in his mind and immediately adapting it to the style of his philosophical works, Arnheim had incidentally not had a moment in which to credit any of it to Ulrich's account, not even as the single solitary credit to be granted to him, so strong was his sense of having made a discovery of his own, something he alone had created; he felt like a maestro spotting a fine voice that had not yet fulfilled its potential. This glow of discovery only began to cool when he caught sight of Soliman's face; Soliman had obviously been staring at him for quite a while, and now believed the time had come again to be able to ask him more questions. His awareness that it was not given to everyone to organize his own mind with the aid of such a mute little semi-savage enhanced Arnheim's joy at being the only one to know his enemy's secret, even if there still were a few points to be cleared up as to their implications for the future. What he felt was the love of the usurer for the victim in whom he has invested his capital. Perhaps it was the sight of Soliman that suddenly inspired him to draw into his own orbit, at any cost, the man whom he had come to see as a different embodiment of the adventure that was his own self, even if he had to adopt him as a son!

He smiled at this overhasty enthusiasm for a notion that would take time to mature, and instantly cut short Soliman, whose face was twitching with a tragic need to know more, saying: "That's all for now. Take the flowers I ordered to Frau Tuzzi. If there's anything else you want to ask, we can deal with it some other time."

113

ULRICH CHATS WITH HANS SEPP AND GERDA
IN THE JARGON OF THE FRONTIER BETWEEN
THE SUPERRATIONAL AND THE SUBRATIONAL

Ulrich had no idea what to do in response to his father's request that he pave the way for a personal talk with His Grace and other high-ranking patriots as a partisan of the sociopragmatic approach to crime and punishment. So he went to see Gerda, to put it all out of his mind. Hans was with her, and Hans instantly took the offensive.

"So now you're standing up for Director Fischel?"

Ulrich dodged the question by asking whether Hans had it from Gerda.

Yes, Gerda had told him.

"What about it? Would you like to know why?"

"Do tell me," Hans demanded.

"That's not so easy, my dear Hans."

"Don't call me your dear Hans."

"Well then, my dear Gerda," Ulrich said, turning to her, "it's far from simple. I've talked about it so exhaustively already that I thought you understood."

"I understand you perfectly, but I don't believe a word of it," Gerda answered, trying hard to soften the blow of her siding with Hans against him by the conciliatory way she said it and looked at him.

"We don't believe you," Hans said, instantly aborting this turn to amiability in the conversation. "We don't believe that you can mean it seriously. You picked it up somewhere."

"What!? I suppose you mean something one can't really put into words . . . ?" Ulrich had instantly realized that Hans's impertinence had to do with what Ulrich and Gerda had discussed in private.

"Oh, it can be put into words, all right, provided one means it."

"I don't seem to have the knack. But let me tell you a story."

"*Another* story! You seem to go in for telling stories like Great Homer himself!" Hans was taking an even ruder and more arrogant tone. Gerda gave him a pleading look. But Ulrich would not let himself be put off, and went on: "I was very much in love myself once, when I was just about the same age as you are now. Actually, I was in love with being in love, with my changed condition, rather than with the woman in the case, and that was when I found out all about the things you, your friends, and Gerda make such great mysteries of. That's the story I wanted to tell you."

They were both startled that it turned out to be so short a story.

"So you were very much in love once . . . ?" Gerda asked haltingly, and hated herself in that instant for having asked the question in front of Hans, with the shivering curiosity of a schoolgirl.

But Hans broke in: "Why are we talking about that sort of thing in the first place? Why don't you tell us instead what your cousin is really up to, now that she has fallen in with all those cultural bankrupts?"

"She is searching for an idea that will give the whole world a splendid image of what our country stands for," Ulrich replied. "Wouldn't you like to help her out with some suggestion of your own? I'd be glad to pass it on to her."

Hans gave a scornful laugh. "Why do you act as if you didn't know that we intend to disrupt the whole show?"

"But why on earth are you so much against it?"

"Because it is an incredibly vicious scheme against all that's German in this country," Hans said. "Is it possible that you really don't know what a strong opposition is developing? The Pan-German League has been alerted to your Count Leinsdorf's machinations. The Physical Culture Clubs have already lodged a protest against this affront to German aspirations. The Federation of Arms-bearing Student Corps throughout our Austrian universities is formulating an appeal against the threat of Slavification, and the League of German Youth, of which I am a member, will not put up with it, even if we have to take to the streets!" Hans had drawn himself up tall and recited this speech with a certain pride. But he could not resist adding: "Not that any of this makes any difference. These people all make too much of externals. What matters is that there's no way of getting anything done to anyone's satisfaction in this country!"

Ulrich asked him to explain.

The great races of mankind had all begun by creating their own mythology. Well, was there such a thing as a great myth of Austria? Hans asked. Did Austria have an ancient religion of its own, or a great epic poem? Neither the Catholic nor the Protestant religion had originated here; the art of printing and the Austrian tradition of painting had all come from Germany. The reigning dynasty had come from Switzerland, Spain, Luxembourg; the technology from England and Germany; our most beautiful cities, Vienna, Prague, Salzburg, had been built by Italians or Germans; the army was organized on the Napoleonic model. Such a country had no business trying to take the lead. Its only possible salvation had to be union with Germany. "Satisfied?" Hans concluded.

Gerda was not sure whether to be proud of him or ashamed. Her attraction to Ulrich had been flaring up again of late, even though the natural human need to be someone in her own right was much better served by her younger friend. This young woman was strangely torn between the contradictory inclinations to grow old as a virgin and to give herself to Ulrich. The second of these inclinations was the natural consequence of a love she had felt for years, though it never burst into flame but only smoldered listlessly inside her, and her feelings were like those of someone infatuated with an inferior, in that her soul was humiliated by her body's contemptible craving for submission to this man. In strange contrast with this, though perhaps tied to it as simply and naturally as a yearning for peace, she suspected that she would never marry but would end up, when all the dreams were over, leading a solitary, quietly busy life of her own. This was not a hope born of conviction, for Gerda had no very clear idea of herself, only a foreboding such as the body may have long before the mind is alerted to it. The influence Hans had on her was part of it. Hans was a colorless young man, bony without being tall or strong, who tended to wipe his hands on his hair or his clothes and peer, whenever possible, into a small round tin-framed pocket mirror because he was always troubled by some new eruption of his muddy skin. But this, with the possible exception of the pocket mirror, was exactly how Gerda pictured the early Roman Christians, forgathering in their underground catacombs in defiance of their persecutors. It was not an exact correspondence of details that she meant, after all, but the basic general feeling of terror shared with the early Christian martyrs, as she saw them. Actually, she found the well-scrubbed and scented pagans more attractive, but taking sides with the Christians was a sacrifice one owed to one's character. For Gerda the lofty demands of conscience had thereby acquired a moldy, slightly revolting smell, which went perfectly with the mystical outlook Hans had opened up to her.

Ulrich was quite conversant with this outlook. We should perhaps feel indebted to spiritualism for satisfying—with its funny rappings from the Beyond so suggestive of the minds of deceased kitchen maids—that crude metaphysical craving for spooning up, if not God, then at least the spirits, like some food icily slipping down one's gullet in the dark. In earlier centuries this longing for personal contact with God or His cohorts, said to occur in a state of ecstasy, did, despite the subtle and sometimes marvelous forms it took, make for a mixture of crude earthliness with experiences of an exceptional and ineffable condition of psychic awareness. The metaphysical was thus the physical, embedded in this intuitive state, a mirror image of earthly longings, believed to reveal whatever the concepts of those times encouraged people to expect that they would see. But it is just such concepts that change with the times and lose their credibility. If nowadays anyone told a story of God speaking to him personally, seizing him painfully by the hair to lift him up to Himself, or slipping into his breast in some numinous, intensely sweet way, no one would take any of these details embodying the experience literally, least of all God's professional functionaries, who, as children of a scientific age, feel an understandable horror of being compromised by hysterical and maniacal adherents. Consequently we must either regard such experiences, of frequent and well-recorded occurrence in the Middle Ages and in classical antiquity, as delusions and pathological phenomena, or face the possibility that there is something to them, something independent of the mythical terms in which it has hitherto been expressed: a pure kernel of experience, in other words, that would have to pass strict empirical tests of credibility, whereupon it would of course become a matter of overriding importance long before anyone could deal with the next question, what conclusions to draw from this with regard to our relationship to the Beyond. And while faith based on theological reasoning is today universally engaged in a bitter struggle with doubt and resistance from the prevailing brand of rationalism, it does seem that the naked fundamental experience itself, that primal seizure of mystic insight, stripped of all the traditional, terminological husks of faith, freed from ancient religious concepts, perhaps no longer to be regarded as a religious experience at all, has undergone an immense expansion and now forms the soul of that complex irrationalism that haunts our era like a night bird lost in the dawn.

An absurd splinter of this manifold movement was in fact represented by the social circle or vortex in which Hans Sepp was playing his part. If one were to tabulate the ideas that ebbed and flowed within that company—though this would be against their principles, as they were against numbering and measuring things—the first one would have been a timid and quite Platonic call for trial or companionate marriage, in fact for the sanctioning of polygamy and polyandry; next, when it came to art, they favored the most abstract, aiming at the universal and the timeless, then called Expressionism, which disdained mere appearances or the shell, the banal externals of things, the faithful, "naturalistic" delineation of which had oddly enough been regarded as revolutionary only one generation earlier. Cheek by jowl with this abstract aim of capturing the essential vision of the mind and the world, without bothering about externals, there was also a taste for the down-to-earth and limited kind of art, the so-called regional and folk arts, the promotion of which these young people regarded as a sacred duty to their Pan-Germanic souls; these and others were just some of the choice straws and grasses picked up beside the road of time to be woven into a nest for the human spirit, most particularly the most luxuriant ideas of the rights, duties, and creative promise of the young, which played so great a role that they must be considered in more detail.

The present era, they argued, was blind to the rights of young peo-

ple; a person had virtually no rights until he or she had come of age.
Fathers, mothers, or guardians could dress, house, feed such a person as they liked, reprimand or punish and even, according to Hans
Sepp, wreck the child's life, so long as they did not overstep some
far-off provision of the law, which granted to a child no more protection than it did to a domestic animal. The child is owned by its parents as a chattel and is, by virtue of its economic dependence on
them, a piece of property, a capitalist object. This "capitalist dehu-
manization of the child," which Hans had picked up somewhere in
his reading and then elaborated for himself, was the first lesson he
taught his astonished disciple, Gerda, who had until then felt quite
well taken care of at home. Christianity had somewhat lightened the
wife's yoke, but not that of the daughter, who was condemned to vegetate at home by being forcibly kept away from real life. After this
prelude, he indoctrinated her in the child's right to educate itself according to the laws of its own personality. The child was creative, it
was growth personified and constantly engaged in creating itself. The
child was regal by nature, born to impose its ideas, feelings, and fantasies on the world; oblivious to the ready-made world of accidentals,
it made up its own ideal world. It had its own sexuality. In destroying
creative originality by stripping the child of its own world, suffocating
it with the dead stuff of traditional learning, and training it for specific utilitarian functions alien to its nature, the adult world committed a barbaric sin. The child was not goal-oriented—it created
through play, its work was play and tender growth; when not deliberately interfered with, it took on nothing that was not utterly absorbed
into its nature; every object it touched was a living thing; the child
was a world, a cosmos unto itself, in touch with the ultimate, the absolute, even though it could not express it. But the child was killed by
being taught to serve worldly purposes and being chained to the vulgar routines so falsely called reality! So said Hans Sepp. He was all of
twenty-one when he brought his doctrines to the House of Fischel,
and Gerda was no younger. In addition, Hans had been fatherless for
a long time by then, and felt free at all times to bully his mother, who
was supporting him and the rest of her children by keeping a small
shop, so that there seemed to be no direct cause for his philosophy of
the child as helpless victim of tyranny.

Gerda, absorbing these teachings of Hans, accordingly wavered between a mild pedagogical urge to raise a future generation in their own light, and putting them to more immediate and direct use in her war upon Leo and Clementine. Hans Sepp, however, stood more firmly on his principles and on his slogan "Let us all be children!" That he clung so fiercely to a child's embattled stance might have originated in an early craving for independence, but he basically owed it to the fact that the language of the youth movement then coming into vogue was the first that helped his soul to find its tongue, and it led him, as any true language does, from one word to the next, each word saying more than the speaker had actually intended. And so the original call for a return to childhood gave rise to the most important insights. For the child should not go counter to its nature, renouncing it for the sake of becoming a father or a mother, which means only becoming a bourgeois, a slave of this world, tied hand and foot, and turned into a "useful" object. What ages people is their social conformism; the child resists being turned into a citizen, and so the objection that a twenty-one-year-old is not supposed to behave like a child is swept away, because this struggle goes on from birth to old age and is ended only when the conventional world is overturned by the world of love. This was the higher aspect of Hans Sepp's doctrine, on all of which Ulrich had been kept informed by Gerda.

It was he who had discovered the link between what these young people called their love, or, alternatively, their community, and the consequences of a peculiar, wildly religious, unmythologically mythical (or merely infatuated) state, and it touched him deeply, though they did not know it, because he confined himself to making fun of its manifestations in them. In the same vein he now answered Hans by asking him point-blank why he would not take advantage of the Parallel Campaign for advancing the cause of his "Community of the Purely Selfless."

"Because it's out of the question," Hans replied.

The resulting conversation between them would have been as baffling to an uninitiated listener as an exchange in criminal street slang, although it was no more than the pidgin of social infatuation. So what follows is more the gist of what was said than a literal transcription of it. The Community of the Purely Selfless was what Hans called it; despite this, it was not devoid of meaning; the more selfless a person feels, the brighter and intenser the things of this world appear; the more weight a person sheds, the more he feels uplifted; everyone has probably experienced this at one time or another, though such experiences must not be confused with mere gaiety, cheerfulness, light-heartedness, or the like, which are simply substitutes for it, serving a lower or even some corrupt purpose. Perhaps the real thing should be called not a state of uplift but rather a shedding of one's armor, that armor in which the ego was encased. You had to distinguish between the two walls pressing in on the human being. Man succeeds in getting over the first rampart every time he does something kind and unselfish, but that is only the lesser rampart. The greater wall equals the selfhood of even the most unselfish person; this is original sin as such; with us, every sensation, every feeling, even that of self-surrender, is more a taking than a giving, and there is hardly any way of shaking off this armor of all-permeating selfishness. Hans ticked off specifics: Knowledge is simply the appropriation of something not our own. We kill, tear, and digest our "object" as an animal does its prey. A concept is a living thought killed, never to stir again. A conviction is an impulse of faith, frozen into some unchanging life-less form. Research confirms the known. Character is inertia, the re-fusal to keep growing. To know a person amounts to no longer being moved by that person. Insight is one-way vision. Truth is the success-ful effort to think impersonally and inhumanly. Everywhere, the in-stinct to kill, to freeze, to clutch, to petrify, is a mixture of self-seeking with a cold, craven, treacherous mock-selflessness. "And when," Hans wanted to know, even though the innocent Gerda was all he had experienced, "when has love ever been anything but pos-session, or the giving of oneself as its quid pro quo?"

Ulrich cautiously and with qualifications professed to agree with all these none too coherent assertions. He allowed that even suffer-ing and renunciation yielded a slight profit for the ego; a faint, as it were grammatical cast of egotism shadowed all we did as long as there was no predicate without a subject.

But Hans would have none of that! He and his friends argued end-lessly about the right way to live. Sometimes they assumed that ev-eryone had to live first and foremost for himself and only then for all the others; or else they agreed that a person could have only one true friend, who, however, needed his own one friend, so that they saw the community as a circular linking of souls, like the spectrum or other chains of being; but what they most liked to believe was that there was such a thing as a communal soul; it might be overshadowed by the forces of egotism, but it was a deep, immense source of vital energy, its potential unimaginable and waiting to be tapped. A tree fighting for its life in the sheltering forest cannot feel more unsure of itself than sensitive people nowadays feel about the dark warmth of the mass, its dynamism, the invisible molecular process of its unconscious cohesion, reminding them with every breath they take that the greatest and the least among them are not alone. Ulrich felt the same. While he perceived clearly that the tamed egotism on which life is built makes for an orderly structure, compared with which the single breath of all mankind is no more than the quintessence of murky thinking, and while for his part he preferred keeping to himself, he could not help feeling oddly moved when Gerda's young friends talked in their extravagant fashion of the great wall that had to be surmounted.

Hans now reeled off the articles of his faith in a drone interspersed with bursts of vehemence, his eyes staring straight ahead without seeing anything. An unnatural crack ran through the cosmos, breaking it in two like the two halves of an apple, which consequently start to shrivel up. Which was why, nowadays, we had to regain by artificial and unnatural means what had once been a natural part of ourselves. But this split could be healed by opening up the self, by a change of attitude, for the more a person could forget himself, blot himself out, get away from himself, the more his energy could be freed for the common good, as though released from a bad chemical combination; and the closer he drew to the community, the more he would realize his true self, because, as Hans saw it, true originality was not a matter of empty uniqueness but came from opening oneself up, degree by degree, to participation and devotion, perhaps all the way to the ultimate degree of total communion with the world achieved by those dissolved in selflessness.

These propositions so devoid of content set Ulrich to wondering how they might possibly be substantiated, but all he did was to ask Hans coolly just how all this opening up of one's self and so forth might be done in actual practice.

Hans came up with some prodigious words for it: the transcendent

ego in place of the sensual ego, the Gothic ego instead of the naturalistic one, the realm of being rather than the realm of phenomena or
appearances, the unconditional experience, and similar formidable
expressions, which had to do duty for his sense of the indescribable
reality he envisioned, as they all too often must, incidentally, to the
detriment of the cause they somehow manage to enhance nonetheless. And because this condition of which he had occasional, perhaps
even frequent, glimpses never stayed in focus for more than a few
brief instants of meditation, he went even further and claimed that
transcendence nowadays simply did not manifest itself other than
sporadically, in flashes of an extracorporeal vision that was naturally
hard to pin down, except perhaps in the traces it left in great works of
art, which led him on to the symbol, his favorite word both for art
and for other supernaturally towering signs of life, and finally to the
Germanic gift, peculiar to those who carried even a smattering of
Germanic blood in their veins, for creating and envisioning said
things. Using this sublime variant of "good old days" nostalgia made
it easy for him to suggest that a lasting perception of the essence of
things was a thing of the past and denied to the present time, an assertion from which the whole debate had after all sprung.

Ulrich found this superstitious claptrap rather irritating. He had
been wondering for a long time what it was that Gerda actually saw in
Hans. There she sat, with her pale look, taking no active part in the
conversation. Hans Sepp had a grandiose theory of love, in which she
probably found the deeper meaning of her own existence. Ulrich
now gave the conversation a new turn by stating—not without a protest against having to carry on this kind of talk in the first place—that
the highest intensity of feeling of which a person was capable did not
arise out of one's usual egotistical appropriation of whatever came
one's way or, as Hans and his friends felt, out of what is called self-
enhancement through self-surrender, but was actually a state of rest,
of changelessness, like still waters.

At this Gerda brightened up and asked what he meant.

Ulrich told her that Hans had actually been talking all this time,
even when he went out of his way to disguise it, about love and nothing but love; saintly love, solitary love, the love that overflows its
banks of desire, the love always described as a loosening, a dissolu-

tion, indeed a reversal of all earthly bonds, in any case no longer a mere emotion but a transformation of a person's whole way of thinking and perceiving.

Gerda looked at him as though she were trying to decide whether this man who knew so much more than she did had somehow discovered this too, or whether this man she was secretly in love with and who sat beside her without revealing much of himself was emitting some strange sympathetic radiation that draws two people together even when their bodies do not touch.

Ulrich felt her probing look. It was as though he were speaking some foreign tongue in which he could go on fluently, but only superficially, because the words had no roots inside him.

"In this state," he said, "in which one oversteps the limits normally imposed on one's actions, one understands everything, because the soul accepts only what is already part of it; in a sense, it already knows all that's coming its way. Lovers have nothing new to say to each other; nor do they actually recognize each other; all that a lover recognizes is the indescribable way in which he is inwardly activated by the beloved. To recognize a person he does not love means drawing that person into the sphere of his love like a blank wall with the sunlight on it. To recognize some inanimate object doesn't mean decoding its characteristics one by one; it means that a veil falls away or a barrier is lifted, somewhere beyond the world of the senses. Even the inanimate, unknown as it is, enters trustfully into the shared life of lovers. Nature and the spirit peculiar to love gaze into each other's eyes, two versions of the same act, a flowing in two directions, a burning at both ends. Awareness of a person or thing apart from oneself then becomes impossible, for to take notice is to take something from the things noticed; they keep their shape but turn to ashes inside; something evaporates from them, leaving only their mummies. For lovers there is no such thing as a truth—it could only be a blind alley, the finish, the death of something that, while it lives, is like the breathing edge of a flame, where light and darkness lie breast-to-breast. How can any one thing light up, in recognition, where all is light? Who needs the beggarly small change of security and proof where everything spills over in superabundance? And how can one still want anything for oneself alone, even the beloved itself, once one knows how those who love no longer belong to themselves but must give themselves freely, four-eyed intertwined creatures that they are, to everything that comes their way?"

Anyone who has mastered the idiom can run on in this vein without even trying. It is like walking with a lighted candle that sheds its tender rays on one aspect of life after another, all of them looking as if their usual appearance in the hard light of common day had been a crude misrepresentation. How impossible it becomes, for instance, to apply that verbal gesture "to possess" to lovers, once one remembers the etymology (from *potis* and *sedere*, i.e., *pos-sess* equals "to sit upon," "be-set"). Does it show desires of a higher order, to aim at "pos-sessing" principles, the respect of one's children, ideas, oneself? But this clumsy ploy of a heavy animal subduing its prey with the full weight of its own body is still, and rightly, the basic and favorite term of capitalism, showing the connection between the possessors of the social world and the possessors of knowledge and skills, which is what it makes of its thinkers and artists, while love and asceticism stand apart in their lonely kinship. How aimless this pair appears, how devoid of a target, compared with the aims and targets of normal life. But the terms "aim" and "target" derive from the language of the marksman. To be without aim or target must have meant, originally, not to be out to kill. So merely by tracking down the clues in language itself—a blurred, but revealing trail!—one can see how a crudely changed meaning has everywhere usurped the function of far subtler messages now quite lost to us, that ever-perceptible but never quite tangible nexus of things. Ulrich gave up pursuing this idea out loud, but Hans could not be blamed for thinking that all he had to do was tug at a certain thread to unravel the whole fabric; the world had merely lost its instinct for the right thread to pull. He had been repeatedly interrupting Ulrich and finishing his sentences for him.

"If you choose to look at all this with a scientific eye, you'll see nothing more in it than any bank teller might. All empirical explanations are deceptive, they never take us beyond the level of crude sensory data. Your need to know would like to reduce the world to nothing more than the so-called forces of nature twiddling their thumbs." These were Hans's objections, his interpolations. He alternated between rudeness and passion. He felt that he had done a poor job of stating his case, and blamed his failure on the presence of this interloper between him and Gerda, for had he been alone with Gerda, eye-to-eye with her, the same words would have risen skyward like a shimmering fountain, like spiraling falcons. He knew it, he felt that this was one of his days. He was also surprised and annoyed to hear Ulrich talking so fluently and so intently in his place.

Actually, Ulrich was not speaking as a scientist at all but was saying far more than he would have been prepared to defend, although he was not saying anything he did not believe. He was carried away by a suppressed fury. To run on like this he had to be in a curiously elevated, a rather inflamed frame of mind, and Ulrich's mood was somewhere between this state and the one induced by seeing Hans, with his greasy, bristling hair, his muddy skin, his repellent emphatic gestures, and his foaming torrent of speech in which some filmy fragment of his true self hung trapped, like the skin from a flayed heart. But strictly speaking, Ulrich had been suspended all his life between two such aspects of this subject, always ready to expound it as he was doing, half believing what he was saying but never going beyond such verbal games, because he did not really take them for real, and so his discomfiture was keeping step with his pleasure in this conversation.

Gerda ignored the mocking asides that he injected into his talk from time to time as a kind of self-parody, overwhelmed as she was by her sense of his opening himself up at last. She looked at him with a touch of anxiety. He's much softer than he'll ever admit, she thought, with a feeling that broke down her own defenses, as if a baby were groping at her breast. Ulrich caught her eye. He knew almost everything that was going on between her and Hans, because in her worry she needed to relieve her heart by at least throwing out hints of her problems, and that made it easy enough for Ulrich to fill in the rest. She and Hans regarded the act of physical possession, the normal preoccupation of young lovers, as a despicable surrender to capitalist urges; they thought they despised physical passion altogether, but they also despised self-control as a middle-class virtue, so what it came to was their always clinging to each other in a nonphysical or semiphysical way. They tried to "accept" each other, as they called it, and felt that trembling, tender merging of two people lost in each other's eyes, slipping into the invisible currents that ripple through each other's heads and hearts, and feeling, at the apparent moment of mutual understanding, that each holds the other inside himself and is at one with the other. At less exalted times they were satisfied with ordinary mutual admiration, seeing in great paintings or dramatic scenes the parallels to their own condition and marveling, when they kissed, at the thought that—as the saying goes—millennia were gazing down upon them. They did kiss, even though they regarded the crude physical sensations of love, that spasm of the bodily self, as no better than a stomach cramp, but their limbs did not pay too much attention to their ideals and pressed hard against each other on their own. Afterward they both felt bewildered. Their budding philosophy was not proof against their heady sense of nobody watching, the dim lights, the furiously mounting attraction of two young bodies nestling close together, and Gerda especially, who as the girl was the more mature of the two, felt the craving to consummate their embrace with the innocent intensity a tree might feel on being prevented from budding in the springtime. This arrested lovemaking, as bland as the kisses of little children and as interminable as the aimless fondlings of the old, always left them feeling shattered. Hans found it easier to take because he could always regard it afterward as a successful test of his convictions.

"It isn't for us to have and to hold," he lectured her. "We are nomads who must keep moving onward, step after step." And when he noticed that Gerda's whole body was quivering with frustrated desire, he made no bones about calling it a weakness, if not actually a residue of her non-Germanic genes, and felt like Adam walking with his God, his manly heart having once more resisted his erstwhile rib's tempting of his faith. At such moments Gerda despised him. Which was probably why she had told Ulrich so much about it, at least in the beginning. She suspected that a full-grown man would do both more and less than Hans, who would bury his tear-stained face in her lap like a child after he had insulted her. Since she was just as proud of her experiences as she was bored with them, she let Ulrich in on all this in the anxious hope that he would find something to say that would put an end to the agonizing beauty of it.

Ulrich, however, seldom spoke to her as she wished he might; instead, he cooled her off with his sardonic tone, because even though it made Gerda more reserved, he knew too well that she longed to submit to him, and that neither Hans nor anyone else had the power over her mind he could have if he chose. He justified himself with the thought that any other real man in his place would have the same effect on Gerda, that of a blessed relief after that woolly-minded dirty little tease Hans. But even as he was thinking it over, suddenly seeing it all in perspective, Hans had collected himself and started a fresh attack.

"All in all," he said, "you've made the biggest possible mistake by trying to express as a concept something that occasionally elevates an idea somewhat above the level of the merely conceptual. But I suppose that's what makes the difference between one of you intellectual people and the likes of us. First," he added proudly, "one must learn to live it before one can, perhaps, learn to think it." When Ulrich smiled at this, he flashed out like a bolt of lightning: "Jesus was a seer at the age of twelve, without first getting his doctorate."

This provoked Ulrich into breaking the silence he owed to Gerda by giving Hans a piece of advice that betrayed his knowledge of facts he could have learned only from her. "I don't know why," he said, "if you want to live it, you don't go all the way. I would take Gerda in my arms, forget all the qualms of my rational mind, and keep her locked in my arms until our bodies either crumbled to ashes or became transformed into the fullness of their own being in a way that is beyond our power of comprehension!"

Hans, feeling a stab of jealousy, looked not at him but at Gerda, who turned pale with embarrassment. Ulrich's words about locking her in his arms had touched her like a secret promise. At the moment she didn't care at all how "the other life" was to be imagined, and she felt sure that Ulrich would do everything just as it should be done, if he really wanted to. Hans, incensed at Gerda's betrayal, argued against Ulrich's proposal, which could not be carried out successfully, he said, because the time was not ripe. The first souls to take flight would have to take off from a mountain, just like the first airplanes, and not from the lowlands of a period like the present. Perhaps there must first come a man who would release mankind from its bondage before it could achieve the heights. It was not unthinkable that he might be the man himself, but that was his own affair, and apart from this, the present low level of spiritual development was incapable of producing such a man.

Now Ulrich remarked on the proliferation of redeemers these

days—indeed, every self-respecting chairman of a social club seemed to be eligible. If Christ were to come again tomorrow, he would certainly fare worse than the first time. The better newspapers and book clubs would find him vulgar, and the great international press would hardly be likely to welcome him to its columns.

With this they were back where they had started, the discussion had come full circle, and Gerda sank back into herself.

Yet something had changed; without giving any outward sign of it, Ulrich had tripped himself up a little. His thoughts had parted company with his words. He looked at Gerda. Her body was angular, her skin looked dull and tired. That faint breath of old-maidishness that hung over her had suddenly become apparent to him, although it had probably always been the major factor holding him back from ever coming to the point with this girl who was in love with him. Of course, Hans also had something to do with it, what with the semi-physical nature of his communal utopia, which had an old-maidish quality of its own. Ulrich did not feel attracted to Gerda, but even so he was inclined to continue his dialogue with her. This reminded him that he had invited her to come to see him. She gave no sign of either remembering this invitation or of having forgotten it, and he got no opportunity to ask her about it privately. It left him with an uneasy sense of regret as well as of relief, such as one feels when one skirts a danger recognized too late.

114

THINGS ARE COMING TO A BOIL. ARNHEIM IS
GRACIOUS TO GENERAL STUMM. DIOTIMA
PREPARES TO MOVE OFF INTO INFINITY.
ULRICH DAYDREAMS ABOUT LIVING ONE'S
LIFE AS ONE READS A BOOK

His Grace had urged Diotima to find out about the famous Makart pageant, which had brought all Austria together in the 1870s in a burst of national fervor; he still had vivid memories of the richly draped carriages, the heavily caparisoned horses, the trumpeters, and the pride people took in their medieval costumes, which lifted them out of their humdrum daily lives. It was this that had brought Diotima, Arnheim, and Ulrich to go through the materials on the period at the Imperial Library, from which they were now emerging together. As Diotima, her lip curling with disdain, had predicted to His Grace, what they had come up with was quite impossible; such frippery could no longer make people forget the monotony of their existence. They were still on the library stairs when the beauty informed her companions that she felt like making the most of the sunny day and the year 1914—which in the few weeks of its existence had already left the moldering past so far behind—by walking home. But they had no sooner stepped out into the light of day when they bumped into the General, on his way in. Proud to be discovered on such a mission of high learning, he instantly offered to turn back and enlarge Diotima's entourage by joining it. This made Diotima realize after only a few steps that she was tired and wanted a cab. With no such vehicle in sight, they all stopped in front of the library, which faced a trough-shaped rectangular square, three sides of which were formed by splendid ancient façades, while on the fourth the asphalt street in front of a long, low palace shimmered like an ice rink, with cars and carriages rushing past, none of which responded to the four people waving and signaling to them like survivors of a shipwreck, until they tired of it and forgot about giving anything but the occasional halfhearted signal in the direction of the traffic.

Arnheim had a big book under his arm. He was pleased with this gesture, both condescending and respectful toward the life of the mind. He greeted the General eagerly: "How nice to see you coming to the library too; men of position nowadays so seldom seek out the life of the mind in its own house."

General Stumm replied that he was quite at home in this library.

Arnheim was impressed. "Almost all we have nowadays is writers, and hardly anyone who reads books anymore," he went on. "Do you realize, General, how many books are printed annually? I think it's over a hundred books a day published in Germany alone. Over a thousand periodicals are founded every year. The whole world is writing! Everyone helps himself to ideas as though they were his own, all the time. Nobody feels any responsibility toward the situation as a whole. Ever since the Church lost its influence, there is no central authority to stem our general chaos. There is no educational model, no educational principle. In these circumstances it is only natural that feeling and morality should drift without an anchor, and the most stable person begins to waver."

The General felt his mouth turning dry. It wasn't as though Dr. Arnheim was actually addressing him in person; he was a man standing in the square and thinking out loud. The General thought of how many people talk to themselves in the street, on their way to somewhere; civilians, of course, because a soldier who did such a thing would be locked up, and an officer would be sent to the psychiatric clinic. Stumm felt embarrassed at the thought of standing there philosophizing in public, as it were, smack-dab in the middle of the Imperial Residential capital. Apart from the two men, there seemed to be only one other, a mute figure of bronze standing on a stone pedestal in the sunny square. The General had only just noticed this monument and did not remember whom it represented, so that he had to apologize for his ignorance when Arnheim asked him.

"And to think that he was put here to be venerated," the great man remarked. "But that's how it is. Every moment of our lives we move among institutions, problems, and challenges of which we have barely caught the tail end, so that the present is constantly reaching into the past. We keep crashing through the floor, if I may put it so, into the cellars of time, even while we imagine ourselves to be occupying the top floor of the present."

Arnheim smiled. He was making conversation. His moving lips flickered in the sunshine, and the lights in his eyes kept changing like those on a signaling steamer. Stumm was growing uneasy; he found it hard to keep acknowledging so many and such unusual turns in the conversation while being served up to the world, in full uniform, on this platter of a square. Grass was growing in the cracks between the cobblestones; it was last year's grass but looked implausibly fresh, like a corpse left lying in the snow; it was, in fact, most peculiar and disturbing that grass should be growing here between the stones, when only a few steps farther on the asphalt was being polished, in keeping with the times, by the passing cars. The General began to be troubled by a nervous fear that if he had to go on listening much longer he might suddenly go down on his knees and eat grass in front of the whole world, without knowing why. He looked around for Ulrich and Diotima for protection.

These two had taken shelter where a thin veil of shade had spun itself around the corner of the wall, and seemed to be involved in an argument, though their voices were too low to be understood.

"You make it sound hopeless," Diotima was saying.

"What do you mean?" Ulrich asked, without real interest.

"There is still such a thing as individuality."

Ulrich tried to catch her eye sideways. "Good heavens, we've been all over this already."

"You have no heart, or you wouldn't always talk like this," she said softly. The sun-heated air was rising from the stone pavement up between her legs, which were encased in long skirts like those of a robed statue, inaccessible and to all intents nonexistent. She showed no awareness of it. It was a caress that had nothing to do with anyone, any man. Her eyes turned pale, but that might have been merely the effect of her reserve in a situation where she was exposed to the glances of the passersby. Turning to Ulrich, she said with an effort:

"When a woman has to choose between duty and passion, what can she rely on if not her character?"

"You don't have to choose," Ulrich replied.

"You go too far; I wasn't speaking of myself," his cousin whispered. As he did not reply, they both stared across the square for a while in a hostile silence. Then Diotima asked: "Do you think that what we call our soul might emerge from the shadows where it usually keeps itself?"

Ulrich gave her a puzzled look.

"In the case of unusual, specially gifted persons," she added.

"Am I to understand that you're interested in establishing a rapport with the Beyond?" Ulrich asked incredulously. "Has Arnheim introduced you to a medium?"

Diotima was disappointed in him. "I would never have thought you capable of such a misunderstanding," she said reproachfully. "When I speak of emerging from the shadows, I mean from the unreality, from that flickering concealment in which we sometimes sense the presence of the unusual. It is spread out like a net that torments us because it will neither hold us nor let us go. Don't you think that there have been times when it was otherwise? When the inner life was a stronger presence, when there were individuals who walked in the light or, as people used to say, walked in holiness, and miracles could happen in reality because they *are* an ever-present form of another reality, and nothing else!"

Diotima surprised herself by the firmness with which it seemed possible to say this sort of thing, without any special elation, as though she were walking on solid ground. Ulrich felt secretly infuriated, but actually he was deeply shocked. Has it come to this, he thought, that this giant hen can talk the way I do? Again he saw Diotima's soul in the shape of a colossal chicken pecking at his own soul, in the shape of a little worm. He was seized by the primal childhood terror of the giantess, mixed with another strange sensation; there was a certain gratification in being spiritually consumed, as it were, in mindless accord with a kinswoman. Their unanimity was a silly coincidence, of course; he did not believe that there was any magic in being related by blood, nor could he possibly have taken his cousin seriously even if he were dead drunk. But he had been changing lately, mellowing perhaps; his characteristic inner readiness to move to the attack was giving way to a need for tenderness, dreams, kinship, whatever, which also manifested itself in sudden outbreaks of the ill will that was its opposite.

Which prompted him to make fun of his cousin now: "If that's how you feel," he said, "then you ought to go all the way and become Arnheim's lover, openly or in secret, as soon as possible."

"You shouldn't say such things; I've given you no right!" Diotima rebuked him.

"But I must speak of it. Until now I wasn't sure what was going on between you and Arnheim. But now I understand, and you look to me like a person who is seriously thinking of flying to the moon. I would never have thought you capable of such madness."

"I've told you that I'm capable of going to extremes." Her upward gaze was meant to be audacious, but the sun made her screw up her eyes, so that she seemed to be twinkling at him.

"These are the ravings of starved love," Ulrich said, "which pass off when hunger is appeased." He wondered what Arnheim's plans might be with regard to her. Did he regret his proposal, and was he covering his retreat by putting on some sort of act? But then he could simply leave and not come back; a man who had been in business all his life would surely have the necessary callousness for that? He remembered noticing certain signs in Arnheim that indicated passion in an older man; his face was sometimes a grayish yellow, slack and tired, like a room with the bed still unmade at noon. The most likely explanation was the havoc caused by two almost equally strong passions fighting each other to a standstill. But since he was incapable of imagining the passion for power in the degree to which it ruled Arnheim, he could not conceive of the measures love had to take in order to fight it.

"You're an odd sort of man," Diotima said. "Always different from what one would expect. Wasn't it you who spoke to me of seraphic love?"

"You regard that as a possibility?" Ulrich asked absentmindedly.

"Not as you described it, of course."

"So Arnheim loves you seraphically?" Ulrich began to laugh softly.

"I wish you wouldn't laugh." Diotima almost hissed at him.

"You don't understand," he apologized. "It's only the excitement. You and Arnheim are sensitive people. You love poetry. I'm sure that you are sometimes touched by a breath . . . a breath of something: the question is just what that is. And now you want to get to the bottom of it, with all the thoroughness of your idealism."

"Aren't you always saying that one must be precise and thorough?" Diotima countered.

It was too much. "You're mad!" he said. "Forgive my saying so, but you are mad. And you of all people mustn't be."

Meanwhile Arnheim had been telling the General that for the last two generations the world had been undergoing the most profound revolution of all: the end of the soul was in sight.

It gave the General a stab. What the devil, here was yet another problem to think about. To be honest, he had thought until this moment, despite Diotima, that there was no such thing as the soul. At military school and in the regiment, nobody gave a hang about this kind of preacher's talk. But here was this manufacturer of guns and tanks, talking about the soul as though he could see it standing there. The General's eyes began to itch and to roll around gloomily, goggling at the translucent air around them.

But Arnheim was not waiting to be asked for particulars; words flowed from his lips, from that pale pink slit between his clipped mustache and his little pointed beard. As he phrased it, the soul had started to shrivel and age ever since the Church began to crumble, around the beginning of the bourgeois era. Since then it had lost God and all solid values and ideals until the present, when men had actually reached the point of living without morals, without principles, without real experiences, in fact.

The General could not quite see why one could not have experiences if one had no morals. Whereupon Arnheim opened the big volume bound in pigskin that he was holding, revealing an expensive facsimile of a manuscript so valuable that even a mortal of Arnheim's extraordinary standing could not be permitted to take the original out of the building. The General saw the depiction of an angel with wings spread horizontally across two pages, against a background of dark earth, golden sky, and marvelous colors layered like clouds; he was looking at a reproduction of one of the most moving and splendid of early medieval paintings, but since he did not know this, while he did know all about bird-hunting and depictions of it, he could only conclude that a creature with wings and a long neck that was neither human nor a snipe must be an aberration to which his companion wished to draw his attention.

Arnheim was pointing his finger at it and saying pensively: "Here you see what that great lady who is creating the Austrian Campaign is trying to bring back into the world. . . ."

"I see, I see," Stumm said, realizing that he had failed to appreciate this thing for what it was and that he had better watch his step.

"The great expressiveness, and with such utter simplicity," Arnheim went on, "bears witness to what our age has lost forever. What is our science compared with this? Patchwork. Our art? Extremes, without a mediating substance to hold them together. We lack the magic key to unity, and this, you see, is why I am so deeply moved by this Austrian plan to set the world an example of unification, of a shared idea, even though I do not quite believe it can be done. I am a German. Everything in the world today is loud and crude, and Germany is the loudest. In every country the people are straining themselves morning, noon, and night, whether at work or at play, but in Germany they start earlier and stop later than anywhere else. In all the world the spirit of cold calculation and brute force has lost touch with the soul, but we in Germany have the most businessmen and the strongest army in the world." He looked around the square with delight. "Here in Austria, things have not yet gone so far. The past is still with you, and the people have kept something of their original intuitiveness. If the German spirit can still be saved from rationalism, this is the only place left from which a start can be made. But I am afraid," he added with a sigh, "we can hardly succeed. A great idea nowadays encounters too much resistance; great ideas just barely help to prevent each other from being misused. We are living in a state of moral truce, as it were, armed to the teeth with ideas."

He smiled at his own joke. Then something more occurred to him: "You know, the difference between Germany and Austria we have just touched on always reminds me of billiards. Even at billiards everything goes wrong if you try to do it all by calculation instead of with feeling."

The General had guessed that he was supposed to feel flattered by the reference to a moral armed truce, and he wanted to show that he had been paying attention. He did know something about billiards, so he said, "I play snooker myself, and skittles too, but I never heard that there's a difference between the Austrian and the German styles of play."

Arnheim shut his eyes and gave it some thought. "I myself never play billiards," he said after a moment, "but I know that you can play the ball high or low, from the right or from the left; that you can strike the second ball head-on or merely graze it; that you can hit it hard or lightly, bluff a little—or a lot—and there must be many more such options. Now, if you imagine each of these elements with all their inherent gradations, you have an almost infinite number of possible combinations. To state them theoretically, I should have to take into account, besides the laws of mathematics and statics, the mechanics of solids, plus the laws of elasticity; I would have to know the coefficients of the materials, the influence of the temperature, the most precise means of measuring the coordination and gradation of my motor impulses, of estimating distances exactly, like a nonius, how to combine the various factors with better than the speed and accuracy of a slide rule, to say nothing of allowing for margins of error, fields of dispersal, and the fact that the aim, which is the correct coincidence of the two balls, is in itself not clearly definable but only a collection of barely adequate data round an average value."

Arnheim spoke slowly, and in a way that compelled attention, as though pouring a liquid drop by drop from a vial to a glass; he did not spare his interlocutor a single detail.

"And so you see," he continued, "that I should need to have all the qualities, and do all the things, I cannot possibly have and do. You must be enough of a mathematician to see that it would take a lifetime to plan a single carom shot in that fashion; it boggles the mind! And yet I step up to the table with a cigarette between my lips, a tune in my ear, and my hat on, as it were, and hardly bothering to look over the board, I take my cue to the ball and the problem is solved! General, this is the sort of thing that happens all the time in real life. You are not only an Austrian, you are a military man, so you're bound to understand me: politics, honor, war, art, all the crucial processes of life, take place beyond the scope of the conscious rational mind. Man's greatness is rooted in the irrational. Even we businessmen don't really operate by calculation—not the leading men, that is. The little fellows may have to count their pennies; we learn to regard our really successful moves as a mystery that defies analysis. A man who doesn't care deeply about feeling, morality, religion, music, poetry, form, discipline, chivalry, generosity, candor, tolerance—believe me, such a man will never make a businessman of real stature. This is why

I have always admired the military, especially the Austrian military, based as it is on age-old traditions, and I am truly delighted that Frau Tuzzi can count on your support. It is a relief to me to know it. Your influence, with that of our younger friend, is extremely important. All great things rest on the same principles; great obligations are a blessing, General."

To his own surprise he suddenly found himself spontaneously shaking Stumm's hand, then he ended by saying: "Hardly anyone realizes that true greatness has no rational basis; I mean to say, everything strong is simple."

Stumm von Bordwehr held his breath; he was not sure he understood a word of it all, and wished he could rush back into the library and spend hours reading up on all these points that the great man had paid him the compliment of making to him. At last, out of this March gale whirling in his mind, there came a piercing ray of lucidity. What the hell, he thought, this fellow wants something from me! He looked up. Arnheim was still holding the book in both hands but was now turning his attention seriously to hailing a cab. His face was slightly flushed with animation, like that of a man who has just been trading ideas with another. The General was silent, like a man awed by a portentous thought. If Arnheim wanted something from him, then General Stumm was free to want something from Arnheim too, to the advantage of His Majesty's service. This perception opened such vistas of possibility that Stumm put off thinking about just what it all really meant. But if the angel in the book had suddenly lifted up a wing to give clever General Stumm a glimpse of what was hidden underneath, the General could not have felt more bewildered and overjoyed.

Over in Diotima's and Ulrich's corner, the following question had meanwhile been posed: Should a woman in Diotima's difficult position make a gesture of renunciation, or let herself be swept into adultery, or take a third, mixed course, such as belonging physically to one man and spiritually to another, or perhaps physically to neither? For this third solution there was as yet no libretto, as it were, only some great harmonic chords. Diotima still wanted it understood that she was absolutely not speaking of herself but speaking only of "a woman"—every time Ulrich tried to fuse the two together he got a warning glance from her.

And so he also chose a devious course. "Have you ever seen a dog?" he asked. "You only think you have. What you see is only something you feel more or less justified in regarding as a dog. It isn't a dog in every respect, and always has some personal quality no other dog has. So how can we ever hope, in this life, to do 'the right thing'? All we can do is something that's never *the* right thing and is always both more and less than that. Has a tile ever fallen off the roof in precise accord with the law of falling bodies? Never. Even in the lab, things never behave just as they should. They diverge from the ideal course in all possible directions, while we keep up a fiction that this is to be blamed on our faulty execution of the experiment, and that somewhere midway a perfect result is obtainable.

"Or else you find certain stones, and because of the properties they have in common they are all regarded as diamonds. But suppose one of them comes from Africa and another from Asia, one is dug out of the ground by a black man and the other by an Oriental. What if these differences in circumstances were to matter so much that they cancel out what the objects have in common? In the equation 'diamond plus circumstances is still diamond,' the use value of the diamond is so great that it makes the value of the circumstances negligible. But it's possible to imagine spiritual circumstances in which the situation is reversed.

"Everything partakes of the universal and also has something special all its own. Everything is both true to type and refuses to conform to type and is in a category all its own, simultaneously. The personal quality of any given creature is precisely that which doesn't coincide with anything else. I once said to you that the more truth we discover, the less of the personal is left in the world, because of the longtime war against individuality that individuality is losing. By the time everything has been rationalized, there's no telling how much of us will be left. Nothing at all, possibly, but then, when the false significance we attach to personality has gone, we may enter upon a new kind of significance as if embarking upon a splendid adventure.

"So how do you decide? Should 'a woman' go by the law? Then she may as well go by the laws of society. Conventional morality is a perfectly valid average and collective value, to be literally adhered to, without deviations, wherever it is acknowledged. But no individual case can be decided on moral grounds alone; morality is irrelevant to it in the precise degree that it shares in the inexhaustible nature of the universe."

"That was quite a speech," Diotima said. She took a certain satisfaction in the loftiness of discourse being imposed upon her, but intended to gain the upper hand by not talking in equally wild generalities. "But what is a woman to do, given the circumstances, in real life?"

"Let things happen," Ulrich answered.

"What things?"

"Whatever happens. Her husband, her lover, her renunciation, her mixed feelings."

"Do you have any idea what you are saying?" Diotima asked, feeling painfully reminded of how her high resolve possibly to give up Arnheim had its wings clipped every night by the mere fact that she slept in Tuzzi's bed. Ulrich must have sensed some of this, because he asked her bluntly: "Would you try your luck with me?"

"With you?" Diotima drawled, then decided to save face by taking a humorous tack. "If this is an offer, just what is it you have in mind?"

"I'll tell you," Ulrich replied seriously. "You read a great deal, don't you?"

"Of course."

"What is it you do, then? I'll tell you: You leave out whatever doesn't suit you. As the author himself has done before you. Just as you leave things out of your dreams or fantasies. By leaving things out, we bring beauty and excitement into the world. We evidently handle our reality by effecting some sort of compromise with it, an in-between state where the emotions prevent each other from reaching their fullest intensity, graying the colors somewhat. Children who haven't yet reached that point of control are both happier and unhappier than adults who have. And yes, stupid people also leave things out, which is why ignorance is bliss. So I propose, to begin with, that we try to love each other as if we were characters in a novel who have met in the pages of a book. Let's in any case leave off all the fatty tissue that plumps up reality."

Diotima felt called upon to argue the case; she wanted to direct the conversation away from this too-personal vein, and she also wanted to show that she understood something of the problems that had been touched upon.

"All well and good," she said, "but art is supposed to afford us a vacation from reality, so that we can return to it with our energies restored."

"And I am opinionated enough to say that there should be no time off," her cousin retorted. "What sort of a life is it that we have to drill holes in it called holidays; would we punch holes in a painting because it makes too strenuous demands on our sense of beauty? Should we look forward to taking time off from eternal bliss in the next world? Even the thought of time taken off my life by having to sleep sometimes seems unacceptable to me."

"Ah, there it is." Diotima seized her opportunity. "You see how unnatural it all is, what you're saying. What human being doesn't need to rest and take a break? It's a perfect illustration of the difference between you and Arnheim. Yours is a mind that will not acknowledge the shadow on things, the dark side, while his has developed out of the fullness of human experience, with sunshine and shadow intermingled."

"Of course I exaggerate," Ulrich admitted coolly. "You will see it even more clearly as we go into more detail. Think of the great writers, for instance. We can model our lives *on* them, but we can't squeeze life out of them, like wine out of grapes. They have given so solid a form to what once moved them that it confronts us like pressed metal even between the lines. But what have they actually said? Nobody knows. They themselves never knew all of it at a time. They're like a field over which bees fly back and forth; they themselves are flying back and forth, as it were. Their thoughts and feelings show all the gradations between truth and even error, as can be demonstrated if necessary, and changeable natures that come close to us at will and then elude us when we try to observe them closely.

"There is no detaching an idea in a book from its context on the page. It catches our eye like the face of a person looming up in a crowd as it is being swept past us. I suppose I'm exaggerating a little again, but tell me, what happens in our lives that is any different from this? Leaving the precise, measurable, and definable sensory data out of account, all the other concepts on which we base our lives are no more than congealed metaphors. Take as simple a concept as manliness, and think how it keeps wavering among its many possible variants. It's like a breath that changes shape at every exhalation, with nothing to hold on to, no firm impression, no logic. So when we simply leave out in art whatever doesn't suit us and our conceptions, we're merely going back to the original condition of life itself."

"My dear friend," Diotima said, "you don't seem to be talking about anything in particular." Ulrich had paused for a moment, and her words fell into that pause.

"Yes, I suppose so. I hope I haven't been talking too loudly."

"You've been talking fast, in a low voice, and at length," she said, with a touch of sarcasm. "Without saying a word of what you meant to say. Do you realize what you've just explained to me all over again? That reality should be abolished! It's true that when I heard you make this point the first time, on one of our trips into the country, I think, it made a lasting impression—I don't know why. But how this is to be done is something you haven't yet revealed, I'm sorry to say."

"Clearly, I'd have to go on talking for at least as long again to do so. But do you really expect it to be that simple? If I'm not mistaken, you spoke of wanting to fly away with Arnheim into some kind of transcendent state. Something you regard as another kind of reality. What I have been saying, on the other hand, is that we must try to recover unreality. Reality no longer makes sense."

"Oh, Arnheim would hardly agree with you there," Diotima said.

"Of course not. That's just the difference between him and me. He is trying to make the fact that he eats, sleeps, is the great Arnheim, and doesn't know whether to marry you or not, mean something, and to this end he has been collecting all the treasures of the mind throughout his life." Ulrich suddenly paused, and the silence lengthened.

After a while he asked, in a different tone: "Can you explain to me why I should be having this conversation with you, of all people? Suddenly I'm reminded of my childhood. You won't believe this, but I was a good child, mild as the air on a warm moonlit night. I could fall madly in love with a dog, a pocketknife . . ." But then he left this statement unfinished too.

Diotima looked at him, wondering what he could mean. She again remembered how he had once hotly advocated "precision of feeling," while just now he was taking the opposite view. He had accused Arnheim of insufficiently clean-cut intentions, while now he favored "letting things happen." And she was troubled by the fact that Ulrich was advocating an intense emotional life without any "time off," compared with Arnheim's ambiguous suggestion never to let oneself in for single-minded hatred or *total love!* These thoughts left her uneasy.

"Do you really believe that there is such a thing as boundless feeling?" Ulrich asked her.

"Oh yes, there is such a thing as boundless emotion," Diotima said, the ground firm under her feet again.

"You see, I don't quite believe that," Ulrich said absently. "Strange how often we talk about it, but we certainly do our best to avoid it throughout our lives, as if we were afraid of drowning in it."

He noticed that Diotima was not listening. She was uneasily watching Arnheim, who was looking around for a cab.

"I'm afraid we ought to rescue him from the General," she said.

"I'll go and get a cab and take the General off your hands," Ulrich offered, and at the moment he turned to go, Diotima laid her hand on his arm and said kindly, as if to reward him for his trouble: "Any feeling that isn't boundless is worthless."

115

THE TIP OF YOUR BREAST IS LIKE
A POPPY LEAF

In accordance with the law that periods of great stability tend to be followed by violent upheavals, Bonadea, too, suffered a relapse. Her attempts to get on closer terms with Diotima had failed, and her fine scheme to get even with Ulrich by making friends with her rival, leaving Ulrich out in the cold—a fantasy she had spent much time in spinning out—had come to nothing. She had to swallow her pride and come knocking on his door again, but when she was there her beloved seemed to have arranged for constant interruptions, and her stories to account for her coming to see him again even though he did not deserve it were wasted on his impervious friendliness. She was longing to make a terrible scene but committed to behaving with absolute propriety, so that in time she came to hate herself for being so good. At night her head, heavy with unappeased cravings, sat on her shoulders like a coconut with its mat of monkeylike hair growing freakishly inside the shell, and she came close to bursting with helpless rage, like a drinker deprived of his bottle. She privately called Diotima every name she could think of, such as fraud and insufferable pompous bitch, and came up with cynical glosses on that noble femininity which was the secret of Diotima's charm. Her aping of Diotima's style, which had delighted her for a while, had now become a prison from which she broke out into an almost licentious freedom; her curling iron and mirror lost the power to turn her into an idealized image of herself, and the artificial state of mind it had supported collapsed as well. Even sleep, which Bonadea had always reveled in despite her chronic inner conflicts, sometimes kept her waiting when she had gone to bed, an experience so new to her that she thought she must be sick with insomnia, and felt what people usually feel when they are seriously ill, that her spirit was deserting her body, leaving it helpless like a wounded soldier on the battlefield. As she lay there in her vexations as if on red-hot sand, all that high-minded talk of Diotima's, which Bonadea had so admired, seemed to her infinitely beside the point, and she honestly despised it.

When she found it impossible to go to Ulrich yet again, she thought of another scheme to bring him back to his senses. It was of course the culmination of the plan that came to her first: a vision of herself effecting an entrance at Diotima's when that siren had Ulrich with her. Bonadea regarded all his visits with Diotima as transparent pretexts for carrying on their flirtation rather than actually doing something for the public good. So it was up to Bonadea to do something for the public good—and this gave her the opening gambit of her plan as well: no one was paying any attention to Moosbrugger anymore, and he was going to his doom, while all the others were pontificating about it. Bonadea never stopped to wonder that it was Moosbrugger once more who came to her rescue in her hour of need. Had she bothered to think about him at all, she would have been horrified, but all she was thinking was that if Ulrich cared so much about Moosbrugger, she would see to it that he would at least not forget the man. As she mulled over her plan, she remembered two things Ulrich had said when they were talking about the murderer: namely, that everyone had a second soul, which was always innocent; and that a responsible person could always choose to do otherwise, but an irresponsible person had no such choice. From this she somehow concluded that she wanted to be irresponsible, which would mean that she would also be innocent, which Ulrich was not, and which he needed to be, for his own salvation.

So motivated, and dressed as for a social occasion, she spent several evenings wandering up and down past Diotima's windows, and never had long to wait before they lit up along the whole front, betokening something going on inside. She had told her husband that she was invited out but would not stay too long, and in the course of a few days, while she was still trying to screw up her courage, her lies and her strolls in front of a house where she had no business to be unleashed a growing impulse that would soon drive her up those steps to the front door. What if she was seen by some acquaintance, or even by her husband if he should pass that way by chance, or what if she was noticed by the doorman, or by a policeman, who might decide to question her—the more often she went out on this expedition, the greater the risks, and the more probable that if she hesitated too long an incident would occur. Now, it was true that Bonadea had more than once slipped into doorways or places where she did not want to be seen, but on those occasions she had been fortified by the thought that it had to be; this time she was about to intrude where she was not expected and could not be sure of her reception. She felt like an assassin who has started out with none too clear an idea of what it would be like, and is then swept by circumstances into a state in which the actual pistol shot or the glitter of vitriol drops flying through the air no longer adds much to the excitement.

Without any such dramatic intentions, Bonadea nevertheless felt similarly benumbed by the time she actually found herself pressing the doorbell and walking inside. Little Rachel had slipped over to Ulrich and told him that someone was waiting out in the hall to see him, not mentioning that this someone was a heavily veiled unknown lady—who, when Rachel shut the door to the salon behind him, flung the veil back from her face. At the moment she was absolutely convinced that Moosbrugger's fate depended on her taking instant action, and she received Ulrich not like a lover plagued by jealousy, but gasping for breath like a marathon runner. With no effort, she lied that her husband had told her yesterday that Moosbrugger would soon be past saving.

"There's nothing I hate so much," she ended, "as this obscene kind of murderer. But even though it goes against my grain, I've taken the risk of being regarded as an intruder here, because you must go straight back to the lady of the house and her very influential guests and get their help if you still want to get anything done." She had no idea what she expected to come of this. Perhaps that Ulrich would be deeply moved and would thank her, then call Diotima, who would then take Bonadea into some private place to talk, away from the other guests. Or else Diotima might be drawn to the hall by the sound of voices, and Bonadea was ready to let her see that she, Bonadea, was far from being the person least qualified to take an interest in Ulrich's noble causes. Her eyes were moist and flashing, her hands trembled, her voice rose out of control. Ulrich, deeply embarrassed, smiled desperately to quiet her down and gain time while he found a way to talk her into leaving as quickly as possible. It was a ticklish situation and could have ended with Bonadea's having a screaming or crying fit, if Rachel had not come to his aid. Little Rachel had been standing close by all this time, with wide-open, shining eyes. When the beautiful stranger, trembling all over, had asked to speak to Ulrich, the maid had instantly divined the romantic nature of the affair. She managed to hear most of what was said, and the syllables of Moosbrugger's name fell on her ear like pistol shots. The sadness, passion, and jealousy throbbing in this lady's voice moved her powerfully, although she knew nothing of what was behind it. She guessed that the woman was Ulrich's mistress, and it doubled her infatuation with him. It was as though the two of them had burst into full-throated song together and made her want to lift up her own voice and join in, or do something to help. And so, with a glance enjoining secrecy, she opened a door and invited the pair into the only room not being used for the gathering this evening. It was Rachel's first conscious act of disloyalty to her mistress, and she knew what would happen if she was found out, but life was so exciting, and romantic passion such an untidy state of mind, that she had no chance to think twice about it.

When the gaslight flamed upward and Bonadea's eyes gradually took in her surroundings, her legs almost gave way under her, and her cheeks flushed red with jealousy: they were inside Diotima's bedroom. There were stockings, hairbrushes, and much else lying around, whatever is left in view when a woman must change hastily from head to foot for a big party and the maid has not had time to put things away or has left it till the next morning, as in this case, because the room was due for a thorough cleaning then anyway; on big-party evenings the bedroom was used to store furnishings from the other rooms where the space was needed. So the air was heavy with the smell of all this furniture jammed together, and of powder, soap, and scent.

"What a silly thing for the girl to do," Ulrich said with a laugh. "We can't stay here. Anyway, you shouldn't have come. There's nothing to be done for Moosbrugger."

"So I shouldn't have bothered, is that it?" Bonadea echoed him almost inaudibly. Her eyes strayed all over the place. How could the girl have even thought of taking Ulrich into the most private room in the house, she wondered in anguish, if she had not done it often before? Yet she could not bring herself to confront him with this proof of his infidelity, but chose instead to say dully: "How can you sleep in peace when such injustice is being done? I haven't been able to sleep at night, which is why I decided to come looking for you." She had turned her back on the room and stood staring out the window into the opaque, glassy darkness outside, at what might be treetops or some deep courtyard down below. Upset as she was, she had enough sense of orientation to know that she was not looking out on the street, and when she considered that here she was in her rival's bedroom, standing in a flood of light in the uncurtained window beside her faithless lover, as on a stage in front of an unseen audience, it threw her mind into turmoil. She had taken off her hat and thrown her coat back; her forehead and the warm tips of her breasts touched the cold windowpane; tenderness and tears moistened her eyes. Slowly she freed herself from the spell and turned back to her friend, but her eyes still held some of that soft, yielding darkness she had gazed into, and were deeper than she knew.

"Ulrich," she said with feeling, "you're not a bad man! You only pretend to be. You go to a lot of trouble to be as good as you can be."

These incongruously perceptive words of Bonadea's made the situation precarious again; for once, they were not the ridiculous desire of a woman to mask her body's demands for consolation with an overlay of lofty sentiment, but the beauty of that body itself claiming its right to the gentle dignity of love. Ulrich went up to her and put his arm around her shoulder; together they turned and looked into the darkness outside. A faint glimmer of light from the house was dissolving in the infinite darkness beyond so that it looked like a dense mist softening the air, and Ulrich felt as if he were staring out into a mildly chilly October night, though it was late winter; the whole city seemed wrapped in a vast woolen blanket. Then it occurred to him that one could just as well say that a woolen blanket resembled a night in October. He felt a gentle uncertainty on his skin and drew Bonadea closer.

"Will you go back to them now?" Bonadea asked.

"And save Moosbrugger from injustice? No; I don't even know whether injustice is being done to him. What do I really know about him? I saw him once, just a glimpse in a courtroom, and I've read a few things that were written about him. It's as though I had dreamed that the tip of your breast is like a poppy leaf. Does that give me the right to think it is any such thing?"

He stopped to think. So did Bonadea. He was thinking, "One human being, when you think of it, means nothing more to another one than a string of similes." Bonadea's thinking concluded with: "Come, let's get away from here."

"That's impossible," Ulrich told her. "They would wonder about my disappearance, and then if something should leak out about your coming here, it could cause quite a scandal."

Again they both fell silent, staring out the window together, into something that could have been a night in October, a night in January, a woolen blanket, sorrow, or joy, though they didn't attempt to define it.

"Why do you never do the natural next thing?" Bonadea asked.

He suddenly remembered a recent dream. He was one of those people who seldom have dreams, or at least never remember their dreams, so that it gave him a queer feeling to have this unexpected memory opening up and letting him in. In the dream, he had kept trying to cross a steep mountainside and was driven back, again and again, by violent dizzy spells. Without trying to interpret it, he now knew that the dream was about Moosbrugger, who never actually appeared in it. Since a dream image often has several meanings, it was also a physical representation of his mind's useless struggles to make some headway, as recently manifested again and again in his conversation and in his affairs, struggles that exactly resembled walking without a path to follow and being unable to get beyond a certain point. He could not help smiling at the ingenuous concreteness of the dream imagery for this: smooth rock and slippery earth underfoot, the occasional lone tree to hold on to or to aim for, the abrupt increase in the steepness of the grade as he went. He had tried and failed to make it on a higher and a lower route and was growing sick with vertigo, when he said to someone with him, Let's give it up; there's the easy road down there in the valley that everyone takes! The meaning was obvious. Incidentally, it occurred to Ulrich that the person with him might very well have been Bonadea. It was quite possible that he had also dreamed of her nipple as a poppy leaf—some unconnected thing that might, to the groping touch, easily seem broad and jagged, the dark purplish hue of a mallow, floating like a mist from some as yet unlit cranny in the dream world.

Now he experienced a moment of that special lucidity that lights up everything going on behind the scenes of oneself, though one may be far from being able to express it. He understood the relationship between a dream and what it expresses, which is no more than analogy, a metaphor, something he often thought about. A metaphor holds a truth and an untruth, felt as inextricably bound up with each other. If one takes it as it is and gives it some sensual form, in the shape of reality, one gets dreams and art; but between these two and real, full-scale life there is a glass partition. If one analyzes it for its rational content and separates the unverifiable from the verifiable, one gets truth and knowledge but kills the feeling. Like certain kinds of bacteria that split an organic substance into two parts, mankind splits the original living body of the metaphor into the firm substance of reality and truth, and the glassy unreality of intuition, faith, and artifact. There seems to be nothing in between; and yet how often a vaguely conceived undertaking does succeed, if only one goes ahead without worrying it too much! Ulrich felt that he had at last emerged from the tangle of streets through which his thoughts and moods had so often taken him, into the central square where all streets had their beginning. And he touched on all this in answering Bonadea's question as to why he never did the natural next thing. She probably did not understand his answer, but this was decidedly one of her good days; after thinking it over, she slipped her arm more firmly into his and summed it all up by saying: "Well, in your dreams you don't think either; you only live through some story or other." This was almost true. He squeezed her hand. Suddenly her eyes filled with tears again. They coursed slowly down her cheeks, and from her skin, bathed in those salty tears, there arose the indefinable scent of desire. Ulrich breathed it in and felt a great longing for this slippery nebulous state, for surrender and forgetfulness. But he pulled himself together and led her tenderly to the door. At this moment he felt sure that there was still something ahead of him and that he must not fritter it away in halfhearted attachments.

"You must go now," he said gently, "and don't be angry with me because I don't know when we can see each other again. I have a great deal to work out for myself just now."

And wonder of wonders! Bonadea put up no resistance and said nothing in anger or wounded pride. Her jealousy was gone. She felt that she was herself part of a story. She felt like taking him in her arms, guessing that he needed to be brought down to earth again, and was tempted to make the sign of the cross over his forehead for his protection, as she did with her children. It was all so romantic that it never occurred to her that it could be the end. She put on her hat and kissed him, and then she kissed him again through her veil, so that the threads seemed to glow like red-hot wires.

With the help of Rachel, who had been guarding the door and listening, Bonadea managed to slip away unseen, even though the party was breaking up and people were coming out. Ulrich pressed a big tip into Rachel's hand and complimented her on her presence of mind, making Rachel so ecstatic that her fingers unconsciously kept clutching his hand with the money. He had to laugh; when she blushed scarlet at this, he patted her on the shoulder.

116

THE TWO TREES OF LIFE AND A PROPOSAL TO ESTABLISH A GENERAL SECRETARIAT FOR PRECISION AND SOUL

That evening at the Tuzzis', there had been fewer guests than formerly; attendance at meetings of the Parallel Campaign was falling off, and people tended to leave earlier. Even the last-minute appearance of His Grace—who incidentally looked worried and preoccupied, and was in a bad mood, in fact, because he had received disturbing news about the nationalist intrigues against his work—could not prevent the party from breaking up. People lingered on for a bit in the expectation that he had brought some special news, but then, when he gave no sign of having anything of the kind to report and paid scant attention to the remaining guests, even the last of them left. By the time Ulrich reappeared, he was shocked to see the rooms almost empty. Shortly afterward only the "innermost circle" was left, joined by Section Chief Tuzzi, who had meanwhile come home.

His Grace had reverted to a favorite topic: "Of course we can regard an eighty-eight-year-old monarch of peace as a symbol; it gives us so much to think about. But it must be given a political content as well. Without that, it is only too natural for people to lose interest. In other words, as far as I am concerned, I've done all I could. The German Nationalists are furious with me for appointing Wisnieczky, whom they regard as a Slavophile, and the Slavs are furious because, as far as they're concerned, when he was in the government he was a wolf in sheep's clothing. All that only goes to show that he is a true patriot who stands above parties, and I wouldn't think of dropping him! However, we must supplement this with all possible speed on the cultural front, so that people have something positive to go on. Our public-opinion survey of what the various population sectors want is moving far too slowly. An Austrian Year or a World Year of Austria is a splendid idea, of course, but I must say that every symbol must in due course turn into something real; that is to say, I can let myself be deeply moved by a symbol without necessarily understanding it, but after a while I am bound to turn away from the mirror of my heart and get something else done, something I have meanwhile found needs doing. I wonder if I have managed to make my point? Our admirable friend the lady of the house is doing her utmost, and the discussions that have been held in this house for months have been most fruitful, I'm sure, but attendance is falling off nevertheless, and I have a feeling that we shall soon have to decide on something definite. I don't know what it will be: perhaps a second steeple on St. Stephen's, or an Imperial and Royal Colony in Africa; it doesn't matter what—it's sure to turn into something else at the last moment anyway. The main thing is to harness the inventiveness of the participants in time, before it all dribbles away."

Count Leinsdorf felt that he had spoken to the point. Arnheim now took the floor on everybody else's behalf. "What you say about the need, at times, to fructify thought by taking action, even if only pro tem, is most realistic and is true to life in general. You will be interested to know that there is a new mood, corresponding to what you say, among those of us meeting here regularly. We are no longer being swamped with an endless stream of considerations; almost no new proposals are being put forward now, and the older proposals are hardly ever mentioned, or at any rate nobody is fighting for them in any persistent way. Everyone seems to realize that in accepting the invitation to take part in this campaign he has obligated himself to come to an agreement, so that any acceptable proposal would now stand a good chance of being approved."

"And how are we coming along, my dear fellow?" said His Grace, turning to Ulrich, whom he had spotted meanwhile. "Can we see our way to winding it up?"

Ulrich had to admit that it was not so. An exchange of views can be drawn out on paper to everyone's pleasure for far longer than in person, and even the influx of proposed reforms had not abated, so that he was still founding organizations and referring them, in His Grace's name, to the various government departments whose readiness to deal with them had, however, shown a marked decline lately. This was what he had to report.

"No wonder," His Grace commented, turning to the others. "There's no dearth of patriotism among the population, but one would have to be as well informed as an encyclopedia to satisfy all the people on every point they bring up. Our government departments simply can't cope, which proves that the time has come for us to intervene from above."

"In this connection"—Arnheim spoke up again—"Your Grace might be interested to note that General von Bordwehr has been attracting increasing interest in the Council of late."

Count Leinsdorf looked at the General for the first time. "In what way?" he asked without in the least bothering to mask the rudeness of his question.

"Oh, how very embarrassing! I never intended anything of the kind," Stumm von Bordwehr demurred bashfully. "The role of the soldier in the council chamber can only be a modest one; that's always been a principle with me. But Your Grace may remember that at the very first meeting, only doing my duty as a soldier, so to speak, I suggested that if the Committee had no better idea, they might remember that our artillery has no up-to-date guns and our navy, for that matter, has no ships—not enough ships, that is, to defend the country if that should ever have to be done—"

"And?" His Grace interrupted him and shot a surprised, questioning look at Diotima that made no secret of his displeasure.

Diotima shrugged her beautiful shoulders in resignation; she had almost become hardened to the fact that wherever she might turn, the pudgy little General popped up like a nightmare, as if sponsored by some sinister forces.

"And lately, you see," Stumm von Bordwehr hastened to say before his modesty could get the better of him in the face of his success, "voices have been raised that would support such a proposal if someone were to come forward with it. It is being said, in fact, that the Army and the Navy are a concept behind which all could rally, and a great concept too, after all, and His Majesty would be pleased as well. Besides, it would be an eye-opener for the Prussians—no offense, I hope, Herr von Arnheim."

"Not at all, General. The Prussians wouldn't be at all disconcerted by it." Arnheim waved this aside with a smile. "Besides, it goes without saying that whenever such Austrian concerns come up I am simply not present, even while I most humbly take the liberty of listening in anyway. . . ."

"Well then, in any case," the General concluded, "opinions have in fact been expressed that the simplest thing would be not to keep talking much longer but to settle for a military solution. For myself, I'd be inclined to think that this could be done in combination with something else, some great civilian concept, perhaps, but as I say, it's not for a soldier to interfere, and views to the effect that nothing better is likely to come out of all this civilian thinking have just been voiced in the most intellectual quarters."

Toward the end of the General's speech, His Grace was listening with a fixed stare, and only involuntary twitchings in the direction of twiddling his thumbs, which he could not quite suppress, betrayed the strain of his painful inner workings.

Section Chief Tuzzi, whose voice was not usually heard on these occasions, now slipped in a comment, speaking slowly and in a low tone: "I don't believe the Ministry of Foreign Affairs would have any objections."

"Aha, so the departments have been in touch on this subject already?" Count Leinsdorf asked ironically, in a tone betraying his irritation. Unshaken, Tuzzi replied affably: "Your Grace is joking. The War Department would sooner welcome universal disarmament than have any truck with the Ministry of Foreign Affairs." He went on to tell a little story. "Your Grace must have heard about the fortifications in the southern Tyrol that have been built during the last ten years at the insistence of the Chief of the General Staff. They are said to be perfectly splendid, quite the latest thing. They have of course also been equipped with electrically charged barbed wire and huge searchlights that get their current from underground diesel engines; no one could say that we're behind the times in this. The only trouble is that the engines were ordered by the Artillery, and the fuel is provided by the War Ministry's Department of Works, according to regulations, which is why the fortifications can't be made operational, because the two authorities can't agree on whether the match that has to be used to start the engine should be regarded as fuel and supplied by the Department of Works, or as a mechanical part for which the Artillery is responsible."

"How delightful!" Arnheim said, though he knew that Tuzzi was confusing a diesel engine with a gas engine and that even with gas it was a long time since matches had been used. It was the kind of story that circulates in government offices, full of enjoyable self-deprecation, and the Section Chief had told it in a tone of tolerant amusement. Everyone smiled or laughed, none more appreciatively than General Stumm. "Of course, it's the civilians in the other departments who are really to blame," he said, to take the joke a little further, "because the minute we order something not regularly provided for in the budget, the Finance Ministry loses no time in reminding us that we don't know the first thing about the workings of constitutional government. So if war were to break out—God forbid!—before the end of the fiscal year we would have to telegraph the commanding officers of these fortifications at dawn, on the first day of mobilization, empowering them to buy matches, and if there were none to be had in those mountain villages, the war would have to be conducted with the matches in the pockets of the officers' orderlies."

The General had probably gone a little too far in his elaboration of the joke; as its humor thinned out, the dire seriousness of the problems facing the Parallel Campaign became apparent again. His Grace said pensively: "As time goes on . . . ," but then he remembered that it is wiser in a difficult situation to let the others do the talking, and did not finish. The six persons present were silent for a moment, as though they were all standing around a deep well, staring down into it.

"No," Diotima said, "that's impossible."

What? all eyes seemed to ask.

"We would only be doing what Germany is accused of: arming for war." Her soul had paid no attention to the anecdotes, or had forgotten them already, arrested at the moment of the General's success.

"But what is to be done?" Count Leinsdorf asked gratefully, but still troubled. "We must look for some temporary expedient, at the very least."

"Germany is a relatively naïve country, bristling with energy," Arnheim said, as though he felt called upon to apologize to his lady on behalf of his country. "It has been handed gunpowder and schnapps."

Tuzzi smiled at this metaphor, which struck him as more than daring.

"There's no denying that Germany is regarded with growing distaste in those circles to which our Campaign is meant to appeal." Count Leinsdorf did not pass up the opportunity to slip this in. "And even, I am sorry to say, in those circles it has already appealed to," he added, for a wonder.

Arnheim surprised him by stating that he was not unaware of it. "We Germans," he said, "are an ill-fated nation. Not only do we live in the heart of Europe; we even suffer the pains of this heart. . . ."

"Heart?" Count Leinsdorf asked involuntarily. He would have been prepared for "brain" and would have more readily acceded to this. But Arnheim insisted on heart. "Do you remember," he asked, "that not so long ago the City Council of Prague awarded a very large order to France, although we had also made a tender, of course, and would have filled our order more efficiently and more cheaply? It is simply an emotional prejudice at work. And I must admit that I fully understand it."

Before he could go on, Stumm von Bordwehr was happy to elucidate. "All over the world," he said, "people are struggling desperately, but in Germany they're struggling even harder. All over the world a lot of noise is being made, but even more in Germany. Business has lost touch with traditional culture everywhere, but most of all in Germany. Everywhere the flower of youth is stuck into barracks as a matter of course, but the Germans have more barracks than anyone else. And so we are bound, in a way, as brothers, not to hang back too far behind Germany," he concluded. "If all this sounds a bit paradoxical, I hope you'll all excuse me, but such are the complications faced by the intellect nowadays."

Arnheim nodded in agreement. "America may be even worse than we are," he added, "but America is at least utterly naïve, without our intellectual conflicts. We Germans are in every respect the nation at the center of things, where all the world's currents crisscross. More than any other we need a synthesis. And we know it. We have a sense of sin, as it were. But admitting this frankly, at the outset, I think it is only fair to acknowledge that we also suffer for the others, that we take their faults upon ourselves, so to speak, and that in a sense we are being cursed or crucified, however you might want to put it, on behalf of the whole world. A change of heart in Germany would probably be the most significant thing that could happen. I rather suspect that some vague idea of this is present in that conflicted and, as it seems, somewhat impassioned opposition to us of which you have just spoken."

Now Ulrich joined in: "You gentlemen underestimate the pro-German elements. I am reliably informed that any day now there is going to be a fierce demonstration against our campaign by those who consider us anti-German. Your Grace will see the people of Vienna demonstrating in the streets. There is to be a protest against the appointment of Baron Wisnieczky. Our friends Tuzzi and Arnheim are assumed to be acting in collusion, while you, sir, are said to be working to undermine the German influence on the Parallel Campaign."

Count Leinsdorf's eyes now reflected something between the impassivity of a frog's gaze and the irritability of a bull's. Tuzzi looked up slowly at Ulrich's face and gave him a warm, questioning look. Arnheim laughed heartily and stood up, trying to catch the Section Chief's eye with an urbane, humorous glance as a way of deprecating the absurd insinuation about the two of them, but as he could not connect with him he turned to Diotima instead. Tuzzi had meanwhile taken Ulrich by the arm and asked where he had got his information. Ulrich told him it was no secret but a widely accepted rumor he had heard at a friend's house. Tuzzi brought his face closer, forcing Ulrich to turn slightly aside from the others, and with this effect of privacy he suddenly whispered: "Don't you know yet why Arnheim is here? He is an intimate friend of Prince Mosyutov and very much persona grata with the Czar. He keeps in touch with Russia and is supposed to influence this Campaign in a pacifist direction. Unofficially, of course, on his Russian Majesty's private initiative, as it were. A matter of ideology. Something for you, my friend," he concluded in a mocking tone. "Leinsdorf has no inkling of it."

Section Chief Tuzzi had this information through official channels. He believed it because he saw pacifism as a movement that was in keeping with the outlook a beautiful woman would have, which would explain Diotima's being so enraptured with Arnheim and Arnheim's spending more time in Tuzzi's house than anywhere else. Before this he had come close to being jealous. He could believe in "intellectual affinities" up to a point, but he did not care to use devious methods to find out whether this point had been passed or not, so he had forced himself to go on trusting his wife. But while this was a victory of his manly self-respect over mere sexual instincts, these could still arouse enough jealousy in him to make him see for the first time that a professional man can never really keep an eye on his wife unless he is willing to neglect his work. Though he told himself that if an engine driver could not keep his woman with him on the job, a man at the controls of an empire could afford even less to be a jealous husband, it went against his character as a diplomat to settle for the noble ignorance in which this left him, and it undermined his professional self-assurance. So he was most thankful to be restored to his old self-confidence by this harmless explanation for everything that had worried him. There was even a little bonus in his feeling that it served his wife right that he knew all about Arnheim, while she saw only the human being and never dreamed that he was an agent of the Czar. Now Tuzzi again enjoyed asking her for little scraps of information, which she undertook to provide with a mixture of graciousness and impatience. He had worked out a whole series of seemingly harmless questions, the answers to which would enable him to draw his own conclusions. The husband would have been glad to take the "cousin" into his confidence, and was just wondering how to go about it without exposing his wife, when Count Leinsdorf again took the lead in the conversation. He alone had remained seated, and nobody had noticed anything of the struggle going on inside him as the problems piled up. But his fighting spirit seemed to be restored. He twirled his Wallenstein mustache and said slowly and firmly: "Something will have to be done."

"Have you come to a decision, Count?" they asked him.

"I haven't been able to come up with anything," he said simply. "Still, something must be done." He sat there like a man who does not intend to move from the spot until his will is done.

The effect was so powerful that everyone present felt the futile straining after an answer rattling inside him like a penny in a piggy bank that no amount of shaking will get out through the slot.

Arnheim said: "Now, really, we can't let ourselves be influenced by that sort of thing."

Leinsdorf did not reply.

The whole litany of proposals intended to give the Parallel Campaign some content was gone over again.

Count Leinsdorf reacted like a pendulum, always in a different position but always swinging the same way: This can't be done because we have to think of the Church. That can't be done, the freethinkers won't like it. The Association of Architects has already protested against this. There are qualms about that in the Department of Finance.

So it went, on and on.

Ulrich kept out of it. He felt as if the five persons taking their turn to speak had just crystallized out of some impure liquid in which his senses had been marinated for months now. Whatever had he meant by telling Diotima that it was necessary to take control of the imaginary, or that other time, when he had said that reality should be abolished? Now she was sitting here, remembering such statements of his, and probably thinking all sorts of things about him. And what on earth had made him say to her that one should live like a character in a book? He felt certain that she had passed all that on to Arnheim by now.

But he also felt sure that he knew what time it was, or the price of eggs, as well as anyone. If he nevertheless happened, just now, to hold a position halfway between his own and that of the others, it did not take some queer shape such as might result from a dim and absent state of mind; on the contrary, he again felt flooded by that illumination he had noticed earlier, in Bonadea's presence. He recalled going with the Tuzzis to a racecourse last fall, not so long ago, when there was an incident involving great, suspicious betting losses, and a peaceful crowd had in a matter of seconds turned into a turbulent sea of people pouring into the enclosure, not only smashing everything within reach but rifling the cash boxes as well, until the police succeeded in transforming them back into an assemblage of people out for a harmless and customary good time. In such a world it was absurd to think in terms of metaphors and the vague borderline shapes life might possibly, or impossibly, assume. Ulrich felt that there was nothing amiss with his perception of life as a crude and needy condition where it was better not to worry too much about tomorrow because it was hard enough to get through today. How could one fail to see that the human world is no hovering, insubstantial thing but craves the most concentrated solidity, for fear that anything out of the way might make it go utterly to pieces? Or, to take it a step further, how could a sound observer fail to recognize that this living compound of anxieties, instincts, and ideas, such as it is, though it uses ideas at most in order to justify itself, or as stimulants, gives those ideas their form and coherence, whatever defines them and sets them in motion? We may press the wine from the grapes, but how much more beautiful than a pool of wine is the sloping vineyard with its inedible rough soil and its endless rows of shining wooden stakes. In short, he reflected, the cosmos was generated not by a theory but—he was about to say "by violence," but a word he had not expected leapt to mind, and so he finished by thinking: but by violence and love, and the usual linkage between these two is wrong.

At this moment violence and love again did not have quite their conventional meaning for Ulrich. Everything that inclined him toward nihilism and hardness was implied in the word "violence." It meant whatever flowed from every kind of skeptical, factual, conscious behavior; a certain hard, cold aggressiveness had even entered into his choice of a career, so that an undercurrent of cruelty might have led to his becoming a mathematician. It was like the dense foliage of a tree hiding the trunk. And if we speak of love not merely in the usual sense but are moved by the word to long for a condition profoundly different, unto the very atoms that make up the body, from the poverty of lovelessness; or when we feel that we can lay claim to every quality as naturally as to none; or when it seems to us that what happens is only semblances prevailing, because life— bursting with conceit over its here-and-now but really a most uncertain, even a downright unreal condition—pours itself headlong into the few dozen cake molds of which reality consists; or that in all the orbits in which we keep revolving there is a piece missing; or that of all the systems we have set up, none has the secret of staying at rest:

then all these things, however different they look, are also bound up with each other like the branches of a tree, completely concealing the trunk on all sides.

These two trees were the shape his life had taken, like a two-pronged fork. He could not say when it had entered into the sign of the tree with the hard, tangled branchwork, but it had happened early on, for even his immature Napoleonic plans had shown him to be a man who looked on life as a problem he had set himself, something it was his vocation to work out. This urge to attack life and master it had always been clearly discernible in him, whether it had manifested itself as a rejection of the existing order or as various forms of striving for a new one, as logical or moral needs or even merely as an urge to keep the body in fighting trim. And everything that, as time went on, he had called essayism, the sense of possibility, and imaginative in contrast with pedantic precision; his suggestions that history was something one had to invent, that one should live the history of ideas instead of the history of the world, that one should get a grip on whatever cannot quite be realized in practice and should perhaps end up trying to live as if one were a character in a book, a figure with all the inessential elements left out, so that what was left would consolidate itself as some magical entity—all these different versions of his thinking, all in their extreme formulations against reality, had just one thing in common: an unmistakable, ruthless passion to influence reality.

Harder to recognize because more shadowy and dreamlike were the ramifications of the other tree that formed an image for his life, rooted perhaps in some primal memory of a childlike relationship to the world, all trustfulness and yielding, which had lived on as a haunting sense of having once beheld the whole vast earth in what normally only fills the flowerpot in which the herbs of morality send up their stunted sprouts. No doubt that regrettably absurd affair of the major's wife was his only attempt to reach a full development on this gentle shadow side of his life; it was also the beginning of a recoil that had never stopped. Since then, the leaves and twigs always drifting on the surface were the only sign that the tree still existed, though it had disappeared from view. This dormant half of his personality perhaps revealed itself most clearly in his instinctive assumption that the active and busy side of him was only standing in for the real self, an assumption that cast a shadow on his active self. In all he did—involving physical passions as well as spiritual—he had always ended up feeling trapped in endless preparations that would never come to fruition in anything, so that as the years went by his life had lost any sense of its own necessity, just as a lamp runs out of oil. His development had evidently split into two tracks, one running on the surface in daylight, the other in the dark below and closed to traffic, so that the state of moral arrest that had oppressed him for a long time, and perhaps more than was strictly necessary, might simply be the result of his failure to bring these two tracks together.

Now, as he realized that this failure to achieve integration had lately been apparent to him in what he called the strained relationship between literature and reality, metaphor and truth, it flashed on Ulrich how much more all this signified than any random insight that turned up in one of those meandering conversations he had recently engaged in with the most inappropriate people. These two basic strategies, the figurative and the unequivocal, have been distinguishable ever since the beginnings of humanity. Single-mindedness is the law of all waking thought and action, as much present in a compelling logical conclusion as in the mind of the blackmailer who enforces his will on his victim step by step, and it arises from the exigencies of life where only the single-minded control of circumstances can avert disaster. Metaphor, by contrast, is like the image that fuses several meanings in a dream; it is the gliding logic of the soul, corresponding to the way things relate to each other in the intuitions of art and religion. But even what there is in life of common likes and dislikes, accord and rejection, admiration, subordination, leadership, imitation, and their opposites, the many ways man relates to himself and to nature, which are not yet and perhaps never will be purely objective, cannot be understood in other than metaphoric or figurative terms. No doubt what is called the higher humanism is only the effort to fuse together these two great halves of life, metaphor and truth, once they have been carefully distinguished from each other. But once one has distinguished everything in a metaphor that might be true from what is mere froth, one usually has gained a little truth, but at the cost of destroying the whole value of the metaphor. The extraction of the truth may have been an inescapable part of our intellectual evolution, but it has had the same effect of boiling down a liquid to thicken it, while the really vital juices and elements escape in a cloud of steam. It is often hard, nowadays, to avoid the impression that the concepts and the rules of the moral life are only metaphors that have been boiled to death, with the revolting greasy kitchen vapors of humanism billowing around the corpses, and if a digression is permissible at this point, it can only be this, that one consequence of this impression that vaguely hovers over everything is what our era should frankly call its reverence for all that is common. For when we lie nowadays it is not so much out of weakness as out of a conviction that a man cannot prevail in life unless he is able to lie. We resort to violence because, after much long and futile talk, the simplicity of violence is an immense relief. People band together in organizations because obedience to orders enables them to do things they have long been incapable of doing out of personal conviction, and the hostility between organizations allows them to engage in the unending reciprocity of blood feuds, while love would all too soon put everyone to sleep. This has much less to do with the question of whether men are good or evil than with the fact that they have lost their sense of high and low. Another paradoxical result of this disorientation is the vulgar profusion of intellectual jewelry with which our mistrust of the intellect decks itself out. The coupling of a "philosophy" with activities that can absorb only a very small part of it, such as politics; the general obsession with turning every viewpoint into a standpoint and regarding every standpoint as a viewpoint; the need of every kind of fanatic to keep reiterating the one idea that has ever come his way, like an image multiplied to infinity in a hall of mirrors: all these widespread phenomena, far from signifying a movement toward humanism, as they wish to do, in fact represent its failure. All in all, it seems that what needs to be excised from human relations is the soul that finds itself misplaced in them. The moment Ulrich realized this he felt that his life, if it had any meaning at all, demonstrated the presence of the two fundamental spheres of human existence in their separateness and in their way of working against each other. Clearly, people like himself were already being born, but they were isolated, and in his isolation he was incapable of bringing together again what had fallen apart. He had no illusions about the value of his philosophical experimentation; even if he observed the strictest logical consistency in linking thought to thought, the effect was still one of piling one ladder upon another, so that the topmost rungs teetered far above the level of natural life. He contemplated this with revulsion.

This could have been the reason he suddenly looked at Tuzzi. Tuzzi was speaking. As though his ear were receiving the first sounds of the morning, Ulrich heard him say: "I am in no position to judge whether our time is devoid of great human and artistic achievements as you say; I can only assure you that foreign policy is nowhere else so hard to determine as in this country of ours. It is fairly safe to predict that even in our great Jubilee Year, French foreign policy will be motivated by the desire to settle scores and by colonialism, the English will be pushing their pawns to advantage on the world's chessboard, as their game has been characterized, and the Germans will be pursuing what they call, not always unambiguously, their Place in the Sun. But our old Empire is so self-contained that it's anyone's guess in what direction we may be driven by circumstances." It was as though Tuzzi were trying to put on the brakes, to utter a warning. That whiff of unintended irony came only from the naïvely factual tone in which he dryly presented to them his conviction that to want for nothing in this world was highly dangerous. The effect on Ulrich was to perk him up, as if he had been chewing on a coffee bean. Meanwhile Tuzzi kept harping on his warning note, and he ended by saying:

"Who can take it upon himself, today, even to think of putting great political ideas into practice? It would take a criminal or a gambler courting bankruptcy. You surely wouldn't want that? The function of diplomacy is to keep what we have."

"Keeping what we have leads to war," Arnheim countered.

"It may, I suppose," Tuzzi conceded. "All one can do, probably, is to choose the most favorable moment for being led into it. Remember Czar Alexander II? His father, Nicholas, was a despot, but he died a natural death. Alexander was a magnanimous ruler who began his reign by instituting sweeping liberal reforms, so that Russian liberalism turned into Russian radicalism, and Alexander survived three attempts to assassinate him, only to succumb to a fourth."

Ulrich looked at Diotima. There she sat, upright, alert, serious, voluptuous, and corroborated her husband: "That's right. From what I have seen of the radical temper in our own discussions, I would say that if you give them an inch they'll take a mile."

Tuzzi smiled with the sense of having won a small victory over Arnheim.

Arnheim looked impassive where he sat, his lips slightly parted, like a bud opening. Diotima, a silent tower of radiant flesh, gazed at him across the moat between them.

The General polished his horn-rimmed glasses.

Ulrich spoke with care: "That's only because those who feel called upon to act, in order to restore some meaning to life, have one thing in common: they despise 'mere' thinking just at the point where it could lead us to truths rather than simple personal opinions; instead, where everything depends on pursuing those views to their inexhaustible wellspring, they opt for shortcuts and half-truths."

Nobody spoke in answer. And why should anyone have answered him? What a man said was only words; after all. What mattered was that there were six people sitting in a room and having an important discussion; what they said or did not say in the course of it, their feelings, apprehensions, possibilities, were all included in this actuality without being on a level with it; they were included in the same way the dark movements of the liver and stomach are included in the actuality of a fully dressed person about to put his signature to an important document. This hierarchical order was not to be disturbed; this was reality itself.

Ulrich's old friend Stumm had now finished cleaning his glasses; he put them on and looked at Ulrich.

Even though Ulrich had always assumed that he was only toying with these people, he suddenly felt quite forlorn among them. He remembered feeling something like it a few weeks or months before, a little puff of Creation's breath asserting itself against the petrified lunar landscape where it had been exhaled; he thought that all the decisive moments of his life had been accompanied by such a sense of wonder and isolation. But was it anxiety that was troubling him this time? He could not quite pin his feeling down, but it suggested that he had never in his life come to a real decision, and that it was high time he did. This occurred to him not in so many words but only as an uneasy feeling, as though something were trying to tear him away from these people he was sitting with, and even though they meant nothing to him, his will suddenly clung to them, kicking and screaming.

Count Leinsdorf was now reminded by the silence in the room of his duties as a political realist, and said in a rallying tone: "Well then, what's to be done? We must do something final, even if it's only temporary, to save our campaign from all those threats against it."

This moved Ulrich to try something preposterous.

"Your Grace," he said, "there is really only one real task for the Parallel Campaign: to make a start at taking stock of our general cultural situation. We must act more or less as if we expected the Day of Judgment to dawn in 1918, when the old spiritual books will be closed and a higher accounting set up. I suggest that you found, in His Majesty's name, a World Secretariat for Precision and Soul. Without that, all our other tasks cannot be solved, or else they are illusory tasks." He now added some of the things that had crossed his mind during the few minutes he had been lost in thought.

As he spoke, it seemed to him not only that everybody's eyes were popping out of their sockets in sheer amazement, but also that their torsos were lifting up from their backsides. They had expected him to follow their host's example and come up with an anecdote, and when the joke failed to materialize he was left sitting there like a child surrounded by leaning towers that looked slightly offended at his silly game. Only Count Leinsdorf managed to put a good face on it. "Quite so," he said, though surprised. "Nevertheless, we are obliged now to go beyond mere suggestions and offer some concrete solution, and in that respect I must say that Property and Culture have left us badly stranded."

Arnheim felt he must save the great nobleman from being taken in by Ulrich's jokes.

"Our friend is caught up in an idea of his own," he explained. "He thinks it is possible to synthesize a right way to live, just like synthetic rubber or nitrogen. But the human mind"—here he gave Ulrich his most chivalrous smile—"is sadly limited in being unable to breed its life forms as white mice are bred in the laboratory; on the contrary, it takes a huge granary to support no more than a few families of mice." He immediately apologized for indulging in so daring an analogy, but was in fact quite pleased with himself for coming up with something in the aristocratic Leinsdorf style of scientific large-scale land management, while so vividly illustrating the difference between ideas with and without the responsibility for carrying them out.

But His Grace shook his head irritably. "I take his point quite well," he said. "People used to grow naturally into the conditions of their lives as they found them, and it was a sound way of coming into their own; but nowadays, with everything being shaken up as it is, everything uprooted from its natural soil, we will have to replace the traditional handicrafts system, even in the raising of souls, as it were, by the intelligence of the factory." It was one of those remarkable statements His Grace occasionally voiced, to his own and everyone else's surprise, all the more so as he had merely been staring at Ulrich with a dumbfounded expression the whole time before he began to speak.

"Still, everything our learned friend is saying is totally impracticable, just the same," Arnheim said firmly.

"Oh, would you say so?" Count Leinsdorf said curtly, full of fighting spirit.

Diotima now tried to make peace. "But, Count," she said, as if asking him for something one doesn't put into words: namely, to come to his senses. "We've long since tried everything my cousin says. What else are these long, strenuous talks, such as the ones we had this evening, about, after all?"

"Indeed?" the annoyed peer huffed. "I had an idea from the first that all these clever fellows won't get us anywhere. All of that psychoanalysis and relativity theory and whatever they call all that stuff is pure vanity. Every one of them is trying to make his own special blueprint of the world prevail over all the others. Let me tell you, even if our Herr Doktor did not express himself as well as he might have, he's basically quite right. People are always trying on something new whenever the times begin to change, and no good ever comes of it."

The nervous strain caused by the abortive meanderings of the Parallel Campaign had now broken through to the surface. Count Leinsdorf had, without being aware of it, switched from twisting his mustache to fretfully twiddling his thumbs. Perhaps something else had also come to the surface: his dislike of Arnheim. While he had been astonished when Ulrich brought up the word "soul," he was quite pleased with what followed. "When a fellow like Arnheim bandies that word about," he thought, "that's a lot of flimflam. We don't need it from him—what else is religion for?" But Arnheim, too, was upset; he had gone white to the lips. Up to now, Count Leinsdorf had spoken in that tone only to the General. Arnheim was not the sort of man to take it lying down. Still, he could not help being impressed with Count Leinsdorf's firmness in taking Ulrich's part, which painfully reminded him of his own divided feelings about Ulrich. He felt at a loss, because he had wanted to talk things out with Ulrich but had not found an opportunity to do so before this fortuitous clash in front of all the others, and so, instead of turning on Count Leinsdorf, whom he simply ignored, he addressed his words to Ulrich, with every sign of intense mental and physical agitation to a degree quite out of character for him.

"Do you actually believe what you have just been saying?" he asked sternly, with no regard to considerations of civility. "Do you believe it can be done? Are you really of the opinion that it is possible to live in accordance with some analogy? If so, what would you do if His Grace were to give you a free hand? Do tell me, I beg you!"

It was an awkward moment. Diotima was oddly enough reminded of a story she had read in the papers a few days before. A woman had received a merciless sentence for giving her lover an opportunity to murder her aged husband, who had not "exercised his marital rights" for years but would not agree to a separation. The case had caught Diotima's attention by its quasi-medical physical detail, and held it by a certain perverse fascination; it was all so understandable that one was not inclined to blame any of the persons involved, limited as they were in their ability to help themselves; it was only some unnatural general state of affairs that gave rise to such situations. She had no idea what made her think of this case just at this moment. But she was also thinking that Ulrich had been talking to her lately about all sorts of things that were "up in the air," and always ended up by annoying her with some outrageous suggestion of a personal kind. She had herself spoken of the soul emerging from its insubstantial state, in the case of a few privileged human beings. She decided that her cousin was just as unsure of himself as she was of herself, and perhaps just as passionate too. All of this was interwoven just now—in her head or in her heart, that abandoned seat of the noble Leinsdorfian amity—with the story of the condemned woman, in a way that caused her to sit there with parted lips, feeling that something terrible would happen if Arnheim and Ulrich were allowed to go on like this, but that it might be even worse if anyone interfered and tried to stop them.

During Arnheim's attack on him, Ulrich had been looking at Tuzzi. It cost Tuzzi an effort to hide his eager curiosity in the brown furrows of his face. He was thinking that all these goings-on in his house were now coming to a head, propelled by their inherent contradictions. Nor had he any sympathy for Ulrich, whose line of talk went quite against Tuzzi's grain, convinced as he was that a man's worth lay in his will or in his work, and certainly not in his feelings or ideas; to talk such nonsense about mere figures of speech, he felt, was positively indecent.

Ulrich might have been sensing some of this, because he remembered telling Tuzzi that he would kill himself if the year he was "taking off" from his life were to pass without results. He had not said it in so many words but had made his meaning painfully clear, and he now felt ashamed of himself. Again he had the impression, without being able to account for it, that his moment of truth was at hand. Suddenly Gerda Fischel came to mind; there was a dangerous possibility of her coming to see him, to continue their last conversation. He realized that even as he had only been toying with her, they had already reached the limit of what words could do, and there was only one last step: he would have to fall in with the girl's unexpressed longings, ungird his intellectual loins, and breach her "inner ramparts." This was crazy; he would never have gone this far with Gerda had he not felt safe with her on this point. He was feeling a strangely sober, irritated exaltation, when he caught sight of Arnheim's angry face and heard himself accused of having no respect for reality, followed by the words "Forgive my saying so, but such a crass Either/Or as yours is really too juvenile," but he had lost the slightest inclination to answer any of it. He glanced at his watch and, with a smile of appeasement, said it had grown much too late for going on with the subject.

In so saying he had regained his contact with the others. Section Chief Tuzzi even stood up, and barely masked this discourtesy by pretending to do something or other. Count Leinsdorf, too, had meanwhile calmed down; he would have been pleased to hear Ulrich put the Prussian in his place but did not mind his doing nothing about it. "When you like a man, you like him, that's that," he thought, "no matter how clever the other fellow's talk may be." And with a daring, though quite unconscious approach to Arnheim's idea of the Mystery of the Whole, he continued cheerfully, as he looked at Ulrich's expression (which was, at the moment, anything but intelligent): "One might even say that a nice, likable person simply can't say or do anything really stupid."

The party quickly broke up. The General slipped his horn-rims into his pistol pocket, after having tried in vain to stick them into the bottom of his tunic; he had not yet found a proper place for this civilian instrument of wisdom. "Here we have an armed truce of the intellect," he said to Tuzzi, like a pleased accomplice, alluding to the speedy dispersal of the last guests.

Only Count Leinsdorf conscientiously held them all back for another moment: "What is the consensus, then?" And when no one found anything to say, he added peaceably: "Oh well, we shall see, we shall see."

117

A DARK DAY FOR RACHEL

Soliman's sexual awakening and his decision to seduce Rachel made him feel as cold-blooded as a hunter sighting game, or a butcher sharpening his knives for the slaughter, but he had no idea how to go about it and what, exactly, a successful seduction was; in short, the more he had a man's will, the more it made him feel the weakness of a boy. Rachel also had her sense of the inevitable next step, and ever since she had so self-forgetfully clung to Ulrich's hand, that evening of the incident with Bonadea, she was quite beside herself, afloat in a state of acute erotic distraction that was also raining flowers on Soliman, as it were. But conditions just then were not favorable and made for delays. The cook had taken sick, Rachel's time off had to be sacrificed, the heavy social schedule in the house was keeping her busy, and although Arnheim continued to visit Diotima often enough, it was as though they had decided that the two youngsters needed watching, for he seldom brought Soliman, and when he did, they saw each other only briefly, in the presence of their employers, with the proper blank and sullen looks on their faces.

At this time they almost learned to hate each other, because they made one another feel the misery of being kept on too short a leash. Soliman was also driven by his mounting ardor to violent escapades; he planned to slip away from the hotel at night unbeknownst to his master, so he stole a bedsheet, which he tried to cut up and twist into a rope ladder; when he made a mess of it, he threw the tortured bed-sheet down a light shaft. Then for a long time he vainly studied ways and means to clamber up and down a housefront, using windowsills and the carved figures on the façade, and on his daytime errands examined the city's fabled architecture solely for the hand- and foot-holds it might offer a cat burglar. Meanwhile Rachel, who had been told of all these plans and setbacks in hasty whispers, would think that she saw the black full moon of his face on the pavement below, looking up at her, or that she heard his chirping call, to which she attempted a shy response, leaning far out her window into the empty night, until she had to admit that the night was indeed empty. She no longer regarded this romantic muddle as a nuisance but surrendered herself to it with a yearning wistfulness. The yearning was actually for Ulrich; Soliman was the man one didn't love but to whom one would give oneself nonetheless, as she never doubted; the fact that they had been kept apart lately, that they had hardly spoken to each other except in stolen whispers and were both in disfavor with their employers, had much the same effect on her as a night full of uncertainty, mystery, and sighs has on all lovers: it concentrated her fantasies like a burning glass, whose intense ray is felt less as a pleasant warmth than as a heat one cannot stand much longer.

In this regard, Rachel, who did not waste any time fantasizing about rope ladders and climbing walls, was the more practical-minded. The nebulous dream of an elopement soon dwindled to a plan for a single night together, and when this could not be arranged, a stolen quarter of an hour would have to do. After all, neither Diotima nor Count Leinsdorf nor Arnheim—staying on together for another hour or two after some crowded and unproductive meeting

with the best minds in town, while they all worried about the progress of their "business," without need of further attentions from their
staff—ever considered that such an hour "at liberty" consists of four
quarter hours. But Rachel had thought about it, and since the cook
was still not quite recovered and had permission to retire early, the
young maid was so overburdened that there was no telling where she
might be at any given time, even as she was spared much of her regular duty as a parlor maid. Experimentally—more or less as a person
afraid of committing suicide outright will go on making halfhearted
attempts until one of them succeeds by mistake—she had smuggled
Soliman into her room several times already, always prepared with
some story of having been on duty if he was caught, while hinting to
him that there were other ways to her bedroom than climbing the
walls. So far, however, the young lovers had not gone beyond yawning together in the front hall while spying out the situation, until one
evening, when the voices inside the meeting room had been heard
endlessly responding to each other, monotonous as the sounds of
threshing, Soliman used a lovely expression he had read in a novel
and said that he could stand it no longer.

Even inside her little room it was he who bolted the door, but then
they did not dare turn on the light but stood there blindly facing each
other as though the loss of sight had deprived them of all their other
senses as well, like two statues in the park at night. Soliman naturally
thought of pressing Rachel's hand or pinching her leg to make her
shriek, his way of conducting his male conquest of her thus far, but
he had to refrain from causing any noise, and when at last he made
some clumsy pass at her, there was only Rachel's impatient indifference in response. For Rachel felt the hand of fate on her spine, pushing her ahead, and her nose and forehead were ice cold, as though
she had already been drained of all her illusions. It made Soliman
feel quite at a loss too; he was all thumbs, and there was no telling
how long it would take them to break the deadlock of their rigid posture face-to-face in the dark. In the end, it had to be the civilized and
more experienced Rachel who took the part of the seducer. What
helped her was the resentment she now felt in place of her former
love for Diotima; ever since she had ceased to be content to enjoy
vicariously her mistress's exaltations and was involved in her own
love affair, she had greatly changed. She not only told lies to cover up

her encounters with Soliman, she even pulled Diotima's hair when she combed it, to revenge herself for the vigilance with which her innocence was being guarded. But what enraged her most was something in which she had formerly delighted: having to wear Diotima's cast-off chemises, panties, and stockings, for even though she cut these things down to a third of their former size and remodeled them, she felt imprisoned in them, as though wearing the yoke of propriety on her bare body. But this lingerie now gave her the inspiration she needed in this situation. For she had told Soliman earlier about the changes she had been noticing for some time in her mistress's underthings, and now she could break their deadlock by simply showing him.

"Here, you can see for yourself what they're really up to," she said in the darkness, showing Soliman the moonbeam frill of her little panties. "And if they're carrying on together like this, then they're certainly also making a fool of the master about that war they're cooking up in our house." And as the boy gingerly fingered the fine-textured and dangerous panties, she added somewhat breathlessly, "I bet that your pants are as black as you are, Soliman; that's what they're all saying." Now Soliman vengefully but gently dug his nails into her thigh, and Rachel had to move closer to free herself, and had to do and say one thing and another, all of which produced no real result, until she finally used her sharp little teeth on Soliman's face (which was pressed childishly against her own and at every movement she made kept on clumsily getting itself in the way), as if it were a large apple. At which point she forgot to feel embarrassed at what she was doing, and Soliman forgot to feel self-conscious, and love raged like a storm through the darkness.

When it was over, it dropped the lovers with a thud, vanished through the walls, and the darkness between them was like a lump of coal with which the sinners had blackened themselves. They had lost track of time, overestimated the time they had taken, and were afraid. Rachel's halfhearted final kiss was a mere annoyance to Soliman; he wanted the light switched on, and behaved like a burglar who has his loot and is now wholly intent upon making his getaway. Rachel, who had quickly and shamefacedly straightened her clothes, gave him a look that was fathomless and aimless at once. Her tousled hair hung down over her eyes, and behind them she saw again all the great images of her ideal self, forgotten until this moment. Her fantasies had been filled with her wish not only for every possible desirable trait in herself but also for a handsome, rich, and exciting lover—and now here in front of her stood Soliman, still half undressed, looking hopelessly ugly, and she didn't believe a single word of all the stories he had told her. She might have liked to take advantage of the dark to cradle his tense, plump face in her arms a little while longer before they let go of each other. But now that the light was on, he was only her new lover, a thousand possibilities shrunken into one somewhat ludicrous little wretch, whose existence excluded all others. And Rachel herself was back to being a servant girl who had let herself be seduced and was now beginning to be terrified of having a baby, which would bring it all to light. She was simply too crushed by this transformation even to give a sigh. She helped Soliman to finish dressing, for in his confusion the boy had flung off his tight little jacket with all those buttons, but she was helping him not out of tenderness but only so that they could hurry downstairs. She had paid far more than it was worth, and to be caught out now would be the last straw. All the same, when they had finished, Soliman turned round and flashed her a dazzling smile that turned into a whinny of self-satisfaction. Rachel quickly picked up a box of matches, turned out the light, softly drew the bolt, and whispered, before opening the door: "You must give me one more kiss." For that was the right way to do things, but it tasted to both of them like toothpowder on their lips.

Back down in the front hall, they were amazed to find they still had time. The voices on the other side of the door were running on as before. By the time the guests were dispersing, Soliman had disappeared, and half an hour later Rachel was combing her mistress's hair with great attentiveness and almost with her former humble devotion.

"I am glad that my little lecture seems to have done you some good," Diotima said with approval, and this woman who in so many ways never quite achieved any real satisfaction kindly patted her little maid's hand.

118

So kill him!

Walter had changed out of his office suit into a better one and was knotting his tie at Clarisse's dresser mirror, which despite its irregularly curving art nouveau frame showed a shallow, distorted image in its cheap glass.

"They're absolutely right," he said gruffly. "The famous campaign is nothing but a fake."

"But what's the point of marching and screaming?" Clarisse said.

"What's the point of anything these days? Marching together, at least they're forming a procession, feeling each other's physical presence. And at least they're not *thinking*, and at least they're not *writing*; something may come of it."

"Do you really think the campaign is worth all that indignation?"

Walter shrugged his shoulders. "Haven't you read that resolution by the German faction in the paper? Haranguing the Prime Minister about defamation and unfairness to the German population and so on? And the sneering proclamation of the Czech League? Or the little item about the Polish delegates returning to their voting districts? For anyone who can read between the lines, that one's the most revealing story, because so much depends on the Poles, and now they've left the government in the lurch! This was no time to provoke everyone by coming out with this patriotic campaign."

"This morning in town," Clarisse said, "I saw mounted police go by, a whole regiment of them. A woman said they're being kept in reserve somewhere."

"Of course. There are troops standing by in the barracks too."

"Do you suppose there'll be trouble?"

"Who can tell?"

"Will they run the people down? How awful, all those horses' bodies jammed in among the people . . ."

Walter had undone his tie and was reknotting it all over again.

"Have you ever been mixed up in anything of this kind?" Clarisse asked.

"As a student."

"Never since then?"

Walter shook his head.

"Didn't you say just now that if there's trouble, it will all be Ulrich's fault?"

"I said nothing of the kind," Walter protested. "He takes no interest at all in politics, unfortunately. All I said was that it's just like him to start up something of this sort; he's involved with the people who are responsible for all this."

"I'd like to come into town with you," Clarisse announced.

"That's out of the question. It would upset you too much." Walter spoke with great firmness. He had heard all sorts of things in the office about what might happen at the demonstration, and he wanted to keep Clarisse away from it. It wouldn't do at all to expose her to the hysteria of a large crowd; Clarisse had to be treated with care, like a pregnant woman. He almost got a lump in his throat at the word "pregnant," even though he did not actually pronounce it, so unexpectedly had it come to mind, warming him with the thought of motherhood, however foolishly, considering his wife's ill-tempered refusal of herself. Well, life is full of such contradictions, he told himself, not without some pride, and offered: "I'll stay home, if you'd rather."

"No," she said. "You should be there, at least."

She wanted to be left to herself. When Walter had told her of the upcoming demonstration and described what it would be like, it had made her think of a huge serpent covered with scales, each in separate motion, and she had wanted to see this for herself, but without the fuss of a long argument about it.

Walter put his arm around her. "I'll stay home too?" he repeated, in a questioning tone.

She brushed his arm off, took a book from the shelf, and ignored him. It was a volume of her Nietzsche. But instead of going, Walter pleaded: "Let me see what you're up to."

The afternoon was ending. A vague foretaste of spring made itself felt in the house, like birdsong muted by walls and glass; an illusory scent of flowers rose from the varnish on the floor, the upholstery, the polished brass doorknobs. Walter held out his hand for her book. Clarisse clutched it with two hands, one finger between the pages where she had opened it.

And now they had one of their "terrible scenes," of which this marriage had seen so many. They were all on the same pattern. Imagine a theater with the stage blacked out, and the lights going on in two boxes on opposite sides of the proscenium, with Walter in one of them and Clarisse in the other, singled out among all the men and women, and between them the deep black abyss, warm with the bodies of invisible human beings. Now Clarisse opens her lips and speaks, and Walter replies, and the whole audience listens in breathless suspense, for never before has human talent produced such a spectacle of son et lumière, sturm und drang.... Such was the scene, once more, with Walter stretching out his arm, imploring her, and Clarisse, a few steps away from him, with her finger wedged between the pages of her book. Opening it at random, she had hit on that fine passage where the master speaks of the impoverishment that follows the decay of the will and manifests itself in every form of life as a proliferation of detail at the expense of the whole. "Life driven back into the most minute forms, leaving the rest devitalized . . ." was what she remembered, though she had only a vague sense of the general drift of the context over which she had run her eye before Walter had again interrupted her; and yet, despite the unfavorable circumstances, she had made a great discovery. For although in this passage the master spoke of all the arts, and even of all the forms taken by human life, his examples were all literary ones, and since Clarisse did not understand generalizations, she saw that Nietzsche had not grasped the full implication of his own ideas—for they applied to music as well! She could hear her husband's morbid piano playing as though he were actually playing there beside her, his exaggerated pauses, choked with emotion, the halting way his notes came from under his fingertips when his thoughts were straying toward her and when—to use another of the master's expressions—"the secondary moral element" overwhelmed the artist in him. Clarisse had come to recognize the sound Walter made when he was full of unuttered desire for her, and she could see the music draining out of his face, leaving only his lips shining, so that he looked as though he had cut his finger and was about to faint. This was how he looked now, with that nervous smile as he held his arm stretched out toward her. Nietzsche, of course, could not have known any of this, and yet it was like a sign that she had been led to open the book, by chance, at the place touching on this very thing, and as she suddenly saw, heard, and grasped it all, she was struck by the lightning flash of inspiration where she stood, on a high mountain called Nietzsche, which had buried Walter although it reached no higher than the soles of her feet. The "practical philosophy and poetry" of most people, who are neither originators nor on the other hand unsusceptible to ideas, consists of just such shimmering fusions of someone else's great thought with their own small private modifications.

Walter had meanwhile stood and was coming toward Clarisse. He had decided to forget the demonstration he had intended to join and stay home with her. He saw her leaning back against the wall in repugnance as he approached her, yet this deliberate gesture of a woman shrinking from a man unfortunately did not infect him with the same abhorrence but only aroused in him those male urges that might have been precisely what she shrank from. For a man must be capable of taking charge and of imposing his will on whoever resists him, and the need to prove his manhood suddenly meant just as much to Walter as the need to fight off the last shreds of his youthful superstition that a man must amount to something special. One doesn't have to be something special! he thought defiantly. It was somehow cowardly not to be able to get along without that illusion. We are all inclined to excesses, he thought dismissively. We all have something morbid, some horror, withdrawal, malevolence, in our makeup; each one of us could do something that he alone could do, but what of it? He resented the mania for fostering the extraordinary in oneself instead of reabsorbing those all too corruptible outgrowths and, by assimilating them organically, injecting some new life into the bloodstream of the civilization, which was far too inclined to grow sluggish. So he thought now, and he was looking forward to the day when music and painting would no longer mean anything more to him than a refined form of amusement. Wanting a child was part of this new sense of mission; the dominant desire of his youth to become a titan, a new Prometheus, had ended in his coming to believe, somewhat overemphatically, that one must first become like everyone else. He was now ashamed of having no children; he would have liked at least five, if Clarisse and his income had permitted it, so that he could be the center of a warm circle of life; he wanted to surpass in mediocrity that great mediocre mass of humanity which transmits life itself, paradoxical as his desire was.

But whether he had taken too long to think, or had slept too late before starting to dress and beginning this conversation, his cheeks were glowing now, and Clarisse showed that she instantly understood why he was moving closer to her book; and this fine attunement to each other's moods, despite the painful signs of her aversion to him, immediately subdued the brute in him and broke down the simplicity of his impulse.

"Why won't you show me what you're reading? Can't we just talk?" he pleaded, intimidated.

"We can't 'just talk'!" Clarisse hissed at him.

"You're hysterical!" Walter exclaimed. He tried to get the book, open as it was, away from her. She stubbornly clung to it. After they had been wrestling over it silently for a while, Walter started wondering, "What on earth do I want the book for?" and let go. At this point the incident would have been closed if Clarisse had not, at the very moment she was released, pressed herself up against the wall even more fiercely than before, as though she had to force her body backward through a stiff hedge to escape some threat of violence. She was fighting for breath, her face white, and hoarsely screamed: "Instead of amounting to something yourself, you just want to make a child to do it for you!"

Her lips spat these words at him venomously, and all Walter could do was gasp his "Let's talk!" at her again.

"I won't talk; you make me sick!" Clarisse answered, suddenly in full possession of her voice again, and using it with such sharpness that it crashed like heavy china to the floor, midway between them. Walter took a step backward and stared at her in amazement.

Clarisse did not really mean it. She was merely afraid of giving in, from good nature or recklessness, and letting Walter bind her to him with swaddling bands, which must not happen, not now when she was ready to settle the whole question once and for all. The situation had come *to a head*. She thought of this term, heavily underlined—it was the one Walter had used to explain why the populace was demonstrating in the streets; for Ulrich, who was linked to Nietzsche by dint of having given her the philosopher's works as a wedding present, was on the other side of the conflict, the side against which this spear*head* would be directed, if there was trouble. Now Nietzsche had just given her a sign, and if she was standing on a high mountain, what was a high mountain other than the earth coming to a point—to a *head?* The way things were interrelated was truly amazing, like a code that hardly anyone could decipher; even Clarisse didn't have too clear a perception of it, but that was just why she needed to be alone and had to get Walter out of the house. The wild hatred that flared up in her face at this point in her thoughts was an expression of a physical rage in which she as a person was only vaguely involved, a kind of pianist's *furioso* such as Walter also had at his fingertips, so that he too, after having stared at his wife in bewilderment, suddenly went white in the face, bared his teeth, and, responding to the loathing of him she had expressed, shouted: "Beware of genius! You in particular, just watch out!"

He was screaming even louder than she had been, and his dark prophecy, which had burst from his throat with a force beyond any he knew himself to have, so horrified him that everything turned black as though there had been an eclipse of the sun.

Clarisse was in shock, too, and struck dumb by it. An emotion with the impact of a solar eclipse is certainly no trifle, and whatever had brought it on, at the heart of it was the quite unexpected explosion of Walter's jealousy of Ulrich. Why was he driven to call Ulrich a genius? All he had meant was hubris, the pride that comes before the fall. Images from the past came to his inner eye: Ulrich returning home in uniform, that barbarian who had already been carrying on with real women when Walter, who was the older, was still writing poems to statues in the park. Later on, Ulrich the engineer bringing home the latest reports on the exact sciences, the world of precision, speed, steel; for Walter, the humanist, it was another invasion by the Mongol horde. With his younger friend, Walter had always felt the obscure uneasiness of being the weaker man, both physically and in initiative, although he had seen himself as the life of the mind incarnate while the other stood merely for raw will. Wasn't Walter always being moved by the Beautiful or the Good, while Ulrich stood by shaking his head? Such impressions leave their mark, they confirm and define the relationship. Had Walter succeeded in seeing that passage in the book for which he had wrestled with Clarisse, he would certainly not have understood it as she did; to her the decadence Nietzsche described as driving the will to life away from the whole and into the realm of detail fitted Walter's tendency to brood over the problems of the artist, while Walter would have seen it as an excellent characterization of his friend Ulrich, beginning with his overestimation of facts, in accord with the modern superstition of empiricism, which led directly to the barbaric fragmentation of the very self that was what made Ulrich a man without qualities, or qualities without a man, according to Walter's diagnosis, which Ulrich, in his megalomania, had had the gall to accept wholeheartedly.

It was this that Walter had meant by denouncing Ulrich as a "genius," for if anyone was entitled to call himself a solitary original it was Walter himself, and yet he had given this up in order to rejoin the rest of the human race in fulfilling its shared mission; in this he was a whole generation ahead of his friend. But as Clarisse did not utter a sound in answer to his violent outburst, he was thinking: "If she says one word in his favor now, I couldn't stand it!" and he shook with hatred, as though it were Ulrich's arm shaking him.

In his fury he imagined himself snatching up his hat and dashing out the door to rush blindly through the streets, the houses bending in the wind as he ran. Only after a while did he slow down and look into the faces of the people he was passing; as they met his stare in a friendly fashion, he began to calm down. At this point he tried, to the extent his consciousness had not been swallowed up altogether by his fantasy, to explain himself to Clarisse. But his words only shone in his eyes instead of coming from his lips. How was a man to describe the joy of being with his own kind, with his brothers? Clarisse would say he was not enough of an individual. But there was something inhuman about Clarisse's towering self-confidence, and he'd had enough of trying to live up to its arrogant demands. He ached to take refuge with her within some broader human order, instead of this lonely drifting in a boundless delusion of love and personal anarchy. "Underneath everything one is and does, and even when one happens to be in opposition to one's fellowmen, one needs to feel that one is basically moving toward union with them" was more or less what he would have liked to say to her now. For Walter had always been lucky in getting along with people; even in the midst of an argument they felt his attraction, and he theirs, and so the somewhat banal notion that there is, inherent in the human community, something that keeps things in balance, that rewards soundness and always comes through in the end, had become a solid conviction in his life. The example came to mind of the kind of person who could make birds come flying to him of their own accord, and who often had a rather birdlike look about them. For every human being there was some animal mysteriously akin to him, he felt; it was a theory he had once worked out for himself, though not scientifically. He believed that musical people are intuitively aware of a great deal that is beyond the ken of science, and from childhood on, Walter's animal kinship had undoubtedly been with fish. Fish had always held a powerful attraction for him, though mixed with dread, and at the start of his school vacations he always acted as if possessed; he would stand for hours at the water's edge angling for fish, pulling them out of their element and laying their corpses beside him on the grass, until it all ended with a fit of revulsion close to panic. Fish in the kitchen, too, were among his earliest passions. There the bones from the filleted fish were put into a boat-shaped receptacle, glazed green and white, like grass and clouds, and half full of water, where, for some reason having to do with the laws of the kitchen, the fish skeletons were kept until after the meal had been prepared, when the fish bones went into the garbage. This dish drew the boy like a magnet; he would always find childish excuses for hovering over it for hours at a time, and when anyone asked him outright what he was doing there, he was struck dumb. When he thought about it now, the answer that occurred to him was that the magic of fish lay in their belonging wholly to one element, never to more than one. Again he saw them as he had often seen them in the deep mirror of the water, moving not as he did both on the earth and within a second, intangible element (and at home in neither the one nor the other, Walter thought, spinning out the image this way and that: one belongs to the earth, with which one shares no more than the bare space occupied by the soles of one's feet; the rest of one's body is upright in air that it merely displaces, that gives no support but lets one fall). The fishes' ground, their air, food, and drink, their recoil from enemies as well as their shadowy advances in love and their grave, were all one, wholly enclosing them; they moved within the element that moved them, something a human being can experience only in a dream or in the longing to return to the sheltering tenderness of the womb (the belief in this universal longing was just coming into fashion). But in that case, why did he rip the fish from their element and kill them? Why did he get such an unutterable, awesome thrill out of that? Well, he did not want to know the answer. He, Walter, could admit that he was an enigma. But Clarisse had once said that fish were the aquatic bourgeoisie. Walter winced at this insult. As he kept hastening through the streets in his ongoing fantasy, looking into the faces of the passersby, it was turning into good fishing weather, not actually raining, but some moisture was coming down, and the streets, as he now saw for the first time, had already been darkly glistening for a while. The men were all dressed in black, with bowler hats but no collars and ties, which did not surprise him, as they were not middle class but were evidently coming from a factory, walking in easy groupings, while others, who had not yet finished their day's work, were hastily pushing through these clusters, just as Walter himself was doing, and it all made him feel very happy, except for those bare necks that reminded him of something troubling and not quite right. Suddenly the rain came pouring down, the people scattered and ran as something came slashing through the air, a flash of white, fish raining down, and then a trembling, tender single voice that seemed to have nothing to do with anything called a little dog by name!

These last images were so independent of him that they took him entirely by surprise. He had not been aware that his thoughts had gone dreaming on their own, drifting along with incredible speed on a flood of images. He raised his eyes and found himself staring into his young wife's face, which was still twisted with dislike. He felt deeply unsure of himself, remembered that he had been about to register a complaint, in detail and at length; his mouth was still open. But he had no idea whether minutes had passed since then, or seconds, or only milliseconds. Yet he also felt a warmth of pride, as after an ice-cold bath an ambiguous shuddering of the skin signalizes more or less: "Look at me, see what I can stand." There was shame as well at such an eruption of buried feeling, when he had been on the point of praising everything that knows its place, keeps a tight rein on itself, and is content with its modest part as a link in the great scheme of things, as being far superior to the deviant—and here his inner-most convictions lay prone with their roots up in the air, mired in life's volcanic mud. Mainly he felt terrified, sure that something horrible was about to befall him. This fear had no rational basis; he was still thinking in images and was obsessed with the notion that Clarisse and Ulrich were intent on tearing him out of his picture. He made an effort to shake off his waking dream and find something to say that would pull the conversation which his loss of control had brought to a a standstill back onto a sensible track, and actually had something on the tip of his tongue, but a suspicion that his words came too late, that meanwhile something else had been said and done without his being aware of it, restrained him, and then, in the midst of catching up with the time-lapse, he suddenly heard Clarisse saying to him:

"If you want to kill Ulrich, why don't you? You're a slave of conscience. An artist can't make good music when he's saddled with a conscience."

It took a long time for this to sink in. Some things are soonest understood by means of one's own answer to them, and Walter was holding back his answer for fear of betraying his absence of mind. And in this moment of indecision he understood, or let himself be persuaded, that Clarisse had actually put into words the source of the terrifying fugue of ideas he had just been through. She was right: if Walter could have had his wish, it would often have been none other than to see Ulrich dead. That sort of thing is not too uncommon in a friendship (which does not dissolve as easily as love) when there is something in it that threatens a person's self-esteem. Nor was there real murder in his heart, for the moment he imagined Ulrich dead, his old boyhood love for his lost friend instantly revived, at least in part, and just as in the theater the civilized inhibition against a monstrous act is temporarily suspended by some pumped-up emotion, Walter almost felt that the thought of a tragic solution ennobled even the intended victim. He felt rather uplifted, despite his physical timidity and his squeamishness at the thought of seeing blood. While he would have liked to see Ulrich's arrogance broken down, he would have done nothing toward bringing even this about. But thoughts are not logical by nature, however much we like to think they are; only the unimaginative resistance of reality alerts us to the paradoxes inherent in the poem called man. So perhaps Clarisse was right in saying that too much of a civilized conscience got in an artist's way. All of this was going through Walter's head as he faced his wife with a baffled, reluctant expression.

"If he hampers you in your work," Clarisse repeated with zeal, "then you have the right to get him out of the way." She seemed to offer this as a stimulating and entertaining idea.

Walter wanted to hold out his hands to her, and although his arms felt pinned to his sides, he seemed to have come closer to her. "Nietzsche and Christ only failed because they were halfhearted in the end," she whispered in his ear. What awful nonsense she was talking. How could she drag Christ into this? What was that supposed to mean—that Christ failed because he was halfhearted? Such analogies were merely embarrassing. And yet Walter felt an indescribable prompting issuing from those moving lips of hers. Evidently his own hard-won resolution to make common cause with the majority was being steadily undermined by the irrepressible need to be someone in his own right. He laid hands on Clarisse and held her fast with all his strength, so that she could not move. Her eyes met his like two tiny disks. "How can you let such ideas enter your head?" he said, over and over, but got no answer. He must have unconsciously drawn her closer to him, for Clarisse now set the nails of her outspread ten fingers on his face like a bird's claws, keeping it from getting any closer to hers. She's crazy, Walter felt, but he couldn't let her go. An ugliness beyond all comprehension distorted her face; he had never seen a lunatic in his life, but this, he thought, must be what they looked like.

And suddenly he groaned: "You're in love with him!" It was not a particularly original remark, nor was this the first time they had argued the point; it was only that he did not want to believe that Clarisse was mad but preferred to believe that she loved Ulrich. This act of self-sacrifice was perhaps not quite uninfluenced by the fact that Clarisse, whose thin-lipped Early Renaissance beauty he had always admired, now for the first time looked ugly to him, an ugliness possibly related to her face being no longer tenderly veiled by love for him but stripped bare by the brutal love for his rival. Here was a sufficiency of complications, trembling between his heart and his eye as something quite new to him, full of meaning both general and personal. But what if his groaning out "You're in love with him!" in that subhuman voice was a sign of his being already infected by Clarisse's madness? The thought gave him a start.

Clarisse had gently freed herself from his grasp but then moved close to him of her own accord and said several times, in answer to his question, as though she were chanting something: "I don't want a child from you! I don't want a child from you!" kissing him lightly and quickly as she spoke.

Then she was gone.

Had she really also said, "He wants a child from me?" Walter could not be sure, but he heard it as a sort of possibility. He stood at the piano, jealous to the bursting point, sensing a breath of something warm and something cold blowing on him from either side. Were these the currents of genius and madness? Of surrender and of hatred? Of love and rationality? He could imagine himself leaving the way open for Clarisse and of laying his heart down on the road for her to walk over, and he could also imagine himself annihilating her and Ulrich with the power of words. He could not decide whether to rush off to Ulrich or begin composing his symphony, which might in this moment become the eternal struggle between the earth and the stars, or whether it might be a good idea to cool himself off first in the water-nymph pool of Wagner's forbidden music. By dint of these considerations, the indescribable state in which he had found himself began to clear up.

He opened the piano and lit a cigarette, and while his thoughts were scattering farther afield, his fingers on the keyboard were beginning to play the billowing, spine-melting music of the Saxon wizard. After this slow discharge of emotion had been going on for a while, he came to realize that he and his wife had both been in a state in which they could not be held responsible for their actions; embarrassing as it was, he knew it was too soon to go after Clarisse and make her understand. Now he needed to be with other people. He clapped on his hat and went off to town to carry out his original intention and immerse himself in the general excitement, if he could find it. As he walked he felt as though he were a captain bringing with him a demonic fighting force to link up with the others. But once he was on the trolley to town, life resumed its ordinary appearance. That Ulrich would have to be among the opposing forces, that

Count Leinsdorf's town house might be stormed by the marchers, that he might see Ulrich hanging from a streetlamp or being trampled by an onrushing mob or, alternatively, being defended by Walter and brought, trembling, to safety—these possibilities were at most fleeting shadows on the bright daylight pattern of the orderly train ride, with its set ticket prices, regular stops, and warning bells, a pattern with which Walter, his breathing now restored to a calmer rhythm, felt so much at home.

119

A COUNTERMINE AND A SEDUCTION

It now looked as though things were coming to a head, and even for Director Leo Fischel, who had been patiently biding his time and laying his countermine against Arnheim, the moment of satisfaction came. Too bad that Frau Clementine happened to be out, so that he had to content himself with walking into his daughter Gerda's room, in his hand the afternoon paper that usually carried the latest news of the Stock Exchange. He settled himself comfortably in a chair, pointed to an item on the page, and asked genially: "Well now, my child, do you know to what we are indebted for the presence of that highbrow financier among us?"

At home he never referred to Arnheim in any other terms, to show that as a serious man of business he was not impressed by his womenfolk's admiration for this rich windbag. Hatred may not give a man second sight, but there's often a grain of truth in a Stock Exchange rumor, and the hint of one in the news item, combined with Fischel's dislike of the man, instantly made him see the whole picture.

"Well, my dear, do you?" he repeated, trying to catch his daughter's eye and hold it in the triumphant beam of his own. "He wants to get control of the Galician oil fields, that's what!"

With this Fischel got up again, grabbed his paper as one might grab a dog by the scruff of his neck, and walked out, because it had just occurred to him that there were several men he might call to check his information. He felt as though what he had just learned from the paper was what he had been thinking all along—which shows that news from the Stock Exchange has quite the same effect as the higher forms of literature—and he now approved of Arnheim as a sensible man of whom nothing less should have been expected, quite forgetting that he had till then been calling him nothing but a windbag. He could not be bothered to elucidate to Gerda the meaning of his announcement; every further word would only have weakened the impact of the facts, which spoke so eloquently for themselves. "He wants control of the Galician oil fields!" With the weight of this blunt statement on his tongue he left the scene, thinking only: "The man who can afford to play a waiting game always wins in the end." This is axiomatic on the Stock Exchange, among other such truths, which most perfectly complement the eternal verities.

Gerda waited until he was out of her room to give vent to her feelings—she would not give her father the satisfaction of seeing her disconcerted or even surprised—but now she hastily flung open the closet, grabbed her hat and coat, and straightened her hair and dress at the mirror, where she sat still for a bit, doubtfully studying her face. She had decided to rush directly to Ulrich with her father's disclosure, which she thought Ulrich of all people should hear as soon as possible, since she knew enough about what was going on in Diotima's circle to realize its importance to him. She sensed a world of feeling coming into motion, like a crowd that has been hesitating on the brink of something for a long time. Up to this point she had forced herself to behave as if she had forgotten Ulrich's invitation, but her first impulses had no sooner begun to detach themselves from the dark mass of feeling and slowly to move forward than the ones farther back were irresistibly impelled to run and push forward, and while she hesitated to make up her mind, her mind made itself up without paying any attention to her.

"He doesn't love me!" she told herself while studying her face, grown even more haggard in the last few days, in the mirror. "How could he love me, when I look like this," she thought listlessly, and added at once, in defiance: "He's not worth it; it's all in my imagination anyway."

She sat there in utter discouragement, feeling drained, feeling also that for years they had both worked hard at complicating something that was basically quite simple. Meanwhile Hans was only adding to her nervous strain with his immature attempts at making love to her. She treated him harshly and sometimes, of late, contemptuously, which only made Hans more violent, behaving like a boy who threatens to do himself in, and when she had to calm him down, he fell back to putting his arms around her and touching her in his vague way, so that her shoulders grew bony and her skin turned dull. All these torments she had put behind her when she opened her closet to take out her hat, and her anxiety in front of the mirror only led to her jumping up again and rushing out, without in the least getting rid of the anxiety itself.

When Ulrich saw her coming in, he saw everything; to top it off, she had even tied on a veil such as Bonadea wore to visit him. Gerda was trembling in every limb and tried to mask her condition by assuming an unnaturally casual manner, which only made her seem absurdly stiff.

"The reason I came, Ulrich, is that I've just had some important information from my father."

"How peculiar," Ulrich thought; "she's never called me by my first name before." Her forced tone of intimacy infuriated him, but he tried to keep her from seeing this by attributing her theatrical behavior to her wish to make her visit look less portentous, more like a normal, if slightly belated, occurrence, though the effort it cost her was bound to have the opposite effect on him, suggesting that her intentions were clearly to go to the limit.

"We've been close friends for a long time," she explained, "and the only reason we never used first names was to avoid the implications." It was a rehearsed entrance, and she was prepared to surprise him with it.

But Ulrich cut it short by putting an arm around her and giving her a kiss. Gerda gave way like a melting candle. Her breathing, her fingers fumbling for him, were those of a person who has lost consciousness. He was instantly moved to behave with the ruthlessness of a seducer who senses the vacillation of a soul being dragged along by its body like a prisoner in the grip of his captors. From the windows a faint glimmer of wintry afternoon light entered the darkening room, where he stood outlined against one of these bright rectangles with the girl in his arms; her head was yellow and sharply contoured against the soft pillow of light, and her complexion had an oily shine, so that the whole effect was corpselike. He had to overcome a slight revulsion as he kissed her slowly everywhere on her bare skin between her hair and her neckline until he came to her lips, which met his in a manner reminiscent of the frail little arms a child puts around a grownup's neck. He thought of Bonadea's beautiful face, which, in the grip of passion, resembled a dove with its feathers ruffled in the claws of a bird of prey, and of Diotima's statuesque loveliness, which he had never enjoyed; how strange that instead of the beauty these two women had to offer he should be looking at Gerda's homely face, grim with passion.

But Gerda did not remain in her waking swoon for long. She had meant to shut her eyes for only a fleeting moment but lost all sense of time while Ulrich was kissing her, as if the stars were standing still in the infinite; as soon as he began to pause in his labors, however, she awakened and got firmly to her feet again. These were the first kisses of real, not merely would-be passion she had ever given and, as she thought, received, and the reverberations in her body were as extraordinary as though this moment had already made a woman of her. It is a process much like having a tooth pulled: although immediately afterward there is less of one's body than before, one actually feels more complete because a source of disquiet has been definitively removed. Hence, when Gerda felt the inner resolution of this chord, she pulled herself up, full of fresh determination.

"You haven't even asked me what I came to tell you," she said.

"That you love me," Ulrich said in some embarrassment.

"Oh no; only that your friend Arnheim is making a fool of your cousin, carrying on like a lover when what he's really after is something quite different," and Gerda told him what her papa had found out.

The news in all its simplicity made a deep impression on Ulrich. He felt obliged to warn Diotima, who was sailing with wings outspread into a ludicrous disappointment. For despite the malicious satisfaction he took in dwelling on this image, he felt sorry for his beautiful cousin. But most of all he was overcome with heartfelt appreciation for Papa Fischel, although he was on the verge of doing him a great wrong; he sincerely admired the man's reliable old-fashioned business sense, with its decorative border of fine sturdy convictions, which had hit on the simplest explanation for all the mysteries surrounding that modish Great Mind. Ulrich's mood had been altered, leaving far behind the tender demands made on him by Gerda's presence. He couldn't believe that only a few days ago he had been able to think that he could open his heart to this girl. Surmounting the inner ramparts, he thought, is what Hans calls his sacrilegious notion of two lovesick angels coming together, and he savored, as though he were running his fingers over it in his mind, the wonderfully smooth, hard surface of the matter-of-fact form life had taken on nowadays, thanks to the good sense of Leo Fischel and his like. All he could find to say was "Your papa is a wonder."

Gerda was so full of the importance of her news that she had expected something more—she didn't know exactly what, but something like the moment when all the instruments in the orchestra, winds and strings, strike up in unison—and Ulrich's indifference was a painful reminder of how he had always made a point of siding with the average, the ordinary, the matter-of-fact aspect of things to deflate her. She had tried to see this as a prickly kind of making advances, something not altogether alien to her own young girl's ways, but now, "when they had really begun to love each other," as her somewhat childish formula went, she felt it as a clear warning that the man to whom she was giving herself so recklessly was not taking her seriously enough. It was a blow to her new self-confidence, and yet she was also oddly pleased by "not being taken seriously enough." It was a relief, compared with the strain in keeping up her relationship with Hans, and while she did not understand Ulrich's praise of her father, it somehow restored an order of things she had disturbed by hurting Papa Leo because of Hans. This mild sense of making a somewhat unusual reentry into the bosom of her family by way of losing her virtue so distracted her that she gently resisted the pressure of Ulrich's arm and said to him: "Let's understand each other first as human beings, and the rest will take care of itself." These words came from a manifesto of her group, the so-called Community in Action, and was all that was left at the moment of Hans Sepp and his circle.

But Ulrich had put his arm around her again because, knowing that he had something important to do since hearing the news about Arnheim, he first had to finish this episode with Gerda. He was not at all reconciled to having to go through everything the situation called for, but he immediately put the rejected arm around her again, this time in that wordless language which, without force, states more firmly than words can do that any further resistance is useless. Gerda felt the virility of that arm all the way down her spine. She had lowered her head, with her eyes fixed on her lap as though it held, gathered as in an apron, all the thoughts that would help her to reach that "human understanding" with Ulrich before anything could be allowed to happen as a crowning act. But she felt her face looking duller and more vacuous by the moment until, like an empty husk, it finally floated upward, with her eyes directly below the eyes of the seducer.

He bent down and covered this face with the ruthless kisses that stir the flesh. Gerda straightened up as if she had no will of her own and let herself be led the ten steps or so to Ulrich's bedroom, leaning heavily on him as though she were wounded or sick. Her feet moved, one ahead of the other, as if she had nothing to do with it, even though she did not let herself be dragged along but went of her own accord. Such an inner void despite all that excitement was something Gerda had never known before; it was as if all the blood had been drained from her; she was freezing, yet in passing a mirror that seemed to reflect her image from a great distance she could see that her face was a coppery red, with flecks of white. Suddenly, as in a street accident when the eye is hypersensitive to the whole scene, she took in the man's bedroom with all its details. It came to her that, had she been wiser and more calculating, she might have moved in here as Ulrich's wife. It would have made her very happy, but she was groping for words to say that she was not out for any advantage and had come only to give herself to him; yet the words did not come, and she told herself that this had to happen, and opened the collar of her dress.

Ulrich had released her. He could not bring himself to help undress her like a fond lover and stood apart, flinging off his own clothes. Gerda saw the man's tall, straight body, powerfully poised between violence and beauty. Panic-stricken, she noticed that her own body, still standing there in her underthings, was covered with gooseflesh. Again she groped for words that might help her, that might make her less of a miserable figure where she stood. She longed to say something that would turn Ulrich into her lover in a way she vaguely imagined as dissolving in infinite sweetness, something one could achieve without having to do what she was about to do, something as blissful as it was indefinable. For an instant she saw herself standing with him in a field of candles growing out of the earth, row upon row to infinity, like so many pansies, all bursting into flame at her feet on signal. But as she could not utter a single word of all this, she went on feeling painfully unattractive and miserable, her arms trembling, unable to finish undressing; she had to clamp her bloodless lips together to keep them from twitching weirdly without a sound.

At this point Ulrich, who saw her agony and realized that the whole struggle up to now might come to nothing, went over to her and slipped off her shoulder straps. Gerda slid into bed like a boy. For an instant Ulrich saw a naked adolescent in motion; it affected him no more, sexually, than the sudden blinking of a fish. He guessed that Gerda had made up her mind to get it over with because it was too late to get out of it, and he had never yet perceived as clearly as in the instant he followed her into bed how much the passionate intrusion into another body is a sequel to a child's liking for secret and forbidden hiding places. His hands encountered the girl's skin, still bristling with fear, and he felt frightened too, instead of attracted. This body, already flabby while still unripe, repelled him; it made no sense to do what he was doing, and he would have liked nothing better than to escape from this bed, so that he had to call to mind everything he could think of that would help him to see it through. In his frantic haste he summoned up all the usual reasons people find nowadays to justify their acting without sincerity, or faith, or scruple, or satisfaction; and in abandoning himself to this effort he found, not, of course, any feeling of love, but a half-crazy anticipation of something like a massacre, a sex murder or, if there is such a thing, a lustful suicide, inspired by the demons of the void who lurk behind all of life's images. This reminded him of his brawl with the hoodlums that night he met Bonadea, and he decided to be quicker this time. But now something awful happened. Gerda had been gathering up all her inner resources to alchemize them into willpower with which to resist the shameful terror she was suffering, as though she were facing her execution; but the instant she felt Ulrich beside her, so strangely naked, his hands on her bare skin, her body flung off all her will. Even while somewhere deep inside her she still felt a friendship beyond words for him, a trembling, tender longing to put her arms around him, kiss his hair, follow his voice to its source with her lips; and imagined that to touch his real self would make her melt like a fragment of snow on a warm hand—but it would have to be the Ulrich she knew, dressed as usual, as he appeared in the familiar setting of her parental home, not this naked stranger whose hostility she sensed and who did not take her sacrifice seriously even as he gave her no time to think what she was doing—Gerda suddenly heard herself screaming. Like a little cloud, a soap bubble, a scream hung in the air, and others followed, little screams expelled from her chest as though she were wrestling with something, a whimpering from which high-pitched cries of *ee-ee* bubbled and floated off, from lips that grimaced and twisted and were wet as if with deadly lust. She wanted to jump up, but she couldn't move. Her eyes would not obey her and kept sending out signals without permission. Gerda was pleading to be let off, like a child facing some punishment or being taken to the doctor, who cannot go one step farther because it is being torn and convulsed by its own shrieks of terror. Her hands were up over her breasts, and she was menacing Ulrich with her nails while frantically pressing her long thighs together. This revolt of her body against herself was frightful. She perceived it with utmost clarity as a kind of theater, but she was also the audience sitting alone and desolate in the dark auditorium and could do nothing to prevent her fate from being acted out before her, in a screaming frenzy; nothing to keep herself from taking the lead in the performance.

Ulrich stared in horror into the tiny pupils of her veiled eyes, with their strangely unbending gaze, and watched, aghast, those weird motions in which desire and taboo, the soul and the soulless, were indescribably intertwined. His eye caught a fleeting glimpse of her pale fair skin and the short black hairs that shaded into red where

they grew more densely. It occurred to him that he was facing a fit of
hysteria, and he had no idea how to handle it. He was afraid that
these horribly distressing screams might get even louder, and remembered that such a fit might be stopped by an angry shout or even
by a sudden, vicious slap. Then the thought that this horror might
have been avoided somehow led him to think that a younger man
might persist in going further with Gerda even in these circumstances. "That might be a way of getting her over it," he thought,
"perhaps it's a mistake to give in to her, now that the silly goose has
let herself in too deep." He did nothing of the sort; it was only that
such irritable thoughts kept zigzagging through his mind while he
was instinctively whispering an uninterrupted stream of comforting
words, promising not to do anything to her, assuring her that nothing
had really happened, asking her to forgive him, at the same time that
all his words, swept up like chaff in his loathing of the scene she was
making, seemed to him so absurd and undignified that he had to
fight off a temptation to grab an armful of pillows to press on her
mouth and choke off these shrieks that wouldn't stop.

At long last her fit began to wear off and her body quieted down.
Her eyes brimming with tears, she sat up in the bed, her little breasts
drooping slackly from a body not yet under the mind's full control.
Ulrich took a deep breath, again overcome with repugnance at the
inhuman, merely physical aspects of the experience. Gerda was re-
gaining normal consciousness; something bloomed in her eyes, like
the first actual awakening after the eyes have been open for some
time, and she stared blankly ahead for a second, then noticed that
she was sitting up stark naked and glanced at Ulrich; the blood came
in great waves back to her face. Ulrich couldn't think of anything better to do than whisper the same reassurances to her again; he put his
arm around her shoulder, drew her to his chest, and told her to think
nothing of it. Gerda found herself back in the situation that had
driven her to hysteria, but now everything looked strangely pale and
forlorn: the tumbled bed, her nude body in the arms of a man intently whispering to her, the feelings that had brought her to this.
She was fully aware of what it all meant, but she also knew that something horrible had happened, something she would rather not focus
on, and while she could tell that Ulrich's voice sounded more tender,
all it meant was that he regarded her as a sick person, but it was he

who had made her sick! Still, it no longer mattered; all she wanted was to be gone from this place, to get away without having to say a word.

She dropped her head and pushed Ulrich away, felt for her camisole, and pulled it over her head like a child or someone who did not care how she looked. Ulrich helped her to dress, he even pulled her stockings up over her legs, and he also felt as though he were dressing a child. Gerda was a bit unsteady on her feet when she stood up. She thought of how she had felt earlier in the day when she left home, the home to which she was about to return, and felt, in deep misery and shame, that she had not passed the test. She did not utter a word in answer to anything Ulrich was saying. A very distant memory came back to her, of Ulrich once saying, as a joke on himself, that solitude sometimes led him into excess. She did not feel angry at him. She simply wanted never again to hear him say anything whatsoever. When he offered to get her a cab she only shook her head, pulled her hat on over her ruffled hair, and left him without a glance. Seeing her walk away with her veil now sadly trailing from her hand, he felt awkward as a schoolboy. He probably should not have let her go in this state, but he could think of no way to stop her, half-dressed as he was because he had been attending to her, unprepared even to confront the serious mood in which he was left, as though he would have to get fully dressed before he could decide what to do with himself.

120

THE PARALLEL CAMPAIGN CAUSES A STIR

When Walter reached the center of town he sensed something in the air. There was no visible difference in the way people moved on the sidewalks or in the carriages and streetcars, and if there was something unusual here and there it faded out before one could tell what it was; nevertheless, everything seemed to be carrying a little sign pointing in one direction, and Walter had barely walked a few steps before he felt such a sign on himself as well. He followed the indicated direction and felt that the Department of Fine Arts official he was, as well as the struggling painter and musician, and even Clarisse's tormented husband, were all giving way to a person who was none of the above. The very streets, with all their bustle and their ornate, pompous buildings, seemed to be in an analogous "expectant state," as though the hard facets of a crystal were being dissolved in some liquid medium and about to fall back into an earlier, more amorphous condition. However conservative he was in rejecting innovations, he was also always ready in his own mind to condemn the present, and the dissolution of the existing order that he was now sensing was positively stimulating. As in his recent daydream, the crowds he ran into had an aura of mobility and haste, and a unity that seemed more unforced than the usual group spirit based on intellect, morality, and sound security measures; more that of a free, informal community. They made him think of a huge bunch of flowers just after it has been untied, opening freely without, however, falling apart; and of a body unclothed, standing free, smiling, naked, having no need of words. Nor was he troubled when, quickening his pace, he ran into a large contingent of police standing by; he enjoyed the sight, like that of a military camp in readiness for the alarm to be given; all those red uniform collars, dismounted riders, movements of small units reporting their arrival or departure, stirred his senses into a warlike mood.

Beyond this point, where a cordon was about to be drawn across the street, the scene was more somber. There were hardly any women on the sidewalks, and even the colorful uniforms of the army officers who normally were seen hereabouts when off duty had somehow been swallowed up by the prevailing uncertainty. There were still many pedestrians like himself coming downtown, but the impression they gave was more that of chaff and litter in the wake of a strong gust of wind. Soon he saw the first groups forming, apparently held together not only by curiosity but just as much by indecision whether to follow the unusual attraction farther or to turn around and go home.

Walter's questions elicited a variety of answers. Some said that there was a great patriotic parade; others thought they had heard of a protest march against certain dangerously nationalistic activists, and opinions were equally split as to whether the general uproar was caused by the Pan-Germans protesting against the government's coddling of the Slavic minorities, as most people thought, or by loyal supporters of the government urging all patriotic Kakanians to march shoulder-to-shoulder in its defense against such continual disorders. They were all tagalongs like himself and knew nothing more than he had already heard rumored at the office, but an irrepressible itch to gossip led Walter on to speak to people, and even though they mostly admitted to having no idea, or laughed the whole thing off as a joke, including their own curiosity, the farther he went the more everyone seemed to be in agreement that it was high time *something* was done, though no one volunteered to tell him just what that should be. As he kept on, he noticed more often on the faces he met something senseless that overflowed and drowned out reason itself, something that told him that no one cared any longer what was happening, wherever they were being drawn to, as long as it was something unusual that would "take them out of themselves," if only in the attenuated form of a common general excitement, suggesting a remote kinship with long-forgotten states of communal ecstasy and transfiguration, a sort of developing unconscious readiness to leap out of their clothes, and even their skins.

Trading speculations and saying things that were not at all in character, Walter fell in with the rest, who were gradually transforming themselves from small crumbling groups of people, just waiting, and other people walking aimlessly along, into a procession that advanced toward the supposed scene of events, still without any definite intent yet visibly growing in density and energy. Emotionally they were still at the stage where they were like rabbits scampering about outside their burrows, ready to scurry back inside at the slightest sign of danger, when from the front of the disordered procession, far ahead and out of sight, a more definite sort of excitement came rippling back toward the rear. Up there a group of students, young men anyway, who had already taken some sort of action and had returned from "the battlefield," joined the vanguard, and sounds of talking and shouting too far away to be understood, garbled messages, and waves of excitement were running through the crowd and, depending on the listeners' temperaments or what scraps of information they snatched up, spread indignation or fear, the itch to fight or some moral imperative, causing the gathering mob to thrust forward in a mood guided by the kind of commonplace notions that take a different form inside every head but are of so little significance, despite being uppermost in the consciousness, that they join in a single vital force that affects the muscles more than the brain. In the midst of this moving throng Walter also became infected and soon found himself in that stimulated but vacuous state rather like the early stages of drunkenness. Nobody really knows the exact nature of the change that turns individuals with a will of their own into a mob with a single will, capable of going to the wildest extremes of good or evil and incapable of stopping to think anything through, even if most of the individuals involved have spent their lives dedicated to moderation and prudence in the conduct of their private affairs. A mob in a state of mounting excitement for which it has no outlet will probably discharge all that energy into the first available channel, and those among its participants who are the most excitable, sensitive, and most vulnerable to pressure, those at the extreme ends of the spectrum who are primed to commit sudden acts of violence or rise to unprecedented levels of sentimental generosity, are most likely to set the example and lead the way; they are the points of least resistance in the mass, but the shout that is uttered through them rather than by them, the stone that somehow finds its way into their hands, the emotion into which they burst, is what opens the way along which the others, who have been generating excitement among themselves to the point where it must be discharged, then come surging in a frenzy, giving to what happens the character of mob action, which is experienced by those involved in it as both compulsion and liberation.

What makes such agitated behavior interesting, incidentally, observable as it is among spectators of any sporting event or among crowds listening to speeches, is not so much the psychology of the emotional release it affords as the question of what it is that primes people to get themselves into such a state in the first place. Assuming that life makes sense, even its senseless manifestations would have some meaning and would not necessarily look like mere demonstrations of mental deficiency. Walter happened to know this better than most and could think of all sorts of remedies for it, so that he was constantly struggling against being swept along by this tidal wave of communal passion, which, demeaning as it was, nevertheless raised his spirits sky-high. The thought of Clarisse flashed through his mind. What a good thing she isn't here, he thought; she'd be crushed flat. A stab of grief kept him from pursuing his thought of her—with it had come the all-too-distinct impression she had given him of being raving mad. Maybe I'm the one that's mad, he thought, because it's taken me so long to notice it. I soon will be, if I go on living with her. I don't believe it, he thought, but there's no doubt about it. Right between my hands her darling face turned into a hideous mask, he thought. But he couldn't think it all through properly; his mind was awash with despair. He could only feel that despite his helpless anguish for her, it was incomparably finer to love Clarisse than to be running with the pack here—and to escape his fears, he pressed himself deeper into the ranks of the marchers.

Meanwhile Ulrich had arrived at the Palais Leinsdorf, though by another route. As he turned into the gate he noticed a double guard at the entrance and a large detachment of police stationed inside the courtyard. His Grace welcomed him with composure, while apparently aware of having become a target of popular disfavor.

"I think I once told you that anything favored by a good many people is sure to turn out to be worthwhile. Well, I have to take that back. Of course, there are exceptions," he said.

His Grace's majordomo now arrived with the latest bulletin: the demonstrators were approaching the Palais, and should he arrange to have the gate and shutters locked? His Grace shook his head. "What an idea!" he said kindly. "They'd like nothing better; it would allow them to think we're afraid of them. Besides, we've got all those men down there from the police looking out for us." Then, turning to Ulrich, he said indignantly: "Let them come and smash our windows! I told you all along that all that intellectual chatter would get us nowhere." Behind his façade of dignified calm, a deep resentment seemed to be working within him.

Ulrich had just walked over to the window when the marchers arrived. They were flanked by police, who dispersed the onlookers lining the avenue like a cloud of dust raised by the firm tread of the marchers. A little farther back, vehicles could be seen wedged in the crowd, while its relentless current flowed around them in endless black waves on which the foam of upturned faces seemed to be dancing. When the spearhead of the mob came within sight of Count Leinsdorf's windows, it looked as though it had been slowed down by some command; an immense ripple ran backward along the column as the advancing ranks jammed up, like a muscle tightening before launching a blow. The next instant this blow came whizzing through the air, in the weird form of a massed shout of indignation made visible by all those wide-open mouths before their roar was heard. In rhythmical succession the rows of faces snapped open as they arrived on the scene, and since the noise of the those in the rear was blotted out by the louder noise of those in the front, the spectacle could be seen repeating itself continually in the distance.

"The maw of the mob," Count Leinsdorf said, just behind Ulrich, as solemnly as if it were some familiar phrase like "our daily bread." "But what is it they're actually yelling? I can't make it out, with all that din."

Ulrich said he thought they were mostly screaming "Boo!"

"Yes, but there's something more, isn't there?"

Ulrich did not tell him that among the indistinct dancing sound waves of boos, a clear, long-drawn-out "Down with Leinsdorf!" could often enough be heard. He even thought he had heard several outcries of "Hurray for Germany!" interspersed with "Long live Arnheim!" but could not be absolutely sure, because the thick glass of the windows muffled the sounds.

Ulrich had come here as soon as Gerda left him, because he felt it was necessary to tell Count Leinsdorf, if no one else, the news that had come to his ears, which exposed Arnheim beyond all expectation. He had not yet had a chance to speak of it. As he looked down at the dark surge of bodies beneath the window, thoughts of his own days in the army made him say to himself: "It would take only one company to make a clean sweep of the square." He could imagine all those gaping mouths turning into a single frothing maw suddenly succumbing to panic, growing slack and drooping at the edges, lips slowly sinking over teeth; his imagination transformed the menacing black crowd into a flock of hens scattering before a dog rushing into their midst. All his anger had contracted again into a hard knot, but the old satisfaction in watching moral man retreat before brute violent man was, as always, a two-edged feeling.

"Are you all right?" Count Leinsdorf was asking. He had been pacing the floor behind Ulrich and had actually received the impression from some odd movement of Ulrich's that he had cut himself, though there was no sharp-edged object anywhere in the vicinity. When he received no answer he stood still, shook his head, and said: "We must not forget, after all, that it is not so very long since His Majesty's generous decision to let the people have a voice in the conduct of their own affairs; so it is understandable that a degree of universal political maturity that would be worthy of our Sovereign's magnanimity is still lacking. I believe I said as much at our very first meeting."

This little speech made Ulrich drop any notion of telling His Grace or Diotima about Arnheim's machinations; despite his antagonism to Arnheim he felt closer to him than to the others, and his memory of himself setting upon Gerda, like a big dog on a howling little one, a memory he now realized had been haunting him all along, troubled him less when he thought of Arnheim's infamous conduct toward Diotima. The episode of the screaming body staging a dramatic scene for a captive audience of two embarrassed souls could also be seen from the farcical side, and the people down there in the street at whom Ulrich was still staring spellbound without taking the slightest notice of Count Leinsdorf were also staging a farce. It was this that fascinated him. They did not really want to attack or rip anyone apart, although they looked as if they did. They made a serious show of being enraged, but it was not the kind of seriousness that drives men into a line of fire, not even that of a fire brigade! They're only going through some kind of ritual, he thought, some time-hallowed display of righteous indignation, the half-civilized, half-barbaric legacy of ancient communal rites no individual need take wholly seriously. He envied them. How appealing they are, even in this state where they are doing their best to be as unappealing as possible, he thought. The warm defense against loneliness that a crowd provides came radiating up from below, and here he was, fated to stand up here, outside its protective shelter—he felt this vividly, for an instant, as if he were looking up from down there and seeing his own image behind the thick pane of glass set in the wall of the building. It would have been better for him and his fate, he felt, had he been able to fly into a rage at this moment, or, on Count

Leinsdorf's behalf, give the alarm to the guard, or alternatively had he been capable of feeling close to the people as their friend; a man who plays cards with his fellows, bargains with them, quarrels with them, and enjoys the same pleasures they do is free to order them shot, too, when the occasion calls for it, without its seeming to be anything unnatural. There is a way of being on good terms with life that allows a man to go about his business with no second thoughts, in a live-and-let-live fashion, Ulrich was thinking. It may have a peculiarity of its own but is no less dependable than a natural instinct, and it is from this that the intimate scent of a healthy personality emanates, while whoever lacks this gift for compromise with life and is solitary, unyielding, and in dead earnest makes the others feel uneasy and unnerves them, as a caterpillar might, not because it is dangerous but because it is repellent. He felt a depressing aversion for the unnaturalness of the solitary man and his mental games, such as may be aroused by the sight of a turbulent crowd in the grip of natural, shared emotions.

The demonstration had been growing more intense. Count Leinsdorf was pacing the room in some agitation, with an occasional glance through the second window. He was in distress, though he would not show it; his eyes protruded like two little marbles from among the soft furrows of his face, and he stretched his arms now and then before he crossed them again behind his back. Ulrich suddenly realized that it was he, who had been standing at the window the whole time, who was being taken for the Count. All the eyes down there seemed focused on his face, and sticks were being brandished at him. A few steps beyond, where the street curved from view as though it were slipping into the wings, the performers were already beginning to take off the greasepaint, as it were; there was no point in looking fierce for no one in particular, so they naturally let their faces relax, and some even began to joke and laugh as if they were on a picnic. Ulrich noticed this and laughed too, but the newcomers took him for the Count laughing and their rage rose to a fearsome pitch, which only made Ulrich laugh all the more and without restraint.

But all at once he broke off in disgust. With his eyes still moving from the threatening open-mouthed faces to the high-spirited ones farther back, and his mind refusing to absorb any more of this spectacle, he was undergoing a strange transformation. I can't go on with this life, and I can't keep on rebelling against it any longer, either, was what he felt, while keenly aware of the room behind him with the large paintings on the wall, the long Empire desk, the stiff perpendicular lines of draperies and bell ropes, like another, smaller stage, with him standing up front on the apron, in the opening between the curtains, facing the drama running its course on the greater stage outside. The two stages had their own way of fusing into one without regard for the fact that he was standing between them. Then his sense of the room behind him contracted and turned inside out, passing through him or flowing past him as if turned to water, making for a strange spatial inversion, Ulrich thought, so that the people were passing behind him. Perhaps he had passed through them and arrived beyond them at some zero point, or else they were moving both before and behind him, lapping against him as the same ever-changing ripples of a stream lap against a stone in their midst. It was an experience beyond his understanding; he was chiefly aware of the glassiness, emptiness, tranquillity of the state in which he found himself. Is it really possible, he wondered, to leave one's own space for some hidden other space? He felt as though chance had led him through a secret door.

He shook these dreams off with so violent a motion of his whole body that Count Leinsdorf stood still in surprise. "Whatever is the matter with you today?" His Grace asked. "You're taking it much too hard. I must stick to my decision: the Germans will have to be won over by way of the non-Germans, whether it hurts or not." At these words Ulrich was at least able to smile again, and was grateful to see the Count's face before him, with all its knots and furrows. He was reminded of that special moment just before a plane lands, when the ground rises up again with all its voluptuous contours out of the maplike flatness to which it had been reduced for hours on end, and things revert to their familiar earthly meanings, which seem to be growing out of the ground itself. At the same moment the incredible idea flashed through his mind to commit some crime, or perhaps it was an unfocused passing image, for he was not thinking of anything in particular. It might have had some reference to Moosbrugger, for he would have liked to help that fool whom fate had chanced to bring his way as two people come to occupy the same park bench. But all this "crime" really amounted to for him was the urge to shut himself out, to abandon the life he had been living companionably with others. His "dissident" or even "misanthropic" attitude, his so variously justified and well-earned position, had not "arisen" from anything, there was nothing to justify it, it simply existed, he had held it all his life, though rarely with such intensity. It is probably safe to say that in all the revolutions that have ever taken place in this world, it has always been the thinking men who have come off worst. They always begin with the promise of a new civilization, make a clean sweep of every advance hitherto achieved by the human mind as though it were enemy property, and are overtaken by the next upheaval before they can surpass the heights previously attained. Our so-called periods of civilization are nothing but a long series of detours, one for every failure of a movement forward; the idea of placing himself outside this series was nothing new for Ulrich. The only new element was the increasing force of the signs that his mind was coming to a decision and that he was, in fact, ready to act on it. He did not make the slightest effort to come down to specifics. For some moments he was content to be permeated with the feeling that this time it would not be something general or theoretical, the sort of thing he had grown so tired of, but that he must do something personal, take an action that would involve him as a man of flesh and blood, with arms and legs. He knew that at the instant of committing his undefined "crime" he would no longer be in a position to defy the world openly, but only God knew why this should arouse in him such a sensation of passionate tenderness. It was somehow linked with his strange spatial experience of a while ago, a faint echo of which he could bring back at will, when what was happening on this side and on the other side of the window fused into one to form an obscurely exciting relationship to the world that might have suggested to Ulrich—if he could have taken the time to think about it—the legendary voluptuousness that overcame mythical heroes on the point of being devoured by the goddesses they had wooed.

Instead, he was interrupted by Count Leinsdorf, who had meanwhile fought his own inner struggle through to a decision.

"I must stay at my post and face down this insurrection," His Grace began, "so I can't leave. But you, my dear fellow, must really go to your cousin as quickly as possible, before she has time to be frightened and possibly moved to say something to some reporter that might not be quite the thing this moment. You might tell her . . ." He paused to consider his message. "Yes, it will be best if you say to her: Strong remedies produce strong reactions. And tell her, too, that those who set out to make life better must not shrink, in a crisis, from using the stake or the knife." He stopped again to think, with an almost alarming look of resolution, as his trim little beard rose and then sank to a downward, vertical position every time he was on the verge of saying something but paused to reconsider. In the end, his innate kindliness broke through and he said: "But tell her not to worry, not to be afraid of the troublemakers. The more of a case they have, the more quickly they adjust themselves to the realities when they are given a chance. I don't know whether you've noticed this, but there has never yet been an opposition party that didn't cease to be in opposition when they took over the helm. This is not merely, as you might think, something that goes without saying. It is, rather, a very important point, because it is, if I may say so, the basic reality, the touchstone, the continuity in politics."

121

TALKING MAN-TO-MAN

When Ulrich arrived at Diotima's, Rachel, who let him in, told him that Madame was out but that Dr. Arnheim was there, waiting for her. Ulrich said he would wait too, not noticing that his little ally of the other night had blushed scarlet at the sight of him.

Arnheim, who had been at the window, watching what unrest there still was in the streets, crossed the room to shake hands with Ulrich. His face lit up at seeing Ulrich unexpectedly, for he had wanted to speak with Ulrich but had hesitated to seek him out; however, he did not want to rush into things, and could not immediately think of a good opening. Ulrich was also reluctant to start off with the

Galician oil fields, and so both men fell silent after their first words of greeting and ended up walking over to the window together, where they stared mutely at the flurries of movement down below.

After a while, Arnheim spoke:

"I really don't understand you. Isn't it a thousand times more important to come to grips with life than to write?"

"But I haven't been writing," Ulrich said crisply.

"I'm glad to hear it." Arnheim adjusted to the fact. "Writing, like the pearl, is a disease. Look down there. . . ." He pointed two of his beautifully manicured fingers at the street, with a movement that for all its rapidity had the air of a papal blessing about it. "See how they come along, singly and in clusters, and from time to time a mouth is torn open and something inside makes it yell something. The same man under different circumstances would write something; I agree with you on that."

"But you are a famous writer yourself, aren't you?"

"Oh, that doesn't mean anything." But after saying this, gracefully leaving the question open, Arnheim turned to face Ulrich, confronting him as it were broadside, and standing chest-to-chest with him, said, carefully spacing his words:

"May I ask you something?"

Ulrich could not say no to that, of course, but as he had instinctively moved back a little, this rhetorical courtesy served to rope him in again.

"I hope," Arnheim began, "that you will not hold our recent little difference of opinion against me but rather credit it to my keen interest in your views even when they seem—as they do often enough—to run counter to mine. So let me ask you whether you really meant what you said—to sum it up, if I may: that we must live with a tight rein on our conscience. Is this a good way of putting it?"

The smile Ulrich gave him in answer said: I don't know; let me wait and see what more you have to say.

"You spoke of having to leave life in a free-floating state, like a certain kind of metaphor that hovers inconclusively between two worlds at once, as it were, did you not? You also said some extremely fascinating things to your cousin. I would be mortified if you were to take me for a Prussian industrial militarist who is unlikely to understand that sort of thing. But you say, for instance, that our reality and our history arise only from those aspects of ourselves that don't matter. I take this to mean that we must change the forms and patterns of what happens, and that it doesn't matter much, in your opinion, what happens meanwhile to Tom, Dick, and Harry."

"What I mean," Ulrich interjected warily and reluctantly, "is that our reality is like a fabric being turned out by the thousands of bales, technically flawless in quality but in antiquated patterns no one bothers to bring up-to-date."

"In other words," Arnheim broke in, "I understand you to say that the present state of the world, which is clearly unsatisfactory, arises from our leaders' concern with making world history instead of turning all our energies to permeating the world of power with new ideas. An even closer analogy to our present state of affairs is the case of the manufacturer who keeps turning out goods in response to the market, instead of regulating it. So you see that your ideas touch me very closely. But just because of this you must see that these ideas at times strike me, a man continually engaged in making decisions that keep vast industries going, as positively monstrous! Such as when you demand that we give up attaching any meaningful reality to our actions! Or propose that we abandon the 'provisionally definitive' character of our behavior, as our friend Leinsdorf so gracefully phrases it, when, in fact, we can do no such thing!"

"I demand nothing at all," Ulrich said.

"Oh, you demand a great deal more! You demand that we live our lives in a scientific, experimental way," Arnheim said with energy and warmth. "You want responsible leaders to regard their job not as making history but as a mandate to draw up reports on experiments as a basis for further experiments. A perfectly delightful idea, of course. But how do wars and revolutions—for instance—fit in with that? Can you raise the dead when your experiment has been carried out and taken off the schedule?"

Ulrich now succumbed after all to the temptation to talk, which is not so very different from the temptation to go on smoking, and conceded that one probably had to tackle everything one wanted to do effectively with the utmost seriousness, even when one knew that in fifty years every experiment would turn out not to have been worthwhile. But such a "punctured seriousness" was nothing so very unusual, after all; people risked their lives every day in sport and for nothing at all. Psychologically, there was nothing impossible about a life conducted as an experiment; all that was needed was the determination to assume a certain unlimited responsibility. "That's the crucial difference," he concluded. "In the old days, people felt as it were deductively, starting from certain assumptions. Those days are gone. Today we live without a guiding principle, but also without any method of conscious, inductive thinking; we simply go on trying this and that like a band of monkeys."

"Splendid!" Arnheim admitted freely. "But allow me one last question. Your cousin tells me that you're taking a great interest in the case of a dangerous psychopath. I happen to understand this very well, incidentally. We really don't know how to handle such cases, and society's method of dealing with them is disgracefully hit-or-miss. But in the circumstances—which leave us no choice but either to kill an 'innocent' man or to let him go on killing innocent people— would you let him escape the night before his execution, if you could?"

"No!" Ulrich said.

"No? Really not?" Arnheim asked with sudden animation.

"I don't know. I don't think so. I might of course talk myself out of it by claiming that in a malfunctioning world I have no right to act freely on my own personal convictions; but I shall simply admit that I don't know what I would do."

"That man must surely be stopped from doing further harm," Arnheim said pensively. "And yet, when he is having one of his seizures, he is certainly a man possessed by the demonic, which in all virile epochs has been felt to be akin to the divine. In the old days such a man would have been sent into the wilderness. Even then he might have committed murder, but perhaps in a visionary state, like Abraham about to slaughter his son Isaac. There it is! We no longer have any idea of how to deal with such things, and there is no sincerity in what we do."

Arnheim might have let himself be carried away in uttering these last words without quite knowing what he meant by them; his ambition might have been spurred on by Ulrich's not mustering up enough "heart and rashness" to answer with an unqualified "yes" when asked whether he would save Moosbrugger. But although Ulrich felt this turn of the conversation to be almost an omen, an unex-

pected reminder of his "resolve" at Count Leinsdorf's, he resented
Arnheim's flamboyance in making the most of the Moosbrugger
problem, and both factors made him ask dryly, but intently: "Would
you set him free?"

"No," Arnheim replied with a smile, "but I'd like to propose something else." And without giving him time to put up resistance, he
added: "It's a suggestion I've been wanting to make to you for some
time, to make you give up your suspicions of me, which, frankly, hurt
my feelings; I want you on my side, in fact. Do you have any conception of what a great industrial enterprise looks like from the inside? It
is controlled by two bodies, the top management and the board of
directors, usually capped by a third body, the executive committee,
as you in Austria call it, made up of representatives of the first two,
which meets almost every day. The board of directors naturally
consists of men who enjoy the confidence of the majority shareholders. . . ." Here he paused for the first time, to give Ulrich a
chance to speak if he wished, as though testing to see whether Ulrich
had already noticed something. "As I was saying, the majority shareholders have their representatives on the board and the executive
committee." He prompted Ulrich. "Have you any idea who this majority is?"

Ulrich had none. He had only a vague general concept of finance,
which to him meant clerks, counters, coupons, and certificates that
looked like ancient documents.

Arnheim cued him in again. "Have you ever helped to elect a
board of directors? No, you haven't," he answered his own question.
"There would be no point in trying to imagine it, since you will never
own the majority of shares in a company." He said this so firmly that
Ulrich very nearly felt ashamed of being found wanting in so important a respect; and it was in fact just like Arnheim to move in one easy
stride from his demons to his board of directors. Smiling, he continued: "There is one person I haven't mentioned yet, the most important of all, in a sense. I spoke of the majority shareholders, which
sounds like a harmless plural but is in fact nearly always a single person, a chief shareholder, unnamed and unknown to the general public, hidden behind those he sends out front in his place."

Ulrich now realized that he was being told things he could read in
the papers every day; still, Arnheim knew how to create suspense.

He was sufficiently interested to ask who was the majority share-holder in Lloyd's of London.

"No one knows," Arnheim replied quietly. "That is to say, there are those in the know, of course, but one doesn't usually hear it spoken of. But let me get to the point. Wherever you find two such forces, a person who really gives the orders and an administrative body that executes them, what automatically happens is that every possible means of increasing profits is used, whether or not it is morally or aesthetically attractive. When I say automatically I mean just that, because the way it works is to a high degree independent of any personal factor. The person who really wields the power takes no hand in carrying out his directives, while the managers are covered by the fact that they are acting not on their own behalf but as functionaries. You will find such arrangements everywhere these days, and by no means exclusively in the world of finance. You may depend on it that our friend Tuzzi would give the signal for war with the clearest conscience in the world, even if as a man he may be incapable of shooting down an old dog, and your friend Moosbrugger will be sent to his death by thousands of people because only three of them need have a hand in it personally. This system of indirection elevated to an art is what nowadays enables the individual and society as a whole to function with a clear conscience; the button to be pressed is always clean and shiny, and what happens at the other end of the line is the business of others, who, for their part, don't press the button. Do you find this revolting? It is how we let thousands die or vegetate, set in motion whole avalanches of suffering, but we always get things done. I might go so far as to say that what we're seeing here, in this form of the social division of labor, is nothing else than the ancient dualism of conscience between the end that is approved and the means that are tolerated, though here we have it in a grandiose and dangerous form."

In answer to Arnheim's question whether he found all this revolting Ulrich had shrugged his shoulders. The split in the moral consciousness that Arnheim spoke of, this most horrifying phenomenon of modern life, was an ancient fact of human history, but it had won its appalling good conscience only in recent times, as a consequence of the universal division of labor with all its magnificent inevitability.

Ulrich did not care to wax indignant over it, especially as it gave him, paradoxically, the funny and gratifying sensation one can get from tearing along at a hundred miles an hour past a dust-bespattered moralist who is standing by the wayside, cursing. When Arnheim came to a stop, Ulrich's first words were: "Every kind of division of labor can be developed further. The question is not whether it repels me but whether I believe that we can attain more acceptable conditions without having to turn back the clock."

"Aha, your general inventory!" Arnheim interjected. "We have organized the division of labor brilliantly but neglected to find ways of correlating the results. We are continuously destroying the old morality and the soul in accordance with the latest patents, and think we can patch them up by resorting to the old household remedies of our religious and philosophical traditions. Levity on such a subject"—he backed off—"is really quite distasteful to me, and I regard jokes on the whole as in dubious taste anyway. But then, I never thought of the suggestion you made to us all in the presence of Count Leinsdorf, that we need to reorganize the conscience itself, as a mere joke."

"It *was* a joke," Ulrich said gruffly. "I don't believe in such a possibility. I would sooner be inclined to believe that the Devil himself built up the European world and that God is willing to let the competition show what he can do."

"A pretty conceit," Arnheim said. "But in that case, why were you so annoyed with me for not wanting to believe you?"

Ulrich did not answer.

"What you said just now," Arnheim calmly persisted, "also contradicts those adventurous remarks of yours, some time ago, about the means toward attaining the right way in life. Besides, quite apart from whether I can agree with you on the details, I can't help noticing the extent to which you are a compound of active tendencies and indifference."

When Ulrich saw no need to reply even on this point, Arnheim said in the civil tone with which such rudeness must be met: "I merely wished to draw your attention to the degree to which we are expected, even in making economic decisions, on which after all everything depends, to work out the problem of our moral responsibility on our own, and how fascinating this makes such decisions." Even in the restraint with which this reproof was expressed there was a faint suggestion of trying to win him over.

"I'm sorry," Ulrich said, "I was totally caught up in what you've been saying." And as though he were still pursuing the same line of thought, he added: "I wonder whether you also regard it as a form of indirect dealing and divided consciousness in keeping with the spirit of the times to fill a woman's soul with mystical feelings while sensibly leaving her body to her husband?"

These words made Arnheim color a little, but he did not lose control of the situation. "I'm not sure I know what you mean," he said quietly, "but if you were speaking of a woman you love, you couldn't say this, because the body of reality is always richer than the mere outline sketch we call principles." He had moved away from the window and invited Ulrich to sit down with him. "You don't give in easily," he went on in a tone of mingled appreciation and regret. "But I know that I represent to you more of an opposing principle than a personal opponent. And those who are privately the bitterest opponents of capitalism are often enough its best servants in the business world; I may even say that to some extent I count myself among them, or I wouldn't presume to say this to you. Uncompromising, passionately committed persons, once they have seen that a concession must be made, usually become its most brilliant champions. And so I want in any case to go ahead with my intended proposal: Will you accept a position in my firm?"

He took care to say this as casually as he could, trying by speaking rapidly and without emphasis to lessen the cheap surprise effect he could be only too sure of causing. Avoiding Ulrich's astonished gaze, he simply proceeded to go into the details without making any effort to indicate his own position.

"You wouldn't, of course, have the necessary training and qualifications at first," he said smoothly, "to assume a leading position, nor would you feel inclined to do so, therefore I would offer you a position at my side, let us say that of my executive secretary, which I would create especially for you. I hope you won't take offense at this: it is not a position I can see as carrying an irresistible salary, to begin with; however, in time, you should be able to aim for any income you might wish. In a year or so, I am sure that you will understand me quite differently from now."

When Arnheim had finished, he felt moved in spite of himself. Actually, he had surprised himself by going so far in making this offer to Ulrich, who only had to refuse in order to put Arnheim at a disadvantage, while if he accepted, there wasn't much in it for Arnheim. Any idea that this man he was talking to could accomplish something that he himself could not do on his own had vanished even as he spoke, and the need to charm Ulrich and get him into his power had become absurd in the very process of finding articulate expression. That he had been afraid of something he called this man's "wit" now seemed unnatural. He, Arnheim, was a man of some consequence, and for such a man life has to be simple! Such a man lives on good terms with other great men and circumstances, he does not act the romantic rebel or cast doubt on existing realities; it would be against his nature. On the other hand, there are, of course, all the things of beauty and ambiguity one wants in one's life as much as possible. Arnheim had never felt as intensely as he did at this moment the permanence of Western civilization, that marvelous network of forces and disciplines. If Ulrich did not recognize this he was nothing but an adventurer, and the fact that Arnheim had almost let himself be tempted to think of him as— At this point words failed him, unformulated as they still were at the back of his mind; he could not bring himself to articulate clearly, even in secret, the fact that he had considered taking Ulrich on as an adopted son. Not that it really mattered; it was only an idea like countless others one need not answer for, probably inspired by the kind of moodiness that afflicts every man of action, because a man is never really satisfied, and perhaps he had not had this idea at all, in so dubious a form, but only some vague impulse that could be so interpreted; still, he shied away from the memory, and only kept painfully in mind that the difference between Ulrich's age and his own was not all that great; and behind this there was a secondary, shadowy sense that Ulrich might serve him as a warning against Diotima! How often he had already felt that his relationship to Ulrich was somehow comparable to a secondary volcanic crater that emits the occasional warning or clue to the strange goings-on in the main crater, and he was somewhat troubled that the eruption had now occurred and his words had come pouring out and were making their way into real life. "What's to be done," flashed through his mind, "if this fellow accepts?" It was in such suspense that an Arnheim had to wait for the decision of a younger man who mattered only insofar as Arnheim's own imagination had lent him significance. Arnheim sat there stiffly, his lips parted in a hostile expression, thinking: "There'll be a way of handling it, in case there's still not a way of getting out of it."

Even while his feelings and thoughts were running their course in this fashion the situation had not come to a standstill; question and answer followed each other without pause.

"And to what qualities of my own," Ulrich asked dryly, "do I owe this offer, which can hardly be justified from a businessman's point of view?"

"You always misjudge this sort of thing," Arnheim replied. "To be businesslike in my position is not the same as counting pennies. What I stand to lose on you is quite immaterial compared to what I hope to gain."

"You certainly pique my curiosity," Ulrich remarked. "Very seldom am I told I represent a gain of any kind. I might perhaps have developed into a minor asset in my special subject, but even there, as you know, I have been a disappointment."

"That you are a man of exceptional intelligence," Arnheim answered, in the same quiet tone of unshakable confidence to which he was outwardly clinging, "is surely something of which you are fully aware without my having to tell you. Still, we may have keener and more dependable minds already working for us. It is actually your character, your human qualities, that, for certain reasons, I wish to have constantly at my side."

"My qualities?" Ulrich could not help smiling at this. "That's funny: I have friends who call me a man without qualities."

Arnheim let slip a faint gesture of impatience that said, more or less: "Tell me about it, as if I didn't know." This twitch that ran across his face all the way to the shoulder betrayed his dissatisfaction, even while his words flowed on as programmed. Ulrich caught the fleeting grimace, and he was so ready to be provoked by Arnheim that he now dropped all restraint against bringing everything out into the open.

They had meanwhile risen from their chairs, and Ulrich moved back a few steps to see his effect all the better as he said:

"You have asked me so many pointed questions, and now there is something I would like to know before I make my decision. . . ." When Arnheim nodded he went on in a frank and matter-of-fact tone: "I've been told that your interest in our Parallel Campaign and everything connected with it, Frau Tuzzi and my humble self thrown in for good measure, has to do with your acquiring major portions of the Galician oil fields."

Despite the failing light, Arnheim could be seen to have turned pale; he walked slowly up to Ulrich, who thought he had brought some rude answer upon himself and regretted his own rash bluntness, which had given the other man a way to break off the conversation when it became inconvenient for him to go on with it. So he said, as affably as he could: "Please don't misunderstand me. I have no wish to offend you, but there is surely no point in our conversation unless we can speak our minds with brutal frankness."

These few words and the time it took him to cover the short distance enabled Arnheim to regain his composure. As he reached Ulrich he smiled, placed his hand—actually, his arm—on Ulrich's shoulder, and said reproachfully: "How can you fall for such a typical Stock Exchange rumor?"

"It reached me not as a rumor but as information from someone who knows what he is talking about."

"Yes, I know, I've heard that such things are being said, but how can you believe it? Of course I'm not here purely for pleasure; it's too bad, but I can never get away entirely from business affairs. And I won't deny that I have talked with some people about these oil fields, though I must ask you to keep this confidential. But what has this to do with anything?"

"My cousin," Ulrich resumed, "hasn't the remotest idea of your interest in oil. She has been asked by her husband to find out whatever she can about the reasons for your stay here, because you are regarded as a confidant of the Czar, but I am convinced that she is not doing justice to this diplomatic mission because she is so sure that she herself is the one and only reason for your continued visit with us."

"How can you be so indelicate?" Arnheim's arm gave Ulrich's shoulder a friendly little nudge. "There are always secondary strings to everything, everywhere, but despite your sardonic intention you have just expressed yourself with the naked rudeness of a schoolboy."

That arm on his shoulder made Ulrich unsure of himself. To stand there in this quasi embrace was ridiculous and unpleasant, a miserable feeling, in fact. Still, it was a long time since Ulrich had known a friend, and perhaps this added an element of bewilderment. He would have liked to shake off the arm, and he instinctively tried to do so, even while Arnheim, for his part, noticed these little signals of Ulrich's restiveness and did his utmost to ignore them. Ulrich, realizing the awkwardness of Arnheim's position, was too polite to move away and forced himself to put up with this physical contact, which felt increasingly like a heavy weight sinking into a loosely mounded dam and breaking it apart. Without meaning to, Ulrich had built up a wall of loneliness around himself, and now life, by way of another man's pulse beat, came pouring in through the breach in that wall, and silly as it was, ridiculous, really, he felt a touch of excitement.

He thought of Gerda. He remembered how even his old friend Walter had aroused in him a longing to find himself once more in total accord with another human being, wholly and without restraint, as if the whole wide world held no differences other than those between like and dislike. Now that it was too late, this longing welled up in him again, as if in silvery waves, as the ripples of water, air, and light fuse into one silvery stream down the whole width of a river. It was so entrancing that he had to force himself to be on his guard and not to give in, lest he cause a misunderstanding in this ambiguous situation. But as his muscles tightened he remembered Bonadea saying to him: "Ulrich, you're not a bad man, you merely make it hard for yourself to be good." Bonadea, who had been so incredibly wise that evening and who had also said: "After all, in dreams you don't think either, you simply live them." And he had said: "I was a child, as soft as the air on a moonlit night . . . ," and he now remembered that at the time he had actually had a different image in mind: the tip of a burning magnesium flare, for in the flying sparks that tore this tip to shreds he thought he recognized his heart; but that was a long time ago, and he had not quite dared to make this comparison and had succumbed to the other; not in conversation with Bonadea, incidentally, but with Diotima, as he now recalled. All the divergences of life begin close together at their roots, he felt, looking at the man who had just now, for reasons not entirely clear, offered him his friendship.

Arnheim had withdrawn his arm. They were standing once more in the window bay where their conversation had begun; on the street below, the lamps were already giving a peaceful light, though there was still a lingering sense of the excitement of earlier in the day. From time to time clusters of people passed by in heated talk, and here and there a mouth would open to shout a threat or some wavering "hoo-hoo," followed by guffaws. One had the impression of semi-consciousness. And in the light from this restless street, between the vertical curtains framing the darkened room, he saw Arnheim's figure and felt his own body standing there, half brightly lit up and half dark, a chiaroscuro sharpening the intense effect. Ulrich remembered the cheers for Arnheim he thought he had heard, and whether or not the man had anything to do with what had happened, in his Caesar-like calm as he stood pensively, gazing down on the street he projected himself as the dominant figure in this momentary light-painting, and he also seemed to feel the weight of his own presence in every glance cast upon him. At Arnheim's side one understood the meaning of self-possession. Consciousness alone cannot impose order on all the world's swarm and glow, since the keener it is, the more boundless the world becomes, at least for the moment; but that consciousness of self that is self-possession enters like a film director who artfully composes a scene into an image of happiness. Ulrich envied the man his happiness. In that instant nothing seemed easier than to do him some violence, for in his need to present an image at center stage this man conjured up all the old tags of melodrama. "Draw your dagger and fulfill his destiny!" Though the words came to mind only in the ranting tone of a ham actor, Ulrich had unconsciously moved so that he stood halfway behind Arnheim. He saw the dark, broad expanse of neck and shoulders before him. The neck in particular was a provocation. His hand groped in his right pocket for a penknife. He rose up on tiptoe and then once more looked over Arnheim's shoulder down on the street. Out there in the twilight, people were still being swept along like sand by an invisible tide pulling their bodies onward. Something would of course have to come of this demonstration, and so the future sent a wave ahead, some sort of suprapersonal fecundation of humanity occurred, though as always in an extremely vague and slipshod manner—or so Ulrich perceived it as it briefly held his attention, but he was tired to the point of nausea at the thought of stopping to analyze it all. Carefully he lowered his heels again, ashamed of the mental byplay that had caused him to raise them just before, though he did not attach too much importance to it, and he now felt greatly tempted to tap Arnheim on the shoulder and say to him: "Thank you. I'm fed up and I would like something new in my life. I accept your offer."

But as he did not really do this, either, the two men let the answer to Arnheim's proposal go by default. Arnheim reverted to an earlier part of their conversation. "Do you ever go to see a film? You should," he said. "In its present form, cinematography may not look like much, but once the big interests get involved—the electro-chemical, say, or the chromochemical concerns—you are likely to see a surging development in just a few decades, which nothing can stop. Every known means of raising and intensifying production will be brought into play, and whatever our writers and aesthetes may suppose to be their own part in it, we will be getting an art based on Associated Electrical or German Dyes, Inc. It's absolutely terrifying; you'll see. Do you write? No, I remember I've asked you that. But why don't you write? Very sensible of you. The poet and philosopher of the future will emerge out of journalism, in any case. Haven't you noticed that our journalists are getting better all the time, while our poets are getting steadily worse? It is unquestionably a process in accordance with the laws of nature. Something is going on, and for my part I haven't the slightest doubt what it is: the age of great individuals is coming to an end." He leaned forward. "I can't see your face in this light; I'm firing all my shots in the dark." He gave a little laugh. "You've proposed a general stocktaking of our spiritual condition: Do you believe in that? Do you really suppose that life can be regulated by the mind? Of course you don't; you've said so. But I don't believe you in any case, because you're someone who would embrace the Devil for being a man without his match in the world."

"Where's that quotation from?"

"From the suppressed preface to *The Robbers*."

Naturally from the suppressed preface, Ulrich thought. He wouldn't bother with the one read by everyone else.

" 'Minds that are drawn to the most loathsome vices for their aura of greatness . . .' " Arnheim continued to quote from his capacious memory. He felt himself to be the master of the situation once more, and that Ulrich, for whatever reasons, had given ground; the antagonistic edge was gone; no need to bring up that offer again; what a narrow escape! But just as a wrestler knows when his opponent is slackening off and then gives it all he's got, so he felt he needed to let the full weight of his offer sink in, and said: "I believe you understand me better now. Quite frankly, there are times when I am keenly aware of being alone. The new men think too much in purely business terms, and those business families in their second or third generation tend to lose their imagination. They produce nothing but impeccable administrators and army officers, and they go in for castles, hunting parties, and titled sons-in-law. I know their kind the world over, fine, intelligent individuals among them, but incapable of coming up with a single idea concomitant with that basic state of restlessness, independence, and possibly unhappiness I referred to with my Schiller quotation just now."

"I'm sorry I can't stay and talk more," Ulrich said. "Frau Tuzzi is probably waiting in some friend's house for things to quiet down out there, but I have to go now. So you suppose me capable, despite my ignorance of business, of that restlessness which is so good for business by making it so much less narrowly businesslike?" He had turned on the light in preparation for saying good-bye, and waited for an answer. With majestic cameraderie, Arnheim laid his arm on Ulrich's shoulder, a gesture that seemed to have proved its usefulness by now, and answered: "Do forgive me if I seem to have said rather too much, in a mood of loneliness. Business and finance are coming into power, and one sometimes asks oneself what to do with this power. I hope you won't take it amiss."

"On the contrary," Ulrich assured him. "I mean to think your proposal over quite seriously." He said it in a rush, which could be interpreted as a sign of excitement. This left Arnheim, who was staying on to wait for Diotima, rather disconcerted and worried that it might not be too easy to find a face-saving way of making Ulrich forget the offer.

122

Going home

Ulrich decided to walk home. It was a fine night, though dark. The houses, tall and compact, formed that strange space "street," open at the top to darkness, wind, and clouds. The road was deserted, as if the earlier unrest had left everything in a deep slumber. Whenever Ulrich did encounter a pedestrian, the sound of his footsteps had preceded him independently for a long time, like some weighty announcement. The night gave one a sense of impending events, as in a theater. One had a notion of oneself as a phenomenon in this world, something that appears bigger than it is, that produces an echo, and, when it passes lighted surfaces, is accompanied by its shadow like a huge spastic clown, rising to full height and the next moment creeping humbly to heel. How happy one can be! he thought.

He walked through a stone archway in a passage some ten paces long, running parallel to the street and separated from it by heavy buttresses; darkness leapt from corners, ambush and sudden death flickered in the dim cloister; a fierce, ancient, grim joy seized the soul. Perhaps this was too much; Ulrich suddenly imagined with what smugness and inward self-dramatization Arnheim would be walking here in his place. It killed the pleasure in his shadow and echo, and the spooky music in the walls faded out. He knew that he would not accept Arnheim's offer, but now he merely felt like a phantom stumbling through life's gallery, dismayed at being unable to find the body it should occupy, and was thoroughly relieved when before long he passed into a district less grand and less oppressive.

Wide streets and squares opened out in the blackness, and the commonplace buildings, peacefully starred with lighted rows of windows, laid no further spell on him. Coming into the open, he breathed this peace and remembered for no special reason some childhood photographs he had recently been looking at, pictures showing him with his mother, who had died young; from what a distance he had regarded the little boy, with the beautiful woman in an old-fashioned dress happily smiling at him. There was that overpowering impression of the good, affectionate, bright little boy they all felt him to be; there were hopes for him that were in no way his own; there were the vague expectations of a distinguished, promising future, like the outspread wings of a golden net opening to enfold him. And though all this had been invisible at the time, there it was for all to see decades afterward in those old photographs, and from the midst of this visible invisibility that could so easily have become reality, there was his tender, blank baby face looking back at him with the slightly forced expression of having to hold still. He had felt not a trace of warmth for that little boy, and even if he did take some pride in his beautiful mother, he had on the whole the impression of having narrowly escaped a great horror.

Anyone who has had the experience of seeing some earlier incarnation of himself gazing at him from an old photograph, wrapped in a bygone moment of self-satisfaction, as if glue had dried up or fallen out, will understand Ulrich's asking himself what sort of glue it was that seemed to hold for other people. He had now reached one of those green spaces bordered by trees, a break in the Ringstrasse, which follows the line of the ancient city walls, and he might have crossed it in a few strides, but the broad strip of sky above the trees made him turn aside and follow where it was leading, seeming to come closer and closer to the festoons of lights so intent upon their privacy in the distant sky above that wintry park, without actually getting any nearer to them. It's a kind of foreshortening of the mind's perspective, he thought, that creates the tranquil sense of the evening, which, from one day to the next, gives one this firm sense of life being in full accord with itself. Happiness, after all, depends for the most part not on one's ability to resolve contradictions but on making them disappear, the way the gaps between trees disappear when we look down a long avenue of them. And just as the visual relationships of things always shift to make a coherent picture for the eye, one in which the immediate and near at hand looks big, while even the big things at a distance look small and the gaps close up and the scene as a whole ends by rounding itself out, so it is with the invisible connections which our minds and feelings unconsciously arrange for us in such a way that we are left to feel we are fully in charge of our affairs. And just this is what I don't seem to be able to achieve the way I should, he said to himself.

A wide puddle blocked his way. Perhaps it was this puddle, or perhaps it was the bare, broomlike trees on either side, that conjured up a country road and a village, and awakened in him that monotonous state of the soul halfway between fulfillment and futility which comes with life in the country, a life that had tempted him more than once to repeat the "escape" he had made as a young man.

Everything becomes so simple, he felt. One's feelings get drowsy, one's thoughts drift off like clouds after bad weather, and suddenly a clear sky breaks out of the soul, and under that sky a cow in the middle of the path may begin to blaze with meaning; things come intensely alive as if there were nothing else in the world. A single cloud drifting past may transform the whole region: the grass darkens, then shines with wetness; nothing else has happened, and yet it's been like a voyage from one seashore to another. Or an old man loses his last tooth, and this trifling event may become a landmark in the lives of his neighbors, from which they date their memories. Every evening the birds sing around the village in the same way, in the stillness of the setting sun, but it feels like something new happening every time, as though the world were not yet seven days old! In the country, he thought, the gods still come to people. A man matters, his experiences matter, but in the city, where experiences come by the thousands, we can no longer relate them to ourselves; and this is of course the beginning of life's notorious turning into abstraction.

But even as he thought all this, he was also aware of how this abstraction extended a man's powers a thousandfold and how, even if from the point of view of any given detail it diluted him tenfold, as a whole it expanded him a hundredfold, and there could be no question of turning the wheel backward. And in one of those apparently random and abstract thoughts that so often assumed importance in his life, it struck him that when one is overburdened and dreams of simplifying one's life, the basic law of this life, the law one longs for, is nothing other than that of narrative order, the simple order that enables one to say: "First this happened and then that happened. . . ." It is the simple sequence of events in which the overwhelmingly manifold nature of things is represented, in a unidimensional order, as a mathematician would say, stringing all that has occurred in space and time on a single thread, which calms us; that celebrated "thread of the story," which is, it seems, the thread of life itself. Lucky the man who can say "when," "before," and "after"! Terrible things may have happened to him, he may have writhed in pain, but as soon as he can tell what happened in chronological order, he feels as contented as if the sun were warming his belly. This is the trick the novel artificially turns to account: Whether the wanderer is riding on the highway in pouring rain or crunching through snow and ice at ten below zero, the reader feels a cozy glow, and this would be hard to understand if this eternally dependable narrative device, which even nursemaids can rely on to keep their little charges quiet, this tried-and-true "foreshortening of the mind's perspective," were not already part and parcel of life itself. Most people relate to themselves as storytellers. They usually have no use for poems, and although the occasional "because" or "in order that" gets knotted into the thread of life, they generally detest any brooding that goes beyond that; they love the orderly sequence of facts because it has the look of necessity, and the impression that their life has a "course" is somehow their refuge from chaos. It now came to Ulrich that he had lost this elementary, narrative mode of thought to which private life still clings, even though everything in public life has already ceased to be narrative and no longer follows a thread, but instead spreads out as an infinitely interwoven surface.

When he resumed his homeward progress, reflecting on this insight, he remembered Goethe writing in an essay on art that "Man is not a teaching animal but one that lives, acts, and influences." He respectfully shrugged his shoulders. "These days," he thought, "a man can only allow himself to forget the uncertainties on which he must base his life and his actions as much as an actor who forgets the scenery and his makeup, and believes that he is really living his part." The thought of Goethe, however, brought back the thought of Arnheim, who was always misusing Goethe as an authority, and Ulrich suddenly remembered with distaste his extraordinary confusion when Arnheim had placed an arm on his shoulder. At this point he had emerged from under the trees and was back on the street, looking for the best way home. Peering upward for a street sign, he almost ran full tilt into a shadowy figure emerging from the darkness, and had to pull up short to avoid knocking down the prostitute who had stepped in his way. She held her ground and smiled instead of revealing her annoyance at his having charged into her like a bull, and Ulrich suddenly felt that her professional smile somehow created a little aura of warmth in the night. She spoke to him, using the threadbare words commonly thrown out as bait, which are like the dirty leavings of other men. She had a child's sloping shoulders, blond hair was showing under her hat, and her face looked pale, even indefinably appealing under the lamplight; beneath her nighttime makeup there was the suggestion of a young girl's freckled skin. She was much shorter than Ulrich and had to look up into his face, yet she said "baby" to him again, too numb to see anything out of place in this sound she uttered hundreds of times in a night.

Ulrich found it touching somehow. He did not brush her off but stopped and let her repeat her offer, as though he had not understood. Here he had unexpectedly found a friend who, for a slight charge, would put herself entirely at his disposal, ready to do her best to please him and avoid anything to put him off. If he showed himself willing, she would slip her arm in his with a gentle trustfulness and faint hesitation, as when old friends meet again for the first time after a separation not of their own making. If he promised to double or treble her usual price, and put the money on the table beforehand, so that she need not think about it but could abandon herself to that carefree, obliging state of mind that goes with having made a good deal, it would be shown that pure indifference has the merit of all pure feeling, which is without personal presumption and functions minus the needless confusion caused by interference from private emotions. Such thoughts went through his mind, half seriously, half flippantly, and he could not bring himself altogether to disappoint the little person, who was waiting for him to strike a deal; he even realized that he wanted her to like him, but clumsily enough, instead of simply exchanging a few words with her in the language of her profession, he fumbled in his pocket, slipped approximately the amount she would have asked into her hand, and walked on. For the space of a moment he had briefly pressed her hand—which had oddly resisted, in her surprise—firmly in his, with a single friendly word. But as he left this willing volunteer behind, he knew that she would rejoin her colleagues, who were whispering nearby in the dark, show them the money, and finally think of some gibe at him to give vent to feelings she could not understand.

The encounter lived on in his mind for a while as though it had been a tender idyll of a minute's duration. He did not romanticize the poverty of his fleeting friend or her debasement, but when he imagined how she would have turned up her eyes and given the fake little moan she had learned to deliver at the right moment, he couldn't help feeling without knowing why that there was something touching about this deeply vulgar, hopelessly inept private performance for an agreed price; perhaps because it was a burlesque version of the human comedy itself. Even while he was still speaking to the girl he had thought fleetingly of Moosbrugger, the pathological comedian, the pursuer and nemesis of prostitutes, who had been out walking on that other, unlucky night just as Ulrich was this evening. When the housefronts on that street had stopped swaying like stage scenery for a moment, Moosbrugger had bumped into the unknown creature who had awaited him by the bridge the night of the murder. What a shock of recognition it must have been, going through him from head to toe: for an instant, Ulrich thought he could feel it himself. Something was lifting him off the ground like a wave; he lost his balance but didn't need it, the movement itself carried him along. His heart contracted, but his imaginings became confused and overran all bounds, until they dissolved in an almost enervating voluptuousness. He made an effort to calm down. He had apparently been living so long without some central purpose that he was actually envying a psychopath his obsessions and his faith in the part he was playing! But Moosbrugger was fascinating, after all, not just to himself but to everyone else as well. Ulrich heard Arnheim's voice asking him: "Would you set him free?" and his own answer: "No! Probably not." Never ever, he now said to himself, and yet he had the hallucinatory image of an act in which the movement of reaching out in some extreme state of excitement and that of being moved by it fused into an ineffable communion, in which desire was indistinguishable from compulsion, meaning from necessity, and the most intense activity from blissful receptiveness. He fleetingly recalled the opinion that such luckless creatures as Moosbrugger were the embodiments of repressed instincts common to all, of all the murders and rapes committed in fantasies. Let those who believed this make their own peace with Moosbrugger, let them justify him to reestablish their own morality, after they had satisfied their dark urges through him! Ulrich's conflict was different; he repressed nothing and could not help seeing that the image of a murderer was no stranger to him than any other of the world's pictures; what they all had in common with his own old images of himself: part crystallization of meaning, part resurgence of the nonsense beneath. A rampant metaphor of order, that was what Moosbrugger meant for him. And suddenly Ulrich said: "All of that—" and made a gesture as though thrusting something aside with the back of his hand. He had not merely thought it, he had said it out loud, and reacted to hearing himself speak by pressing his lips together and finishing his statement in silence: "All of that has to be settled, once and for all!" Never mind what "all of that" was in detail; it was everything he had been preoccupied with, tormented by, sometimes even delighted with, ever since he had taken his "sabbatical"—everything that had tied him up in knots, like a dreamer for whom all things are possible except getting up and moving about; all that had led him from one impossible thing to another, from the very beginning until these last minutes of his homeward walk. Ulrich felt that he would now at long last have to either live like everybody else, for some attainable goal, or come to grips with one of his impossible possibilities. He had reached his own neighborhood, and he quickened his pace through the last street with a peculiar sense of hovering on some threshold. The feeling lent him wings, it moved him to take action, but as it was unspecific, again he was left with only an incomparable sense of freedom.

This might have passed off like so much else, but when he turned the corner into his own street he thought he saw all the windows of his house lit up, and shortly afterward, when he reached his garden gate, he could have no doubt about it. His old servant had asked for permission to spend the night with relatives somewhere; Ulrich had not been home since the episode with Gerda, when it was still daylight, and the gardener couple, who lived on the ground floor, never entered his rooms; yet there were lights on everywhere—intruders must be in the house, burglars he was about to take by surprise. Ulrich was so bewildered, and so disinclined to shake off the spell he was under, that he walked straight up to the house without hesitation. He had no idea what to expect. He saw shadows on the windows that seemed to indicate there was only one person moving about inside, but there could be more, and he wondered whether he might be walking into a bullet as he entered—or should he be prepared to shoot first? In a different state of mind Ulrich would probably have gone looking for a policeman or at least investigated the situation before deciding what to do, but he wanted this adventure to himself, and did not even reach for the pistol he sometimes carried since the night he had been knocked down by the hoodlums. He wanted . . . he didn't know what he wanted; he was willing to see what happened!

But when he pushed open the front door and entered the house, the burglar he had been looking forward to with such mixed feelings was only Clarisse.

123

THE TURNING POINT

Ulrich's recklessness might from the beginning have been motivated in part by an underlying faith in some harmless explanation for everything, that shying away from believing the worst that always leads one into danger; nevertheless, when his old servant unexpectedly came up to him in the hall, he almost knocked him down. Fortunately, he stopped himself in time, and was told that a telegram had come, which Clarisse had signed for and was now holding for him upstairs. The young lady had arrived about an hour ago, just as he, the old man, had been about to leave, and she would not let herself be turned away, so that he had preferred to stay in and give up his night out this once, for if he might be permitted to say so, the young lady seemed to be rather upset.

Ulrich thanked him and went up to his rooms, where he found Clarisse lying on the couch, on her side with her legs drawn up. Her straight, slim figure, her boyish haircut, and the charming oval of her face resting on one hand as she looked at him when he opened the door all made a most seductive picture. He told her that he had taken her for a burglar.

Clarisse's eyes flashed like rapid bursts of machine-gun fire. "Maybe I am a burglar!" she said. "That old fox your servant did his best to make me leave. I sent him off to bed, but I know he's been lurking out of sight downstairs somewhere. Your house is lovely!" She held out the telegram to him without getting up. "I was curious to see what you're like when you come home to be by yourself," she went on. "Walter's gone to a concert. He won't be back till after midnight. But I didn't tell him I was coming to see you."

Ulrich ripped open the telegram and read it while only half listening to Clarisse's words. He turned suddenly pale and read the startling message over again, unable to take it in. Although he had failed to answer several letters from his father asking him about the progress of the Parallel Campaign and the problem of "diminished responsibility," a longish interval had passed, without his noticing it, since any further reminders had come—and now this telegram, obviously drafted in advance with meticulous care by his father himself, informed him punctiliously, and in a funereal tone that did not quite succeed in repressing all reproach, of his own death. There had been little enough affection between them; in fact, the thought of his father had almost always been rather disturbing to Ulrich, and yet, as he now read the quaintly sinister text over again, he was thinking: "Now I am all alone in the world." He did not mean it literally, nor would that have made any sense, considering how things had been between them; what he meant was that he felt, with some amazement, that he was floating free, as though some mooring rope had snapped, or that his state of alienation from a world to which his father had been the last link had now become complete and final.

"My father's dead," he said to Clarisse, holding up the telegram with a touch of unintended solemnity.

"Oh!" Clarisse said. "Congratulations!" And after a slight, thoughtful pause she added: "I suppose you're going to be very rich now?" and looked around with interest.

"I don't believe he was more than moderately well off," Ulrich replied distantly. "I've been living here quite beyond his means."

Clarisse acknowledged the rebuke with a tiny smile, a sort of little curtsy of a smile; many of her expressive movements were as abrupt and disproportionate in a small space as the theatrical bow of a boy who must demonstrate before company how well he has been brought up. She was left alone for a few moments while Ulrich excused himself to go and make preparations for the trip he would have to take. When she had left Walter after their violent scene she had not gone far; outside the door to their apartment there was a seldom-used staircase leading up to the attic, and there she had sat, wrapped in a shawl, until she heard him leave the house. It made her think of the lofts in theaters for the stage machinery, where ropes run on pulleys, and there she sat while Walter made his exit down the stairs. She imagined that actresses might sit on the rafters above the stage between calls, wrapped in shawls, watching the stage from above, enjoying a full view of everything that was going on, just as she was now. It fitted in with a favorite notion of hers, that life was a dramatic role to be played. There was no need to understand one's part rationally, she thought; after all, what did anyone know about it, even those who might know more than she did? It was a matter of having the right instinct for life, like a storm bird. One simply spread out one's arms—and for her that included words, tears, kisses—like wings and took off! This fantasy offered some compensation to her for being no longer able to believe in Walter's future. She looked down the steep staircase Walter had just descended, spread her arms, and kept them raised in that position as long as she could; perhaps she could help him in that way! A steep ascent and a steep descent are strong complementary opposites and belong together, she thought. "Joyful world aslant" was what she named her wingspread arms and her gaze down the stairwell. She changed her mind about sneaking out to watch the demonstrators in town; what did she care about the common herd; the fantastic drama of the elect had begun!

And so Clarisse had gone to see Ulrich. On the way a sly smile would sometimes appear on her face, whenever it occurred to her that Walter thought her crazy each time she let slip any sign of her greater insight into what was going on between them. It tickled her vanity to know that he was afraid of having a child by her even while he impatiently longed for it. "Crazy" to her meant being something like summer lightning, or enjoying so extraordinary a degree of health that it frightened people; it was a quality her marriage had brought out in her, step by step, as her feelings of superiority and control grew. She did realize, all the same, that there were times when other people did not know what to make of her, and when Ulrich reappeared she felt she ought to say something to him that would be in keeping with an event that cut so deeply into his life. She leapt up from the couch, paced through the room and the adjoining rooms, and then said: "Well, my sincere condolences, old fellow!"

Ulrich looked at her in astonishment, although he recognized the tone she fell into when she was nervous. Sometimes she's so hopelessly conventional, he thought; it's like coming upon a page from another book bound in with what one is reading. She had not bothered to watch her words with the appropriate expression but had flung them at him sideways, over her shoulder, which heightened the effect of hearing, not a false note exactly, but the wrong words to the tune, giving the uncanny impression that she herself consisted of many such misplaced texts.

When she received no answer from Ulrich, she stopped in front of him and said: "I have to talk with you!"

"May I offer you some refreshment?" Ulrich said.

Clarisse only fluttered her hand at shoulder height to signal no. She pulled her thoughts together and said: "Walter is dead set on having a child. Can you understand that?" She seemed to be waiting for an answer. But what could Ulrich have said to that?

"But I don't want to!" she cried out violently.

"Well, no need to fly into a rage," Ulrich said. "If you don't want to, it can't happen."

"But it's destroying him!"

"People who are always expecting to die generally live a long time! You and I will be shriveled ancients while Walter will still have his boyish face under his white mane as Director of his Archives."

Clarisse turned pensively on her heel and walked away from Ulrich; at a distance, she wheeled to face him again and "fixed him" with her eye.

"Have you ever seen an umbrella with its shaft removed? Walter falls apart when I turn away from him. I'm his shaft and he's . . ." She was about to say "my umbrella" but thought of something much better: "my shield," she said. "He sees himself as my protector. And the first thing that means is giving me a big belly. Next will be the lectures on breast-feeding the infant because that is nature's way, and then he'll want to bring up the child in his own image. You know him well enough to know all that. All he wants is to have the rights to everything and a terrific excuse for making bourgeois conformists out of both of us. But if I go on saying no, as I have been, he'll be done for. I mean simply everything to him!"

Ulrich smiled incredulously at this sweeping claim.

"He wants to kill you," Clarisse added quickly.

"What? I thought that was your suggestion to him."

"I want the child from you!" Clarisse said.

Ulrich whistled through his teeth in surprise.

She smiled like an adolescent who has misbehaved with deliberate provocation.

"I wouldn't do something so underhanded to such an old friend," Ulrich said slowly. "It goes against my grain."

"Oh? So you're a man of high scruple, are you?" Clarisse seemed to attach some special significance of her own to this that Ulrich didn't understand. She gave it some thought and then returned to the attack: "But if you are my lover, he's got you where he wants you."

"How do you mean?"

"It's obvious; I just don't know quite how to put it. You'll be forced to treat him with consideration. We'll both be feeling sorry for him. You can't just go ahead and cheat on him, of course, so you'll have to try to make it up to him somehow. And so on and so forth. And most important of all, you'll be driving him to bring out the best that's in him. You know perfectly well that we are stuck inside ourselves like statues in a block of stone. We have to sculpt our way out! We have to force each other to do it."

"Maybe so," Ulrich said, "but aren't you getting ahead of yourself? What makes you think any of this will happen?"

Clarisse was smiling again. "Perhaps I am ahead of myself," she said. She sidled up to him and slipped her arm confidingly under his, which hung limply at his side and made no room for hers. "Don't you find me attractive? Don't you like me?" she asked. And when he did not answer, she went on: "But you do find me attractive, I know it; I've seen it often enough, the way you look at me, when you come to see us. Do you remember if I've ever told you that you're the Devil?

That's how I feel. Try to understand, I'm not calling you a poor devil: that's the kind who wants to do evil because he doesn't know any better. You are a great devil: you know what's good and you do the opposite of what you'd like to do! You know the life we lead is abominable, and so you say mockingly that we must go on with it. And you say, full of your high scruples, 'I won't cheat on a friend,' but you only say that because you've thought a hundred times, 'I'd like to have Clarisse.' But just because you're a devil you have something of a god inside you, Ulo! A great god. The kind who lies to try to keep from being recognized. You do want me. . . ."

She had gripped both his arms now, standing before him with her face lifted up to his, her body curving back like a plant responding to a touch on its petals. In a moment her face will be drenched with that look, like the last time, Ulrich thought apprehensively. But nothing of the kind happened; her face remained beautiful. Instead of her usual tight smile there was an open one, which showed a little of her teeth between the rosy flesh of her lips, as though about to bite. Her mouth took on the shape of a double Cupid's bow, a line echoed in the curve of her eyebrows and again in the translucent cloud of her hair.

"For a long time now you've been wanting to pick me up with those teeth in that lying mouth of yours and carry me off, if only you could stand to let me see you as you really are," Clarisse had continued. Ulrich gently freed himself from her grip. She dropped down on the couch as if he had put her there, and pulled him down after her.

"You really shouldn't let your imagination run away with you like this," Ulrich said in reproof.

Clarisse had let go of him. She closed her eyes and supported her head with both hands, her elbows resting on her knees; now that her second attack had been repelled, she decided to resort to icy logic.

"Don't be so literal-minded," she said. "When I speak of the Devil, or of God, it's only a figure of speech. But when I'm alone at home, or walking in the neighborhood, I often think: If I turn to the left, God will come; if I turn to the right, the Devil. Or when I'm about to pick something up with my hand, I have the same feeling about using the right or the left hand. When I tell Walter about it he puts his hands in his pockets, in real panic. He's happy to see a flower in bloom, or even a snail, but don't you think the life we lead is terribly sad? No God comes, or the Devil either. I've been waiting for years now, but what is there to wait for? Nothing. That's all there is, unless art can work a miracle and change everything."

At this moment there was something so gentle and sad about her that Ulrich gave way to an impulse to touch her soft hair with his hand. "You may be right in the details, Clarisse," he said. "But I can never follow your leaps from one point to another, or see how it all hangs together."

"It's quite simple," she said, still in the same posture as before. "As time went on, an idea came to me. Listen!" She straightened up and was suddenly quite vivacious again. "Didn't you once say yourself that the way we live is full of cracks through which we can see the impossible state of affairs underneath, as it were? You needn't say anything, I've known about it for a long time. We all want to have our lives in order, but nobody has! I play the piano or paint a picture, but it's like putting up a screen to hide a hole in the wall. You and Walter also have ideas, and I don't understand much of that, but that doesn't work either, and you said yourself that we avoid looking at the hole out of habit or laziness, or else we let ourselves be distracted from it by bad things. Well, there's a simple answer: That's the hole we have to escape through! And I know how! There are days when I can slip out of myself. Then it's like finding yourself—how shall I put it?— right in the center of things as if peeled out of a shell, and the things have had their dirty rind peeled off too. Or else one feels connected by the air with everything there is, like a Siamese twin. It's an incredible, marvelous feeling; everything turns into music and color and rhythm, and I'm no longer the citizen Clarisse, as I was baptized, but perhaps a shining splinter pressing into some immense unfathomable happiness. But you know all about that. That's what you meant when you said that there's something impossible about reality, and that one's experiences should not be turned inward, as something personal and real, but must be turned outward, like a song or a painting, and so on and so forth. Oh, I could recite it all exactly the way you said it." Her "so on and so forth" recurred like some wild refrain as Clarisse's torrent of words flowed on, regularly interspersed with her assertion "You can do it, but you won't, and I don't know why you won't, but I'm going to shake you up!"

Ulrich had let her go on talking, only shaking his head from time to time when she attributed to him something too unlikely, but he could not bring himself to argue with her and left his hand resting on her hair, where his fingertips could almost sense the confused pulsation of the thoughts inside her skull. He had never yet seen Clarisse in such a state of sensual excitement and was amazed to see that even in her slim, hard young body there was room for all the loosening and soft expansion of a woman's glowing passion; this sudden, always surprising opening up of a woman one has known only as inaccessibly shut away in herself did not fail to have its effect on him. Although they defied all reason, her words did not repel him, for as they came close to touching him in the quick and then again angled off into absurdity, their constant rapid movement, like a buzzing or humming, drowned out the quality of the tone, beautiful or ugly, in the intensity of the vibrations. Listening to her seemed to help him make up his mind, like some wild music, and it was only when she seemed to have lost her way in the maze of her own words and could not find her way out that he shook her head a little with his outspread hand, as though to call her back and set her straight.

But the opposite of what he intended happened, for Clarisse suddenly made a physical assault on him. She flung an arm around his neck and pressed her lips to his so quickly that it took him completely by surprise and he had no time to resist, as she pulled her legs up under her body and slid over to him so that she ended up kneeling in his lap, and he could feel the little hard ball of one breast pressing against his shoulder. He caught barely anything of what she was saying; she stammered something about her power of redemption, his cowardice, and his being a "barbarian," which was why she wanted to conceive the redeemer of the world from him and not from Walter. Actually, her words were no more than a raving murmur at his ear, a hasty muttering under her breath more concerned with itself than with communication, a rippling stream of sound in which he could only catch a word here and there, such as "Moosbrugger" or "Devil's Eye." In self-defense he had grabbed his little assailant by her upper arms and pushed her back on the couch, so that she was now struggling against him with her legs, pushing her hair into his face and trying to get her arms around his neck again.

"I'll kill you if you don't give in," she said loud and clear. Like a boy fighting in affection mixed with anger, who won't be put off, she struggled on in mounting excitement. The effort of restraining her left him with only a faint sense of the current of desire streaming through her body; even so, Ulrich had been strongly affected by it at the moment of putting his arm firmly around her and pressing her down. It was as if her body had penetrated his senses. He had after all known her for such a long time, and had often indulged in a bit of horseplay with her, but he had never been in such close, head-to-toe contact with this little creature, so familiar and yet so strange, its heart wildly bouncing, and when Clarisse's movements quieted down in the grip of his hands, and the relaxation of her muscles was reflected tenderly in the glow of her eyes, what he did not want to happen almost happened. But at this instant he thought of Gerda, as though it were only now that he was facing the challenge to come to terms with himself.

"I don't want to, Clarisse," he said, and let her go. "I need to be by myself now, and I have things to do before I leave."

When Clarisse grasped his refusal, it was as though with a jolt her head had shifted gears. She saw Ulrich standing a few steps away, his face contorted with embarrassment, saw him saying things she did not seem to take in, but as she watched the movement of his lips she felt a growing revulsion. Then she noticed that her skirt was above her knees, and jumped up off the couch. Before she understood what had happened, she was on her feet, shaking her hair and her clothes into place, as if she had been lying on the grass, and said:

"Of course you have to pack now; I won't keep you any longer." She was smiling again, her normal vaguely scoffing smile that was forced through a narrow slit, and wished him a good trip. "By the time you're back we'll probably have Meingast staying with us. He wrote to say he was coming, and that's actually what I came to tell you," she added casually.

Ulrich hesitantly held her hand. She was rubbing his playfully with a finger. She would have given anything to know what in the world she had been saying to him; she must have said all sorts of things, because she had been so worked up that now she had forgotten it all! She did have a general idea of what had happened, and she didn't mind, for her feelings told her that she had been brave or ready to sacrifice herself, and Ulrich timid. She wanted only to part as good friends and not to leave him in any doubt about that. "Better not tell Walter about this visit, and keep what we were talking about between ourselves for the time being," she said lightly. She gave him her hand once more at the garden gate and declined his offer to accompany her beyond it.

When Ulrich went back into the house he was preoccupied. He had to write some letters to let Count Leinsdorf and Diotima know he was leaving and had to attend to various other details, because he foresaw that taking over his inheritance might keep him away for some time. He stuffed various personal articles and a few books into the traveling cases already packed by his servant, whom he had sent off to bed, but when he had finished he no longer felt like going to bed himself. He was both exhausted and overstimulated after his eventful day, yet instead of canceling each other out, these two states of feeling only heightened each other so that, tired as he was, he felt unable to sleep.

Not really thinking, but following the oscillations of his memories, Ulrich began by acknowledging that he could no longer doubt his impression, at various times, that Clarisse was not merely an unusual person but probably already mentally unbalanced—and yet, during her attack just now, or whatever one might call it, she had said things that were too close for comfort to much that he had occasionally said himself. This should have started him really thinking hard, but it only brought the unwelcome reminder, in his half-drowsy state, that he still had much to do. Almost half of the year he had taken off to think was gone, without his having settled any of his problems. It flashed through his mind that Gerda had urged him to write a book about it. But he wanted to live without splitting himself into a real and a shadow self. He remembered speaking to Section Chief Tuzzi about writing. He saw himself and Tuzzi standing in Diotima's drawing room, and there was something theatrical, something stagy, about the scene. He remembered saying casually that he would probably have to either write a book or kill himself. But the thought of death, thinking it over at close range, so to speak, did not in the least correspond to his present state of mind either; when he explored it a little and toyed with the notion of killing himself before morning instead of taking the train, it struck him as an improper conjunction at the moment he had received the news of his father's death! Half asleep as he was, the figures of his imagination raced through his mind; he saw himself peering down the dark barrel of a gun, where he saw a shadowy nothing, the darkness veiling the depths beyond, and mused on the rare coincidence that the same image of a loaded gun had been his favorite metaphor in his youth, when his will was all charged up, waiting to take aim and let fly at some unknown target. His mind was flooded with images such as the pistol and standing with Tuzzi. The look of a meadow in the early morning. A winding river valley filled with dense evening mists, as seen from a moving train. The place at the far end of Europe where he had parted from the woman he loved—he had forgotten what she looked like, but the image of the unpaved village streets and the thatched cottages was as fresh as yesterday. The hair under the arm of another loved woman, all that was left of her. Snatches of forgotten melodies. A characteristic movement. The fragrance of flower beds, unnoticed at the time because of the charged words being forced out by the profound emotion of two souls, and coming back to him now when the words and the people were long forgotten. He saw a man on various paths, almost painful to look at, left over like a row of puppets that had had their springs broken long ago. One would think that such images are the most transient things in the world, but there are moments when all one's life splits up into such images, solitary relics along the road of life, as though the road led only away from them and back to them again, as though a man's fate were obeying not his ideas and his will but these mysterious, half-meaningless pictures.

But while he was moved almost to tears by the pointlessness, the uselessness, of all the efforts he had ever taken pride in, his sleepless, exhausted state gave rise to a feeling, or perhaps one should say that a marvelous feeling diffused itself around him. The lights Clarisse had turned on in all the rooms while she was alone were still on, and an excess of light flowed back and forth between the walls and the objects, filling the space between with an almost living presence. It was probably the tenderness inherent in any painless state of exhaustion that changed his total sense of his body; this ever-present though unheeded physical self-awareness, vaguely enough defined in any case, now passed over into a more yielding and expansive state. It was a loosening up as though a tourniquet were coming undone, and since neither the walls nor the objects underwent any real change and no god entered the rooms of this unbeliever, and since Ulrich himself by no means allowed his clear judgment to become clouded (unless his fatigue deceived him into thinking so), it could only be the relationship between himself and his surroundings that was undergoing such a change. The transformation was not objective; it was a subjective expanse of feeling, deep as groundwater, on which the senses and the intelligence, those pillars of objective perception, normally supported themselves but on which they now were gently separating or merging—the distinction lost its meaning almost as soon as he made it.

"It's a change in attitude; as I change, everything else involved changes too," Ulrich thought, sure that he had himself well under observation. But one could also say that his solitude—a condition that was present within him as well as around him, binding both his worlds—it could be said, and he felt it himself, that this solitude was growing greater or denser all the time. It flowed through the walls, flooded the city, then, without actually expanding, inundated the world. "What world?" he thought. "There is none!" The notion no longer seemed to have any meaning. But Ulrich's good judgment was still sufficiently in charge to make him recoil at once from such an exaggeration; he stopped hunting for more words and moved instead toward a state of full wakefulness. After a few seconds he gave a start. Day was breaking, its gray pallor mingling with the swiftly withering brightness of the artificial light.

Ulrich jumped to his feet and stretched. Something remained in his body that he could not shake off. He passed a finger over his eyelids, but something remained of that gentleness, that fusion of his vision and the things it beheld. And suddenly he recognized in a way hard to describe a sort of draining away of his strength, as though he had lost any power to go on denying that he was again standing exactly where he had stood years before. He shook his head, smiling. "An attack of 'the major's wife,' " he called it mockingly. There was no real danger of that, his rational mind told him, since there was no one with whom he could have repeated that old foolishness. He opened a window. The air outside was neutral, ordinary everyday morning air in which the first sounds of the city's life were striking up. He let its coolness rinse his temples, as the civilized European's distaste for sentimentality began to fill him with its hard clarity and he made up his mind to deal with the situation, if necessary, with the utmost precision. And yet, standing for a long time at the window, staring out into the morning without thinking of anything, he still had a sense of all the feelings that were slipping gleamingly away.

His servant's sudden entrance, with the solemn expression of the early riser, to wake him up, took Ulrich by surprise. He took a bath, rapidly did a few vigorous exercises, and left for the railroad station.

PART III

INTO THE MILLENNIUM

(THE CRIMINALS)

124

THE FORGOTTEN SISTER

On his arrival in ——— toward evening of the same day, as Ulrich came out of the station he saw before him a wide, shallow square that opened into streets at both ends and jolted his memory almost painfully, as happens with a landscape one has seen often and then forgotten again.

"Believe me, income has dropped by twenty percent and prices have gone up twenty percent, that's a total of forty percent!" "Believe *me*, a six-day bike race promotes international goodwill like nothing else!" These voices were still coming out of his ear: train voices. Then he distinctly heard someone saying: "Still, for me, there's nothing to beat opera!" "Is that your hobby?" "It's my passion."

He tilted his head as though to shake water out of his ear. The train had been crowded, the journey long. Driblets of the general conversation around him that had seeped into him during the trip were oozing out again. Ulrich had waited for the joyfulness and bustle of arrival—which had poured into the quiet square from the station exit as from the mouth of a drainpipe—to subside to a trickle; now he was standing in the vacuum of silence left behind by such noise. But even as his hearing was still disturbed from the abrupt change, he was struck by an unaccustomed peace that met his eyes. Everything visible was more intensely so than usual, and when he looked across the square the crossbars of perfectly ordinary windows stood as black against the pale sheen of glass in the dimming light as if they were the crosses of Golgotha. And everything that moved seemed to detach itself from the calm of the street in a way that never happens in very large cities. Whether passing or standing still, things evidently had the space here in which to make their importance felt. He could see this with the curiosity of reacquaintance as he gazed out on the large provincial town where he had spent some brief, not very pleasant, parts of his life. It had, as he well knew, an air of someplace colonial, a place of exile: here a nucleus of ancient German burgher stock, transplanted centuries ago to Slavic soil, had withered away so that hardly anything was left, apart from a few churches and family names, to remind one of it; nor, except for a fine old palace that had been preserved, was there evidence of its having become, later on, the old seat of the Provincial Diet. But in the era of absolute rule this past had been overlaid by a vast apparatus of imperial administration, with its provincial headquarters, schools and universities, barracks, courthouses, prisons, bishop's palace, assembly rooms, and theater, together with the people needed to run them and the merchants and artisans who came in their wake, until finally an industry of entrepreneurs moved in, filling the suburbs with their factories one after the other, with a greater influence on the fate of this piece of earth in the past few generations than anything else had had. This town had a past, and it even had a face, but the eyes did not go with the mouth, or the chin with the hair; over everything lay the traces of a hectic life that is inwardly empty. This could possibly, under special personal circumstances, foster great originality.

To sum it up in a phrase perhaps equally arguable, Ulrich had the sense of something "spiritually insubstantial" in which one lost oneself so entirely as to awaken unbridled imaginings. In his pocket he carried his father's eccentric telegram, which he knew by heart: "This is to inform you that I am deceased" was the old gentleman's message for him—or was it to him? as indicated by the signature at the end: "Your father." His Excellency the Privy Councillor never went in for levity at serious moments. The weird information of the message was consequently infernally logical, since he was himself notifying his son when, in expectation of his end, he wrote or dictated word for word the message that was to be dispatched the instant he had drawn his last breath; the facts could really not be more correctly stated, and yet this act by which the present tried to dominate a future it could not live to see emitted from the grave an uncanny whiff of an angrily decayed will!

This manifestation, which somehow reminded Ulrich of the meticulously undiscriminating taste of small towns, made him think with some misgiving of his sister, who had married in the provinces and whom he was about to meet, in the next few minutes. He had been wondering about her already on the train, for he did not know much about her. From time to time standard items of family news reached him through his father's letters; for example: "Your sister Agathe is married," adding some of the details, since at the time Ulrich had not been able to come home for the wedding. Only about a year later he received notice of the young husband's death; then, three years or so after that, if he was not mistaken, word came that "Your sister Agathe, I am glad to say, has decided to marry again." At this second wedding, five years ago, Ulrich had been present and had seen his sister for a few days, but all he remembered was a ceaseless whirl, like a giant wheel of white cambric and lace. He also remembered the bridegroom, who made a poor impression on him. Agathe must have been twenty-two then, while he was twenty-seven, for he had just received his doctorate, so that his sister had to be twenty-seven now; but he had not seen her since that time, nor exchanged letters with her. He recalled only that his father had later written more than once: "It pains me to report that all does not seem to be going as well as it might in your sister's marriage, although her husband is a capital fellow" and "The latest successes of your sister Agathe's husband have been most gratifying": Such, more or less, were his father's comments in letters to which Ulrich had, regrettably, never paid any attention; but once, as he now remembered quite clearly, in connection with a disapproving comment on his sister's childlessness, their father expressed the hope that she was nevertheless contented in her marriage, although it was not in her character ever to admit it.

"I wonder what she looks like now," he thought.

It had been one of the old gentleman's eccentricities to keep them conscientiously informed about each other after he had sent them away from home at a tender age, right after their mother's death, to be educated in different schools. Ulrich, who got into scrapes, was often not allowed home for school holidays; so that since their childhood, when they had in fact been inseparable, he had hardly seen his sister again, with the exception of one longish visit when Agathe was ten.

In the circumstances, Ulrich had thought it only natural that they did not write. What would they have had to say to each other? At the time of Agathe's first marriage he was, as he now remembered, a lieutenant in the army, and in the hospital recovering from a bullet wound received in a duel: Lord, what an ass he had been! In fact, he had made every kind of ass of himself. For he remembered now that the memory of the wounded lieutenant belonged someplace else. He had been about to qualify as an engineer and had something "important" to do that had kept him from the family ceremony. Later he learned that his sister had been very much in love with her first husband; he could not remember who had told him, but what does "very much in love" mean anyway? It's what people say. She had married again, and Ulrich could not stand her second husband; that was the one thing he was sure of. He disliked him not only for the bad impression he made personally but also for that made by some of his books, which Ulrich had read, so that Ulrich's subsequent forgetting of his sister might not have been quite unintentional. It was nothing to be proud of, but he had to admit that even during this last year, when he had thought of so many things, he had never given her a thought, not even when he had received the news of their father's death. But he did ask the old manservant who came to meet him at the station whether his brother-in-law had arrived yet, and was relieved to hear that Professor Hagauer was not expected until the day of the funeral. Even though it could be no more than two or three days till then, it seemed to him like a respite of indefinite duration, which he would spend alone with his sister as though they were the closest people in the world. There would have been no point in trying to see any logic in this; the thought of "my unknown sister" was evidently one of those roomy abstractions in which many feelings that are not quite at home anywhere could find a place.

Thus preoccupied, Ulrich had walked slowly into the town that opened up before him, at once strange and familiar. He had sent on his luggage, into which he had stuffed quite a number of books at the last minute, in a cab with the old servant, a part of his childhood memories, who had come to combine the functions of caretaker, butler, and clerk in a fashion that over the years made them hard to distinguish from one another. It was probably this self-effacing, taciturn man to whom Ulrich's father had dictated his death notice, and Ulrich's feet led him homeward in pleasurable wonder as his now alert senses curiously took in the fresh impressions that every growing city springs on someone who has not seen it for a long time. At a certain point, which they remembered before he did, Ulrich's feet turned off the main street, and he soon found himself in a narrow lane formed by two garden walls. Diagonally across his path stood the house of barely two stories, the main building higher than the wings, with the old stable to one side and, still pressed against the garden wall, the little house where the servant and his wife lived; it looked as though for all his confidence in them the aged master had wished to keep them as far as possible from him while still embracing them within his walls. Ulrich had absently walked up to the locked garden gate and dropped the big ring-shaped knocker that hung there in lieu of a bell against the low door, black with age, before the servant came running up to correct his error. They had to go back around the wall to the main entrance, where the cab had drawn up, and it was only at this moment, seeing the shuttered façade of the house before him, that it occurred to Ulrich that his sister had not come to meet him at the station. The servant reported that Madame had a migraine and had retired after lunch, ordering them to wake her when the Herr Doktor arrived. Did his sister suffer from migraine often? Ulrich went on to ask, then instantly regretted his slip in drawing the old servant's attention to family matters that were better passed over in silence.

"The young Madame gave orders for tea to be served in half an hour," the well-trained old man replied, with a servant's politely blank expression giving discreet assurance that he understood nothing beyond his duty.

Spontaneously Ulrich glanced up at the windows, supposing that Agathe might be standing there observing his arrival. He wondered whether she would be agreeable, becoming uneasily aware how awkward the visit would be if he happened not to like her. That she had neither come to meet his train nor met him at the house door was distinctly in her favor, however, showing a certain rapport of feeling: rushing to meet him, after all, would have been as uncalled for as it would have been for him on arrival to rush to his father's coffin. He left word for her that he would be down in half an hour, and went to his room to get himself in order. The room he was to stay in was in the mansard-roofed second story of the main house and had been his childhood room, now curiously supplemented by the addition of a few random pieces for an adult's comfort. "It was probably the best they could do as long as the body is still in the house," Ulrich thought, settling in among the ruins of his childhood a little awkwardly, yet also with a rather warm feeling that seemed to rise like mist from the floor. As he started to change it occurred to him to put on a pajama-like lounging suit he came across while unpacking. "She might at least have come down to say hello when I got here," he thought, and there was a hint of rebuke in his casual choice of dress, even as he continued to feel that his sister's reason for acting as she did was likely to be a congenial one, so that he was also complimenting her by his unforced expression of ease.

The loose lounging suit of soft wool he put on was patterned in black and gray squares, almost a Pierrot costume, gathered at the waist, wrists, and ankles; he liked its comfort, which felt pleasant after that sleepless night and the long train journey, as he came down the stairs. But when he entered the room where his sister was waiting, he was amazed at his costume, for by some mysterious directive of chance he found his appearance echoed in that of a tall, blond Pierrot in a pattern of delicate gray and rust stripes and lozenges, who at first glance looked quite like himself.

"I had no idea we were twins!" Agathe said, her face lighting up with a smile.

125

CONFIDENCES

They did not greet each other with a kiss but merely stood amicably facing each other, then moved apart, and Ulrich was able to take a good look at his sister. They were of matching height. Agathe's hair was fairer than his and had the same dry fragrance as her skin, the fragrance that was the only thing he liked about his own body. Instead of being all bosom she had small, firm breasts, and her limbs seemed to have the long, slender spindle shape that combines natural athletic ability and beauty.

"I hope you're over your migraine," Ulrich said. "It doesn't show."

"I never had migraine; it was just the simplest thing to say," Agathe explained. "I couldn't very well send you a long and complicated message through the servants. I was lazy, that's all. I took a nap. In this house I've got into the habit of sleeping every chance I get. I'm basically lazy—out of desperation, I think. And when I heard you were coming I thought, 'Let's hope this is the last time I feel sleepy,' and I gave myself up to a sort of sleep cure. I thought it over carefully and then, for the butler's convenience, decided to call it migraine."

"Don't you go in for any sports?" Ulrich asked.

"Some tennis. But I detest sports."

As she spoke, he studied her face again. It did not seem very like his own, but perhaps he was mistaken; maybe it was like the same face done in pastels and in a woodcut, the difference in the medium obscuring the congruence of line and plane. There was something in this face he found disturbing. After a while, he realized that he simply could not read its expression; what was missing was whatever it is that enables one to draw the usual inferences about the person. It was an expressive face, but nothing in it was emphasized, nothing combined in the way that normally suggests traits of character.

"How did you happen to dress like that?" Ulrich asked.

"No special reason. I thought it would be nice."

"It's very nice!" Ulrich laughed. "But positively a conjuring trick of chance! And Father's death doesn't seem to have greatly upset you either?"

Agathe rose slowly on her toes and then just as slowly sank back on her heels.

"Is your husband here yet?" her brother asked, just to say something.

"Professor Hagauer is coming for the funeral." She seemed to relish the occasion to pronounce that name so formally and to dissociate herself from it as if it were some strange object.

Ulrich was at a loss how to respond. "Oh yes, so I was told," he said.

Again they looked at each other, and then they went, as the proper next step, into the little room where the body lay.

The room had been kept artificially dark for a whole day; it was drenched in black. Flowers and lighted candles glowed and scented the air. The two Pierrots stood straight as they faced the dead man, as if watching him.

"I'll never go back to Hagauer," Agathe said, just to get it out. One could almost think she wanted the dead man to hear it too.

There he lay on his bier, as he had directed: in full evening dress, the pall drawn halfway down his chest to expose the stiff shirtfront with all his decorations, his hands folded without a crucifix. Small, hard-ridged brows, sunken cheeks and lips. Stitched into the horrible, eyeless corpse's skin, which is still a part of the personality and yet already something apart: life's traveling bag. In spite of himself, Ulrich felt shaken at his very core, deep beneath any feeling or thought; but nowhere else. If he had had to put it into words, he would only have been able to say that a tiresome, loveless relationship had come to an end. Just as a bad marriage debases the people who cannot get free of it, so does every burdensome bond meant to last forever when the mortal substance shrivels away from under it.

"I would have liked you to come sooner," Agathe went on, "but Papa wouldn't have it. He made all the arrangements for his death himself. I think he would have been embarrassed to die with you looking on. I've been living here for two weeks now; it's been horrible."

"Did he love *you*, at least?" Ulrich asked.

"Whatever he wanted done he told old Franz to take care of, and from then on he gave the impression of someone who has nothing to do and has no purpose in life. But every fifteen minutes or so he'd lift up his head to check whether I was still in the room. For the first few days, that is. Then it was only every half hour, then every hour, and during that frightful last day it happened only two or three times. And all that time he never said a word to me except when I asked him something."

As she spoke, Ulrich was thinking: "She's really hard. Even as a child she could be incredibly stubborn, in her quiet way. And yet she seems to be amenable enough. . . ." And suddenly he thought of an avalanche. . . . once almost lost his life in a forest that was being devastated by an avalanche. It had been no more than a soft cloud of powdery snow, and yet the irresistible force behind it gave it the impact of a toppling mountain.

"Was it you who sent me the telegram?" he asked.

"That was old Franz, of course. It was all settled beforehand. He wouldn't let me take care of him, either. He certainly never loved me, and I don't know why he sent for me. I felt miserable and shut myself up in my room as often as I could. It was during one of those times that he died."

"He probably did it to prove that you were in the wrong," Ulrich said bitterly. "Come on!" He drew her toward the door. "But maybe he wanted you to stroke his forehead? Or kneel by his bedside? Even if it was only because he had always read that it's the proper way to take leave of a father for the last time. Only he couldn't bring himself to ask you."

"Maybe," she said.

They had stopped for another look at him.

"How horrible it is, all of it!" Agathe said.

"Yes," Ulrich said. "And we know so little about it."

As they were leaving the room Agathe stopped again and said to Ulrich: "I'm springing something on you that can't be of any concern to you, of course, but it was during Father's illness that I decided not to go back to my husband under any circumstances."

Her brother could not help smiling at the stubbornness with which she said this, for Agathe had a vertical furrow between her brows and spoke vehemently; she seemed to fear that he would not be on her side, and reminded him of a terrified cat whose fright makes it leap bravely to the attack.

"Does he consent?" Ulrich asked.

"He knows nothing about it yet," Agathe said. "But he won't consent!"

Her brother gave her a questioning look. She shook her head impatiently. "Oh no, it's not what you think. There's no third person involved," she said.

With this, their conversation came to an end for the time being. Agathe apologized for having been so unmindful of Ulrich's hunger and fatigue, led him to a room where tea had been laid out, then went herself to fetch something that was missing from the tray. Left to himself, Ulrich used the opportunity to concentrate on whatever he could recollect about her husband, the better to understand her. Professor Hagauer was a man of medium height with a ramrod bearing and plump legs in baggy trousers, rather fleshy lips under a bristly mustache, and a fondness for florid neckties, probably as a sign that he was no common schoolmaster but one who was future-oriented. Ulrich felt his cold misgivings about Agathe's choice reawaken, but that Gottlieb Hagauer, with candor shining from his brow and eyes, would harbor secret vices was entirely out of the question. "He's the very model of the industrious, capable person, doing his best for humanity in his own field without meddling in matters beyond his scope," Ulrich decided, remembering Hagauer's writings, as well, and falling into not entirely agreeable thoughts.

Such people can first be recognized for what they are even in their school days. They study not so much conscientiously—as it is called, confusing the effect with the cause—as in an orderly and practical fashion. They lay out every task beforehand, just as one has to lay out every piece of tomorrow's clothing, down to the last collar button, the night before if one wants to dress quickly and without a hitch in the morning. There is no chain of thought they cannot fix in their minds by using half a dozen such laid-out studs, and there is no denying that the results do them credit and stand up to scrutiny. This takes them to the head of the class without their being perceived as prigs by their classmates, while people like Ulrich, who may be far more gifted but are given to overdoing a bit here and falling a bit short there, get gradually left behind in some imperceptibly fated way. It occurred to him that he was secretly somewhat in awe of these favored types, because the precision with which their minds worked made his own romantic enthusiasm for precision seem a bit windy. "They haven't a trace of soul," he thought, "and they're good-natured fellows. After the age of sixteen, when adolescents get worked up about intellectual problems, they seem to fall behind a little, not quite able to catch on to new ideas and feelings, but here, too, they work with their ten studs, and the day comes when they're able to prove that they have always understood everything, of course without going to any untenable extremes, and in the end they are the ones who introduce the new ideas into practical life when for everyone else those ideas have faded away with their long-past adolescence, or have become lonely eccentricities." And so, by the time Agathe came back into the room, Ulrich could still not imagine what had actually happened to her, but he felt that entering the lists against her husband, even if it was unfair, was likely to offer him a most reprehensible pleasure.

Agathe seemed to see no point in trying to explain her decision rationally. Outwardly her marriage was in the most perfect order, as was only to be expected in the case of a man of Hagauer's character. No quarrels, hardly any differences of opinion; if only because Agathe, as she told Ulrich, never confided her opinion to him on any subject. Of course no vices: no drink, no gambling, not even bachelor habits. Income fairly apportioned. Orderly household. Smooth social life as well as unsocial life, when they were alone.

"So if you simply leave him for no reason at all," Ulrich said, "the divorce will be decided in his favor, provided he sues."

"Let him sue!" Agathe said defiantly.

"Wouldn't it be a good idea to offer him a small financial compensation if he'll agree to a friendly settlement?"

"All I took away with me," she replied, "was what I would need during an absence of three weeks, except for a few childish things and mementos from the time before Hagauer. He can keep all the rest; I don't want it. But for the future he's to get nothing more out of me—absolutely nothing!"

Again she had spoken with surprising vehemence. One could perhaps explain it by saying that Agathe wanted to revenge herself on this man for having let him take too much advantage of her in the past. Ulrich's fighting spirit, his sportsmanship, his inventiveness in surmounting obstacles, were now aroused, although he was not especially pleased to feel it; it was too much like the effect of a stimulant that moves the superficial emotions while the deeper ones remain quite untouched. Groping for an overview, he gave the conversation a different turn:

"I've read some of his work, and I've heard of him too," he said. "As far as I can gather, he's regarded as a coming man in pedagogy and education."

"Yes," Agatha said. "So he is."

"Judging by what I know of his work, he's not only a sound educator but a pioneer of reform in higher education. I remember one book of his in which he discussed the unique value of history and the humanities for a moral education on the one hand, and on the other the equally unique value of science and mathematics as intellectual discipline, and then, thirdly, the unique value of that brimming sense of life in sports and military exercise that makes one fit for action. Is that it?"

"I suppose so," Agatha said, "but did you notice his way with quotations?"

"Quotations? Let me see: I dimly remember noticing something there. He uses lots of quotations. He quotes the classics. Of course, he quotes the moderns too. . . . Now I've got it: He does something positively revolutionary for a schoolmaster—he quotes not merely academic sources but even aircraft designers, political figures, and artists of today. . . . But I've already said that, haven't I?" He ended on that uncertain note with which recollection runs into a dead end.

"What he does," Agatha added, "with music, for instance, is to go recklessly as far as Richard Strauss, or with painting as far as Picasso, but he will never, even if only to illustrate something that's wrong, cite a name that hasn't become more or less established currency in the newspapers, even if it's only treated negatively."

That was it. Just what he had been groping for in his memory. He looked up. He was pleased by the taste and the acuity shown in Agathe's reply.

"So he's become a leader, over time, by being among the first to follow in time's train," he commented with a laugh. "All those who come after him see him already ahead of them! But do you like our leading figures yourself?"

"I don't know. In any case, I don't quote them."

"Still, we ought to give him his due," Ulrich said. "Your husband's name stands for a program that many people today regard as the most advanced. His achievement represents a solid small step forward. His rise cannot be long in coming. Sooner or later he will have at least a university chair, even though he has had to toil for his living as a schoolteacher, while as for me, all I ever had to do was go straight along the course laid out for me—and today I've come so far that I probably wouldn't even get a lectureship."

Agathe was disappointed, which was probably why her face took on a blank, porcelain-smooth, ladylike mask as she sweetly said: "Oh, I don't know; perhaps you ought to keep on his good side."

"When do you expect him?" Ulrich asked.

"Not before the funeral; he has no time to spare. But under no circumstances is he to stay in this house—I won't have it!"

"As you like," Ulrich decided unexpectedly. "I shall meet him at the station and drop him off at some hotel. And if you want, I'll tell him, 'This is where you stay.' "

Agathe was surprised and suddenly elated.

"That will make him furious, because he'll have to pay; he was of course counting on staying here with us!" Her expression had instantly changed and regained the look of a wild and mischievous child.

"What is the situation, actually?" her brother asked. "Does the house belong to you, me, or both of us? Is there a will?"

"Papa left a big package for me that's supposed to contain all we need to know." They went to the study, which lay beyond the deceased.

Again they moved through candlelight and the scent of flowers, through the field of vision of those two eyes that no longer saw. In the flickering half-darkness Agathe was for the space of a second a shimmering haze of gold, gray, and pink. They found the package holding the will and took it back with them to the tea table, where they then forgot to open it.

For as they sat down again Agathe told her brother that, to all intents and purposes, she had been living apart from her husband, though under the same roof; she didn't say how long this had been going on.

It made a bad impression on Ulrich at first. When a married woman sees a man as a possible lover, she is likely to treat him to this kind of confidence, and although his sister had come out with it in embarrassment, indeed with defiance, in a clumsy and palpable effort to throw down a challenge, he was annoyed with her for not coming up with something more original; he thought she was making too much of it.

"Frankly," he said, "I have never understood how you could have lived with such a man at all."

Agathe told him that it was their father's idea, and what could she have done to stop it?

"But you were a widow by then, not an underage virgin!"

"That's just it. I had come back to Papa. Everyone was saying that I was still too young to live on my own; even if I was a widow, I was only nineteen. And then I just couldn't stand it here."

"Then why couldn't you have looked for another man? Or studied something and made yourself independent that way?" Ulrich demanded relentlessly.

Agathe merely shook her head. There was a pause before she answered: "I've told you already: I'm lazy."

Ulrich felt that this was no answer. "So you had some special reason for marrying Hagauer?"

"Yes."

"You were in love with someone you couldn't have?"

Agathe hesitated. "I loved my first husband."

Ulrich regretted he had used the word "love" so glibly, as though he regarded the importance of the social arrangement it refers to as inviolable. "Trying to comfort the grieving is no better than handing a dry crust to a beggar," he thought. Nevertheless, he felt tempted to go on in the same vein. "And then you realized what you'd let yourself in for, and you started to make trouble for Hagauer?" he suggested.

"Yes," she admitted, "but not right away—quite late," she added. "Very late, in fact."

At this point they got into a little argument.

These confessions were visibly costing Agathe an effort, even though she was making them of her own accord and evidently, as was to be expected at her age, saw in her sex life an important subject of general conversation. From the first she seemed ready to take her chances on his sympathy or lack of it; she wanted his trust and was determined, not without candor and passion, to win her brother over. But Ulrich, still in the mood to dispense moral guidance, could not yet meet her halfway. For all his strong-mindedness he was by no means always free of those same prejudices he rejected intellectually, having too often let his life go one way and his mind another. For he had more than once exploited and misused his power over women, with a hunter's delight in catching and observing his quarry, so he had almost always seen the woman as the prey struck down by the amorous male spear. The lust of humiliation to which the woman in love subjects herself was fixed in his mind, while the man is very far from feeling a comparable surrender. This masculine notion of female weakness before male power is still quite common today, although with the successive waves of new generations more modern concepts have arisen, and the naturalness with which Agathe treated her dependence on Hagauer offended her brother. It seemed to him that his sister had suffered defilement without being quite aware of it when she subjected herself to the influence of a man he disliked and went on enduring it for years. He did not say so, but Agathe must have read something of the kind in his face, for she suddenly said:

"After all, I couldn't simply bolt the moment I had married him; that would have been hysteria!"

Ulrich was suddenly jerked out of his role as elder brother and dispenser of edifying narrow-mindedness.

"Would it really be hysteria to feel disgusted and draw all the necessary conclusions?" He tried to soften this by following it up with a smile and looking at his sister in the friendliest possible manner.

Agathe looked back at him, her face somehow rendered defenseless with the effort of deciphering the expression on his.

"Surely a normal healthy person is not so sensitive to distasteful circumstances?" she persisted. "What does it matter, after all?"

Ulrich reacted by pulling himself together, not wanting to let his mind be ruled by one part of himself. He was once more all objective intelligence. "You're quite right," he said. "What happens doesn't really matter. What counts is the system of ideas by which we understand it, and the way it fits into our personal outlook."

"How do you mean?" Agathe asked dubiously.

Ulrich apologized for putting it so abstractly, but while he was searching for a more easily accessible formulation, his brotherly jealousy reasserted itself and influenced his choice of terms.

"Suppose that a woman we care about has been raped," he offered. "From a heroic perspective, we would have to be prepared for vengeance or suicide; from a cynical-empirical standpoint, we would expect her to shake it off like a duck shedding water; and what would actually happen nowadays would probably be a mixture of these two. But this lack of a touchstone within ourselves is more sordid than all the rest."

However, Agathe did not accept this way of putting it either. "Does it really seem so horrible to you?" she asked simply.

"I don't know. I thought it must be humiliating to live with a person one doesn't love. But now . . . just as you like."

"Is it worse than a woman who wants to marry less than three months after a divorce having to submit to an examination by an officially appointed gynecologist to see whether she's pregnant, because of the laws of inheritance? I read that somewhere." Agathe's forehead seemed to bulge with defensive anger, and the little vertical furrow between her eyebrows appeared again. "And they all put up with it, if they have to!" she said disdainfully.

"I don't deny it," Ulrich responded. "Everything that actually happens passes over us like rain and sunshine. You're probably being much more sensible than I in regarding that as natural. But a man's nature isn't natural; it wants to change nature, so it sometimes goes to extremes." His smile was a plea for friendship, and his eyes saw how young she looked. When she got excited her face did not pucker up but smoothed out even more under the stress going on behind it, like a glove within which the hand clenches into a fist.

"I've never thought about it in such general terms," she now said. "But after listening to you, I am again reminded that I've been leading a dreadfully wrong kind of life."

"It's only because you've already told me so much, of your own accord, without coming to the point," said her brother, lightly acknowledging this concession in response to his own. "How am I to judge the situation properly when you won't let me know anything about the man for whom you are, after all, really leaving Hagauer?"

Agathe stared at him like a child or a pupil whose teacher is being unfair. "Does there have to be a man? Can't it happen of itself? Did I do something wrong by leaving him without having a lover? I would be lying if I said that I've never had one; I don't want to be so absurd; but I haven't got a lover now, and I'd resent it very much if you thought I'd really need one in order to leave Hagauer!"

Her brother had no choice but to assure her that passionate

women were known to leave their husbands even without having a
lover, and that he even regarded this as the more dignified course.

The tea they had come together to share merged into an informal
and haphazard supper, at Ulrich's suggestion, because he was very
tired and wanted to go to bed early to get a good night's sleep on
account of the next day, which was likely to be busy with bothersome
details. They smoked their final cigarettes before parting, and Ulrich
still did not know what to make of his sister. She did not have anything either emancipated or bohemian about her, even if she was sitting there in those wide trousers in which she had received her
unknown brother. It was more something hermaphroditic, as it now
seemed to him; as she moved and gestured in talking, the light masculine outfit suggested the tender form beneath with the semitrans-
parency of water, and in contrast to the independent freedom of her
legs, she wore her beautiful hair up, in true feminine style. But the
center of this ambivalence was still her face, so rich in feminine
charm yet with something missing, something held in reserve, whose
nature he could not quite make out.

And that he knew so little about her and was sitting with her so
intimately, though not at all as he would with a woman for whom he
would count as a man, was something very pleasant in his present
state of fatigue, to which he was now beginning to succumb.

"What a change from yesterday!" he thought.

He was grateful for it and tried to think of something affectionately brotherly to say to Agathe as they said goodnight, but as all this
was something new to him, he could think of nothing to say. So he
merely put his arm around her and kissed her.

126

START OF A NEW DAY IN A
HOUSE OF MOURNING

The next morning Ulrich woke early as smoothly as a fish leaping out of water, from a dreamless sound sleep that had wiped out every trace of the previous day's fatigue. He prowled through the house looking for breakfast. The ritual of mourning had not yet fully resumed; only a scent of it hung in all the rooms; it made him think of a shop that had opened its shutters early in the day, while the street is still empty of people. Then he got his scientific work out of his suitcase and took it into his father's study. As he sat there, with a fire in the grate, the room looked more human than on the previous evening: Even though a pedantic mind, always weighing all pros and cons, had created it, right up to the plaster busts facing each other symmetrically on the top bookshelves, the many little personal things left lying about—pencils, eyeglass, thermometer, an open book, boxes of pen nibs, and the like—gave the room the touching emptiness of a habitat that had just been abandoned. Ulrich sat, not too far from the window, in the midst of it, at the desk, the room's nerve center, and felt a peculiar listlessness. The walls were hung with portraits of his forebears, and some of the furniture dated from their time. The man who had lived here had formed the egg of his life from the shells of theirs; now he was dead, and his belongings stood as sharply there as if he had been chiseled out of the space; yet already the order of things was about to crumble, adapt itself to his successor, and one sensed all these objects that had outlasted him quickening with a new life as yet almost imperceptible behind their fixedly mournful air.

In this mood Ulrich spread out his work, which he had interrupted weeks and months ago, and his eyes immediately alighted on the equations in hydrodynamics where he had stopped. He dimly remembered having thought of Clarisse as he used the three basic states of water to exemplify a new mathematical operation, and Clarisse having distracted him from it. There is a kind of recollection that evokes not the word itself but the atmosphere in which it was spoken, and so Ulrich suddenly thought: "Carbon . . ." and got the feeling, as if from nowhere, that at this instant all he needed to continue was to know all the various states in which carbon occurred; but he could not remember, and thought instead: "The human being comes in twos. As man and as woman." He paused at this for quite a while, evidently stunned with amazement, as if he had just made some earthshaking discovery. But beneath this stalling of his mind something different was concealed. For one can be hard, selfish, eager, sharply profiled against the world, as it were, and can suddenly feel oneself, the same Ulrich What's-his-name, quite the opposite: deeply absorbed, a selfless, happy creature at one with an ineffably tender and somehow also selfless condition of everything around him. And he asked himself: "How long is it since I last felt like this?" To his surprise it turned out to be hardly more than twenty-four hours. The silence surrounding Ulrich was refreshing, and the condition he was reminded of did not seem as uncommon as he ordinarily thought. "We're all organisms, after all," he thought, relaxing, "who have to strain all their energies and appetites in an unkind world to prevail against each other. But together with his enemies and victims each one of us is also a particle and an offspring of this world, not at all as detached from the others and as independent as he imagines." In which case it was surely not incomprehensible that at times an intimation of oneness and love arises from the world, almost a certainty that the normal exigencies of life keep us from seeing more than half of the great pattern of the interrelationships of being. There was nothing objectionable in this for a man of mathematical-scientific bent and precise feelings; on the contrary, it reminded Ulrich of a study by a psychologist whom he happened to know personally, which dealt with two main opposing groups of concepts, one based on a sense of being enveloped by the content of one's experiences, the other on one's enveloping them, and advanced the connection that such a "being on the inside" and "looking at something from the outside," a feeling of "concavity" and "convexity," a "spatiality" as well as a "corporeality," an "introspection" and an "observation," occurred in so many other pairs of opposites of experience and in their linguistic tropes that one might assume a primal dual form of human consciousness behind it all. It was not one of those strictly factual academic studies but one of the imaginative kind, a speculative groping into the future, that are prompted by some stimulus outside the scope of everyday scientific activity; but it was well grounded and its deductions were persuasive, moving toward a unity of feeling back in the mists of creation, whose tangled wreckage, Ulrich thought, might be the origin of the present-day attitude that vaguely organizes our experience around the contrast between a male and a female mode of experience but is secretly and mysteriously shadowed by ancient dreams.

Here Ulrich tried to secure his footing—literally, as one uses ropes and crampons for a descent down a dangerous rock face—and began to reflect further:

"The most ancient philosophies, obscure and almost incomprehensible as they are to us, often speak of a male and a female principle," he thought.

"The goddesses that existed alongside the gods in primitive religions are in fact no longer within our emotional range," he thought. "Any relationship we might have to such superhuman women would be masochistic!

"But nature," he thought, "provides men with nipples and women with rudimentary male sex organs, which shouldn't lead us to conclude that our ancestors were hermaphrodites. Nor need they have been psychological hybrids either. And so it must have been from outside that they received the double possibility of a giving and a receiving vision, as a dual aspect of nature, and somehow all this is far older than the difference of gender, on which the sexes later drew to fill out their psychological wardrobe. . . ."

As he thought along these lines he remembered a detail from his childhood that distracted him, because—this had not happened for a long time—it gave him pleasure to remember. Here it must be mentioned that his father had in earlier days been a horseman and had even kept riding horses, to which the empty stable by the garden wall, the first sight Ulrich had seen on his arrival, bore witness. Riding was evidently the only aristocratic inclination his father had presumed to adopt, out of admiration for his feudal friends' way of life. But Ulrich had been a little boy; now, in his musings, he experienced anew the sense of the infinite or at least something immeasurable that the horse's high, muscular body aroused in the marveling child, like some awesome legendary mountain range covered with slopes of hair, across which the twitchings of the skin ran like the waves of a great wind. It was the kind of recollection, he realized, that owes its glamour to the child's powerlessness to make its wishes come true; but that hardly counts compared with the greatness of that splendor, which was no less than supernatural, or with the no less miraculous splendor little Ulrich touched shortly afterward with his fingertips in his quest for the first one. For at that time the town was placarded with circus posters showing not only horses but lions and tigers, too, and huge, splendid dogs that lived on good terms with the wild beasts. He had stared at these posters for a long time before he managed to get one of the richly colored pieces of paper for himself, cut the animals out, and stiffen them with little wooden supports so that they could stand up. What happened next can only be compared to drinking that never quenches one's thirst no matter how long one drinks, for there was no end to it, nor, stretching on for weeks, did it get anywhere; he was constantly being drawn to and into these adored creatures with the unutterable joy of the lonely child, who had the feeling every time he looked at them that he owned them, with the same intensity that he felt something ultimate was missing, some unattainable fulfillment the very lack of which gave his yearning the boundless radiance that seemed to flood his whole being. Along with this peculiarly boundless memory there arose unbidden from the oblivion of that early time another, slightly later experience, which now, despite its childish futility, took possession of the grown body dreaming with open eyes. It was the little girl who had only two qualities: one, that she had to belong to him, and the other, the fights with other boys this got him into. And of these two things only the fights were real, because there was no little girl. Strange time, when he used to go out like a knight errant to leap at some boy's throat, preferably when the boy was bigger than he, in some deserted street that might harbor a mystery, and wrestle with the surprised enemy! He had collected quite a few beatings, and sometimes won great victories too, but no matter how it turned out he felt cheated of his satisfaction. Nor would his feelings accept any connection, obvious as it was, between the little girls he actually knew and the secret child he fought for, because, like all boys his age, he froze and became

tongue-tied in the presence of girls until, one day, an exception occurred. And now Ulrich remembered as clearly as if the circular
image in the field of a telescope were trained across the years on that
evening when Agathe was dressed up for a children's party. She wore
a velvet dress, and her hair flowed over it like waves of bright velvet,
so that the sight of her, even though he was himself encased in a
terrifying knight's costume, suddenly filled him, in the same indescribable way as he had longed for the animals on the circus posters,
with the longing to be a girl. At that age he still knew so little about
men and women that he did not regard this as entirely impossible,
but he knew enough not to try immediately, as children usually do, to
force his wish to come true; rather, if he tried to define it now, it had
been as if he were groping in darkness for a door and suddenly came
up against some blood-warm or warmly sweet resistance, pressing
against it time and again as it yielded tenderly to his urge to penetrate it without actually giving way. Perhaps it also resembled some
harmless form of vampire passion, which sucks the desired being
into itself, except that this infant male did not want to draw that infant female into himself but wanted to take her place entirely, and
this happened with that dazzling tenderness present only in the first
intimations of sexuality.

Ulrich stood up and stretched his arms, astonished at his daydreaming. Not ten steps away, on the other side of the wall, his father's body was laid out, and he now noticed for the first time that
around them both the place had been for some time swarming with
people, as though they had shot up out of the ground, bustling about
this dead house that went on living. Old women were laying down
carpets and lighting fresh candles, there was hammering on the staircase, floors were being waxed, flowers delivered, and now he was
about to be drawn into these goings-on. People had come to see him
who were up and about at this early hour because they wanted something, or needed to know something, and from this moment the
chain of people never stopped. There were inquiries from the university about the funeral, a peddler came and shyly asked for clothing, a German firm had commissioned a dealer in local antiquities,
who with profuse apologies made on the firm's behalf an offer for a
rare legal tome that the library of the deceased might contain; a
chaplain needed to see Ulrich about some point that had to be

cleared up in the parish register, a man from the insurance company came with long and complicated questions, someone wanted a piano cheap, a real estate agent left his card in case the house might be for sale, a retired government clerk offered to address envelopes; and so they incessantly came, went, asked, and wanted all through the precious morning hours: at the front door, where the old servant shook off as many as he could, and upstairs, where Ulrich had to see those that managed to slip through, each beginning with a matter-of-fact reference to the death, and each asserting, vocally or in writing, his own claim to life. Ulrich had never before realized how many people were politely waiting for someone to die, and how many hearts are set throbbing the moment one's own stops. It took him somewhat aback, and he saw a dead beetle lying in the woods, and other beetles, birds, and flapping butterflies gathering around.

For all this commotion of profit-seeking was shot through with the flickerings and flutterings of the forest-deep darkness. Through the lenses of eyes veiled with emotion the profit motive gleamed like a lantern left burning in bright daylight, as a man with black crêpe on the black sleeve of something between mourner's garb and business suit entered, stopping at the door; he seemed to expect either Ulrich or himself to burst into tears. When neither happened, after a few seconds he seemed satisfied, for he came forward and like any other businessman introduced himself as the funeral director, come to make sure that Ulrich was satisfied with the arrangements thus far. He assured Ulrich that everything else would be conducted in a manner that even the late lamented, who everyone knew had been a gentleman none too easy to please, was bound to have approved. He pressed into Ulrich's hand a form covered with fine print and rectangles and made him read through what turned out to be a contract drawn to cover all possible classes of funerals, such as: eight horses or two horses . . . wreath carriage . . . number of . . . harness, style of . . . with outrider, silver-plated . . . attendants, style of . . . torches à la Marienburg . . . à la Admont . . . number of attendants . . . style of lighting . . . for how long . . . coffin, kind of wood . . . potted plants . . . name, date of birth, gender, occupation . . . disclaimer of liability . . . Ulrich had no idea where these terms, some of them archaic, came from; he inquired; the funeral director looked at him in surprise; he had no idea either. He stood there facing Ulrich like a synapse in the brain of mankind, linking stimulus and response while failing to generate any consciousness whatever. This merchant of mourning, who had been entrusted with centuries-old traditions which he could use as his stock-in-trade, felt that Ulrich had loosened the wrong screw, and quickly tried to cover this up with a remark intended to expedite the business in hand. He explained that all this terminology was unfortunately required by the statutes of the national association of undertakers, but that it really didn't matter if they were ignored in practice, as indeed they always were, and if Ulrich would just be good enough to sign the form—Madame, his sister, had refused to do so yesterday without consulting her brother—it would simply indicate that the client was in accord with the instructions left by his father, and he would be assured of a first-rate execution of the order.

While Ulrich signed, he asked the man whether he had already seen here in town one of those electrically powered sausage machines with a picture of Saint Luke as patron of the guild of butchers and sausage makers; he himself had seen some once in Brussels—but there was no answer to wait for, because in the place of the funeral director stood another man who wanted something from him, a journalist from the leading local newspaper seeking information for the obituary. Ulrich gave it, dismissing the undertaker with the form; but as soon as he tried to provide an account of the most important aspects of his father's life, he realized that he did not know what was important and what was not, and the reporter had to come to his aid. Only then, in the grip of the forceps of a professional curiosity trained to extract what was worth knowing, did the interview proceed, and Ulrich felt as if he were present at the Creation. The journalist, a young man, asked whether the old gentleman had died after a long illness or unexpectedly, and when Ulrich said that his father had continued lecturing right up to the last week of his life, this was framed as: ". . . working to the very end in the vigorous exercise of all his powers." Then the chips began to fly off the old man's life until nothing was left but a few ribs and joints: Born in Protivin in 1844 . . . educated at . . . and the University of . . . appointed to the post of . . . on [date] . . . until, with the listing of five such appointments and honorary degrees, the basic facts were almost exhausted. Marriage at some point. A few books. Once nearly became Minister of Justice, but someone's opposition prevailed. The reporter took notes, Ulrich checked them, they were in order. The reporter was pleased; he had the necessary number of lines. Ulrich was astonished at the little heap of ashes that remains of a human life. For every piece of information he had received, the reporter had had in readiness some six- or eight-cylinder phrase: distinguished scholar, wide sympathies, forward-looking but statesmanlike, mind of truly universal scope, and so on, as if no one had died for a long time and the phrases had been unemployed for quite a while and were hungering to be used. Ulrich tried to think; he would have liked to add something worth saying about his father, but the chronicler had his facts and was putting his notebook away; what remained was like trying to pick up the contents of a glass of water without the glass.

The comings and goings had meanwhile slackened. All the flood of people who had, the day before, been told by Agathe to see him had now passed; so when the reporter took his leave, Ulrich found himself alone. Something or other had put him in an embittered mood. Hadn't his father been right to drag along his sacks of knowledge, turning the piled grain of that knowledge now and then, and for the rest simply submitting to those powers of life that he regarded as the strongest? Ulrich thought of his own work, lying untouched in a desk drawer. Probably no one would even be able to say of him, someday, as they could of his father, that he had turned the grain pile over! Ulrich stepped into the little room where the dead man lay on his bier. This rigid, geometric cell surrounded by the ceaseless bustle to which it gave rise was incredibly eerie. The body floated stiff as a little wooden stick amid the floods of activity; but now and then for an instant the image would be reversed, and then all the life around him seemed petrified and the body seemed to be gliding along with a peculiarly quiet motion. "What does the traveler care," it said at such moments, "for the cities he has left behind at the landings? Here I once lived, and I did what was expected of me, and now I'm on my way again." Ulrich's heart constricted with the self-doubt of a man who in the midst of others wants something different than they do. He looked his father in the face. What if everything he regarded as his own personality was no more than a reaction against that face, originating in some childish antagonism? He looked around for a mirror, but there was none, only this blank face to reflect the light.

He scrutinized it for resemblances. Perhaps there were some. Perhaps it was all there: their race, their ties with the past, the impersonal element, the stream of heredity in which the individual is only a ripple, the limitations, disillusionments, the endless repetitiveness of the mind going around in circles, which he hated with every fiber of his deepest will to live.

In a sudden fit of discouragement he thought of packing up and leaving even before the funeral. If there really was something he could still achieve in life, what was he doing here?

But in the doorway he bumped into his sister, who had come looking for him.

127

OLD ACQUAINTANCE

For the first time Ulrich saw her dressed as a woman, and after his impression of her yesterday she seemed to be in disguise. Through the open door artificial light mingled with the tremulous gray of midmorning, and this black apparition with blond hair seemed to be standing in an ethereal grotto through which radiant splendor flowed. Agathe's hair was drawn back closer to her head, making her face look more feminine than it had yesterday. Her delicate womanly breasts were embedded in the black of the severe dress in that perfect balance between yielding and resistance characteristic of the feather-light hardness of a pearl; the slim long legs he had seen yesterday as so like his own were now curtained by a skirt. Now that her appearance as a whole was less like his own, he could see how alike their faces were. He felt as if it were his own self that had entered through a door and was coming to meet him, though it was a more beautiful self, with an aura in which he never saw himself. For the first time it flashed on him that his sister was a dreamlike repetition and variant of himself, but as the impression lasted only a moment he forgot it again.

Agathe had come to remind her brother of certain duties that were on the point of being delayed too long, for she had overslept. She held their father's will in her hands and drew Ulrich's attention to some dispositions in it that must be dealt with at once. Most urgent was a rather odd stipulation about the old man's decorations, which was also known to the servant Franz. Agathe had zealously, if somewhat irreverently, underlined this point in the will in red pencil. The deceased had wanted to be buried with his decorations on his chest, and he had quite a few of them, but since it was not from vanity that he wanted this done he had added a long and ruminative justification of this wish. His daughter had read only the beginning, leaving it to her brother to explain the rest to her.

"Now, how shall I put it?" Ulrich said after he had read the passage. "Papa wants to be buried with all his decorations because he considers the individualistic theory of the state to be false! He favors the universalist view: It is only through the creative community of the state that the individual gains a purpose that transcends the merely personal, a sense of value and justice. Alone he is nothing, which is why the monarch personifies a spiritual symbol. In short, when a man dies he should wrap himself in his decorations as a dead sailor is wrapped in the flag when his body is consigned to the sea!"

"But didn't I read somewhere that these medals have to be given back?"

"The heirs are obliged to return the medals to the Chamberlain's Office. So Papa had duplicates made. Still, he seems to feel that the ones he bought are not quite the real thing, so he wants us to substitute them for the originals only when they close the coffin; that's the trouble. Who knows, perhaps that's his silent protest against the regulation, which he wouldn't express any other way."

"But by that time there'll be hundreds of people here, and we'll forget!" Agathe worried.

"We might just as well do it now."

"There's no time now. You'd better read the next part, what he writes about Professor Schwung. Professor Schwung may be here at any moment; I was expecting him all day yesterday."

"Then let's do it after Schwung leaves."

"But it's not very nice," Agathe objected, "not to let him have his wish."

"He'll never know it."

She looked at him doubtfully. "Are you sure of that?"

"Oh?" Ulrich laughed. "Are *you* not quite sure, by any chance?"

"I'm not sure about anything," Agathe answered.

"Even if it weren't sure, he was never satisfied with us anyway."

"That's true," Agathe said. "All right, let's do it later. But tell me something," she added. "Don't you ever bother about what's expected of you?"

Ulrich hesitated. "She has a good dressmaker," he thought. "I needn't have worried that she might be provincial!" But because these words somehow brought back all yesterday evening, he tried to think of an answer that would really be appropriate and helpful to her; but he could not find a way to put it that would not cause misunderstanding, so he ended up with involuntarily youthful brashness:

"It's not only Father who's dead; all the ceremonials around him are dead too. His will is dead. The people who turn up here are dead. I'm not trying to be nasty; God knows we probably ought to be grateful to all those who shore up the world we live in: but all that is the limestone of life, not its oceans!" He noticed a puzzled glance from his sister and realized how obscurely he was talking. "Society's virtues are vices to the saint," he ended with a laugh.

He put his hands on her shoulders, in a gesture that could have been construed as either patronizing or high-spirited but sprang only from embarrassment. Yet Agathe stepped back with a serious face and would not go along.

"Did you make that up yourself?" she asked.

"No; a man whom I love said it."

She had the sullenness of a child forcing itself to think hard as she tried to sum up his responses in one statement: "So you would hardly call a man who is honest out of habit a good man? But a thief who steals for the first time, with his heart pounding, you'll call a good man?"

These odd words took Ulrich aback, and he became more serious.

"I really don't know," he said abruptly. "In some situations I personally don't very much care whether something is considered right or wrong, but I can't give you any rules you could go by."

Agathe slowly turned her questioning gaze away from him and

picked up the will again. "We must get on with this; here's another marked passage," she admonished herself.

Before taking to his bed for the last time the old gentleman had written a number of letters, and his will contained explanations elucidating them and directions for sending them. The marked passage referred to Professor Schwung, one of his old colleagues, who after a lifelong friendship had so galled the last year of his life by opposing his view on the statute relating to diminished responsibility. Ulrich immediately recognized the familiar long-drawn-out arguments about illusion and will, the sharpness of law and the ambiguity of nature, which his father had summarized for him again before his death. Indeed, nothing seemed to have been so much on his mind in his final days as Schwung's denunciation of the social school of thought, which his father had joined, as an emanation of Prussian influence. He had just begun to outline a pamphlet that was to have been titled "The State and the Law; or, Consistency and Denunciation," when he felt his strength beginning to fail and saw with bitterness the enemy left in sole possession of the field. In solemn words such as are inspired only by the imminence of death and the struggle to preserve that sacred possession, one's reputation, he enjoined his children not to let his work fall into oblivion, and most particularly charged his son to cultivate the influential connections he owed to his father's tireless efforts, in order to crush totally all Professor Schwung's hopes of realizing his aims.

Once one has expressed oneself in this fashion, then after one's task is done, or at least the way is paved for its completion, it by no means precludes one's feeling the urge to forgive a former friend such errors as have arisen from gross vanity. When a man is seriously ill and feels his mortal coil quietly uncoiling, he is inclined to forgive and ask forgiveness; but when he feels better he takes it all back, because the healthy body is by nature implacable. The old gentleman must have experienced both these states of mind as his condition fluctuated during his last illness, and the one must have seemed as justified as the other. But such a situation is unbearable for a distinguished jurist, and so his logically trained mind had devised a means of leaving his last will unassailably valid, impervious to the influence of any last-minute emotional waverings: He wrote a letter of forgiveness but left it unsigned and undated, with instructions for Ulrich to date it at the hour of his father's death, then sign it together with his sister Agathe as proxies, as can be done with an oral will when a dying man no longer has the strength to sign his name. Actually, he was, without wanting to admit it, an odd fish, this little old man who had always submitted to the hierarchies of existence and defended them as their most zealous servant while stifling within himself all sorts of rebellious impulses, for which, in his chosen course of life, he could never find an outlet. Ulrich was reminded of the death notice he had received, which had probably been dictated in the same frame of mind; he even almost recognized a certain kinship with himself in it, though not resentfully this time but with compassion, at least in the sense that he could see how the old man's lifelong frustration at not being able to express his feelings must have led to his being infuriated to the point of hatred by this son who made life easy for himself by taking unpardonable liberties. For this is how the ways of sons always appear to fathers, and Ulrich felt a twinge of filial sympathy as he thought of all that was still unresolved inside himself. But he no longer had time to find some appropriate expression for all this that Agathe would also understand; he had just begun when a man swung with great energy into the twilit room. He strode in, hurled forward by his own energy right into the shimmer of the candlelight, before the derailed old servant could catch up to announce him. He lifted his arm in another wide sweep to shield his eyes with his hand, one step from the bier.

"My revered friend!" the visitor intoned sonorously. And the little old man lay with clenched jaws in the presence of his enemy Schwung.

"Ah, my dear young friends," Professor Schwung continued: "Above us the majesty of the starry firmament, within us the majesty of the moral law!" With veiled eyes he gazed down upon his faculty colleague. "Within this breast now cold there lived the majesty of the moral law!" Only then did he turn around to shake hands with the brother and sister.

Ulrich took this first opportunity to acquit himself of his charge.

"You and my father were unfortunately at odds with each other lately, sir?" he opened cautiously.

For a moment the graybeard did not seem to catch his meaning.

"Differences of opinion, hardly worth mentioning!" he replied magnanimously, gazing earnestly at the deceased. But when Ulrich politely persisted, hinting that a last will was involved, the situation in the room suddenly became tense, the way it does in a low-down dive when everyone knows someone has just drawn a knife under the table and in a moment all hell will break loose. So even with his last gasp the old boy had managed to gall his colleague Schwung! Enmity of such long standing had of course long since ceased to be a feeling and become a habit; provided something or other did not happen to stir up the hostility afresh, it simply ceased to exist. There was only the accumulated experience of countless grating episodes in the past, which had coagulated into a contemptuous opinion each held of the other, an opinion as unaffected by the flux of emotion as any unbiased truth would be. Professor Schwung felt this just as his antagonist, now dead, had felt it. Forgiveness seemed to him quite childish and beside the point, for that one relenting impulse before the end—merely a feeling at that, not a professional admission of error—naturally counted for nothing against the experiences of years of controversy and, as Schwung saw it, could only serve, and rather brazenly, to put him in the wrong if he should take advantage of his victory. But this had nothing to do with Professor Schwung's need to take leave of his dead friend. Good Lord, they had known each other back at the start of their academic careers, before either of them was married! Do you remember that evening in the Burggarten, how we drank to the setting sun and argued about Hegel? However many sunsets there may have been since then, that's the one I always remember. And do you remember our first professional disagreement, which almost made enemies of us way back then? Those were the days! Now you are dead, and I'm still on my feet, I'm glad to say, even though I'm standing by your coffin.

Such are the feelings, as everyone knows, of elderly people faced with the death of their contemporaries. When we come into the sere and yellow leaf, poetry breaks out. Many people who have not turned a verse since their seventeenth year suddenly write a poem at seventy-seven, when drawing up their last will. Just as at the Last Judgment the dead shall be called forth one by one, even though they have long been at rest at the bottom of time together with their centuries, like the cargoes of foundered ships, so too, in the last will, things are summoned by name and have their personalities, worn away by use, restored to them: "The Bokhara rug with the cigar burn, in my study . . ." is the sort of thing one reads in such final dispositions, or "The umbrella with the rhinoceros-horn handle that I bought at Sunshine & Winter's in May 1887 . . ." Even the bundles of securities are named and invoked individually by number.

Nor is it chance that, as each object lights up again for the last time, the longing should arise to attach to it a moral, an admonition, a blessing, a principle, to cast one last spell on so many unreckoned things that rise up once more as one feels oneself sinking. And so, together with the poetry of testament-making time, philosophy too awakens; usually an ancient and dusty philosophy, understandably enough, hauled out from where it had been forgotten fifty years earlier. Ulrich suddenly realized that neither of these two old men could possibly have given way. "Let life take care of itself, as long as principles remain intact!" is an appropriate sentiment when a person knows that in a few months or years he will be outlived by those very principles. And it was plain to see how the two impulses were still contending with each other in the old academician: His romanticism, his youth, his poetic side, demanded a fine, sweeping gesture and a noble statement; his philosophy, on the other hand, insisted on keeping the law of reason untainted by sudden eruptions of feeling and sentimental lapses such as his dead opponent had placed on his path like a snare. For the last two days Schwung had been thinking: "Well, now he's dead, and there'll no longer be anything to interfere with the Schwungian view of diminished responsibility"; his feelings flowed in great waves toward his old friend, and he had worked out his scene of farewell like a carefully regulated plan of mobilization, waiting only for the signal to be put into operation. But a drop of vinegar had fallen into his scenario, with sobering effect. Schwung had begun on a great wave of sentiment, but now he felt like someone suddenly coming to his senses in the middle of a poem, and the last lines won't come. And so they confronted each other, a white stubby beard and white beard stubble, each with jaws implacably clenched.

"What's he going to do now?" Ulrich wondered, intent on the scene before him. But finally Hofrat Schwung's happy certainty that Paragraph 318 of the Penal Code would now be formulated in accordance with his own proposals prevailed over his irritation, and freed from angry thoughts, he would most have liked to start singing "Should auld acquaintance be forgot . . ." so as to give vent to his now entirely benevolent and undivided feelings. But since this was out of the question, he turned to Ulrich and said: "Listen to me, my friend's young son: It is the moral crisis that comes first; social decay is its consequence!" Then, turning to Agathe, he added: "It was the mark of greatness in your father that he was always ready to support an idealistic view struggling to prevail in the foundation of our laws."

Then he seized one of Agathe's hands and one of Ulrich's, pressed them both, and exclaimed:

"Your father attached far too much importance to minor differences of opinion, which are sometimes unavoidable in long years of collaboration. I was always convinced that he did so in order not to expose his delicate sense of justice to the slightest reproach. Many eminent scholars will be coming tomorrow to take their leave of him, but none of them will be the man he was!"

And so the encounter ended on a conciliatory note. When he left, Schwung even assured Ulrich that he might count on his father's friends in case he should still decide to take up an academic career.

Agathe had listened wide-eyed, contemplating the uncanny final form life gives to human beings. "It was like being in a forest of plaster trees!" she said to her brother afterward.

Ulrich smiled and said: "I'm feeling as sentimental as a dog in moonlight."

128

THEY DO WRONG

"Do you remember," Agathe asked him after a while, "how once when I was still very small, you were playing with some boys and fell into the water right up to your waist and tried to hide it? You sat at lunch, with your visible top half dry, but your bottom half made your teeth start chattering!"

When he had been a boy home from boarding school on vacation—this had actually been the only instance over a long period—and when the small shriveled corpse here had still been an almost all-powerful man for both of them, it was not uncommon for Ulrich to balk at admitting some fault, and he resisted showing remorse even when he could not deny what he had done. As a result, he had, on one occasion, caught a chill and had to be packed off to bed with an impressive fever.

"And all you got to eat was soup," Agathe said.

"That's true," her brother confirmed with a smile. At this moment the memory of his punishment, something of no concern to him now, seemed no different than if he were seeing on the floor his tiny baby shoes, also of no concern to him now.

"Soup was all you would have got anyway, on account of your fever," Agathe said. "Still, it was also prescribed for you as a punishment."

"That's true," Ulrich agreed again. "But of course it was done not in anger but in fulfillment of some idea of duty." He didn't know what his sister was getting at. He was still seeing those baby shoes. Or not seeing them: he merely saw them *as if* he were seeing them. Feeling likewise the humiliations he had outgrown. And he thought: "This having-nothing-to-do-with-me-anymore somehow expresses the fact that all our lives, we're somehow only half integrated with ourselves!"

"But you wouldn't have been allowed to eat anything but soup anyway!" Agathe reiterated, and added: "I think I've spent my whole life being afraid I might be the only person in the world who couldn't understand that sort of thing."

Can the memories of two people talking of a past familiar to both not only supplement each other but coalesce even before they are uttered? Something of the kind was happening at this moment. A shared state of mind surprised and confused both brother and sister, like hands that come out of coats in places one would never expect and suddenly grasp each other. All at once they both knew more of the past than they had supposed they knew, and Ulrich was again seeing the fever light creeping up the walls like the glittering of the candles in this room where they were now standing. And then his father had come in, waded through the cone of light cast by the table lamp, and sat down by his bed.

"If you did it without realizing the full extent of the consequences, your deed might well appear in a milder light. But in that case you would first have had to admit to yourself that it was so." Perhaps these were phrases from the will or from those letters about Paragraph 318 foisted back onto that memory. Normally he could not remember details or the way things were put, so there was something quite unusual in this recollection of whole sentences in formal array; it had something to do with his sister standing there before him, as though it were her proximity that was bringing about this change in him.

" 'If you were capable, spontaneously and independent of any outward necessity, of choosing to do something wrong, then you must also realize that you have behaved culpably,' " he continued, quoting his father aloud. "He must have talked that way to you too."

"Perhaps not quite the same way," Agathe qualified this. "With me, he usually allowed for mitigating circumstances arising from my psychological constitution. He was always instructing me that an act of the will is linked with a thought, that it is not a matter of acting on instinct."

" 'It is the will,' " Ulrich quoted, " 'that, in the process of the gradual development of the understanding and the reason, must dominate the desires and, relative to them, the instincts, by means of reflection and the resolves consequent thereon.' "

"Is that true?" his sister asked.

"Why do you ask?"

"Because I'm stupid, I suppose."

"You're not stupid!"

"Learning always came hard to me, and I never quite understand."

"That hardly proves anything."

"Then there must be something wrong with me, because I don't assimilate what I do understand."

They were close together, face-to-face, leaning against the jamb of the doorway that had been left open when Professor Schwung took his departure. Daylight and candlelight played over their faces, and their voices intertwined as in a responsory. Ulrich went on intoning his sentences like a liturgy, and Agathe's lips moved quietly in response. The old ordeal of those admonitions, which consisted in imprinting a hard, alien pattern on the tender, uncomprehending mind of childhood, gave them pleasure now, and they played with it.

And then, without having been prompted by anything preceding, Agathe exclaimed: "Just imagine this applied to the whole thing, and you have Gottlieb Hagauer." And she proceeded to mimic her husband like a schoolgirl: " 'You mean to say you really don't know that *Lamium album* is the white dead nettle?' 'But how else can we make progress except through the same hard process of induction that has brought our human race step by step through thousands of years, by painful labor full of error, to our present level of understanding, as at the hand of a faithful guide?' 'Can't you see, my dear Agathe, that thinking is also a moral obligation? To concentrate is a constant struggle against one's indolence.' 'Mental discipline is that training of the mind by means of which a man becomes steadily more capable of working out a growing series of concepts rationally, always consistently questioning his own ideas, that is by means of flawless syllogisms categorical, hypothetical, or disjunctive, or by induction, and finally of submitting the conclusions gained to verification for as long as is necessary to bring all the concepts into agreement!' "

Ulrich marveled at his sister's feat of memory. Agathe seemed to revel in the impeccable recitation of these pedantic dicta she had appropriated from God knew where, some book perhaps. She claimed that this was how Hagauer talked.

Ulrich did not believe it. "How could you remember such long, complicated sentences from only hearing them in conversation?"

"They stuck in my mind," Agathe replied. "That's how I am."

"Do you have any idea," Ulrich asked, astonished, "what a categorical syllogism is, or a verification?"

"Not the slightest!" Agathe admitted with a laugh. "Maybe he only read that somewhere himself. But that's the way he talks. I learned it by heart as a series of meaningless words by listening to him. I think it was out of anger because he talks like that. You're different from me; things lie inert in my mind because I don't know what to do with them—so much for my good memory. Because I'm stupid, I have a terrific memory!" She acted as though this contained a sad truth she would have to shake off in order to go on in her exuberant vein: "It's the same even when he's playing tennis. 'When, in learning to play tennis, I deliberately for the first time place my racket in a certain position in order to give a specific new direction to the ball, which up to that point had been following the precise course I intended, then I intervene in the flow of phenomena: I am experimenting!' "

"Is he a good tennis player?"

"I beat him six–love."

They laughed.

"Do you realize," Ulrich said, "that with all the things you're making Hagauer say, he's actually quite right? It just sounds funny."

"He may be right, for all I know," Agathe replied. "I don't understand any of it. But do you know that a boy in his class once translated a passage from Shakespeare quite literally, and the effect was touching, beginning with 'Cowards die many times before their deaths,' and without any feeling for what the boy had done, Hagauer simply crossed it out and replaced it, word for word, with the old Schlegel version!

"And I remember another instance, a passage from Pindar, I think: 'The law of nature, King of all mortals and immortals, reigns supreme, approving extreme violence, with almighty hand,' and Hagauer polished it: 'The law of nature, that reigns over all mortals and immortals, rules with almighty hand, even approving violence.'

"And wasn't it lovely," she urged, "the way that little boy, whom he criticized, translated the words so literally it gave one the shivers, just the way he found them lying there like a collapsed heap of stones." And she recited: " 'Cowards die so much before they die, / The brave ones just die once. / Among all the miracles, why should men fear death / Because it happens to everyone whenever it comes.' " With her hand high around the doorpost as though it were a tree trunk, she flung out the boy's roughhewn version of Caesar's lines with a splendid wildness, quite oblivious of the poor shriveled body lying there under her youthful gaze alight with pride.

Frowning, Ulrich stared at his sister. "The person who won't try to 'restore' an old poem but leaves it in its decayed state, with half its meaning lost, is the same as the person who will never put a new marble nose on an old statue that has lost its own," he thought. "One could call it a sense of style, but that's not what it is. Nor is it the person whose imagination is so vivid that he doesn't mind when something's missing. It's rather the person who cares nothing for perfection and accordingly doesn't demand that his feelings be 'whole' either. She's capable of kissing," he concluded with a sudden twist, "without her body going all to pieces over it."

At this moment it seemed to him that he need know nothing more of his sister than her passionate declamation to realize that she, too, was only ever "half integrated" with herself, that she, like himself, was a person of "piecemeal passions." This even made him forget the other side of his nature, which yearned for moderation and control. He could now have told his sister with certainty that nothing she did ever fitted in with her surroundings, but that all was dependent on some highly problematic vaster world, a world that begins nowhere and has no limits. This would satisfactorily explain the contradictory impressions of their first evening together. But his habitual reserve was stronger, and so he waited, curious and even slightly skeptical, to see how she would get herself down from the high limb she had got herself out on. She was still standing, with her arm raised against the doorpost, and one instant too many could spoil the whole effect. He detested women who behaved as though they had been brought into the world by a painter or a director, or who do an artful fade-out after such a moment of high excitement as Agathe's. "She could come down," he thought, "from this peak of enthusiasm with the dim-witted look of a sleepwalker, like a medium coming out of a trance. She doesn't have much choice, and it's bound to be awkward." But Agathe seemed to be aware of this herself, or possibly something in her brother's eye had put her on guard. She leapt gaily from her high limb, landed on both feet, and stuck out her tongue at him.

But then she was grave and quiet again, and without saying a word went to fetch the medals. And so brother and sister set about acting in defiance of their father's last will.

It was Agathe who did it. Ulrich felt shy about touching the defenseless old man lying there, but Agathe had a way of doing wrong that undercut any awareness of wrongdoing. Her movements of hand and eye were those of a woman tending a patient, and they had at times the spontaneous and appealing air of young animals who suddenly pause in their romping to make sure that their master is watching. The master took from her the decorations that had been removed and handed her the replicas. He was reminded of a thief whose heart is in his mouth. And if he had the impression that the stars and crosses shone more brightly in his sister's hand than in his own, indeed as if they would turn into magical objects, it might really have been true in the greenish darkness in the room, filled with glimmerings of light reflected off the leaves of the big potted plants; or it might have been that he felt his sister's will, hesitantly taking the lead and youthfully seizing his. But since no conscious motive was to be recognized in this, there again arose in these moments of unalloyed contact an almost dimensionless and therefore intangibly powerful sense of their joint existence.

Now Agathe stopped; it was done. Yet something or other still remained, and after thinking about it for a while she said with a smile: "How about each of us writing something nice on a piece of paper and putting it in his pocket?"

This time, Ulrich instantly knew what she meant, for they did not have many such shared memories, and he recalled how, at a certain age, they had loved sad verses and stories in which someone died and was forgotten by everyone. It might perhaps have been the loneliness of their childhood that had brought this about, and they often made up such stories between them, but even then Agathe had been inclined to act them out, while Ulrich took the lead only in the more manly undertakings, which called for being bold and hard. And so it had been Agathe's idea, one day, that they each should cut off a fingernail to bury in the garden, and she even slipped a small lock of her blond hair in with the parings. Ulrich proudly declared that in a hundred years someone might stumble across these relics and wonder who it might have been, since he was concerned with making an appearance in posterity; but for little Agathe the burial had been an end in itself. She had the feeling that she was hiding a part of herself, permanently removing it from the supervision of a world whose pedagogical demands always intimidated her even though she never thought very highly of them. And because that was when the cottage for the servants was being built at the bottom of the garden, they decided to do something special for it. They would write wonderful poems on two slips of paper, adding their names, to be bricked up in the walls. But when they began writing these poems that were supposed to be so splendid, they couldn't think of anything to say, day after day, and the walls were already rising out of the foundations.

Finally, when it was almost too late, Agathe copied a sentence out of her arithmetic book, and Ulrich wrote: "I am . . ." and added his name. Nevertheless, their hearts were pounding furiously when they sneaked up on the two bricklayers at work in the garden, and Agathe simply threw her piece of paper in the ditch where they were standing and ran off. But Ulrich, as the bigger and as a man even more frightened of being stopped and questioned by the astonished bricklayers, could move neither hand nor foot from excitement; so that Agathe, emboldened because nothing had happened to her, finally came back and took his slip from him. She then sauntered along with it innocently, inspected a brick at the end of a freshly laid row, lifted it, and slipped Ulrich's name into the wall before anyone could turn her away. Ulrich himself had hesitantly followed her and felt at the moment she did it the vise in which in his fright he had been gripped turning into a wheel of sharp knives whirling so rapidly in his chest that it threw off sparks like a flaming catherine wheel.

It was this incident to which Agathe was alluding now, and Ulrich gave no answer for the longest while, but smiled in a way that was meant to deter her, for repeating such a game with the dead man seemed taboo to him. But Agathe had already bent down, slid from her leg a wide silk garter that she wore to relieve the pull on her girdle, lifted the pall, and slipped it into her father's pocket.

And Ulrich? He could hardly believe his eyes to see this childhood memory restored to life. He almost leapt forward to stop her, just because it was so completely out of order. But he caught in his sister's eyes a flash of the dewy fresh innocence of early morning that is still untainted by any of the drab routines of the day, and it held him back.

"What do you think you're doing?" he admonished her softly. He did not know whether she was trying to propitiate the deceased because he had been wronged, or doing him one last kindness because of all the wrong he had done himself. He could have asked, but the barbaric notion of sending the frosty dead man on his way with a garter still warm from his daughter's thigh tightened his throat and muddled his brain.

THE OLD GENTLEMAN IS FINALLY
LEFT IN PEACE

The short time left before the funeral was filled with any number of unaccustomed small chores and passed quickly; in the last half hour before the departure of the deceased, the number of callers in black whose coming had run through all the hours like a black thread finally became a black festival. The undertaker's men had intensified their hammering and scraping—with the gravity of a surgeon to whom one has entrusted one's life and from that moment on surrendered any right to interfere—and had laid, through the untouched normality in the rest of the house, a gangway of ceremonial feeling, which ran from the entrance past the stairs into the room that held the coffin. The flowers and potted plants, the black cloth and crêpe hangings, and the silver candelabra with trembling little golden tongues of flame, which received the visitors, knew their responsibility better than Ulrich and Agathe, who had to represent the family and were obliged to welcome all who had come to pay their last respects, though they hardly knew who any of them were and would have been lost without their father's old servant, who unobtrusively prompted them whenever especially eminent guests appeared. All those who appeared glided up to them, glided past, and dropped anchor somewhere in the room, alone or in little groups, motionlessly observing the brother and sister, whose expressions grew stiff with solemn restraint, until at last the funeral director—the same man who had given Ulrich the printed forms to sign and in this last half hour had dashed up and down the steps at least twenty times— bounded up to Ulrich from the side and, with the studiously modulated self-importance of an adjutant reporting to his general on parade, told him that all was ready.

To conduct the funeral cortège ceremoniously through the town—the mourners would only later be seated in their carriages— Ulrich had to take the lead on foot, flanked on one side by His Imperial and Royal Majesty's representative, the Governor of the province, who had come in person to honor the final sleep of a member of the Upper House, and on the other by an equally high-ranking gentleman, the senior member of three from the Upper House, followed by the two other noblemen of that delegation, then by the Rector and Senate of the University. Only after these, though ahead of the interminable stream of silk hats topping off public figures of slowly diminishing importance and dignity, came Agathe, hemmed in by women in black and personifying the point where, among the peaks of officialdom, the sanctioned private grief had its place. For the unregulated participation of those who had come "merely to show their sympathy" had its place only after those officially in attendance, and it is even possible that it may have consisted solely of the old serving couple trudging along by themselves behind the procession. Thus it was a procession composed mainly of men, and it was not Ulrich who walked at Agathe's side but her husband, Professor Hagauer, whose apple-cheeked face with the bristly caterpillar mustache above the upper lip had been rendered unfamiliar to her by its curious dark-blue cast, produced by the thick black veil that allowed her to observe him unseen. As for Ulrich, who had been spending the many preceding hours with his sister, he could not help feeling that the ancient protocol of funeral precedence, dating back to the medieval beginnings of the University, had torn her from his side, and he missed her without daring to turn around to look for her. He tried to think of something funny to make her laugh when they met again, but his thoughts were distracted by the Governor, pacing along silently beside him with his lordly bearing and occasionally addressing a quiet word to Ulrich, who had to catch it, along with the many other attentions being shown him by all the Excellencies, Lordships, and Worships, for he was looked upon as Count Leinsdorf's shadow, so that even the mistrust with which His Grace's patriotic campaign was gradually coming to be regarded added to Ulrich's prestige.

The curbs and the windows were filled with clusters of the curious, and even though he knew it would all be over in an hour, like a theater performance, he nevertheless experienced everything happening that day with a special vividness, and the universal concern with his personal fate weighed on his shoulders like a heavily braided cape. For the first time he felt the upright attitude of tradition. The involvement that ran like a wave ahead of the procession, among the chatting crowds that lined the pavements, who fell silent and then breathed freely again; the spell cast by the clergy; the thudding of clods of earth on wood that one knew was coming; the dammed-up silence of the procession—all this plucked at the spinal cord as if it were some primordial musical instrument, and Ulrich was amazed to sense within himself an indescribable resonance whose vibrations buoyed up his whole body as though he were actually being borne along by the waves of ceremony around him. And as he was feeling closer to the others on this day, he imagined how it would be if at this moment he were really striding forward in the original sense—half forgotten in the pomp it assumed in its present-day form—as the real heir of a great power. The thought banished the sadness, and death was transmuted from a horrible private affair to a transition that was completed as a public ceremony. Gone was the gaping hole, stared at in dread, that every man whose presence one is accustomed to leaves behind in the first days after his disappearance, for his successor was already striding along in his place, the crowd breathing in homage to him, the funeral being at the same time a coming of age for him who now took up the sword and, for the first time without someone ahead of him, and alone, now walked toward his own end.

"I should have been the one," Ulrich surprised himself by thinking, "to close my father's eyes! Not for his sake, or my own, but . . ." He did not know how to complete the thought. That he had neither liked his father, nor his father him, seemed a petty overestimation of personal importance in the face of this order of things; in the face of death, anyway, personal concerns had the stale taste of meaninglessness, while everything that was of significance now seemed to emanate from the gigantic body of the cortège moving slowly through the streets lined with people, no matter how much idleness, curiosity, and mindless conformity were intermingled with it.

Still, the music played on, it was a light, clear, dazzling day, and Ulrich's feelings wavered this way and that, like the canopy carried in procession above the Holy of Holies. Now and then he would see his own reflection in the glass panes of the hearse in front of him, his head with its hat, his shoulders, and from time to time he glimpsed on the floor of the hearse, beside the armorially resplendent coffin, little droppings of candle wax, never quite cleaned away from previous funerals, and he simply and without thinking felt sorry for his father, as one feels sorry for a dog run over in the street. Then his eyes grew moist, and when he gazed over all the blackness at the onlookers on the curb they looked like colorful sprinkled flowers, and the thought that it was he, Ulrich, who was seeing this, and not the man who had always lived here and who, moreover, loved ceremony so much more than he did, was so peculiar that it seemed downright impossible that his father should miss seeing himself leaving the world, which he had, on the whole, regarded as a good world. Deeply moved as he was, however, Ulrich could not help noticing that the director or undertaker who was leading this Catholic funeral procession to the cemetery and keeping it in good order was a tall, muscular Jew in his thirties: graced with a long blond mustache, carrying papers in his pocket like a courier, he dashed up and down, now straightening a horse's harness, now whispering some instruction to the band. This reminded Ulrich further that his father's body had not been in the house on the last day but had been brought back to it only just before the funeral, in accordance with the old gentleman's testamentary last wish, inspired by the free spirit of humanistic inquiry, to put his body at the disposal of science; after which anatomical intervention it was only natural to assume that the old gentleman had been hurriedly sewn up again. Behind those shiny glass panes that reflected Ulrich's image, then, at the center of this great, beautiful, solemn pageantry, was an untidily recobbled object. "With or without his decorations?" Ulrich wondered in dismay. He had forgotten about it and had no idea whether his father had been dressed again in the lab before the closed coffin was returned to the house. And what about Agathe's garter? It could have been found—and he could imagine the jokes of the medical students. It was all extremely embarrassing, and so the protestations of the present again fragmented his feeling into myriad details, after it had for a moment almost rounded itself out into the smooth shell of a living dream. All he could feel now was the absurdity, the confused wavering nature of human order, and of himself.

"Now I'm all alone in the world," he thought. "A mooring rope has snapped—up I go!" This echo of his first sensation on receiving the news of his father's death now once more expressed his feelings as he walked on between the walls of people.

130

A LETTER FROM CLARISSE ARRIVES

Ulrich had not left his address with anyone, but Clarisse had it from
Walter, who knew it as well as he knew his own childhood.
She wrote:

My dar*ling*—my duck*ling*—my *ling!*
Do you know what a *ling* is? I can't work it out. Could Walter
be a weak*ling?* [All the "lings" were heavily underlined.]
Do you think I was drunk when I came to you? I *can't* get
drunk. (Men get drunk before I do. An *amaz*ing fact.)
But I don't know what I said to you; I can't remember. I'm
afraid you imagine I said things I never said. I never said them.
But this is supposed to be a letter—in a minute! But first: You
know how dreams open up. You know how, when you're
dreaming, sometimes: you've been there before, you've talked
with that person already, or—it's like finding your memory again.
Being awake means knowing I've been awake.
(I have sleepmates.)
Do you still remember who Moosbrugger is? There's
something I have to tell you:
Suddenly, there was his name again.
Those three musical syllables.
But music is fakery. I mean, when it's by itself. Music by itself
is for aesthetes or something like that; no vitality. But music
combined with vision, that makes the walls shake and the life of
those to come rise up out of the grave of the present. Those three
musical syllables, I didn't just hear them, I saw them. They
loomed up in my memory! Then suddenly you know: Where
these appear, there's something more. Why, I once wrote your
Count a letter about Moosbrugger—how could I possibly have
forgotten that! Now I hear-see a world in which the things stand
still and the people move around, just as you've always known it,

but in sound that's visible! I don't know how to describe it exactly, because only three syllables have shown up so far. Can you understand that? It may be too soon to talk about it.

I told Walter: "I must meet Moosbrugger!"

Walter asked: "Who's Moosbrugger?"

I told him: "Ulo's friend the murderer."

We were reading the paper; it was morning, time for Walter to go to the office. Remember how we used to read the paper together, the three of us? (You have a *poor* memory, you *won't* remember!) So I had just unfolded the part of the paper Walter had handed me, one arm left, one right: suddenly I feel hard wood, I'm nailed to the Cross. I ask Walter: "Wasn't it only yesterday that there was something in the paper about a train wreck near Budweis?"

"Yes," he says. "Why do you ask? A minor accident, one person killed, or two."

After a while I say: "Because there's been an accident in America too. Where's Pennsylvania?"

He doesn't know. "In America," he says.

I say: "Those engineers never have a head-on collision on purpose!"

He looks at me. I could tell he didn't understand. "Of course not," he says.

I ask him when Siegmund's coming. He's not sure.

So there you are: of course the engineers don't deliberately drive their locomotives into each other head-on; *but why else do they do it?* I'll tell you why. That monstrous network of tracks, switches, and signals that covers the whole globe drains our conscience of all its power. Because if we had the strength to check ourselves just once more, to go over everything we had to do once more, we would do what was necessary every time and avoid the disaster. *The disaster is that we halt before the next-to-last step!*

Of course we can't expect Walter to realize this at once. I think that I'm capable of achieving this immense power of conscience, and I had to shut my eyes so Walter wouldn't see the lightning flash in them.

For all these reasons I regard it as my duty to get to know Moosbrugger.

You know my brother Siegmund is a doctor. He'll help me.

I was waiting for him.

Last Sunday he came.

When he's introduced to someone he says: "But I'm neither . . . nor musical." That's his sort of joke. Just because his name is Siegmund he doesn't want to be thought to be either a Jew or musical. *He was conceived in a Wagnerian ecstasy*. You can't get him to give a sensible answer to anything. All the time I was talking to him he only muttered some nonsense or other. He threw a rock at a bird, he bored holes in the snow with his stick. He wanted to shovel out a path too; he often comes to work in our garden, because, as he says, he doesn't like staying home with his wife and children. Funny that you've never met him. "You two have the *Fleurs du mal* and a vegetable garden!" he says. I pulled his ears and punched him in the ribs, but it did no good whatsoever.

Then we went indoors to Walter, who of course was sitting at the piano, and Siegmund had his jacket under his arm and his hands were all dirty.

"Siegmund," I said to him in front of Walter, "when do you understand a piece of music?"

He grinned and answered: "Absolutely never."

"When you *play it inside yourself*," I said. "When do you understand another human being? When you feel with him. *Feel with him.*" That's a great mystery, Ulrich! You have to be like him: not by putting yourself *into him* but by taking him *out* into yourself! We redeem *outward:* that's the *strong* way! We fall *in* with people's actions, but *we* fill them *out* and rise above them.

Sorry to be writing so much about this. But the trains collide because our conscience doesn't take that final step. Worlds don't materialize unless we pull them. More of this another time. *The man of genius is duty bound to attack!* He has the mysterious power required. But Siegmund, the coward, looked at his watch and mentioned supper, because he had to go home. You know, Siegmund always tries to find the balance between the blasé attitude of the seasoned physician who has no very high opinion of the ability of his profession, and the blasé attitude of the contemporary person who has transcended the intellectual and already rediscovered the hygiene of the simple life and gardening. But Walter shouted: "Oh, for God's sake, why are you two talking such nonsense? What do you want with this Moosbrugger anyway?" And that was a help.

Because then Siegmund said: "He's neither insane nor a criminal, that's true. But what if Clarisse has a notion that she can do something for him? I'm a doctor, and I have to let the hospital chaplain imagine the same sort of thing! Redeem him, she says! Well, why not let her at least see him?"

He brushed off his trousers, adopted an air of serenity, and washed his hands; we worked it all out over supper.

Now we've already been to see Dr. Friedenthal; he's the deputy medical officer Siegmund knows. Siegmund said straight out that he'd take the responsibility for bringing me in under some sort of false pretenses, as a writer who would like to see the man.

But that was a mistake, because when it was put to him so openly, Dr. Friedenthal could only refuse. "Even if you were Selma Lagerlöf I'd be delighted to see you, of course, as I am in any case, but here we recognize only a scientific interest."

It was rather fun to be called a writer. I looked him straight in the eye and said: "In this situation I count for more than Selma Lagerlöf, because I'm not doing it for 'research.' "

He looked at me, and then he said: "The only thing I can suggest is for you to bring a letter of introduction from your embassy to the superintendent of the clinic." He took me for a foreign writer, not realizing that I was Siegmund's sister.

We finally agreed that I would not be coming to see Moosbrugger the psychiatric patient but Moosbrugger the prisoner. Siegmund got me a letter of introduction from a charitable organization and a permit from the District Court. Afterward Siegmund told me that Dr. Friedenthal regards psychiatry as a science that's half art, and called him the ringmaster of a demons' circus. I rather liked that.

What I liked best was that the clinic is housed in an old

monastery. We had to wait in the corridor, and the lecture hall is in a chapel. It has huge Gothic windows, and I could see inside from across the courtyard. The patients are dressed in white, and they sit up on the dais with the professor. And the professor bends over their chairs in a friendly way. I thought: "Maybe they'll bring Moosbrugger in now." I felt like flying into the lecture hall through that tall window. You'll say I can't fly: jump through the window, then? But I'd never have jumped; that was not how I felt at all.

I hope you'll be coming back soon. One can *never* express things. Least of all in a letter.

This was signed, heavily underlined, *"Clarisse."*

131

A FAMILY OF TWO

Ulrich says: "When two men or women have to share a room for any length of time when traveling—in a sleeping car or a crowded hotel—they're often apt to strike up an odd sort of friendship. Everyone has his own way of using mouthwash or bending over to take off his shoes or bending his leg when he gets into bed. Clothes and underwear are basically the same, yet they reveal to the eye innumerable little individual differences. At first—probably because of the hypertensive individualism of our current way of life—there's a resistance like a faint revulsion that keeps the other person at arm's length, guarding against any invasion into one's own personality. Once that is overcome a communal life develops, which reveals its unusual origin like a scar. At this point many people behave more cheerfully than usual; most become more innocuous; many more talkative; almost all more friendly. The personality is changed; one might almost say that under the skin it has been exchanged for a less idiosyncratic one: the Me is displaced by the beginnings—clearly uneasy and perceived as a diminution, and yet irresistible—of a We."

Agathe replies: "This revulsion from closeness affects women especially. I've never learned to feel at ease with women myself."

"You'll find it between a man and a woman too," Ulrich says. "But there it's covered up by the obligatory rituals of love, which immediately claim all attention. But more often than you might think, those involved wake suddenly from their trance and find—with amazement, irony, or panic, depending on their individual temperament—some totally alien being ensconced at their side; indeed, some people experience this even after many years. Then they can't tell which is more natural: their bond with others or the self's bruised recoil from that bond into the illusion of its uniqueness—both impulses are in our nature, after all. And they're both entangled with the idea of the family. Life within the family is not a full life: Young people feel robbed, diminished, not fully at home with themselves within the circle of the family. Look at elderly, unmarried daughters: they've been sucked dry by the family, drained of their blood; they've become quite peculiar hybrids of the Me and the We."

Clarisse's letter came as a disturbance to Ulrich. The manic outbursts in it bother him much less than the steady and quasi-rational working out of some obviously demented scheme deep within her. He has told himself that after his return he will have to talk to Walter about it, and since then he has deliberately been speaking of other things.

Agathe, stretched out on the couch with one knee drawn up, eagerly picks up what he has just said: "You yourself are explaining, with what you're saying, why I had to marry again!"

"And yet there is also something in the so-called sanctity of the family, in the entering into one another, serving one another, the selfless movement within a closed circle . . . ," Ulrich continues, taking no notice, and Agathe wonders at the way his words so often move away from her again just when they have been so close. "Usually this collective self is only a collective egotist, and then a strong family feeling is the most insufferable thing imaginable. Still, I can also imagine this unconditional leaping into the breach for one another, this fighting shoulder-to-shoulder and licking each other's wounds, as an instinctual feeling of satisfaction rooted deep in the beginnings of the human race, and even marked in herd animals . . . ," she hears him say, without being able to make much of it. Nor can she do more with his next statement: "This condition is subject to rapid degeneration, as it happens, like all ancient conditions whose origin has been lost," and it is only when he ends by saying, "and would presumably have to require that the individuals involved be something quite special if the group they form is not to become some pointless caricature!" that she again feels comfortable with him and tries, as she looks at him, to keep her eyes from blinking so that he won't meanwhile disappear, because it's so amazing that he is sitting there saying things that vanish high into the air and then suddenly drop down again like a rubber ball caught in the branches of a tree.

Brother and sister had met in the late afternoon in the drawing room; many days had already passed since the funeral.

This long room was not only decorated in the Biedermeier taste, it was furnished with genuine pieces of the period. Between the windows hung tall rectangular mirrors in plain gilt frames, and the stiff, sober chairs were ranged along the walls, so that the empty floor seemed to have flooded the room with the darkened gleam of its parquet and filled a shallow basin, into which one hesitantly set foot. At the edge of this salon's elegant barrenness—for the study where Ulrich had settled down on the first morning was set aside for him—about where in a quarried-out niche the tiled stove stood like a severe pillar, wearing a vase on its head (and also a lone candlestick, precisely in the middle of its front, on a shelf running around the stove at waist height), Agathe had created a very personal peninsula for herself. She had had a couch moved here, with a rug beside it, whose ancient reddish blue, in common with the couch's Turkish pattern that repeated itself in infinite meaninglessness, constituted a voluptuous challenge to the subtle grays and sober, unassertive lineaments that were at home in this room by ancestral decree. She had further outraged that chaste and well-bred decree by rescuing a large-leaved man-sized plant complete with tub from the funeral decorations and installing it at the head of the couch, as a "grove," on the other side from the tall, bright floor lamp that would enable her to read in comfort while lying down, and which, in that classicizing setting, had the effect of a searchlight or an antenna pole. This salon, with its coffered ceiling, pilasters, and slender glass cabinets, had not changed much in a hundred years, for it was seldom used and had never really been drawn into the lives of its more recent owners. In their forefathers' day the walls now painted a pale gray might have been covered in fine fabrics, and the upholstery on the chairs had probably looked different too; but Agathe had known this salon as it now was since childhood, without even knowing whether it was her great-grandparents who had furnished it like this or strangers. She had grown up in this house, and the only association she had was the memory that she had always entered this room with the awe that is instilled into children about something they might easily damage or dirty.

But now she had laid aside the last symbol of the past, the mourning she had worn, and put on her lounging pajamas again, and was lying on the rebelliously intruding couch, where since early morning she had been reading all kinds of books, good and bad, whatever she could get her hands on, interrupting herself from time to time to eat or fall asleep; now that the day spent in this fashion was fading into evening, she gazed through the darkening room at the pale curtains that, already quite immersed in twilight, ballooned at the windows like sails, which made her feel that she was voyaging through that stiffly dainty room within the harsh corona of her lamp and had only just come to a halt. So her brother had found her, taking in her well-lit encampment at a glance, for he, too, remembered this salon and could even tell her that the original owner was supposed to have been a rich merchant whose fortunes declined, so that their great-grandfather, an imperial notary, had been in a position to acquire the attractive property at a price well within his means. Ulrich knew all sorts of other things as well about this room, which he had looked over thoroughly; his sister was especially impressed to hear that in their grandparents' day such formal décor had been seen as particularly natural. This was not easy for her to comprehend, since it looked to her like something spawned in a geometry class, and it took a while before she could begin to grasp the outlook of a time so oversaturated with the swirling aggressiveness of the Baroque that its own leaning toward symmetry and somewhat unbending forms was veiled by the tender illusion of being truer to nature in being pure, unadorned, and rational. But when she finally succeeded in grasping this shift of ideas, with the help of all the details Ulrich could supply, she was delighted to know so much about things that every experience in her life up until then had taught her to despise; and when her brother wanted to know what she was reading, she quickly rolled over on top of her supply of books, even though she defiantly said that she enjoyed trashy reading just as much as good.

Ulrich had worked all morning and then gone out. His hope of concentrating, of gaining the new impetus he had expected from the interruption of his customary life, had up to now not been fulfilled; it was outweighed by the distractions resulting from his new circumstances. Only after the funeral had there been a change, when his relations with the outside world, which had begun so actively, had been cut off at a stroke. The brother and sister had been the center of sympathetic attention for a few days, if only as a kind of representation of their father, and had felt the connections attendant upon their position; but apart from Walter's old father they knew no one in town they would have felt like visiting, and in consideration of their mourning no one invited them. Only Professor Schwung had appeared not only at the funeral but again the following day to inquire whether his late friend had not left a manuscript on the problem of diminished responsibility, which one might hope to see published posthumously.

The brusque transition from a constantly seething commotion to the leaden stillness that had followed produced something like a physical shock. Besides, they were still sleeping on camp beds up in the attic, in the rooms they had occupied as children—there were no guest rooms in the house—surrounded by the sparse odds and ends left over from the nursery, their bareness suggesting that of a padded cell, a bareness that, with the insipid sheen of the oilcloth on the tables or the linoleum on the floor—on whose desert the box of building blocks had once spewed forth its rigid ideas of architecture—invaded their dreams. These memories, as senseless and as endless as the life for which they were supposed to have been a preparation, made it a relief that their bedrooms were at least adjacent, separated only by a clothes and storage room; and because the bathroom was on the floor below, they were much in each other's company soon after they got up, meeting on the empty stairs and throughout the empty house, having to show consideration for one another and deal together with all the problems of that unfamiliar household with which they had suddenly been entrusted. In this way they also felt the inevitable comedy of this coexistence, as intimate as it was unexpected: it resembled the adventurous comedy of a shipwreck that had stranded them back on the lonely island of their childhood, and so, after those first few days, over the course of which they had had no control, they strove for independence, although both did so out of altruism more than selfishness.

This was why Ulrich had been up before Agathe had built her peninsula in the drawing room, and had slipped quietly into the study to take up his interrupted mathematical investigation, really more as a way of passing time than with the intention of getting it done. But to his considerable astonishment he all but finished in one morning—except for insignificant details—the work he had left lying untouched for months. He had been helped in this unexpected solution by one of those random ideas of which one might say, not that they turn up only when one has stopped expecting them, but rather that the startling way they flash into the mind is like another sudden recognition—that of the beloved who had always been just another girl among one's friends until the moment when the lover is suddenly amazed that he could ever have put her on the same level as the rest. Such insights are never purely intellectual, but involve an element of passion as well, and Ulrich felt as though he should at this moment have been finished with it and free; indeed, since he could see neither reason nor purpose in it, he had the impression of having finished prematurely, and the leftover energy swept him off into a reverie. He glimpsed the possibility of applying the idea that had solved his problem to other, far more complex problems, and playfully let his imagination stretch the outlines of such a theory. In these moments of happy relaxation he was even tempted to consider Professor Schwung's insinuation that he should return to his career and find the path that leads to success and influence. But when, after a few minutes of intellectual pleasure, he soberly considered what the consequences would be if he were to yield to his ambition and now, as a straggler, take up an academic career, he felt for the first time that he was too old to start anything like that. Since his boyhood he had never felt that the half-impersonal concept of "age" had any independent meaning, any more than he had known the thought: This is something you are no longer able to do!

When Ulrich was telling this to his sister afterward, late that afternoon, he happened to use the word "destiny," and it caught her attention. She wanted to know what "destiny" was.

"Something halfway between 'my toothache' and 'King Lear's daughters,' " Ulrich answered. "I'm not the sort of person who goes in for that word too much."

"But for young people it is part of the song of life; they want to have a destiny but don't know what it is."

"In times to come, when more is known, the word 'destiny' will probably have acquired a statistical meaning," Ulrich responded.

Agathe was twenty-seven. Young enough to have retained some of those hollow, sentimental concepts young people develop first; old enough to already have intimations of the other content that reality pours into them.

"Growing old is probably a destiny in itself!" she answered, but was far from pleased with her answer, which expressed her youthful sadness in a way that seemed to her inane.

But her brother did not notice this, and offered an example: "When I became a mathematician," he said, "I wanted to achieve something in my field and gave it all I had, even though I regarded it only as preliminary to something else. And my first papers—imperfect beginner's work though they were—really did contain ideas that were new at the time, but either remained unnoticed or even met with resistance, though everything else I did was well received. Well, I suppose you could call it destiny that I soon lost patience with having to keep hammering at that wedge."

"Wedge?" Agathe interrupted, as though the mere sound of such a masculine, workmanlike term could mean nothing but trouble. "Why do you call it a wedge?"

"Because it was only my first move; I wanted to drive the wedge further, but then I lost patience. And today, as I completed what may well be the last piece of work that reaches back to that time, I realized that I might actually have had some justification in seeing myself as the leader of a new school of thought, if I'd had better luck then, or shown more persistence."

"You could still make up for it!" Agathe said. "After all, a man doesn't get too old to do things, the way a woman does."

"No," Ulrich replied. "I don't want to go back to that! It's surprising, but true, that objectively—historically, or in the development of science itself—it would have made no difference. I may have been ten years ahead of my time, but others got there without me, even if more slowly or by other means. The most I could have done was to lead them there more quickly, but it remains a question whether such a change in my life would have been enough to give me a fresh impetus that would take me beyond that goal. So there you have a bit of what one calls personal destiny, but what it finally amounts to is something remarkably impersonal.

"Anyway," he went on, "it happens that the older I get, the more often I see something I used to hate that subsequently and in round-about ways takes the same direction as my own road, so that I suddenly can no longer dismiss its right to exist; or it happens that I begin to see what's wrong with ideas or events I used to get excited about. So in the long run it hardly seems to matter whether one gets excited or to what cause one commits one's existence. It all arrives at the same goal; everything serves an evolution that is both unfathomable and inescapable."

"That used to be ascribed to God's working in mysterious ways," Agathe remarked, frowning, with the tone of one speaking from her own experience and not exactly impressed. Ulrich remembered that she had been educated in a convent. She lay on her sofa, as he sat at its foot; she wore her pajama trousers tied at the ankle, and the floor lamp shone on them both in such a way that a large leaf of light formed on the floor, on which they floated in darkness.

"Nowadays," he said, "destiny gives rather the impression of being some overarching movement of a mass; one is engulfed by it and rolled along." He remembered having been struck once before by the idea that these days every truth enters the world divided into its half-truths, and yet this nebulous and slippery process might yield a greater total achievement than if everyone had gone about earnestly trying to accomplish the whole task by himself. He had once even come out with this idea, which lay like a barb in his self-esteem and yet was not without the possibility of greatness, and concluded, tongue-in-cheek, that it meant one could do anything one pleased! Actually, nothing could have been further from his intention than this conclusion, especially now, when his destiny seemed to have set him down and left him with nothing more to do; and at this moment so dangerous to his ambition, when he had been so curiously driven to end, with this belated piece of work, the last thing that had still tied him to his past—precisely at this moment when he felt personally quite bare, what he felt instead of a falling off was this new tension that had begun when he had left his home. He had no name for it, but for the present one could say that a younger person, akin to him, was looking to him for guidance; one could also just as well call it something else. He saw with amazing clarity the radiant mat of bright gold against the black-green of the room, with the delicate lozenges of Agathe's clown costume on it, and himself, and the superlucidly outlined happenstance, cut from the darkness, of their being together.

"Can you say that again?" Agathe asked.

"What we still refer to as a personal destiny," Ulrich said, "is being displaced by collective processes that can finally be expressed in statistical terms."

Agathe thought this over and had to laugh. "I don't understand it, of course, but wouldn't it be lovely to be dissolved by statistics?" she said. "It's been such a long time since love could do it!"

This suddenly led Ulrich to tell his sister what had happened to him when, after finishing his work, he had left the house and walked to the center of town, in order to somehow fill the void left in him by the completion of his paper. He had not intended to speak of it; it seemed too personal a matter. For whenever his travels took him to cities to which he was not connected by business of any kind, he particularly enjoyed the feeling of solitude this gave him, and he had rarely felt this so keenly as he did now. He noticed the colors of the streetcars, the automobiles, shop windows, and archways, the shapes of church towers, the faces and the façades, and even though they all had the usual European resemblances, his gaze flew over them like an insect that has strayed into a field bright with unfamiliar colors and cannot, try as it will, find a place to settle on. Such aimless, purposeless strolling through a town vitally absorbed in itself, the keenness of perception increasing in proportion as the strangeness of the surroundings intensifies, heightened still further by the connection that it is not oneself that matters but only this mass of faces, these movements wrenched loose from the body to become armies of arms, legs, or teeth, to all of which the future belongs—all this can evoke the feeling that being a whole and inviolate strolling human being is positively antisocial and criminal. But if one lets oneself go even further in this fashion, this feeling may also unexpectedly produce a physical well-being and irresponsibility amounting to folly, as if the body were no longer part of a world where the sensual self is enclosed in strands of nerves and blood vessels but belongs to a world bathed in somnolent sweetness. These were the words that Ulrich used to describe to his sister what might perhaps have been the result of a state of mind without goal or ambition, or the result of a diminished ability to maintain an illusory individuality, or perhaps nothing more than that "primal myth of the gods," that "double face of nature," that "giving" and "taking vision," which he was after all pursuing like a hunter.

Now he was waiting curiously to see if Agathe would show by some sign that she understood, that she, too, was familiar with such impressions, but when this did not happen he explained it again: "It's like a slight split in one's consciousness. One feels enfolded, embraced, pierced to the heart by a sense of involuntary dependence; but at the same time one is still alert and capable of making critical judgments, and even ready to start a fight with these people and their stuffy presumptuousness. It's as though there were two relatively independent strata of life within us that normally keep each other profoundly in balance. And we were speaking of destiny: it's as if we had two destinies—one that's all superficial bustle, which takes life over, and one that's motionless and meaningful, which we never find out about."

Now Agathe, who had been listening for a long time without stirring, said out of the blue: "That's like kissing Hagauer!"

Laughing, she had propped herself up on one elbow, her legs still stretched out full length on the couch. And she added: "Of course, it wasn't as beautiful as the way you describe it!"

Ulrich was laughing too. It was not really clear why they were laughing. Somehow this laughter had come upon them from the air, or from the house, or from the traces of bewilderment and uneasiness left behind by the solemnities of the last few days, which had touched so uselessly on the Beyond; or from the uncommon pleasure they found in their conversation. For every human custom that has reached an extreme of cultivation already bears within itself the seeds of change, and every excitement that surpasses the ordinary soon mists over with a breath of sorrow, absurdity, and satiety.

In this fashion and in such a roundabout way they finally end up, as if for relaxation, talking about less demanding matters, about Me and Us and Family, and arriving at the discovery, fluctuating between mockery and astonishment, that the two of them constitute a family. And while Ulrich speaks of the desire for community—once more with the zeal of a man out to mortify his own nature, without knowing whether it is directed against his true nature or his assumed nature—Agathe is listening as his words come close to her and retreat again, and what he notices, looking at her lying quite defenseless in that bright island of light and in her whimsical costume, is that for some time now he has been searching for something about her that would repel him, as he regrettably tends to do, but he has not found anything, and for this he is thankful with a pure and simple affection that he otherwise never feels. And he is thoroughly delighted by the conversation. But when it is over, Agathe asks him casually: "Now, are you actually *for* what you call the family or are you against it?"

Ulrich answers that this is beside the point, because he was talking about an indecision on the part of the world, not his personal indecision.

Agathe thinks it over.

Finally, she says abruptly: "I have no way of judging that. But I wish I could be entirely at one and at peace with myself, and also . . . well, somehow be able to live accordingly. Wouldn't you like to try that too?"

132

Agathe when she can't talk to Ulrich

The moment Agathe got on the train and began the unexpected journey to her father something had happened that bore every resemblance to a sudden rupture, and the two fragments into which the moment of departure exploded flew as far apart as if they had never belonged together. Her husband had seen her off, had raised his hat and held it, that stiff, round, black hat that grew visibly smaller and smaller, in the gesture appropriate to leave-taking, aslant in the air, as her train began to move, so that it seemed to Agathe that the station was rolling backward as fast as the train was rolling forward. At this moment, though an instant earlier she had still been expecting to be away from home no longer than circumstances absolutely required, she made the decision never to return, and her mind became agitated like a heart that realizes suddenly that it has escaped a danger of which it had been wholly unaware.

When Agathe thought it over afterward, she was by no means completely satisfied. What troubled her about her attitude was that its form reminded her of a curious illness she had had as a child, soon after she had begun going to school. For more than a year she had suffered from a not inconsiderable fever that neither rose nor subsided, and she had grown so thin and frail that it worried the doctors, who could not determine the cause. Nor was this illness ever explained later. Actually, Agathe had rather enjoyed seeing the great physicians from the University, who at first entered her room so full of dignity and wisdom, visibly lose some of their confidence from week to week; and although she obediently swallowed all the medicines prescribed for her and really would have liked to get well, because it was expected of her, she was still pleased to see that the doctors could not bring this about with their remedies and felt herself in an unearthly or at least an extraordinary condition, as her physical self diminished. That the grownups' world had no power over her as long as she was sick made her feel proud, though she had no idea how her little body had brought this about. But in the end it recovered of its own accord, and just as mysteriously, too.

Almost all she knew about it today was what the servants had told her later: they maintained that she had been bewitched by a beggar woman who came often to the house but had once been rudely turned away from the door. Agathe had never been able to find out how much truth there was in this story, for although the servants freely dropped hints, they could never be pinned down to explanations and were obviously frightened of violating a strict ban her father was supposed to have issued. Her own memory of that time held only a single, though indeed remarkably lively, image, in which she saw her father in front of her, lashing out in a raging fury at a suspicious-looking woman, the flat of his hand repeatedly making contact with her cheek. It was the only time in her life she had seen that small, usually painfully proper man of reason so utterly changed and beside himself; but to the best of her recollection this had happened not before but during her illness, for she thought she remembered lying in bed, and this bed was not in her nursery but on the floor below, "with the grownups," in one of the rooms where the servants would not have been allowed to let the beggar woman in, even if she had been no stranger to the kitchen and below stairs. Actually, Agathe believed this incident must have occurred rather toward the end of her illness and that she had suddenly recovered a few days later, roused from her bed by a remarkable impatience that ended this illness as unexpectedly as it had begun.

Of course, she could not tell how far these memories stemmed from facts or whether they were fantasies born of the fever. "Probably the only curious thing about it is the way these images have stayed floating in my mind somewhere between reality and illusion," she thought moodily, "without my finding anything unusual about it."

The jolting of the taxi that was driving them over badly paved streets prevented a conversation. Ulrich had suggested taking advantage of the dry winter weather for an outing, and even had an idea where to go, though it was not a specific destination so much as an advance into a half-remembered country of the mind. Now they found themselves in a car that was to take them to the edge of town. "I'm sure that's the only odd thing about it!" Agathe kept saying to herself. This was how she had learned her lessons in school, so that she never knew whether she was stupid or bright, willing or unwilling: she had a facility for coming up with the answers that were demanded of her without ever seeing the point of the questions, from which she felt protected by a deep-seated indifference. After she recovered from her illness she liked going to school as much as before, and because one of the doctors had hit upon the idea that it might help to remove her from the solitary life in her father's house and give her more company of her own age, she had been placed in a convent school. There, and in the secondary school she was sent on to, she was regarded as cheerful and docile. Whenever she was told that something was necessary or true she accommodated herself to it, and she willingly accepted everything required of her, because it seemed the least trouble and it would have seemed foolish to her to do anything against an established system that had no relevance to herself but obviously belonged to a world ordained by fathers and teachers. However, she did not believe a word of what she was learning, and since despite her apparent docility she was no model pupil and, wherever her desires ran counter to her convictions, calmly did as she pleased, she enjoyed the respect of her schoolmates and even that admiring affection won in school by those who know how to make things easy for themselves. It could even be that her mysterious illness had been such an arrangement, for with this one exception she had really always been in good health and hardly ever high-strung. "In short, an idle, good-for-nothing character!" she concluded uncertainly. She remembered how much more vigorously than herself her friends had often mutinied against the strict discipline of the convent, and with what moral indignation they had justified their offenses against the regulations; yet as far as she had been in a position to observe, the very girls who had been most passionate in rebelling against details had eventually succeeded admirably in coming to terms with the whole; they developed into well-situated women who brought up their children not very differently from the way they had been brought up themselves. And so, although dissatisfied with herself as she was, she was not convinced that it was better to have an active and a good character.

Agathe despised the emancipation of women just as she disdained the female's need for a brood in a nest supplied by the male. She remembered with pleasure the time when she had first felt her breasts tightening her dress and had borne her burning lips through the cooling air of the streets. But the fussy erotic busyness of the female sex, which emerges from the guise of girlhood like a round knee from pink tulle, had aroused scorn in her for as long as she could remember. When she asked herself what her real convictions were, a feeling told her that she was destined to experience something extraordinary and of a rare order—even then, when she knew as good as nothing of the world and did not believe the little she had been taught. And it had always seemed to her like a mysterious but active response, corresponding to this impression, to let things go as they had to, without overestimating their importance.

Out of the corner of her eye Agathe glanced at Ulrich, sitting gravely upright, rocking to and fro in the jolting cab, and recalled how hard it had been on their first evening together to make him see why she had not simply run away from her husband on their wedding night, although she didn't like him. She had been so tremendously in awe of her big brother while she was awaiting his arrival, but now she smiled as she secretly recalled her impression of Hagauer's thick lips in those first months, every time they rounded amorously under the bristles of his mustache; his entire face would be drawn in thick-skinned folds toward the corners of his mouth, and she would feel, as if satiated: Oh, what an ugly man he is! She had even suffered his mild pedagogic vanity and kindliness as a merely physical disgust, more outward than inward. After the first surprise was over, she had now and then been unfaithful to him. "If you can call it that," she thought, "when an inexperienced young thing whose sensuality is dormant instantly responds to the advances of a man who is not her husband as if they were thunderclaps rattling her door!" But she had shown little talent for unfaithfulness; lovers, once she had got to know them a little, were no more masterful to her than husbands, and it soon seemed to her that she could take the ritual masks of African tribal dancers as seriously as the love masks put on by European men. Not that she never lost her head; but even in the first attempts to repeat the experience the magic was gone. The world of acted-out fantasies, the theatricality of love, left her unenchanted. These stage directions for the soul, mostly formulated by men, which all came to the conclusion that the rigors of life now and then entitled one to an hour of weakness—with some subcategories of weakening: letting go, going faint, being taken, giving oneself, surrendering, going crazy, and so on—all struck her as smarmy exaggeration, since she had at no time ever felt herself other than weak in a world so superbly constructed by the strength of men.

The philosophy Agathe acquired in this way was simply that of the female person who refuses to be taken in but who automatically observes what the male person is trying to put over on her. Of course, it was no philosophy at all, only a defiantly hidden disappointment, still mingled with a restrained readiness for some unknown release that possibly increased even as her outward defiance lessened. Since Agathe was well-read but not by nature given to theorizing, she often had occasion to wonder, in comparing her own experiences with the ideals in books and plays, that she had never fallen prey to the snares of her seducers, like a wild animal in a trap (which would have accorded with the Don Juanish self-image a man in those days assumed when he and a woman had an affair); nor had her married life, in accord with another fashion, turned into a Strindbergian battle of the sexes in which the imprisoned woman used her cunning and powerlessness to torment her despotic but inept overlord to death. In fact, her relations with Hagauer, in contrast with her deeper feelings about him, had always remained quite good. On their first evening together Ulrich had used strong terms for these relations, such as panic, shock, rape, which completely missed the mark. She was sorry, Agathe thought, rebellious even as she remembered this, but she could not pretend to be an angel; the fact was that everything about the marriage had taken a perfectly natural course. Her father had supported the man's suit with sensible reasons, she herself had decided to marry again; all right, then, it was done, one had to put up with whatever was involved. It was neither especially wonderful nor overly unpleasant! Even now she was sorry to be hurting Hagauer deliberately, though she absolutely wanted to do just that! She had not wanted love, she had thought it would work out somehow, he was after all a good man.

Well, perhaps it was rather that he was one of those people who always do the good thing; they themselves have no goodness in them, Agathe thought. It seems that goodness disappears from the human being to the same extent that it is embodied in goodwill or good deeds! How had Ulrich put it? A stream that turns factory wheels loses its gradient. Yes, he had said that too, but that wasn't what she was looking for. Now she had it: "It seems really that it's only the people who don't do much good who are able to preserve their goodness intact!" But the instant she recalled this sentence, which must have sounded so illuminating when Ulrich said it, it sounded to her like total nonsense. One could not detach it from its now-forgotten context. She tried to reshuffle the words and replace them with similar ones, but that only proved that the first version was the right one, for the others were like words spoken into the wind: nothing was left of them. So that was the way Ulrich had said it. "But how can one call people good who behave badly?" she thought. "That's really nonsense!" But she knew: while Ulrich was saying this, though it had no more real substance when he did so, it had been wonderful! Wonderful wasn't the word for it: she had felt almost ill with joy when she heard him say it. Such sayings illuminated her entire life. This one, for instance, had come up during their last long talk, after the funeral and after Hagauer had left; suddenly she had realized how carelessly she had always behaved, like the time she had simply thought things would "somehow" work out with Hagauer, because he was "a good person." Ulrich often said things that filled her momentarily with joy or misery, although one could not "preserve" those moments. When was it, for example, that Ulrich had said that under certain circumstances it might be possible for him to love a thief but never a person who was honest from habit? At the moment she couldn't quite recall, but then realized with delight that it hadn't been Ulrich but she herself who had said it. As a matter of fact, much of what he said she had been thinking herself, only without words; all on her own, the way she used to be, she would never have made such bold assertions.

Up to now Agathe had been feeling perfectly comfortable between the joggings and joltings as the cab drove over bumpy suburban streets, leaving them incapable of speech, wrapped as they were in a network of mechanical vibrations, and whenever she had used her husband's name in her thoughts, it was as a mere term of reference to a period and its events. But now, for no particular reason, an infinite horror slowly came over her: Hagauer had actually been there with her, in the flesh! The way in which she had tried up to now to be fair to him disappeared, and her throat tightened with bitterness.

He had arrived on the morning of the funeral and had affectionately insisted, late as he was, on seeing his father-in-law, had gone to the autopsy lab and delayed the closing of the coffin. In a tactful, honorable, undemonstrative fashion, he had been truly moved. After the funeral Agathe had excused herself on grounds of fatigue, and Ulrich had to take his brother-in-law out to lunch. As he told her afterward, Hagauer's constant company had made Ulrich as frantic as a tight collar, and for that reason he had done everything to get him to leave as soon as possible. Hagauer had intended to go to the capital for an educators' conference and there devote another day to calling on people at the Ministry and some sightseeing, but he had reserved the two days prior to this to spend with his wife as an attentive husband and to go into the matter of her inheritance. But Ulrich, in collusion with his sister, had made up a story that made it seem impossible for Hagauer to stay at the house, and told him he had booked a room for him at the best hotel in town. As expected, this made Hagauer hesitant: the hotel would be inconvenient and expensive, and he would in all decency have to pay for it himself; instead, he could allot two days to his calls and sightseeing in the capital, and if he traveled at night save the cost of the hotel. So Hagauer expressed fulsome regrets at being unable to take advantage of Ulrich's thoughtfulness, and finally revealed his plan, unalterable by now, to leave that very evening. All that was left to discuss was the question of the inheritance, and this made Agathe smile again, because at her instigation Ulrich had told her husband that the will could not be read for a few days yet. Agathe would be here, after all, he was told, to look after his interests, and he would also receive a proper legal statement. As for whatever concerned furniture, mementos, and the like, Ulrich, as a bachelor, would make no claims to anything his sister might happen to want. Finally, he had asked Hagauer whether he would agree in case they decided to sell the house, which was of no use to them, without committing himself, of course, since none of them had yet seen the will; and Hagauer had agreed, without committing himself, of course, that he could see no objection for the moment, though he must of course reserve the right to determine his position in the light of the actual conditions. Agathe had suggested all this to her brother, and he had passed it on because it meant nothing to him one way or the other, and he wanted to be rid of Hagauer.

Suddenly Agathe felt miserable again, for after they had managed this so well, her husband had after all come to her room, together with her brother, to say goodbye to her. Agathe had behaved as coldly as she could and said that there was no way of telling when she would be returning home. Knowing him as she did, she could tell at once that he had not been prepared for this and resented the fact that his decision to leave right away was now casting him in the role of the unfeeling husband; in retrospect he was suddenly offended at having been expected to stay at a hotel and by the cool reception accorded him. But since he was a man who did everything according to plan he said nothing, decided to have it out with his wife when the time came, and kissed her, after he had picked up his hat, dutifully on the lips.

And this kiss, which Ulrich had seen, now seemed to demolish Agathe. "How could it happen," she asked herself in consternation, "that I stood this man for so long? But then, haven't I put up with things all my life without resisting?" She furiously reproached herself: "If I were any good at all, things could never have gone this far!"

Agathe turned her face away from Ulrich, whom she had been watching, and stared out the window. Low suburban buildings, icy streets, muffled-up people—images of an ugly wilderness rolling past, holding up to her the wasteland of the life into which she felt she had fecklessly allowed herself to drift. She was no longer sitting upright but had let herself slide down into the cab's musty-smelling upholstery; it was easier to look out the window in this position, and she remained in this ungraceful posture, in which she was rudely jolted and shaken to the very bowels. This body of hers, being tossed about like a bundle of rags, gave her an uncanny feeling, for it was the only thing she owned. Sometimes, when as a schoolgirl she awakened in the gray light of dawn, she had felt as though she were drifting into the future inside her body as if inside the hull of a wooden skiff. Now she was just about twice as old as she had been then, and the light in the cab was equally dim. But she still could not picture her life, had no idea what it ought to be. Men were a complement to one's body, but they were no spiritual fulfillment; one took them as they took oneself. Her body told her that in only a few years it would begin to lose its beauty, which meant losing the feelings that, because they arise directly out of its self-assurance, can only barely be expressed in words or thoughts. Then it would be all over, without anything having ever been there. It occurred to her that Ulrich had spoken in a similar vein about the futility of his athletics, and while she doggedly kept her face turned away to the window, she planned to make him talk about it.

133

FURTHER COURSE OF THE EXCURSION TO THE SWEDISH RAMPARTS. THE MORALITY OF THE NEXT STEP

Brother and sister had left the cab at the last, low, and already quite rural-looking houses on the edge of the town and set off along a wide, furrowed country road that rose steadily uphill. The frozen earth of the wheel tracks crumbled beneath their tread. Their shoes were soon covered with the miserable gray of this parquet for carters and peasants, in sharp contrast with their smart city clothes, and although it was not cold, a cutting wind blowing toward them from the top of the hill made their cheeks glow, and the glazed brittleness of their lips made it hard to talk.

The memory of Hagauer drove Agathe to explain herself to her brother. She was convinced that he could not possibly understand her bad marriage from any point of view, not even in the simplest of social terms. The words were already there within her, but she could not make up her mind to overcome the resistance of the climb, the cold, and the wind lashing her face. Ulrich was striding ahead, in a broad track left by a dragging brake, which they were using as their path; looking at his lean, broad-shouldered form, she hesitated. She had always imagined him hard, unyielding, a bit wild, perhaps only because of the critical remarks she had heard from her father and occasionally also from Hagauer; thinking of her brother, estranged and escaped from the family, had made her ashamed of her own subservience. "He was right not to bother about me!" she thought, and her dismay at having continually submitted to demeaning situations returned. But in fact she was full of those same tempestuous, conflicting feelings that had made her break out with those wild lines of poetry between the doorposts of her father's death chamber. She caught up with Ulrich, which left her out of breath, and suddenly questions such as this workaday road had probably never heard before rang out, and the wind was torn to ribbons by words whose sounds no other wind had ever carried in these rural hills.

"You surely remember . . . ," she exclaimed, and named several well-known instances from literature: "You didn't tell me whether you could forgive a thief, but do you mean you'd regard these murderers as good people?"

"Of course!" Ulrich shouted back. "No—wait. Perhaps they're just potentially good people, valuable people. They still are, even afterward, as criminals. But they don't stay good!"

"Then why do you still like them after their crime? Surely not because of their earlier potentiality but because you still find them attractive?"

"But that's always the way it is," Ulrich said. "It's the person who gives character to the deed; it doesn't happen the other way round. We separate good and evil, but in our hearts we know they're a whole!"

Agathe's wind-whipped cheeks flushed an even brighter red because the passion of her questions, which words both revealed and hid, had forced her to resort to books for examples. The misuse of "cultural problems" is so extreme that one could feel them out of place wherever the wind blows and trees stand, as though human culture did not include all of nature's manifestations! But she had struggled bravely, linked her arm through her brother's, and now replied, close to his ear so as not to have to raise her voice anymore and with a flicker of bravado in her face: "I suppose that's why we execute bad men but cordially serve them a hearty breakfast first."

Ulrich, sensing some of the agitation at his side, leaned down to speak in his sister's ear, though in a normal voice: "Everyone likes to think that he couldn't do anything evil, because he himself is good."

With these words they had reached the top, where the road no longer climbed but cut across a rolling, treeless plateau. The wind had suddenly dropped and it was no longer cold, but in this pleasant stillness the conversation stopped as if severed, and would not start up again.

"What on earth got you onto Dostoyevsky and Stendhal in the middle of that gale?" Ulrich asked a while later. "If anybody had seen us they'd have thought we were crazy."

Agathe laughed. "They wouldn't have understood us anymore than the cries of the birds. . . . Anyway, you were talking to me the other day about Moosbrugger."

They walked on.

After a while, Agathe said: "I don't like him at all!"

"And I'd nearly forgotten him," Ulrich replied.

After they had again walked on in silence, Agathe stopped. "Tell me," she asked. "You've surely done some irresponsible things yourself. I remember, for instance, that you were in the hospital once with a bullet wound. You certainly don't always look before you leap . . . ?"

"What a lot of questions you're asking today!" Ulrich said. "What do you expect me to say to that?"

"Are you never sorry for anything you do?" Agathe asked quickly. "I have the impression that you never regret anything. You even said something like that once."

"Good God," Ulrich answered, beginning to walk on again. "There's a plus in every minus. Maybe I did say something like that, but you don't have to take it so literally."

"A plus in every minus?"

"Some good in everything bad. Or at least in much of the bad. A human minus-variant is likely to contain an unrecognized plus-variant—that's probably what I meant to say. Having something to regret may be just the thing to give you the strength to do something far better than you might ever have done otherwise. It's never what one does that counts, but only what one does next!"

"Suppose you've killed someone: what can you do next?"

Ulrich shrugged his shoulders. He was tempted to answer, for the sake of the argument: "It might enable me to write a poem that would enrich the inner life of thousands of people, or to come up with a great invention!" But he checked himself. "That would never happen," he thought. "Only a lunatic could imagine it. Or an eighteen-year-old aesthete. God knows why, but those are ideas that contradict the laws of nature. On the other hand," he conceded, "it did work that way for primitive man. He killed because human sacrifice was a great religious poem!"

He said neither the one thing nor the other aloud, but Agathe went on: "You may regard my objections as silly, but the first time I heard you say that what matters isn't the step one takes but always the next step after that, I thought: So if a person could fly inwardly, fly morally, as it were, and could keep flying at high speed from one improvement to the next, then he would know no remorse! I was madly envious of you!"

"That's nonsense!" Ulrich said emphatically. "What I said was that one false step doesn't matter, only the next step after that. But then what matters after the next step? Evidently the one that follows after *that*. And after the *n*th step, the *n*-plus-one step! Such a person would have to live without ever coming to an end or to a decision, indeed without achieving reality. And yet it is still true that what counts is always only the next step. The truth is, we have no proper method of dealing with this unending series. Dear Agathe," he said abruptly, "I sometimes regret my entire life."

"But that's just what you can't do!" his sister said.

"And why not? Why not that in particular?"

"I have never really done anything," Agathe replied, "and so I've always had time to regret the little I have done. I'm sure you don't know what that's like: such a dim state of mind! The shadows come, and what was has power over me. It's present in the smallest detail, and I can forget nothing and understand nothing. It's an unpleasant state of mind. . . ." Her tone was unemotional, quite unassuming. Ulrich had in fact never known this backwash of life, since his own had always been oriented toward expansion, and it merely reminded him that his sister had several times already expressed dissatisfaction with herself in strong terms. But he failed to question her because they had meanwhile reached a hilltop that he had chosen as their destination and stepped toward its edge. It was a huge mound associated by legend with a Swedish siege in the Thirty Years' War because it looked like a fortification, even though it was far too big for that: a green rampart of nature, without bush or tree, that broke off to a high, bright rock face on the side overlooking the town. A low, empty world of hills surrounded this mound; no village, no house was to be seen, only the shadows of clouds and gray pastures. Once again Ulrich felt the spell of this place, which he remembered from his youth: the town was still lying there, far below in the distance, anxiously huddled around a few churches that looked like hens herding their chicks, so that one suddenly felt like leaping into their midst with one bound and laying about one, or scooping them up in the grip of a giant hand.

"What a glorious feeling it must have been for those Swedish adventurers to reach such a place after trotting relentlessly for weeks, and then from their saddles catch sight of their quarry," he said to his sister after telling her the story of the place. "It is only at such moments that the weight of life, the burden of our secret grievance—that we must all die, that it's all been so brief and probably for nothing—is ever really lifted from us."

"What moments do you mean?"

Ulrich did not know what to answer. He did not want to answer at all. He remembered that as a young man he had always felt the need in this place to clench his teeth and keep silent. Finally, he replied: "Those romantic moments when events run away with us—the senseless moments!" He felt as if his head were a hollow nut on his neck, full of old saws like "Death be not proud" or "I care for nobody, no, not I," and with them the faded fortissimo of those years when there was not yet a boundary between life's expectations and life itself. He thought: "What single-minded and happy experiences have I had since then? None."

Agathe responded: "I've always acted senselessly, and it only makes one unhappy."

She had walked ahead, to the very edge. Her ears were deaf to her brother's words; she did not understand them, and saw a somber, barren landscape before her whose sadness harmonized with her own. When she turned around she said: "It's a place to kill oneself," and smiled. "The emptiness in my head could melt with sweet peace into the emptiness of this view!" She took a few steps back to Ulrich. "All my life," she went on, "I've been reproached with having no willpower, with loving nothing, respecting nothing; in short, for being a person with no real will to live. Papa used to scold me for it, and Hagauer blamed me for it. So now I wish you would tell me, for God's sake, tell me at long last, in which moments does something in life strike us as necessary?"

"When one turns over in bed!" Ulrich said gruffly.

"What does that mean?"

"Excuse the mundane example," he said. "But it's a fact: You're in an uncomfortable position; you incessantly think of changing it and decide on one move and then another, without doing anything; finally, you give up; and then all at once you've turned over! One really should say you've been turned over. That's the one pattern we act on, whether in a fit of passion or after long reflection." He did not look at her as he spoke; he was answering himself. He still had the feeling: Here I stood and longed for something that has never been satisfied.

Agathe smiled again, but the smile twisted her mouth as if in pain. She returned to where she had been standing and stared silently into the romantic distance. Her fur coat made a dark outline against the sky, and her slender form presented a sharp contrast to the broad silence of the landscape and the shadows of the clouds flying over it. Looking at her, Ulrich had an indescribably strong sense that something was happening. He was almost ashamed to be standing there in the company of a woman instead of beside a saddled horse. And although he was perfectly aware that the cause of this was the tranquil image emanating at this moment from his sister, he had the impression that something was happening, not to him, but somewhere in the world, and he was missing it. He felt he was being ridiculous. And yet there had been something true in his blurting out that he regretted the way he had lived his life. He sometimes longed to be wholly involved in events as in a wrestling match, even if they were meaningless or criminal, as long as they were valid, absolute, without the everlasting tentativeness they have when a person is superior to his experiences. "Something an end in itself, authentic," Ulrich thought, seriously looking for the right expression, and, unawares, his thoughts stopped pursuing imaginary events and focused on the sight that Agathe herself now presented, as nothing but the mirror of her self. So brother and sister stood for quite a while, apart and solitary, immobilized by a hesitancy filled with conflicting feelings. Most curious of all, perhaps, was that it never occurred to Ulrich that something had indeed already happened when, at Agathe's behest and in his own desire to get rid of him, he had palmed off on his unsuspecting brother-in-law the lie that there was a sealed testament that could not be opened for several days, and had assured him, also against his better knowledge, that Agathe would look after his interests: something Hagauer would subsequently refer to as "aiding and abetting."

Eventually they did move away from this spot, where each had been sunk in thought, and walked on together without having talked things out. The wind had freshened again, and because Agathe seemed fatigued, Ulrich suggested stopping to rest at a shepherd's cottage he knew of nearby. They soon found the stone cabin, and they had to duck their heads as they went in, while the shepherd's wife, staring, fended them off in embarrassment. In the mixture of German and Slavic that prevailed in this part of the country and that he still vaguely remembered, Ulrich asked if they might come in for a while to warm themselves and eat their provisions indoors, and supported this request with a tip so generous that the involuntary hostess broke out into horrified lamentations that her wretched poverty did not enable her to offer better hospitality to such "fine gentry." She wiped off the greasy table by the window, fanned a fire of twigs on the hearth, and put on some goat's milk to heat. Agathe had immediately squeezed past the table to the window without paying any attention to these efforts, as if it were a matter of course that one would find shelter somewhere, no matter where. She looked out through the dim little square of four panes at the landscape here, on the far side of the rampart, which without the wide extent of the view they had had from the top was more reminiscent of what a swimmer sees, surrounded by green crests. Though it was not yet evening, the day had passed its zenith and the light was fading.

Suddenly Agathe asked: "Why don't you ever talk to me seriously?"

How could Ulrich have found a better answer to this other than to glance up at her with an air of innocence and surprise? He was busy laying out ham, sausage, and boiled eggs on a piece of paper between himself and his sister.

But Agathe continued: "If one accidentally bumps into you it hurts, and one feels a shock at the terrific difference. But when I try to ask you something crucial you dissolve into thin air!"

She did not touch the food he pushed toward her—indeed, in her aversion to winding up the day with a rural picnic, her back was so straight that she was not even touching the table. And now something recurred that was like their climb up the country road. Ulrich shoved aside the mugs of goat's milk that had just been brought to the table from the stove and were emitting a very disagreeable smell to noses unaccustomed to it; the faint nausea it produced in him had a sobering, stimulating effect such as comes from a sudden rush of bitterness.

"I've always spoken seriously to you," he retorted. "If you don't like what I say, it's not my fault; what you don't like in my responses is the morality of our time." He suddenly realized that he wanted to explain to his sister as completely as possible all she would have to know in order to understand herself, and to some extent her brother as well. And with the firmness of a man who will brook no idle interruptions, he launched on a lengthy speech.

"The morality of our time, whatever else may be claimed, is that of achievement. Five more or less fraudulent bankruptcies are acceptable provided the fifth leads to a time of prosperity and patronage. Success can cause everything else to be forgotten. When you reach the point where your money helps win elections and buys paintings, the State is prepared to look the other way too. There are unwritten rules: if you donate to church, charities, and political parties, it needs to be no more than one tenth of the outlay required for someone to demonstrate his goodwill by patronizing the arts. And even success still has its limits; one cannot yet acquire everything in every way; some principles of the Crown, the aristocracy, and society can still to some extent restrain the social climber. On the other hand, the State, for its own suprapersonal person, quite openly countenances the principle that one may rob, steal, and murder if it will provide power, civilization, and glory. Of course, I'm not saying that all this is acknowledged even in theory; on the contrary, the theory of it is quite obscure. I just wanted to sum up the most mundane facts for you. The moral argumentation is just one more means to an end, a weapon used in much the same way as lies. This is the world that men have made, and it would make me want to be a woman—if only women did not love men!

"Nowadays we call good whatever gives us the illusion that it will get us somewhere, but this is precisely what you just called the flying man without remorse, and what I've called a problem we have no method for solving. As a scientifically trained person I feel in every situation that my knowledge is incomplete, no more than a pointer, and that perhaps tomorrow I will have new knowledge that will cause me to think differently. On the other hand, even a person wholly governed by his feelings, 'a person on the way up,' as you have depicted him, will see everything he does as a step upward, from which he is raised to the next step. So there is something in our minds and in our souls, a morality of the 'next-step'—but is that simply the morality of the five bankruptcies, is the entrepreneurial morality of our time so deeply rooted in our inner life? Or is there only the illusion of a connection? Or is the morality of the careerists a monstrosity prematurely born from deeper currents? At this point I really don't know the answer!"

Ulrich's short pause for breath was only rhetorical, for he intended to develop his views further. Agathe, however, who had so far been listening with the curiously passive alertness that was sometimes characteristic of her, switched the conversation onto a totally different track with the simple remark that she wasn't interested in this answer because all she wanted to know was where Ulrich himself stood; she was not in a position to grasp what everyone might think.

"But if you expect me to accomplish anything in any form whatsoever, I'd rather have no principles at all," she added.

"Thank God for that!" Ulrich said. "It's always a pleasure for me, every time I look at your youth, beauty, and strength, to hear from you that you have no energy at all! Our era is dripping with the energy of action. It's not interested in ideas, only in deeds. This fearful activity stems from the single fact that people have nothing to do. Inwardly, I mean. But even outwardly, in the last analysis, everyone spends his whole life repeating the same thing over and over: he gets into some occupation and then goes on with it. I think this brings us back to the question you raised before, out there in the open air. It's so simple to have the energy to act, and so hard to make any sense of it! Almost nobody understands that these days. That's why our men of action look like men bowling; they manage to knock down their nine pins with all the gestures of a Napoleon. It wouldn't even surprise me to see them ending up by assaulting each other in a frenzy, because of their inability to comprehend why all action is inadequate. . . ." He had spoken energetically at first but lapsed again, first into pensiveness, then into silence for a while. At last he just glanced up with a smile and contented himself with saying: "You say that if I expect any moral effort from you, you are bound to disappoint me. I say that if you expect any moral counsel from me, I am bound to disappoint you. I think that we have nothing definite to demand of one another—all of us, I mean; we really shouldn't demand action from one another; we should create the conditions that make action possible; that's how I feel about it."

"But how is that to be done?" Agathe said. She realized that Ulrich had abandoned the big pronouncements he had begun with and had drifted into something closer to himself, but even this was too general for her taste. She had, as we know, no use for general analysis and regarded every effort that extended beyond her own skin, as it were, as more or less hopeless; she was sure of this for her own part, and believed it was probably true of the general assertions of others too. Still, she understood Ulrich quite well. She noticed that as he sat there with his head down, speaking softly against the energy of action, her brother kept absentmindedly carving notches and lines into the table with his pocketknife, and all the sinews of his hand were tense. The unthinking but almost impassioned motion of his hand, and the frank way he had spoken of Agathe's youth and beauty, made for an absurd duet above the orchestra of the other words; nor did she try to give it a meaning other than that she was sitting here watching.

"What's to be done?" Ulrich replied in the same tone as before. "At our cousin's I once proposed to Count Leinsdorf that he should found a World Secretariat for Precision and Soul, so that even the people who don't go to church would know what they had to do. Naturally, I only said it in fun, for while we created science a long time ago for truth, asking for something similar to cope with everything else would still appear so foolish today as to be embarrassing. And yet everything the two of us have been talking about so far would logically call for such a secretariat!" He had dropped the speech and leaned back against his bench. "I suppose I'm dissolving into thin air again if I add: But how would that turn out today?"

Since Agathe did not reply, there was a silence. After a while Ulrich said: "Anyway, I sometimes think that I can't really stand believing that myself! When I saw you before, standing on the rampart," he added in an undertone, "I suddenly had a wild urge to *do* something! I don't know why. I really have done some rash things sometimes. The magic lay in the fact that when it was over, there was something more besides me. Sometimes I'm inclined to think that a person could be happy even as a result of a crime, because it gives him a certain ballast and perhaps keeps him on a steadier course."

This time, too, his sister did not answer right away. He looked at her quietly, perhaps even expectantly, but without reexperiencing the surge he had just described, indeed without thinking of anything at all. After a little while, she asked him: "Would you be angry with me if I committed a crime?"

"What do you expect me to say to that?" Ulrich said; he had bent over his knife again.

"Is there no answer?"

"No; nowadays there is no real answer."

At this point Agathe said: "I'd like to kill Hagauer."

Ulrich forced himself not to look up. The words had entered his ear lightly and softly, but when they had passed they left behind something like broad wheel marks in his mind. He had instantly forgotten her tone; he would have had to see her face to know how to take her words, but he did not want to accord them even that much importance.

"Fine," he said. "Why shouldn't you? Is there anyone left today who hasn't wanted to do something of the kind? Do it, if you really can! It's just as if you had said: 'I would like to love him for his faults!'" Now he straightened up again and looked his sister in the face. It was stubborn and surprisingly excited. Keeping his eyes on her, he said slowly:

"There's something wrong here, you see; on this frontier between what goes on inside us and what goes on outside, some kind of com-

munication is missing these days, and they adapt to each other only
with tremendous losses. One might almost say that our evil desires
are the dark side of the life we lead in reality, and the life we lead in
reality is the dark side of our good desires. Imagine if you actually did
it: it wouldn't at all be what you meant, and you'd be horribly disappointed, to say the least. . . ."

"Perhaps I could suddenly be a different person—you admitted
that yourself!" Agathe interrupted him.

As Ulrich at this moment looked around, he was reminded that
they were not alone; two people were listening to their conversation.
The old woman—hardly over forty, perhaps, but her rags and the
traces of her humble life made her look older—had sat down socia-
bly near the stove, and sitting beside her was the shepherd, who had
come home to his hut during their conversation without their noticing him, absorbed in themselves as they were. The two old people sat
with their hands on their knees and listened, or so it appeared, in
wonder and with pride to the conversation that filled their hut,
greatly pleased even though they did not understand a single word.
They saw that the milk went undrunk, the sausage uneaten; it was all
a spectacle and, for all anyone knew, an edifying one. They were not
even whispering to each other. Ulrich's glance dipped into their
wide-open eyes, and he smiled at them in embarrassment, but of the
two only the woman smiled back, while the man maintained his serious, reverential propriety.

"We must eat," Ulrich said to his sister in English. *"They're wondering about us."*

She obediently toyed with some bread and meat, and he for his
part ate resolutely and even drank a little of the milk. Meanwhile
Agathe went on, aloud and unembarrassed: "The idea of actually
hurting him is repugnant to me when I come to think of it. So maybe
I don't want to kill him. But I do want to wipe him out! Tear him into
little pieces, pound them in a mortar, flush it down the drain; that's
what I'd like to do! Root out everything that's happened!"

"This is a funny way for us to be talking," Ulrich remarked.

Agathe was silent for a while. But then she said: "But you promised me the first day you'd stand by me against Hagauer!"

"Of course I will. But not like that."

Again she was silent. Then she said suddenly: "If you bought or rented a car we could drive to my house by way of Iglau and come back the longer way around, through Tabor, I think. It would never occur to anyone that we'd been there in the night."

"And the servants? Fortunately, I can't drive!" Ulrich laughed, but then he shook his head in annoyance. "Such up-to-date ideas!"

"So you say," Agathe answered. Pensively, she pushed a bit of bacon back and forth on her plate with a fingernail, and it looked as though the fingernail, which had a greasy spot from the bacon, was doing it on its own. "But you've also said that the virtues of society are vices to the saint!"

"But I didn't say that the vices of society are virtues to the saint!" Ulrich pointed out. He laughed, caught hold of Agathe's hand, and cleaned it with his handkerchief.

"You always take everything back!" Agathe scolded him with a dissatisfied smile, the blood rushing to her face as she tried to free her finger.

The two old people by the stove, still watching exactly as before, now smiled broadly in echo.

"When you talk with me first one way, then another," Agathe said in a low but impassioned voice, "it's as if I were seeing myself in a splintered mirror. With you, one never sees oneself from head to toe!"

"No," Ulrich answered without letting go of her hand. "One never sees oneself as a whole nowadays, and one never moves as a whole— that's just it!"

Agathe gave in and suddenly stopped withdrawing her hand. "I'm certainly the opposite of holy," she said softly. "I may have been worse than a kept woman with my indifference. And I'm certainly not spoiling for action, and maybe I'll never be able to kill anyone. But when you first said that about the saint—and it was quite a while ago—it made me see something 'as a whole.' " She bowed her head, in thought or possibly to hide her face. "I saw a saint—maybe a figure on a fountain. To tell the truth, maybe I didn't see anything at all, but I felt something that has to be expressed this way. The water flowed, and what the saint did also came flowing over the rim, as if he were a fountain gently brimming over in all directions. That's how one ought to be, I think; then one would always be doing what was right and yet it wouldn't matter at all what one did."

"Agathe sees herself standing in the world overflowing with holiness and trembling for her sins, and sees with incredulity how the snakes and rhinoceroses, mountains and ravines, silent and even smaller than she is, lie down at her feet," he said, gently teasing her. "But what of Hagauer?"

"That's just it. He doesn't fit in. He has to go."

"Now I have something to tell you," her brother said. "Every time I've had to take part in anything with other people, something of genuine social concern, I've been like a man who steps outside the theater before the final act for a breath of fresh air, sees the great dark void with all those stars, and walks away, abandoning hat, coat, and play."

Agathe gave him a searching look. It was and wasn't an adequate answer.

Ulrich met her gaze. "You, too, are often plagued by a sense that there's always a 'dislike' before there's a 'like,' " he said, and thought: "Is she really like me?" Again he thought: "Perhaps the way a pastel resembles a woodcut." He regarded himself as the more stable. And she was more beautiful than he. Such a pleasing beauty! He shifted his grip from her finger to her whole hand, a warm, long hand full of life, which up to now he had held in his own only long enough for a greeting. His young sister was upset, and while there were no actual tears in her eyes, he saw a moist shimmer there.

"In a few days you'll be leaving me too," she said, "and how can I cope with everything then?"

"We can stay together; you can follow me."

"How do you suppose that would work?" Agathe asked, with the little thoughtful furrow on her forehead.

"I don't suppose at all; it's the first I've thought of it."

He stood up and gave the sheepherders some more money, "for the carved-up table."

Through a haze Agathe saw the country folk grinning, bobbing, and saying something about how glad they were, in short, incomprehensible words. As she went past them, she felt their four hospitable eyes, staring with naked emotion at her face, and realized that she and Ulrich had been taken for lovers who had quarreled and made up.

"They took us for lovers!" she said. Impetuously she slid her arm in his, and a wave of joy welled up in her. "You must give me a kiss!" she demanded, laughing, and pressed her arm in her brother's as they stood on the threshold of the hut and the low door opened into the darkness of evening.

134

HOLY DISCOURSE: BEGINNING

For the rest of Ulrich's stay little more was said about Hagauer; nor for a long time did they again refer to the idea that they should make their reunion permanent and take up life together. Nevertheless, the fire that had flamed up in Agathe's unrestrained desire to do away with her husband still smoldered under the ashes. It spread out in conversations that reached no end and yet burst out again; perhaps one should say: Agathe's feelings were seeking another possibility of burning freely.

She usually began such conversations with a definite, personal question, the inner form of which was: "May I, or may I not . . . ?" The lawlessness of her nature had until now rested on the sad and dispirited principle that "I'm allowed to do anything, but I don't want to anyway," and so his young sister's questions sometimes seemed to Ulrich, not inappropriately, like the questions of a child, which are as warm as the little hands of these helpless beings.

His own answers were different in kind, though no less character-istic: he always enjoyed sharing the yield of his experience and his reflections, and as was his custom expressed himself in a fashion as frank as it was intellectually enterprising. He always arrived quickly at the "moral of the story" his sister was talking about, summed things up in formulas, liked to use himself for illustration, and managed in this fashion to tell Agathe a great deal about himself, especially about his earlier, more eventful life. Agathe told him noth-ing about herself, but she admired his ability to speak about his own life like that, and his way of subjecting every point she raised to moral scrutiny suited her very well. For morality is nothing more than an ordering that embraces both the soul and things, so it is not strange that young people, whose zeal for life has not yet been blunted on every side, talk about it a good deal. But with a man of Ulrich's age and experience some explanation is called for, because men talk of morality only in their working lives, if it happens to be part of their professional jargon; otherwise, the word has been swallowed by the business of living and never manages to regain its freedom. So when Ulrich spoke of morality it was a sign of some profound disorder, which attracted Agathe because it corresponded to something in herself. She was ashamed, now that she heard what complicated preconditions would have to be met, of her naïve proclamation that she intended to live "in complete harmony" with herself, and yet she was impatient for her brother to come more quickly to a conclusion; for it often seemed to her that everything he said brought him closer to it, and with greater precision the further he went, but he always stopped at the last step, just at the threshold, where, every time, he gave up the attempt.

The locus of this deflection and of these last steps—and their paralyzing effect did not escape Ulrich—can most generally be indicated by noting that every proposition in European morality leads to such a point, which one cannot get beyond, so that a person taking stock of himself has first the gestures of wading in shallows, as long as he feels firm convictions underfoot, succeeded by the sudden gestures of horribly drowning when he goes a little farther, as though the solid ground of life had abruptly fallen off from the shallows into a completely imponderable abyss. This had a particular way of manifesting itself as well when brother and sister were talking: Ulrich could speak calmly and clearly on any subject he brought up, so long as his reason was involved, and Agathe felt a similar eagerness in listening; but when they stopped and fell silent, a much greater tension came over their faces. And so it happened once that they were carried across the frontier they had hitherto unconsciously respected. Ulrich had maintained that "the only basic characteristic of our morality is that its commandments contradict each other. The most moral of all propositions is: The exception proves the rule!" He had apparently been moved to this assertion only by his distaste for a system that claims to be unyielding, but in practice must yield to every deflection, which makes it the opposite of a precise procedure that first bases itself on experience and then derives the general law from these observations. He was of course aware of the distinction between natural and moral laws, that the first are derived from observing amoral nature, while the second have to be imposed on less stubborn human nature; but being of the opinion that something about this opposition was today no longer accurate, he had been just about to say that the moral system was intellectually a hundred years behind the times, which was why it was so hard to adapt it to changed conditions. But before he could get that far with his explanation Agathe interrupted him with an answer that seemed very simple, but for the moment took him aback.

"Isn't it good to be good?" she asked her brother, with a gleam in her eye like the one she'd had when she was fiddling with her father's medals, which presumably not everybody would have considered good.

"You're right," he replied eagerly. "One really has to formulate some such proposition if one wants to feel the original meaning again! But children still like being 'good' as if it were some tidbit. . . ."

"And being 'bad' as well," Agathe added.

"But does being good have any part in the passions of adults?" Ulrich asked. "It certainly is part of their principles. Not that they *are* good—they would regard that as childish—but that their behavior is good. A good person is one who has good principles and who does good things: it's an open secret that he can be quite disgusting as well."

"See Hagauer," Agathe volunteered.

"There's an absurd paradox inherent in those good people," Ulrich said. "They turn a condition into an imperative, a state of grace into a norm, a state of being into a purpose! In a whole lifetime this household of good people never serves up anything but leftovers, while keeping up a rumor that these are the scraps from a great feast day that was celebrated once. It's true that from time to time a few virtues come back into fashion, but as soon as that happens they lose their freshness again."

"Didn't you once say that the same act may be either good or bad, depending on circumstances?" Agathe asked.

Ulrich agreed. That was his theory, that moral values were not absolutes but functional concepts. But when we moralize or generalize we separate them out from their natural context: "And that is presumably the point where something goes wrong on the path to virtue."

"Otherwise, how could virtuous people be so dreary," Agathe added, "when their intention to be good ought to be the most delightful, challenging, and enjoyable thing anyone could imagine!"

Her brother hesitated, but suddenly he let slip a remark that was soon to bring them into a most unusual relationship.

"Our morality," he declared, "is the crystallization of an inner movement that is completely different from it. Not one thing we say is right! Take any statement, like the one that just occurred to me: 'Prison is a place for repentance.' It's something we can say with the best conscience in the world, but no one takes it literally, because it would mean hellfire for the prisoners! So how is one to take it? Surely few people know what repentance is, but everybody can tell you where it should reign. Or imagine that something is uplifting—how did that ever get to be part of our morals? When did we ever lie with our faces in the dust, so that it was bliss to be uplifted? Or try to imagine literally being seized by an idea—the moment you were to feel such a thing physically you'd have crossed the border into insanity! Every word demands to be taken literally, otherwise it decays into a lie; but one can't take words literally, or the world would turn into a madhouse! Some kind of grand intoxication rises out of this as a dim memory, and one sometimes wonders whether everything we experience may not be fragmented pieces torn from some ancient entity that was once put together wrong."

The conversation in which this remark occurred took place in the library-study, and while Ulrich sat over several books he had taken along on his trip, his sister was rummaging through the legal and philosophical books, a bequest of which she was the co-inheritor and out of which she picked the notions that led to her questions. Since their outing the pair had rarely left the house. This was how they spent most of their time. Sometimes they strolled in the garden, where winter had peeled the leaves from the bare shrubbery, exposing the earth beneath, swollen with rain. The sight was agonizing. The air was pallid, like something left too long under water. The garden was not large. The paths soon turned back upon themselves. The state of mind induced in both of them by walking on these paths eddied in circles, as a rising current does behind a dam. When they returned to the house the rooms were dark and sheltered, and the windows resembled deep lighting shafts through which the day arrived with all the brittle delicacy of thinnest ivory.

Now, after Ulrich's last, vehement words, Agathe descended from the library ladder on which she had been sitting and put her arms around his shoulders without a word. It was an unaccustomed show of tenderness, for apart from the two kisses, the first on the evening of their first encounter and the other a few days ago when they had set out on their way home from the shepherd's hut, the siblings' natural reserve had released itself in nothing more than words or little acts of attentiveness, and on both those occasions, too, the effect of the intimate contact had been concealed by its unexpectedness and exuberance. But this time Ulrich was instantly reminded of the still-warm garter that his sister had given the deceased as a parting gift instead of a flood of words. The thought shot through his head: "She certainly must have a lover; but she doesn't seem too attached to him, otherwise she wouldn't be staying on here so calmly." Clearly, she was a woman, who had led her life as a woman independently of him and would go on doing so. His shoulder felt the beauty of her arm from the distribution of its resting weight, and on the side turned toward his sister he had a shadowy sense of the nearness of her blond armpit and the outline of her breast. So as not to go on sitting there in mute surrender to that quiet embrace. he placed his hand over her fingers close to his neck, with this contact drowning out the other.

"You know, it's rather childish, talking the way we do," he said, not without some ill humor. "The world is full of energetic resolution, and here we sit in luxuriant idleness, talking about the sweetness of being good and the theoretical pots we could fill with it."

Agathe freed her fingers but let her hand go back to its place. "What's that you've been reading all this time?" she asked.

"You know what it is," he said. "You've been looking at the book behind my back often enough!"

"But I don't know what to make of it."

He could not bring himself to talk about it. Agathe, who had drawn up a chair, was crouching behind him and had simply nestled her face peacefully in his hair as though she were napping. Ulrich was strangely reminded of the moment when his enemy Arnheim had thrown an arm around him and the unregulated current of physical contact with another being had invaded him as through a breach. But this time his own nature did not repel the alien one; on the contrary, something in him advanced toward her, something that had been buried under the rubble of mistrust and resentment that fills the heart of a man who has lived a fairly long time. Agathe's relationship to him, which hovered between sister and wife, stranger and friend, without being equatable to any one of them, was not even based on a far-reaching accord between their thoughts or feelings, as he had often told himself, yet it was in complete accord—as he was now almost astonished to note—with the fact, which had crystallized after relatively few days full of countless impressions not easy to review in a moment, that Agathe's mouth was bedded on his hair with no further claim, and that his hair was becoming warm and moist from her breath. This was as spiritual as it was physical, for when Agathe repeated her question Ulrich was overcome with a seriousness such as he had not felt since the credulous days of his youth; and before this cloud of imponderable seriousness fled again, a cloud that extended from the space behind his back to the book before him, on which his thoughts were resting, he had given an answer that astonished him more for the total absence of irony in its tone than for its meaning:

"I'm instructing myself about the ways of the holy life."

He stood up; not to move away from his sister but in order to be able to see her better from a few steps away.

"You needn't laugh," he said. "I'm not religious; I'm studying the road to holiness to see if it might also be possible to drive a car on it!"

"I only laughed," she replied, "because I'm so curious to hear what you're going to say. The books you brought along are new to me, but I have a feeling that I would find them not entirely incomprehensible."

"You understand that?" her brother asked, already convinced that she did understand. "One may be caught up in the most intense feeling, when suddenly one's eye is seized by the play of some godforsaken, man-forsaken thing and one simply can't tear oneself away. Suddenly one feels borne up by its puny existence like a feather floating weightlessly and powerlessly on the wind."

"Except for the intense feeling you make such a point of, I think I know what you mean," Agathe said, and could not help smiling at the almost ferocious glare of embarrassment on her brother's face, not at all in keeping with the tenderness of his words. "One sometimes forgets to see and to hear, and is struck completely dumb. And yet it's precisely in minutes like these that one feels one has come to oneself for a moment."

"I would say," Ulrich went on eagerly, "that it's like looking out over a wide shimmering sheet of water—so bright it seems like darkness to the eye, and on the far bank things don't seem to be standing on solid ground but float in the air with a delicately exaggerated distinctness that's almost painful and hallucinatory. The impression one gets is as much of intensification as of loss. One feels linked with everything but can't get close to anything. You stand here, and the world stands there, overly subjective and overly objective, but both almost painfully clear, and what separates and unites these normally fused elements is a blazing darkness, an overflowing and extinction, a swinging in and out. You swim like a fish in water or a bird in air, but there's no riverbank and no branch, only this floating!" Ulrich had slipped into poetry, but the fire and firmness of his language stood out in relief against its tender and airy meaning like metal. He seemed to have cast off the caution that usually controlled him, and Agathe looked at him astonished, but also with an uneasy gladness.

"So you think," she asked, "that there's something behind it? More than a 'fit,' or whatever hateful, placating words are used?"

"I should say I do!" He sat down again at his earlier place and leafed through the books that lay there, while Agathe got up to make room for him. Then he opened one of them, with the words: "This is how the saints describe it," and read aloud:

" 'During those days I was exceeding restless. Now I sat awhile, now I wandered back and forth through the house. It was like a torment, and yet it can be called more a sweetness than a torment, for there was no vexation in it, only a strange, quite supernatural contentment. I had transcended all my faculties and reached the obscure power. There I heard without sound, there I saw without light.

And my heart became bottomless, my spirit formless, and my nature immaterial.' "

It seemed to them both that this description resembled the restlessness with which they themselves had been driven through house and garden, and Agathe in particular was surprised that the saints also called their hearts bottomless and their spirits formless. But Ulrich seemed to be caught up again in his irony.

He explained: "The saints say: Once I was imprisoned, then I was drawn out of myself and immersed in God without knowledge. The emperors out hunting, as we read about them in our storybooks, describe it differently: They tell how a stag appeared to them with a cross between its antlers, causing the murderous spear to drop from their hands; and then they built a chapel on the spot so they could get on with their hunting. The rich, clever ladies in whose circles I move will answer immediately, if you should ask them about it, that the last artist who painted such experiences was van Gogh. Or perhaps instead of a painter they might mention Rilke's poetry, but in general they prefer van Gogh, who is a superb investment and who cut his ear off because his painting didn't do enough when measured against the rapture of things. But the great majority of our people will say, on the contrary, that cutting your ear off is not a *German* way of expressing deep feelings; a German way is that unmistakable vacuousness of the elevated gaze one experiences on a mountaintop. For them the essence of human sublimity lies in solitude, pretty little flowers, and murmuring little brooks; and yet even in that bovine exaltation, with its undigested delight in nature, there lurks the misunderstood last echo of a mysterious other life. So when all is said and done, there must be something of the sort, or it must have existed at some time!"

"Then you shouldn't make fun of it," Agathe objected, grim with curiosity and radiant with impatience.

"I only make fun of it because I love it," Ulrich said curtly.

135

Holy discourse: Erratic progress

In the following days there were always many books on the table, some of which he had brought from home, others that he had bought since, and he would either talk extemporaneously or cite a passage, one of many he had marked with little slips of paper, to prove a point or quote the exact wording. The books before him were mostly lives of the mystics, their writings, or scholarly works about them, and he usually deflected the conversation from them by saying: "Now let's take a good hard look and see what's really going on here." This was a cautious attitude he was not prepared to give up easily, and so he said to her once:

"If you could read right through all these accounts that men and women of past centuries have left us, describing their state of divine rapture, you would find much truth and reality in among the printed words, and yet the statements made of these words would go wholly against the grain of your present-day mind." And he went on: "They speak of an overflowing radiance. Of an infinite expanse, a boundless opulence of light. Of an overarching oneness of all things and all the soul's energies. Of an awesome and indescribable uplifting of the heart. Of insights coming so swiftly that it's all simultaneous and like drops of fire falling into the world. And then again they speak of a forgetting and no longer understanding, even of everything falling utterly away. They speak of an immense serenity far removed from all passion. Of growing mute. A vanishing of thoughts and intentions. A blindness in which they see clearly, a clarity in which they are dead and supernaturally alive. They call it a shedding of their being, and yet they claim to be more fully alive than ever. Aren't these the same sensations, however veiled by the difficulty of expressing them, still experienced today when the heart—'greedy and gorged,' as they say!—stumbles by chance into those utopian regions situated somewhere and nowhere between infinite tenderness and infinite loneliness?"

As he paused briefly to think, Agathe's voice joined in: "It's what you once called two layers that overlie each other within us."

"I did? When?"

"When you walked aimlessly into town and felt as though you were dissolving into it, although at the same time you didn't like the place. I told you that this happens to me often."

"Oh yes! You even said 'Hagauer!'" Ulrich exclaimed. "And we laughed—now I remember. But we didn't really mean it. Anyway, it's not the only time I talked to you about the kind of vision that gives and the kind that receives, about the male and female principles, the hermaphroditism of the primal imagination and so on—I can say a lot about these things. As if my mouth were as far away from me as the moon, which is also always on hand for confidential chats in the night! But what these believers have to say about their souls' adventures," he went on, mingling the bitterness of his words with objectivity and even admiration, "is sometimes written with the force and the ruthless analytic conviction of a Stendhal. But only"—he limited this—"as long as they stick to the phenomena and their judgment doesn't enter in, which is corrupted by their flattering conviction that they've been singled out by God to have direct experience of Him. For from that moment on, of course, they no longer speak of their perceptions, which are so hard to describe and have no nouns or verbs, but begin to speak in sentences with subject and object, because they believe in their soul and in God as in the two doorposts between which the miraculous will blossom. And so they arrive at these statements about the soul being drawn out of the body and absorbed into the Lord, or say that the Lord penetrates them like a lover. They are caught, engulfed, dazzled, swept away, raped by God, or else their soul opens to Him, enters into Him, tastes of Him, embraces Him with love and hears Him speak. The earthly model for this is unmistakable, and these descriptions no longer resemble tremendous discoveries but rather a series of fairly predictable images with which an erotic poet decks out his subject, about which only one opinion is permissible. For a person like me, anyway, brought up to maintain reserve, these accounts stretch me on the rack, for the elect, even as they assure me that God has spoken to them, or that they have understood the speech of trees and animals, neglect to tell me what it was that was imparted to them; or if they do, it comes out as purely personal details, or a rehash of the *Clerical News*. It's an everlasting pity that no trained scientists have visions!" he ended his lengthy reply.

"Do you think they could?" Agathe was testing him.

Ulrich hesitated for an instant. Then he answered like a believer: "I don't know; maybe it could happen to me!" When he heard himself saying these words he smiled, as if to mitigate them.

Agathe smiled too; she now seemed to have the answer she had been hankering after, and her face reflected the small moment of letdown that follows the sudden cessation of a tension. Perhaps she now raised an objection only because she wanted to spur her brother on.

"You know," she said, "that I was raised in a very strict convent school. So I have the most scandalous urge to caricature anyone I hear talking about pious ideals. Our teachers wore a habit whose two colors formed a cross, as a sort of enforced reminder of one of the sublimest thoughts we were supposed to have before us all day long; but we never once thought it; we just called the good sisters the cross-spiders, because of the way they looked and their silky way of talking. That's why, while you were reading aloud, I didn't know whether to laugh or cry."

"Do you know what that proves?" Ulrich exclaimed. "Just that the power for good which is somehow present in us eats its way instantly through the walls if it gets locked into solid form, and immediately uses that as a bolt hole to evil! It reminds me of the time I was in the army and upheld throne and altar with my brother officers; never in my life have I heard such loose talk about both as I did in our circle! All emotions refuse to be chained, and some refuse absolutely. I'm convinced your good nuns believed what they preached to you, but faith mustn't ever be more than an hour old! That's the point!"

Although in his haste Ulrich had not expressed himself to his satisfaction, Agathe understood that the faith of those nuns who had taken away the pleasure of faith for her was merely a "bottled" variety, preserved in glass jars, so to speak, in its natural condition and not deprived of any of its qualities of faith but still not fresh; indeed, in some imponderable way it had changed into a different condition from its original one, which now hovered momentarily before this truant and rebellious pupil of holiness as a kind of intimation.

This, with everything else they had been saying about morality, was one of the gripping doubts her brother had implanted in her mind, and also part of that inner reawakening she had been feeling ever since, without rightly knowing what it was. For the attitude of indifference she made such a point of displaying outwardly and encouraging inwardly had not always ruled her life. Something had once happened that had caused her need for self-punishment to spring directly out of a deep depression, which made her appear to herself as unworthy because she believed she had not been granted the ability to keep faith with lofty emotions, and she had despised herself for her heart's sloth ever since.

This episode lay between her life as a young girl in her father's house and her incomprehensible marriage to Hagauer, and was so narrowly circumscribed that even Ulrich, for all his sympathy, had forgotten to ask about it. What had happened is soon told: At the age of eighteen Agathe had married a man only slightly older than herself, and on a trip that began with their wedding and ended in his death, he was snatched away from her within a few weeks, before they had even had time to think about choosing a place to live, by a fatal disease he had caught on their travels. The doctors called it typhus, and Agathe repeated the word after them, finding in it a semblance of order, for that was the side of the event polished smooth for the uses of the world; but on the unpolished side, it was different: until then Agathe had lived with her father, whom everyone respected, so that she reluctantly regarded herself as to blame for not loving him; and the uncertain waiting at school to become herself, through the mistrust it awakened in her mind, had not helped to stabilize her relationship to the world either. Later, on the other hand, when with suddenly aroused vivacity she had united with her childhood playmate to overcome in a matter of months all the obstacles put in the way of such a youthful marriage (even though their families had no objections to each other), she had all at once no longer been isolated and had thereby become herself. This could well be called love; but there are lovers who stare at love as into the sun and merely become blinded by it, and there are lovers who seem to discover life for the first time with astonishment when it is illuminated by love. Agathe was one of the latter kind; she had not even had time to find out whether it was her husband she loved or something else, when something struck that was called, in the language of the unilluminated world, an infectious disease. With primal suddenness horror irrupted upon them from the alien regions of life—a struggle, a flickering, an extinction; a visitation upon two human beings clinging to each other and the disappearance of an innocent world in vomiting, excrement, and fear.

Agathe had never faced up to this event that had annihilated her feelings. Bewildered with despair, she had lain on her knees at the dying man's bedside and persuaded herself that she could conjure up the power that had enabled her as a child to overcome her own illness. When his decline continued nevertheless, and his consciousness was already gone, she kept staring into the vacant face, in that hotel room far from home, unable to understand; she had held the dying body in her arms without considering the danger and without considering the realities being attended to by an indignant nurse. She had done nothing but murmur for hours into his fading ear: "You can't, you can't, you can't!" But when it was all over she had stood up in amazement, and without thinking or believing anything in particular, acting simply from a solitary nature's stubbornness and capacity to dream, she had from that moment on inwardly treated this empty astonishment at what had happened as though it were not final. We see the onset of something similar in everyone who cannot bring himself to believe bad news, or finds a way to soften the irrevocable, but Agathe's attitude was unique in the force and extent of this reaction, which marked the sudden outburst of her disdain for the world. Since then she had conscientiously assimilated anything new as something less actual than extremely uncertain, an attitude greatly facilitated by the mistrust with which she had always confronted reality; the past, on the other hand, was petrified by the blow she had suffered, and eroded by time much more slowly than usually happens with memories. But it had none of the swirl of dreams, the one-sidedness or the skewed sense of proportion that brings the doctor on the scene. On the contrary, Agathe went on living in perfect lucidity, quietly virtuous and merely a little bored, slightly inclined to that reluctance about life that was really like the fever she had suffered so willingly as a child. In her memory, which in any case never let its impressions dissolve into generalizations, every hour of what had been and still was fearful remained vivid, like a corpse under a white sheet; despite all the anguish of remembering so exactly, it made her happy, for it had the effect of a secret, belated indication that all was not yet over, and it preserved in her, despite the decay of her emotional life, a vague but high-minded tension. In truth, all it meant was that she had again lost the sense of meaning in her life and had consciously put herself in a state of mind that did not suit her years; for only old people live by dwelling on the experiences and achievements of a time that is gone and remain untouched by the present. But at the age Agathe was then, fortunately, while resolves are made for eternity a single year feels like half an eternity, and so it was only to be expected that after a time a repressed nature and a fettered imagination would violently free themselves. The details of how it happened are of no consequence in themselves; a man whose advances would in other circumstances never have succeeded in disturbing her equilibrium succeeded, and became her lover, but this attempt at reliving something ended, after a brief period of manic hope, in passionate disenchantment. Agathe now felt herself cast out by both her real life and her unreal life, and unworthy of her own high hopes. She was one of those intense people who can keep themselves motionless and in reserve for a long time, until at some point they suddenly fall prey to total confusion; and so, in her disappointment, she soon took another rash step, which was, in short, to punish herself in a way opposite to the way she had sinned, condemning herself to share her life with a man who inspired in her a mild aversion. And this man whom she had picked out as a penance was Gottlieb Hagauer.

"It was certainly both unfair to him and inconsiderate," Agathe admitted to herself—and it must be admitted that this was the first time she had ever faced up to it, because fairness and consideration are not virtues in high favor with the young. Still, her self-punishment in this marriage was not inconsiderable either, and Agathe now gave it some more thought. She had strayed far from their conversation, and Ulrich, too, was leafing through his books for something and seemed to have forgotten the conversation. "In earlier centuries," she thought, "a person in my state of mind would have entered a convent," and the fact that she had got married instead was not without an innocently comical side, which had previously escaped her. This comedy, which she had then been too young to notice, was simply that of the present day, which satisfies its need for a refuge from the world at worst in some tourist accommodation but usually in an Alpine hotel, and even strives to furnish its prisons tastefully. It expresses the profound European need not to overdo anything. No European any longer scourges himself, smears himself with ashes, cuts out his tongue, really takes part in things or totally withdraws from society, swoons with passion, breaks people on the wheel or impales them, but everyone sometimes feels the need to do so, so that it's hard to say which is more to be avoided: wanting to do it or not doing it. Why should an ascetic, of all people, starve himself? It only gives him disturbing fantasies. A sensible asceticism consists of an aversion to eating while being constantly well nourished. Such an asceticism promises longevity and offers the mind a freedom that is unattainable so long as it remains enslaved to the body in passionate rebellion. Such bitterly humorous reflections, which she had learned from her brother, were now doing Agathe a world of good, for they dissected the "tragic"—a rigid belief that in her inexperience she had long assumed to be a duty—into irony and a passion that had neither name nor aim, and for that reason alone were not bracketed with what she had experienced previously.

It was in this way above all that she had begun to realize, ever since being with her brother, that something was happening to the great split she had suffered between irresponsible living and a spectral fantasy life; there was a movement of release and of recombining what had been released. Now, for instance, in this silence between herself and her brother, which was deepened by the presence of books and memories, she thought of the description Ulrich had given her of his wandering aimlessly into town, and of how the town had entered him as he entered it. It reminded her very exactly of the few weeks of her happiness. And it had also been right for her to laugh, wildly and for no reason, when he told her about it, because it struck her that there was something of this turning of the world inside out, this delicious and funny inversion he was speaking of, even in Hagauer's thick lips when they pursed for a kiss. It made her shudder, of course, but there is a shudder, she thought, even in the bright light of noon, and it made her feel that somehow there was still hope for her. Some mere nothing, some break that had always lain between past and present, had recently vanished. She glanced around covertly. The room she was in had formed part of the space in which her fate had taken shape: it was the first time since her arrival that this had occurred to her. For it was here that she had met with her childhood friend when her father was out, and they made the great decision to love each other; here, too, she had sometimes received her "unworthy" suitor, standing at the window hiding tears of rage or desperation, and here, finally, Hagauer's courting had run its course, with her father's blessing. After having been for so long merely the unnoticed other side of events, the furniture and walls, the peculiarly confined light, now became in this moment of recognition strangely tangible, and the quixotic things that had occurred here assumed a physical and completely unambiguous pastness, as if they were ashes or burned charcoal. What remained, and became almost unbearably powerful, was that funny, shadowy sense of things done with—that strange tickling one feels when confronted with old traces, dried to dust, of one's self—which, the moment one feels it, one can neither grasp nor banish.

Agathe made sure that Ulrich was not paying attention, and carefully opened the top of her dress, where she kept next to her skin the locket with the tiny picture that she had never taken off through the years. She went to the window and pretended to look out. Cautiously, she snapped open the sharp edge of the tiny golden scallop and gazed furtively at her dead love. He had full lips and soft, thick hair, and the cocky expression of the twenty-one-year-old flashed out at her from a face still half in its eggshell. For a long time she did not know what she thought, but then suddenly the thought came: "My God, a twenty-one-year-old!"

What do such youngsters talk about with each other? What meaning do they give to their concerns? How funny and arrogant they often are! How the intensity of their ideas misleads them about the worth of those ideas! Curious, Agathe unwrapped from the tissue paper of memory some sayings that she—thank goodness for her cleverness—had preserved in it. My God, that was almost worth saying, she thought, but she could not really be sure of even that unless she also recalled the garden in which it had been spoken, with the strange flowers whose names she did not know, the butterflies that settled on them like weary drunkards, and the light that flowed over their faces as if heaven and earth were dissolved in it. By that measure she was today an old, experienced woman, even though not that many years had passed. With some confusion she noted the incongruity that she, at twenty-seven, still loved the boy of twenty-one: he had grown much too young for her! She asked herself: "What feelings would I have to have if, at my age, this boyish man were really to be the most important thing in the world to me?" They would certainly have been odd feelings, but she was not even able to imagine them clearly. It all dissolved into nothing.

Agathe recognized in a great upsurge of feeling that the one proud passion of her life had been a mistake, and the heart of this error consisted of a fiery mist she could neither touch nor grasp, no matter whether one were to say that faith could not live more than an hour, or something else. It was always this that her brother had been talking about since they had been together, and it was always herself he was speaking of, even though he hedged it about in his intellectual fashion and his diplomacy was much too slow for her impatience. They kept coming back to the same conversation, and Agathe herself blazed with desire that his flame should not diminish.

When she now spoke to Ulrich he had not even noticed how long the interruption had lasted. But whoever has not already picked up the clues to what was going on between this brother and sister should lay this account aside, for it depicts an adventure of which he will never be able to approve: a journey to the edge of the possible, which led past—and perhaps not always past—the dangers of the impossible and unnatural, even of the repugnant: a "borderline case," as Ulrich later called it, of limited and special validity, reminiscent of the freedom with which mathematics sometimes resorts to the absurd in order to arrive at the truth. He and Agathe happened upon a path that had much in common with the business of those possessed by God, but they walked it without piety, without believing in God or the soul, nor even in the beyond or in reincarnation. They had come upon it as people of this world, and pursued it as such—this was what was remarkable about it. Though at the moment Agathe spoke again Ulrich was still absorbed in his books and the problems they set him, he had not for an instant forgotten their conversation, which had broken off at the moment of her resistance to the devoutness of her teachers and his own insistence on "precise visions," and he immediately answered:

"There's no need to be a saint to experience something of the kind! You could be sitting on a fallen tree or a bench in the mountains, watching a herd of grazing cows, and experience something amounting to being transported into another life! You lose yourself and at the same time suddenly find yourself—you talked about it yourself!"

"But what actually happens?" Agathe asked.

"To know that, you first have to decide what is normal, sister human," Ulrich joked, trying to brake the much too rapid rush of the idea. "What's normal is that a herd of cattle means nothing to us but grazing beef. Or else a subject for a painting, with background. Or it hardly registers at all. Herds of cattle beside mountain paths are part of the mountain paths, and we would only notice what we experience when we see them if a big electric clock or an apartment house were to stand there in their place. For the rest, we wonder whether to get up or stay put; we're bothered by the flies swarming around the cattle; we wonder whether there's a bull in the herd; we wonder where the path goes from here—there are any number of minor deliberations, worries, calculations, and observations that make up the paper, as it were, that has the picture of the cows on it. We have no awareness of the paper, only of the cows!"

"And suddenly the paper tears!" Agathe broke in.

"Right. That is, some tissue of habit in us tears. There's no longer something edible grazing out there, or something paintable; nothing blocks your way. You can't even form the word 'grazing,' because a host of purposeful, practical connotations go along with it, which you have suddenly lost. What is left on the pictorial plane might best be called an ocean swell of sensations that rises and falls, breathes and shimmers, as though it filled your whole field of view without a horizon. Of course, there are still countless individual perceptions contained within it: colors, horns, movements, smells, and all the details of reality; but none of them are acknowledged any longer, even if they should still be recognized. Let me put it this way: the details no longer have their egoism, which they use to capture our attention, but they're all linked with each other in a familiar, literally 'inward' way. And of course the 'pictorial plane' is no longer there either; but everything somehow flows over into you, all boundaries gone."

Again Agathe picked up the description eagerly. "So instead of the egoism of the details, you only need to say the egoism of human beings," she exclaimed, "and you've got what is so hard to put into words. 'Love thy neighbor!' doesn't mean love him on the basis of what you both are; it characterizes a dream state!"

"All moral propositions," Ulrich agreed, "characterize a sort of dream state that has already flown the coop of rules in which we tether it."

"Then there's really no such thing as good and evil, but only faith—or doubt!" cried Agathe, to whom a self-supporting primal condition of faith now seemed so close, as did its disappearance from the morality her brother had spoken of when he said that faith could not live past the hour.

"Yes, the moment one slips away from a life of inessentials, everything enters into a new relationship with everything else," Ulrich agreed. "I would almost go so far as to say into a nonrelationship. For it's an entirely unknown one, of which we have no experience, and all other relationships are blotted out. But despite its obscurity, this one is so distinct that its existence is undeniable. It's strong, but impalpably strong. One might put it this way: ordinarily, we look at something, and our gaze is like a fine wire or a taut thread with two supports—one being the eye and the other what it sees, and there's some such great support structure for every second that passes; but at this particular second, on the contrary, it is rather as though something painfully sweet were pulling our eye beams apart.

"One possesses nothing in the world, one holds on to nothing, one is not held by anything," Agathe said. "It's all like a tall tree on which not a leaf is stirring. And in that condition one could not do anything mean."

"They say that nothing can happen in that condition which is not in harmony with it," Ulrich added. "A desire to 'belong to' it is the only basis, the loving vocation, and the sole form of all acting and thinking that have their place in it. It is something infinitely serene and all-encompassing, and everything that happens in it adds to its quietly growing significance; or it doesn't add to it, in which case it's a bad thing, but nothing bad can happen, because if it did the stillness and clarity would be torn and the marvelous condition would end." Ulrich gave his sister a probing look she was not meant to notice; he had a nagging feeling that it was about time to stop. But Agathe's face was impassive; she was thinking of things long past.

"It makes me wonder at myself," she answered, "but there really was a brief period when I was untouched by envy, malice, vanity, greed, and things like that. It seems incredible now, but it seems to me that they had all suddenly disappeared, not only out of my heart but out of the world! In that state it isn't only oneself who can't behave badly; the others can't either. A good person makes everything that touches him good, no matter what others may do to him; the instant it enters his sphere it becomes transformed."

"No," Ulrich cut in, "not quite. On the contrary, put that way, this would be one of the oldest misconceptions. A good person doesn't make the world good in any way; he has no effect on it whatsoever; all he does is separate himself from it."

"But he stays right in the midst of it, doesn't he?"

"He stays right in its midst, but he feels as if the space were being drawn out of things, or something or other imaginary were happening; it's hard to say."

"All the same, I have the idea that a 'highhearted' person—the word just occurred to me!—never comes in contact with anything base. It may be nonsense, but it does happen."

"It may happen," Ulrich replied, "but the opposite happens too! Or do you suppose that the soldiers who crucified Jesus didn't feel they were doing something base? And they were God's instrument! Incidentally, the mystics themselves testify to the existence of bad feelings—they complain about falling from the state of grace and then enduring unspeakable misery, knowing fear, pain, shame, and perhaps even hatred. Only when the quiet burning begins again do remorse, anger, fear, and misery turn into bliss. It's so hard to know what to make of all this!"

"When were *you* that much in love?" Agathe asked abruptly.

"Me? Oh . . . I've already told you about that: I fled a thousand miles away from the woman I loved, and once I felt safe from any possibility of really embracing her, I howled for her like a dog at the moon!"

Now Agathe confided to him the story of her love. She was excited. Her last question had snapped from her like an overly tightened violin string, and the rest followed in the same vein. She was trembling inwardly as she revealed what had been concealed for many years.

But her brother was not particularly moved. "Memories usually age along with people," he pointed out, "and with time the most passionate experiences take on a comic perspective, as though one were seeing them at the end of ninety-nine doors opened in succession. Still, sometimes certain memories that were tied to strong emotions don't age, but keep a tight grip on whole layers of one's being. That was your case. There are such points in almost everyone, which distort the psychic balance a little. One's behavior flows over them like a river over an invisible boulder—in your case this was very strong, so that it almost amounted to a dam. But you've freed yourself after all; you're moving again!"

He said this with the calm of an almost professional opinion; how easily he was diverted! Agathe was unhappy. Stubbornly she said: "Of course I'm in motion, but that's not what I'm talking about! I want to know where I almost got to back then." She was irritated too, without meaning to be, but simply because her excitement had to express itself somehow. She went on talking, nevertheless, in her original direction and was quite dizzy between the tenderness of her words and the irritation behind them. She was talking about that peculiar condition of heightened receptivity and sensitivity that brings about a rising and falling tide of impressions and creates the feeling of being connected with all things as in the gentle mirror of a sheet of water, giving and receiving without will: that miraculous feeling of the lifting of all bounds, the boundlessness of the outer and inner that love and mysticism have in common. Agathe did not, of course, put it in such terms, which already contain an explanation; she was merely making passionate fragments of her memories into a sequence. But even Ulrich, although he had often thought about it, could not offer any explanation of these experiences; indeed, he did not even know whether he should attempt to deal with such an experience in its own way or according to the usual procedures of rationality; both came naturally to him, but not to the obvious passion of his sister. And so what he said in reply was merely a mediation, a kind of testing of the possibilities. He pointed out how in the exalted state they were speaking of, thought and the moral sense went hand in hand, so that each thought was felt as happiness, event, and gift, and neither lost itself in the storerooms of the brain nor formed attachments to feelings of appropriation and power, of retention and observation; thus in the head no less than in the heart the delight of self-possession is replaced by a boundless self-giving and bonding.

"Once in a lifetime," Agathe replied with passionate decisiveness, "everything one does is done for someone else. One sees the sun shining for him. He is everywhere, oneself nowhere. But there is no egoism à deux, because the same thing must be happening with the other person. In the end, they hardly exist for each other anymore, and what's left is a world for nothing but couples, a world consisting of appreciation, devotion, friendship, and selflessness!"

In the darkness of the room her face glowed with eagerness like a rose standing in the shade.

"Let's be a little more sober again," Ulrich gently proposed. "There can be too much fakery in these matters." There was nothing wrong with that either, she thought. Perhaps it was the irritation, still not quite gone, that somewhat dampened her delight over the reality he was invoking. But this vague trembling of the borderline was a not unpleasant feeling.

Ulrich began by speaking of the mischief of interpreting the kind of experiences they were talking about not as if what was going on in them was merely a peculiar change in thinking, but as if superhuman thinking was taking the place of the ordinary kind. Whether one called it divine illumination or, in the modern fashion, merely intuition, he considered it the main hindrance to real understanding. In his opinion, nothing was to be gained by yielding to notions that would not stand up under careful investigation. That would only be like Icarus's wax wings, which melted with the altitude, he exclaimed. If one wished to fly other than in dreams, one must master it on metal wings.

He paused for a moment, then went on, pointing to his books: "Here you have testimony, Christian, Judaic, Indian, Chinese, some separated by more than a thousand years. Yet one recognizes in all of them the same uniform structure of inner movement, divergent from the ordinary. Almost the only way they differ from each other comes from the various didactic superstructures of theology and cosmic wisdom under whose protective roof they have taken shelter. We therefore may assume the existence of a certain alternative and uncommon condition of great importance, which man is capable of achieving and which has deeper origins than religions.

"On the other hand," he added, qualifying what he had said, "the churches, that is, civilized communities of religious people, have always treated this condition with the kind of mistrust a bureaucrat feels for the spirit of private enterprise. They've never accepted this riotous experience without reservations; on the contrary, they've directed great and apparently justified efforts toward replacing it with a properly regulated and intelligible morality. So the history of this alternative condition resembles a progressive denial and dilution, something like the draining of a swamp.

"And when confessional authority over the spirit and its vocabulary became outmoded, our condition understandably came to be regarded as nothing more than a chimera. Why should bourgeois culture, in replacing the old religious culture, be more religious than its predecessor? Bourgeois culture has reduced this other condition to the status of a dog fetching intuitions. There are hordes of people today who find fault with rationality and would like us to believe that in their wisest moments they were doing their thinking with the help of some special, suprarational faculty. That's the final public vestige of it all, itself totally rationalistic. What's left of the drained swamp is rubbish! And so, except for its uses in poetry, this old condition is excusable only in uneducated people in the first weeks of a love affair, as a temporary aberration, like green leaves that every so often sprout posthumously from the wood of beds and lecterns; but if it threatens to revert to its original luxuriant growth, it is unmercifully dug up and rooted out!"

Ulrich had been talking for about as long as it takes a surgeon to wash his arms and hands so as not to carry any germs into the field of operation, and also with all the patience, concentration, and evenhandedness it paradoxically takes to cope with the excitement attendant on the task ahead. But after he had completely disinfected himself he almost yearned for a little fever or infection—after all, he did not love sobriety for its own sake. Agathe was sitting on the library ladder, and even when her brother fell silent she gave no sign of participation. She gazed out into the endless oceanic gray of the sky and listened to the silence just as she had been listening to the words. So Ulrich took up the thread again, with a slight obstinacy that he barely managed to mask by his lighthearted tone.

"Let's get back to our bench on the mountain, with that herd of cows," he suggested. "Imagine some high bureaucrat sitting there in his brand-new leather shorts with 'Grüss Gott' embroidered on his green suspenders. He represents 'real life' on vacation. Of course, this temporarily alters his consciousness of his existence. When he looks at the herd of cows he neither counts them, classifies them, nor estimates the weight on the hoof of the animals grazing before him; he forgives his enemies and thinks indulgently of his family. For him the herd has been transformed from a practical object into a moral one, as it were. He may also, of course, be estimating and counting a little and not forgiving a whole lot, but then at least it is bathed in woodland murmurs, purling brooks, and sunshine. In a word, what otherwise forms the content of his life seems 'far away' and 'not all that important.' "

"It's a holiday mood," Agathe agreed mechanically.

"Exactly! If he regards his nonvacation life as 'not all that important,' it means only as long as his vacation lasts. So that is the truth today: a man has two modes of existence, of consciousness, and of thought, and saves himself from being frightened to death by ghosts—which this prospect would of necessity induce—by regarding one condition as a vacation from the other, an interruption, a rest, or anything else he thinks he can recognize. Mysticism, on the other hand, would be connected with the intention of going on vacation permanently. Our high official is bound to regard such an idea as disgraceful and instantly feel—as in fact he always does toward the end of his vacation—that *real* life lies in his tidy office. And do we feel any differently? Whether something needs to be straightened out or not will always eventually decide whether one takes it completely seriously, and here these experiences have not had much luck, for over thousands of years they have never got beyond their primordial disorder and incompleteness. And for this we have the ready label of Mania—religious mania, erotomania, take your choice. You can be assured that in our day even most religious people are so infected with the scientific way of thinking that they don't trust themselves to look into what is burning in their inmost hearts but are always ready to speak of this ardor in medical terms as a mania, even though officially they take a different line!"

Agathe gave her brother a look in which something crackled like fire in the rain. "So now you've managed to maneuver us out of it!" she accused him, when he didn't go on.

"You're right," he admitted. "But what's peculiar is that though we've covered it all up like a suspect well, some remaining drop of this unholy holy water burns a hole in all our ideals. None of our ideals is quite right, none of them makes us happy: they all point to something that's not there—we've said enough about that today. Our civilization is a temple of what would be called unsecured mania, but it is also its asylum, and we don't know if we are suffering from an excess or a deficiency."

"Perhaps you've never dared surrender yourself to it all the way," Agathe said wistfully, and climbed down from her ladder; for they were supposed to be busy sorting their father's papers and had let themselves be distracted from what had gradually become a pressing task, first by the books and then by their conversation. Now they went back to checking the dispositions and notes referring to the division of their inheritance, for the day of reckoning with Hagauer was imminent. But before they had seriously settled down to this, Agathe straightened up from her papers and asked him once more: "Just how much do you yourself believe everything you've been telling me?"

Ulrich answered without looking up. "Suppose that while your heart had turned away from the world, there was a dangerous bull among the herd. Try to believe absolutely that the deadly disease you were telling me about would have taken another course if you had not allowed your feelings to slacken for a single instant." Then he raised his head and pointed to the papers he had been sorting: "And law, justice, fair play? Do you really think they're entirely superfluous?"

"So just how much do you believe?" Agathe reiterated.

"Yes and no," Ulrich said.

"That means no," Agathe concluded.

Here chance intervened in their talk. As Ulrich, who neither felt inclined to resume the discussion nor was calm enough to get on with the business at hand, rounded up the scattered papers, something fell to the floor. It was a loose bundle of all kinds of things that had inadvertently been pulled out with the will from a corner of the desk drawer where it might have lain for decades without its owner knowing. Ulrich looked at it distractedly as he picked it up and recognized his father's handwriting on several pages; but it was not the script of his old age but that of his prime. Ulrich took a closer look and saw that in addition to written pages there were playing cards, snapshots, and all sorts of odds and ends, and quickly realized what he had found. It was the desk's "poison drawer." Here were painstakingly recorded jokes, mostly dirty; nude photographs; postcards, to be sent sealed, of buxom dairy maids whose panties could be opened behind; packs of cards that looked quite normal but showed some awful things when held up to the light; mannequins that voided all sorts of stuff when pressed on the belly; and more of the same. The old gentleman had undoubtedly long since forgotten the things lying in that drawer, or he would certainly have destroyed them in good time. They obviously dated from those mid-life years when quite a few aging bachelors and widowers warm themselves with such obscenities, but Ulrich blushed at this exposure of his father's unguarded fantasies, now released from the flesh by death. Their relevance to the discussion just broken off was instantly clear to him. Nevertheless, his first impulse was to destroy this evidence before Agathe could see it. But she had already noticed that something unusual had fallen into his hands, so he changed his mind and asked her to come over.

He was going to wait and hear what she would say. Suddenly the realization possessed him again that she was, after all, a woman who must have had her experiences, a point he had totally lost sight of while they were deep in conversation. But her face gave no sign of what she was thinking; she looked at her father's illicit relics seriously and calmly, at times smiling openly, though not animatedly. So Ulrich, despite his resolve, began.

"Those are the dregs of mysticism!" he said wryly. "The strict moral admonitions of the will in the same drawer as this swill!"

He had stood up and was pacing back and forth in the room. And once he had begun to talk, his sister's silence spurred him on.

"You asked me what I believe," he began. "I believe that all our moral injunctions are concessions to a society of savages.

"I believe none of them are right.

"There's a different meaning glimmering behind them. An alchemist's fire.

"I believe that nothing is ever done with.

"I believe that nothing is in balance but that everything is trying to raise itself on the fulcrum of everything else.

"That's what I believe. It was born with me, or I with it."

He had stood still after each of these sentences, for he spoke softly and had somehow or other to give emphasis to his credo. Now his eye was caught by the classical busts atop the bookshelves; he saw a plaster Minerva, a Socrates; he remembered that Goethe had kept an over-lifesize plaster head of Juno in his study. This predilection seemed alarmingly distant to him; what had once been an idea in full bloom had since withered into a dead classicism. Turned into the rearguard dogmatism of rights and duties of his father's contemporaries. All in vain.

"The morality that has been handed down to us," he said, "is like being sent out on a swaying high wire over an abyss, with no other advice than: 'Hold yourself as stiff as you can!'

"I seem, without having had a say in the matter, to have been born with another kind of morality.

"You asked me what I believe. I believe there are valid reasons you can use to prove to me a thousand times that something is good or beautiful, and it will leave me indifferent; the only mark I shall go by is whether its presence makes me rise or sink.

"Whether it rouses me to life or not.

"Whether it's only my tongue and my brain that speak of it, or the radiant shiver in my fingertips.

"But I can't prove anything, either.

"And I'm even convinced that a person who yields to this is lost. He stumbles into twilight. Into fog and nonsense. Into unarticulated boredom.

"If you take the unequivocal out of our life, what's left is a sheepfold without a wolf.

"I believe that bottomless vulgarity can even be the good angel that protects us.

"And so, I don't believe!

"And above all, I don't believe in the domestication of evil by good as the characteristic of our hodgepodge civilization. I find that repugnant.

"So I believe and don't believe!

"But maybe I believe that the time is coming when people will on the one hand be very intelligent, and on the other hand be mystics. Maybe our morality is already splitting into these two components. I might also say into mathematics and mysticism. Into practical improvements and unknown adventure!"

He had not been so openly excited about anything in years. The "maybe"s in his speech did not trouble him; they seemed only natural.

Agathe had meanwhile knelt down before the stove; she had the bundle of pictures and papers on the floor beside her. She looked at everything once more, piece by piece, before pushing it into the fire. She was not entirely unsusceptible to the vulgar sensuality of the obscenities she was looking at. She felt her body being aroused by them. This seemed to her to have as little to do with her self as the feeling of being on a deserted heath and somewhere a rabbit scutters past. She did not know whether she would be ashamed to tell her brother this, but she was profoundly fatigued and did not want to talk anymore. Nor did she listen to what he was saying; her heart had by now been too shaken by these ups and downs, and could no longer keep up. Others had always known better than she what was right; she thought about this, but she did so, perhaps because she was ashamed, with a secret defiance. To walk a forbidden or secret path: in that she felt superior to Ulrich. She heard him time and again cautiously taking back everything he had let himself be carried away into saying, and his words beat like big drops of joy and sadness against her ear.

136

ULRICH RETURNS AND LEARNS FROM THE GENERAL WHAT HE HAS MISSED

Forty-eight hours later Ulrich was standing in his abandoned house. It was early in the morning. The house was meticulously tidy, dusted and polished; his books and papers lay on the tables precisely as he had left them at his hasty departure, carefully preserved by his servant, open or bristling with markers that had become incomprehensible, this or that paper still with a pencil stuck between the pages. But everything had cooled off and hardened like the contents of a melting pot under which one has forgotten to stoke the fire. Painfully disillusioned, Ulrich stared blankly at these traces of a vanished hour, matrix of the intense excitement and ideas that had filled it. He felt repelled beyond words at this encounter with his own debris. "It spreads through the doors and the rest of the house all the way down to those idiotic antlers in the hall. What a life I've been leading this last year!" He shut his eyes where he stood, so as not to have to see it. "What a good thing she'll soon be following me," he thought. "We'll change everything!" Then he was tempted after all to visualize the last hours he had spent here; it seemed to him that he had been away for a very long time, and he wanted to compare.

Clarisse: that was nothing. But before and after: the strange turmoil in which he had hurried home, and then that nocturnal melting of the world! "Like iron softening under some great pressure," he mused. "It begins to flow, and yet it is still iron. A man forces his way into the world," he thought, "but it suddenly closes in around him, and everything looks different. No more connections. No road on which he came and which he must pursue. Something shimmering enveloping him on the spot where a moment ago he had seen a goal, or actually the sober void that lies before every goal." Ulrich kept his eyes closed. Slowly, as a shadow, his feeling returned. It happened as if it were returning to the spot where he had stood then and was again standing now, this feeling that was more out there in the room than in his consciousness—it was really neither a feeling nor a thought, but some uncanny process. If one were as overstimulated and lonely as he had been then, one could indeed believe that the essence of the world was turning itself inside out; and suddenly it dawned on him—how was it possible that it was happening only now?—and lay there like a peaceful backward glance, that even then his feelings had announced the encounter with his sister, because from that moment on his spirit had been guided by strange forces, until . . . but before he could think "yesterday," Ulrich turned away, awakened as abruptly and palpably from his memories as if he had bumped against some solid edge. There was something here he was not yet ready to think about.

He went over to his desk and without taking off his coat looked through the mail lying there. He was disappointed not to find a telegram from his sister, although he had no reason to expect one. A huge pile of condolence mail lay intermingled with scientific communications and booksellers' catalogs. Two letters had come from Bonadea; both so thick that he did not bother to open them. There was also an urgent request from Count Leinsdorf that he come to see him, and two fluting notes from Diotima, also inviting him to put in an appearance immediately upon his return; perused more closely, one of them, the later one, revealed unofficial overtones of a very warm, wistful, almost tender cast. Ulrich turned to the telephone messages that had come during his absence: General Stumm von Bordwehr, Section Chief Tuzzi, Count Leinsdorf's private secretary (twice), several calls from a lady who would not leave her name, probably Bonadea; Bank Director Leo Fischel; and, for the rest, business calls. While Ulrich was reading all this, still standing at his desk, the phone rang, and when he lifted the receiver a voice said: "War Ministry, Culture and Education, Corporal Hirsch," clearly taken aback at finding itself unexpectedly ricocheting off Ulrich's own voice, but hastening to explain that His Excellency the General had given orders to ring Ulrich every morning at ten, and that His Excellency would speak to him right away.

Five minutes later Stumm was assuring him that he had to attend some "supremely important meetings" that very morning, but absolutely had to speak to Ulrich first. When Ulrich asked what about, and why it could not be taken care of over the phone, Stumm sighed into the receiver and proclaimed "news, worries, problems," but could not be made to say anything more specific. Twenty minutes later a War Ministry carriage drew up at the gate and General Stumm entered the house, followed by an orderly with a large leather briefcase slung from his shoulder. Ulrich, who well remembered this receptacle for the General's intellectual problems from the battle plans and ledger pages of Great Ideas, raised his eyebrows interrogatively. Stumm von Bordwehr smiled, sent the orderly back to the carriage, unbuttoned his tunic to get out the little key for the security lock, which he wore on a fine chain around his neck, unlocked the case, and wordlessly exhumed its sole contents, two loaves of regulation army bread.

"Our new bread," he declared after a dramatic pause. "I've brought you some for a taste!"

"How nice of you," Ulrich said, "bringing me bread after I've spent a night traveling, instead of letting me get some sleep."

"If you have some schnapps in the house, which one may assume," the General retorted, "then there's no better breakfast than bread and schnapps after a sleepless night. You once told me that our regulation bread was the only thing you liked about the Emperor's service, and I'll go so far as to say that the Austrian Army beats any other army in the world at making bread, especially since our Commissariat brought out this new loaf, Model 1914! So I brought you one, though that's not the only reason. The other is that I always do this now on principle. Not that I have to spend every minute at my desk, or account for every step I take out of the room, you understand, but you know that our General Staff isn't called the Jesuit Corps for nothing, and there's always talk when a man is out of the office a lot; also my chief, His Excellency von Frost, may not, perhaps, have a completely accurate idea of the scope of the mind—the civilian mind, I mean—and that's why for some time now I've been taking along this official bag and an orderly whenever I want to go out for a bit; and since I don't want the orderly to think that the bag is empty, I always put two loaves of bread in it."

Ulrich could not help laughing, and the General cheerfully joined in.

"You seem to be less enchanted with the great ideas of mankind than you were?" Ulrich asked.

"Everyone is less enchanted with them," Stumm declared while he sliced the bread with his pocketknife. "The new slogan that's been handed out is 'Action!' "

"You'll have to explain that to me."

"That's what I came for. You're not the true man of action."

"I'm not?"

"No."

"Well, I don't know about that."

"Maybe I don't either. But that's what they say."

"Who's 'they'?"

"Arnheim, for one."

"You're on good terms with Arnheim?"

"Well, of course. We get along famously. If he weren't such a high-brow we could be on a first-name basis by now!"

"Are you involved with the oil fields too?"

To gain time, the General drank some of the schnapps Ulrich had had brought in and chewed on the bread. "Great taste," he brought out laboriously, and kept on chewing.

"Of course you're involved with the oil fields!" Ulrich burst out, suddenly seeing the light. "It's a problem that concerns your naval branch because it needs fuel for its ships, and if Arnheim wants the drilling fields he'll have to concede a favorable price for you. Besides, Galicia is deployment territory and a buffer against Russia, so you have to provide special safeguards in case of war for the oil supply he wants to develop there. So his munitions works will supply you with the cannons you want! Why didn't I see this before? You're positively born for each other!"

The General had taken the precaution of munching on a second piece of bread, but now he could contain himself no longer, and making strenuous efforts to gulp down the whole mouthful at once, he said: "It's easy for you to talk so glibly about an accommodation; you've no idea what a skinflint he is! Sorry—I mean, you have no idea," he amended himself, "what moral dignity he brings to a business deal like this. I never dreamed, for example, that ten pennies per ton per railway mile is an ethical problem you have to read up on in Goethe or the history of philosophy."

"You're conducting these negotiations?"

The General took another gulp of schnapps. "I never said that negotiations were going on! You could call it an exchange of views, if you like."

"And you're empowered to conduct them?"

"Nobody's empowered! We're talking, that's all. Surely one can talk now and then about something besides the Parallel Campaign? And if anyone were empowered, it certainly wouldn't be me; that's no job for the Culture and Education Department, it's a matter for the higher-ups, even the Chiefs of Staff. If I had anything at all to do with it, it would be only as a kind of technical adviser on civilian intellectual questions, an interpreter, so to speak, because of Arnheim being so educated."

"And because you're always running into him, thanks to me and Diotima! My dear Stumm, if you want me to go on being your stalking horse, you'll have to tell me the truth!"

But Stumm had had time to prepare himself for this. "Why are you asking, if you know it already?" he countered indignantly. "Do you think you can nail me down and that I don't know that Arnheim takes you into his confidence?"

"I don't know a thing!"

"But you've just been telling me that you do know."

"I know about the oil fields."

"And then you said that we have a common interest with Arnheim in those oil fields. Give me your word of honor that you know this, then I can tell you everything." Stumm von Bordwehr seized Ulrich's reluctant hand, looked him in the eye, and then said slyly:

"All right, since you're giving me your word of honor that you knew everything already, I give you mine that you know all there is. Agreed? There isn't anything more. Arnheim is trying to use us, and we him. I sometimes have the most complicated spiritual conflicts over Diotima!" he exclaimed. "But you mustn't say a word to anyone; it's a military secret!" The General waxed cheerful. "Do you know, incidentally, what a military secret is?" he went on. "A few years ago, when they were mobilizing in Bosnia, the War Ministry wanted to ax me. I was still a colonel then, and they gave me the command of a territorial battalion; of course, I could have been given a brigade, but since I'm supposed to be Cavalry, and since they wanted to ax me, they sent me to a battalion. And since you need money to fight a war, once I got there they sent me the battalion cashbox too. Did you ever see one of those in your time in the army? It looks like a cross between a coffin and a corn crib; it's made of heavy wood with iron bands all around, like the gate to a fortress. It has three locks, and three officers carry the keys to them, one each, so that no one can unlock it by himself: the commander and his two co-cashbox-key-unlockers. Well, when I got there we congregated as if for a prayer meeting, and one after the other we each opened a lock and reverently took out the bundles of banknotes. I felt like a high priest with two acolytes, only instead of reading the Gospel we read out the figures from the official ledger. When we were done we closed up the box, put the iron bands back on, and locked the locks, the whole thing over again, except in reverse order. I had to say something I can't remember now, and that was the end of the ceremony. Or so I thought, and so you'd have thought, and I was full of respect for the unflagging foresight of the military administration in wartime! But I had a fox terrier in those days, the predecessor to the one I have now; there was no regulation against it. He was a clever little beast, but he couldn't see a hole without starting to dig like mad. So as I was going out I noticed that Spot—that was his name; he was English—was busying himself with the cashbox, and there was no getting him away from it. Well, you keep hearing stories about faithful dogs uncovering the darkest conspiracies, and war was almost upon us too, so I thought to myself, Let's see what's up with Spot. And what do you suppose was the matter with Spot? You must remember that Ordnance doesn't provide the field battalions with the very latest supplies, so our cashbox was a venerable antique, but who would ever have thought that while the three of us were locking up in front, it had a hole in the back, near the bottom, wide enough to put your arm through? There'd been a knot in the wood there, which had fallen out in some previous war. But what was to be done? The whole Bosnian scare was just over when the relief troops we had applied for came, and until then we could go through our ceremony every week, except that I had to leave Spot home so he wouldn't give our secret away. So you see, that's what a military secret sometimes looks like!"

"Hmm . . . it seems to me you're still not quite so open as that cashbox of yours," Ulrich commented. "Are you fellows really closing the deal or not?"

"I don't know. I give you my word of honor as an officer on the General Staff: it hasn't come to that yet."

"And Leinsdorf?"

"He hasn't the faintest idea, of course. Besides, he wouldn't have anything to do with Arnheim. I hear he's still terribly angry about the demonstration—you remember, you were there too. He's now dead set against the Germans."

"Tuzzi?" Ulrich asked, continuing the cross-examination.

"He's the last man we'd want to find out anything! He would ruin the scheme at once. Of course we all want peace, but we military men have a different way of serving it than the bureaucrats."

"And Diotima?"

"Oh, my dear fellow, please! This is altogether a man's affair; she couldn't think of such things even with gloves on! I certainly can't bring myself to burden her with the truth. And I can see why Arnheim wouldn't tell her anything about it. He talks such a lot and so beautifully, it might well be a pleasure for him to hold his tongue about something for once. Like taking a dose of bitters for the stomach, I imagine."

"Do you realize that you've turned into a rogue?" Ulrich asked, and raised his glass. "Here's to your health!"

"No, not a rogue," the General defended himself. "I'm a member of a ministerial council. At a meeting everyone proposes what he would like and thinks right, and in the end something comes out that no one really wanted, the so-called outcome. I don't know if you follow me—I can't express it any better."

"Of course I follow you. But the way you're all treating Diotima is disgraceful, just the same."

"I'd be sorry to think so," Stumm said. "But a hangman, you know, is a disreputable fellow, no question about it; yet the rope manufacturer who supplies the prison with the rope can be a member of the Ethical Society. You don't take that sufficiently into account."

"You got that from Arnheim!"

"Could be. I don't know. One's mind gets so complicated nowadays," the General complained sincerely.

"And where do I come in?"

"Well, you see, I was thinking, here you are, a former army officer . . ."

"Never mind. But what has this to do with being, or not being, a 'man of action'?" Ulrich asked, affronted.

"Man of action?" the General echoed, mystified.

"You began everything by saying I wasn't a man of action."

"Oh, that. That's got nothing at all to do with it; I just happened to start with it. I mean, Arnheim doesn't exactly think of you as a man of action; he once said so. You have nothing to do, he says, and that puts ideas into your head. Or words to that effect."

"Idle ideas, you mean? Ideas that can't be 'introduced in spheres of power'? Ideas for their own sake? In short, true and independent ideas! Is that it? Or possibly the ideas of an 'unworldly aesthete'?"

"Well," Stumm von Bordwehr agreed diplomatically, "something like that."

"Like what? What do you think is more dangerous to the life of the mind—dreams or oil fields? There's no need to stuff your mouth with bread; stop it! I couldn't care less what Arnheim thinks of me. But you started off by saying, 'Arnheim, for one.' So who else is there who doesn't see me as enough of a man of action?"

"Well, you know," Stumm affirmed, "quite a few. I told you that 'Action!' is now the great rallying cry."

"What does that mean?"

"I don't really know either. Old man Leinsdorf said: 'Something has to be done!' That's how it started."

"And Diotima?"

"Diotima calls it a New Spririt. So now lots of people on the Council are saying that. I wonder if you know what it's like, that dizzy feeling in your stomach when a beautiful woman has such a head on her shoulders?"

"I'll take your word for it," Ulrich conceded, refusing to let Stumm wriggle out of it. "But now I'd like to hear what Diotima has to say about this New Spirit."

"It's what people are saying," Stumm answered. "The people on the Council are saying that the times are getting a New Spirit. Not right away, but in a few years; unless something unexpected happens sooner. And this New Spirit won't have many ideas in it. Nor is it a time for feelings. Ideas and feelings—they're more for people who have nothing to do. In short, it's a spirit of action, that's really all I know about it. But it has sometimes occurred to me," the General added pensively, "to wonder if, in the end, that isn't simply the military spirit?"

"An action has to make sense!" Ulrich claimed, and in all seriousness, far beyond this jesters' motley conversation, his conscience reminded him of the first conversation he had had on that subject with
Agathe, on the Swedish rampart.

But the General agreed. "That's what I just said. If someone
doesn't have anything to do, and doesn't know what to do with himself, he becomes energetic. Then he starts boozing, bawling, brawl-
ing, and bullying man and beast. On the other hand, you'll have to
admit that someone who knows exactly what he wants can be an intri-
guer. Just look at any of our youngsters on the General Staff, silently
pressing his lips together and making a face like Moltke: In ten years
he'll have a general's paunch under his tunic buttons—not a benign
one, like mine, but a bellyful of poison. So it's hard to decide how
much sense any action can make." He thought it over, and added: "If
you know how to get hold of it, there's a great deal to be learned in
the army—I'm more and more convinced of it as time goes on—but
don't you think the simplest thing would be if we could still find the
Great Idea?"

"No," Ulrich retorted. "That was nonsense."

"All right, but in that case there's really nothing left but action."
Stumm sighed. "It's almost what I've been saying myself. Do you remember, by the way, my warning you once that all these excessive
ideas only end up in homicide? That's what we've got to prevent!
But," he wheedled, "what we need is someone to take over the leadership."

"And what part have you had the kindness to assign to me in the
matter?" Ulrich asked, yawning openly.

"Very well, I'm leaving," Stumm assured him. "But now that we've
had this heart-to-heart talk, if you wanted to be a true comrade there
is something important you could do. Things are not going too well
between Diotima and Arnheim."

"You don't say!" His host showed some small signs of life.

"You'll see for yourself; no need to take it from me. Besides, she
confides in you more than in me."

"She confides in you? Since when?"

"She seems to have got used to me a little," the General said
proudly.

"Congratulations."

"Thanks. And you ought to look in on Leinsdorf again soon. On account of his antipathy to the Prussians."

"I won't do it."

"Now look, I know you don't like Arnheim. But you'll have to do it anyway."

"That's not why. I have no intention of going back to Leinsdorf."

"But why not? He's such a fine old gentleman. Arrogant, and I can't stand him, but he's been splendid to you."

"I'm getting out of this whole affair."

"But Leinsdorf won't let you go. Nor Diotima either. And I certainly won't! You wouldn't leave me all alone . . .?"

"I'm fed up with the whole stupid business."

"You are, as always, supremely right. But what isn't stupid? Look, without you, I'm pretty dumb. So will you go to Leinsdorf for my sake?"

"But what's this about Diotima and Arnheim?"

"I won't tell you; otherwise you won't go to Diotima either!" Suddenly the General had an inspiration. "If you like, Leinsdorf can get you an assistant to take care of whatever you don't like. Or I can get you one from the War Ministry. Pull out as far as you like, but keep a guiding hand over me!"

"Let me get some sleep first," Ulrich pleaded.

"I won't go till you promise."

"All right, I'll sleep on it," Ulrich conceded. "Don't forget to put the bread of military science back in your bag."

137

WHAT'S NEW WITH WALTER AND CLARISSE. A
SHOWMAN AND HIS SPECTATORS

Toward evening his restlessness drove Ulrich to go out to Walter and Clarisse's. On the way he tried to remember Clarisse's letter, which he had either stowed away irretrievably in his luggage or lost, but he could recall nothing in detail except for a final sentence, "I hope you'll be coming back soon," and his general impression that he would really have to talk with Walter, a feeling tinged not only with regret and uneasiness but also with a certain malice. It was this fleeting and involuntary feeling, of no significance, that he now dwelled on instead of brushing it aside, feeling rather like someone with vertigo who finds relief by getting himself down as low as he can.

When he turned the corner to the house, he saw Clarisse standing in the sun by the side wall where the espaliered peach tree was. She had her hands behind her and was leaning back against the yielding branches, gazing into the distance, oblivious to his approach. There was something self-forgetful and rigid in her attitude, but also something faintly theatrical, apparent only to the friend who knew her ways so well; she looked as if she were acting out a part in the significant drama of her own ideas and one of those ideas had taken hold of her, refusing to let go. He remembered her saying to him: "I want the child from you!" The words did not affect him as disagreeably now as they had at the time; he called out to her softly and waited.

But Clarisse was thinking: "This time Meingast is going through his transformation in our house." He had undergone several rather remarkable transformations in his lifetime, and without reacting to Walter's lengthy answer to his letter, he had, one day, turned the announcement of his coming into reality. Clarisse was convinced that the work he then immediately plunged into in their house had to do with a transformation. The thought of some Indian god who takes up his abode somewhere before each new purification mingled in her mind with the memory of creatures that choose a specific place to change into a pupa, and from this notion, which struck her as tremendously healthy and down-to-earth, she went on to take in the sensuous fragrance of peaches ripening on a sunny wall. The logical result of all this was that she was standing under the window in the glow of the sinking sun, while the prophet had withdrawn into the shadowy cavern behind it. The day before, he had explained to her and Walter that in its original sense "knight" had meant boy, servant, squire, man-at-arms, and hero. Now she said to herself, "I am his knight!" and served him and safeguarded his labors: There was no need to say a word; she simply stood still, dazzled, and faced down the rays of the sun.

When Ulrich spoke to her she slowly turned her face toward the unexpected voice, and he discovered that something had changed. The eyes that looked toward him contained a chill such as the colors of a landscape radiate after the dying of day, and he instantly realized: She no longer wants anything from you! There was no trace anymore in her look of how she had wanted to "force him out of his block of stone," of his having been a great devil or god, of wanting to escape with him through the hole in the music, of wanting to kill him if he would not love her. Not that he cared; it was doubtless a quite ordinary little experience, this extinguished glow of self-interest in a gaze; still, it was like a small rent in the veil of life through which the indifferent void stares out, and it laid the basis for much that was to happen later.

Ulrich was told that Meingast was there, and understood.

They went quietly into the house to fetch Walter, and the three of them just as quietly came back out of doors again so as not to disturb the great man working. Through an open door Ulrich twice caught a glimpse of Meingast's back. Meingast was housed in an empty room detached from the rest of the apartment but belonging to it; Clarisse and Walter had dug up an iron bedstead somewhere for him; a kitchen stool and a tin basin served as a washstand and bath, and in addition to these the room, with its uncurtained window, held only an old kitchen cupboard containing books, and a small, unpainted deal table. Meingast sat at this table writing, and did not turn his head when they passed his door. All this Ulrich either saw for himself or found out from his friends, who had no scruples about providing much more primitive accommodations for the Master than they had themselves; on the contrary, for some reason, they seemed to take pride in his being content with it. It was touching, and it made things easy for them. Walter declared that if one went into this room in Meingast's absence one felt the indescribable aura of a threadbare old glove that had been worn on a noble and forceful hand.

And in fact Meingast greatly enjoyed working in these surroundings, whose spartan simplicity flattered him. It made him feel his will forming the words on paper. And when in addition Clarisse was standing under his window, as she had been just then, or on the landing, or even if she was merely sitting in her room—"wrapped in the cloak of invisible northern lights," as she had confided to him—his pleasure was enhanced by this ambitious disciple on whom he had such a paralyzing effect. Then ideas simply flowed from his pen, and his huge dark eyes above the sharp, quivering nose began to glow. What he intended to complete under these circumstances would be one of the most important sections of his new book, and one ought to be allowed to call it not a book but a call to arms for the spirit of a new breed of men! When he heard an unfamiliar male voice coming from where Clarisse was standing, he had broken off and cautiously peered out; he did not recognize Ulrich, though he dimly remembered him, but he found no reason in the footsteps coming up the stairs to shut his door or turn his head from his work. He wore a heavy wool cardigan under his jacket, showing his imperviousness to weather and people.

Ulrich was taken out for a walk and treated to ecstatic praise of the Master, who was meanwhile devoting himself to his work.

Walter said: "Being friends with a man like Meingast makes one realize how much one has suffered from antipathy to others! Associating with him, one feels . . . let me put it this way: everything seems painted in pure colors, without any grays at all!"

Clarisse said: "Being with him, one feels one has a destiny. There one stands, entirely oneself, fully illuminated."

Walter added: "Today everything splits into hundreds of layers and becomes opaque and blurred—*his* mind is like glass!"

Ulrich's reply to them was: "There are always scapegoats and bellwethers; and then there are sheep who need them!"

Walter flung back at him: "It was to be expected that such a man wouldn't suit you!"

Clarisse cried out: "You once maintained that no one can live by ideas, remember? Well, Meingast can!"

Walter said more soberly: "Not that I always see eye-to-eye with him, of course . . ."

Clarisse broke in: "Listening to him, one feels shudders of light inside."

Ulrich retorted: "A particularly fine head on a man usually means that he's stupid; particularly deep philosophers are usually shallow thinkers; in literature, talents not much above average are usually regarded by their contemporaries as geniuses."

What a curious phenomenon admiration is! In the life of individuals it occurs only in spasms, but it is firmly institutionalized in collective life. Walter would actually have found it more satisfying if he himself could have occupied Meingast's place in his own and Clarisse's esteem, and could not at all understand why this was not so; and yet there was a certain slight advantage in it too. The emotion he was spared in this way was likewise credited to Meingast's account, as when one adopts someone else's child as one's own. On the other hand, it was for this very reason that his admiration for Meingast was not really a pure and wholesome feeling, as Walter himself realized; it was rather an overcharged need to surrender himself to believing in him. There was something assiduous in this admiration; it was a "keyboard emotion," raging without real conviction. Ulrich sensed this too. One of the elementary needs for passion, which life today breaks into fragments and jumbles to the point where they are unrecognizable, was here seeking a way back, for Walter praised Meingast with the ferocity of a theater audience that applauds far beyond the limits of its real opinion the commonplaces that are designed to arouse its need to applaud. He praised him out of one of those desperate urges to admire, which normally find their outlet in festivals and celebrations, in great contemporaries or ideas and the honors bestowed on them, in situations where everyone involved joins in without anybody really knowing for whom or for what, while being inwardly prepared to be twice as mean as usual the next day in order to have nothing to reproach oneself for. This was how Ulrich thought about his friends, and he kept them on their toes by aiming barbed remarks at Meingast from time to time; for like everyone who knows better, he had been annoyed countless times by his contemporaries' capacity for enthusiasms, which almost invariably fasten on the wrong object and so end up destroying even what indifference has let survive.

Dusk had already fallen by the time they had returned, still talking, to the house.

"This Meingast lives on our current confusion of intuition and faith," Ulrich finally said. "Almost everything that isn't science can only be intuited, and for that you need passion and prudence. So a methodology for dealing with what we don't know is almost the same as a methodology for life. But you two 'believe' the minute someone like Meingast comes along! And so does everyone. But this 'belief' is almost as much of a disaster as if you decided to plump your esteemed bodies down on a basket of eggs to hatch their unknown contents!"

They were standing at the foot of the stairs. And suddenly Ulrich realized why he had come here and was talking with them the way he used to. It did not surprise him when Walter answered:

"And the world is supposed to stand still until you've worked out your methodology?"

They evidently did not take him seriously because they did not realize how desolate this area of faith was that stretches between the certainty of knowledge and the mists of intuition! Old ideas swarmed in his head, crowding so thickly they almost suffocated thought. But now he knew that it was no longer necessary to start all over again, like a carpet weaver whose mind has been blinded by a dream, and that this was the only reason he was here again. Everything had become so much simpler lately. The last two weeks had annulled everything that had gone before and had tied up the lines of his inner motions with a powerful knot.

Walter was expecting Ulrich to give him an answer that he could resent. He wanted to pay him back with interest! He had made up his mind to tell Ulrich that people like Meingast were saviors. "Salvation, after all, means the same thing as making one whole," he thought. And: "Saviors may be wrong, but they make us whole again!" he intended to say. And he was going to add: "I don't suppose you have any idea what that means?" The resentment he felt toward Ulrich was like what he felt when he had to go to the dentist.

But Ulrich merely asked him distractedly just what Meingast had actually been writing and doing in the past few years.

"You see!" Walter said, disappointed. "You see, you don't even know that much, but you disparage him!"

"Well," Ulrich said lightly, "I don't have to know; a few lines are sufficient!" He set his foot on the stairs. But Clarisse held him by the jacket and whispered: "Meingast isn't even his real name!"

"Of course it isn't; but is that a secret?"

"He turned into Meingast once, and now that he's here with us he's changing again!" Clarisse whispered intensely and mysteriously, and this whisper had something in common with a blowtorch. Walter flung himself on it to put it out. "Clarisse!" he implored her. "Clarisse, stop this nonsense!"

Clarisse kept quiet and smiled. Ulrich went ahead up the stairs; he wanted at long last to see this messenger who had descended upon Walter and Clarisse's domestic life from Zarathustra's mountains. By the time they got upstairs, Walter was in a temper not only at him but at Meingast as well.

Meingast received his admirers in their dark apartment. He had seen them coming, and Clarisse immediately walked over to him where he stood against the gray windowpane, becoming a small pointed shadow beside his tall gaunt one. There was no introduction, or only a one-sided one in that Ulrich's name was mentioned in order to refresh the Master's memory. Then they were all silent. Ulrich, being curious to see how the situation would develop, positioned himself at the other, unoccupied, window, and Walter made the surprising move of joining him there, probably for no better reason than, being subject to momentarily equal forces of repulsion, he was attracted by the stimulus of the brightness filtering into the room through the less obstructed window.

The calendar said March, but meteorology is not always dependable; it sometimes produces a premature June evening or a belated one, Clarisse thought. The darkness outside the window seemed to her like a summer night. Where the light of the gas lamps fell, the night was lacquered a bright yellow. The bushes nearby were a surging mass of black. Where they hung into the light they became green or whitish—there was no right word for it—scalloped into leaves and floating in the lamplight like laundry spread out in a gently running stream. A narrow iron ribbon on dwarflike posts—a mere reminder and admonition to think of order—ran for a while along the edge of the lawn where the bushes stood, and then vanished in the darkness: Clarisse knew it came to an end there. There might at some time have been a plan to embellish the area with the suggestion of a garden, but it had soon been abandoned.

Clarisse moved close to Meingast, to see as far as possible up the road from his angle; her nose was flat against the windowpane, and their two bodies were touching hard and at as many points as if Clarisse had stretched out full length on the stairs, as she occasionally did. Her right arm had to give way, and was clasped at the elbow by Meingast's long fingers as by the sinewy talons of an extremely absentminded eagle crumpling something like a silk handkerchief in its claws. Clarisse had for a while been watching a man who had something wrong with him, but she couldn't make out what it was. His gait was by turns hesitant and negligent; he gave the impression that something was wrapping itself around his will to walk, and every time he had torn through this he walked for a bit like anyone who was not hurrying but not stopping either. The rhythm of this irregular movement had caught Clarisse's attention; as the man passed a streetlamp she tried to make out his features, which struck her as hollow and numb. When he passed the next-to-last streetlamp she decided that it was an insignificant, unpleasant, and furtive face, but as he approached the nearest lamppost, the one almost beneath her window, his face looked extremely pale, and it floated around on the light as the light floated around on the darkness, so that the thin iron post of the streetlamp looked very straight and aroused beside it, striking the eye with a more penetrating vivid green than it really warranted.

All four had gradually begun to observe this man, who thought himself unseen. He now noticed the bushes bathed in light, and they made him think of the scalloping of a woman's petticoat, more luxurious than any he had ever seen, but one he would like to see. At this moment he was seized by his resolve. He stepped over the low railing, stood on the grass, which reminded him of the green wood shavings in a box of toy trees, stared for a while in bewilderment at his feet, was roused by his head as it cautiously looked around, and concealed himself in the shadows, as was his habit. People lured outdoors by the warm weather were returning home; their noise and their pleasure could be heard from far off. It filled the man with fear, and he sought comfort under the petticoat of leaves. Clarisse still had no idea what was the matter with him. He emerged whenever a group of people had passed by, their eyes blinded to the darkness by the gaslight. Without lifting his feet, he shuffled toward the circle of light, like someone on a shallow bank who will not go into water over the soles of his shoes. Clarisse was struck by how pale the man was; his face was distorted into a white disk. She was overcome with pity for him. But he was making strange little movements that puzzled her for a long time, until, suddenly horrified, she had to grab hold of something; and since Meingast still had a grip on her arm, so that she could not move freely, she grabbed his wide trousers in her search for protection, pulling them taut over the Master's leg like a flag in a gale. So the two of them stood, without letting go.

Ulrich, thinking he was the first to have realized that the man under the windows was one of those sick people who through the abnormality of their sex lives attract the lively curiosity of the sexually normal, worried needlessly for a while about the effect this discovery might have on Clarisse, since she was so unstable. Then he forgot about it, and would have been glad to know for himself what might actually be going on in such a person. The change, he thought, must have been so complete at the moment of stepping over the rail as to defy any attempt to describe it in detail. And as naturally as if it were an appropriate comparison, he was reminded of a singer who has just finished eating and drinking and then steps up to the piano, folds his hands over his stomach, and, opening his mouth to sing, is partly someone else and partly not. Ulrich also thought of His Grace Count Leinsdorf, who was able to switch into a religious-ethical circuit and into a banker's imperial man-of-the-world circuit. He was fascinated by the completeness of this transformation, which takes place inwardly but is confirmed outwardly by the world's acceptance. He did not care how this man down there had got where he was in psychological terms, but he could not help imagining his head gradually filling with tension, like a balloon filling with gas, probably, slowly and for days, but still swaying on the ropes that anchor it to terra firma until there is an inaudible command or some chance occurrence, or simply the set time finally runs its course, at which point anything at all would serve to let the ropes go, and the head, with no connection to the human world, floats off into the emptiness of the abnormal. And there the man actually stood in the shelter of the bushes with his sunken, ordinary face, lurking like a beast of prey. To carry out his purpose he really should have waited for the merrymakers to thin out so that the area might be safer for him. But the moment women passed by, alone in the interval between groups, or sometimes even protected within a group, dancing along and laughing gaily, they were no longer people to him but dolls playing some grotesque part in his consciousness. He was filled with the utter ruthlessness of a killer, immune to their mortal fear; but at the same time he was himself suffering some minor torment at the thought that they might discover him and chase him off like a dog before he could reach the climax of insensibility, and his tongue quivered in his mouth with anxiety. He waited in a stupor, and gradually the last glimmer of twilight faded. Now a solitary woman neared his hiding place, but when he was still separated from her by the streetlamps, he could already see her detached from all her surroundings, bobbing up and down on the waves of light and darkness, a black lump dripping with light before she came closer. Ulrich, too, saw her, a shapeless middle-aged woman approaching. She had a body like a sack filled with gravel, and her expression was not congenial but domineering and cantankerous. But the gaunt pale man in the bushes knew how to get at her without her noticing until it was too late. The dull motions of her eyes and her legs were probably already twitching in his flesh, and he was getting ready to assault her before she had a chance to defend herself, to assault her with the sight of him, which would take her by surprise and enter into her forever, however she might twist and turn. This excitement was whirling and turning in his knees, hands, and larynx, or so it seemed at least to Ulrich as he observed the man groping his way through the bushes where they were already in the half-light, getting ready to step out at the right moment and expose himself. Dazed, the miserable man, leaning into the last slight resistance of the twigs, glued his eyes on the ugly face now pitching up and down toward him in the full light, his breath panting obediently in time with the rhythm of the stranger. "Will she scream?" Ulrich thought. This coarse person was perfectly capable of flying into a rage instead of a panic, and going over to the attack; in which case the demented coward would have to take to his heels, and his frustrated lust would plunge its knife into his own flesh, the squat handle first! But at this tense moment Ulrich heard the casual voices of two men coming down the road, and since he could hear them through the glass they must have penetrated the hissing excitement down below, for the man beneath the window cautiously dropped the nearly opened veil of twigs and withdrew soundlessly back into the midst of the darkness.

"What a swine!" Clarisse whispered to the friend beside her, energetically but not at all indignantly. Back before Meingast's transformation he had often heard her use such terms, provoked by his free-and-easy ways with her, so the word might be considered historical. Clarisse assumed that Meingast would still remember it, despite his transformation, and it really did seem to her that his fingers stirred very faintly on her arm in answer. There was nothing at all accidental about this evening; it was not even by chance that the man had chosen Clarisse's window to stand under. She was firmly convinced that she had a baneful attraction for men who had something wrong with them; it had often proved to be so! Taken all in all, it was not so much that her ideas were confused as that they left out connections, or that they were saturated with affect in many places where other people have no such inner wellspring. Her conviction that she had been the one who had made it possible at the time for Meingast to remake himself was in itself not improbable; if one also considered how independently this change had taken its own course, because there had been no contact over distance and for years, and further how great a change it was—for it had made a prophet out of a superficial worldling—and finally how it was soon after Meingast's departure that the love between Walter and Clarisse had risen to that height of discord where it still remained, then even Clarisse's notion that she and Walter would have had to take on the sins of the still untransformed Meingast to make his rise possible was no worse reasoning than any number of respected ideas people believe in today. This had given rise, however, to the relationship of knightly servitude that Clarisse felt toward the returned Master, and whenever she now spoke of his new "transformation," instead of simply a change, she was only giving fitting expression to the elevated state in which she had since found herself. The awareness of finding herself in a significant relationship could uplift Clarisse in the literal sense. One doesn't quite know whether to paint saints with a cloud under their feet or whether they should be standing on nothing a finger's breadth above the ground, and this was exactly how it now stood with her, since Meingast had chosen her house in which to accomplish his great work, which apparently was grounded in something quite profound. Clarisse was not in love with him as a woman; it was rather like a boy who admires a man: ecstatic when he manages to set his hat at the same angle as his idol, and filled with a secret ambition even to outdo him eventually.

Walter knew this. He could not hear what Clarisse was whispering to Meingast, nor could his eye make out any more of the pair than a heavily fused mass of shadow in the dim light of the window, but he could see through everything. He, too, had recognized what was wrong with the man in the bushes, and the silence that reigned in the room lay most heavily upon him. He managed to make out that Ulrich, who stood motionless beside him, was staring intently out the window, and he assumed that the two at the other window were doing the same. "Why doesn't anyone break this silence?" he thought. "Why doesn't someone open the window and scare this monster off?" It occurred to him that they were obligated to call the police, but there was no telephone in the house, and he lacked the courage to undertake something that might make his companions look down on him. He had no desire whatever to be an "outraged bourgeois," but he was just so exasperated! He could understand very well the "chivalric relationship" in which his wife stood to Meingast, for even in lovemaking it was impossible for her to imagine exaltation without effort: she derived her exaltation not from sensuality, only from ambition. He remembered how incredibly alive she could sometimes be in his arms, at a time when he had still been preoccupied with art; but except by such detours it was impossible to arouse her. "Perhaps ambition is all that really takes people out of themselves," he reflected dubiously. It had not escaped him that Clarisse "stood watch" while Meingast was working, in order to protect his ideas with her body, although she did not even know what these ideas were. Painfully, Walter regarded the lonely egotist in his bush; this wretch offered a warning example for the devastation that can be created in an all-too-isolated mind. That he knew exactly what

Clarisse was feeling as she stood there watching tormented him. "She will be slightly excited, as if she had just run up a flight of stairs," he thought. He himself felt a pressure in the scene that was before his eyes, as if something had been wrapped in a cocoon and was trying to break its envelope, and he felt how within this mysterious pressure, which Clarisse, too, was feeling, the will was aroused not merely to watch but right away, soon, somehow, to do something, to intervene in what was happening in order to set it free. Other people got their ideas from life, but whatever Clarisse experienced came, every time, from ideas: such an enviable madness! And Walter was more inclined to the exaggerations of his wife, even if she was perhaps mentally ill, than to the way of thinking of his friend Ulrich, who fancied himself cautious and cool: somehow the more irrational was closer to him; perhaps it left him personally untouched, it appealed to his sympathy. In any event, many people prefer crazy ideas to difficult ones, and he even derived a certain satisfaction from Clarisse's whispering with Meingast in the dark, while Ulrich was condemned to stand beside him as a mute shadow; it served Ulrich right to be beaten by Meingast. But from time to time Walter was tormented by the expectation that Clarisse would fling open the window or rush down the stairs to the bushes: then he detested both male shadows and their obscene silent watching, which made the situation for the poor little Prometheus he was shielding, who was so vulnerable to every temptation of the spirit, more problematic from one minute to the next.

During this time the afflicted man's shame and frustrated lust had fused into an all-pervasive disappointment that filled his gaunt body with its massive bitterness as he withdrew into his bushes. When he had reached the innermost darkness he collapsed, letting himself fall to the ground, and his head hung from his neck like a leaf. The world stood ready to punish him, and he saw his situation much as it would have appeared to the two passersby had they discovered him. But after this man had wept for himself for a while, dry-eyed, the original change came over him once again, this time mixed with even more vengefulness and spite. And again it miscarried. A girl passed by who might have been around fifteen and was obviously late coming from somewhere; she seemed lovely to him, a small, hastening ideal: the depraved man felt that he now really ought to step out and speak to her in a friendly way, but this plunged him instantly into wild terror. His imagination, ready to conjure up anything that could even be suggested by a woman, became fearful and awkward when confronted with the natural possibility of admiring this defenseless little creature approaching in her beauty. The more she was suited to please his daylight self, the less pleasure she provided his shadow self, and he vainly tried to hate her, since he could not love her. So he stood uneasily at the borderline between shadow and light and exposed himself. When the child noticed his secret she had already passed by him and was about eight paces away; at first she had merely looked at the leaves moving without realizing what was going on, and when she did she could already feel secure enough not to be scared to death: her mouth did stay open for a while, but then she gave a loud scream and began to run; the scamp even seemed to enjoy looking back, and the man felt himself humiliatingly abandoned. He wrathfully hoped that a drop of poison might somehow have fallen into her eyes and would later eat its way through her heart.

This relatively harmless and comical outcome relieved the spectators' sense of humanity; this time they would indeed have intervened if the scene had not resolved itself as it did; and preoccupied with this, they hardly noticed how the business below did come to an end; they could only confirm that it had done so when they observed that the male "hyena," as Walter put it, had suddenly disappeared. The man finally realized his intentions when a perfectly ordinary woman came along who looked at him aghast and with loathing, involuntarily shocked into stopping for a moment, and then tried to pretend that she had not seen anything. During this instant he felt himself, together with his roof of leaves and the whole topsy-turvy world he had come from, sliding deep into the defenseless woman's resisting gaze. That may have been how it happened, or perhaps it was some other way. Clarisse had not been paying attention. With a deep breath she raised herself from her half-crouching position; she and Meingast had let go of each other some time before. It seemed to her that she was suddenly landing on the wooden floor with the soles of her feet, and a whirlpool of inexpressible, horrible desire stilled itself in her body. She was firmly convinced that everything that had just occurred had a special meaning, minted just for her; and strange as it may sound, the repulsive scene left her with the impression that she was a bride who had just been serenaded. In her head, intentions were dancing helter-skelter, some ready to be carried out and others, new ones, just occurring to her.

"Funny!" Ulrich suddenly said into the darkness, the first of the four to break the silence. "What an absurdly twisted notion it is to think how this fellow's fun would have been spoiled if he only knew he was being watched the whole time!"

Meingast's shadow detached itself from the nothingness and stood, a slender compression of darkness, facing in the direction of Ulrich's voice.

"We attach far too much importance to sex," the Master said. "These are in fact the goatlike caperings of our era's will." He said nothing further. But Clarisse, who had winced with annoyance at Ulrich's words, felt borne forward by what Meingast said, although in this darkness there was no telling in what direction.

138

THE TESTAMENT

When Ulrich returned home from what he had experienced, even more dissatisfied than he had been before, he decided that he must not avoid a decision any longer, and tried to recall as best he could the "incident," as he euphemistically called what had happened in his last few hours with Agathe, only a few days after their deep discussion.

He was all packed and ready to leave on a sleeper that came through the town late, and so he and Agathe met for a final meal. They had agreed earlier that she would join him soon, and they somewhat uncertainly estimated this separation at from five days to two weeks.

At dinner Agathe said: "There's something more we have to do before you leave."

"What?" Ulrich asked.

"We have to change the will!"

Ulrich remembered looking at his sister without surprise; despite all their earlier talk he had assumed she was leading up to a joke. But Agathe was gazing down at her plate, with the familiar meditative wrinkle between her eyebrows. Slowly she said:

"He won't keep as much of me between his fingers as would be left if a woolen thread had been burned away between them!"

Something must have been intensely at work in her in the last few days. Ulrich was about to tell her that he regarded such deliberations about how Hagauer's interests could be injured as impermissible and did not want to hear any more about it. But at that moment their father's old servant came in with the next course, and they could only go on talking in veiled allusions.

"Aunt Malvina . . . ," Agathe said, smiling at her brother. "Do you remember Aunt Malvina? She had intended to leave everything she owned to our cousin; it was all arranged and everyone knew about it! Accordingly, all she was left in her parents' will was the legal minimum she was entitled to, all the rest going to her brother, so that neither of the children, whose father was equally devoted to both of them, should inherit more than the other. You remember that, surely? The annuity that Agathe—Alexandra, our cousin, that is"—she corrected herself with a laugh—"had been receiving since her marriage was, for the time being, discounted against her legal share; it was a complicated arrangement, to give Aunt Malvina time to die. . . ."

"I don't understand you," Ulrich muttered.

"Oh, but it's perfectly simple! Aunt Malvina is dead, but before she died she lost all her money; she even had to be supported. Now, if Papa should for some reason have forgotten to revoke that provision in his will, Alexandra gets nothing at all, even if her marriage contract had stipulated joint ownership of property!"

"I don't know about that; it seems very doubtful!" Ulrich said impulsively. "Besides, Father must have given certain assurances. He can't possibly have made such provisions without talking it over with his son-in-law!"

He remembered saying this only too well, because he could not possibly keep silent while listening to his sister's dangerous error. He could still see vividly in his mind the smile with which she had looked at him. "Isn't it just like him?" she seemed to be thinking. "One only has to present a case to him as if it weren't flesh and blood but some abstraction, and one can lead him around by the nose." And then she had asked curtly: "Is there any written evidence of such arrangements?" and answered herself: "I never heard anything about it, and if anyone knew about it, it would certainly be me. But of course Papa was strange about everything."

Now the servant was back at the table, and she took advantage of Ulrich's helplessness to add: "Verbal agreements can always be contested. But if the will was changed again after Aunt Malvina lost everything, then all signs point to this new codicil having been lost."

Again Ulrich let himself be tempted to steer her right: "That still leaves the sizable automatic inheritance that can't be taken away from children of one's body."

"But I've just told you that all of that was paid out during the father's lifetime! After all, Alexandra was married twice." They were alone for a moment, and Agathe hastened to add: "I've looked at that passage very carefully. Only a few words need to be changed to make it look as if my share had already been paid out to me in full. Who knows anything about it now? When Papa went back to leaving us equal shares after Aunt Malvina's losses, he put it in a codicil that can be destroyed. Anyway, there's nothing to have prevented me from having renounced my legal share in your favor for one reason or another."

Ulrich looked at her dumbfounded and missed his opportunity to respond to her inventions as he felt obliged to do; by the time he was ready, they were no longer alone, and he had to resort to circumlocutions.

"One really shouldn't," he began hesitantly, "even think such things!"

"Why not?" Agatha retorted.

Such questions are simple as long as they are left alone, but the moment they rear their heads they are a monstrous serpent that had been curled up into a harmless blob. Ulrich remembered answering: "Even Nietzsche asks the 'free spirits' to observe certain external rules for the sake of a greater internal freedom!" He had said this with a smile, although he felt it was rather cowardly to hide behind someone else's words.

"That's a lame principle!" Agathe said, dismissing it out of hand. "That's the principle behind my marriage!"

And Ulrich thought: "It really is a lame principle." It seems that people who have new and revolutionary answers to particular problems make up for it by compromising on everything else, which enables them to lead highly moral lives in carpet slippers; all the more so as the attempt to keep everything constant except what they are trying to change corresponds totally to the creative economy of thinking in which they feel at home. Even Ulrich had always regarded this more as a strict than as a slack procedure, but when he was having this talk with his sister he felt that she had struck home; he could no longer bear the indecision he had loved, and it seemed to him that it was precisely Agathe who had been given the mission of bringing him to this point. And while he was nevertheless propounding the "rule of the free spirits" to her, she laughed and asked him whether he didn't notice that the moment he tried to formulate general principles a different man appeared in his place.

"And even though you are surely right to admire him, basically he doesn't mean a thing to you!" she declared, giving her brother a willful and challenging look. Again he had no ready answer and said nothing, expecting an interruption at any moment, yet he could not bring himself to drop the subject. This situation emboldened her.

"In the short time we've been together," she went on, "you've given me such wonderful guidelines for my life, things I would never have dared think out for myself, but then you always end up wondering whether they're really true! It seems to me that the truth the way you use it is only a way of mistreating people!"

She was amazed at her own daring in making such reproaches; her own life seemed so worthless to her that she surely ought to have kept quiet. But she drew her courage from Ulrich himself, and there was something so curiously feminine in her way of leaning on him while she attacked him that he felt it too.

"You don't understand the desire to organize ideas in large, articulated masses," Ulrich said. "The battle experiences of the intellect are alien to you; all you see in them is columns marching in some kind of formation, the impersonality of many feet stirring up the truth like a cloud of dust!"

"But didn't you yourself describe to me, far more precisely and clearly than I ever could, the two states of mind in which you can live?" she answered.

A glowing cloud, with ever-changing outlines, flew across her face. She felt the desire to bring her brother to the point where he could no longer retreat. The thought made her feverish, but she did not yet know whether she would have enough courage to carry it through, and so she put off ending the meal.

Ulrich knew all this, he guessed it, but he had pulled himself together and taken up his position. He sat facing her, his eyes focused, absent, his mouth forced to utterance, and had the impression that he was not really there but had remained somewhere behind himself, calling out to himself what he was saying:

"Suppose that, on a trip somewhere, I wanted to steal some stranger's golden cigarette case—I ask you, isn't that simply unthinkable? I don't want to go into the question right now of whether a move such as you're contemplating is or isn't justifiable on grounds of intellectual freedom. For all I know, it may be in order to do Hagauer some injury. But imagine me in a hotel, neither penniless nor a professional thief, nor a mental defective with deformed head or body, nor the offspring of a hysterical mother or a drunkard father, nor confused or stigmatized by anything else in any way at all: yet I steal, nevertheless. I repeat: This couldn't happen anywhere in the world! It's simply impossible! It can be ruled out with absolute scientific certainty!"

Agathe burst out laughing. "But Ulo, what if one does it all the same?"

Ulrich himself had to laugh at this answer, which he had not anticipated. He leapt to his feet and pushed his chair back hastily in order not to encourage her by his concurrence. Agathe got up from the table.

"You cannot do this!" he pleaded with her.

"But Ulo," she said, "do you think even in your dreams, or do you dream something that's happening?"

This question reminded him of his argument, a few days before, that all moral demands pointed to a kind of dream state that had fled from them by the time they were fully postulated. But Agathe had already gone, after her last remark, into her father's study, which now could be seen lamplit beyond two open doors; and Ulrich, who had not followed her, saw her standing in this frame. She was holding a sheet of paper in the light, reading something. "Doesn't she have any idea what it is she's taking on herself?" he wondered. But on that whole key ring of contemporary notions, such as neurotic inferiority, mental deficiency, arrested development, and the like, none fit, and in the lovely picture she made while committing her crime there was no trace of greed or vengefulness or any other inner ugliness. And although with the aid of such concepts Ulrich could have seen even the actions of a criminal or a near psychotic as relatively controlled and civilized, because the distorted and displaced motives of ordinary life shimmer in their depths, his sister's gently fierce determination, an inextricable blend of purity and criminality, left him momentarily speechless. He could not accept the idea that this person, quite openly engaged in committing a bad act, could be a bad person, while at the same time he had to watch how Agathe took one paper after another out of the desk, read it, and laid it aside, seriously searching for a specific document. Her determination gave the impression of having descended from some other planet to the plane of everyday decision.

As he watched, Ulrich was also troubled by the question of why he had talked Hagauer into leaving in good faith. It seemed to him that he had behaved all along as the tool of his sister's will, and to the very last his responses, even when he was disagreeing with her, had only encouraged her. Truth dealt cruelly with people, she had said. "Well put, but she has no idea what truth means!" Ulrich mused. "With the passing of the years it leaves one stiff and gouty, but in one's youth it's a life of hunting and sailing!" He had sat down again. Now he suddenly realized not only that Agathe had somehow got from him what she had said about truth, but that he had sketched out for her in advance what she was doing next door. Had he not said that in the highest state of human awareness there was no such thing as good and evil, but only faith or doubt; that strict rules were contrary to the innermost nature of morality and that faith can never be more than an hour old; that in a state of faith one could never do anything base; that intuition was a more passionate state than truth? And Agathe was now on the point of abandoning the safe enclosure of morality and venturing out upon those boundless deeps where there is no decision other than whether one will rise or fall. She was doing this just as she had the other day when she took her father's medals from his reluctant hand to exchange them for the imitations, and at this moment he loved her in spite of her lack of principle, with the remarkable feeling that it was his own thoughts that had gone from him to her and were now returning from her to him, poorer in deliberation but with that balsamic scent of freedom about them like a creation of the wild. And while he was trembling with the strain of controlling himself, he cautiously made a suggestion:

"I'll put off leaving for a day and sound out a notary or lawyer. Perhaps what you're doing is terribly obvious!"

But Agathe had already ascertained that the notary her father had used was no longer alive. "There's not a soul left who knows anything about this business," she said. "Let it be!"

Ulrich saw that she had taken a piece of paper and was practicing imitating her father's handwriting.

Fascinated, he had drawn closer and stood behind her. There in piles lay the papers on which his father's hand had lived—one could still almost feel its movements—and here Agathe, with an actress's mimicry, conjured up almost the same thing. It was strange to see this happening. The purpose it was serving, the thought that it was a forgery, disappeared. And in truth Agathe had not given this any thought at all. An aura of justice with flames, not with logic, hovered about her. Goodness, decency, abiding by the law, as she had come to know it in people she knew, notably Professor Hagauer, had always seemed to her like removing a spot from a dress; while the wrongdoing that enveloped her at this moment was like the world drowning in the light of a rising sun. It seemed to her that right and wrong no longer constituted a general notion, a compromise devised to serve millions of people, but were a magical encounter between Me and You, the madness of original creation before there was anything to compare it to or anything to measure it by. She was really making Ulrich the present of a crime by putting herself in his hands, trusting him wholeheartedly to understand her rashness, as children do who come up with the most unexpected ideas when they want to give someone a present and have nothing to give. And Ulrich guessed most of this. As his eyes followed her movements he felt a pleasure he had never known before, for it had in it something of the magical absurdity of yielding totally and without remonstrance, for once, to what another being was doing. Even when the thought intervened that this was causing harm to a third person, it flashed only for an instant, like an ax, and he quickly put his mind at rest, since what his sister was doing here was really not anyone else's business; it was not at all certain that these attempts at copying someone's handwriting would actually be used, and what Agathe was doing inside her own four walls was her own affair as long as it had no effect beyond them.

She now called out to her brother, turned around, and was surprised to find him standing behind her. She awoke. She had written all she wanted to write and resolutely singed it over a candle flame in order to make the handwriting look old. She held out her free hand to Ulrich, who did not take it, but he was not able to withdraw entirely behind a somber frown either. She responded by saying: "Listen! If something is a contradiction, and you love both sides of it—really love it!—doesn't that cancel it out, willy-nilly?"

"That's much too frivolous a way of putting it," Ulrich muttered. But Agathe knew how he would judge it in his "second thinking." She took a clean sheet of paper and lightheartedly wrote, in the old-fashioned hand she was so good at imitating: "My bad daughter Agathe proffers no reason to change the above-ordained instructions to the disadvantage of my good son Ulo!" Not yet satisfied, she wrote on the second sheet: "My daughter Agathe is for some time longer to be educated by my good son Uli."

So that was how it had happened, but now that Ulrich had reawakened it down to the last detail, he ended up with just as little knowledge of what to do about it as before.

He ought not to have left without first straightening things out, no doubt about that! And clearly the fashionable superstition that one shouldn't take anything too seriously had played him a trick when it whispered to him to quit the field for a time and not give too much weight to the issue between them by emotional resistance. Heat can't pass from the cooler to the hotter; the most violent extremes, left to themselves, eventually give rise to a new mediocrity; one could hardly take a train or walk in the street without a cocked gun if one could not trust the law of averages, which automatically reduces extreme possibilities to improbability. It was this European faith in empiricism that Ulrich was obeying when, despite all his scruples, he returned home. Deep down he was even glad that Agathe had shown herself to be different.

Nevertheless, the matter could not be properly resolved other than by Ulrich's now taking action, and as soon as possible, to make up for his negligence. He should have sent his sister an immediate special delivery letter or telegram, which should have stated in effect: "I won't have anything to do with you unless you . . . !" But he had absolutely no intention of writing anything of the kind; at the moment he simply could not do it.

Besides, they had decided before that fateful incident that in the next few weeks they would try to live together or at least move in together, and this was what they had mainly talked about in the brief time remaining before his departure. They had agreed that for the moment it would be for "the time it will take to get the divorce," so that Agathe would have a refuge and counsel. But now, in thinking about it, Ulrich also remembered an earlier remark of his sister's about wanting "to kill Hagauer"; this "scheme" had evidently been working in her and taken on a new form. She had insisted vehemently on selling the family property at once, possibly also in the interest of making the inheritance evaporate, although it might seem advisable on other grounds as well. In any case, they had agreed to put the sale in the hands of a broker and had set their terms. And so Ulrich now had to give some thought as well to what was to become of his sister after he returned to his casually interim life, which he did not himself regard as real. It was impossible for her present situation to continue. Amazingly close though they had grown in so short a time—as though their fates were linked, even though this had arisen from all sorts of unconnected details; Agathe probably had a more quixotic view of it—they knew hardly anything of each other in the many and various superficialities on which a shared life depends. When he thought of his sister objectively Ulrich could even perceive numerous unsolved problems, nor could he form a very clear idea of her past; his best guess was that she dealt most casually with everything that happened to her or through her, and that she lived rather vaguely and perhaps with fantasies that ran alongside her actual life;

such an explanation would plausibly account for her having stayed so long with Hagauer and then broken with him so suddenly. And even the carelessness with which she treated the future fitted in with this view: she had left home, and that seemed to satisfy her for the present; and when questions arose about what should happen now, she avoided them. Nor was Ulrich himself capable of either picturing a life for her without a husband, in which she would hover around in vague expectations like a young girl, or imagining what the man would look like who would be right for his sister; he had even told her so shortly before he left.

She had given him a startled look—perhaps she was clowning a bit, pretending to be startled—and then calmly countered with the question: "Can't I just stay with you for the time being, without our having to decide everything?"

It was in this fashion, without anything more definite, that the idea of their moving in together had been ratified. But Ulrich realized that this experiment meant the end of the experiment of his "life on leave." He did not want to think about the possible consequences, but that his life would henceforth be subject to certain restrictions was not unwelcome, and for the first time he again thought of the circle and especially the women of the Parallel Campaign. The idea of cutting himself off from everything, as part of his new life, seemed delightful. Just as it often takes only a trifling alteration in a room to change its dull acoustics to a glorious resonance, so now in his imagination his little house was transformed into a shell within which one heard the roar of the city as a distant river.

And then, toward the end of that conversation, this other special little conversation had taken place:

"We'll live like hermits," Agathe had said with a bright smile, "but of course we'll each be free to pursue any love affairs. For you, at any rate, there's no obstacle!" she assured him.

"Do you realize," Ulrich said by way of an answer, "that we shall be entering into the Millennium?"

"What's that?"

"We've talked so much about the love that isn't a stream flowing toward its goal but a state of being like the ocean. Now tell me honestly: When they told you in school that the angels in heaven did nothing but bask in the presence of the Lord and sing His praises, were you able to imagine this blissful state of doing nothing and thinking nothing?"

"I always thought it must be rather boring, which is certainly due to my imperfection," was Agathe's answer.

"But after everything we've agreed on," Ulrich explained, "you must now imagine this ocean as a state of motionlessness and detachment, filled with everlasting, crystal-clear events. In ages past, people tried to imagine such a life on earth. That is the Millennium, formed in our own image and yet like no world we know. That's how we'll live now! We shall cast off all self-seeking, we shall collect neither goods, nor knowledge, nor lovers, nor friends, nor principles, nor even ourselves! Our spirit will open up, dissolving boundaries toward man and beast, spreading open in such a way that we can no longer remain 'us' but will maintain our identities only by merging with all the world!"

This little interlude had been a joke. He had been sitting with paper and pencil, making notes and talking meanwhile with his sister about what she could expect from the sale of the house and the furniture. He was also still cross, and he himself did not know whether he was blaspheming or dreaming. And with all this they had not got around to talking seriously about the will.

It was probably because of these ambiguities in the way it had happened that Ulrich even now was far from feeling any active regret. There was much about his sister's bold stroke that pleased him, though he was himself the defeated one; he had to admit that it suddenly brought the person living by the "rule of the free spirits," to whom he had given far too much ease within himself, into grave conflict with that deep, undefined person from whom real seriousness emanates. Nor did he want to dodge the consequences of this act by quickly making it good in the usual way; but then, there was no norm, and events had to be allowed to take their course.

139

Reunion with Diotima's diplomatic husband

Next morning Ulrich's mind was no clearer, and late that afternoon he decided to lighten the serious mood that was oppressing him by looking up his cousin who was occupied with liberating the soul from civilization.

To his surprise he was received by Section Chief Tuzzi, who came to greet him even before Rachel had returned from Diotima's room.

"My wife's not feeling well today," the seasoned husband said, with that unconscious tone of tenderness in his voice which regular monthly use has made into a formula that exposes the domestic secret to the world. "I don't know whether she'll be up to a visit." Though dressed to go out, he was quite willing to stay and keep Ulrich company.

Ulrich took the opportunity of inquiring about Arnheim.

"Arnheim's been in England and is now in St. Petersburg," Tuzzi told him. The effect of this trivial and predictable news on Ulrich, depressed as he was by his own experiences, was to make him feel as though world, fullness, and motion were rushing in upon him.

"A good thing too," the diplomat added. "Let him travel here and there as much as he likes. It gives one a chance to make one's observations and pick up some information."

"So you still believe," said Ulrich, amused, "that he's on some pacifist mission for the Czar?"

"I believe it more than ever," was the plain answer from the man who bore official responsibility for carrying out Austro-Hungarian policy. But suddenly Ulrich doubted whether Tuzzi was really so unsuspecting or was only pretending to be and pulling his leg; somewhat annoyed, he dropped Arnheim and asked: "I hear that 'Action!' has become the watchword since I left."

As always when the Parallel Campaign came up, Tuzzi seemed

to relish playing both the innocent and the shrewd insider. He shrugged and grinned.

"I'll let my wife fill you in on that—you'll hear all about it from her as soon as she's able to see you!" But a moment later his little mustache began to twitch and the large dark eyes in the tanned face glistened with a vague distress. "You're a man who has read all the books," he said hesitantly. "Could you perhaps tell me what is meant by a man having soul?"

This was apparently something Tuzzi really wanted to talk about, and it was obviously his insecurity that was responsible for the impression that he was distressed. When Ulrich failed to respond immediately, he went on: "When we speak of someone as 'a good soul,' we mean an honest, conscientious, dependable fellow—I have an administrator in my office like that—but what that amounts to, surely, is the virtues of an underling. Or there's soul as a quality of women, meaning more or less that they cry more easily, or blush more easily, than men do. . . ."

"Your wife has soul," Ulrich corrected him, as gravely as if he were stating that she had raven-black hair.

A faint pallor rushed across Tuzzi's face. "My wife has a mind," he said slowly. "She is rightly regarded as a woman of some intellect. I like to tease her about it and tell her she's an aesthete. That galls her. But that isn't soul. . . ." He thought for a moment. "Have you ever been to a fortune-teller?" he asked. "They read the future in your palm, or from a hair of your head, sometimes amazingly on target. They have a gift for it, or tricks. But can you make any sense of somebody telling you, for instance, that there are signs that a time is coming when our souls will behold each other directly, so to speak, without the mediation of the senses? Let me say at once," he added quickly, "that this is not to be understood only as a figure of speech, but if you're not a good person, then no matter what you do, people today can feel it much more clearly than in earlier centuries, because this is an age of the awakening soul. Do you believe that?"

With Tuzzi, one never knew if his barbs were directed against himself or his listener, so Ulrich answered: "If I were you I'd just let it come to the test."

"Don't make jokes, my dear friend," Tuzzi said plaintively. "It's not decent when you're safely on the sidelines. My wife expects me to take such propositions seriously even if I can't subscribe to them, and I have to surrender without having a chance to defend myself. So in my hour of need I remembered that you're one of those bookish people. . . ."

"Both of these assertions come from Maeterlinck, if I'm not mistaken," Ulrich said helpfully.

"Really? From . . . ? Yes, I can see that. That's the . . . ? I see, that's good; then perhaps he's also the one who claims that there's no such thing as truth—except for people in love! he says. If I am in love with a person, according to him, I participate directly in a secret truth more profound than the common kind. On the other hand, if we say something based on observation and a thorough knowledge of human nature, that's supposed to be worthless, of course. Is that another of this Mae—this man's ideas?"

"I really don't know. It might be. It's what you would expect from him."

"I imagined it came from Arnheim."

"Arnheim has taken a lot from him, as he has from others—they're both gifted eclectics."

"Really? Then it's all old stuff? But in that case can you tell me, for heaven's sake, how it is possible to let that sort of thing be published nowadays?" Tuzzi asked. "When my wife says things like: 'Reason doesn't prove a thing; ideas don't reach as far as the soul!' or 'There's a realm of wisdom and love far beyond your world of facts, and one only desecrates it with considered statements!' I can understand what makes her talk like that: she's a woman, that's all, and this is her way of defending herself against a man's logic! But how can a man say such things?" Tuzzi edged his chair closer and laid a hand on Ulrich's knee. " 'The truth swims like a fish in an invisible principle; the moment you lift it out, it's dead.' What do you make of *that*? Could it maybe have something to do with the difference between an 'eroticist' and a 'sexualist'?"

Ulrich smiled. "Do you really want me to tell you?"

"I can't wait to hear!"

"I don't know how to begin."

"There it is, you see! Men can't bring themselves to utter such things. But if you had a soul, you would now simply be contemplating my soul and marveling at it. We would reach heights where there are no thoughts, no words, no deeds. Nothing but mysterious forces and a shattering silence! May a soul smoke?" he asked, and lit a cigarette, only then recalling his duty as host and offering one to Ulrich. At bottom he was rather proud of now having read Arnheim's books, and precisely because he still found them insufferable he was pleased with himself for having privately discovered the possible usefulness of their puffed-up style for the inscrutable workings of diplomacy. Nor would anyone else have wanted to do such hard labor for nothing, and anyone in his place would have continued making fun of it to his heart's content, only to yield after a while to the temptation of trying out one quotation or another, or dressing up something that could not be stated clearly in any case in one of those annoyingly fuzzy new ideas. This is done reluctantly, because one still considers the new "costume" ridiculous, but one quickly gets used to it, and so the spirit of the times is imperceptibly transformed by its new terminology, and in specific cases Arnheim might in fact have gained a new admirer. Even Tuzzi was ready to concede that the call to unite soul and commerce, despite any hostility to it on principle, could be thought of as a new psychology of economics, and all that kept him unshakably immune from Arnheim's influence was actually Diotima herself. For between her and Arnheim at that time—unknown to anyone—a certain coolness had begun to gain ground, burdening everything Arnheim had ever said about the soul with the suspicion of being a mere evasion; with the result that his sayings were flung in Tuzzi's face with more irritation than ever. Under these circumstances Tuzzi could be forgiven for assuming that his wife's attachment to the stranger was still in the ascendant, though it was not the kind of love against which a husband could take steps, but a "state of love" or "loving state of mind" so far above all base suspicion that Diotima herself spoke openly of the ideas with which it inspired her, and had lately been insisting rather unrelentingly that Tuzzi take spiritual part in them.

He felt inordinately bewildered and vulnerable, surrounded as he was by this state that blinded him like sunlight coming from all sides at once without the sun itself having any fixed position to orient oneself by, so as to find shade and relief.

He heard Ulrich saying: "But let me offer this for your consideration: Within us there is usually a steady inflow and outflow of experiences. The states of excitation that form in us are aroused from outside and flow out of us again as actions or words. Think of it as a mechanical game. But then think of it being disturbed: The flow gets dammed up. The banks are flooded in some fashion. Occasionally it may be no more than a certain gassiness. . . ."

"At least you talk sensibly, even if it's all nonsense . . . ," Tuzzi noted with approval. He could not quite grasp how all this was supposed to explain matters to him, but he had kept his poise, and even though he was inwardly lost in misery, the tiny malicious smile still lingered proudly on his lips, ready for him to slip right back into it.

"What the physiologists say, I think," Ulrich continued, "is that what we call conscious action is the result of the stimulus not just flowing in and out through a reflex arc but being forced into a detour. That makes the world we experience and the world in which we act, which seem to us one and the same, actually more like the water above and below a mill wheel, connected by a sort of dammed-up reservoir of consciousness, with the inflow and the outflow dependent on regulation of level, pressure, and so forth. Or in other words, if something goes wrong on one of the two levels—an estrangement from the world, say, or a disinclination to action—we could reasonably assume that a second, or higher, consciousness might be formed in this fashion. Or don't you think so?"

"Me?" Tuzzi said. "I'd have to say it's all the same to me. Let the professors work that out among themselves, if they think it important. But practically speaking"—he moodily stubbed out his cigarette in the ashtray, then looked up in exasperation—"is it the people with two reservoirs or only one reservoir who run the world?"

"I thought you only wanted to know how I imagine such ideas might arise. . . ."

"If that's what you've been telling me, I'm afraid I don't follow you," Tuzzi said.

"But it's very simple. You have no second reservoir—so you haven't got the principle of wisdom and you don't understand a word of what the people who have a soul are talking about. Do accept my congratulations!"

Ulrich had gradually become aware that he was expressing, in ignominious form and in curious company, ideas that might be not at all unsuited to explain the feelings that obscurely stirred his own heart. The surmise that in a state of enhanced receptivity an overflowing and receding of experiences might arise that would connect the senses boundlessly and gently as a sheet of water with all creation called to mind his long talks with Agathe, and his face involuntarily took on an expression that was partly obdurate, partly forlorn. Tuzzi studied him from under his indolently raised eyelids and gathered from the form of Ulrich's sarcasm that he himself was not the only person present who was "dammed up" in a manner not of his own choice.

Both of them hardly noticed how long Rachel was taking. She had been detained by Diotima, who had needed her help in quickly putting herself and her sickroom into an ordered state of suffering that would be informal, yet proper for receiving Ulrich. Now the maid brought a message that Ulrich should not leave but be patient just a bit longer, and then hurried back to her mistress.

"All those quotations you cited are of course allegories," Ulrich continued after this interruption, to make up to his host for having to keep him company. "A kind of butterfly language! And people like Arnheim give me the impression that they can guzzle themselves potbellied with this vaporous nectar of theirs! I mean . . . ," he hastened to add, remembering just in time that he must not include Diotima in the insult, "I have this impression about Arnheim in particular, just as he also paradoxically gives the impression that he carries his soul in his breast pocket like a wallet!"

Tuzzi put down his briefcase and gloves, which he had picked up when Rachel appeared, and said with some force: "Do you realize what this is? I mean, what you've explained to me so well. It's nothing but the spirit of pacifism!" He paused to let this revelation sink in. "In the hand of amateurs, pacifism can be extremely dangerous!" he added portentously.

Ulrich would have laughed, but Tuzzi was being dead serious; he had, in fact, linked two things that actually were distantly related, funny as it might be to see how love and pacifism were connected for him in an impression of dilettantish debauchery. At a loss for an answer, Ulrich took the occasion to fall back on the Parallel Campaign and its chosen watchword, "Action!"

"That's a Leinsdorf idea," Tuzzi said disdainfully. "Do you recall the last discussion here before you went away? Leinsdorf said: 'Something's got to be done!' That's all there was to it, and that's what they mean by their new watchword, 'Action!' And Arnheim is of course trying to foist his Russian pacifism on it. Do you remember how I warned them about it? I'm afraid they'll have cause to remember me! Nowhere in the world is foreign policy as difficult as it is here, and I said even then: 'Whoever takes it upon himself these days to put fundamental political ideas into practice has to be part gambler and part criminal.' " This time, Tuzzi was really opening up, probably because Ulrich might be called by his wife at any moment, or because in this conversation he did not want to be the only one to have things explained to him.

"The Parallel Campaign is arousing suspicion all over the world," he reported, "and at home, where it's being viewed as both anti-German and anti-Slav, it's also having repercussions in our foreign relations. But if you want to know the difference between amateur and professional pacifism, let me tell you something: Austria could prevent a war for at least thirty years by joining the Entente Cordiale! And this could of course be done on the Emperor's Jubilee with a matchless pacifist flourish, while at the same time we assure Germany of our brotherly love whether or not she follows suit. The majority of our nationalities would be overjoyed. With easy French and English credit we could make our army so strong that Germany couldn't bully us. We'd be rid of Italy altogether. France wouldn't be able to do a thing without us. In short, we would be the key to peace and war, we'd make the big political deals. I'm not giving away any secrets; this is a simple diplomatic calculation that any commercial attaché could work out. So why can't it be done? Imponderables at Court. Where they dislike the Emperor so heartily that they'd consider it almost indecent to let it happen. Monarchies are at a disadvantage today because they're weighed down by decency! Then there are imponderables of so-called public opinion—which brings me to the Parallel Campaign. Why doesn't it educate public opinion? Why doesn't it teach the public to see things objectively? You see"— but at this point Tuzzi's statements lost some of their plausibility and began to sound more like concealed affliction—"this fellow Arnheim really amuses me with those books he writes! He didn't invent writing, and the other night, when I couldn't fall asleep, I had time to

think about it a little. There have always been politicians who wrote
novels or plays, like Clemenceau, for instance, or Disraeli; not Bismarck, but Bismarck was a destroyer. And now look at those French
lawyers who are at the helm today: enviable! Political profiteers, but
with a first-rate diplomatic corps to advise them, to give them guidelines, and all of them have at one time or another dashed off plays or
novels without the slightest embarrassment, at least when they were
young, and even today they're still writing books. Do you think these
books are worth anything? I don't. But I give you my word that last
night I was thinking that our own diplomats are missing out on something because they're not writing books too. And I'll tell you why:
First of all, it's as true for a diplomat as for an athlete that he has to
sweat off his excess water. Secondly, it's good for public security. Do
you know what the European balance of power is?"

They were interrupted by Rachel, who came to tell Ulrich that Diotima was expecting him. Tuzzi let her hand him his hat and coat. "If
you were a patriot . . . ," he said, slipping into the sleeves as Rachel
held his coat for him.

"What would I do then?" Ulrich asked him, looking at the black
pupils of Rachel's eyes.

"If you were a patriot, you'd alert my wife or Count Leinsdorf to
some of these problems. I can't do it myself—coming from a husband it could easily seem narrow-minded."

"But nobody here takes me seriously," Ulrich said calmly.

"Oh, don't say that!" Tuzzi cried out. "They may not take you seriously the way they take other people seriously, but for a long time
now they've all been quite afraid of you. They're afraid that you're
liable to put Leinsdorf up to something crazy. Do you know what the
European balance of power is?" the diplomat probed intently.

"I suppose so; more or less," Ulrich said.

"Then I must congratulate you!" Tuzzi flared up bitterly. "We professional diplomats have no idea—none of us do. It is what mustn't
be disturbed if people are not to be at each other's throats. But what
it is that mustn't be disturbed, no one knows exactly. Just cast your
mind back a little over what's been going on around you these last
few years and is still going on: the Italo-Turkish war, Poincaré in
Moscow, the Baghdad question, armed intervention in Libya, Aus-
tro-Serbian tensions, the Adriatic problem . . . Is that a balance? Our

never-to-be-forgotten Baron Ährenthal— But I mustn't keep you any longer!"

"Too bad," Ulrich said. "If that's what the European balance of power comes to, then it's the best possible expression of the European spirit!"

"Yes, that's what makes it so interesting," Tuzzi replied from the door, with an indulgent smile. "And from that point of view the spiritual achievement of our Parallel Campaign is not to be underestimated!"

"Why don't you put a stop to it?"

Tuzzi shrugged his shoulders. "In this country, if a man in His Grace's position wants something, one can't come out against it. All one can do is just keep one's eyes open."

"And how have you been getting on?" Ulrich asked the little black-and-white sentry who was now taking him to Diotima.

140

DIOTIMA HAS CHANGED THE BOOKS
SHE READS

"My dear friend," Diotima said when Ulrich came in, "I didn't want to let you leave without having a word with you, but to have to receive you in this state . . . !" She was wearing a negligee in which her majestic form, through its accidental position, looked slightly pregnant; this lent the proud body, which had never given birth, something of the lovely abandon of the travail of motherhood. Beside her on the sofa lay a fur collar, which she had obviously been using to keep herself warm, and on her forehead a compress against migraine had been allowed to stay in place because she knew it was decorative, like a Greek headband. Though it was late, no lamp had been lit, and the mingled scent of medications and fresheners for some unknown malaise hung in the air, mixed with a powerful fragrance that had been tossed over all the individual odors like a blanket.

Ulrich bent his face low to kiss Diotima's hand, as if he were trying to make out from the scent of her arm what changes had taken place during his absence. But her skin exuded only the same rich, well-fed, well-bathed aroma it always did.

"Ah, my friend, how good it is to have you back! Oh!" she suddenly moaned, but with a smile. "I'm having the most awful cramps!"

Such information, from a straightforward person as neutral as a weather report, on Diotima's lips took on all the emphasis of a breakdown and a confession.

"Dear cousin!" Ulrich exclaimed, and leaned forward with a smile to look into her face. For an instant Ulrich confused Tuzzi's delicate hint about his wife's indisposition with a conjecture that Diotima had become pregnant, which would have been a momentous turn of events for the household.

Half guessing what was in his mind, she made a languid gesture of denial. What she had was only menstrual cramps, which were, however, something new in her experience; she had begun having them only in the last few months, suggesting an obscure connection with her wavering between Arnheim and her husband. When she heard of Ulrich's return it gave her some comfort, and she welcomed him as the confidant of her struggles, which is why she had received him. She lay there, with only a token pretense of sitting up, abandoned to the pains that raged within her, and was in his company a piece of untrammeled nature, without fences or No Trespassing signs, a rare enough condition with her. She had assumed she could convincingly plead a nervous stomachache, no more than a sign of a sensitive constitution; otherwise, she would not have let him see her.

"Why don't you take something for it?" Ulrich asked her.

"Ah," Diotima sighed, "it's only this excitement. My nerves can't take it much longer!"

There was a little pause, because this was really Ulrich's cue to inquire after Arnheim, but he was more interested in finding out about the things that directly concerned himself, and he could not immediately find a way. Finally, he asked:

"Liberating the soul from civilization is not so easy, I suppose?" and added: "I'm afraid I can flatter myself that I predicted long since that your efforts to blaze a trail for the spirit into the world would come to a painful end!"

Diotima remembered how she had escaped from the reception and sat with Ulrich on the shoe bench in her foyer: she had been almost as depressed then as she was today, and yet there had been countless risings and ebbings of hope since then.

"Wasn't it glorious, dear friend," she said, "when we still believed in the great idea! Today I can say that the world listened, but how deeply disappointed I am myself!"

"But why, actually?" Ulrich asked.

"I don't know. It must be my fault."

She was about to add something about Arnheim, but Ulrich wanted to know what people had made of the great demonstration; the last he remembered of it was not finding Diotima at home after Count Leinsdorf had sent him to prepare her for some firm intervention, while making sure she would not worry.

Diotima made a disdainful gesture. "The police arrested a few young people, and then they let them go; Leinsdorf was very annoyed, but what else could they do? Now he's backing Wisnieczky more than ever, and insists that something must be done. But Wisnieczky can't organize any propaganda if no one knows what it's supposed to be for!"

"I hear it's supposed to be 'Watchword: Action!' " Ulrich interjected. The name of Baron Wisnieczky, who as Cabinet Minister had been wrecked by the opposition of the German nationalist parties—so that putting him at the head of the committee to drum up support for the undefined great patriotic idea of the Parallel Campaign could only arouse intense suspicion—vividly reminded Ulrich of His Grace's political ministrations, whose fruit this was. It seemed that the casual course of Count Leinsdorf's thinking—perhaps confirmed by the predictable failure of all attempts to electrify the spirit of the homeland, and beyond that of all Europe, by a concerted effort of its leading intellects—had now led him to the realization that it would be best to give this spirit a push, no matter from what direction. In His Grace's deliberations this might also have been supported by experiences with cases of possession, whose victims were sometimes supposed to be helped by being ruthlessly screamed at or shaken. But this speculation, which had rushed through Ulrich's mind before Diotima could reply, was now interrupted by her answer. This time, the invalid again addressed him as "dear friend."

"My dear friend," she said, "there is some truth in that! Our century is thirsting for action. An action—"

"But what action? What kind of action?" Ulrich broke in.

"It doesn't matter! In action there is a magnificent pessimism about words. We can't deny that in the past all we have done is talk. We have lived for great and eternal words and ideals; for a heightening of human values; for being true to our inmost selves; for an ever-increasing enrichment of life. We have striven for a synthesis, we have lived for new aesthetic joys and new standards of happiness, and I won't deny that the quest for truth is child's play compared with the immense responsibility of becoming a truth oneself. But we overreached, considering the meager sense of reality the human soul has in our time, and we have lived in a dream of yearning, but for nothing!"

Diotima had urgently risen on one elbow. "It's a healthy sign these days to renounce the search for the buried entrance to the soul and try instead to come to terms with life as it is!" she concluded.

Now Ulrich had a second, authorized version of the slogan "Action!" to set beside the conjectural Leinsdorfian one. Diotima seemed to have changed her library books. He remembered seeing her, as he came in, surrounded by piles of books, but it had grown too dark to make out the titles; besides, some were covered by the meditative young woman's body as by a great serpent that had now reared up higher and was eagerly watching his face. Since girlhood Diotima had been inclined to nourish herself on very sentimental and subjective books, but now, as Ulrich gathered from what she said, she had been seized by that spiritual urge for renewal which is constantly at work, striving to find what it has failed to find in the ideas of the last twenty years in the ideas of the next twenty years. This may turn out to be the root of those great changes of mood in history, which seesaw between humanitarianism and ruthlessness, rage and indifference, or other such contradictions for which there seems to be no adequate explanation. It passed through Ulrich's mind that the little residue of uncertainty left over from every moral experience, about which he had talked so much with Agathe, must really be the cause of this human instability; but because he shied away from the pleasure with which he remembered those conversations, he forced his thoughts to turn aside and focus instead on the General, who had been the first to tell him that the age was receiving a new spirit, and had done so in a tone of healthy irritation that left no room for beguiling oneself with bewitching doubts. And because he was now thinking of the General, the latter's request that Ulrich might look into the ruffled relationship between his cousin and Arnheim came to mind, so that he ended by responding bluntly to Diotima's speech of farewell to the soul:

" 'Boundless love' doesn't seem to have quite agreed with you!"

"Oh, you're incorrigible!" His cousin sighed, letting herself fall back into her pillows, where she closed her eyes; unaccustomed to such straightforward language in Ulrich's absence, she needed time to recollect just how much she had confided in him. But suddenly his nearness brought it back. She dimly remembered a talk with Ulrich about "love beyond measure," which had been continued at their last or penultimate meeting: a conversation in which she had sworn that souls could step outside the prison of the body, or at least lean out of it halfway, as it were, and Ulrich had retorted that these were the delirious ravings of starved love, and that she should concede her "concession" to Arnheim, or himself, or anyone at all; he had even named Tuzzi in that connection, as she now recalled—suggestions of this kind were probably easier to remember than the rest of the things a man like Ulrich talks about. At the time, she had probably been justified in feeling this as impudent, but since past pain is a harmless old friend compared with present pain, it now enjoyed the advantage of being a memory of frankness between friends. So Diotima opened her eyes again and said: "There's probably no perfect love on this earth!"

She said it with a smile, but beneath her compress her brow was sadly furrowed, which gave her face a curiously twisted expression in the dim light. In whatever concerned her personally Diotima was not averse to believing in supernatural possibilities. Even General Stumm's unexpected appearance at the Council meeting had startled her as though it were the doing of spirits, and as a child she had prayed that she might never die. This made it easier for her to believe in a supernatural way in her relationship with Arnheim, or more accurately, to believe with that not quite complete disbelief, that something-that-cannot-be-ruled-out, which today has become the basic attitude in matters of faith. Had Arnheim been capable of doing more than drawing something invisible from her soul and his own, something that touched in midair when they were five yards apart, or had their eyes been able to meet in such a way that something tangible would come of it—a coffee bean, a barleycorn, an ink stain—some trace of some kind of real use or even just a suggestion of progress, then the next thing Diotima would have expected was that someday this connection would go higher still, turning into one of those otherworldly connections that it is just as hard to form an exact idea of as it is of most worldly ones. She could even put up with Arnheim's lately being away more often and for longer periods than before, and his being immersed to a surprising degree in his business affairs even on days when he was present. She permitted herself no doubt that his love for her was still the great event in his life, and whenever they came together again alone, the level of their souls instantly rose so high, and their sense of contact was so powerful, that their feelings were struck dumb, and if they could not find anything impersonal to talk about, a vacuum developed that left a bitter exhaustion in its wake. However little the possibility could be excluded that this was passion, she could just as little bring herself—accustomed as she was by the times she lived in to regard everything not practical as merely a matter of belief, or rather of unsettled unbelief—to exclude the possibility that something more would come of it, which would be contrary to all reasonable expectations. But at this moment, when she had opened her eyes to look straight at Ulrich, of whom she could make out only a dark outline, and who stood there in silence, she asked herself: "What *am* I waiting for? What am I really expecting to happen?"

At length Ulrich said: "But Arnheim wanted to marry you!"

Diotima again propped herself up on her arm, and she said: "Can one solve the problem of love by getting divorced or married?"

"So I was mistaken about the pregnancy," Ulrich noted mentally, unable to think of anything to say in response to his cousin's outburst. Then he said abruptly: "I warned you about Arnheim!" Perhaps he now felt obligated to tell her what he knew about the tycoon's mixing up both their souls in his business deals; but he instantly dropped the idea, for he felt that in this conversation every word had its allotted place, like the objects in his study that he had found carefully dusted on his return, as though he had been dead for the space of a minute.

Diotima chided him: "You shouldn't take it so lightly. There's a deep friendship between Arnheim and me; and if at times there's also something else between us, something I might call a great anxiety, it only comes from our frankness. I don't know whether you've ever experienced this, or whether you can: between two people who reach a certain level of emotional rapport any lie becomes so impossible that they can hardly speak to each other at all anymore!"

In this reproof Ulrich's finely tuned ear heard that his cousin's soul was more accessible to him than usual, and because he was highly amused by her unintended confession that she could not talk with Arnheim without lying, he demonstrated his own openness for a while by not saying anything either. Then, when she had lain back again, he bent over her arm and kissed its hand in a gentle gesture of friendship. Light as the marrow of elder twigs it rested in his own, and remained lying there even after the kiss. Her pulse throbbed on his fingertips. The powder-fine scent of her nearness clung to his face like a puff of cloud. And although this gallant kiss on the hand had been only in jest, it was like infidelity in leaving behind a certain bitter aftertaste of desire, of having leaned so closely over a person that one drank from her like an animal, and no longer saw one's own image rising back up out of the water.

"What are you thinking?" Diotima asked. Ulrich merely shook his head and so gave her a fresh opportunity—in the darkness that was brightened only by a last velvety glimmering—to make comparative studies of silence. She was reminded of a wonderful saying: "There are people with whom not even the greatest hero would trust himself to remain silent." Or it was something like that. She seemed to remember that it was a quotation; Arnheim had used it, and she had applied it to herself. Other than Arnheim's, she had since the first weeks of her marriage never held a man's hand in hers for longer than two seconds; but it was happening now with Ulrich's hand. Wrapped up in herself as she was, she overlooked what the next step might be, but found herself a moment later pleasantly convinced that she had been quite right not to wait idly for the hour of supreme love—perhaps yet to come, perhaps not—but to use the time of temporizing indecision to devote herself somewhat more to her husband. Married people have it easy; where others would be breaking faith with a lover, they can say that they are remembering their duty.

And because Diotima told herself that, come what might, she must do her duty for now at the post where fate had placed her, she had undertaken to improve her husband's shortcomings and infuse him with a little more soul. Again a poet's words came to mind, roughly to the effect that there was no deeper despair than to be entwined in a common fate with a person one did not love; and that also proved that she must make an effort to feel something for Tuzzi as long as their fate had not separated them. In sensible contrast to the incalculable events of the soul, from which she had made him suffer long enough, she set about it systematically; she felt pride in the books on which she was lying, for they concerned themselves with the physiology and psychology of marriage, and somehow everything harmonized: that it was dark, that she had these books by her, that Ulrich was holding her hand, that she had conveyed to him the magnificent pessimism that she might soon be expressing in her public role by renouncing her ideals. So thinking, Diotima pressed Ulrich's hand from time to time as if her suitcases were standing packed for her to take leave of everything that had been. She moaned softly, and the faintest wave of pain ran through her body by way of excuse; but Ulrich reassured her with the pressure of his fingertips. After this had happened several times, Diotima thought it really might be too much, yet she no longer dared to withdraw her hand, because it lay so light and dry in his, even trembling at times, as she herself recognized, like an inadmissible indication of the physiology of love, which she had not the slightest intention of betraying by some awkward movement of flight.

It was "Rachelle," busying herself in the adjoining room—she had been acting in an oddly impertinent fashion lately—who put an end to this scene by suddenly turning on the light on the other side of the open door. Diotima hastily pulled her hand away from Ulrich's, in which a space that had been filled with weightlessness remained lying for a moment longer.

"Rachelle," Diotima called in a hushed voice, "turn the light on in here too!"

When this was done their illumined heads had the look of something just emerged from the depths, as though the darkness had not quite dried off them. Shadows lay around Diotima's mouth, giving it moistness and fullness; the little mother-of-pearl bulges on her neck and under her cheeks, which ordinarily seemed to have been created for the delectation of lovers, were hard as a linocut and shaded with slashes of ink. Ulrich's head, too, loomed up in the unaccustomed light, painted in black and white like that of a savage on the warpath. Blinking, he tried to make out the titles on the books surrounding Diotima, and saw with amazement what his cousin's choice of reading matter revealed about her desire to learn the hygiene of body and soul. "Someday he's going to hurt me!" she suddenly thought, following his glance and troubled by it, but it did not enter her consciousness in the form of that sentence: she merely felt much too defenseless as she lay there in the light under his gaze and struggled to recover her poise. With a gesture meant to be thoroughly superior, as befitted a woman "independent" of everything, she waved her hand over her reading and said in the most matter-of-fact tone: "Would you believe that adultery sometimes strikes me as far too simple a solution for marital conflict?"

"At all events it's the most sparing," Ulrich replied, irritating her with his mocking tone. "I'd say it can do no harm at all."

Diotima gave him a reproachful look and made a sign to warn him that Rachel could hear what they were saying from the next room. Then she said aloud: "That's certainly not what I meant!" and called her maid, who appeared sullenly and accepted with bitter jealousy her being sent out.

This interlude had, however, given their feelings time to put themselves to rights. The illusion, favored by the darkness, that they were committing a tiny infidelity together, though rather indefinably and toward no one in particular, evaporated in the light, and Ulrich now turned to the business that had to be attended to before he could leave.

"I haven't yet told you that I'm resigning as Secretary," he began.

Diotima, however, had heard of it, and told him that he would have to stay on; there was no way out of it. "There's such an immense amount of work still to be done," she pleaded. "Be patient a while longer; we're bound to find a solution soon! A real secretary will be found to place at your disposal."

This impersonal "will be found" aroused Ulrich's curiosity, and he asked for details.

"Arnheim has offered to lend you his own secretary."

"No, thanks," Ulrich replied. "I have the feeling that might not be quite disinterested." Again he was more than strongly tempted to let Diotima in on the simple connection with the oil fields, but she had not even noticed the ambiguity of his answer, and simply continued:

"Apart from that, my husband has also offered to let you have one of the clerks in his office."

"Wouldn't you mind?"

"To be frank, I wouldn't be entirely happy about that," Diotima said more energetically. "Especially as there's no dearth of possibilities. Even your friend the General has given me to understand that he'd be delighted to send you an aide from his department."

"And Leinsdorf?"

"These three offers were made to me spontaneously, so I had no reason to ask Leinsdorf; but I'm sure he wouldn't shrink from making a sacrifice."

"Everyone's spoiling me," Ulrich commented, summing up with these words the amazing readiness of Arnheim, Tuzzi, and Stumm to plant a man of their own inside the Parallel Campaign at such low cost. "But perhaps it would be most advisable for me to take on your husband's clerk."

"My dear friend—" Diotima said, still protesting, but she did not really know how to go on, which was probably why something quite tangled came out. Again she propped herself up on an elbow and said with feeling: "I reject adultery as too crude a solution of marital conflicts—I've told you that! But even so, there's nothing so hard as being linked for life in a single destiny with a person one doesn't love enough!"

This was a most unnatural cry of nature. But Ulrich, unmoved, would not be shaken from his resolve. "No doubt Section Chief Tuzzi would like this way of having a hand in your operation; but so would the others," he pointed out. "All three are in love with you, and each of them has to reconcile this somehow with his duty." How odd, he thought, that Diotima did not understand either the language of facts or that of the comments he made on them, and rising to take his leave, he added with even heavier irony: "The only one who loves you unselfishly is myself—because I have no duties of any kind and no commitments. But feelings without distraction are destructive; you've meanwhile found that out for yourself, and you have

always regarded me with a justifiable, even if only instinctive, mistrust."

Although Diotima did not know why, this was precisely and en-
dearingly the reason that she was pleased to see Ulrich siding with
her own house in this matter of the secretary, and she did not let go
of the hand he offered her.

"And how does this fit in with your affair with 'that' woman?" she
asked, playfully taking her cue from his remark—insofar as Diotima
could be playful; the effect was rather that of a shot-putter playing
with a feather.

Ulrich did not know whom she could mean.

"That judge's wife you introduced to me!"

"You noticed that, cousin?"

"Dr. Arnheim drew my attention to it."

"Oh, did he? How flattering that he should think he can hurt my
standing with you in this fashion. But of course my relations with the
lady are entirely innocent!" Ulrich stated, defending Bonadea's
honor in the conventional fashion.

"She was in your house twice during your absence," Diotima said
with a laugh. "The first time, we happened to be passing by, and we
heard about the second time some other way. So there's no point in
trying to be discreet. But on the other hand, I wish I could understand *you!* I simply *can't!*"

"How on earth could I explain this to you, of all people!"

"Try!" Diotima commanded. She had put on her expression of "official immorality," a sort of bespectacled look she donned whenever
her mind commanded her to speak or hear things that were out of
bounds for her soul as a lady. But Ulrich declined and repeated that
his understanding of Bonadea could only be guesswork.

"All right," Diotima gave in, "even though your lady friend herself
was not sparing with her hints! She seems to feel called upon to justify some wrong or other in my eyes. But do speak of this, if you'd
rather, as if you were merely guessing!"

Now Ulrich felt a thirst for knowledge, and he learned that Bonadea had been to see Diotima several times, and not only in matters
connected with the Parallel Campaign and her husband's position.

"I must admit I find her a beautiful woman," Diotima conceded,
"and she is extraordinarily high-minded. I'm really upset that you're

always eliciting confidences from me but always withholding yours!"

At this moment Ulrich's attitude was approximately "the devil take both of you!" He felt like giving Diotima a scare and paying Bonadea back for her intrusiveness, or else he was suddenly feeling the full distance between himself and the life in which he had been indulging.

"All right," he told her, summoning up a gloomy expression: "The woman is a nymphomaniac and I find that irresistible!"

Diotima knew "academically" what nymphomania was. There was a pause, and then she drawled: "The poor woman! And you find *that* attractive?"

"Isn't it idiotic?" Ulrich said.

Diotima wanted to know "the details"—would he explain this "lamentable phenomenon" and enable her to understand it in "human terms"? He did so without exactly going into detail, but she was nevertheless overcome by a feeling of satisfaction that doubtless rested on that well-known gratitude to God that she was not like the other woman; but at its apex this feeling faded into dismay and curiosity, which was not to be without influence on her subsequent relations with Ulrich. Pensively she said: "But it must be simply awful to embrace a person who doesn't mean anything to you!"

"You think so?" her cousin asked candidly. At this insinuation Diotima felt hurt and indignant to the marrow, but she could not let herself show it; she contented herself with letting go of his hand and sinking back into her pillows with a dismissive gesture. "You never should have told me this!" she said from where she lay. "You treated that poor woman very badly just now, and you've been most indiscreet!"

"I'm never indiscreet!" Ulrich objected, and could not help laughing at his cousin. "You're really being unfair. You are the first woman to whom I've ever confided anything about another woman, and it was you who made me do it!"

Diotima was flattered. She wanted to say something of the same kind, to the effect that without a spiritual transformation one cheated oneself of the best in life; but she could not come out with it because it suddenly seemed too personal. Finally, something from one of the books surrounding her prompted her to answer noncommittally, from within the protection of her official persona: "Like all men," she chided him, "you make the mistake of treating your love partner not as an equal but merely as a complement to yourself, and then you're disappointed. Has it never occurred to you that the only way to a transcendent, harmonious eroticism may lie through stricter self-discipline?"

Ulrich's jaw nearly dropped, but he answered in spontaneous self-defense: "Do you know that Section Chief Tuzzi has already grilled me today on the possibilities of the origin and training of the soul?"

Diotima sat up straight: "What? Tuzzi talks with you about soul?" she asked in amazement.

"Of course he does; he's trying to find out what it is," Ulrich assured her, but he could not be induced to stay any longer. He merely promised to betray a confidence some other time and tell her all about that too.

141

PROBLEMS OF A MORALIST WITH A LETTER TO WRITE

With this visit to Diotima the restless state Ulrich had been in since his return came to an end. On the afternoon of the very next day he sat down at his desk, and in doing so felt at home again, and began writing a letter to Agathe.

It was clear to him—as simple and clear as a windless day sometimes is—that her rash scheme was extremely dangerous. What had happened so far could still be taken as a risky prank, of no concern to anyone but themselves, but that depended entirely on its being rescinded before it acquired connections with reality, and the danger was growing with every passing day. Ulrich had written this much when he stopped, uneasy at the thought of entrusting to the mails a letter in which this was so openly discussed. He told himself that it would be better in every way to take the next train back, in place of the letter; but of course this made no sense to him either, since he had let days go by without doing anything about it. He knew he would not go.

He realized that there was something behind this tantamount to a choice: he simply felt like letting things take their course and seeing what came of this incident. So his problem was just how far he actually, definitely *could* want to risk it, and all sorts of wide-ranging thoughts went through his mind.

It occurred to him right at the start, for instance, that whenever he had taken a "moral" stance so far, he had always been psychologically worse off than when he was doing or thinking something that might usually be considered "immoral." This is a common occurrence, for in situations that are in conflict with their surroundings these ideas and actions develop all their energies, while in the mere doing of what is right and proper they understandably behave as if they were paying taxes. This suggests that all evil is carried out with zest and imagination, while good is distinguished by an unmistakable dreariness and dearth of feeling. Ulrich recalled that his sister had expressed this moral dilemma quite casually by asking him whether being good was no longer a good thing. It ought to be difficult and breathtaking, she had maintained, and wondered why, nevertheless, moral people were almost always bores.

He smiled contentedly, spinning this thought out with the realization that Agathe and he were as one in their particular opposition to Hagauer, which could be roughly characterized as that of people who were bad in a good way to a man who was good in a bad way. Leaving out of account the broad middle of life's spectrum, which is, reasonably enough, occupied by people whose minds have not been troubled by the general terms good and evil since they let go of their mother's apron strings, there remain the two extremes where purposeful moral efforts are still made. Today these are left to just such bad/good and good/bad people, the first kind never having seen good fly or heard it sing, thus expecting their fellowmen to enthuse with them about a moral landscape where stuffed birds perch on dummy trees, while the second kind, the good/bad mortals, exasperated by their competitors, industriously show a penchant for evil, at least in theory, as if they were convinced that only wrongdoing, which is emotionally not quite as threadbare as doing good, still twitches with a bit of moral vitality. And so Ulrich's world—not, of course, that he was fully aware of this—had at that time the option of letting itself be ruined by either its lame morality or its lively immoralists, and to this day it probably does not know which of those two choices it finally embraced with stunning success, unless that majority who can never spare the time to concern themselves with morality in general did pay attention to one case in particular because they had lost confidence in their own situation and, as a result, had of course lost a number of other things as well. For bad/bad people, who can so easily be blamed for everything, were even then as rare as they are today, and the good/good ones represent a mission as far removed as a distant nebula. Still, it was precisely of them that Ulrich was thinking, while everything else he appeared to be thinking about left him cold.

And he gave his thoughts an even more general and impersonal form by setting the relationship that exists between the demands "Do!" and "Don't!" in the place of good and evil. For as long as a particular morality is in the ascendant—and this is just as valid for the spirit of "Love thy neighbor" as it is for a horde of Vandals— "Don't!" is still only the negative and natural corollary of "Do!" Doing and leaving undone are red hot, and the flaws they contain don't count because they are the flaws of heroes and martyrs. In this condition good and evil are identical with the happiness and unhappiness of the whole person. But as soon as the contested system has achieved dominance and spread itself out, and its fulfillment no longer faces any special hurdles, the relationship between imperative and taboo perforce passes through a decisive phase where duty is not born anew and alive each day but is leached and drained and cut up into ifs and buts, ready to serve all sorts of uses. Here a process begins, in the further course of which virtue and vice, because of their common root in the same rules, laws, exceptions, and limitations, come to look more and more alike, until that curious and ultimately unbearable self-contradiction arises which was Ulrich's point of departure: namely, that the distinction between good and evil loses all meaning when weighed against the pleasure of a pure, deep, spontaneous mode of action, a pleasure that can leap like a spark from permissible as well as from forbidden activities. Indeed, whoever takes an unbiased view is likely to find that the negative aspect of morality is more highly charged with this tension than the positive: While it seems relatively natural that certain actions called "bad" must not be allowed to happen, actions such as taking what belongs to others or overindulgence in sensual gratification, or, if they are committed, at least *ought* not to be committed, the corresponding affirmative moral traditions, such as unlimited generosity in giving or the urge to mortify the flesh, have already almost entirely disappeared; and where they are still practiced they are practiced by fools, cranks, or bloodless prigs. In such a condition, where virtue is decrepit and moral conduct consists chiefly in the restraint of immoral conduct, it can easily happen that immoral conduct appears to be not only more spontaneous and vital than its opposite, but actually more moral, if one may use the term not in the sense of law and justice but with regard to whatever passion may still be aroused by matters of conscience. But could anything possibly be more perverse than to incline inwardly toward evil because, with all one has left of a soul, one is seeking good?

Ulrich had never felt this perversity more keenly than at this moment, when the rising arc his reflections had followed led him back to Agathe again. Her innate readiness to act in the good/bad mode—to resort once more to the term they had coined in passing—as so notably exemplified in her tampering with their father's will, offended the same innate readiness in his own nature, which had merely taken on an abstract theoretical form, something like a priest's admiration of the Devil, while as a person he was not only able to lead his life more or less according to the rules but even, as he could see, did not wish to be disturbed in so doing. With as much melancholy satisfaction as ironic clear-sightedness, he noted that all his theoretical preoccupation with evil basically amounted to this, that he wanted to protect the bad things that happened from the bad people who undertook them, and he was suddenly overcome by a longing for goodness, like a man who has been wasting his time in foreign parts dreaming of coming home one day and going straight to the well in his native village for a drink of water. If he had not been caught up in this comparison, he might have noticed that his whole effort to see Agathe as a morally confused person, such as the present age produces in profusion, was only a pretext to screen out a prospect that frightened him a good deal more. For his sister's conduct, which certainly did not pass muster objectively, exerted a remarkable fascination as soon as one dreamed along with it; for then all the controversies and indecisions vanished, and one was left with the impression of a passionate, affirmative virtue lusting for action, which could easily seem, compared with its lifeless daily counterpart, to be some kind of ancient vice.

Ulrich was not the man to indulge himself lightly in such exaltations of his feelings, least of all with this letter to write, so he redirected his mind into general reflections. These would have been incomplete had he not remembered how easily and often, in the times he had lived through, the longing for some duty rooted in completeness had led to first one virtue, then another, being singled out from among the available supply, to be made the focus of noisy glorification. National, Christian, humanistic virtues had all taken their turn; once, it was the virtue of chromium steel, another time, the virtue of kindness; then it was individuality, and then fellowship; today it is the fraction of a second, and yesterday it was historical equilibrium. The changing moods of public life basically depend on the exchange of one such ideal for another: it had always left Ulrich unmoved, and only made him feel that he was standing on the sidelines. Even now all it meant for him was a filling in of the general picture, for only incomplete insight can lead one to believe that one can get at life's moral inexplicability, whose complications have become overwhelming, by means of one of the interpretations already embedded within it. Such efforts merely resemble the movements of a sick person restlessly changing his position, while the paralysis that felled him progresses inexorably. Ulrich was convinced that the state of affairs that gave rise to these efforts was inescapable and characterized the level from which every civilization goes into decline, because no civilization has so far been capable of replacing its lost inner elasticity. He was also convinced that the same thing that had happened to every past moral system would happen to every future one. For the slackening of moral energy has nothing to do with the province of the Commandments or the keeping of them: it is independent of their distinctions; it cannot be affected by any outer discipline but is an entirely inner process, synonymous with the weakening of the significance of all actions and of faith in the unity of responsibility for them.

And so Ulrich's thoughts, without his having intended it, found their way back to the idea he had ironically characterized to Count Leinsdorf as the "General Secretariat for Precision and Soul," and although he had never spoken of it other than flippantly and in jest, he now realized that all his adult life he had consistently behaved as though such a General Secretariat lay within the realm of possibility. Perhaps, he could say by way of excuse, every thoughtful person harbors in himself some such idea of order, just as grown men may still wear next to their skin the picture of a saint that their mother hung around their necks when they were small. And this image of order, which no one dares either to take seriously or to put away, must be more or less something like this: On one hand, it vaguely stands for the longing for some law of right living, a natural, iron law that allows no exceptions and excludes no objections: that is, as liberating as intoxication and sober as the truth. On the other hand, however, it evinces the conviction that one will never behold such a law with one's own eyes, never think it out with one's own thoughts, that no one person's mission or power can bring it about but only an effort by everyone—unless it is only a delusion.

Ulrich hesitated for an instant. He was doubtless a believing person who just didn't believe in anything. Even in his greatest dedication to science he had never managed to forget that people's goodness and beauty come from what they believe, not from what they know. But faith had always been bound up with knowledge, even if that knowledge was illusory, ever since those primordial days of its magic beginnings. That ancient knowledge has long since rotted away, dragging belief down with it into the same decay, so that today the connection must be established anew. Not, of course, by raising faith "to the level of knowledge," but still in some way making it take flight from that height. The art of transcending knowledge must again be practiced. And since no one man can do this, all men must turn their minds to it, whatever else their minds might be on. When Ulrich at this moment thought about the ten-year plan, or the hundred- or thousand-year plan that mankind would have to devise in order to work toward a goal it can have no way of knowing, he soon realized that this was what he had long imagined, under all sorts of names, as the truly experimental life. For what he meant by the term "faith" was not so much that stunted desire to know, the credulous ignorance that is what most people take it to be, but rather a knowledgeable intuition, something that is neither knowledge nor fantasy, but is not faith either; it is just that "something else" which eludes all these concepts.

He suddenly pulled the letter toward him, but immediately pushed it away again.

The stern glow on his face went out, and his dangerous favorite idea struck him as ridiculous. As though with one glance through a suddenly opened window, he felt what was really around him: cannons and business deals. The notion that people who lived in this fashion could ever join in a planned navigation of their spiritual destiny was simply inconceivable, and Ulrich had to admit that historical development had never come about by means of any such coherent combination of ideas as the mind of the individual may just manage in a pinch; the course of history was always wasteful and dissipated, as if it had been flung on the table by the fist of some low-life gambler. He actually felt a little ashamed. Everything he had thought during the last hour was suspiciously reminiscent of a certain "Inquiry for the Drafting of a Guiding Resolution to Ascertain the Desires of the Concerned Sections of the Population"; even the fact that he was moralizing at all, this thinking theoretically that surveyed Nature by candlelight, seemed completely unnatural, while the simple man, accustomed to the clarity of the sun, goes straight for the next item, unbothered by any problem beyond the very definite one of whether he can risk this move and make it work.

At this point Ulrich's thoughts flowed back again from these general considerations to himself, and he felt what his sister meant to him. It was to her he had revealed that curious and unlimited, incredible, and unforgettable state of mind in which everything is an affirmation: the condition in which one is incapable of any spiritual movement except a moral one, therefore the only state in which there exists a morality without interruption, even though it may only consist in all actions floating ungrounded within it. And all Agathe had done was to stretch out her hand toward it. She was the person who stretched out her hand and made Ulrich's reflections give way to the bodies and forms of the real world. All his thoughts now appeared to him a mere delaying and transition. He decided to "take a chance" on what might come of Agathe's idea, and at this moment he could not care less that the mysterious promise it held out had started with what was commonly viewed as a reprehensible act. One could only wait and see whether the morality of "rising or sinking" would show itself as applicable here as the simple morality of honesty. He remembered his sister's passionate question as to whether he himself believed what he was saying, but he could affirm this even now as little as he could then. He admitted to himself that he was waiting for Agathe to be able to answer this question.

The phone rang shrilly, and Walter was suddenly rushing at him with flustered explanations and hasty snatches of words. Ulrich listened indifferently but readily, and when he put down the receiver and straightened up he still felt the ringing of its bell, now finally stopping. Depth and darkness came flooding back into his surroundings to soothe him, though he could not have said whether it happened as sounds or colors; it was a deepening of all his senses. Smiling, he picked up the sheet of paper on which he had begun writing to his sister and, before he left the room, slowly tore it into tiny pieces.

142

ONWARD TO MOOSBRUGGER

Meanwhile Walter, Clarisse, and the prophet Meingast were sitting around a platter loaded with radishes, tangerines, almonds, big Turkish prunes, and cream cheese, consuming this delicious and wholesome supper. The prophet, again wearing only his wool cardigan over his rather bony torso, made a point now and again of praising the natural refreshments offered to him, while Clarisse's brother, Siegmund, sat apart, with his hat and gloves on, reporting on yet another conversation he had "cultivated" with Dr. Friedenthal, the assistant medical officer at the psychiatric clinic, to make arrangements for his "completely crazy" sister Clarisse to see Moosbrugger.

"Friedenthal insists that he can do it only with a permit from the District Court," he wound up dispassionately, "and the District Court is not satisfied with the application I obtained for all of you from the Final Hour Welfare Society but requires a recommendation from the Embassy, because we lied, unfortunately, about Clarisse's being a foreigner. So there's nothing else to be done: Tomorrow Dr. Meingast will have to go to the Swiss Embassy!"

Siegmund, who was the elder, resembled his sister, except that his face was unexpressive. If one looked at them side by side, the nose, mouth, and eyes in Clarisse's pallid face suggested cracks in parched soil, while the same features in Siegmund's face had the soft, slightly blurred contours of rolling grassland, although he was clean-shaven except for a small mustache. He had not shed his middle-class appearance nearly as much as his sister, and it gave him an ingenuous naturalness even at the moment when he was so brazenly disposing of a philosopher's precious time. No one would have been surprised if thunder and lightning had burst from the plate of radishes at this imposition, but the great man took it amiably—which his admirers regarded as an event that would make a great anecdote—and blinked an assenting eye toward Siegmund like an eagle that tolerates a sparrow on the perch beside him.

Nonetheless, the sudden and insufficiently discharged tension made it impossible for Walter to contain himself any longer. He pushed back his plate, reddened like a little cloud at sunrise, and stated emphatically that no sane person who was neither a doctor nor an attendant had any business inside an insane asylum. On him, too, the sage bestowed a barely perceptible nod. Siegmund, who in the course of his life had appropriated quite a few opinions, articulated this assent with the hygienic words: "It is, no doubt, a revolting habit of the affluent middle class to see something demonic in mental cases and criminals."

"But in that case," Walter exclaimed, "please tell me why you all want to help Clarisse do something you don't approve of and that can only make her more nervous than ever?"

His wife did not dignify this with an answer. She made an unpleasant face, whose expression was so remote from reality as to be frightening; two long, arrogant lines ran down alongside her nose, and her chin came to a hard point. Siegmund did not feel himself obliged or authorized to speak for the others, so Walter's question was followed by a short silence, until Meingast said quietly and equably: "Clarisse has suffered too strong an impression. It can't be left at that."

"When?" Walter demanded.

"Just the other day—that evening at the window."

Walter turned pale, because he was the only one who had not been told before—Clarisse had evidently told Meingast and even her brother. Isn't that just like her! he thought.

And although it was not exactly called for, he suddenly had the feeling, across the plate of produce, that they were all about ten years younger. That was the time when Meingast—still the old, untransformed Meingast—was bowing out and Clarisse had opted for Walter. Later she confessed to him that Meingast had still, even though he had already given her up, sometimes kissed and fondled her. The memory was like the large arc of a swing. Walter had been swung higher and higher: he succeeded in everything he did then, even though there were lots of downswings too. Yet even then Clarisse had been unable to speak with Walter when Meingast was present; he had often had to find out from others what she was thinking and doing. With him she froze up. "When *you* touch me, I freeze up!" she had said to him. "My body goes solemn—that's quite different from the way it is with Meingast!" And when he kissed her for the first time she said to him: "I promised Mother never to do anything like this." Later on, though, she admitted to him that in those days Meingast was always secretly playing footsie with her under the dining room table. It was all Walter's doing! The richness of the inner development he had called forth in her had hindered her freedom of movement, as he explained it to himself.

Now he thought of the letters he and Clarisse had written to each other in those days; he still believed that if one were to search through all of literature it would be hard to find anything to match them for passion and originality. In those stormy days he would punish Clarisse, when she was keeping company with Meingast, by running off—and then he would write her a letter; and she wrote him letters, swearing that she was faithful, while candidly reporting that Meingast had kissed her once again on her knee, through her stocking. Walter had wanted to publish these letters as a book, and still thought, off and on, that he would do so someday. So far, unfortunately, nothing had come of it except for a fateful misunderstanding with Clarisse's governess. One day Walter had said to her: "You'll see, soon I shall make up for everything!" He had only meant it in his sense: namely, how splendidly he would be justified in the family's eyes once publication of the letters brought him fame and success; for strictly speaking, things between him and Clarisse at that time were not what they should be. Clarisse's governess—a family heirloom, pensioned off in the honorable guise of serving as an assistant mother, misunderstood him, however, in her sense, and a rumor promptly arose in the family that Walter was about to put himself in a position to ask for Clarisse's hand in marriage; once the word was out, it led to very particular joys and restraints. "Real life" instantly awakened: Walter's father announced that he would no longer pay his son's bills unless Walter began to earn his keep. Walter's prospective father-in-law invited him to his studio, where he spoke to him of the hardships and disillusionments awaiting the practitioner of pure, disinterested art, whether in the visual arts, music, or literature. And finally both Walter and Clarisse began to itch with the suddenly tangible thought of having their own house, children, openly sharing a bedroom: like a crack in the skin that cannot heal because one unconsciously keeps scratching at it. And so it came to pass that Walter, only a few weeks after his impulsive words, actually became engaged to Clarisse, which made both of them very happy but also very tense, because it was the beginning of that search for an established place in life that burdens life with all the problems of Western civilization, since the position Walter was sporadically seeking had to pass muster not only as to income but as to how it would affect six major aspects of his life: Clarisse, himself, their love life, literature, music, and painting. Actually, they had only recently emerged from the whirlwind of complications unleashed as soon as he let his tongue run off with him in the elderly mademoiselle's company, when he accepted his present position in the Department of Works and Monuments and moved with Clarisse into this modest little house, where the rest was up to fate.

In his heart Walter felt it would be quite pleasant if fate were now to call it a day: though the end would not be precisely what the beginning had promised—but then, when apples are ripe they don't fall up the tree, but to the ground. That was what Walter was thinking, and

meanwhile, across the table from him, above the diametrically opposite end of the colorful tray of wholesome vegetarian food, his wife's
small head hovered; Clarisse was trying to supplement Meingast's
explanation with the utmost objectivity, indeed as objectively as
Meingast himself: "I must do something to pulverize the shock. The
shock was too much for me, Meingast says," she specified, and added
on her own: "It was certainly no coincidence that that man stopped
in the bushes right under my window."

"Nonsense!" Walter waved this away as a sleeper waves off a fly.
"It was just as much my window as yours!"

"Our window, then," Clarisse corrected herself, her thin-lipped
smile so pointed that one could not decide whether it expressed bitterness or scorn. *"We* attracted him. But would you like me to tell
you what that man was doing? He was *stealing* sexual pleasure!"

It made Walter's head ache, crammed full as it was of the past, and
now the present was wedging itself in, leaving no clear difference
between past and present. There were still bushes with their bright
patches of foliage in Walter's head, with bicycle paths winding
among them. Their adventurous long trips and walks could have happened only this morning. Girls' skirts were swinging again just as
they had in those years when ankles had been boldly exposed for the
first time and the hems of white petticoats had frothed with the new
movements of a sports-loving generation. In those days, Walter
thought—to put it mildly—that what was going on between him and
Clarisse was not all it should be, because what happened on these
bike trips in the spring of the year they became engaged was in fact
everything that can happen and leave a girl technically still a virgin.
"Almost incredible, for such a nice girl!" Walter thought, reveling in
his memories. Clarisse had called it "taking Meingast's sins upon
ourselves"—he had just gone abroad and was not yet known as Meingast. "It would be cowardly not to be sensual because he was!" was
the way Clarisse phrased it, adding: "But with you and me I want it to
be spiritual!" Walter did at times worry about the fact that these goings-on were too closely connected with the man who had been gone
such a little while, but Clarisse replied: "People who aim at greatness, as we do in art, for instance, can't be bothered with worrying
about this and that." Walter could remember the zeal with which
they set about annihilating the past by repeating it in a new spirit,

and the relish with which they found out how to excuse illicit physical pleasures by magically attributing to them some transcendent purpose. At that time, Clarisse had been as energetic in her lustfulness as she was later in refusing herself to him, Walter admitted, letting his mind wander for a moment to dwell on the refractory thought that her breasts were still as taut today as they had been then. Everyone could see that, even through her clothes. Meingast happened to be staring at her breasts just then; perhaps he didn't realize it. "Her breasts are mute!" Walter declaimed inwardly with all the richness of association of a dream or a poem; and in almost the same way, while this was happening, the reality of the present forced itself through the padding of emotions:

"Come, Clarisse, tell us what you're thinking," he heard Meingast prompting her, like a doctor or a teacher, in that polite, formal tone he sometimes took with her since his return.

Walter also noticed that Clarisse was looking questioningly at Meingast.

"You were telling me about a certain Moosbrugger, that he was a carpenter. . . ."

Clarisse kept her eyes on him.

"Who else was a carpenter? The Savior! Wasn't that what you said? In fact, you even told me that you had written a letter about it to some influential person, didn't you?"

"Stop it!" Walter burst out. His head was spinning. But he had no sooner expressed his protest than it occurred to him that the letter was something else he had not heard about, and growing weak, he asked: "What letter?"

He got no answer from anyone. Meingast, passing over his question, said: "It's one of the most timely ideas. We're incapable of liberating ourselves by our own efforts, no doubt about it; we call it democracy, but that's merely the political term for our psychological state, our 'you can do it this way, but you can also do it another way.' Ours is the era of the ballot. Each year we determine our sexual ideal, the beauty queen, by ballot, and all we have done by making empirical science our intellectual ideal is to let the facts do the voting for us. We are living in an unphilosophical, dispirited age; it doesn't have the courage to decide what is valuable and what isn't, and democracy means, expressed most succinctly: Do whatever is happening! Incidentally, this is one of the most disgraceful vicious circles in all the history of our race."

While he spoke, the prophet had irritably cracked and peeled a nut, the pieces of which he was now shoving into his mouth. Nobody had understood what he was saying. He broke off his speech in favor of a slow chewing motion of his jaws, in which the turned-up tip of his nose also participated, while the rest of his face remained ascetically still, but he did not take his eyes off Clarisse. They remained fixed somewhere in the region of her breast. The eyes of both the other men involuntarily left the master's face to follow his abstracted gaze. Clarisse felt a suction, as though these six eyes might lift her right out of her chair if they remained fastened on her much longer. But the master vigorously gulped down the last of his nut and went on with his lecture:

"Clarisse has found out that Christian legend has decreed that the Savior was a carpenter. That's not quite correct: his foster father was. Nor is she in the least justified in trying to make something of the fact that some criminal she's heard of happens to be a carpenter too. Intellectually that's simply beneath criticism. Morally it is frivolous. But it shows courage! It really does!" Here Meingast paused, to let the force with which he had said "courage" take effect. Then he quietly continued: "She recently saw, as we did also, a psychopath exposing himself. She makes too much of it; there is in general far too much emphasis on sexuality these days. But Clarisse says: 'It is not by chance that this man stopped under my window. . . .' Now, let us try to understand her rightly. She's wrong, for causally the incident is, of course, a coincidence. But what Clarisse is really saying is: If I regard everything as explained, then a person will never be able to change the world. She regards it as inexplicable that a murderer whose name, if I am not mistaken, is Moosbrugger happens to be a carpenter; she regards it as inexplicable that an unknown sufferer from sexual disturbances should have stopped just under her window; and so she has fallen into the habit of regarding all sorts of other things that happen to her as inexplicable and . . ." Again Meingast kept his listeners waiting awhile; his voice had become reminiscent of a man with a resolve who is firmly but warily tiptoeing up to something, and now he pounced: "And so she will do something!" Meingast ended on a strong note.

It gave Clarisse goose pimples.

"I repeat," Meingast said, "this is not subject to intellectual criticism. But intellectuality is, as we know, only the expression or the tool of a life that has dried out, while the point Clarisse is making may arise from another sphere: that of the will. Clarisse may never be able to explain what is happening to her, but she may well be able to solve it, resolve it. So she is quite right to call it 'salvation'—she is instinctively using the right term for it. It would be easy for one of us to speak of delusional thinking, or to say that Clarisse is a person with weak nerves, but what would be the point? The world is currently so undeluded that it doesn't know when to hate or to love anything, and since we're all of two minds about everything, all of us are neurasthenics and weaklings. In short," the prophet concluded abruptly, "although it is not easy for a philosopher to renounce insight, it is probably the great, growing insight of the twentieth century that this is what must be done. For me, in Geneva, it is today of greater spiritual importance that we have a French boxing coach than that the dissector Rousseau did his thinking there!"

Meingast could have continued talking, now that he had hit his stride: To begin with, the idea of salvation had always been anti-intellectual. "What the world today needs more than anything else is a strong, healthy delusion" was what he had been on the point of saying, but he had swallowed it in favor of the other ending. Second, there was the concomitant physical meaning implied in the etymology of *salvation*, its link with "salve" carrying an inference that deeds alone could save, or at least experiences involving the whole person, neck and crop. Third, he had been prepared to say that the overintellectualization of the male could under certain conditions bring woman to the fore as the instinctive leader in action, of which Clarisse was one of the first examples. Finally, there were all the transformations of the salvation idea in the history of peoples, and the present movement from salvation as a purely religious concept, which had been dominant for centuries, toward the realization that salvation must be brought about by resoluteness of will and even, if necessary, by force. Saving the world by force happened to be his central idea at the moment.

Meanwhile, however, the suction of all those eyes on her was becoming more than Clarisse could stand, and she cut off the master's discourse by turning to Siegmund, as the point of least resistance, saying to him rather too loudly:

"That's what I told you: we have to experience something ourselves to understand it. That's why we have to go to the asylum ourselves!"

Walter, who had been peeling a tangerine as a way of keeping steady, at this moment cut too deeply; an acid jet spurted into his eyes, making him start back and grope for his handkerchief. Siegmund, as always well dressed, first contemplated with an expert's concern the acid's effect on his brother-in-law's eye, then moved his gaze to that still life of respectability, the pigskin gloves and bowler hat resting on his knee. It was only when he could not shake off his sister's relentless stare, and no one spoke to save him the trouble, that he looked up with a grave nod and murmured serenely: "I have never doubted that we all belong in an asylum."

Clarisse then turned to Meingast and said: "I've told you about the Parallel Campaign. That could be another tremendous opportunity and obligation for us to do away with all the 'you can do it this way . . . and another way' that is the great evil of our century."

The master waved this off with a smile.

Clarisse, overcome with a heady sense of her own importance, cried out obstinately and somewhat incoherently: "A woman who lets a man have his way with her when it's only going to weaken his mind is a sex murderer too!"

Here Meingast issued a gentle warning: "Let's keep this on a general plane! Incidentally, I can set your mind at rest on one point: As regards those absurd committee meetings where a dying democracy is trying to give birth to one more great mission, I've had my observers and confidential agents for a long time now."

Clarisse simply felt ice at the roots of her hair.

Walter made another vain stab at stemming developments. Deferentially, he took his stand against Meingast, his tone very different from that which he might have used with Ulrich, for example: "What you say probably amounts to much the same thing I've been saying for a long time, that one ought to paint only in pure colors. It's high time to finish with the broken and blurred, with our concessions to the inane, to the fainthearted vision that no longer dares see that each thing has a true outline, true colors. I put it in pictorial terms, you in philosophic terms. But even though we share a point of view . . ." He suddenly became embarrassed, feeling that he could not talk openly in front of the others about why he dreaded Clarisse's involvement with the insane.

"No, I won't have Clarisse doing it!" he exclaimed. "It won't happen with my consent."

The master had listened amiably, and he answered Walter just as pleasantly as if not one of these emphatic words had reached his ear. "Incidentally, there's something Clarisse has expressed beautifully: She claimed that besides the 'sinful form' we inhabit, we all have an 'innocent form.' We could take this in the lovely sense that, apart from the miserable world of experience, our mind has access to a glorious realm where in lucid moments we feel our image moved by dynamics of an infinitely different kind. How did you put it, Clarisse?" he asked her in an encouraging tone. "Didn't you say that if you could stand up for this wretch without disgust, go into his cell and play the piano for him day and night, without tiring, you would draw his sins, as it were, out of him, take them upon yourself, and ascend with them? Naturally," he said, turning back to Walter, "this is to be taken not literally but as a subliminal process in the soul of the age, a process that here assumes the form of a parable about this man, inspiring her will. . . ."

He was at this point uncertain whether to add something about Clarisse's relation to the history of the idea of salvation, or whether it might be more attractive to explain her mission of leadership to her all over again in private. But Clarisse leapt from her chair like an overexcited child, raised her arm, with fist clenched, high above her head, and with a shyly ferocious smile cut short all further praise of herself with the shrill cry: "Onward to Moosbrugger!"

"But we still have nobody who can get us admitted . . . ," Siegmund was heard to say.

"I am not going along with this!" Walter said firmly.

"I cannot accept favors from a state where freedom and equality are to be had at every price and in every quality," Meingast declared.

"Then Ulrich must get us permission!" Clarisse exclaimed.

Meingast and Siegmund, having gone to enough trouble already, gladly agreed to a solution that relieved them, at least temporarily, of the responsibility, and even Walter finally had to give in, in spite of his protest, and take on the mission of going down to the nearby grocery to phone their chosen emissary.

This was the call that made Ulrich break off writing his letter to Agathe. Walter's voice took him by surprise, and so did his proposal. There was certainly room for a difference of opinion about Clarisse's scheme, Walter freely conceded, but it could not be entirely discounted as a whim. Perhaps it was time to somehow make a start somewhere, it didn't matter so much where. Of course, it was only a coincidence that Moosbrugger was involved; but Clarisse was so startlingly direct: her mind looked like those modern paintings in unmixed primary colors, harsh and unwieldy, but if one went along with it, often amazingly right. He couldn't really explain it all on the phone, but he hoped Ulrich wouldn't let him down. . . .

Ulrich was happy to drop what he was doing and agreed to come, although it was a disproportionately long way to go for the sake of talking with Clarisse for a mere fifteen minutes; for Clarisse had been invited for supper at her parents', along with Walter and Siegmund. On the way, Ulrich had time to wonder at his not having given a thought to Moosbrugger in so long and always having to be reminded of him by Clarisse, though the man had been almost constantly on his mind before. Even in the darkness of late evening through which Ulrich had to walk from the last trolley stop to his friends' house, there was no room for such a haunting apparition; a void in which he had occurred had closed. Ulrich noted this with satisfaction and also with that faint self-questioning which is a consequence of changes whose extent is clearer than their cause. He was enjoying the sensation of cutting through the permeable darkness with the solider black of his own body, when Walter came uncertainly toward him, nervous at night in this lonely vicinity but anxious to say a few words to Ulrich before they joined the others. He eagerly took up his explanations from the point where he had broken off. He appeared to be trying to defend himself, and Clarisse as well, from being misunderstood. Even when her notions seemed to be incoherent, he said, one could always detect behind them an element of pathology that was part of the ferment of the times; it was her most curious faculty. She was like a dowsing rod pointing to hidden springs—in this case, the necessity of replacing modern man's passive, merely intellectual, rational attitude with "values." The form of intelligence of the time had destroyed all firm ground, so it was only the will—indeed, if it couldn't be done otherwise, then it was only violence—that could create a new hierarchy of values in which a person could find beginning and end for his inner life. . . . He was repeating, reluctantly and yet with enthusiasm, what he had heard from Meingast.

Guessing this, Ulrich asked him impatiently: "Why are you talking so pompously? Is it that prophet of yours? It used to be you couldn't have enough simplicity and naturalness!"

Walter put up with this for Clarisse's sake, lest his friend decline to help, but had there been just one ray of light in that moonless gloom, the flash of his teeth would have been visible as he bared them in frustration. He said nothing, but his suppressed rage made him weak, and the presence of his muscular friend shielding him from the eerie loneliness of the place made him soft. Suddenly he said: "Imagine loving a woman and then meeting a man you admire and realizing that your wife admires and loves him, too, and that both of you feel, in love, jealousy, and admiration, this man's hopeless superiority—"

"I'd rather not imagine it!" Ulrich should have heard him out, but he squared his shoulders with a laugh and interrupted him.

Walter shot him a venomous glance. He had meant to ask: "What would you do in such a case?" But it was the same game they had been playing since their school days. As they entered the dimly lit hall he said:

"Drop that act of yours! You're not as conceited and thick-skinned as all that!" Then he had to run to catch up with Ulrich on the stairs, where he hastily whispered the rest of what Ulrich needed to know.

"What has Walter been telling you?" Clarisse asked when they got upstairs.

"I can do it, all right," Ulrich said, going straight to the point, "but I don't think it would be sensible."

"Did you hear that? His very first word was 'sensible,'" Clarisse called out to Meingast, laughing. She was rushing back and forth between the clothes closet, the washstand, the mirror, and the half-open door between her room and the one where the men were. They could catch glimpses of her now and then: with a wet face and her hair hanging down; with her hair brushed up; still bare-legged; in stocking feet; in her long-skirted dinner dress below with a dressing jacket above that looked like a white institutional uniform. She enjoyed this appearing and disappearing. Since she had got her way, all her feelings were submerged in an easy sensuality. "I'm dancing on light-ropes!" she shouted into the room. The men smiled, but Siegmund glanced at his watch and dryly asked her to hurry up. He was treating the whole thing as a gymnastic exercise.

Then Clarisse glided on a "light-rope" to the far corner of her room, for a pin, and shut the drawer of her night table with a bang.

"I can change faster than a man," she called back to Siegmund in the other room, but suddenly paused over the double meaning of "change," which right now could mean for her both "dressing for dinner" and "being transformed by mysterious destinies." She quickly finished dressing, stuck her head through the door, and gravely regarded her friends one after the other. Anyone who did not think of it as a game might have been alarmed that something in this solemn countenance had been extinguished that should have been part of a natural, healthy face. She bowed to her friends and said ceremonially: "So now I have put on my destiny!" But when she straightened up again she looked quite normal, even rather charming, and her brother Siegmund cried: "Forward—march! Papa doesn't like people to be late for dinner!"

When the four of them walked to the streetcar—Meingast had disappeared before they left the house—Ulrich fell back a few steps with Siegmund and asked him whether he had not been a bit worried about his sister of late. The glow of Siegmund's cigarette sketched a flatly rising arc in the darkness.

"No doubt she's abnormal," he replied. "But is Meingast normal? Or even Walter? Is playing the piano normal? It's an unusual state of excitement associated with tremors in the wrists and ankles. For a physician, there's no such thing as normal. Still, if you want my serious opinion, my sister is somewhat overwrought, and I think it will pass once the great panjandrum has left. What do you make of him?" There was a hint of malice in "the great panjandrum."

"He's a gasbag," Ulrich said.

"Isn't he, though!" Siegmund was delighted. "Repulsive, repulsive."

"But his ideas are interesting, I wouldn't deny that altogether," he added after a pause.

143

Count Leinsdorf has qualms about "capital and culture"

And so it happened that Ulrich again appeared before Count Leinsdorf.

He found His Grace, enveloped in tranquillity, dedication, solemnity, and beauty, at his desk, reading a newspaper that was lying spread out over a high pile of documents. The Imperial Liege-Count sadly shook his head after once more expressing his condolences to Ulrich.

"Your father was one of the last true representatives of capital and culture," he said. "How well I remember the days when we both sat in the Bohemian Diet. He well deserved the confidence we always placed in him!"

Ulrich inquired out of politeness how the Parallel Campaign had fared in his absence.

"Well, because of that hullabaloo in the street outside my house that afternoon, which you observed, we've set up a Commission to Ascertain the Desires of the Concerned Sections of the Population in Reference to Administrative Reform," Count Leinsdorf told him. "The Prime Minister himself asked us to take this off his shoulders for the time being, because as a patriotic enterprise we enjoy, so to speak, the public's confidence."

With a straight face Ulrich assured him that at any rate the Commission's name had been well chosen and was likely to have a certain effect.

"Yes, a good deal depends on finding the right words," His Grace said pensively, and suddenly asked: "What do you make of this business of the municipal employees in Trieste? I should think it would be high time for the government to pull itself together and take a firm stand." He made as if to hand over the paper he had folded up when Ulrich came in, but at the last moment chose to open it again and read aloud to his visitor, with vivid feeling, from a long-winded article. "Can you imagine this sort of thing happening in any other country in the world?" he asked, when he had finished. "For years the Austrian city of Trieste has been hiring only Italians, subjects of the King of Italy, in its civil service, to make a point that their allegiance is to Italy, not to us. I was there once on His Majesty's birthday: not a single flag in all Trieste except on the administration building, the tax office, the prison, and the roofs of a few barracks! But if you should have any business in some municipal office in Trieste on the King of Italy's birthday, you wouldn't find a clerk anywhere without a flower in his buttonhole!"

"But why has this been tolerated till now?" Ulrich inquired.

"Why shouldn't it be tolerated?" Count Leinsdorf said in a disgruntled tone. "If our government forces the city to discharge its foreign staff, we will immediately be accused of Germanizing. That is just the reproach every government fears. Even His Majesty doesn't like it. After all, we're not Prussians!"

Ulrich seemed to remember that the coastal and port city of Trieste had been founded on Slavic soil by the imperialistic Venetian Republic and today embraced a large Slavic population, so that even if one were to view it as merely the private concern of its inhabitants—without regard to its also being the gateway to the Empire's eastern trade and in every way dependent on the Empire for its prosperity—there was no getting around the fact that its large Slavic lower middle class passionately contested the favored Italian upper class's right to consider the city as its own property. Ulrich said as much to the Count.

"True enough," Count Leinsdorf instructed him, "but once the word is out that we're Germanizing, the Slovenes immediately side with the Italians, even though they have to take time off from tearing each other's hair out, and all the other minorities rally to support them as well! We've been through this often enough. In terms of practical politics, it's the Germans we have to regard as a threat to peace within the Empire, whether we want to or not." This conclusion left Count Leinsdorf deep in thought for a while, for he had touched on the great political scheme that weighed on his mind, though it had not come clearly into focus for him until this moment. But suddenly he livened up again, and continued cheerfully: "Anyway, the others have been told off properly this time." With a tremor of impatience, he replaced his pince-nez and again read aloud to Ulrich with relish all those satisfying passages in the edict issued by His Imperial and Royal Majesty's Governor in Trieste.

" 'Repeated warnings issued by the governmental institutions of public safety to no avail . . . harm done to our people . . . In view of this obstinate resistance to the prescribed official orders, the Governor of Trieste finds himself obliged to take steps toward enforcing the observance of the existing lawful regulations . . .' " He interrupted himself to ask: "Spoken with dignity, don't you think?" He raised his head but immediately lowered it again, eager to get to the final bit, whose official urbane authority underlined his voice with great aesthetic satisfaction:

" 'Furthermore,' " he read, " 'it is reserved to the administration at any time to give careful and sympathetic consideration to each individual case of application for citizenship made by such public functionaries, insofar as these are officially deemed worthy of exceptional regard through long years of public service and an unblemished record, and in such cases the Imperial and Royal Administration is inclined to avoid immediate enforcement of these regulations, while reserving its right to enforce them at such time and in such circumstances as it may think fit.' Now, that's the tone our government should have taken all along!" Count Leinsdorf exclaimed.

"Don't you think, sir, on the basis of this last point, that in the last analysis this leaves things pretty much where they have always been?" Ulrich asked a little later, when the tail end of this long snake of an official sentence had finally vanished inside his ear.

"Yes, that's just it!" His Grace replied, twiddling his thumbs for a while, as he always did when some hard thinking was going on inside. Then he gave Ulrich a searching look and opened his heart to him.

"Do you remember how, when we were at the police exhibition, the Interior Minister announced that there was a new spirit of 'mutual support and strictness' in the offing? Well, I wouldn't expect them to immediately lock up all the troublemakers who were raising such a rumpus on my doorstep, but the Minister could at least have said a few dignified words of repudiation in Parliament!" His feelings were hurt.

"I assumed it was done during my absence," Ulrich cried with feigned astonishment, aware that a genuine distress was roiling the mind of his benevolent friend.

"Not a thing was done!" His Grace said. Again he fixed his worried, protuberant eyes on Ulrich's face with a searching look, and he opened his heart further: "But something will be done!" He straightened up and leaned back in his chair, shutting his eyes as he lapsed into silence.

When he opened them again he began to explain in a calmer tone: "You see, my dear fellow, our Constitution of 1861 entrusted the undisputed leadership in the new experimental governmental scheme to the German element in the population, and in particular to those within that element who represented capital and culture. That was a munificent gift of His Majesty's, a proof of his generosity and his confidence, perhaps not quite in keeping with the times; for what has become of capital and culture since then?" Count Leinsdorf raised one hand and then dropped it in resignation on the other. "When His Majesty ascended the throne in 1848, at Olmütz, that is to say, practically in exile . . . ," he went on slowly, but suddenly becoming impatient or uncertain, he fished a few notes out of his pocket with trembling fingers, struggled in some agitation to set his pince-nez firmly on his nose, and read aloud, his voice sometimes quavering with emotion, as he strained to decipher his own handwriting:

" '. . . he was surrounded by the uproar of the nationalities' wild urge for freedom. He succeeded in quenching the extreme manifestations of this upsurge. Finally, even if after granting some concessions to the demands of his peoples, he stood triumphant as the victor, and a gracious and magnanimous victor, moreover, who forgave his subjects the errors of their ways and held out his hand to them with the offer of a peace honorable for them as well. Although the Constitution and the other liberties had been granted by him under the press of circumstances, it was nevertheless an act of His Majesty's free will, the fruit of his wisdom and compassion, and of hope in the progressive civilization of his peoples. But in recent years this model relationship between the Emperor and his peoples has been tarnished by the work of agitators, demagogues—' " Here Count Leinsdorf broke off reading his exposition of political history, in which every word had been scrupulously weighed and polished, and gazed pensively at the portrait of his ancestor the Grand Marshal and Knight of the Order of Maria Theresa, hanging on the wall facing him. When Ulrich's expectant gaze finally drew his attention, he said: "That's as far as I've come.

"But you can see that I have been giving these problems a great deal of thought lately," he went on. "What I have just read to you is the beginning of the response which the Minister should have presented to Parliament in the matter of the demonstration against me, if he had been doing his job! I've gradually worked it out for myself, and I don't mind telling you that I shall have occasion to present it to His Majesty as soon as I have finished it. You see, it was not without purpose that the Constitution of 1861 entrusted the leadership of our country to capital and culture. It was meant to secure our future. But where are capital and culture today?"

He seemed really put out with the Minister of the Interior, and to divert him Ulrich remarked innocently that one could at least say about capital that it was nowadays not only in the hands of the bankers but also in the time-tested hands of the landed aristocracy.

"I've nothing at all against the Jews," Count Leinsdorf assured Ulrich out of the blue, as though Ulrich had said something that required such a disclaimer. "They are intelligent, hardworking, and reliable. But it was a great mistake to give them those unsuitable names. Rosenberg and Rosenthal, for instance, are aristocratic names; Baer and Wolf and all such creatures are originally heraldic beasts; Meyer derives from landed property; Silver and Gold are armorial colors. All those Jewish names," His Grace disclosed, to Ulrich's surprise, "are nothing but the insolence of our bureaucrats aimed at our nobility. It was the noble families, not the Jews, who were the butt of these officials, which is why the Jews were given other names as well, like Abrahams, Jewison, or Schmucker. You can not infrequently observe this animus of our bureaucracy against the old nobility surfacing even today, if you know how to look for it," he said oracularly, with a gloomy, obstinate air, as though the struggle of the central administration against feudalism had not long since been overtaken by history and vanished completely from sight. In fact, there was nothing His Grace could resent so pureheartedly as the social privileges enjoyed by important bureaucrats by virtue of their position even when their names might be plain Fuchsenbauer or

Schlosser. Count Leinsdorf was no diehard country *Junker;* he wanted to move with the times, and did not mind such a name when it was that of a Member of Parliament or even a cabinet minister or an influential private citizen, nor did he at all object to the political or economic influence of the middle class; what provoked him, with a passion that was the last vestige of venerable traditions, was the social status of high-ranking administrative officials with middle-class names. Ulrich wondered whether Leinsdorf's remarks might have been prompted by his own cousin's husband. It was not out of the question, but Count Leinsdorf continued talking and was, as always happened, soon lifted above all personal concerns by an idea that had apparently been working inside him for a long time.

"The whole so-called Jewish Question would disappear without a trace if the Jews would only make up their minds to speak Hebrew, go back to their old names, and wear Eastern dress," he explained. "Frankly, a Galician Jew who has just recently made his fortune in Vienna doesn't look right on the Esplanade at Ischl, wearing Tyrolean costume with a chamois tuft on his hat. But put him in a long, flowing robe, as rich as you like so long as it covers his legs, and you'll see how admirably his face and his grand sweeping gestures go with his costume! All those things people tend to joke about would then be in their proper place—even the showy rings they like to wear. I am against assimilation the way the English nobility practice it; it's a tedious and uncertain process. But give the Jews back their true character and watch them become a veritable ornament, a genuine aristocracy of a rare and special kind among the nations gratefully thronging around His Majesty's throne—or, if you'd prefer to see it in everyday terms, imagine them strolling along on our Ringstrasse, the only place in the world where you can see, in the midst of Western European elegance at its finest, a Mohammedan with his red fez, a Slovak in sheepskins, or a bare-legged Tyrolean!"

At this point Ulrich could not do otherwise than express his admiration for His Grace's acumen, which had now also enabled him to uncover the "real Jew."

"Well, you know, the true Catholic faith teaches us to see things as they really are," Count Leinsdorf explained benevolently. "But you would never guess what it was that put me on the right track. It wasn't Arnheim—I'm not speaking of the Prussians right now. But I have a banker, a man of the Mosaic faith, of course, whom I've had to see regularly for years now, and at first his intonation always used to bother me a bit, so that I couldn't keep my mind on the business at hand. He speaks exactly as if he wanted me to think he was my uncle—I mean, as if he'd just got out of the saddle, or back from a day's grouse shooting; exactly the way our own kind of people talk, I must say. Well and good; but then, when he gets carried away, he can't keep it up and, to make no bones about it, slips into a kind of Yiddish singsong. It used to bother me considerably, as I believe I've told you already, because it always happened when some important business matter was at stake, so that I was always unconsciously primed for it, and it got so that I couldn't pay attention to what he was talking about, or else I imagined I was listening to something important the whole time. But then I found a way around it: Every time he began to talk like that I imagined he was speaking Hebrew, and you ought to have heard how attractive it sounded then! Positively enchanting—it is, after all, a liturgical language; such a melodious chanting: I'm very musical, I should add. In short, from then on he had me lapping up the most complicated calculations of compound interest or discount positively as if he were at the piano!" As he said this, Count Leinsdorf had for some reason a melancholy smile.

Ulrich took the liberty of pointing out that the people so favored by His Grace's sympathetic interest would be more than likely to turn down his suggestion.

"Oh, of course they won't want to!" the Count said. "But they would have to be forced to for their own good. It would amount to a world mission for the Empire, and it's not a question of whether they want to or not. You see, many people at the beginning have had to be made to do what's best for them. But think, too, what it would mean if we ended up allied with a grateful Jewish State instead of with the Germans and Prussia! Seeing that our Trieste happens to be the Hamburg of the Mediterranean, as it were, apart from the fact that it would make us diplomatically invincible to have not only the Pope on our side but the Jews as well!"

Abruptly, he added: "You must remember that I have to concern myself with problems of the currency, too, these days." And again he smiled in that strangely sad, absentminded way.

It was astonishing that His Grace, who had repeatedly sent out urgent calls for Ulrich, did not discuss the problems of the day now that he had finally come, but lavished his ideas on him. Apparently ideas had come to him in abundance while he had had to do without his confidant, ideas as restless as bees that stream out for miles but are sure to return in their own good time, laden with honey.

"You might perhaps object," Count Leinsdorf resumed, although Ulrich had not said anything, "that I have on earlier occasions often expressed a decidedly low opinion of the financial world. I don't deny it: too much is too much, and we have too much finance in modern life. But that's precisely why we must deal with it! Look, culture has not been pulling its weight alongside capital—there you have the whole secret of developments since 1861. And that's why we must concern ourselves with capital."

His Grace made an almost imperceptible pause, just long enough to let his listener know that now he was coming to the secret of capital, but then went on in his gloomily confidential tone:

"You see, what's most important in a culture is what it forbids people: whatever doesn't belong is out. For instance, a well-bred man will never eat gravy with his knife, only God knows why; they don't teach you these things in school. That's so-called tact, it's based on a privileged class for culture to look up to, a cultural model; in short, if I may say so, an aristocracy. Granted that our aristocracy has not always lived up to that ideal. That's exactly the point, the downright revolutionary experiment, of our 1861 Constitution: Capital and culture were meant to make common cause with the aristocracy. Have they done so? Were they up to taking advantage of the great opportunity His Majesty had so graciously made available to them? I'm sure you'd never claim that the results of your cousin's great efforts that we see every week are in keeping with such hopes." His voice grew more animated as he exclaimed: "You know, it's really most interesting, what sorts of things claim to be 'mind' these days! I was telling His Eminence the Cardinal about it recently, when we were out hunting in Mürzsteg—no, it was Mürzbruck, at the Hostnitz girl's wedding—and he laughed and clapped his hands together: 'Something new every year,' he said. 'Now you can see how modest we are; we've been telling people the same old thing for almost two thousand years.' And that's so true. The main thing about faith is that it keeps believing the same old thing, even if it's heresy to say so. 'You know,' he said, 'I always go out hunting because my predecessor in the days of Leopold von Babanberg did too. But I never kill,' he said—he happens to be known for never firing a shot on the hunt—'because it goes against my grain, something tells me it's not in keeping with my cloth. I can talk about this to you, old friend, because we were boys in dancing class together. But I'd never stand up in public and say: "You shall not shoot while hunting!" Good Lord, who knows whether that would be true, and besides, it's no part of the Church's teaching. But the people who meet at your friend's house make a public issue of things like that the minute it occurs to them! There you have what's called "intelligence" nowadays!' It's easy for him to laugh," Count Leinsdorf went on, speaking for himself again. "He holds that job in perpetuity, but we laymen have the hard task of finding the right path amid perpetual change. I told him as much. I asked him: 'Why did God let literature and painting and all that come into the world anyway, when they're really such a bore?' And he came up with a very interesting explanation. 'You've heard about psychoanalysis, haven't you?' he asked me. I didn't know quite what I was supposed to say. 'Well,' he said, 'you'll probably say it's just a lot of filth. We won't argue about it, it's what everyone says; and yet they all run to these newfangled doctors more than to our Catholic confessional. Take it from me, they rush to them in droves because the flesh is weak! They let their secret sins be discussed because they enjoy it, and if they disparage it, take it from me, we always pick holes in the things we mean to buy! But I could also prove to you that what their atheistic doctors imagine they invented is nothing but what the Church has been doing from the beginning: exorcising the Devil and healing the possessed. It's identical step for step with the ritual of exorcism, for instance, when they try with their own methods to make the person who's possessed talk about what's inside him; according to Church teaching, that's precisely the turning point, where the Devil is getting ready to break out! We merely missed adapting ourselves in time to changing conditions by talking of psychosis, the unconscious, and all that current claptrap instead of filth and the Devil.' Isn't that interesting?" Count Leinsdorf asked. "But what comes next may be even more so. 'Never mind the weakness of the flesh,' the Cardinal said. 'What we need to talk about is that the spirit is weak too. And that's where the Church has kept its wits and not let anything slip by. People aren't nearly so scared of the Devil in the flesh, even if they make a great show of fighting him, as they are of the illumination that comes from the spirit. You never studied theology,' he said to me, 'but at least you respect it, and that's more than a secular philosopher in his blindness ever does. Let me tell you, theology is so difficult that a man can devote himself to studying it and nothing else for fifteen years before he realizes that he hasn't really understood a word of it! If people knew how difficult it is, none of them would have any faith at all; they'd only run us down! They'd run us down exactly the way they run people down—you understand?' he said slyly, '—who are writing their books and painting their pictures and trotting out their theories. And today we're only too glad to let them have plenty of rope to hang themselves with, because, let me tell you, the more earnestly one of those fellows sets about it, the less he's a mere entertainer, or working for his own pocket; the more, in other words, he serves God in his mistaken way, the more he bores people, and the more they run him down. "That's not what life is like!" they say. But we know very well what it's like, and we'll show them too, and because we can also wait, you may yet live to see them come running back to us, full of fury about the time they wasted on all that clever talk. You can see it happening in our own families, even now. And in our fathers' day, God knows, they thought they were going to turn heaven itself into a university.'

"I wouldn't go so far," Count Leinsdorf rounded out this part of his discourse to start on a new topic, "as to say he meant all that literally. The Hostnitzes in Mürzbruck happen to have a celebrated Rhine wine that General Marmont left behind and forgot in 1805 because he had to march on Vienna in such a hurry, and they brought some of it out for the wedding. But in the main I'm sure the Cardinal was right on target. So if I ask myself now what to make of it, all I can say is, I'm sure it's true, but it doesn't work. I mean, there can be no doubt that the people we brought in because we were told they represent the spirit of the times have nothing to do with real life, and the Church can well afford to wait them out. But we civilian politicians can't wait; we must squeeze what good we can out of life as we find it. After all, man doesn't live by bread alone, but by the soul as well. The soul is that which enables him to digest his bread, so to speak. And

that's why it's necessary . . ." Count Leinsdorf was of the opinion that
politics should be a spur to the soul. "In short, something has to happen," he said, "that's what the times demand. Everyone has that feeling, as it were, not just the politically minded. The times have a sort
of interim character that nobody can stand indefinitely." He had the
idea that the trembling balance of ideas upon which the no less trembling balance of power in Europe rested must be given a push.

"It hardly matters what kind of push," he assured Ulrich, who
made a show of being stunned by His Grace's having turned, in the
period since they had last seen each other, into a veritable revolutionary.

"Well, why not?" Count Leinsdorf retorted, flattered. "His Eminence of course also thought that it might be a small step in the right
direction if His Majesty could be persuaded to replace the present
Minister of the Interior, but such petty reforms don't do the trick in
the long run, however necessary they may be. Do you know that as I
mull this over I actually find my thoughts turning to the Socialists?"
He gave his interlocutor time to recover from the amazement he assumed this was bound to cause, and then continued firmly: "You can
take it from me, real socialism wouldn't be nearly as terrible as people seem to think. You may perhaps object that the Socialists are
republicans; that's true, you simply can't listen when they're talking,
but if you consider them in terms of practical politics, you might well
reach the conclusion that a social-democratic republic with a strong
ruler at the helm would not be an impossible solution at all. For my
own part, I'm convinced that if we were to go just a little way to meet
them, they'd be glad to give up the idea of using brute force and
they'd recoil from the rest of their objectionable principles. As it is,
they're already inclined to modify their notion of the class struggle
and their hostility to private property. And there really are people
among them who still place country before party, as compared with
the middle-class parties who've gone radical since the last elections
in putting their conflicting national-minority interests above everything else. Which brings us to the Emperor." He lowered his voice
confidentially. "As I've said already, we must learn to think in economic terms. The one-sided policy of encouraging national minorities has led the Empire into the desert. Now, to the Emperor, all this
Czech-Polish-German-Italian ranting about autonomy . . . I don't

know how to put it: let's just say His Majesty couldn't care less. What His Majesty does care about, deeply, is our getting the defense budget through without any cuts so that the Empire may be strong, and apart from that he feels a hearty distaste for all the pretensions of the middle-class idea-mongers, a distaste he probably acquired in 1848. But these two priorities simply make His Majesty the First Socialist in the land, as it were. You can now see, I think, the magnificent vista I was speaking of? Which leaves only the problem of religiosity, in which there is still an unbridgeable gap between opposing camps, and that's something I'd have to talk over with His Eminence again."

His Grace fell silent, absorbed in his conviction that history, in particular that of his own country, bogged down as it was in fruitless nationalist dissensions, would shortly be called upon to take a step into the future—whereby he perceived the spirit of history as being more or less two-legged, but otherwise a philosophical necessity. Hence it was understandable that he surfaced suddenly with sore eyes, like a diver who had gone too far down. "In any case, we must get ready to do our duty!" he said.

"But where does our duty lie, Your Grace?"

"Why, in doing our duty, of course! It's the only thing we can always do! But to change the subject . . ." It was only now that Count Leinsdorf seemed to remember the pile of newspapers and files on which his fist rested. "Look here, what the people want today is a strong hand. But today a strong hand needs fine words, or the people won't put up with it. And you, and I mean you personally, are eminently qualified in this respect. What you said, for instance, the last time we all met at your cousin's before you left town, was that what we actually need—if you recall—is a central committee for eternal happiness, to bring it in step with our earthly precision in ratiocination. . . . Well, it wouldn't work out quite so easily, but His Eminence laughed heartily when I told him about it; actually, I rubbed it in a bit, as they say, and even though he's always making fun of everything, I can tell pretty well whether his laugh comes from the spleen or from the heart. The fact is, my dear man, we simply can't do without you. . . ."

While all of Count Leinsdorf's other pronouncements that day had had the character of complicated dreams, the wish he now expressed—that Ulrich should give up "definitively, at least for now," any idea of resigning his post as Honorary Secretary of the Parallel Campaign—was so definite and so pointedly fledged, and his hand had come down on Ulrich's arm with such an effect of a surprise maneuver, that Ulrich almost had the not entirely pleasing impression that all the elaborate harangues he had been listening to had only been calculated, far more slyly than he had anticipated, to put him off his guard. At this moment he was quite annoyed with Clarisse, who had got him into this fix. But since he had appealed on her behalf to Count Leinsdorf's kindness the very first time there had been an opening in the conversation, and the request had been granted instantly by the obliging high official, who wanted only to go on talking without interruption, he had no choice now but reluctantly to square the account.

"I've heard from Tuzzi," Count Leinsdorf said, pleased with his success, "that you might decide on a man from his office to take the routine business off your hands. 'Splendid,' I told him, 'if he stays on.' After all, his man has taken his oath of office, which we'll give you too, and my own secretary, whom I'd gladly have put at your disposal, is unfortunately an idiot. All you perhaps shouldn't let him see is the strictly confidential stuff, because he's Tuzzi's man, and that has certain drawbacks; but otherwise, do arrange matters to suit your own convenience," His Grace said, concluding this successful interview with the utmost cordiality.

144

CAST ALL THOU HAST INTO THE FIRE, EVEN UNTO THY SHOES

During this time and from the moment she had stayed behind alone, Agathe had been living in a state of utter release from all ties to the world, in a sweetly wistful suspension of will; a condition that was like a great height, where only the wide blue sky is to be seen. Once a day she treated herself to a short stroll in town; at home, she read, attended to her affairs, and experienced this mild, trivial business of living with grateful enjoyment. Nothing troubled her state: no clinging to the past, no straining for the future; if her eye lit upon some nearby object, it was like coaxing a baby lamb to her: either it came gently closer or it took no notice of her at all—but at no time did her mind deliberately take hold of it with that motion of inner grasping which gives to every act of cold understanding a certain violence as well as a certain futility, for it drives away the joy that is in things. In this fashion everything around her seemed far more intelligible to Agathe than ordinarily, but in the main she was still preoccupied with her conversations with her brother. In keeping with the peculiarity of her unusually exact memory, which did not distort its material with any bias or prejudice, there rose up in her mind more or less at random the living words, the subtle surprises of cadence and gestures, in these conversations, much as they were before she had quite understood them and realized where they were tending. Nevertheless, it all held the utmost significance for her; her memory, so often dominated by remorse, was now suffused with a quiet devotion, and the time just past clung like a caress to the warmth of her body, instead of drifting off as it usually did into the frost and darkness that awaits life lived in vain.

And so, veiled in an invisible light, Agathe also dealt with the lawyers, notaries, brokers, and agents she now had to see. No one refused her; everyone was glad to oblige the attractive young woman—whose father's name was sufficient recommendation—in every way. She conducted herself with as much self-assurance as detachment; she was sure of what she wanted, but it was detached from herself, as it were, and the experience she had acquired in life—also something that can be seen as detached from the personality—went on working in pursuit of that purpose like a shrewd laborer calmly taking advantage for his commission of whatever opportunities presented themselves. That she was engaged in preparing a felony—the significance of her action that would have been strikingly apparent to an outsider—simply did not enter her state of mind during this time. The unity of her conscience excluded it. The pure light of this conscience outshone this dark point, which nevertheless, like the core of a flame, formed its center. Agathe herself did not know how to express it; by virtue of her intention she found herself in a state that was a world away from this same ugly intention.

On the morning after her brother had left, Agathe was already considering her appearance with great care: it had begun by accident with her face, when her gaze had landed on it and not come back out of the mirror. She was held fast, much as one who sometimes has absolutely no desire to walk keeps walking a hundred steps, and then another hundred, all the way toward something one catches sight of only at the end, at which point one definitely intends to turn back and yet does not. In this way she was held captive, without vanity, by this landscape of her self, which confronted her behind the shimmer of glass. She looked at her hair, still like bright velvet; she opened the collar of her reflection's dress and slipped the dress off its shoulders; then she undressed the image altogether and studied it down to the rosy nails, to where the body tapers off into fingers and toes and hardly belongs to itself anymore. Everything was still like the sparkling day approaching its zenith: ascendant, pure, exact, and infused with that forenoon growth that manifests itself in a human being or a young animal as ineffably as in a bouncing ball that has not yet reached its highest point in the air, but is just about to. "Perhaps it is passing through that point this very moment," Agathe thought. The idea frightened her. Still, she was only twenty-seven; it might take a while yet. Her body, as untouched by athletic coaches and masseurs as it was by childbearing and maternal toil, had been formed by nothing but its own growth. If it could have been set down naked in one of those grand and lonely landscapes that mountain ranges form on the side turned toward the sky, the vast, infertile, billowing swell of such heights would have borne it upward like some pagan goddess. In a nature of this kind, noon does not pour down exhalations of light and heat; it merely seems for a while longer to rise above its zenith and then to pass imperceptibly into the sinking, floating beauty of the afternoon. From the mirror came the eerie sense of that undefinable hour.

It occurred to her at this moment that Ulrich, too, was letting his life go by as though it would last forever. "Perhaps it is a mistake that we didn't first meet when we were old," she said to herself, conjuring up the melancholy image of two banks of fog drifting earthward in the evening. "They're not as fine as the blaze of noon, but what do

those formless gray shapes care what people make of them? Their
hour has come, and it is just as tender as the most glowing hour!"

She had now almost turned her back on the mirror, but was provoked by a certain extravagance in her mood to turn around again
before she knew it, and had to laugh at the memory of two fat people
taking the waters at Marienbad years ago; she had watched them as
they sat on one of those green benches, doting on each other with the
sweetest and tenderest feelings. "Their beating hearts are slim under
all that fat, and being lost in their vision of each other, they have no
idea how funny they look to the world," Agathe reminded herself,
and made an ecstatic face while trying to puff up her body with imaginary rolls of fat. When this fit of exuberance had passed, it looked as
if some tiny tears of rage had risen to her eyes, and pulling herself
together, she coolly resumed the point-by-point scrutiny of her appearance. Although she was considered slender, she observed in her
body with some concern a possibility that she could become heavy.
Perhaps she was too broad-chested. In her face, its very white skin
dimmed by her golden hair as if by candles burning in the daytime,
the nose was a bit too wide, and its almost classical line a bit dented
on one side at the tip. It could be that everywhere inside her flame-
like given form a second was lurking, broader and more melancholy,
like a linden leaf that has fallen among twigs of laurel. Agathe felt a
curiosity about herself, as though she were really seeing herself for
the first time. This was how she might well have been perceived by
the men she had become involved with, without her having known
anything about it. It was a rather uncanny feeling. But by some trick
of the imagination, before she could call her memories to account for
it, she kept hearing behind everything she had experienced the ardent, long-drawn-out mating cry of donkeys, which had always curiously aroused her: a hopelessly foolish and ugly sound, which for that
very reason makes no other heroism of love seem so desperately
sweet as theirs. She shrugged her shoulders at her life and resolutely
turned back to her image to discover a place where her appearance
might already be yielding to age. There were those small areas near
the eyes and ears that are the first to change, beginning by looking as
though something had slept on them, or the inner curve under the
breasts, which so easily loses its definition. At this moment it would
have been a satisfaction to her and a promise of peace to come had

she seen such a change, but there was none yet to be seen, and the loveliness of her body floated almost eerily in the depths of the mirror.

It now seemed odd to her that she was actually Frau Hagauer, and the difference between the clear and close relationship that implied and the vagueness with which the fact reached deep into her being was so great that she seemed to herself to be standing there without a body while the body in the mirror belonged to Frau Hagauer, who was the one who would have to learn to cope with its having committed itself to a situation beneath its dignity. Even in this there was some of that elusive pleasure in living that sometimes startles, and it made Agathe, once she had hastily dressed again, go straight to her bedroom to look for a capsule that must be in her luggage. This small airtight capsule, which had been in her possession almost as long as she had been married to Hagauer, and which she always kept within reach, contained a tiny quantity of a drab powder she had been assured was a deadly poison. Agathe recalled certain sacrifices it had cost her to obtain this forbidden stuff, about which she knew only what she had been told of its effect and one of those chemical names the uninitiated must memorize, like a magic formula, without knowing what they mean. But evidently all those means by which the end may be brought a little closer, such as poison or guns, or seeking out survivable dangers, are part of the romantic love of life; and it may be that most people's lives are so oppressed, so fluctuating, with so much darkness in their brightness, and altogether so perverse, that life's inherent joy can be released only by the distant possibility of putting an end to it. Agathe felt better when her eyes lit on the tiny metal object, which she regarded, amid the uncertainty that lay ahead of her, as a bringer of luck, a talisman.

So this did not at all mean that Agathe at this time already intended to kill herself. On the contrary, she feared death just as every young person does to whom, for instance, before falling asleep in bed at night, after a well-spent day, it suddenly occurs that "It's inevitable: sometime, on another fine day just like this, I'll be dead." Nor does one acquire an appetite for dying by having to watch someone else die; her father's death had tormented her with impressions whose horrors had returned since she had been left alone in the house after her brother's departure. But "I'm sort of dead, in a way" was something Agathe felt often; and especially in moments like this, when she had just been conscious of her young body's shapeliness and good health, its taut beauty, equally unfathomable in the mystery of what held it together and what made its elements decompose in death, she tended to fall from her condition of happy confidence into one of anxiety, amazement, and silence: it was like stepping from a noisy, crowded room and suddenly standing under the shimmering stars. Regardless of her awakening intentions and her satisfaction at having extricated herself from a bungled life, she now felt rather detached from herself and only obscurely linked to her own existence. Coolly she thought of death as a state in which one is released from all efforts and illusions, imagined it as a tender inward rocking to sleep: one lies in God's hand, and this hand is like a cradle or a hammock slung between two tall trees swaying faintly in the wind. She thought of death as a great tranquillity and fatigue, the end of all wanting and striving, of all paying attention and having to think, like the pleasant slackening of the fingers one feels when sleep cautiously loosens their hold on whatever last thing of this world they have still been clutching. No doubt she was indulging herself in a rather easy and casual notion of death, typical of someone disinclined to take on the exertions of living; and in the end she was amused to think how this was all of a piece with her moving the couch into her father's austere drawing room to lounge on, reading—the only change she had made in the house on her own initiative.

Still, the thought of giving up life was anything but a game for Agathe. It seemed profoundly believable to her that all this frustrating turmoil must be followed by a state of blissful repose, which she could not help imagining in physical terms. She felt it this way because she had no need of the suspenseful illusion that the world could be improved, and she was always ready to surrender her share in it completely, as long as it could be done in a pleasant fashion. Besides, she had already had a special encounter with death in that extraordinary illness that had befallen her on the borderline between childhood and girlhood. That was when—in an almost imperceptibly gradual loss of energy that seemed to infiltrate each tiniest particle of time, though as a whole it happened with an irresistible rush—more and more parts of her body seemed to dissolve away from her day by day and be destroyed; yet, keeping pace with this decline and this slipping away from life there was an unforgettable fresh striving toward a goal that banished all the unrest and anxiety of her illness, a curiously substantive state that even enabled her to exert a certain domination over the adults around her, who were becoming more and more unsure of themselves. It is not out of the question that this sense of power, gained under such impressive circumstances, could later have been at the heart of her spiritual readiness to withdraw in similar fashion from a life whose allurements for some reason fell short of her expectations. But more probably it was the other way around: that that illness, which enabled her to escape the demands of school and home, was the first manifestation of her attitude to the world, an attitude that was transparent and permeated by the light of an emotion unknown to her. For Agathe felt herself to be a person of a spontaneous, simple temperament, warm, lively, even gay and easy to please; she had in fact adapted herself good-naturedly to a great variety of circumstances, nor had she ever suffered that collapse into indifference that befalls women who can no longer bear their disillusionment. But in the midst of her laughter or the tumult of some sensual adventure that continued nonetheless, there lived a disenchantment that made every fiber of her body tired and nostalgic for something else, something best described as nothingness.

This nothingness had a definite, if indefinable, content. For a long time she had been in the habit of repeating to herself, on all sorts of occasions, words of Novalis: "What then can I do for my soul, that lives within me like an unsolved riddle, even while it grants the visible man the utmost license, because there is no way it can control him?" But the flickering light of this utterance always went out again, like a flash of lightning that only left her in darkness, for she did not believe in a soul, as it was something too presumptuous and in any case much too definite for her own person. On the other hand, she could not believe in the earthly here and now either. To understand this rightly, one need only realize that this turning away from an earthly order when there is no faith in a supernatural order is a profoundly natural response, because in every head, alongside the process of logical thought, with its austere and simple orderliness reflecting the conditions of our external world, there is an affective world, whose logic, insofar as it can be spoken of at all, corresponds to feelings, passions, moods. The laws governing these two bear roughly the same relation to each other as those of a lumberyard, where chunks of wood are hewn into rectangular shapes and stacked ready for transport, bear to the dark tangled laws of the forest, with its mysterious workings and rustlings. And since the objects of our thought are in no way quite independent of its conditions, these two modes of thinking not only mingle in each person but can, to a certain extent, even present him with two worlds, at least immediately before and after that "first mysterious and indescribable moment" of which a famous religious thinker has said that it occurs in every sensory perception before vision and feeling separate and fall into the places in which one is accustomed to find them: one of them an object in space and the other a mental process enclosed within the observer.

And so, whatever the relationship may be between objects and feeling in the civilized person's mature view of the world, everyone surely knows those ecstatic moments in which a split has not yet occurred, as though water and land had not yet been divided and the waves of feeling still shared the same horizon as the hills and valleys that form the shape of things. There is even no need to assume that Agathe experienced such moments unusually often or with unusual intensity; she merely perceived them more vividly or, if you like, more superstitiously, for she was always willing to trust the world and then again not really trust it, just as she had done ever since her school days, and she had not unlearned it even later, when she had come in closer contact with masculine logic. In this sense, which is not to be confused with whim and willfulness, Agathe could have claimed—given more self-confidence than she had—to be the most illogical of women. But it had never occurred to her to regard the alienated feelings she experienced as more than a personal eccentricity. It was only through the encounter with her brother that a transformation occurred within her. In these empty rooms, all hollowed out in the shadows of solitude, rooms so recently filled with talk and a fellowship that reached to the innermost soul, the distinction between physical separation and mental presence unwittingly lost itself; and as the days glided by without a trace, Agathe felt with a hitherto unknown intensity the curious charm of that sense of omnipresence and omnipotence which occurs when the felt world makes the transition to perceptions. Her attention now seemed to be not with the senses but already opened wide deep inside her emotions, where no light could enter that did not already glow like the light in her heart, and it seemed to her, remembering her brother's words, that regardless of the ignorance she normally complained of she could understand everything that mattered without having to reflect on it. And as in this way her spirit was so filled with itself that even the liveliest idea had something of the soundless floating quality of a memory about it, everything that came her way spread out into a limitless present. Even when she did something, only a dividing line melted between herself, the doer, and the thing done, and her movements seemed to be the path by which things came to her when she stretched out her arms to them. This gentle power, this knowledge, and the world's speaking presence were, however, whenever she wondered with a smile what she *was* doing after all, hardly distinguishable from absence, helplessness, and a profound muteness of the spirit. With only a slight exaggeration of what she was feeling, Agathe could have said that she no longer knew where she was. On all sides she was in a state of suspension in which she felt both lifted up and lost to sight. She might have said: I am in love, but I don't know with whom. She was filled with a clear will, something she had always felt the lack of, but she did not know what she should undertake in its clarity, since all that her life had ever held of good and evil was now meaningless.

So it was not only when she looked at the poison capsule but every day that Agathe thought she would like to die, or that the happiness of death must be like the happiness in which she was spending her days while she was waiting to go and join her brother, meanwhile doing exactly what he had pleaded with her to stop doing. She could not imagine what would happen after she was with her brother in the capital. She remembered almost reproachfully that he had sometimes nonchalantly given signs of assuming that she would be successful there and would soon find a new husband or at least a lover; it would be nothing like that, that much she knew. Love, children, fine days, gay social gatherings, travel, a little art—the good life was so easy; she understood its appeal and was not immune to it. But ready as she was to regard herself as useless, Agathe felt the total contempt of the born rebel for this easy way out. She recognized it as a fake. The life supposedly lived to the full is in truth a life "without rhyme or reason"; in the end—and truly at the real end, death—something is always missing. It is—how should she put it?—like things piled up without being ordered by some guiding principle; unfulfilled in its fullness, the opposite of easy or simple, a jumble one accepts with the cheerfulness of habit! And suddenly going off at a tangent, she thought: "It's like a bunch of strange children you look at with conventional friendliness, with growing anxiety because you can't find your own child among them!"

She took some comfort in her resolve to put an end to her life if the new turn it was about to take should prove to have changed nothing. Like fermenting wine, she felt hope streaming in her that death and terror would not be the final word of truth. She felt no need to think about it. Actually, she feared this need, which Ulrich was always so glad to indulge, and she feared it aggressively. For she did feel that everything that moved her so strongly was not entirely free of a persistent hint that it was merely illusion. But it was just as true that every illusion contained a reality, however fluid and dissolved: perhaps a reality not yet solidified into earth, she thought; and in one of those wonderful moments when the place where she was standing seemed to melt away, she was able to believe that behind her, in that space into which one could never see, God might be standing. This was too much, and she recoiled from it. An awesome immensity and emptiness suddenly flooded through her, a shoreless radiance darkened her mind and overwhelmed her heart with fear. Her youth, easily prone to such anxieties as come with a lack of experience, whispered to her that she might be in danger of allowing an incipient madness to grow in her; she struggled to back away. Fiercely, she reminded herself that she did not believe in God at all. And she really did not believe, ever since she had been taught belief; it was part of her mistrust of everything she was taught. She was anything but religious if it meant faith in the supernatural, or at least some moral conviction. But after a while, exhausted and trembling, she still had to admit to herself that she had felt "God" as distinctly as if he were a man standing behind her and putting a coat on her shoulders.

When she had thought this over and recovered her nerve, she discovered that the meaning of her experience did not lie in that "solar eclipse" of her physical sensations, but was mainly a moral matter. A sudden change of her inmost condition, and hence of all her relations with the world, had for a moment given her that "unity of the con-science with the senses" which she had so far experienced so fleet-ingly that it was barely sufficient to impart to her ordinary life a tinge of something disconsolate and murkily passionate, whether Agathe tried to behave well or badly. This change seemed to her an incom-parable outpouring that emanated as much from her surroundings toward her as from herself toward them, a oneness of the highest significance through the smallest mental motion, a motion that was barely distinguishable from the objects themselves. The objects were perfused by her sensations and the sensations by the objects in a way so convincing that Agathe felt she had never before been remotely touched by anything for which she had formerly used the word "con-vincing." And this had happened in circumstances that would nor-mally be expected to rule out the possibility of her being convinced.

So the meaning of what she experienced in her solitude did not lie in its possible psychological import, as an indication of a high-strung or overly fragile personality, for it did not lie in the person at all but in something general, or perhaps in the link between his generality and the person, something Agathe not unjustly regarded as a moral conclusion in the sense that it seemed to the young woman—disap-pointed as she was in herself—that if she could always live as she did in such exceptional moments, and if she was not too weak to keep it up, she could love the world and willingly accommodate herself to it—something she would never be able to do otherwise! Now she was filled with a fierce longing to recover that mood, but such mo-ments of highest intensity cannot be willed by force. It was only when her furious efforts proved useless that she realized, with the clarity which a pale day takes on after sunset, that the only thing she could hope for, and what in fact she was waiting for, with an impa-tience merely masked by her solitude, was the strange prospect that her brother had once half-humorously called the Millennium. He could just as well have chosen another word for it, for what it meant to Agathe was the convincing and confident ring of something that was coming. She would never have dared make this assertion. Even now she did not know whether it was truly possible. She had no idea what it could be. She had at the moment again forgotten all the words with which her brother had proved to her that beyond what filled her spirit with nebulous light, possibility stretched onward into the uncharted. As long as she had been in his company she had simply felt that a country was crystallizing out of his words, crystallizing not in her head but actually under her feet. The very fact that he often spoke of it only ironically, and his usual way of alternating between coolness and emotion, which had so often confused her in the beginning, now gladdened her in her loneliness, and she took it as a kind of guarantee that he meant it—antagonistic states of soul being more convincing than rapturous ones. "I was apparently thinking of death only because I was afraid he was not being serious enough," she confessed to herself.

The last day she had to spend in absentia took her by surprise. All at once everything in the house was cleared out and tidied up; nothing was left to do but hand the keys over to the old couple who were being pensioned off under the provisions of the will and were to go on living in the servants' lodge until the property found a new owner. Agathe refused to go to a hotel, intending to stay at her post until her train left in the small hours. The house was packed up and shrouded. One naked bulb was lit. Some crates, pushed together, served as table and chair. She had them set her table for supper on the edge of a ravine on a terrace of crates. Her father's old factotum juggled a loaded tray through light and shadow; he and his wife had insisted on cooking a dinner in their own kitchen, so that, as they expressed it, "the young lady" should be properly taken care of for her last meal at home. Suddenly Agathe thought, completely outside the state of mind in which she had spent the last few days: "Can they possibly have noticed anything?" She could easily have neglected to destroy every last scrap of paper on which she had practiced changing the will. She felt cold terror, a nightmarish weight that hung on all her limbs: the miserly dread of reality that holds no nourishment for the spirit but only consumes it. Now she perceived with fierce intensity her newly awakened desire to live; it furiously resisted the possibility of anything getting in her way. When the old servant returned, she scrutinized his face intently. But the old man, with his discreet smile, went about his business unsuspecting, seeming to feel something or other that was mute and ceremonious. She could not see into him any more than she could see into a wall, and did not know what else there might be in him behind his blank polish. Now she, too, felt something muted, ceremonious, and sad. He had always been her father's confidant, unfailingly ready to betray to him his children's every secret as soon as he had discovered it. But Agathe had been born in this house, and everything that had happened since was coming to an end this day: Agathe was moved to find herself and him here now, solemnly alone. She made up her mind to give him a special little gift of money, and in a fit of sudden weakness she planned to tell him that it came from Professor Hagauer; not from some calculating motive but as an act of atonement, with the intention of leaving nothing undone, even though she realized this was as unnecessary as it was superstitious. Before the old man returned again, she also took out her locket and capsule. The locket with the portrait of her never-forgotten beloved she slipped, after one last frowning look at his face, under the loosely nailed lid of a crate destined to go into storage indefinitely; it appeared to contain kitchen utensils or lamps, for she heard the clink of metal on metal, like branches falling from a tree. Then she placed the capsule with the poison where she had formerly worn the portrait.

"How old-fashioned of me!" she thought with a smile as she did this. "I'm sure there are things more important than one's love life!" But she did not believe it.

At this moment it would have been as untrue to say that she was disinclined to enter into illicit relations with her brother as that she desired to. That might depend on how things turned out; but in her present state of mind nothing corresponded to the clarity of such a problem.

The light painted the bare boards of the crates between which she was sitting a glaring white and deep black. And a similar tragic mask gave an eerie touch to the otherwise simple thought that she was now spending her last evening in the house where she had been born of a woman she had never been able to remember, who had also given birth to Ulrich. An old impression came to her of clowns with dead-serious faces and strange instruments standing around her. They began to play. Agathe recognized it as a childhood daydream of hers. She could not hear the music, but all the clowns were looking at her. She told herself that at this moment her death would be no loss to anyone or anything, and for herself it would mean no more than the outward end of an inner dying. So she thought while the clowns were sending their music up to the ceiling and she seemed to be sitting on a circus floor strewn with sawdust, tears dropping on her finger. It was a feeling of utter futility she had known often as a girl, and she thought: "I suppose I've remained childish to this day," which did not prevent her from thinking at the same time of something that loomed vastly magnified by her tears: how, in the first hour of their reunion, she and her brother had come face-to-face in just such clown costumes. "What does it mean that it is my brother, of all people, who seems to hold the key to what's inside me?" she wondered. And suddenly she was really weeping. It seemed to be happening for no other reason she knew of but sheer pleasure, and she shook her head hard, as though there were something here she could neither undo nor put together.

At the same time she was thinking with a native ingenuousness that Ulrich would find the answers to all problems . . . until the old man came back again and was moved at seeing her so moved. "Oh my, the dear young lady!" he said, also shaking his head.

Agathe looked at him in confusion, but when she realized the misunderstanding behind this compassion, that it had been aroused by her appearance of childlike grief, her youthful high spirits rose again.

"Cast all thou hast into the fire, even unto thy shoes. When thou has nothing left, think not even on thy shroud, but cast thyself naked into the fire!" she said to him.

It was an ancient saying that Ulrich had read to her delightedly, and the old man showed the stumps of his teeth in a smile at the grave and mellow lilt of the words she recited to him, her eyes aglow with tears; with his eyes he followed her hand pointing at the high-piled crates—she was trying to help his understanding by misleading it—suggesting something like a pyre. He had nodded at the word "shroud," eager to follow even though the path of the words was none too smooth, but he'd stiffened from the word "naked" on, and when she repeated her maxim, his face had reverted to the mask of the well-trained servant whose expression gives assurance that he can be trusted not to hear, see, or judge his betters.

In all his years with his old master that word had never once been uttered in his hearing; "undressed" would have been the closest permissible. But young people were different nowadays, and he would probably not be able to give them satisfaction in any case. Serenely, as one who has earned his retirement, he felt that his career was over.

But Agathe's last thought before she left was: "Would Ulrich really cast everything into the fire?"

145

FROM KONIATOWSKI'S CRITIQUE OF
DANIELLI'S THEOREM TO THE FALL OF MAN.
FROM THE FALL OF MAN TO THE EMOTIONAL
RIDDLE POSED BY A MAN'S SISTER

The state in which Ulrich emerged into the street on leaving the Palais Leinsdorf was rather like the down-to-earth sensation of hunger. He stopped in front of a billboard and stilled his hunger for bourgeois normality by taking in the announcements and advertisements. The billboard was several yards wide and covered with words.

"Actually," it occurred to him, "one might assume that these particular words, which are met with in every corner of the city, have a great deal to tell us." The language seemed to him akin to the clichés uttered by the characters in popular novels at important points in their lives. He read: "Have you ever worn anything so flattering yet so durable as Topinam silk stockings?" "His Excellency Goes Out on the Town!" *"Saint Bartholomew's Night*—A Brand-New Production!" "For Fun and Food Come to the Black Pony!" "Hot Sex Show & Dancing at the Red Pony!" Next to this he noticed a political poster: "Criminal Intrigues!" but it referred to the price of bread, not to the Parallel Campaign. He turned away and, a few steps farther along, looked into the window of a bookshop. "The Great Author's Latest Work," said a cardboard sign beside a row of fifteen copies of the same book. In the opposite corner of the display window, a sign accompanying another book read: *"Love's Tower of Babel* by ——— makes gripping reading for men and women."

"The Great Author?" Ulrich thought. He remembered having read one book by him and resolved never to read another; but since then the man had nevertheless become famous. Considering the window display of German intellect, Ulrich was reminded of an old army joke: "Mortadella!" During Ulrich's military service this had been the nickname of an unpopular general, after the popular Italian sausage, and if anyone wondered why, the answer was: "Part pig, part donkey." He was prevented from pursuing this stimulating analogy by the voice of a woman asking him:

"Are you waiting for the streetcar too?" Only then did he realize that he was no longer standing in front of the bookshop. He also had not realized that he was now standing immobile at a streetcar stop. The woman who had called this to his attention wore a knapsack and glasses, and turned out to be an acquaintance from the staff of the Astronomical Institute, one of the few women of accomplishment in this man's profession. He looked at her nose and the bags under her eyes, which the strain of unremitting intellectual effort had turned into something resembling underarm dress shields made of gutta-percha. Then he glanced down and noticed her short tweed skirt, then up and saw a black rooster feather in a green mountaineer's hat that floated over her learned features, and he smiled.

"Are you off to the mountains?" he asked.

Dr. Strastil was going to the mountains for three days to "relax." "What do you think of Koniatowski's paper?" she asked Ulrich. Ulrich had nothing to say. "Kneppler will be furious," she said, "but Koniatowski's critique of Kneppler's deduction from Danielli's theorem is interesting, don't you agree? Do *you* think Kneppler's deduction is possible?"

Ulrich shrugged his shoulders.

He was one of those mathematicians called logicians, for whom nothing was ever "correct" and who were working out new theoretical principles. But he was not entirely satisfied with the logic of the logicians either. Had he continued his work, he would have gone right back to Aristotle; he had his own views of all that.

"For my part, I don't think Kneppler's deduction is mistaken, it's just that it's wrong," Dr. Strastil confessed. She might have said with the same firmness that she did consider the deduction mistaken but nevertheless not essentially wrong. She knew what she meant, but in ordinary language, where the terms are undefined, one cannot express oneself unequivocally. Using this holiday language under her tourist hat made her feel something of the timid haughtiness that might be aroused in a cloistered monk who was rash enough to let himself come in contact with the sensual world of the laity.

Ulrich got into the streetcar with Fräulein Strastil; he didn't know why. Perhaps it was because she cared so much about Koniatowski's criticism of Kneppler. Perhaps he felt like talking to her about literature, about which she knew nothing.

"What will you do in the mountains?" he asked.

She was going up to the Hochschwab.

"There'll still be too much snow up there." He knew the mountains. "It's too late for skis, and too early to go up there without them."

"Then I'll stay down," Fräulein Strastil declared. "I once spent three days in a cabin at the foot of the Farsenalm. I only want to get back to nature for a bit!"

The expression on the worthy astronomer's face as she uttered the word "nature" provoked Ulrich to ask her what she needed nature for.

Dr. Strastil was sincerely indignant. She could lie on the mountain meadow for three whole days without stirring—"just like a boulder!" she declared.

"That's because you're a scientist," Ulrich pointed out. "A peasant would be bored."

Dr. Strastil did not see it that way. She spoke of the thousands who sought nature every holiday, on foot, on wheels, or by boat.

Ulrich spoke of the peasants deserting the countryside in droves for the attractions of the city.

Fräulein Strastil doubted that he was feeling on a sufficiently elementary level.

Ulrich claimed that the only elementary level, besides eating and love, was to make oneself comfortable, not to seek out an alpine meadow. The natural feeling that was supposed to drive people to do such things was actually a modern Rousseauism, a complicated and sentimental attitude.

He was not at all pleased with the way he was expressing himself, but he did not care what he said, and merely kept on talking because he had not yet come to what he wanted to get out of his system. Fräulein Strastil gave him a mistrustful look. She could not make him out. Here her considerable experience in abstract thinking was of no use to her; she could neither keep separate nor fit together the ideas he seemed merely to be juggling so nimbly; she guessed that he was talking without thinking. She took some comfort in listening to him with a rooster feather on her hat, and it reinforced her joy in the solitude she was heading for.

At this point Ulrich's eye happened to light on the newspaper of the man opposite him, and he read the opening line of an advertisement, in heavy type: "Our time asks questions—Our time gives answers." It could have been the announcement of a new arch support or of a forthcoming lecture—who could tell these days?—but his mind suddenly leapt onto the track he had been seeking.

His companion struggled to be objective. "I'm afraid," she admitted with some hesitation, "that I don't know much about literature; people like us never have time. Perhaps I don't know the right things, either. But ————"—she mentioned a popular name— "means a great deal to me. A writer who can make us feel things so intensely is surely what we mean by a great writer!"

However, since Ulrich felt he had now profited enough from Dr. Strastil's combination of an exceptionally developed capacity for abstract thought and a notably retarded understanding of the soul, he stood up cheerfully, treated his colleague to a bit of outrageous flattery, and hastily got off, excusing himself on the grounds that he had gone two stops past his destination. When he stood on the street, raising his hat to her once more, Fräulein Strastil remembered that she had recently heard some disparaging remarks about his own work; but she also felt herself blushing in response to his charming parting words to her, which, to her way of thinking, was not exactly to his credit. But he now knew, without yet being fully conscious of it, why his thoughts were revolving on the subject of literature and what it was they were after, from the interrupted "Mortadella" comparison to his unintentionally leading the good Strastil on to those confidences. After all, literature had been no concern of his since he had written his last poem, at twenty; still, before that, writing secretly had been a fairly regular habit, which he had given up not because he had grown older or had realized he didn't have enough talent, but for reasons that now, with his current impressions, he would have liked to define by some kind of word suggesting much effort culminating in a void.

For Ulrich was one of those book-lovers who do not want to go on reading because they feel that the whole business of reading and writing is a nuisance. "If the sensible Strastil wants to be 'made to feel,'" he thought ("Quite right too! If I had objected she'd have brought up music as her trump card!")—and as one so often does, he was partly thinking in words, partly carrying on a wordless argument in his head—so if this reasonable Dr. Strastil wants to be made to feel, it only amounts to what everyone wants from art, to be moved, overwhelmed, entertained, surprised, to be allowed a sniff of noble ideas; in short, to be made to experience something "alive," have a "living" experience. Ulrich was certainly not against it. Somewhere at the back of his mind he was thinking something that ended in a mingling of a touch of sentiment and ironic resistance: "Feeling is rare enough. To keep feeling at a certain temperature, to keep it from cooling down, probably means preserving the body warmth from which all intellectual development arises. And whenever a person is momentarily lifted out of his tangle of rational intentions, which involve him with countless alien objects, whenever he is raised to a state wholly without purpose, such as listening to music, for instance, he is almost in the biological condition of a flower on which the rain and the sunshine fall." He was willing to admit that there is a more eternal eternity in the mind's pauses and quiescence than in its activity; but he had been thinking first "feeling" and then "experiencing": a contradiction was implied here. For there were experiences of the will! There were experiences of action at its peak! Though one could probably assume that by the time each experience had reached its acme of radiant bitterness it was sheer feeling; which would bring up an even greater contradiction: that in its greatest purity the state of feeling is a quiescence, a dying away of all activity. Or was it not a contradiction, after all? Was there some curious connection by which the most intense activity was motionless at the core? At this point he realized that this sequence of ideas had begun not so much as a thought at the back of his mind as one that was unwelcome, for with a sudden stiffening of resistance against the sentimental turn it had taken, Ulrich repudiated the whole train of thought into which he had slipped. He had absolutely no intention of brooding over certain states of mind and, when he was thinking about feeling, succumbing to feelings.

He suddenly realized that what he was getting at could best be defined, without much ado, as the futile actuality or the eternal momentariness of literature. Does it lead to anything? Literature is either a tremendous detour from experience to experience, ending back where it came from, or an epitome of sensations that leads to nothing at all definite. "A puddle," he now thought, "has often made a stronger impression of depth on someone than the ocean, for the simple reason that we have more occasion to experience puddles than oceans." It seemed to him that it was the same with feelings, which was the only reason commonplace feelings are regarded as the deepest. Putting the ability to feel above the feeling itself—the characteristic of all sensitive people—like the wanting to make others feel and be made to feel that is the common impulse behind all our arrangements concerning the emotional life, amounts to downgrading the importance and nature of the feelings compared with their fleeting presence as a subjective state, and so leads to that shallowness, stunted development, and utter irrelevance, for which there is no lack of examples. "Of course," Ulrich added mentally, "this view will repel all those people who feel as cozy in their feelings as a rooster in his feathers and who even preen themselves on the idea that eternity starts all over again with every separate 'personality'!" He had a clear mental image of an immense perversity of a scope involving all mankind, but he could not find a way to express it that would satisfy him, probably because its ramifications were too intricate.

While busy with all this he was watching the passing trolley cars, waiting for the one that would take him back as close as possible to the center of town. He saw people climbing in and out of the cars, and his technically trained eye toyed distractedly with the interplay of welding and casting, rolling and bolting, of engineering and hand finishing, of historical development and the present state of the art, which combined to make up these barracks-on-wheels that these people were using.

"As a last step, a committee from the municipal transportation department comes to the factory and decides what kind of wood to use as veneer, the color of the paint, upholstery, arms on the seats and straps for standees, ashtrays, and the like," he thought idly, "and it is precisely these trivial details, along with the red or green color of the exterior, and how they swing themselves up the steps and inside, that for tens of thousands of people make up what they remember, all they experience, of all the genius that went into it. This is what forms their character, endows it with speed or comfort; it's what makes them perceive red cars as home and blue ones as foreign, and adds up to that unmistakable odor of countless details that clings to the clothing of the centuries." So there was no denying—and this suddenly rounded out Ulrich's main line of thought—that life itself largely peters out into trivial realities or, to put it technically, that the power of its spiritual coefficient is extremely small.

And suddenly, as he felt himself swinging aboard the trolley, he said to himself: "I shall have to make Agathe see that morality is the subordination of every momentary state in our life to one enduring one!" This principle had come to him all at once in the form of a definition. But this highly polished concept had been preceded and was followed by others which, though not so fully developed and articulated, rounded out its meaning. The innocuous business of feeling was here set in an austere conceptual framework, it was given a job to do, with a strict hierarchy of values, vaguely foreshortened, in the offing: feelings must either be functional or refer to a still-undefined condition as immense as the open sea. Should it be called an idea or a longing? Ulrich had to leave it at that, for from the moment his sister's name had occurred to him her shadow had darkened his thoughts. As always when he thought of her, he felt that he had shown himself in her company in a different frame of mind than usual. And he knew, too, that he was longing passionately to get back into that frame of mind. But the same memory overcame him with humiliation when he thought of himself carrying on in a presumptuous, ludicrous, and drunken fashion, no better than a man who sinks to his knees in a frenzy in front of people he won't be able to look in the face the next day. Considering how balanced and controlled the intellectual exchange between brother and sister had been this was a wild exaggeration, and if it was not completely unfounded, it was probably no more than a reaction to feelings that had not yet taken shape. He knew Agathe was bound to arrive in a few days, and he had done nothing to stop her. Had she actually done anything wrong? One might suppose that as she cooled off she had gone back on it all. But a lively premonition assured him that Agathe had not abandoned her scheme. He could have tried to find out by asking her. Again he felt duty bound to write and warn her against it. But instead of giving this even a moment's serious consideration, he tried to imagine what could have prompted Agathe to do something so irregular: he saw it as an incredibly vehement gesture meant to show her trust in him and to put herself entirely in his hands. "She has very little sense of reality," he thought, "but a wonderful way of doing what she wants. Rash, I suppose, but just for that reason spontaneous! When she's angry, she sees red with a vengeance." He smiled indulgently and looked around at the other passengers. Every one of them had evil thoughts, of course, and every one suppressed them, and nobody blamed himself overmuch; but no one else had these thoughts outside himself, in another person, who would give them the enchanting inaccessibility of an experience in a dream.

Since Ulrich had left his letter unfinished, he realized for the first time that he no longer had a choice but was already in the state he was still hesitating to enter. According to its laws—he indulged himself in the overweening ambiguity of calling them "holy"—Agathe's misstep could not be undone by repentance but only be made *good* by actions that followed it, which incidentally was doubtless in keeping with the original meaning of repentance as a state of purifying fire, not a state of being impaired. To repair the damage done to Agathe's inconvenient husband, or indemnify him, would have meant only to undo the damage done, that is, it would only have been that double and crippling negation of which ordinary good conduct consists, which inwardly cancels out to zero. But what should be done for Hagauer, how a looming burden should be "lifted," was possible only if one could marshal a great sympathy for him, a prospect Ulrich could not face without dismay. Keeping within the framework of this logic that Ulrich was trying to adapt to, all that could ever be made good was something other than the damage done, and he did not doubt for an instant that this would have to be his and his sister's whole life.

"Putting it presumptuously," he thought, "this means: Saul did not make good each single consequence of his previous sins; he turned into Paul!" Against this curious logic, however, both feeling and judgment raised the customary objection that it would nevertheless be more decent—and no deterrent to more romantic future possibilities—to straighten out accounts with one's brother-in-law first, and only then to plan one's new life. The kind of morality to which he was so attracted was not, after all, suited in the least to dealing with money matters and business and the resulting conflicts. So insoluble and conflicting situations were bound to arise on the borderline between that other life and everyday life, which it would be better not to allow to develop into borderline cases; they should be dispatched at the outset, in the normal, unemotional way of simple decency. But here again Ulrich felt it was impossible to take one's bearings from the normal conditions of goodness if one wanted to press on into the realm of unconditional goodness. The mission laid upon him, to take the first step into uncharted territory, would apparently suffer no abatement.

His last line of defense was his strong aversion to the terms he had been using so lavishly, such as "self," "feeling," "goodness," "alternative goodness," "evil," for being so subjective and at the same time presumptuous, gauzy abstractions, which really corresponded to the moral ponderings of very much younger people. He found himself doing what any number of those who are following his story are likely to do, irritably picking out individual words and phrases, asking himself such questions as: " 'Production and results of feelings?' What a machinelike, rationalistic, humanly unrealistic notion! 'Morality as the problem of a permanent state to which all individual states are subordinate'—and that's all? The inhumanity of it!" Looked at through a rational person's eyes, it all seemed extraordinarily perverse. "The essence of morality virtually hinges on the important feelings remaining constant," Ulrich thought, "and all the individual has to do is act in accord with them!"

But just at this point the rolling locale that enclosed him and that had been created with T-square and compass came to a halt, at a spot where his eye, peering out from the body of modern transportation and still an involuntary part of it, lit on a stone column that had been standing beside this roadway since the period of the Baroque, so that the engineered comfort of this calculated artifact, unconsciously taken for granted, suddenly clashed with the passion erupting from the statue's antiquated pose, which suggested something not unlike a petrified bellyache. The effect of this optical collision was to powerfully confirm the ideas from which Ulrich had just been trying to escape. Could anything have illustrated life's confusion more clearly than this chance spectacle? Without taking sides with either the Now or the Then in matters of taste, as one usually does when faced with such a juxtaposition, he felt his mind abandoned by both sides without an instant's hesitation, and saw in it only the great demonstration of a problem that is at bottom a moral problem. He could not doubt that the transience of what is regarded as style, culture, the will of the time, or the spirit of an era, for which it is admired, was a moral weakness. For in the great scale of the ages this instability means exactly what it would mean on the smaller scale of personal life: to have developed one's potential one-sidedly, to have dissipated it in extravagant exaggerations, never taking the measure of one's own will, never achieving a complete form, and in disjointed passions doing now this, now that. Even the so-called succession or progress of the ages seemed to him to be only another term for the fact that none of these experiments ever reach the point where they would all meet and move on together toward a comprehensive understanding that would at last offer a basis for a coherent development, a lasting enjoyment, and that seriousness of great beauty of which nowadays hardly more than a shadow occasionally drifts across our life.

Ulrich of course saw the preposterous arrogance of assuming that everything had in effect come to nothing. And yet it was nothing. Immeasurable as existence; confusion as meaning. At least, judging by the results, it was no more than the stuff of which the soul of the present is made, which is not much. While Ulrich was thinking this he was nevertheless savoring the "not much," as if it were the last meal at the table of life his outlook would permit him to have. He had left the streetcar and taken a route that would bring him quickly to the city's center. He felt as if he were coming out of a cellar. The streets were screeching with gaiety and filled with unseasonable warmth like a summer day. The sweet poisonous taste of talking to oneself had left his mouth: everything was expansive and out in the sun. Ulrich stopped at almost every shop window. Those tiny bottles in so many colors, stoppered scents, countless variants of nail scissors—what quantities of genius there were even in a hairdresser's window! A glove shop: what connections, what inventions, before a goat's skin is drawn up on a lady's hand and the animal's pelt has become more refined than her own! He was astonished at the luxuries one took for granted, the countless cozy trappings of the good life, as though he were seeing them for the first time. Trap-pings! What a charming word, he felt. And what a boon, this tremendous contract to get along together! Here there was no reminder of life's earth crust, of the unpaved roads of passion, of—he truly felt this—the *uncivilized* nature of the soul! One's attention, a bright and narrow beam, glided over a flower garden of fruits, gemstones, fabrics, forms and allurements whose gently persuasive eyes were opened in all the colors of the rainbow. Since at that time a white skin was prized and guarded from the sun, a few colorful parasols were already floating above the crowd, laying silky shadows on women's pale faces. Ulrich's glance was even enchanted by the pale-golden beer seen in passing through the plate-glass windows of a restaurant, on tablecloths so white that they formed blue patches at the edges of shadows. Then the Archbishop's carriage drove by, a gently rocking, heavy carriage, whose dark interior showed red and purple. It had to be the Archbishop's carriage, for this horse-drawn vehicle that Ulrich followed with his eyes had a wholly ecclesiastical air, and two policemen sprang to attention and saluted this follower of Christ without thinking of their predecessors who had run a lance into *his* predecessor's side.

He gave himself up with such zest to these impressions, which he had just been calling "life's futile actuality," that little by little, as he sated himself with the world, his earlier revulsion against it began to reassert itself. Ulrich now knew exactly where his speculations fell short. "What's the point, in the face of all this vainglory, of looking for some result beyond, behind, beneath it all? Would that be a philosophy? An all-embracing conviction, a law? Or the finger of God? Or, instead of that, the assumption that morality has up to now lacked an 'inductive stance,' that it is much harder to be good than we had believed, and that it will require an endless cooperative effort, like every other science? I think there is no morality, because it cannot be deduced from anything constant; all there are are rules for uselessly maintaining transitory conditions. I also assume that there can be no profound happiness without a profound morality; yet my thinking about it strikes me as an unnatural, bloodless state, and it is absolutely not what I want!" Indeed, he might well have asked himself much more simply, "What is this I have taken upon myself?" which is what he now did. However, this question touched his sensibility more than his intellect; in fact, the question stopped his thinking and diminished bit by bit his always keen delight in strategic planning before he had even formulated it. It began as a dark tone close to his ear, accompanying him; then it sounded inside him, an octave lower than everything else; finally, Ulrich had merged with his question and felt as though he himself were a strangely deep sound in the bright, hard world, surrounded by a wide interval. So what was it he had really taken on himself, what had he promised?

He thought hard. He knew that he had not merely been joking when he used the expression "the Millennium," even if it was only a figure of speech. If one took this promise seriously, it meant the desire to live, with the aid of mutual love, in a secular condition so transcendent that one could only feel and do whatever heightened and maintained that condition. He had always been certain that human beings showed hints of such a disposition. It had begun with the "affair of the major's wife," and though his subsequent experiences had not amounted to much, they had always been of the same kind. In sum, what it more or less came to was that Ulrich believed in the "Fall of Man" and in "Original Sin." That is, he was inclined to think that at some time in the past, man's basic attitude had undergone a fundamental change that must have been roughly comparable to the moment when a lover regains his sobriety; he may then see the whole truth, but something greater has been torn to shreds, and the truth appears everywhere as a mere fragment left over and patched up again. Perhaps it was even the apple of "knowledge" that had caused this spiritual change and expelled mankind from a primal state to which it might find its way back only after becoming wise through countless experiences and through sin. But Ulrich believed in such myths not in their traditional form, but only in the way he had discovered them; he believed in them like an arithmetician who, with the system of his feelings spread out before him, concludes, from the fact that none of them could be justified, that he would have to introduce a fantastic hypothesis whose nature could be arrived at only intuitively. That was no trifle! He had turned over such thoughts in his mind often enough, but he had never yet been in the situation of having to decide within a few days whether to stake his life on it. A faint sweat broke out under his hat and collar, and he was bothered by the proximity of all the people jostling by him. What he was thinking amounted to taking leave of most of his living relationships; he had no illusions about that. For today our lives are divided, and parts are entangled with other people; what we dream has to do with dreaming and also with what other people dream; what we do has sense, but more sense in relation with what others do; and what we believe is tied in with beliefs only a fraction of which are our own. It is therefore quite unrealistic to insist upon acting out of the fullness of one's own personal reality. Especially for a man like himself, who had been imbued all his life with the thought that one's beliefs had to be shared, that one must have the courage to live in the midst of moral contradictions, because that was the price of great achievement. Was he at least convinced of what he had just been thinking about the possibility and significance of another kind of life? Not at all! Nevertheless, he could not help being emotionally drawn to it, as though his feelings were facing the unmistakable signs of a reality they had been looking forward to for years.

At this point he did have to ask himself what, if anything, entitled him, like a veritable Narcissus, to wish not to do ever again anything that left his soul unmoved. Such a resolve runs counter to the principles of the active life with which everyone is today imbued, and even if God-fearing times could have fostered such ambitions, they have melted away like the half-light of dawn as the sun grows stronger. There was an odor of something reclusive and syrupy clinging to him that Ulrich found increasingly distasteful. He tried to rein in his unruly thoughts as quickly as possible, and told himself—if not quite sincerely—that the promise of a Millennium he had so oddly given his sister, rationally considered, boiled down to no more than a kind of social work: living with Agathe would probably call for all the delicacy and selflessness he could muster—qualities that had been all too lacking in him. He recalled, the way one recalls an unusually transparent cloud flitting across the sky, certain moments of their recent time together that had already been of this kind. "Perhaps the content of the Millennium is merely the burgeoning of this energy, which at first shows itself in two people, until it grows into a resounding universal communion," he wondered in some embarrassment. Again he resorted to his own "affair of the major's wife" for more light on the subject. Leaving aside the delusions of love, since immaturity had been at the root of that aberration, he focused all his attention on the feelings of tender care and adoration of which he had been capable in his solitude at the time, and it seemed to him that feeling trust and affection, or living for another person, must be a happiness that could move one to tears, as lovely as the lambent sinking of day into the peace of evening and also, just a little, an impoverishing of spirit and intellect to the point of tears. For there was also a funny side to their project, as of two elderly bachelors setting up house together, and such twitchings of his imagination warned him how little the notion of a life of service in brotherly love was likely to offer him fulfillment. With some detachment he could see that from the first there had been a large measure of the asocial intermingled in his relationship with Agathe. Not only the business with Hagauer and the will, but the whole emotional tone of their association, pointed to something impetuous, and there was no doubt that what brought them together was not so much love for each other as a repelling of the rest of the world.

"No!" Ulrich thought. "Wanting to live for another person is no more than egoism going bankrupt and then opening a new shop next door, with a partner!"

Actually, his inner concentration, despite this brilliantly honed insight, had already passed its peak at the moment when he had been tempted to confine the diffuse illumination that filled him inside an earthly lamp, and now that this had shown itself to be a mistake, his thinking had lost the urge to press for a decision and was eager for some distraction. Not far from him two men had just collided and were shouting unpleasant remarks at each other as if getting ready to fight; Ulrich watched with a renewed interest, and had hardly turned away when his glance struck that of a woman giving him a look like a fat flower nodding on its stem. In that pleasant mood which is an equal blend of feeling and extroverted attention, he noted that real people pursue the ideal commandment to love one another in two parts, the first consisting in their detesting one another and the second in making up for it by entering into sexual relations with the half that is excepted. Without stopping to think he too turned, after a few steps, to follow the woman; it was a quite mechanical consequence of their eye contact. He could see her body beneath her dress like a big white fish just under the surface of the water. He felt the male urge to harpoon the fish and watch it flap and struggle, and there was in this as much repugnance as desire. Some hardly perceptible signs made him certain this woman knew he was prowling after her and was interested. He tried to work out her place on the social scale and decided on "upper-middle class," where it is hard to pinpoint the position with precision. "Business family? Government service?" he speculated. Various random images came to him, even including that of a pharmacy: he could feel the pungently sweet smell of the husband coming home, the compact atmosphere of the household betraying no sign of the shifting beam from the burglar's flashlight that had just recently moved through it. It was vile, no doubt, but shamefully exciting.

As Ulrich kept following the woman, actually afraid that she might stop at some shop window and so force him either to stumble foolishly past her or to pick her up, something in him was still undistracted and wide awake. "What exactly might Agathe want from *me*?" he asked himself for the first time. He did not know. He assumed that it would be something like what he wanted of her, but he had nothing to base this on but intuition. Wasn't it amazing how quickly and unexpectedly it had all happened? Other than a few childhood memories he had known nothing about her, and the little he had heard, such as her connection of some years with Hagauer, he found rather distasteful. He now recalled the curious hesitancy, almost reluctance, with which he had approached his father's house on his arrival. Suddenly the idea took hold of him: "My feeling for Agathe is just imagination!" In a man who continually wanted something other than what those around him wanted—he was thinking seriously again—in such a man, who always felt strong dislikes and never got as far as liking, the usual kindliness and lukewarm human goodness can easily separate and turn into a cold hardness with a mist of impersonal love floating above it. Seraphic love, he had once named it. It could also, he thought, be called love without a partner. Or, just as well, love without sex. Sexual love was all the love there was nowadays: those alike in gender repelled each other, and in the sexual crossover people loved with a growing resentment of the overestimation of this compulsion. But seraphic love was free of both these defects. It was love cleansed of the crosscurrents of social and sexual aversions. This love, which makes itself felt everywhere in company with the cruelty of modern life, could truly be called the sisterly love of an age that has no room for brotherly love, he said to himself, wincing in irritation.

Yet having finally arrived at this conclusion, alongside it and alternately with it he went on dreaming of a woman who could not be attained at all. He had a vision of her like late-autumn days in the mountains, when the air is as if drained of its lifeblood to the point of death, while the colors are aflame with fierce passion. He saw the blue vistas, without end in their mysterious gradations. He completely forgot the woman who was actually walking ahead of him; he was far from desire and perhaps close to love.

He was distracted only by the lingering gaze of another woman, like that of the first, yet not so brazen and obvious; this one was well-bred and delicate as a pastel stroke that leaves its stamp in a fraction of a second. He looked up and in a state of utmost emotional exhaustion beheld a very beautiful lady in whom he recognized Bonadea.

The glorious day had lured her out for a walk. Ulrich glanced at his watch: he had been strolling along only fifteen minutes, and no more than forty-five had passed since he left the Palais Leinsdorf.

Bonadea said: "I'm not free today."

Ulrich thought: "How long, by comparison, is a whole day, a year, not to mention a resolution for a lifetime!" It was beyond calculation.

146

BONADEA; OR, THE RELAPSE

And so it happened that Ulrich received a visit soon afterward from his abandoned mistress. Their encounter on the street had not provided him with an opportunity to call her to account for misusing his name to win Diotima's friendship, nor had it given Bonadea enough time to reproach him for his long silence and not only defend herself from the charge of indiscretion and call Diotima "an ignoble snake" but even make up a story to prove it. Hence she and her retired lover had hurriedly agreed that they must meet once again and have it all out.

The visitor who appeared was no longer the Bonadea who coiled her hair until it gave her head something of a Grecian look when she studied it in the mirror with eyes narrowed, intending to be just as pure and noble as Diotima, nor was she the one who raved in the night, maddened by the withdrawal pains of such a cure for her addiction, cursing her exemplar shamelessly and with a woman's instinct for the lethal thrust; she was once again the dear old Bonadea whose curls hung down over her none-too-wise brow or were swept back from it, depending on the dictates of fashion, and in whose eyes there was always something reminiscent of the air rising above a fire. While Ulrich started to reprove her for having betrayed their relationship to his cousin, she was carefully removing her hat before the mirror, and when he wanted to know exactly how much she had said, she smugly and in great detail told him a story she claimed to have made up for Diotima about having had a letter from him in which he asked her to see that Moosbrugger was not overlooked entirely, whereupon she had thought the best thing to do was to turn to the woman of whose high-mindedness the writer of the letter had so often spoken to her. Then she perched on the arm of Ulrich's chair, kissed his forehead, and meekly insisted that it was all perfectly true, except for the letter.

Her bosom emitted a great warmth.

"Then why did you call my cousin a snake? You were one yourself!" Ulrich said.

Bonadea pensively shifted her gaze from him to the wall. "Oh, I don't know," she answered. "She's so nice to me. She takes so much interest in me!"

"What is that supposed to mean?" Ulrich asked. "Are you participating in her efforts for the Good, the True, and the Beautiful?"

Bonadea replied: "She explained to me that no woman can live for her love with all her might, she no more than I. And that is why every woman must do her duty in the place appointed to her by fate. She really is so very decent," Bonadea went on, even more thoughtfully. "She keeps telling me to be more patient with my husband, and she insists that a superior woman can find considerable happiness in making the most of her marriage; she puts far more value in that than in adultery. And after all, it's exactly what I've always thought myself!"

It happened to be true, in fact; for Bonadea had never thought otherwise, she had merely always acted otherwise, and so she could agree with a good conscience. When Ulrich said as much to her, it earned him another kiss, this time somewhat lower than the forehead. "You happen to upset my polygamous balance," she said with a little sigh of apology for the discrepancy that had arisen between her principles and her conduct.

It turned out, after some cross-examination, that she had meant to say "polyglandular balance"—a new physiological term at that time comprehensible only to initiates, which might be translated as balance of secretions, on the assumption that certain glands which affected the blood had a stimulating or inhibiting effect, thereby influencing character and, more specifically, a person's temperament, especially the kind of temperament Bonadea had to a degree that caused her much suffering in certain circumstances.

Ulrich raised his eyebrows in curiosity.

"Well, something to do with glands," Bonadea said. "It's rather a relief to know one can't help it!" She gave the lover she had lost a wistful smile. "A person who loses her balance easily is liable to have unsuccessful sexual experiences."

"My dear Bonadea," Ulrich marveled, "what kind of talk is this?"

"It's what I've been learning to say. You are an unsuccessful sexual experience, your cousin says. But she also says that a person can escape the shattering physical and emotional effects by bearing in mind that nothing we do is merely our own personal affair. She's very nice to me. She says that *my* mistake is that I make too much of a single aspect of love instead of taking in the whole spectrum of the experience. You see, what she means by a single aspect is what she also calls 'the crude mechanics': it's often very interesting to see things in her light. But there's one thing about her I don't like. She may say that a strong woman sees her life's work in monogamy and should love it like an artist, but she does have three men, and, counting you, possibly four, on her string, and I have none at all now to make me happy!"

The gaze with which she scrutinized her AWOL reservist was warm and questioning. Ulrich did his best to ignore it.

"So the two of you talk about me?" he asked with some foreboding.

"Oh, only on and off," Bonadea replied. "When your cousin needs to exemplify something, or when your friend the General is present."

"I suppose Arnheim is in on this too?"

"He lends a dignified ear to what the gracious ladies have to say." Bonadea made fun of him, not without talent for unobtrusive mimicry, but she added seriously: "I don't like the way he treats your cousin at all. Most of the time he's off on some trip or other, and when he's present he talks too much to everyone, and when she is quoting Frau von Stern, for example—"

"Frau von Stein?" Ulrich corrected her by asking.

"Of course, I meant Stein: it isn't as if Diotima didn't talk about her often enough. Well, when she talks about Frau von Stein and Goethe's other woman, the Vul . . . What's her name? It sounds a little obscene, I think. . . ."

"Vulpius."

"Oh yes. You know, I get to hear so many foreign words there that I'm beginning to forget the simplest ones! So when she's making her comparisons between Frau von Stein and the other, Arnheim keeps staring at me as if, compared with his idol, I was no better than the kind you just said."

Now Ulrich insisted on an explanation of these new developments.

It turned out that since Bonadea had claimed the status of Ulrich's confidante she had made great strides in her intimacy with Diotima.

Her alleged nymphomania, which Ulrich had carelessly mentioned to Diotima in a moment of pique, had had a far-reaching effect on his cousin. She had begun by inviting the newcomer to her gatherings, in the role of a lady vaguely active in social welfare, and watched her covertly. This intruder, soaking up Diotima's domestic interiors with eyes soft as blotting paper, not only had been downright uncanny but had also aroused in her as much feminine curiosity as dread. To tell the truth, when Diotima pronounced the term "venereal disease" she felt the same vague sensations as when she tried to imagine what her new acquaintance actually did, and from one occasion to the next she was expecting, with an uneasy conscience, some impossible behavior, outrage, or scandal from her. Bonadea succeeded, however, in calming these suspicions by cloaking her ambition in the kind of especially well-bred behavior that naughty children affect when their moral zeal is aroused by the tone of their surroundings. In the process she even managed to forget that she was jealous of Diotima, who was surprised to find that her disturbing protégée was just as much given over to "ideals" as she was herself. For the "fallen sister," as she thought of her, had soon become a protégée, in whom Diotima was moved to take an especially active interest because her own situation made her see the ignoble mystery of nymphomania as a kind of female sword of Damocles which, she said, might hang by a thin thread even over the head of a vestal virgin. "I know, my child," she consolingly instructed Bonadea, who was about her own age, "there is nothing so tragic as embracing a man of whom one is not entirely convinced!" and kissed her on that unchaste mouth with a heroic effort that would have been enough to make her press her lips on the blood-dripping bristles of a lion's beard.

Diotima's position at that time was midway between Arnheim and Tuzzi: a seesaw position, metaphorically speaking, one end of which was weighted down too much, the other not enough. Even Ulrich had found her, on his return, with hot towels around her head and stomach; but these female complaints, the intensity of which she sensed to be her body's protest against the contradictory orders it was receiving from her soul, had also awakened in Diotima that noble resolve that was characteristic of her as soon as she refused to be just like every other woman. It was of course hard to decide, at first, whether it was her soul or her body that was called upon to take action, or whether a change in her attitude toward Arnheim or toward Tuzzi would be the better response; but this was settled with the world's help, for while her soul with its enigmas eluded her like a fish one tries to hold bare-handed, the suffering seeker was surprised to find plenty of advice in the books of the *zeitgeist,* once she had decided to deal with her fate from the physical angle, as represented by her husband. She had not known that our time, which has presumably distanced itself from the concept of passionate love because it is more of a religious than a sexual concept, regards love contemptuously as being too childish to still bother about, devoting all its energies instead to marriage, the bodily operations of which in all their variants it investigates with zestful specificity. There was already at that time a spate of books that discussed the "sexual revolution" with the clean-mindedness of a gym teacher, and whose aim was to help people be happy though married. In these books man or wife were referred to only as "male and female procreators," and the boredom they were supposed to exorcise by all manner of mental and physical diversions was labeled "the sexual problem." When Diotima first immersed herself in this literature she furrowed her brow, but it soon smoothed out again; for it was a spur to her ambition to discover that a great new movement of the *zeitgeist* was under way, which had so far escaped her notice. Transported, she finally clapped hands to brow in amazement that she who had it in her to set the world a great goal (though it was not yet clear what) had never before realized that even the unnerving discomfitures of marriage could be dealt with by using one's intellectual resources. This possibility coincided with her inclinations and suddenly opened the prospect of treating her relationship with her husband, which she had so far regarded as something to be endured, as a science and an art.

"Wherever we may roam, there's no place like home," Bonadea said, with her characteristic taste for platitudes and quotations. For it came about that Diotima, in the role of guardian angel, soon took on Bonadea as a pupil in these matters, in accordance with the pedagogical principle that one learns best by teaching. This enabled Diotima to go on extracting, from the still undirected and unclear impressions she gained from her new reading, points she could really believe in—guided as she was by the happy secret of "intuition," that you are sure to hit the bull's-eye if you talk about anything long enough. At the same time it worked to Bonadea's advantage that she could bring to the dialogue that response without which the student remains barren soil for even the best teacher: her rich practical experience, doled out with restraint, had served the theoretician Diotima as an anxiously studied source of information ever since she had set out to put her marriage in order with the aid of textbooks.

"Look, I'm sure I'm not nearly as bright as she is," Bonadea explained, "but often there are things in her books that even I never dreamed of, and that makes her so discouraged sometimes, and then she'll say things like: This can't be decided at the council table of the marriage bed, I'm afraid; it would, unfortunately, take an immense amount of trained sexual experience, a lot of real physical practice on living material!"

"But for heaven's sake," Ulrich exclaimed, convulsed with laughter at the mere idea of his chaste cousin's straying into "sexology," "what on earth is she after?"

Bonadea gathered her memories of the happy conjunction between the scientific interests of the time and unthinking utterance. "It's a question of how best to develop and manage her sex instinct," she finally responded, in the spirit of her teacher. "And she stands for the principle that a joyous and harmonious sex life has to be achieved through the most severe self-discipline."

"So you two are in training? Endurance training, at that? I'm impressed, I must say," Ulrich exclaimed. "But now will you kindly explain just what it is Diotima is training for?"

"To begin with, she's training her husband, of course," Bonadea corrected him.

"The poor devil!" Ulrich could not help thinking. "In that case," he said, "I'd like to know how she does it. Please don't turn prudish on me all of a sudden."

Under this grilling Bonadea did, in fact, feel inhibited by her ambition to shine, like a prize pupil in an exam.

"Her sexual atmosphere is poisoned," she explained cautiously. "The only way to save it is for her and Tuzzi to make a most careful study of their behavior. There are no general rules for this. Each of them has to observe how the other reacts to life. To be a good observer, a person has to have some insight into sexual life. One has to be able to compare one's practical experience with the results of theoretical research, Diotima says. Woman today happens to have a new and different attitude to the sex problem; she expects a man not only to act but to act with a real understanding of the feminine!" And for Ulrich's entertainment or even just to amuse herself, she gaily added: "Just imagine what it must be like for her husband, who hasn't the faintest inkling of all this new stuff and gets to hear about it mostly at bedtime while they're undressing—let's say when Diotima is taking her hair down and fishing for hairpins, with her petticoats tucked between her knees, and then suddenly she starts talking about all that. I tried it out on my husband, and it drove him almost to apoplexy. One thing you must admit: If marriage is to be for a lifetime, at least there's the advantage that you have the opportunity of getting all the erotic possibilities in it out of your spouse. Which is what Diotima is trying to do with Tuzzi, who happens to be a bit crude!"

"Sounds like hard times for your husbands!" Ulrich teased.

Bonadea laughed, and he could tell how glad she would be to occasionally play truant from the oppressive earnestness of her school of love.

But Ulrich's probing instincts would not let go; he sensed that his greatly changed friend was keeping quiet about something she would much rather have talked about. He professed to be mystified because, from what he had heard, the two husbands involved had so far rather erred in overdoing the "erotic possibilities."

"Of course, that's all you ever think!" Bonadea said reproachfully, giving him a long, pointed glance with a little hook at its end that could easily be interpreted as regret for the innocence she had acquired. "You take advantage of a woman's physiological feeblemindedness yourself!"

"What do I take advantage of? You've found a splendid expression for the history of our love!"

Bonadea slapped his face lightly and, nervously, patted her hair in front of the mirror. Glancing at him out of the mirror, she said: "That's from a book."

"Of course. A very well known book."

"But Diotima disputes it. She found something in another book that speaks of 'the physiological inferiority of the male.' The author is a woman. Do you think it really makes much difference?"

"How can I tell, since I've no idea what we're talking about?"

"Well then, listen! Diotima's starting point is the discovery that she calls 'a woman's constant readiness for sex.' Can you see that?"

"Not in Diotima!"

"Don't be so crude!" she rebuked him. "It's a delicate theory, and it's hard for me to explain it to you so that you don't draw false conclusions from the fact that I happen to be here alone with you in your house while I'm talking about it. So this theory has it that a woman

can be made love to even when she doesn't feel like it. Now do you
see?"

"I do."

"Unfortunately, it can't be denied either. On the other hand, they
say that quite often a man can't make love even when he wants to.
Diotima says this has been scientifically established. Do you believe
that?"

"It's been known to happen."

"Oh, I don't know," Bonadea said doubtfully. "But Diotima says
that if you regard it in the light of science, it's obvious. For in contrast
with a woman's constant readiness for sex, a man—well, in a word, a
man's manliest part is easily discouraged." Her face was the color of
bronze as she now turned it away from the mirror.

"I never would have guessed it about Tuzzi," Ulrich said tactfully.

"I don't think it used to be the case, either," Bonadea said. "It's
only happening now, as a belated confirmation of the theory, because she lectures him on it day in, day out. She calls it the theory of
the 'fiasco.' Because the male procreator is so prone to this fiasco, he
only feels sexually secure if he doesn't have to be afraid of a woman's
being in some way or other spiritually superior, and that's why men
hardly ever have the courage to try a relationship with a woman
who's their equal as a human being. At least, they try right away to
put them down. Diotima says that the guiding principle of all male
love transactions, and especially of male arrogance, is fear. Great
men show it—she means Arnheim, of course. Lesser men hide it behind brutal physical aggression and abusing a woman's soul—I mean
you! And she means Tuzzi. That sort of 'Now or never!' you men so
often use to make us give in is only a kind of overcomp—" She was
about to say "compress"; "overcompensation," Ulrich said, coming
to the rescue.

"Right. That's how you men manage to overcome the impression
of your physiological inferiority!"

"What have you two decided to do, then?" Ulrich said meekly.

"We have to make an effort to be nice to men! That's why I've
come to see you. We'll see how you take it."

"And Diotima?"

"Heavens, what do you care about Diotima? Arnheim's eyes pop

out like a snail's when she tells him that the most intellectually superior men unfortunately seem to find full satisfaction only with inferior women and fail with women who are their equals, as attested
scientifically by the case of Frau von Stein and the Vulpius woman.
You see, now I've got her name right, but of course I've always
known she was the noted sex partner of the aging Olympian!"

Ulrich tried to steer the conversation away from himself and back
to Tuzzi. Bonadea began to laugh; she was not without sympathy for
the sorry predicament of the diplomat, whom she found quite attractive as a man, and felt a certain malicious and conspiratorial glee
about his having to suffer under the castigations of the soul. She reported that Diotima was basing her treatment of Tuzzi on the assumption that she must cure him of his fear of her, which had also
enabled her to come to terms somewhat with his "sexual brutality."
The great blunder of her life, she admitted, was in achieving an eminence too great for her male marriage partner's naïve need to feel
superior, so she had set about toning it down by hiding her spiritual
superiority behind a more suitable erotic coquetry.

Ulrich broke in to ask, with lively interest, what she understood by
that.

Bonadea's glance bored deeply into his face. "She might say to
him, for instance, 'Up to now our life has been spoiled by our competing for status.' And then she admits to him that the poisonous effect of the male struggle for power dominates all of public life as
well. . . ."

"But that's neither coquettish nor sexy!" Ulrich objected.

"Oh, but it is! You have to remember that a man in the grip of
passion will behave toward a woman like an executioner toward his
victim. That's part of his struggle for self-assertion, as it's now called.
On the other hand, you won't deny that the sex drive is important to a
woman too?"

"Certainly not!"

"Good. But a happy sexual relationship demands an equal give-
and-take. To get a really rapturous response from the love partner,
the partner must be respected as an equal and not just as a will-less
extension of oneself," she went on, caught up in her mentor's mode
of expression like someone sliding helplessly and anxiously across a
polished surface, carried along by his own momentum. "If no other

human relationship is able to endure unremitting pressure and counterpressure, how much less can a sexual—"

"Oho!" Ulrich disagreed.

Bonadea pressed his arm, and her eye glittered like a falling star.
"Hold your tongue!" she cried. "None of you have any firsthand experience of the feminine psyche! And if you want me to go on telling
you about your cousin . . ." But her energy was spent, and her eyes
now had the glitter of a tigress's as she watches fresh meat being carried past her cage. "No, I can't listen to any more of this myself!" she
cried.

"Does she really talk like that?" Ulrich asked. "Did she actually say
these things?"

"But it's all I hear every day, nothing but sexual practice, successful embraces, key principles of eroticism, glands, secretions, repressed urges, erotic training, and regulation of the sex drive!
Apparently everyone has the sexuality he deserves, at least that's
what your cousin claims, but do I deserve to be so overloaded with
it?"

Her gaze firmly held his.

"I don't think so," Ulrich said slowly.

"After all, couldn't one just as easily say that my strong capacity for
experiencing represents a physiological superiority?" Bonadea asked
with a gaily suggestive burst of laughter.

There was no more discussion. When, some considerable time
later, Ulrich became aware of a certain resistance in himself, living
daylight was spraying through the chinks in the curtains, and if one
glanced in that direction the darkened room resembled the sepul-
cher of an emotion that had shriveled past the point of recognition.
Bonadea lay there with her eyes closed, giving no sign of life. The
feeling she now had of her body was not unlike that of a child whose
defiance had been broken by a whipping. Every inch of that body,
which was both completely satiated and battered, cried out for the
tenderness of moral forgiveness. From whom? Certainly not from
the man in whose bed she lay and whom she had implored to kill her,
because her lust could not be appeased by any repetition or intensification. She kept her eyes shut to avoid having to see him. She tried
thinking: "I'm in his bed." This—and "I'll never let myself be driven
out of it again!"—was what she had been shouting inwardly just a

short time before; now it merely expressed a situation she could not get out of without having to go through an embarrassing performance, which was still ahead of her. Bonadea slowly and indolently picked up her thoughts where she had dropped them.

She thought of Diotima. Gradually, words came to mind, then whole sentences and fragments of sentences, but mainly only a sense of satisfaction at being where she was while words as incomprehensible and hard to remember as hormones, lymphatic glands, chromosomes, zygotes, and inner secretions thundered past her ear in a cascade of talk. For her mentor's chastity recognized no boundaries as soon as they were effaced by the glare of scientific illumination. Diotima was capable of saying to her listeners: "One's sex life is not a craft that is to be learned; it should always be the highest art we may acquire in life!" while feeling as little unscientific emotion as when in her zeal she spoke of a "point of reference" or "a central point." Her disciple now recalled these expressions exactly. Critical analysis of the embrace, clarification of the physical elements, erogenous zones, the way to highest fulfillment for the woman, men who have themselves well under control and are considerate of their partner . . . Just an hour ago Bonadea, who normally admired these scientific, intellectual, and highly refined terms, had felt grossly deceived by them. To her surprise she had just now realized with returning consciousness that this jargon was meaningful not only for science but for the emotions too, when the flames were already licking out from the unsupervised emotional side. At that point she hated Diotima. "Talking that way about such things, it's enough to kill your appetite!" she had thought, feeling horribly vindictive toward Diotima, who evidently, with four men of her own, begrudged Bonadea anything at all and was deliberately hoodwinking her in this fashion. Indeed, Bonadea had actually considered the enlightenment with whose help sexual science cleans up the occult ways of the sexual process as a plot of Diotima's. Now she could not understand that any more than she could understand her passionate longing for Ulrich. She tried to remember the moments in which all her thoughts and feelings had gone wild; it was as incomprehensible as if a man bleeding to death were to try to think back on the impatience that had led him to tear off his protective bandages. Bonadea thought of Count Leinsdorf, who had called marriage a high office and had compared Diotima's

books on the subject with a manual for organizing official procedures. She thought of Arnheim, who was a multimillionaire and who
had called the revival of marital fidelity, based on the idea of the
body, a true necessity of the times. And she thought of all the other
famous men she had recently met, without even remembering
whether they had short legs or long ones, were fat or lean, for all she
saw in them was the radiance of their celebrity rounded out by a
vague physical mass, much as the delicate frame of a young roast pigeon is given substance by a solid mass of herb stuffing. Sunk in
these memories, Bonadea vowed that she would never again let herself be prey to one of those sudden hurricanes that mix up above and
below, and she swore this to herself so fervently that she could already see herself—if only she could hold firmly enough to her resolve—in fantasy and without physical particulars, as the mistress of
the finest of all her great friend's admirers, hers for the choosing. But
since for the present there was no getting around the fact that she
was still lying in Ulrich's bed with very little on, reluctant to open her
eyes, this rich sense of eager contrition, instead of developing further
into a comfort to her, turned into a wretched state of exasperation.

The passion whose workings split Bonadea's life into such opposing elements had its deepest roots not in sensuality but in ambition.
Ulrich, who knew her well, thought about this but said nothing, to
avoid bringing on her complaints, as he studied her face, while her
eyes hid from him. The root of all her desires seemed to him a desire
for distinction that had got on the wrong track, quite literally the
wrong nerve track. And why shouldn't, really, an ambition to break
social records that can be celebrated with triumph, such as drinking
the most beer or hanging the most diamonds on one's neck, sometimes manifest itself, as in Bonadea's case, as nymphomania? Now
that it was over, she regretted this form of expression and wished she
could undo it, he could see that; and he could also appreciate the fact
that Diotima's elaborate artificiality must impress Bonadea, whom
the devil had always ridden bareback, as divine. He looked at her
lidded eyeballs resting exhausted and heavy in their sockets; he saw
before him her tawny nose, turned decidedly upward at the tip, with
its pink, pointed nostrils; he noticed in some bewilderment the various lines of her body, its large round breasts spreading on the
straight corset of her ribs, the bulbous curve of hips, the hollow

sweep of the back rising from them, the hard pointed nails shielding the soft tips of the fingers. And finally, as he gazed for some time in revulsion at a few tiny hairs sprouting before his eyes from his mistress's nostrils, he, too, wondered at recalling how his desires had been aroused only a short while ago by this person's seductive charms. The bright, mischievous smile with which Bonadea had arrived for their "talk," the natural ease with which she had fended off any rebukes or told the latest story about Arnheim, indeed her new, almost witty keenness of observation: she really had changed for the better; she seemed to have grown more independent, to have achieved a finer balance between the forces in her nature that pulled her up and those that pulled her down, and Ulrich found this lack of moral ponderousness particularly refreshing after his own recent bouts of seriousness. He still could feel the pleasure with which he had listened to her and watched the play of expression on her face, like sun and waves. Suddenly, while his gaze was still on Bonadea's now sulky face, it struck him that only serious people could really be evil. "One might safely say," he thought, "that lighthearted people are proof against wickedness. On the same principle that the villain in opera is always a bass!" Somehow this also implied an uncomfortable link in his own case between "deep" and "dark." Guilt is certainly mitigated when incurred "lightly" by a cheerful person, but on the other hand this may apply only to love, where impassioned seducers seem to act far more destructively and unforgivably than frivolous ones, even when they are doing the same thing. So his thoughts went this way and that, and if this hour of love, so lightly begun, left him a little downhearted, it had also unexpectedly stimulated him.

So thinking, he forgot, without quite knowing how, the Bonadea who was there; resting his head on his arm, he had pensively turned his back to Bonadea and was gazing through the walls at distant things, when his total silence moved her to open her eyes. All unaware, he was at this moment remembering how he had once on a journey got off a train before reaching his destination; a translucent day that had mysteriously, seductively, swept the veils from the landscape had lured him away from the station for a walk, only to desert him at nightfall, when he found himself without his luggage in a hamlet hours away. Indeed, he seemed to recall that he had always had the quality of staying out for unpredictable lengths of time and never returning by the same road; and this suddenly brought back a far distant memory, from a period in his childhood that he normally could not recall, which cast a light on his life. Through a tiny chink in time he seemed to feel again the mysterious yearning by which a child is drawn toward some object it sees, to touch it or even put it in its mouth, at which point the magic comes to a stop as in a blind alley. Just as briefly, he regarded it as possible that the longing of adults, which drives them toward any distance merely to transform it into nearness, is no better or worse—the same sort of longing that dominated him, a compulsion, to judge by a certain aimlessness that was merely masked by curiosity; and finally, this basic image changed to a third, emerging as this hasty and disappointing episode with Bonadea, which neither of them had wanted to turn out as it had. Lying side by side in bed seemed utterly childish to him. "But what does its opposite mean, that motionless, hushed love at a great distance, as incorporeal as an early autumn day?" he wondered. "Probably only another version of child's play," he thought skeptically, and remembered the colorful animal prints he had loved more rapturously as a child than he had loved his mistress today.

Bonadea at this point had seen just about enough of his back to gauge her unhappiness, and she spoke up: "It was your fault!"

Ulrich turned to her with a smile and said spontaneously: "My sister is coming here in a few days to stay with me—did I tell you? We'll hardly be able to see each other then."

"For how long?" Bonadea asked.

"To stay," Ulrich answered, smiling again.

"Well?" Bonadea said. "What difference will it make? Unless you're trying to tell me that your sister won't let you have a lover?"

"That's just what I am trying to tell you," Ulrich said.

Bonadea laughed. "Here I came to see you today in all innocence, and you never even let me finish my story!" she complained.

"I seem to have been designed as a machine for the relentless devaluation of life! I want to be different for once," Ulrich retorted. This was quite beyond her, but it made her remember defiantly that she loved Ulrich. All at once she stopped being the helpless victim of her nerves and found a convincing naturalness; she said, simply: "You've started an affair with her!"

Ulrich warned her not to say such things; a little more grimly than he had meant to. "I intend for a long time to love no woman other-wise than if she were my sister," he said, and stopped. The length of his silence impressed Bonadea with a greater sense of his determination than was perhaps justified by his words.

"You're really perverse!" she cried in a tone of prophetic warning, and leapt out of bed in order to hurry back to Diotima's academy of love, whose unsuspecting portals stood wide open to receive its repentant and refreshed disciple.

147

AGATHE ACTUALLY ARRIVES

That evening there was a telegram, and the next afternoon Agathe arrived.

Ulrich's sister brought only a few suitcases, in accordance with her plan to leave everything behind—not that the quantity of her luggage was wholly in keeping with the precept "Cast all thou hast into the fire, even unto thy shoes." When he heard about the precept, Ulrich laughed; there were even two hatboxes that had escaped the fire.

Agathe's forehead showed the charming furrow denoting hurt feelings and futile brooding over them.

Whether it was fair of Ulrich to find fault with the imperfect expression of a grand and sweeping emotion was left undetermined, for Agathe did not raise the question. The cheerful fuss and upheaval that of necessity attended her arrival made an uproar in her ears and eyes like a dance swaying around a brass band. She was in fine spirits but faintly disappointed, although she had not been expecting anything in particular and had even made a point during her journey of not forming any expectations. It was only that when she remembered that she had stayed up all the previous night she was suddenly overcome with fatigue. She didn't mind when Ulrich had to tell her, after a while, that her telegram had come too late for him to postpone an appointment he had for the afternoon. He promised to be back in an hour, and settled his sister on the sofa in his study with such elaborate care that they both had to laugh.

When Agathe woke up, the hour was long gone, and Ulrich was not there. The room was sunk in deep twilight and was so alien that she felt suddenly dismayed at finding herself in the midst of the new life to which she had been looking forward. As far as she could make out, the walls were lined with books just as her father's had been, and the tables covered with papers. Curiosity led her to open a door and enter the adjacent room: here she found clothes closets, shoe boxes, the punching bag, barbells, and parallel bars. Beyond these were more books, the bathroom with its eau de cologne, bath salts, brushes, and combs, her brother's bedroom, and the hall, with its hunting trophies. Her passage was marked by lights flashing on and off, but as chance would have it, Ulrich noticed none of this, even though he was home by now. He had put off waking her to let her rest a while longer, and now he ran into her on the landing as he was coming up from the little-used basement kitchen. He had gone there to look around for a snack to bring her; since he had not planned ahead, there was no one to wait on them that day. It was only when they stood side by side that Agathe's random impressions began to coalesce into a perception that left her so disconcerted and disheartened that she felt it would be best to bolt as soon as she could. There was something so impersonal, so indifferent about the spirit in which things had been thrown together here that it frightened her.

Ulrich noticed this and apologized, explaining the situation lightheartedly. He told her how he had come to acquire his house and gave its history in detail, beginning with the antlers he had come to own without ever going hunting and ending with the punching bag, which he set bobbing for her benefit. Agathe looked at everything again with disquieting seriousness, and even turned her head for another look whenever they left a room. Ulrich tried to make this examination entertaining, but as it went on he began to feel embarrassed about his house. It turned out—something habit had made him overlook—that he had used only the few rooms he needed, leaving the rest dangling from them like a neglected decoration. When they sat down together after this survey Agathe asked: "But why did you do it, if you don't like it?"

Her brother provided her with tea and every refreshment he could find in the house, and insisted on giving a hospitable welcome, belated though it was, so that their second reunion should not be inferior to the first in material comforts. Dashing back and forth on these errands, he confessed: "I've done everything so carelessly and wrong that the place doesn't have anything at all to do with me."

"But it's all really very attractive," Agathe now consoled him.

Ulrich responded that it would probably have been even worse if he had done it differently. "I can't stand houses with interiors tailored to express one's personality," he declared. "It would make me feel that I had ordered myself from an interior decorator too."

And Agathe said: "I shy away from that kind of house also."

"Even so, it can't be left the way it is," Ulrich rectified. He was sitting at the table with her, and the very fact that they would now be having their meals together raised a number of problems. The realization that all sorts of things would have to be changed took him by surprise; it would take a quite unprecedented effort on his part, and he reacted to this at first with the zeal of a beginner.

"A person living alone," he said, when his sister seemed considerately willing to leave everything as it was, "can afford to have a weakness; it will merge with his other qualities and hardly be noticeable. But when two people share a weakness it becomes twice as conspicuous in comparison with the qualities they don't share, and approaches a public confession."

Agathe could not see it.

"In other words, as brother and sister there are things that each of us could indulge in on our own but we cannot do together; that's exactly why we have come together."

This appealed to Agathe. Still, his negative formulation, that they had come together in order *not* to do something, left something to be desired, and after a while she asked, returning to the way his furnishings had been assembled by the best firms: "I'm afraid I still don't understand. Why did you let the place be done like this if you didn't think it was right?"

Ulrich met her cheerful gaze and let his eyes rest on her face, which, above the slightly crumpled traveling dress she was still wearing, now looked smooth as silver and so amazingly *present* that it felt equally near and far from him; or perhaps the closeness and the remoteness in his presence canceled each other out, just as, out of the infinity of sky, the moon suddenly appears behind the neighboring roof.

"Why did I do it?" he answered, smiling. "I forget now. Probably because I could just as well have done it some other way. I felt no responsibility. I'd be less sure of myself if I were to tell you that the irresponsible way in which we're conducting ourselves now may well be the first step toward a new responsibility."

"How so?"

"Oh, in all sorts of ways. You know: the life of an individual person may be only a slight variant of the most probable average value in the series, and so on."

All Agathe took in of this was what made sense to her. She said: "Which comes to: 'Quite nice' and 'Very nice indeed.' Soon one stops realizing what a revolting life one is leading. But sometimes it gives one the creeps, like waking up to find oneself on a slab in the mortuary!"

"What was your place like?" Ulrich asked.

"Middle-class respectable, à la Hagauer. 'Quite nice.' Just as counterfeit as yours!"

Ulrich had meanwhile found a pencil and was sketching the plan of his house on the tablecloth, reallotting the rooms. That was easy, and so quickly done that Agathe's housewifely gesture of protecting the tablecloth came too late and ended uselessly with her hand resting on his. Problems arose again only over the principles of how the place should be furnished.

"We happen to have a house," Ulrich argued, "and we do have to make some changes to accommodate the two of us. But by and large it's an outdated and idle question these days. 'Setting up house' is putting up a façade with nothing behind it: social and personal relations are no longer solid enough for homes; no one takes any real pleasure now in keeping up a show of durability and permanence. In the old days people did that, to show who they were by the number of rooms and servants and guests they had. Today almost everyone feels that only a formless life corresponds to the variety of purposes and possibilities life is filled with, and young people either prefer stark simplicity, which is like a bare stage, or else they dream of wardrobe trunks and bobsled championships, tennis cups and luxury hotels along great highways, with golf course scenery and music on tap in every room."

He spoke in a light conversational tone, as if playing host to a stranger, but was actually talking himself up to the surface because he was self-conscious about their being together in a situation that combined finality with a new beginning.

After she had let him have his say, his sister asked:

"Are you suggesting that we ought to live in a hotel?"

"Not at all!" Ulrich hastened to assure her. "Except now and then when traveling."

"And for the rest of the time, should we build ourselves a bower on an island or a log cabin in the mountains?"

"We'll be settling in here, of course," Ulrich answered, more seriously than the nature of their conversation warranted. There was a brief lull in the exchange. He had stood up and was pacing up and down the room. Agathe pretended to be picking at a thread on the hem of her dress, bending her head below the line on which their eyes had been meeting. Suddenly Ulrich stopped and said, with some effort in his voice but going straight to the point:

"My dear Agathe, there's a whole circle of questions here, which has a large circumference and no center, and all these questions are: 'How should I live?' "

Agathe had risen, too, but still did not look at him. She shrugged her shoulders.

"We'll have to try!" she said. Her face was flushed from bending over, but when she lifted her head, her eyes were alight with high spirits, the flush only lingering on her cheek like a passing cloud. "If we're going to stay together," she declared, "you'll have to start by helping me unpack and put my things away and change, because I haven't seen a maid anywhere!"

His bad conscience traveled into his arms and legs and made them galvanically mobile, under Agathe's direction and with her help, to make up for his negligence. He cleared out closets like a hunter disemboweling an animal, abandoning his bedroom to Agathe, swearing to her that it was hers and that he would find a sofa somewhere. Eagerly he moved to and fro all objects of daily use that had hitherto lived in their places like flowers in a flower bed, waiting to be picked one at a time by a selecting hand. Suits were piled up on chairs; on the glass shelves in the bathroom, cosmetics were carefully separated into men's and women's departments. By the time order had more or less been transformed into disorder, only Ulrich's gleaming leather slippers remained, abandoned on the floor like an offended lapdog evicted from its basket: a pitiful symbol of disrupted comfort in all its pleasant triviality. But there was no time to take this to heart, for Agathe's suitcases were next, and however few there seemed to be, they were inexhaustibly crammed with exquisitely folded things that spread open as they were lifted out, blossoming in the air just like the hundreds of roses a magician pulls from his hat. These things had to be hung up or laid down, shaken out and put in piles, and because Ulrich was helping, it proceeded with slip-ups and laughter.

But in the midst of all this activity, he could only think, incessantly, that for his whole life, and up to a few hours ago, he had lived alone. And now Agathe was here. This little sentence, "Agathe is here now," repeated itself in waves, like the astonishment of a boy who has received a new plaything; there was something mind-numbing about it and, on the other hand, a quite overwhelming sense of presence too, all of which expressed itself again and again in the words: Agathe is here now.

"So she's tall and slender?" Ulrich thought as he watched her covertly. But she wasn't at all; she was shorter than he, and had broad, athletic shoulders. "Is she attractive?" he mused. That was hard to say too. Her proud nose, for instance, was slightly tilted up from one side; there was far more potent charm in this than attractiveness. "Could she be a beauty?" Ulrich wondered in a rather strange way, for he was not quite at ease with this question even though, leaving aside all convention, Agathe was a stranger to him. There is, after all, no such thing as a natural inhibition against looking at a blood relation with sexual interest; it is only a matter of custom, or to be explained by the detours of morality or eugenics. Also, the circumstance that they had not grown up together had prevented the sterilized brother-sister relationship that is prevalent in European families. Even so, their origin and their feeling toward each other were enough to take the edge off even the harmless question of how beautiful she might be, a missing excitement Ulrich now noticed with distinct surprise. To find something beautiful surely means, first of all, to *find* it: whether it is a landscape or a lover, there it is, looking at the pleased finder, and it seems to have been waiting for him alone. And so, delighted that she was now his and ready to be discovered by him, he was hugely pleased with his sister. But he still thought: "One can't regard one's own sister as truly beautiful; at most one can be pleased by the admiration she evokes in others." But then he was hearing her voice for minutes at a time, where no voice had been before, and what was her voice like? Waves of scent accompanied the movement of her clothing, and what was this scent like? Her movements were now knee, now delicate finger, now rebelliousness of a curl. All one could say about it was: it was there. It was there where before there had been nothing. The difference in intensity between the most vivid moment of thinking about the sister he had left behind and the emptiest present moment was still so great and distinct a pleasure that it was like a shady spot filling up with the warmth of the sun and the scent of wild herbs unfurling.

Agathe was aware of her brother's watching her, but she did not let him know it. During the pauses, when she felt his eyes following her movements while the interval between a response and the next remark was not so much a complete stop as like a car coasting over some deep and risky patch of road with its motor switched off, she, too, enjoyed the supercharged air and the calm intensity that surrounded their reunion. When they had finished unpacking and putting things away and Agathe was alone in her bath, an adventure threatened to break into these peaceful pastures like a wolf, for she had undressed down to her underclothes in the room where Ulrich, smoking a cigarette, was now keeping watch over her abandoned things. Soaking in the water, she wondered what she should do. There was no maid, so ringing was as pointless as calling out; there was evidently nothing to be done but to wrap herself in Ulrich's bathrobe, which was hanging on the wall, knock on the door, and send him out of the room. But considering the serious intimacy that, if not already flourishing, had just been born between them, Agathe cheerfully doubted whether it was appropriate to play the young lady and beg Ulrich to withdraw, so she decided to ignore the ambivalence of femininity and simply appear before him as the natural, familiar companion he should see in her, dressed or not.

Yet when she resolutely entered the room again, both felt an unexpected quickening of the heart. They each tried not to feel embarrassed. For an instant they could not shake off the conventional inconsistency that permits virtual nakedness on the beach while indoors the hem of a chemise or a panty becomes the smuggler's path to romantic intimacy. Ulrich smiled awkwardly as Agathe, with the light of the anteroom behind her, stood in the open door like a silver statue lightly veiled in a haze of batiste and, in a voice much too emphatically casual, asked for her dress and stockings, which turned out to be in the next room. Ulrich showed her the way, and saw to his secret delight that she strode off in a manner that was a little too boyish, taking a sort of defiant pleasure in it, as women tend to do when they don't feel themselves protected by their skirts. Then something new came up, when a little later Agathe found herself stuck midway getting into her dress and had to call Ulrich for help. While he was busy at her back she sensed, without sisterly jealousy but rather, if anything, with pleasure, that he clearly knew his way around women's clothing, and she moved with agility to make it easier for him when the nature of the procedure made it necessary.

Bending over close to the moving, delicate, yet full and fresh skin of her shoulders, intent upon the unaccustomed task, which raised a flush on his brow, Ulrich felt himself lapped by a pleasing sensation not easily put into words, unless one might say that his body was equally affected by having a woman and yet not having a woman so close to him; or one could just as easily have said that though he was unquestionably standing there in his own shoes, he nevertheless felt drawn out of himself and over to her as though he had been given a second, far more beautiful, body for his own.

This was why the first thing he said to his sister when he had straightened up again was: "Now I know what you are: you are my self-love!" It may have sounded odd, but it really expressed what it was that moved him so. "In a sense," he explained, "I've always lacked the right sort of love for myself that others seem to have in abundance. And now," he added, "by some mistake or by fate, it has been embodied in you instead of myself!"

It was his first attempt that evening to pass a verdict on the meaning of his sister's arrival.

148

THE SIAMESE TWINS

Later that evening he came back to this.

"You should know," he started to tell his sister, "that there's a kind of self-love that's foreign to me, a certain tenderness toward oneself that seems to come naturally to most other people. I don't know how best to describe it. I could say, for instance, that I've always had lovers with whom I've had a skewed relationship. They've been illustrations of some sudden idea, caricatures of my mood—in effect, just instances of my inability to be on easy terms with other people. That in itself reveals something about one's relationship to oneself. Basically, lovers I have chosen were always women I didn't like. . . ."

"There's nothing wrong with that!" Agathe interrupted. "If I were a man, I wouldn't have any qualms about trifling with women in the most irresponsible way. And I'd desire them only out of absentmindedness and wonder."

"Oh? Would you really? How nice of you!"

"They're such absurd parasites. Women share a man's life on the same level as his dog!" There was no hint of moral indignation in Agathe's statement. She was pleasantly tired and kept her eyes closed, for she had gone to bed early and Ulrich, who had come to say good night, saw her lying in his place in his bed. But it was also the bed in which Bonadea had lain thirty-six hours earlier, which was probably why Ulrich reverted to the subject of his mistresses.

"All I was trying to describe was my own incapacity for a reasonably forgiving relationship to myself," he repeated, smiling. "For me to take a real interest in something it must be part of some context, it must be controlled by an idea. The experience itself I'd really prefer to have behind me, as a memory; the emotional effort it exacts strikes me as unpleasant and absurdly beside the point. That's how it is with me, to describe myself to you bluntly. Now, the simplest, most instinctive idea one can have, at least when one is young, is that one's a hell of a fellow, the new man the world's been waiting for. But that doesn't last beyond thirty!" He reflected for a moment and then said: "That's not it. It's so hard to talk about oneself. What I would have to say is that I have never subjected myself to an idea with staying power. One never turned up. One should love an idea like a woman; be overjoyed to get back to it. And one always has it inside oneself! And always looks for it in everything outside! I never formed such ideas. My relationship to the so-called great ideas, and perhaps even to those that really are great, has always been man-to-man: I never felt I was born to submit to them; they always provoked me to overthrow them and put others in their place. Perhaps it was precisely this jealousy that drove me to science, whose laws are established by teamwork and never regarded as immutable!" Again he paused and laughed, at either himself or his argument. "But however that may be," he went on seriously, "by connecting no idea or every idea with myself, I got out of the habit of taking life seriously. I get much more out of it when I read about it in a novel, where it's wrapped up in some point of view, but when I'm supposed to experience it in all its fullness it always seems already obsolete, overdone in an old-fashioned way, and intellectually outdated. And I don't think that's peculiar to me. Most people today feel much the same. Lots of people feign an urgent love of life, the way schoolchildren are taught to hop about merrily among the daisies, but there's always a certain premeditation about it, and they feel it. Actually, they're as capable of killing each other in cold blood as they are of being the best of friends. Our time certainly does not take all the adventures and goings-on it's full of at all seriously. When they happen, there's a fuss. They immediately set off more happenings, a kind of vendetta of happenings, a whole compulsive alphabet of sequels, from B to Z, and all because someone said A. But these happenings in our lives have less life than a book, because they have no coherent meaning."

So Ulrich talked, loosely, his moods changing. Agathe offered no response; she still had her eyes closed but was smiling.

Ulrich said: "Now I've forgotten what I'm telling you. I don't think I know my way back to the beginning."

They were silent for a while. He was able to scrutinize his sister's face at leisure, since it was not defended by the gaze of her eyes. It lay there, a piece of naked body, the way women are when they're together in a women's public bath. The feminine, unguarded, natural cynicism of this sight, not intended for men's eyes, still had an unusual effect on Ulrich, though no longer quite as powerful as in their first days together, when Agathe had from the start claimed her right as a sister to talk to him without any mental beating around the bush, since for her he was not a man like others. He remembered the mixture of surprise and horror he had experienced as a boy when he saw a pregnant woman on the street, or a woman nursing her child; secrets from which the boy had been carefully shielded suddenly bulged out full-blown and unembarrassed in the light of day. Perhaps he had long been carrying vestiges of such reactions about with him, for all at once he seemed to feel entirely free of them. That Agathe was a woman with many experiences behind her was a pleasant and comfortable thought; there was no need to be on his guard in talking with her, as he would be with a young girl; indeed, it was touchingly natural that everything was morally relaxed with a mature woman. It also made him feel protective toward her, to make up to her for something by being good to her in some way. He decided to do all he could for her. He even decided to look for another husband for her. This need to be kind restored to him, although he barely noticed, the lost thread of his discourse.

"Our self-love probably undergoes a change during adolescence," he said without transition. "That's when a whole meadow of tenderness in which one had been playing gets mowed down to provide the fodder for one particular instinct."

"So that the cow can give milk!" Agathe added, after the slightest pause, pertly and with dignity but without opening her eyes.

"Yes, it's all connected, I suppose," Ulrich agreed, and went on: "So there's a moment when the tenderness goes out of our lives and concentrates on that one particular operation, which then remains overcharged with it. It's as though there were a terrible drought everywhere on earth except for one place where it never stops raining, don't you think?"

Agathe said: "I think that as a child I loved my dolls more fiercely than I have ever loved a man. After you'd gone I found a whole trunkful of my old dolls in the attic."

"What did you do with them?" Ulrich asked. "Did you give them away?"

"Who was there to give them to? I gave them a funeral in the kitchen stove," she said.

Ulrich responded with animation: "When I remember as far back as I can, I'd say that there was hardly any separation between inside and outside. When I crawled toward something, it came on wings to meet me; when something important happened, the excitement was not just in us, but the things themselves came to a boil. I won't claim that we were happier then than we were later on. After all, we hadn't yet taken charge of ourselves. In fact, we didn't really yet exist; our personal condition was not yet separated from the world's. It sounds strange, but it's true: our feelings, our desires, our very selves, were not yet quite inside ourselves. What's even stranger is that I might as easily say: they were not yet quite taken away from us. If you should sometime happen to ask yourself today, when you think you're entirely in possession of yourself, who you really are, you will discover that you always see yourself from the outside, as an object. You'll notice that one time you get angry, another time you get sad, just as your coat will sometimes be wet and sometimes too warm. No matter how intensely you try to look at yourself, you may at most find out something about the outside, but you'll never get inside yourself. Whatever you do, you remain outside yourself, with the possible exception of those rare moments when a friend might say that you're beside yourself. It's true that as adults we've made up for this by being able to think at any time that 'I am'—if you think that's fun. You see a car, and somehow in a shadowy way you also see: 'I am seeing a car.' You're in love, or sad, and see that it's you. But neither the car, nor your sadness, nor your love, nor even yourself, is quite fully there. Nothing is as completely there as it once was in childhood; everything you touch, including your inmost self, is more or less congealed from the moment you have achieved your 'personality,' and what's left is a ghostly hanging thread of self-awareness and murky self-regard, wrapped up in a wholly external existence. What's gone wrong? There's a feeling that something might still be salvaged. Surely you can't claim that a child's experience is all that different from a man's? I don't know any real answer, even if there may be this or that idea about it. But for a long time I've responded by having lost my love for this kind of 'being myself' and for this kind of world."

Ulrich was glad that Agathe listened to him without interrupting, for he was not expecting an answer from her any more than he was from himself, and was convinced that for the present, nobody could give him the kind of answer he had in mind. Yet he did not fear for an instant that anything he was talking about might be above her head. He did not see it as philosophizing, nor even as an unusual subject for a conversation, any more than a young man—and he was behaving like one, in this situation—will let the difficulty of groping for the right words keep him from finding everything simple when he is exchanging views on the eternal problems of "Who are you? This is who I am" with someone else. He derived the assurance that his sister was able to follow him word for word not from having reflected on it but from her inner being. His eyes rested on her face, and there was something in it that made him happy. This face, its eyes closed, did not thrust back at him. The attraction it held for him was bottomless, even in the sense that it seemed to draw him into never-ending depths. Submerging himself in contemplation of this face, he nowhere found that muddy bottom of dissolved resistances from which the diver into love kicks off, to rebound to the surface and reach dry ground again. But since he was accustomed to experience every inclination toward a woman as a forcibly reversed disinclination against human beings, which—even though he found it regrettable—did offer some guarantee against losing himself in her, the pure inclination as he bent even deeper toward her in curiosity alarmed him almost as if he were losing his balance, so that he soon drew back from this state, and from pure happiness took refuge in a boy's trick for recalling Agathe to everyday reality: with the most delicate touch he could manage, he tried to open her eyes. Agathe opened them wide with a laugh and cried: "Isn't this pretty rough treatment for someone who's supposed to be your self-love?"

This response was as boyish as his attack, and their looks collided hard, like two little boys who want to tussle but are laughing too much to begin. Suddenly Agathe dropped this and asked seriously: "You know that myth Plato tells, following some ancient source, that the gods divided the original human being into two halves, male and female?" She had propped herself up on one elbow and unexpectedly blushed, feeling awkward at having asked Ulrich if he knew so familiar a story; then she resolutely charged ahead: "Now those two pathetic halves do all kinds of silly things to come together again. It's in all the schoolbooks for older children; unfortunately, they never tell you why it doesn't work!"

"I can tell you that," Ulrich broke in, glad to see how well she had understood him. "Nobody knows which of so many halves running around in the world is his missing half. He grabs one that seems to be his, vainly trying to become one with her, until the futility of it becomes hopelessly clear. If a child results, both halves believe for a few youthful years that they've at least become one in the child. But the child is merely a third half, which soon shows signs of trying to get as far away from the other two as it possibly can and look for a fourth half. In this way human beings keep 'halving' themselves physiologically, while the ideal of oneness remains as far away as the moon outside the bedroom window."

"You'd think that siblings might have succeeded halfway already!" Agathe interjected in a voice that had become husky.

"Twins, possibly."

"Aren't we twins?"

"Certainly!" Ulrich suddenly became evasive. "Twins are rare; twins of different gender especially so. But when, into the bargain, they differ in age and have hardly known each other for the longest time, it's quite a phenomenon—one really worthy of us!" he declared, struggling to get back into a shallower cheeriness.

"But we met as twins!" Agathe challenged him, ignoring his tone.

"Because we unwittingly dressed alike?"

"Maybe. And in all sorts of ways! You may say it was chance; but what is chance? *I* think it's fate or destiny or providence, or whatever you want to call it. Haven't you ever thought it was by chance that you were born as yourself? Our being brother and sister doubles that chance!" That was how Agathe put it, and Ulrich submitted to this wisdom.

"So we declare ourselves to be twins," he agreed. "Symmetrical creatures of a whim of nature, henceforth we shall be the same age, the same height, with the same hair, walking the highways and byways of the world in identical striped clothes with the same bow tied under our chins. But I warn you that people will turn around and look after us, half touched and half scornful, as always happens when something reminds them of the mysteries of their own beginnings."

"Why can't we dress for contrast?" Agathe said lightly. "One in yellow when the other is in blue, or red alongside green, and we can dye our hair violet or purple, and I can affect a hump and you a paunch: yet we'd still be twins!"

But the joke had gone stale, the pretext worn out, and they fell silent for a while.

"Do you realize," Ulrich then said suddenly, "that this is something very serious we're talking about?"

No sooner had he said this than his sister again dropped the fan of her lashes over her eyes and, veiling her consent, let him talk alone. Or perhaps it only looked as if she had shut her eyes. The room was dark; what light there was did not so much clarify outlines as pour over them in bright patches. Ulrich had said: "It's not only the myth of the human being divided in two; we could also mention Pygmalion, the Hermaphrodite, or Isis and Osiris—all different forms of the same theme. It's the ancient longing for a doppelgänger of the opposite sex, for a lover who will be the same as yourself and yet someone else, a magical figure that is oneself and yet remains magical, with the advantage over something we merely imagine of having the breath of autonomy and independence. This dream of a quintessential love, unhampered by the body's limitations, coming face-to-face in two identical yet different forms, has been concocted countless times in solitary alchemy in the alembic of the human skull. . . ."

Here he broke off; evidently something disturbing had occurred to him, and he ended with the almost unfriendly words: "There are traces of this in even the most commonplace situations of love: the charm of every change of clothing, every disguise, the meaning two people find in what they have in common, the way they see themselves repeated in the other. This little magic is always the same, whether one's seeing an elegant lady naked for the first time or a naked girl formally dressed for the first time in a dress buttoned up to the neck, and great reckless passions all have something to do with the fact that everyone thinks it's his own secret self peering out at him from behind the curtains of a stranger's eyes."

It sounded as though he were asking her not to attach too much importance to what they were saying. But Agathe was again thinking of the lightning flash of surprise she had felt when they first met, disguised, as it were, in their lounging suits. And she answered:

"So this has been going on for thousands of years. Is it any easier to understand as a case of shared self-delusion?"

Ulrich was silent.

And after a while, Agathe said delightedly: "But it does happen in one's sleep! There you do sometimes see yourself transformed into something else. Or meet yourself as a man. And then you're much kinder to him than you are to yourself. You'll probably say that these are sexual dreams, but I think they are much older."

"Do you often have that sort of dream?" Ulrich asked.

"Sometimes. Not often."

"I almost never do," he confessed. "It must be ages since I had such a dream."

"And yet you once explained to me," Agathe now said, "—it must have been at the very beginning, back in our old house—that people really did experience life differently thousands of years ago."

"Oh, you mean the 'giving' and the 'receiving' vision?" Ulrich replied, smiling at her although she could not see him. "The 'embracing' and 'being embraced' of the spirit? Yes, of course I should have talked about this mysterious dual sexuality of the soul too. And how much else besides! There's a hint of it wherever you look. Every analogy contains a remnant of that magic of being identical and not identical. But haven't you noticed? In all these cases we've been talking about, in dream, in myth, poem, childhood, even in love, feeling more comes at the cost of understanding less, and that means: through a loss of reality."

"Then you don't really believe in it?" Agathe asked.

Ulrich did not answer. But after a while he said: "Translated into the ghastly jargon of our times, we could call this faculty we all lack to such a frightening degree nowadays 'the percentual share' of an individual's experiences and actions. In dreams it's apparently a hundred percent, in our waking life not even half as much. You noticed it today at once in my house; but it's exactly the same with my relations to the people you'll meet. I also once called it—if I'm not mistaken, in conversation with a woman where it was truly relevant, I must admit—the acoustics of the void. If a pin drops in an empty room, the sound it makes is somehow disproportionate, even incommensurable; but it's the same when there's a void between people. There's no way to tell: is one screaming, or is there a deathly silence? For everything out of place and askew acquires the magnetic attraction of a tremendous temptation when there's nothing with which to counteract it. Don't you agree? . . . But I'm sorry," he interrupted himself, "you must be tired, and I'm not letting you have your rest. It seems there are many things in my surroundings and my social life that won't be much to your liking, I'm afraid."

Agathe had opened her eyes. After coming out of hiding at last, her glance contained something uncommonly hard to define, which Ulrich felt coursing sympathetically through his whole body. He suddenly started to talk again: "When I was younger I tried to see just that as a source of strength. And if one doesn't have anything to pit against life? Fine, then life flees from man into his works! That's more or less what I thought. And I suppose there's something daunting about the lovelessness and irresponsibility of today's world. At the very least there's something in it of adolescence, which centuries can go through as well as teenagers, years of rapid, uneven growth. And like every young man I began by plunging into work, adventures, amusements; what difference did it make what one did, as long as one did it wholeheartedly? Do you remember that we once spoke of 'the morality of achievement'? We're born with that image, and orient ourselves by it. But the older one gets, the more clearly one finds out that this apparent exuberance, this independence and mobility in everything, this sovereignty of the driving parts and the partial drives—both your own against yourself and yours against the world—in short, everything that we 'people of the present' have regarded as a strength and a special distinction of our species, is basically nothing but a weakness of the whole as against its parts. Passion and willpower can do nothing about it. The moment you're ready to go all out into the middle of something, you find yourself washed back to the periphery. Today this is the experience in all experiences!"

Agathe, with her eyes now open, was waiting for something to happen in his voice; when nothing changed and her brother's words simply came to an end like a path turning off a road into a dead end, she said: "So your experience tells you that one can never really act with conviction and will never be able to. By conviction," she explained, "I don't mean whatever knowledge or moral training have been drilled into us, but simply feeling entirely at home with oneself and with everything, feeling replete now where there's emptiness, something one starts out from and returns to—" She broke off. "Oh, I don't really know *what* I mean! I was hoping you'd explain it to me."

"You mean just what we were talking about," Ulrich answered gently. "And you're also the only person I can talk to about these things. But there'd be no point in starting over just to add a few more seductive words. I'd have to say, rather, that being 'at the inner core' of things, in a state of unmarred 'inwardness'—using the word not in any sentimental sense but with the meaning we just gave it—is apparently not a demand that can be satisfied by rational thinking." He had leaned forward and was touching her arm and gazing steadily into her eyes. "Human nature is probably averse to it," he said in a low voice. "All we really know is that we feel a painful need for it! Perhaps it's connected with the need for sibling love, an addition to ordinary love, moving in an imaginary direction toward a love unmixed with otherness and not-loving." And after a pause he added: "You know how popular those babes-in-the-wood games are in bed: people who could murder their real siblings fool around as brother-and-sister babies under the same blanket."

In the dim light his face twitched in self-mockery. But Agathe put her trust in his face and not in his confused words. She had seen faces quivering like this a moment before they plunged; this one did not come nearer; it seemed to be moving at infinitely great speed over an immense distance. Tersely she answered: "Being brother and sister isn't really enough, that's all."

"Well, we've already spoken of being twins," Ulrich responded, getting noiselessly to his feet, because he thought that she was finally being overwhelmed by fatigue.

"We'd have to be Siamese twins," Agathe managed to say.

"Right, Siamese twins!" her brother echoed, gently disengaging her hand from his and carefully placing it on the coverlet. His words had a weightless sound, light and volatile, expanding in widening circles even after he had left the room.

Agathe smiled and gradually sank into a lonely sadness, whose darkness imperceptibly turned into that of sleep. Ulrich meanwhile tiptoed into his study and stayed there, unable to work, for another two hours, until he, too, grew tired, learning for the first time what it was like to be cramped out of considerateness. He was amazed at how much he would have wanted to do during this time that would involve making noise and so had to be suppressed. This was new for him. And it almost irritated him a little, although he did his best to imagine sympathetically what it would be like to be really physically attached to another person. He knew hardly anything about how such nervous systems worked in tandem, like two leaves on a single stalk, united not only through a single bloodstream but still more by the effect of their total interdependence. He assumed that every agitation in one soul would also be felt by the other, even though whatever evoked it was going on in a body that was not, in the main, one's own. "An embrace, for instance—you are embraced by way of the other body," he thought. "You may not even want it, but your other self floods you with an overwhelming wave of acceptance! What do you care who's kissing your sister? But her excitement is something you must love jointly. Or suppose it's you who are making love, and you have to find a way to 'ensure' her participation; you can't just let her be flooded with senseless physiological processes . . . !" Ulrich felt a strong arousal and a great uneasiness at this idea; it was hard for him to draw the line between a new way of looking at something and a distortion of the ordinary way.

149

SPRING IN THE VEGETABLE GARDEN

The praise Meingast bestowed on her and the new ideas she was getting from him had deeply impressed Clarisse.

Her mental unrest and excitability, which sometimes worried even her, had eased, but they did not give way this time, as they so often did, to dejection, frustration, and hopelessness; they were succeeded

instead by an extraordinary taut lucidity and a transparent inner atmosphere. Once again she took stock of herself and arrived at a critical estimate. Without questioning it, and even with a certain
satisfaction, she noted that she was not overly bright; she had not
been educated enough. Ulrich, on the other hand, whenever she
thought of him by comparison, was like a skater gliding to and fro at
will on a surface of intellectual ice. There was no telling where it
came from when he said something, or when he laughed, when he
was irritable, when his eyes flashed, when he was there and with his
broad shoulders preempting Walter's space in the room. Even when
he merely turned his head in curiosity, the sinews of his neck taut-
ened like the rigging of a sailboat taking off with the wind into the
blue. There was always more to him than she could grasp, which
acted as a spur to her desire to fling herself on him bodily to catch
hold of it. But the tumult in which this sometimes happened, so that
once nothing in the world had mattered except that she wanted to
bear Ulrich's child, had now receded far into the distance, leaving
behind not even that flotsam and jetsam that incomprehensibly
keeps bobbing up in the memory after the tide of passion has ebbed.
When she thought of her failure at Ulrich's house, insofar as she ever
still did, Clarisse felt cross, at most, but her self-confidence was hale
and hearty thanks to the new ideas supplied by her philosophic guest,
not to mention the sheer excitement of again seeing this old friend
who had been transported into the sublime. Thus many days passed
in all kinds of suspense while everyone in the little house, now
bathed in spring sunshine, waited to see whether Ulrich would or
would not bring the permit to visit Moosbrugger in his eerie
domicile.

There was one idea in particular that seemed important to Clarisse
in this connection: The Master had called the world "so thoroughly
stripped of illusions" that people could no longer say about anything
whether they ought to love it or hate it. Since then Clarisse felt that
one was obliged to surrender oneself to an illusion if one received the
grace of having one. For an illusion is a mercy. How was anyone at
that time to know whether to turn right or left on leaving the house,
unless he had a job, like Walter, which then cramped him, or, like
herself, had a visit to pay to her parents or brothers and sisters, who
bored her! It's different in an illusion! There life is arranged as effi-

ciently as a modern kitchen: you sit in the middle and hardly need stir to set all the gadgets going. That had always been Clarisse's sort of thing. Besides, she understood "illusion" to mean nothing other than what was called "the will," only with added intensity. Up to now Clarisse had felt intimidated by being able to understand so little of what was going on in the world. But since Meingast's return she saw this as a veritable advantage that freed her to love, hate, and act as she pleased. For according to the Master's word mankind needed nothing so much as willpower, and when it came to wanting something with a will, Clarisse had always had that inner power! When Clarisse thought about it she was chilled with joy and hot with responsibility. Of course, what was meant by will here was not the grim effort it took to learn a piano piece or win an argument; it meant being powerfully steered by life itself, being deeply moved within oneself, being swept away with happiness!

Eventually she could not help telling Walter something about it. She informed him that her conscience was growing stronger day by day. But despite his admiration for Meingast, the suspected instigator of this deed, Walter answered angrily: "It's probably lucky for us that Ulrich doesn't seem able to get the permit!"

Clarisse's lips merely quivered slightly, betraying sympathy for his ignorance and stubbornness.

"What is it you want from this criminal, anyway, who has nothing whatever to do with any of us?" Walter demanded manfully.

"It'll come to me when I get there!" she said.

"I should think you ought to know it already," Walter asserted.

His little wife smiled the way she always did when she was about to hurt him to the quick. But then she merely said: "I'm going to do something."

"Clarisse!" Walter remonstrated firmly. "You may not do anything without my permission. I am your lawful husband and guardian."

This tone was new to her. She turned away and took a few steps in confusion.

"Clarisse!" Walter called after her, getting up to follow her. "I intend to take steps to deal with the insanity that's going around in this house!"

Now she realized that the healing power of her resolve was already manifesting itself, even in the strengthening of Walter's character. She turned on her heel: "What steps?" she asked, and a flash of lightning from her narrowed eyes struck into the moist, wide-open brown of his.

"Now look," he said to mollify her, backing away a little, in surprise at her demanding such a concrete response. "We've all got this in our system, this intellectual taste for the unhealthy, the problematic, for making our flesh creep; every thinking person has it; but—"

"But we let the philistines have their way!" Clarisse interrupted triumphantly. Now she advanced on him without taking her eyes off him; felt how a sense of her own healing power held him in its strong embrace and overpowered him. Her heart was filled with an odd and inexpressible joy.

"But we won't make such a to-do over it," Walter muttered sulkily, finishing his sentence. Behind him, at the hem of his jacket, he felt an obstacle; reaching backward, he identified it as the edge of one of those light, thin-legged little tables they had, which suddenly seemed spooky to him; he realized that if he kept backing away he would make it slide backward, which would be ludicrous. So he resisted the sudden desire to get far away from this struggle, to some dark-green meadow under blossoming fruit trees, among people whose healthy cheerfulness would wash his wounds clean. It was a quiet, stout wish, graced with women hanging on his words and paying their toll of grateful admiration. At the moment Clarisse came up close he actually felt rudely molested, in a nightmarish way. But to his surprise Clarisse did not say: "You're a coward!" Instead, she said: "Walter? Why are we unhappy?"

At the sound of her appealing, clairvoyant voice he felt that happiness with any other woman could never take the place of his unhappiness with Clarisse. "We have to be!" he answered with an equally noble upsurge.

"No, we shouldn't have to be," she said obligingly. She let her head droop to one side, trying to find a way to convince him. It didn't matter what it was: They stood there facing each other like a day without an evening, pouring out its fire hour after hour without lessening.

"You'll have to admit," she said finally, at once shyly and stubbornly, "that really great crimes come about not because somebody commits them but because we let them happen."

Now Walter knew, of course, what was coming, and felt a shock of disappointment.

"Oh God!" he cried out impatiently. "I know as well as you do that far more people's lives are ruined by indifference and by the ease with which most of us today can square our conscience than by the evil intentions of isolated individuals. And of course it's admirable that you're now going to say that this is why we must all quicken our conscience and carefully weigh in advance every step we take."

Clarisse interrupted him by opening her mouth, but thought better of it and did not respond.

"Of course I think about poverty too, and hunger, and all the corruption that's allowed to go on in this world, or mines caving in because the management economized on safety measures," Walter went on in a deflated tone, "and I've agreed with you about it already."

"But in that case two lovers mustn't love each other either, as long as they're not in a state of 'pure happiness,' " Clarisse said. "And the world will never improve until there are such lovers!"

Walter struck his hands together. "Don't you understand how unfair to life such great, dazzling, uncompromising demands are?" he exclaimed. "And it's the same with this Moosbrugger, who keeps popping into your head like something on a turntable. Of course you're right to claim that no stone should be left unturned as long as such miserable human creatures are simply killed off because society doesn't know what to do with them. But of course it's even more right that the healthy, normal conscience is justified in simply refusing to bother with such overrefined scruples. A healthy way of thinking is recognizable, in fact, by certain signs; one can't prove it but has to have it in one's blood."

"In *your* blood," Clarisse replied, " 'of course' always means 'of course not.' "

Nettled, Walter shook his head to show that he would not answer this. He was fed up with always being the one to warn that a diet of one-sided ideas was unhealthy; in the long run, it was probably also making him unsure of himself.

But Clarisse read his thoughts with that nervous sensitivity that never failed to amaze him. With her head high, she jumped over all the intermediate stages and landed on his main point with the subdued but intense question: "Can you imagine Jesus as boss of a coal mine?" He could see in her face that by "Jesus" she really meant him, through one of those exaggerations in which love is indistinguishable from madness. He waved this off with a gesture at once indignant and discouraged. "Not so direct, Clarisse!" he pleaded. "Such things mustn't be said so directly!"

"Yes, they must," she answered. "It's the only way! If we don't have the strength to save him, we will never have the strength to save ourselves!"

"And what difference will it make if they do string him up?" Walter burst out. The brutality of it made him believe he felt the liberating taste of life itself on his tongue, gloriously blended with the taste of death and the doom of their entanglement with it that Clarisse was conjuring up with her hints.

Clarisse looked at him expectantly. But Walter said nothing more, either from relief after his outburst or from indecision. And like someone forced to play an unbeatable final trump card, she said: "I've had a sign!"

"But that's just one of your fantasies!" Walter shouted at the ceiling, which represented heaven. But with those last airy words Clarisse had ended their tête-à-tête, giving him no chance to say anything more.

Yet he saw her only a short while later talking eagerly with Meingast, who was rightly troubled by a feeling that they were being watched but was too nearsighted to be sure of it. Walter was not really participating in the gardening being done so zestfully by his visiting brother-in-law, Siegmund, who with rolled-up shirtsleeves was kneeling in a furrow doing something or other that Walter had insisted must be done in the spring if one wanted to be a human being and not a bookmark in the pages of a gardening book. Instead of gardening, Walter was sneaking glances at the pair talking in the far corner of the open kitchen garden.

Not that he suspected anything untoward in the corner he was observing. Still, his hands felt unnaturally cold in the spring air; his legs were cold too, what with the wet places on his trousers from occasionally kneeling to give Siegmund instructions. He took a high tone with his brother-in-law, the way weak, downtrodden people will whenever they get a chance to work off their frustrations on someone. He knew that Siegmund, who had taken it into his head to revere Walter, would not be easily shaken in his loyalty. But this did not prevent him from feeling a veritable after-sunset loneliness, a graveyard chill, as he watched Clarisse; she never cast a glance in his direction but was all eyes for Meingast, hanging on the Master's words. Moreover, Walter actually took a certain pride in this. Ever since Meingast had come to stay in his house, he was just as proud of the chasms that suddenly opened up in it as he was anxious to cover them up again. From his standing height he had dispatched to the kneeling Siegmund the words: "Of course we all feel and are familiar with a certain hankering for the morbid and problematic!" He was no sneaking coward. In the short time since Clarisse had called him a philistine for saying the same thing to her, he had formulated a new phrase: "life's petty dishonesty."

"A little dishonesty is good, like sweet or sour," he now instructed his brother-in-law, "but we are obligated to refine it in ourselves to the point where it would do credit to a healthy life! What I mean by a little dishonesty," he went on, "is as much the nostalgic flirting with death that seizes us when we listen to *Tristan* as the secret fascination that's in most sex crimes, even though we don't succumb to it. For there's something dishonest and antihuman, you see, both in elemental life when it overpowers us with want and disease, and in exaggerated scruples of mind and conscience trying to do violence to life. Everything that tries to overstep the limits set for us is dishonest! Mysticism is just as dishonest as the conceit that nature can be reduced to a mathematical formula! And the plan to visit Moosbrugger is just as dishonest as"—here Walter paused for a moment—"as if you were to invoke God at a patient's bedside!"

There was certainly something in what he had said, and he had even managed to take Siegmund by surprise with his appeal to the physician's professional and spontaneous humanitarianism, to make him see Clarisse's scheme and her overwrought motivation as an impermissible overstepping of bounds. However, Walter was a genius compared with Siegmund, as may be seen in Walter's healthy outlook having led him to confess such ideas as these, while his brother-in-law's even healthier outlook manifested itself in his dogged silence in the face of such dubious subject matter. Siegmund patted the soil with his fingers while tilting his head now to one side, now to the other, without opening his lips, as if he were trying to pour something out of a test tube, or then again, as if he had just heard enough with that ear. And when Walter had finished there was a fearfully profound silence, in which Walter now heard a statement that Clarisse must have called out to him once, for without being as vivid as a hallucination, it was as if the hollow space were punctuated by these words: "Nietzsche and Christ both perished of their incompleteness!" Somehow, in some uncanny fashion reminiscent of the "coal mine boss," he felt flattered. It was a strange position that he, health personified, should be standing here in the cool garden between a man he regarded condescendingly and two unnaturally overheated people just out of earshot, whose mute gesticulations he watched with a superior air and yet with longing. For Clarisse was the slightly dishonest element his own health needed to keep from flagging, and a secret voice told him that Meingast was at this very moment engaged in immeasurably increasing the permissible limits of this dishonesty. He admired Meingast as an obscure relation admires a famous one, and seeing Clarisse whispering conspiratorially with him aroused his envy more than his jealousy—a feeling, that is, that ate into him even more deeply than jealousy would have, and yet it was also somehow uplifting; the consciousness of his own dignity forbade him to get angry or to go over there and disturb them; in view of their agitation he felt himself superior, and from all this arose, he did not know how, some vague, mongrel notion, spawned outside all logic, that the two of them over there were in some reckless and reprehensible fashion invoking God.

If such a curiously mixed state of mind must be called thinking, it was of a kind that cannot possibly be put into words, because the chemistry of its darkness is instantly ruined by the luminous influence of language. Besides, as his remark to Siegmund had shown, Walter did not associate belief of any sort with the word "God," and when the word occurred to him it generated an abashed void around itself. And so it happened that the first thing Walter said to his brother-in-law, after a long silence, had nothing to do with this. "You're an idiot to think you have no right to talk her out of this visit in the strongest possible terms," he said bitterly. "What are you a doctor for?"

Siegmund wasn't in the least offended. "You're the one who will have to have it out with her," he replied, glancing up calmly before turning back to what he was doing.

Walter sighed, then started over again. "Clarisse is an extraordinary person, of course. I can understand her very well. I'll even admit that she's not all wrong to be as austere in her views as she is. Just thinking of the poverty, hunger, misery of every kind the world is so full of, the disasters in coal mines, for instance, because the management wouldn't spend enough on timbering . . ."

Siegmund gave no sign that he was giving it any thought.

"Well, *she* does!" Walter continued sternly. "And I think it's wonderful of her. The rest of us get ourselves a good conscience much too easily. And she's better than we are for insisting that we all ought to change and have a more active conscience, the kind with no limit to it, ever. But what I'm asking you is whether this isn't bound to lead to a pathological state of moral scrupulousness, if it isn't something like that already. You must have an opinion!"

Siegmund responded to this pressing challenge by propping himself up on one knee and giving his brother-in-law a searching look. "Crazy!" he said. "But not, strictly speaking, in a medical sense."

"And what do you say," Walter continued, forgetting his superior stance, "to her claim that she's being sent signs?"

"She says she's being sent signs?" Siegmund said dubiously.

"Signs, I tell you. That crazy killer, for instance. And that crazy swine outside our window the other day!"

"A swine?"

"No, a kind of exhibitionist."

"I see," Siegmund said, turning it over in his mind. "You're sent signs too, when you find something to paint. She just expresses herself in a more high-strung way than you," he concluded.

"And what about her claim that she has to take these people's sins on herself, and yours and mine as well, and I don't know whose else's?" Walter pressed him.

Siegmund had risen to his feet and was brushing the dirt from his hands. "She feels oppressed by sin, does she?" he asked, again superfluously, politely agreeing as if glad to be able at last to support his brother-in-law. "That's a symptom!"

"That's a symptom?" Walter echoed, crushed.

"Fixed ideas about sin are a symptom," Siegmund affirmed with the detachment of a professional.

"But it's like this," Walter added, instantly appealing against the judgment he had just been suing for: "You must first ask yourself: Does sin exist? Of course it does. But in that case there's also a fixed idea of sin that is no delusion. You might not understand that, because it's beyond empiricism! It's a human being's aggrieved sense of responsibility toward a higher life!"

"But she insists she's receiving signs?" Siegmund persisted.

"But you just said that signs are sent to me too!" Walter cried. "And I can tell you there are times when I would like to go down on my knees and beg fate to leave me in peace; but it keeps sending signs, and it sends the most inspiring signs through Clarisse!" Then he continued more calmly: "She now claims, for instance, that this man Moosbrugger represents her and me in our 'sinful body' and has been sent to us as a warning; but it can be understood as a symbol of our neglecting the higher possibilities of our lives, our 'astral body,' as it were. Years ago, when Meingast left us—"

"But an obsession with sin *is* a symptom of specific disorders," Siegmund reminded him, with the relentless equanimity of the expert.

"Symptoms, that's all you know!" Walter said in animated defense of his Clarisse. "Anything beyond that is outside your experience! But perhaps this superstition, which regards everything that doesn't accord with the most pedestrian experience as a disorder, is itself the true sin and sinful form of our life. Clarisse demands spiritual action against this! Many years ago, when Meingast left and we . . ." He thought of how he and Clarisse had "taken Meingast's sins upon themselves," but realized it was hopeless to try telling Siegmund the process of a spiritual awakening, so he ended vaguely by saying: "Anyway, I don't suppose you'll deny that there have always been people who have, so to speak, drawn humanity's sins on themselves or even concentrated them in themselves."

His brother-in-law looked at him complacently. "There you are!"

he said amiably. "You yourself prove just what I've been saying. That she regards herself as oppressed by sin is a characteristic attitude of certain disorders. But there are also untypical modes of behavior in life: I never claimed anything more."

"And the exaggerated stringency with which she carries things out?" Walter asked after a while, with a sigh. "Surely to be so rigorous can hardly be called normal?"

Clarisse, meanwhile, was having an important conversation with Meingast.

"You've said," she reminded him, "that the kind of people who pride themselves on understanding and explaining the world will never change anything in it, isn't that so?"

"Yes," the Master replied. " 'True' and 'false' are the evasions of people who never want to arrive at a decision. Truth is something without end."

"So that's why you said one must have the courage to choose between 'worth' and 'worthless'?" she pressed on.

"Right," the Master said, somewhat bored.

"And then there's your marvelously contemptuous formulation," Clarisse cried, "that in modern life people only do what is happening anyway."

Meingast stopped and looked down; one might have said that he was either inclining an ear or studying a pebble lying before him on the path, slightly to the right. But Clarisse did not go on proffering honeyed praises; she, too, had now bent her head, so that her chin almost rested in the hollow of her neck, and her gaze bored into the ground between the tips of Meingast's boots. A gentle flush rose to her pale cheeks as, cautiously lowering her voice, she continued:

"You said all sexuality was nothing but goatish caperings."

"Yes, I did say that in a particular context. Whatever our age lacks in willpower it expends, apart from its so-called scientific endeavors, in sexuality."

After some hesitation, Clarisse said: "I have plenty of willpower myself, but Walter is for capering."

"What's really the matter between you two?" the Master asked with some curiosity, but almost immediately added in a tone of disgust: "I can guess, I suppose."

They were standing in a corner of the treeless garden that lay under the full spring sun, almost diametrically opposite the corner where Siegmund was squatting on the ground with Walter standing over and haranguing him. The garden formed a rectangle parallel with and against the long wall of the house, with a gravel path running around its vegetable and flower beds, and two others forming a bright cross on the still-bare ground in the middle. Warily glancing in the direction of the two men, Clarisse replied: "Perhaps he can't help it; you see, I attract Walter in a way that's not quite right."

"I can imagine," the Master answered, this time with a sympathetic look. "There is something boyish about you."

At this praise Clarisse felt happiness bouncing through her veins like hailstones. "Did you notice *before*," she eagerly asked him, "that I can change clothes faster than a man?"

A blank expression came over the philosopher's benevolently seamed face. Clarisse giggled. "That's a double word," she explained. "There are others too: sex murder, for instance."

The Master probably thought it would be wise not to show surprise at anything. "Oh yes, I know," he replied. "You did say once that to satisfy desire in the usual embrace is a kind of sex murder." But what did she mean by "changing," he wanted to know.

"To offer no resistance is murder," Clarisse explained with the speed of someone going through one's paces on slippery ground and losing one's footing through overagility.

"Now you've really lost me," Meingast admitted. "You must be talking about that fellow the carpenter again. What is it you want from him?"

Clarisse moodily scraped the gravel with the tip of her shoe. "It's all part of the same thing," she said. And suddenly she looked up at the Master. "I think Walter should learn to deny me," she said in an abruptly cut-off sentence.

"I can't judge that," Meingast remarked, after waiting in vain for her to go on. "But certainly radical solutions are always best."

He said this only to cover all contingencies. But Clarisse dropped her head again so that her gaze burrowed somewhere in Meingast's suit, and after a while her hand reached slowly for his forearm. She suddenly had an uncontrollable impulse to take hold of that hard, lean arm under the broad sleeve and touch the Master, who was pretending to have forgotten all those illuminating things he had said about the carpenter. While this was happening she was dominated by the feeling that she was pushing a part of herself over to him, and in the slowness with which her hand disappeared inside his sleeve, in this flooding slowness, there eddied fragments of a mysterious lust, which derived from her perception that the Master was keeping still and letting her touch him.

But Meingast for some reason stared aghast at the hand clutching his arm this way and creeping up it like some many-legged creature mounting its female. Under the little woman's lowered eyelids he caught a flash of something peculiar and realized the dubious character of what was taking place, although he was moved by her doing it so publicly.

"Come!" he said gently, removing her hand from his arm. "We're too conspicuous, standing here like this; let's go on walking."

As they strolled up and down the path, Clarisse said: "I can dress quickly, faster than a man if I have to. Clothes come flying onto my body when I'm—what shall I call it?—when I'm like that! Maybe it's a kind of electricity. I attract things that belong to me. But it's usually a sinister attraction."

Meingast smiled at her puns, which he still did not understand, and fished haphazardly in his mind for an impressive retort. "So you put on your clothes like a hero his destiny?" he responded.

To his surprise, Clarisse stopped short and cried: "Yes, that's it exactly! Whoever lives like this feels it even in a dress, shoes, knife and fork!"

"There's some truth in that," the Master confirmed her obscurely credible assertion. Then he asked point-blank: "But how do you do it with Walter, actually?"

Clarisse failed to understand. She looked at him, and suddenly saw in his eyes yellow clouds that seemed to be driven on a desert wind.

"You said," Meingast went on with some reluctance, "that you attract him in a way that 'isn't right.' You mean, I suppose, not right for a woman? How do you mean? Are you frigid with men?"

Clarisse did not know the word.

"Being frigid," the Master explained, "is when a woman is unable to enjoy the act of love with men."

"But I only know Walter," Clarisse objected timidly.

"Even so, it does seem a fair assumption, after what you've been telling me."

Clarisse was nonplussed. She had to think about it. She didn't know. "Me? But I'm not supposed to—I'm the one who must put a stop to it!" she said. "I can't permit it to happen!"

"You don't say?" The Master's laugh was vulgar. "You have to prevent yourself from feeling anything? Or prevent Walter from getting satisfaction?"

Clarisse blushed. But now she understood more clearly what she had to say. "When you give in, everything gets swamped in lust," she replied seriously. "I won't let a man's lust leave him and become my lust. That's why I've attracted men ever since I was a little girl. There's something wrong with the lust of men."

For various reasons Meingast preferred not to go into that.

"Do you have that much self-control?" he asked.

"Well, yes and no," Clarisse said candidly. "But I told you, if I let him have his way, I'd be a sex murderer!" Warming to her subject, she went on: "My woman friends say they 'pass out' in the arms of a man. I don't know what that is. I've never passed out in a man's arms. But I do know what it's like to 'pass out' *without* being in a man's arms. You must know about that too; after all, you did say that the world is too devoid of illusions . . . !"

Meingast waved this off with a gesture, as if to say she had misunderstood him. But now it was all too clear to her.

"When you say, for instance, that one must decide against the lesser value for the sake of the higher value," she cried, "it means that there's a life in an immense and boundless ecstasy! Not sexual ecstasy but the ecstasy of genius! Against which Walter would commit treason if I don't prevent him!"

Meingast shook his head. Denial filled him on hearing this altered and impassioned version of his words; it was a startled, almost frightened denial, but of all the things it prompted him to say, he chose the most superficial: "But who knows whether he could do anything else?"

Clarisse stopped, as if rooted to the ground by a bolt of lightning. "He must!" she cried. "You yourself taught us that!"

"So I did," the Master granted reluctantly, trying in vain to get her to keep walking by setting an example. "But what do you really want?"

"There was nothing I wanted before you came, don't you see?" Clarisse said softly. "But it's such an awful life, to take nothing more than the little bit of sexual pleasure out of the vast ocean of the possible joys in life! So now I want something."

"That's just what I am asking you about," Meingast prompted.

"One has to be here for a purpose. One has to be 'good' for something. Otherwise everything is horribly confused," Clarisse answered.

"Is what you want connected with Moosbrugger?" Meingast probed.

"That's hard to say. We'll have to see what comes of it," Clarisse replied. Then she said thoughtfully: "I'm going to abduct him. I'm going to create a scandal!" As she said this, her expression took on an air of mystery. "I've been watching you!" she said suddenly. "You have strange people coming to see you. You invite them when you think we're not home. Boys and young men! You don't talk about what they want!" Meingast stared at her, speechless. "You're working up to something," Clarisse went on, "you're getting something going! But I," she uttered in a forceful whisper, "I'm also strong enough to have several different friends at the same time. I've gained a man's character and a man's responsibilities. Living with Walter, I've learned masculine feelings!" Again her hand groped for Meingast's arm; it was evident she was unaware of what she was doing. Her fingers came out of her sleeve curved like claws. "I'm two people in one," she whispered, "you must know that! But it's not easy. You're right that one mustn't be afraid to use force in a case like this!"

Meingast was still staring at her in embarrassment. He had never known her in such a state. The import of her words was incomprehensible. For Clarisse herself at the moment, the concept of being two people in one was self-evident, but Meingast wondered whether she had guessed something of his secret life and was alluding to that. There was nothing much to guess at yet; he had only recently begun to perceive a shift in his feelings that accorded with his male-oriented philosophy, and begun to surround himself with young men who meant more to him than disciples. But that might have been why he had changed his residence and come here, where he felt safe from observation; he had never thought of such a possibility, and this little person, who had turned uncanny, was apparently capable of guessing what was going on in him. Somehow more and more of her arm was emerging from the sleeve of her dress without reducing the distance between the two bodies it connected, and this bare, skinny forearm, together with its attached hand, which was clutching Meingast, seemed at this moment to have such an unusual shape that everything in the man's imagination that had hitherto been distinct became wildly muddled.

But Clarisse no longer came out with what she had been just about to say, even though it was perfectly clear inside her. The double words were signs, scattered throughout the language like snapped-off twigs or leaves strewn on the ground, to mark a secret path. "Sex murder" and "changing" and even "quick" and many other words—perhaps all others—exhibited double meanings, one of which was secret and private. But a double language means a double life. Ordinary language is evidently that of sin, the secret one that of the astral body. "Quick," for instance, in its sinful form meant ordinary, everyday, tiring haste, while in its joyous form everything flew off it in joyful leaps and bounds. But then the joyous form can also be called the form of energy or of innocence, while the sinful form can be called all the names having to do with the depression, dullness, and irresolution of ordinary life. There were these amazing connections between the self and things, so that something one did had an effect where one would never have expected it; and the less Clarisse could express all this, the more intensely the words kept coming inside her, too fast for her to gather them in. But for quite some time she had been convinced of one thing: the duty, the privilege, the mission of whatever it is we call conscience, illusion, will, is to find the vital form, the light form. This is the one where nothing is accidental, where there is no room for wavering, where happiness and compulsion coincide. Other people have called this "living authentically" and spoken of the "intelligible character"; they have referred to instinct as innocence and to the intellect as sin. Clarisse could not think in these terms, but she had made the discovery that one could set something in motion, and then sometimes parts of the astral body would attach themselves to it of their own accord and in this fashion become embodied in it. For reasons primarily rooted in Walter's hypersensitive inaction, but also because of heroic aspirations she never had the means of satisfying, she had been led to think that by taking forceful action one could set up a memorial to oneself in advance, and the memorial would then draw one into itself. So she was not at all clear about what she intended to do with Moosbrugger, and could not answer Meingast's question.

Nor did she want to. While Walter had forbidden her to say that the Master was about to undergo another transformation, there was no doubt that his spirit was moving toward secret preparations for some action, she did not know what, but one which could be as magnificent as his spirit was. He was therefore bound to understand her, even if he pretended not to. The less she said, the more she showed him how much she knew. She also had a right to take hold of him, and he could not forbid it. Thus he accorded recognition to her undertaking and she entered into his and took part in it. This, too, was a kind of being-two-people-in-one, and so forceful that she could hardly grasp it. All her strength, more than she could know she had, was flowing through her arm in an inexhaustible stream from her to her mysterious friend, draining the very marrow from her bones and leaving her faint with sensations surpassing any of those from making love. She could do nothing but look at her hand, smiling, or alternately look into his face. Meingast, too, was doing nothing but gaze now at her, now at her hand.

All at once, something happened that at first took Clarisse by surprise and then threw her into a whirl of bacchantic ecstasy:

Meingast had been trying to keep a superior smile fixed on his face in order not to betray his uncertainty. But this uncertainty was growing from moment to moment, constantly reborn from something apparently incomprehensible. For every act undertaken with doubts is preceded by a brief span of weakness, corresponding to the moments of remorse after the thing is done, though in the normal course of events it may barely be apparent. The convictions and vivid illusions that protect and justify the completed act have not yet been fully formed and are still wavering in the mounting tide of passion, vague and formless as they will probably be when they tremble and collapse afterward in the outgoing tide of passionate remorse. It was in just this state of his intentions that Meingast had been surprised. It was doubly painful for him because of the past and because of the regard in which he was now held by Walter and Clarisse, and then, every intense excitement changes the sense of one's image of reality so that it can rise to new heights. His own frightened state made Clarisse frightening to Meingast, and the failure of his efforts to get back to sober reality only increased his dismay. So instead of projecting superior strength, the smile on his face stiffened from one minute to the next; indeed, it became a sort of floating stiffness, which ended by floating away stiffly, as if on stilts. At this moment the Master was behaving no differently than a large dog facing some much smaller creature he does not dare to attack, like a caterpillar, toad, or snake; he reared up higher and higher on his long legs, drew back his lips and arched his back, and found himself suddenly swept away by the currents of discomfort from the place where they had their source, without being able to conceal his flight by any word or gesture.

Clarisse did not let go of him. As he took his first, hesitant steps, her clinging might have been taken for ingenuous eagerness, but after that he was dragging her along with him while barely finding the necessary words to explain that he was in a hurry to get back to his room and work. It was only in the front hall that he managed to shake her off completely; up till then he had been driven only by his urge to escape, paying no attention to what Clarisse was saying and choked by his caution not to attract the attention of Walter and Siegmund. Walter had actually been able to guess at the general pattern of what was going on. He could see that Clarisse was passionately demanding something that Meingast was refusing her, and jealousy bored into his breast like a double-threaded screw. For although he suffered agonies at the thought that Clarisse was offering her favors to their friend, he was even more furious at the insult of seeing her apparently disdained. If that feeling were taken to its logical conclusion, he would have to force Meingast to take Clarisse, only to be plunged into despair by the sweep of that same impulse. He felt deeply sad and heroically excited. It was insufferable, with Clarisse poised on the razor's edge of her destiny, that he should have to listen to Siegmund asking whether the seedlings should be planted loosely in the soil or if it had to be patted firmly around them. He had to say something, and felt like a piano in the fraction of a second between the moment when the ten-fingered crash of an incredible blow hits it and the cry of pain. Light was in his throat, words that would surely put a wholly new and different face on everything. Yet all he managed to say was something quite different from what he expected. "I won't have it!" he said, again and again, more to the garden than to Siegmund.

But it turned out that Siegmund, intent as he had seemed to be on the seedlings and on pushing the soil this way and that, had also noticed what was going on and even given it some thought. For now he rose to his feet, brushed the dirt from his knees, and gave his brother-in-law some advice.

"If you feel she's going too far, you'll have to give her something else to think about," he said in a tone that implied he had of course been thinking all this time, with a doctor's sense of responsibility, about everything Walter had confided in him.

"And how am I to do that?" Walter asked, disconcerted.

"Like any man!" Siegmund said. "All a woman's fuss and fury is to be cured in one place, to quote Mephistopheles more or less!"

Siegmund put up with a great deal from Walter. Life is full of such relationships, in which one partner keeps the upper hand and constantly suppresses the other, who never rebels. In fact, and in accordance with Siegmund's own convictions, this is the way normal, healthy life is. The world would probably have come to an end in the Bronze Age if everyone had stood up for himself to the last drop of his blood. Instead, the weaker have always moved away and looked around for neighbors they in their turn could push around; the majority of human relationships follow this model to this day, and with time these things take care of themselves.

In his family circle, where Walter passed for a genius, Siegmund had always been treated as a bit of a blockhead; he had accepted it, and even today would have been the one who yielded and did homage wherever it was a matter of precedence in the family hierarchy. That old hierarchical structure had ceased to matter years ago, compared with the new status each of them had acquired, and precisely for that reason it could be left undisturbed. Siegmund not only had a very respectable practice as a physician—and the doctor's power, unlike that of the bureaucrat, is not imposed from above but is owed to his personal ability; people come to him for help and submit to him willingly—but also had a wealthy wife, who had presented him within a brief period with herself and three children, and to whom he was unfaithful with other women, not often but regularly, whenever it pleased him. So he was certainly in a position, if he chose, to give Walter confident and reliable advice.

At this moment Clarisse came back out of the house. She no longer remembered what had been said during their tempestuous rush indoors. She realized that the Master had been trying to get away from her, but the memory of it had lost its details, had folded up and closed. Something had happened! With this one notion in her head, Clarisse felt like someone emerging from a thunderstorm, still charged from head to toe with sensual energy. In front of her, a few yards beyond the bottom of the small flight of stone steps she had come out by, she saw a shiny blackbird with a flame-colored beak, dining on a fat caterpillar. There was an immense energy in the creature, or in the two contrasting colors. One could not say that Clarisse was thinking anything about it; it was more like a response coming from behind and all around her. The blackbird was a sinful body in the act of committing violence. The caterpillar the sinful form of a butterfly. Fate had placed the two creatures in her path, as a sign that she must act. One could see how the blackbird assumed the caterpillar's sins through its flaming orange-red beak. Wasn't the bird a "black genie"? Just as the dove is the "white spirit"? Weren't these signs linked in a chain? The exhibitionist with the carpenter, with the Master's flight . . . ? Not one of these notions was clearly formed in her; they lodged invisibly in the walls of the house, summoned but still keeping their answer to themselves. But what Clarisse really felt as she stepped out on the stairs and saw the bird that was eating the caterpillar was an ineffable correspondence of inner and outer happenings.

She conveyed it in some curious way to Walter. The impression he received instantly corresponded with what he had called "invoking God"; there was no mistaking it this time. He could not make out what was going on inside Clarisse, she was too far away, but there was something in her bearing that was not happenstance, as she stood facing the world into which the little flight of stairs descended like steps leading down to a swimming pool. It was something exalted. It was not the attitude of ordinary life. And suddenly he understood; this was what Clarisse meant when she said: "It's not by chance that this man is under my window!" Gazing at his wife, he himself felt how the pressure of strange forces came flooding in to fill appearances. In the fact that he was standing here and Clarisse there, at such an angle to him that he had to turn his eyes away from the direction they had automatically taken, along the length of the garden, in order to see her clearly—even in this simple juxtaposition, the mute emphasis of life suddenly outweighed natural contingency. Out of the fullness of images thrusting themselves upon the eye something geometrically linear and extraordinary reared up. This must be how it could happen that Clarisse found a meaning in almost empty correlations, such as the circumstance of one man stopping under her window while another was a carpenter. Events seemed to have a way of arranging themselves that was different from the usual pattern, as elements in some strange entity that revealed them in unexpected aspects, and because it brought these aspects out from their obscure hiding places, it justified Clarisse's claim that it was she herself who was attracting events toward herself. It was hard to express this without sounding fanciful, but then it occurred to Walter that it came closest to something he knew very well—what happens when you paint a picture. A painting, too, has its own inexplicable way of excluding every color or line not in accord with its basic form, style, and palette of colors, while on the other hand it extracts from the painter's hand whatever it needs, thanks to the laws of genius, which are not the same as the usual laws of nature. At this point he no longer had in him any of that easy, healthy self-assurance which scrutinizes life's excrescences for anything that might come in handy and which he had been extolling only a little while ago; what he felt was more the misery of a little boy too timid to join in a game.

But Siegmund was not the man to let go of something so easily once he had taken it up. "Clarisse is high-strung," he declared. "She's always been ready to run her head through a wall, and now she's got it stuck in one. You'll have to get a good grip on her, even if she resists you."

"You doctors don't have a clue about human psychology!" Walter cried. He looked for a second point of attack and found it. "You talk of 'signs,'" he went on, his irritation overlaid by his pleasure in being able to speak about Clarisse, "and you carefully examine when signs indicate a disorder and when they don't, but I tell you this: the true human condition is the one in which everything is a sign! But everything! You may be able to look truth in the eye, but truth will never look you in the eye; this divine, uncertain feeling is something you'll never know!"

"You're obviously both crazy," Siegmund remarked dryly.

"Yes, of course we are!" Walter cried out. "You're not a creative man, after all; you've never learned what it means to 'express oneself,' which means first of all, for an artist, to *understand* something. The expression we impart to things is what develops our ability to perceive them aright. I can only understand what I want, or someone else wants, by carrying it out! This is our living experience, as distinct from your dead experience! Of course you'll say it's paradoxical, a confusion of cause and effect; you and your medical causality!"

But Siegmund did not say this; he merely reiterated doggedly: "It will definitely be for her own good if you won't put up with too much. Excitable people need a certain amount of strictness."

"And when I play the piano at the open window," Walter asked, as if he had not heard his brother-in-law's warning, "what am I doing? People are passing by, some of them young girls, perhaps anyone who feels like it stops to listen; I play for young lovers and lonely old people. Clever people, stupid people. I'm not giving them something to *think* about. What I'm playing isn't rational information. I'm giving them myself. I sit invisible in my room and give them signs: just a few notes, and it's their life, and it's my life. You could certainly call this crazy too . . . !" Suddenly he fell silent. That feeling: "Oh, I could tell all of you a thing or two!"—that basic ambitious urge of every inhabitant of earth who feels the need to communicate something but has no more than an average creative capacity—had fallen to pieces. Every time Walter sat in the soft emptiness of the room behind his open window and released his music into the air with the proud awareness of the artist giving happiness to unknown thousands, this feeling was like an open umbrella, and the instant he stopped playing, it was like a sloppily closed one. All the airiness was gone, it was as if everything that had happened had not happened, and all he could say was that art had lost its connection to the people and everything was no good. He thought of this and felt dejected. He tried to fight it off. After all, Clarisse had said: music must be played "through to the end." Clarisse had said: "We understand something only as long as we ourselves are part of it!" But Clarisse had also said: "That's why we have to go to the madhouse ourselves!" Walter's "inner umbrella" flapped halfway closed in irregular stormy gusts.

Siegmund said: "Excitable people need a certain amount of guidance, for their own good. You yourself said you wouldn't put up with it anymore. Professionally and personally, I can only give you the same advice: Show her that you're a man. I know she balks at that, but she'll come around." Siegmund was like a dependable machine tirelessly reiterating the "answer" he had come up with.

Walter, in a "stormy gust," replied: "This medical exaggeration of a well-adjusted sex life is old hat! When I make music or paint or think, I am affecting both an immediate and a distant audience, without depriving the ones of what I give to the others. On the contrary! Take it from me, there's probably no sphere of life in which one remains justified in living only for oneself, thinking of life as a private matter! Not even marriage!"

But the heavier pressure was on Siegmund's side, and Walter sailed before the wind across to Clarisse, of whom he had not lost sight during this conversation. He did not relish anyone's being able to say of him that he was not a man; he turned his back on this suggestion by letting it drive him over to Clarisse. And halfway there he felt the certainty, between nervously bared teeth, that he would have to begin with the question: "What do you mean, talking about signs?"

But Clarisse saw him coming. She had already seen him wavering while he was still standing there. Then his feet were pulled from the ground and bore him toward her. She participated in this with wild elation. The blackbird, startled, flew off, hastily taking its caterpillar with it. The way was now clear for her power of attraction. Yet she suddenly thought better of it and eluded the encounter for the time being by slowly slipping along the side of the house into the open, not turning away from Walter but moving faster than he, hesitant as he was, could move out of the realm of telepathic effect into that of statement and response.

150

AGATHE IS QUICKLY DISCOVERED AS A SOCIAL ASSET BY GENERAL STUMM

Since Agathe had joined forces with him, Ulrich's relations with the extensive social circle of the Tuzzis had been making great demands on his time. For although it was late in the year the winter's busy social season was not yet over, and the least he could do in return for the great show of sympathy he had received upon his father's death was not hide Agathe away, even though their being in mourning relieved them of having to attend large affairs. Had Ulrich chosen to take full advantage of it, their mourning would actually have allowed them to avoid attending all social functions for a long time, so that he could have dropped out of a circle of acquaintances that he had fallen into only through curious circumstances. However, since Agathe had put her life into his charge Ulrich acted against his own inclination, and assigned to a part of himself labeled with the traditional concept "duties of an elder brother" many decisions that his whole person was undecided about, even when he did not actually disapprove of them. The first of these duties of an elder brother was to see that Agathe's flight from her husband's house should end only in the house of a better husband.

"If things continue this way," he would say, whenever they touched on the subject of what arrangements needed to be made in setting up house together, "you will soon be getting some offers of marriage, or at least of love," and if Agathe planned something for more than a few weeks ahead he would say: "By that time everything will be different." This would have wounded her even more had she not perceived the conflict in her brother, so that for the present she refrained from making an issue of it when he chose to widen their social circle to the limit. And so after Agathe's arrival they became far more involved in social obligations than Ulrich would have been on his own.

Their constant appearances together, when for a long time Ulrich had always been seen alone and without ever uttering a word about a sister, caused no slight sensation. One day General Stumm von Bordwehr had shown up at Ulrich's with his orderly, his briefcase, and his loaf of bread, and started to sniff the air suspiciously. Then Stumm discovered a lady's stocking hanging over a chair, and said reproachfully: "Oh, you young fellows!"

"My sister," Ulrich declared.

"Oh, come on—you haven't got a sister!" the General protested. "Here we are, tormented by the most serious problems, and you're hiding out with a little playmate!"

Just then Agathe came in, and the General lost his composure. He saw the family resemblance, and could tell by the casual air with which Agathe wandered in that Ulrich had told the truth, yet he could not shake off the feeling that he was looking at one of Ulrich's girlfriends, who incomprehensibly and misleadingly happened to look like him.

"I really don't know what came over me, dear lady," he told Diotima later, "but I couldn't have been more amazed if he'd suddenly stood before me as a cadet again!" For at the sight of Agathe, to whom he was instantly attracted, Stumm had been overcome by that stupor he had learned to recognize as a sign of being deeply moved. His tender plumpness and sensitive nature inclined the General to hasty retreat from such a tricky situation, and despite all Ulrich's efforts to make him stay, he did not learn much more about the serious problems that had brought the educated General to him.

"No!" Stumm blamed himself. "Nothing is so important as to justify my disturbing you like this."

"But you haven't disturbed us at all," Ulrich assured him with a smile. "What's there to be disturbed?"

"No, of course not," Stumm assured him, now completely confused. "Of course not, in a sense. But all the same . . . look, why don't I come back another time?"

"You might at least tell me what brought you here, before you dash off again," Ulrich demanded.

"Nothing, not a thing! A trifle!" the General cried in his eagerness to take to his heels. "I think the Great Event is about to start!"

"A horse! A horse! Take ship for France!" Ulrich threw in in fun.

Agathe looked at him in surprise.

"I do apologize," the General said, turning to her. "You can't have any idea what this is all about."

"The Parallel Campaign has found its crowning idea!" Ulrich filled her in.

"No, I never said that," the General demurred. "All I meant was that the great event everyone was waiting for is now on its way."

"I see," Ulrich said. "Well, it's been on its way from the start."

"No, not quite like this," the General earnestly assured him. "There is now a quite definite nobody-knows-what in the air. There's soon to be a decisive gathering at your cousin's. Frau Drangsal—"

"Who's she?" Ulrich had never heard of her.

"That only shows how much you've been out of touch," the General said reproachfully, and turned immediately to Agathe to mend matters. "Frau Drangsal is the lady who has taken the poet Feuermaul under her wing. I suppose," he said, turning his round body back again to the silent Ulrich, "you don't know him either?"

"Yes, I do. The lyric poet."

"Writes verses," the General said, mistrustfully avoiding the unaccustomed word.

"Good verse, in fact. And all sorts of plays."

"I don't know about plays. And I haven't got my notes with me. But he's the one who says: Man is good. In short, Frau Drangsal is backing the hypothesis that man is good, and they say it is a great European idea and that Feuermaul has a great future. She was married to a man who was a world-famous doctor, and she means to make Feuermaul world-famous too. Anyway, there's a danger that your cousin may lose the leadership to Frau Drangsal, whose salon has also been attracting all the celebrities."

The General mopped the sweat from his brow, though Ulrich did not find the prospect at all alarming.

"You surprise me!" Stumm scolded him. "As an admirer of your cousin like everyone else, how can you say such things? Don't you agree, dear lady," he appealed to Agathe, "that your brother is being incredibly disloyal and ungrateful toward an inspiring woman?"

"I've never met my cousin," Agathe admitted.

"Oh!" said Stumm, and in words that turned a chivalrous intention into a rather backhanded compliment which involved an obscure concession to Agathe, he added: "Though she hasn't been at her best lately!"

Neither Ulrich nor Agathe had anything to say to this, so the General felt he had to elucidate. "And you know why, too," he said meaningfully to Ulrich. He disapproved of Diotima's current absorption in sexology, which was distracting her mind from the Parallel Campaign, and he was worried because her relationship with Arnheim was not improving, but he did not know how far he might go in speaking of such matters in the presence of Agathe, whose expression was now growing steadily cooler. But Ulrich answered calmly: "I suppose you're not making any progress with your oil affair if our Diotima no longer has her old influence on Arnheim?"

Stumm made a pathetically pleading gesture, as if to stop Ulrich from making a joke not fit for a lady's ear, but at the same time threw him a sharp glance of warning. He even found the energy, despite his weight, to bounce to his feet like a young man, and tugged his tunic straight. Enough of his original suspicion about Agathe's background lingered to keep him from exposing the secrets of the War Ministry in her presence. It was only when Ulrich had escorted him out to the hall that he clutched his arm and whispered hoarsely, through a smile: "For God's sake, man, don't talk open treason!" and enjoined Ulrich from uttering a word about the oil fields in front of any third person, even one's own sister. "Oh, all right," Ulrich promised. "But she's my *twin* sister."

"Not even in front of a twin sister!" the General asseverated, still so incredulous about the sister that he could take the addition of "twin" in stride. "Give me your word!"

"But it's no use making me promise such a thing." Ulrich was even more outrageous. "We're Siamese twins, don't you see?" Stumm finally caught on that Ulrich, whose manner was never to give a straight answer to anything, was making fun of him. "Your jokes used to be better," he protested, "than to suggest the unappetizing notion that such a delightful person, even if she's ten times your sister, is fused together with you!" But this had reawakened his lively mistrust of the reclusiveness in which he had found Ulrich, and so he appended a few more questions to find out what he had been up to. Has the new secretary turned up yet? Have you been to see Diotima? Have you kept your promise to visit Leinsdorf? Have you found out how things are between your cousin and Arnheim? Since the plump skeptic was of course already informed on all these points, he was merely testing Ulrich's truthfulness, and was satisfied with the result.

"In that case, do me a favor and don't be late for this crucial session," he pleaded while buttoning up his greatcoat, slightly out of breath from mastering the traversal through the sleeves. "I'll call you again beforehand and fetch you in my carriage, agreed?"

"And when will this boredom take place?" Ulrich asked, not exactly with enthusiasm.

"In a couple of weeks or so, I think," the General said. "We want to bring the rival party to Diotima's, but we want Arnheim to be there too, and he's still abroad." With one finger he tapped the golden sword knot dangling from his coat pocket. "Without him, it's not much fun for *us*, as you can understand. But believe me"—he sighed—"there's nothing I personally desire more than that our spiritual leadership should stay with your cousin; it would be horrible for me, if I had to adapt to an entirely new situation!"

Thus it was this visit that brought Ulrich, now accompanied by his sister, back into the fold he had deserted when he was still alone. He would have had to resume his social obligations even if he had not wanted to, as he could not possibly stay in hiding with Agathe a day longer and expect Stumm to keep to himself a discovery so ripe for gossip. When "the Siamese" called on Diotima, she had apparently already heard of this curious and dubious epithet, if she was not yet charmed with it. For the divine Diotima, famed for the distinguished and remarkable people always to be met under her roof, had at first taken Agathe's unheralded debut very badly; a kinswoman who might not be a social success could be far more damaging to her own position than a male cousin, and she knew just as little about this new cousin as she had previously known about Ulrich, which in itself caused the all-knowing Diotima some annoyance when she had to admit her ignorance to the General. So she had decided to refer to Agathe as "the orphan sister," partly to help reconcile herself to the situation and partly to prepare wider circles for it. It was in this spirit that she received the cousins.

She was agreeably surprised by the socially impeccable manners

Agathe was able to produce, while Agathe, mindful of her good education in a pious boarding school and always ready, with a mixture of
irony and wonder, to take life as it came—an attitude she deplored to
Ulrich—from the first managed almost unconsciously to win the gracious sympathies of the stupendous young woman whose ambition
for "greatness" left Agathe quite cold and indifferent. She marveled
at Diotima with the same guilelessness with which she would have
marveled at a gigantic power station in whose mysterious function of
spreading light one did not meddle. Once Diotima had been won
over, especially as she could soon see that Agathe was generally liked,
she laid herself out to extend Agathe's social success, which she arranged to throw greater credit on herself. The "orphan sister"
aroused much sympathetic interest, which among Diotima's intimates began on a note of frank amazement that nobody had ever
heard of her before, and in wider circles was transformed into that
vague pleasure at everything new and surprising which is shared by
princes and the press alike.

And so it happened that Diotima, with her dilettante's knack for
choosing instinctively, among several options, that which was both
the worst and the most promising of public success, made the move
that assured Ulrich and Agathe of their permanent place in the
memory of that distinguished circle by promptly passing on the delightful story—as she now suddenly found it to be—that the cousins,
reunited under romantic circumstances after an almost lifelong separation, called themselves Siamese twins, even though they had been
blindly fated thus far to be almost the opposite. It would be hard to
say why Diotima first, and then everyone else, was so taken with this
circumstance, and why it made the "twins" ' resolve to live together
appear both extraordinary and natural; such was Diotima's gift for
leadership; and this outcome—for both things happened—proved
that she still exerted her gentle sway despite all her rivals' maneuvers. Arnheim, when he heard of it on his return from abroad, delivered an elaborate address to a select circle, rounding it off with a
homage to aristocratic-popular forces. Somehow the rumor arose
that Agathe had taken refuge with her brother from an unhappy marriage with a celebrated foreign savant. And since the arbiters of good
form at that time had the landowners' antipathy to divorce and made
do with adultery, many older persons perceived Agathe's choice in

that double halo of the higher life composed of willpower and piety which Count Leinsdorf, who looked upon the "twins" with special favor, at one point characterized with the words: "Our theaters are always treating us to displays of the most awful excesses of passion. Now here's a story the Burgtheater could use as a good example!"

Diotima, in whose presence this was uttered, responded: "It's become fashionable for many people to say that man is good. But anyone who knows, as I have learned in my studies, the confusions of our sex life will know how rare such examples are!"

Did she mean to qualify His Grace's praise or reinforce it? She had not yet forgiven Ulrich what she called his lack of confidence in her, since he had not given her advance notice of his sister's arrival; but she was proud of the success in which she had a part, and this entered into her reply.

151

TOO MUCH GAIETY

Agathe proved naturally adept at making use of the advantages social life offered, and her brother was pleased to see her moving with so much poise in these demanding social circles. The years she had spent as the wife of a secondary-school principal in the provinces seemed to have fallen from her without leaving a trace. For the present, however, Ulrich summed it all up with a shrug, saying: "Our high nobility find it amusing that we should be called the Siamese twins. They've always gone in more for menageries than, say, for art."

By tacit agreement they treated all that was happening as a mere interlude. There was much that needed changing or rearranging in their household, as they had seen from the very first day; but they did nothing about it, because they shied away from another discussion whose limits could not be foreseen. Ulrich had given up his bedroom to Agathe and settled himself in the dressing room, with the bathroom between them, and had gradually given up most of his closet space to her. He declined her offer of sympathy for these hardships with an allusion to Saint Lawrence and his grille; and anyway it did not occur to Agathe that she might be interfering with her brother's bachelor life, because he assured her that he was very happy and because she could have only the vaguest idea of the degrees of happiness he might have enjoyed previously. She had come to like this house with its unconventional arrangements, its useless extravagance of anterooms and reception rooms around the few habitable rooms, which were now overcrowded; there was about it something of the elaborate civilities of a bygone age left defenseless against the self-indulgent and churlish high-handedness of the present. Sometimes the mute protest of the handsome rooms against the disorderly invasion seemed mournful, like broken, tangled strings hanging from the exquisitely carved frame of an old instrument. Agathe now saw that her brother had not really chosen this secluded house without interest or feeling, as he pretended, and from its ancient walls emerged a language of passion that was not quite mute, but yet not quite audible. But neither she nor Ulrich admitted to anything more than enjoying its casualness. They lived in some disarray, had their meals sent in from a hotel, and derived from everything a sort of wild fun that comes with eating a meal more awkwardly on the grass at a picnic than one would have had to do at one's table.

In these circumstances they also did not have the right domestic help. The well-trained servant Ulrich had taken on temporarily when he moved in—an old man about to retire and only waiting for some technicality to be settled first—could not be expected to do more than the minimum Ulrich expected of him; the part of lady's maid fell to Ulrich himself, since the room where a regular maid might be lodged was, like everything else, still in the realm of good intentions, and a few efforts in that direction had not brought good results. Instead, Ulrich was making great strides as a squire arming his lady knight to set forth on her social conquests. In addition, Agathe had done some shopping to supplement her wardrobe, and her acquisitions were strewn all over the house, which was nowhere equipped for the demands of a lady. She had acquired the habit of using the entire house as a dressing room, so that Ulrich willy-nilly took part in her new purchases. The doors between rooms were left open, his gymnastic apparatus served as clotheshorse and coatrack, and he would be called away from his desk for conferences like Cincinnatus from his plow. This interference with his latent but at least potential will to work was something he put up with not merely because he thought it would pass but because he enjoyed it; it was something new and made him feel young again. His sister's vivacity, idle as it might appear to be, crackled in his loneliness like a small fire in a long-unused stove. Bright waves of charming gaiety, dark waves of warm trustfulness, filled the space in which he lived, taking from it the nature of a space in which he up till then had moved only at the dictates of his own will. But what was most amazing about this inexhaustible fountain of another presence was that the sum of the countless trifles of which it consisted added up to a non-sum that was of a quite different kind: his impatience with wasting his time, that unquenchable feeling that had never left him since he could remember, no matter what he had taken up that was supposed to be great and important, was to his astonishment totally gone, and for the first time he loved his day-to-day life without thinking.

He even overdid it a little, gasping in delight when Agathe, with the seriousness women feel in these matters, offered for his admiration the thousand charming things she had been buying. He acted as if the quaint workings of a woman's nature—which, on the same level of intelligence, is more sensitive than the male and therefore more susceptible to the suggestion of dressing up to a point of crass self-display that is even further removed from the ideal of a cultivated humanity than the man's nature—irresistibly compelled his participation. And perhaps it really was so. For the many small, tender, absurd notions he became involved with—tricking oneself out with glass beads, crimping the hair, the mindless arrangements of lace and embroidery, the ruthless seductive colors: charms so akin to the tinfoil stars at the fairgrounds that every intelligent woman sees right through them without in the least losing her taste for them—began to entangle him in the network of their glittering madness. For the moment one begins to take anything, no matter how foolish or tasteless, seriously and puts oneself on its level, it begins to reveal a rationale of its own, the intoxicating scent of its love for itself, its innate urge to play and to please. This was what happened to Ulrich when he helped equip Agathe with her new outfits. He fetched and carried, admired, appraised, was asked for advice, helped with trying on. He stood with Agathe in front of the mirror. Nowadays, when a woman's appearance suggests that of a well-plucked fowl ready for the oven, it is hard to imagine her predecessor's appearance in all its charm of endlessly titillated desire, which has meanwhile become ridiculous: the long skirt, to all appearances sewn to the floor by the dressmaker and yet miraculously in motion, enclosing other, secret gossamer skirts beneath it, pastel-shaded silk flower petals whose softly fluttering movements suddenly turned into even finer tissues of white, which were the first to touch the body itself with their soft foam. And if these clothes resembled waves in that they drew the eye seductively and yet repulsed it, they were also an ingenious contrivance of way stations and intermediate fortifications around expertly guarded marvels and, for all their unnaturalness, a cleverly curtained theater of the erotic, whose breathtaking darkness was lit only by the feeble light of the imagination. It was these quintessential preliminaries that Ulrich now saw removed daily, taken apart, as it were from the inside. Even though a woman's secrets had long since lost their mystery for him, or just because he had always only rushed through them as anterooms or outer gardens, they had quite a different effect on him now that there was no gateway or goal for him. The tension that lies in all these things struck back. Ulrich could hardly have said what changes it wrought. He rightly regarded himself as a man of masculine temperament, and he could understand being attracted by seeing what he so often desired from its other side, for once, but at times it was almost uncanny, and he warded it off with a laugh.

"As if the walls of a girls' boarding school had sprouted all around me in the night, completely locking me in!" he protested.

"Is that so terrible?" Agathe asked.

"I don't know," he replied.

Then he called her a flesh-eating plant and himself a miserable insect that had crawled into her shimmering calyx. "You've closed it around me," he said, "and now I'm sitting surrounded by colors, perfume, and radiance, already a part of you in spite of myself, waiting for the males we're going to attract!"

And it really was uncanny for him to witness the effect his sister had on men, considering his concern to "get her a husband." He was not jealous—in what capacity could he have been?—and put her interests ahead of his, hoping that the right man would soon come along to release her from this interim phase in which leaving Hagauer had placed her; and yet, when he saw her surrounded by men paying her attentions, or when a man on the street, attracted by her beauty and ignoring her escort, gave her a bold stare, Ulrich did not know what to make of his feelings. Here too, natural male jealousy being forbidden him, he often felt somehow caught up in a world he had never entered before. He knew from experience all about the male mating dance as well as the female's warier technique in love, and when he saw Agathe being treated to the one and responding with the other, it pained him; he felt as if he were watching the courtship of horses or mice, the sniffing and whinnying, the pouting and baring of teeth, with which strangers parade their self-regard and regard of the opposite sex; to Ulrich, observing this without empathy, it was nauseating, like some stupefaction welling up from within the body. And if he nevertheless tried to put himself in his sister's place, prompted by some deep-seated emotional need, it sometimes would not have taken much afterward for him to feel, not just bewilderment at such tolerance, but the sort of shame a normal man feels when deviously approached by one who is not. When he let Agathe in on this, she laughed.

"There are also several women among our friends who take an interest in you," she said.

What was going on here?

Ulrich said: "Basically it's a protest against the world!" And then he said: "You know Walter: It's been a long time since we've liked each other. But even when I'm annoyed with him and know that I irritate him too, I nevertheless often feel, at the mere sight of him, a certain warmth as if we understood each other perfectly, as in fact we don't. Look, there's so much in life we understand without agreeing with it; that's why accepting someone from the beginning, before understanding him, is pure mindless magic, like water in spring running down all the hillsides to the valley!"

What he felt was: "That's the way it is now!" And what he thought was: "Whenever I succeed in shedding all my selfish and egocentric feelings toward Agathe, and every single hateful feeling of indifference too, she draws all the qualities out of me the way the Magnetic

Mountain draws the nails out of a ship! She leaves me morally dissolved into a primary atomic state, one in which I am neither myself nor her. Could this be bliss?"

But all he said was: "Watching you is so much fun!"

Agathe blushed deeply and said: "Why is that 'fun'?"

"Oh, I don't know. Sometimes you're self-conscious with me in the room," Ulrich said. "But then you remember that, after all, I'm 'only your brother.' And at other times you don't seem to mind at all when I catch you in circumstances that would be most interesting for a stranger, but then it suddenly occurs to you that I shouldn't be looking at you, and you make me look the other way. . . ."

"And why is *that* fun?" Agathe asked.

"Maybe it's a form of happiness to follow another person with one's eyes for no reason at all," Ulrich said. "It's like a child's love for its possessions, without the child's intellectual helplessness. . . ."

"Maybe it's fun for you to play at brother-and-sister only because you've had more than enough of playing at man-and-woman?"

"That too," Ulrich said, watching her. "Love is basically a simple urge to come close, to grab at something that has been split into two poles, lady and gentleman, with incredible tensions, frustrations, spasms, and perversions arising in between. We've now had enough of this inflated ideology; it's become nearly as ridiculous as a science of eating. I'm convinced most people would be glad if this connection between an epidermic itch and the entire personality could be revoked. And sooner or later there will be an era of simple sexual companionship in which boy and girl will stand in perfectly tuned incomprehension, staring at an old heap of broken springs that used to be Man and Woman."

"But if I were to tell you that Hagauer and I were pioneers of that era you would hold it against me!" Agathe retorted, with a smile as astringent as good dry wine.

"I no longer hold things against people," Ulrich said. He smiled. "A warrior unbuckled from his armor. For the first time since God knows when, he feels nature's air instead of hammered iron on his skin and sees his body growing so lax and frail that the birds might carry him off," he assured her.

And still smiling, simply forgetting to stop smiling, he contemplated his sister as she sat on the edge of a table, swinging one leg in its black silk stocking; aside from her chemise, she was wearing only short panties. But these were somehow fragmentary impressions, detached, solitary images, as it were. "She's my friend, in the delightful guise of a woman," Ulrich thought. "Though this *is* complicated by her really being a woman!"

And Agathe asked him: "Is there really no such thing as love?"

"Yes, there is," Ulrich said. "But it's the exception. You have to make distinctions. There is first of all a physical experience, to be classed with other irritations of the skin, a purely sensory indulgence without any requisite moral or emotional accessories. Second, emotions are usually involved, which become intensely associated with the physical experience, but in such a way that with slight variations they are the same for everyone; so that even the compulsory sameness of love's climax belongs on the physical-mechanical level rather than on that of the soul. Finally, there is also the real spiritual experience of love, which doesn't necessarily have anything to do with the other two. One can love God, one can love the world; perhaps one can *only* love God and the world. Anyway, it's not necessary to love a person. But if one does, the physical element takes over the whole world, so that it turns everything upside down, as it were. . . ." Ulrich broke off.

Agathe had flushed a dark red. If Ulrich had deliberately chosen and ordered his words with the hypocritical intention of suggesting to Agathe's imagination the physical act of love inevitably associated with them, he could not have succeeded better.

He looked around for a match, simply to undo the unintended effect of his speech by some diversion. "Anyway," he said, "love, if that is love, is an exceptional case, and can't serve as a model for everyday action."

Agathe had reached for the corners of the tablecloth and wrapped them around her legs. "Wouldn't strangers, who saw and heard us, talk about a perverse feeling?" she asked suddenly.

"Nonsense!" Ulrich maintained. "What each of us feels is the shadowy doubling of his own self in the other's opposite nature. I'm a man, you're a woman; it's widely believed that every person bears within him the shadowy or repressed opposite inclination; at least each of us has this longing, unless he's disgustingly self-satisfied. So my counterpart has come to light and slipped into you, and yours into me, and they feel marvelous in their exchanged bodies, simply because they don't have much respect for their previous environment and the view from it!"

Agathe thought: "He's gone into all that more deeply before. Why is he attenuating it now?"

What Ulrich was saying did, of course, fit quite well with the life they were leading as two companions who occasionally, when the company of others leaves them free, take time to marvel at the fact that they are man and woman but at the same time twins. Once two people find themselves in such an accord their relations with the world as individuals take on the charm of an invisible game of hide-and-seek, each switching bodies and costumes with the other, practicing their carefree two-in-one deception for an unsuspecting world behind two kinds of masks. But this playful and overemphatic fun—as children sometimes make noise instead of being noisy—was not in keeping with the gravity that sometimes, from a great height, laid its shadow on the hearts of this brother and sister, making them fall unexpectedly silent. So it happened one evening, as they exchanged a few chance words more before going to bed, that Ulrich saw his sister in her long nightgown and tried to joke about it, saying: "A hundred years ago I would have cried out: 'My angel!' Too bad the term has become obsolete!" He fell silent, disconcerted by the thought: "Isn't that the only word I should be using for her? Not friend, not wife! 'Heavenly creature!' was another term they used. Ridiculously high-flown, of course, but nevertheless better than not having the courage of one's convictions."

Agathe was thinking: "A man in pajamas doesn't look like an angel!" But he did look fierce and broad-shouldered, and she suddenly felt ashamed of her wish that this strong face framed in tousled hair might cast its shadow over her eyes. In some physically innocent way she was sensually aroused; her blood was pulsing through her body in wild waves, spreading over her skin while leaving her drained and weak inside. Since she was not such a fanatical person as her brother, she simply felt what she felt. When she was tender, she was tender, not lit up with ideas or moral impulses, even though this was something she loved in him as much as she shrank from it.

Again and again, day after day, Ulrich summed it all up in the idea: Basically, it's a protest against life! They walked arm in arm through the city: well matched in height, well matched in age, well matched in their attitude to things. Strolling along side by side, they could not see much of each other. Tall figures, pleasing to one another, they walked together for the sheer enjoyment of it, feeling at every step the breath of their contact in the midst of all the strangeness surrounding them. We belong together! This feeling, far from uncommon, made them happy, and half within it, half in resistance to it, Ulrich said: "It's funny we should be so content to be brother and sister. The world in general regards it as a commonplace relationship, but we're making something special of it!"

Perhaps he had hurt her feelings in saying this. He added: "But it's what I've always wished for. When I was a boy I made up my mind to marry only a woman I'd have adopted as a child and brought up myself. I think plenty of men have such fantasies; they're pretty banal, I suppose. But as an adult I actually once fell in love with such a child, though it was only for two or three hours!" And he went on to tell her about it:

"It happened on a streetcar. A little girl of about twelve got on, with her very young father or her older brother. The way she got on, sat down, and casually handed the fare to the conductor for both of them, she was every inch a lady, without a trace of childish affectation. It was the same when she talked to her companion, or quietly listened to him. She was extraordinarily beautiful: brunette, with full lips, strong eyebrows, a slightly turned-up nose; perhaps a dark-haired Polish girl, or a southern Slav. As I recall, the dress she was wearing suggested some national costume: long jacket, tight waist, laced bodice, and frills at the throat and wrists, all in its way as perfect as the little person herself. Perhaps she was Albanian. I was sitting too far away to be able to hear what she was saying. It struck me that the features of her grave little face were mature beyond her years, so that she seemed fully adult; yet it was not the face of a dwarfishly tiny woman, but unquestionably that of a child. On the other hand, it was not at all the immature stage of an adult's face. It seems that a woman's face may sometimes be complete at the age of twelve, formed even spiritually like a perfect first sketch from the hand of a master, so that everything added later to develop the picture only spoils its original greatness. One can fall passionately in love with such a phenomenon, mortally so, and really without any physical desire. I remember I glanced around nervously at the other passengers, because I felt as if I were falling apart. When she got off, I got off, too, but lost her in the crowded street," he ended his little story.

After giving it a moment or two, Agathe asked with a smile: "And how does that fit in with the time for love being over, leaving only sex and companionship?"

"It doesn't fit in at all!" Ulrich laughed.

His sister thought about it, and remarked with a noticeable harshness—it seemed to be an intentional repetition of the words he had used the evening of her arrival: "All men like to play at little-brother-and-little-sister. There must really be some stupid idea behind it. These little brothers and sisters call each other 'father' and 'mother' when they're not quite sober."

Ulrich was taken aback. It was not merely that Agathe was right, for gifted women are merciless observers of the men they love in their lives; but not being inclined to theorize, they make no use of their discoveries except when provoked. He felt somewhat affronted.

"Of course they've got a psychological explanation for it," he said hesitantly. "It's pretty obvious that the two of us are psychologically suspect. Incestuous tendencies, demonstrable in early childhood, together with antisocial dispositions and a rebellious attitude toward life. Possibly even a not sufficiently rooted gender identification, although I—"

"Nor I, either!" Agathe broke in, laughing, if possibly somewhat against her will. "I have no use for women at all!"

"It really doesn't matter anyway," Ulrich said. "Psychic entrails, in any case. You might also say that there's a sultanesque need to be the only one who adores and is adored, to the exclusion of the rest of the world. In the ancient Orient it produced the harem, and today we have family, love, and the dog. And I don't mind saying that the mania to possess another person so entirely that no one else can come anywhere near is a sign of personal loneliness within the human community, which even the socialists rarely deny. If you'd like to see it that way, we represent nothing but a bourgeois extravagance! Oh, look at that! How splendid!" He broke off, pulling on her arm.

They were standing at the edge of a small marketplace surrounded by old houses. Around the neoclassical statue of some intellectual giant, colorful vegetables were spread out, the big canvas umbrellas of the market stands had been set up, fruits tumbled, baskets were being dragged along, dogs chased away from the outspread treasures, and one saw the red faces of rough men and women. The air throbbed and pounded with industriously loud voices and smelled of the sun that shines on the earthly hodgepodge.

"Can we help loving the world when we simply see it and smell it?" Ulrich asked spiritedly. "Yet we can't love it, because we don't agree with what's inside people's heads," he added.

This did not happen to be a reservation entirely to Agathe's taste, and she did not reply. But she pressed her brother's arm, and both of them understood that this was as if she had gently laid her hand over his mouth.

Ulrich laughed, saying: "Not that I like myself either! That's what happens when one is always finding fault with other people. But even I have to be able to love something, and a Siamese sister who's neither me nor herself, but just as much me as herself, is clearly the only point where everything comes together for me!"

He had cheered up again. And Agathe usually went along with his mood. But they never again talked as they had on the first night of their reunion, or before. That was gone, like castles in the clouds, which, when they hover over city streets teeming with life instead of over the deserted countryside, are hard to believe in. Perhaps the cause of this was only that Ulrich did not know what degree of substantiality he should ascribe to the experiences that moved him, while Agathe often thought that he regarded them solely as excesses of fantasy. And she could not prove to him that it was not so; she always spoke less than he did, she could not hit the right note, and did not feel confident enough to try. She merely felt that he was avoiding coming to grips with it, and that he should not be doing that. So they were actually both hiding in their lighthearted happiness, which had no depth or weight, and Agathe became sadder day by day, although she laughed quite as often as her brother.

152

PROFESSOR HAGAUER TAKES PEN IN HAND

But thanks to Agathe's disregarded husband, this changed.

On a morning that brought these joyful days to an end, Agathe received a fat, official-looking letter with a great round yellow seal imprinted with the white insignia of the Imperial and Royal Rudolfsgymnasium in ———. Instantly, while she was still holding the letter unopened in her hand, there arose out of nothing two-story houses with the mute mirrors of well-polished windows; with white thermometers on the outside of their brown frames, one for each story, to tell what the weather was; with classical pediments and Baroque scallops above the windows, heads projecting from the walls, and other such mythological sentinels, which looked as if they had been produced in a wood-carving shop and painted as stone. The streets ran through the town brown and wet, just like the country roads they were on the way in, with deep ruts, and lined on both sides by shops with their brand-new display windows, looking for all that like gentlewomen of thirty years earlier who have lifted up their long skirts but cannot make up their mind to step from the sidewalk into the muddy street: the provinces in Agathe's head! Apparition in Agathe's head! Something incomprehensible still inside her, which she had been so sure of having shaken off forever! Even more incomprehensible: that she had ever been tied to it! She saw the way from her front door, past familiar housefronts, to the school, the way taken four times daily by her husband, Hagauer, which in the beginning she had often taken with him, accompanying him from his home to his work, in those days when she conscientiously did not let a drop of her bitter medicine escape. "Is Hagauer taking his lunches at the hotel these days?" she wondered. "Does he tear a page off the calender each morning, which I used to do?" It had all suddenly come back to life, so surreally vivid as if it could never die, and with a mute shudder she recognized that familiar craven feeling awakening in her that consisted of indifference, of lost courage, of saturation with ugliness, and of her own insecure volatility. With a kind of avidity, she opened the thick letter her husband had addressed to her.

When Professor Hagauer had returned to his home and workplace from his father-in-law's funeral and a brief visit to the capital, his surroundings welcomed him exactly as they always did after one of his short trips: with the agreeable awareness of his having properly accomplished his mission; and changing from his shoes into the house slippers in which a man works twice as well, he turned his attention to his environment. He went off to his school, was respectfully greeted by the porter, felt welcomed back when he met the teachers who were under him. In the administration office the files and problems no one had dared to deal with in his absence awaited him. When he hastened through the corridors he was accompanied by the feeling that his steps lent wings to the whole building: Gottlieb Hagauer was somebody, and he knew it. Encouragement and good cheer beamed from his brow throughout the educational establishment under his wing, and when anyone outside school inquired after the health and whereabouts of his wife, he replied with the serenity of a man conscious of having married creditably. Everyone knows that the male of the species, so long as he is still capable of procreation, reacts to brief interruptions of his married life as if an easy yoke has been lifted from his shoulders, even when he does not think of illicit associations in connection with it and at the end of this interlude, refreshed, resumes his happy lot. In this manner Hagauer at first accepted his wife's absence, and for a while did not even notice how long she was staying away.

What actually first drew his attention to it was that same wall calendar that had figured in Agathe's memory as such a hateful symbol of life by its needing to have a page torn off every morning. It hung in the dining room as a spot that did not belong on the wall, stranded there as a New Year's greeting from a stationery shop brought home from school by Hagauer, and because of its dreariness not only tolerated but actually cultivated by Agathe. It would have been quite true to form for Hagauer to have taken over the chore of ripping off the daily page in Agathe's absence, for it was not in keeping with his habits to let that part of the wall run wild, as it were. On the other hand, he was also a man who always knew precisely on what latitude of the week or month he found himself upon the ocean of infinity; moreover, he of course had a proper calendar in his office at school; and lastly, just as he was nevertheless about to lift his hand so as to properly regulate the time in his household, and inwardly smiling, he felt something peculiar stop him—one of those impulses through which, as it would later turn out, fate declares itself, but which at the time he merely took for a tender, chivalrous sentiment that surprised him and made him feel pleased with himself: he decided to leave untouched the page marking the day on which Agathe had left the house as a token of homage and a reminder, until her return.

So the wall calendar became in time a festering wound, reminding Hagauer at every glance how long his wife was avoiding her home. A man thrifty with his emotions as with his household, he wrote her postcards to let her know how he was and to ask her, with gradually increasing urgency, when she would be coming back. He received no answer. Now he no longer beamed in answer to sympathetic inquiries whether his wife would be away much longer in fulfillment of her sad duties. But luckily he always had a great deal to keep him busy, apart from his duties at school and the various clubs to which he belonged, since the mail daily brought him a pile of invitations, inquiries, letters from admiring readers, attacks, proofs, periodicals, and important books. Hagauer's human self might be living in the provinces, as an element in the unendearing impressions these might make on a stranger passing through, but his spirit called Europe its home, and this kept him for a long time from grasping the full significance of Agathe's prolonged absence. There came a day, however, when the mail brought him a letter from Ulrich, curtly informing him that Agathe no longer intended to return to him and asking him to agree to a divorce. Politely worded as it was, this letter was so laconic and was written with such a lack of consideration as to make Hagauer feel indignantly that Ulrich cared about his, the recipient's, feelings about as much as if he were an insect to be flicked off a leaf. His first reaction of inner defense was: Don't take it seriously, a whim! There the letter lay, like a grinning specter in the bright daylight of pressing correspondence and showers of professional recognition.

It was not until evening, when Hagauer entered his empty house again, that he sat down at his desk and in dignified brevity wrote to Ulrich that it would be best to pretend his communication had never been written. But he soon received a new letter from Ulrich, reject-ing this view of the matter, reiterating Agathe's request (without her knowledge), and merely asking Hagauer in somewhat more courte-ous detail to do all he could toward keeping the necessary legal steps simple as befitted a man of his high moral principles, and as was also desirable if the deplorable concomitants of a public dispute were to be avoided. Hagauer now grasped the seriousness of the situation, and allowed himself three days' time to compose an answer that would leave nothing to be either desired or regretted afterward.

For the first two days he felt as though someone had struck him a blow in the solar plexus. "A bad dream!" he said plaintively to himself several times, and it took great self-discipline not to let himself forget that he had really received such a request. He felt a deep discomfort in his breast very much like injured love, and an indefinable jealousy as well, which was directed not so much against a lover—which he assumed to be the cause of Agathe's behavior—as against some in-comprehensible Something that had shunted him aside. It was a kind of humiliation, similar to that of an extremely orderly man when he has broken or forgotten something; something that had had its fixed place in his mind since time immemorial and that he no longer no-ticed, but on which much depended, was suddenly smashed. Pale and distraught, in real anguish—not to be underestimated merely because it was lacking in beauty—Hagauer made his rounds, avoid-ing people, shrinking from the explanations he would have to give and the humiliations to be borne. It was only on the third day that his condition finally stabilized. Hagauer's natural dislike for Ulrich was just as great as Ulrich's for him, and while this had never before come out into the open it did so now, all at once, when he intuitively imputed all the blame for Agathe's conduct to her will-o'-the-wisp gypsy brother, who must have turned her head. He sat down at his desk and demanded in a few words the immediate return of his wife, resolutely declaring that as her husband he would only discuss any-thing further with her.

From Ulrich came a refusal, equally terse and resolute.

Now Hagauer decided to work on Agathe herself; he made copies of his correspondence with Ulrich and added a long, carefully con-sidered letter; all of this was what Agathe saw before her when she opened the large envelope with the official seal.

Hagauer himself was unable to believe that these things were really happening. Back from his daily obligations, he had sat that evening in his "deserted home," facing a blank sheet of paper much as Ulrich had faced one, not knowing how to begin. But in Hagauer's experience the tried and true "buttons method" had worked more than once, and he resorted to it again in this case. It consists in taking a systematic approach to one's problems, even problems that cause great agitation, on the same principle on which a man has buttons sewn on his clothes to save the time that would be lost if he acted on the assumption that he could get out of his clothes faster without buttons. The English writer Surway, for example, whose work on the subject Hagauer now consulted, for even in his depressed state it was important for him to compare Surway's work with his own views, distinguishes five such buttons in the process of successful reasoning: (a) close observation of an event, in which the observation immediately reveals problems of interpretation; (b) establishing such problems and defining them more narrowly; (c) hypothesis of a possible solution; (d) logically developing the consequences of this hypothesis; and (e) further observations, leading to acceptance or rejection of the hypothesis and thereby to a successful outcome of the thinking process. Hagauer had already profitably applied a similar method to so worldly an enterprise as lawn tennis when he was learning the game at the Civil Service Club, and it had lent considerable intellectual charm to the game for him; but he had never yet resorted to this method for purely emotional matters, since his ordinary inner life consisted mainly of professional concerns, and for personal events he relied on that "sound instinct" which is a mix of all the possible feelings acceptable and customary to the Caucasian race in any given situation, with a certain bias toward the most proximate local, professional, or class feelings. Applying the buttons to so extraordinary a situation as his wife's extraordinary demand was not going to be easy given his lack of practice, and in cases of personal problems even the "sound instinct" shows a tendency to split in two: It told Hagauer on the one hand that much obliges a man who moved with the times as he did to put no obstacles in the way of a proposal to dissolve a relationship based on trust; but on the other hand, if this goes against the grain, much also absolves him of such an obligation, for the widespread irresponsibility in such matters nowadays should in no way be encouraged. In such a case, as Hagauer had learned, it behooves a modern man to "relax," i.e., disperse his attention, loosen up physically, and listen intently for whatever may be audible of his deepest inner self. So he cautiously stopped thinking, stared at the orphaned wall calendar, and hearkened to his inner voice; after a while it answered, coming from a depth beneath his conscious mind, and told him what he had already thought: the voice said that he had no reason whatsoever to put up with anything so unjustifiable as Agathe's preposterous demand.

But at this point Professor Hagauer's mind found itself set down willy-nilly in front of Surway's buttons *a* to *e*, or some equivalent series of buttons, and he felt afresh all the difficulties of interpreting the event under his observation. "Can I, Gottlieb Hagauer, possibly be to blame for this embarrassing business?" he asked himself. He examined himself and could not find a single point on which he could be faulted. "Is the cause another man she is in love with?" was his second hypothesis toward a possible solution. It was an assumption he had difficulty accepting, for if he forced himself to look at the matter objectively, he could not really see what another man could offer Agathe that was better than what he did. Still, this problem was especially susceptible to being muddied by personal vanity, so he studied it in exacting detail; and here he found vistas opening up that he had never even thought of. Suddenly, from Surway's point *c*, Hagauer found himself on the track of a possible solution via *d* and *e*: for the first time since his marriage, he was struck by a complex of phenomena reported, as far as he knew, only in women whose erotic response to the opposite sex was never deep or passionate. It pained him to find nowhere in his memories any indication of that completely openhearted, dreamy surrender he had experienced earlier, in his bachelor years, with females about whose sensual bent there could be no doubt; but this offered the advantage of enabling him to rule out, with absolute scientific detachment, the destruction of his marital bliss by a third party. Agathe's conduct was reduced, in consequence, to a purely idiosyncratic rebellion against their happiness, all the more so because she had left without giving the slightest hint of such intentions, and there simply had not been enough time since then for her to develop a rational basis for changing her mind! Hagauer had to conclude, and this conviction never left him, that

Agathe's incomprehensible behavior could only be understood as one of those slowly building temptations to turn one's back on life, known to occur in characters who do not know what they want.

But was Agathe really that sort of person? That still remained to be investigated, and Hagauer pensively weeded his whiskers with the end of his pen. Though she usually seemed companionable enough, easy to live with, as he put it, still, when it came to what most preoccupied him, she tended to show a marked indifference, not to say apathy! There was in fact something in her that did not fit in with himself or other people and their interests; not that she set herself up against them. She laughed along with them and looked serious in the right places, but she had always, now that he came to think of it, made a somewhat distracted impression through all these years. She seemed to be listening attentively to what she was told, yet never to believe it. There was something downright unhealthy about her indifference, the more he thought about it. Sometimes one got the impression that she was not taking in what was going on around her at all. . . . And all at once, before he was aware of it himself, his pen had begun to race over the paper with his purposeful motion. "Who can guess what may be going on in your mind," he wrote, "if you think yourself too good to love the life I am in a position to offer you, which I can say in all modesty is a pure and full life; you've always handled it as if with fire tongs, as it now seems to me. You have shut yourself off from the riches of human and moral values that even an unassuming life has to offer, and even if I had to believe that you could somehow have felt justified in doing this, there is still your lack of the moral will to change; instead, you have chosen an artificial way out, a fantasy!"

He mulled it over once more. He mustered the schoolboys who had passed through his guiding hands, searching for a case that might be instructive. But even before he had got into this, there popped into his mind the missing bit that had been uneasily hovering in the back of his mind. At this point Agathe ceased to be a completely personal problem for him, without any clues to its general nature, for when he thought how much she was ready to give up in life without being blinded by any specific passion he was led inescapably, to his joy, to that basic assumption so familiar to modern pedagogy, that she lacked the capacity for objective thought and for keeping in firm intellectual touch with the world of reality! Swiftly he wrote: "Probably you are even at this moment far from being aware of what it is, exactly, that you are about to do; but I warn you, before you come to a decisive conclusion! You are perhaps the absolute opposite of the kind of person, such as I represent, who knows life and knows how to face it, but that is precisely why you should not lightly divest yourself of the support I offer you!"

Actually, Hagauer had meant to write something else. For human intelligence is not a self-contained and unrelated faculty; its flaws involve moral flaws—we speak of moral idiocy—just as moral flaws, though so much less attention is paid to them, often misdirect or totally confuse the rational power in whatever direction they choose. And so Hagauer had formed in his mind an image of a fixed type that he was now inclined, in the course of these reflections, to define as "an adequately intelligent variant of moral idiocy that expresses itself only in certain irregular forms of behavior." But he could not bring himself to use this illuminating phrase, partly to avoid provoking his runaway wife even more, and partly because a layperson usually misunderstands such terms when applied to himself. Objectively, however, it was now established that the forms of behavior that Hagauer deprecated came under the great inclusive genus of the "subnormal," and in the end Hagauer hit upon a way out of this conflict between conscience and chivalry: the irregularities in his wife's conduct could be classified with a fairly general pattern of female behavior and termed "socially deficient."

In this spirit he concluded his letter in words charged with feeling. With the prophetic ire of the scorned lover and pedagogue, he depicted Agathe's asocial, solipsistic, and morbid temperament as a "minus factor" that never permitted her to grapple vigorously and creatively with life's problems, as "our era" demands of "its people," but "shielded her instead from reality behind a pane of glass," mired in deliberate isolation and always on the edge of pathological peril. "If there was something about me you didn't like, you ought to have done something about it," he wrote, "but the truth is that your mind is not equipped to cope with the energies of our time, and evades its demands! Now that I have warned you about your character," he concluded, "I repeat: You, more urgently than most people, need someone strong to lean on. In your own interest I urge you to come back immediately, and I assure you that the responsibility I bear as your husband forbids me to accede to your wish."

Before signing this letter Hagauer read it through once more. Although not satisfied with his description of the psychological type under discussion, he made no changes except at the end—expelling as a gusty sigh through his mustache the unaccustomed, proudly mastered strain of thinking hard about his wife as he pondered how much more still needed to be said about "our modern age"—where he inserted beside the word "responsibility" a chivalrous phrase about his venerated late father-in-law's precious bequest to him.

When Agathe had read all this, a strange thing happened: the content of these arguments did not fail to make an impression on her. After reading it word for word a second time, where she stood, without bothering to sit down, she slowly lowered the letter and handed it to Ulrich, who had been observing his sister's agitation with astonishment.

153

ULRICH AND AGATHE LOOK FOR A REASON AFTER THE FACT

While Ulrich was reading, Agathe dispiritedly watched his face. It was bent over the letter, and its expression seemed to be irresolute, as though he could not decide between ridicule, gravity, sadness, or contempt. Now a heavy weight descended on Agathe from all sides, as if the air that had been so unnaturally light and delicious were becoming unbearably dense and sultry; what she had done to her father's will oppressed her conscience for the first time. To say that she suddenly realized the full measure of her culpability would not be sufficient; what she realized rather was her guilt toward everything, even her brother, and she was overcome with an indescribable disillusionment. Everything she had done seemed incomprehensible to her. She had talked of killing her husband, she had falsified a will, and she had imposed herself on her brother without asking whether she would be disrupting his life: she had done this in a state of being drunk on her own fantasies. What she was most ashamed of at this moment was that it had never occurred to her to do the obvious, the most natural thing: any other woman who wanted to leave a husband she did not like would either look for a better man or arrange for something else, something equally natural. Ulrich himself had pointed this out often enough, but she had paid no attention. And now here she stood and did not know what he would say. Her behavior seemed to her so much that of a being who was not entirely mentally competent that she thought Hagauer was right; he was only holding up the mirror to her in his own way. Seeing his letter in Ulrich's hand struck her dumb in the same way a person might be struck dumb who had been charged with a crime and on top of that receives a letter from a former teacher excoriating him. She had of course never allowed Hagauer to have any influence over her; nevertheless, it now looked as if he had the right to say: "I'm disappointed in you!" or else: "I'm afraid I've never been disappointed in you but always had the feeling you'd come to a bad end!" In her need to shake off this absurd and distressing feeling she impatiently interrupted Ulrich, who was still absorbed in reading the letter without giving any sign of coming to the end, by saying: "His description of me is really quite accurate." She spoke in an apparently casual tone but with a note of defiance, clearly betraying some hope of hearing the opposite. "And even if he doesn't say it in so many words, it's true; either I was not mentally competent when I married him for no compelling reason, or I am not so now, when I'm leaving him for just as little reason."

Ulrich, who was rereading for the third time those passages that made his vivid imagination an involuntary witness of her close relations with Hagauer, absently muttered something she did not catch.

"Do please listen to me!" Agathe pleaded. "Am I the up-to-date woman, active somehow either economically or intellectually? No. Am I a woman in love? No again. Am I the good, nest-building wife and mother who simplifies things and smooths over the rough spots? That least of all. What else is there? Then what in the world am I good for? The social life we're caught up in, I can tell you frankly, basically means nothing at all to me. And I almost think I could get along without whatever it is in music, art, and literature that sends the cognoscenti into raptures. Hagauer, for instance, is different: he needs all that, if only for his quotations and allusions. He at least has the pleasure and satisfaction of a collector. So isn't he right when he accuses me of doing nothing at all, of rejecting the 'wealth of the beautiful and moral,' and tells me that it's only with Professor Hagauer that I can find any sympathy and tolerance?"

Ulrich handed the letter back to her and replied with composure. "Let's face it, the term for you is 'socially retarded,' isn't it?" He smiled, but there was in his tone a hint of irritation left from his having been made privy to this intimate letter.

But her brother's answer did not sit well with Agathe. It made her feel worse. Shyly she tried to turn the tables on him: "In that case why did you insist, if that is what you did, without telling me anything, that I must get a divorce and lose my only protector?"

"Well," he said evasively, "probably because it is so delightfully easy to adopt a firm, manly tone in our exchanges. I bang *my* fist on the table, he bangs *his* fist on the table; so of course I have to bang mine twice as hard the next time around. That's why I think I did it."

Up to now—although her dejection kept her from realizing it herself—Agathe had been really glad, overjoyed in fact, at her brother's secretly doing the opposite of what he had outwardly advocated during the time of their humorous brother-sister flirtation, since offending Hagauer could only have the effect of erecting a barrier to her ever returning to him. Yet even in the place of that secret joy there was now only a hollow sense of loss, and Agathe fell silent.

"We mustn't overlook," Ulrich went on, "how well Hagauer succeeds in misunderstanding you so accurately, if I may say so. Just wait, you'll see that in his own way—without hiring detectives, just by cogitating over the weaknesses of your attachment to the human race—he'll find out what you did to Father's will. How are we going to defend you then?"

So it happened that for the first time since they had been together again the subject came up of the blissful but horrible prank Agathe had played on Hagauer. She fiercely shrugged her shoulders, with a vague gesture of waving it aside.

"Hagauer is in the right, of course," Ulrich offered, with gentle emphasis, for her consideration.

"He's not in the right!" she answered vehemently.

"He's partly right," Ulrich compromised. "In so risky a situation we must start off by facing things openly, including ourselves. What you've done can put us both in jail."

Agathe stared at him with startled eyes. She had known this, of course, but it had never been so straightforwardly stated.

Ulrich responded with a reassuring gesture. "But that's not the worst of it," he continued. "How do we keep what you've done, and the way you did it, from being perceived as"—he groped for the right word and failed to find it—"well, let's just say that to some extent it's the way Hagauer sees it, that it's all a bit on the shadowy side, the side of abnormality and the kind of flaw that comes from something already flawed. Hagauer voices what the world thinks, even though it sounds ridiculous coming from him."

"Now we're getting to the cigarette case," Agathe said in a small voice.

"Right, here it comes," Ulrich said firmly. "I have to tell you something that's been on my mind for a long time."

Agathe tried to stop him. "Wouldn't it be better to undo the whole thing?" she asked. "Suppose I have a friendly talk with him and make some sort of apology?"

"It's already too late for that. He might use it to blackmail you into coming back to him," Ulrich declared.

Agathe was silent.

Ulrich returned to his hypothetical cigarette case, stolen on a whim by a man who is well off. He had worked out a theory that there could be only three basic motivations for such a theft of property: poverty, profession, or, if it was neither of these, a damaged psyche. "You pointed out when we talked about it once that it might be done out of conviction too," he added.

"I said one might just do it!" Agathe interjected.

"Right, on principle."

"No, not on principle!"

"But that's just it!" Ulrich said. "If one does such a thing at all, there has to be at least some conviction behind it! There's no getting away from that. Nobody 'just does' anything; there has to be a reason, either an external or an internal one. It may be hard to know one from the other, but we won't philosophize about that now. I'm only saying that if one feels one is doing the right thing with absolutely no basis for it, or some decision arises out of the blue, then there's good reason to suspect some sickness, something constitutionally wrong."

This was certainly far more and much worse than Ulrich had meant to say; it merely converged with the drift of his qualms.

"Is that all you have to say to me about it?" Agathe asked very quietly.

"No, it's not all," Ulrich replied grimly. "When one has no reason, one must look for one!"

Neither of them was in any doubt where to look for it. But Ulrich was after something else, and after a slight pause he continued thoughtfully: "The moment you fall out of step with the rest of the world, you can never ever know what's good and what's evil. If you want to be good you have to be convinced that the world is good. And neither one of us is. We're living at a time when morality is either dissolving or in convulsions. But for the sake of a world yet to come, one should keep oneself pure."

"Do you really think that will have any effect on whether it comes or not?" Agathe asked skeptically.

"No, I'm afraid I don't think that. Or at most I think like this: If even those people who understand don't act as they should, it certainly won't come at all, and there's no way to stop everything from falling apart!"

"And what do you care whether it's any different five hundred years from now or not?"

Ulrich hesitated. "I'm doing my duty, don't you see? Maybe like a soldier."

Probably because on that miserable morning Agathe needed a more comforting, more affectionate kind of answer than Ulrich was giving, she said: "No different from your General, then?"

Ulrich said nothing.

Agathe was not inclined to stop. "You don't even know for sure whether it's your duty," she went on. "You do it because that's how you are and because you enjoy it. And that's all I did!"

Suddenly she lost her self-control. Something was terribly sad.

Tears sprang to her eyes, and a violent sob rose in her throat. To hide it from her brother's eyes, she threw her arms around his neck and hid her face against his shoulder. Ulrich felt her crying and the trembling of her back. A burdensome embarrassment came over him: he was aware of turning cold. At this moment, when he should have been sympathetic, all the tender and happy feelings he thought he had for his sister deserted him; his sensibility was disturbed and wouldn't function. He stroked Agathe's back and whispered some comforting words, but it went against his grain. Since he did not share her agitation, the contact of their two bodies seemed to him like that of two wisps of straw. He put an end to it by leading Agathe to a chair and himself sitting down in another, some distance away. Then he gave her his answer: "You're not enjoying this business with the will at all. And you never shall, because it's all been a disorderly mess!"

"Order?" Agathe exclaimed through her tears. "Duty?"

She was really quite beside herself because Ulrich had behaved so coldly. But she was already smiling again. She realized that she would have to work things out for herself. She felt that the smile she had forced seemed to be hovering somewhere out there, far from her icy lips. Ulrich meanwhile had shaken off his embarrassment; he was even pleased not to have felt the usual physical stirring; he realized that this, too, would have to be different between them. But he did not have time to think about that now, because he could see that Agathe was deeply troubled, and so he began to talk.

"Don't be upset by the words I used," he pleaded, "and don't hold them against me. I suppose I'm wrong to use words such as 'order' and 'duty'—they sound too much like preaching. But why"—he now went off at a tangent—"why the devil is preaching contemptible? It really ought to be our greatest joy!"

Agathe had no desire to answer this.

Ulrich let it drop.

"Please don't think I'm trying to set myself up as morally superior!" he begged. "I didn't mean to say that I never do anything bad. What I don't like is having to do it in secret. I like the good highway robbers of morality, not the sneak thieves. I'd like to make a moral robber out of you," he joked, "and not let you err out of weakness."

"It's not a point of honor with me," his sister said from behind her distantly hovering smile.

"It's really extremely funny that there are times like ours, when all young people are infatuated with whatever's bad," he said with a laugh, to distance the conversation from the personal level. "This current preference for the morally gruesome is a weakness, of course. Probably middle-class gorging on goodness; being all sucked dry. I myself originally thought one had to say no to everything; everyone thinks so who is between twenty-five and forty-five today; but of course it was only a kind of fashion. I can imagine a reaction setting in soon, and with it a new generation that will again stick morality instead of immorality in its buttonhole. The oldest donkeys, who never in their lives felt any moral fervor, who merely uttered moral platitudes when the occasion called for them, will then suddenly be hailed as precursors and pioneers of a new character!"

Ulrich had risen to his feet and was restlessly pacing the room.

"We might put it this way," he suggested. "Good has become a cliché almost by its very nature, while evil remains criticism. The immoral achieves its divine right by being a drastic critique of the moral! It shows us that life has other possibilities. It shows us up for liars. For this we show our gratitude by a certain forbearance. That there are truly delightful people who forge wills should prove that there is something amiss with the sanctity of private property. Even if this doesn't need proving, it is where our task begins: for every kind of crime, we must be able to conceive of criminals who can be excused, even including infanticide or whatever other horrors there may be. . . ."

He had been trying in vain to catch his sister's eye, even though he was teasing her by bringing up the will. Now she made an involuntary gesture of protest. She was no theoretician; the only crime she regarded as excusable was her own, and she was insulted all over again by his comparison.

Ulrich laughed. "It looks like an intellectual game, but this kind of juggling does mean something," he assured her. "It goes to show that there's something amiss in the way we judge our conduct. And there really is, you know. In a company of will-forgers you would certainly stand up for the inviolability of the legal regulations; it's only in the company of the righteous that it all gets blurred and perverted. If only Hagauer were a rogue, you would be flamingly just; it's too bad he's such a decent fellow! That's the seesaw we're on."

He waited for a response but none came, so he shrugged his shoulders and came back to the point:

"We're looking to justify what you did. We have established that respectable people are deeply attracted to crime, though of course only in their imagination. We might add that criminals, to hear them talk, would almost without exception like to be regarded as respectable people. So we might arrive at a definition: Crimes are the concentrated form, within sinners, of everything other people work off in little irregularities, in their imagination and in innumerable petty everyday acts and attitudes of spite and viciousness. We could also say: Crimes are in the air and simply seek the path of least resistance, which leads them to certain individuals. We could even say that while they are the acts of individuals who are incapable of behaving morally, in the main they're the condensed expression of some kind of general human maladjustment where the distinction between good and evil is concerned. This is what has imbued us from our youth with the critical spirit our contemporaries have never been able to get beyond!"

"But what is good and evil?" Agathe tossed off the question, while Ulrich remained oblivious to the pain his banter was causing her.

"Well, how would I know?" he answered with a laugh. "I've only just noticed for the first time that I loathe evil. Until today I really didn't know how much. My dear Agathe, you have no idea what it's like," he complained moodily. "Take science, for instance! For a mathematician, to put it very simply, minus five is no worse than plus five. A scientist researching a problem mustn't recoil in horror from anything, and under certain conditions he might get more excited by a lovely cancer than a lovely woman. A man of knowledge knows that nothing is true and that the whole truth will be revealed only at the end of time. Science is amoral. All our glorious thrusting of ourselves into the Unknown gets us out of the habit of being personally concerned with our conscience; in fact, it doesn't even give us the satisfaction of taking our conscience entirely seriously. And art? Doesn't it amount to a creation of images that don't correspond to the realities of life? I'm not talking about bogus idealism, or the paintings of voluptuous nudes in a period when everyone goes around covered up to the eyeballs," he joked again. "But think of a real work of art: have you never had the feeling that something about it is reminiscent of the smell of burning metal you get from a knife you're whetting on a grindstone? It's a cosmic, meteoric, lightning-and-thunder smell, something divinely uncanny!"

This was the only point at which Agathe interrupted him with real interest: "Didn't you once write poetry yourself?" she asked him.

"You still remember that? When did I let you in on it?" Ulrich asked. "Yes; we all write verses at one time or another. I even went on doing it when I was a mathematician," he admitted. "But the older I got, the worse they became; not so much because of lack of talent, I think, as from a growing aversion to the disorderly and bohemian romanticism of that sort of emotional excess. . . ."

His sister shook her head almost imperceptibly, but Ulrich noticed it. "Yes," he insisted, "a poem should be no more of an exceptional phenomenon than an act of goodness! But what, if I may ask, becomes of the moment of inspiration the moment after? You love poetry, I know; but what I'm saying is that it isn't enough to breathe out one great puff of fire and let it fade away. This kind of sporadic performance is the counterpart of the kind of morality that exhausts itself in half-baked criticism." And abruptly returning to his main subject, he said to his sister: "If I were to behave in this Hagauer matter the way you're expecting me to today, I would have to be skeptical, casual, and ironic. The exemplary children you or I might yet have would then be able to say truthfully of us that we belonged to a very secure period of middle-class values that was never plagued by doubts, or plagued at most by superficial doubts. But in fact you and I have already gone to such trouble over our philosophy . . . !"

Ulrich probably wanted to say a great deal more; he was actually only leading up to some way of coming down on his sister's side, which he had already worked out, and it would have been good if he had revealed it to her. For she suddenly stood up and on some vague pretext got her outdoor things.

"So we're leaving it that I'm morally retarded?" she asked with a forced attempt at humor. "I can't keep up with all you've been saying to the contrary!"

"We're both morally retarded!" Ulrich gallantly assured her. "Both of us!" And he was rather proud of the haste with which his sister left him without saying when she would return.

154

AGATHE WANTS TO COMMIT SUICIDE AND
MAKES A GENTLEMAN'S ACQUAINTANCE

In truth she had rushed off to spare her brother the sight of the tears she could barely hold back. She was as sad as a person who has lost everything. She did not know why. It had come over her while Ulrich was talking. Why? She didn't know that either. He should have done something other than talk. What? She didn't know. He was right, of course, not to take seriously the "stupid coincidence" of her being upset and the arrival of that letter, and to go on talking as he always did. But Agathe had to get away.

At first she felt only the need to walk. She rushed headlong from their house. Where the layout of the streets forced her to detour, she always kept to the same general direction. She fled, in the way people and animals flee from a catastrophe. Why, she did not ask herself. It was only when she grew tired that she realized what she intended to do: never go back!

She would keep walking until dusk. Farther from home with every step. She assumed that by the time she came up against the barricade of evening her decision would be made. The decision was to kill herself. It was not an actual decision to kill herself, but the expectation that by evening it would be. Behind this expectation was a desperate seething and whirling inside her head. She did not even have anything with her to kill herself with. Her little poison capsule lay somewhere in a drawer or in a suitcase. The only clear thing about her death was the longing never to have to go back again. She wanted to walk out of life. That was where the walking came from. It was as if every step she took was already a step out of life.

As she tired she began to long for green fields and woods, for walking in silence and the open air. She could not get there on foot. She took a streetcar. She had been brought up to control herself in public. So her voice betrayed no emotion when she bought her ticket and asked for directions. She sat straight-backed and impassive, with not

a finger twitching. And as she sat there the thoughts started coming.
She would of course have felt better had she been able to let herself
go; with her limbs fettered as they were, these thoughts came in
large bundles that she vainly tried to force through an opening. She
bore Ulrich a grudge for what he had said. She didn't want to hold it
against him. She gave up her right to. What had she done for him?
She was only taking up his time, and doing nothing for him in return;
she was in the way of his work and his habits. When she thought of
his habits she felt a pang. It seemed that no woman had entered his
house in all the time she'd been there. Agathe was convinced that her
brother always had to have a woman in his life. So he was depriving
himself for her sake. At this moment she would have liked to turn
back and tenderly beg his forgiveness. As there was no way she could
make it up to him, she was being selfish and bad. But then she remembered again how cold he had been. He was obviously sorry he
had taken her in. To think of all he had planned and said before he
got tired of her! Now he no longer mentioned any of it. Agathe's
heart was again tormented with the great disillusionment her husband's letter had brought her. She was jealous. Senselessly and commonly jealous. She would have liked to force herself on her brother;
she felt the passionate and helpless friendship of the person throwing
himself against his own rejection. "I could steal or walk the streets
for him!" she thought, knowing this was ridiculous but not able to
help it. Ulrich's conversations, with their humor and sovereign air of
being above the battle, made a mockery of this idea. She admired his
superiority and all his intellectual needs, which surpassed her own.
But she didn't see why every idea always had to be equally true for
everyone! In her humbled state she needed some personal comforting, not edifying sermons! She did not want to be brave! And after a
while, she reproached herself for being the way she was, and en-
larged her pain by imagining that she deserved nothing better than
Ulrich's indifference.

This self-denigration, for which neither Ulrich's conduct nor even
Hagauer's upsetting letter was sufficient cause, was a temperamental
outburst. Ever since Agathe had outgrown her childhood, not so very
long ago, everything she regarded as her failure in the face of society's demands had had to do with her sense of not living in accord
with her own deepest inclinations, or even in opposition to them. She

inclined to devotion and trustfulness, for she had never become so
much at home in solitude as her brother; and if she had found it impossible to yield herself heart and soul to a person or a cause, it was
because she had the capacity for some greater devotion, whether it
reached out to the whole world or to God. There is the well-known
path of devotion to all mankind that begins with an inability to get
along with one's neighbor, and just so may a deep latent yearning for
God arise in an antisocial character equipped with a great capacity
for love; in that sense, the religious criminal is no greater paradox
than the religious old woman who never found a husband. Agathe's
behavior toward Hagauer, which had the absurd appearance of a
selfish action, was as much the outburst of an impatient will as was
the intensity with which she accused herself of losing life by her own
weakness just when she had been awakened to it by her brother.

She soon lost patience with the slow, rumbling streetcar. When
the buildings along the way grew lower and more rural, she got off
and continued the rest of the way on foot. The courtyards were open;
through archways and over low fences came glimpses of handymen
at their chores, animals, children at play. The air was filled with a
peace in whose distances voices sounded and tools banged; sounds
moved in the bright air with the irregular, gentle motions of a butterfly, while Agathe felt herself gliding like a shadow past them toward
the rising ground of vineyards and woodland. Just once she paused,
in front of a yard where coopers were at work and there was the good
noise of mallets hammering on barrel staves. She had always liked
watching such honest work and taken pleasure in the modest, sensible, well-considered labor of the workmen. This time, too, she could
not get enough of the rhythm of the mallets and the men's moving
round and round the barrel. For a few moments it made her forget
her misery and plunged her into a pleasant, unthinking oneness with
the world. She always admired people who could do this kind of task,
with skills developed so variously and naturally out of a generally acknowledged need. But there was nothing she wanted to do herself,
although she had all kinds of mental and practical aptitudes. Life was
complete without her. And suddenly, before she saw the connection,
she heard church bells ringing, and could barely restrain herself from
bursting into tears again. Both bells of the little local church had
probably been chiming the whole time, but Agathe just now noticed

it and was instantly overcome by how these useless chimes, excluded from the good, lavish earth and flying passionately through the air, were related to her own existence.

She hastily resumed walking, and accompanied by the chimes, which now would not leave her ears, she passed swiftly between the last of the houses and emerged where the road climbed the hillside with its vineyards and scattered bushes lining the paths below, while above, the bright green of the woods beckoned. Now she knew where she was going, and it was a beautiful feeling, as though with every step she were sinking more deeply into nature. Her heart pounded with joy and effort when she sometimes stopped and found the bells still accompanying her, though now hidden high in the air and scarcely audible. It seemed to her she had never heard bells chiming like this in the midst of an ordinary day, for no apparent festive reason, mingling democratically with the natural and self-sufficient affairs of men. But of all the tongues of this thousand-voiced city, this was the last to speak to her, and something in it seized hold of her as if to lift her high and swing her up the hill, only to drop her again as it faded into a slight metallic sound no better than all the chirping, rumbling, and rustling sounds of the countryside. So Agathe climbed and walked upward for perhaps another hour, until she suddenly found herself facing the little shrubby wilderness she had carried in her memory. It enclosed a neglected grave at the edge of the woods, where nearly a hundred years before a poet had killed himself and where, in accordance with his last wish, he had also been laid to rest. Ulrich had said that he was not a good poet, even if he was famous. Ulrich was sharply critical of the rather shortsighted poetics that expressed a longing to be *buried high up with a view*. But Agathe had loved the inscription on the big stone slab since the day they had come this way and together deciphered the beautiful, rain-worn Biedermeier lettering, and she leaned over the black chain fence with its great angular links, which marked off the rectangle of death from life.

"I meant nothing to all of you" were the words the disgruntled poet had had inscribed on his gravestone, and Agathe thought that this could equally well be said of herself. This thought, here on the edge of the wooded pulpit above the greening vineyards and the alien, immeasurable city that was slowly waving its trails of smoke in the morning sun, moved her afresh. Impulsively she knelt down to press her forehead against one of the stone posts that held the chains; the unaccustomed position and the cool touch of the stone feigned the rather stiff and passive tranquillity of the death that was awaiting her. She tried to pull herself together, but was not immediately successful; bird calls intruded on her ear, so many and such various bird calls that it surprised her; branches stirred, and since she did not feel the wind she had the impression that the trees were waving their branches of their own accord. In a sudden hush, a faint pattering could be heard; the stone she was resting against, touching, was so smooth that she felt that a piece of ice between it and her forehead was keeping her from quite touching it. Only after a while did she realize that what distracted her was precisely what she was trying to hold on to, that fundamental sense of being superfluous which, reduced to its simplest terms, could be expressed only in the words that life was so complete without her that she had no business being in it. This cruel feeling contained, at bottom, neither despair nor offense, but was rather a listening and looking on that Agathe had always known; it was just that she had no impulse, indeed no possibility, of taking a hand in her own fate. This state of exclusion was almost a shelter, just as there is a kind of astonishment that forgets to ask questions. She could just as well go away. Where to? There really must be a Somewhere. Agathe was not one of those people who can find satisfaction in their conviction of the emptiness of all illusions, which, as a way of accepting a disappointing fate, is equivalent to a militant and spiteful asceticism. She was generous and uncritical in such matters, unlike Ulrich, who subjected all his feelings to the most relentless scrutiny in order to outlaw any that did not pass the test. She was simply stupid! That's what she told herself. She didn't want to think things over! Defiantly she pressed her forehead against the iron chains, which gave a little and then stiffened in resistance. During these last weeks she had somehow begun to believe in God again, but without thinking of Him. Certain states of mind, in which she perceived the world differently from what it appeared to be, in such a way that even she lived no longer shut out but completely enveloped in a radiant certainty, had been brought, under Ulrich's influence, to something akin to an inward metamorphosis, a total transformation.

She would have been willing to imagine a God who opens up His world like a hiding place. But Ulrich said that this was not necessary, it could only do harm to imagine more than one could experience. And it was for him to decide in these matters. But then, it was also for him to guide her without abandoning her. He was the threshold between two lives, and all her longing for the one and all her flight from the other led first to him. She loved him as shamelessly as one loves life. When she opened her eyes in the morning, he awoke in every limb of her body. He was looking at her even now, from the dark mirror of her anguish: which made Agathe remember that she wanted to kill herself. She had a feeling that it was to spite him that she had run away to God when she had left home to kill herself. But that intention now seemed exhausted, to have sunk back to its source, which was that Ulrich had hurt her feelings. She was angry with him, she still felt that, but the birds were singing, and now she heard them again. She was just as confused as before, but it was now a joyful confusion. She wanted to do something, but it should strike out at Ulrich, not just at herself. The endless stupor in which she had been kneeling gave way to the warmth of the blood streaming back into her limbs as she rose to her feet.

When she looked up, a man was standing beside her. She was embarrassed, not knowing how long he had been watching her. As her glance, still dark with agitation, met his, she saw that he was looking at her with unconcealed sympathy, manifestly hoping to inspire her with wholehearted confidence. The man was tall and lean and wore dark clothes, and a short blond beard covered his cheeks and chin. Beneath his mustache one could easily make out full, soft lips, which were in remarkably youthful contrast to the many gray hairs already scattered among the blond ones, as if age had forgotten them in the growth of hair. It was altogether not an easy face to read. The first impression led one to think of a secondary-school teacher; the severity in this face was not carved in hardwood but rather resembled something soft that had hardened under petty daily frustrations. But if one started with this softness, on which the manly beard seemed to have been planted in order to adjust it to a system with which the wearer concurred, then one realized that this originally rather effeminate face showed hard, almost ascetic details, clearly the work of a relentlessly active will upon the soft basic material.

Agathe did not know what to make of this face, which left her suspended between attraction and repulsion; all she understood was that this man wanted to help her.

"Life offers us just as much opportunity to strengthen the will as to weaken it," the stranger said, wiping his glasses, which had been misted over, in order to see her better. "One should never run away from problems, but try to master them!" Agathe stared at him in surprise. He had obviously been watching her for quite some time, because his words were emerging from the middle of some interior monologue. Startled by his own voice, he raised his hat, his manners belatedly catching up with this essential gesture of courtesy, then quickly regained his composure and went straight on: "Do forgive my asking whether I may be of some help," he said. "It seems to me that it is truly easier to speak of one's pain to a stranger, even concerning a grave shock to the self, such as I believe I am witnessing here?"

Evidently it was not without effort that the stranger spoke to her; apparently he had felt called upon to do so out of duty, as an act of charity; and now that he found himself walking beside this beautiful woman, he was literally struggling for words. For Agathe had simply stood up and begun slowly to walk with him away from the grave and out from under the trees into the open space at the edge of the hills, neither of them deciding whether they wanted to choose one of the paths leading downward, or which one. Instead, they walked along the hilltop for quite a distance, talking, then turned back, and then turned back to walk in the original direction once more; neither of them knew where the other had meant to go originally, and neither wanted to interfere with the other's plans.

"Won't you tell me why you were crying?" the stranger persisted, in the mild tones of a physician asking where it hurts.

Agathe shook her head. "It wouldn't be easy to explain," she said, and suddenly asked him: "But tell me something else: What makes you so sure you can help me without knowing me? I'd be inclined to think that one can't help anyone!"

Her companion did not answer right away. He opened his mouth to speak several times, but seemed to force himself to hold back. Finally, he said: "One can probably only help someone who is suffering from something one has experienced oneself."

He fell silent. Agathe laughed at the thought that this man could suppose himself to have been through what she was suffering, which would have been repellent to him had he known what it was. But her companion seemed not to hear this laugh, or to regard it as a rudeness born of nerves. After a pause, he said calmly: "Of course, I don't mean that anyone has a right to imagine that he can tell anyone else what to do. But you see, fear in a catastrophe is infectious—and successful escape is also infectious! I mean just having escaped as from a fire, when everyone has lost his head and run into the flames: what an immense help when a single person stands outside, waving, does nothing but wave and shout incomprehensibly that there is a way out. . . ."

Agathe nearly laughed again at the horrible ideas this kindly man harbored; but just because they seemed so out of character, they molded his wax-soft face almost uncannily.

"You talk like a fireman!" she retorted, deliberately adopting the teasing, frivolous tone of high society to hide her curiosity. "Still, you must have formed some notion of the kind of catastrophe I'm involved in, surely?" Unintentionally, the seriousness of her scorn showed through, for the simple idea that this man presumed to offer her help aroused her indignation by the equally simple gratitude that welled up in her. The stranger looked at her in astonishment, then collected himself and said almost in rebuke: "You are probably still too young to know how simple life is. It only becomes hopelessly confused when one is thinking of oneself; but as soon as one stops thinking of oneself and asks oneself how to help someone else, it's quite simple!"

Agathe thought it over in silence. And whether it was her silence or the inviting distance into which his words took wing, the stranger went on, without looking at her:

"It's a modern superstition to overestimate the personal. There's so much talk today about cultivating one's personality, living one's life to the full, and affirming life. But all this fuzzy and ambiguous verbiage only betrays the user's need to befog the real meaning of his protest. What, exactly, is to be affirmed? Anything and everything, higgledy-piggledy? Evolution is always associated with resistance, an American thinker has said. We cannot develop one side of our nature without stunting another. Then what's to be lived to the full? The mind or the instincts? Every passing whim or one's character? Self-ishness or love? If our higher nature is to fulfill itself, the lower must learn renunciation and obedience!"

Agathe was considering why it should be simpler to take care of others than of oneself. She was one of those completely nonegotistical characters who may always be thinking about themselves, but not for their own benefit, which differs far more from the usual selfishness, which is always on the lookout for its own advantage, than does the complacent unselfishness of those who are always worrying about their fellow human beings. So what her companion was saying was at bottom foreign to her nature, and yet it somehow moved her, and the words he seized hold of so forcefully sailed alarmingly before her eyes as though their meaning were more to be seen in the air than heard. Also, they happened to be walking along a ridge that gave Agathe a marvelous view of the deep curving valley below, a position that evidently gave her companion the sense of being in a pulpit or on a lecture platform. She stopped and with her hat, which all this time she had been swinging carelessly in her hand, she drew a line through the stranger's argument: "So you *have* formed your own picture of me," she said. "I can see it shining through your words, and it isn't flattering."

The tall gentleman seemed dismayed, for he hadn't meant to hurt her, and Agathe looked at him with a friendly laugh. "You seem to be confusing me with the cause of the liberated personality, and a rather neurotic and unpleasant personality at that!" she maintained.

"I was only speaking of the underlying principle of the personal life," he said apologetically. "I must confess that the situation in which I found you suggested to me that you might want some helpful advice. The underlying principle of life is so widely misunderstood nowadays. Our entire modern neurosis, with all its excesses, arises solely from a flabby inner state in which the will is lacking, for without a special effort of will no one can achieve the integrity and stability that lifts a person above the obscure confusion of the organism!"

Here again were two words, "integrity" and "stability," that echoed her old longings and self-accusations. "Do tell me what you mean by that," she asked him. "Surely there can only really be a will when one has a goal?"

"What I mean doesn't matter," was the answer she received, in a tone both mild and brusque. "Don't all the great ancient scriptures of mankind tell us with utmost clarity what to do and not to do?"

Agathe was disconcerted.

"To set up fundamental ideals of life," her companion explained, "requires such a penetrating knowledge of life and of people, and such a heroic mastery of the passions and egotism, as has been granted to only very few individuals in the course of thousands of years. And these teachers of mankind have throughout the ages always taught the same truths."

Agathe instinctively resisted, as would anyone who considers her young flesh and blood better than the bones of dead sages.

"But precepts formulated thousands of years ago can't possibly apply to conditions today!" she cried.

"Those precepts are not nearly as foreign as is claimed by skeptics, who are out of touch with living experience and self-knowledge," her chance companion answered, with bitter satisfaction. "Life's deepest truths are not arrived at in debate, as Plato already said. Man hears them as the living meaning and fulfillment of his self. Believe me, what makes the human being truly free, and what takes away his freedom, what gives him true bliss and what destroys it, isn't subject to 'progress'—it is something every genuinely alive person knows perfectly well in his own heart, if he will just listen to it!"

Agathe liked the expression "living meaning," but then something suddenly occurred to her: "Are you religious?" she asked him. She looked at her companion with curiosity. He gave no answer.

"You're not a priest, by any chance . . . ?" she continued, but was reassured by his beard, for the rest of his appearance suddenly suggested that surprising possibility. It must be said to her credit that she would not have been more astounded had he casually referred to "our sublime ruler, the divine Augustus." She knew that religion plays a great role in politics, but one is so used to not taking ideas bandied about in public life seriously that to expect the "Christian" parties to be composed of true believers is the same kind of exaggeration as expecting every postal clerk to be a philatelist.

After a lengthy, somewhat wavering pause, the stranger replied: "I would prefer not to answer your question; you are too remote from all that."

But Agathe was seized with a lively curiosity.

"I'd like to know who you are!" she demanded to be told, and this was, after all, a feminine privilege that was not to be denied. He showed the same, slightly comical hesitation as before, when he had belatedly raised his hat to her. His arm seemed to twitch as if he were thinking of thus saluting her again, but then something in him stiffened, as though one army of thoughts had battled another and won, instead of a trifling gesture being playfully performed.

"My name is Lindner, and I teach at the Franz Ferdinand Gymnasium," he said, adding after a moment's thought: "I also lecture at the University."

"Then you might know my brother?" Agathe asked in relief, adding Ulrich's name. "He read a paper there recently, if I'm not mistaken, at the Pedagogical Society, on Mathematics and the Humanities, or something like that."

"Only by name. We've never met. Oh yes, I did attend that lecture," Lindner admitted. He seemed to say it with a certain reserve, but Agathe's attention was caught by his next question:

"Your father must have been the distinguished jurist?"

"Yes. He died recently, and I'm now staying with my brother," Agathe said freely. "Won't you come and see us?"

"I'm afraid I have no time for social calls," Lindner replied brusquely, his eyes cast down in uncertainty.

"In that case I hope you won't have any objections if I come to see you sometime," Agathe said, paying no attention to his reluctance. "I do need your advice." And since he had been calling her "Fräulein," she said: "I'm married; Hagauer is my name."

"Then you're the wife of the noted Professor of Education Hagauer . . . !" Lindner cried. He had begun the sentence on a note of high enthusiasm, but it wavered and became hesitant. For Hagauer was two things: he was in education and he was a progressive in education. Lindner was actually opposed to his ideas, but how bracing it was to recognize, through the uncertain mists of a female psyche, which has just proposed the impossible notion of inviting herself to a man's house, the familiar form of an enemy; it was the drop from the second to the first of these sentiments that was reflected in his change of tone.

Agathe had noticed it. She did not know whether to tell Lindner of the situation between her husband and herself. If she told him, it might put an immediate end to everything between herself and this new friend, that much was clear. And she would have been sorry; precisely because there was so much about Lindner that made her laugh at him, he also made her feel that she could trust him. The impression, borne out by his appearance, that this man seemed to want nothing for himself oddly moved her to be forthright with him: he quieted all longing, and that made frankness quite natural.

"I'm about to get a divorce," she finally admitted.

A silence followed. Lindner now had a downcast look. It put Agathe out of all patience with him. Finally, Lindner said with an offended smile: "I thought it must be something like that when I first caught sight of you!"

"Does that mean you're opposed to divorce too?" Agathe cried, giving free rein to her irritation with him. "Of course, you're bound to be against it. But it really does put you rather behind the times!"

"At least I can't regard it as matter-of-factly as you do." Lindner defended himself pensively, took off his glasses, polished them, put them on again, and contemplated Agathe. "It seemed to me you have too little willpower," he stated.

"Willpower? My will, for what it's worth, is to get a divorce!" Agathe cried, knowing it was not a very sensible answer.

"Please don't misunderstand me," Lindner gently corrected her. "I am of course willing to believe that you have good reasons. It's only that I see things in a different light. The free and easy morals prevailing nowadays amount, in effect, to nothing more than a sign that the individual is chained hand and foot to his own ego and incapable of living and acting from any wider perspective. Our esteemed poets," he added jealously, with an attempt at humor about Agathe's perfervid pilgrimage to the poet's grave, an attempt that only turned sour on his lips, "who play up to the sentiments of young ladies, and are therefore overestimated by them, have a far easier role to play than I, when I tell you that marriage is an institution of responsibility and the mastery of the human being over its passions! Before anyone dissociates himself from the external safeguards that mankind has wisely set up against its own undependability, he should recognize that isolation from and disobedience to the greater whole do far more harm than the physical disappointments we so fear!"

"That sounds like a military code for archangels," Agathe said, "but I'm not inclined to agree with you. Let me walk with you part-way. You must explain how it is possible to think as you do. Which way are you going now?"

".I must get home," Lindner answered.

"Would your wife mind very much if I walked home with you? When we get back down to town we can take a taxi. I have plenty of time."

"My son will be coming home from school," Lindner said with de-fensive dignity. "Mealtimes are on a strict schedule with us, which is why I must be home on time. My wife died suddenly, some years ago," he added, correcting Agathe's mistaken assumption, and with a glance at his watch he said with nervous impatience: "I must hurry!"

"Then you must explain it to me some other time. It is important to me!" Agathe insisted with feeling. "If you won't come to see us, I shall look you up."

Lindner caught his breath, but nothing came of it. Finally, he said: "But as a lady you can't come calling on a man!"

"Oh, yes I can!" Agathe assured him. "I shall simply arrive one day, you'll see. Though I can't say when. There is no harm in it!"

With this, she said good-bye and took a path diverging from his.

"You have no willpower!" she said under her breath, trying to imi-tate Lindner, but the word "willpower" tasted fresh and cool in her mouth. It had overtones of pride, toughness, and confidence; her heart beat higher; the man had done her good.

155

THE GENERAL MEANWHILE TAKES ULRICH AND CLARISSE TO THE MADHOUSE

While Ulrich was alone at home, the War Ministry telephoned to ask whether His Excellency the Chief of the Department for Military, Educational, and Cultural Affairs could see him privately in half an hour, and thirty-five minutes later General Stumm von Bordwehr's official carriage came dashing up the little drive.

"A fine kettle of fish!" the General cried out to his friend, who instantly noticed that this time the orderly with the intellectual bread was absent. The General was in full dress, decorations and all. "A fine mess you've got me into!" he reiterated. "There's a plenary session at your cousin's this evening. I haven't even had a chance to see my chief about it. And now suddenly the bombshell bursts—we have to be at the madhouse within an hour!"

"But why?" Ulrich asked, not unnaturally. "Usually that sort of thing is arranged ahead of time!"

"Don't ask so many questions!" the General implored him. "Just go and telephone your little friend or cousin or whatever she is, and tell her we're coming to call for her!"

Ulrich telephoned the grocery store where Clarisse was in the habit of doing her local shopping, and while he was waiting for her to come to the phone he heard about the misfortune the General was bemoaning. To make the arrangements for Clarisse to visit Moosbrugger, as a favor to Ulrich, Stumm had turned to the Chief of the Medical Corps, who then got in touch with his celebrated colleague the head of the University Clinic, where Moosbrugger was awaiting a top-level opinion on his psychiatric status. However, through a misunderstanding by both these gentlemen, the appointment for the date and time of Clarisse's visit had been made on the spot, as Stumm had been told with many apologies at the last minute, along with the error that he himself had been named as one of the visiting party that the famous psychiatrist was expecting with great pleasure.

"I feel quite ill!" he declared. This was a time-honored formula for his needing a schnapps. After he had tossed it off, he relaxed a little. "What's a madhouse to me! It's only because of you that I have to go!" he lamented. "Whatever will I say to that idiot professor when he asks me why I came along?"

At this moment a jubilant war whoop sounded at the other end of the line.

"Fine!" the General said fretfully. "But I also must absolutely talk to you about tonight. And I still have to report to my chief about it too. And he leaves the office at four!" He glanced at his watch and out of sheer hopelessness did not budge from his chair.

"Well, I'm ready," Ulrich said.

"Your lovely sister isn't coming?" Stumm asked in surprise.

"My sister is out."

"Too bad." The General sighed. "Your sister is the most remarkable woman I have ever met."

"I thought that was Diotima," Ulrich said.

"She's another," Stumm replied. "Diotima is admirable too. But since she's been going in for sex education I feel like a schoolboy. I'm happy to look up to her—God knows, a soldier's trade is a simple and crude kind of manual labor, as I always say, but precisely in the realm of sex it goes against one's honor as an officer to let oneself be treated as a novice!"

By now they were in the carriage and being driven off at a brisk trot.

"Is your young lady pretty, at least?" Stumm inquired suspiciously.

"She's quite an original, as you'll see," Ulrich replied.

"Now, as regards tonight"—the General sighed—"something is brewing. I expect something to happen."

"That's what you say every time you come to see me," Ulrich protested, smiling.

"Maybe, but it's true just the same. And tonight you'll be present at the encounter between your cousin and Frau Professor Drangsal. I hope you haven't forgotten everything I've told you about that. The Drangsal pest—that's what your cousin and I call her between ourselves—has been pestering your cousin for such a long time that she's got what she wanted: she's been haranguing everyone, and tonight will be the showdown between them. We were only waiting for Arnheim, so that he can form an opinion too."

"Oh?" Ulrich had not seen Arnheim for a long time, and had not known that he was back.

"Of course. Just for a few days," Stumm said. "So we had to set it up—" He broke off suddenly, bounding up from the swaying upholstery toward the driver's box with an agility no one would have expected of him. "Idiot!" he barked into the ear of the orderly disguised as a civilian coachman who was driving the ministerial horses, and he rocked helplessly back and forth with the carriage as he clung to the back of the man he was insulting, shouting: "You're taking the long way round!" The soldier in civvies held his back stiff as a board, numb to the General's extramilitary use of his body to save himself from falling, turned his head exactly ninety degrees, so that he could not see either his general or his horses, and smartly reported to a vertical that ended in the air that the shortest route was blocked off by street repairs, but he would soon be back on it. "There you are—so I was right!" Stumm cried as he fell back, glossing over his futile outburst of impatience, partly for the orderly's benefit and partly for Ulrich's. "So now the fellow has to take a detour, when I'm supposed to report to my chief this very afternoon, and he wants to go home at four o'clock, by which time he should have briefed the Minister himself! . . . His Excellency the Minister has sent word to the Tuzzis to expect him in person tonight," he added in a low voice, just for Ulrich's ear.

"You don't say!" Ulrich showed himself properly impressed by this news.

"I've been telling you for a long time there's something in the air."

Now Ulrich wanted to know what was in the air. "Come out with it, then," he demanded. "What does the Minister want?"

"He doesn't know himself," Stumm answered genially. "His Excellency has a feeling that the time has come. Old Leinsdorf also has a feeling that the time has come. The Chief of the General Staff likewise has a feeling that the time has come. When a lot of people have such a feeling, there may be something in it."

"But the time for what?" Ulrich persisted.

"Well, we don't need to know that yet," the General instructed him. "These are simply reliable indications! By the way," he asked abstractedly, or perhaps thoughtfully, "how many of us will there be today?"

"How would I know?" Ulrich asked in surprise.

"All I meant," Stumm explained, "is how many of us are going to the madhouse? Excuse me! Funny, isn't it, that kind of misunderstanding? There are days when there's too much coming at one from all sides. So: how many are coming?"

"I don't know who else will be coming—somewhere between three and six people."

"What I meant," the General said earnestly, "was that if there are more than three of us, we'll have to get another cab—you understand, because I'm in uniform."

"Oh, of course," Ulrich reassured him.

"I can't very well drive in a sardine can."

"Of course not. But tell me, what's this about reliable indications?"

"But will we be able to get a cab out there?" Stumm worried. "It's so far out you can hear the animals snoring."

"We'll pick one up on the way," Ulrich said firmly. "Now will you please tell me how you have reliable indications that it's time for something to happen?"

"There's nothing to tell," Stumm replied. "When I say about something that that's the way it is and it can't be otherwise, what I'm really saying is that I can't explain it! At most one might add that this Drangsal is one of those pacifists, probably because Feuermaul, who's her protégé, writes poems about 'Man is good.' Lots of people believe that sort of thing now."

Ulrich was not convinced. "Didn't you tell me the opposite just a little while ago? That they're now all in favor of taking action, taking a strong line, and all that?"

"True too," the General granted. "And influential circles are backing Drangsal; she has a great knack for that sort of thing. They expect the patriotic campaign to come up with a humanitarian action."

"Really?" Ulrich said.

"You know, you really don't seem to care about anything anymore! The rest of us are worried. Let me remind you, for instance, that the fratricidal Austro-German war of 1866 only happened because all the Germans in the Frankfurt Parliament declared themselves to be brothers. Not, of course, that I'm suggesting that the War Minister or the Chief of the General Staff might be worrying along those lines; that would be nonsense. But one thing does lead to another. That's how it is! See what I mean?"

It was not clear, but it made sense. And the General went on to make a very wise observation:

"Look, you're always wanting things to be clear and logical," he remonstrated with his seatmate. "And I do admire you for it, but you must for once try to think in historical terms. How can those directly involved in what's happening know beforehand whether it will turn out to be a great event? All they can do is pretend to themselves that it is! If I may indulge in a paradox, I'd say that the history of the world is written before it happens; it always starts off as a kind of gossip. So that people who have the energy to act are faced with a very serious problem."

"You have a point," Ulrich said appreciatively. "But now tell me all about it."

Although the General wanted to expand on it, there was so much on his mind in these moments, when the horse's hooves had begun to hit softer ground, that he was suddenly seized by other anxieties.

"Here I am, decked out like a Christmas tree in case the Minister calls for me," he cried, underlining it by pointing to his light-blue tunic and the medals hanging from it. "Don't you think it could lead to awkward incidents if I appear like this, in full dress, in front of loonies? What do I do, for instance, if one of them decides to insult the Emperor's uniform? I can hardly draw my sword, but it would be really dangerous for me *not* to say anything, either!"

Ulrich calmed him down by pointing out that he would be likely to wear a doctor's white coat over his uniform. But before Stumm had time to declare himself fully satisfied with this solution they met Clarisse, impatiently coming to meet them in a smart summer dress, escorted by Siegmund. She told Ulrich that Walter and Meingast had refused to join them. And after they had managed to find a second carriage, the General was pleased to say to Clarisse: "As you were coming down the road toward us, my dear young lady, you looked positively like an angel!"

But by the time he left the carriage at the hospital gate, Stumm von Bordwehr appeared rather flushed and ill at ease.

156

THE LUNATICS GREET CLARISSE

Clarisse was twisting her gloves in her hands, looking up at the windows, and fidgeting constantly while Ulrich paid for the cab. Stumm von Bordwehr protested Ulrich's doing this, and the cabbie sat on his box with a flattered smile as the two gentlemen kept each other back. Siegmund brushed specks off his coat with his fingertips, as usual, or stared into space.

In a low voice, the General said to Ulrich: "There's something odd about your lady friend. She lectured me the whole way about what will is. I didn't understand a word!"

"That's the way she is," Ulrich said.

"Pretty, though," the General whispered. "Like a fourteen-year-old ballerina. But why does she say that we came here in order to follow our 'hallucination'? The world is 'too free of hallucinations,' she says. D'you know anything about that? It was so distressing, I simply couldn't think of a word to say."

The General was obviously holding up the departure of the cab only because he wanted to ask these questions, but before Ulrich could answer he was relieved of the responsibility by an emissary who welcomed the visitors in the name of the director of the clinic, and apologizing to the General for having to keep them waiting because of some urgent business, he led the company upstairs to a waiting room. Clarisse took in every inch of the staircase and the corridors with her eyes, and even in the little waiting room, with its chairs upholstered in threadbare green velvet so reminiscent of an old-fashioned first-class waiting room in a railway station, her gaze roved about slowly almost the whole time. There the four of them sat, after the emissary had left, and found nothing to say until Ulrich, to break the silence, teased Clarisse by asking her whether the thought of meeting Moosbrugger face-to-face wasn't making her blood run cold.

"Bah!" Clarisse said. "He's only known ersatz women; it had to come to this."

The General had come up with a face-saving idea, something having belatedly occurred to him: "The will is now very up-to-date," he said. "We're very much concerned with this problem in our patriotic action too!"

Clarisse gave him a smile and stretched her arms to ease the tension in them. "Having to wait like this, one can feel what's coming in one's arms and legs, as if one were looking through a telescope," she replied.

Stumm von Bordwehr gave it some thought, careful not to put a foot wrong again. "That's true!" he said. "It may have something to do with the current cult of exercise and bodybuilding. We're concerned with that also."

At this point the Medical Director swept in with his cavalcade of assistants and nurses and a gracious word for everyone, especially Stumm; mumbled about something pressing, which would, regrettably, prevent him from taking them around himself, as he had intended; and introduced Dr. Friedenthal, who would take good care of them in his stead.

Dr. Friedenthal was a tall, slender man with a somewhat effeminate body and a thick mop of hair, who smiled at them, as he was introduced, like an acrobat climbing a ladder for a death-defying performance. When the director had gone, the white lab coats were brought in. "We don't want to get the patients excited," Dr. Friedenthal explained.

As Clarisse slipped into hers she experienced a strange surge of power. She stood there like a little doctor. She felt very much a man, and very white.

The General looked around for a mirror. It was hard to find a lab coat to fit his idiosyncratic proportion of girth to height; when they finally managed to get him into something that covered him completely, he looked like a child in an adult's nightshirt. "Don't you think I should take my spurs off?" he asked Dr. Friedenthal.

"Army doctors wear spurs too," Ulrich pointed out.

Stumm made one last feeble and laborious effort to see what he looked like from behind, where the medical coverall was caught up in heavy folds above his spurs. Then they set out. Dr. Friedenthal enjoined them to keep calm no matter what they might see.

"So far so good!" Stumm whispered to his friend. "But I'm not really interested in any of this. Could use the time much better to talk with you about tonight's meeting. Now look, you said you wanted me to tell you frankly what's going on. It's quite simple: the whole world is arming. The Russians have a brand-new field artillery. Are you listening? The French are using their two-year conscription law to build up an enormous army. The Italians . . ."

They had descended the same old-fashioned princely staircase they had climbed before and, after somehow turning off the main corridor, found themselves in a maze of small rooms and twisting passages with whitewashed beams protruding from the ceiling. These were mostly utility rooms and offices, cramped and dreary because of a shortage of space in the ancient building. Sinister figures, only some of whom wore institutional uniforms, populated them. One door bore the inscription "Reception"; another, "Men." The General's talk dried up. He had a premonition that things could happen at any moment, requiring by their unprecedented nature great presence of mind. He could not help wondering what he would do if an irresistible need forced him to leave the group and he were to stumble, alone and without an expert guide in a place where all men are equal, upon a madman.

Clarisse, on the other hand, was walking a step ahead of Dr. Friedenthal. His having said that they had to wear these white coats so as not to alarm the patients buoyed her up like a life vest on the current of her impressions. She was mulling over some of her pet ideas. Nietzsche: "Is there a pessimism of strength? An intellectual predisposition to whatever is hard, sinister, evil, problematic in life? A yearning for the terrible as a worthy foe? Perhaps madness is not necessarily a symptom of degeneracy." She was not thinking this in so many words, but she remembered it as a whole; her thoughts had compressed it all into a tiny packet, admirably fitted to the smallest space, like a burglar's tool. For her this excursion was half philosophy and half adultery.

Dr. Friedenthal stopped in front of an iron door and took a flat key from his pants pocket. When he opened the door they stepped out from the shelter of the building and were blinded by the brightness. At the same moment Clarisse heard a frightful shriek such as she had never heard before in her life. For all her pluckiness, she winced.

"Just a horse!" Dr. Friedenthal said, smiling.

And in fact they were on a road that led from the front gate, along the side of the administration building, and around to the kitchen yard of the institution. It was no different from other such roads, with old wheel tracks and homely weeds on which the sun was blazing hotly. And yet all the others too, with the exception of Dr. Friedenthal, felt oddly disconcerted and—in a startled, confused fashion—almost indignant, to find themselves on a wholesome and ordinary road after having already survived a long, arduous passage. Freedom, at first blush, had something disconcerting about it, even though it was incredibly comforting; it actually took some getting used to again. With Clarisse, who was more vulnerable to the clash of contrasts, the tension shattered in a loud giggle.

Still smiling, Dr. Friedenthal strode ahead across the road and on the other side opened a small but heavy iron door in the high wall of a park. "This is where it begins," he said gently.

And now they really found themselves inside that world to which Clarisse had felt herself inexplicably attracted for weeks, not only with the shudder at something incommensurable and impenetrable, but as though she were fated to experience something there that she could not imagine beforehand. At first there was nothing to differentiate this world from any other big old park, with the greensward sloping up in one direction toward groups of tall trees, among which small white villa-like buildings could be seen. The sweep of the sky behind them gave promise of a lovely view, and from one such lookout point Clarisse saw patients with attendants standing and sitting in groups, looking like white angels.

General Stumm took this as the right moment to resume his conversation with Ulrich. "Now, let me prime you a bit more for this evening," he began. "The Italians, the Russians, the French, and the English too, you know, are all arming, and we—"

"You want your artillery; I know that already," Ulrich interrupted.

"Among other things!" the General continued. "But if you don't ever let me finish, we'll soon be among the loonies and won't be able to talk in peace. So, as I was saying, we're in the middle of all this, in a very risky position from the military point of view. And in this fix we're being badgered—I'm referring to the Parallel Campaign—to think of nothing but the goodness of man!"

"And your people are against it! I understand."

"Not at all, on the contrary!" Stumm protested. "We're not against it! We take pacifism very seriously! But we must get our artillery budget through. And if we could do that hand in hand with pacifism, so to speak, it would be the best safeguard against all those imperialistic misunderstandings that are so quick to assert that we're endangering world peace! It's true, if you like, that we're in bed with La Drangsal, just a little. But we also have to proceed with caution because her opposition, the nationalist movements, who now have their people inside the Campaign too, are against pacifism and in favor of getting our army up to scratch!"

The General had to cut himself short, with an expression of bitterness, for they had almost reached the top of the incline, where Dr. Friedenthal was awaiting his troop. The angels' gathering place turned out to be lightly fenced in; their guide crossed it without paying it much attention, as a mere prelude. "A 'quiet' ward," he explained.

They were all women; their hair hung loose down to their shoulders, and their faces were repellent, with fat, blurred, puffy features. One of them came rushing up to the doctor and forced a letter on him. "It's always the same thing," Dr. Friedenthal explained to his visitors and read aloud: " 'Adolf, my love! When are you coming to see me? Have you forgotten me?' " The woman, about sixty, stood there with an apathetic face and listened. "You'll send it out right away, won't you?" she begged. "Of course!" Dr. Friedenthal promised, then he tore the letter into pieces in front of her eyes and smiled at the nurse. Clarisse instantly challenged him: "How could you do this?" she asked. "These patients must be taken seriously!"

"Come along," Dr. Friedenthal said. "There's no point in wasting our time here. If you like, I'll show you hundreds of such letters later. You must have noticed that the old woman didn't react at all when I tore it up?"

Clarisse was disconcerted, because what Dr. Friedenthal said was true, but it confused her thoughts. And before she could straighten them out again, they were further disturbed when, on their way out, another old woman, who had been lying in wait for them, lifted up her skirt and exposed to the passing gentlemen her ugly old-woman's thighs up to her belly, above coarse woolen stockings.

"The old sow," Stumm von Bordwehr muttered, sufficiently outraged and disgusted to forget politics for a while.

But Clarisse had discovered a resemblance between the thigh and the face. The thigh probably showed the same stigmata of fatty physical degeneration as the face, but this gave Clarisse for the first time an impression of strange correspondences and a world that worked differently from what one could grasp with the usual categories. She also now realized that she had not noticed the transformation of the white angels into these women, and indeed that even while walking through their midst she had not been able to distinguish the patients from the nurses. She turned around and looked back, but because the path had curved behind a building, she could no longer see anything and stumbled after the others like a child that turns its head away. From this point on, her impressions no longer formed the transparent flow of events that one accepts life to be, but became a foaming torrent with only occasional smooth patches that stuck in the memory.

"Another quiet ward, this time for men," Dr. Friedenthal announced, gathering his flock at the entrance to a building, and when they paused at the first bed he presented its occupant to them in a considerately lowered voice as a case of "depressive dementia paralytica."

"An old syphilitic. Delusions of sin and nihilistic obsessions," Siegmund whispered, translating the terms for his sister. Clarisse found herself face-to-face with an old gentleman who, to all appearances, had once belonged to the upper reaches of society. He sat upright in bed, was perhaps in his late fifties, and had a very white skin. His well-cared-for and highly intelligent face was framed in thick white hair and looked as improbably distinguished as the faces one finds described only in the cheapest novels.

"Couldn't one do a portrait of him?" Stumm von Bordwehr asked. "The very model of intellectual beauty! I'd love to give the portrait to your cousin!" he said to Ulrich.

Dr. Friedenthal gave a sad smile and commented: "The noble expression is caused by a slackening of tension in the facial muscles."

He demonstrated with a quick movement the unresponsive fixity of the man's pupils, then led them onward. There was not enough time for all the available material. The old gentleman, who had nodded mournfully to everything said at his bedside, was still muttering in a low, troubled voice when the five of them stopped again, several beds farther on, to consider the next case Dr. Friedenthal had chosen for them.

This time it was someone who was himself engaged in art, a cheerful, fat painter whose bed stood close to a sunny window. He had paper and many pencils on his blanket, and busied himself with them all day long. Clarisse was immediately struck by the happy restlessness of his movements. "That's the way Walter should be painting!" she thought. Friedenthal, seeing her interest, quickly snatched a sheet of paper from the fat man and handed it to Clarisse; the painter snickered and behaved like a serving girl who'd just been pinched. But Clarisse was amazed to see a sketch for a large composition, drawn with sure, accomplished strokes, entirely sensible to the point of banality, with many figures woven together in accurate perspective and a large hall, everything executed in meticulous detail, so that the whole effect was of something so salutary and professorial that it could have come from the National Academy. "What amazing craftsmanship!" she cried impulsively.

Dr. Friedenthal responded with a flattered smile.

The artist gleefully made a rude noise at him.

"You see, that gentleman likes it! Show him some more, go on! Amazing how good it is, he said! Go on, show him! I know you're only laughing at me, but he likes it!" He spoke good-humoredly, holding out the rest of his drawings to the doctor, with whom he seemed to be on easy terms although the doctor didn't appreciate his work.

"We don't have time for you today," Dr. Friedenthal told him and, turning to Clarisse, summed up the case by saying: "He's not schizophrenic; sorry he's the only one we have here at the moment. Schizophrenics are often fine artists, quite modern."

"And insane?" Clarisse said dubiously.

"Why not?" Dr. Friedenthal answered sadly.

Clarisse bit her lip.

Meanwhile Stumm and Ulrich were already on the threshold to the next ward, and the General was saying: "Looking at this, I'm really sorry I called my orderly an idiot this morning. I'll never do it again!" For the ward they were facing was a room with extreme cases of idiocy.

Clarisse had not yet seen this and was thinking: "So even academic art, so respectably and widely recognized, has a sister in Bedlam—a sister denied, deprived, and yet so much a twin one can barely tell the difference!" This almost impressed her more than Friedenthal's remark that another time he might be able to show her expressionist artists. She made up her mind to take him up on it. Her head was down, and she was still biting her lip. There was something wrong with all this. It seemed to her clearly wrong to lock up such gifted people; the doctors might know about diseases, she thought, but probably did not understand art and all it stood for. Something would have to be done, she felt. But it was not clear to her what. Yet she did not lose heart, for the fat painter had immediately called her "that gentleman"—it seemed to her a good omen.

Friedenthal scrutinized her with curiosity.

When she felt his gaze she looked up with her thin-lipped smile and moved toward him, but before she could say anything an appalling sight made her mind a blank. In this new ward a series of horrible apparitions crouched and sat in their beds, everything about their bodies crooked, unclean, twisted, or paralyzed. Decayed teeth. Waggling heads. Heads too big, too small, totally misshapen. Slack, drooping jaws from which saliva was dribbling, or brutish grinding motions of the mouth, without food or words. Yard-wide leaden barriers seemed to lie between these souls and the world, and after the low chuckling and buzzing in the other room, the silence here, broken only by obscure grunting and muttering sounds, was oppressive. Such wards for severe mental deficiency are among the most horrifying sights to be found in the hideousness of a mental institution, and Clarisse felt herself plunged headlong into a ghastly darkness that blotted out all distinctions.

But their guide, Friedenthal, could see even in the dark, and pointing to various beds, he explained: "That's idiocy over there, and over here you have cretinism."

Stumm von Bordwehr pricked up his ears. "A cretin is not the same as an idiot?" he asked.

"No," the doctor said, "there's a medical distinction."

"Interesting," Stumm said. "In ordinary life one would never think of such a thing."

Clarisse moved from bed to bed. Her eyes bored into the patients, as she tried with all her might to understand, without succeeding in the least in gleaning anything from these faces that took no cognizance of her. All thought in them was extinguished. Dr. Friedenthal followed her softly and explained: "congenital amaurotic idiocy"; "tubercular hypertrophic sclerosis"; "idiotia thymica . . ."

The General, who meanwhile felt that he had seen enough of these "morons" and assumed that Ulrich felt the same way, glanced at his watch and said: "Now, where were we? We mustn't waste time!" And rather unexpectedly he resumed: "So, if you'll bear in mind: the War Ministry finds itself flanked by the pacifists on one side and the nationalists on the other. . . ."

Ulrich, not so quick to tear his mind away from his surroundings, gave him a blank stare.

"This is no joke, my friend!" Stumm explained. "I'm talking politics! Something's got to be done. We've come to a stop once before already. If we don't do something soon, the Emperor's birthday will be upon us before we know it, and we'll look like fools. But *what* is to be done? It's a logical question, isn't it? And summing up rather bluntly what I told you, we're being pushed by one crowd to help them love mankind, and by the other to let them bully the rest of the world so that the nobler blood will prevail, or however you want to call it. There's something to be said for both sides. Which is why, in a word, you should somehow bring them together so there'll be no damage!"

"Me?" Ulrich protested at his friend's bombshell, and would have burst out laughing in other circumstances.

"Certainly you—who else?" the General replied decisively. "I'll do all I can to help, but you're the campaign's secretary and Leinsdorf's right hand!"

"I can get you admitted here!" Ulrich announced firmly.

"Fine!" The General knew from the art of war that it was best to avoid unexpected resistance in the most unruffled manner possible. "If you get me in here I might meet someone who has found the Greatest Idea in the world. Outside they seem to have lost their taste for great ideas anyway." He glanced at his watch again. "I hear they've got some people here who are the Pope, or the universe. We haven't met a single one, and they're the ones I was most looking forward to getting acquainted with. Your little friend's terribly conscientious," he complained.

Dr. Friedenthal gently eased Clarisse away from the defectives.

Hell is not interesting, it is terrifying. If it has not been humanized—as by Dante, who populated it with writers and other prominent figures, thereby distracting attention from the technicalities of punishment—but an attempt has been made to represent it in some original fashion, even the most fertile minds never get beyond childish tortures and unimaginative distortions of physical realities. But it is precisely the bare idea of an unimaginable and therefore inescapable everlasting punishment and agony, the premise of an inexorable change for the worse, impervious to any attempt to reverse it, that has the fascination of an abyss. Insane asylums are also like that. They are poorhouses. They have something of hell's lack of imagination. But many people who have no idea of the causes of mental illness are afraid of nothing so much, next to losing their money, as that they might one day lose their minds; an amazing number of people are plagued by the notion that they could suddenly lose themselves. It is apparently an overestimation of their self-worth that leads to the overestimation of the horror with which the sane imagine mental institutions to be imbued. Even Clarisse suffered a faint disappointment, which stemmed from some vague expectation implanted by her upbringing. It was quite the contrary with Dr. Friedenthal. He was used to these rounds. Order as in a military barracks or another mass institution, alleviation of conspicuous pains or complaints, prevention of avoidable deterioration, a slight improvement or a cure: these were the elements of his daily activity. Observing a good deal, knowing a good deal, without having a sufficient explanation for the overall problems, was his intellectual portion. These rounds through the wards, prescribing a few sedatives besides the usual medications for coughs, colds, constipation, and bedsores, were his daily work of healing. He felt the ghostly horror of the world he lived in only when the contrast was awakened through contact with the normal world, which did not happen every day, but visits are such occasions, and that was why what Clarisse got to see had been prepared not without a certain sense of theatrical production, so that no sooner had he aroused her from her absorption with one phenomenon that he immediately went on to something new and even more dramatic.

They had hardly left this ward when they were joined by several large men in crisp white uniforms, with hulking shoulders and jovial corporals' faces. It happened so silently that it had the effect of a drum roll.

"Now we're coming to a disturbed ward," Dr. Friedenthal announced, and they approached a screaming and squawking that seemed to issue from an immense birdcage. They stood in front of a door that had no handle, which had to be opened with a special key by one of the attendants. Clarisse started to enter first, as she had done up until now, but Dr. Friedenthal pulled her back roughly.

"Wait!" he said with emphasis, wearily, without apology.

The attendant who had opened the door had opened it only a crack, while covering the open space with his powerful body; after first listening and then peering inside, he hastily slipped in, followed by a second attendant, who took up a position at the other side of the entrance. Clarisse's heart started to pound.

"Advance guard, rear guard, cover flank!" the General said appreciatively. And thus covered, they walked in and were escorted from bed to bed by the two attending giants. What were sitting in the beds thrashed about, agitated and screaming, with arms and eyes, as if each of them was shouting into some private space that was for himself alone, and yet they all seemed to be caught up in a raging conversation, like alien birds locked in the same cage, each speaking the dialect of its own island. Some of them sat without restraints, while others were tied down to their beds with straps that allowed only limited movement of the hands.

"To keep them from attempting suicide," the doctor explained, and listed the diseases: paralysis, paranoia, manic depression, were the species to which these strange birds belonged.

Clarisse again felt intimidated at first by her confused impressions and could not get her bearings. And so it came as a friendly sign when she saw someone waving to her excitedly from a distance, calling out something to her while she was still many beds away. He was moving back and forth in his bed as if desperately trying to free himself in order to dash over to her, outshouting the chorus with his complaints and fits of rage, and succeeding in concentrating Clarisse's attention on himself. The closer she came to him, the more she was troubled by her sense of his addressing himself only to her, while she was completely unable to understand a word of what he was trying to say. When they finally reached his bed, the senior attendant told the doctor something so softly that Clarisse could not hear, and Friedenthal, looking very grave, gave some instructions. But then he said something in a light vein to the patient, who was slow to react but then suddenly asked: "Who's that man?" with a gesture indicating Clarisse.

Friedenthal nodded toward Siegmund and answered that it was a doctor from Stockholm.

"No, that one!" The patient insisted on Clarisse. Friedenthal smiled and said she was a woman doctor from Vienna.

"No. That's a man," the patient contradicted him, and fell silent. Clarisse felt her heart thudding. Here was another who took her for a man!

Then the patient intoned slowly: "It is the seventh son of our Emperor."

Stumm von Bordwehr nudged Ulrich.

"That is not so," Friedenthal told him, and continued the game by turning to Clarisse, saying: "Do tell him yourself that he's mistaken."

"It's not true, my friend," Clarisse said in a low voice to the patient, so moved she could barely speak.

"You *are* the seventh son," the patient replied stubbornly.

"No, no," Clarisse assured him, smiling at him in her excitement as if she were playing a love scene, her lips stiff with stage fright.

"Yes you are!" the patient repeated, and looked at her in a way she could not find words for. She could not think of another thing to say, and just kept gazing helplessly with a fixed smile into the eyes of the lunatic who took her for a prince. Something remarkable was happening in her mind: the possibility was forming that he might be right. The force of his repeated assertion dissolved some resistance in her; in some way she lost control over her thoughts, new patterns took shape, their outlines looming from mist: he was not the first who wanted to know who she was and to take her for a "gentleman." But while she was still gazing at his face, caught up in this strange bond, taking no account of his age or of any other vestiges of a normal life still left in his countenance, something quite incomprehensible was beginning to happen in that face and in the whole person. It looked as though her gaze was too heavy for the eyes on which it rested; they began to slide away and fall. His lips, too, began to quiver, and like heavy drops merging more and more quickly, audible obscenities mixed themselves with a rush of jabbering. Clarisse was as stunned by this slithering transformation as if something were slipping away from her; she impulsively reached out to the miserable creature with both arms, and before anyone could interfere, the patient leapt to meet her: he cast off his bedclothes, knelt at the foot of the bed, and began to masturbate like a caged monkey.

"Don't be such a pig!" the doctor said quickly and sternly, while the attendants instantly grabbed the man and his bedclothes and in a flash reduced both to a lifeless bundle on the bed. Clarisse had turned dark red. She felt as dizzy as when the floor of an elevator all at once seems to drop away from under one's feet. Suddenly it seemed to her that all the patients they had already passed were shouting at her back and the others, whom they had not yet seen, were shouting at her from in front. And as chance would have it, or the infectious power of excitement, a friendly old man in the next bed, who had been making good-natured little jokes while the visitors stood nearby, leapt up the instant Clarisse hurried past him, and began raving at them in foul language that formed a disgusting foam on his lips. On him, too, the attendants' fists descended like a heavy press, crushing all resistance.

But the magician Friedenthal had even more tricks to conjure up. Under guard at the exit as they had been at the entrance, the visitors left this ward at the far end, and suddenly their ears seemed plunged into healing silence. They found themselves in a clean, cheerful corridor with a linoleum floor, and encountered people in their Sunday best and attractive children, all greeting the doctor confidently and politely. They were visitors, waiting to get to see their relatives, and once again the impact of this healthy world was disconcerting; for a moment all these discreet and well-behaved people in their best clothes seemed like dolls, or extremely well-made artificial flowers. But Friedenthal passed through them hurriedly and announced to his friends that he was now about to take them to the ward for murderers and others of the criminally insane. The watchful looks and behavior of the attendants at the next iron gate did not bode at all well. They entered a cloistered courtyard surrounded by a gallery, resembling one of those gardens of modern design that have many stones and few plants. The empty air first seemed like a cube of silence; it was only after a while that one noticed figures sitting mutely along the walls. Near the entrance some retarded boys were squatting, runny-nosed, dirty, motionless, as if a sculptor had had the grotesque idea of attaching them to the pillars flanking the gate. Near them, the first figure by the wall, sitting apart from the others, was an ordinary-looking man still in his dark Sunday suit, but without a collar; he must have just been admitted, and was indescribably moving in his impression of not belonging anywhere. Clarisse suddenly imagined the anguish she would cause Walter if she left him, and almost burst into tears. It was the first time this had ever happened, but she quickly suppressed it, for the other men past whom she was being escorted merely gave the impression of habitual submission to be expected in prisons: They greeted the doctor with shy politeness and made minor requests. Only one made a nuisance of himself with his complaints, a young man who emerged from heaven knew what oblivion. He demanded to be released at once, and why was he here in the first place? When Dr. Friedenthal replied evasively that such requests were handled by the superintendent, not by him, the young man persisted; his pleas became repetitive, like links in a chain rattling past faster and faster; gradually, a note of urgency came into his voice and grew threatening, finally turning into brutish, mindless danger. At that point the giants pushed him back down on the bench, and he crept back into his silence like a dog, without having received an answer. By now Clarisse was used to this, and it merely became part of her general excitement.

There would have been no time for anything else, since they had reached the armored door at the far end of the courtyard, and the guards were banging on it. This was something new, for up to this point they had used great caution in opening doors but had not announced themselves. On this door they banged their fists four times, and listened to the stirrings from the other side.

"That's the signal for everyone inside to line up against the walls," Dr. Friedenthal explained, "or sit on the benches along the walls."

And indeed, as the door turned slowly, inch by inch, they could see that all the men who had been milling around quietly or noisily were behaving obediently, like well-drilled prisoners. Even so, the guards were so cautious as they entered that Clarisse suddenly clutched at Dr. Friedenthal's sleeve and asked excitedly whether Moosbrugger was here. Friedenthal only shook his head. He had no time. He hastily admonished the visitors to stay at least two paces away from every prisoner. His responsibilities in this situation seemed to cause him some anxiety. They were seven against thirty, in a remote, walled courtyard full of insane men almost all of whom had committed a murder.

Those who are accustomed to carrying a weapon feel more exposed without it than others, so one could not hold it against the General, who had left his saber in the waiting room, that he asked the doctor: "Don't you have a weapon on you?" "Alertness and experience!" Dr. Friedenthal replied, pleased at the flattering question. "It's all a matter of nipping any potential disturbance in the bud."

And in fact at the slightest move among the inmates to break ranks, the guards rushed in and thrust the offender back into place so swiftly that these attacks seemed to be the only acts of violence occurring. Clarisse did not approve of them. "What the doctors don't seem to understand," she thought, "is that although these men are shut in here together all day long without supervision, they don't do anything to each other; it's only we, coming from the world that is foreign to them, who may be in danger." She wanted to speak to one of them, suddenly imagining that she could certainly find a way to communicate properly with him. In a corner right near the entrance was a sturdy-looking man of medium height, with a full brown beard and piercing eyes; he was leaning against the wall with his arms folded, silently surveying the visitors' activity with an angry expression. Clarisse stepped toward him, but Dr. Friedenthal instantly restrained her with a hand on her arm. "Not this one," he said in a low voice. He chose another murderer for Clarisse and spoke to him. This was a short, squat fellow with a pointy head, shaved convict fashion, apparently known to the doctor as tractable, who instantly stood at attention and, answering smartly, showed two rows of teeth that dubiously suggested two rows of gravestones.

"Ask him why he's here," Dr. Friedenthal whispered to Clarisse's brother, and Siegmund asked the broad-shouldered man with the pointy head: "Why are you here?"

"You know that very well!" was the curt reply.

"No, I don't know," Siegmund—who did not like to give up too easily—said rather foolishly. "So tell me why you're here."

"You know that very well!" The response was repeated with a stronger emphasis.

"Why are you being rude to me?" Siegmund asked. "I honestly don't know why!"

"This lying!" Clarisse thought, and she was glad when the patient simply answered: "Because I choose! I can do as I like!" he insisted, and bared his teeth at them.

"Well, there's no need to be rude for no reason," the hapless Siegmund persisted, just as unable as the insane man to come up with anything new.

Clarisse was furious with him for playing the stupid role of someone teasing a caged animal in a zoo.

"It's none of your business! I do as I like, get it? Whatever I like!" The mental patient barked like a sergeant and produced a laugh from somewhere in his face, but not his mouth or eyes, which were both charged with uncanny anger.

Even Ulrich was thinking: "I wouldn't care to be alone with this fellow just now." Siegmund was having a hard time standing his ground, since the madman had stepped up close to him, and Clarisse was wishing he would seize her brother by the throat and bite him in the face. Friedenthal complacently let the scene take its course, for after all, as a medical colleague Siegmund ought to be able to handle it, and Friedenthal was rather enjoying the other's discomfiture. With his sense of theater, he waited for the scene to reach a climax, and only when Siegmund was beyond uttering another word did he give the signal to break it off. But the desire to meddle was back in Clarisse; it had somehow grown stronger and stronger as the man drummed out his answers. Suddenly she could no longer hold back and, walking up to the man, said:

"I'm from Vienna!"

It made as little sense as a random sound one might entice from a bugle. She neither knew what she meant by saying it nor where the idea had come from, nor had she stopped to wonder whether the man knew what town he was in, and if he did know, her remark would be even more pointless. But she felt tremendously sure of herself as she said it. And in fact miracles still do happen, occasionally, and they have a partiality for insane asylums. As she spoke, flaming with excitement, a glow came over him; his rock-grinder teeth withdrew behind his lips, and benevolence spread over the glare in his eyes.

"Ah, Vienna, city of dreams! A beautiful place!" he said with the smugness of the former petit bourgeois who has his clichés in order.

"Congratulations!" Dr. Friedenthal laughed.

But for Clarisse the episode had become an event.

"Now let's go on to Moosbrugger!" Friedenthal said.

But this was not to be. They moved cautiously back through the two courtyards and were walking up an incline toward what appeared to be a distant isolated pavilion, when a guard who seemed to have been looking for them everywhere came running up to them. He whispered to Friedenthal at some length, something important and disagreeable, to judge by the doctor's expression as he listened and asked an occasional question. Finally, Dr. Friedenthal turned back to the others with a grave, apologetic air and told them that he had to go to another ward, to deal with an incident that would take some time, so that he would, regretfully, have to curtail their tour. He addressed himself primarily to the official personage in the General's uniform beneath the lab coat; Stumm von Bordwehr gratefully assured him that he had seen enough of the outstanding organization and discipline of this institution, and that after what they had been through, one murderer more or less did not matter. Clarisse, however, had such a disappointed, stricken face that Friedenthal proposed to make up the visit to Moosbrugger, along with some other interesting cases, some other time; he would give Siegmund a call as soon as a date could be arranged.

"Very kind of you"—the General thanked him on behalf of the group—"though for my part, I really can't say whether other obligations will allow me to be present."

With this reservation, a future visit was agreed upon, and Friedenthal set off along a path that soon took him over the rise and out of sight, while the others, accompanied by the attendant Friedenthal had left with them, headed back to the gate. They left the path and took a shortcut across the grassy slope between fine beeches and plane trees. The General had slipped out of his lab coat and carried it jauntily over his arm, as one might carry a raincoat on an outing, but nobody seemed to feel like talking. Ulrich showed no interest in being coached further for the evening's reception, and Stumm was himself too preoccupied with what was awaiting him at his office, though he felt called upon to make some amusing remarks to Clarisse, whom he was gallantly escorting. But Clarisse was absent-minded and quiet. "Perhaps she's still embarrassed over that filthy pig," he mused, feeling the need to apologize somehow for not having been in a position to offer his chivalric protection, but on the other hand, it was probably best to say no more about it. So the walk back passed in silence and constraint.

It was only when Stumm von Bordwehr had entered his carriage, leaving it to Ulrich to see Clarisse and her brother home, that his good spirits returned, and with them an idea that gave a certain shape to the whole depressing episode. He had taken a cigarette out of the big leather case in his pocket, and leaning back in the cushions and blowing the first little blue clouds into the sunny air, he thought comfortably: "Terrible thing, to be out of one's mind like that. Come to think of it, all the time we were there I didn't see a single one of them having a smoke! People don't realize how well off they are as long as they're still in their right mind!"

157

A GREAT EVENT IS IN THE MAKING. COUNT LEINSDORF AND THE INN RIVER

This eventful day culminated in a gala reception at the Tuzzis'.

The Parallel Campaign was on parade, in glory and brilliance: eyes blazed, jewels blazed, prominence blazed, wit blazed. A lunatic might conceivably conclude from this that on such a social occasion eyes, jewels, prominent names, and wit amount to the same thing, and he would not be far off the mark: everyone who did not happen to be on the Riviera or the north Italian lakes was there, except for those few who refused on principle to recognize any "events" so late in the season.

In their place were quite a number of people whom no one had ever seen before. A long respite had torn holes in the guest list, and to fill it up again new people had been invited more hastily than was consonant with Diotima's circumspect ways: Count Leinsdorf himself had turned over to her a list of people he wanted invited for political reasons, and once the principle of her salon's exclusiveness had thus been sacrificed to higher considerations, she had no longer attached the same importance to it. His Grace was, in fact, the sole begetter of this festive gathering: Diotima was of the opinion that humanity could be helped only in pairs. But Count Leinsdorf held firmly to his assertion that "capital and culture have not done their duty by our historical development; we must give them one last chance!"

Count Leinsdorf was always coming back to this point.

"Tell me, my dear, haven't you come to a decision yet?" he would ask. "It's high time. All sorts of people are coming to the fore with destructive tendencies. We must give the cultural sector one last opportunity to restore the balance." But Diotima, deflected by the wealth of variation in the forms of human coupling, was deaf to all else.

Finally, Count Leinsdorf had to call her to order.

"You know, my dear, I hardly seem to know you anymore! We've given out the password 'Action!' to all and sundry; I myself had a hand—surely I may tell you in confidence that it was I who was behind the Minister of the Interior's resignation. It had to be done on a high level, you understand; a very high level! But it had really become a scandal, and nobody had the courage to put a stop to it. So this is just for your own ears," he continued, "and now the Premier has asked us to bestir ourselves a bit with our Inquiry Concerning the Desires of the Concerned Sections of the Population with Respect to the Conduct of Home Affairs, because the new Minister naturally can't be expected to have it at his fingertips; and now you want to leave me in the lurch, you who have always been the last to give up? We *must* give capital and culture a last chance! You know, it's either that or . . ."

This somewhat incomplete final sentence was uttered so menacingly that there was no mistaking that he knew what he wanted, and

Diotima obediently promised to hurry; but then she forgot again and did nothing.

And then one day Count Leinsdorf was seized by his well-known energy and drove straight to her door, propelled by forty horse-power.

"Has anything happened yet?" he asked, and Diotima had to admit that nothing had.

"Do you know the Inn River, my dear?" he asked.

Of course Diotima knew the Inn, second only to the Danube as Kakania's most famous river, richly interwoven with the country's geography and history. She observed her visitor rather dubiously, while doing her best to smile.

But Count Leinsdorf was in deadly earnest. "Apart from Innsbruck," he said, "what ridiculous backwoods places all those little towns in the Inn Valley are, and what an imposing river the Inn is in our culture! And to think I never realized it before!" He shook his head. "You see, I happened by chance to look at a highway map today," he said, finally coming to the point, "and I noticed that the Inn rises in Switzerland. I must have known it before, of course, we all know it, but we never give it a thought. It rises at Majola, I've seen it there myself; a ridiculous little creek no wider than the Kamp or the Morava in our country. But what have the Swiss made of it? The Engadine! The world-famous Engadine! The Engad-Inn, my dear! Has it ever occurred to you that the whole Engadine comes from the name Inn? That's what I hit upon today. While we, with our insufferable Austrian modesty, of course never make anything out of what belongs to us!"

After this chat Diotima hastened to arrange for the desired reception, partly because she realized that she had to stand by Count Leinsdorf, and partly because she was afraid of driving her high-ranking friend to some extreme if she continued to refuse.

But when she gave him her promise, Leinsdorf said:

"And this time, I beg of you, dearest lady, don't fail to invite—er— that x you call Drangsal. Her friend Frau Wayden has been pestering me about this person for weeks, and won't leave me in peace!"

Diotima promised this too, although at other times she would have regarded putting up with her rival as a dereliction of duty to her country.

158

A GREAT EVENT IS IN THE MAKING. PRIVY COUNCILLOR MESERITSCHER

When the rooms were filled with the radiance of festive illumination and the assembled company, an observer could note among those present not only His Excellency, together with other leading members of the high aristocracy for whose appearance he had arranged, but also His Excellency the Minister of War, and in the latter's entourage the intensely intellectual, somewhat overworked head of General Stumm von Bordwehr. One observed Paul Arnheim (without the "Dr.": simple and most effective; the observer had thought it over carefully—it's called "litotes," an artful understatement, like removing some trifle from one's body, as when a king removes a ring from his finger to place it on someone else's). Then one observed everyone worth mentioning from the various ministries (the Minister of Education and Culture had apologized to His Excellency in the Upper House for not coming in person; he had to go to Linz for the consecration of a great altar screen). Then one noted that the foreign embassies and legations had sent an "elite." There were well-known names "from industry, art, and science," and a time-honored allegory of diligence lay in this invariable combination of three bourgeois activities, a combination that seized hold of the scribbling pen all by itself. That same adept pen then presented the ladies: beige, pink, cherry, cream . . . ; embroidered, draped, triple-tiered, or dropped from the waist. . . . Between Countess Adlitz and Frau Generaldirektor Weghuber was listed the well-known Frau Melanie Drangsal, widow of the world-famous surgeon, "in her own right a charming hostess, who provides in her house a hearth for the leading lights of our times." Finally, listed separately at the end of this section, was the name of Ulrich von So-and-so and sister. The observer had hesitated about adding "whose name is widely associated with his selfless service on behalf of that high-minded and patriotic undertaking," or even "a coming man." Word had gone around long since that one of these days this protégé of Count Leinsdorf was widely expected to involve his patron in some rash misstep, and the temptation to go on record early as someone in the know was great. However, the deepest satisfaction for those in the know is always silence, especially when it proceeds from caution. It was to this that Ulrich and Agathe owed the mere mention of their names as stragglers, immediately preceding those leaders of society and the intelligentsia who are not named individually but simply destined for the mass grave of "all those of rank and station." Many people fell into this category, among them the well-known professor of jurisprudence Councillor Herr Professor Schwung, who happened to be in the capital as a member of a government commission of inquiry, and also the young poet Friedel Feuermaul, for although his was known to be among the moving spirits behind this evening's gathering, that was a far cry from the more substantial significance of a title or the triumphs of haute couture. People such as Acting Bank Director Leo Fischel and family—who had won admittance thanks to Gerda's grueling efforts, without any help from Ulrich, in other words because of Diotima's momentarily flagging attention—were simply buried in the corner of one's eye. And the wife of an eminent jurist (who was well known but on such an occasion still below the threshold of public notice), a lady whose name, Bonadea, was unknown even to the observer, was later exhumed for listing among the wearers of noteworthy gowns because her sensational looks aroused great admiration.

This impersonal seeing eye, the surveying curiosity of the public, was of course a person. There are usually quite a lot of them, but in the Kakanian metropolis at that time there was one who overtopped all the rest: Privy Councillor Meseritscher. Born in the Wallachian town of Meseritsch, whence his name, this publisher, editor, and news correspondent of the *Parliamentary and Social Gazette*, which he had founded in the sixties of the last century, had come to the capital as a young man, sacrificing his expectation of taking over his parents' tavern in his native town in order to become a journalist, having been attracted by the political promise of liberalism that was then at its zenith. And before long he had made his contribution to that era by founding a news agency, which began by supplying small local items of a police nature to the newspapers. Thanks to the industry, reliability, and thoroughness of its owner, this rudimentary agency not only earned the esteem of the papers and the police but was soon noticed by other high authorities as well, and used by them for placing items they wanted to publicize without taking responsibility, so that the agency soon found itself in a privileged position for tapping unofficial information from official sources. A man of great enterprise and a tireless worker, Meseritscher, as he saw this success developing, extended his activity to include news from the Court and Society; indeed, he would probably never have left Meseritsch for the capital if this had not been his guiding vision. Flawless reporting of "those present" was regarded as his specialty. His memory for people and what was said about them was extraordinary, and this assured him of the same splendid relationship with the salon that he had with the prison. He knew Society better than it knew itself, and his unflagging devotion enabled him to make people who had met at a gathering properly acquainted with each other the very next morning, like some old cavalier in whom everyone has for decades been confiding all their marriage plans and the problems they were having with their dressmakers. And so, on every sort of great occasion, the zealous, nimble, ever-obliging, affable little man was a familiar institution, and in his later years it was only he and his presence that conferred indisputable prestige to such occasions.

Meseritscher's career had reached a peak when the title Privy Councillor was bestowed upon him, and this involves an interesting peculiarity. Kakania was the most peace-loving of countries, but at some time or other it had decided, in the profound innocence of its convictions, that, wars being a thing of the past, its civil service should be organized as a hierarchy corresponding to military ranks, complete with similar uniforms and insignia. Since then the rank of Privy Councillor corresponded to that of a lieutenant colonel in His Majesty's Imperial and Royal Army. But even though this was not in itself an exalted rank, the peculiarity was that according to an immutable tradition, which, like everything immutable in Kakania, was modified only in exceptional cases, Meseritscher should really have been named an Imperial Councillor. An Imperial Councillor was not, as one might suppose from the term, superior to a Privy Councillor, but inferior: it only corresponded to the rank of captain. Meseritscher should have been an Imperial Councillor because that title was given, other than to certain civil servants, only to those engaged in independent professions such as, for example, court barber or coach builder, and, by the same token, writers and artists; while Privy Councillor was at the time an actual high-ranking title in the civil service. That Meseritscher was nevertheless the first and only member of his profession to be so honored expressed something more than the high honor of the title itself—indeed, even more than the daily reminder not to take too seriously whatever happens in this country of ours; the unjustified title was a subtle and discreet way of assuring the indefatigable chronicler his close association with Court, State, and Society.

Meseritscher had been a model for many journalists in his time, and was on the boards of leading literary associations. The story also went around that he had had made for himself a uniform with a gold collar, but only put it on, sometimes, at home. Chances are the rumor was untrue, because deep down Meseritscher had always preserved certain memories of the tavern trade in Meseritsch, and a good tavernkeeper also knows the secrets of all his guests but doesn't make use of everything he knows; he never brings his own opinions into a discussion but enjoys noting and telling everything in the way of fact, anecdote, or joke. And so Meseritscher, whom one met on every social occasion as the acknowledged memorializer of beautiful women and distinguished men, had himself never even thought of going to a good tailor; he knew all the behind-the-scenes intricacies of politics, yet had never dabbled in politics in even a single line of print; he knew about all the discoveries and inventions of his time without understanding any of them. He was perfectly satisfied to know that they existed and were "present." He honestly loved his time, and his time reciprocated his affection to a certain degree, because he daily reported its presence to the world.

When Diotima caught sight of him as he entered, she immediately beckoned him to her side.

"My dear Meseritscher," she said, as sweetly as she knew how. "You surely didn't take His Excellency's speech in the Upper House today as an expression of our position—you couldn't have taken it literally?"

His Excellency, in the context of the Minister's downfall and exasperated by his cares, had made a widely noticed speech in the Upper House in which he not only charged his victim with having failed to show the true constructive spirit of cooperation and strictness of principle, but also let his zeal carry him to making general observations that in some inexplicable fashion culminated in a recognition of the importance of the press, in which he reproached this "institution risen to the status of a world power" with pretty much everything with which a feudal-minded, independent, nonpartisan, Christian gentleman could charge an institution that in his view is the dead opposite of himself. It was this that Diotima was diplomatically trying to smooth over, and Meseritscher listened pensively as she found increasingly fine and unintelligible language for Count Leinsdorf's real point of view. Then suddenly he laid a hand on her arm and magnanimously interrupted her:

"My dear lady, how can you upset yourself like this?" he summed up. "His Excellency is a good friend to us, isn't he? What if he did exaggerate? Why shouldn't he, a gallant gentleman like him?" And to prove that his relationship to the Count was unruffled, he added: "I'll just go and greet him now!"

That was Meseritscher! But before he moved off he turned to Diotima once more and asked confidentially:

"What about Feuermaul, dear lady?"

Smiling, Diotima shrugged her beautiful shoulders. "Nothing so very earthshaking, my dear Councillor. We wouldn't like it to be said that we rebuffed anyone who came to us in good faith!"

"Good faith—that's rich," Meseritscher thought on his way to Count Leinsdorf. But before he reached him, indeed even before his thoughts had reached a conclusion, his host stepped amicably into his path.

"My dear Meseritscher, my official sources have let me down again," Section Chief Tuzzi began with a smile. "So I'm turning to you as our semi-official source of information. Can *you* tell me anything about this Feuermaul who's here this evening?"

"What would I have to tell you, Herr Section Chief?" Meseritscher deprecated.

"I'm told he's a genius."

"Glad to hear it!" Meseritscher answered.

If the news is to be reported with speed and confidence, today's news should not be too different from yesterday's, or what one knows already. Even genius is no exception: real, acknowledged genius, that is, whose significance can be readily assessed in its own time. Not so the genius that is not instantly recognized by all and sundry! This sort of genius has something distinctly ungenial about it, a quality, moreover, that is not even solely its own, so that it is possible to misjudge it in every respect. Privy Councillor Meseritscher had a solid inventory of geniuses, which he tended with care and attention, but he was not keen on adding new items. The older and more experienced he grew, in fact, the more he had even formed the habit of regarding any rising artistic genius, especially in his neighboring field of literature, merely as a frivolous interference with his own work of reportage, and he hated it in all righteousness until it became ripe for inclusion in his lists of "those present." At that time Feuermaul still had a long way to go, and his way had yet to be smoothed for him. Privy Councillor Meseritscher was not quite sure he was in favor.

"They say he's supposed to be a great poet," Tuzzi repeated hesitantly, and Meseritscher retorted firmly: "Who says so? The critics on the book page? I ask you, Section Chief, what difference does that make? The specialists say these things, and what of it? Many of them say the opposite. We've even known the same experts to say one thing one day and something else the next. Does it really matter what they say? A real literary reputation has to have reached the illiterates; only then can you depend on it! Would you like to know what I think? What a great man does, apart from his arriving and leaving, is nobody's business!"

He had worked himself up into a gloomy fervor, and his eyes were glued to Tuzzi's. Tuzzi gave up and said nothing.

"What's really going on here this evening, Section Chief?" Meseritscher asked him.

Tuzzi smiled absently and shrugged his shoulders. "Nothing. Nothing, really. A little ambition. Have you ever read any of Feuermaul's books?"

"I know what he writes about: peace, friendship, goodness, et cetera."

"So you don't think too much of him?" Tuzzi said.

"Good Lord!" Meseritscher started wriggling. "Who am I to say . . . ?" At this point Frau Drangsal came bearing down on them, and Tuzzi had to take a courteous step or two in her direction. Meseritscher saw the chance to slip into a breach he had espied in the circle around Count Leinsdorf, and seizing it before anyone else could waylay him, he dropped anchor beside His Grace.

Count Leinsdorf was talking with the Minister and some other men, but as soon as Meseritscher had paid them all his devout respects, His Grace turned slightly and drew him aside.

"Meseritscher," he said intently. "Promise me that there will be no misunderstandings; the gentlemen of the press never seem to know what to write. Now then: Nothing whatsoever has changed in our position since the last time. Something may change. We don't know about that. For the time being there must be no interference. So please, even if one of your colleagues should ask you, remember that this whole evening here is nothing more than a private party given by Frau Tuzzi."

Meseritscher's eyelids slowly and solicitously conveyed that he had understood these top-level commands. And since one confidence deserves another, he moistened his lips, which then gleamed as his eyes should have done, and asked: "And what about Feuermaul, Your Excellency, if I may be permitted to ask?"

"Why on earth shouldn't you?" Count Leinsdorf replied in surprise. "There's nothing whatever to be said about Feuermaul! He was invited because Baroness Wayden wouldn't leave us in peace until he was! What else should there be? Perhaps you know something?"

Up to this point Privy Councillor Meseritscher had not been inclined to take the Feuermaul question too seriously, but regarded it as one of the many social rivalries he ran into every day. But now that even Count Leinsdorf denied so energetically that there was anything in it, Meseritscher had to think again, and came to the conclusion that something important was in the wind. "What can they be up to now?" he brooded as he wandered through the throng, pondering one by one the most daring possibilities of domestic and foreign policy. But after a while he decided abruptly: "There's probably nothing to it," and refused to let himself be distracted any longer from his job of reporting the news.

For however much it appeared to be in conflict with his mission in life, Meseritscher did not believe in great events; indeed, he did not hold with them. When one believes that one is living in a very important, very splendid, and very great period, one does not welcome the idea that anything especially important, splendid, and great has yet to happen in it. Meseritscher was no alpinist, but if he had been he would have said that his attitude was as correct as it was to put lookout towers on middling-high mountains but never on the really high peaks. Since such analogies did not occur to him, it was enough to register a certain uneasiness and make up his mind that he would not mention Feuermaul in his column at all, not even by name.

159

A GREAT EVENT IS IN THE MAKING. MEETING SOME OLD ACQUAINTANCES

Ulrich, who had been standing beside his cousin while she was speaking with Meseritscher, asked her as soon as they were alone for a moment:

"I'm sorry I arrived too late; how was your first encounter with La Drangsal?"

Diotima raised her heavy eyelashes to give him a single worldweary glance and dropped them again.

"Delightful, of course. She'd been to see me. We'll arrange something or other this evening. As if it made any difference!"

"You see!" Ulrich said, in the tone of their old conversations, as if to draw a final line under all that.

Diotima turned her head and gave her cousin a quizzical look.

"I told you already," Ulrich said. "Now it's almost all over, as if nothing had happened." He needed to talk: when he had got home that afternoon, Agathe had been there but soon left again; they had spoken only a few brief words before they came to Diotima's; Agathe had dressed with the aid of the gardener's wife. "I did warn you!" Ulrich said.

"Against what?" Diotima asked slowly.

"Oh, I don't know. Against everything!"

In fact, he no longer knew himself what he had *not* warned her against: her ideas, her ambition, the Parallel Campaign, love, intellect, the Jubilee Year, the world of business, her salon, her passions; against the dangers of sensibility and of casually letting things take their course, against letting herself go too far and holding herself too much in check, against adultery and marriage. There was nothing he had not warned her against. "That's how she is," he thought. Everything she did looked ridiculous to him, yet she was so beautiful it made him sad.

"I warned you," Ulrich repeated. "I hear that you're no longer interested in anything but the scientific approach to sexual problems."

Diotima ignored this. "Do you think this Drangsal's protégé is really gifted?" she asked.

"Certainly," Ulrich replied. "Gifted, young, undeveloped. His success and this woman will be the ruin of him. In this country newborn babies are ruined by being told that they are people with fabulous instincts that intellectual development would only rob them of. He sometimes comes up with good ideas, but can't let ten minutes go by without making an ass of himself." He leaned over to say in her ear: "Do you know anything specific about that woman?"

Diotima shook her head almost imperceptibly.

"She's dangerously ambitious," Ulrich said. "But not uninteresting from the point of view of your current researches. Where beautiful women used to wear a fig leaf, she wears a laurel leaf! I hate women like that!"

Diotima did not laugh, nor even smile; she merely inclined her head toward the "cousin."

"And how do you find him as a man?" he asked.

"Pathetic," Diotima whispered. "Like a lambkin running to premature fat."

"What of it? The beauty of the male is only a secondary sexual characteristic," Ulrich said. "What's primarily exciting about him is the expectation of his success. Ten years from now Feuermaul will be an international celebrity; Drangsal's connections will take care of that, and then she'll marry him. If he remains a celebrity, it'll be a happy marriage."

Diotima bethought herself and gravely corrected him: "Happiness in marriage depends on factors one cannot judge without first subjecting oneself to a certain discipline!" Then she abandoned him as a proud ship abandons the quay alongside which it has lain. Her duties as hostess bore her away from him with the barest nod, not even a glance, as she cast off her moorings. But she did not mean it unkindly; on the contrary, Ulrich's voice had affected her like an old tune from her youth. She even wondered privately what she might learn about him by subjecting his sexuality to the illumination of a scientific study. Oddly enough, in all her detailed research into these problems, she had never thought of connecting them with him.

Ulrich looked up, and through a gap in the festive tumult—a kind of optical channel through which Diotima's gaze might have preceded his own just before she had taken her somewhat abrupt departure—he saw, in the room beyond the next, Paul Arnheim in conversation with Feuermaul, with Frau Drangsal standing benignly by. She had brought the two men together. Arnheim was holding the hand with the cigar raised, as though in an unconscious gesture of self-defense, but he was smiling most engagingly; Feuermaul was talking vivaciously, holding his cigar with two fingers and sucking at it between sentences with the greed of a calf butting its muzzle at the maternal udder. Ulrich could have imagined what they were talking about, but he didn't bother; he stayed where he was, in happy isolation, looking around for his sister. He discovered her in a group of men who were mostly strangers to him, and a cool chill ran through him despite his distractedness. But just then Stumm von Bordwehr poked him gently in the ribs with a fingertip, and at the same moment Hofrat Professor Schwung approached him on the other side but was stopped a few steps away by the intervention of one of his colleagues from the capital.

"So there you are at last!" the General murmured in relief. "The Minister wants to know what an 'ethos' is."

"Why an ethos?"

"I don't know. What's an ethos?"

"An eternal truth," Ulrich defined, "that is neither eternal nor true, but valid for a time to serve as a standard for people to go by. It's a philosophical and sociological term, and not often used."

"Aha, that'll be it," the General said. "Arnheim, you see, was claiming that the proposition 'Man is good' is only an ethos. Feuermaul replied that he didn't know what an ethos was, but man is good, and that's an eternal truth! Then Leinsdorf said, 'Quite right. There can't really be any evil people, since no one can possibly will evil; these people are only misguided. People are rather nervous these days because in times like these we have so many skeptics who won't believe in anything solid.' I couldn't help thinking he should have been with us this afternoon. Anyway, he also thinks that people who won't realize what's good for them have to be forced to. And so the Minister wants to know what an ethos is. I'll just dash over to him and come right back. Don't budge, so I can find you again! There's something else I must talk with you about, urgently, and then I'll take you to the Minister."

Before Ulrich could ask for particulars, Tuzzi slipped a hand around his arm in passing, saying: "We haven't seen you here in ages!" Then he went on: "Do you remember my prediction that we'd have a pacifist invasion to deal with?" So saying, he gazed cordially into the General's eyes, but Stumm was in a hurry and merely said that though his ethos as an officer was of another kind, any sincere conviction . . . The rest of this sentence vanished with him, because he always found Tuzzi irritating, which is not conducive to good thinking.

The Section Chief blinked gaily at the General's retreating form and then turned back to the "cousin." "That business with the oil fields is only a blind, of course," he said.

Ulrich looked at him in surprise.

"You don't mean to say you haven't heard about the oil fields?" Tuzzi asked.

"I have," Ulrich answered. "I was merely surprised that you knew about them," and, not to be impolite, added, "You really understood how to keep quiet about it!"

"I've known about them for quite some time," Tuzzi said, flattered. "That this fellow Feuermaul is here this evening is of course Arnheim's doing, by way of Leinsdorf. Have you read his books, incidentally?"

Ulrich admitted that he had.

"A dyed-in-the-wool pacifist!" Tuzzi said. "And La Drangsal, as my wife calls her, mothers him so ambitiously that she'll kill for pacifism if she has to, even though it's not really her line—artists are her line." Tuzzi paused to consider, then revealed to Ulrich: "Pacifism is the main thing, of course; the oil fields are only a red herring; that's why they're pushing Feuermaul, with his pacifism, to make everyone think: 'Aha, that's the red herring!' and believe that what's behind it is the oil fields! Neatly done, but much too clever to fool anybody. For if Arnheim has the Galician oil fields and a contract to supply the Army, we naturally have to protect our frontier. We also have to install oil bases for the Navy on the Adriatic, which will upset the Italians. But if we provoke our neighbors this way, the outcry for peace goes up, and so does the peace propaganda, and then when the Czar steps forward with some idea about Perpetual Peace, he'll find the ground psychologically prepared for it. That's Arnheim's real objective!"

"And you've something against it?"

"Of course we have nothing against it," Tuzzi said. "But as you may remember, I've already explained to you why there's nothing so dangerous as peace at any price. We must defend ourselves against the dilettantes!"

"But Arnheim is a munitions maker!" Ulrich objected, smiling.

"Of course he is!" Tuzzi murmured with some exasperation. "For heaven's sake, how can you be so naïve about these things? He'll have his contract in his pocket. At most, our neighbors will arm too. Mark my words: at the crucial moment, he'll show his hand as a pacifist! Pacifism is a safe, dependable business for munitions makers; war is a risk!"

"It seems to me the military doesn't really mean any harm," Ulrich said, trying to mollify him. "They're only using the business with Arnheim to bring their artillery up-to-date, nothing more. Today the whole world is only arming for peace, after all, so it only seems right to let the pacifists help."

"And how do these people imagine that's to be done?" Tuzzi inquired, ignoring the joke.

"I don't think they've got that far yet; for the present they're still searching their hearts."

"Naturally!" Tuzzi agreed crossly, as though this were just what he had expected. "The military ought to stick to thinking about war and leave everything else to the department responsible. But before doing that, these gentlemen with their dilettantism would rather endanger the whole world! I tell you again: Nothing is so dangerous in diplomacy as loose talk about peace! Every time the demand for peace has reached a certain pitch and was no longer to be contained, it's led straight to war! I can document that for you!"

Now Hofrat Professor Schwung had rid himself of his colleague and turned with great warmth to Ulrich for an introduction to their host. Ulrich obliged with the remark that one might say that this distinguished jurist condemned pacifism in the sphere of the penal code as ardently as the authoritative Section Chief did in the political arena.

"But good gracious," Tuzzi protested, laughing, "you've misunderstood me entirely!"

And Schwung too, after a moment's hesitation, was sufficiently reassured to join forces with him, saying that he would not like his view of diminished responsibility to be regarded as in any way bloodthirsty or inhumane.

"Quite the opposite!" he said, spreading his voice in place of his arms like an old actor on the lecture platform. "It is precisely the pacification of the human being that requires us to be strict! May I assume that the Herr Section Chief has heard something about my most recent current efforts in this matter?" And he now turned directly to his host, who had heard nothing about the dispute as to whether the diminished responsibility of an insane criminal is based exclusively in his ideas or exclusively in his will, and thus hastened all the more politely to agree with everything Schwung said. Schwung, well satisfied with the effect he had produced, then began to praise the serious view of life to which this evening's gathering gave witness, and reported that he had often overheard in conversations here and there such expressions as "manly severity" and "moral soundness." "Our culture is far too infested with inferior types and moral imbeciles," he added by way of his own contribution, and asked: "But what is the real purpose of this evening? As I passed some of the groups, I've been struck by how often I've heard positively Rousseauistic sentiments about the innate goodness of man."

Tuzzi, to whom this question was principally addressed, merely smiled, but just then the General came back to Ulrich, and Ulrich, who wanted to give him the slip, introduced him to Schwung and called him the man best qualified among all those present to answer the question. Stumm von Bordwehr vehemently denied this, but neither Schwung nor even Tuzzi would let him go. Ulrich was already beating a jubilant retreat, when he was grabbed by an old acquaintance, who said:

"My wife and daughter are also here." It was Bank Director Leo Fischel.

"Hans Sepp has passed his State Exam," he said. "What do you say to that? All he has to do now is pass one more exam for his doctorate! We're all sitting in that corner over there. . . ." He pointed toward the farthest room. "We know too few people here. Nor have we seen anything of you for a long time! Your father, wasn't it . . . ? Hans Sepp got us the invitation for this evening—my wife was dead set on it—so you see the fellow isn't entirely hopeless. They're semi-officially engaged now, he and Gerda. You probably didn't know that, did you? But Gerda, you see, that girl, I don't even know whether she's in love with him or has just got it into her head that she is. Won't you come over and join us for a bit?"

"I'll be along later," Ulrich promised.

"Please do," Fischel urged, and fell silent. Then he whispered: "Isn't that our host? Won't you introduce me? We haven't had the opportunity. We don't know either him or her."

But when Ulrich made a move in that direction, Fischel held him back. "And how is the great philosopher? What's he up to?" he asked. "My wife and Gerda are of course mad about him. But what's this about the oil fields? The word now is that it was a false rumor, but I don't believe it. They always deny it! You know, it's the same as when my wife is annoyed with a maid, then I keep hearing that the maid is untruthful, immoral, impertinent—nothing but defects of character, you see? But when I quietly promise the girl a raise, just to have peace in the house, then her character suddenly disappears. No more talk about character, everything's suddenly in order, and my wife doesn't know why. Isn't it always like that? There's too much economic probability in those oil fields for the denials to be believed."

And because Ulrich held his peace, while Fischel wanted to return to his wife as the glorious bearer of inside information, he began once more:

"One has to admit it's very nice here. But my wife would like to know what all the strange talk is about. And who is this Feuermaul anyway?" he added. "Gerda says he's a great poet; Hans Sepp says he's nothing but a careerist who's taken everyone in!"

Ulrich allowed that the truth probably lay somewhere in between.

"Now, that's well put!" Fischel said gratefully. "The truth always lies somewhere in between, which everyone forgets nowadays, they're all so extreme! I keep telling Hans Sepp that everyone's entitled to his opinions, but the only opinions that count are the ones that enable you to earn a living, because that means that other people appreciate your opinions too!"

There had been an impalpable but important change in Leo Fischel, but Ulrich unfortunately passed up the opportunity to look into it and merely hastened to leave Gerda's father with the group around Section Chief Tuzzi. Here Stumm von Bordwehr had meanwhile grown eloquent, frustrated at his inability to pin Ulrich down, and so highly charged with things to say that they burst out by the shortest path.

"How to account for this gathering tonight?" he cried, reiterating Hofrat Schwung's question. "I would assert, in the same judicious spirit in which it was asked: Not at all! I'm not joking, gentlemen," he went on, not without a touch of pride. "This very afternoon I happened to ask a young lady whom I had to show around the psychiatric clinic of our University what it was she was actually interested in seeing, so we could explain it properly, and she gave me a very witty answer, exceptionally thought-provoking. What she said was: 'If we stop to explain everything, we will never change anything in the world.' "

Schwung shook his head in disapproval.

"What she meant by that I don't really know"—Stumm defended himself—"and I won't take responsibility for it, but you can't help feeling there is some truth in it. You see, I am, for instance, indebted to my friend here"—he gave a polite nod in Ulrich's direction—"who has so often given His Grace, and thereby the Parallel Campaign too, the benefit of his thoughts, for a great deal of instruction. But what is taking shape here tonight is a certain distaste for instruction. Which brings me back to my first assertion."

"But isn't what you want . . . ?" Tuzzi said. "I mean, the word is that colleagues from the War Ministry hope to stimulate a patriotic decision here, a collection of public funds or some such thing, in order to bring our artillery up to strength. Naturally, a mere token demonstration, just to put some pressure on Parliament through public opinion."

"That is certainly my understanding of some things I've heard tonight!" Hofrat Schwung concurred.

"It's much more complicated, Herr Section Chief," the General said.

"And what about Dr. Arnheim?" Tuzzi said bluntly. "If I may be quite candid: Are you sure that Arnheim wants nothing more than the Galician oil fields, which are tied up, as it were, with the artillery problem?"

"I can only speak of myself and my part in it, Section Chief," Stumm said, warding him off, then repeated: "And it's all much more complicated!"

"Naturally it's more complicated," Tuzzi said, smiling.

"Of course we need the guns," the General said, warming to the subject, "and it may indeed be advantageous to work with Arnheim along the lines you suggest. But I repeat that I can only speak from my point of view as a cultural officer, and as such I put it to you: 'What's the use of cannons without the spirit to go with them?'"

"And why, in that case, was so much importance attached to bringing in Herr Feuermaul?" Tuzzi asked ironically. "That is defeatism pure and simple!"

"Permit me to disagree," the General said firmly, "but that is the spirit of the times! Nowadays the spirit of the times has two separate currents. His Grace—he's standing over there with the Minister; I've just come from talking with them—His Grace, for instance, says that the call has to go out for action, that's what the times demand. And in fact people are much less enchanted with the great idea of humanity than they were, say, a hundred years ago. On the other hand, there is of course something to be said for the point of view of loving mankind, but about that His Grace says that those who do not want what is good for them must in certain circumstances be forced to accept it! So His Grace is in favor of the one current, but without turning his back on the other."

"I don't quite follow that," Professor Schwung demurred.

"It's not easy to follow," Stumm readily admitted. "Suppose we go back to the point that I see two currents at work in the mind of our period. The one states that man is good by nature, when he is left to himself, as it were—"

"How do you mean good?" Schwung interrupted. "Who can possibly think in such naïve terms nowadays? We're not living in the world of eighteenth-century idealism!"

"Well, I don't know about that." The General sounded rather nettled. "Just think of the pacifists, the vegetarians, the enemies of violence, the back-to-nature people, the anti-intellectuals, the conscientious objectors—I can't call them all to mind offhand—and all the people who put their faith in mankind, as it were; they all form one big current. But if you prefer," he added in that obliging way he had that made him so likable, "we can just as easily start out from the opposite point of view. Suppose we start with the fact that people must be regimented because they never do the right thing of their own accord; we might find it easier to agree on that. The masses need a strong hand, they need leaders who can be tough with them and don't just talk; in a word, they need to be guided by the spirit of action. Human society consists, as it were, of only a small number of volunteers, who also have the necessary training, and of millions without any higher ambitions, who serve only because they must. Isn't that so, roughly speaking? And because experience has gradually forced us to recognize this fact even here in our campaign, the first current—for what I've just been talking about is the second current—the first current, I say, is alarmed at the possibility that the great idea of love and faith in mankind might get lost altogether. Hence there were forces at work, you see, that have sent Feuermaul into our midst to save what can still be saved at the eleventh hour. Which makes it all much easier to understand than we first thought, no?"

"And what's going to happen then?" Tuzzi wanted to know.

"Nothing, I imagine," Stumm replied. "We've had lots of currents in the campaign by now."

"But there's an intolerable contradiction between your two currents," protested Professor Schwung, who as a jurist could not bear such ambiguity.

"Not if you look at it closely," Stumm countered. "The one current is of course also in favor of loving mankind, provided you change it first by force. They differ on a technicality, you might say."

Now Director Fischel spoke up: "As a latecomer to the discussion, I'm afraid I don't have a complete picture. But if I may say so, it seems to me that respect for humanity is basically on a higher level than its opposite. This evening I've heard some incredible sentiments—not representative of this gathering, I'm sure, but still—incredible sentiments about people of different convictions and above all of differing nationalities." With his chin clean-shaven between muttonchop whiskers and his tilted pince-nez, he looked like an English lord upholding the freedom of humanity and free trade; he did not mention that the disreputable sentiments in question were those of Hans Sepp, his prospective son-in-law, who was in his element in "the second current" of our times.

"Savage sentiments?" the General asked helpfully.

"Extraordinarily savage," Fischel confirmed.

"Could they have been talking about 'toughening up'? It's easy to misconstrue that kind of talk," Stumm said.

"No, no," Fischel exclaimed. "Utterly nihilistic, positively revolutionary views! Perhaps you're out of touch with our rebellious younger generation, Herr Major General. I'm surprised that such people are admitted here at all."

"Revolutionary views?" Stumm asked, not at all pleased, and smiling in as chilly a manner as his plump face would allow. "I'm afraid I must admit, Herr Direktor, that I'm by no means an out-and-out opponent of revolutionary views. Short of an actual revolution, of course. There's often a good deal of idealism in that sort of thing. And as for admitting them here, our campaign, which is intended to draw the whole country together, has no right to turn away constructive forces, in whatever mode they may express themselves!"

Leo Fischel was silent. Professor Schwung was not much interested in the views of a dignitary who was outside the ranks of the civilian bureaucracy. Tuzzi had been dreaming: "first current . . . second current." It reminded him of two similar expressions, "first reservoir . . . second reservoir," but he could not remember them precisely, or the conversation with Ulrich in which they had come up; yet it stirred in him an incomprehensible jealousy of his wife, which was connected to this harmless General by intangible links he could not begin to disentangle. Awakened to reality by the silence, he wanted to show the representative of the military that he was not to be sidetracked by digressions.

"All in all, General," he began, "the military party wants—"

"But, my dear Section Chief, there *is* no military party!" Stumm immediately broke in. "People are always talking about a military party, but by its very nature the military is above party!"

"Let's say the military hierarchy, then," Tuzzi replied, chafing at the interruption. "You were saying that what the army needs is not just guns but the spirit to go with them; by what spirit will you be pleased to have your guns loaded?"

"That's going too far, Section Chief!" Stumm protested. "It all started with my being asked to explain tonight's gathering to these gentlemen, and I said one really couldn't explain anything; that's all I'm taking my stand on! If the spirit of the times really has two such currents as I have described, neither of them favors 'explanation'; today we favor instinctual energies, dark forces in the blood, and the like. I certainly don't go along with that, but there's something in it!"

At these words Fischel began to fume again, finding it immoral for the military to even consider making terms with the anti-Semites in order to get their guns.

"Come now, Herr Director," Stumm tried to pacify him. "In the first place, a little anti-Semitism more or less hardly matters when people are already so anti to begin with: the Germans anti the Czechs and the Magyars, the Czechs anti the Magyars and the Germans, and so on, everybody against everybody else. Second, if anyone has always been international, it has been the Austrian Army Officers Corps: you need only look at the many Italian, French, Scottish, and Lord knows what other names; we even have an Infantry General von Kohn, he's a corps commandant in Olmütz!"

"All the same, I'm afraid you've bitten off more than you can chew," Tuzzi broke in on this diversion. "You're both internationalist and war-minded, but you want to deal with the nationalist movements and the pacifists as well: that's almost more than a professional diplomat could manage. Conducting military politics with pacifism is the task confronting the greatest diplomatic experts in Europe at this moment!"

"But we're not at all the ones who are playing politics!" Stumm protested again, in a tone of weary complaint over so much misunderstanding. "His Grace simply wanted to give capital and culture one last chance to join forces—that's the whole reason for this evening. Of course, if the civilian sector can't come to some kind of accord, we would find ourselves in a position—"

"In what position? That would be interesting to hear, indeed!" Tuzzi cried, a bit too eager to fan the flame.

"Well, in a difficult position, of course," Stumm said with caution and modesty.

While the four gentlemen were engaged in this discussion, Ulrich had long since unobtrusively slipped away to find Gerda, giving a wide berth to the group around His Grace and the Minister to avoid a summons from that quarter.

He caught sight of her from some way off, sitting by the wall beside her mother, who was gazing stiffly into the salon. Hans Sepp was standing at her other side, with an uneasy, defiant look. Since her last miserable encounter with Ulrich, Gerda had grown even thinner, looking more barren of feminine charms the closer he came, and yet, by the same measure, more banefully attractive, her head on those slack shoulders standing out against the room. When she caught sight of Ulrich her face flushed scarlet, only to turn paler than ever, and she made an involuntary movement with her upper body like someone with a sharp pain in the heart who is somehow unable to press a hand to the spot. He had a fleeting vision of the scene when, wildly intent on his animal advantage in having aroused her physically, he had abused her confusion. There that body was sitting, visible to him beneath her dress, receiving orders from her humiliated will to hold itself proudly high, but trembling the while. Gerda was not angry at him, he could see, but she wanted to be done with him at all costs. He unobtrusively slowed down, trying to savor this to the full, and this sensuous tarrying seemed in keeping with the relationship between these two people, who could never quite come together. When Ulrich was very close to her, aware of nothing now but the quivering in the uplifted face awaiting him, he felt in passing something weightless, like a shadow or a gust of warmth; and he perceived Bonadea, who had passed by him in silence but hardly without intent, and in all probability had been following him. He bowed to her. The world is beautiful if one takes it as it is: For a second the naïve contrast between the voluptuous and the meager, as expressed in these two women, loomed as large to him as that between pasture and rock at the timberline, and he felt himself stepping down from the Parallel Campaign, even though with a guilty smile. When Gerda saw this smile slowly sinking down toward her outstretched hand, her eyelids quivered.

At this moment Diotima noticed that Arnheim was taking young Feuermaul to meet His Grace and the War Minister, and, skilled tactician that she was, she thwarted all encounters by ordering the servants in with trays of refreshments.

160

A COMPARISON

Such conversations as those just reported went on by the dozen, and they all had something in common, which is not easy to describe but that cannot be passed over if one lacks Privy Councillor Meseritscher's flair for giving a dazzling account of a party just by making lists: who was there, wearing what, and saying this and that—all those things that are, in fact, considered by many to be the truest narrative art. So Friedel Feuermaul was not really being a miserable toady, which he never was, but merely finding the right word for the time and place when he said of Meseritscher, while standing in front of him: "He's really the Homer of our era! No, I mean it," he added, when Meseritscher tried to brush it off. "That epic, imperturbable 'and' with which you link all persons and events strikes me as having real greatness!" He had got hold of Meseritscher because the editor of the *Parliamentary and Social Gazette* had been reluctant to leave without paying his respects to Arnheim; but this still did not get Feuermaul's name into print "among those present."

Without going into the finer distinctions between idiots and cretins, suffice it to say that an idiot of a certain degree is not up to forming the concept "parents," even though he has no trouble with the idea of "father and mother." This same simple additive, "and," was Meseritscher's device for relating social phenomena to one another. Another point about idiots is that in the basic concreteness of their thinking they have something that is generally agreed to appeal to the emotions in a mysterious way; and poets appeal directly to the emotions in very much the same way, insofar as their minds run to palpable realities. And so, when Friedel Feuermaul addressed Meseritscher as a poet, he could just as well—that is, out of the same obscure, hovering feeling, which, in his case, was also tantamount to a sudden illumination—have called him an idiot, in a way that would have had considerable significance for all mankind. For the element common to both is a mental condition that cannot be spanned by far-reaching concepts, or refined by distinctions and abstractions, a mental state of the crudest pattern, expressed most clearly in the way it limits itself to the simplest of coordinating conjunctions, the helplessly additive "and," which for those of meager mental capacity replaces more intricate relationships; and it may be said that our world, regardless of all its intellectual riches, is in a mental condition akin to idiocy; indeed, there is no avoiding this conclusion if one tries to grasp as a totality what is going on in the world.

Not that those who are the first to propound or who come to share such a view have a monopoly on intelligence! It simply doesn't depend in the least on the individual, or on the pursuits he is engaged in—and which were indeed being engaged in, with more or with less shrewdness, by all those who had come to Diotima's on this evening. For when General Stumm von Bordwehr, for instance, during the pause caused by the arrival of refreshments, got into a conversation with His Grace in the course of which he argued in a genially obstinate and respectfully daring tone: "With all due respect, Your Grace, permit me to disagree most strongly; there is more than mere presumption in people who are proud of their race; there is also something appealingly aristocratic!" he knew precisely what he meant by these words, but not so precisely what he conveyed by them, for such civilities are wrapped in an extra something that is like a pair of thick gloves in which one must struggle to pick up a single match out of a full box. And Leo Fischel, who had not budged from Stumm's side after he noticed that the General was moving impatiently toward His Grace, added:

"People must be judged not by their race but on their merit!"

What His Grace replied was logical; disregarding Director Fischel, who had only just been introduced to him, he answered Stumm:

"What does the middle class need race for? They've always been up in arms about a court chamberlain needing sixteen noble ancestors, and now what are they doing themselves? Trying to ape it, and exaggerating it to boot! More than sixteen ancestors is sheer snobbery!" For His Grace was upset, and therefore it was quite logical for him to express himself in this fashion. Man is indisputably endowed with reason; the problem is only how he uses his reason in the company of others.

His Grace was vexed by the intrusion of "national" elements into the Parallel Campaign, although he himself had brought it about. Various political and social considerations had driven him to it; he himself recognized only "the national populace." His political friends had advised him: "There's no harm in listening to what they have to say about race and purity and blood—who takes what anyone says seriously anyway?"

"But they're talking about human beings as if they were beasts!" Count Leinsdorf had objected; he had a Catholic view of human dignity, which prevented him from seeing that the principles of the chicken farm and of horse breeding could be equally well applied to God's children, even though he was a great landowner. To this his friends had replied: "Come now, you've no need to brood about it. And anyhow it's probably better than their talking about the good of mankind and all that revolutionary drivel from abroad, as they've been doing." His Grace had finally seen the light on this point. But His Grace was also vexed because this fellow Feuermaul, whom he had forced Diotima to invite, was merely bringing fresh confusion into the Parallel Campaign and was a disappointment to him. Baroness Wayden had praised Feuermaul to the skies, and he had finally yielded to her insistence. "You're quite right," Leinsdorf had conceded. "The way things are going just now, we can easily be accused of Germanizing. And there may be no harm, as you say, in inviting a poet who says that we *have* to love all mankind. But don't you see, I can't really spring that on Frau Tuzzi!" But the Baroness would not give an inch and must have found new and effective arguments, for at the end of their conversation Leinsdorf had promised to make Diotima invite Feuermaul. "Not that I like doing it," he had said, "but a strong hand does need the right word to get its message across; I must agree with you there. And it's also true that things have been moving too slowly recently; we haven't had the right spirit!"

But now he was dissatisfied. His Grace was far from thinking that other people were stupid, even if he did think himself more intelligent than they were, and he could not comprehend why all these intelligent people taken together made such a poor impression on him. Indeed, life as a whole made this impression on him, as though all the intelligence in individuals and in official institutions—among which he was known to count religion and science—somehow added up to a state of total unaccountability. New ideas that one had not heard of before kept popping up, aroused passions, and then vanished again after running their course; people were always chasing after some leader or another, and stumbling from one superstition to the next, cheering His Majesty one day and giving the most disgusting incendiary speeches in Parliament the next, and none of it ever amounted to anything in the end! If this could be miniaturized by a factor of a million and reduced, as it were, to the dimensions of a single head, the result would be precisely the image of the unaccountable, forgetful, ignorant conduct and the demented hopping around that had always been Count Leinsdorf's image of a lunatic, although he had hitherto had little occasion to think about it. Glumly he stood here now, in the midst of the men surrounding him, and reflected that the whole idea of the Parallel Campaign had been to bring out the truth behind all this, and he found himself unable to formulate some vague idea about faith that was there in his mind; all he could feel was something as pleasantly soothing as the shade of a high wall—a church wall, presumably.

"Funny," he said to Ulrich, giving up his thought after a while. "If you look at all this with some detachment, it somehow reminds you of starlings—you know, the way they flock together in autumn in the fruit trees."

Ulrich had come back after seeing Gerda. Their conversation had not lived up to its promising beginning; Gerda had not managed to utter more than brief, laborious answers hacked off from something that stuck like a hard wedge in her breast, while Hans Sepp talked all the more; he had set himself up as her watchdog and let it be known at once that he was not to be intimidated by his decadent surroundings.

"You don't know the great racial theorist Bremshuber?" he had asked Ulrich.

"Where does he live?" Ulrich had asked.

"In Schärding on the Laa," Hans Sepp had told him.

"What does he do?" Ulrich had asked.

"What difference does that make?" Hans had said. "New people are coming to the top! He's a druggist."

Ulrich had said to Gerda: "I hear you're now formally engaged."

And Gerda had replied: "Bremshuber demands the ruthless suppression of all alien races; that's surely less cruel than toleration and contempt!" Her lip had trembled again as she forced out this sentence that was so badly patched together from broken bits of thought.

Ulrich had merely looked at her and shaken his head. "I don't understand that," he had said, holding out his hand to say good-bye, and now, standing beside Leinsdorf, he felt as innocent as a star in the infinity of space.

"But if you don't regard it with detachment"—Count Leinsdorf slowly continued his new thought, after a pause—"then it keeps circling around in your head like a dog trying to catch its tail! Now I've let my friends have their way with me," he added, "and I've let the Baroness Wayden have her way, and if you go around listening to what we're saying here, each separate bit sounds quite sensible, but in the nobler spiritual context we're looking for, it sounds really rambling and incoherent!"

Around the War Minister and Feuermaul, whom Arnheim had brought over, a group had formed in which Feuermaul was holding forth, loving all mankind, while a second, more distant group was collecting around Arnheim, who had moved away; in it Ulrich saw Hans Sepp and Gerda some while later. Feuermaul could be heard proclaiming: "We don't learn about life by studying it in books, but through kindness. We must believe in life!" Frau Professor Drangsal stood ramrod straight behind him and pressed his point home by saying:

"After all, Goethe was no Ph.D.!"

In her eyes, Feuermaul bore a strong resemblance to Goethe. The War Minister also held himself very straight and smiled tenaciously, as he was accustomed to doing when graciously acknowledging the salute of parading troops.

Count Leinsdorf asked Ulrich: "Tell me, who is this Feuermaul?"

"His father owns some factories in Hungary," Ulrich answered. "I think it has something to do with phosphorus, since none of the workers lives past forty. Occupational disease: necrosis of the bone."

"Hmm, I see, but the son?" Leinsdorf was unmoved by the factory workers' fate.

"He was slated to go to the university; law, I believe. The father is a self-made man, and he took it hard that his son was not interested in studying."

"Why wasn't he interested in studying?" Count Leinsdorf persisted; he was being very thorough today.

"Who knows?" Ulrich shrugged. "Probably *Fathers and Sons.* When the father is poor, the sons love money; when Papa has money, the sons love mankind. Hasn't Your Grace heard about the father-son problem in our day?"

"Yes, I've heard about it. But why is Arnheim playing the patron to this young man? Has it anything to do with those oil fields?"

"Your Grace knows about that?" Ulrich exclaimed.

"Of course; I know everything," Leinsdorf said patiently. "But what I still don't understand is this: That people should love each other, and that it takes a firm hand in government to make them do it, is nothing new. So why should it suddenly be a case of either/or?"

Ulrich answered: "Your Grace has always wanted a spontaneous rallying cry arising from the entire nation; this is the form it's bound to take!"

"Oh, that's not true!" Count Leinsdorf disagreed spiritedly, but before he could go on they were interrupted by Stumm von Bordwehr, coming from the Arnheim group with a burning question for Ulrich.

"Excuse me for interrupting, Your Grace," he said. "But tell me," he turned to Ulrich, "can one really claim that people are motivated entirely by their feelings and never by their reason?"

Ulrich stared at him blankly.

"There's one of those Marxists over there," Stumm explained, "who seems to be claiming that a person's economic substructure entirely determines his ideological superstructure. And there's a psychoanalyst denying it and insisting that the ideological superstructure is entirely the product of man's instinctual substructure."

"It's not that simple," Ulrich said, hoping to wriggle out of it.

"That's just what I always say! It didn't do me a bit of good, though," the General answered promptly, keeping his eyes fixed on Ulrich. But now Leinsdorf entered the discussion.

"Now there, you see," he said to Ulrich, "is something rather like the question I was about to raise myself. No matter whether the substructure is economic or sexual, well, what I wanted to say before is: Why are people so unreliable in their superstructure? You know the common saying that the world is crazy; it is getting all too easy to believe it's true!"

"That's the psychology of the masses, Your Grace," the learned General interposed again. "So far as it applies to the masses it makes sense to me. The masses are moved only by their instincts, and of course that means by those instincts most individuals have in common; that's logical. That's to say, it's illogical, of course. The masses are illogical; they only use logic for window dressing. What they really let themselves be guided by is simply and solely *suggestion!* Give me the newspapers, the radio, the film industry, and maybe a few other avenues of cultural communication, and within a few years—as my friend Ulrich once said—I promise I'll turn people into cannibals! That's precisely why mankind needs strong leadership, as Your Grace knows far better than I do. But that even highly cultivated individuals are not motivated by logic in some circumstances is something I find it hard to believe, though Arnheim says so."

What on earth could Ulrich have offered his friend by way of support in this scattered debate? Like a bunch of weeds an angler catches on his hook instead of a fish, the General's question was baited with a tangled bunch of theories. Does a man follow only his feelings, doing, feeling, even thinking only that to which he is moved by unconscious currents of desire, or even by the milder breeze of pleasure, as we now assume? Or does he not rather act on the basis of reasoned thought and will, as we also widely assume? Does he primarily follow certain instincts, such as the sexual instinct, as we assume? Or is it above all not the sexual instinct that dominates, but rather the psychological effect of economic conditions, as we also assume today? A creature as complicated as man can be seen from many different angles, and whatever one chooses as the axis in the theoretical picture one gets only partial truths, from whose interpretation the level of truth slowly rises higher—or does it? Whenever a partial truth has been regarded as the only valid one, there has been a high price to pay. On the other hand, this partial truth would hardly have been discovered if it had not been overestimated. In this fashion the history of truth and the history of feeling are variously linked, but that of feeling remains obscure. Indeed, to Ulrich's way of thinking it was no history at all, but a wild jumble. Funny, for instance, that the religious ideas, meaning the passionate ideas, of the Middle Ages about the nature of man were based on a strong faith in man's reason and his will, while today many scholars, whose only passion is smoking too much, consider the emotions as the basis for all human activity. Such were the thoughts going through Ulrich's head, and he naturally did not feel like saying anything in response to the oratory of Stumm, who was in any case not waiting for an answer but only cooling off a bit before returning to Arnheim's group.

"Count Leinsdorf," Ulrich said mildly. "Do you remember my old suggestion to establish a General Secretariat for all those problems that need the soul as much as the mind for a solution?"

"Indeed I do," Leinsdorf replied. "I remember telling His Eminence about it, and his hearty laugh. But he did say that you had come too late!"

"And yet it's the very thing you were feeling the lack of, Your Grace," Ulrich continued. "You notice that the world no longer remembers today what it wanted yesterday, that its mood keeps changing for no perceptible reason, that it's in a constant uproar and never resolves anything, and if we imagined all this chaos of humanity brought together in a single head, we'd have a really unmistakable case of recognizable pathological symptoms that one would count as mental insufficiency. . . ."

"Absolutely right!" cried Stumm von Bordwehr, whose pride in everything he had learned that afternoon had welled up again. "That's precisely the configuration of . . . well, I can't think of the name of that mental disease at the moment, but that's it exactly!"

"No," Ulrich said with a smile. "It's surely not the description of any specific disease; the difference between a normal person and an insane one is precisely that the normal person has all the diseases of the mind, while the madman has only one!"

"Brilliantly put!" Stumm and Leinsdorf cried as with one voice, though in slightly different words, and then added in the same way: "But what does that mean exactly?"

"It means this," Ulrich stated. "If I understand by morality the ordering of all those interrelations that include feeling, imagination, and the like, each of these takes its relative position from the others and in that way attains some sort of stability; but all of them together, in moral terms, don't get beyond the state of delusion!"

"Come, that's going too far," Count Leinsdorf said good-naturedly. And the General said: "But surely every man has to have his own morals; you can't order anyone to prefer a cat to a dog . . . ?"

"Can one prescribe it, Your Grace?" Ulrich asked intently.

"Well, in the old days," Count Leinsdorf said diplomatically, although he had been challenged in his religious conviction that "the truth" existed in every sphere. "It was easier in the old days. But today . . . ?"

"Then that leaves us in a permanent state of religious war," Ulrich pointed out.

"You call that a religious war?"

"What else?"

"Hmm . . . not bad. Quite a good characterization of modern life. Incidentally, I always knew that there's not such a bad Catholic secretly tucked away inside you."

"I'm a very bad one," Ulrich said. "I don't believe that God has been here yet, but that He is still to come. But only if we pave the way for Him more than we have so far!"

His Grace rejected this with the dignified words: "That's over my head."

161

A GREAT EVENT IS IN THE MAKING. BUT NO ONE HAS NOTICED

The General, however, cried: "I'm afraid I must get back to His Excellency the Minister at once, but you absolutely will have to explain all that to me—I won't let you off! I'll join you gentlemen again soon, if I may."

Leinsdorf gave the impression of wanting to say something—his mind was clearly hard at work—but he and Ulrich had hardly been left alone for a moment when they found themselves surrounded by people borne toward them by the constant circulation of the guests and the charisma of His Grace. There could, of course, be no more talk about what Ulrich had just said, and no one besides him was giving it a thought, when an arm slipped into his from behind; it was Agathe.

"Have you found grounds for my defense yet?" she asked in a maliciously caressing tone.

Ulrich took a grip on her arm and drew her aside from the crowd around them.

"Can't we go home?" Agathe asked.

"No," Ulrich said. "I can't leave yet."

"I suppose," she teased him, "that times to come, for whose sake you're keeping yourself pure here, won't let you go?"

Ulrich pressed her arm.

"Isn't it greatly in my favor that I don't belong here but in jail?" she whispered in his ear.

They looked for a place where they could be alone. The party had reached the boiling point and was impelling the guests to constantly circulate. On the whole, however, the twofold grouping was still distinguishable: around the Minister of War the talk was of peace and love, and around Arnheim, at the moment, about how the German love of peace flourished best in the shadow of German power.

Arnheim lent a benevolent ear to this, because he never snubbed an honest opinion and was especially interested in new ones. He was worried that the deal for the oil fields might run into opposition in Parliament. He was certain of the unavoidable opposition of the Slavic contingent, and hoped he could count on the pro-German faction to support him. On the Ministry level all seemed to be going well, except for a certain antagonism in the Ministry of Foreign Affairs, but he did not regard this as particularly significant. Tomorrow he was going to Budapest.

There were plenty of hostile "observers" around him and other leading personages. They were easily spotted in that they always said yes to everything and were unfailingly polite, while the others tended to have different opinions.

Tuzzi was trying to win one of them over by asserting: "What they're saying doesn't mean a thing. It never means anything!" His listener, a member of Parliament, believed him. But this did not change his mind, made up before he had come, that something fishy was going on here.

His Grace, on the other hand, spoke up on behalf of the evening's seriousness by saying to another skeptic: "My dear sir, ever since 1848 even the revolutions have been brought about by nothing more than a lot of talk!"

It would be wrong to regard such differences as no more than acceptable variants on the otherwise usual monotony of life; and yet this error, with all its grave consequences, occurs almost as frequently as the expression "It's a matter of feeling," without which our mental economy would be unthinkable. This indispensable phrase divides what *must* be in life from what *can* be.

"It sets apart," Ulrich said to Agathe, "the given order of things from a private, personal preserve. It separates what has been rationalized from what is held to be irrational. As commonly used, it is an admission that we are forced to be humane on major counts, but being humane on minor counts is suspiciously arbitrary. We think life would be a prison if we were not free to choose between wine or water, religion or atheism, but nobody believes in the least that we have any real option in matters of feeling; on the contrary, we draw a line, ambiguous though it may be, between legitimate and illegitimate feelings."

The feelings between Ulrich and Agathe were of the illegitimate kind, although they did no more than talk about the party as, still arm in arm, they looked in vain for a private corner, while experiencing a wild and unacknowledged joy in being reunited after their estrangement. By contrast, the choice between loving all one's fellow human beings, or first annihilating some of them, obviously involved doubly legitimate feelings, or it would not have been so eagerly debated in Diotima's house and in the presence of His Grace, even though it also split the company into two spiteful parties. Ulrich maintained that invention of "a matter of feeling" had rendered the worst possible service to the cause of feeling, and as he undertook to describe to his sister the curious impression this evening's affair had awakened in him, he soon found himself saying things that unintentionally took up where their talk of the morning had broken off and were apparently intended to justify it.

"I hardly know where to start," he said, "without boring you. May I tell you what I understand by 'morality'?"

"Please do," Agathe said.

"Morality is regulation of conduct within a society, beginning with regulation of its inner impulses, that is, feelings and thoughts."

"That's a lot of progress in a few hours!" Agathe replied with a laugh. "This morning you were still saying you didn't know what morality was!"

"Of course I don't. That doesn't stop me from giving you a dozen explanations. The oldest reason for it is that God revealed the order of life to us in all its details. . . ."

"That would be the best," Agathe said.

"But the most probable," Ulrich said emphatically, "is that morality, like every other form of order, arises through force and violence! A group of people that has seized power simply imposes on the rest those rules and principles that will secure their power. Morality thereby tends to favor those who brought it to power. At the same time, it sets an example in so doing. And at the same time reactions set in that cause it to change—this is of course too complicated to be described briefly, and while it by no means happens without thought, but then again not by means of thought, either, but rather empirically, what you get in the end is an infinite network that seems to span everything as independently as God's firmament. Now, everything relates to this self-contained circle, but this circle relates to nothing. In other words: Everything is moral, but morality itself is not!"

"How charming of morality," Agathe said. "But do you know that I encountered a good person today?"

The change of subject took Ulrich by surprise, but when Agathe began telling him of her meeting with Lindner, he first tried to find a place for it in his train of thought. "You can find good people here by the dozen too," he said, "but I'll tell you why the bad people are here as well, if you'll let me go on."

As they talked they gradually edged their way out of the throng and reached the anteroom, and Ulrich had to think where they might turn for refuge: Diotima's bedroom occurred to him, and also Rachel's little room, but he did not want to set foot in either of them again, so he and Agathe remained for the time being among the unpeopled coats that were hanging there. Ulrich could not find a way to pick up the thread. "I really ought to start again from the beginning," he said, with an impatient, helpless gesture. Then suddenly he said:

"You don't want to know whether you've done something good or bad; you're uneasy because you do both without a solid reason!"

Agathe nodded.

He had taken both her hands in his.

The matte sheen of his sister's skin, with its fragrance of plants unknown to him, rising before his eyes from the low neckline of her gown, lost for a moment all earthly connection. The motion of the blood pulsed from one hand into the other. A deep moat from some other world seemed to enclose them both in a nowhere world of their own.

He suddenly could not find the ideas to characterize it; he could not even get hold of those that had often served him before: "Let's not act on the impulse of the moment but act out of the condition that lasts to the end." "In such a way that it takes us to the center from which one cannot return to take anything back." "Not from the periphery and its constantly changing conditions, but out of the one, immutable happiness." Such phrases did come to mind, and he might well have used them if it had only been as conversation. But in the direct immediacy with which they were to be applied to this very moment between him and his sister, it was suddenly impossible. It left him helplessly agitated. But Agathe understood him clearly. And she should have been happy that for the first time the shell encasing her "hard brother" had cracked, exposing what was inside, like an egg that has fallen to the floor. To her surprise, however, her feelings this time were not quite ready to fall into step with his. Between morning and evening lay her curious encounter with Lindner, and although this man had merely aroused her wonder and curiosity, even this tiny grain sufficed to keep the unending mirroring of reclusive love from coming into play.

Ulrich felt it in her hands even before she said anything—and Agathe made no answer.

He guessed that this unexpected self-denial had something to do with the experience he had just had to listen to her describing. Abashed and confused by the rejection of his unanswered feelings, he said, shaking his head:

"It's annoying how much you seem to expect from the goodness of such a man!"

"I suppose it is," Agathe admitted.

He looked at her. He realized that this encounter meant more to his sister than the attentions paid to her by other men since she had been under his protection. He even knew this man slightly. Lindner was a public figure of sorts; he was the man who, at the very first session of the Parallel Campaign, had made the brief speech, received with embarrassing silence, hailing the "historical moment" or something similar: awkward, sincere, and pointless. . . . On impulse Ulrich glanced around, but he did not recall seeing the man tonight, for he had not been asked again, as Ulrich knew. He must have come across him elsewhere from time to time, probably at some learned society, and have read one or another of his publications, for as he concentrated his memory, ultramicroscopic traces of images from the past condensed like a repulsive viscous drop into his verdict: "That dreary ass! The more anyone wants to be taken seriously, the less one can take such a man seriously, any more than Professor Hagauer!" So he said to Agathe.

Agathe met it with silence. She even pressed his hand.

He felt: There is something quite contradictory here, but there's no stopping it.

At this point people came into the anteroom, and the siblings drew slightly apart.

"Shall I take you back in?" Ulrich asked.

Agathe said no and looked around for an escape.

It suddenly occurred to Ulrich that the only way they could get away from the other guests was by retreating to the kitchen. Three batteries of glasses were being filled and trays loaded with cakes. The cook was bustling about with great zeal; Rachel and Soliman were waiting to be loaded up, standing apart and motionless and not whispering to each other as they used to do on such occasions. Little Rachel dropped a curtsy as they came in, Soliman merely saluted with his dark eyes, and Ulrich said: "It's too stuffy in there; can we get something to drink here?"

He sat down with Agathe on the window seat and put a glass and a plate down for show so that in case anyone should see them it would look as if two old friends of the family were having a private chat. When they were seated, he said with a little sigh: "So it's merely a matter of feeling whether one finds such a Professor Lindner good or insufferable?"

Agathe was concentrating on unwrapping a piece of candy.

"Which is to say," Ulrich went on, "that the feeling is neither true nor false. Feeling has remained a private matter! It remains at the mercy of suggestion, fantasy, or persuasion. You and I are no different from those people in there. Do you know what these people want?"

"No. But does it matter?"

"Perhaps it does. They are forming two parties, each of which is as right or as wrong as the other."

Agathe said she could not help thinking that it was better to believe in human goodness than only in guns and politics, even if the manner of the belief was absurd.

"What's he like, this man you met?"

"Oh, that's impossible to say. He's good!" his sister answered with a laugh.

"You can no more depend on what looks good to you than on what looks good to Leinsdorf," Ulrich responded testily.

Both their faces were tense with excitement and laughter; the easy flow of humorous civility blocked deeper countercurrents. Rachel sensed it at the roots of her hair, under her little cap, but she was feeling so miserable herself that her perception was much dimmer than it used to be, like a memory of better days. The lovely curve of her cheeks was a shade hollow, the black blaze of her eyes dulled with discouragement. Had Ulrich been in a mood to compare her beauty with that of his sister, he would have been bound to notice that Rachel's former dark brilliance had crumbled like a piece of coal that had been run over by a heavy truck. But he had no eyes for her now. She was pregnant, and no one knew it except Soliman, who showed no understanding of the disastrous reality and responded with nothing but childish romantic schemes.

"For centuries now," Ulrich went on, "the world has known truth in thinking and accordingly, to a certain degree, rational freedom of thought. But during this same time the emotional life has had neither the strict discipline of truth nor any freedom of movement. For every moral system has, in its time, regulated the feelings, and rigidly too, but only insofar as certain basic principles and feelings were needed for whatever action it favored; the rest was left to individual whim, to the private play of emotions, to the random efforts of art, and to academic debate. So morality has adapted our feelings to the needs of moral systems and meanwhile neglected to develop them, even though it depends on feelings: morality is, after all, the order and integrity of the emotional life." Here he broke off. He felt Rachel's fascinated stare on his animated face, even if she could no longer quite muster her former enthusiasm for the concerns of important people.

"I suppose it's funny how I go on talking about morality even here in the kitchen," he said in embarrassment.

Agathe was gazing at him intently and thoughtfully. He leaned over closer to his sister and added softly, with a flickering smile: "But it's only another way of expressing an impassioned state that takes up arms against the whole world!"

Without intending to, he was reenacting their confrontation of the morning, in which he had played the unpleasant role of the lecturing schoolmaster. He could not help it. For him morality was neither conformism nor philosophic wisdom, but living the infinite fullness of possibilities. He believed in morality's capacity for intensification, in stages of moral experience, and not merely, as most people do, in stages of moral understanding, as if it were something cut-and-dried for which people were just not pure enough. He believed in morality without believing in any specific moral system. Morality is generally understood to be a sort of police regulations for keeping life in order, and since life does not obey even these, they come to look as if they were really impossible to live up to and accordingly, in this sorry way, not really an ideal either. But morality must not be reduced to this level. Morality is imagination. This was what he wanted to make Agathe see. And his second point was: Imagination is not arbitrary. Once the imagination is left to caprice, there is a price to pay.

The words twitched in his mouth. He was on the verge of bringing up the neglected difference between the way in which various historical periods have developed the rational mind in their own fashion and the way they have kept the moral imagination static and closed off, also in their own fashion. He was on the verge of talking about this because it results in a line that rises, despite all skepticism, more or less steadily through all of history's transformations, representing the rational mind and its patterns, and contrasting with a mound of broken shards of feelings, ideas, and potentials of life that were heaped up in layers just the way they were when they came into being, as eternal side issues, and that were always discarded. And also because a further result is that this finally adds up to any number of possibilities for forming an opinion one way or another, as soon as they are extended into the realm of principles; but that there is never a possibility of bringing them together. And because it follows that the various opinions lash out at each other since they have no way of communicating. And because it follows, finally, that the emotional life of mankind slops back and forth like water in an unsteady tub. Ulrich had an idea that had been haunting him all evening, an old idea of his, incidentally, but everything that had happened this evening had somehow simply confirmed it, and he wanted to show Agathe where her error lay and how it could be put right, if everyone agreed. Actually, it was only his painful intention to prove that one could not, on the whole, even trust the discoveries of one's own imagination.

Agathe now said, with a little sigh, as a hard-pressed woman gets in one last, quick defensive move before surrendering:

"So one has to do everything 'on principle,' is that it?"

And she looked at him, responding to his smile.

But he answered: "Yes, but only on *one* principle!"

This was something quite different from what he had meant to say. It again came from the realm of the Siamese twins and the Millennium, where life grows in magical stillness like a flower, and even if it were not a mere flight of fancy, it pointed to the frontiers of thought, which are solitary and treacherous. Agathe's eyes were like split agate. If at this instant he had said only a little more, or touched her with his hand, something would have happened—something that was gone a moment later, before she even knew what it was. For Ulrich did not want to say any more. He took a knife and a piece of fruit and began to peel. He was happy because the distance that had separated him from his sister shortly before had melted into an immeasurable closeness; but he was also glad that at this moment they were interrupted.

It was the General, who came peering into the kitchen with the sly glance of a patrol leader surprising the enemy encampment. "Please forgive the intrusion," he called out as he entered, "but as it's only a tête-à-tête with your brother, dear lady, it can't be too great a crime!" And turning to Ulrich, he said: "They're looking for you high and low."

And Ulrich told the General what he had meant to say to Agathe. But first he asked: "Who are *they*?"

"I was supposed to bring you to the Minister!" Stumm said reproachfully.

Ulrich waved that aside.

"Well, it's too late anyway," the good-natured General said. "The old boy just left. But on my own account, as soon as Madame has chosen some better company than yours, I shall have to interrogate you about what you meant with that 'religious war'—if you'll be so kind as to remember your own words."

"We were just talking about that," Ulrich said.

"How very interesting!" the General exclaimed. "Your sister is also interested in moral systems?"

"It's all my brother talks about," Agathe corrected him, smiling.

"That was virtually the whole agenda this evening!" Stumm sighed. "Leinsdorf, for instance, said only a few minutes ago that morality is just as important as eating. I can't see it myself." So saying, he bent with relish over the candies Agathe handed him. It was supposed to be a joke. Agathe said, to comfort him: "Neither can I."

"An officer and a woman must have morals, but they don't like to talk about it," the General went on improvising. "Don't you agree, dear lady?"

Rachel had brought him a kitchen chair, which she was zealously dusting off with her apron when these words of his stabbed her to the heart; she nearly broke into tears.

Stumm was prompting Ulrich again: "Now then, what's this about the religious war?" But before Ulrich could say anything, he forestalled him, saying: "Actually, I have the feeling that your cousin is also prowling around looking for you, and I have my military training to thank for finding you first. So I must make the most of my time. Things are not going well in there! It's supposed to be our fault. And your cousin—how shall I put it? She's simply let go of the reins. Do you know what they've decided?"

"Who decided?"

"A lot of people have already left. Some have stayed and are paying very close attention," the General described the situation. "There's no telling who is deciding."

"In that case it might be better if you told me first what they've decided," Ulrich said.

Stumm von Bordwehr shrugged his shoulders. "All right. But luckily it's not a resolution in the sense of committee business," he elucidated. "Since all the responsible people had left in time, thank heaven. So it's only what you might call a special-interest proposal, a suggestion, or a minority vote. I shall take the line that we have no official knowledge of it. But you'd better tell your secretary to watch the minutes so none of this gets into the record. Do forgive me," he said to Agathe, "for talking business like this!"

"But what happened?" she urged him on.

Stumm made a wide, sweeping gesture. "Feuermaul . . . if you remember the young man we really only invited because—how shall I put it?—because he is an exponent of the spirit of the times, and because we had to invite the opposing exponents anyway. We had hoped that nevertheless, and with the added stimulus of intellectual debate, we'd be able to get down to talking about the things that, unfortunately, really matter. Your brother knows about it, dear lady; the idea was to get the Minister together with Leinsdorf and Arnheim, to see whether Leinsdorf has any objections to . . . certain patriotic views. And all in all I'm not really dissatisfied." He turned confidentially to Ulrich. "So far so good. But while this was going on, Feuermaul and the others . . ." Here Stumm felt obliged to add for Agathe's benefit: ". . . that is, the exponent of the view that man is basically a good and peace-loving creature who responds best to kindness, and those who expound approximately the opposite view, that it takes a strong hand and all that to keep order in the world. This Feuermaul got into an argument with these others, and before anyone could stop them they had agreed on a joint proposal!"

"A joint proposal?" Ulrich was incredulous.

"That's right. Perhaps I seem to be making light of it"—Stumm sounded rather pleased with himself at the unintended comic effect of his story—"but nobody could have predicted anything of the sort. And if I tell you what their resolution was, you won't believe it! Since I was supposed to visit Moosbrugger this afternoon in a semi-official capacity, the whole Ministry will refuse to believe that I wasn't the one who put them up to it!"

Here Ulrich burst out laughing, and he interrupted him the same way from time to time as Stumm went on with his story; only Agathe understood why, while his friend commented somewhat huffily each time that he seemed to be wrought up. But what had happened corresponded far too much to the pattern Ulrich had just laid out for his sister for him not to find it hilarious.

The Feuermaul group had appeared on the scene at the very last moment to save what could still be saved. In such cases the object tends to be less clear than the intention. The young poet Friedel Feuermaul—who was called Pepi by his intimates, and who went about trying to look like the young Schubert, for he doted on everything having to do with Old Vienna, though he had been born in a small provincial town in Hungary—happened to believe in Austria's mission, and he believed besides in mankind. It was obvious that an undertaking like the Parallel Campaign that did not include him would from the beginning have made him uneasy. How could a humanitarian project in an Austrian key, or an Austrian project in a humanitarian key, flourish without him? It is true that he had said this, with a shrug, only in private to his friend Frau Drangsal, but she, the widow of a celebrity and a credit to her country, as the hostess presiding over a spiritual beauty salon overshadowed only during the last year by Diotima's, had repeated it to every influential person with whom she came in contact. Hence a rumor had begun to make the rounds that the Parallel Campaign was in peril, unless . . . This "unless" and the peril naturally enough remained rather undefined, for first Diotima had to be made to invite Feuermaul, and after that one would see. But the news of some danger apparently connected with the patriotic campaign was noted by those alert politicians who acknowledged no fatherland, but only an ethnic motherfolk living in enforced wedlock with the State as an abused wife; they had long suspected that the Parallel Campaign would only produce some new form of oppression. And even though they were civil enough to conceal this suspicion, they attached far less importance to the intention of diverting it—for there had always been despairing humanists among the Germans, but as a whole they would always be oppressors and bureaucratic parasites!—than to the useful hint that even Germans admitted how dangerous their people's nationalism was. Consequently Frau Drangsal and the poet Feuermaul felt buoyed up by sympathies for their aims, which they accepted without bothering to investigate, and Feuermaul, who was a recognized man of feeling, was obsessed with the notion that something compelling about love and peace had to be said to the Minister of War in person. Why the Minister of War, and what he was expected to do about it, remained unclear; but the idea itself was so dazzlingly original and dramatic that it really needed no additional support. On this point they had even won the approval of Stumm von Bordwehr, the fickle General, whose devotion to culture sometimes took him to Frau Drangsal's salon, unbeknownst to Diotima; it was his doing, moreover, that the original perception of Arnheim the munitions maker as part of the danger gave way to the view of Arnheim the thinker as an important element of everything good.

So far all had gone as befitted the participants, even including the fact that, despite Frau Drangsal's help, the Minister's encounter with Feuermaul unfolded as is usual in the course of human events, producing nothing more than some flashes of Feuermaulian brilliance, to which His Excellency lent a tolerant ear. But Feuermaul was far from spent, and because the troops he could summon to arms consisted of literary men young and old, councillors, Hofräte, librarians, and some pacifists, in short, people of all ages and in all sorts of positions, united in their feeling for their old Fatherland and its mission in the world—a sentiment as readily marshaled in the cause of bringing back the historic three-horse omnibus as in that of Viennese porcelain—and because all these faithful had in the course of the evening made many diverse contacts with their opponents, who also did not go around showing their claws, many discussions had sprung up in which opinions crisscrossed wildly in all directions. Such was the temptation facing Feuermaul when the Minister of War had finished with him and Frau Drangsal's attention had been distracted for a while through some unknown occurrence. Stumm von Bordwehr could only report that Feuermaul had got into an extremely lively exchange with a young man who, from his description, might well have been Hans Sepp. The young man was in any case one of those who find a scapegoat on which to blame all the evils they cannot cope with themselves; nationalist arrogance is only that special case of it in which honest conviction makes one choose a scapegoat not of one's own breed and as unlike oneself as possible. Now, everyone knows what a great relief it is when one is upset to work off one's anger on someone, even if it has nothing to do with him; but it is less well known that this also applies to love. For love, too, must often be worked off in the same way on someone not really involved, for lack of a more suitable outlet. Feuermaul, for instance, was an industrious young man who could be quite unpleasant in the struggle for his own advantage, but his lovegoat happened to be "Man," and the moment he thought of Man in general, there was no restraining his unsatisfied benevolence. Hans Sepp, on the other hand, was basically a decent fellow who could not even bring himself to deceive Director Fischel, and so his scapegoat was "non-German man," on whom he blamed everything beyond his power to change. Lord knows what they had started to talk to each other about; they must have instantly mounted their respective goats and charged at each other, for as Stumm put it:

"I've really no idea how it happened; suddenly they were surrounded, and the next minute there was a real crowd, and finally everyone still here was standing around them."

"Do you know what they were arguing about?" Ulrich asked him.

Stumm shrugged his shoulders. "Feuermaul shouted at the other fellow: 'You want to hate, but you can't do it! Because we're all born with love inside!' or something like that. And the other one shouted back at him: 'And you want to love? But that's something you're even less capable of, you—you—' Well, I can't really say exactly; I had to hold myself a bit apart, because of my uniform."

"Oh," Ulrich said. "I see the point." He turned to Agathe, trying to catch her eye.

"No—the point was the resolution!" Stumm reminded him. "There they were, ready to bite each other's heads off, and then, as if nothing had happened, they agreed to make common cause, and I do mean common!"

With his rounded figure, Stumm gave the impression of unwavering gravity. "The Minister left on the spot," he reported.

"But what was it they agreed on?" Ulrich and Agathe asked.

"I can't exactly say," Stumm replied, "because of course I took off myself before they were finished. Besides, it's always hard to remember that sort of thing clearly. It's something in favor of Moosbrugger and against the army."

"Moosbrugger? How on earth . . ." Ulrich laughed again.

"How on earth?" the General echoed venomously. "It's easy for you to laugh, but I'm the one who's going to be called on the carpet for it! At the very least it'll mean days of paperwork! How does anyone know 'how on earth' with such people? Maybe it was that old professor's fault, the one who was talking to everyone in favor of hanging and against leniency. Or it could have been because the papers have been making such a fuss again lately about the problem of that monster. Anyway, they were suddenly talking about him. This has got to be undone again!" he declared with unwonted severity.

At this moment the kitchen was invaded in quick succession by Arnheim, Diotima, and even Tuzzi and Count Leinsdorf. Arnheim had heard voices in the foyer. He had been on the point of slipping away quietly, hoping that the disturbance would enable him to escape another heart-to-heart talk with Diotima; and tomorrow he would be leaving town again for some time. But his curiosity made him glance into the kitchen, and since Agathe had seen him, politeness prevented him from withdrawing. Stumm instantly besieged him with questions about how things stood.

"I can even give it to you verbatim," Arnheim replied with a smile. "Some of it was so quaint that I simply had to write it down on the sly."

He drew a small card from his wallet and slowly read, deciphering his shorthand, the contents of the proposed manifesto:

" 'The patriotic campaign has passed the following resolution, as proposed by Herr Feuermaul and Herr—' I didn't catch the other name. 'Any man may choose to die for his own ideas, but whoever induces men to die for ideas not their own is a murderer!' That was the proposal," he added, "and my impression was that it was final."

"That's it!" the General exclaimed. "That's the way I heard it too! They're enough to make you sick, these intellectual debates!"

Arnheim said gently: "It's the desire of young people today for stability and leadership."

"But it wasn't only young people," Stumm said in disgust. "Even baldheads were agreeing!"

"Then it's a need for leadership in general," Arnheim said with a friendly nod. "It's widespread these days. Incidentally, the resolution was borrowed from a recent book, if I remember rightly."

"Indeed?" Stumm said.

"Yes," Arnheim said. "And of course we'll pretend it never happened. But if we could find a way to direct the sentiment it expresses into some useful channel, it would certainly be of help."

The General appeared somewhat relieved and, turning to Ulrich, asked:

"Do you have any idea what could be done?"

"Of course!" Ulrich said.

Arnheim's attention was diverted by Diotima.

"In that case," the General said in a low voice, "fire away! I would prefer it if we could remain in control."

"You have to focus on what actually happened," Ulrich said, taking his time. "These people aren't so far wrong, you know, when one of them accuses the other of wanting to love if he only could, and the other retorts that it's the same with wanting to hate. It's true of all the feelings. Hatred today has something companionable about it, and on the other hand, in order to feel what would really be love for another human being—I maintain," Ulrich said abruptly, "that two such people have never yet existed!"

"That's certainly most interesting," the General interrupted quickly, "especially as I completely fail to understand how you can assert such a thing. But I have to write a protocol tomorrow about everything that happened here tonight, and I implore you to bear this in mind! In the army, what counts most is being able to report progress; a certain optimism is indispensable even in defeat—that's part of the profession. So how can I report what happened here as a step forward?"

"Write," Ulrich advised him with a wink, "that the moral imagination has taken its revenge!"

"But you can't write that sort of thing in the military!" Stumm replied indignantly.

"Then let's put it another way," Ulrich said seriously, "and write: All creative periods have been serious. There is no profound happiness without a profound ethos. There is no morality that is not derived from a firm basis. There is no happiness that does not rest on a strong belief. Not even animals live without morality. But today human beings no longer know on what—"

Stumm broke in on this calmly flowing dictation too: "My dear friend, I can speak of a troop's morale, or morale in battle, or a woman's morals; but always only in specific instances. I cannot discuss morality without such a restriction in a military report, any more than I could imagination or God Almighty. You know that as well as I do!"

Diotima saw Arnheim standing at the window of her kitchen, an oddly domestic sight after they had exchanged only a few circumspect words during the entire evening. Paradoxically, it only made her suddenly wish to continue her unfinished chat with Ulrich. Her mind was dominated by that comforting despair which, breaking in from several directions at once, had almost become sublimated into an amiable and serene state of expectation. The long-foreseen collapse of her Council left her cold. Arnheim's faithlessness also left her, as she thought, almost equally indifferent. He looked at her as she came in, and for a moment it brought back the old feeling of a living space in which they were united. But she remembered that he had been avoiding her for weeks, and the thought "Sexual coward!" stiffened her knees again so that she could move toward him regally.

Arnheim saw it: her seeing him, her faltering, the distance between them melting; over frozen roads connecting them in innumerable ways hovered an intimation that they might thaw out again. He had moved away from the others, but at the last moment both he and Diotima made a turn that brought them together with Ulrich, General Stumm, and the rest, who were on the other side.

In all its manifestations, from the inspired ideas of original thinkers to the kitsch that unites all peoples, what Ulrich called the moral imagination, or, more simply, feeling, has for centuries been in a state of ferment without turning into wine. Man is a being who cannot survive without enthusiasm. And enthusiasm is that state of mind in which all his feelings and thoughts have the same spirit. You think it is rather the opposite, that it is a condition in which one overpowering feeling—of being carried away!—sweeps all the others along with it? You weren't going to say anything at all? Anyway, that's how it is. Or one way it is. But there is nothing to sustain such an enthusiasm. Feelings and thoughts become lasting only with each other's help, in their totality; they must somehow be aligned with each other and carry each other onward. And by every available means, through drugs, liquor, fantasies, hypnosis, faith, conviction, often even through the simplifying effect of stupidity, man is always trying to achieve a condition like it. He believes in ideas not because they are sometimes true but because he needs to believe; because he has to keep his feelings in order. Because he must have an illusion to stop up the gap between the walls of his life, through which his feelings would otherwise fly off in every direction. The answer is probably at least to seek the conditions of an authentic enthusiasm, instead of giving oneself up to transient delusory states. But although, all in all, the number of choices based on feeling is infinitely greater than those based on clear logic, and every event that moves mankind arises from the imagination, only the purely rational problems have achieved an objective order, while nothing deserving the name of a joint effort, or even hinting at any insight into the desperate need for it, has been done for the world of feeling and imagination.

This was more or less what Ulrich said, interspersed with understandable protests from the General.

All Ulrich saw in the events of the evening, even though they had been impetuous enough and were destined through malicious misrepresentation to have grave consequences, was the example of an infinite disorder. Feuermaul seemed at this moment to matter to him as little as the love of mankind, nationalism as little as Feuermaul, and Stumm was asking him in vain how to distill a sense of some tangible progress out of an attitude so very personal.

"Why don't you simply report," Ulrich responded, "that it's the Millennial War of Religion. And that people have never been as unprepared to fight it as now, when the rubble of 'ineffectual feelings,' which every period bequeaths to the next, has grown into mountains without anything being done about it. So the War Ministry can sit back and serenely await the next mass catastrophe."

Ulrich was foretelling the future, with no inkling of it. His concern was not with real events at all; he was struggling for his salvation. He was trying to throw in everything that could get in its way, and it was for that reason that he laughed so much and tried to mislead them into thinking he was joking and exaggerating. He was exaggerating for Agathe's benefit, carrying on his long-standing dialogue with her, not just this most recent one. Actually, he was throwing up a bulwark of ideas against her, knowing that in a certain place there was a little bolt, and that if this bolt were drawn back, everything would be flooded and buried by feeling. In truth he was thinking incessantly of this bolt.

Diotima was standing near him and smiling. She sensed something of Ulrich's efforts on behalf of his sister, and was sadly moved; she forgot sexual enlightenment, and something in her opened up: it was doubtless the future, but in any case, her lips were slightly open too.

Arnheim asked Ulrich: "And you think . . . that something might be done about it?" The tone of his question suggested that he had caught the seriousness behind the exaggeration, but that he regarded even the seriousness as an exaggeration.

Tuzzi said to Diotima: "Something must in any case be done to prevent this affair from leaking out."

"Isn't it obvious?" Ulrich said in reply to Arnheim. "Today we are facing too many possibilities of feeling, too many possible ways of living. But isn't it like the kind of problem our intellect deals with whenever it is confronted with a vast number of facts and a history of the relevant theories? And for the intellect we have developed an open-ended but precise procedure, which I don't need to describe to you. Now tell me whether something of the kind isn't equally possible for the feelings. We certainly need to find out what we're here for; it's one of the main sources of all violence in the world. Earlier centuries tried to answer it with their own inadequate means, but the great age of empiricism has done nothing of its own, so far. . . ."

Arnheim, who caught on quickly and liked to interrupt, laid his hand on Ulrich's shoulder as if to restrain him. "This implies an increasing relationship with God!" he said in a low tone of warning.

"Would that be so terrible?" Ulrich asked, not without a hint of mockery at such premature alarm. "But I haven't gone that far yet!"

Arnheim promptly checked himself and smiled. "How delightful after a long absence to find someone unchanged. Such a rarity, these days!" he said. He was genuinely glad, in fact, once he felt safe again behind his defensive front of benevolence. Ulrich might, after all, have very well taken him up on that rash offer of a position, and Arnheim was grateful that Ulrich, in his irresponsible intransigence, disdained touching the earth with his feet. "We must have a talk about this sometime," he added cordially. "It's not clear to me how you conceive of applying our theoretical attitude to practical affairs."

Ulrich knew very well that it was still unclear. What he meant was not a life of "research," or a life "in the light of science," but a "quest for feeling" similar to a quest for truth, except that truth was not the issue here. He watched Arnheim moving over to Agathe. Diotima was standing there too; Tuzzi and Count Leinsdorf came and went. Agathe was chatting with everyone and thinking: "Why is he talking with all these people? He ought to have left with me! He's cheapening what he said to me!" She liked many of the things she heard him say from across the room, and yet they hurt her. Everything that came from Ulrich was hurting her again, and for the second time that day she suddenly felt the need to get away from him. She despaired of ever being able, with her limitations, to be what he wanted, and the prospect that they would soon be going home like any other couple, gossiping about the evening behind them, was intolerable.

Meanwhile Ulrich was thinking: "Arnheim will never understand that." And he added: "It is precisely in his feelings that the scientist is limited, and the practical man even more so. It's as necessary as having your legs firmly planted if you intend to lift something with your arms." In ordinary circumstances he was that way himself; the moment he began thinking about anything, even if it was about feeling itself, he was very cautious about letting any feeling into it. Agathe called this coldness, but he knew that in order to be wholly otherwise one has to be prepared to renounce life, as if on a mortal adventure, for one has no idea what its course will be! He was in the mood for it, and for the moment no longer feared it. He gazed for a long time at his sister: the lively play of conversation on the deeper, untouched face. He was about to ask her to leave with him, but before he could move, Stumm had come back and was intent on talking with him.

The good General was fond of Ulrich. He had already forgiven him his witticisms about the War Ministry, and was actually rather taken with the phrase "religious war": it had such a festively military air, like oak leaves on a helmet, or shouts of hurrah on the Emperor's birthday. With his arm pressed to Ulrich's, he steered him out of earshot of the others. "You know, I like what you said about all events originating in the imagination," he said. "Of course, that's more my private opinion than my official attitude," and he offered Ulrich a cigarette.

"I've got to go home," Ulrich said.

"Your sister is having a fine time; don't disturb her," Stumm said. "Arnheim's outdoing himself to pay court to her. But what I was going to say: the joy seems to have gone out of mankind's great ideas. You ought to put some life back into them. I mean, there's a new spirit in the air, and you're the man to take charge!"

"What gives you that idea?" Ulrich asked guardedly.

"That's how it strikes me." Stumm passed over it and went on intently: "You're for order too; everything you say shows it. And so then I ask myself: which is more to the point—that man is good, or that he needs a firm hand? It's all tied in with our present-day need to take a stand. I've already told you it would put my mind at rest if you would take charge of the campaign again. With all this talk, there's simply no knowing what may happen otherwise!"

Ulrich laughed. "Do you know what I'm going to do now? I'm not coming here anymore!" he said happily.

"But why?" Stumm protested hotly. "All those people will be right who've been saying that you've never been a real power!"

"If I told them what I really think, they would *really* say so." Ulrich answered, laughing, and disengaged himself from his friend.

Stumm was vexed, but then his good humor prevailed, and he said in parting: "These things are so damned complicated. Sometimes I've actually thought it would be best if a real idiot came along to tackle all these insoluble problems—I mean some sort of Joan of Arc. A person like that might be able to help!"

Ulrich's eyes searched for his sister but did not find her. While he was asking Diotima about her, Leinsdorf and Tuzzi returned from the salon and announced that everyone was leaving.

"I said all along," His Grace remarked cheerfully to the lady of the house, "that what those people were saying was not what they really meant. And Frau Drangsal has come up with a really saving idea; we've decided to continue this evening's meeting another time. Feuermaul, or whatever his name is, will read us some long poem he has written, so things will be much quieter. I of course took it upon myself, on account of the urgency, to say I was sure you'd agree!"

It was only then that Ulrich learned that Agathe had suddenly said good-bye and left the house without him. She had left word that she had not wanted to disturb him.

picador.com

blog
videos
interviews
extracts